MW00686071

Tarzan at the Earth's Core

An urgent message from Pellucidar, that world of primitive men and primeval jungles that lies inside the crust of the Earth, called on Tarzan of the Apes for assistance. Now all Tarzan's skill in the jungle, all his talents with beasts and primitive men, would be put to the extreme test. For in that land at the Earth's core, under the eternal day of the Central Sun, his terrific talents were needed just to stay alive – let alone to fulfil the mission that had called him there!

Tarzan The Invincible

Tarzan: the mighty hunter, the peerless fighter! Tarzan the Invincible, embroiled in a thrilling communist plot for the domination of savage Africa. Here, in his own grim jungle and in the wild wastes of mysterious Abyssinia, he meets high adventure – and clashes with cruel, relentless, unscrupulous enemies.

Tarzan Triumphant

A lost aviatrix, a professor, a gangster and the golden-haired goddess of the Midianites are brought together in the heart of the Dark Continent to create an explosive situation. Once again, only the incomparable figure of the Lord of the Jungle can surmount the mountains and mysteries that stand between these four people and disaster.

Tarzan and the City of Gold

In the fabled land of Onthar lie the twin cities of Cathne and Athne – one a city of gold, the other a city of ivory. For generations the Cathneans and Athneans have warred with one another, using armies of trained lions and elephants. When Tarzan rescues Valthor, an Athnean, the Ape-Man is taken captive by Nemone, the mad Queen of Cathne – as a pawn to be used in the savage games conducted for her amusement.

Tarzan and the Lion Man

A great safari had come to Africa to make a movie. It had struggled across the veldt and through the jungle in great ten-ton trucks, equipped with all the advantages of civilisation. But now it was halted, almost destroyed by the poisoned arrows of the savage Bansuto tribe. There was no way to return. Their only hope, now, was Tarzan …

Tarzan and the Leopard Men

The steel-clawed Leopard Men were looking for victims for their savage rites. The secret cult struck terror in the hearts of all the villagers. Only Orando of the Utengi dared to resist them. And with Orando went Tarzan of the Apes. But this was a strangely changed Tarzan – who now believed that he was Muzimo, the spirit or demon who had been Orando's ancestor …

Also by Edgar Rice Burroughs

Tarzan
1. Tarzan of the Apes (1912)
2. The Return of Tarzan (1913)
3. The Beasts of Tarzan (1914)
4. The Son of Tarzan (1914)
5. Tarzan and the Jewels of Opar (1916)
6. Jungle Tales of Tarzan (1916, 1917)
7. Tarzan the Untamed (1919, 1921)
8. Tarzan the Terrible (1921)
9. Tarzan and the Golden Lion (1922, 1923)
10. Tarzan and the Ant Men (1924)
11. Tarzan, Lord of the Jungle (1927, 1928)
12. Tarzan and the Lost Empire (1928)
13. Tarzan at the Earth's Core (1929)
14. Tarzan the Invincible (1930–1)
15. Tarzan Triumphant (1931)
16. Tarzan and the City of Gold (1932)
17. Tarzan and the Lion Man (1933, 1934)
18. Tarzan and the Leopard Men (1935)
19. Tarzan's Quest (1935, 1936)
20. Tarzan the Magnificent (1936, 1937)
21. Tarzan and the Forbidden City (1938)
22. Tarzan and the Foreign Legion (1947)
23. Tarzan and the Madman (1964)
24. Tarzan and the Castaways (1965)
25. Tarzan and the Valley of Gold (1965)
    (authorized sequel by Fritz Leiber)

Martian Tales*
1. A Princess of Mars (1917)
   (aka Under The Moons Of Mars, 1912)
2. The Gods of Mars (1918)
3. The Warlord of Mars (1919)
4. Thuvia, Maid of Mars (1920)
5. The Chessmen of Mars (1922)
6. The Master Mind of Mars (1927)
7. A Fighting Man of Mars (1930)
8. Swords of Mars (1934)
9. Synthetic Men of Mars (1938)
10. Llana of Gathol (1948)
11. John Carter of Mars (1941)

Pellucidar
1. At the Earth's Core (1914)
2. Pellucidar (1923)
3. Tanar of Pellucidar (1928)
4. Back to the Stone Age (1937)
5. Land of Terror (1944)
6. Savage Pellucidar (1963)

Venus
1. Pirates of Venus (1934)
2. Lost on Venus (1935)

3. Carson of Venus (1939)
4. Escape on Venus (1946)
5. The Wizard of Venus (1970)

The Land That Time Forgot
1. The Land That Time Forgot (1918)
2. The People That Time Forgot (1918)
3. Out of Time's Abyss (1918)

Other Science Fiction
The Moon Maid (1926)
(aka The Moon Men)
Beyond the Farthest Star (1941)
The Lost Continent (1916)
The Monster Men (1929)
The Resurrection of Jimber-Jaw (1937)

The Mucker
1. The Mucker (1914)
2. The Return of the Mucker (1916)
3. The Oakdale Affair (1917)

Jungle Adventure Novels
The Man-Eater (1915)
The Cave Girl (1925)
The Eternal Lover (1925)
(aka The Eternal Savage)
Jungle Girl (1932)
(aka Land of the Hidden Men)
The Lad and the Lion (1938)

* Not available as SF Gateway eBooks

Tarzan at the Earth's Core and Other Tales

SF GATEWAY OMNIBUS

TARZAN AT THE EARTH'S CORE
TARZAN THE INVINCIBLE
TARZAN TRIUMPHANT
TARZAN AND THE CITY OF GOLD
TARZAN AND THE LION MAN
TARZAN AND THE LEOPARD MEN

Edgar Rice Burroughs

GOLLANCZ

LONDON

First published in Great Britain in 2014 by
Gollancz
An imprint of the Orion Publishing Group
Orion House, 5 Upper St Martin's Lane,
London WC2H 9EA

An Hachette UK Company

A CIP catalogue record for this book is
available from the British Library

ISBN 978 0 575 12918 4

1 3 5 7 9 10 8 6 4 2

Typeset by Jouve (UK), Milton Keynes

Printed and bound by CPI Group (UK) Ltd, Croydon, CR0 4YY

The Orion Publishing Group's policy is to use papers
that are natural, renewable and recyclable products and
made from wood grown in sustainable forests. The logging
and manufacturing processes are expected to conform to
the environmental regulations of the country of origin.

www.orionbooks.co.uk
www.gollancz.co.uk

CONTENTS

ENTER THE SF GATEWAY . . .

Towards the end of 2011, in conjunction with the celebration of fifty years of coherent, continuous science fiction and fantasy publishing, Gollancz launched the SF Gateway.

Over a decade after launching the landmark SF Masterworks series, we realised that the realities of commercial publishing are such that even the Masterworks could only ever scratch the surface of an author's career. Vast troves of classic SF and fantasy were almost certainly destined never again to see print. Until very recently, this meant that anyone interested in reading any of those books would have been confined to scouring second-hand bookshops. The advent of digital publishing changed that paradigm for ever.

Embracing the future even as we honour the past, Gollancz launched the SF Gateway with a view to utilising the technology that now exists to make available, for the first time, the entire backlists of an incredibly wide range of classic and modern SF and fantasy authors. Our plan, at its simplest, was – and still is! – to use this technology to build on the success of the SF and Fantasy Masterworks series and to go even further.

The SF Gateway was designed to be the new home of classic science fiction and fantasy – the most comprehensive electronic library of classic SFF titles ever assembled. The programme has been extremely well received and we've been very happy with the results. So happy, in fact, that we've decided to complete the circle and return a selection of our titles to print, in these omnibus editions.

We hope you enjoy this selection. And we hope that you'll want to explore more of the classic SF and fantasy we have available. These are wonderful books you're holding in your hand, but you'll find much, much more ... through the SF Gateway.

www.sfgateway.com

INTRODUCTION

from The Encyclopedia of Science Fiction

Edgar Rice Burroughs (1875–1950) was a US writer whose early life was marked by numerous false starts and failures – at the time he began to write, at the age of 36, he was a pencil-sharpener salesman – but it would seem that the impulse to create the psychically charged Science-Fantasy dream-worlds that became his trademark territory was deep-set and powerful. Once he began to write, with a great rush of built-up energy, within two years he had initiated three of his four most important series. He never stopped.

Certainly the first of his published works has ever since its first appearance served as a successful escape from mid-life burdens and frustrations. *A Princess of Mars* (1917), which was originally published February–July 1912 in *All-Story* as "Under the Moons of Mars" as by Norman Bean, opens the long Barsoom sequence of novels set on Mars (Barsoom). (Many of Burroughs's novels appeared first in magazines; we are giving only first book publications here). The long array of Barsoom tales established that planet as a venue for dream-like and interminable Planetary Romance sagas in which sf and fantasy protocols mixed indiscriminately as an enabling pretext and human men were preternaturally strong, due to the manly intensity of their native Earth gravity. *The Gods of Mars* (1918) and *The Warlord of Mars* (1919) further recount the exploits of John Carter as he variously befriends and battles various green, yellow and black Martians without the law, and wins the hand of the red-skinned (and oviparous) princess Dejah Thoris. The standard of storytelling and invention is high in the Barsoom books, *Chessmen* and *Swords* being particularly fine; but it has always been difficult for some critics to accept the Planetary Romance as being, in any cognitive sense, sf. Although Carter's adventures take place on another planet, he incontrovertibly travels there by magical means, and Barsoom itself is inconsistent and scientifically implausible to modern eyes. It is clear, however, that Burroughs's immense popularity has nothing to do with conventional sf virtues, for it depends on storylines and venues as malleable as dreams, exotic and dangerous and unending.

The long Tarzan saga came next (see below), occupying much of his time before the creation of his third major series. The Pellucidar novels based on the Hollow-Earth theory of John Cleves Symmes, began with *At the Earth's Core* (1922) and continued in *Pellucidar* (1923), *Tanar of Pellucidar* (1930),

Tarzan at the Earth's Core (1930) – a notable 'overlap' volume – *Back to the Stone Age* (1937), *Land of Terror* (1944) and *Savage Pellucidar* (1963). Pellucidar is perhaps the best of Burroughs's locales – a world without time where Dinosaurs and beast-men roam circularly forever – and is a perfect setting for bloodthirsty romantic adventure. The first of the series was filmed disappointingly as At the Earth's Core (*1976*).

His fourth series, the Venus sequence – created much later in Burroughs's career – concerns the exploits of spaceman Carson Napier on Venus, and consists of *Pirates of Venus* (1934), *Lost on Venus* (1935), *Carson of Venus* (1939) and *Escape on Venus* (1946). These books are not as stirring and vivid as the Barsoom series. A posthumous story, 'The Wizard of Venus', was published in *Tales of Three Planets* (1964) and subsequently as the title story of a separate paperback, *The Wizard of Venus* (1970). Two of the stories from *Tales of Three Planets*, 'Beyond the Farthest Star' (January 1942 *Blue Book*) and the posthumous 'Tangor Returns' (in *Tales of Three Planets* 1964), form the opening of a fifth series which Burroughs abandoned. They are of particular sf interest because they are his only tales with an interstellar setting. The two stories were subsequently republished as a paperback entitled *Beyond the Farthest Star* (1965).

Of Burroughs's non-series tales, perhaps the finest is *The Land that Time Forgot* (1924; revised in three volumes under the original magazine titles: *The Land that Time Forgot* 1962, *The People that Time Forgot* 1962 and *Out of Time's Abyss* 1962), set in the lost world of Caspak near the South Pole, and cunningly presenting in literal form – for animals here metamorphose through evolutionary stages – the dictum that ontogeny recapitulates phylogeny. The book was loosely adapted into two films, *The Land That Time Forgot* (*1975*) and *The People That Time Forgot* (*1977*). Also of interest is *The Moon Maid* 1926), which describes a civilization in the hollow interior of the Moon and a future Invasion of the Earth.

Among Burroughs's other books, those which can be claimed as sf include: *The Eternal Lover* (1925), a prehistoric adventure involving Time Travel featuring a character, Barney Custer, who reappears in the Ruritanian *The Mad King* (1926); *The Monster Men* (1929), a reworking of the Frankenstein theme, which should not be confused with *The Man without a Soul* (1922), which is not fantasy or sf; *The Cave Girl* (1925), another prehistoric romance; *Jungle Girl* (1932), about a lost civilization in Cambodia; and *Beyond Thirty* (1956), a story set in the twenty-second century after the collapse of European civilization.

It cannot be claimed that Burroughs's works aim at literary polish, or that their merits are intellectual. His lovers and his critics agree on this. Nevertheless, because of their efficient narrative style, and because Burroughs had a genius for highly-energized literalizations of dream-worlds, they have endured. Tarzan is a figure with the iconic density of Sherlock Holmes or Dracula. His 'rediscovery' during the 1960s was an astonishing publishing phenomenon, with the majority of his books being reprinted regularly. He had never been forgotten, however. Burroughs has probably had more imitators than any other sf writer, ranging from Otis Adelbert Kline in the 1930s to Kenneth Bulmer (writing as Alan Burt Akers) in the 1970s, with homages from much later writers like Terry Bisson in *Voyage to the Red Planet* (1990) and Hitoshi Yoshioka in *Nangun Kihei Taii John Carter* ['Southern Cavalry Captain John Carter'] (2005). Serious sf writers who owe a debt to Burroughs include Leigh Brackett, Ray Bradbury, Michael Moorcock and, above all, Philip José Farmer, whose Lord Grandrith and Ancient Opar novels are among the most enjoyable of latter-day Burroughs-inflected romances. Burroughs was posthumously inducted into the Science Fiction Hall of Fame in 2003. It was clear he belonged there.

The massive Tarzan saga, which begins with *Tarzan of the Apes and Other Tales* (Gollancz centenary omnibus, 2012), is just as much sf (or non-sf) as the Barsoom series. Though clearly influenced by H. Rider Haggard, Burroughs did not attempt to imitate one of that writer's prime virtues: Haggard's effort to embed his tales in a vision of history, even though (to modern eyes) his work seems almost dementedly dated, certainly in its imperialist assumptions about race. Allan Quatermain's Africa, even though it is romantically exaggerated, can distress modern readers; but Tarzan's Africa is a Never Never Land, and must accepted as being no more governed by the reality principle than Barsoom. *Tarzan of the Apes* (1914), the story of an English aristocrat's son raised in the jungle by 'great apes' (of a non-existent species) as a kind of feral child or Noble Savage, was immensely popular from the beginning, and Burroughs continued producing sequels to the end of his career. In most of them Tarzan has unashamedly fantastic adventures, some of which – discovering lost cities and live Dinosaurs, being reduced to 18 inches (46 cm) in height, visiting the Earth's core – marvellously evoke the conventions of Pulp sf. Burroughs did not perhaps entirely grasp the iconic power of his aristocrat/barbarian lord in *Tarzan of the Apes* itself – which continues with *The Return of Tarzan* (1915), *The Beasts of Tarzan* (1916), *The Son of Tarzan* (1917) and *Tarzan and the Jewels of Opar* (1918), all relatively uninspired. *Jungle Tales of Tarzan* (1919) gains creative fire through its clever reminders of Rudyard Kipling's two *Jungle Books* (1894, 1895); and in 'Tarzan's First Love' (September 1916 *Blue Book*) Burroughs invokes Apes-as-Human material otherwhere left tacit: which is to say Tarzan falls in love with an ape.

Tarzan at the Earth's Core (1930), which also comprises part of the Pellucidar sequence, is the first of the six tales assembled in this third Tarzan omnibus, followed by *Tarzan the Invincible* (1931), *Tarzan Triumphant* (1932),

Tarzan and the City of Gold (1933), *Tarzan and the Lion Man* (1934) and *Tarzan and the Leopard Men* (1935). Tarzan travels more widely now, and into deeper realms. *Tarzan at the Earth's Core* (1930) fits effortless into the Pellucidar sequence, and is the fourth volume set in a Hollow Earth occupying the interior of our own planet (see *The Pellucidar SF Gateway Omnibus,* Gollancz, 2013). When these stories were first published, Burroughs's compulsive assurance as a storyteller had become taken for granted, and new episodes of Tarzan, however ingeniously they explored the territory, were treated as routine. Perhaps it is time to rediscover the true stories.

For a more detailed version of the above, see Edgar Rice Burroughs' author entry in *The Encyclopedia of Science Fiction*: http://sf-encyclopedia.com/entry/burroughs_edgar_rice

Some terms above are capitalised when they would not normally be so rendered; this indicates that the terms represent discrete entries in *The Encyclopedia of Science Fiction*.

TARZAN AT THE EARTH'S CORE

FOREWORD

Pellucidar, as every schoolboy knows, is a world within a world, lying, as it does, upon the inner surface of the hollow sphere, which is the Earth.

It was discovered by David Innes and Abner Perry upon the occasion when they made the trial trip upon the mechanical prospector invented by Perry, wherewith they hoped to locate new beds of anthracite coal. Owing, however, to their inability to deflect the nose of the prospector, after it had started downward into the Earth's crust, they bored straight through for five hundred miles, and upon the third day, when Perry was already unconscious owing to the consumption of their stock of oxygen, and David was fast losing consciousness, the nose of the prospector broke through the crust of the inner world and the cabin was filled with fresh air.

In the years that have intervened, weird adventures have befallen these two explorers. Perry has never returned to the outer crust, and Innes but once – upon that occasion when he made the difficult and dangerous return trip in the prospector for the purpose of bringing back to the empire he had founded in the inner world the means to bestow upon his primitive people of the stone age the civilization of the twentieth century.

But what with battles with primitive men and still more primitive beasts and reptiles, the advance of the empire of Pellucidar toward civilization has been small; and in so far as the great area of the inner world is concerned, or the countless millions of its teeming life of another age than ours, David Innes and Abner Perry might never have existed.

When one considers that these land and water areas upon the surface of Pellucidar are in opposite relationship to the same areas upon the outer crust, some slight conception of the vast extent of this mighty world within a world may be dreamed.

The land area of the outer world comprises some fifty-three million square miles, or one-quarter of the total area of the earth's surface; while within Pellucidar three-quarters of the surface is land, so that jungle, mountain, forest and plain stretch interminably over 124,110,000 square miles; nor are the oceans with their area of 41,370,000 square miles of any mean or niggardly extent.

Thus, considering the land area only, we have the strange anomaly of a larger world within a smaller one, but then Pellucidar is a world of deviation from what we of the outer crust have come to accept as unalterable laws of nature.

In the exact center of the earth hangs Pellucidar's sun, a tiny orb compared with ours, but sufficient to illuminate Pellucidar and flood her teeming jungles with warmth and life-giving rays. Her sun hanging thus perpetually at zenith, there is no night upon Pellucidar, but always an endless eternity of noon.

There being no stars and no apparent movement of the sun, Pellucidar has no points of compass; nor has she any horizon since her surface curves always upward in all directions from the observer, so that far above one's line of vision, plain or sea or distant mountain range go onward and upward until lost in the haze of the distance. And again, in a world where there is no sun, no stars and no moon, such as we know, there can be no such thing as time, as we know it. And so, in Pellucidar, we have a timeless world which must necessarily be free from those pests who are constantly calling our attention to 'the busy little bee' and to the fact that 'time is money.' While time may be 'the soul of this world' and the 'essence of contracts,' in the beatific existence of Pellucidar it is nothing and less than nothing.

Thrice in the past have we of the outer world received communication from Pellucidar. We know that Perry's first great gift of civilization to the stone age was gunpowder. We know that he followed this with repeating rifles, small ships of war upon which were mounted guns of no great caliber, and finally we know that he perfected a radio.

Knowing Perry as something of an empiric, we were not surprised to learn that his radio could not be tuned in upon any known wave or wave length of the outer world, and it remained for young Jason Gridley of Tarzana, experimenting with his newly discovered Gridley Wave, to pick up the first message from Pellucidar.

The last word that we received from Perry before his messages faltered and died out was to the effect that David Innes, first Emperor of Pellucidar, was languishing in a dark dungeon in the land of the Korsars, far across continent and ocean from his beloved land of Sari, which lies upon a great plateau not far inland from the Lural Az.

I
The O-220

Tarzan of the Apes paused to listen and to sniff the air. Had you been there you could not have heard what he heard, or had you you could not have interpreted it. You could have smelled nothing but the mustiness of decaying vegetation, which blended with the aroma of growing things.

The sounds that Tarzan heard came from a great distance and were faint even to his ears; nor at first could he definitely ascribe them to their true source, though he conceived the impression that they heralded the coming of a party of men.

Buto the rhinoceros, Tantor the elephant or Numa the lion might come and go through the forest without arousing more than the indifferent interest of the Lord of the Jungle, but when man came Tarzan investigated, for man alone of all creatures brings change and dissension and strife wheresoever he first sets foot.

Reared to manhood among the great apes without knowledge of the existence of any other creatures like himself, Tarzan had since learned to anticipate with concern each fresh invasion of his jungle by these two-footed harbingers of strife. Among many races of men he had found friends, but this did not prevent him from questioning the purposes and the motives of whose ever entered his domain. And so today he moved silently through the middle terrace of his leafy way in the direction of the sounds that he had heard.

As the distance closed between him and those he went to investigate, his keen ears cataloged the sound of padding, naked feet and the song of native carriers as they swung along beneath their heavy burdens. And then to his nostrils came the scent spoor of black men and with it, faintly, the suggestion of another scent, and Tarzan knew that a white man was on safari before the head of the column came in view along the wide, well marked game trail, above which the Lord of the Jungle waited.

Near the head of the column marched a young white man, and when Tarzan's eyes had rested upon him for a moment as he swung along the trail they impressed their stamp of approval of the stranger within the ape-man's brain, for in common with many savage beasts and primitive men Tarzan possessed an uncanny instinct in judging aright the characters of strangers whom he met.

Turning about, Tarzan moved swiftly and silently through the trees until he was some little distance ahead of the marching safari, then he dropped down into the trail and awaited its coming.

Rounding a curve in the trail the leading askari came in sight of him and when they saw him they halted and commenced to jabber excitedly, for these were men recruited in another district – men who did not know Tarzan of the Apes by sight.

'I am Tarzan,' announced the ape-man. 'What do you in Tarzan's country?'

Immediately the young man, who had halted abreast of his askari, advanced toward the ape-man. There was a smile upon his eager face. 'You are Lord Greystoke?' he asked.

'Here, I am Tarzan of the Apes,' replied the foster son of Kala.

'Then luck is certainly with me,' said the young man, 'for I have come all the way from Southern California to find you.'

'Who are you,' demanded the ape-man, 'and what do you want of Tarzan of the Apes?'

'My name is Jason Gridley,' replied the other. 'And what I have come to talk to you about will make a long story. I hope that you can find the time to accompany me to our next camp and the patience to listen to me there until I have explained my mission.'

Tarzan nodded. 'In the jungle,' he said, 'we are not often pressed for time. Where do you intend making camp?'

'The guide that I obtained in the last village complained of being ill and turned back an hour ago, and as none of my own men is familiar with this country we do not know whether there is a suitable campsite within one mile or ten.'

'There is one within half a mile,' replied Tarzan, 'and with good water.'

'Good,' said Gridley; and the safari resumed its way, the porters laughing and singing at the prospect of an early camp.

It was not until Jason and Tarzan were enjoying their coffee that evening that the ape-man reverted to the subject of the American's visit.

'And now,' he said, 'what has brought you all the way from Southern California to the heart of Africa?'

Gridley smiled. 'Now that I am actually here,' he said, 'and face to face with you, I am suddenly confronted with the conviction that after you have heard my story it is going to be difficult to convince you that I am not crazy, and yet in my own mind I am so thoroughly convinced of the truth of what I am going to tell you that I have already invested a considerable amount of money and time to place my plan before you for the purpose of enlisting your personal and financial support, and I am ready and willing to invest still more money and all of my time. Unfortunately I cannot wholly finance the expedition that I have in mind from my personal resources, but that is not primarily my reason for coming to you. Doubtless I could have raised the necessary money elsewhere, but I believe that you are peculiarly fitted to lead such a venture as I have in mind.'

'Whatever the expedition may be that you are contemplating,' said Tarzan, 'the potential profits must be great indeed if you are willing to risk so much of your own money.'

'On the contrary,' replied Gridley, 'there will be no financial profit for anyone concerned in so far as I now know.'

'And you are an American?' asked Tarzan, smiling.

'We are not all money mad,' replied Gridley.

'Then what is the incentive? Explain the whole proposition to me.'

'Have you ever heard of the theory that the earth is a hollow sphere, containing a habitable world within its interior?'

'The theory that has been definitely refuted by scientific investigation,' replied the ape-man.

'But has it been refuted satisfactorily?' asked Gridley.

'To the satisfaction of the scientists,' replied Tarzan.

'And to my satisfaction, too,' replied the American, 'until I recently received a message direct from the inner world.'

'You surprise me,' said the ape-man.

'And I, too, was surprised, but the fact remains that I have been in radio communication with Abner Perry in the inner world of Pellucidar and I have brought a copy of that message with me and also an affidavit of its authenticity from a man with whose name you are familiar and who was with me when I received the message; in fact, he was listening in at the same time with me. Here they are.'

From a portfolio he took a letter which he handed to Tarzan and a bulky manuscript bound in board covers.

'I shall not take the time to read you all of the story of Tanar of Pellucidar,' said Gridley, 'because there is a great deal in it that is not essential to the exposition of my plan.'

'As you will,' said Tarzan. 'I am listening.'

For half an hour Jason Gridley read excerpts from the manuscript before him. 'This,' he said, when he had completed the reading, 'is what convinced me of the existence of Pellucidar, and it is the unfortunate situation of David Innes that impelled me to come to you with the proposal that we undertake an expedition whose first purpose shall be to rescue him from the dungeon of the Korsars.'

'And how do you think this may be done?' asked the ape-man. 'Are you convinced of the correctness of Innes' theory that there is an entrance to the inner world at each pole?'

'I am free to confess that I do not know what to believe,' replied the American. 'But after I received this message from Perry I commenced to investigate and I discovered that the theory of an inhabitable world at the center of the earth with openings leading into it at the north and south poles is no new one and that there is much evidence to support it. I found a very complete exposition of the theory in a book written about 1830 and in another work of more recent time. Therein I found what seemed to be a reasonable explanation of many well known phenomena that have not been satisfactorily explained by any hypothesis endorsed by science.'

'What, for example?' asked Tarzan.

'Well, for example, warm winds and warm ocean currents coming from the north are encountered and reported by practically all arctic explorers; the presence of the limbs and branches of trees with green foliage upon them floating southward from the far north, far above the latitude where any such trees are found upon the outer crust; then there is the phenomenon of the northern lights, which in the light of David Innes' theory may easily be explained as rays of light from the central sun of the inner world, breaking occasionally through the fog and cloud banks above the polar opening. Again there is the pollen, which often thickly covers the snow and ice in portions of the polar regions. This pollen could not come from elsewhere than the inner world. And in addition to all this is the insistence of the far northern tribes of Eskimos that their forefathers came from a country to the north.'

'Did not Amundson and Ellsworth in the Norge expedition definitely disprove the theory of a north polar opening in the earth's crust, and have not airplane flights been made over a considerable portion of the hitherto unexplored regions near the pole?' demanded the ape-man.

'The answer to that is that the polar opening is so large that a ship, a dirigible or an airplane could dip down over the edge into it a short distance and return without ever being aware of the fact, but the most tenable theory is that in most instances explorers have merely followed around the outer rim of the orifice, which would largely explain the peculiar and mystifying action of compasses and other scientific instruments at points near the so-called north pole – matters which have greatly puzzled all arctic explorers.'

'You are convinced then that there is not only an inner world but that there is an entrance to it at the north pole?' asked Tarzan.

'I am convinced that there is an inner world, but I am not convinced of the existence of a polar opening,' replied Gridley. 'I can only say that I believe there is sufficient evidence to warrant the organization of an expedition such as I have suggested.'

'Assuming that a polar opening into an inner world exists, by just what means do you purpose accomplishing the discovery and exploration of it?'

'The most practical means of transportation that exists today for carrying out my plan would be a specially constructed rigid airship, built along the lines of the modern Zeppelin. Such a ship, using helium gas, would show a higher factor of safety than any other means of transportation at our disposal. I have given the matter considerable thought and I feel sure that if there is such a polar opening, the obstacles that would confront us in an attempt to enter the inner world would be far less than those encountered by the Norge in its famous trip across the pole to Alaska, for there is no question in my mind but that it made a wide detour in following the rim of the polar orifice and covered a far greater distance than we shall have to cover to reach a reasonably safe anchorage below the cold, polar sea that David Innes discovered north of the land of the Korsars before he was finally taken prisoner by them.

'The greatest risk that we would have to face would be a possible inability to return to the outer crust, owing to the depletion of our helium gas that might be made necessary by the maneuvering of the ship. But that is only the same chance of life or death that every explorer and scientific investigator must be willing to assume in the prosecution of his labors. If it were but possible to build a hull sufficiently light, and at the same time sufficiently strong, to withstand atmospheric pressure, we could dispense with both the dangerous hydrogen gas and the rare and expensive helium gas and have the assurance of the utmost safety and maximum of buoyancy in a ship supported entirely by vacuum tanks.'

'Perhaps even that is possible,' said Tarzan, who was now evincing increasing interest in Gridley's proposition.

The American shook his head. 'It may be possible some day,' he said, 'but not at present with any known material. Any receptacle having sufficient strength to withstand the atmospheric pressure upon a vacuum would have a weight far too great for the vacuum to lift.'

'Perhaps,' said Tarzan, 'and, again, perhaps not.'

'What do you mean?' inquired Gridley.

'What you have just said,' replied Tarzan, 'reminds me of something that a young friend of mine recently told me. Erich von Harben is something of a scientist and explorer himself, and the last time that I saw him he had just returned from a second expedition into the Wiramwazi Mountains, where he told me that he had discovered a lake-dwelling tribe using canoes made of a metal that was apparently as light as cork and stronger than steel. He brought some samples of the metal back with him, and at the time I last saw him he was conducting some experiments in a little laboratory he has rigged up at his father's mission.'

'Where is this man?' demanded Gridley.

'Dr von Harben's mission is in the Urambi country,' replied the ape-man, 'about four marches west of where we now are.'

Far into the night the two men discussed plans for the project, for Tarzan was now thoroughly interested, and the next day they turned back toward the Urambi country and von Harben's mission where they arrived on the fourth day and were greeted by Dr von Harben and his son, Erich, as well as by the latter's wife, the beautiful Favonia of Castrum Mare.

It is not my intention to weary you with a recital of the details of the organization and equipment of the Pellucidarian expedition, although that portion of it which relates to the search for and discovery of the native mine containing the remarkable metal now known as Harbenite, filled as it was with adventure and excitement, is well worth a volume by itself.

While Tarzan and Erich von Harben were locating the mine and transporting the metal to the seacoast, Jason Gridley was in Friedrichshafen in consultation with the engineers of the company he had chosen to construct the specially designed airship in which the attempt was to be made to reach the inner world.

Exhaustive tests were made of the samples of Harbenite brought to Friedrichshafen by Jason Gridley. Plans were drawn, and by the time the shipment of the ore arrived everything was in readiness to commence immediate construction, which was carried on secretly. And six months later, when the O-220, as it was officially known, was ready to take the air, it was generally considered to be nothing more than a new design of the ordinary type of rigid airship, destined to be used as a common carrier upon one of the already numerous commercial airways of Europe.

The great cigar-shaped hull of the O-220 was 997 feet in length and 150 feet in diameter. The interior of the hull was divided into six large, air-tight compartments, three of which, running the full length of the ship, were above the medial line and three below. Inside the hull and running along each side of the ship, between the upper and lower vaccum tanks, were long corridors in which were located the engines, motors and pumps, in addition to supplies of gasoline and oil.

The internal location of the engine room was made possible by the elimination of fire risk, which is an ever-present source of danger in airships which depend for their lifting power upon hydrogen gas, as well as to the absolutely fireproof construction of the O-220; every part of which, with the exception of a few cabin fittings and furniture, was of Harbenite, this metal being used throughout except for certain bushings and bearings in motors, generators and propellers.

Connecting the port and starboard engine and fuel corridors were two transverse corridors, one forward and one aft, while bisecting these transverse corridors were two climbing shafts extending from the bottom of the ship to the top.

The upper end of the forward climbing shaft terminated in a small gun and observation cabin at the top of the ship, along which was a narrow walkingway extending from the forward cabin to a small turret near the tail of the ship, where provision had been made for fixing a machine gun.

The main cabin, running along the keel of the ship, was an integral part of the hull, and because of this entirely rigid construction, which eliminated the necessity for cabins suspended below the hull, the O-220 was equipped with landing gear in the form of six, large, heavily tired wheels projecting below the bottom of the main cabin. In the extreme stern of the keel cabin a small scout monoplane was carried in such a way that it could be lowered through the bottom of the ship and launched while the O-220 was in flight.

Eight air-cooled motors drove as many propellers, which were arranged in pairs upon either side of the ship and staggered in such a manner that the air from the forward propellers would not interfere with those behind.

The engines, developing 5600 horsepower, were capable of driving the ship at a speed of 105 miles per hour.

In the O-220 the ordinary axial wire, which passes the whole length of the ship through the center, consisted of a tubular shaft of Harbenite from which smaller tubular braces radiated, like the spokes of a wheel, to the tubular girders, to which the Harbenite plates of the outer envelope were welded.

Owing to the extreme lightness of Harbenite, the total weight of the ship was 75 tons, while the total lift of its vacuum tanks was 225 tons.

For purposes of maneuvering the ship and to facilitate landing, each of the vacuum tanks was equipped with a bank of eight air valves operated from the control cabin at the forward end of the keel; while six pumps, three in the starboard and three in the port engine corridors, were designed to expel the air from the tanks when it became necessary to renew the vacuum. Special rudders and elevators were also operated from the forward control cabin as well as from an auxiliary position aft in the port engine corridor, in the event that the control cabin steering gear should break down.

In the main keel cabin were located the quarters for the officers and crew, gun and ammunition room, provision room, galley, additional gasoline and oil storage tanks, and water tanks, the latter so constructed that the contents of any of them might be emptied instantaneously in case of an emergency, while a proportion of the gasoline and oil tanks were slip tanks that might be slipped through the bottom of the ship in cases of extreme emergency when it was necessary instantaneously to reduce the weight of the load.

This, then, briefly, was the great, rigid airship in which Jason Gridley and Tarzan of the Apes hoped to discover the north polar entrance to the inner world and rescue David Innes, Emperor of Pellucidar, from the dungeons of the Korsars.

II

Pellucidar

Just before daybreak of a clear June morning, the O-220 moved slowly from its hangar under its own power. Fully loaded and equipped, it was to make its test flight under load conditions identical with those which would obtain when it set forth upon its long journey. The three lower tanks were still filled with air and she carried an excess of water ballast sufficient to overcome her equilibrium, so that while she moved lightly over the ground she moved with entire safety and could be maneuvered almost as handily as an automobile.

As she came into the open her pumps commenced to expel the air from the three lower tanks, and at the same time a portion of her excess water ballast was slowly discharged, and almost immediately the huge ship rose slowly and gracefully from the ground.

The entire personnel of the ship's company during the test flight was the same that had been selected for the expedition. Zuppner, who had been chosen as captain, had been in charge of the construction of the ship and had a considerable part in its designing. There were two mates, Von Horst and Dorf, who had been officers in the Imperial air forces, as also had the navigator, Lieutenant Hines. In addition to these there were twelve engineers and eight mechanics, a negro cook and two Filipino cabin-boys.

Tarzan was commander of the expedition, with Jason Gridley as his lieutenant, while the fighting men of the ship consisted of Muviro and nine of his Waziri warriors.

As the ship rose gracefully above the city, Zuppner, who was at the controls, could scarce restrain his enthusiasm.

'The sweetest thing I ever saw!' he exclaimed. 'She responds to the lightest touch.'

'I am not surprised at that,' said Hines; 'I knew she'd do it. Why, we've got twice the crew we need to handle her.'

'There you go again. lieutenant,' said Tarzan, laughing; 'but do not think that my insistence upon a large crew was based upon any lack of confidence in the ship. We are going into a strange world. We may be gone a long time. If we reach our destination we shall have fighting, as each of you men who volunteered has been informed many times, so that while we may have twice as many men as we need for the trip in, we may yet find ourselves short handed on the return journey, for not all of us will return.'

'I suppose you are right,' said Hines; 'but with the feel of this ship permeating me and the quiet peacefulness of the scene below, danger and death seem remote.'

'I hope they are,' returned Tarzan, 'and I hope that we shall return with every man that goes out with us, but I believe in being prepared and to that end Gridley and I have been studying navigation and we want you to give us a chance at some practical experience before we reach our destination.'

Zuppner laughed. 'They have you marked already, Hines,' he said.

The Lieutenant grinned. 'I'll teach them all I know,' he said; 'but I'll bet the best dinner that can be served in Berlin that if this ship returns I'll still be her navigator.'

'That is a case of heads-I-win, tails-you-lose,' said Gridley.

'And to return to the subject of preparedness,' said Tarzan, 'I am going to ask you to let my Waziri help the mechanics and engineers. They are highly intelligent men, quick to learn, and if some calamity should overtake us we cannot have too many men familiar with the engines, and other machinery of the ship.'

'You are right,' said Zuppner, 'and I shall see that it is done.'

The great, shining ship sailed majestically north; Ravensburg fell astern and half an hour later the somber gray ribbon of the Danube lay below them.

The longer they were in the air the more enthusiastic Zuppner became. 'I had every confidence in the successful outcome of the trial flight,' he said; 'but I can assure you that I did not look for such perfection as I find in this ship. It marks a new era in aeronautics, and I am convinced that long before we cover the four hundred miles to Hamburg that we shall have established the entire air worthiness of the O-220 to the entire satisfaction of each of us.'

'To Hamburg and return to Friedrichshafen was to have been the route of the trial trip,' said Tarzan, 'but why turn back at Hamburg?'

The others turned questioning eyes upon him as the purport of his query sank home.

'Yes, why?' demanded Gridley.

Zuppner shrugged his shoulders. 'We are fully equipped and provisioned,' he said.

'Then why waste eight hundred miles in returning to Friedrichshafen?' demanded Hines.

'If you are all agreeable we shall continue toward the north,' said Tarzan. And so it was that the trial trip of the O-220 became an actual start upon its long journey toward the interior of the earth, and the secrecy that was desired for the expedition was insured.

The plan had been to follow the Tenth Meridian east of Greenwich north to the pole. But to avoid attracting unnecessary notice a slight deviation from this course was found desirable, and the ship passed to the west of Hamburg and out across the waters of the North Sea, and thus due north, passing to the west of Spitzbergen and out across the frozen polar wastes.

Maintaining an average cruising speed of about 75 miles per hour, the O-220 reached the vicinity of the north pole about midnight of the second day, and excitement ran high when Hines announced that in accordance with his calculation they should be directly over the pole. At Tarzan's suggestion the ship circled slowly at an altitude of a few hundred feet above the rough, snow-covered ice.

'We ought to be able to recognize it by the Italian flags,' said Zuppner, with a smile. But if any reminders of the passage of the Norge remained below them, they were effectually hidden by the mantle of many snows.

The ship made a single circle above the desolate ice pack before she took up her southerly course along the 170th East Meridian.

From the moment that the ship struck south from the pole Jason Gridley remained constantly with Hines and Zuppner eagerly and anxiously watching the instruments, or gazing down upon the bleak landscape ahead. It was Gridley's belief that the north polar opening lay in the vicinity of 85 north latitude and 170 east longitude. Before him were compass, aneroids, bubble statoscope, air speed indicator, inclinometers, rise and fall indicator, bearing plate, clock and thermometers; but the instrument that commanded his closest attention was the compass, for Jason Gridley held a theory and upon the correctness of it depended their success in finding the north polar opening.

For five hours the ship flew steadily toward the south, when she developed an apparent tendency to fall off toward the west.

'Hold her steady, Captain,' cautioned Gridley, 'for if I am correct we are now going over the lip of the polar opening, and the deviation is in the compass only and not in our course. The further we go along this course the more erratic the compass will become and if we were presently to move upward, or in other words, straight out across the polar opening toward its center, the needle would spin erratically in a circle. But we could not reach the center of the polar opening because of the tremendous altitude which this would require. I believe that we are now on the eastern verge of the opening and if whatever deviation from the present course you make is to the starboard we shall slowly spiral downward into Pellucidar, but your compass will be useless for the next four to six hundred miles.'

Zuppner shook his head, dubiously. 'If this weather holds, we may be able to do it,' he said, 'but if it commences to blow I doubt my ability to keep any sort of a course if I am not to follow the compass.'

'Do the best you can,' said Gridley, 'and when in doubt put her to starboard.'

So great was the nervous strain upon all of them that for hours at a time scarcely a word was exchanged.

'Look!' exclaimed Hines suddenly. 'There is open water just ahead of us.'

'That, of course, we might expect,' said Zuppner, 'even if there is no polar opening, and you know that I have been sceptical about that ever since Gridley first explained his theory to me.'

'I think,' said Gridley, with a smile, 'that really I am the only one in the party who has had any faith at all in the theory, but please do not call it my theory for it is not, and even I should not have been surprised had the theory proven to be a false one. But if any of you has been watching the sun for the last few hours, I think that you will have to agree with me that even though there may be no polar opening into an inner world, there must be a great depression at this point in the earth's crust and that we had gone down into it for a considerable distance, for you will notice that the midnight sun is much lower than it should be and that the further we continue upon this course the lower it drops – eventually it will set completely, and if I am not much mistaken we shall soon see the light of the eternal noonday sun of Pellucidar.'

Suddenly the telephone rang and Hines put the receiver to his ear. 'Very good, sir,' he said, after a moment, and hung up. 'It was Von Horst, Captain, reporting from the observation cabin. He has sighted land dead ahead.'

'Land!' exclaimed Zuppner. 'The only land our chart shows in this direction is Siberia.'

'Siberia lies over a thousand miles south of 85, and we cannot be over three hundred miles south of 85,' said Gridley.

'Then we have either discovered a new arctic land, or we are approaching the northern frontiers of Pellucidar,' said Lieutenant Hines

'And that is just what we are doing,' said Gridley. 'Look at your thermometer.'

'The devil!' exclaimed Zuppner. 'It is only twenty degrees above zero Fahrenheit.'

'You can see the land plainly now,' said Tarzan. 'It looks desolate enough, but there are only little patches of snow here and there.'

'This corresponds with the land Innes described north of Korsar,' said Gridley.

Word was quickly passed around the ship to the other officers and the crew that there was reason to believe that the land below them was Pellucidar. Excitement ran high, and every man who could spare a moment from his duties was aloft on the walkingway, or peering through portholes for a glimpse of the inner world.

Steadily the O-220 forged southward and just as the rim of the midnight sun disappeared from view below the horizon astern, the glow of Pellucidar's central sun was plainly visible ahead.

The nature of the landscape below was changing rapidly. The barren land had fallen astern, the ship had crossed a range of wooded hills and now before it lay a great forest that stretched on and on, seemingly curving upward to be lost eventually in the haze of the distance. This was indeed Pellucidar – the Pellucidar of which Jason Gridley had dreamed.

Beyond the forest lay a rolling plain dotted with clumps of trees, a well-watered plain through which wound numerous streams, which emptied into a large river at its opposite side.

Great herds of game were grazing in the open pasture land and nowhere was there sight of man.

'This looks like heaven to me,' said Tarzan of the Apes. 'Let us land, Captain.'

Slowly the great ship came to earth as air was taken into the lower vacuum tanks.

Short ladders were run out, for the bottom of the cabin was only six feet above the ground, and presently the entire ship's company, with the exception of a watch of an officer and two men, were knee deep in the lush grasses of Pellucidar.

'I thought we might get some fresh meat,' said Tarzan, 'but the ship has frightened all the game away.'

'From the quantity of it I saw, we shall not have to go far to bag some,' said Dorf.

'What we need most right now, however, is rest,' said Tarzan. 'For weeks every man has been working at high pitch in completing the preparation for the expedition and I doubt if one of us has had over two hours sleep in the last three days. I suggest that we remain here until we are all thoroughly rested and then take up a systematic search for the city of Korsar.'

The plan met with general approval and preparations were made for a stay of several days.

'I believe,' said Gridley to Captain Zuppner, 'that it would be well to issue strict orders that no one is to leave the ship, or rather its close vicinity, without permission from you and that no one be allowed to venture far afield except in parties commanded by an officer, for we have every assurance that we shall meet with savage men and far more savage beasts everywhere within Pellucidar.'

'I hope that you will except me from that order,' said Tarzan, smiling.

'I believe that you can take care of yourself in any country,' said Zuppner.

'And I can certainly hunt to better effect alone than I can with a party,' said the ape-man.

'In any event,' continued Zuppner, 'the order comes from you as commander, and no one will complain if you exempt yourself from its provisions since I am sure that none of the rest of us is particularly anxious to wander about Pellucidar alone.'

Officers and men, with the exception of the watch, which changed every four hours, slept the clock around.

Tarzan of the Apes was the first to complete his sleep and leave the ship. He had discarded the clothing that had encumbered and annoyed him since he had left his own African jungle to join in the preparation of the O-220, and it was no faultlessly attired Englishman that came from the cabin and dropped to the ground below, but instead an almost naked and primitive warrior, armed with hunting knife, spear, a bow and arrows, and the long rope which Tarzan always carried, for in the hunt he preferred the weapons of his youth to the firearms of civilization.

Lieutenant Dorf, the only officer on duty at the time, saw him depart and watched with unfeigned admiration as the black-haired jungle lord moved across the open plain and disappeared in the forest.

There were trees that were familiar to the eyes of the ape-man, and trees such as he had never seen before, but it was a forest and that was enough to lure Tarzan of the Apes and permit him to forget the last few weeks that had been spent amidst the distasteful surroundings of civilization. He was happy to be free from the ship, too, and, while he liked all his companions, he was yet glad to be alone.

In the first flight of his new-found freedom Tarzan was like a boy released from school. Unhampered by the hated vestments of civilization, out of sight of anything that might even remotely remind him of the atrocities with which man scars the face of nature, he filled his lungs with the free air of Pellucidar, leaped into a nearby tree and swung away through the forest, his only concern for the moment the joyousness of exultant vitality and life. On he sped through the primeval forest of Pellucidar. Strange birds, startled by his swift and silent passage, flew screaming from his path, and strange beasts slunk to cover beneath him. But Tarzan did not care; he was not hunting; he was not even searching for the new in this new world. For the moment he was only living.

While this mood dominated him Tarzan gave no thought to the passage of time any more than he had given thought to the timelessness of Pellucidar, whose noonday sun, hanging perpetually at zenith, gives a lie to us of the outer crust who rush frantically through life in mad and futile effort to beat the earth in her revolutions. Nor did Tarzan reckon upon distance or direction, for such matters were seldom the subjects of conscious consideration upon the part of the ape-man, whose remarkable ability to meet every and any emergency he unconsciously attributed to powers that lay within himself, not stopping to consider that in his own jungle he relied upon the friendly sun and moon and stars as guides by day and night, and to the myriad familiar things that spoke to him in a friendly, voiceless language that only the jungle people can interpret.

As his mood changed Tarzan reduced his speed, and presently he dropped to the ground in a well-marked game trail. Now he let his eyes take in the

new wonders all about him. He noticed the evidences of great age as betokened by the enormous size of the trees and the hoary stems of the great
vines that clung to many of them – suggestions of age that made his own
jungle seem modern – and he marvelled at the gorgeous flowers that bloomed
in riotous profusion upon every hand, and then of a sudden something
gripped him about the body and snapped him high into the air.

Tarzan of the Apes had nodded. His mind occupied with the wonders of
this new world had permitted a momentary relaxation of that habitual wari-
ness that distinguishes creatures of the wild.

Almost in the instant of its occurrence the ape-man realized what had
befallen him. Although he could easily imagine its disastrous sequel, the suggestion of a smile touched his lips – a rueful smile – and one that was perhaps
tinged with disgust for himself, for Tarzan of the Apes had been caught in as
primitive a snare as was ever laid for unwary beasts.

A rawhide noose, attached to the downbent limb of an overhanging tree,
had been buried in the trail along which he had been passing and he had
struck the trigger – that was the whole story. But its sequel might have had
less unfortunate possibilities had the noose not pinioned his arms to his sides
as it closed about him.

He hung about six feet above the trail, caught securely about the hips, the
noose imprisoning his arms between elbows and wrists and pinioning them
securely to his sides. And to add to his discomfort and helplessness, he swung
head downward, spinning dizzily like a human plumb-bob.

He tried to draw an arm from the encircling noose so that he might reach
his hunting knife and free himself, but the weight of his body constantly
drew the noose more tightly about him and every effort upon his part seemed
but to strengthen the relentless grip of the rawhide that was pressing deep
into his flesh.

He knew that the snare meant the presence of men and that doubtless they
would soon come to inspect their noose, for his own knowledge of primitive
hunting taught him that they would not leave their snares long untended,
since in the event of a catch, if they would have it at all, they must claim it
soon lest it fall prey to carnivorous beasts or birds. He wondered what sort of
people they were and if he might not make friends with them, but whatever
they were he hoped that they would come before the beasts of prey came.
And while such thoughts were running through his mind, his keen ears
caught the sound of approaching footsteps, but they were not the steps of
men. Whatever was approaching was approaching across the wind and he
could detect no scent spoor; nor, upon the other hand, he realized, could the
beast scent him. It was coming leisurely and as it neared him, but before it
came in sight along the trail, he knew that it was a hoofed animal and, therefore, that he had little reason to fear its approach unless, indeed, it might

prove to be some strange Pellucidarian creature with characteristics entirely unlike any that he knew upon the outer crust.

But even as he permitted these thoughts partially to reassure him, there came strongly to his nostrils a scent that always caused the short hairs upon his head to rise, not in fear but in natural reaction to the presence of an hereditary enemy. It was not an odor that he had ever smelled before. It was not the scent spoor of Numa the lion, nor Sheeta the leopard, but it was the scent spoor of some sort of great cat. And now he could hear its almost silent approach through the underbrush and he knew that it was coming down toward the trail, lured either by knowledge of his presence or by that of the beast whose approach Tarzan had been awaiting.

It was the latter who came first into view – a great ox-like animal with widespread horns and shaggy coat – a huge bull that advanced several yards along the trail after Tarzan discovered it before it saw the ape-man dangling in front of it. It was the thag of Pellucidar, the Bos Primigenus of the paleontologist of the outer crust, a long extinct progenitor of the bovine races of our own world.

For a moment it stood eyeing the man dangling in its path.

Tarzan remained very quiet. He did not wish to frighten it away for he realized that one of them must be the prey of the carnivore sneaking upon them, but if he expected the thag to be frightened he soon realized his error in judgment for, uttering low grumblings, the great bull pawed the earth with a front foot, and then, lowering his massive horns, gored it angrily, and the ape-man knew that he was working his short temper up to charging pitch; nor did it seem that this was to take long for already he was advancing menacingly to the accompaniment of thunderous bellowing. His tail was up and his head down as he broke into the trot that preluded the charge.

The ape-man realized that if he was ever struck by those massive horns or that heavy head, his skull would be crushed like an eggshell.

The dizzy spinning that had been caused by the first stretching of the rawhide to his weight had lessened to a gentle turning motion, so that sometimes he faced the thag and sometimes in the opposite direction. The utter helplessness of his position galled the ape-man and gave him more concern than any consideration of impending death. From childhood he had walked hand in hand with the Grim Reaper and he had looked upon death in so many forms that it held no terror for him. He knew that it was the final experience of all created things, that it must as inevitably come to him as to others and while he loved life and did not wish to die, its mere approach induced within him no futile hysteria. But to die without a chance to fight for life was not such an end as Tarzan of the Apes would have chosen. And now, as his body slowly revolved and his eyes were turned away from the charging thag his heart sank at the thought that he was not even to be vouchsafed the meager satisfaction of meeting death face to face.

In the brief instant that he waited for the impact, the air was rent by as horrid a scream as had ever broken upon the ears of the ape-man and the bellowing of the bull rose suddenly to a higher pitch and mingled with that other awesome sound.

Once more the dangling body of the ape-man revolved and his eyes fell upon such a scene as had not been vouchsafed to men of the outer world for countless ages.

Upon the massive shoulders and neck of the great thag clung a tiger of such huge proportions that Tarzan could scarce credit the testimony of his own eyes. Great saber-like tusks, projecting from the upper jaw, were buried deep in the neck of the bull, which, instead of trying to escape, had stopped in its tracks and was endeavoring to dislodge the great beast of prey, swinging its huge horns backward in an attempt to rake the living death from its shoulders, or again shaking its whole body violently for the same purpose and all the while bellowing in pain and rage.

Gradually the saber-tooth changed its position until it had attained a hold suited to its purpose. Then with lightning-like swiftness it swung back a great forearm and delivered a single, terrific blow on the side of the thag's head – a titanic blow that crushed that mighty skull and dropped the huge bull dead in its tracks. And then the carnivore settled down to feast upon its kill.

During the battle the saber-tooth had not noticed the ape-man; nor was it until after he had commenced to feed upon the thag that his eye was attracted by the revolving body swinging above the trail a few yards away. Instantly the beast stopped feeding; his head lowered and flattened, his upper lip turned back in a hideous snarl. He watched the ape-man. Low, menacing growls rumbled from his cavernous throat; his long, sinuous tail lashed angrily as slowly he arose from the body of his kill and advanced toward Tarzan of the Apes.

III

The Great Cats

The ebbing tide of the great war had left human flotsam stranded upon many an unfamiliar beach. In its full flow it had lifted Robert Jones, high private in the ranks of a labor battalion, from uncongenial surroundings and landed him in a prison camp behind the enemy line. Here his good nature won him friends and favors, but neither one nor the other served to obtain his freedom. Robert Jones seemed to have been lost in the shuffle. And finally, when the evacuation of the prison had been completed, Robert Jones still remained, but he was not downhearted. He had learned the language of his captors and had made many friends among them. They found him a job and Robert Jones of Alabama was content to remain where he was. He had been graduated from body servant to cook of an officers' mess and it was in this capacity that he had come under the observation of Captain Zuppner, who had drafted him for the O-220 expedition.

Robert Jones yawned, stretched, turned over in his narrow berth aboard the O-220, opened his eyes and sat up with an exclamation of surprise. He jumped to the floor and stuck his head out of an open port.

'Lawd, niggah!' he exclaimed; 'you all suah done overslep' yo'sef.'

For a moment he gazed up at the noonday sun shining down upon him and then, hastily dressing, hurried into his galley.

''S funny,' he soliloquized; 'dey ain't no one stirrin' – mus' all of overslep' demsef.' He looked at the clock on the galley wall. The hour hand pointed to six. He cocked his ear and listened. 'She ain't stopped,' he muttered. Then he went to the door that opened from the galley through the ship's side and pushed it back. Leaning far out he looked up again at the sun. Then he shook his head. 'Dey's sumpin wrong,' he said. 'Ah dunno whether to cook breakfas', dinner or supper.'

Jason Gridley, emerging from his cabin, sauntered down the narrow corridor toward the galley. 'Good morning, Bob!' he said, stopping in the open doorway. 'What's the chance for a bite of breakfast?'

'Did you all say breakfas', suh?' inquired Robert.

'Yes,' replied Gridley; 'just toast and coffee and a couple of eggs – anything you have handy.'

'Ah knew it!' exclaimed the black. 'Ah knew dat ol' clock couldn't be wrong, but Mistah Sun he suah gone haywire.'

Gridley grinned. 'I'll drop down and have a little walk,' he said. 'I'll be back in fifteen minutes. Have you seen anything of Lord Greystoke?'

'No suh, Ah ain't seen nothin' o' Massa Ta'zan sence yesterday.'

'I wondered,' said Gridley; 'he is not in his cabin.'

For fifteen minutes Gridley walked briskly about in the vicinity of the ship. When he returned to the mess room he found Zuppner and Dorf awaiting breakfast and greeted them with a pleasant 'good morning.'

'I don't know whether it's good morning or good evening,' said Zuppner.

'We have been here twelve hours,' said Dorf, 'and it is just the same time that it was when we arrived. I have been on watch for the last four hours and if it hadn't been for the chronometer I could not swear that I had been on fifteen minutes or that I had not been on a week.'

'It certainly induces a feeling of unreality that is hard to explain,' said Gridley.

'Where is Greystoke?' asked Zuppner. 'He is usually an early riser.'

'I was just asking Bob,' said Gridley, 'but he has not seen him.'

'He left the ship shortly after I came on watch,' said Dorf. 'I should say about three hours ago, possibly longer. I saw him cross the open country and enter the forest.'

'I wish he had not gone out alone,' said Gridley.

'He strikes me as a man who can take care of himself,' said Zuppner.

'I have seen some things during the last four hours,' said Dorf, 'that make me doubt whether any man can take care of himself alone in this world, especially one armed only with the primitive weapons that Greystoke carried with him.'

'You mean that he carried no firearms?' demanded Zuppner.

'He was armed with a bow and arrows, a spear and a rope,' said Dorf, 'and I think he carried a hunting knife as well. But he might as well have had nothing but a peashooter if he met some of the things I have seen since I went on watch.'

'What do you mean?' demanded Zuppner. 'What have you seen?'

Dorf grinned sheepishly. 'Honestly, Captain, I hate to tell you,' he said, 'for I'm damned if I believe it myself.'

'Well, out with it,' exclaimed Zuppner. 'We will make allowances for your youth and for the effect that the sun and horizon of Pellucidar may have had upon your eyesight or your veracity.'

'Well,' said Dorf, 'about an hour ago a bear passed within a hundred yards of the ship.'

'There is nothing remarkable about that,' said Zuppner.

'There was a great deal that was remarkable about the bear, however,' said Dorf.

'In what way?' asked Gridley.

'It was fully as large as an ox,' said Dorf, 'and if I were going out after bear in this country I should want to take along field artillery.'

'Was that all you saw – just a bear?' asked Zuppner.

'No,' said Dorf, 'I saw tigers, not one but fully a dozen, and they were as much larger than our Bengal tigers as the bear was larger than any bear of the outer crust that I have ever seen. They were perfectly enormous and they were armed with the most amazing fangs you ever saw – great curved fangs that extended from their upper jaws to lengths of from eight inches to a foot. They came down to this stream here to drink and then wandered away, some of them toward the forest and some down toward that big river yonder.'

'Greystoke couldn't do much against such creatures as those even if he had carried a rifle,' said Zuppner.

'If he was in the forest, he could escape them,' said Gridley.

Zuppner shook his head. 'I don't like the looks of it,' he said. 'I wish that he had not gone out alone.'

'The bear and the tigers were bad enough,' continued Dorf, 'but I saw another creature that to me seemed infinitely worse.'

Robert, who was more or less a privileged character, had entered from the galley and was listening with wide-eyed interest to Dorf's account of the creatures he had seen, while Victor, one of the Filipino cabin-boys, served the officers.

'Yes,' continued Dorf, 'I saw a mighty strange creature. It flew directly over the ship and I had an excellent view of it. At first I thought that it was a bird, but when it approached more closely I saw that it was a winged reptile. It had a long, narrow head and it flew so close that I could see its great jaws, armed with an infinite number of long, sharp teeth. Its head was elongated above the eyes and came to a sharp point. It was perfectly immense and must have had a wing spread of at least twenty feet. While I was watching it, it dropped suddenly to earth only a short distance beyond the ship, and when it arose again it was carrying in its talons some animal that must have been fully as large as a good sized sheep, with which it flew away without apparent effort. That the creature is carnivorous is evident as is also the fact that it has sufficient strength to carry away a man.'

Robert Jones covered his large mouth with a pink palm and with hunched and shaking shoulders turned and tiptoed from the room. Once in the galley with the door closed, he gave himself over to unrestrained mirth.

'What is the matter with you?' asked Victor.

'Lawd-a-massy!' exclaimed Robert. 'Ah allus thought some o' dem gem'n in dat dere Adventurous Club in Bummingham could lie some, but, shucks, dey ain't in it with this Lieutenant Dorf. Did you all heah him tell about dat flyin' snake what carries off sheep?'

But back in the mess room the white men took Dorf's statement more seriously.

'That would be a pterodactyl,' said Zuppner.

'Yes,' replied Dorf. 'I classified it as a Pteranodon.'

'Don't you think we ought to send out a search party?' asked Gridley.

'I am afraid Greystoke would not like it,' replied Zuppner.

'It could go out under the guise of a hunting party,' suggested Dorf.

'If he has not returned within an hour,' said Zuppner, 'we shall have to do something of the sort.'

Hines and Von Horst now entered the mess room, and when they learned of Tarzan's absence from the ship and had heard from Dorf a description of some of the animals that he might have encountered, they were equally as apprehensive as the others of his safety.

'We might cruise around a bit, sir,' suggested Von Horst to Zuppner.

'But suppose he returns to this spot during our absence?' asked Gridley.

'Could you return the ship to this anchorage again?' inquired Zuppner.

'I doubt it,' replied the Lieutenant. 'Our instruments are almost worthless under the conditions existing in Pellucidar.'

'Then we had better remain where we are,' said Gridley, 'until he returns.'

'But if we send a searching party after him on foot, what assurance have we that it will be able to find its way back to the ship?' demanded Zuppner.

'That will not be so difficult,' said Gridley. 'We can always blaze our trail as we go and thus easily retrace our steps.'

'Yes, that is so,' agreed Zuppner.

'Suppose,' said Gridley, 'that Von Horst and I go out with Muviro and his Waziri. They are experienced trackers, prime fighting men and they certainly know the jungle.'

'Not this jungle,' said Dorf.

'But at least they know any jungle better than the rest of us,' insisted Gridley.

'I think your plan is a good one,' said Zuppner, 'and anyway as you are in command now, the rest of us gladly place ourselves under your orders.'

'The conditions that confront us here are new to all of us,' said Gridley. 'Nothing that any one of us can suggest or command can be based upon any personal experience or knowledge that the rest do not possess, and in matters of this kind I think that we had better reach our decision after full discussion rather than to depend blindly upon official priority of authority.'

'That has been Greystoke's policy,' said Zuppner, 'and it has made it very easy and pleasant for all of us. I quite agree with you, but I can think of no more feasible plan than that which you have suggested.'

'Very good,' said Gridley. 'Will you accompany me, Lieutenant?' he asked, turning to Von Horst.

The officer grinned. 'Will I?' he exclaimed. 'I should never have forgiven you if you had left me out of it.'

'Fine,' said Gridley. 'And now, I think, we might as well make our preparations at once and get as early a start as possible. See that the Waziri have eaten, Lieutenant, and tell Muviro that I want them armed with rifles. These fellows can use them all right but they rather look with scorn upon anything more modern than their war spears and arrows.'

'Yes, I discovered that,' said Hines. 'Muviro told me a few days ago that his people consider firearms as something of an admission of cowardice. He told me that they use them for target practice, but when they go out after lions or rhino they leave their rifles behind and take their spears and arrows.'

'After they have seen what I saw,' said Dorf, 'they will have more respect for an express rifle.'

'See that they take plenty of ammunition, Von Horst,' said Gridley, 'for from what I have seen in this country we shall not have to carry any provisions.'

'A man who could not live off this country would starve to death in a meat market,' said Zuppner.

Von Horst left to carry out Gridley's orders while the latter returned to his cabin to prepare for the expedition.

The officers and crew remaining with the O-220 were all on hand to bid farewell to the expedition starting out in search of Tarzan of the Apes, and as the ten stalwart Waziri warriors marched away behind Gridley and Von Horst, Robert Jones, watching from the galley door, swelled with pride. 'Dem niggahs is sho nuf hot babies,' he exclaimed. 'All dem flyin' snakes bettah clear out de country now.' With the others Robert watched the little party as it crossed the plain and until it had disappeared within the dark precincts of the forest upon the opposite side. Then he glanced up at the noonday sun, shook his head, elevated his palms in resignation and turned back into his galley.

Almost immediately after the party had left the ship, Gridley directed Muviro to take the lead and watch for Tarzan's trail since, of the entire party, he was the most experienced tracker; nor did the Waziri chieftain have any difficulty in following the spoor of the ape-man across the plain and into the forest, but here, beneath a great tree, it disappeared.

'The Big Bwana took to the trees here,' said Muviro, 'and no man lives who can follow his spoor through the lower, the middle or the upper terraces.'

'What do you suggest, then, Muviro?' asked Gridley.

'If this were his own jungle,' replied the warrior, 'I should feel sure that when he took to the trees he would move in a straight line toward the place he wished to go; unless he happened to be hunting, in which case his direction would be influenced by the sign and scent of game.'

'Doubtless he was hunting here,' said Von Horst.

'If he was hunting,' said Muviro, 'he would have moved in a straight line until he caught the scent spoor of game or came to a well-beaten game trail.'

'And then what would he do?' asked Gridley.

'He might wait above the trail,' replied Muviro, 'or he might follow it. In a new country like this, I think he would follow it, for he has always been interested in exploring every new country he entered.'

'Then let us push straight into the forest in this same direction until we strike a game trail,' said Gridley.

Muviro and three of his warriors went ahead, cutting brush where it was necessary and blazing the trees at frequent intervals that they might more easily retrace their steps to the ship. With the aid of a small pocket compass Gridley directed the line of advance, which otherwise it would have been difficult to hold accurately beneath that eternal noonday sun, whose warm rays filtered down through the foliage of the forest.

'God! What a forest!' exclaimed Von Horst. 'To search for a man here is like the proverbial search for the needle in a haystack.'

'Except,' said Gridley, 'that one might stand a slight chance of finding the needle.'

'Perhaps we had better fire a shot occasionally,' suggested Von Horst.

'Excellent,' said Gridley. 'The rifles carry a much heavier charge and make a louder report than our revolvers.'

After warning the others of his intention, he directed one of the blacks to fire three shots at intervals of a few seconds, for neither Gridley nor Von Horst was armed with rifles, each of the officers carrying two 45 caliber Colts. Thereafter, at intervals of about half an hour, a single shot was fired, but as the searching party forced its way on into the forest each of its members became gloomily impressed with the futility of their search.

Presently the nature of the forest changed. The trees were set less closely together and the underbrush, while still forming an almost impenetrable screen, was less dense than it had been heretofore and here they came upon a wide game trail, worn by countless hoofs and padded feet to a depth of two feet or more below the surface of the surrounding ground, and here Jason Gridley blundered.

'We won't bother about blazing the trees as long as we follow this trail,' he said to Muviro, 'except at such places as it may fork or be crossed by other trails.'

It was, after all, a quite natural mistake since a few blazed trees along the trail would not serve any purpose in following it back when they wished to return.

The going here was easier and as the Waziri warriors swung along at a brisk pace, the miles dropped quickly behind them and already had the noonday sun so cast its spell upon them that the element of time seemed not to enter into their calculations, while the teeming life about them absorbed the attention of blacks and whites alike.

Strange monkeys, some of them startlingly man-like in appearance and of large size, watched them pass. Birds of both gay and somber plumage scattered protestingly before their advance, and again dim bulks loomed through the undergrowth and the sound of padded feet was everywhere.

At times they would pass through a stretch of forest as silent as the tomb, and then again they seemed to be surrounded by a bedlam of hideous growls and roars and screams.

'I'd like to see some of those fellows,' said Von Horst, after a particularly savage outburst of sound.

'I am surprised that we haven't,' replied Gridley; 'but I imagine that they are a little bit leery of us right now, not alone on account of our numbers but because of the, to them, strange and unfamiliar odors which must surround us. These would naturally increase the suspicion which must have been aroused by the sound of our shots.'

'Have you noticed,' said Von Horst, 'that most of the noise seems to come from behind us; I mean the more savage, growling sounds. I have heard squeals and noises that sounded like the trumpeting of elephants to the right and to the left and ahead, but only an occasional growl or roar seems to come from these directions and then always at a considerable distance.'

'How do you account for it?' asked Gridley.

'I can't account for it,' replied Von Horst. 'It is as though we were moving along in the center of a procession with all the savage carnivores behind us.'

'This perpetual noonday sun has its compensations,' remarked Gridley with a laugh, 'for at least it insures that we shall not have to spend the night here.'

At that instant the attention of the two men was attracted by an exclamation from one of the Waziri behind them. 'Look, Bwana! Look!' cried the man, pointing back along the trail. Following the direction of the Waziri's extended finger, Gridley and Von Horst saw a huge beast slinking slowly along the trail in their rear.

'God!' exclaimed Von Horst, 'and I thought Dorf was exaggerating.'

'It doesn't seem possible,' exclaimed Gridley, 'that five hundred miles below our feet automobiles are dashing through crowded streets lined by enormous buildings; that there the telegraph, the telephone and the radio are so commonplace as to excite no comment; that countless thousands live out their entire lives without ever having to use a weapon in self-defense, and yet at the same instant we stand here facing a saber-tooth tiger in surroundings that may not have existed upon the outer crust for a million years.'

'Look at them!' exclaimed Von Horst. 'If there is one there are a dozen of them.'

'Shall we fire, Bwana?' asked one of the Waziri.

'Not yet,' said Gridley. 'Close up and be ready. They seem to be only following us.'

Slowly the party fell back, a line of Waziri in the rear facing the tigers and backing slowly away from them. Muviro dropped back to Gridley's side.

'For a long time, Bwana,' he said, 'there has been the spoor of many elephants in the trail, or spoor that looked like the spoor of elephants, though it was different. And just now I sighted some of the beasts ahead. I could not make them out distinctly, but if they are not elephants they are very much like them.'

'We seem to be between the devil and the deep sea,' said Von Horst.

'And there are either elephants or tigers on each side of us,' said Muviro. 'I can hear them moving through the brush.'

Perhaps the same thought was in the minds of all these men, that they might take to the trees, but for some reason no one expressed it. And so they continued to move slowly along the trail until suddenly it broke into a large, open area in the forest, where the ground was scantily covered with brush and there were few trees. Perhaps a hundred acres were included in the clearing and then the forest commenced again upon all sides.

And into the clearing, along numerous trails that seemed to center at this spot, came as strange a procession as the eyes of these men had ever rested upon. There were great ox-like creatures with shaggy coats and wide-spreading horns. There were red deer and sloths of gigantic size. There were mastodon and mammoth, and a huge, elephantine creature that resembled an elephant and yet did not seem to be an elephant at all. Its great head was four feet long and three feet wide. It had a short, powerful trunk and from its lower jaw mighty tusks curved downward, their points bending inward toward the body. At the shoulder it stood at least ten feet above the ground, and in length it must have been fully twenty feet. But what resemblance it bore to an elephant was lessened by its small, pig-like ears.

The two white men, momentarily forgetting the tigers behind them in their amazement at the sight ahead, halted and looked with wonder upon the huge gathering of creatures within the clearing.

'Did you ever see anything like it?' exclaimed Gridley.

'No, nor anyone else,' replied Von Horst.

'I could catalog a great many of them,' said Gridley, 'although practically all are extinct upon the outer crust. But that fellow there gets me,' and he pointed to the elphantine creature with the downward pointing tusks.

'A dinotherium of the Miocene,' said Von Horst.

Muviro had stopped beside the two whites and was gazing in wide-eyed astonishment at the scene before him.

'Well,' asked Gridley, 'what do you make of it, Muviro?'

'I think I understand now, Bwana,' replied the black, 'and if we are ever going to escape our one chance is to cross that clearing as quickly as possible. The great cats are herding these creatures here and presently there will be such a killing as the eyes of man have never before seen. If we are not killed by the cats, we shall be trampled to death by these beasts in their efforts to escape or to fight the tigers.'

'I believe you are right, Muviro,' said Gridley.

'There is an opening just ahead of us,' said Von Horst.

Gridley called the men around him and pointed out across the clearing to the forest upon the opposite side. 'Apparently our only chance now,' he said, 'is to cross before the cats close in on these beasts. We have already come into the clearing too far to try to take refuge in the trees on this side for the saber-tooths are too close. Stick close together and fire at nothing unless we are charged.'

'Look!' exclaimed Von Horst. 'The tigers are entering the clearing from all sides. They have surrounded their quarry.'

'There is still the one opening ahead of us, Bwana,' said Muviro.

Already the little party was moving slowly across the clearing, which was covered with nervous beasts moving irritably to and fro, their whole demeanor marked by nervous apprehension. Prior to the advent of the tigers the animals had been moving quietly about, some of them grazing on the short grass of the clearing or upon the leaves and twigs of the scattered trees growing in it; but with the appearance of the first of the carnivores their attitude changed. A huge bull mastodon raised his trunk and trumpeted shrilly, and instantly every herbivore was on the alert. And as eyes or nostrils detected the presence of the great cats, or the beasts became excited by the excitement of their fellows, each added his voice to the pandemonium that now reigned. To the squealing, trumpeting and bellowing of the quarry were added the hideous growls and roars of the carnivores.

'Look at those cats!' cried Von Horst. 'There must be hundreds of them.' Nor was his estimate an exaggeration for from all sides of the clearing, with the exception of a single point opposite them, the cats were emerging from the forest and starting to circle the herd. That they did not rush it immediately evidenced their respect for the huge beasts they had corraled, the majority of which they would not have dared to attack except in superior numbers.

Now a mammoth, a giant bull with tail raised and ears up-cocked, curled his trunk above his head and charged. But a score of the great cats, growling hideously, sprang to meet him, and the bull, losing his nerve, wheeled in a wide circle and returned to the herd. Had he gone through that menacing line of fangs and talons, as with his great size and weight and strength he might have done, he would have opened a hole through which a stampede of the other animals would have carried the bulk of them to safety.

The frightened herbivores, their attention centered upon the menacing tigers, paid little attention to the insignificant man-things passing among them. But there were some exceptions. A thag, bellowing and pawing the earth directly in their line of march, terrified by the odor of the carnivores and aroused and angered by the excited trumpeting and squealing of the creatures about him, seeking to vent his displeasure upon something, lowered his head and charged them. A Waziri warrior raised his rifle to his shoulder and fired, and a prehistoric Bos Primigenus crashed to the impact of a modern bullet.

As the report of the rifle sounded above the other noises of the clearing, the latter were momentarily stilled, and the full attention of hunters and hunted was focused upon the little band of men, so puny and insignificant in the presence of the mighty beasts of another day. A dinotherium, his little ears up-cocked, his tail stiffly erect, walked slowly toward them. Almost immediately others followed his example until it seemed that the whole aggregation was converging upon them. The forest was yet a hundred yards away as Jason Gridley realized the seriousness of the emergency that now confronted them.

'We shall have to run for it,' he said. 'Give them a volley, and then beat it for the trees. If they charge, it will have to be every man for himself.'

The Waziri wheeled and faced the slowly advancing herd and then, at Gridley's command, they fired. The thunderous volley had its effect upon the advancing beasts. They hesitated and then turned and retreated; but behind them were the carnivores. And once again they swung back in the direction of the men, who were now moving rapidly toward the forest.

'Here they come!' cried Von Horst. And a backward glance revealed the fact that the entire herd, goaded to terror by the tigers behind them, had broken into a mad stampede. Whether or not it was a direct charge upon the little party of men is open to question, but the fact that they lay in its path was sufficient to seal their doom if they were unable to reach the safety of the forest ahead of the charging quadrupeds.

'Give them another volley!' cried Gridley. And again the Waziri turned and fired. A dinotherium, a thag and two mammoths stumbled and fell to the ground, but the remainder of the herd did not pause. Leaping over the carcasses of their fallen comrades they thundered down upon the fleeing men.

It was now, in truth, every man for himself, and so close pressed were they that even the brave Waziri threw away their rifles as useless encumbrances to flight.

Several of the red deer, swifter in flight than the other members of the herd, had taken the lead, and, stampeding through the party, scattered them to left and right.

Gridley and Von Horst were attempting to cover the retreat of the Waziri and check the charge of the stampeding animals with their revolvers. They succeeded in turning a few of the leaders, but presently a great red stag passed between them, forcing them to jump quickly apart to escape his heavy antlers, and behind him swept a nightmare of terrified beasts forcing them still further apart. Not far from Gridley grew a single, giant tree, a short distance from the edge of the clearing, and finding himself alone and cut off from further retreat, the American turned and ran for it, while Von Horst was forced to bolt for the jungle which was now almost within reach.

Bowled over by a huge sloth, Gridley scrambled to his feet, and, passing in front of a fleeing mastodon, reached the tree just as the main body of the stampeding herd closed about it. Its great bole gave him momentary protection and an instant later he had scrambled among its branches.

Instantly his first thought was for his fellows, but where they had been a moment before was now only a solid mass of leaping, plunging, terrified beasts. No sign of a human being was anywhere to be seen and Gridley knew that no living thing could have survived the trampling of those incalculable tons of terrified flesh.

Some of them, he knew, must have reached the forest, but he doubted that all had come through in safety and he feared particularly for Von Horst, who had been some little distance in rear of the Waziri.

The eyes of the American swept back over the clearing to observe such a scene as probably in all the history of the world had never before been vouchsafed to the eyes of man. Literally thousands of creatures, large and small, were following their leaders in a break for life and liberty, while upon their flanks and at their rear hundreds of savage saber tooth tigers leaped upon them, dragging down the weaker, battling with the stronger, leaving the maimed and crippled behind that they might charge into the herd again and drag down others.

The mad rush of the leaders across the clearing had been checked as they entered the forest, and now those in the rear were forced to move more slowly, but in their terror they sought to clamber over the backs of those ahead. Red deer leaped upon the backs of mastodons and fled across the heaving bodies beneath them, as a mountain goat might leap from rock to rock. Mammoths raised their huge bulks upon lesser animals and crushed them to the ground. Tusks and horns were red with gore as the maddened beasts battled for their lives. The scene was sickening in its horror, and yet fascinating in its primitive strength and savagery – and everywhere were the great, savage cats.

Slowly they were cutting into the herd from both sides in an effort to encircle a portion of it and at last they were successful, though within the circle there remained but a few scattered beasts that were still unmaimed or uncrippled. And then the great tigers turned upon these, closing in and drawing tighter their hideous band of savage fury.

In twos and threes and scores they leaped upon the remaining beasts and dragged them down until the sole creature remaining alive within their circle was a gigantic bull mammoth. His shaggy coat was splashed with blood and his tusks were red with gore. Trumpeting, he stood at bay, a magnificent picture of primordial power, of sagacity, of courage.

The heart of the American went out to that lone warrior trumpeting his challenge to overwhelming odds in the face of certain doom.

By hundreds the carnivores were closing in upon the great bull; yet it was evident that even though they outnumbered him so overwhelmingly, they still held him in vast respect. Growling and snarling, a few of them slunk in stealthy circles about him, and as he wheeled about with them, three of them charged him from the rear. With a swiftness that matched their own, the pachyderm wheeled to meet them. Two of them he caught upon his tusks and tossed them high into the air, and at the same instant a score of others rushed him from each side and from the rear and fastened themselves to his back and flanks. Down he went as though struck by lightning, squatting quickly upon his haunches and rolling over backward, crushing a dozen tigers before they could escape.

Gridley could scarce repress a cheer as the great fellow staggered to his feet and threw himself again upon the opposite side to the accompaniment of hideous screams of pain and anger from the tigers he pinioned beneath him. But now he was gushing blood from a hundred wounds, and other scores of the savage carnivores were charging him.

Though he put up a magnificent battle the end was inevitable and at last they dragged him down, tearing him to pieces while he yet struggled to rise again and battle with them.

And then commenced the aftermath as the savage beasts fought among themselves for possession of their prey. For even though there was flesh to more than surfeit them all, in their greed, jealousy and ferocity, they must still battle one with another.

That they had paid heavily for their meat was evident by the carcasses or the tigers strewn about the clearing and as the survivors slowly settled down to feed, there came the jackals, the hyaenodons and the wild dogs to feast upon their leavings.

IV

The Sagoths

As the great cat slunk toward him, Tarzan of the Apes realized that at last he faced inevitable death, yet even in that last moment of life the emotion which dominated him was one of admiration for the magnificent beast drawing angrily toward him.

Tarzan of the Apes would have preferred to die fighting, if he must die; yet he felt a certain thrill as he contemplated the magnificence of the great beast that Fate had chosen to terminate his earthly career. He felt no fear, but a certain sense of anticipation of what would follow after death. The Lord of the Jungle subscribed to no creed. Tarzan of the Apes was not a church man; yet like the majority of those who have always lived close to nature he was, in a sense, intensely religious. His intimate knowledge of the stupendous forces of nature, of her wonders and her miracles had impressed him with the fact that their ultimate origin lay far beyond the conception of the finite mind of man, and thus incalculably remote from the farthest bounds of science.

When he thought of God he liked to think of Him primitively, as a personal God. And while he realized that he knew nothing of such matters, he liked to believe that after death he would live again.

Many thoughts passed quickly through his mind as the saber-tooth advanced upon him. He was watching the long, glistening fangs that so soon were to be buried in his flesh when his attention was attracted by a sound among the trees about him. That the great cat had heard too was evident, for it stopped in its tracks and gazed up into the foliage of the trees above. And then Tarzan heard a rustling in the branches directly overhead, and looking up he saw what appeared to be a gorilla glaring down upon him.

Two more savage faces showed through the foliage above him and then in other trees about he caught glimpses of similar shaggy forms and fierce faces. He saw that they were like gorillas, and yet unlike them; that in some respects they were more man than gorilla, and in others more gorilla than man. He caught glimpses of great clubs wielded by hairy hands, and when his eyes returned to the saber-tooth he saw that the great beast had hesitated in its advance and was snarling and growling angrily as its eyes roved upward and around at the savage creatures glaring down upon it.

It was only for a moment that the cat paused in its advance upon the ape-man. Snarling angrily, it moved forward again and as it did so, one of the creatures in the tree above Tarzan reached down, and seizing the rope that held him dangling in mid-air, drew him swiftly upward. Then several things occurred simultaneously – the saber-tooth leaped to retrieve its prey and a dozen heavy cudgels hurtled through the air from the surrounding trees, striking the great cat heavily upon head and body with the result that the talons that must otherwise have inevitably been imbedded in the flesh of the ape-man grazed harmlessly by him, and an instant later he was drawn well up among the branches of the tree, where he was seized by three hairy brutes whose attitude suggested that he might have been as well off had he been left to the tender mercies of the saber-tooth.

Two of them, one on either side, seized an arm and the third grasped him by the throat with one hand while he held his cudgel poised above his head in the other. And then from the lips of the creature facing him came a sound that fell as startlingly upon the ears of the ape-man as had the first unexpected roar of the saber-tooth, but with far different effect.

'Ka-goda!' said the creature facing Tarzan.

In the language of the apes of his own jungle Ka-goda may be roughly interpreted according to its inflection as a command to surrender, or as an interrogation, 'do you surrender?' or as a declaration of surrender.

This word, coming from the lips of a hairy gorilla man of the inner world, suggested possibilities of the most startling nature. For years Tarzan had considered the language of the great apes as the primitive root language of created things. The great apes, the lesser apes, the gorillas, the baboons and the monkeys utilized this with various degrees of refinement and many of its words were understood by jungle animals of other species and by many of the birds; but, perhaps, after the fashion that our domestic animals have learned many of the words in our vocabulary, with this difference that the language of the great apes has doubtless persisted unchanged for countless ages.

That these gorilla men of the inner world used even one word of this language suggested one of two possibilities – either they held an origin in common with the creatures of the outer crust, or else that the laws of evolution and progress were so constant that this was the only form of primitive language that could have been possible to any creatures emerging from the lower orders toward the estate of man. But the suggestion that impressed Tarzan most vividly was that this single word, uttered by the creature grasping him by the throat, postulated familiarity on the part of his fierce captors with the entire ape language that he had used since boyhood.

'Ka-goda?' inquired the bull.

'Ka-goda,' said Tarzan of the Apes.

The brute, facing Tarzan, half lowered his cudgel as though he were surprised to hear the prisoner answer in his own tongue. 'Who are you?' he demanded in the language of the great apes.

'I am Tarzan – mighty hunter, mighty fighter,' replied the ape-man.

'What are you doing in M'wa-lot's country?' demanded the gorilla man.

'I come as a friend,' replied Tarzan. 'I have no quarrel with your people.'

The fellow had lowered his club now, and from other trees had come a score more of the shaggy creatures until the surrounding limbs sagged beneath their weight.

'How did you learn the language of the Sagoths?' demanded the bull. 'We have captured gilaks in the past, but you are the first one who ever spoke or understood our language.'

'It is the language of my people,' replied Tarzan. 'As a little balu, I learned it from Kala and other apes of the tribe of Kerchak.'

'We never heard of the tribe of Kerchak,' said the bull.

'Perhaps he is not telling the truth,' said another. 'Let us kill him; he is only a gilak.'

'No,' said a third. 'Take him back to M'wa-lot that the whole tribe of M'wa-lot may join in the killing.'

'That is good,' said another. 'Take him back to the tribe, and while we are killing him we shall dance.'

The language of the great apes is not like our language. It sounds to man like growling and barking and grunting, punctuated at times by shrill screams, and it is practically untranslatable to any tongue known to man; yet it carried to Tarzan and the Sagoths the sense that we have given it. It is a means of communicating thought and there its similarity to the languages of men ceases.

Having decided upon the disposition of their prisoner, the Sagoths now turned their attention to the saber-tooth, who had returned to his kill, across the body of which he was lying. He was not feeding, but was gazing angrily up into the trees at his tormentors.

While three of the gorilla men secured Tarzan's wrists behind his back with a length of buckskin thong, the others renewed their attention to the tiger. Three or four of them would cast well-aimed cudgels at his face at intervals so nicely timed that the great beast could do nothing but fend off the missiles as they sped toward him. And while he was thus occupied, the other Sagoths, who had already cast their clubs, sprang to the ground and retrieved them with an agility and celerity that would have done credit to the tiniest monkey of the jungle. The risk that they took bespoke great self-confidence and high courage since often they were compelled to snatch their cudgels from almost beneath the claws of the saber-tooth.

Battered and bruised, the great cat gave back inch by inch until, unable to stand the fusillade longer, it suddenly turned tail and bounded into the underbrush, where for some time the sound of its crashing retreat could be distinctly heard. And with the departure of the carnivore, the gorilla men leaped to the ground and fell upon the carcass of the thag. With heavy fangs they tore its flesh, oftentimes fighting among themselves like wild beasts for some particularly choice morsel; but unlike many of the lower orders of man upon similar occasions they did not gorge themselves, and having satisfied their hunger they left what remained to the jackals and wild dogs that had already gathered.

Tarzan of the Apes, silent spectator of this savage scene, had an opportunity during the feast to examine his captors more closely. He saw that they were rather lighter in build than the gorillas he had seen in his own native jungle, but even though they were not as heavy as Bolgani, they were yet mighty creatures. Their arms and legs were of more human conformation and proportion than those of a gorilla, but the shaggy brown hair covering their entire body increased their beast-like appearance, while their faces were even more brutal than that of Bolgani himself, except that the development of the skull denoted a brain capacity seemingly as great as that of man.

They were entirely naked, nor was there among them any suggestion of ornamentation, while their only weapons were clubs. These, however, showed indications of having been shaped by some sharp instrument as though an effort had been made to insure a firm grip and a well-balanced weapon.

Their feeding completed, the Sagoths turned back along the game trail in the same direction that Tarzan had been going when he had sprung the trigger of the snare. But before departing several of them reset the noose, covered it carefully with earth and leaves and set the trigger that it might be sprung by the first passing animal.

So sure were all their movements and so deft their fingers, Tarzan realized that though these creatures looked like beasts they had long since entered the estate of man. Perhaps they were still low in the scale of evolution, but unquestionably they were men with the brains of men and the faces and skins of gorillas.

As the Sagoths moved along the jungle trail they walked erect as men walk, but in other ways they reminded Tarzan of the great apes who were his own people, for they were given neither to laughter nor song and their taciturnity suggested the speechlessness of the alali. That certain of their sense faculties were more highly developed than in man was evidenced by the greater dependence they placed upon their ears and noses than upon their eyes in their unremitting vigil against surprise by an enemy.

While by human standards they might have been judged ugly and even hideous, they did not so impress Tarzan of the Apes, who recognized in them a certain primitive majesty of bearing and mien such as might well have been expected of pioneers upon the frontiers of humanity.

It is sometimes the custom of theorists to picture our primordial progenitors as timid, fearful creatures, fleeing from the womb to the grave in constant terror of the countless, savage creatures that beset their entire existence. But as it does not seem reasonable that a creature so poorly equipped for offense and defense could have survived without courage, it seems far more consistent to assume that with the dawning of reason came a certain superiority complex – a vast and at first stupid egotism – that knew caution, perhaps, but not fear; nor is any other theory tenable unless we are to suppose that from the loin of a rabbit-hearted creature sprang men who hunted the bison, the mammoth and the cave bear with crude spears tipped with stone.

The Sagoths of Pellucidar may have been analogous in the scale of evolution to the Neanderthal men of the outer crust, or they may, indeed, have been even a step lower; yet in their bearing there was nothing to suggest to Tarzan that they had reached this stage in evolution through the expedience of flight. Their bearing as they trod the jungle trail bespoke assurance and even truculence, as though they were indeed the lords of creation, fearing nothing. Perhaps Tarzan understood their attitude better than another might have since it had been his own always in the jungle – unquestioning fearlessness – with which a certain intelligent caution was not inconsistent.

They had come but a short distance from the scene of Tarzan's capture when the Sagoths stopped beside a hollow log, the skeleton of a great tree that had fallen beside the trail. One of the creatures tapped upon the log with his club – one, two; one, two; one, two, three. And then, after a moment's pause, he repeated the same tapping. Three times the signal boomed through the jungle and then the signaler paused, listening, while others stopped and put their ears against the ground.

Faintly through the air, more plainly through the ground, came an answering signal – one, two; one, two; one, two, three.

The creatures seemed satisfied and, climbing into the surrounding trees, disposed themselves comfortably as though settling down to a wait. Two of them carried Tarzan easily aloft with them, as with his hands bound behind his back he could not climb unassisted.

Since they had started on the march Tarzan had not spoken, but now he turned to one of the Sagoths near him. 'Remove the bonds from my wrists,' he said. 'I am not an enemy.'

'Tar-gash,' said he whom Tarzan had addressed, 'the gilak wants his bonds removed.'

Tar-gash, a large bull with noticeably long, white canine fangs, turned his savage eyes upon the ape-man. For a long time he glared unblinkingly at the prisoner and it seemed to Tarzan that the mind of the half-brute was struggling with a new idea. Presently he turned to the Sagoth who had repeated Tarzan's request. 'Take them off,' he said.

'Why?' demanded another of the bulls. The tone was challenging.

'Because I, Tar-gash, say "take them off,"' growled the other.

'You are not M'wa-lot. He is king. If M'wa-lot says take them off, we will take them off.'

'I am not M'wa-lot, To-yad; I am Tar-gash, and Tar-gash says "take them off."'

To-yad swung to Tarzan's side. 'M'wa-lot will come soon,' he said. 'If M'wa-lot says take them off, we shall take them off. We do not take orders from Tar-gash.'

Like a panther, quickly, silently, Tar-gash sprang straight for the throat of To-yad. There was no warning, not even an instant of hesitation. In this Tarzan saw that Tar-gash differed from the great apes with whom the Lord of the Jungle had been familiar upon the outer crust, for among them two bulls ordinarily must need have gone through a long preliminary of stiff-legged strutting and grumbled invective before either one launched himself upon the other in deadly combat. But the mind of Tar-gash had functioned with like celerity, so much so that decision and action had appeared to be almost simultaneous.

The impact of the heavy body of Tar-gash toppled To-yad from the branch upon which he had been standing, but so naturally arboreal were the two great creatures that even as they fell they reached out and seized the same branch and still fighting, each with his free hand and his heavy fangs, they hung there a second breaking their fall, and then dropped to the ground.

They fought almost silently except for low growls, Tar-gash seeking the jugular of To-yad with those sharp, white fangs that had given him his name. To-yad, his every faculty concentrated upon defense, kept the grinning jaws from his flesh and suddenly twisting quickly around, tore loose from the powerful fingers of his opponent and sought safety in flight. But like a football player, Tar-gash launched himself through the air; his long hairy arms encircled the legs of the fleeing To-yad, bringing him heavily to the ground, and an instant later the powerful aggressor was on the back of his opponent and To-yad's jugular was at the mercy of his foe, but the great jaws of Tar-gash did not close.

'Ka-goda?' he inquired.

'Ka-goda,' growled To-yad, and instantly Tar-gash arose from the body of the other bull.

With the agility of a monkey the victor leaped back into the branches of the tree. 'Remove the bonds from the wrists of the gilak,' he said, and at the same time he glared ferociously about him to see if there was another so mutinously minded as To-yad; but none spoke and none objected as one of the Sagoths who had dragged Tarzan up into the tree untied the bonds that secured his wrists.

'If he tries to run away from us,' said Tar-gash, 'kill him.'

When his bonds were removed Tarzan expected that the Sagoths would take his knife away from him. He had lost his spear and bow and most of his arrows at the instant that the snare had snapped him from the ground, but though they had lain in plain view in the trail beneath the snare the Sagoths had paid no attention to them; nor did they now pay any attention to his knife. He was sure they must have seen it and he could not understand their lack of concern regarding it, unless they were ignorant of its purpose or held him in such contempt that they did not consider it worth the effort to disarm him.

Presently To-yad sneaked back into the tree, but he huddled sullenly by himself, apart from the others.

Faintly, from a distance, Tarzan heard something approaching. He heard it just a moment before the Sagoths heard it.

'They come!' announced Tar-gash.

'M'wa-lot comes,' said another, glancing at To-yad. Now Tarzan knew why the primitive drum had been sounded, but he wondered why they were gathering.

At last they arrived, nor was it difficult for Tarzan to recognize M'wa-lot, the king among the others. A great bull walked in front – a bull with so much gray among the hairs on his face that the latter had a slightly bluish complexion, and instantly the ape-man saw how the king had come by his name.

As soon as the Sagoths with Tarzan were convinced of the identity of the approaching party, they descended from the trees to the ground and when M'wa-lot had approached within twenty paces of them, he halted. 'I am M'wa-lot,' he announced. 'With me are the people of my tribe.'

'I am Tar-gash,' replied the bull who seemed to be in charge of the other party. 'With me are other bulls of the tribe of M'wa-lot.'

This precautionary preliminary over, M'wa-lot advanced, followed by the bulls, the shes and the balus of his tribe.

'What is that?' demanded M'wa-lot, as his fierce eyes espied Tarzan.

'It is a gilak that we found caught in our snare,' replied Tar-gash.

'That is the feast that you called us to?' demanded M'wa-lot, angrily. 'You should have brought it to the tribe. It can walk.'

'This is not the food of which the drum spoke,' replied Tar-gash. 'Nearby is the body of a thag that was killed by a tarag close by the snare in which this gilak was caught.'

'Ugh!' grunted M'wa-lot. 'We can eat the gilak later.'

'We can have a dance,' suggested one of Tarzan's captors. 'We have eaten and slept many times since we have danced, M'wa-lot.'

As the Sagoths, guided by Tar-gash, proceeded along the trail towards the body of the thag, the shes with balus growled savagely when one of the little ones chanced to come near to Tarzan. The bulls eyed him suspiciously and all seemed uneasy because of his presence. In these and in other ways the Sagoths were reminiscent of the apes of the tribe of Kerchak and to such an extent was this true that Tarzan, although a prisoner among them, felt strangely at home in this new environment.

A short distance ahead of the ape-man walked M'wa-lot, king of the tribe, and at M'wa-lot's elbow was To-yad. The two spoke in low tones and from the frequent glances they cast at Tar-gash, who walked ahead of them, it was evident that he was the subject of their conversation, the effect of which upon M'wa-lot seemed to be highly disturbing.

Tarzan could see that the shaggy chieftain was working himself into a frenzy of rage, the inciting cause of which was evidently the information that To-yad was imparting to him. The latter seemed to be attempting to goad him to greater fury, a fact which seemed to be now apparent to every member of the tribe with the exception of Tar-gash, who was walking in the lead, ahead of M'wa-lot and To-yad, for practically every other eye was turned upon the king, whose evident excitement had imparted a certain fierce restlessness to the other members of his party. But it was not until they had come within sight of the body of the thag that the storm broke and then, without warning, M'wa-lot swung his heavy club and leaped forward toward Tar-gash with the very evident intention of braining him from behind.

If the life of the ape-man in his constant battle for survival had taught him to act quickly, it also had taught him to think quickly. He knew that in all his savage company he had no friends, but he also knew that Tar-gash, from very stubbornness and to spite To-yad, might alone be expected to befriend him and now it appeared that Tar-gash himself might need a friend, for it was evident that no hand was to be raised in defense of him nor any voice in warning. And so Tarzan of the Apes, prompted both by considerations of self-interest and fair play, took matters into his own hands with such suddenness that he had already acted before any hand could be raised to stop him.

'Kreeg-ah, Tar-gash!' he cried, and at the same instant he sprang quickly forward, brushing To-yad aside with a single sweep of a giant arm that sent the Sagoth headlong into the underbrush bordering the trail.

At the warning cry of 'Kreeg-ah,' which in the language of the great apes is synonymous to beware, Tar-gash wheeled about to see the infuriated M'wa-lot with upraised club almost upon him and then he saw something else which made his savage eyes widen in surprise. The strange gilak, whom he had taken prisoner, had leaped close to M'wa-lot from behind. A smooth, bronzed arm slipped quickly about the king's neck and tightened. The gilak turned and stooped and surging forward with the king across his hip threw the great, hairy bull completely over his head and sent him sprawling at the feet of his astonished warriors. Then the gilak leaped to Tar-gash's side and, wheeling, faced the tribe with Tar-gash.

Instantly a score of clubs were raised against the two.

'Shall we remain and fight, Tar-gash?' demanded the ape-man.

'They will kill us,' said Tar-gash. 'If you were not a gilak, we might escape through the trees, but as you cannot escape we shall have to remain and fight.'

'Lead the way,' said Tarzan. 'There is no Sagoth trail that Tarzan cannot follow.'

'Come then,' said Tar-gash, and as he spoke he hurled his club into the faces of the oncoming warriors and, turning, fled along the trail. A dozen mighty bounds he took and then leaped to the branch of an overhanging tree, and close behind him came the hairless gilak.

M'wa-lot's hairy warrior bulls pursued the two for a short distance and then gave up the chase as Tarzan was confident that they would, since among his own people it had usually been considered sufficient to run a recalcitrant bull out of the tribe and, unless he insisted upon returning, no particular effort was made to molest him.

As soon as it became evident that pursuit had been abandoned the Sagoth halted among the branches of a huge tree. 'I am Tar-gash,' he said, as Tarzan stopped near him.

'I am Tarzan,' replied the ape-man.

'Why did you warn me?' asked Tar-gash.

'I told you that I did not come among you as an enemy,' replied Tarzan, 'and when I saw that To-yad had succeeded in urging M'wa-lot to kill you, I warned you because it was you that kept the bulls from killing me when I was captured.'

'What were you doing in the country of the Sagoths?' asked Tar-gash.

'I was hunting,' replied Tarzan.

'Where do you want to go now?' asked the Sagoth.

'I shall return to my people,' replied Tarzan.

'Where are they?'

Tarzan of the Apes hesitated. He looked upward toward the sun, whose rays were filtering down through the foliage of the forest. He looked about him – everywhere was foliage. There was nothing in the foliage nor upon the boles or branches of the trees to indicate direction. Tarzan of the Apes was lost!

V

Brought Down

Jason Gridley, looking down from the branches of the tree in which he had found sanctuary, was held by a certain horrible fascination as he watched the feast of the great cats.

The scene that he had just witnessed – this stupendous spectacle of savagery – suggested to him something of what life upon the outer crust must have been at the dawn of humanity.

The suggestion was borne in upon him that perhaps this scene which he had witnessed might illustrate an important cause of the extinction of all of these animals upon the outer crust.

The action of the great saber-tooth tigers of Pellucidar in rounding up the other beasts of the forest and driving them to this clearing for slaughter evidenced a development of intelligence far beyond that attained by the carnivores of the outer world of the present day, such concerted action by any great number for the common good being unknown.

Gridley saw the vast number of animals that had been slaughtered and most of them uselessly, since there was more flesh there than the surviving tigers could consume before it reached a stage of putrefaction that would render it unpalatable even to one of the great cats. And this fact suggested the conviction that the cunning of the tigers had reached a plane where it might reasonably be expected to react upon themselves and eventually cause their extinction, for in their savage fury and lust for flesh they had slaughtered indiscriminately males and females, young and old. If this slaughter went on unchecked for ages, the natural prey of the tigers must become extinct and then, goaded by starvation, they would fall upon one another.

The last stage of the ascendancy of the great cats upon the outer crust must have been short and terrible and so eventually it would prove here in Pellucidar.

And just as the great cats may have reached a point where their mental development had spelled their own doom, so in the preceding era the gigantic, carnivorous dinosaurs of the Jurassic may similarly have caused the extinction of their own contemporaries and then of themselves. Nor did Jason Gridley find it difficult to apply the same line of reasoning to the evolution of man upon the outer crust and to his own possible extinction in the not far remote future. In fact, he recalled quite definitely that statisticians had shown that within two hundred years or less the human race would have so greatly increased and the natural resources of the outer world would have been so depleted that the last generation must either starve to death or turn to cannibalism to prolong its hateful existence for another short period.

Perhaps, thought Gridley, in nature's laboratory each type that had at some era dominated all others represented an experiment in the eternal search for perfection. The invertebrate had given way to fishes, the fishes to the reptiles, the reptiles to the birds and mammals, and these, in turn, had been forced to bow to the greater intelligence of man.

What would be next? Gridley was sure that there would be something after man, who is unquestionably the Creator's greatest blunder, combining as he does all the vices of preceding types from invertebrates to mammals, while possessing few of their virtues.

As such thoughts were forced upon his mind by the scene below him they were accompanied by others of more immediate importance, first of which was concern for his fellows.

Nowhere about the clearing did he see any sign of a human being alive or dead. He called aloud several times but received no reply, though he realized that it was possible that above the roaring and the growling of the feeding beasts his voice might not carry to any great distance. He began to have hopes that his companions had all escaped, but he was still greatly worried over the fate of Von Horst.

The subject of second consideration was that of his own escape and return to the O-220. He had it in his mind that at nightfall the beasts might retire and unconsciously he glanced upward at the sun to note the time, when the realization came to him that there would never be any night, that forever throughout all eternity it would be noon here. And then he began to wonder how long he had been gone from the ship, but when he glanced at his watch he realized that that meant nothing. The hour hand might have made an entire circle since he had last looked at it, for in the excitement of all that had transpired since they had left the O-220 how might the mind of man, unaided, compute time?

But he knew that eventually the beasts must get their fill and leave. After them, however, there would be the hyaenodons and the jackals with their fierce cousins, the wild dogs. As he watched these, sitting at a respectful distance from the tigers or slinking hungrily in the background, he realized that they might easily prove as much of a bar to his escape as the saber-tooth tigers themselves.

The hyaenodons especially were most discouraging to contemplate. Their bodies were as large as that of a full grown mastiff. They walked upon short, powerful legs and their broad jaws were massive and strong. Dark, shaggy hair covered their backs and sides, turning to white upon their breasts and bellies.

Gnawing hunger assailed Jason Gridley and also an overpowering desire to sleep, convincing him that he must have been many hours away from the O-220, and yet the beasts beneath him continued to feed.

A dead thag lay at the foot of the tree in which the American kept his lonely vigil. So far it had not been fed upon and the nearest tiger was fifty yards away. Gridley was hungry, so hungry that he eyed the thag covetously. He glanced about him, measuring the distance from the tree to the nearest tiger and trying to compute the length of time that it would take him to clamber back to safety should he descend to the ground. He had seen the tigers in action and he knew how swiftly they could cover ground and that one of them could leap almost as high as the branch upon which he sat.

Altogether the chance of success seemed slight for the plan he had in mind in the event that the nearest tiger took exception to it. But great though the danger was, hunger won. Gridley drew his hunting knife and lowered himself gently to the ground, keeping an alert eye upon the nearest tiger. Quickly he sliced several long strips of flesh from the thag's hind quarter.

The tarag feeding fifty yards away looked up. Jason sliced another strip, returned his knife to its sheath and climbed quickly back to safety. The tarag lowered its head upon its kill and closed its eyes.

The American gathered dead twigs and small branches that still clung to the living tree and with them he built a small fire in a great crotch.

Here he cooked some of the meat of the thag; the edges were charred, the inside was raw, but Jason Gridley could have sworn that never before in his life had he tasted such delicious food.

How long his culinary activities employed him, he did not know, but when he glanced down again at the clearing he saw that most of the tigers had quitted their kills and were moving leisurely toward the forest, their distended bellies proclaiming how well they had surfeited themselves. And as the tigers retired, the hyaenodons, the wild dogs and the jackals closed in to the feast.

The hyaenodons kept the others away and Gridley saw another long wait ahead of him; nor was he mistaken. And when the hyaenodons had had their fill and gone, the wild dogs came and kept the jackals away.

In the meantime Gridley had fashioned a rude platform among the branches of the tree, and here he had slept, awakening refreshed but assailed by a thirst that was almost overpowering.

The wild dogs were leaving now and Gridley determined to wait no longer. Already the odor of decaying flesh was warning him of worse to come and there was the fear too that the tigers might return to their kills.

Descending from the tree he skirted the clearing, keeping close to the forest and searching for the trail by which his party had entered the clearing. The wild dogs, slinking away, turned to growl at him, baring menacing fangs. But knowing how well their bellies were filled, he entertained little fear of them; while for the jackals he harbored that contempt which is common among all creatures.

Gridley was dismayed to note that many trails entered the clearing; nor could he recognize any distinguishing mark that might suggest the one by which he had come. Whatever footprints his party had left had been entirely obliterated by the pads of the carnivores.

He tried to reconstruct his passage across the clearing to the tree in which he had found safety and by this means he hit upon a trail to follow, although he had no assurance that it was the right trail. The baffling noonday sun shining down upon him seemed to taunt him with his helplessness.

As he proceeded alone down the lonely trail, realizing that at any instant he might come face to face with some terrible beast of a long dead past, Jason Gridley wondered how the ape-like progenitors of man had survived to transmit any of their characteristics however unpleasant to a posterity. That he could live to reach the O-220 he much doubted. The idea that he might live to take a mate and raise a family was preposterous.

While the general aspect of the forest through which he was passing seemed familiar, he realized that this might be true no matter what trail he was upon and now he reproached himself for not having had the trees along the trail blazed. What a stupid ass he had been, he thought; but his regrets were not so much for himself as for the others, whose safety had been in his hands.

Never in his life had Jason Gridley felt more futile or helpless. To trudge ceaselessly along that endless trail, having not the slightest idea whether it led toward the O-220 or in the opposite direction was depressing, even maddening; yet there was naught else to do. And always that damned noonday sun staring unblinkingly down upon him – the cruel sun that could see his ship, but would not lead him to it.

His thirst was annoying, but not yet overpowering, when he came to a small stream that was crossed by the trail. Here he drank and rested for a while, built a small fire, cooked some more of his thag meat, drank again and took up his weary march – but much refreshed.

Aboard the O-220, as the hours passed and hope waned, the spirit of the remaining officers and members of the crew became increasingly depressed as apprehension for the safety of their absent comrades increased gradually until it became eventually an almost absolute conviction of disaster.

'They have been gone nearly seventy-two hours now,' said Zuppner, who, with Dorf and Hines, spent most of his time in the upper observation cabin or pacing the narrow walkingway along the ship's back. 'I never felt helpless before in my life,' he continued ruefully, 'but I am free to admit that I don't know what in the devil to do.'

'It just goes to show,' said Hines, 'how much we depend upon habit and custom and precedence in determining all our action even in the face of what we are pleased to call emergency. Here there is no custom, habit or precedence to guide us.'

'We have only our own resources to fall back upon,' said Dorf, 'and it is humiliating to realize that we have no resources.'

'Not under the conditions that surround us,' said Zuppner. 'On the outer crust there would be no question but that we should cruise around in search of the missing members of our party. We could make rapid excursions, returning to our base often; but here in Pellucidar if we should lose sight of our base there is not one of us who believes he could return the ship to this same anchorage. And that is a chance we cannot take for the only hope those men have is that the ship shall be here when they return.'

One hundred and fifty feet below them Robert Jones leaned far out of the galley doorway in an effort to see the noonday sun shining down upon the ship. His simple, good-natured face wore a puzzled expression not untinged with awe, and as he drew back into the galley he extracted a rabbit's foot from his trousers pocket. Gently he touched each eye with it and then rubbed it vigorously upon the top of his head at the same time muttering incoherently below his breath.

From the vantage point of the walkingway far above, Lieutenant Hines scanned the landscape in all directions through powerful glasses as he had done for so long that it seemed he knew every shrub and tree and blade of grass within sight. The wildlife of savage Pellucidar that crossed and re-crossed the clearing had long since become an old story to these three men. Again and again as one animal or another had emerged from the distant forest the glasses had been leveled upon it until it could be identified as other than man; but now Hines voiced a sudden, nervous exclamation.

'What is it?' demanded Zuppner. 'What do you see?'

'It's a man!' exclaimed Hines. 'I'm sure of it.'

'Where?' asked Dorf, as he and Zuppner raised their glasses to their eyes.

'About two points to port.'

'I see it,' said Dorf. 'It's either Gridley or Von Horst, and whoever it is he is alone.'

'Take ten of the crew at once, Lieutenant,' said Zuppner, turning to Dorf. 'See that they are well armed and go out and meet him. Lose no time,' he shouted after the Lieutenant, who had already started down the climbing shaft.

The two officers upon the top of the O-220 watched Dorf and his party as it set out to meet the man they could see trudging steadily toward the ship. They watched them as they approached one another, though, owing to the contour of the land, which was rolling, neither Dorf nor the man he had gone to meet caught sight of one another until they were less than a hundred yards apart. It was then that the Lieutenant recognized the other as Jason Gridley.

As they hastened forward and clasped hands it was typical of the man that Gridley's first words were an inquiry relative to the missing members of the party.

Dorf shook his head. 'You are the only one that has returned,' he said.

The eager light died out of Gridley's eyes and he suddenly looked very tired and much older as he greeted the engineers and mechanics who made up the party that had come to escort him back to the ship.

'I have been within sight of the ship for a long time,' he said. 'How long, I do not know. I broke my watch back in the forest a way trying to beat a tiger up a tree. Then another one treed me just on the edge of the clearing in plain view of the ship. It seems as though I have been there a week. How long have I been gone, Dorf?'

'About seventy-two hours.'

Gridley's face brightened. 'Then there is no reason to give up hope yet for the others,' he said. 'I honestly thought I had been gone a week. I have slept several times, I never could tell how long; and then I have gone for what seemed long periods without sleep because I became very tired and excessively hungry and thirsty.'

During the return march to the ship Jason insisted upon hearing a detailed account of everything that had happened since his departure, but it was not until they had joined Zuppner and Hines that he narrated the adventures that had befallen him and his companions during their ill-fated expedition.

'The first thing I want,' he told them after he had been greeted by Zuppner and Hines, 'is a bath, and then if you will have Bob cook a couple of cows I'll give you the details of the expedition while I am eating them. A couple of handfuls of Bos Primigenus and some wild fruit have only whetted my appetite.'

A half hour later, refreshed by a bath, a shave and fresh clothing, he joined them in the mess room.

As the three men seated themselves, Robert Jones entered from the galley, his black face wreathed in smiles.

'Ah'm suttinly glad to see you all, Mas' Jason,' said Robert. 'Ah knew sumpin was a-goin' to happen though – Ah knew we was a-goin' to have good luck.'

'Well, I'm glad to be back, Bob,' said Gridley, 'and I don't know of anyone that I am any happier to see than you, for I sure have missed your cooking. But what made you think that we're going to have good luck?'

'Ah jes had a brief conversation with mah rabbit's foot. Dat ole boy he never fails me. We suah be out o' luck if Ah lose him.'

'Oh, I've seen lots of rabbits around, Bob,' said Zuppner. 'We can get you a bushel of them in no time.'

'Yes suh, Cap'n, but you can't get 'em in de dahk of de moon where dey ain't no dahk an' dey ain't no moon, an' othe'wise dey lacks efficiency.'

'It's a good thing, then, that we brought you along,' said Jason, 'and a mighty good thing for Pellucidar, for she never has had a really effective rabbit's foot before in all her existence. But I can see where you're going to need that rabbit's foot pretty badly yourself in about a minute, Bob.'

'How's dat, suh?' demanded Robert.

'The spirits tell me that something is going to happen to you if you don't get food onto this table in a hurry,' laughed Gridley.

'Yes suh, comin' right up,' exclaimed the black as he hastened into the galley.

As Gridley ate, he went over the adventures of the last seventy-two hours in careful detail and the three men sought to arrive at some definite conjecture as to the distance he had covered from the ship and the direction.

'Do you think that you could lead another party to the clearing where you became separated from Von Horst and the Waziri?' asked Zuppner.

'Yes, of course I could,' replied Gridley, 'because from the point that we entered the forest we blazed the trees up to the time we reached the trail, which we followed to the left. In fact I would not be needed at all and if we decide to send out such a party, I shall not accompany it.'

The other officers looked at him in surprise and for a moment there was an embarrassed silence.

'I have what I consider a better plan,' continued Gridley. 'There are twenty-seven of us left. In the event of absolute necessity, twelve men can operate the ship. That will leave fifteen to form a new searching party. Leaving me out, you would have fourteen, and after you have heard my plan, if you decide upon sending out such a party, I suggest that Lieutenant Dorf command it, leaving you, Captain Zuppner, and Hines to navigate the ship in the event that none of us returns, or that you finally decide to set out in search of us.'

'But I thought that you were not going,' said Zuppner.

'I am not going with the searching party. I am going alone in the scout plane, and my advice would be that you send out no searching party for at least twenty-four hours after I depart, for in that time I shall either have located those who are missing or have failed entirely.'

Zuppner shook his head, dubiously. 'Hines, Dorf and I have discussed the feasibility of using the scout plane,' he said. 'Hines was very anxious to make the attempt, although he realizes better than any of us that once a pilot is out of sight of the O-220 he may never be able to locate it again, for you must remember that we know nothing concerning any of the landmarks of the country in the direction that our search must be prosecuted.'

'I have taken all that into consideration,' replied Gridley, 'and I realize that it is at best but a forlorn hope.'

'Let me undertake it,' said Hines. 'I have had more flying experience than any of you with the possible exception of Captain Zuppner, and it is out of the question that we should risk losing him.'

'Any one of you three is probably better fitted to undertake such a flight than I,' replied Gridley; 'but that does not relieve me of the responsibility. I am more responsible than any other member of this party for our being where we are and, therefore, my responsibility for the safety of the missing members of the expedition is greater than that of any of the rest of you. Under the circumstances, then, I could not permit anyone else to undertake this flight. I think that you will all understand and appreciate how I feel and that you will do me the favor to interpose no more objection.'

It was several minutes thereafter before anyone spoke, the four seeming to be immersed in the business of sipping their coffee and smoking their cigarettes. It was Zuppner who broke the silence.

'Before you undertake this thing,' he said, 'you should have a long sleep, and in the meantime we will get the plane out and have it gone over thoroughly. You must have every chance for success that we can give you.'

'Thank you!' said Gridley. 'I suppose you are right about the sleep. I hate to waste the time, but if you will call me the moment that the ship is ready I shall go to my cabin at once and get such sleep as I can in the meantime.'

While Gridley slept, the scout plane, carried aft in the keel cabin, was lowered to the ground, where it underwent a careful inspection and test by the engineers and officers of the O-220.

Even before the plane was ready Gridley appeared at the cabin door of the O-220 and descended to the ground.

'You did not sleep long,' said Zuppner.

'I do not know how long,' said Gridley, 'but I feel rested and anyway I could not have slept longer, knowing that those fellows are out there somewhere waiting and hoping for succour.'

'What route do you expect to follow,' asked Zuppner, 'and how are you planning to insure a reasonable likelihood of your being able to return?'

'I shall fly directly over the forest as far as I think it at all likely that they could have marched in the time that they have been absent, assuming that they became absolutely confused and have traveled steadily away from the ship. As soon as I have gained sufficient altitude to make any observation I shall try and spot some natural landmark, like a mountain or a body of water, near the ship and from time to time, as I proceed, I shall make a note of similar landmarks. I believe that in this way I can easily find my way back, since at the furthest I cannot proceed over two hundred and fifty miles from the O-220 and return to it with the fuel that I can carry.

'After I have reached the furthest possible limits that I think the party could have strayed, I shall commence circling, depending upon the noise of the motor to attract their attention and, of course, assuming that they will find some means of signaling their presence to me, which they can do even in wooded country by building smudges.'

'You expect to land?' inquired Zuppner, nodding at the heavy rifle which Gridley carried.

'If I find them in open country, I shall land; but even if I do not find them it may be necessary for me to come down and my recent experiences have taught me not to venture far in Pellucidar without a rifle.'

After a careful inspection, Gridley shook hands with the three remaining officers and bid farewell to the ship's company, all of whom were anxious observers of his preparation for departure.

'Goodbye, old man,' said Zuppner, 'and may God and luck go with you.'

Gridley pressed the hand of the man he had come to look upon as a staunch and loyal friend, and then took his seat in the open cockpit of the scout plane. Two mechanics spun the propeller, the motor roared and a moment later the block was kicked away and the plane rolled out across the grassy meadowland towards the forest at the far side. The watchers saw it rise swiftly and make a great circle and they knew that Gridley was looking for a landmark. Twice it circled above the open plain and then darted away across the forest.

It had not been until he had made that first circle that Jason Gridley had realized the handicap that this horizonless landscape of Pellucidar had placed upon his chances of return. He had thought of a mountain standing boldly out against the sky, for such a landmark would have been almost constantly within the range of his vision during the entire flight.

There were mountains in the distance, but they stood out against no background of blue sky nor upon any horizon. They simply merged with the landscape beyond them, curving upward in the distance. Twice he circled, his keen eyes searching for any outstanding point in the topography of the country beneath him, but there was nothing that was more apparent than the grassy plain upon which the O-220 rested.

He felt that he could not waste time and fuel by searching longer for a landmark that did not exist, and while he realized that the plain would be visible for but a comparatively short distance he was forced to accept it as his sole guide in lieu of a better one.

Roaring above the leafy roof of the primeval forest, all that transpired upon the ground below was hidden from him and it was tantalizing to realize that he might have passed directly over the heads of the comrades he sought, yet there was no other way. Returning, he would either circle or hold an exaggerated zig-zag course, watching carefully for sign of a signal.

For almost two hours Jason Gridley held a straight course, passing over forest, plain and rolling, hilly country, but nowhere did he see any sign of those he sought. Already he had reached the limit of the distance he had planned upon coming when there loomed ahead of him in the distance a range of lofty mountains. These alone would have determined him to turn back, since his judgment told him that the lost members of the party, should they have chanced to come this far, would be now have realized that they were traveling in the wrong direction.

As he banked to turn he caught a glimpse out of the corner of an eye of something in the air above him and looking quickly back, Jason Gridley caught his breath in astonishment.

Hovering now, almost above him, was a gigantic creature, the enormous spread of whose wings almost equalled that of the plane he was piloting. The man had a single glimpse of tremendous jaws, armed with mighty teeth, in the very instant that he realized that this mighty anachronism was bent upon attacking him.

Gridley was flying at an altitude of about three thousand feet when the huge pteranodon launched itself straight at the ship. Jason sought to elude it by diving. There was a terrific crash, a roar, a splintering of wood and a grinding of metal as the pteranodon swooped down upon its prey and full into the propeller.

What happened then happened so quickly that Jason Gridley could not have reconstructed the scene five seconds later.

The plane turned completely over and at the same instant Gridley jumped. He jerked the rip cord of his parachute. Something struck him on the head and he lost consciousness.

VI

A Phororhacos of the Miocene

'Where are your people?' Tar-gash asked again.

Tarzan shook his head. 'I do not know,' he said.

'Where is your country?' asked Tar-gash.

'It is a long way off,' replied the ape-man. 'It is not in Pellucidar;' but that the Sagoth could not understand any more than he could understand that a creature might be lost at all, for inherent in him was that same homing instinct that marked all the creatures of Pellucidar and which constitutes a wise provision of nature in a world without guiding celestial bodies.

Had it been possible to transport Tar-gash instantly to any point within that mighty inner world, elsewhere than upon the surface of an ocean, he could have unerringly found his way to the very spot where he was born, and because that power was instinctive he could not understand why Tarzan did not possess it.

'I know where there is a tribe of men,' he said, presently. 'Perhaps they are your people. I shall lead you to them.'

As Tarzan had no idea as to the direction in which the ship lay and as it was remotely possible that Tar-gash was referring to the members of the O-220 expedition, he felt that he was as well off following where Tar-gash led as elsewhere, and so he signified his readiness to accompany the Sagoth.

'How long since you saw this tribe of men,' he asked after a while, 'and how long have they lived where you saw them?'

Upon the Sagoth's reply to these questions, the ape-man felt that he might determine the possibility of the men to whom Tar-gash referred being the members of his own party, for if they were newcomers in the district then the chances were excellent that they were the people he sought; but his questions elicited no satisfactory reply for the excellent reason that time meant nothing to Tar-gash. And so the two set out upon a leisurely search for the tribe of men that Tar-gash knew of. It was leisurely because for Tar-gash time did not exist; nor had it ever been a very important factor in the existence of the ape-man, except in occasional moments of emergency.

They were a strangely assorted pair – one a creature just standing upon the threshold of humanity, the other an English Lord in his own right, who was, at the same time, in many respects as primitive as the savage, shaggy bull into whose companionship chance had thrown him.

At first Tar-gash had been inclined to look with contempt upon this creature of another race, which he considered far inferior to his own in strength, agility, courage and woodcraft, but he soon came to hold the ape-man in vast respect. And because he could respect his prowess he became attached to him in bonds of loyalty that were as closely akin to friendship as the savage nature of his primitive mind permitted.

They hunted together and fought together. They swung through the trees when the great cats hunted upon the ground, or they followed game trails ages old beneath the hoary trees of Pellucidar or out across her rolling, grassy, flower-spangled meadowland.

They lived well upon the fat of the land for both were mighty hunters.

Tarzan fashioned a new bow and arrows and a stout spear, and these, at first, the Sagoth refused even to notice, but presently when he saw how easily and quickly they brought game to their larder he evinced a keen interest and Tarzan taught him how to use the weapons and later how to fashion them.

The country through which they traveled was well watered and was alive with game. It was partly wooded with great stretches of open land, where tremendous herds of herbivores grazed beneath the eternal noonday sun, and because of these great herds the beasts of prey were numerous – and such beasts!

Tarzan had thought that there was no world like his own world and no jungle like his own jungle, but the more deeply he dipped into the wonders of Pellucidar the more enamored he became of this savage, primitive world, teeming with the wildlife he loved best. That there were few men was Pellu-cidar's chiefest recommendation. Had there been none the ape-man might have considered this the land of ultimate perfection, for who is there more conversant with the cruelty and inconsideration of man than the savage beasts of the jungle?

The friendship that had developed between Tarzan and the Sagoth – and that was primarily based upon the respect which each felt for the prowess of the other – increased as each seemed to realize other admirable personal qualities and characteristics in his companion, not the least of which being a common taciturnity. They spoke only when conversation seemed necessary, and that, in reality, was seldom.

If man spoke only when he had something worthwhile to say and said that as quickly as possible, ninety-eight per cent of the human race might as well be dumb, thereby establishing a heavenly harmony from pate to tonsil.

And so the companionship of Tar-gash, coupled with the romance of strange sights and sounds and odors in this new world, acted upon the ape-man as might a strong drug, filling him with exhilaration and dulling his sense of responsibility, so that the necessity of finding his people dwindled to a matter of minor importance. Had he known that some of them were in trouble his attitude would have changed immediately, but this he did not know. On the contrary he was only aware that they had every facility for insuring their safety and their ultimate return to the outer world and that his absence would not handicap them in any particular. However, when he did give the matter thought he knew that he must return to them, that he must find them, and that sooner or later he must go back with them to the world from which they had come.

But all such considerations were quite remote from his thoughts as he and Tar-gash were crossing a rolling, tree-dotted plain in their search for the tribe of men to which the Sagoth was guiding him. By comparison with other plains they had crossed, this one seemed strangely deserted, but the reason for this was evident in the close-cropped grass which suggested that great herds had grazed it off before moving on to new pastures. The absence of life and movement was slightly depressing and Tarzan found himself regretting the absence of even the dangers of the teeming land through which they had just come.

They were well out toward the center of the plain and could see the solid green of a great forest curving upward into the hazy distance when the attention of both was attracted by a strange, droning noise that brought them to a sudden halt. Simultaneously both turned and looked backward and up into the sky from which the sound seemed to come.

Far above and just emerging from the haze of the distance was a tiny speck. 'Quick!' exclaimed Tar-gash. 'It is a thipdar,' and motioning Tarzan to follow him he ran swiftly to concealment beneath a large tree.

'What is a thipdar?' asked Tarzan, as the two halted beneath the friendly shade.

'A thipdar,' said the Sagoth, 'is a thipdar;' nor could he describe it more fully other than to add that the thipdars were sometimes used by the Mahars either to protect them or to hunt their food.

'Is the thipdar a living thing?' demanded Tarzan.

'Yes,' replied Tar-gash. 'It lives and is very strong and very fierce.'

'Then that is not a thipdar,' said Tarzan.

'What is it then?' demanded the Sagoth.

'It is an aeroplane,' replied Tarzan.

'What is that?' inquired the Sagoth.

'It would be hard to explain it to you,' replied the ape-man. 'It is something that the men of my world build and in which they fly through the air,' and as he spoke he stepped out into the opening, where he might signal the pilot of the plane, which he was positive was the one carried by the O-220 and which, he assumed, was prosecuting a search for him.

'Come back,' exclaimed Tar-gash. 'You cannot fight a thipdar. It will swoop down and carry you off if you are out in the open.'

'It will not harm me,' said Tarzan. 'One of my friends is in it.'

'And you will be in it, too, if you do not come back under the tree,' replied Tar-gash.

As the plane approached, Tarzan ran around in a small circle to attract the pilot's attention, stopping occasionally to wave his arms, but the plane sped on above him and it was evident that its pilot had not seen him.

Until it faded from sight in the distance, Tarzan of the Apes stood upon the lonely plain, watching the ship that was bearing his comrade away from him.

The sight of the ship awakened Tarzan to a sense of his responsibility. He realized now that someone was risking his life to save him and with this thought came a determination to exert every possible effort to locate the O-220.

The passage of the plane opened many possibilities for conjecture. If it was circling, which was possible, the direction of its flight as it passed over him would have no bearing upon the direction of the O-220, and if it were not circling, then how was he to know whether it was traveling away from the ship in the beginning of its quest, or was returning to it having concluded its flight.

'That was not a thipdar,' said Tar-gash, coming from beneath the tree and standing at Tarzan's side. 'It is a creature that I have never seen before. It is larger and must be even more terrible than a thipdar. It must have been very angry, for it growled terribly all the time.'

'It is not alive,' said Tarzan. 'It is something that the men of my country build that they may fly through the air. Riding in it is one of my friends. He is looking for me.'

The Sagoth shook his head. 'I am glad he did not come down,' he said. 'He was either very angry or very hungry, otherwise he would not have growled so loudly.'

It was apparent to Tarzan that Tar-gash was entirely incapable of compre-hending his explanation of the aeroplane and that he would always believe it was a huge, flying reptile; but that was of no importance – the thing that troubled Tarzan being the question of the direction in which he should now prosecute his search for the O-220, and eventually he determined to follow in the direction taken by the airship, for as this coincided with the direction in which Tar-gash assured him he would find the tribe of human beings for which they were searching, it seemed after all the wisest course to pursue.

The drone of the motor had died away in the distance when Tarzan and Tar-gash took up their interrupted journey across the plain and into broken country of low, rocky hills.

The trail, which was well marked and which Tar-gash said led through the hills, followed the windings of a shallow canyon, which was rimmed on one side by low cliffs, in the face of which there were occasional caves and crevices. The bottom of the canyon was strewn with fragments of rock of various sizes. The vegetation was sparse and there was every indication of an aridity such as Tarzan had not previously encountered since he left the O-220, and as it seemed likely that both game and water would be scarce here, the two pushed on at a brisk, swinging walk.

It was very quiet and Tarzan's ears were constantly upon the alert to catch the first sound of the hum of the motor of the returning aeroplane, when suddenly the silence was shattered by the sound of hoarse screeching which seemed to be coming from a point further up the canyon.

Tar-gash halted. 'Dyal,' he said.

Tarzan looked at the Sagoth questioningly.

'It is a Dyal,' repeated Tar-gash, 'and it is angry.'

'What is a Dyal?' asked Tarzan.

'It is a terrible bird,' replied the Sagoth; 'but its meat is good, and Tar-gash is hungry.'

That was enough. No matter how terrible the Dyal might be, it was meat and Tar-gash was hungry, and so the two beasts of prey crept warily forward, stalking their quarry. A vagrant breeze, wafting gently down the canyon, brought to the nostrils of the ape-man a strange, new scent. It was a bird scent, slightly suggestive of the scent of an ostrich, and from its volume Tarzan guessed that it might come from a very large bird, a suggestion that was borne out by the loud screeching of the creature, intermingled with which was a scratching and a scraping sound.

Tar-gash, who was in the lead and who was taking advantage of all the natural shelter afforded by the fragments of rock with which the canyon bed was strewn, came to a halt upon the lower side of a great boulder, behind which he quickly withdrew, and as Tarzan joined him he signalled the ape-man to look around the corner of the boulder.

Following the suggestion of his companion, Tazan saw the author of the commotion that had attracted their attention. Being a savage jungle beast, he exhibited no outward sign of the astonishment he felt as he gazed upon the mighty creature that was clawing frantically at a crevice in the cliffside.

To Tarzan it was a nameless creature of another world. To Tar-gash it was simply a Dyal. Neither knew that he was looking upon a Phororhacos of the Miocene. They saw a huge creature whose crested head, larger than that of a horse, towered eight feet above the ground. Its powerful, curved beak gaped wide as it screeched in anger. It beat its short, useless wing in a frenzy of rage as it struck with its mighty three-toed talons at something just within the fissure before it. And then it was that Tarzan saw that the thing at which it struck was a spear, held by human hands – a pitifully inadequate weapon with which to attempt to ward off the attack of the mighty Dyal.

As Tarzan surveyed the creature he wondered how Tar-gash, armed only with his puny club, might hope to pit himself in successful combat against it. He saw the Sagoth creep stealthily out from behind their rocky shelter and move slowly to another closer to the Dyal and behind it, and so absorbed was the bird in its attack upon the man within the fissure that it did not notice the approach of the enemy in its rear.

The moment that Tar-gash was safely concealed behind the new shelter, Tarzan followed him and now they were within fifty feet of the great bird.

The Sagoth, grasping his club firmly by the small end, arose and ran swiftly from his concealment, straight toward the giant Dyal, and Tarzan followed, fitting an arrow to his bow.

Tar-gash had covered but half the distance when the sound of his approach attracted the attention of the bird. Wheeling about, it discovered the two rash creatures who dared to interfere with its attack upon its quarry, and with a loud screech and wide distended beak it charged them.

The instant that the Dyal had turned and discovered them, Tar-gash had commenced whirling his club about his head and as the bird charged he launched it at one of those mighty legs, and on the instant Tarzan understood the purpose of the Sagoth's method of attack. The heavy club, launched by the mighty muscles of the beast man, would snap the leg bone that it struck, and then the enormous fowl would be at the mercy of the Sagoth. But if it did not strike the leg, what then? Almost certain death for Tar-gash.

Tarzan had long since had reason to appreciate his companion's savage disregard of life in the pursuit of flesh, but this seemed the highest pinnacle to which rashness might ascend and still remain within the realm of sanity.

And, indeed, there happened that which Tarzan had feared – the club missed its mark. Tarzan's bow sang and an arrow sank deep into the breast of the Dyal. Tar-gash leaped swiftly to one side, eluding the charge, and another arrow pierced the bird's feathers and hide. And then the ape-man sprang quickly to his right as the avalanche of destruction bore down upon him, its speed undiminished by the force of the two arrows buried so deeply within it.

Before the Dyal could turn to pursue either of them, Tar-gash hurled a rock, many of which were scattered upon the ground about them. It struck the Dyal upon the side of the head, momentarily dazing him, and Tarzan drove home two more arrows. As he did so, the Dyal wheeled drunkenly toward him and as he faced about a great spear drove past Tarzan's shoulder and plunged deep into the breast of the maddened creature, and to the impact of this last missile it went down, falling almost at the feet of the ape-man.

Ignorant though he was of the strength and the methods of attack and defense of this strange bird, Tarzan nevertheless hesitated not an instant and as the Dyal fell he was upon it with drawn hunting knife.

So quickly was he in and out that he had severed its windpipe and was away again before he could become entangled in its death struggle, and then it was that for the first time he saw the man who had cast the spear.

Standing erect, a puzzled expression upon his face, was a tall, stalwart warrior, his slightly bronzed skin gleaming in the sunlight, his shaggy head of hair bound back by a deerskin band.

For weapons, in addition to his spear, he carried a stone knife, thrust into the girdle that supported his G string. His eyes were well set and intelligent. His features were regular and well cut. Altogether he was as splendid a specimen of manhood as Tarzan had ever beheld.

Tar-gash, who had recovered his club, was advancing toward the stranger. 'I am Tar-gash,' he said. 'I kill.'

The stranger drew his stone knife and waited, looking first at Tar-gash and then at Tarzan.

The ape-man stepped in front of Tar-gash. 'Wait,' he commanded. 'Why do you kill?'

'He is a gilak,' replied the Sagoth.

'He saved you from the Dyal,' Tarzan reminded Tar-gash. 'My arrows would not stop the bird. Had it not been for his spear, one or both of us must have died.'

The Sagoth appeared puzzled. He scratched his head in perplexity. 'But if I do not kill him, he will kill me,' he said finally.

Tarzan turned toward the stranger. 'I am Tarzan,' he said. 'This is Tar-gash,' and he pointed at the Sagoth and waited.

'I am Thoar,' said the stranger.

'Let us be friends,' said Tarzan. 'We have no quarrel with you.'

Again the stranger looked puzzled.

'Do you understand the language of the Sagoths?' asked Tarzan, thinking that possibly the man might not have understood him.

Thoar nodded. 'A little,' he said; 'but why should we be friends?'

'Why should we be enemies?' countered the ape-man.

Thoar shook his head. 'I do not know,' he said. 'It is always thus.'

'Together we have slain the Dyal,' said Tarzan. 'Had we not come it would have killed you. Had you not cast your spear it would have killed us. Therefore, we should be friends, not enemies. Where are you going?'

'Back to my own country,' replied Thoar, nodding in the direction that Tarzan and Tar-gash had been travelling.

'We, too, are going in that direction,' said Tarzan. 'Let us go together. Six hands are better than four.'

Thoar glanced at the Sagoth.

'Shall we all go together as friends, Tar-gash?' demanded Tarzan.

'It is not done,' said the Sagoth, precisely as though he had behind him thousands of years of civilization and culture.

Tarzan smiled one of his rare smiles. 'We shall do it, then,' he said. 'Come!'

As though taking it for granted that the others would obey his command, the ape-man turned to the body of the Dyal and, drawing his hunting knife, fell to work cutting off portions of the meat. For a moment Thoar and Tar-gash hesitated, eyeing each other suspiciously, and then the bronzed warrior walked over to assist Tarzan and presently Tar-gash joined them.

Thoar exhibited keen interest in Tarzan's steel knife, which slid so easily through the flesh while he hacked and hewed laboriously with his stone implement; while Tar-gash seemed not particularly to notice either of the implements as he sunk his strong fangs into the breast of the Dyal and tore away a large hunk of the meat, which he devoured raw. Tarzan was about to do the same, having been raised exclusively upon a diet of raw meat, when he saw Thoar preparing to make fire, which he accomplished by the primitive expedient of friction. The three ate in silence, the Sagoth carrying his meat to a little distance from the others, perhaps because in him the instinct of the wild beast was stronger.

When they had finished they followed the trail upward toward the pass through which it led across the hills, and as they went Tarzan sought to question Thoar concerning his country and its people, but so limited is the primitive vocabulary of the Sagoths and so meager Thoar's knowledge of this language that they found communication difficult and Tarzan determined to master Thoar's tongue.

Considerable experience in learning new dialects and languages rendered the task far from difficult and as the ape-man never for a moment relinquished a purpose he intended to achieve, nor ever abandoned a task that he had set himself until it had been successfully concluded, he made rapid progress which was greatly facilitated by the interest which Thoar took in instructing him.

As they reached the summit of the low hills, they saw, hazily in the far distance, what appeared to be a range of lofty mountains.

'There,' said Thoar, pointing, 'lies Zoram.'

'What is Zoram?' asked Tarzan.

'It is my country,' replied the warrior. 'It lies in the Mountains of the Thipdars.'

This was the second time that Tarzan had heard a reference to thipdars. Tar-gash had said the aeroplane was a thipdar and now Thoar spoke of the Mountains of the Thipdars. 'What is a thipdar?' he asked.

Thoar looked at him in astonishment. 'From what country do you come,' he demanded, 'that you do not know what a thipdar is and do not speak the language of the gilaks?'

'I am not of Pellucidar,' said Tarzan.

'I could believe that,' said Thoar, 'if there were any other place from which you could be, but there is not, except Molop Az, the flaming sea upon which Pellucidar floats. But the only inhabitants of the Molop Az are the little demons, who carry the dead who are buried in the ground, piece by piece, down to Molop Az, and while I have never seen one of these little demons I am sure that they are not like you.'

'No,' said Tarzan, 'I am not from Molop Az, yet sometimes I have thought that the world from which I come is inhabited by demons, both large and small.'

As they hunted and ate and slept and marched together, these three creatures found their confidence in one another increasing so that even Tar-gash looked no longer with suspicion upon Thoar, and though they represented three distinct periods in the ascent of man, each separated from the other by countless thousands of years, yet they had so much in common that the advance which man had made from Tar-gash to Tarzan seemed scarcely a fair recompense for the time and effort which Nature must have expended.

Tarzan could not even conjecture the length of time he had been absent from the O-220, but he was confident that he must be upon the wrong trail, yet it seemed futile to turn back since he could not possibly have any idea as to what direction he should take. His one hope was that either he might be sighted by the pilot of the plane, which he was certain was hunting for him, or that the O-220, in cruising about, would eventually pass within signaling distance of him. In the meantime he might as well be with Tar-gash and Thoar as elsewhere.

The three had eaten and slept again and were resuming their journey when Tarzan's keen eyes espied from the summit of a low hill something lying upon an open plain at a considerable distance ahead of them. He did not know what it was, but he was sure that whatever it was, it was not a part of the natural landscape, there being about it that indefinable suggestion of discord, or, more properly, lack of harmony with its surroundings that every man whose perception has not been dulled by city dwelling will understand. And as it was almost instinctive with Tarzan to investigate anything that he did not understand, he turned his footsteps in the direction of the thing that he had seen.

The object that had aroused his curiosity was hidden from him almost immediately after he started the descent of the hill upon which he had stood when he discovered it; nor did it come again within the range of his vision until he was close upon it, when to his astonishment and dismay he saw that it was the wreck of an aeroplane.

VII

The Red Flower of Zoram

Jana, The Red Flower of Zoram, paused and looked back across the rocky crags behind and below her. She was very hungry and it had been long since she had slept, for behind her, dogging her trail, were the four terrible men from Pheli, which lies at the foot of the Mountains of the Thipdars, beyond the land of Zoram.

For just an instant she stood erect and then she threw herself prone upon the rough rock, behind a jutting fragment that partially concealed her, and here she looked back along the way she had come, across a pathless waste of tumbled granite. Mountain-bred, she had lived her life among the lofty peaks of the Mountains of the Thipdars, considering contemptuously the people of the lowland to which those who pursued her belonged. Perchance, if they followed her here she might be forced to concede them some measure of courage and possibly to look upon them with a slightly lessened contempt, yet even so she would never abate her effort to escape them.

Bred in the bone of The Red Flower was loathing of the men of Pheli, who ventured occasionally into the fastnesses of the Mountains of the Thipdars to steal women, for the pride and the fame of the mountain people lay in the beauty of their girls, and so far had this fame spread that men came from far countries, out of the vast river basin below their lofty range, and risked a hundred deaths in efforts to steal such a mate as Jana, The Red Flower of Zoram.

The girl's sister, Lana, had been thus stolen, and within her memory two other girls of Zoram, by the men from the lowland, and so the fear, as well as the danger, was ever present. Such a fate seemed to The Red Flower worse than death, since not only would it take her forever from her beloved mountains, but make her a low-country woman and her children low-country children than which, in the eyes of the mountain people, there could be no deeper disgrace, for the mountain men mated only with mountain women, the men of Zoram, and Clovi, and Daroz taking mates from their own tribes or stealing them from their neighbors.

Jana was beloved by many of the young warriors of Zoram, and though, as yet, there had been none who had fired her own heart to love she knew that some day she would mate with one of them, unless in the meantime she was stolen by a warrior from another tribe.

Were she to fall into the hands of one from either Clovi or Daroz she would not be disgraced and she might even be happy, but she was determined to die rather than to be taken by the men from Pheli.

Long ago, it seemed to her now, who had no means for measuring time, she had been searching for thipdar eggs among the lofty crags above the caverns that were the home of her people when a great hairy man leaped from behind a rock and endeavored to seize her. Active as a chamois, she eluded him with ease, but he stood between her and the village and when she sought to circle back she discovered that he had three companions who effectually barred her way, and then had commenced the flight and the pursuit that had taken her far from Zoram among lofty peaks where she had never been before.

Not far below her, four squat, hairy men had stopped to rest. 'Let us turn back,' growled one. 'You can never catch her, Skruk, in country like this, which is fit only for thipdars and no place for men.'

Skruk shook his bullet head. 'I have seen her,' he said, 'and I shall have her if I have to chase her to the shores of Molop Az.'

'Our hands are torn by the sharp rock,' said another. 'Our sandals are almost gone and our feet bleed. We cannot go on. We shall die.'

'You may die,' said Skruk, 'but until then you shall go on. I am Skruk, the chief, and I have spoken.'

The others growled resentfully, but when Skruk took up the pursuit again they followed him. Being from a low country they found strenuous exertion in these high altitudes exhausting, it is true, but the actual basis for their disinclination to continue the pursuit was the terror which the dizzy heights inspired in them and the perilous route along which The Red Flower of Zoram was leading them.

From above Jana saw them ascending, and knowing that they were again upon the right trail she stood erect in plain view of them. Her single, soft garment, made from the pelt of tarag cubs, whipped about her naked legs, half revealing, half concealing the rounded charms of her girlish figure. The noonday sun shone down upon her light, bronzed skin, glistening from the naked contours of a perfect shoulder and imparting golden glints to her hair that was sometimes a lustrous brown and again a copper bronze. It was piled loosely upon her head and held in place by slender, hollow bones of the dimorphodon, a little long-tailed cousin of the thipdar. The upper ends of these bone pins were ornamented with carving and some of them were colored. A fillet of soft skin ornamented in colors encircled her brow and she wore bracelets and anklets made of the vertebrae of small animals, strung upon leather thongs. These, too, were carved and colored. Upon her feet were stout, little sandals, soled with the hide of the mastodon and from the center of her headband rose a single feather. At her hip was a stone knife and in her right hand a light spear.

She stooped and picking up a small fragment of rock hurled it down at Skruk and his companions. 'Go back to your swamps, jaloks of the low country,' she cried. 'The Red Flower of Zoram is not for you,' and then she turned and sped away across the pathless granite.

To her left lay Zoram, but there was a mighty chasm between her and the city. Along its rim she made her way, sometimes upon its very verge, but unshaken by the frightful abyss below her. Constantly she sought for a means of descent, since she knew that if she could cross it she might circle back toward Zoram, but the walls rose sheer for two thousand feet offering scarce a handhold in a hundred feet.

As she rounded the shoulder of the peak she saw a vast country stretching away below her – a country that she had never seen before – and she knew that she had crossed the mighty range and was looking on the land that lay beyond. The fissure that she had been following she could see widening below her into a great canyon that led out through foothills to a mighty plain. The slopes of the lower hills were wooded and beyond the plain were forests.

This was a new world to Jana of Zoram, but it held no lure for her; it did not beckon to her for she knew that savage beasts and savage men of the low countries roamed its plains and forests.

To her right rose the mountains she had rounded; to her left was the deep chasm, and behind her were Skruk and his three companions.

For a moment she feared that she was trapped, but after advancing a few yards she saw that the sheer wall of the abyss had given way to a tumbled mass of broken ledges. But whether there were any means of descent, even here, she did not know – she could only hope.

From pausing often to search for a way down into the gorge, Jana had lost precious time and now she became suddenly aware that her pursuers were close behind her. Again she sprang forward, leaping from rock to rock, while they redoubled their speed and stumbled after her in pursuit, positive now that they were about to capture her.

Jana glanced below, and a hundred feet beneath her she saw a tumbled mass of granite that had fallen from above and formed a wide ledge. Just ahead the mountain jutted out forming an overhanging cliff.

She glanced back. Skruk was already in sight. He was stumbling awkwardly along in a clumsy run and breathing heavily, but he was very near and she must choose quickly.

There was but one way – over the edge of the cliff lay temporary escape or certain death. A leather thong, attached a foot below the point of her spear, she fastened around her neck, letting the spear hang down her back, threw herself upon the ground and slid over the edge of the cliff. Perhaps there were handholds; perhaps not. She glanced down. The face of the cliff was rough and not perpendicular, leaning in a little toward the mountain. She felt about with her toes and finally she located a protuberance that would hold her weight. Then she relinquished her hold upon the top of the cliff with one hand and searched about for a crevice in which to insert her fingers, or a projection to which she could cling.

She must work quickly for already the footsteps of the Phelians were sounding above her. She found a hold to which she might cling with scarcely more than the tips of her fingers, but it was something and the horror of the lowland was just above her and only death below.

She relinquished her hold upon the cliff edge with her other hand and lowered herself very slowly down the face of the cliff, searching with her free foot for another support. One foot, two, three she descended, and then attracted by a noise above her she glanced up and saw the hairy face of Skruk just above her.

'Hold my legs,' he shouted to his companions, at the same time throwing himself prone at the edge of the cliff, and as they obeyed his command he reached down a long, hairy arm to seize Jana, and the girl was ready to let go all holds and drop to the jagged rocks beneath when Skruk's hand should touch her. Still looking upward she saw the fist of the Phelian but a few inches from her face.

The outstretched fingers of the man brushed the hair of the girl. One of her groping feet found a tiny ledge and she lowered herself from immediate danger of capture. Skruk was furious, but that one glance into the upturned face of the girl so close beneath him only served to add to his determination to possess her. No lengths were too far now to go to achieve his heart's desire, but as he glanced down that frightful escarpment his savage heart was filled with fear for the safety of his prize. It seemed incredible that she had descended as far as she had without falling and she had only commenced the descent. He knew that he and his companions could not follow the trail that she was blazing and he realized, too, that if they menaced her from above she might be urged to a greater haste that would spell her doom.

With these thoughts in his mind Skruk arose to his feet and turned to his companions. 'We shall seek an easier way down,' he said in a low voice, and then leaning over the cliff edge, he called down to Jana. 'You have beaten me, mountain girl,' he said. 'I go back now to Pheli in the lowland. But I shall return and then I shall take you with me as my mate.'

'May the thipdars catch you and tear out your heart before ever you reach Pheli again,' cried Jana. But Skruk made no reply and she saw that they were going back the way that they had come, but she did not know that they were merely looking for an easier way into the bottom of the gorge toward which she was descending, or that Skruk's words had been but a ruse to throw her off her guard.

The Red Flower of Zoram, relieved of immediate necessity for haste, picked her way cautiously down the face of the cliff to the first ledge of tumbled granite. Here, by good fortune, she found the egg of a thipdar, which furnished her with both food and drink.

It was a long, slow descent to the bottom of the gorge, but finally the girl accomplished it, and in the meantime Skruk and his companions had found an easier way and had descended into the gorge several miles above her.

For a moment after she reached the bottom Jana was undecided as to what course to pursue. Instinct urged her to turn upward along the gorge in the general direction of Zoram, but her judgment prompted her to descend and skirt the base of the mountain to the left in search of an easier route back across them. And so she came leisurely down toward the valley, while behind her followed the four men from Pheli.

The canyon wall at her left, while constantly lessening in height as she descended, still presented a formidable obstacle, which it seemed wiser to circumvent than to attempt to surmount, and so she continued on downward toward the mouth of the canyon, where it debauched upon a lovely valley.

Never before in all her life had Jana approached the lowland so closely. Never before had she dreamed how lovely the lowland country might be, for she had always been taught that it was a horrid place and no fit abode for the stalwart tribes of the mountains.

The lure of the beauties and the new scenes unfolding before her, coupled with a spirit of exploration which was being born within her, led her downward into the valley much farther than necessity demanded.

Suddenly her attention was attracted by a strange sound coming suddenly from on high – a strange, new note in the diapason of her savage world, and glancing upward she finally descried the creature that must be the author of it.

A great thipdar, it appeared to be, moaning dismally far above her head – but what a thipdar! Never in her life had she seen one as large as this.

As she watched she saw another thipdar, much smaller, soaring above it. Suddenly the lesser one swooped upon its intended prey. Faintly she heard sounds of shattering and tearing and then the two combatants plunged earthward. As they did so she saw something separate itself from the mass and as the two creatures, partially supported by the wings of the larger, fell in a great, gliding spiral a most remarkable thing happened to the piece that had broken loose. Something shot out of it and unfolded above it in the air – something that resembled a huge toadstool, and as it did so the swift flight of the falling body was arrested and it floated slowly earthward, swinging back and forth as she had seen a heavy stone do when tied at the end of a buckskin thong.

As the strange thing descended nearer, Jana's eyes went wide in surprise and terror as she recognized the dangling body as that of a man.

Her people had few superstitions, not having advanced sufficiently in the direction of civilization to have developed a priesthood, but here was something that could be explained according to no natural logic. She had seen two great, flying reptiles meet in battle, high in the air and out of one of them had come a man. It was incredible, but more than all it was terrifying. And so The Red Flower of Zoram, reacting in the most natural way, turned and fled.

Back toward the canyon she raced, but she had gone only a short distance when, directly in front of her, she saw Skruk and his three companions.

They, too, had seen the battle in mid-air and they had seen the thing floating downward toward the ground, and while they had not recognized it for what it was they had been terrified and were themselves upon the point of fleeing when Skruk descried Jana running toward them. Instantly every other consideration was submerged in his desire to have her and growling commands to his terrified henchmen he led them toward the girl.

When Jana discovered them she turned to the right and tried to circle about them, but Skruk sent one to intercept her and when she turned in the opposite direction, the four spread out across her line of retreat so as to effectually bar her escape in that direction.

Choosing any fate rather than that which must follow her capture by Skruk, Jana turned again and fled down the valley and in pursuit leaped the four squat, hairy men of Pheli.

At the instant that Jason Gridley had pulled the rip cord of his parachute a fragment of the broken propeller of his plane had struck him a glancing blow upon the head, and when he regained consciousness he found himself lying upon a bed of soft grasses at the head of a valley, where a canyon, winding out of lofty mountains, opened onto leveller land.

Disgusted by the disastrous end of his futile search for his companions, Gridley arose and removed the parachute harness. He was relieved to discover that he had suffered no more serious injury than a slight abrasion of the skin upon one temple.

His first concern was for his ship and though he knew that it must be a total wreck he hoped against hope that he might at least salvage his rifle and ammunition from it. But even as the thought entered his mind it was forced into the background by a chorus of savage yelps and growls that caused him to turn his eyes quickly to the right. At the summit of a little rise of ground a short distance away he saw four of the ferocious wolf dogs of Pellucidar. As hyaenodons they were known to the paleontologists of the outer crust, and as jaloks to the men of the inner world. As large as full grown mastiffs they stood there upon their short, powerful legs, their broad, strong jaws parted in angry growls, their snarling lips drawn back to reveal their powerful fangs.

As he discovered them Jason became aware that their attention was not directed upon him – that they seemed not as yet to have discovered him – and as he looked in the direction that they were looking he was astounded to see a girl running swiftly toward them, and at a short distance behind the girl four men, who were apparently pursuing her.

As the vicious growls of the jaloks broke angrily upon the comparative silence of the scene, the girl paused and it was evident that she had not before been aware of the presence of this new menace. She glanced at them and then back at her pursuers.

The hyaenodons advanced toward her at an easy trot. In piteous bewilderment she glanced about her. There was but one way open for escape and then as she turned to flee in that direction her eyes fell upon Jason Gridley, straight ahead in her path of flight and again she hesitated.

To the man came an intuitive understanding of her quandary. Menaced from the rear and upon two sides by known enemies, she was suddenly faced by what might indeed by another, cutting off all hope of retreat.

Acting impulsively and in accordance with the code that dominates his kind, Gridley ran toward the girl, shouting words of encouragement and motioning her to come to him.

Skruk and his companions were closing in upon her from behind and from her right, while upon her left came the jaloks. For just an instant longer, she hesitated and then seemingly determined to place her fate in the hands of an unknown, rather than surrender it to the inevitable doom which awaited her either at the hands of the Phelians or the fangs of the jaloks, she turned and sped toward Gridley, and behind her came the four beasts and the four men.

As Gridley ran forward to meet the girl he drew one of his revolvers, a heavy 45 caliber Colt.

The hyaenodons were charging now and the leader was close behind her, and at that instant Jana tripped and fell, and simultaneously Jason reached her side, but so close was the savage beast that when Jason fired the hyaenodon's body fell across the body of the girl.

The shot, a startling sound to which none of them was accustomed, brought the other hyaenodons to a sudden stop, as well as the four men, who were racing rapidly forward under Skruk's command in an effort to save the girl from the beasts.

Quickly rolling the body of the jalok from its intended victim, Jason lifted the girl to her feet and as he did so she snatched her stone knife from its scabbard. Jason Gridley did not know how near he was to death at that instant. To Jana, every man except the men of Zoram was a natural enemy. The first law of nature prompted her to kill lest she be killed, but in the instant before she struck the blade home she saw something in the eyes of this man, something in the expression upon his face that she had never seen in the eyes or face of any man before. As plainly as though it had been spoken in words she understood that this stranger was prompted by solicitousness for her safety; that he was prompted by a desire to befriend rather than to harm her, and though in common with the jaloks and the Phelians she had been terrified by the loud noise and the smoke that had burst from the strange stick in his hand she knew that this had been the means that he had taken to protect her from the jaloks.

Her knife hand dropped to her side, and, as a slow smile lighted the face of the stranger, The Red Flower of Zoram smiled back in response.

They stood as they had when he had lifted her from the ground, his left arm about her shoulders supporting her and he maintained this unconscious gesture of protection as he turned to face the girl's enemies, who, after their first fright, seemed on the point of returning to the attack.

Two of the hyaenodons, however, had transferred their attention to Skruk and his companions, while the third was slinking bare fanged, toward Jason and Jana.

The men of Pheli stood ready to receive the charge of the hyaenodons, having taken positions in line, facing their attackers, and at sufficient intervals to permit them properly to wield their clubs. As the beasts charged two of the men hurled their weapons, each singling out one of the fierce carnivores. Skruk hurled his weapon with the greater accuracy, breaking one of the forelegs of the beast attacking him, and as it went down the Phelian standing next to Skruk leaped forward and rained heavy blows upon its skull.

The cudgel aimed at the other beast struck it a glancing blow upon the shoulder, but did not stop it and an instant later it was upon the Phelian whose only defense now was his crude stone knife. But his companion, who had reserved his club for such an emergency, leaped in and swung lustily at the savage brute, while Skruk and the other, having disposed of their adversary, came to the assistance of their fellows.

The savage battle between men and beast went unnoticed by Jason, whose whole attention was occupied by the fourth wolf dog as it moved forward to attack him and his companion.

Jana, fully aware that the attention of each of the men was fully centered upon the attacking beasts, realized that now was the opportune moment to make a break for freedom. She felt the arm of the stranger about her shoulders, but it rested there lightly – so lightly that she might easily disengage herself by a single, quick motion. But there was something in the feel of that arm about her that imparted to her a sense of greater safety than she had felt since she had left the caverns of her people – perhaps the protective instinct which dominated the man subconsciously exerted its natural reaction upon the girl to the end that instead of fleeing she was content to remain, sensing greater safety where she was than elsewhere.

And then the fourth hyaenodon charged, growling, to be met by the roaring bark of the Colt. The creature stumbled and went down, stopped by the force of the heavy charge – but only for an instant – again it was up, maddened by pain, desperate in the face of death. Bloody foam crimsoned its jowls as it leaped for Jason's throat.

Again the Colt spoke, and then the man went down beneath the heavy body of the wolf dog, and at the same instant the Phelians dispatched the second of the beasts which had attacked them.

Jason Gridley was conscious of a great weight upon him as he was borne to the ground and he sought to fend those horrid jaws from his throat by interposing his left forearm, but the jaws never closed and when Gridley struggled from beneath the body of the beast and scrambled to his feet he saw the girl tugging upon the shaft of her crude, stone-tipped spear in an effort to drag it from the body of the jalok.

Whether his last bullet or the spear had dispatched the beast the man did not know, and he was only conscious of gratitude and admiration for the brave act of the slender girl, who had stood her ground at his side, facing the terrible beast without loss of poise or resourcefulness.

The four jaloks lay dead, but Jason Gridley's troubles were by no means over, for scarcely had he arisen after the killing of the second beast when the girl seized him by the arm and pointed toward something behind him.

'They are coming,' she said. 'They will kill you and take me. Oh, do not let them take me!'

Jason did not understand a word that she had said, but it was evident from her tone of voice and from the expression upon her beautiful face that she was more afraid of the four men approaching them than she had been of the hyaenodons, and as he turned to face them he could not wonder, for the men of Pheli looked quite as brutal as the hyaenodons and there was nothing impressive or magnificent in their appearance as there had been in the mien of the savage carnivores – a fact which is almost universally noticeable when a comparison is made between the human race and the so-called lower orders.

Gridley raised his revolver and levelled it at the leading Phelian, who happened to be another than Skruk. 'Beat it!' he said. 'Your faces frighten the young lady.'

'I am Gluf,' said the Phelian. 'I kill.'

'If I could understand you I might agree with you,' replied Jason, 'but your exuberant whiskers and your diminutive forehead suggest that you are all wet.'

He did not want to kill the man, but he realized that he could not let him approach too closely. But if he had any compunction in the matter of manslaughter, it was evident that the girl did not for she was talking volubly, evidently urging him to some action, and when she realized that he could not understand her she touched his pistol with a brown forefinger and then pointed meaningly at Gluf.

The fellow was now within fifteen paces of them and Jason could see that his companions were starting to circle them. He knew that something must be done immediately and prompted by humanitarian motives he fired his

Colt, aiming above the head of the approaching Phelian. The sharp report stopped all four of them, but when they realized that none of them was injured they broke into a torrent of taunts and threats, and Gluf, inspired only by a desire to capture the girl so that they might return to Pheli, resumed his advance, at the same time commencing to swing his club menacingly. Then it was that Jason Gridley regretfully shot, and shot to kill. Gluf stopped in his tracks, stiffened, whirled about and sprawled forward upon his face.

Wheeling upon the others, Gridley fired again, for he realized that those menacing clubs were almost as effective at short range as was his Colt. Another Phelian dropped in his tracks, and then Skruk and his remaining companion turned and fled.

'Well,' said Gridley, looking about him at the bodies of the four hyaenodons and the corpses of the two men, 'this is a great little country, but I'll be gosh-darned if I see how anyone grows up to enjoy it.'

The Red Flower of Zoram stood looking at him admiringly. Everything about this stranger aroused her interest, piqued her curiosity and stimulated her imagination. In no particular was he like any other man she had ever seen. Not one item of his strange apparel corresponded to anything that any other human being of her acquaintance wore. The remarkable weapon, which spat smoke and fire to the accompaniment of a loud roar, left her dazed with awe and admiration; but perhaps the outstanding cause for astonishment, when she gave it thought, was the fact that she was not afraid of this man. Not only was the fear of strangers inherent in her, but from earliest childhood she had been taught to expect only the worst from men who were not of her own tribe and to flee from them upon any and all occasions. Perhaps it was his smile that had disarmed her, or possibly there was something in his friendly, honest eyes that had won her immediate trust and confidence. Whatever the cause, however, the fact remained that The Red Flower of Zoram made no effort to escape from Jason Gridley, who now found himself completely lost in a strange world, which in itself was quite sad enough without having added to it responsibilities for the protection of a strange, young woman, who could understand nothing that he said to her and whom, in turn, he could not understand.

VIII

Jana and Jason

Tar-gash and Thoar looked with wonder upon the wreckage of the plane and Tarzan hastily searched it for the body of the pilot. The ape-man experienced at least temporary relief when he discovered that there was no body there, and a moment later he found footprints in the turf upon the opposite side of the plane – the prints of a booted foot which he recognized immediately as having been made by Jason Gridley – and this evidence assured him that the American had not been killed and apparently not even badly injured by the fall. And then he discovered something else which puzzled him exceedingly. Mingling with the footprints of Gridley and evidently made at the same time were those of a small sandaled foot.

A further brief examination revealed the fact that two persons, one of them Gridley and the other apparently a female or a youth of some Pellucidarian tribe, who had accompanied him, had approached the plane after it had crashed, remained in its vicinity for a short time and then returned in the direction from which they had come. With the spoor plain before him there was nothing for Tarzan to do other than to follow it.

The evidence so far suggested that Gridley had been forced to abandon the plane in the air and that he had safely made a parachute descent, but where and under what circumstances he had picked up his companion, Tarzan could not even hazard a guess.

He found it difficult to get Thoar away from the aeroplane, the strange thing having so fired his curiosity and imagination that he must need remain near it and ask a hundred questions concerning it.

With Tar-Gash, however, the reaction was entirely different. He had glanced at it with only a faint show of curiosity or interest, and then he had asked one question, 'What is it?'

'This is the thing that passed over us and which you said was a flying reptile,' replied Tarzan. 'I told you at that time that one of my friends was in it. Something happened and the thing fell, but my friend escaped without injury.'

'It has no eyes,' said Tar-gash. 'How could it see to fly?'

'It was not alive,' replied Tarzan.

'I heard it growl,' said the Sagoth; nor was he ever convinced that the thing was not some strange form of living creature.

They had covered but a short distance along the trail made by Gridley and Jana, after they had left the aeroplane, when they came upon the carcass of a huge pteranodon. Its head was crushed and battered and almost severed from its body and a splinter of smooth wood projected from its skull – a splinter that Tarzan recognized as a fragment of an aeroplane propeller – and instantly he knew the cause of Gridley's crash.

Half a mile further on the three discovered further evidence, some of it quite startling. An opened parachute lay stretched upon the ground where it had fallen and at short distances from it lay the bodies of four hyaenodons and two hairy men.

An examination of the bodies revealed the fact that both of the men and two of the hyaenodons had died from bullet wounds. Everywhere upon the trampled turf appeared the imprints of the small sandals of Jason's companion. It was evident to the keen eyes of Tarzan that two other men, both natives, had taken part in the battle which had been waged here. That they were of the same tribe as the two that had fallen was evidenced by the imprints of their sandals, which were of identical make, while those of Tarzan's companion differed materially from all the others.

As he circled about, searching for further evidence, he saw that the two men who had escaped had run rapidly for some distance toward the mouth of a large canyon, and that, apparently following their retreat, Jason and his companion had set out in search of the plane. Later they had returned to the scene of the battle, and when they had departed they also had gone toward the mountains, but along a line considerably to the right of the trail made by the fleeing natives.

Thoar, too, was much interested in the various tracks that the participants in the battle by the parachute had left, but he said nothing until after Tarzan had completed his investigation.

'There were four men and either a woman or a youth here with my friend,' said Tarzan.

'Four of them were low countrymen from Pheli,' said Thoar, 'and the other was a woman of Zoram.'

'How do you know?' asked Tarzan, who was always anxious to add to his store of woodcraft.

'The low country sandals are never shaped to the foot as closely as are those of the mountain tribes,' replied Thoar, 'and the soles are much thinner, being made usually of the hides of the thag, which is tough enough for people who do not walk often upon anything but soft grasses or in soggy marshland. The sandals of the mountain tribes are soled with the thick hide of Maj, the cousin of Tandor. If you will look at the spoor you will see that they are not worn at all, while there are holes in the sandals of these dead men of Pheli.'

'Are we near Zoram?' asked Tarzan.

'No,' replied Thoar. 'It lies across the highest range ahead of us.'

'When we first met, Thoar, you told me that you were from Zoram.'

'Yes, that is my country,' replied Thoar.

'Then, perhaps, this woman is someone whom you know?'

'She is my sister,' replied Thoar.

Tarzan of the Apes looked at him in surprise. 'How do you know?' he demanded.

'I found an imprint where there was no turf, only soft earth, and there the spoor was so distinct that I could recognize the sandals as hers. So familiar with her work am I that I could recognize the stitching alone, where the sole is joined to the upper part of the sandal, and in addition there are the notches, which indicate the tribe. The people of Zoram have three notches in the underside of the sole at the toe of the left sandal.'

'What was your sister doing so far from her own country and how is it that she is with my friend?'

'It is quite plain,' replied Thoar. 'These men of Pheli sought to capture her. One of them wanted her for his mate, but she eluded them and they pursued her across the Mountains of the Thipdars and down into this valley, where she was set upon by jaloks. The man from your country came and killed the jaloks and two of the Phelians and drove the other two away. It is evident that my sister could not escape him, and he captured her.'

Tarzan of the Apes smiled. 'The spoor does not indicate that she ever made any effort to escape him,' he said.

Thoar scratched his head. 'That is true,' he replied, 'and I cannot understand it, for the women of my tribe do not care to mate with the men of other tribes and I know that Jana, my sister, would rather die than mate outside the Mountains of the Thipdars. Many times has she said so and Jana is not given to idle talk.'

'My friend would not take her by force,' said Tarzan. 'If she has gone with him, she has gone with him willingly. And I think that when we find them you will discover that he is simply accompanying her back to Zoram, for he is the sort of man who would not permit a woman to go alone and unprotected.'

'We shall see,' said Thoar, 'but if he has taken Jana against her wishes, he must die.'

As Tarzan, Tar-gash and Thoar followed the spoor of Jason and Jana a disheartened company of men rounded the end of the great Mountains of the Thipdars, fifty miles to the east of them, and entered the Gyor Cors, or great Plains of the Gyors.

The party consisted of ten black warriors and a white man, and, doubtless, never in the history of mankind had eleven men been more completely and hopelessly lost than these.

Muviro and his warriors, than whom no better trackers ever lived, were totally bewildered by their inability even to back-track successfully.

The stampeding of the maddened beasts, from which they had barely escaped with their lives and then only by what appeared nothing short of a miracle, had so obliterated all signs of the party's former spoor that though they were all confident that they had gone but a short distance from the clearing, into which the beasts had been herded by the tarags, they had never again been able to locate the clearing, and now they were wandering hopelessly and, in accordance with Von Horst's plans, keeping as much in the open as possible in the hope that the cruising O-220 might thus discover them, for Von Horst was positive that eventually his companions would undertake a search for them.

Aboard the O-220 the grave fear that had been entertained for the safety of the thirteen missing members of the ship's company had developed into a conviction of disaster when Gridley failed to return within the limit of the time that he might reasonably be able to keep the scout plane in the air.

Then it was that Zuppner had sent Dorf out with another searching party, but at the end of seventy hours they had returned to report absolute failure. They had followed the trail to a clearing where jackals fed upon rotting carrion, but beyond this there was no sign of spoor to suggest in what direction their fellows had wandered.

Going and coming they had been beset by savage beasts and so ruthless and determined had been the attacks of the giant tarags that Dorf reported to Zuppner that he was confident that all of the missing members of the party must by this time have been destroyed by these great cats.

'Until we have proof of that, we must not give up hope,' replied Zuppner, 'nor may we relinquish our efforts to find them, whether dead or alive, and that we cannot do by remaining here.'

There was nothing now to delay the start. While the motors were warming up, the anchor was drawn in and the air expelled from the lower vacuum tanks. As the giant ship rose from the ground Robert Jones jotted down a brief note in a greasy memorandum book: 'We sailed from here at noon.'

When Skruk and his companion had left the field to the victorious Jason, the latter had returned his six-gun to its holster and faced the girl. 'Well,' he inquired, 'what now?'

She shook her head. 'I cannot understand you,' she said. 'You do not speak the language of gilaks.'

Jason scratched his head. 'That being the case,' he said, 'and as it is evident that we are never going to get anywhere on conversation which neither one of us understands, I am going to have a look around for my ship, in the meantime, praying to all the gods that my thirty-thirty and ammunition are safe. It's a cinch that she did not burn for she must have fallen close by and I could have seen the smoke.'

Jana listened attentively and shook her head.

'Come on,' said Jason, and started off in the direction that he thought the ship might lie.

'No, not that way,' exclaimed Jana, and running forward she seized his arm and tried to stop him, pointing back to the tall peaks of the Mountains of the Thipdars, where Zoram lay.

Jason essayed the difficult feat of explaining in a weird sign language of his own invention that he was looking for an aeroplane that had crashed somewhere in the vicinity, but the conviction soon claimed him that that would be a very difficult thing to accomplish even if the person to whom he was trying to convey the idea knew what an aeroplane was, and so he ended up by grinning good naturedly, and, seizing the girl by the hand, gently leading her in the direction he wished to go.

Again that charming smile disarmed The Red Flower of Zoram and though she knew that this stranger was leading her away from the caverns of her people, yet she followed docilely, though her brow was puckered in perplexity as she tried to understand why she was not afraid, or why she was willing to go with this stranger, who evidently was not even a gilak, since he could not speak the language of men.

A half hour's search was rewarded by the discovery of the wreck of the plane, which had suffered far less damage than Jason had expected.

It was evident that in its plunge to earth it must have straightened out and glided to a landing. Of course, it was wrecked beyond repair, even if there had been any facilities for repairs, but it had not burned and Jason recovered his thirty-thirty and all his ammunition.

Jana was intensely interested in the plane and examined every portion of it minutely. Never in her life had she wished so much to ask questions, for never in her life had she seen anything that had so aroused her wonder. And here was the one person in all the world who could answer her questions, but she could not make him understand one of them. For a moment she almost hated him, and then he smiled at her and pressed her hand, and she forgave him and smiled back.

'And now,' said Jason, 'where do we go from here? As far as I am concerned one place is as good as another.'

Being perfectly well aware that he was hopelessly lost, Jason Gridley felt that the only chance he had of being reunited with his companions lay in the possibility that the O-220 might chance to cruise over the very locality where he happened to be, and no matter whither he might wander, whether north or south or east or west, that chance was as slender in one direction as another, and, conversely, equally good. In an hour the O-220 would cover a distance fully as great as he could travel in several days of outer earthly time. And so even if he chanced to be moving in a direction that led away from the ship's first anchorage, he could never go so far that it might not easily and quickly overtake him, if its search should chance to lead it in his direction. Therefore he turned questioningly to the girl, pointing first in one direction, and then in another, while he looked inquiringly at her, attempting thus to convey to her the idea that he was ready and willing to go in any direction she chose, and Jana, sensing his meaning, pointed toward the lofty Mountains of the Thipdars.

'There,' she said, 'lies Zoram, the land of my people.'

'Your logic is unavailable,' said Jason, 'and I only wish I could understand what you are saying, for I am sure that anyone with such beautiful teeth could never be uninteresting.'

Jana did not wait to discuss the matter, but started forthwith for Zoram and beside her walked Jason Gridley of California.

Jana's active mind had been working rapidly and she had come to the conclusion that she could not for long endure the constantly increasing pressure of unsatisfied curiosity. She must find some means of communicating with this interesting stranger and to the accomplishment of this end she could conceive of no better plan than teaching the man her language. But how to commence! Never in her experience or that of her people had the necessity arisen for teaching a language. Previously she had not dreamed of the existence of such a means. If you can feature such a state, which is doubtful, you must concede to this primitive girl of the stone age a high degree of intelligence. This was no accidental blowing off of the lid of the teapot upon which might be built a theory. It required, as a matter of fact, a greater reasoning ability. Give a steam engine to a man who had never heard of steam and ask him to make it go – Jana's problem was almost as difficult. But the magnitude of the reward spurred her on, for what will one not do to have one's curiosity satisfied, especially if one happens to be a young and beautiful girl and the object of one's curiosity an exceptionally handsome young man. Skirts may change, but human nature never.

And so The Red Flower of Zoram pointed at herself with a slim, brown forefinger and said, 'Jana.' She repeated this several times and then she pointed at Jason, raising her eyebrows in interrogation.

'Jason,' he said, for there was no misunderstanding her meaning. And so the slow, laborious task began as the two trudged upward toward the foothills of the Mountains of the Thipdars.

There lay before them a long, hard climb to the higher altitudes, but there was water in abundance in the tumbling brooks, dropping down the hillside, and Jana knew the edible plants, and nuts, and fruits which grew in riotous profusion in many a dark, deep ravine, and there was game in plenty to be brought down, when they needed meat, by Jason's thirty-thirty.

As they proceeded in their quest for Zoram, Jason found greater opportunity to study his companion and he came to the conclusion that nature had attained the pinnacle of physical perfection with the production of this little savage. Every line and curve of that lithe, brown body sang of symmetry, for

The Red Flower of Zoram was a living poem of beauty. If he had thought that her teeth were beautiful he was forced to admit that they held no advantage in that respect over her eyes, her nose or any other of her features. And when she fell to with her crude stone knife and helped him skin a kill and prepare the meat for cooking, when he saw the deftness and celerity with which she made fire with the simplest and most primitive of utensils, when he witnessed the almost uncanny certitude with which she located nests of eggs and edible fruit and vegetables, he was conscious that her perfections were not alone physical and he became more than ever anxious to acquire a sufficient understanding of her tongue to be able to communicate with her, though he realized that he might doubtless suffer a rude awakening and disillusionment when, through an understanding of her language, he might be able to judge the limitations of her mind.

When Jana was tired she went beneath a tree, and, making a bed of grasses, curled up and fell asleep immediately, and, while she slept, Gridley watched, for the dangers of this primitive land were numerous and constant. Fully as often as he shot for food he shot to protect them from some terrible beast, until the encounters became as prosaic and commonplace as does the constant eluding of death by pedestrians at congested traffic corners in cities of the outer crust.

When Jason felt the need of sleep, Jana watched and sometimes they merely rested without sleeping, usually beneath a tree for there they found the greatest protection from their greatest danger, the fierce and voracious thipdars from which the mountains took their name. These hideous, flying reptiles were a constant menace, but so thoroughly had nature developed a defense against them that the girl could hear their wings at a greater distance than either of them could see the creatures.

Jason had no means for determining how far they had travelled, or how long they had been upon their way, but he was sure that considerable outer earthly time must have elapsed since he had met the girl, when they came to a seemingly insurmountable obstacle, for already he had made considerable progress toward mastering her tongue and they were exchanging short sentences, much to Jana's delight, her merry laughter, often marking one of Jason's more flagrant errors in pronunciation or construction.

And now they had come to a deep chasm with overhanging walls that not even Jana could negotiate. To Jason it resembled a stupendous fault that might have been caused by the subsidence of the mountain range for it paralleled the main axis of the range. And if this were true he knew that it might extend for hundreds of miles, effectually barring the way across the mountains by the route they were following.

For a long time Jana sought a means of descent into the crevice. She did not want to turn to the left as that route might lead her eventually back to the canyon that she had descended when pursued by Skruk and his fellows and she well knew how almost unscalable were the perpendicular sides of this terrific gorge. Another thing, perhaps, which decided her against the left hand route was the possibility that in that direction they might again come in contact with the Phelians, and so she led Jason toward the right and always she searched for a way to the bottom of the rift.

Jason realized that they were consuming a great deal of time in trying to cross, but he became also aware of the fact that time meant nothing in timeless Pellucidar. It was never a factor with which to reckon for the excellent reason that it did not exist, and when he gave the matter thought he was conscious of a mild surprise that he, who had been always a slave of time, so easily and naturally embraced the irresponsible existence of Pellucidar. It was not only the fact that time itself seemed not to matter but that the absence of this greatest of all task masters singularly affected one's outlook upon every other consideration of existence. Without time there appeared to be no accountability for one's acts since it is to the future that the slaves of time have learned to look for their reward or punishment. Where there is no time, there is no future. Jason Gridley found himself affected much as Tarzan had been in that the sense of his responsibility for the welfare of his fellows seemed deadened. What had happened to them had happened and no act of his could alter it. They were not there with him and so he could not be of assistance to them, and as it was difficult to visualize the future beneath an eternal noonday sun how might one plan ahead for others or for himself?

Jason Gridley gave up the riddle with a shake of his head and found solace in contemplation of the profile of The Red Flower of Zoram.

'Why do you look at me so much?' demanded the girl; for by now they could make themselves understood to one another.

Jason Gridley flushed slightly and looked quickly away. Her question had been very abrupt and surprising and for the first time he realized that he had been looking at her a great deal. He started to answer, hesitated and stopped. Why *had* he been looking at her so much? It seemed silly to say that it was because she was beautiful.

'Why do you not say it, Jason?' she inquired.

'Say what?' he demanded.

'Say the thing that is in your eyes when you look at me,' she replied.

Gridley looked at her in astonishment. No one but an imbecile could have misunderstood her meaning, and Jason Gridley was no imbecile.

Could it be possible that he had been looking at her *that* way? Had he gone stark mad that he was even subconsciously entertaining such thoughts of this little barbarian who seized her meat in both hands and tore pieces from it with her flashing, white teeth, who went almost as naked as the beasts of the field and with all their unconsciousness of modesty? Could it be that his eyes had told this untutored savage that he was harboring thoughts of love for her? The artificialities of a thousand years of civilization rose up in horror against such a thought.

Upon the screen of his memory there was flashed a picture of the haughty Cynthia Furnois of Hollywood, daughter of the famous director, Abelard Furnois, né Abe Fink. He recalled Cynthia's meticulous observance of the minutest details of social usages and the studied perfection of her deportment that had sometimes awed him. He saw, too, the aristocratic features of Barbara Green, daughter of old John Green, the Los Angeles realtor, from Texas. It is true that old John was no purist and that his total disregard of the social precedence of forks often shocked the finer sensibilities that Mrs Green and Barbara had laboriously achieved in the universities of Montmarte and Cocoanut Grove, but Barbara had had two years at Marlborough and knew her suffixes and her hardware.

Of course Cynthia was a rotten little snob, not only on the surface but to the bottom of her shallow, selfish soul, while Barbara's snobbishness, he felt, was purely artificial, the result of mistaking for the genuine the silly artificialities and affectations of the almost celebrities and sudden rich that infest the public places of Hollywood.

But nevertheless these two did, after a fashion, reflect the social environment to which he was accustomed and as he tried to answer Jana's question he could not but picture her seated at dinner with a company made up of such as these. Of course, Jana was a bully companion upon an adventure such as that in which they were engaged, but modern man cannot go adventuring forever in the Stone Age. If his eyes had carried any other message to Jana than that of friendly comradeship he felt sorry, for he realized that in fairness to her, as well as to himself, there could never be anything more than this between them.

As Jason hesitated for a reply, the eyes of The Red Flower of Zoram searched his soul and slowly the half expectant smile faded from her lips. Perhaps she was a savage little barbarian of the Stone Age, but she was no fool and she was a woman.

Slowly she drew her slender figure erect as she turned away from him and started back along the rim of the rift toward the great gorge through which she had descended from the higher peaks when Skruk and his fellows had been pursuing her.

'Jana,' he exclaimed, 'don't be angry. Where are you going?'

She stopped and with her haughty little chin in air turned a withering look back upon him across a perfect shoulder. 'Go your way, jalok,' she said, 'and Jana will go hers.'

IX

To the Thipdar's Nest

Heavy clouds formed about the lofty peaks of the Mountains of the Thipdars – black, angry clouds that rolled down the northern slopes, spreading far to east and west.

'The waters have come again,' said Thoar. 'They are falling upon Zoram. Soon they will fall here too.'

It looked very dark up there above them and presently the clouds swept out across the sky, blotting out the noonday sun.

It was a new landscape upon which Tarzan looked – a sullen, bleak and forbidding landscape. It was the first time that he had seen Pellucidar in shadow and he did not like it. The effect of the change was strikingly apparent in Thoar and Tar-gash. They seemed depressed, almost fearful. Nor was it man alone that was so strangely affected by the blotting out of the eternal sunlight, for presently from the upper reaches of the mountains the lower animals came, pursuing the sunlight. That they, too, were strangely affected and filled with terror was evidenced by the fact that the carnivores and their prey trotted side by side and that none of them paid any attention to the three men.

'Why do they not attack us, Thoar?' asked Tarzan.

'They know that the water is about to fall,' he replied, 'and they are afraid of the falling water. They forget their hunger and their quarrels as they seek to escape the common terror.'

'Is the danger so great then?' asked the ape-man.

'Not if we remain upon high ground,' replied Thoar. 'Sometimes the gulleys and ravines fill with water in an instant, but the only danger upon the high land is from the burning spears that are hurled from the black clouds. But if we stay in the open, even these are not dangerous for, as a rule, they are aimed at trees. Do not go beneath a tree while the clouds are hurling their spears of fire.'

As the clouds shut off the sunlight, the air became suddenly cold. A raw wind swept down from above and the three men shivered in their nakedness.

'Gather wood,' said Tarzan. 'We shall build a fire for warmth.' And so the three gathered firewood and Tarzan made fire and they sat about it, warming their naked hides; while upon either side of them the brutes passed on their way down toward the sunlight.

The rain came. It did not fall in drops, but in great enveloping blankets that seemed to beat them down and smother them. Inches deep it rolled down the mountainside, filling the depressions and the gulleys, turning the canyons into raging torrents.

The wind lashed the falling water into a blinding maelstrom that the eye could not pierce a dozen feet. Terrified animals stampeded blindly, constituting themselves the greatest menace of the storm. The lightning flashed and the thunder roared, and the beasts progressed from panic to an insanity of fear.

Above the roar of the thunder and the howling of the wind rose the piercing shrieks and screams of the monsters of another day, and in the air above flapped shrieking reptiles fighting toward the sunlight against the pounding wrath of the elements. Giant pteranodons, beaten to the ground, staggered uncertainly upon legs unaccustomed to the task, and through it all the three beast-men huddled at the spot where their fire had been, though not even an ash remained.

It seemed to Tarzan that the storm lasted a great while, but like the others he was enured to the hardships and discomforts of primitive life. Where a civilized man might have railed against rate and cursed the elements, the three beast-men sat in stoic silence, their backs hunched against the storm, for each knew that it would not last forever and each knew that there was nothing he could say or do to lessen its duration or abate its fury.

Had it not been for the example set by Tarzan and Thoar, Tar-gash would have fled toward the sunlight with the other beasts, not that he was more fearful than they, but that he was influenced more by instinct than by reason. But where they stayed, he was content to stay, and so he squatted there with them, in dumb misery, waiting for the sun to come again.

The rain lessened; the howling wind died down; the clouds passed on and the sun burst forth upon a steaming world. The three beast-men arose and shook themselves.

'I am hungry,' said Tarzan.

Thoar pointed about them to where lay the bodies of lesser beasts that had been crushed in the mad stampede for safety.

Now even Thoar was compelled to eat his meat raw, for there was no dry wood wherewith to start a fire, but to Tarzan and Tar-gash this was no hardship. As Tarzan ate, the suggestion of a smile smoldered in his eyes. He was recalling a fussy old nobleman with whom he had once dined at a London club and who had almost suffered a stroke of apoplexy because his bird had been slightly underdone.

When the three had filled their bellies, they arose to continue their search for Jana and Jason, only to discover that the torrential rain had effectually erased every vestige of the spoor that they had been following.

'We cannot pick up their trail again,' said Thoar, 'until we reach the point where they continued on again after the waters ceased to fall. To the left is a deep canyon, whose walls are difficult to scale. In front of us is a fissure, which extends along the base of the mountains for a considerable distance in both directions. But if we go to the right we shall find a place where we can descend into it and cross it. This is the way that they should have gone. Perhaps there we shall pick up their trail again.' But though they continued on and crossed the fissure and clambered upward toward the higher peaks, they found no sign that Jana or Jason had come this way.

'Perhaps they reached your country by another route,' suggested Tarzan.

'Perhaps,' said Thoar. 'Let us continue on to Zoram. There is nothing else that we can do. There we can gather the men of my tribe and search the mountains for them.'

In the ascent toward the summit Thoar sometimes followed trails that for countless ages the rough pads of the carnivores had followed, or again he led them over trackless wastes of granite, taking such perilous chances along dizzy heights that Tarzan was astonished that any of them came through alive.

Upon a bleak summit they had robbed a thipdar's nest of its eggs and the three were eating when Thoar became suddenly alert and listening. To the ears of the ape-man came faintly a sound that resembled the dismal flapping of distant wings.

'A thipdar,' said Thoar, 'and there is no shelter for us.'

'There are three of us,' said Tarzan. 'What have we to fear?'

'You do not know them,' said Thoar. 'They are hard to kill and they are never defeated until they are killed. Their brains are very small. Sometimes when we have cut them open it has been difficult to find the brain at all, and having no brain they have no fear of anything, not even death, for they cannot know what death is; nor do they seem to be affected much by pain, it merely angers them, making them more terrible. Perhaps we can kill it, but I wish that there were a tree.'

'How do you know that it will attack us?' asked Tarzan.

'It is coming in this direction. It cannot help but see us, and whatever living thing they see they attack.'

'Have you ever been attacked by one?' asked Tarzan.

'Yes,' replied Thoar; 'but only when there was no tree or cave. The men of Zoram are not ashamed to admit that they fear the mighty thipdars.'

'But if you have killed them in the past, why may we not kill this one?' demanded the ape-man.

'We may,' replied Thoar, 'but I have never chanced to have an encounter with one, except when there were a number of my tribesmen with me. The lone hunter who goes forth and never returns is our reason for fearing the thipdar. Even when there are many of us to fight them, always there are some killed and many injured.'

'It comes,' said Tar-gash, pointing.

'It comes,' said Thoar, grasping his spear more firmly.

Down to their ears came a sound resembling the escaping of steam through a petcock.

'It has seen us,' said Thoar.

Tarzan laid his spear upon the ground at his feet, plucked a handful of arrows from his quiver and fitted one to his bow. Tar-gash swung his club slowly to and fro and growled.

On came the giant reptile, the dismal flapping of its wings punctuated occasionally by a loud and angry hiss. The three men waited, poised, ready, expectant.

There were no preliminaries. The mighty pteranodon drove straight toward them. Tarzan loosed a bolt which drove true to its mark, burying its head in the breast of the pterodactyl. The hiss became a scream of anger and then in rapid succession three more arrows buried themselves in the creature's flesh.

That this was a warmer reception than it had expected was evidenced by the fact that it rose suddenly upward, skimmed above their heads as though to abandon the attack, and then, quite suddenly and with a speed incomprehensible in a creature of its tremendous size, wheeled like a sparrow hawk and dove straight at Tarzan's back.

So quickly did the creature strike that there could be no defense. The ape-man felt sharp talons half buried in his naked flesh and simultaneously he was lifted from the ground.

Thoar raised his spear and Tar-gash swung his cudgel, but neither dared strike for fear of wounding their comrade. And so they were forced to stand there futilely inactive and watch the monster bear Tarzan of the Apes away across the tops of the Mountains of the Thipdars.

In silence they stood watching until the creature passed out of sight beyond the summit of a distant peak, the body of the ape-man still dangling in its talons. Then Tar-gash turned and looked at Thoar.

'Tarzan is dead,' said the Sagoth. Thoar of Zoram nodded sadly. Without another word Tar-gash turned and started down toward the valley from which they had ascended. The only bond that had united these two hereditary enemies had parted, and Tar-gash was going his way back to the stamping grounds of his tribe.

For a moment Thoar watched him, and then, with a shrug of his shoulders, he turned his face toward Zoram.

As the pteranodon bore him off across the granite peaks, Tarzan hung limply in its clutches, realizing that if Fate held in store for him any hope of escape it could not come in midair and if he were to struggle against his adversary, or seek to battle with it, death upon the jagged rocks below would be the barren reward of success. His one hope lay in retaining consciousness and the power to fight when the creature came to the ground with him. He knew that there were birds of prey that kill their victims by dropping them from great heights, but he hoped that the pteranodons of Pellucidar had never acquired this disconcerting habit.

As he watched the panorama of mountain peaks passing below him, he realized that he was being carried a considerable distance from the spot at which he had been seized; perhaps twenty miles.

The flight at last carried them across a frightful gorge and a short distance beyond the pteranodon circled a lofty granite peak, toward the summit of which it slowly dropped, and there, below him, Tarzan of the Apes saw a nest of small thipdars, eagerly awaiting with wide distended jaws the flesh that their savage parent was bringing to them.

The nest rested upon the summit of a lofty granite spire, the entire area of the summit encompassing but a few square yards, the walls dropping perpendicularly hundreds of feet to the rough granite of the lofty peak the spire surmounted. It was, indeed, a precarious place at which to stage a battle for life. Cautiously, Tarzan of the Apes drew his keen hunting knife from its sheath. Slowly his left hand crept upward against his body and passed over his left shoulder until his fingers touched the thipdar's leg. Cautiously, his fingers encircled the scaly, bird-like ankle just above the claws.

The reptile was descending slowly toward its nest. The hideous demons below were screeching and hissing in anticipation. Tarzan's feet were almost in their jaws when he struck suddenly upward with his blade at the breast of the thipdar.

It was no random thrust. What slender chance for life the ape-man had depended upon the accuracy and the strength of that single blow. The giant pteranodon emitted a shrill scream, stiffened convulsively in mid-air and, as it collapsed, relaxed its hold upon its prey, dropping the ape-man into the nest among the gaping jaws of its frightful brood.

Fortunately for Tarzan there were but three of them and they were still very young, though their teeth were sharp and their jaws strong.

Striking quickly to right and left with his blade he scrambled from the nest with only a few minor cuts and scratches upon his legs.

Lying partially over the edge of the spire was the body of the dead thipdar. Tarzan gave it a final shove and watched it as it fell three hundred feet to the rocks below. Then he turned his attention to a survey of his surroundings, but almost hopelessly since the view that he had obtained of the spire while the thipdar was circling it assured him that there was little or no likelihood that he could find any means of descent.

The young thipdars were screaming and hissing, but they had made no move to leave their nest as Tarzan started a close investigation of the granite spire upon the lofty summit of which it seemed likely that he would terminate his adventurous career.

Lying flat upon his belly he looked over the edge, and thus moving slowly around the periphery of the lofty aerie he examined the walls of the spire with minute attention to every detail.

Again and again he crept around the edge until he had catalogued within his memory every projection and crevice and possible handhold that he could see from above.

Several times he returned to one point and then he removed the coils of his grass rope from about his shoulders and, holding the two ends in one hand, lowered the loop over the edge of the spire. Carefully he noted the distance that it descended from the summit and what a pitiful span it seemed – that paltry twenty-five feet against the three hundred that marked the distance from base to apex.

Releasing one end of the rope, he let that fall to its full length, and when he saw where the lower end touched the granite wall he was satisfied that he could descend at least that far, and below that another twenty-five feet. But it was difficult to measure distances below that point and from there on he must leave everything to chance.

Drawing the rope up again he looped the center of it about a projecting bit of granite, permitting the ends to fall over the edge of the cliff. Then he seized both strands of the rope tightly in one hand and lowered himself over the edge. Twenty feet below was a projection that gave him precarious foothold and a little crevice into which he could insert the fingers of his left hand. Almost directly before his face was the top of a buttress-like projection and below him he knew that there were many more similar to it. It was upon these that he had based his slender hope of success.

Gingerly he pulled upon one strand of the rope with his right hand. So slender was his footing upon the rocky escarpment that he did not dare draw the rope more than a few inches at a time lest the motion throw him off his balance. Little by little he drew it in until the upper end passed around the projection over which the rope had been looped at the summit and fell upon him. And as it descended he held his breath for fear that even this slight weight might topple him to the jagged rocks below.

And now came the slow process of drawing the rope unaided through one hand, fingering it slowly an inch at a time until the center was in his grasp. This he looped over the top of the projection in front of him, seating it as securely as he could, and then he grasped both strands once more in his right hand and was ready to descend another twenty-five feet.

This stage of the descent was the most appalling of all, since the rope was barely seated upon a shelving protuberance from which he was aware it might slip at any instant. And so it was with a sense of unspeakable relief that

he again found foothold near the end of the frail strands that were supporting him.

At this point the surface of the spire became much rougher. It was broken
by fissures and horizontal cracks that had not been visible from above, with
the result that compared with the first fifty feet the descent from here to the
base was a miracle of ease, and it was not long before Tarzan stood again
squarely upon his two feet and level ground. And now for the first time he
had an opportunity to take stock of his injuries.

His legs were scratched and cut by the teeth and talons of the young thipdars, but these wounds were as nothing to those left by the talons of the adult
reptile upon his back and shoulders. He could feel the deep wounds, but he
could not see them; nor the clotted blood that had dried upon his brown skin.

The wounds pained and his muscles were stiff and sore, but his only fear
lay in the possibility of blood poisoning and that did not greatly worry the
ape-man, who had been repeatedly torn and mauled by carnivores since
childhood.

A brief survey of his position showed him that it would be practically
impossible for him to recross the stupendous gorge that yawned between
him and the point at which he had been so ruthlessly torn from his companions. And with that discovery came the realization that there was little or no
likelihood that the people toward which Tar-gash had been attempting to
guide him could be the members of the O-220 expedition. Therefore it
seemed useless to attempt the seemingly impossible feat of finding Thoar and
Tar-gash again among this maze of stupendous peaks, gorges and ravines.
And so he determined merely to seek a way out of the mountains and back
to the forests and plains that held a greater allure for him than did the rough
and craggy contours of inhospitable hills. And to the accomplishment of this
end he decided to follow the line of least resistance, seeking always the easiest
avenues of descent.

Below him, in various directions, he could see the timber line and toward
this he hastened to make his way.

As he descended the way became easier, though on several occasions he
was again compelled to resort to his rope to lower himself from one level to
another. Then the steep crags gave place to leveler land upon the shoulders of
the mighty range and here, where earth could find lodgment, vegetation
commenced. Grasses and shrubs, at first, then stunted trees and finally what
was almost a forest, and here he came upon a trail.

It was a trail that offered infinite variety. For a while it wound through a
forest and then climbed to a ledge of rock that projected from the face of a
cliff and overhung a stupendous canyon.

He could not see the trail far ahead for it was continually rounding the
shoulders of jutting crags.

As he moved along it, sure-footed, silent, alert, Tarzan of the Apes became aware that somewhere ahead of him other feet were treading probably the same trail.

What wind there was was eddying up from the canyon below and carrying the scent spoor of the creature ahead of him as well as his own up toward the mountain top, so that it was unlikely that either might apprehend the presence of the other by scent; but there was something in the sound of the footsteps that even at a distance assured Tarzan that they were not made by man, and it was evident too that they were going in the same direction as he for they were not growing rapidly more distinct, but very gradually as though he was slowly overhauling the author of them.

The trail was narrow and only occasionally, where it crossed some ravine or shallow gulley, was there a place where one might either descend or ascend from it.

To meet a savage beast upon it, therefore, might prove, to say the least, embarrassing but Tarzan had elected to go this way and he was not in the habit of turning back whatever obstacles in the form of man or beast might bar his way. And, too, he had the advantage over the creature ahead of him whatever it might be, since he was coming upon it from behind and was quite sure that it had no knowledge of his presence, for Tarzan well knew that no creature could move with greater silence than he, when he elected to do so, and now he passed along that trail as noiselessly as the shadow of a shadow.

Curiosity caused him to increase his speed that he might learn the nature of the thing ahead, and as he did so and the sound of its footsteps increased in volume, he knew that he was stalking some heavy, four-footed beast with padded feet – that much he could tell, but beyond that he had no idea of the identity of the creature; nor did the winding trail at any time reveal it to his view. Thus the silent stalker pursued his way until he knew that he was but a short distance behind his quarry when there suddenly broke upon his ears the horrid snarling and growling of an enraged beast just ahead of him.

There was something in the tone of that awful voice that increased the ape-man's curiosity. He guessed from the volume of the sound that it must come from the throat of a tremendous beast, for the very hills seemed to shake to the thunder of its roars.

Guessing that it was attacking or was about to attack some other creature, and spurred, perhaps, entirely by curiosity, Tarzan hastened forward at a brisk trot, and as he rounded the shoulder of a buttressed crag his eyes took in a scene that galvanized him into instant action.

A hundred feet ahead the trail ended at the mouth of a great cave, and in the entrance to the cave stood a boy – a lithe, handsome youth of ten or twelve – while between the boy and Tarzan a huge cave bear was advancing angrily upon the former.

The boy saw Tarzan and at the first glance his eyes lighted with hope, but an instant later, evidently recognizing that the newcomer was not of his own tribe, the expression of hopelessness that had been there before returned to his face, but he stood his ground bravely, his spear and his crude stone knife ready.

The scene before the ape-man told its own story. The bear, returning to its cave, had unexpectedly discovered the youth emerging from it, while the latter, doubtless equally surprised, found himself cornered with no avenue of escape open to him.

By the primitive jungle laws that had guided his youth, Tarzan of the Apes was under no responsibility to assume the dangerous rôle of savior, but there had always burned within his breast the flame of chivalry, bequeathed him by his English parents, that more often than not found him jeopardizing his own life in the interests of others. This child of a nameless tribe in an unknown world might hold no claim upon the sympathy of a savage beast, or even of savage men who were not of his tribe. And perhaps Tarzan of the Apes would not have admitted that the youth had any claim upon him, yet in reality he exercised a vast power over the ape-man – a power that lay solely in the fact that he was a child and that he was helpless.

One may analyze the deeds of a man of action and speculate upon them, whereas the man himself does not appear to do so at all – he merely acts; and thus it was with Tarzan of the Apes. He saw an emergency confronting him and he was ready to meet it, for since the moment that he had known that there was a beast upon the trail ahead of him he had had his weapons in readiness, years of experience with primitive men and savage beasts having taught him the value of preparedness.

His grass rope was looped in the hollow of his left arm and in the fingers of his left hand were grasped his spear, his bow and three extra arrows, while a fourth arrow was ready in his right hand.

One glance at the beast ahead of him had convinced him that only by a combination of skill and rare luck could he hope to destroy this titanic monster with the relatively puny weapons with which he was armed, but he might at least divert its attention from the lad and by harassing it draw it away until the boy could find some means of escape. And so it was that within the very instant that his eyes took in the picture his bow twanged and a heavy arrow sank deeply into the back of the bear close to its spine, and at the same time Tarzan voiced a savage cry intended to apprise the beast of an enemy in its rear.

Maddened by the pain and surprised by the voice behind it, the creature evidently associated the two, instantly whirling about on the narrow ledge.

Tarzan's first impression was that in all his life he had never gazed upon such a picture of savage bestial rage as was depicted upon the snarling countenance of the mighty cave bear as its fiery eyes fell upon the author of its hurt.

In quick succession three arrows sank into its chest as it charged, howling, down upon the ape-man.

For an instant longer Tarzan held his ground. Poising his heavy spear he carried his spear hand far back behind his right shoulder, and then with all the force of those giant muscles, backed by the weight of his great body, he launched the weapon.

At the instant that it left his hand the bear was almost upon him and he did not wait to note the effect of his throw, but turned and leaped swiftly down the trail; while close behind him the savage growling and the ponderous footfalls of the carnivore proved the wisdom of his strategy.

He was sure that upon this narrow, rocky ledge, if no obstacle interposed itself, he could outdistance the bear, for only Ara, the lightning, is swifter than Tarzan of the Apes.

There was the possibility that he might meet the bear's mate coming up to their den, and in that event his position would be highly critical, but that, of course, was only a remote possibility and in the meantime he was sure that he had inflicted sufficiently severe wounds upon the great beast to sap its strength and eventually to prove its total undoing. That it possessed an immense reserve of vitality was evidenced by the strength and savagery of its pursuit. The creature seemed tireless and although Tarzan was equally so he found fleeing from an antagonist peculiarly irksome, and to a considerable degree obnoxious to his self esteem. And so he cast about him for some means of terminating the flight and to that end he watched particularly the cliff walls rising above the trail down which he sped, and at last he saw that for which he had hoped – a jutting granite projection protruding from the cliff about twenty-five feet above the trail.

His coiled rope was ready in his left hand, the noose in his right, and as he came within throwing distance of the projection, he unerringly tossed the latter about it. The bear tore down the trail behind him. The ape-man pulled heavily once upon the end of the rope to assure himself that it was safely caught above, and then with the agility of Manu, the monkey, he clambered upward.

X

Only a Man May Go

It required no Sherlockian instinct to deduce that Jana was angry, and Jason was not so dense as to be unaware of the cause of her displeasure, which he attributed to natural feminine vexation induced by the knowledge that she had been mistaken in assuming that her charms had effected the conquest of his heart. He judged Jana by his own imagined knowledge of feminine psychology. He knew that she was beautiful and he knew that she knew it, too. She had told him of the many men of Zoram who had wanted to take her as their mate, and he had saved her from one suitor, who had pursued her across the terrible Mountains of the Thipdars, putting his life constantly in jeopardy to win her. He felt that it was only natural, therefore, that Jana should place a high valuation upon her charms and believe that any man might fall a victim to their spell, but he saw no reason why she should be angry because she had not succeeded in enthralling him. They had been very happy together. He could not recall when ever before he had been for so long a time in the company of any girl, or so enjoyed the companionship of one of her sex. He was sorry that anything had occurred to mar the even tenor of their friendship and he quickly decided that the manly thing to do was to ignore her tantrum and go on with her as he had before, until she came to her senses. Nor was there anything else that he might do for he certainly could not permit Jana to continue her journey to Zoram without protection. Of course it was not very nice of her to have called him a jalok, which he knew to be a Pellucidarian epithet of high insult, but he would overlook that for the present and eventually she would relent and ask his forgiveness.

And so he followed her, but he had taken scarcely a dozen steps when she wheeled upon him like a young tiger, whipping her stone knife from its sheath. 'I told you to go your way,' she cried. 'I do not want to see you again. If you follow me I shall kill you.'

'I cannot let you go on alone, Jana,' he said quietly.

'The Red Flower of Zoram wants no protection from such as you,' she replied haughtily.

'We have been such good friends, Jana,' he pleaded. 'Let us go on together as we have in the past. I cannot help it if—' He hesitated and stopped.

'I do not care that you do not love me,' she said. 'I hate you. I hate you because your eyes lie. Sometimes lips lie and we are not hurt because we have learned to expect that from lips, but when eyes lie then the heart lies and the whole man is false. I cannot trust you. I do not want your friendship. I want nothing more of you. Go away.'

'You do not understand, Jana,' he insisted.

'I understand that if you try to follow me I will kill you,' she said.

'Then you will have to kill me,' he replied, 'for I shall follow you. I cannot let you go on alone, no matter whether you hate me or not,' and as he ceased speaking he advanced toward her.

Jana stood facing him, her little feet firmly planted, her crude stone dagger grasped in her right hand, her eyes flashing angrily.

His hands at his sides, Jason Gridley walked slowly up to her as though offering his breast as a target for her weapon. The stone blade flashed upward. It poised a moment above her shoulder and then The Red Flower of Zoram turned and fled along the rim of the rift.

She ran very swiftly and was soon far ahead of Jason, who was weighted down by clothes, heavy weapons and ammunition. He called after her once or twice, begging her to stop, but she did not heed him and he continued doggedly along her trail, making the best time that he could. He felt hurt and angry, but after all the emotion which dominated him was one of regret that their sweet friendship had been thus wantonly blasted.

Slowly the realization was borne in upon him that he had been very happy with Jana and that she had occupied his thoughts almost to the exclusion of every other consideration of the past or future. Even the memory of his lost comrades had been relegated to the hazy oblivion of temporary forgetfulness in the presence of the responsibility which he had assumed for the safe conduct of the girl to her home land.

'Why, she has made a regular monkey out of me,' he mused. 'Odysseus never met a more potent Circe. Nor one half so lovely,' he added, as he regretfully recalled the charms of the little barbarian.

And what a barbarian she had proven herself – whipping out her stone knife and threatening to kill him. But he could not help but smile when he realized how in the final extremity she had proven herself so wholly feminine. With a sigh he shook his head and plodded on after The Red Flower of Zoram.

Occasionally Jason caught a glimpse of Jana as she crossed a ridge ahead of him and though she did not seem to be travelling as fast as at first, yet he could not gain upon her. His mind was constantly harassed by the fear that she might be attacked by some savage beast and destroyed before he could come to her rescue with his rifle. He knew that sooner or later she would have to stop and rest and then he was hopeful of overtaking her, when he might persuade her to forget her anger and resume their former friendly comradeship.

But it seemed that The Red Flower of Zoram had no intention of resting,

though the American had long since reached a state of fatigue that momentarily threatened to force him to relinquish the pursuit until outraged nature
could recuperate. Yet he plodded on doggedly across the rough ground,
while the weight of his arms and ammunition seemed to increase until his
rifle assumed the ponderous proportions of a field gun. Determined not to
give up, he staggered down one hill and struggled up the next, his legs seeming to move mechanically as though they were some detached engine of
torture over which he had no control and which were bearing him relentlessly onward, while every fiber of his being cried out for rest.

Added to the physical torture of fatigue were hunger and thirst, and
knowing that only thus might time be measured, he was confident that he
had covered a great distance since they had last rested and then he topped
the summit of a low rise and saw Jana directly ahead of him.

She was standing on the edge of the rift where it opened into a mighty
gorge that descended from the mountains and it was evident that she was
undecided what course to pursue. The course which she wished to pursue
was blocked by the rift and gorge. To her left the way led back down into the
valley in a direction opposite to that in which lay Zoram, while to retrace her
steps would entail another encounter with Jason.

She was looking over the edge of the precipice, evidently searching for
some avenue of descent when she became aware of Jason's approach.

She wheeled upon him angrily. 'Go back,' she cried, 'or I shall jump.'

'Please, Jana,' he pleaded, 'let me go with you. I shall not annoy you. I shall
not even speak to you unless you wish it, but let me go with you to protect
you from the beasts.'

The girl laughed. 'You protect me!' she exclaimed, her tone caustic with
sarcasm. 'You do not even know the dangers which beset the way. Without
your strange spear, which spits fire and death, you would be helpless before
the attack of even one of the lesser beasts, and in the high Mountains of the
Thipdars there are beasts so large and so terrible that they would devour you
and your fire spear in a single gulp. Go back to your own people, man of
another world; go back to the soft women of which you have told me. Only a
man may go where The Red Flower of Zoram goes.'

'You half convince me,' said Jason with a rueful smile, 'that I am only a caterpillar, but nevertheless even a caterpillar must have guts of some sort and
so I am going to follow you, Red Flower of Zoram, until some goggle-eyed
monstrosity of the Jurassic snatches me from this vale of tears.'

'I do not know what you are talking about,' snapped Jana; 'but if you follow
me you will be killed. Remember what I told you – only a man may go where
goes The Red Flower of Zoram,' and as though to prove her assertion she
turned and slid quickly over the edge of the precipice, disappearing from his
view.

Running quickly forward to the edge of the chasm, Jason Gridley looked down and there, a few yards below him, clinging to the perpendicular face of the cliff, Jana was working her way slowly downward. Jason held his breath. It seemed incredible that any creature could find hand or foothold upon that dizzy escarpment. He shuddered and cold sweat broke out upon him as he watched the girl.

Foot by foot she worked her way downward, while the man, lying upon his belly, his head projecting over the edge of the cliff, watched her in silence. He dared not speak to her for fear of distracting her attention and when, after what seemed an eternity, she reached the bottom, he fell to trembling like a leaf and for the first time realized the extent of the nervous strain he had been undergoing.

'God!' he murmured. 'What a magnificent display of nerve and courage and skill!'

The Red Flower of Zoram did not look back or upward once as she resumed her way, following the gorge upward, searching for some point where she might clamber out of it above the rift.

Jason Gridley looked down into the terrible abyss.

' "Only a man may go where goes The Red Flower of Zoram," ' he mused.

He watched the girl until she disappeared behind a mass of fallen rock, where the gorge curved to the right, and he knew that unless he could descend into the gorge she had passed out of his life forever.

'Only a man may go where goes The Red Flower of Zoram!'

Jason Gridley arose to his feet. He readjusted the leather sling upon his rifle so that he could carry the weapon hanging down the center of his back. He slipped the holsters of both of his six-guns to the rear so that they, too, were entirely behind him. He removed his boots and dropped them over the edge of the cliff. Then he lay upon his belly and lowered his body slowly downward, and from a short distance up the gorge two eyes watched him from behind a pile of tumbled granite. There was anger in them at first, then scepticism, then surprise, and then terror.

As gropingly the man sought for some tiny foothold and then lowered himself slowly a few inches at a time, the eyes of the girl, wide in horror, never left him for an instant.

'Only a man may go where goes The Red Flower of Zoram!'

Cautiously, Jason Gridley groped for each handhold and foothold – each precarious support from which it seemed that even his breathing might dislodge him. Hunger, thirst and fatigue were forgotten as he marshalled every faculty to do the bidding of his iron nerve.

Hugging close to the face of the cliff he did not dare turn his head sufficiently to look downward and though it seemed he had clung there, lowering himself inch by inch, for an eternity, yet he had no idea how much further he had to descend. And so impossible of accomplishment did the task that he had set himself appear that never for an instant did he dare to hope for a successful conclusion. Never for an instant did any new hold impart to him a feeling of security, but each one seemed, if possible, more precarious than its predecessor, and then he reached a point where, grope as he would, he could find no foothold. He could not move to right or left; nor could he ascend. Apparently he had reached the end of his resources, but still he did not give up. Replacing his torn and bleeding feet upon the last, slight hold that they had found, he cautiously sought for new handholds lower down, and when he had found them – mere protuberances of rough granite – he let his feet slip slowly from their support as gradually he lowered his body to its full length, supported only by his fingers, where they clutched at the tiny projections that were his sole support.

As he clung there, desperately searching about with his feet for some slight projection, he reproached himself for not having discarded his heavy weapons and ammunition. And why? Because his life was in jeopardy and he feared to die? No, his only thought was that because of them he would be unable to cling much longer to the cliff and that when his hands slipped from their holds and he was dashed into eternity, his last, slender hope of ever again seeing The Red Flower of Zoram would be gone. It is remarkable, perhaps, that as he clung thus literally upon the brink of eternity, no visions of Cynthia Furnois or Barbara Green impinged themselves upon his consciousness.

He felt his fingers weakening and slipping from their hold. The end came suddenly. The weight of his body dragged one hand loose and instantly the other slipped from the tiny knob it had been clutching, and Jason Gridley dropped downward, perhaps eighteen inches, to the bottom of the cliff.

As he came to a stop, his feet on solid rock, Jason could not readily conceive the good fortune that had befallen him. Almost afraid to look, he glanced downward and then the truth dawned upon him – he had made the descent in safety. His knees sagged beneath him and as he sank to the ground, a girl, watching him from up the gorge, burst into tears.

A short distance below him a spring bubbled from the canyon side, forming a little brooklet which leaped downward in the sunlight toward the bottom of the canyon and the valley, and after he had regained his composure he found his boots and hobbled down to the water. Here he satisfied his thirst and washed his feet, cleansing the cuts as best he could, bandaged them crudely with strips torn from his handkerchief, pulled his boots on once more and started up the canyon after Jana.

Far above, near the summit of the stupendous range, he saw ominous clouds gathering. They were the first clouds that he had seen in Pellucidar, but only for this reason did they seem remarkable or important. That they presaged rain, he could well imagine; but how could he dream of the catastrophic proportions of their menace.

Far ahead of him The Red Flower of Zoram was clambering upward along a precarious trail that gave promise of leading eventually over the rim of the gorge to the upper reaches that she wished to gain. When she had seen Jason's life in imminent jeopardy, she had been filled with terror and remorse, but when he had safely completed the descent her mood changed, and with the perversity of her sex she still sought to elude him. She had almost gained the summit of the escarpment when the storm broke and with it came a realization that the man behind her was ignorant of the danger which now more surely menaced him than had the descent of the cliff.

Without an instant's hesitation The Red Flower of Zoram turned and fled swiftly down the steep trail she had just so laboriously ascended. She must reach him before the waters reached him. She must guide him to some high place upon the canyon's wall, for she knew that the bottom of this great gorge would soon be a foaming, boiling torrent, spreading from side to side, its waters, perhaps, two hundred feet in depth. Already the water was running deep in the canyon far below her and. spilling over the rim above her, racing downward in torrents and cataracts and waterfalls that carried earth and stone with them. Never in her life had Jana witnessed a storm so terrible. The thunder roared and the lightning flashed; the wind howled and the water fell in blinding sheets, and yet constantly menaced by instant death the girl groped her way blindly downward upon her hopeless errand of mercy. How hopeless it was she was soon to see, for the waters in the gorge had risen, she saw them just below her now, nor was the end in sight. Nothing down there could have survived. The man must long since have been washed away.

Jason was dead! The Red Flower of Zoram stood for an instant looking at the rising waters below her. There came to her an urge to throw herself into them. She did not want to live, but something stayed her; perhaps it was the instinct of primeval man, whose whole existence was a battle against death, who knew no other state and might not conceive voluntary surrender to the enemy, and so she turned and fought her way upward as the waters rising below her climbed to overtake her and the waters from above sought to hurl her backward to destruction.

Jason Gridley had witnessed cloudbursts in California and Arizona and he knew how quickly gulleys and ravines may be transformed into raging torrents. He had seen a river a mile wide formed in a few hours in the San Simon Flats, and when he saw the sudden rush of waters in the bottom of the gorge below him and realized that no storm that he had ever previously witnessed could compare in magnitude with this, he lost no time in seeking higher ground; but the sides of the canyon were steep and his upward progress discouragingly slow, as he saw the waters rising rapidly behind him. Yet there was hope, for just ahead and above him he saw a gentle acclivity rising toward the summit of the canyon rim.

As he struggled toward safety the boiling torrent rose and lapped his feet, while from above the torrential rain thundered down upon him, beating him backward so that often for a full minute at a time he could make no headway.

The raging waters that were filling the gorge reached his knees and for an instant he was swept from his footing. Clutching at the ground above him with his hands, he lost his rifle, but as it slid into the turgid waters he clambered swiftly upward and regained momentary safety.

Onward and upward he fought until at last he reached a spot above which he was confident the flood could not reach and there he crouched in the partial shelter of an overhanging granite ledge as Tarzan and Thoar and Tar-gash were crouching in another part of the mountains, waiting in dumb misery for the storm to spend its wrath.

He wondered if Jana had escaped the flood and so much confidence did he have in her masterful ability to cope with the vagaries of savage Pellucidarian life that he harbored few fears for her upon the score of the storm.

In the cold and the dark and the wet he tried to plan for the future. What chance had he to find The Red Flower of Zoram in this savage chaos of stupendous peaks when he did not even know the direction in which her country lay and where there were no roads or trails and where even the few tracks that she might have left must have been wholly obliterated by the torrents of water that had covered the whole surface of the ground?'

To stumble blindly on, then, seemed the only course left open to him, since he knew neither the direction of Zoram, other than in a most general way, nor had any idea as to the whereabouts of his fellow members of the O-220 expedition.

At last the rain ceased; the sun burst forth upon a steaming world and beneath the benign influence of its warm rays Jason felt the cold ashes of hope rekindled within his breast. Revivified, he took up the search that but now had seemed so hopeless.

Trying to bear in mind the general direction in which Jana had told him Zoram lay, he set his face toward what appeared to be a low saddle between two lofty peaks, which appeared to surmount the summit of the range. Thirst no longer afflicted him and the pangs of hunger had become deadened. Nor did it seem at all likely that he might soon find food since the storm seemed to have driven all animal life from the higher hills, but fortune smiled upon him. In a water worn rocky hollow he found a nest of eggs that had withstood the onslaught of the elements. The nature of the creature that had laid them he did not know; nor whether they were the eggs of fowl or reptile did he care. They were fresh and they were food and so large were they that the contents of two of them satisfied his hunger.

A short distance from the spot where he had found them grew a low stunted tree, and having eaten he carried the three remaining eggs to this meager protection from the prying eyes of soaring reptiles and birds of prey. Here he removed his clothing, hanging it upon the branches of the tree where the sunlight might dry it, and then he lay down beneath the tree to sleep, and in the warmth of Pellucidar's eternal noon he found no discomfort.

How long a time he slept he had no means of estimating, but when he awoke he was completely rested and refreshed. He was imbued with a new sense of self-confidence as he arose, stretching luxuriously, to don his clothes. His stretch half completed, he froze with consternation – his clothes were gone! He looked hastily about for them or for some sign of the creature that had purloined them, but never again did he see the one, nor ever the other.

Upon the ground beneath the tree lay a shirt that, having fallen, evidently escaped the eye of the marauder. That, his revolvers and belts of ammunition, which had lain close to him while he slept, were all that remained to him.

The temperature of Pellucidar is such that clothing is rather a burden than a necessity, but so accustomed is civilized man to the strange apparel with which he has encumbered himself for generations that, bereft of it, his efficiency, self-reliance and resourcefulness are reduced to a plane approximating the vanishing point.

Never in his life had Jason Gridley felt so helpless and futile as he did this instant as he contemplated the necessity which stared him in the face of going forth into this world clothed only in a torn shirt and an ammunition belt. Yet he realized that with the exception of his boots he had lost nothing that was essential either to his comfort or his efficiency, but perhaps he was appalled most by the realization of the effect that this misfortune would have upon the pursuit of the main object of his quest – how could he prosecute the search for The Red Flower of Zoram thus scantily appareled?

Of course The Red Flower had not been overburdened with wearing apparel; yet in her case this seemed no reflection upon her modesty, but the anticipation of finding her was now dampened by a realization of the ridiculousness of the figure he would cut, and already the mere contemplation of such a meeting caused a flush to overspread him.

In his dreams he had sometimes imagined himself walking abroad in some ridiculous state of undress, but now that such a dream had become an actuality he appreciated that in the figment of the subconscious mind he had never fully realized such complete embarrassment and loss of self-confidence as the actuality entailed.

Ruefully he tore his shirt into strips and devised a G string; then he buckled his ammunition belt around him and stepped forth into the world, an Adam armed with two Colts.

As he proceeded upon his search for Zoram he found that the greatest hardship which the loss of his clothing entailed was the pain and discomfort attendant upon travelling barefoot on soles already lacerated by his descent of the rough granite cliff. This discomfort, however, he eventually partially overcame when with the return of the game to the mountains he was able to shoot a small reptile, from the hide of which he fashioned two crude sandals.

The sun, beating down upon his naked body, had no such effect upon his skin as would the sun of the outer world under like conditions, but it did impart to him a golden bronze color, which gave him a new confidence similar to that which he would have felt had he been able to retrieve his lost apparel, and in this fact he saw what he believed to be the real cause of his first embarrassment at his nakedness – it had been the whiteness of his skin that had made him seem so naked by contrast with other creatures, for this whiteness had suggested softness and weakness, arousing within him a disturbing sensation of inferiority; but now as he took on his heavy coat of tan and his feet became hardened and accustomed to the new conditions, he walked no longer in constant realization of his nakedness.

He slept and ate many times and was conscious, therefore, that considerable outer earthly time had passed since he had been separated from Jana. As yet he had seen no sign of her or any other human being, though he was often menaced by savage beasts and reptiles, but experience had taught him how best to elude these without recourse to his weapons, which he was determined to use only in extreme emergencies for he could not but anticipate with misgivings the time, which must sometime come, when the last of his ammunition would have been exhausted.

He had crossed the summit of the range and found a fairer country beyond. It was still wild and tumbled and rocky, but the vegetation grew more luxuriantly and in many places the mountain slopes were clothed in forests that reached far upward toward the higher peaks. There were more streams and a greater abundance of smaller game, which afforded him relief from any anxiety upon the score of food.

For the purpose of economizing his precious ammunition he had fashioned other weapons; the influence of his association with Jana being reflected in his spear, while to Tarzan of the Apes and the Waziri he owed his crude bow and arrows. Before he had mastered the intricacies of either of his new weapons he might have died of starvation had it not been for his Colts, but eventually he achieved a sufficient degree of adeptness to insure him a full larder at all times.

Jason Gridley had long since given up all hope of finding his ship or his companions and had accepted with what philosophy he could command the future lot from which there seemed no escape in which he visioned a lifetime spent in Pellucidar, battling with his primitive weapons for survival amongst the savage creatures of the inner world.

Most of all he missed human companionship and he looked forward to the day that he might find a tribe of men with which he could cast his lot. Although he was quite aware from the information that he had gleaned from Jana that it might be extremely difficult, if not impossible, for him to win either the confidence or the friendship of any Pellucidarian tribe whose attitude towards strangers was one of habitual enmity; yet he did not abandon hope and his eyes were always on the alert for a sign of man; nor was he now to have long to wait.

He had lost all sense of direction in so far as the location of Zoram was concerned and was wandering aimlessly from camp to camp in the idle hope that some day he would stumble upon Zoram, when a breeze coming from below brought to his nostrils the acrid scent of smoke. Instantly his whole being was surcharged with excitement, for smoke meant fire and fire meant man.

Moving cautiously down the mountain in the direction from which the wind was blowing, his eager, searching eyes were presently rewarded by sight of a thin wisp of smoke arising from a canyon just ahead. It was a rocky canyon with precipitous walls, those upon the opposite side from him being lofty, while that which he was approaching was much lower and in many places so broken down by erosion or other natural causes as to give ready ingress to the canyon bottom below.

Creeping stealthily to the rim Jason Gridley peered downward into the canyon. Along the center of its grassy floor tumbled a mountain torrent. Giant trees grew at intervals, lending a park-like appearance to the scene; a similarity which was further accentuated by the gorgeous blooms which starred the sward or blossomed in the trees themselves.

Beside a small fire at the edge of a brook squatted a bronzed warrior, his attention centered upon a fowl which he was roasting above the fire. Jason, watching the warrior, deliberated upon the best method of approaching him, that he might convince him of his friendly intentions and overcome the natural suspicion of strangers that he knew to be inherent in these savage tribesmen. He had decided that the best plan would be to walk boldly down to the stranger, his hands empty of weapons, and he was upon the point of putting his plan into action when his attention was attracted to the summit of the cliff upon the opposite side of the narrow canyon.

There had been no sound that had been appreciable to his ears and the top of the opposite cliff had not been within the field of his vision while he had been watching the man in the bottom of the canyon. So what had attracted his attention he did not know, unless it had been the delicate powers of perception inherent in that mysterious attribute of the mind which we are sometimes pleased to call a sixth sense.

But be that as it may, his eyes moved directly to a spot upon the summit of the opposite cliff where stood such a creature as no living man upon the outer crust had ever looked upon before – a giant armored dinosaur it was, a huge reptile that appeared to be between sixty and seventy feet in length, standing at the rump, which was its highest point, fully twenty-five feet above the ground. Its relatively small, pointed head resembled that of a lizard. Along its spine were thin, horny plates arranged alternately, the largest of which were almost three feet high and equally as long, but with a thickness of little more than an inch. The stout tail, which terminated in a long, horny spine, was equipped with two other such spines upon the upper side and toward the tip. Each of these spines was about three feet in length. The creature walked upon four lizard-like feet, its short, front legs bringing its nose close to the ground, imparting to it an awkward and ungainly appearance.

It appeared to be watching the man in the canyon, and suddenly, to Jason's amazement, it gathered its gigantic hind legs beneath it and launched itself straight from the top of the lofty cliff.

Jason's first thought was that the gigantic creature would be dashed to pieces upon the ground in the canyon bottom, but to his vast astonishment he saw that it was not falling but was gliding swiftly through the air, supported by its huge spinal plates, which it had dropped to a horizontal position, transforming itself into a gigantic animate glider.

The swish of its passage through the air attracted the attention of the warrior squatting over his fire. The man leaped to his feet, snatching up his spear as he did so, and simultaneously Jason Gridley sprang over the edge of the cliff and leaped down the rough declivity toward the lone warrior, at the same time whipping both his six-guns from their holsters.

XI

The Cavern of Clovi

As Tarzan swarmed up the rope the bear, almost upon his heels and running swiftly, squatted upon its haunches to overcome its momentum and came to a stop directly beneath him. And then it was that there occurred one of those unforeseen accidents which no one might have guarded against.

It chanced that the granite projection across which Tarzan had cast his noose was at a single point of knife-like sharpness upon its upper edge, and with the weight of the man dragging down upon it the rope parted where it rested upon this sharp bit of granite, and the Lord of the Jungle was precipitated upon the back of the cave bear.

With such rapidity had these events transpired it is a matter of question as to whether the bear or Tarzan was the more surprised, but primitive creatures who would survive cannot permit surprise to disconcert them. In this instance both of the creatures accepted the happening as though it had been planned and expected.

The bear reared up and shook itself in an effort to dislodge the man-thing from its back, while Tarzan slipped a bronzed arm around the shaggy neck and clung desperately to his hold while he dragged his hunting knife from its sheath. It was a precarious place in which to stage a struggle for life. On one side the cliff rose far above them, and upon the other it dropped away dizzily into the depth of a gloomy gorge, and here the efforts of the cave bear to dislodge its antagonist momentarily bade fair to plunge them both into eternity.

The growls and roars of the quadruped reverberated among the mighty peaks of the Mountains of the Thipdars, but the ape-man battled silently, driving his blade repeatedly into the back of the lunging beast, which was seeking by every means at its command to dislodge him, though ever wary against precipitating itself over the brink into the chasm.

But the battle could not go on forever and at last the blade found the spinal cord. The creature stiffened spasmodically and Tarzan slipped quickly from its back. He found safe footing upon the ledge as the mighty carcass stumbled forward and rolled over the edge to hurtle downward to the gorge's bottom, carrying with it four of Tarzan's arrows and his spear.

The ape-man found his rope lying upon the ledge where it had fallen, and gathering it up he started back along the trail in search of the bow that he had been forced to discard in his flight, as well as to find the boy.

He had taken only a few steps when, upon rounding the shoulder of a crag, he came face to face with the youth. At sight of him the latter stopped, his spear ready, his stone knife loosened in its sheath. He had been carrying Tarzan's bow, but at sight of the ape-man he dropped it at his feet, the better to defend himself in the event that he was attacked by the stranger.

'I am Tarzan of the Apes,' said the Lord of the Jungle. 'I come as a friend, and not to kill.'

'I am Ovan,' said the boy. 'If you did not come to our country to kill, then you came to steal a mate, and thus it is the duty of every warrior of Clovi to kill you.'

'Tarzan seeks no mate,' said the ape-man.

'Then why is he in Clovi?' demanded the youth.

'He is lost,' replied the ape-man. 'Tarzan comes from another world that is beyond Pellucidar. He has become separated from his friends and he cannot find his way back to them. He would be friend with the people of Clovi.'

'Why did you attack the bear?' demanded Ovan, suddenly.

'If I had not attacked it it would have killed you,' replied the ape-man.

Ovan scratched his head. 'It seemed to me,' he said presently, 'that there could be no other reason. It is what one of the men of my own tribe would have done, but you are not of my tribe. You are an enemy and so I could not understand why you did it. Do you tell me that though I am not of your tribe you would have saved my life?'

'Certainly,' replied Tarzan.

Ovan looked long and steadily at the handsome giant standing before him. 'I believe you,' he said presently, 'although I do not understand. I never heard of such a thing before, but I do not know that the men of my tribe will believe. Even after I have told them what you have done for me they may still wish to kill you, for they believe that it is never safe to trust an enemy.'

'Where is your village?' asked Tarzan.

'It is not at a great distance,' replied Ovan.

'I will go there with you,' said Tarzan, 'and talk with your chief.'

'Very well,' said the boy. 'You may talk with Avan the chief. He is my father. And if they decide to kill you I shall try to help you, for you saved my life when the ryth would have destroyed me.'

'Why were you in the cave?' demanded Tarzan. 'It was plainly apparent that it was the den of a wild beast.'

'You, too, were upon the same trail,' said the boy, 'while you chanced to be behind the ryth. It was my misfortune that I was in front of it.'

'I did not know where the trail led,' said the ape-man.

'Neither did I,' said Ovan. 'I have never hunted before except in the company of older men, but now I have reached an age when I would be a warrior myself, and so I have come out of the caves of my people to make my first kill alone, for only thus may a man hope to become a warrior. I saw this trail and, though I did not know where it led, I followed it; nor had I been long upon it when I heard the footsteps of the ryth behind me and when I came to the cave and saw that the trail ended there, I knew that I should never again see the caves of my people, that I should never become a warrior. When the great ryth came and saw me standing there he was very angry, but I should have fought him. Perhaps I might have killed him, though I do not believe that that is at all likely.

'And then you came and with this bent stick cast a little spear into the back of the ryth, which so enraged him that he forgot me and turned to pursue you as you knew that he would. They must indeed be brave warriors who come from the land from which you come. Tell me about your country. Where is it? Are your warriors great hunters and is your chief powerful in the land?'

Tarzan tried to explain that his country was not in Pellucidar, but that was beyond Ovan's powers of conception, and so Tarzan turned the conversation from himself to the youth and as they followed a winding trail toward Clovi, Ovan discoursed upon the bravery of the men of his tribe and the beauty of its women.

'Avan, my father, is a great chief,' he said, 'and the men of my tribe are mighty warriors. Often we battle with the men of Zoram and we have even gone as far as Daroz, which lies beyond Zoram, for always there are more men than women in our tribe and the warriors must seek their mates in Zoram and Daroz. Even now Carb has gone to Zoram with twenty warriors to steal women. The women of Zoram are very beautiful. When I am a little larger I shall go to Zoram and steal a mate.'

'How far is it from Clovi to Zoram?' asked Tarzan.

'Some say that it is not so far, and others that it is farther,' replied Ovan. 'I have heard it said that going to Zoram is much farther than returning inasmuch as the warriors usually eat six times on the journey from Clovi to Zoram, but returning a strong man may make the journey eating only twice and still retain his strength.'

'But why should the distance be shorter returning than going?' demanded the ape-man.

'Because when they are returning they are usually pursued by the warriors of Zoram,' replied Ovan.

Inwardly Tarzan smiled at the naïveté of Ovan's reasoning, while it again impressed upon him the impossibility of measuring distances or computing time under the anomalous condition obtaining in Pellucidar.

As the two made their way toward Clovi, the boy gradually abandoned his suspicious attitude toward Tarzan and presently seemed to accept him quite as he would have a member of his own tribe. He noticed the wound made by the talons of the thipdar on Tarzan's back and shoulders and when he had wormed the story from his companion he marvelled at the courage resourcefulness and strength that had won escape for this stranger from what a Pellucidarian would have considered an utterly hopeless situation.

Ovan saw that the wounds were inflamed and realized that they must be causing Tarzan considerable pain and discomfort, and so when first their way led near a brook he insisted upon cleansing them thoroughly, and collecting the leaves of a particular shrub he crushed them and applied the juices to the open wounds.

The pain of the inflammation had been as nothing compared to the acute agony caused by the application thus made by Ovan and yet the boy noticed that not even by the tremor of a single muscle did the stranger evidence the agony that Ovan well knew he was enduring, and once again his admiration for his new-found companion was increased.

'It may hurt,' he said, 'but it will keep the wounds from rotting and afterward they will heal quickly.'

For a short time after they resumed their march the pain continued to be excruciating, but it lessened gradually until it finally disappeared, and thereafter the ape-man felt no discomfort.

The way led to a forest where there were straight, tough, young saplings, and here Tarzan tarried long enough to fashion a new spear and to split and scrape half a dozen additional arrows.

Ovan was much interested in Tarzan's steel-bladed knife and in his bow and arrows, although secretly he looked with contempt upon the latter, which he referred to as little spears for young children. But when they became hungry and Tarzan bowled over a mountain sheep with a single shaft, the lad's contempt was changed to admiration and thereafter he not only evinced great respect for the bow and arrows, but begged to be taught how to make and to use them.

The little Clovian was a lad after the heart of the ape-man and the two became fast friends as they made their way toward the land of Clovi, for Ovan possessed the quiet dignity of the wild beast; nor was he given to that garrulity which is at once the pride and the curse of civilized man – there were no boy orators in the peaceful Pliocene.

'We are almost there,' announced Ovan, halting at the brink of a canyon. 'Below lie the caves of the Clovi. I hope that Avan, the chief, will receive you as a friend, but that I cannot promise. Perhaps it might be better for you to go your way and not come to the caves of the Clovi. I do not want you to be killed.'

'They will not kill me,' said Tarzan. 'I come as a friend.' But in his heart he knew that the chances were that these primitive savages might never accept a stranger among them upon an equal or a friendly footing.

'Come, then,' said Ovan, as he started the descent into the canyon. Part way down the trail turned up along the canyon side in the direction of the head of the gorge. It was a level trail here, well kept and much used, with indications that no little engineering skill had entered into its construction. It was by no means the haphazard trail of beasts, but rather the work of intelligent, even though savage and primitive men.

They had proceeded no great distance along the trail when Ovan sounded a low whistle, which, a moment later, was answered from around the bend in the trail ahead, and when the two had passed this turn Tarzan saw before him a wide, natural ledge of rock entirely overhung by beetling cliffs and in the depth of the recess thus formed in the cliffside he saw the dark mouth of a cavern.

Upon the flat surface of the ledge, which comprised some two acres, were congregated fully a hundred men, women and children.

All eyes were turned in their direction as they came into view and on sight of Tarzan the warriors sprang to their feet, seizing spears and knives. The women called their children to them and moved quickly toward the entrance to the cavern.

'Do not fear,' cried the boy. 'It is only Ovan and his friend, Tarzan.'

'We kill,' growled some of the warriors.

'Where is Avan the chief?' demanded the boy.

'Here is Avan the chief,' announced a deep gruff voice, and Tarzan shifted his gaze to the figure of a stalwart, brawny savage emerging from the mouth of the cavern.

'What have you there, Ovan?' demanded the chief. 'If you have brought a prisoner of war, you should have disarmed him first.'

'He is no prisoner,' replied Ovan. 'He is a stranger in Pellucidar and he comes as a friend and not as an enemy.'

'He is a stranger,' replied Avan, 'and you should have killed him. He has learned the way to the caverns of Clovi and if we do not kill him he will return to his people and lead them against us.'

'He has no people and he does not know how to return to his own country,' said the boy.

'Then he does not speak true words, for that is not possible,' said Avan. 'There can be no man who does not know the way to his own country. Come! Stand aside, Ovan, while I destroy him.'

The lad drew himself stiffly erect in front of Tarzan. 'Who would kill the friend of Ovan,' he said, 'must first kill Ovan.'

A tall warrior, standing near the chief, laid his hand upon Avan's arm. 'Ovan has always been a good boy,' he said. 'There is none in Clovi near his age whose words are as full of wisdom as his. If he says that this stranger is his friend and if he does not wish us to kill him, he must have a reason and we should listen to him before we decide to destroy the stranger.'

'Very well,' said the chief; 'perhaps you are right, Ulan. We shall see. Speak, boy, and tell us why we should not kill the stranger.'

'Because at the risk of his life he saved mine. Hand to hand he fought with a great ryth from which I could not have escaped had it not been for him; nor did he offer to harm me, and what enemy of the Clovi is there, even among the people of Zoram or Daroz who are of our own blood, that would not slay a Clovi youth who was so soon to become a warrior? Not only is he very brave, but he is a great hunter. It would be well for the tribe of Clovi if he came to live with us as a friend.'

Avan bowed his head in thought. 'When Carb returns we shall call a council and decide what to do,' he said. 'In the meantime the stranger must remain here as a prisoner.'

'I shall not remain as a prisoner,' said Tarzan. 'I came as a friend and I shall remain as a friend, or I shall not remain at all.'

'Let him stay as a friend,' said Ulan. 'He has marched with Ovan and has not harmed him. Why should we think that he will harm us when we are many and he only one?'

'Perhaps he has come to steal a woman,' suggested Avan.

'No,' said Ovan, 'that is not so. Let him remain and with my life I will guarantee that he will harm no one.'

'Let him stay,' said some of the other warriors, for Ovan had long been the pet of the tribe so that they were accustomed to humoring him and so unspoiled was he that they still found pleasure in doing so.

'Very well,' said Avan. 'Let him remain. But Ovan and Ulan shall be responsible for his conduct.'

There were only a few of the Clovians who accepted Tarzan without suspicion, and among these was Maral, the mother of Ovan, and Rela, his sister. These two accepted him without question because Ovan had accepted him. Ulan's friendship, too, had been apparent from the first; nor was it without great value for Ulan, because of his intelligence, courage and ability was a force in the councils of the Clovi.

Tarzan, accustomed to the tribal life of primitive people, took his place naturally among them, paying no attention to those who paid no attention to him, observing scrupulously the ethics of tribal life and conforming to the customs of the Clovi in every detail of his relations with them. He liked to talk with Maral because of her sunny disposition and her marked intelligence. She told him that she was from Zoram, having been captured by Avan when, as a young warrior, he had decided to take a mate. And to her nativity he attributed her great beauty, for it seemed to be an accepted fact among the Clovis that the women of Zoram were the most beautiful of all women.

Ulan he had liked from the first, being naturally attracted to him because he had been the first of the Clovians to champion his cause. In many ways Ulan differed from his fellows. He seemed to have been the first among his people to discover that a brain may be used for purposes other than securing the bare necessities of existence. He had learned to dream and to exercise his brain along pleasant paths that gave entertainment to himself and others – fantastic stories that sometimes amused and sometimes awed his eager audiences; and, too, he was a maker of pictures and these he exhibited to Tarzan with no small measure of pride. Leading the ape-man into the rocky cavern that was the shelter, the storehouse and the citadel of the tribe, he lighted a crude torch which illuminated the walls, revealing the pictures that Ulan had drawn there. Mammoth and saber-tooth and cave bear were depicted, with the red deer, the hyaenodon and other familiar beasts, and in addition thereto were some with which Tarzan was unfamiliar and one that he had never seen elsewhere than in Pal-ul-don, where it had been known as a gryf. Ulan told him that it was a gyor and that it was found upon the Gyor

Cors, or Gyor Plains, which lie at the end of the range of the Mountains of the Thipdars beyond Clovi.

The drawings were in outline and were well executed. The other members of the tribe thought they were very wonderful for Ulan was the first ever to have made them and they could not understand how he did it. Perhaps if he had been a weakling he would have lost caste among them because of this gift, but inasmuch as he was also a noted hunter and warrior his talents but added to his fame and the esteem in which he was held by all.

But though these and a few others were friendly toward him, the majority of the tribe looked upon Tarzan with suspicion, for never within the memory of one of them had a strange warrior entered their village other than as an enemy. They were waiting for the return of Carb and the warriors who had accompanied him, when, the majority of them hoped, the council would sentence the stranger to death.

As they became better acquainted with Tarzan, however, others among them were being constantly won to his cause and this was particularly true when he accompanied them upon their hunts, his skill and his prowess winning their admiration, and his strange weapons which they had at first viewed with contempt, soon commanding their unqualified respect.

And so it was that the longer that Carb remained away the better Tarzan's chances became of being accepted into the tribe upon an equal footing with its other members; a contingency for which he hoped since it would afford him a base from which to prosecute his search for his fellows and allies familiar with the country, whose friendly services he could enlist to aid him in his search.

He was confident that Jason Gridley, if he still lived, was lost somewhere among these stupendous mountains and if he could but find him they might eventually, with the assitance of the Clovians, locate the camp of the O-220.

He had eaten and slept with the Clovi many times and had accompanied them upon several hunts. It had been noon when he arrived and it was still noon, so whether a day or a month had passed he did not know. He was squatting by the cookfire of Maral, talking with her and with Ulan, when from down the gorge there sounded the whistled signal of the Clovians announcing the approach of a friendly party and an instant later a youth rounded the shoulder of the cliff and entered the village.

'It is Tomar,' announced Maral. 'Perhaps he brings news of Carb.'

The youth ran to the center of the ledge upon which the village stood and halted. For a moment he stood there dramatically with upraised hand, commanding silence, and then he spoke. 'Carb is returning,' he cried. 'The victorious warriors of Clovi are returning with the most beautiful woman of Zoram. Great is Carb! Great are the warriors of Clovi!'

Cookfires and the routine occupations of the moment were abandoned as the tribe advanced to await the coming of the victorious war party.

Presently it came into sight, rounding the shoulder of the cliff and filing on to the ledge – twenty warriors led by Carb and among them a girl, her wrists bound behind her back, a rawhide leash around her neck, the free end held by a brawny warrior.

The ape-man's greatest interest lay in Carb, for his position in the tribe, perhaps even his life itself might rest with the decision of this man, whose influence, he had learned, was great in the councils of his people.

Carb was evidently a man of great physical strength; his regular features imparted to him much of the physical beauty that is an attribute of his people, but an otherwise handsome countenance was marred by thin, cruel lips and cold, unsympathetic eyes.

From contemplation of Carb the ape-man's eyes wandered to the face of the prisoner, and there they were arrested by the startling beauty of the girl. Well, indeed, thought Tarzan, might she be acclaimed the most beautiful woman of Zoram, for it was doubtful that there existed many in this world or the outer who might lay claim to greater pulchritude than she.

Avan, the chief, standing in the center of the ledge, received the returning warriors. He looked with favor upon the prize and listened attentively while Carb narrated the more important details of the expedition.

'We shall hold the council at once,' announced Avan, 'to decide who shall possess the prisoner, and at the same time we may settle another matter that has been awaiting the return of Carb and his warriors.'

'What is that?' demanded Carb.

Avan pointed at Tarzan. 'There is a stranger who would come into the tribe and be as one of us.'

Carb turned his cold eyes in the direction of the ape-man and his face clouded. 'Why has he not been destroyed?' he asked. 'Let us do away with him at once.'

'That is not for you to decide,' said Avan, the chief. 'The warriors in council alone may say what shall be done.'

Carb shrugged. 'If the council does not destroy him, I shall kill him myself,' he said. 'I, Carb, will have no enemy living in the village where I live.'

'Let us hold the council at once, then,' said Ulan, 'for if Carb is greater than the council of the warriors we should know it.' There was a note of sarcasm in his voice.

'We have marched for a long time without food or sleep,' said Carb. 'Let us eat and rest before the council is held, for matters may arise in the council which will demand all of our strength,' and he looked pointedly at Ulan.

The other warriors, who had accompanied Carb, also wished to eat and rest before the council was held, and Avan, the chief, acceded to their just demands.

The girl captive had not spoken since she had arrived in the village and she was now turned over to Maral, who was instructed to feed her and permit her to sleep. The bonds were removed from her wrists and she was brought to the cookfire of the chief's mate, where she stood with an expression of haughty disdain upon her beautiful face.

None of the women revealed any inclination to abuse the prisoner – an attitude which rather surprised Tarzan until the reason for it had been explained to him, for he had upon more than one occasion witnessed the cruelties inflicted upon female prisoners by the women of native African tribes into whose hands the poor creatures had fallen.

Maral, in particular, was kind to the girl. 'Why should I be otherwise?' she asked when Tarzan commented upon the fact. 'Our daughters, or even any-one of us, may at any time be captured by the warriors of another tribe, and if it were known that we had been cruel to their women, they would doubt-less repay us in kind; nor, aside from this, is there any reason why we should be other than kind to a woman who will live among us for the rest of her life. We are few in numbers and we are constantly together. If we har-bored enmities and if we quarreled our lives would be less happy. Since you have been here you have never seen quarreling among the women of Clovi; nor would you if you remained here for the rest of your life. There have been quarrelsome women among us, just as at some time there have been crippled children, but as we destroy the one for the good of the tribe we destroy the others.'

She turned to the girl. 'Sit down,' she said pleasantly. 'There is meat in the pot. Eat, and then you may sleep. Do not be afraid; you are among friends. I, too, am from Zoram.'

At that the girl turned her eyes upon the speaker. 'You are from Zoram?' she asked. 'Then you must have felt as I feel. I want to go back to Zoram. I would rather die than live elsewhere.'

'You will get over that,' said Maral. 'I felt the same way, but when I became acquainted I found that the people of Clovi are much like the people of Zoram. They have been kind to me; they will be kind to you, and you will be happy as I have been. When they have given you a mate you will look upon life very differently.'

'I shall not mate with one of them,' cried the girl, stamping her sandaled foot. 'I am Jana, The Red Flower of Zoram, and I choose my own mate.'

Maral shook her head sadly. 'Thus spoke I once,' she said; 'but I have changed, and so will you.'

'Not I,' said the girl. 'I have seen but one man with whom I would mate and I shall never mate with another.'

'You are Jana,' asked Tarzan, 'the sister of Thoar?'

The girl looked at him in surprise, and as though she had noticed him now for the first time her eyes quickly investigated him. 'Ah,' she said, 'you are the stranger whom Carb would destroy.'

'Yes,' replied the ape-man.

'What do you know of Thoar, my brother?'

'We hunted together. We were travelling back to Zoram when I became separated from him. We were following the tracks made by you and a man who was with you when a storm came and obliterated them. Your companion was the whom I was seeking.'

'What do you know of the man who was with me?' demanded the girl.

'He is my friend,' replied Tarzan. 'What has become of him?'

'He was caught in a canyon during the storm and he must have been drowned,' replied Jana sadly. 'You are from his country?'

'Yes.'

'How did you know he was with me?' she demanded.

'I recognized his tracks and Thoar recognized yours.'

'He was a great warrior,' she said, 'and a very brave man.'

'Are you sure that he is dead?' asked Tarzan.

'I am sure,' replied The Red Flower of Zoram.

For a time they were silent, both occupied with thoughts of Jason Gridley. 'You were his friend,' said Jana. She had moved close to him and had seated herself at his side. Now she leaned still closer. 'They are going to kill you,' she whispered. 'I know the people of these tribes better than you and I know Carb. He will have his way. You were Jason's friend and so was I. If we can escape I can lead the way back to Zoram, and if you are Thoar's friend and mine the people of Zoram will have to accept you.'

'Why do you whisper?' asked a gruff voice behind them, and turning they saw Avan, the chief. Without waiting for a reply, he turned to Maral. 'Take the woman to the cavern,' he said. 'She will remain there until the council has decided who shall have her as mate, and in the meantime I will place warriors at the entrance to the cavern to see that she does not escape.'

As Maral motioned Jana toward the cavern, the latter arose, and as she did so she cast an appealing glance at Tarzan. The ape-man, who was already upon his feet, looked quickly about him. Perhaps a hundred members of the tribe were scattered about the ledge, while near the opening to the trail which led down the canyon and which afforded the only avenue of escape, fully a dozes warriors loitered. Alone he might have won his way through, but with the girl it would have been impossible. He shook his head and his lips, which were turned away from Avan, formed the word, 'Wait,' and a moment later The Red Flower of Zoram had entered the dark cavern of the Clovians.

'And as for you, man of another country,' said Avan, addressing Tarzan, 'until the council has decided upon your fate, you are a prisoner. Go, therefore, into the cavern and remain there until the council of warriors has spoken.'

A dozen warriors barred his way to freedom now, but they were lolling idly, expecting no emergency. A bold dash for freedom might carry him beyond them before they could realize that he was attempting escape. He was confident that the voice of the council would be adverse to him and when its decision was announced he would be surrounded by all the warriors of Clovi, alert and ready to prevent his escape. Now, therefore, was the most propitious moment; but Tarzan of the Apes made no break for liberty; instead he turned and strode toward the entrance to the cavern, for The Red Flower of Zoram had appealed to him for aid and he would not desert the sister of Thoar and the friend of Jason.

XII

The Phelian Swamp

As Jason Gridley leaped down the canyon side toward the lone warrior who stood facing the attack of the tremendous reptile gliding swiftly through the air from the top of the opposite cliff side, there flashed upon the screen of his recollection the picture of a restoration of a similar extinct reptile and he recognized the creature as a stegosaurus of the Jurassic; but how inadequately had the picture that he had seen carried to his mind the colossal proportions of the creature, or but remotely suggested its terrifying aspect.

Jason saw the lone warrior standing there facing inevitable doom, but in his attitude there was no outward sign of fear. In his right hand he held his puny spear, and in his left his crude stone knife. He would die, but he would give a good account of himself. There was no panic of terror, no futile flight.

The distance between Jason and the stegosaurus was over great for a revolver shot, but the American hoped that he might at least divert the attention of the reptile from its prey and even, perhaps, frighten it away by the unaccustomed sound of the report of the weapon, and so he fired twice in rapid succession as he leaped downward toward the bottom of the canyon. That at least one of the shots struck the reptile was evidenced by the fact that it veered from its course, simultaneously emitting a loud, screaming sound.

Attracted to Jason by the report of the revolver and evidently attributing its hurt to this new enemy, the reptile, using its tail as a rudder and tilting its spine plates up on one side, veered in the direction of the American.

As the two shots shattered the silence of the canyon, the warrior turned his eyes in the direction of the man leaping down the declivity toward him, and then he saw the reptile veer in the direction of the newcomer.

Heredity and training, coupled with experience, had taught this primitive savage that every man's hand was against him, unless that man was a member of his own tribe. Only upon a single occasion in his life had experience controverted these teachings, and so it seemed inconceivable that this stranger, whom he immediately recognized as such, was deliberately risking his life in an effort to succour him; yet there seemed no other explanation, and so the perplexed warrior, instead of seeking to escape now that the attention of the reptile was diverted from him, ran swiftly toward Jason to join forces with him in combatting the attack of the creature.

From the instant that the stegosaurus had leaped from the summit of the cliff, it had hurtled through the air with a speed which seemed entirely out of proportion to its tremendous bulk, so that all that had transpired in the meantime had occupied but a few moments of time, and Jason Gridley found himself facing this onrushing death almost before he had had time to speculate upon the possible results of his venturesome interference.

With wide distended jaws and uttering piercing shrieks, the terrifying creature shot toward him, but now at last it presented an easy target and Jason Gridley was entirely competent to take advantage of the altered situation.

He fired rapidly with both weapons, trying to reach the tiny brain, at the location of which he could only guess and for which his bullets were searching through the roof of the opened mouth. His greatest hope, however, was that the beast could not for long face that terrific fusillade of shots, and in this he was right. The strange and terrifying sound and the pain and shock of the bullets tearing into its skull proved too much for the stegosaurus. Scarcely half a dozen feet from Gridley it swerved upward and passed over his head, receiving two or three bullets in its belly as it did so.

Still shrieking with rage and pain it glided to the ground beyond him.

Almost immediately it turned to renew the attack. This time it came upon its four feet, and Jason saw that it was likely to prove fully as formidable upon the ground as it had been in the air, for considering its tremendous bulk it moved with great agility and speed.

As he stood facing the returning creature, the warrior reached his side.

'Get on that side of him,' said the warrior, 'and I will attack him on this. Keep out of the way of his tail. Use your spear; you cannot frighten a dyrodor away by making a noise.'

Jason Gridley leaped quickly to one side to obey the suggestions of the warrior, smiling inwardly at the naive suggestion of the other that his Colt had been used solely to frighten the creature.

The warrior took his place upon the opposite side of the approaching reptile, but before he had time to cast his spear or Jason to fire again the creature stumbled forward, its nose dug into the ground and it rolled over upon its side dead.

'It is dead!' said the warrior in a surprised tone. 'What could have killed it? Neither one of us has cast a spear.'

Jason slipped his Colts into their holsters. 'These killed it,' he said, tapping them.

'Noises do not kill,' said the warrior sceptically. 'It is not the bark of the jalok or the growl of the ryth that rends the flesh of man. The hiss of the thipdar kills no one.'

'It was not the noise that killed it,' said Jason, 'but if you will examine its head and especially the roof of its mouth you will see what happened when my weapons spoke.'

Following Jason's suggestion the warrior examined the head and mouth of the dyrodor and when he had seen the gaping wounds he looked at Jason with a new respect. 'Who are you,' he asked, 'and what are you doing in the land of Zoram?'

'My God!' exclaimed Jason. 'Am I in Zoram?'

'You are.'

'And you are one of the men of Zoram?' demanded the American.

'I am; but who are you?'

'Tell me, do you know Jana, The Red Flower of Zoram?' insisted Jason.

'What do you know of The Red Flower of Zoram, stranger?' demanded the other. And then suddenly his eyes widened to a new thought. 'Tell me,' he cried, 'by what name do they call you in the country from which you come?'

'My name is Gridley,' replied the American; 'Jason Gridley.'

'Jason!' exclaimed the other; 'yes, Jason Gridley, that is it. Tell me, man, where is The Red Flower of Zoram? What did you with her?'

'That is what I am asking you,' said Jason. 'We became separated and I have been searching for her. But what do you know of me?'

'I followed you for a long time,' replied the other, 'but the waters fell and obliterated your tracks.'

'Why did you follow me?' asked Jason.

'I followed because you were with The Red Flower of Zoram,' replied the other. 'I followed to kill you, but he said you would not harm her; he said that she went with you willingly. Is that true?'

'She came with me willingly for a while,' replied Jason, 'and then she left me; but I did not harm her.'

'Perhaps he was right then,' said the warrior. 'I shall wait until I find her and if you have not harmed her, I shall not kill you.'

'Whom do you mean by "he"?' asked Jason. 'There is no one in Pellucidar who could possibly know anything about me, except Jana.'

'Do you not know Tarzan?' asked the warrior.

'Tarzan!' exclaimed Jason. 'You have seen Tarzan? He is alive?'

'I saw him. We hunted together and we followed you and Jana, but he is not alive now; he is dead.'

'Dead! You are sure that he is dead?'

'Yes, he is dead.'

'How did it happen?'

'We were crossing the summit of the mountains when he was seized by a thipdar and carried away.'

Tarzan dead! He had feared as much and yet now that he had proof it seemed unbelievable. His mind could scarcely grasp the significance of the words that he had heard as he recalled the strength and vitality of that man of steel. It seemed incredible that that giant frame should cease to pulsate with life; that those mighty muscles no longer rolled beneath the sleek, bronzed hide; that that courageous heart no longer beat.

'You were very fond of him?' asked the warrior, noticing the silence and dejection of the other.

'Yes,' said Jason.

'So was I,' said the warrior; 'but neither Tar-gash nor I could save him, the thipdar struck so swiftly and was gone before we could cast a weapon.'

'Who is Tar-gash?' asked Jason.

'A Sagoth – one of the hairy men,' replied the warrior. 'They live in the forest and are often used as warriors by the Mahars.'

'And he was with you and Tarzan?' inquired Jason.

'Yes. They were together when I first saw them, but now Tarzan is dead and Tar-gash has gone back to his own country and I must proceed upon my search for The Red Flower of Zoram. You have saved my life, man from another country, but I do not know that you have not harmed Jana. Perhaps you have slain her. How am I to know? I do not know what I should do.'

'I, too, am looking for Jana,' said Jason. 'Let us look for her together.'

'Then if we find her, she shall tell me whether or not I shall kill you,' said the warrior.

Jason could not but recall how angry Jana had been with him. She had almost killed him herself. Perhaps she would find it easier to permit this warrior to kill him. Doubtless the man was her sweetheart and if he knew the truth he would need no urging to destroy a rival, but neither by look nor word did he reveal any apprehension as he replied.

'I will go with you,' he, said, 'and if I have harmed The Red Flower of Zoram you may kill me. What is your name?'

'Thoar,' replied the warrior.

Jana had spoken of her brother to Jason, but if she had ever mentioned his name, the American had forgotten it, and so he continued to think that Thoar was the sweetheart and possibly the mate of The Red Flower and his reaction to this belief was unpleasant; yet why it should have been he could not have explained. The more he thought of the matter the more certain he was that Thoar was Jana's mate, for who was there who might more naturally desire to kill one who had wronged her. Yes, he was sure that the man was Jana's mate. The thought made him angry for she had certainly led him to believe that she was not mated. That was just like a woman, he meditated; they were all flirts; they would make a fool of a man merely to pass an idle hour, but she had not made a fool of him. He had not fallen victim to her lures, that is why she had been so angry – her vanity had been piqued – and being a very primitive young person the first thought that had come to her mind had been to kill him. What a little devil she was to try to get him to make love to her when she already had a mate, and thus Jason almost succeeded in working himself into a rage until his sense of humor came to his rescue; yet even though he smiled, way down deep within him something hurt and he wondered why.

'Where did you last see Jana?' asked Thoar. 'We can return there and try and locate her tracks.'

'I do not know that I can explain,' replied Jason. 'It is very difficult for me to locate myself or anything else where there are no points of compass.'

'We can start together at the point where we found your tracks with Jana's,' Said Thoar.

'Perhaps that will not be necessary if you are familiar with the country on the other side of the range,' said Jason. 'Returning toward the mountains from the spot where I first saw Jana, there was a tremendous gorge upon our left. It was toward this gorge that the two men of the four that had been pursuing her ran after I had killed two of their number. Jana tried to find a way to the summit, far to the right of this gorge, but our path was blocked by a deep rift which paralleled the base of the mountains, so that she was compelled to turn back again toward the gorge, into which she descended. The last I saw of her she was going up the gorge, so that if you know where this gorge lies it will not be necessary for us to go all the way back to the point at which I first met her.'

'I know the gorge,' said Thoar, 'and if the two Phelians entered it it is possible that they captured her. We will search in the direction of the gorge then and if we do not find any trace of her, we shall drop down to the country of the Phelians in the lowland.'

Through a maze of jagged peaks Thoar led the way. To him time meant nothing; to Jason Gridley it was little more than a memory. When they found food they ate; when they were tired they slept, and always just ahead there were perilous crags to skirt and stupendous cliffs to scale. To the American it would have seemed incredible that a girl ever could find her way here had he not had occasion to follow where The Red Flower of Zoram led.

Occasionally they were forced to take a lower route which led into the forests that climbed high along the slopes of the mountains, and here they found more game and with Thoar's assistance Jason fashioned a garment from the hide of a mountain goat. It was at best but a sketchy garment; yet it sufficed for the purpose for which it was intended and left his arms and legs free. Nor was it long before he realized its advantages and wondered why civilized man of the outer crust should so encumber himself with useless clothing, when the demands of temperature did not require it.

As Jason became better acquainted with Thoar he found his regard for him changing from suspicion to admiration, and finally to a genuine liking for the savage Pellucidarian, in spite of the fact that this sentiment was tinged with a feeling that, while not positive animosity, was yet akin to it. It was difficult for Jason to fathom the sentiment which seemed to animate him. There could be no rivalry between him and this primitive warrior and yet Jason's whole demeanor and attitude toward Thoar was such as might be scrupulously observed by any honorable man toward an honorable opponent or rival.

They seldom, if ever, spoke of Jana; yet thoughts of her were uppermost in the mind of each of them. Jason often found himself reviewing every detail of his association with her; every little characteristic gesture and expression was indelibly imprinted upon his memory, as were the contours of her perfect figure and the radiant loveliness of her face. Not even the bitter words with which she had parted with him could erase the memory of her joyous comradeship. Never before in his life had he missed the companionship of any woman. At times he tried to crowd her from his thoughts by recalling incidents of his friendship with Cynthia Furnois or Barbara Green, but the vision of The Red Flower of Zoram remained persistently in the foreground, while that of Cynthia and Barbara always faded gradually into forgetfulness.

This state of mental subjugation to the personality of an untutored savage, however beautiful, annoyed his ego and he tried to escape it by dwelling upon the sorrow entailed by the death of Tarzan; but somehow he never could convince himself that Tarzan was dead. It was one of those things that it was simply impossible to conceive.

Failing in this, he would seek to occupy his mind with conjectures concerning the fate of Von Horst, Muviro and the Waziri warriors, or upon what was transpiring aboard the great dirigible in search of which his eyes were often scanning the cloudless Pellucidarian sky. But travel where it would, even to his remote Tarzana hills in far off California, it would always return to hover around the girlish figure of The Red Flower of Zoram.

Thoar, upon his part, found in the American a companion after his own heart – a dependable man of quiet ways, always ready to assume his share of the burden and responsibilities of the savage trail they trod.

So the two came at last to the rim of the great gorge and though they followed it up and down for a great distance in each direction they found no trace of Jana, nor any sign that she had passed that way.

'We shall go down to the lowlands,' said Thoar, 'to the country that is called Pheli and even though we may not find her, we shall avenge her.'

The idea of primitive justice suggested by Thoar's decision aroused no opposing question of ethics in the mind of the civilized American; in fact, it seemed quite the most natural thing in the world that he and Thoar should constitute themselves a court of justice as well as the instrument of its punishment, for thus easily does man slough off the thin veneer of civilization, which alone differentiates him from his primitive ancestors.

Thus a gap of perhaps a hundred thousand years which yawned between Thoar of Zoram and Jason Gridley of Tarzana was closed. Imbued with the same hatred, they descended the slopes of the Mountains of the Thipdars toward the land of Pheli, and the heart of each was hot with the lust to kill. No greedy munitions manufacturer was needed here to start a war.

Down through stately forests and across rolling foothills went Thoar and Jason toward the land of Pheli. The country teemed with game of all descriptions and their way was beset by fierce carnivores, by stupid, irritable herbivores of ponderous weight and short tempers or by gigantic reptiles beneath whose charging feet the earth trembled. It was by the exercise of the superior intelligence of man combined with a considerable share of luck that they passed unscathed to the swamp land where Pheli lies. Here the world seemed dedicated to the reptilia. They swarmed in countless thousands and in all sizes and infinite varieties. Aquatic and amphibious, carnivorous and herbivorous, they hissed and screamed and fought and devoured one another constantly, so that Jason wondered in what intervals they found the time to propagate their kind and he marvelled that the herbivores among them could exist at all. A terrific orgy of extermination seemed to constitute the entire existence of a large proportion of the species and yet the tremendous size of many of them, including several varieties of the herbivores, furnished ample evidence that considerable numbers of them lived to a great age, for unlike mammals, reptiles never cease to grow while they are living.

The swamp, in which Thoar believed the villages of the Phelians were to be found, supported a tremendous forest of gigantic trees and so interlaced were their branches that oftentimes the two men found it expedient to travel among them rather than upon the treacherous, boggy ground. Here, too, the reptiles were smaller, though scarcely less numerous. Among these, however, there were exceptions, and those which caused them the greatest anxiety were snakes of such titanic proportions that when he first encountered one Jason could not believe the testimony of his own eyes. They came upon the creature suddenly as it was in the act of swallowing a trachodon that was almost as large as an elephant. The huge herbivorous dinosaur was still alive and battling bravely to extricate itself from the jaws of the serpent, but not even its giant strength nor its terrific armament of teeth, which included a reserve supply of over four hundred in the lower jaw alone, availed it in its unequal struggle with the colossal creature that was slowly swallowing it alive.

Perhaps it was their diminutive size as much as their brains or luck that saved the two men from the jaws of these horrid creatures. Or, again, it may have been the dense stupidity of the reptiles themselves, which made it comparatively easy for the men to elude them.

Here in this dismal swamp of horrors not even the giant tarags or the equally ferocious lions and leopards of Pellucidar dared venture, and how man existed there it was beyond the power of Jason to conceive. In fact he doubted that the Phelians or any other race of men made their homes here. 'Men could not exist in such a place,' he said to Thoar. 'Pheli must lie elsewhere.'

'No,' said his companion, 'members of my tribe have come down here more than once in the memory of man to avenge the stealing of a woman and the stories that they have brought back have familiarized us all with the conditions existing in the land of Pheli. This is indeed it.'

'You may be right,' said Jason, 'but, like these snakes that we have seen, I shall have to see the villages of the Phelians before I will believe that they exist here and even then I won't know whether to believe it or not.'

'It will not be long now,' said Thoar, 'before you shall see the Phelians in their own village.'

'What makes you think so?' asked Jason.

'Look down below you and you will see what I have been searching for,' replied Thoar, pointing.

Jason did as he was bid and discovered a small stream meandering through the swamp. 'I see nothing but a brook,' he said.

'That is what I have been searching for,' replied Thoar. 'All of my people who have been here say that Phelians live upon the banks of a river that runs through the swamp. In places the land is high and upon these hills the Phelians build their homes. They do not live in caverns as do we, but they make houses of great trees so strong that not even the largest reptiles can break into them.'

'But why should anyone choose to live in such a place?' demanded the American.

'To eat and to breed in comparative peace and contentment,' replied Thoar. 'The Phelians, unlike the mountain people, are not a race of warriors. They do not like to fight and so they have hidden their villages away in this swamp where no man would care to come and thus they are practically free from human enemies. Also, here, meat abounds in such quantities that food lies always at their doors. For them then the conditions are ideal and here, more than elsewhere in Pellucidar, may they find contentment.'

As they advanced now they exercised the greatest caution, knowing that any moment they might come within sight of a Phelian village. Nor was it long before Thoar halted and drew back behind the bole of a tree through which they were passing, then he pointed forward. Jason, looking, saw a bare hill before them, just a portion of which was visible through the trees. It was evident that the hill had been cleared by man, for many stumps remained. Within the range of his vision was but a single house, if such it might be called.

It was constructed of logs, a foot or two in diameter. Three or four of these logs, placed horizontally and lying one upon the other, formed the wall that was presented to Jason's view. The other side wall paralleled it at a distance of five or six feet, and across the top of the upper logs were laid sections of smaller trees, about six inches in diameter, and placed not more than a foot apart. These supported the roof, which consisted of several logs, a little longer than the logs constituting the walls. The roof logs were laid close together, the interstices being filled with mud. The front of the building was formed by shorter logs set upright in the ground, a single small aperture being left to form a doorway. But the most noticeable feature of Phelian architecture consisted of long pointed stakes, which protruded diagonally from the ground at an angle of about forty-five degrees, pointing outward from the base of the walls entirely around the building at intervals of about eighteen inches. The stakes themselves were six or eight inches in diameter and about ten feet long, being sharpened at the upper end, and forming a barrier against which few creatures, however brainless they might be, would venture to hurl themselves.

Drawing closer the two men had a better view of the village, which contained upon that side of the hill they were approaching and upon the top four buildings similar to that which they had first discovered. Close about the base of the hill grew the dense forest, but the hill itself had been entirely denuded of vegetation so that nothing, either large or small, could approach the habitation of the Phelians without being discovered.

No one was in sight about the village, but that did not deceive Thoar, who guessed that anything which transpired upon the hillside would be witnessed by many eyes peering through the openings between the wall logs from the dim interiors of the long buildings, beneath whose low ceilings Phelians must spend their lives either squatting or lying down, since there was not sufficient headroom to permit an adult to stand erect.

'Well,' said Jason, 'here we are. Now, what are we going to do?'

Thoar looked longingly at Jason's two Colts. 'You have refused to use those for fear of wasting the deaths which they spit from their blue mouths,' he said, 'but with one of those we might soon find Jana if she was here or quickly avenge her if she is not.'

'Come on then,' said Jason. 'I would sacrifice more than my ammunition for The Red Flower of Zoram.' As he spoke he descended from the tree and started toward the nearest Phelian dwelling. Close behind him was Thoar and neither saw the eyes that watched them from among the trees that grew thickly upon the river side of the hill – cruel eyes that gleamed from whiskered faces.

XIII

The Horibs

Avan, chief of the Clovi, had placed warriors before the entrance to the cavern and as Tarzan approached it to enter they halted him.

'Where are you going?' demanded one.

'Into the cavern,' replied Tarzan.

'Why?' asked the warrior.

'I wish to sleep,' replied the ape-man. 'I have entered often before and no one has ever stopped me.'

'Avan has issued orders that no strangers are to enter or leave the cavern until after the council of the warriors,' exclaimed the guard.

At this juncture Avan approached. 'Let him enter,' he said. 'I sent him hither, but do not let him come out again.'

Without a word of comment or question the Lord of the Jungle passed into the interior of the gloomy cavern of Clovi. It was several moments before his eyes became accustomed to the subdued light within and permitted him to take account of his surroundings.

That portion of the cavern which was visible and with which he was familiar was of considerable extent. He could see the walls on either side, and, very vaguely, a portion of the rear wall, but adjoining that was utter darkness, suggesting that the cavern extended further into the mountainside. Against the walls upon pallets of dry grasses covered with hide lay many warriors and a few women and children, almost all of whom were wrapped in slumber. In the greater light near the entrance a group squatted engaged in whispered conversation as, silently, he moved about the cavern searching for the girl from Zoram. It was she who recognized him first, attracting his attention by a low whistle.

'You have a plan of escape?' she asked as Tarzan seated himself upon a skin beside her.

'No,' he said, 'all that we may do is to await developments and take advantage of any opportunity that may present itself.'

'I should think that it would be easy for you to escape,' said the girl; 'they do not treat you as a prisoner; you go about among them freely and they have permitted you to retain your weapons.'

'I am a prisoner now,' he replied. 'Avan just instructed the warriors at the entrance not to permit me to leave here until after the council of warriors had decided my fate.'

'Your future does not look very bright then,' said Jana, 'and as for me I already know my fate, but they shall not have me, Carb nor any other!'

They talked together in low tones with many periods of long silence, but when Jana turned the conversation upon the world from which Jason had come, the silences were few and far between. She would not let Tarzan rest, but plied him with questions, the answers to many of which were far beyond her powers to understand. Steam and electricity and all the countless activities of civilized existence which are dependent upon them were utterly beyond her powers of comprehension, as were the heavenly bodies or musical instruments or books, and yet despite what appeared to be the darkest depth of ignorance, to the very bottom of which she had plumbed, she was intelligent and when she spoke of those things pertaining to her own world with which she was familiar, she was both interesting and entertaining.

Presently a warrior near them opened his eyes, sat up and stretched. He looked about him and then he arose to his feet. He walked around the apartment awakening the other warriors.

'Awaken,' he said to each, 'and attend the council of the warriors.'

When he approached Tarzan and Jana he recognized the former and stopped to glare down at him.

'What are you doing here?' he demanded.

Tarzan arose and faced the Clovian warrior, but he did not reply to the other's question.

'Answer me,' growled Carb. 'Why are you here?'

'You are not the chief,' said Tarzan. 'Go and ask your question of women and children.'

Carb sputtered angrily. 'Go!' said Tarzan, pointing toward the exit. For an instant the Clovian hesitated, then he continued on around the apartment, awakening the remaining warriors.

'Now he will see that you are killed,' said the girl.

'He had determined on that before,' replied Tarzan. 'We are no worse off than we were.'

Now they lapsed into silence, each waiting for the doom that was to be pronounced upon them. They knew that outside upon the ledge the warriors were sitting in a great circle and that there would be much talking and boasting and argument before any decision was reached, most of it unnecessary, for that has been the way with men who make laws from time immemorial, a great advantage, however, lying with our modern lawmakers in that they know more words than the first ape-men.

As Tarzan and Jana waited a youth entered the cavern. He bore a torch in the light of which he searched about the interior. Presently he discovered Tarzan and came swiftly toward him. It was Ovan.

'The council has reached its decision,' he said. 'They will kill you and the girl goes to Carb.'

Tarzan of the Apes rose to his feet. 'Come,' he said to Jana, 'now is as good a time as any. If we can cross the ledge and reach the trail only a swift warrior can overtake us. And if you are my friend,' he continued, turning to Ovan, 'and you have said that you are, you will remain silent and give us our chance.'

'I am your friend,' replied the youth; 'that is why I am here, but you would never live to cross the ledge to the trail, there are too many warriors and they are all prepared. They know that you are armed and they expect that you will try to escape.'

'There is no other way,' said Tarzan.

'There is another way,' replied the boy, 'and I have come to show it to you.'

'Where?' asked Jana.

'Follow me,' replied Ovan, and he started back into the remote recesses of the cavern, which were fitfully illumined by his flickering torch, while behind him followed Jana and the ape-man.

The walls of the cavern narrowed, the floor rose steeply ahead of them, so that in places it was only with considerable difficulty that they ascended in the semi-darkness. At last Ovan halted and held his torch high above his head, revealing a small, natural chamber, at the far end of which there was a dark fissure.

'In that dark hole,' he said, 'lies a trail that leads to the summit of the mountains. Only the chief and the chief's first son ever know of this trail. If my father learns that I have shown it to you, he will have to kill me, but he shall never know for when next they find me I shall be asleep upon a skin in the cavern far below. The trail is steep and rough, but it is the only way. Go now. This is the return I make you for having saved my life.' With that he dashed the torch to the floor, leaving them in utter darkness. He did not speak again, but Tarzan heard the soft falls of his sandaled feet groping their way back down toward the cavern of the Clovi.

The ape-man reached out through the darkness and found Jana's hand. Carefully he led her through the Stygian darkness toward the mouth of the fissure. Feeling his way step by step, groping forward with his free hand, the ape-man finally discovered the entrance to the trail.

Clambering upward over broken masses of jagged granite through utter darkness, it seemed to the two fugitives that they made no progress whatever. If time could be measured by muscular effort and physical discomfort, the two might have guessed that they passed an eternity in this black fissure, but at length the darkness lessened and they knew that they were approaching the opening in the summit of the mountains; nor was it long thereafter before they emerged into the brilliant light of the noonday sun.

'And now,' said Tarzan, 'in which direction lies Zoram?'

The girl pointed. 'But we cannot reach it by going back that way,' she said, 'for every trail will be guarded by Carb and his fellows. Do not think that they will let us escape so easily. Perhaps in searching for us they may even find the fissure and follow us here.'

'This is your world,' said Tarzan. 'You are more familiar with it than I. What, then, do you suggest?'

'We should descend the mountains, going directly away from Clovi,' replied Jana, 'for it is in the mountains that they will look for us. When we have reached the lowland we can turn back along the foot of the range until we are below Zoram, but not until then should we come back to the mountains.'

The descent of the mountains was slow because neither of them was familiar with this part of the range. Oftentimes, their way barred by yawning chasms, they were compelled to retrace their steps to find another way around. They ate many times and slept thrice and thus only could Tarzan guess that they had consumed considerable time in the descent, but what was time to them?

During the descent Tarzan had caught glimpses of a vast plain, stretching away as far as the eye could reach. The last stage of their descent was down a long, winding canyon, and when, at last, they came to its mouth they found themselves upon the edge of the plain that Tarzan had seen. It was almost treeless and from where he stood it looked as level as a lake.

'This is the Gyor Cors,' said Jana, 'and may we not have the bad fortune to meet a Gyor.'

'And what is a Gyor?' asked Tarzan.

'Oh, it is a terrible creature,' replied Jana. 'I have never seen one, but some of the warriors of Zoram have been to the Gyor Cors and they have seen them. They are twice the size of a tandor and their length is more than that of four tall men, lying upon the ground. They have a curved beak and three great horns, two above their eyes and one above their nose. Standing upright at the backs of their heads is a great collar of bony substance covered with thick, horny hide, which protects them from the horns of their fellows and spears of men. Thy do not eat flesh, but they are irritable and short tempered, charging every creature that they see and thus keeping the Gyor Cors for their own use.'

'Theirs is a vast domain,' said Tarzan, letting his eyes sweep the illimitable expanse of pasture land that rolled on and on, curving slowly upward into the distant haze, 'and your description of them suggests that they have few enemies who would care to dispute their dominion.'

'Only the Horibs,' replied Jana. 'They hunt them for their flesh and hide.'

'What are Horibs?' asked Tarzan.

The girl shuddered. 'The snake people,' she whispered in an awed tone.

'Snake people,' repeated Tarzan, 'and what are they?'

'Let us not speak of them. They are horrible. They are worse than the Gyors. Their blood is cold and men say that they have no hearts, for they do not possess any of the characteristics that men admire, knowing not friendship or sympathy or love.'

Along the bottom of the canyon through which they had descended a mountain torrent had cut a deep gorge, the sides of which were so precipitous that they found it expedient to follow the stream down into the plain in order to discover an easier crossing, since the stream lay between them and Zoram.

They had proceeded for about a mile below the mouth of the canyon; around them were low, rolling hills which gradually merged with the plain below; here and there were scattered clumps of trees; to their knees grew the gently waving grasses that rendered the Gyor Cors a paradise for the huge herbivorous dinosaurs. The noonday sun shone down upon a scene of peace and quiet, yet Tarzan of the Apes was restless. The apparent absence of animal life seemed almost uncanny to one familiar with the usual teeming activity of Pellucidar; yet the ape-man knew that there were creatures about and it was the strange and unfamiliar scent spoors carried to his nostrils that aroused within him a foreboding of ill omen. Familiar odors had no such effect upon him, but here were scents that he could not place, strangely disagreeable in the nostrils of man. They suggested the scent spoor of Histah the snake, but they were not his.

For Jana's sake Tarzan wished that they might quickly find a crossing and ascend again to the higher levels on their journey to Zoram, for there the creatures would be well known to them, and the dangers which they portended familiar dangers with which they were prepared to cope, but the vertical banks of the raging torrent as yet offered no means of descent and now they saw that the appearance of flatness which distance had imparted to the great Gyor Cors was deceptive, since it was cut by ravines and broken by depressions, some of which were of considerable extent and depth. Presently a lateral ravine, opening into the now comparatively shallow gorge of the river, necessitated a detour which took them directly away from Zoram. They had proceeded for about a mile in this direction when they discovered a crossing and as they emerged upon the opposite side the girl touched Tarzan's arm and pointed. The thing that she saw he had seen simultaneously.

'A Gyor,' whispered the girl. 'Let us lie down and hide in this tall grass.'

'He has not seen us yet,' said Tarzan, 'and he may not come in this direction.'

No description of the beast looming tremendously before them could convey an adequate impression of its titanic proportions or its frightful mien. At the first glance Tarzan was impressed by its remarkable likeness to the Gryfs of Pal-ul-don. It had the two large horns above the eyes, a medial horn on the nose, a horny beak and a great, horny hood or transverse crest over the neck, and its coloration was similar but more subdued, the predominant note being a slaty gray with yellowish belly and face. The blue bands around the eyes were less well marked and the red of the hood and the bony protuberances along the spine were less brilliant than in the Gryf. That it was herbivorous, a fact that he had learned from Jana, convinced him that he was looking upon an almost unaltered type of the gigantic triceratops that had, with its fellow dinosaurs, ruled the ancient Jurassic world.

Jana had thrown herself prone among the grasses and was urging Tarzan to do likewise. Crouching low, his eyes just above the grasses, Tarzan watched the huge dinosaur.

'I think he has caught our scent,' he said. 'He is standing with his head up, looking about him; now he is trotting around in a circle. He is very light on his feet for a beast of such enormous size. There, he has caught a scent, but it is not ours; the wind is not in the right direction. There is something approaching from our left, but it is still at a considerable distance. I can just hear it, a faint suggestion of something moving. The Gyor is looking in that direction now. Whatever is coming is coming swiftly. I can tell by the rapidly increasing volume of sound, and there are more than one – there are many. He is moving forward now to investigate, but he will pass at a considerable distance to our left.' Tarzan watched the Gyor and listened to the sound coming from the, as yet, invisible creatures that were approaching. 'Whatever is approaching is coming along the bottom of the ravine we just crossed,' he whispered. 'They will pass directly behind us.'

Jana remained hiding low in the grasses. She did not wish to tempt Fate by revealing even the top of her head to attract the attention of the Gyor. 'Perhaps we had better try to crawl away while his attention is attracted elsewhere,' she suggested.

'They are coming out of the ravine,' whispered Tarzan. 'They are coming up over the edge – a number of men – but in the name of God what is it that they are riding?'

Jana raised her eyes above the level of the grasses and looked in the direction that Tarzan was gazing. She shuddered. 'They are not men,' she said; 'they are the Horibs and the things upon the backs of which they ride are Gorobors. If they see us we are lost. Nothing in the world can escape the

Gorobors, for there is nothing in all Pellucidar so swift as they. Lie still. Our only chance is that they may not discover us.'

At sight of the Horibs the Gyor emitted a terrific bellow that shook the ground and, lowering his head, he charged straight for them. Fully fifty of the Horibs on their horrid mounts had emerged from the ravine. Tarzan could see that the riders were armed with long lances – pitiful and inadequate weapons, he thought, with which to face an enraged triceratop. But it soon became apparent that the Horibs did not intend to meet that charge head-on. Wheeling to their right they formed in single file behind their leader and then for the first time Tarzan had an exhibition of the phenomenal speed of the huge lizards upon which they were mounted, which is comparable only to the lightning-like rapidity of a tiny desert lizard known as a swift.

Following tactics similar to those of the plains Indians of western America, the Horibs were circling their prey. The bellowing Gyor, aroused to a frenzy of rage, charged first in one direction and then another, but the Gorobors darted from his path so swiftly that he never could overtake them. Panting and blowing, he presently came to bay and then the Horibs drew their circle closer, whirling dizzily about him, while Tarzan watched the amazing scene, wondering by what means they might ever hope to dispatch the ten tons of incarnate fury that wheeled first this way and then that at the center of their circle.

As swiftly as they had darted in all three wheeled and were out again, part of the racing circle, but in the sides of the Gyor they had left two lances deeply imbedded. The fury of the wounded triceratop transcended any of his previous demonstrations. His bellowing became a hoarse, coughing scream as once again he lowered his head and charged.

This time he did not turn and charge in another direction as he had in the past, but kept on in a straight line, possibly in the hope of breaking through the encircling Horibs, and to his dismay the ape-man saw that he and Jana were directly in the path of the charging beast. If the Horibs did not turn him, they were lost.

A dozen of the reptile-men darted in upon the rear of the Gyor. A dozen more lances sank deeply into its body, proving sufficient to turn him in an effort to avenge himself upon those who had inflicted these new hurts.

This charge had carried the Gyor within fifty feet of Tarzan and Jana. It had given the ape-man an uncomfortable moment, but its results were almost equally disastrous for it brought the circling Horibs close to their position.

The Gyor stood now with lowered head, breathing heavily and bleeding from more than a dozen wounds. A Horib now rode slowly toward him, approaching him directly from in front. The attention of the triceratop was centered wholly upon this single adversary as two more moved toward him diagonally from the rear, one on either side, but in such a manner that they were concealed from his view by the great transverse crest encircling his neck behind the horns and eyes. The three approached thus to within about fifty feet of the brute and then those in the rear darted forward simultaneously at terrific speed, leaning well forward upon their mounts, their lances lowered. At the same instant each struck heavily upon either side of the Gyor, driving their spears far in. So close did they come to their prey that their mounts struck the shoulders of the Gyor as they turned and darted out again.

For an instant the great creature stood reeling in its tracks and then it slumped forward heavily and rolled over upon its side – the final lances had pierced its heart.

Tarzan was glad that it was over as he had momentarily feared discovery by the circling Horibs and he was congratulating himself upon their good fortune when the entire band of snake-men wheeled their mounts and raced swiftly in the direction of their hiding place. Once more they formed their circle, but this time Tarzan and Jana were at its center. Evidently the Horibs had seen them, but had temporarily ignored them until after they had dispatched the Gyor.

'We shall have to fight,' said Tarzan, and as concealment was no longer possible he arose to his feet.

'Yes,' said Jana, arising to stand beside him. 'We shall have to fight, but the end will be the same. There are fifty of them and we are but two.'

Tarzan fitted an arrow to his bow. The Horibs were circling slowly about them inspecting their new prey. Finally they came closer and halted their mounts, facing the two.

Now for the first time Tarzan was able to obtain a good view of the snake-men and their equally hideous mounts. The conformation of the Horibs was almost identical to man insofar as the torso and extremities were concerned. Their three-toed feet and five-toed hands were those of reptiles. The head and face resembled a snake, but pointed ears and two short horns gave a grotesque appearance that was at the same time hideous. The arms were better proportioned than the legs, which were quite shapeless. The entire body was covered with scales, although those upon the hands, feet and face were so minute as to give the impression of bare skin, a resemblance which was further emphasized by the fact that these portions of the body were a much lighter color, approximating the shiny dead whiteness of a snake's belly. They wore a single apron-like garment fashioned from a piece of very heavy hide, apparently that of some gigantic reptile. This garment was really a piece of armor, its sole purpose being, as Tarzan later learned, to cover the soft, white bellies of the Horibs. Upon the breast of each garment was a strange device – an eight-pronged cross with a circle in the center. Around his waist each Horib wore a leather belt, which supported a scabbard in which was inserted a bone knife. About each wrist and above each elbow was a band or bracelet.

These completed their apparel and ornaments. In addition to his knife each Horib carried a long lance shod with bone. They sat on their grotesque mounts with their toes locked behind the elbows of the Gorobors, anomodont reptiles of the Triassic, known to paleontologists as Pareiasuri. Many of these creatures measured ten feet in length, though they stood low upon squat and powerful legs.

As Tarzan gazed in fascination upon the Horibs, whose 'blood ran cold and who had no hearts,' he realized that he might be gazing upon one of the vagaries of evolution, or possibly upon a replica of some form that had once existed upon the outer crust and that had blazed the trail that some, to us, unknown creature must have blazed from the age of reptiles to the age of man. Nor did it seem to him, after reflection, any more remarkable that a man-like reptile might evolve from reptiles than that birds should have done so or, as scientific discoveries are now demonstrating, mammals must have.

These thoughts passed quickly, almost instantaneously, through his mind as the Horibs sat there with their beady, lidless eyes fastened upon them, but if Tarzan had been astounded by the appearance of these creatures the emotion thus aroused was nothing compared with the shock he received when one of them spoke, addressing him in the common language of the gilaks of Pellucidar.

'You cannot escape,' he said. 'Lay down your weapons.'

XIV

Through the Dark Forest

Jason Gridley ran swiftly up the hill toward the Phelian village in which he hoped to find The Red Flower of Zoram and at his side was Thoar, ready with spear and knife to rescue or avenge his sister, while behind them, concealed by the underbrush that grew beneath the trees along the river's bank, a company of swarthy, bearded men watched the two.

To Thoar's surprise no defending warriors rushed from the building they were approaching, nor did any sound come from the interior. 'Be careful,' he cautioned Jason, 'we may be running into a trap,' and the American, profiting by the advice of his companion, advanced more cautiously. To the very entrance of the building they came and as yet no opposition to their advance had manifested itself.

Jason stopped and looked through the low doorway, then, stooping, he entered with Thoar at his heels.

'There is no one here,' said Jason; 'the building is deserted.'

'Better luck in the next one then,' said Thoar; but there was no one in the next building, nor in the next, nor in any of the buildings of the Phelian village.

'They have all gone,' said Jason.

'Yes,' replied Thoar, 'but they will return. Let us go down among the trees at the riverside and wait for them there in hiding.'

Unconscious of danger, the two walked down the hillside and entered the underbrush that grew luxuriantly beneath the trees. They followed a narrow trail, worn by Phelian sandals.

Scarcely had the foliage closed about them when a dozen men sprang upon them and bore them to the ground. In an instant they were disarmed and their wrists bound behind their backs; then they were jerked roughly to their feet and Jason Gridley's eyes went wide as they got the first glimpse of his captors.

'Well, for Pete's sake!' he exclaimed. 'I have learned to look with comparative composure upon woolly rhinoceroses, mammoths, trachodons, pterodactyls and dinosaurs, but I never expected to see Captain Kidd, Lafitte and Sir Henry Morgan in the heart of Pellucidar.'

In his surprise he reverted to his native tongue, which, of course, none of the others understood.

'What language is that?' demanded one of their captors. 'Who are you and from what country do you come?'

'That is good old American, from the U.S.A.,' replied Jason; 'but who the devil are you and why have you captured us?' and then turning to Thoar, 'these are not the Phelians, are they?'

'No,' replied Thoar. 'These are strange men, such as I have never before seen.'

'We know who you are,' said one of the bearded men. 'We know the country from which you come. Do not try to deceive us.'

'Very well, then, if you know, turn me loose, for you must know that we haven't a war on with anyone.'

'Your country is always at war with Korsar,' replied the speaker. 'You are a Sarian. I know it by the weapons that you carry. The moment I saw them, I knew that you were from distant Sari. The Cid will be glad to have you and so will Bulf. Perhaps,' he added, turning to one of his fellows, 'this is Tanar, himself. Did you see him when he was a prisoner in Korsar?'

'No, I was away upon a cruise,' replied the other. 'I did not see him, but if this is indeed he we shall be well rewarded.'

'We might as well return to the ship now,' said the first speaker. 'There is no use waiting any longer for these flat-footed natives with but one chance in a thousand of finding a good looking woman among them.'

'They told us further down the river that these people sometimes captured women from Zoram. Perhaps it would be well to wait.'

'No,' said the other, 'I should like well enough to see one of these women from Zoram that I have heard of all my life, but the natives will not return as long as we are in the vicinity. We have been gone from the ship too long now and if I know the captain, he will be wanting to slit a few throats by the time we get back.'

Moored to a tree along the shore and guarded by five other Korsars was a ship's longboat, but of a style that was reminiscent of Jason's boyhood reading as were the bearded men with their bizarre costumes, their great pistols and cutlasses and their ancient arquebuses.

The prisoners were bundled into the boat, the Korsars entered and the craft was pushed off into the stream, which here was narrow and swift.

As the current bore them rapidly along Jason had an opportunity to examine his captors. They were as villainous looking a crew as he had ever imagined outside of fiction and were more typically piratical than the fiercest pirates of his imagination. What with earrings and, in some instances, nose rings of gold, with the gay handkerchiefs bound about their heads and body sashes around their waists, they would have presented a gorgeous and colorful picture at a distance sufficiently great to transform their dirt and patches into a pleasing texture.

Although in the story of Tanar of Pellucidar that Jason had received by radio from Perry, he had become familiar with the appearance and nature of the Korsars, yet he now realized that heretofore he had accepted them more as he had accepted the pirates of history and of his boyhood reading – as fictional or, at best, legendary – and not men of flesh and bone such as he saw before him, their mouths filled with oaths and coarse jokes, the grime and filth of reality marking them as real human beings.

In these savage Korsars, their boat, their apparel and their ancient firearms, Jason saw conclusive proof of their descent from men of the outer crust and realized how they must have carried to the mind of David Innes an overwhelming conviction of the existence of a polar opening leading from Pellucidar to the outer world.

While Thoar was disheartened by the fate that had thrown them into the hands of these strange people, Jason was not at all sure but that it might prove a stroke of fortune for himself, as from the conversation and comments that he had heard since their capture it seemed reasonable to assume that they were to be taken to Korsar, the city in which David Innes was confined and which was, therefore, the first goal of their expedition to effect the rescue of the Emperor of Pellucidar.

That he would arrive there alone and a prisoner were not in themselves causes for rejoicing; yet, on the whole, he would be no worse off than to remain wandering aimlessly through a country filled with unknown dangers without the faintest shadow of a hope of ever being able to locate his fellows. Now, at least, he was almost certain of being transported to a place that they also were attempting to reach and thus the chances of a reunion were so much the greater.

The stream down which they floated wound through a swampy forest, crossing numerous lagoons that sometimes were a size that raised them to the dignity of lakes. Everywhere the waters and the banks teemed with reptilian life, suggesting to Jason Gridley that he was reviewing a scene such as might have been enacted in a Mesozoic paradise countless ages before upon the outer crust. So numerous and oftentimes so colossal and belligerent were the savage reptiles that the descent of the river became a running fight, during which the Korsars were constantly upon the alert and frequently were compelled to discharge their arquebuses in defense of their lives. More often than not the noise of the weapons frightened off the attacking reptiles, but occasionally one would persist in its attack until it had been killed; nor was the possibility ever remote that in one of these encounters some fierce and brainless saurian might demolish their craft and with its fellows devour the crew.

Jason and Thoar had been placed in the middle of the boat, where they squatted upon the bottom, their wrists still secured behind their backs. Close to Jason was a Korsar whose fellows addressed him as Lajo. There was something about this fellow that attracted Jason's particular attention. Perhaps it was his more open countenance or a less savage and profane demeanor. He had not joined the others in the coarse jokes that were directed against their captives; in fact, he paid little attention to anything other than the business of defending the boat against the attacking monsters.

There seemed to be no one in command of the party, all matters being discussed among them and in this way a decision arrived at; yet Jason had noticed that the others listened attentively when Lajo spoke, which was seldom, though always intelligently and to the point. Guided by the result of these observations he selected Lajo as the most logical Korsar through whom to make a request. At the first opportunity, therefore, he attracted the man's attention.

'What do you want?' asked Lajo.

'Who is in command here?' asked Jason.

'No one,' replied the Korsar. 'Our officer was killed on the way up. Why do you ask?'

'I want the bonds removed from our wrists,' replied Jason. 'We cannot escape. We are unarmed and outnumbered and, therefore, cannot harm you; while in the event that the boat is destroyed or capsized by any of these reptiles we shall be helpless with our wrists tied behind our backs.'

Lajo drew his knife.

'What are you going to do?' asked one of the other Korsars who had been listening to the conversation.

'I am going to cut their bonds,' replied Lajo. 'There is nothing to be gained by keeping them bound.'

'Who are you to say that their bonds shall be cut?' demanded the other belligerently.

'Who are you to say that they shall not?' returned Lajo quietly, moving toward the prisoners.

'I'll show you who I am,' shouted the other, whipping out his knife and advancing toward Lajo.

There was no hesitation. Like a panther Lajo swung upon his adversary, striking up the other's knife-hand with his left forearm and at the same time plunging his villainous looking blade to the hilt in the other's breast. Voicing a single bloodcurdling scream the man sank lifeless to the bottom of the boat. Lajo wrenched his knife from the corpse, wiped it upon his adversary's shirt and quietly cut the bonds that confined the wrists of Thoar and Jason. The other Korsars looked on, apparently unmoved by the killing of their fellow, except for a coarse joke or two at the expense of the dead man and a grunt of approbation for Lajo's act.

The killer removed the weapons from the body of the dead man and cast them aft out of reach of the prisoners, then he motioned to the corpse. 'Throw it overboard,' he commanded, addressing Jason and Thoar.

'Wait,' cried another member of the crew. 'I want his boots.'

'His sash is mine,' cried another, and presently half a dozen of them were quarreling over the belongings of the corpse like a pack of dogs over a bone. Lajo took no part in this altercation and presently the few wretched belongings that had served to cover the nakedness of the dead man were torn from his corpse and divided among them by the simple expedient of permitting the stronger to take what they could; then Jason and Thoar eased the naked body over the side, where it was immediately seized upon by voracious denizens of the river.

Interminable, to an unknown destination, seemed the journey to Jason. They ate and slept many times and still the river wound through the endless swamp. The luxuriant vegetation and flowering blooms which lined the banks long since had ceased to interest, their persistent monotony making them almost hateful to the eyes.

Jason could not but wonder at the superhuman efforts that must have been necessary to row this large, heavy boat upstream in the face of all the terrific assaults which must have been launched upon it by the reptilian hordes that contested every mile of the downward journey.

But presently the landscape changed, the river widened and the low swamp gave way to rolling hills. The forests, which still lined the banks, were freer from underbrush, suggesting that they might be the feeding grounds of droves of herbivorous animals, a theory that was soon substantiated by sight of grazing herds, among which Jason recognized red deer, bison, bos and several other species of herbivorous animals. The forest upon the right bank was open and sunny and with its grazing herds presented a cheerful aspect of warmth and life, but the forest upon the left bank was dark and gloomy. The foliage of the trees, which grew to tremendous proportions, was so dense as practically to shut out the sunlight, the space between the boles giving the impression of long, dark aisles, gloomy and forbidding.

There were fewer reptiles in the stream here, but the Korsars appeared unusually nervous and apprehensive of danger after they entered this stretch of the river. Previously they had been drifting with the current, using but a single oar, scull fashion, from the stern to keep the nose, of the boat pointed downstream, but now they manned the oars, pressing Jason and Thoar into service to row with the others. Loaded arquebuses lay beside the oarsmen, while in the bow and stern armed men were constantly upon watch. They paid little attention to the right bank of the river, but toward the dark and gloomy left bank they directed their nervous, watchful gaze. Jason wondered what it was that they feared, but he had no opportunity to inquire and there was no respite from the rowing, at least not for him or Thoar, though the Korsars alternated between watching and rowing.

Between oars and current they were making excellent progress, though whether they were close to the end of the danger zone or not, Jason had no means of knowing any more than he could guess the nature of the menace which must certainly threaten them if aught could be judged by the attitude of the Korsars.

The two prisoners were upon the verge of exhaustion when Lajo noticed their condition and relieved them from the oars. How long they had been rowing, Jason could not determine, although he knew that while no one had either eaten or slept, since they had entered this stretch of the river, the time must have been considerable. The distance they had come he estimated roughly at something over a hundred miles, and he and Thoar had been continuously at the oars during the entire period, without food or sleep, but they had barely thrown themselves to the bottom of the boat when a cry, vibrant with excitement, arose from the bow. 'There they are!' shouted the man, and instantly all was excitement aboard the boat.

'Keep to the oars!' shouted Lajo. 'Our best chance is to run through them.'

Although almost too spent with fatigue to find interest even in impending death, Jason dragged himself to a sitting position that raised his eyes above the level of the gunwales of the boat. At first he could not even vaguely classify the horde of creatures swimming out upon the bosom of the placid river with the evident intention of intercepting them, but presently he saw that they were man-like creatures riding upon the backs of hideous reptiles. They bore long lances and their scaly mounts sped through the waters at incredible speed. As the boat approached them he saw that the creatures were not men, though they had the forms of men, but were grotesque and horrid reptiles with the heads of lizards to whose naturally frightful mien, pointed ears and short horns added a certain horrid grotesquery.

'My God!' he exclaimed. 'What are they?'

Thoar, who had also dragged himself to a sitting posture, shuddered. 'They are the Horibs,' he said. 'It is better to die than to fall into their clutches.'

Carried downward by the current and urged on by the long sweeps and its own terrific momentum, the heavy boat shot straight toward the hideous horde. The distance separating them was rapidly closing; the boat was almost upon the leading Horib when an arquebus in the bow spoke. Its loud report broke the menacing silence that had overhung the river like a pall. Directly in front of the boat's prow the horde of Horibs separated and a moment later they were racing along on either side of the craft. Arquebuses were belching smoke and fire, scattering the bits of iron and pebbles with which they were loaded among the hissing enemy, but for every Horib that fell there were two to take its place.

Now they withdrew to a little distance, but with apparently no effort whatever their reptilian mounts kept pace with the boat and then, one after another on either side, a rider would dart in and cast his lance; nor apparently ever did one miss its mark. So deadly was their aim that the Korsars were compelled to abandon their oars and drop down into the bottom of the boat, raising themselves above the gunwales only long enough to fire their arquebuses, when they would again drop down into concealment to reload. But even these tactics could not preserve them for long, since the Horibs, darting in still closer to the side of the boat, could reach over the edge and lance the inmates. Straight to the muzzles of the arquebuses they came, apparently entirely devoid of any conception of fear; great holes were blown entirely through the bodies of some, others were decapitated, while more than a score lost a hand or an arm, yet still they came.

Presently exhausted and without weapons to defend themselves, Jason and Thoar had remained lying upon the bottom of the boat almost past caring what fate befell them. Half covered by the corpses of the Korsars that had fallen, they lay in a pool of blood. About them arquebuses still roared amid screams and curses, and above all rose the shrill, hissing screech that seemed to be the war cry of the Horibs.

The boat was dragged to shore and the rope made fast about the bole of a tree, though three times the Korsars had cut the line and three times the Horibs had been forced to replace it.

There was only a handful of the crew who had not been killed or wounded when the Horibs left their mounts and swarmed over the gunwales to fall upon their prey. Cutlasses, knives and arquebuses did their deadly work, but still the slimy snake-men came, crawling over the bodies of their dead to fall upon the survivors until the latter were practically buried by greater numbers.

When the battle was over there were but three Korsars who had escaped death or serious wounds – Lajo was one of them. The Horibs bound their wrists and took them ashore, after which they started unloading the dead and wounded from the boat, killing the more seriously wounded with their knives. Coming at last upon Jason and Thoar and finding them unwounded, they bound them as they had the living Korsars and placed them with the other prisoners on the shore.

The battle over, the prisoners secured, the Horibs now fell upon the corpses of the dead, nor did they rest until they had devoured them all, while Jason and his fellow prisoners sat nauseated with horror during the grizzly feast. Even the Korsars, cruel and heartless as they were, shuddered at the sight.

'Why do you suppose they are saving us?' asked Jason.

Lajo shook his head. 'I do not know,' he said.

'Doubtless to feed us to their women and children,' said Thoar. 'They say that they keep their human prisoners and fatten them.'

'You know what they are? You have seen them before?' Lajo asked Thoar.

'Yes, I know what they are,' said Thoar, 'but these are the first that I have ever seen. They are the Horibs, the snake people. They dwell between the Rela Am and the Gyor Cors.'

As Jason watched the Horibs at their grizzly feast, he became suddenly conscious of a remarkable change that was taking place in their appearance. When he had first seen them and all during the battle they had been of a ghastly bluish color, the hands, feet and faces being several shades paler than the balance of the body, but as they settled down to their gory repast this hue gradually faded to be replaced by a reddish tinge, which varied in intensity in different individuals, the faces and extremities of a few of whom became almost crimson as the feast progressed.

If the appearance and bloodthirsty ferocity of the creatures appalled him, he was no less startled when he first heard them converse in the common language of the men of Pellucidar.

The general conformation of the creatures, their weapons, which consisted of long lances and stone knives, the apron-like apparel which they wore and the evident attempt at ornamentation as exemplified by the insignia upon the breasts of their garments and the armlets which they wore, all tended toward establishing a suggestion of humanity that was at once grotesque and horrible, but when to these other attributes was added human speech the likeness to man created an impression that was indescribably repulsive.

So powerful was the fascination that the creatures aroused in the mind of Jason that he could divert neither his thoughts nor his eyes from them. He noticed that while the majority of them were about six feet in height, there were many much smaller, ranging downward to about four feet, while there was one tremendous individual that must have been fully nine feet tall; yet all were proportioned identically and the difference in height did not have the appearance of being at all related to a difference in age, except that the scales upon the largest of them were considerably thicker and coarser. Later, however, he was to learn that differences in size predicated differences in age, the growth of these creatures being governed by the same law which governs the growth of reptiles, which, unlike mammals, continue to grow throughout the entire duration of their lives.

When they had gorged themselves upon the flesh of the Korsars, the Horibs lay down, but whether to sleep or not Jason never knew since their lidless eyes remained constantly staring. And now a new phenomenon occurred. Gradually the reddish tinge faded from their bodies to be replaced by a dull brownish gray, which harmonized with the ground upon which they lay.

Exhausted by his long tour at the oars and by the horrors that he had witnessed, Jason gradually drifted off into deep slumber, which was troubled by hideous dreams in which he saw Jana in the clutches of a Horib. The creature was attempting to devour The Red Flower of Zoram, while Jason struggled with the bonds that secured him.

He was awakened by a sharp pain in his shoulder and opening his eyes he saw one of the homosaurians, as he had mentally dubbed them, standing over him, prodding him with the point of his sharp lance. 'Make less noise,' said the creature, and Jason realized that he must have been raving in his sleep.

The other Horibs were rising from the ground, voicing strange whistling hisses, and presently from the waters of the river and from the surrounding aisles of the gloomy forest their hideous mounts came trooping in answer to the summons.

'Stand up!' said the Horib who had awakened Jason. 'I am going to remove your bonds,' he continued. 'You cannot escape. If you try to you will be killed. Follow me,' he then commanded after he had removed the thongs which secured Jason's wrists.

Jason accompanied the creature into the midst of the herd of periosauri that was milling about, snapping and hissing, along the shore of the river.

Although the Gorobors all looked alike to Jason, it was evident that the Horibs differentiated between individuals among them for he who was leading Jason threaded his way through the mass of slimy bodies until he reached the side of a particular individual.

'Get up,' he said, motioning Jason to mount the creature. 'Sit well forward on its neck.'

It was with a sensation of the utmost disgust that Jason vaulted onto the back of the Gorobor. The feel of its cold, clammy, rough hide against his naked legs sent a chilly shudder up his spine. The reptileman mounted behind him and presently the entire company was on the march, each of the other prisoners being mounted in front of a Horib.

Into the gloomy forest the strange cavalcade marched, down dark, winding corridors overhung with dense vegetation, much of which was of a dead pale cast through lack of sunlight. A clammy chill, unusual in Pellucidar, pervaded the atmosphere and a feeling of depression weighed heavily upon all the prisoners.

'What are you going to do with us?' asked Jason after they had proceeded in silence for some distance.

'You will be fed upon eggs until you are fit to be eaten by the females and the little ones,' replied the Horib. 'They tire of fish and Gyor flesh. It is not often that we get as much gilak meat as we have just had.'

Jason relapsed into silence, discovering that, as far as he was concerned, the Horib was conversationally a total loss and for long after the horror of the creature's reply weighed upon his mind. It was not that he feared death; it was the idea of being fattened for slaughter that was peculiarly abhorrent.

As they rode between the never ending trees he tried to speculate as to the origin of these grewsome creatures. It seemed to him that they might constitute a supreme effort upon the part of Nature to reach a higher goal by a less devious route than that which evolution had pursued upon the outer crust from the age of reptiles upwards to the age of man.

During the march Jason caught occasional glimpses of Thoar and the other prisoners, though he had no opportunity to exchange words with them, and after what seemed an interminable period of time the cavalcade emerged from the forest into the sunlight and Jason saw in the distance the shimmering blue water of an inland lake. As they approached its shores he discerned throngs of Horibs, some swimming or lolling in the waters of the lake, while others lay or squatted upon the muddy bank. As the company arrived among them they showed only a cold, reptilian interest in the returning warriors, though some of the females and young evinced a suggestive interest in the prisoners.

The adult females differed but slightly from the males. Aside from the fact that they were hornless and went naked Jason could discover no other distinguishing feature. He saw no signs of a village, nor any indication of arts or crafts other than those necessary to produce their crude weapons and the simple apron-like armor that the warriors wore to protect the soft skin of their bellies.

On the way they passed a number of females laying eggs which they deposited in the soft, warm mud just above the water line, covering them lightly with mud, afterwards pushing a slender stake into the ground at the spot to mark the nest. All along the shore at this point were hundreds of such stakes and further on Jason saw several tiny Horibs, evidently but just hatched, wriggling upward out of the mud. No one paid the slightest attention to them as they stumbled and reeled about trying to accustom themselves to the use of their limbs, upon all four of which they went at first, like tiny, grotesque lizards.

Arrived at the higher bank the warrior in charge of Thoar, who was in the lead, suddenly clapped his hand over the prisoner's mouth, pinching Thoar's nose tightly between his thumb and first finger, and, without other preliminaries, dove head foremost into the waters of the lake carrying his victim with him.

Jason was horrified as he saw his friend and companion disappear beneath the muddy waters, which, after a moment of violent agitation, settled down again, leaving only an ever widening circular ripple to mark the spot where the two had disappeared. An instant later another Horib dove in with Lajo and in rapid succession the other two Korsars shared a similar fate.

With a superhuman effort Jason sought to tear himself free from the clutches of his captor, but the cold, clammy hands held him tightly. One of them was suddenly clapped over his mouth and nose and an instant later he felt the warm waters of the lake close about him.

Still struggling to free himself he was conscious that the Horib was carrying him swiftly beneath the surface. Presently he felt slimy mud beneath him, along which his body was being dragged. His lungs cried out in tortured agony for air, his senses reeled and momentarily all went black before him, though no blacker than the Stygian darkness of the hole into which he was being dragged, and then the hand was removed from his mouth and nose; mechanically his lungs gasped for air and as consciousness slowly returned Jason realized that he was not drowned, but that he was lying upon a bed of mud inhaling air and not water.

Total darkness surrounded him; he felt a clammy body scrape against his, and then another and another. There was a sound of splashing, gurgling water and then silence – the silence of the tomb.

XV

Prisoners

Standing upon the edge of the great Gyor plains surrounded by armed crea-tures, who had but just demonstrated their ability to destroy one of the most powerful and ferocious creatures that evolution has ever succeeded in pro-ducing, Tarzan of the Apes was yet loath to lay down his weapons as he had been instructed and surrender, without resistance, to an unknown fate.

'What do you intend to do with us?' he demanded of the Horib who had ordered him to lay down his weapons.

'We shall take you to our village where you will be well fed,' replied the creature. 'You cannot escape us; no one escapes the Horibs.'

The ape-man hesitated. The Red Flower of Zoram moved closer to his side. 'Let us go with them,' she whispered. 'We cannot escape them now; there are too many of them. Possibly if we go with them we shall find an opportunity later.'

Tarzan nodded and then he turned to the Horib. 'We are ready,' he said.

Mounted upon the necks of Gorobors, each in front of a Horib warrior, they were carried across a corner of the Gyor Cors to the same gloomy forest through which Jason and Thoar had been taken, though they entered it from a different direction.

Rising at the east end of the Mountains of the Thipdars, a river flows in a southeasterly direction entering upon its course the gloomy forest of the Horibs, through which it runs down to the Rela Am, or River of Darkness. It was near the confluence of these two rivers that the Korsars had been attacked by the Horibs and it was along the upper reaches of the same river that Tar-zan and Jana were being conducted downstream toward the village of the lizard-men.

The lake of the Horibs lies at a considerable distance from the eastern end of the Mountains of the Thipdars, perhaps five hundred miles, and where there is no time and distances are measured by food and sleep it makes little difference whether places are separated by five miles or five hundred. One man might travel a thousand miles without mishap, while another, in attempting to go one mile, might be killed, in which event the one mile would be much further than the thousand miles, for, in fact, it would have proved an interminable distance to him who had essayed it in this instance.

As Tarzan and Jana rode through the dismal forest, hundreds of miles away Jason Gridley drew himself to a sitting position in such utter darkness that he could almost feel it. 'God!' he exclaimed.

'Who spoke?' asked a voice out of the darkness, and Jason recognized the voice as Thoar's.

'It is I, Jason,' replied Gridley.

'Where are we?' demanded another voice. It was Lajo.

'It is dark. I wish they had killed us,' said a fourth voice.

'Don't worry,' said a fifth, 'we shall be killed soon enough.'

'We are all here,' said Jason. 'I thought we were all done for when I saw them drag you into the water one by one.'

'Where are we?' demanded one of the Korsars. 'What sort of hole is this into which they have put us?'

'In the world from which I come,' said Jason, 'there are huge reptiles, called crocodiles, who build such nests or retreats in the banks of rivers, just above the water line, but the only entrance leads down below the waters of the river. It is such a hole as that into which we have been dragged.'

'Why can't we swim out again?' asked Thoar.

'Perhaps we could,' replied Jason, 'but they would see us and bring us back again.'

'Are we going to lie here in the mud and wait to be slaughtered?' demanded Lajo.

'No,' said Jason; 'but let us work out a reasonable plan of escape. It will gain us nothing to act rashly.'

For some time the men sat in silence, which was finally broken by the American. 'Do you think we are alone here?' he asked in a low tone. 'I have listened carefully, but I have heard no sound other than our own breathing.'

'Nor I,' said Thoar.

'Come closer then,' said Jason, and the five men groped through the darkness and arranged themselves in a circle, where they squatted leaning forward till their heads touched. 'I have a plan,' continued Jason. 'When they were bringing us here I noticed that the forest grew close to the lake at this point. If we can make a tunnel into the forest, we may be able to escape.'

'Which way is the forest?' asked Lajo.

'That is something that we can only guess at,' replied Jason. 'We may guess wrong, but we must take the chance. But I think that it is reasonable to assume that the direction of the forest is directly opposite the entrance through which we were carried into this hole.'

'Let us start digging at once,' exclaimed one of the Korsars.

'Wait until I locate the entrance,' said Thoar.

He crawled away upon his hands and knees, groping through the darkness and the mud. Presently he announced that he had found the opening, and from the direction of his voice the others knew where to start digging.

All were filled with enthusiasm, for success seemed almost within the range of possibility, but now they were confronted with the problem of the disposal of the dirt which they excavated from their tunnel. Jason instructed Lajo to remain at the point where they intended excavating and then had the others crawl in different directions in an effort to estimate the size of the chamber in which they were confined. Each man was to crawl in a straight line in the direction assigned him and count the number of times that his knees touched the ground before he came to the end of the cavern.

By this means they discovered that the cave was long and narrow and, if they were correct in the directions they had assumed, it ran parallel to the lake shore. For twenty feet it extended in one direction and for over fifty in the other.

It was finally decided that they should distribute the earth equally over the floor of the chamber for a while and then carry it to the further end, piling it against the further wall uniformly so as not to attract unnecessary attention in the event that any of the Horibs visited them.

Digging with their fingers was slow and laborious work, but they kept steadily at it, taking turns about. The man at work would push the dirt behind him and the others would gather it up and distribute it, so that at no time was there a fresh pile of earth upon the ground to attract attention should a Horib come. Horibs did come; they brought food, but the men could hear the splash of their bodies in the water as they dove into the lake to reach the tunnel leading to the cave and being thus warned they grouped themselves in front of the entrance to their tunnel effectually hiding it from view. The Horibs who came into the chamber at no time gave any suggestion of suspicion that all was not right. While it was apparent that they could see in the dark it was also quite evident that they could not discern things clearly and thus the greatest fear that their plot might be discovered was at least partially removed.

After considerable effort they had succeeded in excavating a tunnel some three feet in diameter and about ten feet long when Jason, who was excavating at the time, unearthed a large shell, which greatly facilitated the process of excavation. From then on their advance was more rapid, yet it seemed to them all that it was an endless job; nor was there any telling at what moment the Horibs would come to take them for the feast.

It was Jason's wish to get well within the forest before turning their course upward toward the surface, but to be certain of this he knew that they must first encounter roots of trees and pass beyond them, which might necessitate a detour and delay; yet to come up prematurely would be to nullify all that they had accomplished so far and to put a definite end to all hope of escape.

And while the five men dug beneath the ground in the dark hole that was stretching slowly out beneath the dismal forest of the Horibs a great ship rode majestically high in air above the northern slopes of the Mountains of the Thipdars.

'They never passed this way,' said Zuppner. 'Nothing short of a mountain goat could cross this range.'

'I quite agree with you, sir,' said Hines. 'We might as well search in some other direction now.'

'God!' exclaimed Zuppner, 'if I only knew in what direction to search.'

Hines shook his head. 'One direction is as good as another, sir,' he said.

'I suppose so,' said Zuppner, and, obeying his light touch upon the helm, the nose of the great dirigible swung to port. Following an easterly course she paralleled the Mountains of the Thipdars and sailed out over the Gyor Cors. A slight turn of the wheel would have carried her to the southeast, across the dismal forest through whose gloomy corridors Tarzan and Jana were being borne to a horrible fate. But Captain Zuppner did not know and so the O-220 continued on toward the east, while the Lord of the Jungle and The Red Flower of Zoram rode silently toward their doom.

From almost the moment that they had entered the forest Tarzan had known that he might escape. It would have been the work of but an instant to have leaped from the back of the Gorobor upon which he was riding to one of the lower branches of the forest, some of which barely grazed their heads as they passed beneath, and once in the trees he knew that no Horib nor any Gorobor could catch him, but he could not desert Jana; nor could he acquaint her with his plans for they were never sufficiently close together for him to whisper to her unheard by the Horibs. But even had he been able to lay the whole thing before her, he doubted her ability to reach the safety of the trees before the Horibs recaptured her.

If he could but get near enough to take hold of her, he was confident that he could effect a safe escape for both of them and so he rode on in silence, hoping against hope that the opportunity he so desired would eventually develop.

They had reached the upper end of the lake and were skirting its western shore and, from remarks dropped by the Horibs in their conversations, which were far from numerous, the ape-man guessed that they were almost at their destination, and still escape seemed as remote as ever.

Chafing with impatience Tarzan was on the point of making a sudden break for liberty, trusting that the unexpectedness of his act would confuse the lizard-men for just the few seconds that would be necessary for him to throw Jana to his shoulder and swing to the lower terrace that beckoned invitingly from above.

The nerves and muscles of Tarzan of the Apes are trained to absolute obedience to his will; they are never surprised into any revelation of emotion, nor are they often permitted to reveal what is passing in the mind of the ape-man when he is in the presence of strangers or enemies, but now, for once, they were almost shocked into revealing the astonishment that filled him as a vagrant breeze carried to his nostrils a scent spoor that he had never thought to know again.

The Horibs were moving almost directly upwind so that Tarzan knew that the authors of the familiar odors that he had sensed were somewhere ahead of them. He thought quickly now, but not without weighing carefully the plan that had leaped to his mind the instant that that familiar scent spoor had impinged upon his nostrils. His major consideration was for the safety of the girl, but in order to rescue her he must protect himself. He felt that it would be impossible for them both to escape simultaneously, but there was another way now – a way which seemed to offer excellent possibilities for success. Behind him, upon the Gorobor, and so close that their bodies touched, sat a huge Horib. In one hand he carried a lance, but the other hand was free. Tarzan must move so quickly that the fellow could not touch him with his free hand before he was out of reach. To do this would require agility of an almost superhuman nature, but there are few creatures who can compare in this respect with the ape-man. Low above them swung the branches of the dismal forest; Tarzan waited, watching for the opportunity he sought. Presently he saw it – a sturdy branch with ample head room above it – a doorway in the ceiling of somber foliage. He leaned forward, his hands resting lightly upon the neck of the Gorobor. They were almost beneath the branch he had selected when he sprang lightly to his feet and almost in the same movement sprang upward into the tree. So quickly had he accomplished the feat that he was gone before the Horib that had been guarding him realized it. When he did it was too late – the prisoner had gone. With others, who had seen the escape, he raised a cry of warning to those ahead, but neither by sight nor sound could they locate the fugitive, for Tarzan travelled through the upper terrace and all the foliage beneath hid him from the eyes of his enemies.

Jana, who had been riding a little in the rear of Tarzan, saw his escape and her heart sank for in the presence of the Horibs The Red Flower of Zoram had come as near to experiencing fear as she ever had in her life. She had derived a certain sense of comfort from the presence of Tarzan and now that he was gone she felt very much alone. She did not blame him for escaping when he had the opportunity, but she was sure in her own heart that Jason would not thus have deserted her.

Following the scent spoor that was his only guide, Tarzan of the Apes moved rapidly through the trees. At first he climbed high to the upper terraces and here he found a new world – a world of sunlight and luxuriant foliage, peopled by strange birds of gorgeous plumage which darted swiftly hither and thither. There were flying reptiles, too, and great gaudy moths. Snakes coiled upon many a branch and because they were of varieties unknown to him, he did not know whether they constituted a real menace or not. It was at once a beautiful and a repulsive world, but the feature of it which attracted him most was its silence, for its denizens seemed to be voiceless. The presence of the snakes and the dense foliage rendered it an unsatisfactory world for one who wished to travel swiftly and so the ape-man dropped to a lower level, and here he found the forest more open and the scent spoor clearer in his nostrils.

Not once had he doubted the origin of that scent, although it seemed preposterously unbelievable that he should discover it here in this gloomy wood in vast Pellucidar.

He was moving very rapidly for he wished, if possible, to reach his destination ahead of the Horibs. He hoped that his escape might delay the lizard-men and this was, in fact, the case, for they had halted immediately while a number of them had climbed into the trees searching for Tarzan. There was little in their almost expressionless faces to denote their anger, but the sickly bluish cast which overspread their scales denoted their mounting rage at the ease with which this gilak prisoner had escaped them, and when, finally, thwarted in their search, they resumed their interrupted march, they were in a particularly ugly mood.

Far ahead of them now Tarzan of the Apes dropped to the lower terraces. Strong in his nostrils was the scent spoor he had been following, telling him in a language more dependable than words that he had but little further to go to find those he sought, and a moment later he dropped down into one of the gloomy aisles of the forest, dropping as from heaven into the astonished view of ten stalwart warriors.

For an instant they stood looking at him in wide-eyed amazement and then they ran forward and threw themselves upon their knees about him, kissing his hands as they shed tears of happiness. 'Oh, Bwana, Bwana,' they cried; 'it is indeed you! Mulungu has been good to his children; he has given their Big Bwana back to them alive.'

'And now I have work for you, my children,' said Tarzan; 'the snake people are coming and with them is a girl whom they have captured. I thank God that you are armed with rifles and I hope that you have plenty of ammunition.'

'We have saved it, Bwana, using our spears and our arrows whenever we could.'

'Good,' said Tarzan; 'we shall need it now. How far are we from the ship?'

'I do not know,' said Muviro.

'You do not know?' repeated Tarzan.

'No, Bwana, we are lost. We have been lost for a long while,' replied the chief of the Waziri.

'What were you doing away from the ship alone?' demanded Tarzan.

'We were sent out with Gridley and Von Horst to search for you, Bwana.'

'Where are they?' asked Tarzan.

'A long time ago, I do not know how long, we became separated from Gridley and never saw him again. At that time it was savage beasts that separated us, but how Von Horst became separated from us we do not know. We had found a cave and had gone into it to sleep; when we awoke Von Horst was gone; we never saw him again.'

'They are coming!' warned Tarzan.

'I hear them, Bwana,' replied Muviro.

'Have you seen them – the snake people?' asked Tarzan.

'No, Bwana, we have seen no people for a long time; only beasts – terrible beasts.'

'You are going to see some terrible men now,' Tarzan warned them; 'but do not be frightened by their appearance. Your bullets will bring them down.'

'When, Bwana, have you seen a Waziri frightened?' asked Muviro proudly.

The ape-man smiled. 'One of you let me take his rifle,' he said, 'and then spread out through the forest. I do not know exactly where they will pass, but the moment that any of you makes contact with them commence shooting and shoot to kill, remembering, however, that the girl rides in front of one of them. Be careful that you do not harm her.'

He had scarcely ceased speaking when the first of the Horibs rode into view. Tarzan and the Waziri made no effort to seek concealment and at sight of them the leading Horib gave voice to a shrill cry of pleasure. Then a rifle spoke and the leading Horib writhed convulsively and toppled sideways to the ground. The others in the lead, depending upon the swiftness of their mounts, darted quickly toward the Waziri and the tall, white giant who led them, but swifter than the Gorobors were the bullets of the outer world. As fast as Tarzan and the Waziri could fire the Horibs fell. Never before had they known defeat. They blazed blue with rage, which faded to a muddy gray when the bullets found their hearts and they rolled dead upon the ground.

So swiftly did the Gorobors move and so rapidly did Tarzan and the Waziri fire that the engagement was decided within a few minutes of its inception, and now the remaining Horibs, discovering that they could not hope to overcome and capture gilaks armed with these strange weapons that hit them more swiftly than they could hurl their lances, turned and scattered in an effort to pass around the enemy and continue on their way.

As yet Tarzan had not caught a glimpse of Jana, though he knew that she must be there somewhere in the rear of the remaining Horibs, and then he saw her as she flashed by in the distance, borne swiftly upon the back of a fleet Gorobor. What appeared to be the only chance to save her now was to shoot down the swift beast upon which she was being borne away. Tarzan swung his rifle to his shoulder and at the same instant a riderless Gorobor struck him in the back and sent him sprawling upon the ground. By the time he had regained his feet, Jana and her captor were out of sight, hidden by the boles of intervening trees.

Milling near the Waziri were a number of terrified, riderless Gorobors. It was from this number that the fellow had broken who had knocked Tarzan down. The beasts seemed to be lost without the guidance of their masters, but when they saw one of their number start in pursuit of the Horibs who had ridden away, the others followed and in their mad rush these savage beasts constituted as great a menace as the Horibs themselves.

Muviro and his warriors leaped nimbly behind the boles of large trees to escape them, but to the mind of the ape-man they carried a new hope, offering as they did the only means whereby he might overtake the Horib who was bearing away The Red Flower of Zoram, and then, to the horror and astonishment of the Waziri, Tarzan leaped to the back of one of the great lizards as it scuttled abreast of him. Locking his toes beneath its elbows, as he had seen the Horibs do, he was carried swiftly in the mad rush of the creature to overtake its fellows and its masters. No need to urge it on, if he had known what means to employ to do so, for probably still terrified and excited by the battle it darted with incredible swiftness among the boles of the gray trees, outstripping its fellows and leaving them behind.

Presently, just ahead of him, Tarzan saw the Horib who was bearing Jana away and he saw, too, that he would soon overtake him, but so swiftly was his own mount running that it seemed quite likely that he would be carried past Jana without being able to accomplish anything toward her rescue, and with this thought came the realization that he must stop the Horib's mount.

There was just an instant in which to decide and act, but in that instant he raised his rifle and fired. Perhaps it was a wonderful bit of marksmanship, or perhaps it was just luck, but the bullet struck the Gorobor in the spine and a moment later its hind legs collapsed and it rolled over on its side, pitching Jana and the Horib heavily to the ground. Simultaneously Tarzan's mount swept by and the ape-man, risking a bad fall, slipped from its back to go tumbling head over heels against the carcass of the Horib's mount.

Leaping to his feet, he faced the lizard-man and as he did so the ground gave way beneath him and he dropped suddenly into a hole, almost to his armpits. As he was struggling to extricate himself something seized him by the ankles and dragged him downward – cold fingers that clung relentlessly to him dragging him into a dark, subterranean hole.

XVI

Escape

The O-220 cruised slowly above the Gyor Cors, watchful eyes scanning the ground below, but the only living things they saw were huge dinosaurs. Disturbed by the motors of the dirigible, the great beasts trotted angrily about in circles and occasionally an individual, sighting the ship above him, would gallop after it, bellowing angrily, or again one might charge the elliptical shadow that moved along the ground directly beneath the O-220.

'Sweet tempered little fellows,' remarked Lieutenant Hines, who had been watching them from a messroom port.

'Jes' which *am* dem bad dreams, Lieutenant?' asked Robert Jones.

'Triceratops,' replied the officer.

'Ah'll try most anything once, suh, but not dem babies,' replied Robert.

Unknown to the bewildered navigating officer, the ship was taking a southeasterly course. Far away, on its port side, loomed a range of mountains, hazily visible in the up-curving distance, and now a river cut the plain – a river that came down from the distant mountains – and this they followed, knowing that men lost in a strange country are prone to follow the course of a river, if they are so fortunate as to find one.

They had followed the river for some distance when Lieutenant Dorf telephoned down from the observation cabin. 'There is a considerable body of water ahead, sir,' he reported to Captain Zuppner. 'From its appearance I should say that we might be approaching the shore of a large ocean.'

All eyes were now strained ahead and presently a large body of water became visible to all on board. The ship cruised slowly up and down the coast for a short distance, and as it had been some time since they had had fresh water or fresh meat, Zuppner decided to land and make camp, selecting a spot just north of the river they had been following, where it emptied into the sea. And as the great ship settled gently to rest upon a rolling, grassy meadow, Robert Jones made an entry in his little black diary.

'Arrived here at noon.'

While the great ship settled down beside the shore of the silent Pellucidarian sea, Jason Gridley and his companions, hundreds of miles to the west, pushed their tunnel upward toward the surface of the ground. Jason was in front, laboriously pushing the earth backward a few handfuls at a time to those behind him. They were working frantically now because the length of the tunnel already was so great that it was with difficulty that they could return to the cavern in time to forestall discovery when they heard Horibs approaching.

As Jason scraped away at the earth above him, there broke suddenly upon his ears what sounded like the muffled reverberation of rifle shots. He could not believe that they were such, and yet what else could they be? For so long had he been separated from his fellows that it seemed impossible that any freak of circumstance had brought them to this gloomy corner of Pellucidar, and though hope ran high yet he cast this idea from his mind, substituting for it a more natural conclusion – that the shots had come from the arque-buses of Korsars, who had come up from the ship that Lajo had told him was anchored somewhere below in the Rela Am. Doubtless the captain had sent an expedition in search of the missing members of his crew, but even the prospects of falling again into the hands of the fierce Korsars appeared a heavenly one by comparison to the fate with which they were confronted.

Now Jason redoubled his efforts, working frantically to drive his narrow shaft upward toward the surface. The sound of the shots, which had lasted but a few minutes, had ceased, to be followed by the rapidly approaching thunder of many feet, as though heavy animals were racing in his direction. He heard them passing almost directly overhead and they seemed so close that he was positive he must be near the surface of the ground. Another shot sounded almost directly above him; he heard the thud of a heavy body and the earth about him shook to the impact of its fall. Jason's excitement had arisen to the highest pitch when suddenly the earth gave way above him and something dropped into the shaft upon his head.

His mind long imbued with the fear that their plan for escape would be discovered by the Horibs, Jason reacted instinctively to the urge of self-preservation, the best chance for the accomplishment of which seemed to be to drag the discoverer of their secret out of sight as quickly as possible, and with this end in view he backed quickly into the tunnel, dragging the inter-loper with him, and to a certain point this was not difficult, but it so happened that Tarzan had clung to his rifle. The rifle chanced to strike the ground in a horizontal position, as the ape-man was dragged into the tunnel, and the muzzle and butt lodged upon opposite sides of the opening, thus forming a rigid bar across the mouth of the aperture, to which the ape-man clung as Jason dragged frantically upon his ankles, and then slowly the steel thews of the Jungle Lord tensed and as he drew himself upward, he drew Jason Grid-ley with him. Strain and struggle as he would, the American could not overcome the steady pull of those giant thews. Slowly, irresistibly, he was dragged into the shaft and upward toward the surface of the ground.

By this time, of course, he knew that the creature to which he clung was no Horib, for his fingers were closed upon the smooth skin of a human being, and not upon the scaly hide of a lizard-man, but yet he felt that he must not let the fellow escape.

The Horib, who had been expecting Tarzan's attack, had seen him disappear mysteriously into the ground; nor did he wait to investigate the miracle, but seizing Jana by the wrist he hurried after his fellows, dragging the struggling girl with him.

The two were just disappearing among the boles of the trees down a gloomy aisle of the somber forest when Tarzan, emerging from the shaft, caught a single fleeting glimpse of them. It was almost the growl of an enraged beast that escaped his lips as he realized that this last calamity might have definitely precluded the possibility of effecting the girl's rescue. Chafing at the restraint of the clutching fingers clinging desperately to his ankles, the ape-man kicked violently in an effort to dislodge them and with such good effect that he sent Jason tumbling back into his tunnel, while he leaped to the solid ground and freedom to spring into pursuit of the Horib and The Red Flower of Zoram.

Calling back to his companions to hurry after him, Jason clambered swiftly to the surface of the ground just in time to see a half-naked bronzed giant before he disappeared from view behind the bole of a large tree, but that single glimpse awakened familiar memories and his heart leaped within him at the suggestion it implied. But how could it be? Had not Thoar seen the Lord of the Jungle carried to his doom? Whether the man was Tarzan or not was of less import than the reason for his haste. Was he escaping or pursuing? But in either event something seemed to tell Jason Gridley that he should not lose sight of him; at least he was not a Horib, and if not a Horib, then he must be an enemy of the lizard-men. So rapidly had events transpired that Jason was confused in his own mind as to the proper course to pursue; yet something seemed to urge him not to lose sight of the stranger and acting upon this impulse, he followed at a brisk run.

Through the dark wood ran Tarzan of the Apes, guided only by the delicate and subtle aroma that was the scent spoor of The Red Flower of Zoram and which would have been perceptible to no other human nostrils than those of the Lord of the Jungle. Strong in his nostrils, also, was the sickening scent of the Horibs and fearful less he come upon them unexpectedly in numbers, he swung lightly into the trees and, with undiminished speed, raced in the direction of his quarry; nor was it long before he saw them beneath him – a single Horib dragging the still-struggling Jana.

There was no hesitation, there was no diminution in his speed as he launched himself like a living projectile straight for the ugly back of the Horib. With such force he struck the creature that it was half stunned as he bore it to the ground. A sinewy arm encircled its neck as Tarzan arose dragging the creature up with him. Turning quickly and bending forward, Tarzan swung the body over his head and hurled it violently to the ground, still retaining his hold about its neck. Again and again he whipped the mighty body over his head and dashed it to the gray earth, while the girl, wide-eyed with astonishment at this exhibition of Herculean strength, looked on.

At last, satisfied that the creature was dead or stunned, Tarzan released it. Quickly he appropriated its stone knife and picked up its fallen lance, then he turned to Jana. 'Come,' he said, 'there is but one safe place for us,' and lifting her to his shoulder he leaped to the low hanging branch of a nearby tree. 'Here, at least,' he said, 'you will be safe from Horibs, for I doubt if any Goro-bor can follow us here.'

'I always thought that there were no warriors like the warriors of Zoram,' said Jana, 'but that was before I had known you and Jason;' nor could she, as Tarzan well knew, have voiced a more sincere appreciation of what he had done for her, for to the primitive woman there are no men like her own men. 'I wish,' she continued sadly after a pause, 'that Jason had lived. He was a great man and a mighty warrior, but above all he was a kind man. The men of Zoram are never cruel to their women, but they are not always thoughtful and considerate. Jason seemed always to think of my comfort before every-thing except my safety.'

'You were very fond of him, were you not?' asked Tarzan.

The Red Flower of Zoram did not answer. There were tears in her eyes and in her throat so that she could only nod her head.

Once in the trees, Tarzan had lowered Jana to her feet, presently discover-ing that she could travel quite without assistance, as might have been expected of one who could leap lightly from crag to crag upon the dizzy slopes of Thipdars' heights. They moved without haste back to the point where they had last seen Muviro, and his Waziri warriors, but as the way took them downwind Tarzan could not hope to pick up the scent spoor of his hench-men and so his ears were constantly upon the alert for any slightest sound that might reveal their whereabouts. Presently they were rewarded by the sound of footsteps hurrying through the forest toward them.

The ape-man drew the girl behind the bole of a large tree and waited, silent, motionless, for all footfalls are not the footfalls of friends.

They had waited for but a moment when there came into view upon the ground below them an almost naked man clothed in a bit of filthy goatskin, which was almost undistinguishable as such beneath a coating of mud, while the original color of his skin was hidden beneath a similar covering. A great mass of tousled black hair surmounted his head. He was quite the filthiest appearing creature that Tarzan had ever looked upon, but he was evidently no Horib and he was unarmed. What he was doing there alone in the grim forest, the ape-man could not imagine, so he dropped to the ground imme-diately in front of the surprised wayfarer.

At sight of the ape-man, the other stopped his eyes wide with astonishment and incredulity. 'Tarzan!' he exclaimed. 'My God, it is really you. You are not dead. Thank God you are not dead.'

It was an instant before the ape-man could recognize the speaker, but not so the girl hiding in the tree above. The instant that she had heard his voice she had known him.

A slow smile overspread the features of the Lord of the Jungle. 'Gridley!' he exclaimed. 'Jason Gridley! Jana told me that you were dead.'

'Jana!' exclaimed Jason. 'You know her? You have seen her? Where is she?'

'She is here with me,' replied Tarzan.

The Red Flower of Zoram had slipped to the ground upon the opposite side of the tree and now she stepped from behind its trunk.

'Jana!' cried Jason, coming eagerly toward her.

The girl drew herself to her full height and turned a shoulder toward him. 'Jalok!' she cried contemptuously. 'Must I tell you again to keep away from The Red Flower of Zoram?'

Jason halted in his tracks, his arms dropped limply to his sides, his attitude one of utter dejection.

Tarzan looked silently on, his brows momentarily revealing his perplexity; but it was not his way to interfere in affairs that were wholly the concern of others. 'Come,' he said, 'we must find the Waziri.'

Suddenly loud voices just ahead apprised them of the presence of other men and in the babel of excited voices Tarzan recognized the tones of his Waziri. Hurrying forward the three came upon a scene that was momentarily ludicrous, but which might soon have developed into tragedy had they not arrived in time.

Ten Waziri warriors armed with rifles had surrounded Thoar and the three Korsars and each party was jabbering volubly in a language unknown to the other.

The Pellucidarians, never before having seen human beings of the rich, deep, black color of the Waziri and assuming that all strangers were enemies, apprehended only the worst and were about to make a concerted effort to escape their captors, while Muviro, believing that these men might have some sinister connection with the disappearance of his master, was determined to hold and question them; nor would he have hesitated to kill them had they resisted him. It was, therefore, a relief to both parties when Tarzan, Jason and Jana appeared, and the Waziri saw their Big Bwana greet one of their captives with every indication of friendship.

Thoar was even more suprised to find Tarzan alive than Jason had been, and when he saw Jana the natural reserve which ordinarily marked his bearing was dissipated by the joy and relief which he felt in finding her safe and well; nor any less surprised and happy was Jana as she rushed forward and threw herself into her brother's arms.

His breast filled with emotion such as he had never experienced before, Jason Gridley stood apart, a silent witness of this loving reunion, and then, probably for the first time, there came to him an acute realization of the fact that the sentiment which he entertained for this little barbarian was nothing less than love.

It galled him even to admit it to himself and he felt that he was contemptible to harbor jealousy of Thoar, not only because Thoar was his friend, but because he was only a primitive savage, while he, Jason Gridley, was the product of ages of culture and civilization.

Thoar, Lajo and the other two Korsars were naturally delighted when they found that the strange warriors whom they had looked upon as enemies were suddenly transformed into friends and allies, and when they heard the story of the battle with the Horibs they knew that the greatest danger which threatened them was now greatly minimized because of the presence of these warriors armed with death-dealing weapons that made the ancient arquebuses of the Korsars appear as inadequate as slingshots, and that escape from this horrible country was as good as accomplished.

Resting after their recent exertion, each party briefly narrated the recent adventures that had befallen them and attempts were made to formulate plans for the future, but here difficulties arose. Thoar wished to return to Zoram with Jana. Tarzan, Jason and the Waziri desired only to find the other members of their expedition; while Lajo and his two fellows were principally concerned with getting back to their ship.

Tarzan and Jason, realizing that it might not be expedient to acquaint the Korsars with the real purpose of their presence in Pellucidar and finding that the men were familiar with the story of Tanar, gave them to believe that they were merely searching for Sari in order to pay a friendly visit to Tanar and his people.

'Sari is a long way,' said Lajo. 'He who would go to Sari from here must sleep over a hundred times upon the journey, which would take him across the Korsar Az and then through strange countries filled with enemies, even as far as The Land of Awful Shadow. Maybe one would never reach it.'

'Is there no way overland?' asked Tarzan.

'Yes,' replied Lajo, 'and if we were at Korsar, I might direct you, but that, too, would be a terrible journey, for no man knows what savage tribes and beasts beset the long marches that must lie between Korsar and Sari.'

'And if we went to Korsar,' said Jason, 'we could not hope to be received as friends. Is this not true, Lajo?'

The Korsar nodded. 'No,' he said. 'You would not be received as friends.'

'Nevertheless,' said Tarzan to Jason, 'I believe that if we are ever to find the O-220 again our best chance is to look for it in the vicinity of Korsar.'

Jason nodded in acquiescence. 'But that will not accord with Thoar's plans,' he said, 'for, if I understand it correctly, we are much nearer to Zoram now than we are to Korsar and if we decide to go to Korsar, our route will lead directly away from Zoram. But unless we accompany them with the Waziri, I doubt if Thoar and Jana could live to reach Zoram if they returned by the route that he and I have followed since we left the Mountains of the Thipdars.'

Tarzan turned to Thoar. 'If you will come with us, we can return you very quickly to Zoram if we find our ship. If we do not find it within a reasonable time, we will accompany you back to Zoram. In either event you would have a very much better chance of reaching your own country than you would if you and Jana set out alone from here.'

'We will accompany you, then,' said Thoar, and then his brow clouded as some thought seemed suddenly to seize upon his mind. He looked for a moment at Jason, and then he turned to Jana. 'I had almost forgotten,' he said. 'Before we can go with these people as friends, I must know if this man offered you any injury or harm while you were with him. If he did, I must kill him.'

Jana did not look at Jason as she replied. 'You need not kill him,' she said. 'Had that been necessary The Red Flower of Zoram would have done it herself.'

'Very well,' said Thoar, 'I am glad because he is my friend. Now we may all go together.'

'Our boat is probably in the river where the Horibs left it after they captured us,' said Lajo. 'If it is we can soon drop down to our ship, which is anchored in the lower waters of the Rela Am.'

'And be taken prisoners by your people,' said Jason. 'No, Lajo, the tables are turned now and if you go with us, it is you who will be the prisoners.'

The Korsar shrugged. 'I do not care,' he said. 'We will doubtless get a hundred lashes apiece when the captain finds that we have been unsuccessful, that we have brought back nothing and that he has lost an officer and many members of his crew.'

It was finally decided that they would return to the Rela Am and look for the longboat of the Korsars. If they found it they would float down in search of the ship, when they would at least make an effort to persuade the captain to receive them as friends and transport them to the vicinity of Korsar.

On the march back to the Rela Am they were not molested by the Horibs, who had evidently discovered that they had met their masters in the Waziri. During the march Jason made it a point to keep as far away from Jana as possible. The very sight of her reminded him of his hopeless and humiliating infatuation, and to be very near her constituted a form of refined agony which he could not endure. Her contempt, which she made no effort to conceal, galled him bitterly, though it was no greater than his own self-contempt when he realized that in spite of every reason that he had to dislike her, he still loved her – loved her more than he had thought it was possible for him to love any woman.

The American was glad when a glimpse of the broad waters of the Rela Am ahead of them marked the end of this stage of their journey, which his own unhappy thoughts, combined with the depressing influence of the gloomy forest, had transformed into one of the saddest periods of his life.

To the relief of all, the boat was found still moored where the Horibs had left it; nor did it take them long to embark and push out upon the waters of the River of Darkness.

The river widened as they floated down toward the sea until it became possible to step a mast and set sail, after which their progress was still more rapid. Though the way was often beset by dangers in the form of angry and voracious saurians, the rifles of the Waziri proved adequate protection when other means of defense had failed.

The river became very wide so that but for the current they might have considered it an arm of the sea and at Lajo's direction they kept well in toward the left bank, near which, he said, the ship was anchored. Dimly visible in the distance was the opposite shore, but only so because the surface of Pellucidar curved upward. At the same distance upon the outer crust, it would have been hidden by the curvature of the earth.

As they neared the sea it became evident that Lajo and the two other Korsars were much concerned because they had not sighted their ship.

'We have passed the anchorage,' said Lajo at last. 'That wooded hill, which we just passed, was directly opposite the spot where the ship lay. I cannot be mistaken because I noted it particularly and impressed it upon my memory as a landmark against the time when we should return from our expedition up the river.'

'He has sailed away and left us,' growled one of the Korsars, applying a vile epithet to the captain of the departed ship.

Continuing on down to the ocean they sighted a large island directly off the mouth of the river, which Lajo told them afforded good hunting with plenty of fresh water and as they were in need of meat they landed there and made camp. It was an ideal spot inasmuch as that part of the island at which they had touched seemed to be peculiarly free from the more dangerous forms of carnivorous mammals and reptiles; nor did they see any sign of the presence of man. Game, therefore, was abundant.

Discussing their plans for the future, it was finally decided that they would push on toward Korsar in the longboat, for Lajo assured them that it lay upon the coast of the same landmass that loomed plainly from their island refuge.

'What lies in that direction,' he said, pointing south, 'I do not know, but there lies Korsar, upon this same coast,' and he pointed in a direction a little east of north. 'Otherwise I am not familiar with this sea, or with this part of Pellucidar, since never before has an expedition come as far as the Rela Am.'

In preparation for the long cruise to Korsar, great quantities of meat were cut into strips and dried in the sun, or smoked over slow fires, after which it was packed away in bladders that had been carefully cleaned and dried. These were stowed in the boat together with other bladders filled with fresh water, for, although it was their intention to hug the coast on the way to Korsar, it might not always be expedient to land for water or food and there was always the possibility that a storm arising they might be blown out to sea.

At length, all preparations having been made, the strangely assorted company embarked upon their hazardous journey toward distant Korsar.

Jana had worked with the others preparing the provisions and the containers and though she had upon several occasions worked side by side with Jason, she had never relaxed toward him; nor appeared to admit that she was cognizant of his presence.

'Can't we be friends, Jana?' he asked once. 'I think we would both be very much happier if we were.'

'I am as happy as I can be,' she replied lightly, 'until Thoar takes me back to Zoram.'

XVII

Reunited

As favorable winds carried the longboat and its company up the sunlit sea, the O-220, following the same route, made occasional wide circles inland upon what Zuppner now considered an almost hopeless quest for the missing members of the expedition, and not only was he hopeless upon this score, but he also shared the unvoiced hopelessness of the balance of the company with regard to the likelihood of their ever being able to find the polar opening and return again to the outer world. With them, he knew that even their tremendous reserve of fuel and oil would not last indefinitely and if they were unable to find the polar opening, while they still had sufficient in reserve to carry them back to civilization, they must resign themselves to remaining in Pellucidar for the rest of their lives.

Lieutenant Hines finally broached this subject and the two officers, after summoning Lieutenant Dorf to their conference, decided that before their fuel was entirely exhausted they would try to locate some district where they might be reasonably free from attacks by savage tribesmen, or the even more dangerous menace of the mighty carnivores of Pellucidar.

While the remaining officers of the O-220 pondered the serious problems that confronted them, the great ship moved serenely through the warm Pellucidarian sunlight and the members of the crew went quietly and efficiently about their various duties.

Robert Jones of Alabama, however, was distressed. He seemed never to be able to accustom himself to the changed conditions of Pellucidar. He often mumbled to himself, shaking his head vehemently, and frequently he wound a battered alarm clock or took it down from the hook upon which it hung and held it to his ear.

Below the ship there unrolled a panorama of lovely sea coast, indented by many beautiful bays and inlets. There were rolling hills and plains and forests and winding rivers blue as turquoise. It was a scene to inspire the loftiest sentiments in the lowliest heart nor was it without its effect upon the members of the ship's company, which included many adventurous spirits, who would experience no regret should it develop that they must remain forever in this, to them, enchanted land. But there were others who had left loved ones at home and these were already beginning to discuss the possibilities and the probabilities of the future. With few exceptions, they were keen and intelligent men and fully as cognizant of the possible plight of the O-220 as was its commander, but they had been chosen carefully and there was not one who waivered even momentarily in loyalty to Zuppner, for they well knew that whatever fate was to be theirs, he would share it with them and, too, they had confidence that if any man could extricate them from their predicament, it was he. And so the great ship rode its majestic way between the sun and earth and each part, whether mechanical or human, functioned perfectly.

The Captain and his Lieutenant discussed the future as Robert Jones laboriously ascended the climbing shaft to the walkingway upon the ship's back, a hundred and fifty feet above his galley. He did not come entirely out of the climbing shaft onto the walkingway, but merely looked about the blue heaven and when his gaze had completed the circle, he hesitated a moment and then looked straight up, where, directly overhead, hung the eternal noonday sun of Pellucidar.

Robert Jones blinked his eyes and retreated into the shaft, closing the hatch after him. Muttering to himself, he descended carefully to the galley, crossed it, took the clock off its hook and, walking to an open port, threw it overboard.

To the occupants of the longboat dancing over the blue waves, without means of determining either time or distance, the constant expectation of nearing their journey's end lessened the monotony as did the oft recurring attacks of the frightful denizens of this Mesozoic sea. To the highly civilized American the utter timelessness of Pellucidarian existence brought a more marked nervous reaction than to the others. To a lesser degree Tarzan felt it, while the Waziri were only slightly conscious of the anomalous conditions. Upon the Pellucidarians, accustomed to no other state, it had no effect whatever. It was apparent when Tarzan and Jason discussed the matter with them that they had practically no conception of the meaning of time.

But time did elapse, leagues of ocean passed beneath them and conditions changed.

As they moved along the coast their course changed; though without instruments or heavenly bodies to guide them they were not aware of it. For a while they had moved northeast and then, for a long distance, to the east, where the coast curved gradually until they were running due north.

Instinct told the Korsars that they had come about three quarters of the distance from the island where they had outfitted to their destination. A land breeze was blowing stiffly and they were tacking briskly up the coast at a good clip. Lajo was standing erect in the bow apparently sniffing the air, as might a hunting dog searching out a scent spoor. Presently he turned to Tarzan.

'We had better put in to the coast,' he said. 'We are in for a stiff blow.' But it was too late, the wind and the sea mounted to such proportions that finally they had to abandon the attempt and turn and flee before the storm. There was no rain nor lightning, for there were no clouds – just a terrific wind that rose to hurricane violence and stupendous seas that threatened momentarily to engulf them.

The Waziri were frankly terrified, for the sea was not their element. The mountain girl and her brother seemed awed, but if they felt fear they gave no outward indication of it. Tarzan and Jason were convinced that the boat could not live and the latter made his way to where Jana sat huddled upon a thwart. The howling of the wind made speech almost impossible, but he bent low placing his lips close to her ear.

'Jana,' he said, 'it is impossible for this small boat to ride out such a storm. We are going to die, but before we die, whether you hate me or not, I am going to tell you that I love you,' and then before she could reply, before she could humiliate him further, he turned away and moved forward to where he had been before.

He knew that he had done wrong; he knew that he had no right to tell Thoar's sweetheart that he loved her; it had been an act of disloyalty and yet a force greater than loyalty, greater than pride, had compelled him to speak those words – he could not die with them unspoken. Perhaps it had been a little easier because he could not help but have noticed the seemingly platonic relationship which existed between Thoar and Jana and being unable to picture Jana as platonic in love, he had assumed that Thoar did not appreciate her. He was always kind to her and always pleasant, but he had never been quite as thoughtful of her as Jason thought that he should have been. He felt that perhaps it was one of the strange inflections of Pellucidarian character, but it was difficult to know either Jana or Thoar and also to believe that, for they were evidently quite as normal human beings as was he, and though they had much of the natural primitive reserve and dignity that civilized man now merely affects; yet it seemed unlikely that either one of them could have been for so long a time in close association without inadvertently, at least, having given some indication of their love. 'Why,' mused Jason, 'they might be brother and sister from the way they act.'

By some miracle of fate the boat lived through the storm, but when the wind diminished and the seas went down there were only tumbling waters to be seen on every hand; nor any sign of land.

'Now that we have lost the coast, Lajo, how are we going to set our course for Korsar?' asked Tarzan.

'It will not be easy,' replied Lajo. 'The only guide that we have is the wind. We are well out on the Korsar Az and I know from which direction the wind usually blows. By keeping always on the same tack we shall eventually reach land and probably not far from Korsar.'

'What is that?' asked Jana, pointing, and all eyes turned in the direction that she indicated.

'It is a sail,' said Lajo presently. 'We are saved.'

'But suppose the ship is manned by unfriendly people?' asked Jason.

'It is not,' said Lajo. 'It is manned by Korsars, for no other ships sail the Korsar Az.'

'There is another,' exclaimed Jana. 'There are many of them.'

'Come about and run for it,' said Tarzan; 'perhaps they have not seen us yet.'

'Why should we try to escape?' asked Lajo.

'Because we have not enough men to fight them,' replied Tarzan. 'They may not be your enemies, but they will be ours.'

Lajo did as he was bid, nor had he any alternative since the Korsars aboard were only three unarmed men, while there were ten Waziri with rifles.

All eyes watched the sails in the distance and it soon became apparent that they were coming closer, for the longboat, with its small sail, was far from fast. Little by little the distance between them and the ships decreased until it was evident that they were being pursued by a considerable fleet.

'Those are no Korsars,' said Lajo. 'I have never seen ships like those before.'

The longboat wallowed through the sea making the best headway that it could, but the pursuing ships, stringing out as far as the eye could reach until their numbers presented the appearance of a vast armada, continued to close up rapidly upon it.

The leading ship was now closing up so swiftly upon them that the occupants of the longboat had an excellent view of it. It was short and broad of beam with rather a high bow. It had two sails and in addition was propelled by bars, which protruded through ports along each side, there being some fifty oars all told. Above the line of oars, over the sides of the ship, were hung the shields of the warriors.

'Lord!' exclaimed Jason to Tarzan; 'Pellucidar not only boasts Spanish pirates, but vikings as well, for if those are not viking ships they certainly are an adaptation of them.'

'Slightly modernized, however,' remarked the Lord of the Jungle. 'There is a gun mounted on a small deck built in the bow.'

'So there is,' exclaimed Jason, 'and I think we had better come about. There is a fellow up there turning it on us now.'

Presently another man appeared upon the elevated bow deck of the enemy. 'Heave to,' he cried, 'or I'll blow you out of the water.'

'Who are you?' demanded Jason.

'I am Ja of Anoroc,' replied the man, 'and this is the fleet of David I, Emperor of Pellucidar.'

'Come about,' said Tarzan to Lajo.

'Someone in this boat must have been born on Sunday,' exclaimed Jason. 'I never knew there was so much good luck in the world.'

'Who are you?' demanded Ja as the longboat came slowly about.

'We are friends,' replied Tarzan.

'The Emperor of Pellucidar can have no friends upon the Korsar Az,' replied Ja.

'If Abner Perry is with you, we can prove that you are wrong,' replied Jason.

'Abner Perry is not with us,' said Ja; 'but what do you know of him?'

By this time the two boats were alongside and the bronzed Mezop warriors of Ja's crew were gazing down curiously upon the occupants of the boat.

'This is Jason Gridley,' said Tarzan to Ja, indicating the American. 'Perhaps you have heard Abner Perry speak of him. He organized an expedition in the outer world to come here to rescue David Innes from the dungeons of the Korsars.'

The three Korsars of the longboat made Ja suspicious, but when a full explanation had been made and especially when he had examined the rifles of the Waziri, he became convinced of the truth of their statements and welcomed them warmly aboard his ship, about which were now gathered a considerable number of the armada. When word was passed among them that two of the strangers were friends from the outer world who had come to assist in the rescue of David Innes, a number of the captains of other ships came aboard Ja's flagship to greet Tarzan and Jason. Among these captains were Dacor the Strong One, brother of Dian the Beautiful, Empress of

Pellucidar; Kolk, son of Goork, who is chief of the Thurians; and Tanar, son of Ghak, the Hairy One, King of Sari.

From these Tarzan and Jason learned that this fleet was on its way to effect the rescue of David. It had been building for a great while, so long that they had forgotten how many times they had eaten and slept since the first keel was laid, and then they had had to find a way into the Korsar Az from the Lural Az, where the ships were built upon the island of Anoroc.

'Far down the Sojar Az beyond the Land of Awful Shadow we found a passage that led to the Korsar Az. The Thurians had heard of it and while the fleet was building they sent warriors out to see if it was true and they found the passage and soon we shall be before the city of Korsar.'

'How did you expect to rescue David with only a dozen men?' asked Tanar.

'We are not all here,' said Tarzan. 'We became separated from our companions and have been unable to find them. However, there were not very many men in our expedition. We depended upon other means than manpower to effect the rescue of your Emperor.'

At this moment a great cry arose from one of the ships. The excitement rose and spread. The warriors were all looking into the air and pointing. Already some of them were elevating the muzzles of their cannons and all were preparing their rifles, and as Tarzan and Jason looked up they saw the O-220 far above them.

The dirigible had evidently discovered the fleet and was descending toward it in a wide spiral.

'Now I *know* someone was born on Sunday,' said Jason. 'That is our ship. Those are our friends.' he added, turning to Ja.

All that transpired on board the flagship passed quickly from ship to ship until every member of the armada knew that the great thing hovering above them was no gigantic flying reptile, but a ship of the air in which were friends of Abner Perry and their beloved Emperor, David I.

Slowly the great ship settled toward the surface of the sea and as it did so Jason Gridley borrowed a spear from one of the warriors and tied Lajo's head handkerchief to its tip. With this improvised flag he signalled, 'O-220 ahoy! This is the war fleet of David I, Emperor of Pellucidar, commanded by Ja of Anoroc; Lord Greystoke, ten Waziri and Jason Gridley aboard.'

A moment later a gun boomed from the rear turret of the O-220, marking the beginning of the first international salute of twenty-one guns that had ever reverberated beneath the eternal sun of Pellucidar, and when the significance of it was explained to Ja he returned the salute with the bow gun of his flagship.

The dirigible dropped lower until it was within speaking distance of the flagship.

'Are you all well aboard?' asked Tarzan.

'Yes,' came back the reassuring reply in Zuppner's booming tone.

'Is Von Horst with you?' asked Jason.

'No,' replied Zuppner.

'Then he alone is missing,' said Jason sadly.

'Can you drop a sling and take us aboard?' asked Tarzan.

Zuppner maneuvered the dirigible to within fifty feet of the deck of Ja's flagship, a sling was lowered and one after another the members of the party were taken on board the O-220, the Waziri first and then Jana and Thoar, followed by Jason and Tarzan the three Korsars being left prisoners with Ja with the understanding that they were to be treated humanely.

Before Tarzan left the deck of the flagship he told Ja that if he would proceed toward Korsar, the dirigible would keep in touch with him and in the meantime they would be perfecting plans for the rescue of David Innes.

As Thoar and Jana were hoisted aboard the O-220, they were filled with a boundless amazement. To them such a creation as the giant dirigible was inconceivable. As Jana expressed it afterward: 'I knew that I was dreaming, but yet at the same time I knew that I could not dream about such a thing as this because no such thing existed.'

Jason introduced Jana and Thoar to Zuppner and Hines, but Lieutenant Dorf did not come to the cabin until after Tarzan had boarded the ship, and it was the latter who introduced them to Dorf.

He presented Lieutenant Dorf to Jana and then, indicating Thoar, 'This is Thoar, the brother of The Red Flower of Zoram.'

As those words broke upon the ears of Jason Gridley he reacted almost as to the shock of a physical blow. He was glad that no one chanced to be looking at him at the time and instantly he regained his composure, but it left him with a distinct feeling of injury. They had all known it and none of them had told him. He was almost angry at them until it occurred to him that they had all probably assumed that he had known it too, and yet try as he would he could not quite forgive Jana. But, really, what difference did it make, for, whether sister or mate of Thoar or another, he knew that The Red Flower of Zoram was not for him. She had made that definitely clear in her attitude toward him, which had convinced him even more definitely than had her bitter words.

The reunited officers of the expedition had much to discuss and many reminiscences to narrate as the O-220 followed above the slowly moving fleet. It was a happy reunion, clouded only by the absence of Von Horst.

As the dirigible moved slowly above the waters of the Korsar Az, Zuppner dropped occasionally to within speaking distance of Ja of Anoroc, and when the distant coast of Korsar was sighted a sling was lowered and Ja was taken aboard the O-220, where plans for the rescue of David were discussed, and when they were perfected Ja was returned to his ship, and Lajo and the two other Korsars were taken aboard the dirigible.

The three prisoners were filled with awe and consternation as Jason and Tarzan personally conducted them throughout the giant craft. They were shown the armament, which was carefully explained to them, special stress being laid upon the destructive power of the bombs which the O-220 carried. 'One of these,' said Jason to Lajo, 'would blow The Cid's palace a thousand feet into the air and, as you see, we have many of them. We could destroy all of Korsar and all the Korsar ships.'

While Ja's fleet was still a considerable distance off the coast, the O-220 raced ahead at full speed toward Korsar, for the plan which they had evolved was such that, if successful, David's release would be effected without the shedding of blood – a plan which was especially desirable since if it was necessary to attack Korsar either from the sea or the air, the Emperor's life would be placed in jeopardy from the bombs and cannons of his friends, as well as from a possible spirit of vengeance which might animate The Cid.

As the dirigible glided almost silently over the city of Korsar, the streets and courtyards filled with people staring upward in awe-struck wonder.

Three thousand feet above the city the ship stopped and Tarzan sent for the three Korsar prisoners.

'As you know,' he said to them, 'we are in a position to destroy Korsar. You have seen the great fleet coming to the rescue of the Emperor of Pellucidar. You know that every warrior manning those ships is armed with a weapon far more effective than your best; even with their knives and spears and their bows and arrows they might take Korsar without their rifles, but they have the rifles and they have better ammunition than yours and in each ship of the fleet cannons are mounted. Alone the fleet could reduce Korsar, but in addition to the fleet there is this airship. Your shots could never reach it as it sailed back and forth above Korsar, dropping bombs upon the city. Do you think, Lajo, that we can take Korsar?'

'I know it,' replied the Korsar.

'Very well,' said Tarzan. 'I am going to send you with a message to The Cid. Will you tell him the truth?'

'I will,' replied Lajo.

'The message is simple,' continued Tarzan. 'You may tell him that we have come to effect the release of the Emperor of Pellucidar. You may explain to him that the means that we have to enforce our demands, and then you may say to him that if he will place the Emperor upon a ship and take him out to our fleet and deliver him unharmed to Ja of Anoroc, we will return to Sari without firing a shot. Do you understand?'

'I do,' said Lajo.

'Very well, then,' said Tarzan. He turned to Dorf, 'Lieutenant, will you take him now?' he asked.

Dorf approached with a bundle in his hand. 'Slip into this,' he said.

'What is it?' asked Lajo.

'It is a parachute,' said Dorf.

'What is that?' demanded Lajo.

'Here,' said Dorf, 'put your arms through here.' A moment later he had the parachute adjusted upon the Korsar.

'Now,' said Jason, 'a great distinction is going to be conferred upon you – you are going to make the first parachute jump that has ever been witnessed in Pellucidar.'

'I don't understand what you mean,' said Lajo.

'You will presently,' said Jason. 'You are going to take Lord Greystoke's message to The Cid.'

'But you will have to bring the ship down to the ground before I can,' objected Lajo.

'On the contrary we are going to stay right where we are,' said Jason; 'you are going to jump overboard.'

'What?' exclaimed Lajo. 'You are going to kill me?'

'No,' said Jason with a laugh. 'Listen carefully to what I tell you and you will land safely. You have seen some wonderful things on board this ship so you must have some conception of what we of the outer world can do. Now you are going to have a demonstration of another very wonderful invention and you may take my word for it that no harm will befall you if you do precisely as I tell you to. Here is an iron ring,' and he touched the ring opposite Lajo's left breast; 'take hold of it with your right hand. After you jump from the ship, pull it; give it a good jerk and you will float down to the ground as lightly as a feather.'

'I will be killed,' objected Lajo.

'If you are a coward,' said Jason, 'perhaps one of these other men is braver than you. I tell you that you will not be hurt.'

'I am not afraid,' said Lajo. 'I will jump.'

'Tell The Cid,' said Tarzan, 'that if we do not presently see a ship sail out alone to meet the fleet, we shall start dropping bombs upon the city.'

Dorf led Lajo to a door in the cabin and flung it open. The man hesitated.

'Do not forget to jerk the ring,' said Dorf, and at the same time he gave Lajo a violent push that sent him headlong through the doorway and a moment later the watchers in the cabin saw the white folds of the parachute streaming in the air. They saw it open and they knew that the message of Tarzan would be delivered to The Cid.

What went on in the city below we may not know, but presently a great crowd was seen to move from the palace down toward the river, where the ships were anchored, and a little later one of the ships weighed anchor and as it drifted slowly with the current its sails were set and presently it was moving directly out to sea toward the fleet from Sari.

The O-220 followed above it and Ja's flagship moved forward to meet it, and thus David Innes, Emperor of Pellucidar, was returned to his people.

As the Korsar ship turned back to port the dirigible dropped low above the flagship of the Sarian fleet and greetings were exchanged between David and his rescuers – men from another world whom he had never seen.

The Emperor was half starved and very thin and weak from his long period of confinement, but otherwise he had been unharmed, and great was the rejoicing aboard the ships of Sari as they turned back to cross the Korsar Az toward their own land.

Tarzan was afraid to accompany the fleet back to Sari for fear that their rapidly diminishing store of fuel would not be sufficient to complete the trip and carry them back to the outer world. He followed the fleet only long enough to obtain from David explicit directions for reaching the polar opening from the city of Korsar.

'We have another errand to fulfill first,' said Jason to Tarzan. 'We must return Thoar and Jana to Zoram.'

'Yes,' said the ape-man, 'and drop these two Korsars off near their city. I have thought of all that and we shall have fuel enough for that purpose.'

'I am not going to return with you,' said Jason. 'I wish to be put aboard Ja's flagship.'

'What?' exclaimed Tarzan. 'You are going to remain here?'

'This expedition was undertaken at my suggestion. I feel responsible for the life and safety of every man in it and I shall never return to the outer world while the fate of Lieutenant Von Horst remains a mystery.'

'But how can you find Von Horst if you go back to Sari with the fleet?' asked Tarzan.

'I shall ask David Innes to equip an expedition to go in search of him,' replied Jason, 'and with such an expedition made up of native Pellucidarians I shall stand a very much better chance of finding him than we would in the O-220.'

'I quite agree with you,' said Tarzan, 'and if you are unalterably determined to carry out your project, we will lower you to Ja's ship immediately.'

As the O-220 dropped toward Ja's flagship and signaled it to heave to, Jason gathered what belongings he wished to take with him, including rifles and revolvers and plenty of ammunition. These were lowered first to Ja's ship, while Jason bid farewell to his companions of the expedition.

'Goodbye, Jana,' he said, after he had shaken hands with the others.

The girl made no reply, but instead turned to her brother.

'Goodbye, Thoar,' she said.

'Goodbye?' he asked. 'What do you mean?'

'I am going to Sari with the man I love,' replied The Red Flower of Zoram.

TARZAN THE INVINCIBLE

CHAPTER I
Little Nkima

I am no historian, no chronicler of facts, and, furthermore, I hold a very definite conviction that there are certain subjects which fiction writers should leave alone, foremost among which are politics and religion. However, it seems to me not unethical to pirate an idea occasionally from one or the other, provided that the subject be handled in such a way as to impart a definite impression of fictionizing.

Had the story that I am about to tell you broken in the newspapers of two certain European powers, it might have precipitated another and a more terrible world war. But with that I am not particularly concerned. What interests me is that it is a good story that is particularly well adapted to my requirements through the fact that Tarzan of the Apes was intimately connected with many of its most thrilling episodes.

I am not going to bore you with dry political history, so do not tax your intellect needlessly by attempting to decode such fictitious names as I may use in describing certain people and places, which, it seems to me, to the best interest of peace and disarmament, should remain incognito.

Take the story simply as another Tarzan story in which, it is hoped, you will find entertainment and relaxation. If you find food for thought in it, so much the better.

Doubtless very few of you saw, and still fewer will remember having seen, a news dispatch that appeared inconspicuously in the papers some time since, reporting a rumour that French Colonial troops stationed in Somaliland, on the north-east coast of Africa, had invaded an Italian African colony. Back of that news item is a story of conspiracy, intrigue, adventure and love – a story of scoundrels and of fools, of brave men, of beautiful women, a story of the beasts of the forest and the jungle.

If there were few who saw the newspaper account of the invasion of Italian Somaliland upon the north-east coast of Africa, it is equally a fact that none of you saw a harrowing incident that occurred in the interior some time previous to this affair. That it could possibly have any connection whatsoever with European international intrigue, or with the fate of nations, seems not even remotely possible, for it was only a very little monkey fleeing through the tree tops and screaming in terror. It was little Nkima, and pursuing him was a large, rude monkey – a much larger monkey than little Nkima.

Fortunately for the peace of Europe and the world, the speed of the pursuer was in no sense proportionate to his unpleasant disposition, and so Nkima escaped him; but for long after the larger monkey had given up the chase, the smaller one continued to flee through the tree tops, screeching at the top of his shrill little voice, for terror and flight were the two major activities of little Nkima.

Perhaps it was fatigue, but more likely it was a caterpillar or a bird's nest that eventually terminated Nkima's flight and left him scolding and chattering upon a swaying bough, far above the floor of the jungle.

The world into which little Nkima had been born seemed a very terrible world, indeed, and he spent most of his waking hours scolding about it, in which respect he was quite as human as he was simian. It seemed to little Nkima that the world was populated with large, fierce creatures that liked monkey meat. There were Numa the lion, and Sheeta the panther, and Histah the snake – a triumvirate that rendered unsafe his entire world from the loftiest tree top to the ground. And then there were the great apes, and the lesser apes, and the baboons, and countless species of monkeys, all of which God had made larger than He had made little Nkima, and all of which seemed to harbour a grudge against him.

Take, for example, the rude creature which had just been pursuing him. Little Nkima had done nothing more than throw a stick at him while he was asleep in the crotch of a tree, and just for that he had pursued little Nkima with unquestionable homicidal intent – I use the word without purposing any reflection upon Nkima. It had never occurred to Nkima, as it never seems to occur to some people, that, like beauty, a sense of humour may sometimes be fatal.

Brooding upon the injustices of life, little Nkima was very sad. But there was another and more poignant cause of sadness that depressed his little heart. Many, many moons ago his master had gone away and left him. True, he had left him in a nice, comfortable home with kind people who fed him, but little Nkima missed the great Tarmangani whose naked shoulder was the one harbour of refuge from which he could, with perfect impunity, hurl insults at the world. For a long time now little Nkima had braved the dangers of the forest and the jungle in search of his beloved Tarzan.

Because hearts are measured by content of love and loyalty, rather than by diameters in inches, the heart of little Nkima was very large – so large that the average human being could hide his own heart and himself, as well, behind it – and for a long time it had been just one great ache in his diminutive breast. But fortunately for the little Manu his mind was so ordered that it might easily be distracted even from a great sorrow. A butterfly or a luscious grub might suddenly claim his attention from the depths of brooding, which was well, since otherwise he might have grieved himself to death.

And now, therefore, as his melancholy thoughts returned to contemplation of his loss, their trend was suddenly altered by the shifting of a jungle breeze that brought to his keen ears a sound that was not primarily of the jungle sounds that were a part of his hereditary instincts. It was a discord. And who is it that brings discord into the jungle as well as into everywhere else that he enters? Man. It was the voices of men that Nkima heard.

Silently the little monkey glided through the trees into the direction from which the sounds had come; and presently, as the sounds grew louder, there came also that which was the definite, final proof of the identity of the noise makers, as far as Nkima, or, for that matter, any other of the jungle folk, might be concerned – the scent spoor.

You have seen a dog, perhaps your own dog, half recognize you by sight; but was he ever entirely satisfied until the evidence of his eyes had been tested and approved by his sensitive nostrils?

And so it was with Nkima. His ears had suggested the presence of men, and now his nostrils definitely assured him that men were near. He did not think of them as men, but as great apes. There were Gomangani, Great Black Apes, negroes, among them. This his nose told him. And there were Tarmangani, also. These, which to Nkima would be Great White Apes, were white men.

Eagerly his nostrils sought for the familiar scent spoor of his beloved Tarzan, but it was not there – that he knew even before he came within sight of the strangers.

The camp upon which Nkima presently looked down from a nearby tree was well established. It had evidently been there for a matter of days and might be expected to remain still longer. It was no overnight affair. There were the tents of the white men and the byut of Arabs neatly arranged with almost military precision and behind these the shelters of the negroes, lightly constructed of such materials as nature had provided upon the spot.

Within the open front of an Arab beyt sat several white burnoosed Bedouins drinking their inevitable coffee; in the shade of a great tree before another tent four white men were engrossed in a game of cards; among the native shelters a group of stalwart Galla warriors were playing at minkala. There were blacks of other tribes too – men of East Africa and of Central Africa, with a sprinkling of West Coast negroes.

It might have puzzled an experienced African traveller or hunter to catalogue this motley aggregation of races and colours. There were far too many blacks to justify a belief that all were porters, for with all the impedimenta of the camp ready for transportation there would have been but a small fraction of a load for each of them, even after more than enough had been included among the askaris, who do not carry any loads beside their rifles and ammunition.

Then, too, there were more rifles than would have been needed to protect even a larger party. There seemed, indeed, to be a rifle for every man. But these were minor details which made no impression upon Nkima. All that impressed him was the fact that here were many strange Tarmangani and Gomangani in the country of his master; and as all strangers were, to Nkima, enemies, he was perturbed. Now, more than ever he wished that he might find Tarzan.

A swarthy, turbaned East Indian sat cross-legged upon the ground before a tent, apparently sunk in meditation; but could one have seen his dark sensuous eyes, one would have discovered that their gaze was far from introspective – they were bent constantly upon another tent that stood a little apart from its fellows – and when a girl emerged from this tent, Raghunath Jafar arose and approached her. He smiled an oily smile as he spoke to her, but the girl did not smile as she replied. She spoke civilly, but she did not pause, continuing her way toward the four men at cards.

As she approached their table they looked up; and upon the face of each was reflected some pleasurable emotion, but whether it was the same in each the masks that we call faces, and which are trained to conceal our true thoughts, did not divulge. Evident it was, however, that the girl was popular.

'Hello, Zora!' cried a large, smooth-faced fellow. 'Have a good nap?'

'Yes, Comrade,' replied the girl; 'but I am tired of napping. This inactivity is getting on my nerves.'

'Mine, too,' agreed the man.

'How much longer will you wait for the American, Comrade Zveri?' asked Raghunath Jafar.

The big man shrugged. 'I need him,' he replied. 'We might easily carry on without him, but for the moral effect upon the world of having a rich and highborn American identified actively with the affair it is worth waiting.'

'Are you quite sure of this gringo, Zveri?' asked a swarthy young Mexican sitting next to the big, smooth-faced man who was evidently the leader of the expedition.

'I met him in New York and again in San Francisco,' replied Zveri. 'He has been very carefully checked and favourably recommended.'

'I am always suspicious of these fellows who owe everything they have to capitalism,' declared Romero. 'It is in their blood – at heart they hate the proletariat, just as we hate them.'

'This fellow is different, Miguel,' insisted Zveri. 'He has been won over so completely that he would betray his own father for the good of the cause – and already he is betraying his country.'

A slight, involuntary sneer, that passed unnoticed by the others, curled the lip of Zora Drinov as she heard this description of the remaining member of the party, who had not yet reached the rendezvous.

Miguel Romero, the Mexican, was still unconvinced. 'I have no use for gringos of any sort,' he said.

Zveri shrugged his heavy shoulders. 'Our personal animosities are of no importance,' he said, 'as against the interests of the workers of the world. When Colt arrives we must accept him as one of us; nor must we forget that however much we may detest America and Americans nothing of any moment may be accomplished in the world of today without them and their filthy wealth.'

'Wealth ground out of the blood and sweat of the working class,' growled Romero.

'Exactly,' agreed Raghunath Jafar, 'but how appropriate that this same wealth should be used to undermine and overthrow capitalistic America and bring the workers eventually into their own.'

'That is precisely the way I feel about it,' said Zveri. 'I would rather use American gold in furthering the cause than any other – and after that British.'

'But what do the puny resources of this single American mean to us?' demanded Zora. 'A mere nothing compared to what America is already pouring into Soviet Russia. What is his treason compared with the treason of those others who are already doing more to hasten the day of world communism than the Third Internationale itself – it is nothing, not a drop in the bucket.'

'What do you mean, Zora?' asked Miguel.

'I mean the bankers, and manufacturers, and engineers of America, who are selling their own country and the world to us in the hope of adding more gold to their already bursting coffers. One of their most pious and lauded citizens is building great factories for us in Russia, where we may turn out tractors and tanks; their manufacturers are vying with one another to furnish us with engines for countless thousands of airplanes; their engineers are selling us their brains and their skill to build a great modern manufacturing city in which ammunitions and engines of war may be produced. These are the traitors, these are the men who are hastening the day when Moscow shall dictate the policies of a world.'

'You speak as though you regretted it,' said a dry voice at her shoulder.

The girl turned quickly. 'Oh, it is you, Sheikh Abu Batn?' she said, as she recognized the swart Arab who had strolled over from his coffee. 'Our own good fortune does not blind me to the perfidiousness of the enemy, nor cause me to admire treason in anyone, even though I profit by it.'

'Does that include me?' demanded Romero, suspiciously.

Zora laughed. 'You know better than that, Miguel,' she said, 'You are of the working class – you are loyal to the workers of your own country – but these others are of the capitalistic class; their government is a capitalistic government that is so opposed to our beliefs that it has never recognized our government; yet, in their greed, these swine are selling out their own kind and their own country for a few more rotten dollars. I loathe them.'

Zveri laughed. 'You are a good Red, Zora,' he cried; 'you hate the enemy as much when he helps us as when he hinders.'

'But hating and talking accomplish so little,' said the girl. 'I wish we might do something. Sitting here in idleness seems so futile.'

'And what would you have us do?' demanded Zveri, good naturedly.

'We might at least make a try for the gold of Opar,' she said. 'If Kitembo is right, there should be enough there to finance a dozen expeditions such as you are planning, and we do not need this American – what do they call them, cake eaters? – to assist us in that venture.'

'I have been thinking along similar lines,' said Raghunath Jafar.

Zveri scowled. 'Perhaps some of the rest of you would like to run this expedition,' he said, crustily. 'I know what I am doing and I don't have to discuss all my plans with anyone. When I have orders to give, I'll give them. Kitembo has already received his, and preparations have been underway for several days for the expedition to Opar.'

'The rest of us are as much interested and are risking as much as you, Zveri,' snapped Romero. 'We were to work together – not as master and slaves.'

'You'll soon learn that I am master,' snarled Zveri in an ugly tone.

'Yes,' sneered Romero, 'the czar was master, too, and Obregon. You know what happened to them?'

Zveri leaped to his feet and whipped out a revolver, but as he levelled it at Romero the girl struck his arm up and stepped between them. 'Are you mad, Zveri?' she cried.

'Do not interfere, Zora; this is my affair and it might as well be settled now as later. I am chief here and I am not going to have any traitors in my camp. Stand aside.'

'No!' said the girl with finality. 'Miguel was wrong and so were you, but to shed blood now – our own blood – would utterly ruin any chance we have of success. It would sow the seed of fear and suspicion and cost us the respect of the blacks, for they would know that there was dissension among us. Furthermore, Miguel is not armed; to shoot him would be cowardly murder that would lose you the respect of every decent man in the expedition.' She had spoken rapidly in Russian, a language that was understood by only Zveri and herself, of those who were present; then she turned again to Miguel and addressed him in English. 'You were wrong, Miguel,' she said gently. 'There must be one responsible head, and Comrade Zveri was chosen for the responsibility. He regrets that he acted hastily. Tell him that you are sorry for what you said, and then the two of you shake hands and let us all forget the matter.'

For an instant Romero hesitated; then he extended his hand toward Zveri. 'I am sorry,' he said.

The Russian took the proffered hand in his and bowed stiffly. 'Let us forget it, Comrade,' he said; but the scowl was still upon his face, though no darker than that which clouded the Mexican's.

Little Nkima yawned and swung by his tail from a branch far overhead. His curiosity concerning these enemies was sated. They no longer afforded him entertainment, but he knew that his master should know about their presence; and that thought, entering his little head, recalled his sorrow and his great yearning for Tarzan, to the end that he was again imbued with a grim determination to continue his search for the ape-man. Perhaps in half an hour some trivial occurrence might again distract his attention, but for the moment it was his life work. Swinging through the forest, little Nkima held the fate of Europe in his pink palm, but he did not know it.

The afternoon was waning. In the distance a lion roared. An instinctive shiver ran up Nkima's spine. In reality, however, he was not much afraid, knowing, as he did, that no lion could reach him in the tree tops.

A young man marching near the head of a safari cocked his head and listened. 'Not so very far away, Tony,' he said.

'No, sir; much too close,' replied the Filipino.

'You'll have to learn to cut out that "sir" stuff, Tony, before we join the others,' admonished the young man.

The Filipino grinned. 'All right, Comrade,' he assented. 'I got so used calling everybody "sir" it hard for me to change.'

'I'm afraid you're not a very good Red then, Tony.'

'Oh, yes I am,' insisted the Filipino emphatically. 'Why else am I here? You think I like come this God forsaken country full of lion, ant, snake, fly, mosquito just for the walk? No, I come lay down my life for Philippine independence.'

'That's noble of you all right, Tony,' said the other gravely; 'but just how is it going to make the Philippines free?'

Antonio Mori scratched his head. 'I don't know,' he admitted; 'but it make trouble for America.'

High among the tree tops a little monkey crossed their path. For a moment he paused and watched them; then he resumed his journey in the opposite direction.

A half hour later the lion roared again, and so disconcertingly close and unexpected rose the voice of thunder from the jungle beneath him that little Nkima nearly fell out of the tree through which he was passing. With a scream of terror he scampered as high aloft as he could go and there he sat, scolding angrily.

The lion, a magnificent full-maned male, stepped into the open beneath the tree in which the trembling Nkima clung. Once again he raised his mighty voice until the ground itself trembled to the great, rolling volume of his challenge. Nkima looked down upon him and suddenly ceased to scold. Instead he leaped about excitedly, chattering and grimacing. Numa, the lion, looked up; and then a strange thing occurred. The monkey ceased its chattering and voiced a low, peculiar sound. The eyes of the lion, that had been glaring balefully upward, took on a new and almost gentle expression. He arched his back and rubbed his side luxuriously against the bole of the tree, and from those savage jaws came a soft, purring sound. Then little Nkima dropped quickly downward through the foliage of the tree, gave a final nimble leap, and alighted upon the thick mane of the king of beasts.

CHAPTER II

The Hindu

With the coming of a new day came a new activity to the camp of the conspirators. Now were the Bedauwy drinking no coffee in the muk'aad; the cards of the whites were put away and the Galla warriors no longer played at minkala.

Zveri sat behind his folding camp table directing his aides and with the assistance of Zora and Raghunath Jafar issued ammunition to the file of armed men marching past them. Miguel Romero and the two remaining whites were supervising the distribution of loads among the porters. Savage black Kitembo moved constantly among his men, hastening laggards from belated breakfast fires and forming those who had received their ammunition into companies. Abu Batn, the sheikh, squatted aloof with his sun-bitten warriors. They, always ready, watched with contempt the disorderly preparations of their companions.

'How many are you leaving to guard the camp?' asked Zora.

'You and Comrade Jafar will remain in charge here,' replied Zveri. 'Your boys and ten askaris also will remain as camp guard.'

'That will be plenty,' replied the girl. 'There is no danger.'

'No,' agreed Zveri, 'not now, but if that Tarzan were here it would be different. I took pains to assure myself as to that before I chose this region for our base camp, and I have learned that he has been absent for a great while – went on some fool dirigible expedition that has never been heard from. It is almost certain that he is dead.'

When the last of the blacks had received his issue of ammunition, Kitembo assembled his tribesmen at a little distance from the rest of the expedition and harangued them in a low voice. They were Basembos, and Kitembo, their chief, spoke to them in the dialect of their people.

Kitembo hated all whites. The British had occupied the land that had been the home of his people since before the memory of man; and because Kitembo, hereditary chief, had been irreconcilable to the domination of the invaders they had deposed him, elevating a puppet to the chieftaincy.

To Kitembo, the chief – savage, cruel and treacherous – all whites were anathema, but he saw in his connection with Zveri an opportunity to be avenged upon the British; and so he had gathered about him many of his tribesmen and enlisted in the expedition that Zveri promised him would rid the land forever of the British and restore Kitembo to even greater power and glory than had formerly been the lot of Basembo chiefs.

It was not, however, always easy for Kitembo to hold the interest of his people in this undertaking. The British had greatly undermined his power and influence so that warriors, who formerly might have been as subservient to his will as slaves, now dared openly to question his authority. There had been no demur so long as the expedition entailed no greater hardships than short marches, pleasant camps, and plenty of food, with West Coast blacks, and members of other tribes less warlike than the Basembos, to act as porters, carry the loads, and do all of the heavy work; but now, with fighting looming ahead, some of his people had desired to know just what they were going to get out of it, having, apparently, little stomach for risking their hides for the gratification of the ambitions or hatreds of either the white Zveri or the black Kitembo.

It was for the purpose of mollifying these malcontents that Kitembo was now haranguing his warriors, promising them loot on the one hand and ruthless punishment on the other as a choice between obedience and mutiny. Some of the rewards he dangled before their imaginations might have caused Zveri and the other white members of the expedition considerable perturbation could they have understood the Basembo dialect; but perhaps a greater argument for obedience to his commands was the genuine fear that most of his followers still entertained for their pitiless chieftain.

Among the other blacks of the expedition were outlaw members of several tribes and a considerable number of porters hired in the ordinary manner to accompany what was officially described as a scientific expedition.

Abu Batn and his warriors were animated to temporary loyalty to Zveri by two motives – a lust for loot and hatred for all Nasrâny as represented by the British influence in Egypt and out in to the desert, which they considered their hereditary domain.

The members of other races accompanying Zveri were assumed to be motivated by noble, humanitarian aspirations; but it was, nevertheless, true that their leader spoke to them more often of the acquisition of personal riches and power than of the advancement of the brotherhood of man or the rights of the proletariat.

It was, then, such a loosely knit, but nonetheless formidable, expedition that set forth this lovely morning upon the sack of the treasure vaults of mysterious Opar.

As Zora Drinov watched them depart, her beautiful, inscrutable eyes remained fixed steadfastly upon the person of Peter Zveri until he had disappeared from view along the river trail that led into the dark forest.

Was it a maid watching in trepidation the departure of her lover upon a mission fraught with danger, or—

'Perhaps he will not return,' said an oily voice at her shoulder.

The girl turned her head to look into the half-closed eyes of Raghunath Jafar. 'He will return, Comrade,' she said. 'Peter Zveri always returns to me.'

'You are very sure of him,' said the man, with a leer.

'It is written,' replied the girl as she started to move toward her tent.

'Wait,' said Jafar.

She stopped and turned toward him. 'What do you want?' she asked.

'You,' he replied. 'What do you see in that uncouth swine, Zora? What does he know of love or beauty? I can appreciate you, beautiful flower of the morning. With me you may attain the transcendant bliss of perfect love, for I am an adept in the cult of love. A beast like Zveri would only degrade you.'

The sickening disgust that the girl felt she hid from the eyes of the man, for she realized that the expedition might be gone for days and that during that time she and Jafar would be practically alone together, except for a handful of savage black warriors whose attitude toward a matter of this nature between an alien woman and an alien man she could not anticipate; but she was nonetheless determined to put a definite end to his advances.

'You are playing with death, Jafar,' she said quietly. 'I am here upon no mission of love, and if Zveri should learn of what you have said to me he would kill you. Do not speak to me again on this subject.'

'It will not be necessary,' replied the Hindu, enigmatically. His half-closed eyes were fixed steadily upon those of the girl. For perhaps less than half a minute the two stood thus, while there crept through Zora Drinov a sense of growing weakness, a realization of approaching capitulation. She fought against it, pitting her will against that of the man. Suddenly she tore her eyes from his. She had won, but victory left her weak and trembling as might be one who had but just experienced a stubbornly contested physical encounter. Turning quickly away, she moved swiftly toward her tent, not daring to look back for fear that she might again encounter those twin pools of vicious and malignant power that were the eyes of Raghunath Jafar; and so she did not see the oily smile of satisfaction that twisted the sensuous lips of the Hindu, nor did she hear his whispered repetition – 'It will not be necessary.'

*

As the expedition wound along the trail that leads to the foot of the barrier cliffs that hem the lower frontier of the arid plateau beyond which stand the ancient ruins that are Opar, Wayne Colt, far to the west, pushed on toward the base camp of the conspirators. To the south, a little monkey rode upon the back of a great lion, shrilling insults now with perfect impunity at every jungle creature that crossed their path; while, with equal contempt for all lesser creatures, the mighty carnivore strode haughtily downwind, secure in the knowledge of his unquestioned might. A herd of antelope, grazing in his path, caught the acrid scent of the cat and moved nervously about; but when he came within sight of them they trotted only a short distance to one side, making a path for him; and, while he was still in sight, they resumed their feeding, for Numa the lion had fed well and the herbivores knew, as creatures of the wild know many things that are beyond the dull sensibilities of man, and felt no fear of Numa with a full belly.

To others, yet far off, came the scent of the lion; and they, too, moved nervously, though their fear was less than had been the first fear of the antelopes. These others were the great apes of the tribe of To-yat, whose mighty bulls had little cause to fear even Numa himself, though their shes and their balus might well tremble.

As the cat approached, the Mangani became more restless and more irritable. To-yat, the king ape, beat his breast and bared his great fighting fangs. Ga-yat, his powerful shoulders hunched, moved to the edge of the herd nearest the approaching danger. Zu-tho thumped a warning menace with his calloused feet. The shes called their balus to them, and many took to the lower branches of the larger trees or sought positions close to an arboreal avenue of escape.

It was at this moment that an almost naked white man dropped from the dense foliage of a tree and alighted in their midst. Taut nerves and short tempers snapped. Roaring and snarling, the herd rushed upon the rash and hated man-thing. The king ape was in the lead.

'To-yat has a short memory,' said the man in the tongue of the Mangani.

For an instant the ape paused, surprised perhaps to hear the language of his kind issuing from the lips of a man-thing. 'I am To-yat!' he growled. 'I kill.'

'I am Tarzan,' replied the man, 'mighty hunter, mighty fighter. I come in peace.'

'Kill! Kill!' roared To-yat, and the other great bulls advanced, bare-fanged, menacingly.

'Zu-tho! Ga-yat!' snapped the man, 'it is I, Tarzan of the Apes;' but the bulls were nervous and frightened now, for the scent of Numa was strong in their nostrils, and the shock of Tarzan's sudden appearance had plunged them into a panic.

'Kill! Kill!' they bellowed, though as yet they did not charge, but advanced slowly, working themselves into the necessary frenzy of rage that would terminate in a sudden, blood-mad rush that no living creature might withstand and which would leave naught but torn and bloody fragments of the object of their wrath.

And then a shrill scream broke from the lips of a great, hairy mother with a tiny balu on her back. 'Numa!' she shrieked, and, turning, fled into the safety of the foliage of a nearby tree.

Instantly the shes and balus remaining upon the ground took to the trees. The bulls turned their attention for a moment from the man to the new menace. What they saw upset what little equanimity remained to them. Advancing straight toward them, his round, yellow-green eyes blazing in ferocity, was a mighty, yellow lion; and upon his back perched a little monkey, screaming insults at them. The sight was too much for the apes of To-yat, and the king was the first to break before it. With a roar, the ferocity of which may have salved his self esteem, he leaped for the nearest tree; and instantly the others broke and fled, leaving the white giant to face the angry lion alone.

With blazing eyes the king of beasts advanced upon the man, his head lowered and flattened, his tail extended, the brush flicking. The man spoke a single word in a low tone that might have carried but a few yards. Instantly the head of the lion came up, the horrid glare died in his eyes; and at the same instant the little monkey, voicing a shrill scream of recognition and delight, leaped over Numa's head and in three prodigious bounds was upon the shoulder of the man, his little arms encircling the bronzed neck.

'Little Nkima!' whispered Tarzan, the soft cheek of the monkey pressed against his own.

The lion strode majestically forward. He sniffed the bare legs of the man, rubbed his head against his side and lay down at his feet.

'Jad-bal-ja!' greeted the ape-man.

The great apes of the tribe of To-yat watched from the safety of the trees. Their panic and their anger had subsided. 'It is Tarzan,' said Zu-tho.

'Yes, it is Tarzan,' echoed Ga-yat.

To-yat grumbled. He did not like Tarzan, but he feared him; and now, with this new evidence of the power of the great Tarmangani, he feared him even more.

For a time Tarzan listened to the glib chattering of little Nkima. He learned of the strange Tarmangani and the many Gomangani warriors who had invaded the domain of the Lord of the Jungle.

The great apes moved restlessly in the trees, wishing to descend; but they feared Numa, and the great bulls were too heavy to travel in safety upon the high flung leafy trails along which the lesser apes might pass with safety, and so could not depart until Numa had gone.

'Go away!' cried To-yat, the King. 'Go away, and leave the Mangani in peace.'

'We are going,' replied the ape-man, 'but you need not fear either Tarzan or the Golden Lion. We are your friends. I have told Jad-bal-ja that he is never to harm you. You may descend.'

'We shall stay in the trees until he has gone,' said To-yat; 'he might forget.'

'You are afraid,' said Tarzan contemptuously. 'Zu-tho or Ga-yat would not be afraid.'

'Zu-tho is afraid of nothing,' boasted that great bull.

Without a word Ga-yat climbed ponderously from the tree in which he had taken refuge and, if not with marked enthusiasm, at least with slight hesitation, advanced toward Tarzan and Jad-bal-ja, the Golden Lion. His fellows eyed him intently, momentarily expecting to see him charged and mauled by the yellow-eyed destroyer that lay at Tarzan's feet watching every move of the shaggy bull. The Lord of the Jungle also watched great Numa, for none knew better than he that a lion, however accustomed to obey its master, is still a lion. The years of their companionship, since Jad-bal-ja had been a little, spotted, fluffy ball, had never given him reason to doubt the loyalty of the carnivore, though there had been times when he had found it both difficult and dangerous to thwart some of the beast's more ferocious hereditary instincts.

Ga-yat approached, while little Nkima scolded and chattered from the safety of his master's shoulder; and the lion, blinking lazily, finally looked away. The danger, if there had been any, was over – it is the fixed, intent gaze of the lion that bodes ill.

Tarzan advanced and laid a friendly hand upon the shoulder of the ape. 'This is Ga-yat,' he said, addressing Jad-bal-ja, 'friend of Tarzan; do not harm him.' He did not speak in any language of man. Perhaps the medium of communication that he used might not properly be called a language at all, but the lion and the great ape and the little Manu understood him.

'Tell the Mangani that Tarzan is the friend of little Nkima,' shrilled the monkey. 'He must not harm little Nkima.'

'It is as Nkima has said,' the ape-man assured Ga-yat.

'The friends of Tarzan are the friends of Ga-yat,' replied the great ape.

'It is well,' said Tarzan, 'and now I go. Tell To-yat and the others what we have said and tell them also that there are strange men in this country which is Tarzan's. Let them watch them, but do not let the men see them, for these are bad men, perhaps, who carry the thunder sticks that hurl death with smoke and fire and a great noise. Tarzan goes now to see why these men are in his country.'

Zora Drinov had avoided Jafar since the departure of the expedition to Opar. Scarcely had she left her tent, feigning a headache as an excuse, nor had the

Hindu made any attempt to invade her privacy. Thus passed the first day. Upon the morning of the second, Jafar summoned the headman of the askaris that had been left to guard them and to procure meat.

'Today,' said Raghunath Jafar, 'would be a good day to hunt. The signs are propitious. Go, therefore, into the forest, taking all your men, and do not return until the sun is low in the west. If you do this there will be presents for you, besides all the meat you can eat from the carcases of your kills. Do you understand?'

'Yes, Bwana,' replied the black.

'Take with you the boy of the woman. He will not be needed here. My boy will remain to cook for us.'

'Perhaps he will not come,' suggested the negro.

'You are many, he is only one; but do not let the woman know that you are taking him.'

'What are the presents?' demanded the headman.

'A piece of cloth and cartridges,' replied Jafar.

'And the curved sword that you carry when we are on the march.'

'No,' said Jafar.

'This is not a good day to hunt,' replied the black, turning away.

'Two pieces of cloth and fifty cartridges,' suggested Jafar.

'And the curved sword,' and thus, after much haggling, the bargain was made.

The headman gathered his askaris and bade them prepare for the hunt, saying that the brown bwana had so ordered, but he said nothing about any presents. When they were ready, he dispatched one to summon the white woman's servant.

'You are to accompany us on the hunt,' he said to the boy.

'Who said so?' demanded Wamala.

'The brown bwana,' replied Kahiya, the headman.

Wamala laughed. 'I take my orders from my mistress – not from the brown bwana.'

Kahiya leaped upon him and clapped a rough palm across his mouth as two of his men seized Wamala upon either side. 'You take your orders from Kahiya,' he said. Hunting spears were pressed against the boy's trembling body. 'Will you go upon the hunt with us?' demanded Kahiya.

'I go,' replied Wamala. 'I did but joke.'

As Zveri led his expedition toward Opar, Wayne Colt, impatient to join the main body of the conspirators, urged his men to greater speed in their search for the camp. The principal conspirators had entered Africa at different points that they might not arouse too much attention by their numbers. Pursuant to this plan Colt had landed on the west coast and had travelled inland a short distance by train to rail-head, from which point he had had a long and arduous journey on foot; so that now, with his destination almost in sight, he was anxious to put a period to this part of his adventure. Then, too, he was curious to meet the other principals in this hazardous undertaking, Peter Zveri being the only one with whom he was acquainted.

The young American was not unmindful of the great risks he was inviting in affiliating himself with an expedition which aimed at the peace of Europe and at the ultimate control of a large section of north-eastern Africa through the disaffection by propaganda of large and warlike native tribes, especially in view of the fact that much of their operation must be carried on within British territory, where British power was considerably more than a mere gesture. But, being young and enthusiastic, however misguided, these contingencies did not weigh heavily upon his spirits, which, far from being depressed, were upon the contrary eager and restless for action.

The tedium of the journey from the coast had been unrelieved by pleasurable or adequate companionship, since the childish mentality of Tony could not rise above a muddy conception of Philippine independence and a consideration of the fine clothes he was going to buy when, by some vaguely visualized economic process, he was to obtain his share of the Ford and Rockefeller fortunes.

However, notwithstanding Tony's mental shortcomings, Colt was genuinely fond of the youth, and as between the companionship of the Filipino or Zveri he would have chosen the former, his brief acquaintance with the Russian in New York and San Francisco having convinced him that as a playfellow he left everything to be desired; nor had he any reason to anticipate that he would find any more congenial associates among the conspirators.

Plodding doggedly onward Colt was only vaguely aware of the now familiar sights and sounds of the jungle both of which by this time, it must be admitted, had considerably palled upon him. Even had he taken particular note of the latter, it is to be doubted that his untrained ear would have caught the persistent chatter of a little monkey that followed in the trees behind him; nor would this have particularly impressed him, unless he had been able to know that this particular little monkey rode upon the shoulder of a bronzed Apollo of the forest who moved silently in his wake along a leafy highway of the lower terraces.

Tarzan had guessed that perhaps this white man, upon whose trail he had come unexpectedly, was making his way toward the main camp of the party of strangers for which the Lord of the Jungle was searching; and so, with the persistence and patience of the savage stalker of the jungle, he followed Wayne Colt; while little Nkima, riding upon his shoulder, berated his master for not immediately destroying the Tarmangani and all his party, for little Nkima was a bloodthirsty soul when the spilling of blood was to be accomplished by someone else.

And while Colt impatiently urged his men to greater speed and Tarzan followed and Nkima scolded, Raghunath Jafar approached the tent of Zora Drinov. As his figure darkened the entrance, casting a shadow across the book she was reading, the girl looked up from the cot upon which she was lying.

The Hindu smiled his oily, ingratiating smile. 'I came to see if your headache was better,' he said.

'Thank you, no,' said the girl coldly; 'but perhaps with undisturbed rest I may be better soon.'

Ignoring the suggestion, Jafar entered the tent and seated himself in a camp chair. 'I find it lonely,' he said, 'since the others have gone. Do you not also?'

'No,' replied Zora. 'I am quite content to be alone and resting.'

'Your headache developed very suddenly,' said Jafar. 'A short time ago you seemed quite well and animated.'

The girl made no reply. She was wondering what had become of her boy, Wamala, and why he had disregarded her explicit instructions to permit no one to disturb her. Perhaps Raghunath Jafar read her thoughts, for to East Indians are often attributed uncanny powers, however little warranted such a belief may be. However that may be, his next words suggested the possibility.

'Wamala has gone hunting with the askaris,' he said.

'I gave him no such permission,' said Zora.

'I took the liberty of doing so,' said Jafar.

'You had no right,' said the girl angrily, sitting up upon the edge of her cot. 'You have presumed altogether too far, Comrade Jafar.'

'Wait a moment, my dear,' said the Hindu soothingly. 'Let us not quarrel. As you know, I love you and love does not find confirmation in crowds. Perhaps I have presumed, but it was only for the purpose of giving me an opportunity to plead my cause without interruption; and then, too, as you know, all is fair in love and war.'

'Then we may consider this as war,' said the girl, 'for it certainly is not love, either upon your side or mine. There is another word to describe what animates you, Comrade Jafar, and that which animates me now is loathing. I could not abide you if you were the last man on earth, and when Zveri returns, I promise you that there shall be an accounting.'

'Long before Zveri returns I shall have taught you to love me,' said the Hindu, passionately. He arose and came toward her. The girl leaped to her feet, looking about quickly for a weapon of defence. Her cartridge belt and revolver hung over the chair in which Jafar had been sitting, and her rifle was upon the opposite side of the tent.

'You are quite unarmed,' said the Hindu. 'I took particular note of that when I entered the tent. Nor will it do you any good to call for help; for there is no one in camp but you and me, and my boy; and he knows that, if he values his life, he is not to come here unless I call him.'

'You are a beast,' said the girl.

'Why not be reasonable, Zora?' demanded Jafar. 'It would not harm you any to be kind to me, and it will make it very much easier for you. Zveri need know nothing of it, and once we are back in civilization again, if you still feel that you do not wish to remain with me I shall not try to hold you; but I am sure that I can teach you to love me and that we shall be very happy together.'

'Get out!' ordered the girl. There was neither fear nor hysteria in her voice. It was very calm and level and controlled. To a man not entirely blinded by passion, that might have meant something – it might have meant a grim determination to carry self-defence to the very length of death – but Raghunath Jafar saw only the woman of his desire, and stepping quickly forward he seized her.

Zora Drinov was young and lithe and strong, yet she was no match for the burly Hindu, whose layers of greasy fat belied the great physical strength beneath them. She tried to wrench herself free and escape from the tent, but he held her and dragged her back. Then she turned upon him in a fury and struck him repeatedly in the face, but he only enveloped her more closely in his embrace and bore her backward upon the cot.

CHAPTER III

Out of the Grave

Wayne Colt's guide, who had been slightly in advance of the American, stopped suddenly and looked back with a broad smile. Then he pointed ahead. 'The camp, Bwana!' he exclaimed triumphantly.

'Thank the Lord!' exclaimed Colt with a sigh of relief.

'It is deserted,' said the guide.

'It does look that way, doesn't it?' agreed Colt. 'Let's have a look around,' and, followed by his men, he moved in among the tents. His tired porters threw down their loads and, with the askaris, sprawled at full length beneath the shade of the trees while Colt, followed by Tony, commenced an investigation of the camp.

Almost immediately the young American's attention was attracted by the violent shaking of one of the tents. 'There is someone or something in there,' he said to Tony, as he walked briskly toward the entrance.

The sight within that met his eyes brought a sharp ejaculation to his lips – a man and woman struggling upon the ground, the former choking the bare throat of his victim while the girl struck feebly at his face with clenched fists.

So engrossed was Jafar in his unsuccessful attempt to subdue the girl that he was unaware of Colt's presence until a heavy hand fell upon his shoulder and he was jerked violently aside.

Consumed by maniacal fury, he leaped to his feet and struck at the American only to be met with a blow that sent him reeling backward. Again he charged and again he was struck heavily upon the face. This time he went to the ground, and, as he staggered to his feet, Colt seized him, wheeled him around and hurtled him through the entrance of the tent, accelerating his departure with a well-timed kick. 'If he tries to come back, Tony, shoot him,' he snapped at the Filipino, and then turned to assist the girl to her feet. Half carrying her, he laid her on the cot and then, finding water in a bucket, bathed her forehead, her throat and her wrists.

Outside the tent Raghunath Jafar saw the porters and the askaris lying in the shade of a tree. He also saw Antonio Mori with a determined scowl upon his face and a revolver in his hand, and with an angry imprecation he turned and made his way toward his own tent, his face livid with anger and murder in his heart.

Presently Zora Drinov opened her eyes and looked up into the solicitous face of Wayne Colt, bending over her.

From the leafy seclusion of a tree above the camp, Tarzan of the Apes overlooked the scene below. A single, whispered syllable had silenced Nkima's scolding. Tarzan had noted the violent shaking of the tent that had attracted Colt's attention, and he had seen the precipitate ejection of the Hindu from its interior and the menacing attitude of the Filipino preventing Jafar's return to the conflict. These matters were of little interest to the ape-man. The quarrelings and defections of these people did not even arouse his curiosity. What he wished to learn was the reason for their presence here, and for the purpose of obtaining this information he had two plans. One was to keep them under constant surveillance until their acts divulged that which he wished to know. The other was to determine definitely the head of the expedition and then to enter the camp and demand the information he desired. But this he would not do until he had obtained sufficient information to give him an advantage. What was going on within the tent he did not know, nor did he care.

For several seconds after she opened her eyes Zora Drinov gazed intently into those of the man bent upon her. 'You must be the American,' she said finally.

'I am Wayne Colt,' he replied, 'and I take it from the fact that you guessed my identity that this is Comrade Zveri's camp.'

She nodded. 'You came just in time, Comrade Colt,' she said.

'Thank God for that,' he said.

'There is no God,' she reminded him.

Colt flushed. 'We are creatures of heredity and habit,' he explained.

Zora Drinov smiled. 'That is true,' she said, 'but it is our business to break a great many bad habits not only for ourselves, but for the entire world.'

Since he had laid her upon the cot, Colt had been quietly appraising the girl. He had not known that there was a white woman in Zveri's camp, but had he it is certain that he would not have anticipated one at all like this girl. He would rather have visualized a female agitator capable of accompanying a band of men to the heart of Africa as a coarse and unkempt peasant woman of middle age; but this girl, from her head of glorious, wavy hair to her small, well-shaped foot, suggested the antithesis of a peasant origin and, far from being unkempt, was as trig and smart as it were possible for a woman to be under such circumstances and, in addition, she was young and beautiful.

'Comrade Zveri is absent from camp?' he asked.

'Yes, he is away on a short expedition.'

'And there is no one to introduce us to one another?' he asked, with a smile.

'Oh, pardon me,' she said. 'I am Zora Drinov.'

'I had not anticipated such a pleasant surprise,' said Colt. 'I expected to find nothing but uninteresting men like myself. And who was the fellow I interrupted?'

'That was Raghunath Jafar, a Hindu.'

'He is one of us?' asked Colt.

'Yes,' replied the girl, 'but not for long – not after Peter Zveri returns.'

'You mean—?'

'I mean that Peter will kill him.'

Colt shrugged. 'It is what he deserves,' he said. 'Perhaps I should have done it.'

'No,' said the girl, 'leave that for Peter.'

'Were you left alone here in this camp without any protection?' demanded Colt.

'No. Peter left my boy and ten askaris, but in some way Jafar got them all out of camp.'

'You will be safe now,' he said. 'I shall see to that until Comrade Zveri returns. I am going now to make my camp, and I shall send two of my askaris to stand guard before your tent.'

'That is good of you,' she said, 'but I think now that you are here it will not be necessary.'

'I shall do it anyway,' he said. 'I shall feel safer.'

'And when you have made camp, will you come and have supper with me?'

she asked, and then, 'Oh, I forgot, Jafar has sent my boy away, too. There is no one to cook for me.'

'Then, perhaps, you will dine with me,' he said. 'My boy is a fairly good cook.'

'I shall be delighted, Comrade Colt,' she replied.

As the American left the tent, Zora Drinov lay back upon the cot with half-closed eyes. How different the man had been from what she had expected. Recalling his features, and especially his eyes, she found it difficult to believe that such a man could be a traitor to his father or to his country, but then, she realized, many a man has turned against his own for a principle. With her own people it was different. They had never had a chance. They had always been ground beneath the heel of one tyrant or another. What they were doing they believed implicitly to be for their own and for their country's good. Among those of them who were motivated by honest conviction there could not fairly be brought any charge of treason, and yet, Russian though she was to the core, she could not help but look with contempt upon the citizens of other countries who turned against their governments to aid the ambitions of a foreign power. We may be willing to profit by the act of foreign mercenaries and traitors, but we cannot admire them.

As Colt crossed from Zora's tent to where his men lay to give the necessary instructions for the making of his camp, Raghunath Jafar watched him from the interior of his own tent. A malignant scowl clouded the countenance of the Hindu, and hatred smouldered in his eyes.

Tarzan, watching from above, saw the young American issuing instructions to his men. The personality of this young stranger had impressed Tarzan favourably. He liked him as well as he could like any stranger, for deeply ingrained in the fibre of the ape-man was the wild beast suspicion of all strangers and especially of all white strangers. As he watched him now nothing else within the range of his vision escaped him. It was thus that he saw Raghunath Jafar emerge from his tent, carrying a rifle. Only Tarzan and little Nkima saw this, and only Tarzan placed any sinister interpretation upon it.

Raghunath Jafar walked directly away from camp and entered the jungle. Swinging silently through the trees, Tarzan of the Apes followed him. Jafar made a half circle of the camp just within the concealing verdure of the jungle, and then he halted. From where he stood the entire camp was visible to him, but his own position was concealed by foliage.

Colt was watching the disposition of his loads and the pitching of his tent. His men were busy with the various duties assigned to them by their headman. They were tired and there was little talking. For the most part they worked in silence, and an unusual quiet pervaded the scene – a quiet that was suddenly and unexpectedly shattered by an anguished scream and the report of a rifle, blending so closely that it was impossible to say which had preceded the other. A bullet whizzed by Colt's head and nipped the lobe off the ear of one of his men standing behind him. Instantly the peaceful activities of the camp were supplanted by pandemonium. For a moment there was a difference of opinion as to the direction from which the shot and the scream had come, and then Colt saw a wisp of smoke rising from the jungle just beyond the edge of camp.

'There it is,' he said, and started towards the point.

The headman of the askaris stopped him. 'Do not go, Bwana,' he said. 'Perhaps it is an enemy. Let us fire into the jungle first.'

'No,' said Colt, 'we will investigate first. Take some of your men in from the right, and I'll take the rest in from the left. We'll work around slowly through the jungle until we meet.'

'Yes, Bwana,' said the headman, and calling his men he gave the necessary instructions.

No sound of flight or any suggestion of a living presence greeted the two parties as they entered the jungle; nor had they discovered any signs of a marauder when, a few moments later, they made contact with one another. They were now formed in a half circle that bent back into the jungle and, at a word from Colt, they advanced toward the camp.

It was Colt who found Raghunath Jafar lying dead just at the edge of camp. His right hand grasped his rifle. Protruding from his heart was the shaft of a sturdy arrow.

The negroes gathering around the corpse looked at one another questioningly and then back into the jungle and up into the trees. One of them examined the arrow. 'It is not like any arrow I have ever seen,' he said. 'It was not made by the hand of man.'

Immediately the blacks were filled with superstitious fears. 'The shot was meant for the bwana,' said one; 'therefore the demon who shot the arrow is a friend of our bwana. We need not be afraid.'

This explanation satisfied the blacks, but it did not satisfy Wayne Colt. He was puzzling over it as he walked back into camp, after giving orders that the Hindu be buried.

Zora Drinov was standing in the entrance to her tent, and as she saw him she came to meet him. 'What was it?' she asked. 'What happened?'

'Comrade Zveri will not kill Raghunath Jafar,' he said.

'Why?' she asked.

'Because Raghunath Jafar is already dead.'

'Who could have shot the arrow?' she asked, after he had told her of the manner of the Hindu's death.

'I haven't the remotest idea,' he admitted. 'It is an absolute mystery, but it means that the camp is being watched and that we must be very careful not to go into the jungle alone. The men believe that the arrow was fired to save me from an assassin's bullet; and while it is entirely possible that Jafar may have been intending to kill me, I believe that if I had gone into the jungle alone instead of him it would have been I that would be lying out there dead now. Have you been bothered at all by natives since you made camp here, or have you had any unpleasant experiences with them at all?'

'We have not seen a native since we entered this camp. We have often commented upon the fact that the country seems to be entirely deserted and uninhabited, notwithstanding the fact that it is filled with game.'

'This thing may help to account for the fact that it is uninhabited,' suggested Colt, 'or rather apparently uninhabited. We may have unintentionally invaded the country of some unusually ferocious tribe that takes this means of acquainting newcomers with the fact that they are *persona non grata*.'

'You say one of our men was wounded?' asked Zora.

'Nothing serious. He just had his ear nicked a little.'

'Was he near you?'

'He was standing right behind me,' replied Colt.

'I think there is no doubt that Jafar meant to kill you,' said Zora.

'Perhaps,' said Colt, 'but he did not succeed. He did not even kill my appetite; and if I can succeed in calming the excitement of my boy, we shall have supper presently.'

From a distance Tarzan and Nkima watched the burial of Raghunath Jafar and a little later saw the return of Kayiha and his askaris with Zora's boy Wamala, who had been sent out of camp by Jafar.

'Where,' said Tarzan to Nkima, 'are all the many Tarmangani and Gomangani that you told me were in this camp?'

'They have taken their thundersticks and gone away,' replied the little Manu. 'They are hunting for Nkima.'

Tarzan of the Apes smiled one of his rare smiles. 'We shall have to hunt them down and find out what they are about, Nkima,' he said.

'But it grows dark in the jungle soon,' pleaded Nkima, 'and then will Sabor, and Sheeta, and Numa, and Histah be abroad, and they, too, search for little Nkima.'

Darkness had fallen before Colt's boy announced supper, and in the meantime Tarzan, changing his plans, had returned to the trees above the camp. He was convinced that there was something irregular in the aims of the expedition whose base he had discovered. He knew from the size of the camp that it had contained many men. Where they had gone and for what purpose were matters that he must ascertain. Feeling that this expedition, whatever its purpose, might naturally be a principal topic of conversation in the camp, he sought a point of vantage wherefrom he might overhear the conversations that passed between the two white members of the party beneath him; and so it was that as Zora Drinov and Wayne Colt seated themselves at the supper table, Tarzan of the Apes crouched amid the foliage of a great tree just above them.

'You have passed through a rather trying ordeal today,' said Colt, 'but you do not appear to be any the worse for it. I should think that your nerves would be shaken.'

'I have passed through too much already in my life, Comrade Colt, to have any nerves left at all,' replied the girl.

'I suppose so,' said Colt. 'You must have passed through the revolution in Russia.'

'I was only a little girl at the time,' she explained, 'but I remember it quite distinctly.'

Colt was gazing at her intently. 'From your appearance,' he ventured, 'I imagine that you were not by birth of the proletariat.'

'My father was a labourer. He died in exile under the Tzarist régime. That was how I learned to hate everything monarchistic and capitalistic. And when I was offered this opportunity to join Comrade Zveri, I saw another field in which to encompass my revenge while at the same time advancing the interests of my class throughout the world.'

'When I last saw Zveri in the United States,' said Colt, 'he evidently had not formulated the plans he is now carrying out, as he never mentioned any expedition of this sort. When I received orders to join him here, none of the details were imparted to me; and so I am rather in the dark as to what his purpose is.'

'It is only for good soldiers to obey,' the girl reminded him.

'Yes, I know that,' agreed Colt, 'but at the same time even a poor soldier may act more intelligently sometimes if he knows the objective.'

'The general plan, of course, is no secret to any of us here,' said Zora, 'and I shall betray no confidence in explaining it to you. It is a part of a larger plan to embroil the capitalistic powers in wars and revolutions to such an extent that they will be helpless to unite against us.

'Our emissaries have been labouring for a long time toward the culmination of the revolution in India that will distract the attention and the armed forces of Great Britain. We are not succeeding so well in Mexico as we had planned, but there is still hope, while our prospects in the Philippines are very bright. The conditions in China you well know. She is absolutely helpless, and we have hope that with our assistance she will eventually constitute a real menace to Japan. Italy is a very dangerous enemy, and it is largely for the purpose of embroiling her in war with France that we are here.'

'But just how can that be accomplished in Africa?' asked Colt.

'Comrade Zveri believes that it will be simple,' said the girl. 'The suspicion and jealousy that exist between France and Italy are well known; their race for naval supremacy amounts almost to a scandal. At the first overt act of either against the other, war might easily result, and a war between Italy and France would embroil all of Europe.'

'But just how can Zveri, operating in the wilds of Africa, embroil Italy and France in war?' demanded the American.

'There is now in Rome a delegation of French and Italian Reds engaged in this very business. The poor men know only a part of the plan, and unfortunately for them, it will be necessary to martyr them in the cause for the advancement of our world plan. They have been furnished with papers outlining a plan for the invasion of Italian Somaliland by French troops. At the proper time one of Comrade Zveri's secret agents in Rome will reveal the plot to the Fascist Government; and almost simultaneously a considerable number of our own blacks, disguised in the uniforms of French native troops, led by the white men of our expedition, uniformed as French officers, will invade Italian Somaliland.

'In the meantime our agents are carrying on in Egypt and Abyssinia and among the native tribes of North Africa, and already we have definite assurance that with the attention of France and Italy distracted by war and Great Britain embarrassed by a revolution in India the natives of North Africa will arise in what will amount almost to a holy war for the purpose of throwing off the yoke of foreign domination and the establishment of autonomous soviet states throughout the entire area.'

'A daring and stupendous undertaking,' exclaimed Colt, 'but one that will require enormous resources in money as well as men.'

'It is Comrade Zveri's pet scheme,' said the girl. 'I do not know, of course, all the details of his organization and backing; but I do know that while he is already well financed for the initial operations, he is depending to a considerable extent upon this district for furnishing most of the necessary gold to carry on the tremendous operations that will be necessary to ensure final success.'

'Then I am afraid he is foredoomed to failure,' said Colt, 'for he surely cannot find enough wealth in this savage country to carry on any such stupendous programme.'

'Comrade Zveri believes to the contrary,' said Zora; 'in fact, the expedition that he is now engaged upon is for the purpose of obtaining the treasure he seeks.'

Above them, in the darkness, the silent figure of the ape-man lay stretched at ease upon a great branch, his keen ears absorbing all that passed between them, while curled in sleep upon his bronzed back lay little Nkima, entirely oblivious of the fact that he might have listened to words well calculated to shake the foundations of organized government throughout the world.

'And where,' demanded Colt, 'if it is no secret, does Comrade Zveri expect to find such a great store of gold?'

'In the famous treasure vaults of Opar,' replied the girl. 'You certainly must have heard of them.'

'Yes,' answered Colt, 'but I never considered them other than purely legendary. The folklore of the entire world is filled with these mythical treasure vaults.'

'But Opar is no myth,' replied Zora.

If the startling information divulged to him affected Tarzan, it induced no outward manifestation. Listening in silence imperturbable, trained to the utmost refinement of self-control, he might have been part and parcel of the great branch upon which he lay, or of the shadowy foliage which hid him from view.

For a time Colt sat in silence, contemplating the stupendous possibilities of the plan that he had just heard unfolded. It seemed to him little short of the dream of a mad man, and he did not believe that it had the slightest chance for success. What he did realize was the jeopardy in which it placed the members of the expedition, for he believed that there would be no escape for any of them once Great Britain, France and Italy were apprised of their activities; and, without conscious volition, his fears seemed centred upon the safety of the girl. He knew the type of people with whom he was working and so he knew that it would be dangerous to voice a doubt as to the practicability of the plan, for scarcely without exception the agitators whom he had met had fallen naturally into two separate categories, the impractical visionary, who believed everything that he wanted to believe, and the shrewd knave, actuated by motives of avarice, who hoped to profit either in power or riches by any change that he might be instrumental in bringing about in the established order of things. It seemed horrible that a young and beautiful girl should have been enticed into such a desperate situation. She seemed far too intelligent to be merely a brainless tool, and even his brief association with her made it most difficult for him to believe that she was a knave.

'The undertaking is certainly fraught with grave dangers,' he said, 'and as it is primarily a job for men I cannot understand why you were permitted to face the dangers and hardships that must of necessity be entailed by the carrying out of such a perilous campaign.'

'The life of a woman is of no more value than that of a man,' she declared, 'and I was needed. There is always a great deal of important and confidential clerical work to be done which Comrade Zveri can entrust only to one in whom he has implicit confidence. He reposes such trust in me and, in addition, I am a trained typist and stenographer. Those reasons in themselves are sufficient to explain why I am here, but another very important one is that I desire to be with Comrade Zveri.'

In the girl's words Colt saw the admission of a romance; but to his American mind this was all the greater reason why the girl should not have been brought along, for he could not conceive of a man exposing the girl he loved to such dangers.

Above them Tarzan of the Apes moved silently. First he reached over his shoulder and lifted little Nkima from his back. Nkima would have objected, but the veriest shadow of a whisper silenced him. The ape-man had various methods of dealing with enemies – methods that he had learned and practised long before he had been cognizant of the fact that he was not an ape. Long before he had ever seen another white man he had terrorized the Gomangani, the black men of the forest and the jungle, and had learned that a long step toward defeating an enemy may be taken by first demoralizing its morale. He knew now that these people were not only the invaders of his own domain and, therefore, his own personal enemies, but that they threatened the peace of Great Britain, which was dear to him, and of the rest of the civilized world, with which, at least, Tarzan had no quarrels. It is true that he held civilization in general in considerable contempt, but in even greater contempt he held those who interfered with the rights of others or with the established order of jungle or city.

As Tarzan left the tree in which he had been hiding, the two below him were no more aware of his departure than they had been of his presence. Colt found himself attempting to fathom the mystery of love. He knew Zveri, and it appeared inconceivable to him that a girl of Zora Drinov's type could be attracted by a man of Zveri's stamp. Of course it was none of his affair, but it bothered him nevertheless because it seemed to constitute a reflection upon the girl and to lower her in his estimation. He was disappointed in her, and Colt did not like to be disappointed in people to whom he had been attracted.

'You knew Comrade Zveri in America, did you not?' asked Zora.

'Yes,' replied Colt.

'What do you think of him?' she demanded.

'I found him a very forceful character,' replied Colt. 'I believe him to be a man who would carry on to a conclusion anything that he attempted. No better man could have been chosen for this mission.'

If the girl had hoped to surprise Colt into an expression of personal regard or dislike for Zveri, she had failed, but if such was the fact she was too wise to pursue the subject further. She realized that she was dealing with a man from whom she would get little information that he did not wish her to have; but on the other hand a man who might easily wrest information from others, for he was that type which seemed to invite confidences, suggesting as he did, in his attitude, his speech and his manner, a sterling uprightness of character that could not conceivably abuse a trust. She rather liked this upstanding young American, and the more she saw of him the more difficult she found it to believe that he had turned traitor to his family, his friends and his country. However, she knew that many honourable men had sacrificed everything to a conviction and, perhaps, he was one of these. She hoped that this was the explanation.

Their conversation drifted to various subjects – to their lives and experiences in their native lands – to the happenings that had befallen them since they had entered Africa, and, finally, to the experiences of the day. And while they talked, Tarzan of the Apes returned to the tree above them, but this time he did not come alone.

'I wonder if we shall ever know,' she said, 'who killed Jafar.'

'It is a mystery that is not lessened by the fact that none of the askaris could recognize the type of arrow with which he was slain, though that, of course, might be accounted for by the fact that none of them are of this district.'

'It has considerably shaken the nerves of the men,' said Zora, 'and I sincerely hope that nothing similar occurs again. I have found that it does not take much to upset these natives, and while most of them are brave in the face of known dangers, they are apt to be entirely demoralized by anything bordering on the supernatural.'

'I think they felt better when they got the Hindu planted under ground,' said Colt, 'though some of them were not at all sure that he might not return anyway.'

'There is not much chance of that,' rejoined the girl, laughing.

She had scarcely ceased speaking when the branches above them rustled, and a heavy body plunged downward to the table top between them, crushing the flimsy piece of furniture to earth.

The two sprang to their feet, Colt whipping out his revolver and the girl stifling a cry as she stepped back. Colt felt the hairs rise upon his head and goose flesh form upon his arms and back, for there between them lay the dead body of Raghunath Jafar upon its back, the dead eyes rolled backward staring up into the night.

CHAPTER IV

Into the Lion's Den

Nkima was angry. He had been awakened from the depth of a sound sleep, which was bad enough, but now his master had set out upon such foolish errands through the darkness of the night that, mingled with Nkima's scoldings, were the whimperings of fear, for in every shadow he saw Sheeta the panther lurking, and in each gnarled limb of the forest the likeness of Histah the snake. While Tarzan had remained in the vicinity of the camp, Nkima had not been particularly perturbed, and when he had returned to the tree with his burden the little Manu was sure that he was going to remain there for the rest of the night; but instead he had departed immediately and now was swinging through the black forest with an evident fixity of purpose that boded ill for either rest or safety for little Nkima during the remainder of the night.

Whereas Zveri and his party had started slowly along winding jungle trails, Tarzan moved almost in an air line through the jungle toward his destination, which was the same as that of Zveri. The result was that before Zveri reached the almost perpendicular crag which formed the last and greatest natural barrier to the forbidden valley of Opar, Tarzan and Nkima had disappeared beyond the summit and were crossing the desolate valley, upon the far side of which loomed the great walls and lofty spires and turrets of ancient Opar. In the bright light of the African sun, domes and minarets shone red and gold above the city; and once again the ape-man experienced the same feeling that had impressed him upon the occasion, now years gone, when his eyes had first alighted upon the splendid panorama of mystery that had unfolded before them.

No evidence of ruin was apparent at this great distance. Once again, in imagination, he beheld a city of magnificent beauty, its streets and temples thronged with people; and once again his mind toyed with the mystery of the city's origin, when back somewhere in the dim vista of antiquity a race of rich and powerful people had conceived and built this enduring monument to a vanished civilization. It was possible to conceive that Opar might have existed when a glorious civilization flourished upon the great continent of Atlantis, which, sinking beneath the waves of the ocean, left this lost colony to death and decay.

That its few inhabitants were direct descendants of its once powerful builders seemed not unlikely in view of the rites and ceremonies of the ancient religion which they practised, as well as by the fact that by scarcely any other hypothesis could the presence of a white-skinned people be accounted for in this remote and inaccessible African fastness.

The peculiar laws of heredity, which seemed operative in Opar as in no other portion of the world, suggested an origin differing materially from that of other men; for it is a peculiar fact that the men of Opar bear little or no resemblance to the females of their kind. The former are short, heavy set, hairy, almost ape-like in their conformation and appearance, while the women are slender, smooth skinned and often beautiful. There were certain physical and mental attributes of the men that had suggested to Tarzan the possibility that at some time in the past the colonists had, either by choice or necessity, interbred with the great apes of the district; and he also was aware that owing to the scarcity of victims for the human sacrifice which their rigid worship demanded that it was common practice among them to use for this purpose either males or females who deviated considerably from the standard time had established for each sex, with the result that through the laws of natural selection an overwhelming majority of the males would be grotesque and the females normal and beautiful.

It was with such reveries that the mind of the ape-man was occupied as he crossed the desolate valley of Opar, which lay shimmering in the bright sunlight that was relieved only by the shade of an occasional gnarled and stunted tree. Ahead of him and to his right was the small rocky hillock, upon the summit of which was located the outer entrance to the treasure vaults of Opar. But with this he was not now interested, his sole object being to forewarn La of the approach of the invaders that she might prepare her defence.

It had been long since Tarzan had visited Opar; but upon that last occasion, when he had restored La to her loyal people and re-established her supremacy following the defeat of the forces of Cadj, the high priest, and the death of the latter beneath the fangs and talons of Jad-bal-ja, he had carried away with him for the first time a conviction of the friendliness of all of the people of Opar. He had for years known that La was secretly his friend, but her savage, grotesque retainers always heretofore had feared and hated him; and so it was now that he approached Opar as one might approach any citadel of one's friends, without stealth and without any doubt but that he would be received in friendship.

Nkima, however, was not so sure. The gloomy ruins terrified him. He scolded and pleaded, but all to no avail; and at last terror overcame his love and loyalty so that, as they were approaching the outer wall which loomed high above them, he leaped from his master's shoulder and scampered away from the ruins that confronted him, for deep in his little heart was an abiding fear of strange and unfamiliar places that not even his confidence in Tarzan could overcome.

Nkima's keen eyes had noted the rocky hillock which they had passed a short time before, and to the summit of this he scampered as a comparatively safe haven from which to await the return of his master from Opar.

As Tarzan approached the narrow fissure which alone gave entrance through the massive outer walls of Opar he was conscious, as he had been years before on the occasion of his first approach to the city, of unseen eyes upon him, and at any moment he expected to hear a greeting when the watchers recognized him.

Without hesitation, however, and with no apprehensiveness, Tarzan entered the narrow cleft and descended a flight of concrete steps that led to the winding passage through the thick outer wall. The narrow court, beyond which loomed the inner wall, was silent and deserted; nor was the silence broken as he crossed it to another narrow passage which led through it; at the end of this he came to a broad avenue, upon the opposite side of which stood the crumbling ruins of the great temple of Opar.

In silence and solitude he entered the frowning portal, flanked by its rows of stately pillars, from the capitals of which grotesque birds glared down upon him as they had stared through all the countless ages since forgotten hands had carved them from the solid rock of the monoliths. On through the temple toward the inner courtyard, where he knew the activities of the city were carried on, Tarzan made his way in silence. Perhaps another man would have given notice of his coming, voicing a greeting to apprise them of his approach; but Tarzan of the Apes in many respects is less man than beast. He goes the silent way of most beasts, wasting no breath in useless mouthing. He had not sought to approach Opar stealthily, and he knew that he had not arrived unseen. Why a greeting was delayed he did not know, unless it was that, after carrying word of his coming to La, they were waiting for her instructions.

Through the main corridor Tarzan made his way, noting again the tablets of gold with their ancient and long undeciphered hieroglyphics. Through the chamber of the seven golden pillars he passed and across the golden floor of an adjoining room, and still only silence and emptiness, yet with vague suggestions of figures moving in the galleries that overlooked the apartment through which he was passing; and then at last he came to a heavy door beyond which he was sure he would find either priests or priestesses of this great temple of the Flaming God. Fearlessly he pushed it open and stepped across the threshold, and in the same instant a knotted club descended heavily upon his head, felling him senseless to the floor.

Instantly he was surrounded by a score of gnarled and knotted men; their matted beards fell low upon their hairy chests as they rolled forward upon their short, crooked legs. They chattered in low, growling gutturals as they bound their victim's wrists and ankles with stout thongs, and then they lifted him and carried him along other corridors and through the crumbling glories of magnificent apartments to a great tiled room, at one end of which a young woman sat upon a massive throne, resting upon a dais a few feet above the level of the floor.

Standing beside the girl upon the throne was another of the gnarled and knotted men. Upon his arms and legs were bands of gold and about his throat many necklaces. Upon the floor beneath these two was a gathering of men and women – the priests and priestesses of the Flaming God of Opar.

Tarzan's captors carried their victim to the foot of the throne and tossed his body upon the tile floor. Almost simultaneously the ape-man regained consciousness and, opening his eyes, looked about him.

'Is it he?' demanded the girl upon the throne.

One of Tarzan's captors saw that he had regained consciousness and with the help of others dragged him roughly to his feet.

'It is he, Oah,' exclaimed the man at her side.

An expression of venomous hatred convulsed the face of the woman. 'God has been good to His high priestess,' she said. 'I have prayed for this day to come as I prayed for the other, and as the other came so has this.'

Tarzan looked quickly from the woman to the man at her side. 'What is the meaning of this, Dooth?' he demanded. 'Where is La? Where is your high priestess?'

The girl rose angrily from her throne. 'Know, man of the outer world, that I am high priestess. I, Oah, am high priestess of the Flaming God.'

Tarzan ignored her. 'Where is La?' he demanded again of Dooth.

Oah flew into a frenzy of rage. 'She is dead!' she screamed, advancing to the edge of the dais as though to leap upon Tarzan, the jewelled handle of her sacrificial knife gleaming in the sunlight, which poured through a great aperture where a portion of the ancient roof of the throne room had fallen in. 'She is dead!' she repeated. 'Dead as you will be when next we honour the Flaming God with the life blood of a man. La was weak. She loved you, and thus she betrayed her God, who had chosen you for sacrifice. But Oah is strong – strong with the hate she has nursed in her breast since Tarzan and La stole the throne of Opar from her. Take him away!' she screamed to his captors, 'and let me not see him again until I behold him bound to the altar in the court of sacrifice.'

They now cut the bonds that secured Tarzan's ankles so that he might walk; but even though his wrists were tied behind him it was evident that they still held him in great fear, for they put ropes about his neck and his arms and led him as a man might lead a lion. Down into the familiar darkness of the pits of Opar they led him, lighting the way with torches; and when finally they had brought him to the dungeon in which he was to be confined it was some time before they could muster sufficient courage to cut the bonds that held his wrists, and even then they did not do so until they had again bound his ankles securely so that they might escape from the chamber and bolt the door before he could release his feet and pursue them. Thus greatly had the prowess of Tarzan impressed itself upon the brains of the crooked priests of Opar.

Tarzan had been in the dungeons of Opar before and, before, he had escaped; and so he set to work immediately seeking for a means of escape from his present predicament, for he knew that the chances were that Oah would not long delay the moment for which she had prayed – the instant when she should plunge the gleaming sacrificial knife into his breast. Quickly removing the thongs from his ankles, Tarzan groped his way carefully along the walls of his cell until he had made a complete circuit of it; then, similarly, he examined the floor. He discovered that he was in a rectangular chamber about ten feet long and eight wide and that by standing upon his tiptoes he could just reach the ceiling. The only opening was the door through which he had entered, in which an aperture, protected by iron bars, gave the cell its only ventilation but, as it opened upon a dark corridor, admitted no light. Tarzan examined the bolts and the hinges of the door, but they were, as he had conjectured, too substantial to be forced; and then, for the first time, he saw that a priest sat on guard in the corridor without, thus putting a definite end to any thoughts of surreptitious escape.

For three days and nights priests relieved each other at intervals; but upon the morning of the fourth day Tarzan discovered that the corridor was empty, and once again he turned his attention actively to thoughts of escape.

It had so happened that at the time of Tarzan's capture his hunting knife had been hidden by the tail of the leopard skin that formed his loin cloth; and, in their excitement, the ignorant, half-human priests of Opar had overlooked it when they took his other weapons away from him. Doubly thankful was Tarzan for this good fortune, since, for sentimental reasons, he cherished the hunting knife of his long dead sire – the knife that had started him upon the upward path to ascendancy over the beasts of the jungle that day, long gone, when, more by accident than intent, he had plunged it into the heart of Bolgani, the gorilla. But for more practical reasons it was, indeed, a gift from the gods, since it afforded him not only a weapon of defence, but an instrument wherewith he might seek to make good his escape.

Years before had Tarzan of the Apes escaped from the pits of Opar, and so he well knew the construction of their massive walls. Granite blocks of various sizes, hand hewn to fit with perfection, were laid in courses without mortar, the one wall that he had passed through having been fifteen feet in thickness. Fortune had favoured him upon that occasion in that he had been placed in a cell which, unknown to the present inhabitants of Opar, had a secret entrance, the opening of which was closed by a single layer of loosely laid courses that the ape-man had been able to remove without great effort.

Naturally he sought for a similar condition in the cell in which he now found himself, but his search was not crowned with success. No single stone could be budged from its place, anchored as each was by the tremendous weight of the temple walls they supported; and so, perforce, he turned his attention toward the door.

He knew that there were few locks in Opar since the present degraded inhabitants of the city had not developed sufficient ingenuity either to repair old ones or construct new. Those locks that he had seen were ponderous affairs opened by huge keys and were, he guessed, of an antiquity that reached back to the days of Atlantis; but, for the most part, heavy bolts and bars secured such doors as might be fastened at all, and he guessed that it was such a crude contrivance that barred his way to freedom.

Groping his way to the door, he examined the small opening that let in air.

It was about shoulder high and perhaps ten inches square and was equipped with four vertical iron bars half an inch square, set an inch and a half apart – too close to permit him to insert his hands between them, but this fact did not entirely discourage the ape-man. Perhaps there was another way.

His steel thewed fingers closed upon the centre of one of the bars. With his left hand he clung to another, and bracing one knee high against the door he slowly flexed his right elbow. Rolling like plastic steel, the muscles of his forearm and his biceps swelled, until gradually the bar bent inward toward him. The ape-man smiled as he took a new grip upon the iron bar. Then he surged backward with all his weight and all the strength of that mighty arm, and the bar bent to a wide U as he wrenched it from its sockets. He tried to insert his arm through the new opening, but it still was too small. A moment later another bar was torn away, and now, his arm through the aperture to its full length, he groped for the bar or bolts that held him prisoner.

At the fullest extent to which he could reach his fingertips downward against the door, he just touched the top of the bar, which was a timber about three inches in thickness. Its other dimensions, however, he was unable to ascertain, or whether it would release by raising one end or must be drawn back through keepers. It was most tantalizing! To have freedom almost within one's grasp and yet to be denied it was maddening.

Withdrawing his arm from the aperture, he removed his hunting knife from his scabbard and, again reaching outward, pressed the point of the blade into the wood of the bar. At first he tried lifting the bar by this means, but his knife point only pulled out of the wood. Next, he attempted to move the bar backward in a horizontal plane, and in this he was successful. Though the distance that he moved it in one effort was small, he was satisfied, for he knew that patience would win its reward. Never more than a quarter of an inch, sometimes only a sixteenth of an inch at a time, Tarzan slowly worked the bar backward. He worked methodically and carefully, never hurrying, never affected by nervous anxiety, although he never knew at what moment a savage warrior priest of Opar might make his rounds; and at last his efforts were rewarded, and the door swung upon its hinges.

Stepping quickly out, Tarzan shut the bar behind him and, knowing no other avenue of escape, turned back up the corridor along which his captors had conducted him to his prison cell. Faintly in the distance he discerned a lessening darkness, and toward this he moved upon silent feet. As the light increased slightly, he saw that the corridor was about ten feet wide and that at irregular intervals it was pierced by doors, all of which were closed and secured by bolts or bars.

A hundred yards from the cell in which he had been incarcerated he crossed a transverse corridor, and here he paused an instant to investigate with palpitating nostrils and keen eyes and ears. In neither direction could he discern any light, but faint sounds came to his ears indicating that life existed somewhere behind the doors along this corridor, and his nostrils were assailed by a medley of scents – the sweet aroma of incense, the odour of human bodies and the acrid scent of carnivores; but there was nothing there to attract his further investigation, so he continued on his way along the corridor toward the rapidly increasing light ahead.

He had advanced but a short distance when his keen ears detected the sound of approaching footsteps. Here was no place to risk discovery. Slowly he fell back toward the transverse corridor, seeking to take concealment there until the danger had passed; but it was already closer than he had imagined, and an instant later half a dozen priests of Opar turned into the corridor from one just ahead of him. They saw him instantly and halted, peering through the gloom.

'It is the ape-man,' said one. 'He has escaped,' and with their knotted cudgels and their wicked knives they advanced upon him.

That they came slowly evidenced the respect in which they held his prowess, but still they came; and Tarzan fell back, for even he, armed only with a knife, was no match for six of these savage half-men with their heavy cudgels. As he retreated, a plan formed quickly in his alert mind, and when he reached the transverse corridor he backed slowly into it. Knowing that now that he was hidden from them they would come very slowly, fearing that he might be lying in wait for them, he turned and ran swiftly along the corridor. He passed several doors, not because he was looking for any door in particular, but because he knew that the more difficult it was for them to find him the greater his chances of eluding them; but at last he paused before one secured by a huge wooden bar. Quickly he raised it, opened the door and stepped within just as the leader of the priests came into view at the intersection of the corridor.

The instant that Tarzan stepped into the dark and gloomy chamber beyond he knew that he had made a fatal blunder. Strong in his nostrils was the acrid scent of Numa, the lion; the silence of the pit was shattered by a savage roar; in the dark background he saw two yellow-green eyes flaming with hate, and then the lion charged.

CHAPTER V

Before the Walls of Opar

Peter Zveri established his camp on the edge of the forest at the foot of the barrier cliff that guards the desolate valley of Opar. Here he left his porters and a few askaris as guards and then, with his fighting men, guided by Kitembo, commenced the arduous climb to the summit.

None of them had ever come this way before, not even Kitembo, though he had known the exact location of Opar from one who had seen it; and so when the first view of the distant city broke upon them they were filled with awe, and vague questionings arose in the primitive minds of the black men.

It was a silent party that filed across the dusty plain toward Opar; nor were the blacks the only members of the expedition to be assailed with doubt, for in their black tents on distant deserts the Arabs had imbibed with the milk of their mothers the fear of jân and ghrôl and had heard, too, of the fabled city of Nimmr, which it was not well for men to approach. With such thoughts and forebodings were the minds of the men filled as they approached the towering ruins of the ancient Atlantean city.

From the top of the great boulder that guards the outer entrance to the treasure vaults of Opar a little monkey watched the progress of the expedition across the valley. He was a very much distraught little monkey, for in his heart he knew that his master should be warned of the coming of these many Gomangani and Tarmangani with their thundersticks; but fear of the forbidding ruins gave him pause, and so he danced about upon the top of the rock, chattering and scolding. The warriors of Peter Zveri marched right past and never paid any attention to him; and as they marched, other eyes were upon them, peering from out of the foliage of the trees that grew rank among the ruins.

If any member of the party saw a little monkey scampering quickly past upon their right, or saw him clamber up the ruined outer wall of Opar, he doubtless gave the matter no thought; for his mind, like the minds of all his fellows, was occupied by speculation as to what lay within that gloomy pile.

Kitembo did not know the location of the treasure vaults of Opar. He had but agreed to guide Zveri to the city, but, like Zveri, he entertained no doubt but that it would be easy to discover the vaults if they were unable to wring its location from any of the inhabitants of the city. Surprised, indeed, would they have been had they known that no living Oparian knew either of the location of the treasure vaults or of their existence and that, among all living men, only Tarzan and some of his Waziri warriors knew their location or how to reach them.

'The place is nothing but a deserted ruin,' said Zveri to one of his white companions.

'It is an ominous looking place though,' replied the other, 'and it has already had its effect upon the men.'

Zveri shrugged. 'This might frighten them at night, but not in broad daylight; they are certainly not that yellow.'

They were close to the ruined outer wall now, which frowned down upon them menacingly, and here they halted while several searched for an opening. Abu Batn was the first to find it – the narrow crevice with the flight of concrete steps leading upward. 'Here is a way through, Comrade,' he called to Zveri.

'Take some of your men with you and reconnoitre,' ordered Zveri.

Abu Batn summoned a half-dozen of his black men, who advanced with evident reluctance.

Gathering the skirt of his thôb about him, the sheikh entered the crevice, and at the same instant a piercing screech broke from the interior of the ruined city – a long drawn, high pitched shriek that ended in a series of low moans. The Bedaùwy halted. The blacks froze in terrified rigidity.

'Go on!' yelled Zveri. 'A scream can't kill you!'

'Wullah!' exclaimed one of the Arabs; 'But jân can.'

'Get out of there, then!' cried Zveri angrily. 'If you damned cowards are afraid to go, I'll go in myself.'

There was no argument. The Arabs stepped aside. And then a little monkey, screaming with terror, appeared upon the top of the wall from the inside of the city. His sudden and noisy appearance brought every eye to bear upon him. They saw him turn an affrighted glance backward over his shoulder and then, with a loud scream, leap far out to the ground below. It scarcely seemed that he could survive the jump, yet it barely sufficed to interrupt his flight, for he was on his way again in an instant as, with prodigious leaps and bounds, he fled screaming out across the barren plains.

It was the last straw. The shaken nerves of the superstitious blacks gave way to the sudden strain; and almost with one accord they turned and fled the dismal city, while close upon their heels were Abu Batn and his desert warriors in swift and undignified retreat.

Peter Zveri and his three white companions, finding themselves suddenly deserted, looked at one another questioningly. 'The dirty cowards!' exclaimed Zveri angrily. 'You go back, Mike, and see if you can rally them. We are going on in, now that we are here.'

Michael Dorsky, only too glad of any assignment that took him farther away from Opar, started at a brisk run after the fleeing warriors, while Zveri turned once more into the fissure with Miguel Romero and Paul Ivitch at his heels.

The three men passed through the outer wall and entered the courtyard, across which they saw the lofty inner wall rising before them. Romero was the first to find the opening that led to the city proper and, calling to his fellows, he stepped boldly into the narrow passage. Then once again the hideous scream shattered the brooding silence of the ancient temple.

The three men halted. Zveri wiped the perspiration from his brow. 'I think we have gone as far as we can alone,' he said. 'Perhaps we had all better go back and rally the men. There is no sense in doing anything foolhardy.' Miguel Romero threw him a contemptuous sneer, but Ivitch assured Zveri that the suggestion met with his entire approval.

The two men crossed the court quickly without waiting to see whether the Mexican followed them or not and were soon once again outside the city.

'Where is Miguel?' asked Ivitch.

Zveri looked around. 'Romero!' he shouted in a loud voice, but there was no reply.

'It must have got him,' said Ivitch with a shudder.

'Small loss,' grumbled Zveri.

But whatever the thing was that Ivitch feared, it had not, as yet, got the young Mexican, who, after watching his companions' precipitate flight, had continued on through the opening in the inner wall determined to have at least one look at the interior of the ancient city of Opar that he had travelled so far to see and of the fabulous wealth of which he had been dreaming for weeks.

Before his eyes spread a magnificent panorama of stately ruins, before which the young and impressionable Latin-American stood spellbound; and then once again the eerie wail rose from the interior of a great building before him, but if he was frightened Romero gave no evidence of it. Perhaps he grasped his rifle a little more tightly; perhaps he loosened his revolver in his holster, but he did not retreat. He was awed by the stately grandeur of the scene before him, where age and ruin seemed only to enhance its pristine magnificence.

A movement within the temple caught his attention. He saw a figure emerge from somewhere, the figure of a gnarled and knotted man that rolled on short crooked legs; and then another and another came until there were fully a hundred of the savage creatures approaching slowly toward him. He saw their knotted bludgeons and their knives, and he realized that here was a menace more effective than an unearthly scream.

With a shrug he backed into the passageway. 'I cannot fight an army single-handed,' he muttered. Slowly he crossed the outer court, passed through the first great wall and stood again upon the plain outside the city.

In the distance he saw the dust of the fleeing expedition and, with a grin, he started in pursuit, swinging along at an easy walk as he puffed upon a cigarette. From the top of the rocky hill at his left a little monkey saw him pass – a little monkey which still trembled from fright, but whose terrified screams had become only low, pitiful moans. It had been a hard day for little Nkima.

So rapid had been the retreat of the expedition that Zveri, with Dorsky and Ivitch, did not overtake the main party until the greater part of it was already descending the barrier cliffs; nor could any threats or promises stay the retreat, which ended only when camp was reached.

Immediately Zveri called Abu Batn, together with Dorsky and Ivitch, into council. The affair had been Zveri's first reverse, and it was a serious one inasmuch as he had relied heavily upon the inexhaustible store of gold to be found in the treasure vaults of Opar. First, he berated Abu Batn, Kitembo, their ancestors and all their followers for cowardice; but all that he accomplished was to arouse the anger and resentment of these two.

'We came with you to fight the white men, not demons and ghosts,' said Kitembo. 'I am not afraid. I would go into the city, but my men will not accompany me and I cannot fight the enemy alone.'

'Nor I,' said Abu Batn, a sullen scowl still further darkening his swart countenance.

'I know,' sneered Zveri, 'you are both brave men, but you are much better runners than you are fighters. Look at us. We were not afraid. We went in and we were not harmed.'

'Where is Comrade Romero?' demanded Abu Batn.

'Well, perhaps, he is lost,' admitted Zveri. 'What do you expect? To win a battle without losing a man?'

'There was no battle,' said Kitembo, 'and the man who went farthest into the accursed city did not return.'

Dorsky looked up suddenly. 'There he is now!' he exclaimed, and as all eyes turned up the trail toward Opar, they saw Miguel Romero strolling jauntily into camp.

'Greeting, my brave comrades!' he cried to them. 'I am glad to find you alive. I feared that you might all succumb to heart failure.'

Sullen silence greeted his raillery, and no one spoke until he had approached and seated himself near them.

'What detained you?' demanded Zveri presently.

'I wanted to see what was beyond the inner wall,' replied the Mexican.

'And you saw?' asked Abu Batn.

'I saw magnificent buildings in splendid ruin,' replied Romero; 'a dead and mouldering city of the dead past.'

'And what else?' asked Kitembo.

'I saw a company of strange warriors, short, heavy men on crooked legs, with long powerful arms and hairy bodies. They came out of a great building that might have been a temple. There were too many of them for me. I could not fight them alone, so I came away.'

'Did they have weapons?' asked Zveri.

'Clubs and knives,' replied Romero.

'You see,' exclaimed Zveri, 'just a band of savages armed with clubs. We could take the city without the loss of a man.'

'What did they look like?' demanded Kitembo. 'Describe them to me,' and when Romero had done so, with careful attention to details, Kitembo shook his head. 'It is as I thought,' he said. 'They are not men; they are demons.'

'Men or demons, we are going back there and take their city,' said Zveri angrily. 'We must have the gold of Opar.'

'You may go, white man,' returned Kitembo, 'but you will go alone. I know my men, and I tell you that they will not follow you there. Lead us against white men, or brown men, or black men, and we will follow you. But we will not follow you against demons and ghosts.'

'And you, Abu Batn?' demanded Zveri.

'I have talked with my men on the return from the city, and they tell me that they will not go back there. They will not fight the jân and ghrôl. They heard the voice of the jin warning them away, and they are afraid.'

Zveri stormed and threatened and cajoled, but all to no effect. Neither the Arab sheikh nor the African chief could be moved.

'There is still a way,' said Romero.

'And what is that?' asked Zveri.

'When the gringo comes and the Philippine, there will be six of us who are neither Arabs nor Africans. We six can take Opar.' Paul Ivitch made a wry face, and Zveri cleared his throat.

'If we are killed,' said the latter, 'our whole plan is wrecked. There will be no one left to carry on.'

Romero shrugged. 'It was only a suggestion,' he said, 'but, of course, if you are afraid—'

'I am not afraid,' stormed Zveri, 'but neither am I a fool.'

An ill-concealed sneer curved Romero's lips. 'I am going to eat,' he said, and, rising, he left them.

The day following his advent into the camp of his fellow conspirators, Wayne Colt wrote a long message in cipher and dispatched it to the coast by one of his boys. From her tent Zora Drinov had seen the message given to the boy. She had seen him place it in the end of a forked stick and start off upon his long journey. Shortly after, Colt joined her in the shade of a great tree beside her tent.

'You sent a message this morning, Comrade Colt,' she said.

He looked up at her quickly. 'Yes,' he replied.

'Perhaps you should know that only Comrade Zveri is permitted to send messages from the expedition,' she told him.

'I did not know,' he said. 'It was merely in relation to some funds that were to have been awaiting me when I reached the coast. They were not there. I sent the boy back after them.'

'Oh,' she said, and then their conversation drifted to other topics.

That afternoon he took his rifle and went out to look for game and Zora went with him, and that evening they had supper together again, but this time she was the hostess. And so the days passed until an excited native aroused the camp one day with an announcement that the expedition was returning. No words were necessary to apprise those who had been left behind that victory had not perched upon the banner of their little army. Failure was clearly written upon the faces of the leaders. Zveri greeted Zora and Colt, introducing the latter to his companions, and when Tony had been similarly presented the returning warriors threw themselves down upon cots or upon the ground to rest.

That night, as they gathered around the supper table, each party narrated the adventures that had befallen them since the expedition had left camp. Colt and Zora were thrilled by the stories of weird Opar, but no less mysterious was their tale of the death of Raghunath Jafar and his burial and uncanny resurrection.

'Not one of the boys would touch the body after that,' said Zora. 'Tony and Comrade Colt had to bury him themselves.'

'I hope you made a good job of it this time,' said Miguel.

'He hasn't come back again,' rejoined Colt with a grin.

'Who could have dug him up in the first place?' demanded Zveri.

'None of the boys certainly,' said Zora. 'They were all too much frightened by the peculiar circumstances surrounding his death.'

'It must have been the same creature that killed him,' suggested Colt, 'and whoever or whatever it was must have been possessed of almost superhuman strength to carry that heavy corpse into a tree and drop it upon us.'

'The most uncanny feature of it to me,' said Zora, 'is the fact that it was accomplished in absolute silence. I'll swear that not even a leaf rustled until just before the body hurtled down upon our table.'

'It could have been only a man,' said Zveri.

'Unquestionably,' said Colt, 'but what a man!'

As the company broke up later, repairing to their various tents, Zveri detained Zora with a gesture. 'I want to talk to you a minute, Zora,' he said, and the girl sank back into the chair she had just quitted. 'What do you think of this American? You have had a good opportunity to size him up.'

'He seems to be all right. He is a very likable fellow,' replied the girl.

'He said or did nothing, then, that might arouse your suspicion?' demanded Zveri.

'No,' said Zora, 'nothing at all.'

'You two have been alone here together for a number of days,' continued Zveri. 'Did he treat you with perfect respect?'

'He was certainly much more respectful than your friend, Raghunath Jafar.'

'Don't mention that dog to me,' said Zveri. 'I wish that I had been here to kill him myself.'

'I told him that you would when you got back, but someone beat you to it.'

They were silent for several moments. It was evident that Zveri was trying to frame into words something that was upon his mind. At last he spoke. 'Colt is a very prepossessing young man. See that you don't fall in love with him, Zora.'

'And why not?' she demanded. 'I have given my mind and my strength and my talent to the cause and, perhaps, most of my heart. But there is a corner of it that is mine to do with as I wish.'

'You mean to say that you are in love with him?' demanded Zveri.

'Certainly not. Nothing of the kind. Such an idea had not entered my head. I just want you to know, Peter, that in matters of this kind you may not dictate to me.'

'Listen, Zora. You know perfectly well that I love you, and what is more, I am going to have you. I get what I go after.'

'Don't bore me, Peter. I have no time for anything so foolish as love now. When we are well through with this undertaking, perhaps I shall take the time to give it a little thought.'

'I want you to give it a lot of thought right now, Zora,' he insisted. 'There are some details in relation to this expedition that I have not told you. I have not divulged them to anyone, but I am going to tell you now because I love you and you are going to become my wife. There is more at stake in this for us than you dream. After all the thought and all the risks and all the hardships, I do not intend to surrender all of the power and the wealth that I shall have gained to anyone.'

'You mean not even to the cause?' she asked.

'I mean not even to the cause, except that I shall use them both for the cause.'

'Then what do you intend? I do not understand you,' she said.

'I intend to make myself emperor of Africa,' he declared, 'and I intend to make you my empress.'

'Peter!' she cried. 'Are you crazy?'

'Yes, I am crazy for power, for riches, and for you.'

'You can never do it, Peter. You know how far-reaching are the tentacles of the power we serve. If you fail it, if you turn traitor, those tentacles will reach you and drag you down to destruction.'

'When I win my goal, my power will be as great as theirs, and then I may defy them.'

'But how about these others with us, who are loyally serving the cause which they think you represent? They will tear you to pieces, Peter.'

The man laughed. 'You do not know them, Zora. They are all alike. All men and women are alike. If I offered to make them grand dukes and give them each a palace and a harem, they would slit their own mothers' throats to obtain such a prize.'

The girl arose. 'I am astounded, Peter. I thought that you, at least, were sincere.'

He arose quickly and grasped her by the arm. 'Listen, Zora,' he hissed in her ear, 'I love you, and because I love you I have put my life in your hands. But understand this, if you betray me, no matter how well I love you, I shall kill you. Do not forget that.'

'You did not have to tell me that, Peter. I was perfectly well aware of it.'

'And you will not betray me?' he demanded.

'I never betray a friend, Peter,' she said.

The next morning Zveri was engaged in working out the details of a second expedition to Opar based upon Romero's suggestions. It was decided that this time they would call for volunteers; and as the Europeans, the two Americans and the Filipino had already indicated their willingness to take part in the adventure, it remained now only to seek to enlist the services of some of the blacks and Arabs, and for this purpose Zveri summoned the entire company to a palaver. Here he explained just what they purposed doing. He stressed the fact that Comrade Romero had seen the inhabitants of the city and that they were only members of a race of stunted savages, armed only with sticks. Eloquently he explained how easily they might be overcome with rifles.

Practically the entire party was willing to go as far as the walls of Opar; but there were only ten warriors who would agree to enter the city with the white men, and all of these were from the askaris who had been left behind to guard camp and from those who had accompanied Colt from the coast, none of whom had been subjected to the terrors of Opar. Not one of those who had heard the weird screams issuing from the ruins would agree to enter the city, and it was admitted among the whites that it was not at all unlikely that their ten volunteers might suddenly develop a change of heart when at last they stood before the frowning portals of Opar and heard the weird warning cry from its defenders.

Several days were spent in making careful preparations for the new expedition, but at last the final detail was completed; and early one morning Zveri and his followers set out once more upon the trail to Opar.

Zora Drinov had wished to accompany them, but as Zveri was expecting messages from a number of his various agents throughout northern Africa, it had been necessary to leave her behind. Abu Batn and his warriors were left to guard the camp, and these, with a few black servants, were all who did not accompany the expedition.

Since the failure of the first expedition and the fiasco at the gates of Opar, the relations of Abu Batn and Zveri had been strained. The sheikh and his warriors, smarting under the charges of cowardice, had kept more to themselves than formerly; and though they would not volunteer to enter the city of Opar, they still resented the affront of their selection to remain behind as camp guards; and so it was that as the others departed, the Arabs sat in the muk'aad of their sheikh's beyt es-sh'ar, whispering over their thick coffee, their swart scowling faces half hidden by their thorrîbs.

They did not deign even to glance at their departing comrades, but the eyes of Abu Batn were fixed upon the slender figure of Zora Drinov as the sheikh sat in silent meditation.

CHAPTER VI

Betrayed

The heart of little Nkima had been torn by conflicting emotions, as from the vantage point of the summit of the rocky hillock he had watched the departure of Miguel Romero from the city of Opar. Seeing these brave Tarmangani, armed with death-dealing thundersticks, driven away from the ruins, he was convinced that something terrible must have befallen his master within the grim recesses of that crumbling pile. His loyal heart prompted him to return and investigate, but Nkima was only a very little Manu – a little Manu who was very much afraid; and though he started twice again toward Opar, he could not muster his courage to the sticking point; and at last, whimpering pitifully, he turned back across the plains toward the grim forest, where, at least, the dangers were familiar ones.

The door of the gloomy chamber which Tarzan had entered swung inward, and his hands were still upon it as the menacing roar of the lion apprised him of the danger of his situation. Agile and quick is Numa, the lion, but with even greater celerity functioned the mind and muscles of Tarzan of the Apes.

In the instant that the lion sprang toward him a picture of the whole scene flashed to the mind of the ape-man. He saw the gnarled priests of Opar advancing along the corridor in pursuit of him. He saw the heavy door that swung inward. He saw the charging lion, and he pieced these various factors together to create a situation far more to his advantage than they normally presented. Drawing the door quickly inward, he stepped behind it as the lion charged, with the result that the beast, either carried forward by his own momentum or sensing escape, sprang into the corridor full in the faces of the advancing priests, and at the same instant Tarzan closed the door behind him.

Just what happened in the corridor without he could not see, but from the growls and screams that receded quickly into the distance he was able to draw a picture that brought a quiet smile to his lips; and an instant later a piercing shriek of agony and terror announced the fate of at least one of the fleeing Oparians.

Realizing that he would gain nothing by remaining where he was, Tarzan decided to leave the cell and seek a way out of the labyrinthine mazes of the pits beneath Opar. He knew that the lion upon its prey would doubtless bar his passage along the route he had been following when his escape had been interrupted by the priests and though, as a last resort, he might face Numa he was of no mind to invite such an unnecessary risk; but when he sought to open the heavy door he found that he could not budge it, and in an instant he realized what had happened and that he was now in prison once again in the dungeons of Opar.

The bar that secured this particular door was not of the sliding type but, working upon a pin at the inner end, dropped into heavy wrought iron keepers bolted to the door itself and to its frame. When he had entered, he had raised the bar, which had dropped into place of its own weight when the door slammed to, imprisoning him as effectually as though the work had been done by the hand of man.

The darkness of the corridor without was less intense than that of the passage upon which his former cell had been located; and though not enough light entered the cell to illuminate its interior, there was sufficient to show him the nature of the ventilating opening in the door, which he found to consist of a number of small round holes, none of which was of sufficient diameter to permit him to pass his hand through in an attempt to raise the bar.

As Tarzan stood in momentary contemplation of his new predicament, the sound of stealthy movement came to him from the black recesses at the rear of the cell. He wheeled quickly, drawing his hunting knife from its sheath. He did not have to ask himself what the author of this sound might be, for he knew that the only other living creature that might have occupied this cell with its former inmate was another lion. Why it had not joined in the attack upon him he could not guess, but that it would eventually seize him was a foregone conclusion. Perhaps even now it was preparing to sneak upon him. He wished that his eyes might penetrate the darkness, for if he could see the lion as it charged he might be better prepared to meet it. In the past he had met the charges of other lions, but always before he had been able to see their swift spring and to elude the sweep of their mighty talons as they reared upon their hind legs to seize him. Now it would be different, and for once in his life Tarzan of the Apes felt death was inescapable. He knew that his time had come.

He was not afraid. He simply knew that he did not wish to die and that the price at which he would sell his life would cost his antagonist dearly. In silence he waited. Again he heard that faint, yet ominous sound. The foul air of the cell reeked with the stench of the carnivores. From somewhere in a distant corridor he heard the growling of a lion at its kill; and then a voice broke the silence.

'Who are you?' it asked. It was the voice of a woman, and it came from the back of the cell in which the ape-man was imprisoned.

'Where are you?' demanded Tarzan.

'I am here at the back of the cell,' replied the woman.

'Where is the lion?'

'It went out when you opened the door.' she replied.

'Yes, I know,' said Tarzan, 'but the other one. Where is it?'

'There is no other one. There was but one lion here and it is gone. Ah, now I know you!' she exclaimed. 'I know the voice. It is Tarzan of the Apes.'

'La!' exclaimed the ape-man, advancing quickly across the cell. 'How could you be here with the lion and still live?'

'I am in an adjoining cell that is separated from this one by a door made of iron bars,' replied La. Tarzan heard metal hinges creak. 'It is not locked,' she said. 'It was not necessary to lock it, for it opens into this other cell where the lion was.'

Groping forward through the dark, the two advanced until their hands touched one another.

La pressed close to the man. She was trembling. 'I have been afraid,' she said, 'but I shall not be afraid now.'

'I shall not be of much help to you,' said Tarzan. 'I also am a prisoner.'

'I know it,' replied La, 'but I always feel safe when you are near.'

'Tell me what has happened,' demanded Tarzan. 'How is it that Oah is posing as high priestess and you a prisoner in your own dungeons?'

'I forgave Oah her former treason when she conspired with Cadj to wrest my power from me,' explained La, 'but she could not exist without intrigue and duplicity. To further her ambitions, she made love to Dooth, who has been high priest since Jad-bal-ja killed Cadj. They spread stories about me through the city; and as my people have never forgiven me for my friendship for you, they succeeded in winning enough to their cause to overthrow and imprison me. All the ideas were Oah's, for Dooth and the other priests, as you well know, are stupid beasts. It was Oah's idea to imprison me thus with a lion for company, merely to make my suffering more terrible, until the time should come when she might prevail upon the priests to offer me in sacrifice to the Flaming God. In that she has had some difficulty, I know, as those who have brought my food have told me.'

'How could they bring food to you here?' asked Tarzan. 'No one could pass through the outer cell while the lion was there.'

'There is another opening in the lion's cell, that leads into a low, narrow corridor into which they can drop meat from above. Thus they would entice the lion from this outer cell, after which they would lower a gate of iron bars across the opening of the small corridor into which he went, and while he was thus imprisoned they brought my food to me. But they did not feed him much. He was always hungry and often growling and pawing at the bars of my cell. Perhaps Oah hoped that some day he would batter them down.'

'Where does this other corridor, in which they feed the lion, lead?' asked Tarzan.

'I do not know,' replied La, 'but I imagine that it is only a blind tunnel built in ancient times for this very purpose.'

'We must have a look at it,' said Tarzan. 'It may offer a means of escape.'

'Why not escape through the door by which you entered?' asked La; and when the ape-man had explained why this was impossible, she pointed out the location of the entrance to the small tunnel.

'We must get out of here as quickly as possible, if it is possible at all,' said Tarzan, 'for if they are able to capture the lion, they will certainly return him to this cell.'

'They will capture him,' said La. 'There is no question as to that.'

'Then I had better hurry and make my investigation of the tunnel, for it might prove embarrassing were they to return him to the cell while I was in the tunnel, if it proved to be a blind one.'

'I will listen at the outer door while you investigate,' offered La. 'Make haste.'

Groping his way toward the section of the wall that La had indicated, Tarzan found a heavy grating of iron closing an aperture leading into a low and narrow corridor. Lifting the barrier, Tarzan entered and with his hands extended before him moved forward in a crouching position, since the low ceiling would not permit him to stand erect. He had progressed but a short distance when he discovered that the corridor made an abrupt right-angle turn to the left, and beyond the turn he saw at a short distance a faint luminosity. Moving quickly forward, he came to the end of the corridor, at the bottom of a vertical shaft, the interior of which was illuminated by subdued daylight. The shaft was constructed of the usual rough-hewn granite of the foundation walls of the city, but here set with no great nicety or precision, giving the interior of the shaft a rough and uneven surface.

As Tarzan was examining it, he heard La's voice coming along the tunnel from the cell in which he had left her. Her tone was one of excitement, and her message one that presaged a situation fraught with extreme danger to them both.

'Make haste, Tarzan. They are returning with the lion!'

The ape-man hurried quickly back to the mouth of the tunnel.

'Quick!' he cried to La, as he raised the gate that had fallen behind him after he had passed through.

'In there?' she demanded in an affrighted voice.

'It is our only chance of escape,' replied the ape-man.

Without another word La crowded into the corridor beside him. Tarzan lowered the grating and, with La following closely behind him, returned to the opening leading into the shaft. Without a word, he lifted La in his arms and raised her as high as he could, nor did she need to be told what to do. With little difficulty she found both hand and footholds upon the rough surface of the interior of the shaft, and with Tarzan just below her, assisting and steadying her, she made her way slowly aloft.

The shaft led directly upward into a room in the tower, which overlooked the entire city of Opar; and here, concealed by the crumbling walls, they paused to formulate their plans.

They both knew that their greatest danger lay in discovery by one of the numerous monkeys infesting the ruins of Opar, with which the inhabitants of the city are able to converse. Tarzan was anxious to be away from Opar that he might thwart the plans of the white men who had invaded his domain. But first he wished to bring about the downfall of La's enemies and reinstate her upon the throne of Opar, or if that should prove impossible, to ensure the safety of her flight.

As he viewed her now in the light of day he was struck again by the matchlessness of her deathless beauty that neither time, nor care, nor danger seemed capable of dimming, and he wondered what he should do with her; where he could take her; where this savage priestess of the Flaming God could find a place in all the world, outside the walls of Opar, with the environments of which she would harmonize. And as he pondered, he was forced to admit to himself that no such place existed. La was of Opar, a savage queen born to rule a race of savage half-men. As well introduce a tigress to the salons of civilization as La of Opar. Two or three thousand years earlier she might have been a Cleopatra or a Sheba, but today she could be only La of Opar.

For some time they had sat in silence, the beautiful eyes of the high priestess resting upon the profile of the forest god. 'Tarzan!' she said.

The man looked up. 'What is it, La?' he asked.

'I still love you, Tarzan,' she said in a low voice.

A troubled expression came into the eyes of the ape-man. 'Let us not speak of that.'

'I like to speak of it,' she murmured. 'It gives me sorrow, but it is a sweet sorrow – the only sweetness that has ever come into my life.'

Tarzan extended a bronzed hand and laid it upon her slender, tapering fingers. 'You have always possessed my heart, La,' he said, 'up to the point of love. If my affection goes no further than this, it is through no fault of mine or yours.'

La laughed. 'It is certainly through no fault of mine, Tarzan,' she said, 'but I know that such things are not ordered by ourselves. Love is a gift of the gods. Sometimes it is awarded as a recompense; sometimes as a punishment. For me it has been a punishment, perhaps, but I would not have it otherwise. I have nurtured it in my breast since first I met you; and without that love, however hopeless it may be, I should not care to live.'

Tarzan made no reply, and the two relapsed into silence, waiting for night to fall that they might descend into the city unobserved. Tarzan's alert mind was occupied with plans for reinstating La upon her throne, and presently they fell to discussing these.

'Just before the Flaming God goes to his rest at night,' said La, 'the priests and the priestesses all gather in the throne room. There they will be tonight before the throne upon which Oah will be seated. Then may we descend to the city.'

'And then what?' asked Tarzan.

'If we can kill Oah in the throne room,' said La, 'and Dooth at the same time, they would have no leaders; and without leaders they are lost.'

'I cannot kill a woman,' said Tarzan.

'I can,' returned La, 'and you can attend to Dooth. You certainly would not object to killing him?'

'If he attacked, I would kill him,' said Tarzan, 'but not otherwise. Tarzan of the Apes kills only in self-defence and for food, or when there is no other way to thwart an enemy.'

In the floor of the ancient room in which they were waiting were two openings; one was the mouth of the shaft through which they had ascended from the dungeons, the other opened into a similar but larger shaft, to the bottom of which ran a long wooden ladder set in the masonry of its sides. It was this shaft which offered them a means of escape from the tower, and as

Tarzan sat with his eyes resting idly upon the opening, an unpleasant thought suddenly obtruded itself upon his consciousness.

He turned toward La. 'We have forgotten,' he said, 'that whoever casts the meat down the shaft to the lion must ascend by this other shaft. We may not be as safe from detection here as we had hoped.'

'They do not feed the lion very often,' said La; 'not every day.'

'When did they feed him last?' asked Tarzan.

'I do not recall,' said La. 'Time dragged so heavily in the darkness of the cell that I lost count of days.'

'S-st!' cautioned Tarzan. 'Someone is ascending now.'

Silently the ape-man arose and crossed the floor to the opening, where he crouched upon the side opposite the ladder. La moved stealthily to his side, so that the ascending man, whose back would be toward them as he emerged from the shaft, would not see them. Slowly the man ascended. They could hear his shuffling progress coming nearer and nearer to the top. He did not climb as the ape-like priests of Opar are wont to climb. Tarzan thought perhaps he was carrying a load either of such weight or cumbersomeness as to retard his progress, but when finally his head came into view the ape-man saw that he was an old man, which accounted for his lack of agility; and then powerful fingers closed about the throat of the unsuspecting Oparian, and he was lifted bodily out of the shaft.

'Silence!' said the ape-man. 'Do as you are told and you will not be harmed.'

La had snatched a knife from the girdle of their victim, and now Tarzan forced him to the floor of the room and slightly released his hold upon the fellow's throat, turning him around so that he faced them.

An expression of incredulity and surprise crossed the face of the old priest as his eyes fell upon La.

'Darus!' exclaimed La.

'All honour to the Flaming God who has ordered your escape!' exclaimed the priest.

La turned to Tarzan. 'You need not fear Darus,' she said; 'he will not betray us. Of all the priests of Opar, there never lived one more loyal to his queen.'

'That is right,' said the old man, shaking his head.

'Are there many more loyal to the high priestess, La?' demanded Tarzan.

'Yes, very many,' replied Darus, 'but they are afraid. Oah is a she-devil and Dooth is a fool. Between the two of them there is no longer either safety or happiness in Opar.'

'How many are there whom you absolutely know may be depended upon?' demanded La.

'Oh, very many,' replied Darus.

'Gather them in the throne room tonight then, Darus; and as the Flaming

God goes to his couch, be ready to strike at the enemies of La, your priestess.'

'You will be there?' asked Darus.

'I shall be there,' replied La. 'This, your dagger, shall be the signal. When you see La of Opar plunge it into the breast of Oah, the false priestess, fall upon those who are the enemies of La.'

'It shall be done, just as you say,' Darus assured her, 'and now I must throw this meat to the lion and be gone.'

Slowly the old priest descended the ladder, gibbering and muttering to himself, after he had cast a few bones and scraps of meat into the other shaft to the lion.

'You are quite sure you can trust him, La?' demanded Tarzan.

'Absolutely,' replied the girl. 'Darus would die for me, and I know that he hates Oah and Dooth.'

The slow remaining hours of the afternoon dragged on, the sun was low in the west, and now the two must take their greatest risk, that of descending into the city while it was still light and making their way to the throne room, although the risk was greatly minimized by the fact that the inhabitants of the city were all supposed to be congregated in the throne room at this time, performing the age-old rite with which they speeded the Flaming God to his night of rest. Without interruption they descended to the base of the tower, crossed the courtyard and entered the temple. Here, through devious and round-about passages, La led the way to a small doorway that opened into the throne room at the back of the dais upon which the throne stood. Here she paused, listening to the services being conducted within the great chamber, waiting for the cue that would bring them to a point when all within the room, except the high priestess, were prostrated with their faces pressed against the floor.

When that instant arrived, La swung open the door and leaped silently upon the dais behind the throne in which her victim sat. Close behind her came Tarzan, and in that first instant both realized that they had been betrayed, for the dais was swarming with priests ready to seize them.

Already one had caught La by an arm, but before he could drag her away Tarzan sprang upon him, seized him by the neck and jerked his head backward so suddenly and with such force that the sound of his snapping vertebra could be heard across the room. Then he raised the body high above his head and cast it into the faces of the priests charging upon him. As they staggered back, he seized La and swung her into the corridor along which they had approached the throne room.

It was useless to stand and fight, for he knew that even though he might hold his own for awhile they must eventually overcome him, and that once they laid their hands upon La they would tear her limb from limb.

Down the corridor behind them came the yelling horde of priests, and in their wake, screaming for the blood of her victim, was Oah.

'Make for the outer walls by the shortest route, La,' directed Tarzan, and the girl sped on winged feet, leading him through the labyrinthine corridors of the ruins, until they broke suddenly into the chamber of the seven pillars of gold, and then Tarzan knew the way.

No longer needing his guide, and realizing that the priests were overtaking them, being fleeter of foot than La, he swept the girl into his arms and sped through the echoing chambers of the temple toward the inner wall. Through that, across the courtyard and through the outer wall they passed, and still the priests pursued, urged on by screaming Oah. Out across the deserted valley they fled; and now the priests were losing ground, for their short, crooked legs could not compete with the speed of Tarzan's clean-limbed stride, even though he was burdened by the weight of La.

The sudden darkness of the near tropics that follows the setting of the sun soon obliterated the pursuers from their sight; and a short time thereafter the sounds of pursuit ceased, and Tarzan knew that the chase had been abandoned, for the men of Opar have no love for the darkness of the outer world.

Then Tarzan paused and lowered La to the ground; but as he did so her soft arms encircled his neck and she pressed close to him, her cheek against his breast, and burst into tears.

'Do not cry, La,' he said. 'We shall come again to Opar, and when we do you shall be seated upon your throne again.'

'I am not crying for that,' she replied.

'Then why do you cry?' he asked.

'I am crying for joy,' she said, 'joy that perhaps I shall be alone with you now for a long time.'

In pity, Tarzan pressed her to him for a moment, and then they set off once more towards the barrier cliff.

That night they slept in a great tree in the forest at the foot of the cliff, after Tarzan had constructed a rude couch for La between two branches, while he settled himself in a crotch of the tree a few feet below her.

It was dawn when Tarzan awoke. The sky was overcast, and he sensed an approaching storm. No food had passed his lips for many hours, and he knew that La had not eaten since the morning of the previous day. Food, therefore, was a prime essential and he must find it and return to La before the storm broke. Since it was meat that he craved, he knew that he must be able to make fire and cook it before La could eat it, though he himself still preferred it raw. He looked into La's cot and saw that she was still asleep. Knowing that she must be exhausted from all that she had passed through the previous day, he let her sleep on; and swinging to a nearby tree, he set out upon his search for food.

As he moved upwind through the middle terrace, every faculty of his deli-cately attuned senses was alert. Like the lion, Tarzan particularly relished the flesh of Pacco, the zebra, but either Bara, the antelope, or Horta, the boar, would have proved an acceptable substitute; but the forest seemed to be des-erted by every member of the herds he sought. Only the scent spoor of the great cats assailed his nostrils, mingled with the lesser and more human odour of Manu, the monkey. Time means little to a hunting beast. It meant little to Tarzan, who, having set out in search of meat, would return only when he had found meat.

When La awakened, it was some time before she could place her sur-roundings; but when she did, a slow smile of happiness and contentment parted her lovely lips, revealing an even row of perfect teeth. She sighed, and then she whispered the name of the man she loved. 'Tarzan!' she called.

There was no reply. Again she spoke his name, but this time louder, and again the only answer was silence. Slightly troubled, she arose upon an elbow and leaned over the side of her sleeping couch. The tree beneath her was empty.

She thought, correctly, that perhaps he had gone to hunt, but still she was troubled by his absence, and the longer she waited the more troubled she became. She knew that he did not love her, and that she must be a burden to him. She knew, too, that he was as much a wild beast as the lions of the forest and that the same desire for freedom, which animated them, must animate him. Perhaps he had been unable to withstand the temptation longer and while she slept, he had left her.

There was not a great deal in the training or ethics of La of Opar that could have found exception to such conduct, for the life of her people was a life of ruthless selfishness and cruelty. They entertained few of the finer sensibilities of civilized man, or the great nobility of character that marked so many of the wild beasts. Her love for Tarzan had been the only soft spot in La's savage life, and realizing that she would think nothing of deserting a creature she did not love, she was fair enough to cast no reproaches upon Tarzan for hav-ing done the thing that she might have done, nor to her mind did it accord illy with her conception of his nobility of character.

As she descended to the ground, she sought to determine some plan of action for the future, and in this moment of her loneliness and depression she saw no alternative but to return to Opar, and so it was toward the city of her birth that she turned her steps; but she had not gone far before she real-ized the danger and futility of this plan, which could but lead to certain death while Oah and Dooth ruled in Opar. She felt bitterly toward Darus, who she believed had betrayed her; and accepting his treason as an index of what she might expect from others whom she had believed to be friendly to her, she realized the utter hopelessness of regaining the throne of Opar without outside help. La had no happy life to which she might look forward; but the will to live was yet strong within her, the result more, perhaps, of the courageousness of her spirit than of any fear of death, which, to her, was but another word for defeat.

She paused in the trail that she had reached a short distance from the tree in which she had spent the night; and there, with almost nothing to guide her, she sought to determine in what direction she should break a new trail into the future, for wherever she went, other than back to Opar, it would be a new trail, leading among peoples and experiences as foreign to her as though she had suddenly stepped from another planet, or from the long-lost continent of her progenitors.

It occurred to her that perhaps there might be other people in this strange world as generous and chivalrous as Tarzan. At least in this direction there lay hope. In Opar there was none, and so she turned back away from Opar; and above her black clouds rolled and billowed as the storm king marshalled his forces, and behind her a tawny beast with gleaming eyes slunk through the underbrush beside the trail that she followed.

CHAPTER VII
In Futile Search

Tarzan of the Apes, ranging far in search of food, caught at length the welcome scent of Horta, the boar. The man paused and, with a deep and silent inhalation, filled his lungs with air until his great bronzed chest expanded to the full. Already he was tasting the fruits of victory. The red blood coursed through his veins, as every fibre of his being reacted to the exhilaration of the moment – the keen delight of the hunting beast that has scented its quarry. And then swiftly and silently he sped in the direction of his prey.

Presently he came upon it, a young tusker, powerful and agile, his wicked tusks gleaming as he tore bark from a young tree. The ape-man was poised just above him, concealed by the foliage of a great tree.

A vivid flash of lightning broke from the blllowing black clouds above. Thunder crashed and boomed. The storm broke, and at the same instant the man launched himself downward upon the back of the unsuspecting boar, in one hand the hunting knife of his long-dead sire.

The weight of the man's body crushed the boar to the earth, and before it could struggle to its feet again the keen blade had severed its jugular. Its life blood gushing from the wound, the boar sought to rise and turn to fight; but the steel thews of the ape-man dragged it down, and an instant later, with a last convulsive shudder, Horta died.

Leaping to his feet, Tarzan placed a foot upon the carcase of his kill and, raising his face to the heavens, gave voice to the victory cry of the bull-ape.

Faintly to the ears of marching men came the hideous scream. The blacks in the party halted, wide-eyed.

'What the devil was that?' demanded Zveri.

'It sounded like a panther,' said Colt.

'That was no panther,' said Kitembo. 'It was the cry of a bull-ape who has made a kill, or—'

'Or what?' demanded Zveri.

Kitembo looked fearfully in the direction from which the sound had come. 'Let us get away from here,' he said.

Again the lightning flashed and the thunder crashed, and as the torrential rain deluged them, the party staggered on in the direction of the barrier cliffs of Opar.

Cold and wet, La of Opar crouched beneath a great tree that only partly protected her almost naked body from the fury of the storm, and in the dense underbrush a few yards from her a tawny carnivore lay with unblinking eyes fixed steadily upon her.

The storm, titanic in its brief fury, passed on, leaving the deep worn trail a tiny torrent of muddy water; and La, thoroughly chilled, hastened onward in an effort to woo new warmth to her chilled body.

She knew that trails must lead somewhere, and in her heart she hoped that this one would lead to the country of Tarzan. If she could live there, seeing him occasionally, she would be content. Even knowing that he was near her would be better than nothing. Of course she had no conception of the immensity of the world she trod. A knowledge of even the extent of the forest that surrounded her would have appalled her. In her imagination she visualized a small world, dotted with the remains of ruined cities like Opar, in which dwelt creatures like those she had known; gnarled and knotted men like the priests of Opar, white men like Tarzan, black men such as she had seen, and great shaggy gorillas like Bolgani, who had ruled in the Valley of the Palace of Diamonds.

And thinking these thoughts, she came at last to a clearing into which the unbroken rays of the warm sun poured without interruption. Near the centre of the clearing was a small boulder; and toward this she made her way with the intention of basking in the warm rays of the sun until she should be thoroughly dried and warmed, for the dripping foliage of the forest had kept her wet and cold even after the rain had ceased.

As she seated herself she saw a movement at the edge of the clearing ahead of her, and an instant later a great leopard bounded into view. The beast paused at sight of the woman, evidently as much surprised as she; and then, apparently realizing the defencelessness of this unexpected prey, the creature crouched and with twitching tail slowly wormed itself forward.

La rose and drew from her girdle the knife that she had taken from Darus. She knew that flight was futile. In a few bounds the great beast could overtake her, and even had there been a tree that she could have reached before she was overtaken, it would have proved no sanctuary from a leopard. Defence, too, she knew to be futile, but surrender without battle was not within the fibre of La of Opar.

The metal discs, elaborately wrought by the hands of some long-dead goldsmith of ancient Opar, rose and fell above her firm breasts as her heart beat, perhaps a bit more rapidly, beneath them. On came the leopard. She knew that in an instant he would charge; and then of a sudden he rose to his feet, his back arched, his mouth grinning in a fearful snarl; and simultaneously a tawny streak whizzed by her from behind, and she saw a great lion leap upon her would-be destroyer.

At the last instant, but too late, the leopard had turned to flee; and the lion seized him by the back of the neck, and with his jaws and one great paw he twisted the head back until the spine snapped. Then, almost contemptuously, he cast the body from him and turned toward the girl.

In an instant La realized what had happened. The lion had been stalking her, and seeing another about to seize his prey, he had leaped to battle in its defence. She had been saved, but only to fall victim immediately to another and more terrible beast.

The lion stood looking at her. She wondered why he did not charge and claim his prey. She did not know that within that little brain the scent of the woman had aroused the memory of another day, when Tarzan had lain bound upon the sacrificial altar of Opar with Jad-bal-ja, the golden lion, standing guard above him. A woman had come – this same woman – and Tarzan, his master, had told him not to harm her, and she had approached and cut the bonds that secured him.

This Jad-bal-ja remembered, and he remembered, too, that he was not to harm this woman; and if he was not to harm her, then nothing must harm her. For this reason he had killed Sheeta, the leopard.

But all this, La of Opar did not know, for she had not recognized Jad-bal-ja. She merely wondered how much longer it would be; and when the lion came closer she steeled herself, for still she meant to fight; yet there was something in his attitude that she could not understand. He was not charging; he was merely walking toward her, and when he was a couple of yards from her he half turned away and lay down and yawned.

For what seemed an eternity to the girl she stood there watching him. He paid no attention to her. Could it be that, sure of his prey and not yet hungry, he merely waited until he was quite ready to make his kill? The idea was horrible, and even La's iron nerves commenced to weaken beneath the strain.

She knew that she could not escape, and so better instant death than this suspense. She determined, therefore, to end the matter quickly and to discover once and for all whether the lion considered her already his prey or would permit her to depart. Gathering all the forces of self-control that she possessed, she placed the point of her dagger to her heart and walked boldly past the lion. Should he attack her, she would end the agony instantly by plunging the blade into her heart.

Jad-bal-ja did not move, but with lazy, half-closed eyes he watched the woman cross the clearing and disappear beyond the turn of the trail that wound its way back into the jungle.

All that day La moved on with grim determination, looking always for a ruined city like Opar, astonished by the immensity of the forest, appalled by its loneliness. Surely, she thought, she must soon come to the country of Tarzan. She found fruits and tubers to allay her hunger, and as the trail descended a valley in which a river ran she did not want for water. But night came again, and still no sight of man or city. Once again she crept into a tree to sleep, but this time there was no Tarzan of the Apes to fashion a couch for her or to watch over her safety.

After Tarzan had slain the boar, he cut off the hind quarters and started back to the tree in which he had left La. The storm made his progress much slower than it otherwise would have been, but notwithstanding this he realized long before he reached his destination that his hunting had taken him much farther afield than he had imagined.

When at last he reached the tree and found that La was not there he was slightly disconcerted, but thinking that perhaps she had descended to stretch her limbs after the storm, he called her name aloud several times. Receiving no answer, he became genuinely apprehensive for her safety and, dropping to the ground, sought some sign of her spoor. It so happened that beneath the tree her footprints were still visible, not having been entirely obliterated by the rain. He saw that they led back in the direction of Opar, so that, although he lost them when they reached the trail in which water still was running, he was nonetheless confident that he knew her intended destination; and so he set off in the direction of the barrier cliff.

It was not difficult for him to account for her absence and for the fact that she was returning to Opar, and he reproached himself for his thoughtlessness in having left her for so long a time without first telling her of his purpose. He guessed, rightly, that she had imagined herself deserted and had turned back to the only home she knew, to the only place in the world where La of

Opar might hope to find friends; but that she would find them even there Tarzan doubted, and he was determined that she must not go back until she could do so with a force of warriors sufficiently great to ensure the overthrow of her enemies.

It had been Tarzan's plan first to thwart the scheme of the party whose camp he had discovered in his dominion and then to return with La to the country of his Waziri, where he would gather a sufficient body of those redoubtable warriors to ensure the safety and success of La's return to Opar. Never communicative, he had neglected to explain his purposes to La; and this he now regretted, since he was quite certain that had he done so she would not have felt it necessary to have attempted to return alone to Opar.

But he was not much concerned with the outcome since he was confident that he could overtake her long before she reached the city; and, enured as he was to the dangers of the forest and the jungle, he minimized their import-ance, as we do those which confront us daily in the ordinary course of our seemingly humdrum existence, where death threatens us quite as constantly as it does the denizens of the jungle.

At any moment expecting to catch sight of her whom he sought, Tarzan traversed the back trail to the foot of the rocky escarpment that guards the plain of Opar; and now he commenced to have his doubts, for it did not seem possible that La could have covered so great a distance in so short a time. He scaled the cliff and came out upon the summit of the flat mountain that over-looked distant Opar. Here only a light rain had fallen, the storm having followed the course of the valley below, and plain in the trail were the foot-prints of himself and La where they had passed down from Opar the night before; but nowhere was there any sign of spoor to indicate that the girl had returned, nor, as he looked out across the valley, was there any moving thing in sight.

What had become of her? Where could she have gone? In the great forest that spread below him there were countless trails. Somewhere below, her spoor must be plain in the freshly-wet earth, but he realized that even for him it might prove a long and difficult task to pick it up again.

As he turned back rather sorrowfully to descend the barrier cliff, his atten-tion was attracted by a movement at the edge of the forest below. Dropping to his belly behind a low bush, Tarzan watched the spot to which his atten-tion had been attracted; and as he did so the head of a column of men debouched from the forest and moved toward the foot of the cliff.

Tarzan had known nothing of what had transpired upon the occasion of Zveri's first expedition to Opar, which had occurred while he had been incar-cerated in the cell beneath the city. The apparent mysterious disappearance of the party that he had known to have been marching on Opar had mystified him; but here it was again, and where it had been in the meantime was of no moment.

Tarzan wished that he had his bow and arrows, which the Oparians had taken from him and which he had not had an opportunity to replace since he had escaped. But if he did not have them, there were other ways of annoying the invaders. From his position he watched them approach the cliff and commence the ascent.

Tarzan selected a large boulder, many of which were strewn about the flat top of the mountain, and when the leaders of the party were about halfway to the summit and the others were strung out below them, the ape-man pushed the rock over the edge of the cliff just above them. In its descent it just grazed Zveri, struck a protuberance beyond him, bounded over Colt's head, and carried two of Kitembo's warriors to death at the base of the escarpment.

The ascent stopped instantly. Several of the blacks who had accompanied the first expedition started a hasty retreat; and utter disorganization and rout faced the expedition, whose nerves had become more and more sensitive the nearer that they approached Opar.

'Stop the damn cowards!' shouted Zveri to Dorsky and Ivitch, who were bringing up the rear. 'Who will volunteer to go over the top and investigate?'

'I'll go,' said Romero.

'And I'll go with him,' offered Colt.

'Who else?' demanded Zveri; but no one else volunteered, and already the Mexican and the American were climbing upward.

'Cover our advance with a few rifles,' Colt shouted back to Zveri. 'That ought to keep them away from the edge.'

Zveri issued instructions to several of the askaris who had not joined in the retreat; and when their rifles commenced popping, it put new heart into those who had started to flee, and presently Dorsky and Ivitch had rallied the men and the ascent was resumed.

Perfectly well aware that he might not stop the advance single-handed, Tarzan had withdrawn quickly along the edge of the cliff to a spot where tumbled masses of granite offered concealment and where he knew that there existed a precipitous trail to the bottom of the cliff. Here he could remain and watch, or, if necessary, make a hasty retreat. He saw Romero and Colt reach the summit and immediately recognized the latter as the man he had seen in the base camp of the invaders. He had previously been impressed by the appearance of the young American, and now he acknowledged his unquestioned bravery and that of his companion in leading a party over the summit of the cliff in the face of an unknown danger.

Romero and Colt looked quickly about them, but there was no enemy in sight, and this word they passed back to the ascending company.

From his point of vantage Tarzan watched the expedition surmount the summit of the cliff and start on its march toward Opar. He believed that they could never find the treasure vaults; and now that La was not in the city he was not concerned with the fate of those who had turned against her. Upon the bare and inhospitable Oparian plain, or in the city itself, they could accomplish little in furthering the objects of the expedition he had overheard Zora Drinov explaining to Colt. He knew that eventually they must return to their base camp, and in the meantime he would prosecute his search for La; and so, as Zveri led his expedition once again toward Opar, Tarzan of the Apes slipped over the edge of the barrier cliff and descended swiftly to the forest below.

Just inside the forest and upon the bank of the river was an admirable camp site; and having noticed that the expedition was not accompanied by porters, Tarzan naturally assumed that they had established a temporary camp within striking distance of the city, and it occurred to him that in this camp he might find La a prisoner.

As he had expected, he found the camp located upon the spot where, upon other occasions, he had camped with his Waziri warriors. An old thorn boma that had encircled it for years had been repaired by the newcomers, and within it a number of rude shelters had been erected, while in the centre stood the tents of the white men. Porters were dozing in the shade of the trees; a single askari made a pretence of standing guard, while his fellows lolled at their ease, their rifles at their sides; but nowhere could he see La of Opar.

He moved downwind from the camp, hoping to catch her scent spoor if she was a prisoner there, but so strong was the smell of smoke and the body odours of the blacks that he could not be sure but that these drowned La's scent. He decided, therefore, to wait until darkness had fallen when he might make a more careful investigation, and he was further prompted to this decision by the sight of weapons, which he sorely needed. All of the warriors were armed with rifles, but some, clinging through force of ancient habit to the weapons of their ancestors, carried also bows and arrows, and, in addition, there were many spears.

As a few mouthfuls of the raw flesh of Horta had constituted the only food that had passed Tarzan's lips for almost two days, he was ravenously hungry. With the discovery that La had disappeared, he had cached the hind quarter of the boar in the tree in which they had spent the night and set out upon his fruitless search for her; so now, while he waited for darkness, he hunted again, and this time Bara, the antelope, fell a victim to his prowess, nor did he leave the carcass of his kill until he had satisfied his hunger. Then he lay up in a nearby tree and slept.

The anger of Abu Batn against Zveri was rooted deeply in his inherent racial antipathy for Europeans and their religion, and its growth was stimulated by the aspersions which the Russian had cast upon the courage of the Arab and his followers.

'Dog of a Nasrâny!' ejaculated the sheikh. 'He called us cowards, we Bedaùwy, and he left us here like old men and boys to guard the camp and the woman.'

'He is but an instrument of Allah,' said one of the Arabs, 'in the great cause that will rid Africa of all Nasrany.'

'Wellah-billah!' ejaculated Abu Batn. 'What proof have we that these people will do as they promise? I would rather have my freedom on the desert and what wealth I can gather by myself than to lie longer in the same camp with these Nasrâny pigs.'

'There is no good in them,' muttered another.

'I have looked upon their woman,' said the sheikh, 'and I find her good. I know a city where she would bring many pieces of gold.'

'In the trunk of the chief Nasrâny there are many pieces of gold and silver.' said one of the men. 'His boy told that to a Galla, who repeated it to me.'

'The plunder of the camp is rich besides,' suggested a swarthy warrior.

'If we do this thing, perhaps the great cause will be lost,' suggested he who had first answered the sheikh.

'It is the cause of the Nasrâny,' said Abu Batn, 'and it is only for profit. Is not the huge pig always reminding us of the money, and the women, and the power that we shall have when we have thrown out the English? Man is moved only by his greed. Let us take our profits in advance and be gone.'

Wamala was preparing the evening meal for his mistress. 'Before, you were left with the brown bwana,' he said, 'and he was no good; nor do I like any better the sheikh Abu Batn. He is no good. I wish that Bwana Colt were here.'

'So do I,' said Zora. 'It seems to me that the Arabs have been sullen and surly ever since the expedition returned from Opar.'

'They have sat all day in the tent of their chief talking together,' said Wamala, 'and often Abu Batn looked at you.'

'That is your imagination, Wamala,' replied the girl. 'He would not dare to harm me.'

'Who would have thought that the brown bwana would have dared to?' Wamala reminded her.

'Hush, Wamala, the first thing you know you will have me frightened,' said Zora, and then, suddenly, 'Look, Wamala! Who is that?'

The black boy turned his eyes in the direction toward which his mistress was looking. At the edge of the camp stood a figure that might have wrung an exclamation of surprise from a Stoic. A beautiful woman stood there regarding them intently. She had halted just at the edge of camp – an almost naked woman whose gorgeous beauty was her first and most striking characteristic. Two golden discs covered her firm breasts, and a narrow stomacher of gold and precious stones encircled her hips, supporting in front and behind a broad strip of soft leather, studded with gold and jewels, which formed the pattern of a pedestal on the summit of which was seated a grotesque bird. Her feet were shod in sandals that were covered with mud, as were her shapely legs upward to above her knees. A mass of wavy hair, shot with golden bronze lights by the rays of the setting sun, half surrounded an oval face, and from beneath narrow pencilled brows fearless grey eyes regarded them.

Some of the Arabs had caught sight of her, too, and they were coming forward now toward her. She looked quickly from Zora and Wamala toward the others. Then the European girl arose quickly and approached her that she might reach her before the Arabs did; and as she came nearer the stranger with outstretched hands, Zora smiled. La of Opar came quickly to meet her as though sensing in the smile of the other an index to the friendly intent of this stranger.

'Who are you,' asked Zora, 'and what are you doing here alone in the jungle?'

La shook her head and replied in a language that Zora did not understand.

Zora Drinov was an accomplished linguist but she exhausted every language in her repertoire, including a few phrases from various Bantu dialects, and still found no means of communicating with the stranger, whose beautiful face and figure but added to the interest of the tantalizing enigma she presented to pique the curiosity of the Russian girl.

The Arabs addressed her in their own tongue and Wamala in the dialect of his tribe, but all to no avail. Then Zora put an arm about her and led her toward her tent; and there, by means of signs, La of Opar indicated that she would bathe. Wamala was directed to prepare a tub in Zora's tent, and by the time supper was prepared the stranger reappeared, washed and refreshed.

As Zora Drinov seated herself opposite her strange guest, she was impressed with the belief that never before had she looked upon so beautiful a woman, and she marvelled that no one who must have felt so utterly out of place in her surroundings should still retain a poise that suggested the majestic bearing of a queen rather than of a stranger ill at ease.

By signs and gestures, Zora sought to converse with her guest until even the regal La found herself laughing; and then La tried it too until Zora knew that her guest had been threatened with clubs and knives and driven from her home, that she had walked a long way, that either a lion or a leopard had attacked her and that she was very tired.

When supper was over, Wamala prepared another cot for La in the tent with Zora, for something in the faces of the Arabs had made the European girl fear for the safety of her beautiful guest.

'You must sleep outside the tent door tonight, Wamala,' she said. 'Here is an extra pistol.'

In his goat hair beyt Abu Batn, the sheikh, talked long into the night with the principal men of his tribe. 'The new one,' he said, 'will bring a price such as has never been paid before.'

Tarzan awoke and glanced upward through the foliage at the stars. He saw that the night was half gone, and he arose and stretched himself. He ate again sparingly of the flesh of Bara and slipped silently into the shadows of the night.

The camp at the foot of the barrier cliff slept. A single askari kept guard and tended the beast fire. From a tree at the edge of the camp two eyes watched him, and when he was looking away a figure dropped silently into the shadows. Behind the huts of the porters it crept, pausing occasionally to test the air with dilated nostrils. It came at last, among the shadows, to the tents of the Europeans, and one by one it ripped a hole in each rear wall and entered. It was Tarzan searching for La, but he did not find her and, disappointed, he turned to another matter.

Making a half circuit of the camp, moving sometimes only inch by inch as he wormed himself along on his belly, lest the askari upon guard might see him, he made his way to the shelters of the other askaris, and there he selected a bow and arrows, and a stout spear, but even yet he was not done.

For a long time he crouched waiting – waiting until the askari by the fire should turn in a certain direction.

Presently the sentry arose and threw some dry wood upon the fire, after which he walked toward the shelter of his fellows to awaken the man who was to relieve him. It was this moment for which Tarzan had been waiting. The path of the askari brought him close to where Tarzan lay in hiding. The man approached and passed, and in the same instant Tarzan leaped to his feet and sprung upon the unsuspecting black. A strong arm encircled the fellow from behind and swung him to a broad, bronzed shoulder. As Tarzan had anticipated, a scream of terror burst from the man's lips, awaking his fellows; and then he was borne swiftly through the shadows of the camp away from the beast fire as, with his prey struggling futilely in his grasp, the ape-man leaped the thorn boma and disappeared into the black jungle beyond.

So sudden and violent was the attack, so complete the man's surprise, that he had loosened his grasp upon his rifle in an effort to clutch his antagonist as he was thrown lightly to the shoulder of his captor.

His screams, echoing through the forest, brought his terrified companions from their shelters in time to see an indistinct form leap the boma and vanish into the darkness. They stood temporarily paralyzed by fright, listening to the diminishing cries of their comrade. Presently these ceased as suddenly as they had commenced. Then the headman found his voice.

'Simba!' he said.

'It was not Simba,' declared another. 'It ran high upon two legs, like a man. I saw it.'

Presently from the dark jungle came a hideous, long-drawn cry. 'That is the voice of neither man nor lion,' said the headman.

'It is a demon,' whispered another, and then they huddled about the fire, throwing dry wood upon it until the blaze had crackled high into the air.

In the darkness of the jungle Tarzan paused and laid aside his spear and bow, possession of which had permitted him to use but one hand in his abduction of the sentry. Now the fingers of his free hand closed upon the throat of his victim, putting a sudden period to his screams. Only for an instant did Tarzan choke the man; and when he relaxed his grasp upon the fellow's throat the black made no further outcry, fearing to invite again the ungentle grip of those steel fingers. Quickly Tarzan jerked the fellow to his feet, relieved him of his knife and, grasping him by his thick wool, pushed him ahead of him into the jungle, after stooping to retrieve his spear and bow. It was then that he voiced the victory cry of the bull-ape, for the value of the effect that it would have not only upon his victim, but upon his fellows in the camp behind them.

Tarzan had no intention of harming the fellow. His quarrel was not with the innocent black tools of the white men; and, while he would not have hesitated to take the life of the black had it been necessary, he knew them well enough to know that he might effect his purpose with them as well without bloodshed as with it.

The whites could not accomplish anything without their black allies, and if Tarzan could successfully undermine the morale of the latter, the schemes of their masters would be as effectually thwarted as though he had destroyed them, since he was confident that they would not remain in a district where they were constantly reminded of the presence of a malign, supernatural enemy. Furthermore, this policy accorded better with Tarzan's grim sense of humour and, therefore, amused him, which the taking of life never did.

For an hour he marched his victim ahead of him in an utter silence, which he knew would have its effect upon the nerves of the black man. Finally he halted him, stripped his remaining clothing from him, and, taking the fellow's loin cloth, bound his wrists and ankles together loosely. Then, appropriating his cartridge belt and other belongings, Tarzan left him, knowing that the black would soon free himself from his bonds; yet, believing that he had made his escape, would remain for life convinced that he had narrowly eluded a terrible fate.

Satisfied with his night's work, Tarzan returned to the tree in which he had cached the carcass of Bara, ate once more and lay up in sleep until morning, when he again took up his search for La, seeking trace of her up the valley beyond the barrier cliff of Opar, in the general direction that her spoor had indicated she had gone, though, as a matter of fact, she had gone in precisely the opposite direction, down the valley.

CHAPTER VIII

The Treachery of Abu Batn

Night was falling when a frightened little monkey took refuge in a tree top. For days he had been wandering through the jungle, seeking in his little mind a solution for his problem during those occasional intervals that he could concentrate his mental forces upon it. But in an instant he might forget it to go swinging and scampering through the trees, or again a sudden terror would drive it from his consciousness, as one or another of the hereditary menaces to his existence appeared within the range of his perceptive faculties.

While his grief lasted, it was real and poignant, and tears welled in the eyes of little Nkima as he thought of his absent master. Lurking always within him upon the borderland of conviction was the thought that he must obtain succour for Tarzan. In some way he must fetch aid to his master. The great black Gomangani warriors, who were also the servants of Tarzan, were many darknesses away, but yet it was in the general direction of the country of the Waziri that he drifted. Time was in no sense the essence of the solution of this or any other problem in the mind of Nkima. He had seen Tarzan enter Opar alive. He had not seen him destroyed, nor had he seen him come out of the city; and, therefore, by the standards of his logic Tarzan must still be alive and in the city, but because the city was filled with enemies Tarzan must be in danger. As conditions were they would remain. He could not readily visualize any change that he did not actually witness, and so, whether he found and fetched the Waziri today or tomorrow would have little effect upon the result. They would go to Opar and kill Tarzan's enemies, and then little Nkima would have his master once more, and he would not have to be afraid of Sheeta, or Sabor, or Histah.

Night fell, and in the forest Nkima heard a gentle tapping. He aroused himself and listened intently. The tapping grew in volume until it rolled and moved through the jungle. Its source was at no great distance, and as Nkima became aware of this, his excitement grew.

The moon was well up in the heavens, but the shadows of the jungle were dense. Nkima was upon the horns of a dilemma, between his desire to go to the place from which the drumming emanated and his fear of the dangers that might lie along the way; but at length the urge prevailed over his terror, and keeping well up in the relatively greater safety of the tree tops, he swung quickly in the direction from which the sound was coming to halt at last, above a little natural clearing that was roughly circular in shape.

Below him, in the moonlight, he witnessed a scene that he had spied upon before, for here the great apes of To-yat were engaged in the death dance of the Dum-Dum. In the centre of the amphitheatre was one of those remarkable earthen drums, which from time immemorial primitive man has heard, but which few have seen. Before the drum were seated two old shes, who beat upon its resounding surface with short sticks. There was a rough rhythmic cadence to their beating, and to it, in a savage circle, danced the bulls; while encircling them in a thin outer line, the females and the young squatted upon their haunches, enthralled spectators of the savage scene. Close beside the drum lay the dead body of Sheeta, the leopard, to celebrate whose killing the Dum-Dum had been organized.

Presently the dancing bulls would rush in upon the body and beat it with heavy sticks and, leaping out again, resume their dance. When the hunt, and the attack, and the death had been depicted at length, they would cast away their bludgeons and with bared fangs leap upon the carcass, tearing and rending it as they fought among themselves for large pieces or choice morsels.

Now Nkima and his kind are noted neither for their tact nor judgment. One wiser than little Nkima would have remained silent until the dance and the feast were over and until a new day had come and the great bulls of the tribe of To-yat had recovered from the hysterical frenzy that the drum and the dancing always induced within them. But little Nkima was only a monkey. What he wanted, he wanted immediately, not being endowed with that mental poise which results in patience, and so he swung by his tail from an overhanging branch and scolded at the top of his voice in an effort to attract the attention of the great apes below.

'To-yat! Ga-yat! Zu-tho!' he cried. 'Tarzan is in danger! Come with Nkima and save Tarzan!'

A great bull stopped in the midst of the dancing and looked up. 'Go away, Manu,' he growled. 'Go away or we kill!' But little Nkima thought that they could not catch him, and so he continued to swing from the branch and yell and scream at them until finally To-yat sent a young ape, who was not too heavy to clamber into the upper branches of the tree, to catch little Nkima and kill him.

Here was an emergency which Nkima had not foreseen. Like many people, he had believed that everyone would be as interested in what interested him as he; and when he had first heard the booming of the drums of the Dum-Dum, he thought that the moment the apes learned of Tarzan's peril they would set out upon the trail to Opar.

Now, however, he knew differently, and as the real menace of his mistake became painfully apparent with the leaping of a young ape into the tree below him, little Nkima emitted a loud shriek of terror and fled through the night; nor did he pause until, panting and exhausted, he had put a good mile between himself and the tribe of To-yat.

When La of Opar awoke in the tent of Zora Drinov she looked about her, taking in the unfamiliar objects that surrounded her, and presently her gaze rested upon the face of her sleeping hostess. These, indeed, she thought, must be the people of Tarzan, for had they not treated her with kindness and courtesy? They had offered her no harm and had fed her and given her shelter. A new thought crossed her mind now and her brows contracted, as did the pupils of her eyes into which there came a sudden, savage light. Perhaps this woman was Tarzan's mate. La of Opar grasped the hilt of Darus' knife where it lay ready beside her. But then, as suddenly as it had come, the mood passed, for in her heart she knew that she could not return evil for good, nor could she harm whom Tarzan loved, and when Zora opened her eyes La greeted her with a smile.

If the European girl was a cause for astonishment to La, she herself filled the other with profoundest wonder and mystification. Her scant, yet rich and gorgeous apparel harked back to an ancient age, and the gleaming whiteness of her skin seemed as much out of place in the heart of an African jungle as did her trappings in the twentieth century. Here was a mystery that nothing in the past experience of Zora Drinov could assist in solving. How she wished that she could converse with her, but all that she could do was to smile back at the beautiful creature regarding her so intently.

La, accustomed as she had been to being waited upon all her life by the lesser priestesses of Opar, was surprised by the facility with which Zora Drinov attended to her own needs as she rose to bathe and dress, the only service she received being in the form of a pail of hot water that Wamala fetched and poured into her folding tub; yet though La had never before been expected to lift a hand in the making of her toilet, she was far from helpless, and perhaps she found pleasure in the new experience of doing for herself.

Unlike the customs of the men of Opar, those of its women required scrupulous bodily cleanliness, so that in the past much of La's time had been devoted to her toilet, to the care of her nails, and her teeth, and her hair, and to the massaging of her body with aromatic unguents – customs, handed down from a cultured civilization of antiquity, to take on in ruined Opar the significance of religious rites.

By the time the two girls were ready for breakfast, Wamala was prepared to serve it; and as they sat outside the tent beneath the shade of a tree, eating the coarse fare of the camp, Zora noted unwonted activity about the byût of the Arabs, but she gave the matter little thought, as they had upon other occasions moved their tents from one part of the camp to another.

Breakfast over, Zora took down her rifle, wiped out the bore and oiled the breech mechanism, for today she was going out after fresh meat, the Arabs having refused to hunt. La watched her with evident interest and later saw her depart with Wamala and two of the black porters; but she did not attempt to accompany her since, although she had looked for it, she had received no sign to do so.

Ibn Dammuk was the son of a sheikh of the same tribe as Abu Batn, and upon this expedition he was the latter's right-hand man. With the fold of his thob drawn across the lower part of his face, leaving only his eyes exposed, he had been watching the two girls from a distance. He saw Zora Drinov quit the camp with a gun-bearer and two porters and knew that she had gone to hunt.

For some time after she had departed he sat in silence with two companions. Then he arose and sauntered across the camp toward La of Opar, where she sat buried in reverie in a camp chair before Zora's tent. As the three men approached, La eyed them with level gaze, her natural suspicion of strangers aroused in her breast. As they came closer and their features became distinct, she felt a sudden distrust of them. They were crafty, malign looking men, not at all like Tarzan, and instinctively she distrusted them.

They halted before her and Ibn Dammuk, the son of a sheikh, addressed her. His voice was soft and oily, but it did not deceive her.

La eyed him haughtily. She did not understand him and she did not wish to, for the message that she read in his eyes disgusted her. She shook her head to signify that she did not understand and turned away to indicate that the interview was terminated, but Ibn Dammuk stepped closer and laid a hand familiarly upon her naked shoulder.

Her eyes flaming with anger, La leaped to her feet, one hand moving swiftly to the hilt of her dagger. Ibn Dammuk stepped back, but one of his men leaped forward to seize her.

Misguided fool! Like a tigress she was upon him; and before his friends could intervene the sharp blade of the knife of Darus, the priest of the Flaming God, had sunk thrice into his breast, and with a gasping scream he had slumped to the ground dead.

With flaming eyes and bloody knife, the high priestess of Opar stood above her kill, while Abu Batn and the other Arabs, attracted by the death cry of the stricken man, ran hurriedly toward the little group.

'Stand back!' cried La. 'Lay no profaning hand upon the person of the high priestess of the Flaming God.'

They did not understand her words, but they understood her flashing eyes and her dripping blade. Jabbering volubly, they gathered around her, but at a safe distance. 'What means this, Ibn Dammuk?' demanded Abu Batn.

'Dogman did but touch her, and she flew at him like el adrea, lord of the broad head.'

'A lioness she may be,' said Abu Batn, 'but she must not be harmed.'

'Wullah!' exclaimed Ibn Dammuk, 'but she must be tamed.'

'Her taming we may leave to him who will pay many pieces of gold for her,' replied the sheikh. 'It is necessary only for us to cage her. Surround her, my children, and take the knife from her. Make her wrists secure behind her back, and by the time the other returns we shall have struck camp and be ready to depart.'

A dozen brawny men leaped upon La simultaneously. 'Do not harm her! Do not harm her!' screamed Abu Batn, as, fighting like a lioness indeed, La sought to defend herself. Slashing right and left with her dagger, she drew blood more than once before they overpowered her; nor did they accomplish it before another Arab fell with a pierced heart, but at length they succeeded in wrenching the blade from her and securing her wrists.

Leaving two warriors to guard her, Abu Batn turned his attention to gathering up the few black servants that remained in camp. These he forced to prepare loads of such of the camp equipment and provisions as he required. While this work was going on under Ibn Dammuk's supervision the sheikh ransacked the tents of the Europeans, giving special attention to those of Zora Drinov and Zveri, where he expected to find the gold that the leader of the expedition was reputed to have in large quantities; nor was he entirely disappointed since he found in Zora's tent a box containing a considerable amount of money, though by no means the great quantity that he had expected, a fact which was due to the foresight of Zveri, who had personally buried the bulk of his funds beneath the floor of his tent.

Zora met with unexpected success in her hunting, for within a little more than an hour of her departure from camp she had come upon antelope, and two quick shots had dropped as many members of the herd. She waited while the porters skinned and dressed them and then returned leisurely toward camp. Her mind was occupied to some extent with the disquieting attitude of the Arabs, but she was not at all prepared for the reception that she met when she approached camp about noon.

She was walking in advance immediately followed by Wamala, who was carrying both of her rifles, while behind them were the porters staggering under their heavy loads. Just as she was about to enter the clearing, Arabs leaped from the underbrush on either side of the trail. Two of them seized Wamala and wrenched the rifles from his grasp, while others laid heavy hands upon Zora. She tried to free herself from them and draw her revolver, but the attack had so taken her by surprise that, before she could accomplish anything in defence, she was overpowered and her hands bound at her back.

'What is the meaning of this?' she demanded. 'Where is Abu Batn, the sheikh?'

The men laughed at her. 'You shall see him presently,' said one. 'He has another guest whom he is entertaining, so he could not come to meet you,' at which they all laughed again.

As she stepped into the clearing where she could obtain an unobstructed view of the camp, she was astounded by what she saw. Every tent had been struck. The Arabs were leaning on their rifles ready to march, each of them burdened with a small pack, while the few black men, who had been left in camp, were lined up before heavy loads. All the rest of the paraphernalia of the camp, which Abu Batn had not men enough to transport, was heaped in a pile in the centre of the clearing, and even as she looked she saw men setting torches to it.

As she was led across the clearing toward the waiting Arabs, she saw her erstwhile guest between two warriors, her wrists confined by thongs even as her own. Near her, scowling malevolently, was Abu Batn.

'Why have you done this thing, Abu Batn?' demanded Zora.

'Allah was wroth that we should betray our land to the Nasrâny,' said the sheikh. 'We have seen the light, and we are going back to our own people.'

'What do you intend to do with this woman and with me?' asked Zora.

'We shall take you with us for a little way,' replied Abu Batn. 'I know a kind man who is very rich, who will give you both a good home.'

'You mean that you are going to sell us to some black sultan?' demanded the girl.

The sheikh shrugged. 'I would not put it that way,' he said. 'Rather let us say that I am making a present to a great and good friend and saving you and this other woman from certain death in the jungle should we depart without you.'

'Abu Batn, you are a hypocrite and a traitor,' cried Zora, her voice vibrant with contempt.

'The Nasrâny like to call names,' said the sheikh with a sneer. 'Perhaps if the pig, Zveri, had not called us names, this would not have happened.'

'So this is your revenge,' asked Zora, 'because he reproached you for your cowardice at Opar?'

'Enough!' snapped Abu Batn. 'Come, my children, let us be gone.'

As the flames licked at the edges of the great pile of provisions and equipment that the Arabs were forced to leave behind, the deserters started upon their march toward the west.

The girls marched near the head of the column, the feet of the Arabs and the carriers behind them totally obliterating their spoor from the motley record of the trail. They might have found some comfort in their straits had they been able to converse with one another; but La could understand no one and Zora found no pleasure in speaking to the Arabs, while Wamala and the other blacks were so far toward the rear of the column that she could not have communicated with them had she cared to.

To pass the time away, Zora conceived the idea of teaching her companion in misery some European language, and because in the original party there had been more who were familiar with English than any other tongue, she selected that language for her experiment.

She began by pointing to herself and saying 'woman' and then to La and repeating the same word, after which she pointed to several of the Arabs in succession and said 'man' in each instance. It was evident that La understood her purpose immediately, for she entered into the spirit of it with eagerness and alacrity, repeating the two words again and again, each time indicating either a man or a woman.

Next the European girl again pointed to herself and said 'Zora.' For a moment La was perplexed, and then she smiled and nodded.

'Zora,' she said, pointing to her companion, and then, swiftly, she touched her own breast with a slender forefinger and said, 'La.'

And this was the beginning. Each hour La learned new words, all nouns at first, that described each familiar object that appeared oftenest to their view. She learned with remarkable celerity, evidencing an alert and intelligent mind and a retentive memory, for once she learned a word she never forgot it. Her pronunciation was not always perfect, for she had a decidedly foreign accent that was like nothing Zora Drinov had ever heard before, and so altogether captivating that the teacher never tired of hearing her pupil recite.

As the march progressed, Zora realized that there was little likelihood that they would be mistreated by their captors, it being evident to her that the sheikh was impressed with the belief that the better the condition in which they could be presented to their prospective purchaser the more handsome the return that Abu Batn might hope to receive.

Their route lay to the north-west through a section of the Galla country of

Abyssinia, and from scraps of conversation Zora overheard she learned that Abu Batn and his followers were apprehensive of danger during this portion of the journey. And well they may have been, since for ages the Arabs have conducted raids in Galla territory for the purpose of capturing slaves, and among the negroes with them was a Galla slave that Abu Batn had brought with him from his desert home.

After the first day the prisoners had been allowed the freedom of their hands, but always Arab guards surrounded them, though there seemed little likelihood that an unarmed girl would take the risk of escaping into the jungle, where she would be surrounded by the dangers of wild beasts or almost certain starvation. However, could Abu Batn have read their thoughts, he might have been astonished to learn that in the mind of each was a determination to escape to any fate rather than to march docilely on to an end that the European girl was fully conscious of and which La of Opar unquestionably surmised in part.

La's education was progressing nicely by the time the party approached the border of the Galla country, but in the meantime both girls had become aware of a new menace threatening La of Opar. Ibn Dammuk often marched beside her and in his eyes, when he looked at her, was a message that needed no words to convey. But when Abu Batn was near Ibn Dammuk ignored the fair prisoner, and this caused Zora the most apprehension, for it convinced her that the wily Ibn was but biding his time until he might find conditions favourable to the carrying out of some scheme that he already had decided upon, nor did Zora harbour any doubts as to the general purpose of his plan.

At the edge of the Galla country they were halted by a river in flood. They could not go north into Abyssinia proper, and they dared not go south where they might naturally have expected pursuit to follow. So perforce they were compelled to wait where they were.

And while they waited Ibn Dammuk struck.

CHAPTER IX

In the Death Cell of Opar

Once again Peter Zveri stood before the walls of Opar, and once again the courage of his black soldiers was dissipated by the weird cries of the inmates of the city of mystery. The ten warriors, who had not been to Opar before and who had volunteered to enter the city, halted trembling as the first of the bloodcurdling screams rose, shrill and piercing, from the forbidding ruins.

Miguel Romero once more led the invaders, and directly behind him was Wayne Colt. According to the plan the blacks were to have followed closely behind these two, with the rest of the whites bringing up the rear, where they might rally and encourage the negroes, or, if necessary, force them on at the points of their pistols. But the blacks would not even enter the opening of the outer wall, so demoralized were they by the uncanny warning screams which their superstitious minds attributed to malignant demons, against which there could be no defence and whose animosity meant almost certain death for those who disregarded their wishes.

'In with you, you dirty cowards!' cried Zveri, menacing the blacks with his revolver in an effort to force them into the opening.

One of the warriors raised his rifle threateningly. 'Put away your weapon, white man,' he said. 'We will fight men, but we will not fight the spirits of the dead.'

'Lay off, Peter,' said Dorsky. 'You will have the whole bunch on us in a minute and we shall all be killed. Every nigger in the outfit is in sympathy with these men.'

Zveri lowered his pistol and commenced to plead with the warriors, promising them rewards that amounted to riches to them if they would accompany the whites into the city; but the volunteers were obdurate – nothing could induce them to venture into Opar.

Seeing failure once again imminent and with a mind already obsessed by the belief that the treasures of Opar would make him fabulously wealthy and ensure the success of his secret scheme of empire, Zveri determined to follow Romero and Colt with the remainder of his aides, which consisted only of Dorsky, Ivitch and the Filipino boy. 'Come on,' he said, 'we will have to make a try at it alone, if these yellow dogs won't help us.'

By the time the four men had passed through the outer wall, Romero and Colt were already out of sight beyond the inner wall. Once again the warning scream broke menacingly upon the brooding silence of the ruined city.

'God!' ejaculated Ivitch. 'What do you suppose it could be?'

'Shut up,' exclaimed Zveri irritably. 'Stop thinking about it, or you'll go yellow like those damn niggers.'

Slowly they crossed the court toward the inner wall, nor was there much enthusiasm manifest among them other than for an evident desire in the breast of each to permit one of the others the glory of leading the advance. Tony had reached the opening when a bedlam of noise from the opposite side of the wall burst upon their ears – a hideous chorus of war cries, mingled with the sound of rushing feet. There was a shot, and then another and another.

Tony turned to see if his companions were following him. They had halted and were standing with blanched faces, listening.

Then Ivitch turned. 'To hell with the gold!' he said, and started back toward the outer wall at a run.

'Come back, you lousy cur,' cried Zveri, and went after him with Dorsky at his heels. Tony hesitated for a moment and then scurried in pursuit, nor did any of them halt until they were beyond the outer wall. There Zveri overtook Ivitch and seized him by the shoulder. 'I ought to kill you,' he cried in a trembling voice.

'You were as glad to get out of there as I was,' growled Ivitch. 'What was the sense of going in there? We should only have been killed like Colt and Romero. There were too many of them. Didn't you hear them?'

'I think Ivitch is right,' said Dorsky. 'It's all right to be brave, but we have got to remember the cause – if we are killed everything is lost.'

'But the gold!' exclaimed Zveri. 'Think of the gold!'

'Gold is no good to dead men,' Dorsky reminded him.

'How about our comrades?' asked Tony. 'Are we to leave them to be killed?'

'To hell with the Mexican,' said Zveri, 'and as for the American I think his funds will still be available as long as we can keep the news of his death from getting back to the coast.'

'You are not even going to try to rescue them?' asked Tony.

'I cannot do it alone,' said Zveri.

'I will go with you,' said Tony.

'Little good two of us can accomplish,' mumbled Zveri, and then in one of his sudden rages, he advanced menacingly upon the Filipino, his great figure towering above that of the other.

'Who do you think you are anyway?' he demanded. 'I am in command here. When I want your advice I'll ask for it.'

When Romero and Colt passed through the inner wall, that part of the interior of the temple which they could see appeared deserted, and yet they were conscious of movement in the darker recesses and the apertures of the ruined galleries that looked down into the courtway.

Colt glanced back. 'Shall we wait for the others?' he asked.

Romero shrugged. 'I think we are going to have this glory all to ourselves, comrade,' he said with a grin.

Colt smiled back at him. 'Then let's get on with the business,' he said. 'I don't see anything very terrifying yet.'

'There is something in there though,' said Romero. 'I've seen things moving.'

'So have I,' said Colt.

With their rifles ready, they advanced boldly into the temple; but they had not gone far when, from shadowy archways and from numerous gloomy doorways there rushed a horde of horrid men, and the silence of the ancient city was shattered by hideous war cries.

Colt was in advance and now he kept on moving forward, firing a shot above the heads of the grotesque warrior priests of Opar. Romero saw a number of the enemy running along the side of the great room which they had entered, with the evident intention of cutting off their retreat. He swung about and fired, but not over their heads. Realizing the gravity of their position, he shot to kill, and now Colt did the same, with the result that the screams of a couple of wounded men mingled now with the war cries of their fellows.

Romero was forced to drop back a few steps to prevent the Oparians from surrounding him. He shot rapidly now and succeeded in checking the advance around their flank. A quick glance at Colt showed him standing his ground, and at the same instant he saw a hurled club strike the American on the head. The man dropped like a log, and instantly his body was covered by the terrible little men of Opar.

Miguel Romero realized that his companion was lost, and even if not now already dead, he, single-handed, could accomplish nothing toward his rescue. If he escaped with his own life he would be fortunate, and so, keeping up a steady fire, he fell back toward the aperture in the inner wall.

Having captured one of the invaders, seeing the other falling back, and fearing to risk further the devastating fire of the terrifying weapon in the hand of their single antagonist, the Oparians hesitated.

Romero passed through the inner wall, turned and ran swiftly to the outer and a moment later had joined his companions upon the plain.

'Where is Colt?' demanded Zveri.

'They knocked him out with a club and captured him,' said Romero. 'He is probably dead by this time.'

'And you deserted him?' asked Zveri.

The Mexican turned upon his chief in fury. 'You ask me that?' he demanded. 'You turned pale and ran even before you saw the enemy. If you fellows had backed us up Colt might not have been lost, but to let us go in there alone the two of us didn't have a Chinaman's chance with that bunch of wild men. And you accuse me of cowardice?'

'I didn't do anything of the kind,' said Zveri sullenly. 'I never said you were a coward.'

'You meant to imply it though,' snapped Romero, 'but let me tell you, Zveri, that you can't get away with that with me or anyone else who has been to Opar with you.'

From behind the walls rose a savage cry of victory; and while it still rumbled through the tarnished halls of Opar, Zveri turned dejectedly away from the city. 'It's no use,' he said. 'I can't capture Opar alone. We are returning to camp.'

The little priests, swarming over Colt, stripped him of his weapons and secured his hands behind his back. He was still unconscious, and so they lifted him to the shoulder of one of their fellows and bore him away into the interior of the temple.

When Colt regained consciousness he found himself lying on the floor of a large chamber. It was the throne room of the temple of Opar, where he had been fetched that Oah, the high priestess, might see the prisoner.

Perceiving that their captive had regained consciousness, his guards jerked him roughly to his feet and pushed him forward toward the foot of the dais upon which stood Oah's throne.

The effect of the picture bursting suddenly upon him imparted to Colt the definite impression that he was the victim of an hallucination or a dream. The outer chamber of the ruin, in which he had fallen, had given no suggestion of the size and semi-barbaric magnificence of this great chamber, the grandeur of which was scarcely dimmed by the ruin of ages.

He saw before him, upon an ornate throne, a young woman of exceptional physical beauty, surrounded by the semi-barbaric grandeur of an ancient civilization. Grotesque and hairy men and beautiful maidens formed her entourage. Her eyes, resting upon him, were cold and cruel; her mien haughty and contemptuous. A squat warrior, more ape-like in his conformation than human, was addressing her in a language unfamiliar to the American.

When he had finished, the girl rose from the throne and, drawing a long knife from her girdle, raised it high above her head as she spoke rapidly and almost fiercely, her eyes fixed upon the prisoner.

From among a group of priestesses at the right of Oah's throne, a girl, just come into womanhood, regarded the prisoner through half-closed eyes, and beneath the golden plates that confined her smooth, white breasts, the heart of Nao palpitated to the thoughts that contemplation of this strange warrior engendered within her.

When Oah had finished speaking, Colt was led away, quite ignorant of the fact that he had been listening to the sentence of death imposed upon him by the high priestess of the Flaming God. His guards conducted him to a cell just within the entrance of a tunnel leading from the sacrificial court to the pits beneath the city, and because it was not entirely below ground, fresh air and light had access to it through a window and the grated bars of its doorway. Here the escort left him, after removing the bonds from his wrists.

Through the small window in his cell Wayne Colt looked out upon the inner court of the Temple of the Sun at Opar. He saw the surrounding galleries rising tier upon tier to the summit of a lofty wall. He saw the stone altar standing in the centre of the court, and the brown stains upon it and upon the pavement at its foot told him what the unintelligible words of Oah had been unable to convey. For an instant he felt his heart sink within his breast, and a shudder passed through his frame as he contemplated his inability to escape the fate which confronted him. There could be no mistaking the purpose of that altar when viewed in connection with the grinning skulls of former human sacrifices which stared through eyeless sockets upon him from their niches in the surrounding walls.

Fascinated by the horror of his situation he stood staring at the altar and skulls, but presently he gained control of himself and shook the terror from him, yet the hopelessness of his situation continued to depress him. His thoughts turned to his companion. He wondered what Romero's fate had been. There, indeed, had been a brave and gallant comrade, in fact, the only member of the party who had impressed Colt favourably, or in whose society he had found pleasure. The others had seemed either ignorant fanatics or avaricious opportunists, while the manner and speech of the Mexican had stamped him as a light-hearted soldier of fortune, who might gaily offer his life in any cause which momentarily seized his fancy with an eye more singly for excitement and adventure than for any serious purpose. He did not know, of course, that Zveri and the others had deserted him; but he was confident that Romero had not before his cause had become utterly hopeless, or until the Mexican himself had been killed or captured.

In lonely contemplation of his predicament, Colt spent the rest of the long afternoon. Darkness fell, and still there came no sign from his captors. He wondered if they intended leaving him there without food or water, or if, perchance, the ceremony that was to see him offered in sacrifice upon that grim, brown-stained altar was scheduled to commence so soon that they felt it unnecessary to minister to his physical needs.

He had lain down upon the hard cement-like surface of the cell floor and was trying to find momentary relief in sleep, when his attention was attracted by the shadow of a sound coming from the courtyard where the altar stood. As he listened he was positive that someone was approaching, and rising quietly he went to the window and looked out. In the shadowy darkness of the night, relieved only by the faint light of distant stars, he saw something moving across the courtyard toward his cell, but whether man or beast he could not distinguish; and then, from somewhere high up among the lofty ruins, there pealed out upon the silent night the long drawn scream, which seemed now to the American as much a part of the mysterious city of Opar as the crumbling ruins themselves.

It was a sullen and discouraged party that made its way back to the camp at the edge of the forest below the barrier cliffs of Opar, and when they arrived it was to find only further disorganization and discouragement.

No time was lost in narrating to the members of the returning expedition the story of the sentry who had been carried off into the jungle at night by a demon, from whom the man had managed to escape before being devoured.

Still fresh in their minds was the uncanny affair of the death of Raghunath Jafar, nor were the nerves of those who had been before the walls of Opar inclined to be at all steadied by that experience, so that it was a nervous company that bivouacked that night beneath the dark trees at the edge of the gloomy forest and, with sighs of relief, witnessed the coming of dawn.

Later, after they had taken up the march toward the base camp, the spirit of the blacks gradually returned to normal, and presently the tension under which they had been labouring for days was relieved by song and laughter, but the whites were gloomy and sullen. Zveri and Romero did not speak to one another while Ivitch, like all weak characters, nursed a grievance against everyone because of his own display of cowardice during the fiasco at Opar.

From the interior of a hollow tree in which he had been hiding, little Nkima saw the column pass; and after it was safely by he emerged from his retreat and, dancing up and down upon a limb of the tree, shouted dire threats after them and called them many names.

Tarzan of the Apes lay stretched upon his belly upon the back of Tantor, the elephant, his elbows upon the broad head, his chin resting in his cupped hands. Futile had been his search for the spoor of La of Opar. Had the earth opened and swallowed her she could not more effectually have disappeared.

Today Tarzan had come upon Tantor and, as had been his custom from childhood, he had tarried for that silent communion with the sagacious old patriarch of the forest, which seemed always to impart to the man something of the beast's great strength of character and poise. There was an atmosphere of restful stability about Tantor that filled the ape-man with a peace and tranquillity that he found restful; and Tantor, upon his part, welcomed the companionship of the Lord of the Jungle, whom, alone, of all two-legged creatures, he viewed with friendship and affection.

The beasts of the jungle acknowledge no master, least of all the cruel tyrant that drives civilized man throughout his headlong race from the cradle to the grave – Time, the master of countless millions of slaves. Time, the measurable aspect of duration, was measureless to Tarzan and Tantor. Of all the vast resources that Nature had placed at their disposal, she had been most profligate with Time, since she had awarded to each all that he could use during his lifetime, no matter how extravagant of it he might be. So great was the supply of it that it could not be wasted, since there was always more, even up to the moment of death, after which it ceased, with all things, to be essential to the individual. Tantor and Tarzan, therefore, were wasting no time as they communed together in silent meditation; but though Time and space go on forever, whether in curves or straight lines, all other things must end; and so the quiet and the peace that the two friends were enjoying were suddenly shattered by the excited screams of a diminutive monkey in the foliage of a great tree above them.

It was Nkima. He had found his Tarzan, and his relief and joy aroused the jungle to the limit of his small, shrill voice. Lazily Tarzan rolled over and looked up at the jabbering simian above him; and then Nkima, satisfied now beyond peradventure of a doubt that this was, indeed, his master, launched himself downward to alight upon the bronzed body of the ape-man. Slender, hairy little arms went around Tarzan's neck as Nkima hugged close to this haven of refuge which imparted to him those brief moments in his life when he might enjoy the raptures of a temporary superiority complex. Upon Tarzan's shoulder he felt almost fearless and could, with impunity, insult the entire world.

'Where have you been, Nkima?' asked Tarzan.

'Looking for Tarzan,' replied the monkey.

'What have you seen since I left you at the walls of Opar?' demanded the ape-man.

'I have seen many things. I have seen the great Mangani dancing in the moonlight around the dead body of Sheeta. I have seen the enemies of Tarzan marching through the forest. I have seen Histah, gorging himself on the carcass of Bara.'

'Have you seen a Tarmangani she?' demanded Tarzan.

'No,' replied Nkima. 'There were no shes among the Gomangani and Tarmangani enemies of Tarzan. Only bulls, and they marched back toward the place where Nkima first saw them.'

'When was this?' asked Tarzan.

'Kudu had climbed into the heavens but a short distance out of the darkness when Nkima saw the enemies of Tarzan marching back to the place where he first saw them.'

'Perhaps we had better see what they are up to,' said the ape-man. He slapped Tantor affectionately with his open palm in farewell, leaped to his feet and swung nimbly into the overhanging branches of a tree; while far away Zveri and his party plodded through the jungle toward their base camp.

Tarzan of the Apes follows no earth-bound trails where the density of the forest offers him the freedom of leafy highways, and thus he moves from point to point with a speed that has often been disconcerting to his enemies.

Now he moved in an almost direct line so that he overtook the expedition as it made camp for the night. As he watched them from behind a leafy screen of high-flung foliage, he noticed, though with no surprise, that they were not burdened with any treasure from Opar.

As the success and happiness of jungle dwellers, nay, even life itself, is largely dependent upon their powers of observation, Tarzan had developed his to a high degree of perfection. At his first encounter with this party he had made himself familiar with the faces, physiques and carriages of all of its principals and of many of its humble warriors and porters, with the result that he was immediately aware that Colt was no longer with the expedition. Experience permitted Tarzan to draw a rather accurate picture of what had happened at Opar and of the probable fate of the missing man.

Years ago he had seen his own courageous Waziri turn and flee upon the occasion of their first experience of the weird warning screams from the ruined city, and he could easily guess that Colt, attempting to lead the invaders into the city, had been deserted and found either death or capture within the gloomy interior. This, however, did not greatly concern Tarzan. While he had been rather drawn toward Colt by that tenuous and invisible power known as personality, he still considered him as one of his enemies, and if he were either dead or captured Tarzan's cause was advanced by that much.

From Tarzan's shoulder Nkima looked down upon the camp, but he kept silent as Tarzan had instructed him to do. Nkima saw many things that the would have liked to have possessed, and particularly he coveted a red calico shirt worn by one of the askaris. This, he thought, was very grand, indeed, being set off as it was by the unrelieved nakedness of the majority of the blacks. Nkima wished that his master would descend and slay them all, but particularly the man with the red shirt; for, at heart, Nkima was bloodthirsty, which made it fortunate for the peace of the jungle that he had not been born a gorilla. But Tarzan's mind was not set upon carnage. He had other means for thwarting the activities of these strangers. During the day he had made a kill, and now he withdrew to a safe distance from the camp and satisfied his hunger, while Nkima searched for birds' eggs, fruit, and insects.

And so night fell and when it had enveloped the jungle in impenetrable darkness, relieved only by the beast fires of the camp, Tarzan returned to a tree where he could overlook the activities of the bivouacked expedition. He watched them in silence for a long time, and then suddenly he raised his voice in a long scream that perfectly mimicked the hideous warning cry of Opar's defenders.

The effect upon the camp was instantaneous. Conversation, singing, and laughter ceased. For a moment the men sat as in a paralysis of terror. Then, seizing their weapons, they came closer to the fire.

With the shadow of a smile upon his lips, Tarzan melted away into the jungle.

CHAPTER X
The Love of a Priestess

Ibn Dammuk had bided his time and now, in the camp by the swollen river at the edge of the Galla country, he at last found the opportunity he had so long awaited. The surveillance over the two prisoners had somewhat relaxed, due largely to the belief entertained by Abu Batn that the women would not dare to invite the perils of the jungle by attempting to escape from captors who were, at the same time, their protectors from even greater dangers. He had, however, reckoned without a just estimation of the courage and resourcefulness of his two captives, who, had he but known it, were constantly awaiting the first opportunity for escape. It was this fact, as well, that played into the hands of Ibn Dammuk.

With great cunning he enlisted the services of one of the blacks who had been forced to accompany them from the base camp and who was virtually a prisoner. By promising him his liberty Ibn Dammuk had easily gained the man's acquiescence in the plan that he had evolved.

A separate tent had been pitched for the two women, and before it sat a single sentry, whose presence Abu Batn considered more than sufficient for this purpose, which was, perhaps, even more to protect the women from his own followers than to prevent a very remotely possible attempt at escape.

This night, which Ibn Dammuk had chosen for his villainy, was one for which he had been waiting, since it found upon duty before the tent of the captives one of his own men, a member of his own tribe, who was bound by laws of hereditary loyalty to serve and obey him. In the forest, just beyond the camp, waited Ibn Dammuk, with two more of his own tribesmen, four slaves that they had brought from the desert and the black porter who was to win his liberty by this night's work.

The interior of the tent that had been pitched for Zora and La was illuminated by a paper lantern, in which a candle burned dimly; and in this subdued light the two sat talking in La's newly acquired English, which was at best most fragmentary and broken. However, it was far better than no means of communication and gave the two girls the only pleasure that they enjoyed. Perhaps it was not a remarkable coincidence that this night they were speaking of escape and planning to cut a hole in the back of their tent through which they might sneak away into the jungle after the camp had settled down for the night and their sentry should be dozing at his post. And while they conversed the sentry before their tent rose and strolled away, and a moment later they heard a scratching upon the back of the tent. Their conversation ceased, and they sat with eyes riveted upon the point where the fabric of the tent moved to the pressure of the scratching without.

Presently a voice spoke in a low whisper. 'Memsahib Drinov!'

'Who is it? What do you want?' asked Zora in a low voice.

'I have found a way to escape. I can help you if you wish.'

'Who are you?' demanded Zora.

'I am Bukula,' and Zora at once recognized the name as that of one of the blacks that Abu Batn had forced to accompany him from the base camp.

'Put out your lantern,' whispered Bukula. 'The sentry has gone away. I will come in and tell you my plans.'

Zora rose and blew out the candle, and a moment later the two captives saw Bukula crawling into the interior of the tent. 'Listen, Memsahib,' he said, 'the boys that Abu Batn stole from Bwana Zveri are running away tonight. We are going back to the safari. We will take you two with us, if you want to come.'

'Yes,' said Zora, 'we will come.'

'Good!' said Bukula. 'Now listen well to what I tell you. The sentry will not come back, but we cannot all go out at once. First I will take this other Memsahib with me out into the jungle where the boys are waiting; then I will return for you. You can make talk to her. Tell her to follow me and to make no noise.'

Zora turned to La. 'Follow Bukula,' she said. 'We are going tonight. I will come after you.'

'I understand,' replied La.

'It is all right, Bukula,' said Zora. 'She understands.'

Bukula stepped to the entrance to the tent and looked quickly about the camp. 'Come!' he said, and, followed by La, disappeared quickly from Zora's view.

The European girl fully realized the risk that they ran in going into the jungle alone with these half-savage blacks, yet she trusted them far more implicitly than she did the Arabs and, too, she felt that she and La together might circumvent any treachery upon the part of any of the negroes, the majority of whom she knew would be loyal and faithful. Waiting in the silence and loneliness of the darkened tent, it seemed to Zora that it took Bukula an unnecessarily long time to return for her; but when minute after minute dragged slowly past until she felt that she had waited for hours and there was no sign either of the black or the sentry, her fears were aroused in earnest. Presently she determined not to wait any longer for Bukula, but to go out into the jungle in search of the escaping party. She thought that perhaps Bukula had been unable to return without risking detection and that they were all waiting just beyond the camp for a favourable opportunity to return to her. As she arose to put her decision into action she heard footsteps approaching the tent, and, thinking that they were Bukula's, she waited; but instead she saw the flapping robe and the long-barrelled musket of an Arab silhouetted against the lesser darkness of the exterior as the man stuck his head inside the tent. 'Where is Hajellan?' he demanded, giving the name of the departed sentry.

'How should we know?' retorted Zora in a sleepy voice. 'Why do you awaken us thus in the middle of the night? Are we keepers of your fellows?'

The fellow grumbled something in reply and then, turning, called aloud across the camp, announcing to all who might hear that Hajellan was missing and inquiring if any had seen him. Other warriors strolled over then, and there was a great deal of speculation as to what had become of Hajellan. The name of the missing man was called aloud many times, but there was no response, and finally the sheikh came and questioned everyone. 'The women are in the tent yet?' he demanded of the new sentry.

'Yes,' replied the man. 'I have talked with them.'

'It is strange,' said Abu Batn, and then, 'Ibn Dammuk!' he cried. 'Where art thou, Ibn? Hajellan was one of thy men.' There was no answer. 'Where is Ibn Dammuk?'

'He is not here,' said a man standing near the sheikh.

'Nor are Fodil and Dareyem,' said another.

'Search the camp and see who is missing,' commanded Abu Batn; and when the search had been made they found that Ibn Dammuk, Hajellan, Fodil, and Dareyem were missing with five of the blacks.

'Ibn Dammuk has deserted us,' said Abu Batn. 'Well, let it go. There will be fewer with whom to share the reward we shall reap when we are paid for the two women,' and thus reconciling himself to the loss of four good fighting men, Abu Batn repaired to his tent and resumed his interrupted slumber.

Weighted down by apprehension as to the fate of La and disappointment occasioned by her own failure to escape, Zora spent an almost sleepless night, yet fortunate for her peace of mind was it that she did not know the truth.

Bukula moved silently into the jungle, followed by La; and when they had gone a short distance from the camp, the girl saw the dark forms of men standing in a little group ahead of them. The Arabs, in their tell-tale thobs, were hidden in the underbrush, but their slaves had removed their own white robes and, with Bukula, were standing naked but for G strings, thus carrying conviction to the mind of the girl that only black prisoners of Abu Batn awaited her. When she came among them, however, she learned her mistake; but too late to save herself, for she was quickly seized by many hands and effectually gagged before she could give the alarm. Then Ibn Dammuk and his Arab companions appeared, and silently the party moved on down the river through the dark forest, though not before they had subdued the enraged high priestess of The Flaming God, secured her wrists behind her back, and placed a rope about her neck.

All night they fled, for Ibn Dammuk well guessed what the wrath of Abu Batn would be when, in the morning, he discovered the trick that had been played upon him; and when morning dawned they were far away from camp, but still Ibn Dammuk pushed on, after a brief halt for a hurried breakfast.

Long since had the gag been removed from La's mouth, and now Ibn Dammuk walked beside her gloating upon his prize. He spoke to her, but La could not understand him and only strode on in haughty disdain, biding her time against the moment when she might be revenged and inwardly sorrowing over her separation from Zora, for whom a strange affection had been aroused in her savage breast.

Toward noon the party withdrew from the game trail which they had been following and made camp near the river. It was here that Ibn Dammuk made a fatal blunder. Goaded to passion by close proximity to the beautiful woman for whom he had conceived a mad infatuation, the Arab gave way to his desire to be alone with her; and leading her along a little trail that paralleled the river, he took her away out of sight of his companions; and when they had gone perhaps a hundred yards from camp, he seized her in his arms and sought to kiss her lips.

With equal safety might Ibn Dammuk have embraced a lion. In the heat of his passion he forgot many things, among them the dagger that hung always at his side. But La of Opar did not forget. With the coming of daylight she had noticed that dagger, and ever since she had coveted it; and now as the man pressed her close, her hand sought and found its hilt. For an instant she seemed to surrender. She let her body go limp in his arms, while her own, firm and beautifully rounded, crept about him, one to his right shoulder, the other beneath his left arm. But as yet she did not give him her lips, and then as he struggled to possess them the hand upon his shoulder seized him suddenly by the throat. The long, tapered fingers that seemed so soft and white were suddenly claws of steel that closed upon his windpipe; and simultaneously the hand that had crept so softly beneath his left arm drove his own long dagger into his heart from beneath his shoulder blade.

The single cry that he might have given was choked in his throat. For an instant the tall form of Ibn Dammuk stood rigidly erect; then it slumped forward, and the girl let it slip to the earth. She spurned it once with her foot, then removed from it the girdle and sheath for the dagger, wiped the bloody blade upon the man's thob and hurried on up the little river trail until she found an opening in the underbrush that led away from the stream. On and on she went until exhaustion overtook her; and then, with her remaining strength, she climbed into a tree in search of much needed rest.

*

Wayne Colt watched the shadowy figure approach the mouth of the corridor where his cell lay. He wondered if this was a messenger of death, coming to lead him to sacrifice. Nearer and nearer it came until presently it stopped before the bars of his cell door; and then a soft voice spoke to him in a low whisper and in a tongue which he could not understand, and he knew that his visitor was a woman.

Prompted by curiosity, he came close to the bars. A soft hand reached in and touched him, almost caressingly. A full moon rising above the high walls that ring the sacrificial court suddenly flooded the mouth of the corridor and the entrance to Colt's cell in silvery light, and in it the American saw the figure of a young girl pressed against the cold iron of the grating. She handed him food, and when he took it she caressed his hand and drawing it to the bars pressed her lips against it.

Wayne Colt was nonplussed. He could not know that Nao, the little priestess, had been the victim of love at first sight, that to her mind and eyes, accustomed to the sight of males only in the form of the hairy, grotesque priests of Opar, this stranger appeared a god indeed.

A slight noise attracted Nao's attention toward the court and, as she turned, the moonlight flooded her face, and the American saw that she was very lovely. Then she turned back toward him, her dark eyes wells of adoration, her full, sensitive lips trembling with emotion as, still clinging to his hand, she spoke rapidly in low liquid tones.

She was trying to tell Colt that at noon of the second day he was to be offered in sacrifice to the Flaming God, that she did not wish him to die and if it were possible she would help him, but that she did not know how that would be possible.

Colt shook his head. 'I cannot understand you, little one,' he said, and Nao, though she could not interpret his words, sensed the futility of her own. Then, raising one of her hands from his, she made a great circle in a vertical plane from east to west with a slender index finger, indicating the path of the sun across the heavens; and then she started a second circle, which she stopped at zenith, indicating high noon of the second day. For an instant her raised hand poised dramatically aloft; and then, the fingers closing as though around the hilt of an imaginary sacrificial knife, she plunged the invisible point deep into her bosom.

'Thus will Oah destroy you,' she said, reaching through the bars and touching Colt over the heart.

The American thought that he understood the meaning of her pantomime, which he then repeated, plunging the imaginary blade into his own breast and looking questioningly at Nao.

In reply she nodded sadly, and the tears welled to her eyes.

As plainly as though he had understood her words, Colt realized that here was a friend who would help him if she could, and reaching through the bars, he drew the girl gently toward him and pressed his lips against her forehead. With a low sob Nao encircled his neck with her arms and pressed her face to his. Then, as suddenly, she released him and, turning, hurried away on silent feet, to disappear in the gloomy shadows of an archway at one side of the court of sacrifice.

Colt ate the food that she had brought him and for a long time lay pondering the inexplicable forces which govern the acts of men. What train of circumstances leading down out of a mysterious past had produced this single human being in a city of enemies in whom, all unsuspecting, there must always have existed a germ of potential friendship for him, an utter stranger and alien, of·whose very existence she could not possibly have dreamed before this day. He tried to convince himself that the girl had been prompted to her act by pity for his plight, but he knew in his heart that a more powerful motive impelled her.

Colt had been attracted to many women, but he had never loved; and he wondered if that was the way that love came and if some day it would seize him as it had seized this girl; and he wondered also if, had conditions been different, he might have been as strongly attracted to her. If not, then there seemed to be something wrong in the scheme of things; and still puzzling over this riddle of the ages, he fell asleep upon the hard floor of his cell.

With morning a hairy priest came and gave him food and water, and during the day others came and watched him, as though he were a wild beast in a menagerie. And so the long day dragged on, and once again night came – his last night.

He tried to picture what the final ceremony would be like. It seemed almost incredible that in the twentieth century he was to be offered as a human sacrifice to some heathen deity, but yet the pantomime of the girl and the concrete evidence of the bloody altar and the grinning skulls assured him that such must be the very fate awaiting him upon the morrow. He thought of his family and his friends at home; they would never know what had become of him. He weighed his sacrifice against the mission that he had undertaken and he had no regret, for he knew that it had not been in vain. Far away, already near the coast, was the message he had dispatched by the runner. That would ensure that he had not failed in his part for the sake of a great principle for which, if necessary, he was glad to lay down his life. He was glad that he had acted promptly and sent the message when he had for now, upon the morrow, he could go to his death without vain regrets.

He did not want to die, and he made many plans during the day to seize upon the slightest opportunity that might be presented to him to escape.

He wondered what had become of the girl and if she would come again now that it was dark. He wished that she would, for he craved the companionship of a friend during his last hours; but as the night wore on, he gave up the hope and sought to forget the morrow in sleep.

As Wayne Colt moved restlessly upon his hard couch, Firg, a lesser priest of Opar, snored upon his pallet of straw in the small, dark recess that was his bed chamber. Firg was the keeper of the keys, and so impressed was he with the importance of his duties that he never would permit anyone even to touch the sacred emblems of his trust, and probably because it was well known that Firg would die in defence of them they were entrusted to him. Not with justice could Firg have laid any claim to intellectuality, if he had known that such a thing existed. He was only an abysmal brute of a man and, like many men, far beneath the so-called brutes in many of the activities of mind. When he slept, all his faculties were asleep, which is not true of wild beasts when they sleep.

Firg's cell was in one of the upper stories of the ruins that still remained intact. It was upon a corridor that encircled the main temple court – a corridor that was now in dense shadow, since the moon, touching it early in the night, had now passed on; so that the figure creeping stealthily toward the entrance to Firg's chamber would have been noticeable only to one who happened to be quite close. It moved silently, but without hesitation, until it came to the entrance beyond which Firg lay. There it paused, listening, and when it heard Firg's noisy snoring, it entered quickly. Straight to the side of the sleeping man it moved, and there it knelt, searching with one hand lightly over his body, while the other grasped a long, sharp knife that hovered constantly above the hairy chest of the priest.

Presently it found what it wanted – a great ring, upon which were strung several enormous keys. A leather thong fastened the ring to Firg's girdle, and with the keen blade of the dagger the nocturnal visitor sought to sever the thong. Firg stirred, and instantly the creature at his side froze to immobility. Then the priest moved restlessly and commenced to snore again, and once more the dagger sawed at the leather thong. It passed through the strand unexpectedly and touched the metal of the ring lightly, but just enough to make the keys jangle ever so slightly.

Instantly Firg was awake, but he did not rise. He was never to rise again.

Silently, swiftly, before the stupid creature could realize his danger, the keen blade of the dagger had pierced his heart.

Soundlessly, Firg collapsed. His slayer hesitated a moment with poised dagger as though to make certain that the work had been well done. Then, wiping the tell-tale stains from the dagger's blade with the victim's loin cloth, the figure arose and hurried from the chamber, in one hand the great keys upon their golden ring.

Colt stirred uneasily in his sleep and then awakened with a start. In the waning moonlight he saw a figure beyond the grating of his cell. He heard a key turn in the massive lock. Could it be that they were coming for him? He rose to his feet, the urge of his last conscious thought strong upon him – escape. And then as the door swung open, a soft voice spoke, and he knew that the girl had returned.

She entered the cell and threw her arms about Colt's neck, drawing his lips down to hers. For a moment she clung to him, and then she released him and, taking one of his hands in hers, urged him to follow her; nor was the American loath to leave the depressing interior of the death cell.

On silent feet Nao led the way across the corner of the sacrificial court, through a dark archway into a gloomy corridor. Winding and twisting, keeping always in dark shadows, she led him along a circuitous route through the ruins, until, after what seemed an eternity to Colt, the girl opened a low, strong wooden door and led him into the great entrance hall of the temple, through the mighty portal of which he could see the inner wall of the city.

Here Nao halted, and coming close to the man looked up into his eyes. Again her arms stole about his neck, and again she pressed her lips to his. Her cheeks were wet with tears, and her voice broke with little sobs that she tried to stifle as she poured her love into the ears of the man who could not understand.

She had brought him here to offer him his freedom, but she could not let him go yet. She clung to him, caressing him and crooning to him.

For a quarter of an hour she held him there, and Colt had not the heart to tear himself away, but at last she released him and pointed toward the opening in the inner wall.

'Go!' she said, 'taking the heart of Nao with you. I shall never see you again, but at least I shall always have the memory of this hour to carry through life with me.'

Wayne stopped and kissed her hand, the slender, savage little hand that had but just killed that her lover might live. Though of that, Wayne knew nothing.

She pressed her dagger with its sheath upon him that he might not go out into the savage world unarmed, and then he turned away from her and moved slowly toward the inner wall. At the entrance of the opening he paused and turned about. Dimly, in the moonlight, he saw the figure of the little priestess standing very erect in the shadows of the ancient ruins. He raised his hand and waved a final, silent farewell.

A great sadness depressed Colt as he passed through the inner wall and crossed the court to freedom, for he knew that he had left behind him a sad and hopeless heart, in the bosom of one who must have risked death, perhaps, to save him – a perfect friend of whom he could but carry a vague memory of a half-seen lovely face, a friend whose name he did not know, the only tokens of whom he had carried away with him were the memory of hot kisses and a slender dagger.

And thus, as Wayne Colt walked across the moonlit plain of Opar, the joy of his escape was tempered by sadness as he recalled the figure of the forlorn little priestess standing in the shadows of the ruins.

CHAPTER XI

Lost in the Jungle

It was some time after the uncanny scream had disturbed the camp of the conspirators before the men could settle down to rest again.

Zveri believed that they had been followed by a band of Oparian warriors, who might be contemplating a night attack, and so he placed a heavy guard about the camp; but his blacks were confident that that unearthly cry had broken from no human throat.

Depressed and dispirited, the men resumed their march the following morning. They made an early start and by dint of much driving arrived at the base camp just before dark. The sight that met their eyes there filled them with consternation. The camp had disappeared, and in the centre of the clearing where it had been pitched a pile of ashes suggested that disaster had overtaken the party that had been left behind.

This new misfortune threw Zveri into a maniacal rage, but there was no one present upon whom he might lay the blame, and so he was reduced to the expedient of tramping back and forth while he cursed his luck in loud tones and several languages.

From a tree Tarzan watched him. He, too, was at a loss to understand the nature of the disaster that seemed to have overtaken the camp during the absence of the main party, but as he saw that it caused the leader intense anguish, the ape-man was pleased.

The blacks were confident that this was another manifestation of the anger of the malign spirit that had been haunting them, and they were all for deserting the ill-starred white man, whose every move ended in failure or disaster.

Zveri's powers of leadership deserve full credit, since from the verge of almost certain mutiny he forced his men by means of both cajolery and threat to remain with him. He set them to building shelters for the entire party, and immediately he dispatched messengers to his various agents, urging them to forward necessary supplies at once. He knew that certain things he needed already were on the way from the coast – uniforms, rifles, ammunition. But now he particularly needed provisions and trade goods. To ensure discipline, he kept the men working constantly, either in adding to the comforts of the camp, enlarging the clearing, or hunting fresh meats.

And so the days passed and became weeks, and meanwhile Tarzan watched in waiting. He was in no hurry, for hurry is not a characteristic of the beasts. He roamed the jungle, often at a considerable distance from Zveri's camp, but occasionally he would return, though not to molest them, preferrring to let them lull themselves into a stupor of tranquil security, the shattering of which in his own good time would have dire effect upon their morale. He understood the psychology of terror, and it was with terror that he would defeat them.

To the camp of Abu Batn, upon the border of the Galla country, word had come from spies that he had sent out that the Galla warriors were gathering to prevent his passage through their territory. Being weakened by the desertion of so many men, the sheikh dared not defy the bravery and numbers of the Galla warriors, but he knew that he must make some move, since it seemed inevitable that pursuit must overtake him from the rear, if he remained where he was much longer.

At last scouts that he had sent far up the river on the opposite side returned to report that a way to the west seemed clear along a more northerly route, and so, breaking camp, Abu Batn moved north with his lone prisoner.

Great had been his rage when he discovered that Ibn Dammuk had stolen La, and now he redoubled his precaution to prevent the escape of Zora Drinov. So closely was she guarded that any possibility of escape seemed almost hopeless. She had learned the fate for which Abu Batn was reserving her, and now, depressed and melancholy, her mind was occupied with plans for self-destruction. For a time she had harboured the hope that Zveri would overtake the Arabs and rescue her, but this she had long since discarded, as day after day passed without bringing the hoped-for succour.

She could not know, of course, the straits in which Zveri had found himself. He had not dared to detach a party of his men to search for her, fearing that, in their mutinous state of mind, they might murder any of his lieutenants that he placed in charge of them and return to their own tribe, where, through the medium of gossip, word of his expedition and its activities might reach his enemies; nor could he lead all of his force upon such an expedition in person, since he must remain at the base camp to receive the supplies that he knew would presently be arriving.

Perhaps, had he known definitely the danger that confronted Zora, he would have cast aside every other consideration and gone to her rescue; but being naturally suspicious of the loyalty of all men, he had persuaded himself that Zora had deliberately deserted him – a half-hearted conviction that had at least the effect of rendering his naturally unpleasant disposition infinitely more unbearable, so that those who should have been his companions and his support in his hour of need contrived as much as possible to keep out of his way.

And while these things were transpiring, little Nkima sped through the jungle upon a mission. In the service of his beloved master, little Nkima could hold to a single thought and a line of action for considerable periods of time at a stretch; but eventually his attention was certain to be attracted by some extraneous matter and then, for hours, perhaps, he would forget all about whatever duty had been imposed upon him; but when it again occurred to him, he would carry on entirely without any appreciation of the fact that there had been a break in the continuity of his endeavour.

Tarzan, of course, was entirely aware of this inherent weakness in his little friend; but he knew, too, from experience that, however many lapses might occur, Nkima would never entirely abandon any design upon which his mind had been fixed; and having himself none of civilized man's slavish sub-servience to time, he was prone to overlook Nkima's erratic performance of a duty as a fault of almost negligible consequence. Some day Nkima would arrive at his destination. Perhaps it would be too late. If such a thought occurred at all to the apeman, doubtless he passed it off with a shrug.

But time is of the essence of many things to civilized man. He fumes and frets, and reduces his mental and physical efficiency if he is not accomplish-ing something concrete during the passage of every minute of that medium which seems to him like a flowing river, the waters of which are utterly wasted if they are not utilized as they pass by.

Imbued by some such insane conception of time, Wayne Colt sweated and stumbled through the jungle, seeking his companions as though the very fate of the universe hung upon the slender chance that he should reach them without the loss of a second.

The futility of his purpose would have been entirely apparent to him could he have known that he was seeking his companions in the wrong direction. Wayne Colt was lost. Fortunately for him he did not know it; at least not yet. That stupefying conviction was to come later.

Days passed and still his wanderings revealed no camp. He was hard put to it to find food, and his fare was meagre and often revolting, consisting of such fruits as he had already learned to know and of rodents, which he man-aged to bag only with the greatest difficulty and an appalling waste of that precious time which he still prized above all things. He had cut himself a stout stick and would lie in wait along some tiny runway where observation had taught him he might expect to find his prey, until some unwary little creature came within striking distance. He had learned that dawn and dusk were the best hunting hours for the only animals that he could hope to bag, and he learned other things as he moved through the grim jungle, all of which pertained to his struggle for existence. He had learned, for instance, that it was wiser for him to take to the trees whenever he heard a strange noise. Usually the animals got out of his way as he approached; but once a rhinoceros charged him, and again he almost stumbled upon a lion at his kill. Providence intervened in each instance and he escaped unkilled, but thus he learned caution.

About noon one day he came to a river that effectually blocked his further progress in the direction that he had been travelling. By this time the conviction was strong upon him that he was utterly lost, and not knowing which direction he should take, he decided to follow the line of least resistance and travel downhill with the river, upon the shore of which he was positive that sooner or later he must discover a native village.

He had proceeded no great distance in the new direction, following a hardpacked trail, worn deep by the countless feet of many beasts, when his attention was arrested by a sound that reached his ears dimly from a distance. It came from somewhere ahead of him and his hearing, now far more acute than it ever had been before, told him that something was approaching. Following the practice that he had found most conducive to longevity since he had been wandering alone and ill-armed against the dangers of the jungle, he flung himself quickly into a tree and sought a point of vantage from where he could see the trail below him. He could not see it for any distance ahead, so tortuously did it wind through the jungle. Whatever was coming would not be visible until it was almost directly beneath him, but that now was of no importance. This experience of the jungle had taught him patience, and perchance he was learning, too, a little of the valuelessness of time, for he settled himself comfortably to wait at his ease.

The noise that he heard was little more than an imperceptible rustling, but presently it assumed a new volume and a new significance, so that now he was sure that it was someone running rapidly along the trail, and not one but two – he distinctly heard the footfalls of the heavier creature mingling with those he had first heard.

And then he heard a man's voice cry 'Stop!' and now the sounds were very close to him, just around the first bend ahead. The sound of running feet stopped, to be followed by that of a scuffle and strange oaths in a man's voice.

And then a woman's voice spoke, 'Let me go! You will never get me where you are taking me alive.'

'Then I'll take you for myself now,' said the man.

Colt had heard enough. There had been something familiar in the tones of the woman's voice. Silently he dropped to the trail, drawing his dagger, and stepped quickly toward the sounds of the altercation. As he rounded the bend in the trail, he saw just before him only a man's back – by thôb and thorîb an Arab – but beyond the man and in his clutches Colt knew the woman was hidden by the flowing robes of her assailant.

Leaping forward, he seized the fellow by the shoulder and jerked him suddenly about; and as the man faced him Colt saw that it was Abu Batn, and now, too, he saw why the voice of the woman had seemed familiar – she was Zora Drinov.

Abu Batn purpled with rage at the interruption, but great as was his anger so, too, was his surprise as he recognized the American. Just for an instant he thought that possibly this was the advance guard of a party of searchers and avengers from Zveri's camp, but when he had time to observe the unkempt, disheveled, unarmed condition of Colt he realized that the man was alone and doubtless lost.

'Dog of a Nasrâny!' he cried, jerking away from Colt's grasp. 'Lay not your filthy hand upon a true believer.' At the same time he moved to draw his pistol, but in that instant Colt was upon him again, and the two men went down in the narrow trail, the American on top.

What happened then, happened very quickly. As Abu Batn drew his pistol, he caught the hammer in the folds of his thôb, so that the weapon was discharged. The bullet went harmlessly into the ground, but the report warned Colt of his imminent danger, and in self defence he ran his blade through the sheikh's throat.

As he rose slowly from the body of the sheikh, Zora Drinov grasped him by the arm. 'Quick!' she said. 'That shot will bring the others. They must not find us.'

He did not wait to question her, but, stooping, quickly salvaged Abu Batn's weapons and ammunition, including a long musket that lay in the trail beside him; and then with Zora in the lead they ran swiftly up the trail down which he had just come.

'Can you climb?' he asked.

'Yes,' she replied. 'Why?'

'We are going to take to the trees,' he said. 'We can go into the jungle a short distance and throw them off the trail.'

'Good!' she said, and with his assistance clambered into the branches of a tree beneath which they stood.

Fortunately for them, several large trees grew close together so that they were able to make their way with comparative ease a full hundred feet from the trail, where, climbing high into the branches of a great tree, they were effectually hidden from sight in all directions.

When at last they were seated side by side in a great crotch, Zora turned toward Colt. 'Comrade Colt!' she said. 'What has happened? What are you doing here alone? Were you looking for me?'

The man grinned. 'I was looking for the whole party,' he said. 'I have seen no one since we entered Opar. Where is the camp, and why was Abu Batn pursuing you?'

'We are a long way from the camp,' replied Zora. 'I do not know how far, though I could return to it if it were not for the Arabs.' And then briefly she told the story of Abu Batn's treachery and of her captivity. 'The sheikh made a temporary camp shortly after noon today. The men were very tired, and for the first time in days they relaxed their vigilance over me. I realized that at last the moment I had been awaiting so anxiously had arrived, and while they slept I escaped into the jungle. My absence must have been discovered shortly after I left, and Abu Batn overtook me. The rest you witnessed.'

'Fate functioned deviously and altogether wonderfully,' he said. 'To think that your only chance of rescue hinged upon the contingency of my capture at Opar!'

She smiled. 'Fate reaches back further than that,' she said. 'Suppose you had not been born?'

'Then Abu Batn would have carried you off to the harem of some black sultan, or perhaps another man would have been captured at Opar.'

'I am glad that you were born,' said Zora.

'Thank you,' said Colt.

While listening for signs of pursuit, they conversed in low tones, Colt narrating in detail the events leading up to his capture, though some of the details of his escape he omitted through a sense of loyalty to the nameless girl who had aided him. Neither did he stress Zveri's lack of control over his men, or what Colt considered his inexcusable cowardice in leaving himself and Romero to their fate within the walls of Opar without attempting to succour them, for he believed that the girl was Zveri's sweetheart and he did not wish to offend her.

'What became of Comrade Romero?' she asked.

'I do not know,' he said. 'The last I saw of him he was standing his ground, fighting off those crooked little demons.'

'Alone?' she asked.

'I was pretty well occupied myself,' he said.

'I do not mean that,' she replied. 'Of course, I know you were there with Romero, but who else?'

'The others had not arrived,' said Colt.

'You mean you two went in alone?' she asked.

Colt hesitated. 'You see,' he said, 'the blacks refused to enter the city, so the rest of us had to go in or abandon the attempt to get the treasures.'

'But only you and Miguel did go in. Is that not true?' she demanded.

'I passed out so soon, you see,' he said with a laugh, 'that really I do not know exactly what did happen.'

The girl's eyes narrowed. 'It was beastly,' she said.

As they talked, Colt's eyes were often upon the girl's face. How lovely she was, even beneath the rags and the dirt that were the outward symbols of her captivity among the Arabs. She was a little thinner than when he had last seen her, and her eyes were tired and her face drawn from privation and worry. But, perhaps, by very contrast her beauty was the more startling. It seemed incredible that she could love the coarse, loud-mouthed Zveri, who was her antithesis in every respect.

Presently she broke a short silence. 'We must try to get back to the base camp,' she said. 'It is vital that I be there. So much must be done, so much that no one else can do.'

'You think only of the cause,' he said; 'never of yourself. You are very loyal.'

'Yes,' she said in a low voice. 'I am loyal to the thing I have sworn to accomplish.'

'I am afraid,' he said, 'that for the past few days I have been thinking more of my own welfare than of that of the proletariat.'

'I am afraid that at heart you are still bourgeois,' she said, 'and that you cannot yet help looking upon the proletariat with contempt.'

'What makes you say that?' he asked. 'I am sure that I said nothing to warrant it.'

'Often a slight unconscious inflection in the use of a word alters the significance of a whole statement, revealing a speaker's secret thoughts.'

Colt laughed good naturedly. 'You are a dangerous person to talk to,' he said. 'Am I to be shot at sunrise?'

She looked at him seriously. 'You are different from the others,' she said. 'I think you could never imagine how suspicious they are. What I have said is only in the way of warning you to watch your every word when you are talking with them. Some of them are narrow and ignorant, and they are already suspicious of you because of your antecedents. They are sensitively jealous of a new importance which they believe their class has attained.'

'*Their* class?' he asked. 'I thought you told me once that you were of the proletariat?'

If he had thought that he had surprised her and that she would show embarrassment, he was mistaken. She met his eyes squarely and without wavering. 'I am,' she said, 'but I can still see the weaknesses of my class.'

He looked at her steadily for a long moment, the shadow of a smile touching his lips. 'I do not believe—'

'Why do you stop?' she asked. 'What is it that you do not believe?'

'Forgive me,' he said. 'I was starting to think aloud.'

'Be careful, Comrade Colt,' she warned him. 'Thinking aloud is sometimes fatal;' but she tempered her words with a smile.

Further conversation was interrupted by the sound of the voices of men in the distance. 'They are coming,' said the girl.

Colt nodded, and the two remained silent, listening to the sounds of approaching voices and footsteps. The men came abreast of them and halted and Zora, who understood the Arab tongue, heard one of them say, 'The trail stops here. They have gone into the jungle.'

'Who can the man be who is with her?' asked another.

'It is a Nasrâny. I can tell by the imprint of his feet,' said another.

'They would go toward the river,' said a third. 'That is the way that I should go if I were trying to escape.'

'Wullah! You speak words of wisdom,' said the first speaker. 'We will spread out here and search toward the river; but look out for the Nasrâny. He has the pistol and the musket of the sheikh.'

The two fugitives heard the sound of pursuit diminishing in the distance as the Arabs forced their way into the jungle toward the river. 'I think we had better get out of this,' said Colt; 'and while it may be pretty hard going, I believe that we had better stick to the brush for awhile and keep on away from the river.'

'Yes,' replied Zora, 'for that is the general direction in which the camp lies.' And so they commenced their long and weary march in search of their comrades.

They were still pushing through dense jungle when night overtook them. Their clothes were in rags and their bodies scratched and torn, mute and painful reminders of the thorny way that they had traversed.

Hungry and thirsty they made a dry camp among the branches of a tree, where Colt built a rude platform for the girl, while he prepared to sleep upon the ground at the foot of the great bole. But to this, Zora would not listen.

'That will not do at all,' she said. 'We are in no position to permit ourselves to be victims of every silly convention that would ordinarily order our lives in civilized surroundings. I appreciate your thoughtful consideration, but I would rather have you up here in the tree with me than down there where the first hunting lion that passed might get you,' And so with the girl's help Colt built another platform close to the one that he had built for her; and as darkness fell, they stretched their tired bodies on their rude couches and sought to sleep.

Presently Colt dozed, and in his dream he saw the slender figure of a star-eyed goddess, whose cheeks were wet with tears, but when he took her in his arms and kissed her he saw that she was Zora Drinov; and then a hideous sound from the jungle below awakened him with a start, so that he sat up, seizing the musket of the sheikh in readiness.

'A hunting lion,' said the girl in a low voice.

'Phew!' exclaimed Colt. 'I must have been asleep, for that certainly gave me a start.'

'Yes, you were asleep,' said the girl. 'I heard you talking,' and he felt that he detected laughter in her voice.

'What was I saying?' asked Colt.

'Maybe you wouldn't want to hear. It might embarrass you,' she told him.

'No. Come ahead. Tell me.'

'You said "I love you".'

'Did I, really?'

'Yes. I wonder whom you were talking to,' she said, banteringly.

'I wonder,' said Colt, recalling that in his dream the figure of one girl had merged into that of another.

The lion, hearing their voices, moved away growling. He was not hunting the hated man-things.

CHAPTER XII

Down Trails of Terror

Slow days dragged by for the man and woman searching for their comrades – days filled with fatiguing effort, most of which was directed toward the procuring of food and water for their sustenance. Increasingly was Colt impressed by the character and personality of his companion. With apprehension he noticed that she was gradually weakening beneath the strain of fatigue and the scant and inadequate food that he had been able to procure for her. But yet she kept a brave front and tried to hide her condition from him. Never once had she complained. Never by word or look had she reproached him for his inability to procure sufficient food, a failure which he looked upon as indicative of inefficiency. She did not know that he himself often went hungry that she might eat, telling her when he returned with food that he had eaten his share where he had found it, a deception that was made possible by the fact that when he hunted he often left Zora to rest in some place of comparative security, that she might not be subjected to needless exertion.

He left her thus today, safe in a great tree beside a winding stream. She was very tired. It seemed to her that now she was always tired. The thought of continuing the march appalled her, and yet she knew that it must be undertaken. She wondered how much longer she could go on before she sank exhausted for the last time. It was not, however, for herself that she was most concerned, but for this man – this scion of wealth, and capitalism, and power, whose constant consideration and cheerfulness and tenderness had been a revelation to her. She knew that when she could go no further, he would not leave her and that thus his chances of escape from the grim jungle would be jeopardized and perhaps lost forever because of her. She hoped, for his sake, that death would come quickly to her that, thus relieved of responsibility, he might move on more rapidly in search of that elusive camp that seemed to her now little more than a meaningless myth. But from the thought of death she shrank, not because of the fear of death, as well might have been the case, but for an entirely new reason, the sudden realization of which gave her a distinct shock. The tragedy of this sudden self-awakening left her numb with terror. It was a thought that must be put from her, one that she must not entertain even for an instant; and yet it persisted – persisted with a dull insistency that brought tears to her eyes.

Colt had gone farther afield than usual this morning in his search for food, for he had sighted an antelope; and, his imagination inflamed by the contemplation of so much meat in a single kill and what it would mean for Zora, he clung doggedly to the trail, lured further on by an occasional glimpse of his quarry in the distance.

The antelope was only vaguely aware of an enemy, for he was upwind from Colt and had not caught his scent, while the occasional glimpses he had had of the man had served mostly to arouse his curiosity; so that though he moved away he stopped often and turned back in an effort to satisfy his wonderment. But presently he waited a moment too long. In his desperation, Colt chanced a long shot; and as the animal dropped, the man could not stifle a loud cry of exultation.

As time, that she had no means of measuring, dragged on, Zora grew increasingly apprehensive on Colt's account. Never before had he left her for so long a time, so that she began to construct all sorts of imaginary calamities that might have overtaken him. She wished now that she had gone with him. If she had thought it possible to track him, she would have followed him; but she knew that that was impossible. However, her forced inactivity made her restless. Her cramped position in the tree became unendurable; and then, suddenly assailed by thirst, she lowered herself to the ground and walked toward the river.

When she had drunk and was about to return to the tree, she heard the sound of something approaching from the direction in which Colt had gone. Instantly her heart leaped with gladness, her depression and even much of her fatigue seemed to vanish, and she realized suddenly how very lonely she had been without him. How dependent we are upon the society of our fellow-men, we seldom realize until we become the victims of enforced solitude. There were tears of happiness in Zora Drinov's eyes as she advanced to meet Colt. Then the bushes before her parted and there stepped into view, before her horrified gaze, a monstrous, hairy ape.

To-yat, the king, was as much surprised as the girl but his reactions were almost opposite. It was with no horror that he viewed this soft, white she Mangani. To the girl there was naught but ferocity in his mien, though in his breast was an entirely different emotion. He lumbered toward her; and then, as though released from a momentary paralysis, Zora turned to flee. But how futilely, she realized an instant later as a hairy paw gripped her roughly by the shoulder. For an instant she had forgotten the sheikh's pistol that Colt always left with her for self-protection. Jerking it from its holster, she turned upon the beast; but To-yat, seeing in the weapon a club with which she intended to attack him, wrenched it from her grasp and hurled it aside; and then, though she struggled and fought to regain her freedom, he lifted her lightly to his hip and lumbered off into the jungle in the direction that he had been going.

Colt tarried at his kill only long enough to remove the feet, the head and the viscera, that he might by that much reduce the weight of the burden that he must carry back to camp, for he was quite well aware that his privation had greatly reduced his strength.

Lifting the carcass to his shoulder, he started back toward camp, exulting in the thought that for once he was returning with an ample quantity of strength-giving flesh. As he staggered along beneath the weight of the small antelope, he made plans that imparted a rosy hue to the future. They would rest now until their strength returned; and while they were resting they would smoke all of the meat of his kill that they did not eat at once, and thus they would have a reserve supply of food that he felt would carry them a great distance. Two days' rest with plenty of food would, he was positive, fill them with renewed hope and vitality.

As he started laboriously along the back trail, he commenced to realize that he had come much farther than he had thought, but it had been well worthwhile. Even though he reached Zora in a state of utter exhaustion, he did not fear for a minute but that he would reach her, so confident was he of his own powers of endurance and the strength of his will.

As he staggered at last to his goal, he looked up into the tree and called her by name. There was no reply. In that first brief instant of silence, a dull and sickening premonition of disaster crept over him. He dropped the carcass of the deer and looked hurriedly about.

'Zora! Zora!' he cried; but only the silence of the jungle was his answer. Then his searching eyes found the pistol of Abu Batn where To-yat had dropped it; and his worst fears were substantiated, for he knew that if Zora had gone away of her own volition she would have taken the weapon with her. She had been attacked by something and carried off, of that he was positive; and presently as he examined the ground closely he discovered the imprints of a great man-like foot.

A sudden madness seized Wayne Colt. The cruelty of the jungle, the injustice of nature aroused within his breast a red rage. He wanted to kill the thing that had stolen Zora Drinov. He wanted to tear it with his hands and rend it with his teeth. All the savage instincts of primitive man were reborn within him as, forgetting the meat that the moment before had meant so much to him, he plunged headlong into the jungle upon the faint spoor of To-yat, the king ape.

La of Opar made her way slowly through the jungle after she had escaped from Ibn Dammuk and his companions. Her native city called to her, though she knew that she might not enter it in safety; but what place was there in all the world that she might go to? Something of a conception of the immensity of the great world had been impressed upon her during her wandering since she had left Opar, and the futility of searching further for Tarzan had been indelibly impressed upon her mind. So she would go back to the vicinity of Opar, and perhaps some day again Tarzan would come there. That great dangers beset her way she did not care, for La of Opar was indifferent to life that had never brought her much of happiness. She lived because she lived; and it is true that she would strive to prolong life because such is the law of nature, which imbues the most miserable unfortunates with as powerful an urge to prolong their misery as it gives to the fortunate few who are happy and contented a similar desire to live.

Presently she became aware of pursuit, and so she increased her speed and kept ahead of those who were following her. Finding a trail she followed it, knowing that if it permitted her to increase her speed it would permit her pursuers also to increase theirs, nor would she be able to hear them now as plainly as she had before, when they were forcing their way through the jungle. Still she was confident that they could not overtake her; but as she was moving swiftly on, a turn in the trail brought her to a sudden stop for there, blocking her retreat, stood a great, maned lion. This time La remembered the animal, not as Jad-bal-ja the hunting mate of Tarzan, but as the lion that had rescued her from the leopard, after Tarzan had deserted her.

Lions were familiar creatures to La of Opar, where they were often captured by the priests while cubs, and where it was not unusual to raise some of them occasionally as pets until their growing ferocity made them unsafe. Therefore, La knew that lions could associate with people without devouring them; and having had experience of this lion's disposition and having as little sense of fear as Tarzan himself, she quickly made her choice between the lion and the Arabs pursuing her and advanced directly toward the great beast, in whose attitude she saw there was no immediate menace. She was sufficiently a child of nature to know that death came quickly and painlessly in the embrace of a lion, and so she had no fear, but only a great curiosity.

Jad-bal-ja had long had the scent spoor of La in his nostrils, as she had moved with the wind along the jungle trails; and so he had awaited her, his curiosity aroused by the fainter scent spoor of the men who trailed her. Now as she came toward him along the trail, he stepped to one side that she might pass and, like a great cat, rubbed his maned neck against her legs.

La paused and laid a hand upon his head and spoke to him in low tones in the language of the first man – the language of the great apes that was the common language of her people, as it was Tarzan's language.

Hajellan, leading his men in pursuit of La, rounded a bend in the trail and stopped aghast. He saw a great lion facing him, a lion that bared its fangs now in an angry snarl; and beside the lion, one hand tangled in its thick black mane, stood the white woman.

The woman spoke a single word to the lion in a language that Hajellan did not understand. 'Kill!' said La in the language of the great apes.

So accustomed was the high priestess of the Flaming God to command that it did not occur to her that Numa might do other than obey; and so, although she did not know that it was thus that Tarzan had been accustomed to command Jad-bal-ja, she was not surprised when the lion crouched and charged.

Fodil and Dareyem had pushed close behind their companion as he halted, and great was their horror when they saw the lion leap forward. They turned and fled, colliding with the blacks behind them; but Hajellan only stood paralyzed with fright as Jad-bal-ja reared upon his hind feet and seized him, the great jaws crunching through the man's head and shoulders, cracking his skull like an egg shell. He gave the body a vicious shake and dropped it. Then he turned and looked inquiringly at La.

In the woman's heart was no more sympathy for her enemies than in the heart of Jad-bal-ja; she only wished to be rid of them. She did not care whether they lived or died, and so she did not urge Jad-bal-ja after those who had escaped. She wondered what the lion would do now that he had made his kill; and knowing that the vicinity of a feeding lion was no safe place, she turned and moved on along the trail. But Jad-bal-ja was no eater of man, not because he had any moral scruples, but because he was young and active and had no difficulty in killing prey that he relished far more than he did the salty flesh of man. Therefore, he left Hajellan lying where he had fallen and followed La along the shadowy jungle trails.

A black man, naked but for a G string, bearing a message from the coast for Zveri, paused where two trails crossed. From his left the wind was blowing, and to his sensitive nostrils it bore the faint stench that announced the presence of a lion. Without a moment's hesitation, the man vanished into the foliage of a tree that overhung the trail. Perhaps Simba was not hungry, perhaps Simba was not hunting; but the black messenger was taking no chances. He was sure that the lion was approaching, and he would wait here where he could see both trails until he discovered which one Simba took.

Watching with more or less indifference because of the safety of his sanctuary, the negro was ill-prepared for the shock which the sight that presently broke upon his vision induced. Never in the lowest depths of his superstition had he conceived such a scene as he now witnessed, and he blinked his eyes repeatedly to make sure that he was awake; but, no, there could be no mistake. It was indeed a white woman almost naked but for golden ornaments and a soft strip of leopard skin beneath her narrow stomacher – a white woman who walked with the fingers of one hand tangled in the black mane of a great golden lion.

Along the trail they came, and at the crossing they turned to the left into the trail that he had been following. As they disappeared from his view, the black man fingered the fetish that was suspended from a cord about his neck and prayed to Mulungo, the god of his people; and when he again set out toward his destination he took another and more circuitous route.

Often, after darkness had fallen, Tarzan had come to the camp of the conspirators and, perched in a tree above them, listened to Zveri outlining his plans to his companions; so that the ape-man was familiar with what they intended, down to the minutest detail.

Now, knowing that they would not be prepared to strike for some time, he was roaming the jungle far away from the sight and stench of man, enjoying to the full the peace and freedom that were his life. He knew that Nkima should have reached his destination by this time and delivered the message that Tarzan had dispatched by him. He was still puzzled by the strange disappearance of La and piqued by his inability to pick up her trail. He was genuinely grieved by her disappearance, for already he had his plans well formulated to restore her to her throne and punish her enemies; but he gave himself over to no futile regrets as he swung through the trees in sheer joy of living, or, when hunger overtook him, stalked his prey in the grim and terrible silence of the hunting beast.

Sometimes he thought of the good-looking young American, to whom he had taken a fancy in spite of the fact that he considered him an enemy. Had he known of Colt's now almost hopeless plight, it is possible that he would have gone to his rescue but he knew nothing of it.

So, alone and friendless, sunk to the uttermost depths of despair, Wayne Colt stumbled through the jungle in search of Zora Drinov and her abductor. But already he had lost the faint trail; and To-yat, far to his right, lumbered along with his captive safe from pursuit.

Weak from exhaustion and shock, thoroughly terrified now by the hopelessness of her hideous position, Zora had lost consciousness. To-yat feared that she was dead; but he carried her on, nevertheless, that he might at least have the satisfaction of exhibiting her to his tribe as evidence of his prowess and, perhaps, to furnish an excuse for another Dum-Dum. Secure in his might, conscious of few enemies that might with safety to themselves molest him, To-yat did not take the precaution of silence, but wandered on through the jungle heedless of all dangers.

Many were the keen ears and sensitive nostrils that carried the message of his passing to their owners, but to only one did the strange mingling of the scent spoor of the bull ape with that of a she-Mangani suggest a condition worthy of investigation. So as To-yat pursued his careless way another creature of the jungle, moving silently on swift feet, bore down upon him; and when, from a point of vantage, keen eyes beheld the shaggy bull and the slender, delicate girl, a lip curled in a silent snarl. A moment later To-yat, the king ape, was brought to a snarling, bristling halt as the giant figure of a bronzed Tarmangani dropped lightly into the trail before him, a living threat to his possession of his prize.

The wicked eyes of the bull shot fire and hate. 'Go away,' he said. 'I am To-yat. Go away or I kill.'

'Put down the she,' demanded Tarzan.

'No,' bellowed To-yat. 'She is mine.'

'Put down the she,' repeated Tarzan, 'and go your way; or I kill. I am Tarzan of the Apes, Lord of the Jungle!'

Tarzan drew the hunting knife of his father and crouched as he advanced towards the bull. To-yat snarled; and seeing that the other meant to give battle, he cast the body of the girl aside that he might not be handicapped. As they circled, each looking for an advantage, there came a sudden, terrific crashing sound in the jungle downwind from them.

Tantor, the elephant, asleep in the security of the depth of the forest, had been suddenly awakened by the growling of the two beasts. Instantly his nostrils caught a familiar scent spoor – the scent spoor of his beloved Tarzan – and his ears told him that he was facing in battle the great Mangani, whose scent was also strong in the nostrils of Tantor.

To the snapping and bending of trees, the great bull rushed through the forest; and as he emerged suddenly, towering above them, To-yat, the king ape, seeing death in those angry eyes and gleaming tusks, turned and fled into the jungle.

CHAPTER XIII
The Lion-Man

Peter Zveri was, in a measure, regaining some of the confidence that he had lost in the ultimate success of his plan, for his agents were succeeding at last in getting to him some of his much needed supplies, together with contingents of disaffected blacks wherewith to recruit his forces to sufficient numbers to ensure the success of his contemplated invasion of Italian Somaliland. It was his plan to make a swift and sudden incursion, destroying native villages and capturing an outpost or two, then retreating quickly across the border, pack away the French uniforms for possible future use and undertake the overthrow of Ras Tafari in Abyssinia, where his agents had assured him conditions were ripe for a revolution. With Abyssinia under his control to serve as a rallying point, his agents assured him that the native tribes of all Northern Africa would flock to his standards.

In distant Bokhara a fleet of two hundred planes – bombers, scouts, and fighting planes – made available through the greed of American capitalists, were being mobilized for a sudden dash across Persia and Arabia to his base in Abyssinia. With these to support his great native army, he felt that his position would be secure, the malcontents of Egypt would join forces with him and, with Europe embroiled in a war that would prevent any concerted action against him, his dream of empire might be assured and his position made impregnable for all time.

Perhaps it was a mad dream; perhaps Peter Zveri was mad – but, then, what great world conqueror has not been a little mad?

He saw his frontiers pushed towards the south as, little by little, he extended his dominion until one day he should rule a great continent – Peter I, Emperor of Africa.

'You seem happy, Comrade Zveri,' said little Antonio Mori.

'Why should I not be, Tony?' demanded the dreamer. 'I see success just before us. We should all be happy, but we are going to be very much happier later on.'

'Yes,' said Tony, 'when the Philippines are free, I shall be very happy. Do you not think that I should be a very big man back there, then, Comrade Zveri?'

'Yes,' said the Russian, 'but you can be a bigger man if you stay here and work for me. How would you like to be a Grand Duke, Tony?'

'A Grand Duke!' exclaimed the Filipino. 'I thought there were no more Grand Dukes.'

'But perhaps there may be again.'

'They were wicked men who ground down the working classes,' said Tony.

'To be a Grand Duke who grinds down the rich and takes money from them might not be so bad,' said Peter. 'Grand Dukes are very rich and powerful. Would you not like to be rich and powerful, Tony?'

'Well, of course, who would not?'

'Then always do as I tell you, Tony; and some day I shall make you a Grand Duke,' said Zveri.

The camp was filled with activity now at all times, for Zveri had conceived the plan of whipping his native recruits into some semblance of military order and discipline. Romero, Dorsky, and Ivitch having had military experience, the camp was filled with marching men, deploying, charging and assembling, practising the Manual of Arms, and being instructed in the rudiments of fire discipline.

The day following his conversation with Zveri, Tony was assisting the Mexican, who was sweating over a company of black recruits.

During a period of rest, as the Mexican and Filipino were enjoying a smoke, Tony turned to his companion. 'You have travelled much, Comrade,' said the Filipino. 'Perhaps you can tell me what sort of uniform a Grand Duke wears.'

'I have heard,' said Romero, 'that in Hollywood and New York many of them wear aprons.'

Tony grimaced. 'I do not think,' he said, 'that I want to be a Grand Duke.'

The blacks in the camp, held sufficiently interested and busy in drills to keep them out of mischief, with plenty of food and with the prospects of fighting and marching still in the future, were a contented and happy lot. Those who had undergone the harrowing experiences of Opar and those other untoward incidents that had upset their equanimity had entirely regained their self confidence, a condition for which Zveri took all the credit to himself, assuming that it was due to his remarkable gift for leadership. And then a runner arrived in camp with a message for him and with a weird story of having seen a white woman hunting in the jungle with a black-maned golden lion. This was sufficient to recall to the blacks the other weird occurrences and to remind them that there were supernatural agencies at work in this territory, that it was peopled by ghosts and demons, and that at any moment some dire calamity might befall them.

But if this story upset the equanimity of the blacks, the message that the runner brought to Zveri precipitated an emotional outbreak in the Russian that bordered closely upon the frenzy of insanity. Blaspheming in a loud voice, he strode back and forth before his tent; nor would he explain to any of his lieutenants the cause of his anger.

And while Zveri fumed, other forces were gathering against him. Through the jungle moved a hundred ebon warriors, their smooth, sleek skin, their rolling muscles and elastic step bespeaking their physical fitness. They were naked but for narrow loin cloths of leopard or lion skin and a few of those ornaments that are dear to the hearts of savages – anklets and arm bands of copper and necklaces of the claws of lions or leopards – while above the head of each floated a white plume. But here the primitiveness of their equipment ceased, for their weapons were the weapons of modern fighting men; high-powered service rifles, revolvers, and bandoleers of cartridges. It was, indeed, a formidable appearing company that swung steadily and silently through the jungle, and upon the shoulder of the black chief who led them rode a little monkey.

Tarzan was relieved when Tantor's sudden and unexpected charge drove To-yat into the jungle; for Tarzan of the Apes found no pleasure in quarrelling with the Mangani, which he considered above all other creatures his brothers. He never forgot that he had been nursed at the breast of Kala, the she-ape, nor that he had grown to manhood in the tribe of Kerchak, the king. From infancy to manhood he had thought of himself only as an ape, and even now it was often easier for him to understand and appreciate the motives of the great Mangani than those of man.

At a signal from Tarzan, Tantor stopped; and assuming again his custom-ary composure, though still alert to any danger that might threaten his friend, he watched while the ape-man turned and knelt beside the prostrate girl. Tarzan had at first thought her dead, but he soon discovered that she was only in a swoon. Lifting her in his arms, he spoke a half-dozen words to the great pachyderm, who turned about and, putting down his head, started off straight into the dense jungle, making a pathway along which Tarzan bore the unconscious girl.

Straight as an arrow moved Tantor, the elephant, to halt at last upon the bank of a considerable river. Beyond this was a spot that Tarzan had in mind to which he wished to convey To-yat's unfortunate captive, whom he had recognized immediately as the young woman he had seen in the base camp of the conspirators and a cursory examination of whom convinced him was upon the verge of death from starvation, shock, and exposure.

Once again he spoke to Tantor; and the great pachyderm, twining his trunk around their bodies, lifted the two gently to his broad back. Then he waded into the river and set out for the opposite shore. The channel in the centre was deep and swift, and Tantor was swept off his feet and carried downstream for a considerable distance before he found footing again, but eventually he won to the opposite bank. Here again he went ahead, making trail, until at last he broke into a broad, well marked game trail.

Now Tarzan took the lead, and Tantor followed. While they moved thus silently toward their destination, Zora Drinov opened her eyes. Instantly recollection of her plight filled her consciousness; and then almost simultaneously she realized that her cheek, resting upon the shoulder of her captor, was not pressing against a shaggy coat, but against the smooth skin of a human body, and then she turned her head and looked at the profile of the creature that was carrying her.

She thought at first that she was the victim of some strange hallucination of terror; for, of course, she could not measure the time that she had been unconscious, nor recall any of the incidents that had occurred during that period. The last thing that she remembered was that she had been in the arms of a great ape, who was carrying her off to the jungle. She had closed her eyes; and when she opened them again, the ape had been transformed into a handsome demigod of the forest.

She closed her eyes and turned her head so that she faced back over the man's shoulder. She thought that she would keep her eyes tightly closed for a moment, then open them and turn them stealthily once more toward the face of the creature that was carrying her so lightly along the jungle trail. Perhaps this time he would be an ape again, and then she would know that she was indeed mad, of dreaming.

And when she did open her eyes, the sight that met them convinced her that she was experiencing a nightmare; for plodding along the trail directly behind her was a giant bull elephant.

Tarzan, apprised of her returning consciousness by the movement of her head upon his shoulder, turned his own to look at her and saw her gazing at Tantor in wide-eyed astonishment. Then she turned toward him, and their eyes met.

'Who are you?' she asked in a whisper. 'Am I dreaming?' But the ape-man only turned his eyes to the front and made no reply.

Zora thought of struggling to free herself; but realizing that she was very weak and helpless, she at last resigned herself to her fate and let her cheek fall again to the bronzed shoulder of the ape-man.

When Tarzan finally stopped and laid his burden upon the ground, it was in a little clearing through which ran a tiny stream of clear water. Immense trees arched overhead, and through their foliage the great sun dappled the grass beneath them.

As Zora Drinov lay stretched upon the soft turf, she realized for the first time how weak she was; for when she attempted to rise, she found that she could not. As her eyes took in the scene about her, it seemed more than ever like a dream – the great bull elephant standing almost above her and the bronzed figure of an almost naked giant squatting upon his haunches beside the little stream. She saw him fold a great leaf into the shape of a cornucopia and, after filling it with water, rise and come toward her. Without a word he stooped, and putting an arm beneath her shoulders and raising her to a sitting position, he offered her the water from his improvised cup.

She drank deeply, for she was very thirsty. Then, looking up into the handsome face above her, she voiced her thanks; but when the man did not reply, she thought, naturally, that he did not understand her. When she had satisfied her thirst and he had lowered her gently to the ground again, he swung lightly into a tree and disappeared into the forest. But above her the great elephant stood, as though on guard, his huge body swaying gently to and fro.

The quiet and peace of her surroundings tended to soothe her nerves, but deeply rooted in her mind was the conviction that her situation was most precarious. The man was a mystery to her; and while she knew, of course, that the ape that had stolen her had not been transformed miraculously into a handsome forest god, yet she could not account in any way for his presence or for the disappearance of the ape, except upon the rather extravagant hypothesis that the two had worked together, the ape having stolen her for this man, who was its master. There had been nothing in the man's attitude to suggest that he intended to harm her, and yet so accustomed was she to gauge all men by the standards of civilized society that she could not conceive that he had other than ulterior designs.

To her analytical mind the man presented a paradox that intrigued her imagination, seeming, as he did, so utterly out of place in this savage African jungle; while at the same time he harmonized perfectly with his surroundings, in which he seemed absolutely at home and assured of himself, a fact that was still further impressed upon her by the presence of the wild bull elephant, to which the man paid no more attention than one would to a lap dog. Had he been unkempt, filthy, and degraded in appearance, she would have catalogued him immediately as one of those social outcasts, usually half demented, who are occasionally found far from the haunts of men, living the life of wild beasts, whose high standards of decency and cleanliness they uniformly fail to observe. But this creature had suggested more the trained athlete in whom cleanliness was a fetish, nor did his well shaped head and intelligent eyes even remotely suggest mental or moral degradation.

And as she pondered him the man returned, bearing a great load of straight branches from which the twigs and leaves had been removed. With a celerity and adeptness that bespoke long years of practice, he constructed a shelter upon the bank of the rivulet. He gathered broad leaves to thatch its roof, and leafy branches to enclose it upon three sides, so that it formed a protection against the prevailing winds. He floored it with leaves and small twigs and dry grasses. Then he came and, lifting the girl in his arms, bore her to the rustic bower he had fabricated.

Once again he left her; and when he returned he brought a little fruit which he fed to her sparingly, for he guessed that she had been long without food and knew that he must not overtax her stomach.

Always he worked in silence; and though no word had passed between them, Zora Drinov felt growing within her consciousness a conviction of his trustworthiness.

The next time that he left her he was gone a considerable time, but still the elephant stood in the clearing, like some titanic sentinel upon guard.

When next the man returned, he brought the carcass of a deer; and then Zora saw him make fire, after the manner of primitive men. As the meat roasted above it, the fragrant aroma came to her nostrils bringing consciousness of a ravening hunger. When the meat was cooked the man came and squatted beside her, cutting small pieces with his keen hunting knife and feeding her as though she had been a helpless baby. He gave her only a little at a time, making her rest often; and while she ate he spoke for the first time, but not to her, nor in any language that she had ever heard. He spoke to the great elephant and the huge pachyderm wheeled slowly about and entered the jungle, where she could hear the diminishing noise of his passage until it was lost in the distance. Before the meal was over, it was quite dark; and she finished it in the fitful light of the fire that shone redly on the bronzed skin of her companion and shot back from mysterious gray eyes that gave the impression of seeing everything, even her inmost thoughts. Then he brought her a drink of water, after which he squatted down beside her shelter and proceeded to satisfy his own hunger.

Gradually the girl had been lulled to a feeling of security by the seeming solicitude of her strange protector. But now distinct misgivings assailed her, and suddenly she felt a strange new fear of the silent giant in whose power she was; for when he ate she saw that he ate his meat raw, tearing the flesh like a wild beast. When there came the sound of something moving in the jungle just beyond the fire light and he raised his head and looked and there came a low and savage growl of warning from his lips, the girl closed her eyes and buried her face in her arms in sudden terror and revulsion. From the darkness of the jungle there came an answering growl; but the sound moved on, and presently all was silent again.

It seemed a long time before Zora dared open her eyes again, and when she did she saw that the man had finished his meal and was stretched out on the grass between her and the fire. She was afraid of him, of that she was quite certain; yet, at the same time, she could not deny that his presence there imparted to her a feeling of safety that she had never before felt in the jungle. As she tried to fathom this, she dozed and presently was asleep.

The young sun was already bringing renewed warmth to the jungle when she awoke. The man had replenished the fire and was sitting before it, grilling small fragments of meat. Beside him were some fruits, which he must have gathered since he had awakened. As she watched him, she was still further impressed by his great physical beauty, as well as by a certain marked nobility of bearing that harmonized well with the dignity of his poise and the intelligence of his keen gray eyes. She wished that she had not seen him devour his meat like a – ah, that was it – like a lion. How much like a lion he was, in his strength, and dignity, and majesty, and with all the quiet suggestion of ferocity that pervaded his every act. And so it was that she came to think of him as her lion-man and, while trying to trust him, always fearing him not a little.

Again he fed her and brought her water before he satisfied his own hunger; but before he started to eat, he arose and voiced a long, low call. Then once more he squatted upon his haunches and devoured his food. Although he held it in his strong, brown hands and ate the flesh raw, she saw now that he ate slowly and with the same quiet dignity that marked his every act, so that presently she found him less revolting. Once again she tried to talk with him, addressing him in various languages and several African dialects, but as for any sign he gave that he understood her she might as well have been addressing a dumb brute. Doubtless her disappointment would have been replaced by anger could she have known that she was addressing an English lord who understood perfectly every word that she uttered, but who, for reasons which he himself best knew, preferred to remain the dumb brute to this woman whom he looked upon as an enemy.

However, it was well for Zora Drinov that he was what he was, for it was the prompting of the English lord and not that of the savage carnivore that had moved him to succour her because she was alone, and helpless, and a woman. The beast in Tarzan would not have attacked her, but would merely have ignored her, letting the law of the jungle take its course as it must with all its creatures.

Shortly after Tarzan had finished his meal, a crashing in the jungle announced the return of Tantor; and when he appeared in the little clearing, the girl realized that the great brute had come in response to the call of the man, and marvelled.

And so the days wore on; and slowly Zora Drinov regained her strength, guarded by night by the silent forest god and by day by the great bull elephant. Her only apprehension now was for the safety of Wayne Colt, who was seldom from her thoughts. Nor was her apprehension groundless, for the young American had fallen upon bad days.

Almost frantic with concern for the safety of Zora, he had exhausted his strength in futile search for her and her abductor, forgetful of himself until hunger and fatigue had taken their toll of his strength. He had awakened at last to the realization that his condition was dangerous; and now when he needed food most, the game that he had formerly found reasonably plentiful seemed to have deserted the country. Even the smaller rodents that had once sufficed to keep him alive were either too wary for him or not present at all. Occasionally he found fruits that he could eat, but they seemed to impart little or no strength to him; and at last he was forced to the conviction that he had reached the end of his endurance and his strength and that nothing short of a miracle could preserve him from death. He was so weak that he could only stagger a few steps at a time and then, sinking to the ground, was forced to lie there for a long time before he could arise again; and always there was the knowledge that eventually he would not arise.

Yet he would not give up. Something more than the urge to live drove him on. He could not die, he must not die while Zora Drinov was in danger. He had found a well beaten trail at last where he was sure that sooner or later he must meet a native hunter, or, perhaps, find his way to the camp of his fellows. He could only crawl now, for he had not the strength to rise; and then suddenly the moment came that he had striven so long to avert – the moment that marked the end, though it came in a form that he had only vaguely anticipated as one of several that might ring the curtain upon his earthly existence.

As he lay in the trail resting before he dragged himself on again, he was suddenly conscious that he was not alone. He had heard no sounds, for doubtless his hearing had been dulled by exhaustion; but he was aware through the medium of that strange sense, the possession of which each of us has felt at some time in his existence, that told him eyes were upon him.

With an effort he raised his head and looked, and there, before him in the trail, stood a great lion, his lips drawn back in an angry snarl, his yellow-green eyes glaring balefully.

CHAPTER XIV

Shot Down

Tarzan went almost daily to watch the camp of his enemy, moving swiftly through the jungle by trails unknown to man. He saw that preparations for the first bold stroke were almost completed, and finally he saw uniforms being issued to all members of the party – uniforms which he recognized as those of French colonial troops – and he realized that the time had come when he must move. He hoped that little Nkima had carried his message safely, but if not Tarzan would find some other way.

Zora Drinov's strength was slowly returning. Today she had arisen and taken a few steps out into the sunlit clearing. The great elephant regarded her.

She had long since ceased to fear him, as she had ceased to fear the strange white man who had befriended her. Slowly the girl approached the great bull, and Tantor regarded her out of his little eyes as he waved his trunk to and fro.

He had been so docile and harmless all the days that he had guarded her that it had grown to be difficult for Zora to conceive him capable of inflicting injury upon her. But as she looked into his little eyes now, there was an expression there that brought her to a sudden halt; and as she realized that after all he was only a wild bull elephant, she suddenly appreciated the rashness of her act. She was already so close to him that she could have reached out and touched him, as had been her intention, having thought that she would thus make friends with him.

It was in her mind to fall back with dignity, when the waving trunk shot suddenly out and encircled her body. Zora Drinov did not scream. She only closed her eyes and waited. She felt herself lifted from the ground, and a moment later the elephant had crossed the little clearing and deposited her in her shelter. Then he backed off slowly and resumed his post of duty.

He had not hurt her. A mother could not have lifted her baby more gently, but he had impressed upon Zora Drinov that she was a prisoner and that he was her keeper. As a matter of fact, Tantor was only carrying out Tarzan's instructions, which had nothing to do with the forcible restraint of the girl, but were only a measure of precaution to prevent her wandering into the jungle where other dangers might overtake her.

Zora had not fully regained her strength, and the experience left her trembling. Though she now realized that her sudden fears for her safety had been groundless, she decided that she would take no more liberties with her mighty warden.

It was not long after that Tarzan returned, much earlier in the day than was his custom. He spoke only to Tantor; and the great beast, touching him almost caressingly with his trunk, turned and lumbered off into the forest. Then Tarzan advanced to where Zora sat in the opening of her shelter. Lightly he lifted her from the ground and tossed her to his shoulder; and then, to her infinite surprise at the strength and agility of the man, he swung into a tree and was off through the jungle in the wake of the pachyderm.

At the edge of the river that they had crossed before, Tantor was awaiting them, and once more he carried Zora and Tarzan safely to the other bank.

Tarzan himself had crossed the river twice a day since he had made the camp for Zora; but when he went alone he needed no help from Tantor or any other, for he swam the swift stream, his eye alert and his keen knife ready should Gimla, the crocodile, attack him. But for the crossing of the woman, he had enlisted the services of Tantor that she might not be subjected to the danger and hardship of the only other means of crossing that was possible.

As Tantor clambered up the muddy bank, Tarzan dismissed him with a word, as with the girl in his arms he leaped into a nearby tree.

That flight through the jungle was an experience that might long stand vividly in the memory of Zora Drinov. That a human being could possess the strength and agility of the creature that carried her seemed unbelievable, and she might easily have attributed a supernatural origin to him had she not felt the life in the warm flesh that was pressed against hers. Leaping from branch to branch, swinging across breathless voids, she was borne swiftly through the middle terrace of the forest. At first she had been terrified, but gradually fear left her, to be replaced by that utter confidence which Tarzan of the Apes has inspired in many a breast. At last he stopped and, lowering her to the branch upon which he stood, pointed through the surrounding foliage ahead of them. Zora looked and to her astonishment saw the camp of her companions lying ahead and below her. Once more the ape-man took her in his arms and dropped lightly to the ground into a wide trail that swept past the base of the tree in which he had halted. With a wave of his hand he indicated that she was free to go to the camp.

'Oh, how can I thank you!' exclaimed the girl. 'How can I ever make you understand how splendid you have been and how I appreciate all that you have done for me?' But his only reply was to turn and swing lightly into the tree that spread its green foliage above them.

With a rueful shake of her head, Zora Drinov started along the trail toward camp, while above her Tarzan followed through the trees to make certain that she arrived in safety.

Paul Ivitch had been hunting, and he was just returning to camp when he saw something move in a tree at the edge of the clearing. He saw the spots of a leopard, and, raising his rifle, he fired; so that at the moment that Zora entered the camp, the body of Tarzan of the Apes lunged from a tree almost at her side, blood trickling from a bullet wound in his head as the sunshine played upon the leopard spots of his loin cloth.

The sight of the lion growling above him might have shaken the nerves of a man in better physical condition than was Wayne Colt, but the vision of a beautiful girl running quickly toward the savage beast from the rear was the final stroke that almost overwhelmed him.

Through his brain ran a medley of recollection and conjecture. In a brief instant he recalled that men had borne witness to the fact that they had felt no pain while being mauled by a lion – neither pain nor fear – and he also recalled that men went mad from thirst and hunger. If he were to die, then, it would not be painful, and of that he was glad; but if he were not to die, then surely he was mad, for the lion and the girl must be the hallucination of a crazed mind.

Fascination held his eyes fixed upon the two. How real they were! He heard the girl speak to the lion, and then he saw her brush past the great savage beast and come and bend over him where he lay helpless in the trail. She touched him, and then he knew that she was real.

'Who are you?' she asked, in limping English that was beautiful with a strange accent. 'What has happened to you?'

'I have been lost,' he said, 'and I am about done up. I have not eaten for a long while,' and then he fainted.

Jad-bal-ja, the golden lion, had conceived a strange affection for La of Opar. Perhaps it was the call of one kindred savage spirit to another. Perhaps it was merely the recollection that she was Tarzan's friend. But be that as it may, he seemed to find the same pleasure in her company that a faithful dog finds in the company of his master. He had protected her with fierce loyalty, and when he made his kill he shared the flesh with her. She, however, after cutting off a portion that she wanted, had always gone away a little distance to build her primitive fire and cook the flesh; nor ever had she ventured back to the kill after Jad-bal-ja had commenced to feed, for a lion is yet a lion, and the grim and ferocious growls that accompanied his feeding warned the girl against presuming too far upon the new found generosity of the carnivore.

They had been feeding when the approach of Colt had attracted Numa's attention and brought him into the trail from his kill. For a moment La had feared that she might not be able to keep the lion from the man, and she had wanted to do so; for something in the stranger's appearance reminded her of Tarzan, whom he more nearly resembled than he did the grotesque priests of Opar. Because of this fact she thought that possibly the stranger might be from Tarzan's country. Perhaps he was one of Tarzan's friends and, if so, she must protect him. To her relief, the lion had obeyed her when she had called upon him to halt, and now he evinced no further desire to attack the man.

When Colt regained consciousness, La tried to raise him to his feet; and, with considerable difficulty and some slight assistance from the man, she succeeded in doing so. She put one of his arms across her shoulders and, supporting him thus, guided him back along the trail, while Jad-bal-ja followed at their heels. She had difficulty in getting him through the brush to the hidden glen where Jad-bal-ja's kill lay and her little fire was burning a short distance away. But at last she succeeded and when they had come close to her fire, she lowered the man to the ground, while Jad-bal-ja turned once more to his feeding and his growling.

La fed the man tiny pieces of the meat that she had cooked, and he ate ravenously all that she would give him. A short distance away ran the river, where La and the lion would have gone to drink, after they had fed; but doubting whether she could get the man so great a distance through the jungle, she left him there with the lion and went down to the river; but first she told Jad-bal-ja to guard him, speaking in the language of the first men, the language of the Mangani, that all creatures of the jungle understand to a greater or lesser extent. Near the river La found what she sought – a fruit with a hard rind. With her knife she cut an end from one of these fruits and scooped out the pulpy interior, producing a primitive but entirely practical cup, which she filled with water from the river.

The water, as much as the food, refreshed and strengthened Colt; and though he lay but a few yards from a feeding lion, it seemed an eternity since he had experienced such a feeling of contentment and security, clouded only by his anxiety concerning Zora.

'You feel stronger now?' asked La, her voice tinged with concern.

'Very much,' he replied.

'Then tell me who you are and if this is your country.'

'This is not my country,' replied Colt. 'I am an American. My name is Wayne Colt.'

'You are perhaps a friend of Tarzan of the Apes?' she asked.

He shook his head. 'No,' he said. 'I have heard of him, but I do not know him.'

La frowned. 'You are his enemy, then?' she demanded.

'Of course not,' replied Colt. 'I do not even know him.'

A sudden light flashed in La's eyes. 'Do you know Zora?' she asked.

Colt came to his elbow with a sudden start. 'Zora Drinov?' he demanded. 'What do you know of her?'

'She is my friend,' said La.

'She is my friend also,' said Colt.

'She is in trouble,' said La.

'Yes, I know it; but how did you know?'

'I was with her when she was taken prisoner by the men of the desert. They took me also, but I escaped.'

'How long ago was that?'

'The Flaming God has gone to rest many times since I saw Zora,' replied the girl.

'Then I have seen her since.'

'Where is she?'

'I do not know. She was with the Arabs when I found her. We escaped from them; and then, while I was hunting in the jungle something came and carried her away. I do not know whether it was a man or a gorilla; for though I saw its footprints, I could not be sure. I have been searching for her for a long time; but I could not find food, and it has been some time since I have had water; so I lost my strength, and you found me as I am.'

'You will not want for food or water now,' said La, 'for Numa, the lion, will hunt for us; and if we can find the camp of Zora's friends, perhaps they will go out and search for her.'

'You know where the camp is?' he asked. 'Is it near?'

'I do not know where it is. I have been searching for it to lead her friends after the men of the desert.'

Colt had been studying the girl as they talked. He had noted her strange, barbaric apparel and the staggering beauty of her face and figure. He knew almost intuitively that she was not of the world that he knew, and his mind was filled with curiosity concerning her.

'You have not told me who you are,' he said.

'I am La of Opar,' she replied, 'high priestess of the Flaming God.'

Opar! Now indeed he knew that she was not of his world. Opar, the city of mystery, the city of fabulous treasures. Could it be that the same city that housed the grotesque warriors with whom he and Romero had fought produced also such beautiful creatures as Nao and La, and only these? He wondered why he had not connected her with Opar at once, for now he saw that her stomacher was similar to that of Nao and of the priestess that he had seen upon the throne in the great chamber of the ruined temple. Recalling his attempt to enter Opar and loot it of its treasures, he deemed it expedient to make no mention of any familiarity with the city of the girl's birth, for he guessed that Opar's women might be as primitively fierce in their vengeance as he had found Nao in her love.

The lion, and the girl, and the man lay up that night beside Jad-bal-ja's kill, and in the morning Colt found that his strength had partially returned. During the night Numa had finished his kill; and after the sun had risen, La found fruits which she and Colt ate, while the lion strolled to the river to drink, pausing once to roar, that the world might know the king was there.

'Numa will not kill again until tomorrow,' she said, 'so we shall have no meat until then, unless we are fortunate enough to kill something ourselves.'

Colt had long since abandoned the heavy rifle of the Arabs, to the burden of which his growing weakness had left his muscles inadequate; so he had nothing but his bare hands and La only a knife with which they might make a kill.

'Then I guess we shall eat fruit until the lion kills again,' he said. 'In the meantime we might as well be trying to find the camp.'

She shook her head. 'No,' she said, 'you must rest. You were very weak when I found you, and it is not well that you should exert yourself until you are strong again. Numa will sleep all day. You and I will cut some sticks and lie beside a little trail, where the small things go. Perhaps we shall have luck; but if we do not, Numa will kill again tomorrow, and this time I shall take a whole hind quarter.'

'I cannot believe that a lion would let you do that,' said the man.

'At first I did not understand it myself,' said La, 'but after awhile I remembered. It is because I am Tarzan's friend that he does not harm me.'

When Zora Drinov saw her lion-man lying lifeless on the ground, she ran quickly to him and knelt at his side. She had heard the shot, and now seeing the blood running from the wound upon his head, she thought that someone had killed him intentionally and when Ivitch came running out, his rifle in his hand, she turned upon him like a tigress.

'You have killed him,' she cried. 'You beast! He was worth more than a dozen such as you.'

The sound of the shot and the crashing of the body to the ground had brought men running from all parts of the camp; so that Tarzan and the girl were soon surrounded by a curious and excited throng of blacks, among whom the remaining whites were pushing their way.

Ivitch was stunned, not only by the sight of the giant white man lying apparently dead before him, but also by the presence of Zora Drinov, whom all within the camp had given up as irretrievably lost. 'I had no idea, Comrade Drinov,' he explained, 'that I was shooting at a man. I see now what caused my mistake. I saw something moving in a tree and thought that it was a leopard, but instead it was the leopard skin that he wears about his loins.'

By this time Zveri had elbowed his way to the centre of the group. 'Zora!' he cried in astonishment as he saw the girl. 'Where did you come from? What has happened? What is the meaning of this?'

'It means that this fool, Ivitch, has killed the man who saved my life,' cried Zora.

'Who is he?' asked Zveri.

'I do not know,' replied Zora. 'He has never spoken to me. He does not seem to understand any language with which I am familiar.'

'He is not dead,' cried Ivitch. 'See, he moved.'

Romero knelt and examined the wound in Tarzan's head. 'He is only stunned,' he said. 'The bullet struck him a glancing blow. There are no indications of a fracture of the skull. I have seen men hit thus before. He may be unconscious for a long time, or he may not, but I am sure that he will not die.'

'Who the devil do you suppose he is?' asked Zveri.

Zora shook her head. 'I have no idea,' she said. 'I only know that he is as splendid as he is mysterious.'

'I know who he is,' said a black who had pushed forward to where he could see the figure of the prostrate man, 'and if he is not already dead, you had better kill him, for he will be your worst enemy.'

'What do you mean?' demanded Zveri. 'Who is he?'

'He is Tarzan of the Apes.'

'You are certain?' snapped Zveri.

'Yes, Bwana,' replied the black. 'I saw him once before, and one never forgets Tarzan of the Apes.'

'Yours was a lucky shot, Ivitch,' said the leader, 'and now you may as well finish what you started.'

'Kill him, you mean?' demanded Ivitch.

'Our cause is lost and our lives with it, if he lives!' replied Zveri. 'I thought that he was dead, or I should never have come here; and now that Fate has thrown him into our hands we would be fools to let him escape, for we could not have a worse enemy than he.'

'I cannot kill him in cold blood,' said Ivitch.

'You always were a weak minded fool,' said Zveri, 'but I am not. Stand aside, Zora,' and as he spoke he drew his revolver and advanced toward Tarzan.

The girl threw herself across the ape-man, shielding his body with hers. 'You cannot kill him,' she cried. 'You must not.'

'Don't be a fool, Zora,' snapped Zveri.

'He saved my life and brought me back here to camp. Do you think I am going to let you murder him?' she demanded.

'I am afraid you can't help yourself, Zora,' replied the man. 'I do not like to do it, but it is his life or the cause. If he lives, we fail.'

The girl leaped to her feet and faced Zveri. 'If you kill him, Peter, I shall kill you – I swear it by everything that I hold most dear. Hold him prisoner if you will, but as you value your life, do not kill him.'

Zveri went pale with anger. 'Your words are treason,' he said. 'Traitors to the cause have died for less than what you have said.'

Zora Drinov realized that the situation was extremely dangerous. She had little reason to believe that Zveri would make good his threat toward her, but she saw that if she would save Tarzan she must act quickly. 'Send the others away,' she said to Zveri. 'I have something to tell you before you kill this man.'

For a moment the leader hesitated. Then he turned to Dorsky, who stood at his side. 'Have the fellow securely bound and taken to one of the tents,' he commanded. 'We shall give him a fair trial after he has regained consciousness and then place him before a firing squad,' and then to the girl, 'Come with me, Zora, and I will listen to what you have to say.'

In silence the two walked to Zveri's tent. 'Well?' inquired Zveri, as the girl halted before the entrance. 'What have you to say to me that you think will change my plans relative to your lover?'

Zora looked at him for a long minute, a faint sneer of contempt curling her lips. '*You* would think such a thing,' she said, 'but you are wrong. However you may think, though, you shall not kill him.'

'And why not?' demanded Zveri.

'Because if you do I shall tell them all what you plans are; that you yourself are a traitor to the cause, and that you have been using them all to advance your own selfish ambition to make yourself Emperor of Africa.'

'You would not dare,' cried Zveri; 'nor would I let you; for as much as I love you, I shall kill you here on the spot, unless you promise not to interfere in any way with my plans.'

'You do not dare kill me,' taunted the girl. 'You have antagonized every man in the camp, Peter, and they all like me. Some of them, perhaps, love me a little. Do you think that I should not be avenged within five minutes after you had killed me? You will have to think of something else, my friend; and the best thing that you can do is to take my advice. Keep Tarzan of the Apes a prisoner if you will, but on your life do not kill him or permit anyone else to do so.'

Zveri sank into a camp chair. 'Everyone is against me,' he said. 'Even you, the woman I love, turn against me.'

'I have not changed toward you in any respect, Peter,' said the girl.

'You mean that?' he asked, looking up.

'Absolutely,' she replied.

'How long were you alone in the jungle with that man?' he demanded.

'Don't start that, Peter,' she said. 'He could not have treated me differently if he had been my own brother; and, certainly, all other considerations aside, you should know me well enough to know that I have no such weakness in the direction that your tone implied.'

'You have never loved me – that is the reason,' he declared. 'But I would not trust you or any other woman with a man she loves or with whom she was temporarily infatuated.'

'That,' she said, 'has nothing to do with what we are discussing. Are you going to kill Tarzan of the Apes, or are you not?'

'For your sake, I shall let him live,' replied the man, 'even though I do not trust you,' he added. 'I trust no one. How can I? Look at this,' and he took a code message from his pocket and handed it to her. 'This came a few days ago – the damn traitor. I wish I could get my hands on him. I should like to have killed him myself, but I suppose I shall have no such luck, as he is probably already dead.'

Zora took the paper. Below the message, in Zveri's scrawling hand, it had been decoded in Russian script. As she read it her eyes grew large with astonishment. 'It is incredible,' she cried.

'It is the truth, though,' said Zveri. 'I always suspected the dirty hound,' and he added with an oath, 'I think that damn Mexican is just as bad.'

'At least,' said Zora, 'his plan has been thwarted, for I take it that his message did not get through.'

'No,' said Zveri. 'By error it was delivered to our agents instead of his.'

'Then no harm has been done.'

'Fortunately, no; but it has made me suspicious of everyone, and I am going to push the expedition through at once before anything further can occur to interfere with my plans.'

'Everything is ready, then?' she asked.

'Everything is ready,' he replied. 'We march tomorrow morning. And now tell me what happened while I was at Opar. Why did the Arabs desert, and why did you go with them?'

'Abu Batn was angry and resentful because you left him to guard the camp. The Arabs felt that it was a reflection upon their courage, and I think that they would have deserted you anyway, regardless of me. Then, the day after you left, a strange woman wandered into camp. She was a very beautiful white woman from Opar; and Abu Batn, conceiving the idea of profiting through the chance that Fate had sent him, took us with him with the intention of selling us into captivity on his return march to his own country.'

'Are there no honest men in the world?' demanded Zveri.

'I am afraid not,' replied the girl; but as he was staring moodily at the ground, he did not see the contemptuous curl of her lip that accompanied her reply.

She described the luring of La from Abu Batn's camp and of the sheikh's anger at the treachery of Ibn Dammuk; and then she told him of her own escape, but she did not mention Wayne Colt's connection with it and led him to believe that she wandered alone in the jungle until the great ape had captured her. She dwelt at length upon Tarzan's kindness and consideration and told of the great elephant who had guarded her by day.

'Sounds like a fairy story,' said Zveri, 'but I have heard enough about this ape-man to believe almost anything concerning him, which is one reason why I believe we shall never be safe while he lives.'

'He cannot harm us while he is our prisoner; and, certainly, if you loved me as you say you do, the man who saved my life deserves better from you than ignominious death.'

'Speak no more of it,' said Zveri. 'I have already told you that I would not kill him,' but in his treacherous mind he was formulating a plan whereby Tarzan might be destroyed while still he adhered to the letter of his promise to Zora.

CHAPTER XV
'Kill, Tantor, Kill!'

Early the following morning the expedition filed out of camp, the savage black warriors arrayed in the uniforms of French colonial troops; while Zveri, Romero, Ivitch, and Mori wore the uniforms of French officers. Zora Drinov accompanied the marching column; for though she had asked to be permitted to remain and nurse Tarzan, Zveri would not permit her to do so, saying that he would not again let her out of his sight. Dorsky and a handful of blacks were left behind to guard the prisoner and watch over the store of provisions and equipment that were to be left in the base camp.

As the column had been preparing to march, Zveri gave his final instructions to Dorsky. 'I leave this matter entirely in your hands,' he said. 'It must appear that he escaped, or, at worst, that he met an accidental death.'

'You need give the matter no further thought, Comrade,' replied Dorsky. 'Long before you return, this stranger will have been removed.'

A long and difficult march lay before the invaders, their route lying across south-eastern Abyssinia into Italian Somaliland, along five hundred miles of rough and savage country. It was Zveri's intention to make no more than a demonstration in the Italian colony, merely sufficient to arouse the anger of the Italians still further against the French and to give the fascist dictator the excuse which Zveri believed was all that he awaited to carry his mad dream of Italian conquest across Europe.

Perhaps Zveri was a little mad, but then he was a disciple of mad men whose greed for power wrought distorted images in their minds, so that they could not differentiate between the rational and the bizarre; and then, too, Zveri had for so long dreamed his dream of empire that he saw now only his goal and none of the insurmountable obstacles that beset his path. He saw a new Roman emperor ruling Europe, and himself as Emperor of Africa making an alliance with this new European power against all the balance of the world. He pictured two splendid golden thrones; upon one of them sat the Emperor Peter I, and upon the other the Empress Zora; and so he dreamed through the long, hard marches toward the east.

It was the morning of the day following that upon which he had been shot before Tarzan regained consciousness. He felt weak and sick, and his head ached horribly. When he tried to move, he discovered that his wrists and ankles were securely bound. He did not know what had happened, and at first he could not imagine where he was; but, as recollection slowly returned and he recognized about him the canvas walls of a tent, he understood that in some way his enemies had captured him. He tried to wrench his wrists free from the cords that held them, but they resisted his every effort.

He listened intently and sniffed the air, but he could detect no evidence of the teeming camp that he had seen when he had brought the girl back. He knew, however, that at least one night had passed; for the shadows that he could see though the tent opening indicated that the sun was high in the heavens, whereas had been low in the west when last he saw it. Hearing voices, he realized that he was not alone, though he was confident that there must be comparatively few men in camp.

Deep in the jungle he heard an elephant trumpeting, and once, from far off, came faintly the roar of a lion. Tarzan strove again to snap the bonds that held him, but they would not yield. Then he turned his head so that he faced the opening in the tent, and from his lips burst a long, low cry; the cry of a beast a distress.

Dorsky, who was lolling in a chair before his own tent, leaped to his feet. The blacks, who had been talking animatedly before their own shelters, went quickly quiet and seized their weapons.

'What was that?' Dorsky demanded of his black boy.

The fellow, wide-eyed and trembling, shook his head. 'I do not know, Bwana,' he said. 'Perhaps the man in the tent has died, for such a noise may well have come from the throat of a ghost.'

'Nonsense,' said Dorsky. 'Come, we'll have a look at him.' But the black held back, and the white man went on alone.

The sound, which had come apparently from the tent in which the captive lay, had had a peculiar effect upon Dorsky, causing the flesh of his scalp to creep and a strange foreboding to fill him; so that as he neared the tent, he went more slowly and held his revolver ready in his hand.

When he entered the tent, he saw the man lying where he had been left; but now his eyes were open, and when they met those of the Russian, the latter had a sensation similar to that which one feels when he comes eye to eye with a wild beast that has been caught in a trap.

'Well,' said Dorsky, 'so you have come to, have you? What do you want?' The captive made no reply, but his eyes never left the other's face. So steady was the unblinking gaze that Dorsky became uneasy beneath it. 'You had better learn to talk,' he said gruffly, 'if you know what is good for you.' Then it occurred to him that perhaps the man did not understand him so he turned in the entrance and called to some of the blacks, who had advanced, half in curiosity, half in fear, toward the tent of the prisoner. 'One of you fellows come here,' he said.

At first no one seemed inclined to obey, but presently a stalwart warrior advanced. 'See if this fellow can understand your language. Come in and tell him that I have a proposition to make to him and that he had better listen to it.'

'If this is indeed Tarzan of the Apes,' said the black, 'he can understand me,' and he came warily to the entrance of the tent.

The black repeated the message in his own dialect, but by no sign did the ape-man indicate that he understood.

Dorsky lost his patience. 'You damned ape,' he said. 'You needn't try to make a fool of me. I know perfectly well that you understand this fellow's gibberish, and I know, too, that you are an Englishman and that you understand English. I'll give you just five minutes to think this thing over, and then I am coming back. If you have not made up your mind to talk by that time, you can take the consequences.' Then he turned on his heel and left the tent.

Little Nkima had travelled far. Around his neck was a stout thong, supporting a little bag of leather, in which reposed a message. This eventually he had brought to Muviro, war chief of the Waziri; and when the Waziri had started out upon their long march, Nkima had ridden proudly upon the shoulder of Muviro. For some time he had remained with the black warriors; but then, at last, moved perhaps by some caprice of his erratic mind, or by a great urge that he could not resist, he had left them and, facing alone all the dangers that he feared most, had set out by himself upon business of his own.

Many and narrow were the escapes of Nkima as he swung through the giants of the forest. Could he have resisted temptation, he might have passed with reasonable safety, but that he could not do; and so he was forever getting himself into trouble by playing pranks upon strangers, who, if they possessed any sense of humour themselves, most certainly failed to appreciate little Nkima's. Nkima could not forget that he was friend and confidant of Tarzan, Lord of the Jungle, though he seemed often to forget that Tarzan was not there to protect him when he hurled taunts and insults at other monkeys less favoured. That he came through alive speaks more eloquently for his speed than for his intelligence or courage. Much of the time he was fleeing in terror, emitting shrill screams of mental anguish; yet he never seemed to learn from experience, and having barely eluded one pursuer intent upon murdering him he would be quite prepared to insult or annoy the next creature he met, especially selecting, it would seem, those that were larger and stronger than himself.

Sometimes he fled in one direction, sometimes in another, so that he occupied much more time than was necessary in making his journey. Otherwise he would have reached his master in time to be of service to him at a moment that Tarzan needed a friend as badly, perhaps, as ever he had needed one before in his life.

And now, while far away in the forest Nkima fled from an old dog baboon, whom he had hit with a well-aimed stick, Michael Dorsky approached the tent where Nkima's master lay bound and helpless. The five minutes were up, and Dorsky had come to demand Tarzan's answer. He came alone, and as he entered the tent his simple plan of action was well formulated in his mind.

The expression upon the prisoner's face had changed. He seemed to be listening intently. Dorsky listened then, too, but could hear nothing; for by comparison with the hearing of Tarzan of the Apes Michael Dorsky was deaf. What Tarzan heard filled him with quiet satisfaction.

'Now,' said Dorsky, 'I have come to give you your last chance. Comrade Zveri has led two expeditions to Opar in search of the gold that we know is stored there. Both expeditions failed. It is well known that you know the location of the treasure vaults of Opar and can lead us to them. Agree that you will do this when Comrade Zveri returns, and not only will you not be harmed, but you will be released as quickly as Comrade Zveri feels that it would be safe to have you at liberty. Refuse and you die.' He drew a long, slender stiletto from its sheath at his belt. 'If you refuse to answer me, I shall accept that as evidence that you have not accepted my proposition.' And as the ape-man maintained his stony silence, the Russian held the thin blade low before his eyes. 'Think well, ape,' he said, 'and remember that when I slip this between your ribs there will be no sound. It will pierce your heart, and I shall leave it there until the blood has ceased to flow. Then I shall remove it and close the wound. Later in the day you will be found dead, and I shall tell the blacks that you died from the accidental gunshot. Thus your friends will never learn the truth. You will not be avenged, and you will have died uselessly.' He paused for a reply, his evil eyes glinting menacingly into the cold, gray eyes of the ape-man.

The dagger was very near Tarzan's face now; and of a sudden, like a wild beast, he raised his body, and his jaws closed like a steel trap upon the wrist of the Russian. With a scream of pain Dorsky drew back. The dagger dropped from his nerveless fingers. At the same instant Tarzan swung his legs around the feet of the would-be assassin; and as Dorsky rolled over on his back, he dragged Tarzan of the Apes on top of him.

The ape-man knew from the snapping of Dorsky's wrist bones between his teeth that the man's right hand was useless, and so he released it. Then to the Russian's horror, the ape-man's jaws sought his jugular as, from his throat, there rumbled the growl of a savage beast at bay.

Screaming for his men to come to his assistance, Dorsky tried to reach the revolver at his right hip with his left hand, but he soon saw that unless he could rid himself of Tarzan's body he would be unable to do so.

Already he heard his men running toward the tent, shouting among themselves, and then he heard exclamations of surprise and screams of terror. The next instant the tent vanished from above them, and Dorsky saw a huge bull elephant towering above him and his savage antagonist.

Instantly Tarzan ceased his efforts to close his teeth on Dorsky's throat and at the same time rolled quickly from the body of the Russian. As he did so Dorsky's hand found his revolver.

'Kill, Tantor!' shouted the ape-man. 'Kill!'

The sinuous trunk of the pachyderm twined around the Russian. The little eyes of the elephant flamed red with hate, and he trumpeted shrilly as he raised Dorsky high above his head and, wheeling about, hurled him out into the camp; while the terrified blacks, casting affrighted glances over their shoulders, fled into the jungle. Then Tantor charged his victim. With his great tusks he gored him; and then, in a frenzy of rage, trumpeting and squealing, he trampled him until nothing remained of Michael Dorsky but a bloody pulp.

From the moment that Tantor had seized the Russian, Tarzan had sought ineffectually to stay the great brute's fury, but Tantor was deaf to commands until he had wreaked his vengeance upon this creature that had dared to attack his friend. But when his rage had spent its force and nothing remained against which to vent it, he came quietly to Tarzan's side and at a word from the ape-man lifted his brown body gently in his powerful trunk and bore him away into the forest.

Deep into the jungle to a hidden glade, Tantor carried his helpless friend, and there he placed him gently on soft grasses beneath the shade of a tree. Little more could the great bull do other than to stand guard. As a result of the excitement attending the killing of Dorsky and his concern for Tarzan, Tantor was nervous and irritable. He stood with upraised ears, alert for any menacing sound, waving his sensitive trunk to and fro, searching each vagrant air current for the scent of danger.

The pain of his wound annoyed Tarzan far less than the pangs of thirst.

To little monkeys watching him from the trees he called, 'Come, Manu, and untie the thongs that bind my wrists.'

'We are afraid,' said an old monkey.

'I am Tarzan of the Apes,' said the man reassuringly. 'Tarzan has been your friend always. He will not harm you.'

'We are afraid,' repeated the old monkey. 'Tarzan deserted us. For many moons the jungle has not known Tarzan; but other Tarmangani and strange Gomangani came and with thundersticks they hunted little Manu and killed him. If Tarzan had still been our friend, he would have driven these strange men away.'

'If I had been here, the strange men-things would not have harmed you,' said Tarzan. 'Still would Tarzan have protected you. Now I am back, but I cannot destroy the strangers or drive them away until the thongs are taken from my wrists.'

'Who put them there?' asked the monkey.

'The strange Tarmangani,' replied Tarzan.

'Then they must be more powerful than Tarzan,' said Manu, 'so what good would it do to set you free? If the strange Tarmangani found out that we had done it, they would be angry and come and kill us. Let Tarzan, who for many rains has been Lord of the Jungle, free himself.'

Seeing that it was futile to appeal to Manu, Tarzan, as a forlorn hope, voiced the long, plaintive, uncanny help call of the great apes. With slowly increasing crescendo it rose to a piercing shriek that drove far and wide through the silent jungle.

In all directions, beasts, great and small, paused as the weird note broke upon their sensitive eardrums. None was afraid, for the call told them that a great bull was in trouble and, therefore, doubtless harmless; but the jackals interpreted the sound to mean the possibility of flesh and trotted off through the jungle in the direction from which it had come; and Dango, the hyena, heard and slunk on soft pads, hoping that he would find a helpless animal that would prove easy prey. And far away, and faintly, a little monkey heard the call, recognizing the voice of the caller. Swiftly, then, he flew through the jungle, impelled as he was upon rare occasions by a directness of thought and a tenacity of purpose that brooked no interruption.

Tarzan had sent Tantor to the river to fetch water in his trunk. From a distance he caught the scent of the jackals and the horrid scent of Dango, and he hoped that Tantor would return before they came creeping upon him. He felt no fear, only an instinctive urge toward self-preservation. The jackals he held in contempt, knowing that, though bound hand and foot, he still could keep the timid creatures away; but Dango was different, for once the filthy brute realized his helplessness, Tarzan knew that those powerful jaws would make quick work of him. He knew the merciless savagery of the beast; knew that in all the jungle there was none more terrible than Dango.

The jackals came first, standing at the edge of the little glade watching him. Then they circled slowly, coming nearer; but when he raised himself to a sitting position they ran yelping away. Three times they crept closer, trying to force their courage to the point of actual attack; and then a horrid, slinking form appeared upon the edge of the glade, and the jackals withdrew to a safe distance. Dango, the hyena, had come.

Tarzan was still sitting up, and the beast stood eyeing him, filled with curiosity and with fear. He growled, and the man-thing facing him growled back; and then from above them came a great chattering, and Tarzan, looking up, saw little Nkima dancing upon the limb of a tree above him.

'Come down, Nkima,' he cried, 'and untie the thongs that bind my wrists.'

'Dango! Dango!' shouted Nkima. 'Little Nkima is afraid of Dango.'

'If you come now,' said Tarzan, 'it will be safe; but if you wait too long, Dango will kill Tarzan; and then to whom may little Nkima go for protection?'

'Nkima comes,' shouted the little monkey, and dropping quickly through the trees, he leaped to Tarzan's shoulder.

The hyena bared his fangs and laughed his horrid laugh. Tarzan spoke. 'Quick, the thongs, Nkima,' urged Tarzan; and the little monkey, his fingers trembling with terror, went to work upon the leather thongs at Tarzan's wrists.

Dango, his ugly head lowered, made a sudden rush; and from the deep lungs of the ape-man came a thunderous roar that might have done credit to Numa himself. With a yelp of terror the cowardly Dango turned and fled to the extremity of the glade, where he stood bristling and growling.

'Hurry, Nkima,' said Tarzan. 'Dango will come again. Maybe once, maybe twice, maybe many times before he closes on me; but in the end he will realize that I am helpless, and then he will not stop or turn back.'

'Little Nkima's fingers are sick,' said the Manu. 'They are weak and they tremble. They will not untie the knot.'

'Nkima has sharp teeth,' Tarzan reminded him. 'Why waste your time with sick fingers over knots that they cannot untie? Let your sharp teeth do the work.'

Instantly Nkima commenced to gnaw upon the strands. Silent perforce because his mouth was otherwise occupied, Nkima strove diligently and without interruption.

Dango, in the meantime, made two short rushes, each time coming a little closer, but each time turning back before the menace of the ape-man's roars and savage growls, which by now had aroused the jungle.

Above them, in the tree tops, the monkeys chattered, scolded and screamed, and in the distance the voice of Numa rolled like far thunder, while from the river came the squealing and trumpeting of Tantor.

Little Nkima was gnawing frantically at the bonds, when Dango charged again, evidently convinced by this time that the great Tarmangani was helpless, for now, with a growl, he rushed in and closed upon the man.

With a sudden surge of the great muscles of his arms that sent little Nkima sprawling, Tarzan sought to tear his hands free that he might defend himself against the savage death that menaced him in those slavering jaws; and the thongs, almost parted by Nkima's sharp teeth, gave to the terrific strain of the ape-man's efforts.

As Dango leaped for the bronzed throat, Tarzan's hand shot forward and seized the beast by the neck, but the impact of the heavy body carried him backward to the ground. Dango twisted, struggled and clawed in a vain effort to free himself from the death grip of the ape-man, but those steel fingers closed relentlessly upon his throat, until, gasping for breath, the great brute sank helplessly upon the body of its intended victim.

Until death was assured, Tarzan did not relinquish his grasp; but when at last there could be no doubt, he hurled the carcass from him and, sitting up, fell quickly to the thongs that secured his ankles.

During the brief battle, Nkima had taken refuge among the topmost branches of a lofty tree, where he leaped about, screaming frantically at the battling beasts beneath him. Not until he was quite sure that Dango was dead did he descend. Warily he approached the body lest, perchance, he had been mistaken; but again convinced by closer scrutiny, he leaped upon it and struck it viciously, again and again, and then he stood upon it shrieking his defiance at the world with all the assurance and bravado of one who has overcome a dangerous enemy.

Tantor, startled by the help cry of his friend, had turned back from the river without taking water. Trees bent beneath his mad rush as, ignoring winding trails, he struck straight through the jungle toward the little glade in answer to the call of the ape-man; and now, infuriated by the sounds of battle, he came charging into view, a titanic engine of rage and vengeance.

Tantor's eyesight is none too good, and it seemed that in his mad charge he must trample the ape-man, who lay directly in his path; but when Tarzan spoke to him the great beast came to a sudden stop at his side and, pivoting, wheeled about in his tracks, his ears forward, his trunk raised, trumpeting a savage warning as he searched for the creature that had been menacing his friend.

'Quiet, Tantor; it was Dango. He is dead,' said the ape-man. As the eyes of the elephant finally located the carcass of the hyena he charged and trampled it, as he had trampled Dorsky, to a bloody pulp; as Nkima fled, shrieking, to the trees.

His ankles freed of their bonds, Tarzan was upon his feet; and, when Tantor had vented his rage upon the body of Dango, he called the elephant to him. Tantor came then quietly to his side and stood with his trunk touching the ape-man's body, his rage quieted and his nerves soothed by the reassuring calm of the ape-man.

And now Nkima came, making an agile leap from a swaying bow to the back of Tantor and then to the shoulder of Tarzan, where, with his little arms about the ape-man's neck, he pressed his cheek close against the bronzed cheek of the great Tarmangani, who was his master and his god.

Thus the three friends stood in the silent communion that only beasts know as the shadows lengthened and the sun set behind the forest.

CHAPTER XVI
'Turn Back!'

The privations that Wayne Colt had endured had weakened him far more than he had realized, so that before his returning strength could bring renewed powers of resistance, he was stricken with fever.

The high priestess of the Flaming God, versed in the lore of ancient Opar, was conversant with the medicinal properties of many roots and herbs and, as well, with the mystic powers of incantation that drove demons from the bodies of the sick. By day she gathered and brewed, and at night she sat at the feet of her patient, intoning weird prayers, the origin of which reached back through countless ages to vanished temples, above which now rolled the waters of a mighty sea; and while she wrought with every artifice at her command to drive out the demon of sickness that possessed this man of an alien world, Jad-bal-ja, the golden lion, hunted for all three, and, though at times he made his kill at a distance, he never failed to carry the carcass of his prey back to the hidden lair where the woman nursed the man.

Days of burning fever, days of delirium, shot with periods of rationality, dragged their slow length. Often Colt's mind was confused by a jumble of bizarre impressions, in which La might be Zora Drinov one moment, a ministering angel from heaven the next, and then a Red Cross nurse; but in whatever guise he found her it seemed always a pleasant one, and when she was absent, as she was sometimes forced to be, he was depressed and unhappy.

When, upon her knees at his feet, she prayed to the rising sun, or to the sun at zenith, or to the setting sun, as was her wont, or when she chanted strange, weird songs in an unknown tongue, accompanying them with the mysterious gestures that were a part of the ritual, he was sure that the fever was worse and that he had become delirious again.

And so the days dragged on, and while Colt lay helpless, Zveri marched toward Italian Somaliland; and Tarzan, recovered from the shock of his wound, followed the plain trail of the expedition, and from his shoulder little Nkima scolded and chattered through the day.

Behind him Tarzan had left a handful of terrified blacks in the camp of the conspirators. They had been lolling in the shade, following their breakfast, a week after the killing of Dorsky and the escape of his captive. Fear of the ape-man at liberty, that had so terrified them at first, no longer concerned them greatly. Psychologically akin to the brutes of the forest, they happily soon forgot their terrors; nor did they harass their minds by anticipating those which might assail them in the future, as it is the silly custom of civilized man to do.

And so it was this morning that a sight which burst suddenly upon their astonished eyes found them entirely unprepared. They heard no noise, so silently go the beasts of the jungle, however large or heavy they may be; yet suddenly, in the clearing at the edge of the camp, appeared a great elephant, and upon his head sat the recent captive, whom they had been told was Tarzan of the Apes, and upon the man's shoulder perched a little monkey. With exclamations of terror, the blacks leaped to their feet and dashed into the jungle upon the opposite side of the camp.

Tarzan leaped lightly to the ground and entered Dorsky's tent. He had returned for a definite purpose; and his effort was crowned with success, for in the tent of the Russian he found his rope and his knife, which had been taken away from him at the time of his capture. For bow and arrows and a spear he had only to look to the shelters of the blacks; and, having found what he wanted, he departed as silently as he had come.

Now the time had arrived when Tarzan must set out rapidly upon the trail of his enemy, leaving Tantor to the peaceful paths that he loved best.

'I go, Tantor,' he said. 'Search out the forest where the young trees have the tenderest bark and watch well against the men-things, for they alone in all the world are the enemies of all living creatures.' He was off through the forest then, with little Nkima clinging tightly to his bronzed neck.

Plain lay the winding trail of Zveri's army before the eyes of the ape-man, but he had no need to follow any trail. Long weeks before, as he had kept vigil above their camp, he had heard the principals discussing their plans; and so he knew their objectives, and he knew, too, how rapidly they could march and, therefore, about where he might hope to overtake them. Unhampered by files of porters sweating under heavy loads, earthbound to no winding trails, Tarzan was able to travel many times faster than the expedition. He saw their trail only when his own chanced to cross it as he laid a straight course for a point far in advance of the sweating column.

When he overtook the expedition night had fallen, and the tired men were in camp. They had eaten and were happy and many of the men were singing. To one who did not know the truth it might have appeared to be a military camp of French colonial troops; for there was a military precision about the arrangement of the fires, the temporary shelters, and the officer's tents that would not have been undertaken by a hunting or scientific expedition, and, in addition, there were the uniformed sentries pacing their beats. All this was the work of Miguel Romero, to whose superior knowledge of military matters Zveri had been forced to defer in all matters of this nature, though with no dimunition of the hatred which each felt for the other.

From his tree Tarzan watched the scene below, attempting to estimate as closely as possible the number of armed men that formed the fighting force of the expedition, while Nkima, bent upon some mysterious mission, swung nimbly through the trees toward the east. The ape-man realized that Zveri had recruited a force that might constitute a definite menace to the peace of Africa, since among its numbers were represented many large and warlike tribes, who might easily be persuaded to follow this mad leader were success to crown his initial engagement. It was, however, to prevent this very thing that Tarzan of the Apes had interested himself in the activities of Peter Zveri; and here, before him, was another opportunity to undermine the Russian's dream of empire while it was still only a dream and might be dissipated by trivial means; by the grim and terrible jungle methods of which Tarzan of the Apes was a past-master.

Tarzan fitted an arrow to his bow. Slowly his right hand drew back the feathered end of the shaft until the point rested almost upon his left thumb. His manner was marked by easy, effortless grace. He did not appear to be taking conscious aim; and yet when he released the shaft, it buried itself in the fleshy part of a sentry's leg precisely as Tarzan of the Apes had intended that it should.

With a yell of surprise and pain the black collapsed upon the ground, more frightened, however, than hurt; and as his fellows gathered around him, Tarzan of the Apes melted away into the shadows of the jungle night.

Attracted by the cry of the wounded man, Zveri, Romero, and the other leaders of the expedition hastened from their tents and joined the throng of excited blacks that surrounded the victim of Tarzan's campaign of terrorism.

'Who shot you?' demanded Zveri when he saw the arrow protruding from the sentry's leg.

'I do not know,' replied the man.

'Have you an enemy in camp who might want to kill you?' asked Zveri.

'Even if he had,' said Romero, 'he couldn't have shot him with an arrow because no bows or arrows were brought with the expedition.'

'I hadn't thought of that,' said Zveri.

'So it must have been someone outside camp,' declared Romero.

With difficulty, and to the accompaniment of the screams of the victim, Ivitch and Romero cut the arrow from the sentry's leg, while Zveri and Kitembo discussed various conjectures as to the exact portent of the affair.

'We have evidently run into hostile natives,' said Zveri.

Kitembo shrugged non-committally. 'Let me see the arrow,' he said to Romero. 'Perhaps that will tell us something.'

As the Mexican handed the missile to the black chief, the latter carried it close to a campfire and examined it closely, while the white men gathered about him waiting for his findings.

At last Kitembo straightened up. The expression upon his face was serious, and when he spoke his voice trembled slightly. 'This is bad,' he said, shaking his bullet head.

'What do you mean?' demanded Zveri.

'This arrow bears the mark of a warrior who was left behind in our base camp,' replied the chief.

'That is impossible,' cried Zveri.

Kitembo shrugged. 'I know it,' he said, 'but it is true.'

'With an arrow out of the air the Hindu was slain,' suggested a black headman, standing near Kitembo.

'Shut up, you fool,' snapped Romero, 'or you'll have the whole camp in a blue funk.'

'That's right,' said Zveri. 'We must hush this thing up.' He turned to the headman. 'You and Kitembo,' he commanded, 'must not repeat this to your men. Let us keep it to ourselves.'

Both Kitembo and the headman agreed to guard the secret, but within half an hour every man in camp knew that the sentry had been shot with an arrow that had been left behind in the base camp, and immediately their minds were prepared for other things that lay ahead of them upon the long trail.

The effect of the incident upon the minds of the black soldiers was apparent during the following day's march. They were quieter and more thoughtful, and there was much low voiced conversation among them; but if they had given signs of nervousness during the day, it was nothing as compared with their state of mind after darkness fell upon their camp that night. The sentries evidenced their terror plainly by their listening attitudes and nervous attention to the sounds that came out of the blackness surrounding the camp. Most of them were brave men who would have faced a visible enemy with courage, but to a man they were convinced that they were confronted by the supernatural, against which they knew that neither rifle nor bravery might avail. They felt that ghostly eyes were watching them, and the result was as demoralizing as would an actual attack have been; in fact, far more so.

Yet they need not have concerned themselves so greatly, as the cause of all their superstitious apprehension was moving rapidly through the jungle, miles away from them, and every instant the distance between him and them was increasing.

Another force, that might have caused them even greater anxiety had they been aware of it, lay still further away upon the trail that they must traverse to reach their destination.

Around tiny cooking fires squatted a hundred black warriors, whose white plumes nodded and trembled as they moved. Sentries guarded them; sentries who were unafraid, since these men had little fear of ghosts or demons.

They wore their amulets in leather pouches that swung from cords about their necks and they prayed to strange gods, but deep in their hearts lay a growing contempt for both. They had learned from experience and from the advice of a wise leader to look for victory more to themselves and their weapons than to their god.

They were a cheerful, happy company, veterans of many an expedition and, like all veterans, took advantage of every opportunity for rest and relaxation, the value of both of which is enhanced by the maintenance of a cheerful frame of mind; and so there was much laughing and joking among them, and often both the cause and butt of this was a little monkey, now teasing, now caressing, and in return being himself teased or caressed. That there was a bond of deep affection between him and these clean-limbed black giants was constantly apparent. When they pulled his tail they never pulled it very hard, and when he turned upon them in apparent fury, his sharp teeth closing upon their fingers or arms, it was noticeable that he never drew blood. Their play was rough, for they were all rough and primitive creatures; but it was all playing, and it was based upon a foundation of mutual affection.

These men had just finished their evening meal when a figure, materializing as though out of thin air, dropped silently into their midst from the branches of a tree which overhung their camp.

Instantly a hundred warriors sprang to arms, and then, as quickly, they relaxed, as with shouts of 'Bwana! Bwana!' they ran toward the bronzed giant standing silently in their midst.

As to an emperor or a god they went upon their knees before him, and those that were nearest him touched his hands and his feet in reverence; for to the Waziri Tarzan of the Apes, who was their king, was yet something more and of their own volition they worshipped him as their living god.

But if the warriors were glad to see him, little Nkima was frantic with joy. He scrambled quickly over the bodies of the kneeling blacks and leaped to Tarzan's shoulder, where he clung about his neck, jabbering excitedly.

'You have done well, my children,' said the ape-man, 'and little Nkima has done well. He bore my message to you, and I find you ready where I had planned that you should be.'

'We have kept always a day's march ahead of the strangers, Bwana,' replied Muviro, 'camping well off the trail that they might not discover our fresh camp sites and become suspicious.'

'They do not suspect your presence,' said Tarzan. 'I listened above their camp last night, and they said nothing that would indicate that they dreamed that another party was preceding them along the trail.'

'Where the dirt of the trail was soft a warrior, who marched at the rear of the column, brushed away the freshness of our spoor with a leafy bough,' explained Muviro.

'Tomorrow we shall wait here for them,' said the ape-man, 'and tonight you shall listen to Tarzan while he explains the plans that you will follow.'

As Zveri's column took up the march upon the following morning, after a night of rest that had passed without incident, the spirits of all had risen to an appreciable degree. The blacks had not forgotten the grim warning that had sped out of the night surrounding their previous camp, but they were of a race whose spirits soon rebound from depression.

The leaders of the expedition were encouraged by the knowledge that over a third of the distance to their goal had been covered. For various reasons they were anxious to complete this part of the plan. Zveri believed that upon its successful conclusion hinged his whole dream of empire. Ivitch, a natural born trouble maker, was happy in the thought that the success of the expedition would cause untold annoyance to millions of people and perhaps, also, by the dream of his return to Russia as a hero; perhaps a wealthy hero.

Romero and Mori wanted to have it over for entirely different reasons. They were thoroughly disgusted with the Russian. They had lost all confidence in the sincerity of Zveri, who, filled as he was with his own importance and his delusions of future grandeur, talked too much, with the result that he had convinced Romero that he and all his kind were frauds, bent upon accomplishing their selfish ends with the assistance of their silly dupes and at the expense of the peace and prosperity of the world. It had not been difficult for Romero to convince Mori of the truth of his deductions, and now, thoroughly disillusioned, the two men continued on with the expedition because they believed that they could not successfully accomplish their intended desertion until the party was once more settled in the base camp.

The march had continued uninterruptedly for about an hour after camp had been broken, when one of Kitembo's black scouts, leading the column, halted suddenly in his tracks.

'Look!' he said to Kitembo, who was just behind him.

The chief stepped to the warrior's side; and there, before him in the trail sticking upright in the earth, was an arrow.

'It is a warning,' said the warrior.

Gingerly, Kitembo plucked the arrow from the earth and examined it. He would have been glad to have kept the knowledge of his discovery to himself, although not a little shaken by what he had seen; but the warrior at his side had seen, too. 'It is the same,' he said. 'It is another of the arrows that were left behind in the base camp.'

When Zveri came abreast of them, Kitembo handed him the arrow. 'It is the same,' he said to the Russian, 'and it is a warning for us to turn back.'

'Pooh!' exclaimed Zveri contemptuously. 'It is only an arrow sticking in the dirt and cannot stop a column of armed men. I did not think that you were a coward, too, Kitembo.'

The black scowled. 'Nor do men with safety call me a coward,' he snapped; 'but neither am I a fool, and better than you do I know the danger signals of the forest. We shall go on because we are brave men, but many will never come back. Also, your plans will fail.'

At this Zveri flew into one of his frequent rages; and though the men continued the march, they were in a sullen mood, and many were the ugly glances that were cast at Zveri and his lieutenants.

Shortly after noon the expedition halted for the noonday rest. They had been passing through dense woods, gloomy and depressing; and there was neither song nor laughter, nor a great deal of conversation as the men squatted together in little knots while they devoured the cold food that constituted their midday meal.

Suddenly, from somewhere far above, a voice floated down to them. Weird and uncanny, it spoke to them in a Bantu dialect that most of them could understand. 'Turn back, children of Mulungu,' it cried. 'Turn back before you die. Desert the white men before it is too late.'

That was all. The men crouched fearfully, looking up into the trees. It was Zveri who broke the silence. 'What the hell was that?' he demanded. 'What did it say?'

'It warned us to turn back,' said Kitembo.

'There will be no turning back,' snapped Zveri.

'I do not know about that,' replied Kitembo.

'I thought you wanted to be a king,' cried Zveri. 'You'd make a hell of a king.'

For the moment Kitembo had forgotten the dazzling prize that Zveri had held before his eyes for months – to be the king of Kenya. That was worth risking much for.

'We will go on,' he said.

'You may have to use force,' said Zveri, 'but stop at nothing. We must go on, no matter what happens,' and then he turned to his other lieutenants. 'Romero, you and Mori go to the rear of the column and shoot every man who refuses to advance.'

The men had not as yet refused to go on, and when the order to march was given, they sullenly took their places in the column. For an hour they marched thus; and then, far ahead, came the weird cry that many of them had heard before at Opar, and a few minutes later a voice out of the distance called to them. 'Desert the white men,' it said.

The blacks whispered among themselves, and it was evident that trouble was brewing; but Kitembo managed to persuade them to continue the march, a thing that Zveri never could have accomplished.

'I wish we could get that trouble-maker,' said Zveri to Zora Drinov, as the two walked together near the head of the column. 'If he would only show himself once, so that we could get a shot at him; that's all I want.'

'It is someone familiar with the workings of the native mind,' said the girl. 'Probably a medicine man of some tribe through whose territory we are marching.'

'I hope that it is nothing more than that,' replied Zveri. 'I have no doubt that the man is a native, but I am afraid that he is acting on instructions from either the British or the Italians, who hope thus to disorganize and delay us until they can mobilize a force with which to attack us.'

'It has certainly shaken the morale of the men,' said Zora, 'for I believe that they attribute all of the weird happenings, from the mysterious death of Jafar to the present time, to the same agency, to which their superstitious minds naturally attribute a supernatural origin.'

'So much the worse for them then,' said Zveri, 'for they are going on whether they wish to or not; and when they find that attempted desertion means death, they will wake up to the fact that it is not safe to trifle with Peter Zveri.'

'They are many, Peter,' the girl reminded him, 'and we are few; in addition they are, thanks to you, well armed. It seems to me that you may have created a Frankenstein that will destroy us all in the end.'

'You are as bad as the blacks,' growled Zveri, 'making a mountain out of a mole hill. Why if I—'

Behind the rear of the column and again apparently from the air above them sounded the warning voice. 'Desert the whites.' Silence fell again upon the marching column, but the men moved on exhorted by Kitembo and threatened by the revolvers of their white officers.

Presently the forest broke at the edge of a small plain, across which the trail led through buffalo grass that grew high above the heads of the marching men. They were well into this when, ahead of them, a rifle spoke, and then another and another, seemingly in a long line across their front.

Zveri ordered one of the blacks to rush Zora to the rear of the column into a position of safety, while he followed close behind her, ostensibly searching for Romero and shouting words of encouragement to the men.

As yet no one had been hit; but the column had stopped, and the men were rapidly losing all semblance of formation.

'Quick, Romero,' shouted Zveri, 'take command up in front. I will cover the rear with Mori and prevent desertions.'

The Mexican sprang past him and with the aid of Ivitch and some of the black chiefs he deployed one company in a long skirmish line, with which he advanced slowly; while Kitembo followed with half the rest of the expedition acting as a support, leaving Ivitch, Mori, and Zveri to organize a reserve from the remainder.

After the first widely scattered shots the firing had ceased, to be followed by a silence even more ominous to the overwrought nerves of the black soldiers. The utter silence of the enemy, the lack of any sign of movement in the grasses ahead of them coupled with the mysterious warnings which still rang in their ears, convinced the blacks that they faced no mortal foe.

'Turn back!' came mournfully from the grasses ahead. 'This is the last warning. Death will follow disobedience.'

The line wavered, and to steady it Romero gave the command to fire. In response came a rattle of musketry out of the grasses ahead of them, and this time a dozen men went down, killed or wounded.

'Charge!' cried Romero, but instead the men wheeled about and broke for the rear and safety.

At sight of the advance line bearing down upon them, throwing away their rifles as they ran, the support turned and fled, carrying the reserve with it, and the whites were carried along in the mad rout.

In disgust, Romero fell back alone. He saw no enemy, for none pursued him and this fact induced within him an uneasiness that the singing bullets had been unable to arouse. As he plodded on alone far in the rear of his companions, he began to share to some extent the feeling of unreasoning terror that had seized his black companions, or at least, if not to share it, to sympathize with them. It is one thing to face a foe that you can see, and quite another to be beset by an invisible enemy, of whose very appearance, even, one is ignorant.

Shortly after Romero re-entered the forest, he saw someone walking along the trail ahead of him; and presently, when he had an unobstructed view, he saw that it was Zora Drinov.

He called to her then, and she turned and waited for him.

'I was afraid that you had been killed, Comrade,' she said.

'I was born under a lucky star.' he replied smiling. 'Men were shot down on either side of me and behind me. Where is Zveri?'

Zora shrugged. 'I do not know,' she answered.

'Perhaps he is trying to reorganize the reserve,' suggested Romero.

'Doubtless,' said the girl shortly.

'I hope he is fleet of foot then,' said the Mexican, lightly.

'Evidently he is,' replied Zora.

'You should not have been left alone like this,' said the man.

'I can take care of myself,' replied Zora.

'Perhaps,' he said, 'but if you belonged to me—'

'I belong to no one, Comrade Romero,' she replied icily.

'Forgive me, Señorita,' he said. 'I know that. I merely chose an unfortunate way of trying to say that if the girl I loved were here she would not have been left alone in the forest, especially when I believe, as Zveri must believe, that we are being pursued by an enemy.'

'You do not like Comrade Zveri, do you, Romero?'

'Even to you, Señorita,' he replied, 'I must admit, since you ask me, that I do not.'

'I know that he has antagonized many.'

'He has antagonized all – except you, Señorita.'

'Why should I be excepted?' she asked. 'How do you know that he has not antagonized me also?'

'Not deeply, I am sure,' he said, 'or else you would not have consented to become his wife.'

'And how do you know that I have?' she asked.

'Comrade Zveri boasts of it often,' replied Romero.

'Oh, he does?' nor did she make any other comment.

CHAPTER XVII

A Gulf that was Bridged

The general rout of Zveri's forces ended only when their last camp had been reached and even then only for part of the command, for as night fell it was discovered that fully twenty-five per cent. of the men were missing, and among the absentees were Zora and Romero. As the stragglers came in, Zveri questioned each about the girl, but no one had seen her. He tried to organize an expedition to go back in search of her, but no one would accompany him. He threatened and pleaded, only to discover that he had lost all control of his men. Perhaps he would have gone back alone, as he insisted that he intended doing; but he was relieved of this necessity when, well after dark, the two walked into camp together.

At sight of them Zveri was both relieved and angry. 'Why didn't you remain with me?' he snapped at Zora.

'Because I cannot run so fast as you,' she replied, and Zveri said no more.

From the darkness of the trees above the camp came the now familiar warning. 'Desert the whites!' A long silence followed this, broken only by the nervous whisperings of the blacks, and then the voice spoke again. 'The trails to your own countries are free from danger, but death walks always with the white men. Throw away your uniforms and leave the white men to the jungle and to me.'

A black warrior leaped to his feet and stripped the French uniform from his body, throwing it upon a cooking fire that burned near him. Instantly others followed his example.

'Stop that!' cried Zveri.

'Silence, white man!' growled Kitembo.

'Kill the whites!' shouted a naked Basembo warrior.

Instantly there was a rush toward the whites, who were gathered near Zveri, and then from above them came a warning cry. 'The whites are mine!' it cried. 'Leave them to me.'

For an instant the advancing warriors halted; and then, he who had constituted himself their leader, maddened perhaps by his hatred and his blood lust, advanced again grasping his rifle menacingly.

From above a bowstring twanged. The black, dropping his rifle, screamed as he tore at an arrow protruding from his chest; and, as he fell forward upon his face, the other blacks fell back, and the whites were left alone, while the negroes huddled by themselves in a far corner of the camp. Many of them would have deserted that night, but they feared the darkness of the jungle and the menace of the thing hovering above them.

Zveri strode angrily to and fro, cursing his luck, cursing the blacks, cursing everyone. 'If I had had any help, if I had had any co-operation,' he grumbled, 'this would not have happened, but I cannot do everything alone.'

'You have done this pretty much alone,' said Romero.

'What do you mean?' demanded Zveri.

'I mean that you have made such an overbearing ass of yourself that you have antagonized everyone in the expedition, but even so they might have carried or if they had had any confidence in your courage – no man likes to follow a coward.'

'You call me that, you yellow greaser,' shouted Zveri, reaching for his revolver.

'Cut that,' snapped Romero. 'I have you covered. And let me tell you now that if it weren't for Señorita Drinov I would kill you on the spot and rid the world of at least one crazy mad dog that is threatening the entire world with the hydrophobia of hate and suspicion. Señorita Drinov saved my life once. I have not forgotten that; and because, perhaps, she loves you, you are safe, unless I am forced to kill you in self-defence.'

'This is utter insanity,' cried Zora. 'There are five of us here alone with a band of unruly blacks who fear and hate us. Tomorrow, doubtless, we shall be deserted by them. If we hope ever to get out of Africa alive, we must stick together. Forget your quarrels, both of you, and let us work together in harmony hereafter for our mutual salvation.'

'For your sake, Señorita, yes,' said Romero.

'Comrade Drinov is right,' said Ivitch.

Zveri dropped his hand from his gun and turned sulkily away; and for the rest of the night peace, if not happiness, held sway in the disorganized camp of the conspirators.

When morning came the whites saw that the all blacks had discarded their

French uniforms, and from the concealing foliage of a nearby tree other eyes had noted this same fact – gray eyes that were touched by the shadow of a grim smile. There were no black boys now to serve the whites, as even their personal servants had deserted them to foregather with the men of their own blood, and so the five prepared their own breakfast, after Zveri's attempt to command the services of some of their boys had met with surly refusal.

While they were eating, Kitembo approached them accompanied by the headmen of the different tribes that were represented in the personnel of the expedition. 'We are leaving with our people for our own countries,' said the Basembo chief. 'We leave food for your journey to your own camp. Many of our warriors wish to kill you, and that we cannot prevent if you attempt to accompany us, for they fear the vengeance of the ghosts that have followed you for many moons. Remain here until tomorrow. After that you are free to go where you will.'

'But,' expostulated Zveri, 'you can't leave us like this without porters or askaris.'

'No longer can you tell us what we can do, white man,' said Kitembo, 'for you are few and we are many, and your power over us is broken. In everything you have failed. We do not follow such a leader.'

'You can't do it,' growled Zveri. 'You will all be punished for this, Kitembo.'

'Who will punish us?' demanded the black. 'The English? The French? The Italians? You do not dare go to them. They would punish you, not us. Perhaps you will go to Ras Tafari. He would have your heart cut out and your body thrown to the dogs, if he knew what you were planning.'

'But you can't leave this white woman alone here in the jungle without servants, or porters, or adequate protection,' insisted Zveri, realizing that his first argument had made no impression upon the black chief who now held their fate in his hands.

'I do not intend to leave the white woman,' said Kitembo. 'She is going with me,' and then it was that, for the first time, the whites realized that the headmen had surrounded them and that they were covered by many rifles.

As he had talked, Kitembo had come closer to Zveri, at whose side stood Zora Drinov, and now the black chief reached out quickly and grasped her by the wrist. 'Come!' he said, and as he uttered the word something hummed above their heads, and Kitembo, chief of the Basembos, clutched at an arrow in his chest.

'Do not look up,' cried a voice from above. 'Keep your eyes upon the ground, for whosoever looks up dies. Listen well to what I have to say, black men. Go your way to your own countries, leaving behind you all of the white people. Do not harm them. They belong to me. I have spoken.'

Wide-eyed and trembling, the black headmen fell back from the whites, leaving Kitembo writhing upon the ground. They hastened to cross the camp to their fellows, all of whom were now thoroughly terrified; and before the chief of the Basembos ceased his death struggle, the black tribesmen had seized the loads which they had previously divided amongst them and were pushing and elbowing for precedence along the game trail that led out of camp toward the west.

Watching them depart, the whites sat in stupefied silence, which was not broken until after the last black had gone and they were alone.

'What do you suppose that thing meant by saying we belong to him?' asked Ivitch in a slightly thickened voice.

'How could I know?' growled Zveri.

'Perhaps it is a man-eating ghost,' suggested Romero with a smile.

'It has done about all the harm it can do now.' said Zveri. 'It ought to leave us alone for awhile.'

'It is not such a malign spirit,' said Zora. 'It can't be, for it certainly saved me from Kitembo.'

'Saved you for itself,' said Ivitch.

'Nonsense!' said Romero. 'The purpose of that mysterious voice from the air is just as obvious as is the fact that it is the voice of a man. It is the voice of someone who wanted to defeat the purposes of this expedition, and I imagine Zveri guessed close to the truth yesterday when he attributed it to English or Italian sources that were endeavouring to delay us until they could mobilize a sufficient force against us.'

'Which proves,' declared Zveri, 'what I have suspected for a long time; that there is more than one traitor among us,' and he looked meaningly at Romero.

'What it means,' said Romero, 'is that crazy, hare-brained theories always fail when they are put to the test. You thought that all the blacks in Africa would rush to your standard and drive all the foreigners into the ocean. In theory, perhaps, you were right, but in practice one man, with a knowledge of native psychology which you did not have, burst your entire dream like a bubble, and for every other hare-brained theory in the world there is always a stumbling block of fact.'

'You talk like a traitor to the cause,' said Ivitch threateningly.

'And what are you going to do about it?' demanded the Mexican. 'I am fed up with all of you and your whole rotten, selfish plan. There isn't an honest hair in your head nor in Zveri's. I can accord Tony and Señorita Drinov the benefit of a doubt, for I cannot conceive either of them as knaves. As I was deluded, so may they have been deluded, as you and your kind have striven for years to delude countless millions of others.'

'You are not the first traitor to the cause,' cried Zveri, 'nor will you be the first traitor to pay the penalty of his treason.'

'That is not a good way to talk now,' said Mori. 'We are not already too many. If we fight and kill one another, perhaps none of us will come out of

Africa alive. But if you kill Miguel, you will have to kill me, too, and perhaps you will not be successful. Perhaps it is you who will be killed.'

'Tony is right,' said the girl. 'Let us call a truce until we reach civilization.' And so it was that under something of the nature of an armed truce, the five set forth the following morning on the back trail toward their base camp; while upon another trail, a full day ahead of them, Tarzan and his Waziri warriors took a short cut for Opar.

'La may not be there,' Tarzan explained to Muviro, 'but I intend to punish Oah and Dooth for their treachery and thus make it possible for the high priestess to return in safety, if she still lives.'

'But how about the white enemies in the jungle back of us, Bwana?' asked Muviro.

'They shall not escape us,' said Tarzan. 'They are weak and inexperienced to the jungle. They move slowly. We may always overtake them when we will. It is La who concerns me most, for she is a friend, while they are only enemies.'

Many miles away, the object of his friendly solicitude approached a clearing in the jungle, a man-made clearing that was evidently intended for a camp site for a large body of men, though now only a few rude shelters were occupied by a handful of blacks.

At the woman's side walked Wayne Colt, his strength now fully regained, and at their heels paced Jad-bal-ja, the golden lion.

'We have found it at last,' said the man; 'thanks to you.'

'Yes, but it is deserted,' replied La. 'They have all left.'

'No,' said Colt, 'I see some blacks over by those shelters at the right.'

'It is well,' said La, 'and now I must leave you.' There was a note of regret in her voice.

'I hate to say goodbye,' said the man, 'but I know where your heart is and that all your kindness to me has only delayed your return to Opar. It is futile for me to attempt to express my gratitude, but I think that you know what is in my heart.'

'Yes,' said the woman, 'and it is enough for me to know that I have made a friend, I who have so few loyal friends.'

'I wish that you would let me go with you to Opar,' he said. 'You are going back to face enemies, and you may need whatever little help I should be able to give you.'

She shook her head. 'No, that cannot be,' she replied. 'All the suspicion and hatred of me that was engendered in the hearts of my people was caused by my friendship for a man of another world. Were you to return with me and assist me in regaining my throne, it would but arouse their suspicions still further. If Jad-bal-ja and I cannot succeed alone, three of us could accomplish no more.'

'Won't you at least be my guest for the rest of the day?' he asked. 'I can't offer you much hospitality,' he added with a rueful smile.

'No, my friend,' she said. 'I cannot take the chance of losing Jad-bal-ja; nor could you take the chance of losing your blacks, and I fear that they would not remain together in the same camp. Goodbye, Wayne Colt. But do not say that I go alone, at whose side walks Jad-bal-ja.'

From the base camp La knew the trail back to Opar; and as Colt watched her depart, he felt a lump rise in his throat, for the beautiful girl and the great lion seemed personifications of loveliness, and strength, and loneliness.

With a sigh he turned into camp and crossed to where the blacks lay sleeping through the midday heat. He awoke them, and at sight of him they were all very much excited, for they had been members of his own safari from the coast and recognized him immediately. Having long given him up for lost, they were at first inclined to be a little bit frightened until they had convinced themselves that he was, indeed, flesh and blood.

Since the killing of Dorsky they had had no master, and they confessed to him that they had been seriously considering deserting the camp and returning to their own countries; for they had been unable to rid their minds of the weird and terrifying occurrences that the expedition had witnessed in this strange country, in which they felt very much alone and helpless without the guidance and protection of a white master.

Across the plain of Opar, toward the ruined city, walked a girl and a lion; and behind them, at the summit of the escarpment which she had just scaled, a man halted, looking out across the plain, and saw them in the distance.

Behind him a hundred warriors swarmed up the rocky cliff. As they gathered about the tall, bronzed, gray-eyed figure that had preceded them, the man pointed. 'La!' he said.

'And Numa!' said Muviro. 'He is stalking her. It is strange, Bwana, that he does not charge.'

'He will not charge,' said Tarzan. 'Why, I do not know; but I know that he will not because it is Jad-bal-ja.'

'The eyes of Tarzan are like the eyes of the eagle,' said Muviro. 'Muviro sees only a woman and a lion, but Tarzan sees La and Jad-bal-ja.'

'I do not need my eyes for those two,' said the ape-man. 'I have a nose.'

'I too, have a nose,' said Muviro, 'but it is only a piece of flesh that sticks out from my face. It is good for nothing.'

Tarzan smiled. 'As a little child you did not have to depend upon your nose for your life and your food,' he said, 'as I have always done, then and since. Come, my children, La and Jad-bal-ja will be glad to see us.'

It was the keen ears of Jad-bal-ja that caught the first faint warning noises from the rear. He halted and turned, his great head raised majestically, his ears forward, the skin of his nose wrinkling to stimulate his sense of smell. Then he voiced a low growl, and La stopped and turned back to discover the cause of his displeasure.

As her eyes noted the approaching column, her heart sank. Even Jad-bal-ja could not protect her against so many. She thought then to attempt to outdistance them to the city; but when she glanced again at the ruined walls at the far side of the valley she knew that that plan was quite hopeless, as she would not have the strength to maintain a fast pace for so great a distance, while among those black warriors there must be many trained runners who could easily outdistance her. And so, resigned to her fate, she stood and waited; while Jad-bal-ja, with flattened head and twitching tail, advanced slowly to meet the oncoming men; and as he advanced, his savage growls rose to the tumult of tremendous roars that shook the earth as he sought to frighten away this menace to his loved mistress.

But the men came on; and then, of a sudden, La saw that one who came in advance of the others was lighter in colour, and her heart leaped in her breast; and then she recognized him, and tears came to the eyes of the savage high priestess of Opar.

'It is Tarzan! Jad-bal-ja, it is Tarzan!' she cried, the light of her great love illuminating her beautiful features.

Perhaps at the same instant the lion recognized his master, for the roaring ceased, the eyes no longer glared, no longer was the great head flattened as he trotted forward to meet the ape-man. Like a great dog, he reared up before Tarzan. With a scream of terror little Nkima leaped from the ape-man's shoulder and scampered, screaming, back to Muviro, since bred in the fibre of Nkima was the knowledge that Numa was always Numa. With his great paws on Tarzan's shoulder Jad-bal-ja licked the bronzed cheek, and then Tarzan pushed him aside and walked rapidly toward La; while Nkima, his terror gone, jumped frantically up and down on Muviro's shoulder calling the lion many jungle names for having frightened him.

'At last!' exclaimed Tarzan, as he stood face to face with La.

'At last,' repeated the girl, 'you have come back from your hunt.'

'I came back immediately,' replied the man, 'but you had gone.'

'You came back?' she asked.

'Yes, La,' he replied. 'I travelled far before I made a kill, but at last I found meat and brought it to you, and you were gone and the rain had obliterated your spoor and though I searched for days I could not find you.'

'Had I thought that you intended to return,' she said, 'I should have remained there forever.'

'You should have known that I would not have left you thus,' replied Tarzan.

'La is sorry,' she said.

'And you have not been back to Opar since?' he asked.

'Jad-bal-ja and I are on our way to Opar now,' she said. 'I was lost for a long time. Only recently did I find the trail to Opar, and then, too, there was the white man who was lost and sick with fever. I remained with him until the fever left him and his strength came back, because I thought that he might be a friend of Tarzan's.'

'What was his name?' asked the ape-man.

'Wayne Colt,' she replied.

The ape-man smiled. 'Did he appreciate what you did for him?' he asked.

'Yes, he wanted to come to Opar with me and help me regain my throne.'

'You liked him then, La?' he asked.

'I liked him very much,' she said, 'but not in the same way that I like Tarzan.'

He touched her shoulder in a half caress. 'La, the immutable!' he murmured, and then, with a sudden toss of his head as though he would clear his mind of sad thoughts, he turned once more toward Opar. 'Come,' he said, 'the queen is returning to her throne.'

The unseen eyes of Opar watched the advancing column. They recognized La, Tarzan, and the Waziri, and some there were who guessed the identity of Jad-bal-ja; and Oah was frightened, and Dooth trembled, and little Nao, who hated Oah, was almost happy, as happy as one may be who carries a broken heart in one's bosom.

Oah had ruled with a tyrant hand, and Dooth had been a weak fool whom no one longer trusted; and there were whisperings now among the ruins, whisperings that would have frightened Oah and Dooth had they heard them, and the whisperings spread among the priestesses and the warrior priests, with the result that when Tarzan and Jad-bal-ja led the Waziri into the courtyard of the outer temple there was no one there to resist them; but, instead, voices called down to them from the dark arches of surrounding corridors pleading for mercy and voicing earnest assurance of their future loyalty to La.

As they made their way into the city, they heard far in the interior of the temple a sudden burst of noise. High voices were punctuated by loud screams, and then came silence; and when they came to the throne room the cause of it was apparent to them, for lying in a welter of blood were the bodies of Oah and Dooth, with those of a half-dozen priests and priestesses who had remained loyal to them; and, but for these the great throne room was empty.

Once again did La, the high priestess of the Flaming God, resume her throne as Queen of Opar.

That night Tarzan, Lord of the Jungle, ate again from the golden platters of Opar, while young girls, soon to become priestesses of the Flaming God, served meats and fruits, and wines so old that no living man knew their vintage, nor in what forgotten vineyard grew the grapes that went into their making.

But in such things Tarzan found little interest, and he was glad when the new day found him at the head of his Waziri crossing the plain of Opar toward the barrier cliffs. Upon his bronzed shoulder sat Nkima, and at the ape-man's side paced the golden lion, while in column behind him marched his hundred Waziri warriors.

It was a tired and disheartened company of whites that approached their base camp after a long, monotonous and uneventful journey. Zveri and Ivitch were in the lead, followed by Zora Drinov, while a considerable distance to the rear Romero and Mori walked side by side, and such had been the order in which they had marched all these long days.

Wayne Colt was sitting in the shade of one of the shelters, and the blacks were lolling in front of another, a short distance away, as Zveri and Ivitch came into sight.

Colt rose and came forward, and it was then that Zveri spied him. 'You damned traitor!' he cried. 'I'll get you if it's the last thing I do on earth,' and as he spoke he drew his revolver and fired point blank at the unarmed American.

His first shot grazed Colt's side without breaking the skin, but Zveri fired no second shot, for almost simultaneously with the report of his own shot another rang out behind him, and Peter Zveri, dropping his pistol and clutching at his back, staggered drunkenly upon his feet.

Ivitch wheeled about. 'My God, Zora, what have you done?' he cried.

'What I have been waiting to do for twelve years,' replied the girl. 'What I have been waiting to do ever since I was little more than a child.'

Wayne Colt had run forward and seized Zveri's gun from the ground where it had fallen, and Romero and Mori now came up at a run.

Zveri had sunk to the ground and was glaring savagely about him. 'Who shot me?' he screamed. 'I know. It was that damned greaser.'

'It was I,' said Zora Drinov.

'You!' gasped Zveri.

Suddenly she turned to Wayne Colt as though only he mattered. 'You might as well know the truth,' she said. 'I am not a Red and never have been. This man killed my father, and my mother, and an older brother and sister. My father was – well, never mind who he was. He is avenged now.' She turned fiercely upon Zveri. 'I could have killed you a dozen times in the last few years,' she said, 'but I waited because I wanted more than your life. I wanted to help kill the hideous schemes with which you and your kind are seeking to wreck the happiness of the world.'

Peter Zveri sat on the ground, staring at her, his wide eyes slowly glazing. Suddenly he coughed and a torrent of blood gushed from his mouth. Then he sank back dead.

Romero had moved close to Ivitch. Suddenly he poked the muzzle of a revolver into the Russian's ribs. 'Drop your gun,' he said. 'I'm taking no chances on you either.'

Ivitch, paling, did as he was bid. He saw his little world tottering, and he was afraid.

Across the clearing a figure stood at the edge of the jungle. It had not been there an instant before. It had appeared silently as though out of thin air. Zora Drinov was the first to perceive it. She voiced a cry of surprised recognition; and as the others turned to follow the direction of her eyes, they saw a bronzed white man, naked but for a loin cloth of leopard skin, coming toward them. He moved with the easy, majestic grace of a lion and there was much about him that suggested the king of beasts.

'Who is that?' asked Colt.

'I do not know who he is,' replied Zora, 'other than that he is the man who saved my life when I was lost in the jungle.'

The man halted before them.

'Who are you?' demanded Wayne Colt.

'I am Tarzan of the Apes,' replied the other. 'I have seen and heard all that has occurred here. The plan that was fostered by this man,' he nodded at the body of Zveri, 'has failed and he is dead. This girl has avowed herself. She is not one of you. My people are camped a short distance away. I shall take her to them and see that she reaches civilization in safety. For the rest of you I have no sympathy. You may get out of the jungle as best you may. I have spoken.'

'They are not all what you think them, my friend,' said Zora.

'What do you mean?' demanded Tarzan.

'Romero and Mori have learned their lesson. They avowed themselves openly during a quarrel when our blacks deserted us.'

'I heard them,' said Tarzan.

She looked at him in surprise. 'You heard them?' she asked.

'I have heard much that has gone on in many of your camps,' replied the ape-man, 'but I do not know that I may believe all that I hear.'

'I think you may believe what you heard them say,' Zora assured him. 'I am confident that they are sincere.'

'Very well,' said Tarzan. 'If they wish they may come with me also, but these other two will have to shift for themselves.'

'Not the American,' said Zora.

'No? And why not?' demanded the ape-man.

'Because he is a special agent in the employ of the United States Government,' replied the girl.

The entire party, including Colt, looked at her in astonishment. 'How did you learn that?' demanded Colt.

'The message that you sent when you first came to camp and we were here alone was intercepted by one of Zveri's agents. Now do you understand how I know?'

'Yes,' said Colt. 'It is quite plain.'

'That is why Zveri called you a traitor and tried to kill you.'

'And how about this other?' demanded Tarzan, indicating Ivitch. 'Is he, also, a sheep in wolf's clothing?'

'He is one of those paradoxes who are so numerous,' replied Zora. 'He is one of those Reds who is all yellow.'

Tarzan turned to the blacks who had come forward and were standing, listening questioningly to a conversation they could not understand. 'I know our country,' he said to them in their own dialect. 'It lies near the end of the railroad that runs to the coast.'

'Yes, master,' said one of the blacks.

'You will take this white man with you as far as the railroad. See that he has enough to eat and is not harmed, and then tell him to get out of the country. Start now.' Then he turned back to the whites. 'The rest of you will follow me to my camp.' And with that he turned and swung away toward the trail by which he had entered the camp. Behind him followed the four who owed to his humanity more than they could ever know, nor had they known could have guessed that his great tolerance, courage, resourcefulness and the protective instinct that had often safeguarded them sprang not from his human progenitors, but from his lifelong association with the natural beasts of the forest and the jungle, who have these instinctive qualities far more strongly developed than do the unnatural beasts of civilization, in whom the greed and lust of competition have dimmed the lustre of these noble qualities where they have not eradicated them entirely.

Behind the others walked Zora Drinov and Wayne Colt, side by side.

'I thought you were dead,' she said.

'And I thought that you were dead,' he replied.

'And worse than that,' she continued, 'I thought that, whether dead or alive, I might never tell you what was in my heart.'

'And I thought that a hideous gulf separated us that I could never span to ask you the question that I wanted to ask you,' he answered in a low tone.

She turned toward him, her eyes filled with tears, her lips trembling. 'And I thought that, alive or dead, I could never say yes to that question, if you did ask me,' she replied.

A curve in the trail hid them from the sight of the others as he took her in his arms and drew her lips to his.

THE END

TARZAN TRIUMPHANT

PROLOGUE

Time is the warp of the tapestry which is life. It is eternal, constant, unchanging. But the woof is gathered together from the four corners of the earth and the twenty-eight seas and out of the air and the minds of men by that master artist, Fate, as she weaves the design that is never finished.

A thread from here, a thread from there, another from out of the past that has waited years for the companion thread without which the picture must be incomplete.

But Fate is patient. She waits a hundred or a thousand years to bring together two strands of thread whose union is essential to the fabrication of her tapestry, to the composition of the design that was without beginning and is without end.

A matter of someone thousand eight hundred sixty-five years ago (scholars do not agree as to the exact year), Paul of Tarsus suffered martyrdom at Rome.

That a tragedy so remote should seriously affect the lives and destinies of an English aviatrix and an American professor of geology, neither of whom was conscious of the existence of the other at the time this narrative begins – when it does begin, which is not yet, since Paul of Tarsus is merely by way of prologue – may seem remarkable to us, but not to Fate, who has been patiently waiting these nearly two thousand years for these very events I am about to chronicle.

But there is a link between Paul and these two young people. It is Angustus the Ephesian. Angustus was a young man of moods and epilepsy, a nephew of the house of Onesiphorus. Numbered was he among the early converts to the new faith when Paul of Tarsus first visited the ancient Ionian city of Ephesus.

Inclined to fanaticism, from early childhood an epileptic, and worshipping the apostle as the representative of the Master on earth, it is not strange that news of the martyrdom of Paul should have so affected Angustus as to seriously imperil his mental balance.

Conjuring delusions of persecution, he fled Ephesus, taking ship for Alexandria; and here we might leave him, wrapped in his robe, huddled, sick and frightened, on the deck of the little vessel, were it not for the fact that at the Island of Rhodus, where the ship touched, Angustus, going ashore, acquired in some manner (whether by conversion or purchase we know not) a fair haired slave girl from some far northern barbarian tribe.

And here we bid Angustus and the days of the Caesars adieu, and not without some regrets upon my part for I can well imagine adventure, if not romance, in the flight of Angustus and the fair haired slave girl down into Africa from the storied port of Alexandria, through Memphis and Thebae into the great unknown.

I

Gathering the Threads

As far as I know the first Earl of Whimsey has nothing to do with this story, and so we are not particularly interested in the fact that it was not so much the fine grade of whiskey that he manufactured that won him his earldom as the generous contribution he made to the Liberal party at the time that it was in power a number of years ago.

Being merely a simple historian and no prophet, I cannot say whether we shall see the Earl of Whimsey again or not. But if we do not find the Earl particularly interesting, I can assure you that the same may not be said of his fair daughter, Lady Barbara Collis.

The African sun, still an hour high, was hidden from the face of the earth by solid cloud banks that enveloped the loftier peaks of the mysterious, impenetrable fastnesses of the forbidding Ghenzi Mountain range that frowned perpetually upon a thousand valleys little known to man.

From far above this seeming solitude, out of the heart of the densely banked clouds, there came to whatever ears there might be to hear a strange and terrifying droning, suggesting the presence of a preposterous gargantuan bumblebee circling far above the jagged peaks of Ghenzi. At times it grew in volume until it attained terrifying proportions; and then gradually it diminished until it was only a suggestion of a sound, only to grow once again in volume and to again retreat.

For a long time, invisible and mysterious, it had been describing its great circles deep in the concealing vapors that hid it from the earth and hid the earth from it.

Lady Barbara Collis was worried. Her petrol was running low. At the crucial moment her compass had failed her, and she had been flying blind through the clouds looking for an opening for what now seemed an eternity of hours to her.

She had known that she must cross a lofty range of mountains, and she had kept at a considerable altitude above the clouds for this purpose; but presently they had risen to such heights that she could not surmount them; and, foolishly, rather than turn back and give up her projected non-stop flight from Cairo to the Cape, she had risked all in an effort to penetrate them.

For an hour Lady Barbara had been indulging in considerable high powered thinking, intermingled with the regret that she had not started thinking a little more heavily before she had taken off, as she had, against the explicit command of her sire. To say that she was terrified in the sense that fear had impaired any of her faculties would not be true. However, she was a girl of keen intelligence, fully competent to understand the grave danger of her situation; and when there loomed suddenly close to the tip of her left wing a granite escarpment that was lost immediately above and below her in the all enveloping vapor, it is no reflection upon her courage that she involuntarily caught her breath in a quick gasp and simultaneously turned the nose of her ship upwards until her altimeter registered an altitude that she knew must be far higher than the loftiest peak that reared its head above any part of Africa.

Rising in a wide spiral, she was soon miles away from that terrifying menace that had seemingly leaped out of the clouds to seize her. Yet even so, her plight was still as utterly hopeless as it well could be. Her fuel was practically exhausted. To attempt to drop below the cloud banks, now that she knew positively that she was among lofty mountains, would be utter madness; and so she did the only thing that remained to her.

Alone in the cold wet clouds, far above an unknown country, Lady Barbara Collis breathed a little prayer as she bailed out. With the utmost meticulosity she counted ten before she jerked the rip cord of her chute.

At the same instant Fate was reaching out to gather other threads – far flung threads – for his tiny fragment of her tapestry.

Kabariga, chief of the Bangalo people of Bungalo, knelt before Tarzan of the Apes many weary marches to the south of the Ghenzi Mountain.

In Moscow, Leon Stabutch entered the office of Stalin, the dictator of Red Russia.

Ignorant of the very existence of Kabariga, the black chief, or of Leon Stabutch or Lady Barbara Collis, Lafayette Smith, A.M., Ph. D., Sc. D., professor of geology at the Phil Sheridan Military Academy, boarded a steamship in the harbor of New York.

Mr Smith was a quiet, modest, scholarly looking young man with horn-rimmed spectacles, which he wore not because of any defect of eyesight but in the belief that they added a certain dignity and semblance of age to his appearance. That his spectacles were fitted with plain glass was known only to himself and his optician.

Graduated from college at seventeen the young man had devoted four additional years to acquiring further degrees, during which time he optimistically expected the stamp of dignified maturity to make itself evident in his face and bearing; but, to his intense dismay, his appearance seemed quite as youthful at twenty-one as it had at seventeen.

Lafe Smith's great handicap to the immediate fulfillment of his ambition (to occupy the chair of geology in some university of standing) lay in his possession of the unusual combination of brilliant intellect and retentive memory with robust health and a splendid physique. Do what he might he could not look sufficiently mature and scholarly to impress any college board. He tried whiskers, but the result was humiliating; and then he conceived the idea of horn-rimmed spectacles and pared his ambition down, temporarily, from a university to a prep school.

For a school year, now, he had been an instructor in an inconspicuous western military academy, and now he was about to achieve another of his cherished ambitions – he was going to Africa to study the great rift valleys of the Dark Continent, concerning the formation of which there are so many theories propounded and acclaimed by acknowledged authorities on the subject as to leave the layman with the impression that a fundamental requisite to success in the science of geology is identical to that required by weather forecasters.

But be that as it may, Lafayette Smith was on his way to Africa with the financial backing of a wealthy father and the wide experience that might be gained from a number of weekend field excursions into the back pastures of accommodating farmers, plus considerable ability as a tennis player and a swimmer.

We may leave him now, with his note books and seasickness, in the hands of Fate, who is leading him inexorably toward sinister situations from which no amount of geological knowledge nor swimming nor tennis ability may extricate him.

When it is two hours before noon in New York it is an hour before sunset in Moscow and so it was that as Lafe Smith boarded the liner in the morning, Leon Stabutch, at the same moment, was closeted with Stalin late in the afternoon.

'That is all,' said Stalin; 'you understand?'

'Perfectly,' replied Stabutch. 'Peter Zveri shall be avenged, and the obstacle that thwarted our plans in Africa shall be removed.'

'The latter is most essential,' emphasized Stalin, 'but do not belittle his abilities. He may be, as you have said, naught but an ape-man; but he utterly routed a well organized Red expedition that might have accomplished much in Abyssinia and Egypt but for his interference. And,' he added, 'I may tell you, comrade, that we contemplate another attempt; but it will not be made until we have a report from you that – the obstacle has been removed.'

Stabutch swelled his great chest. 'Have I ever failed?' he asked.

Stalin rose and laid a hand upon the other's shoulder. 'Red Russia does not look to the OGPU for failures,' he said. Only his lips smiled as he spoke.

That same night Leon Stabutch left Moscow. He thought that he left secretly and alone, but Fate was at his side in the compartment of the railway carriage.

As Lady Barbara Collis bailed out in the clouds above the Ghenzi range, and Lafayette Smith trod the gangplank leading aboard the liner, and Stabutch stood before Stalin, Tarzan, with knitted brows, looked down upon the black kneeling at his feet.

'Rise!' he commanded, and then; 'Who are you and why have you sought Tarzan of the Apes?'

'I am Kabariga, O Great Bwana,' replied the black. 'I am chief of the Bangalo people of Bungalo. I come to the Great Bwana because my people suffer much sorrow and great fear and our neighbors, who are related to the Gallas, have told us that you are the friend of those who suffer wrongs at the hands of bad men.'

'And what wrongs have your people suffered?' demanded Tarzan, 'and at whose hands?'

'For long we lived at peace with all men,' explained Kabariga; 'we did not make war upon our neighbors. We wished only to plant and harvest in security. But one day there came into our country from Abyssinia a band of *shiftas* who had been driven from their own country. They raided some of our villages, stealing our grain, our goats and our people, and these they sold into slavery in far countries.

'They do not take everything, they destroy nothing; but they do not go away out of our country. They remain in a village they have built in inaccessible mountains, and when they need more provisions or slaves they come again to other villages of my people.

'And so they permit us to live and plant and harvest that they may continue to take toll of us.'

'But why do you come to me?' demanded the ape-man. 'I do not interfere among tribes beyond the boundaries of my own country, unless they commit some depredation against my own people.'

'I come to you, Great Bwana,' replied the black chief, 'because you are a white man and these *shiftas* are led by a white man. It is known among all men that you are the enemy of bad white men.'

'That,' said Tarzan, 'is different. I will return with you to your country.'

And thus Fate, enlisting the services of the black chief, Kabariga, led Tarzan of the Apes out of his own country, toward the north. Nor did many of his own people know whither he had gone nor why – not even little Nkima, the close friend and confidant of the ape-man.

II

The Land of Midian

Abraham, the son of Abraham, stood at the foot of the towering cliff that is the wall of the mighty crater of a long extinct volcano. Behind and above him were the dwellings of his people, carved from the soft volcanic ash that rose from the bottom of the crater part way up the encircling cliffs; and clustered about him were the men and women and children of his tribe.

One and all, they stood with faces raised toward the heavens, upon each countenance reflected the particular emotion that the occasion evoked – wonder, questioning, fear, and always rapt, tense listening, for from the low clouds hanging but a few hundred feet above the rim of the great crater, the floor of which stretched away for fully five miles to its opposite side, came a strange, ominous droning sound, the like of which not one of them had ever heard before.

The sound grew in volume until it seemed to hover just above them, filling all the heavens with its terrifying threat; and then it diminished gradually until it was only a suggestion of a sound that might have been no more than a persistent memory rumbling in their heads; and when they thought that it had gone it grew again in volume until once it thundered down upon them where they stood in terror or in ecstasy, as each interpreted the significance of the phenomenon.

And upon the opposite side of the crater a similar group, actuated by identical fears and questionings, clustered about Elija, the son of Noah.

In the first group a woman turned to Abraham, the son of Abraham. 'What is it, Father?' she asked. 'I am afraid.'

'Those who trust in the Lord,' replied the man, 'know no fear. You have revealed the wickedness of your heresy, woman.'

The face of the questioner blenched and now, indeed, did she tremble. 'Oh, Father, you know that I am no heretic!' she cried piteously.

'Silence, Martha!' commanded Abraham. 'Perhaps this is the Lord Himself, come again to earth as was prophesied in the days of Paul, to judge us all.' His voice was high and shrill, and he trembled as he spoke.

A half grown child, upon the outskirts of the assemblage, fell to the ground, where he writhed, foaming at the mouth. A woman screamed and fainted.

'Oh, Lord, if it is indeed Thee, Thy chosen people await to receive Thy blessing and Thy commands,' prayed Abraham; 'but,' he added, 'if it is not Thee, we beseech that Thou savest us whole from harm.'

'Perhaps it is Gabriel!' suggested another of the long bearded men.

'And the sound of his trump,' wailed a woman – 'the trump of doom!'

'Silence!' shrilled Abraham, and the woman shrank back in fear.

Unnoticed, the youth floundered and gasped for breath as, with eyes set as in death, he struggled in the throes of agony; and then another lurched and fell and he, too, writhed and foamed.

And now they were dropping on all sides – some in convulsions and others in deathlike faints – until a dozen or more sprawled upon the ground, where their pitiable condition elicited no attention from their fellows unless a stricken one chanced to fall against a neighbor or upon his feet, in which case the latter merely stepped aside without vouchsafing so much as a glance at the poor unfortunate.

With few exceptions those who suffered the violent strokes were men and boys, while it was the women who merely fainted; but whether man, woman or child, whether writhing in convulsions or lying quietly in coma, no one paid the slightest attention to any of them. As to whether this seeming indifference was customary, or merely induced by the excitement and apprehension of the moment, as they stood with eyes, ears, and minds focussed on the clouds above them, only a closer acquaintance with these strange people may enlighten us.

Once more the terrifying sound, swollen to hideous proportions, swept toward them; it seemed to stop above them for a moment and then—

Out of the clouds floated a strange apparition – a terrifying thing – a great, white thing above, below which there swung to and fro a tiny figure. At sight of it, dropping gently toward them, a dozen of the watchers collapsed, frothing, in convulsions.

Abraham, the son of Abraham, dropped to his knees, raising his hands in supplication toward the heavens. His people, those of them who were still upon their feet, followed his example. From his lips issued a torrent of strange sounds – a prayer perhaps, but if so not in the same language as that in which he had previously spoken to his people nor in any language known to man, and as he prayed, his followers knelt in terrified silence.

Closer and closer floated the mysterious apparition until, at length, expectant eyes recognized in the figure floating beneath the small, white cloud the outlines of a human form.

A great cry arose as recognition spread – a cry that was a mingling of terror born wail and ecstatic hosanna. Abraham was among the last to recognize the form of the dangling figure for what it was, or, perhaps, among the last to admit the testimony of his eyes. When he did he toppled to the ground, his muscles twitching and jerking his whole body into horrid contortions, his eyes rolled upward and set as in death, his breath expelled in painful gasps between lips flecked with foam.

Abraham, the son of Abraham, never an Adonis, was at this moment anything but a pretty sight; but no one seemed to notice him any more than they had the score or more of lesser creatures who had succumbed to the nervous excitation of the experiences of the past half hour.

Some five hundred people, men, women and children, of which thirty, perhaps, lay quietly or writhed in convulsions upon the ground, formed the group of watchers toward which Lady Barbara Collis gently floated. As she landed in, if the truth must be told (and we historians are proverbially truthful, except when we are chronicling the lives of our national heroes, or living rulers within whose grasp we may be, or of enemy peoples with whom our country has been at war, and upon other occasions) – but, as I was recording, as Lady Barbara landed in an awkward sprawl within a hundred yards of the assemblage all those who had remained standing up to this time went down upon their knees.

Hastily scrambling to her feet, the girl disengaged the harness of her parachute and stood gazing in perplexity upon the scene about her. A quick glance had revealed the towering cliffs that formed the encircling walls of the gigantic crater, though at the time she did not suspect the true nature of the valley spreading before her. It was the people who claimed her surprised attention.

They were white! In the heart of Africa she had landed in the midst of a settlement of whites. But this thought did not wholly reassure her. There was something strange and unreal about these prone and kneeling figures; but at least they did not appear ferocious or unfriendly – their attitudes, in fact, were quite the opposite, and she saw no evidence of weapons among them.

She approached them, and, as she did so, many of them began to wail and press their faces against the ground, while others raised their hands in supplication – some toward the heavens and others toward her.

She was close enough now to see their features and her heart sank within her, for she had never conceived the existence of an entire village of people of such unprepossessing appearance, and Lady Barbara was one of those who are strongly impressed by externals.

The men were particularly repulsive. Their long hair and beards seemed as little acquainted with soap, water and combs as with shears and razors.

There were two features that impressed her most strongly and unfavorably – the huge noses and receding chins of practically the entire company. The noses were so large as to constitute a deformity, while in many of those before her, chins were almost non-existent.

And then she saw two things that had diametrically opposite effects upon her – the scores of epileptics writhing upon the ground and a singularly beautiful, golden haired girl who had risen from the prostrate herd and was slowly approaching her, a questioning look in her large grey eyes.

Lady Barbara Collis looked the girl full in the eyes and smiled, and when Lady Barbara smiled stone crumbled before the radiant vision of her face – or so a poetic and enthralled admirer had once stated in her hearing. The fact that he lisped, however, had prejudiced her against his testimony.

The girl return the smile with one almost as gorgeous, but quickly erased it from her features, at the same time glancing furtively about her as though fearful that someone had detected her in the commission of a crime; but when Lady Barbara extended both her hands toward her, she came forward and placed her own within the grasp of the English girl's.

'Where am I?' asked Lady Barbara. 'What country is this? Who are these people?'

The girl shook her head. 'Who are you?' she asked. 'Are you an angel that the Lord God of Hosts has sent to His chosen people?'

It was now the turn of Lady Barbara to shake her head to evidence her inability to understand the language of the other.

An old man with a long white beard arose and came toward them, having seen that the apparition from Heaven had not struck the girl dead for her temerity.

'Get thee gone, Jezebel!' cried the old man to the girl. 'How durst thou address this Heavenly visitor?'

The girl stepped back, dropping her head; and though Lady Barbara had understood no word that the man spoke, his tone and gesture, together with the action of the girl, told her what had transpired between them.

She thought quickly. She had realized the impression that her miraculous appearance had made upon these seemingly ignorant people, and she guessed that their subsequent attitude toward her would be governed largely by the impression of her first acts; and being English, she held to the English tradition of impressing upon lesser people the authority of her breed. It would never do, therefore, to let this unkempt patriarch order the girl from her if Lady Barbara chose to retain her; and, after glancing at the faces about her, she was quite sure that if she must choose a companion from among them the fair haired beauty would be her nominee.

With an imperious gesture, and a sinking heart, she stepped forward and took the girl by the arm, and, as the latter turned a surprised glance upon her, drew her to her side.

'Remain with me,' she said, although she knew her words were unintelligible to the girl.

'What did she say, Jezebel?' demanded the old man.

The girl was about to reply that she did not know, but something stopped her. Perhaps the very strangeness of the question gave her pause, for it must have been obvious to the old man that the stranger spoke in a tongue unknown to him and, therefore, unknown to any of them.

She thought quickly, now. Why should he ask such a question unless he might entertain a belief that she might have understood? She recalled the smile that the stranger had brought to her lips without her volition, and she recalled, too, that the old man had noted it.

The girl called Jezebel knew the price of a smile in the land of Midian, where any expression of happiness is an acknowledgment of sin; and so, being a bright girl among a people who were almost uniformly stupid, she evolved a ready answer in the hope that it might save her from punishment.

She looked the ancient one straight in the eye. 'She said, Jobab,' she replied, 'that she cometh from Heaven with a message for the chosen people and that she will deliver the message through me and through no other.'

Now much of this statement had been suggested to Jezebel by the remarks of the elders and the apostles as they had watched the strange apparition descending from the clouds and had sought to find some explanation for the phenomenon. In fact, Jobab himself had volunteered the very essence of this theory and was, therefore, the more ready to acknowledge belief in the girl's statement.

Lady Barbara stood with an arm about the slim shoulders of the golden haired Jezebel, her shocked gaze encompassing the scene before her – the degraded, unkempt people huddled stupidly before her, the inert forms of those who had fainted, the writhing contortions of the epileptics. With aversion she appraised the countenance of Jobab, noting the watery eyes, the huge monstrosity of his nose, the long, filthy beard that but half concealed his weak chin. With difficulty she stemmed the involuntary shudder that was her natural nervous reaction to the sight before her.

Jobab stood staring at her, an expression of awe on his stupid, almost imbecile face. From the crowd behind him several other old men approached, almost fearfully, halting just behind him. Jobab looked back over his shoulder. 'Where is Abraham, the son of Abraham?' he demanded.

'He still communeth with Jehovah,' replied one of the ancients.

'Perhaps even now Jehovah revealeth to him the purpose of his visitation,' suggested another hopefully.

'She hath brought a message,' said Jobab, 'and she will deliver it only through the girl called Jezebel. I wish Abraham, the son of Abraham, was through communing with Jehovah,' he added; but Abraham, the son of Abraham, still writhed upon the ground, foaming at the mouth.

'Verily,' said another old man, 'if this be indeed a messenger from Jehovah let us not stand thus idly staring, lest we arouse the anger of Jehovah, that he bring a plague upon us, even of flies or of lice.'

'Thou speaketh true words, Timothy,' agreed Jobab, and, turning to the crowd behind them; 'Get thee hence quickly and fetch offerings that may be good in the sight of Jehovah, each in accordance with his ability.'

Stupidly the assemblage turned away toward the caves and hovels that constituted the village, leaving the small knot of ancients facing Lady Barbara and the golden Jezebel and, upon the ground, the stricken ones, some of whom were evidencing symptoms of recovery from their seizures.

Once again a feeling of revulsion gripped the English girl as she noted the features and carriages of the villagers. Almost without exception they were disfigured by enormous noses and chins so small and receding that in many instances the chin seemed to be lacking entirely. When they walked they ordinarily leaned forward, giving the impression that they were upon the verge of pitching headlong upon their faces.

Ocassionally among them appeared an individual whose countenance suggested a much higher mentality than that possessed by the general run of the villagers, and without exception these had blond hair, while the hair of all the others was black.

So striking was this phenomenon that Lady Barbara could not but note it almost in her first brief survey of these strange creatures, yet she was never to discover an indusputable explanation, for there was none to tell her of Angustus and the fair haired slave girl from some barbarian horde of the north, none who knew that Angustus had had a large nose, a weak chin and epilepsy, none to guess the splendid mind and the radiant health of the little slave girl, dead now for almost nineteen centuries, whose blood, even now, arose occasionally above the horrid decadence of all those long years of enforced inbreeding to produce such a creature as Jezebel in an effort, however futile, to stem the tide of degeneracy.

Lady Barbara wondered now why the people had gone to their dwellings – what did it portend? She looked at the old men who had remained behind; but their stupid, almost imbecile faces revealed nothing. Then she turned to the girl. How she wished that they might understand one another. She was positive that the girl was actively friendly, but she could not be so sure of these others. Everything about them repelled her, and she found it impossible to have confidence in their intentions toward her.

But how different was the girl! She, too, doubtless, was an alien among them; and that fact gave the English girl hope, for she had seen nothing to indicate that the golden haired one was being threatened or mistreated; and at least she was alive and uninjured. Yes, she must be of another breed. Her simple, and scant, apparel, fabricated apparently from vegetable fibre, was clean, as were those parts of her body exposed to view, while the garments of all the others, especially the old men, were filthy beyond words, as were their hair and beards and every portion of their bodies not concealed by the mean garments that scarce half covered their nakedness.

As the old men whispered among themselves, Lady Barbara turned slowly to look about her in all directions. She saw precipitous cliffs completely hemming a small circular valley, near the center of which was a lake. Nowhere could she see any indication of a break in the encircling walls that rose hundreds of feet above the floor of the valley; and yet she felt that there must be an entrance from the outer world, else how had these people gained entrance?

Her survey suggested that the valley lay at the bottom of the crater of a great volcano, long extinct, and if that were true the path to the outer world must cross the summit of those lofty walls; yet these appeared, insofar as she could see, utterly unscalable. But how to account for the presence of these people? The problem vexed her, but she knew that it must remain unsolved until she had determined the attitude of the villagers and discovered whether she were to be a guest or a prisoner.

Now the villagers were returning, and she saw that many of them carried articles in their hands. They came slowly, timidly nearer her, exhorted by the ancients, until at her feet they deposited the burdens they had carried – bowls of cooked food, raw vegetables and fruits, fish, and pieces of the fibre cloth such as that from which their crude garments were fabricated, the homely offerings of a simple people.

As they approached her many of them displayed symptoms of great nervousness and several sank to the ground, victims of the convulsive paroxysms that marked the seizures to which so many of them appeared to be subject.

To Lady Barbara it appeared that these simple folk were either bringing gifts attesting their hospitality or were offering their wares, in barter, to the stranger within their gates; nor did the truth once occur to her at the moment – that the villagers were, in fact, making votive offerings to one they believed the messenger of God, or even, perhaps, a goddess in her own right. When, after depositing their offerings at her feet, they turned and hastened away, the simple faces of some evidencing fear caused her to abandon the idea that the goods were offered for sale; and she determined that, if not gifts of hospitality, they might easily be considered as tribute to appease the wrath of a potential enemy.

Abraham, the son of Abraham, had regained consciousness. Slowly he raised himself to a sitting position and looked about him. He was very weak. He always was after these seizures. It required a minute or two before he could collect his wits and recall the events immediately preceding the attack. He saw the last of those bringing offerings to Lady Barbara deposit them at her feet. He saw the stranger. And then he recalled the strange droning that had come out of the heavens and the apparition that he had seen floating down toward them.

Abraham, the son of Abraham, arose. It was Jobab, among the ancients, who saw him first. 'Hallelujah!' he exclaimed. 'Abraham, the son of Abraham, walketh no longer with Jehovah. He hath returned to our midst. Let us pray!' Whereupon the entire assemblage, with the exception of Lady Barbara and the girl called Jezebel, dropped to its knees. Among them, Abraham, the son of Abraham, moved slowly, as though in a trance, toward the stranger, his mind still lethargic from the effects of his seizure. About him arose a strange, weird babel as the ancients prayed aloud without concord or harmony, interrupted by occasional cries of 'Hallelujah' and 'Amen.'

Tall and thin, with a long grey beard still flecked with foam and saliva, his scant robe ragged and filthy, Abraham, the son of Abraham, presented a most repulsive appearance to the eyes of the English girl as, at last, he stopped before her.

Now his mind was clearing rapidly, and as he halted he seemed to note the presence of the girl Jezebel, for the first time. 'What doest thou here, wanton?' he demanded. 'Why art thou not upon thy knees praying with the others?'

Lady Barbara was watching the two closely. She noted the stern and accusing attitude and tones of the man, and she saw the appealing glance that the girl cast toward her. Instantly she threw an arm about the latter's shoulder. 'Remain here!' she said, for she feared that the man was ordering the girl to leave her.

If Jezebel did not understand the words of the strange, heavenly visitor, she could not mistake the detaining gesture; and, anyway, she did not wish to join the others in prayer. Perhaps it was only that she might cling a few brief minutes longer to the position of importance to which the incident had elevated her out of a lifetime of degradation and contempt to which her strange inheritance of beauty had condemned her.

And so, nerved by the pressure of the arm about her, she faced Abraham, the son of Abraham, resolutely, although, withal, a trifle fearfully, since who knew better than she what a terrible man Abraham, the son of Abraham, might become when crossed by anyone.

'Answer me, thou – thou—' Abraham, the son of Abraham, could not find an epithet sufficiently excoriating to meet the emergency.

'Let not thy anger blind thee to the will of Jehovah,' warned the girl.

'What meanest thou?' he demanded.

'Canst thou not see that His messenger hath chosen me to be her mouthpiece?'

'What sacrilege is this, woman?'

'It is no sacrilege,' she replied sturdily. 'It is the will of Jehovah, and if thou believest me not, ask Jobab, the apostle.'

Abraham, the son of Abraham, turned to where the ancients prayed. 'Jobab!' he cried in a voice that arose above the din of prayer.

Instantly the devotions ceased with a loud 'Amen!' from Jobab. The old men arose, their example being followed by those others of the villagers who were not held earthbound by epilepsy; and Jobab, the apostle, approached the three who were now the goal of every eye.

'What transpired while I walked with Jehovah?' demanded Abraham, the son of Abraham.

'There came this messenger from heaven,' replied Jobab, 'and we did her honor, and the people brought offerings, each according to his ability, and laid them at her feet, and she did not seem displeased – nor either did she seem pleased,' he added. 'And more than this we knew not what to do.'

'But this daughter of Satan!' cried Abraham, the son of Abraham. 'What of her?'

'Verily I say unto you that she speaks with the tongue of Jehovah,' replied Jobab, 'for He hath chosen her to be the mouthpiece of His messenger.'

'Jehovah be praised,' said Abraham, the son of Abraham; 'the ways of the Almighty passeth understanding.' He turned now to Jezebel, but when he spoke there was a new note in his tones – a conciliatory note – and, perhaps, not a little of fear in his eyes. 'Beseech the messenger to look upon us poor servants of Jehovah with mercy and forgiveness; beg of her that she open her mouth to us poor sinners and divulge her wishes. We await her message, trembling and fearful in the knowledge of our unworthiness.'

Jezebel turned to Lady Barbara.

'But wait!' cried Abraham, the son of Abraham, as a sudden questioning doubt assailed his weak mind, 'How can you converse with her? You speak only the language of the land of Midian. Verily, if thou canst speak with her, why may not I, the Prophet of Paul, the son of Jehovah?'

Jezebel had a brain worth fifty such brains as that possessed by the Prophet of Paul; and now she used it to advantage, though, if the truth were known, not without some misgivings as to the outcome of her rash proposal, for, although she had a bright and resourceful mind, she was nonetheless the ignorant child of an ignorant and superstitious people.

'Thou hast a tongue, Prophet,' she said. 'Speak thou then to the messenger of Jehovah, and if she answers thee in a language of the land of Midian thou canst understand her as well as I.'

'That,' said Abraham, the son of Abraham, 'is scarce less than an inspiration.'

'A miracle!' exclaimed Jobab. 'Jehovah must have put the words in her mouth.'

'I shall address the messenger,' said the Prophet. 'O angel of light!' he cried, turning toward Lady Barbara, 'look with compassion upon an old man, upon Abraham, the son of Abraham, the Prophet of Paul, the son of Jehovah, and deign to make known to him the wishes of Him who sent you to us.'

Lady Barbara shook her head. 'There is something that one does when one is embarrassed,' she said. 'I have read it repeatedly in the advertising sections of American periodicals, but I haven't that brand. However, any port in a storm,' and she extracted a gold cigarette case from a pocket of her jacket and lighted one of the cigarettes.

'What didst she say, Jezebel?' demanded the Prophet – 'and, in the name of Paul, what miracle is this? "Out of his nostrils goeth smoke" is said of the behemoth of holy writ. What can be the meaning of this?'

'It is a warning,' said Jezebel, 'because thou didst doubt my words.'

'Nay, nay,' exclaimed Abraham, the son of Abraham, 'I doubted thee not. Tell her that I did not doubt thee, and then tell me what she said.'

'She said,' replied Jezebel, 'that Jehovah is not pleased with thee or thy people. He is angry because thou so mistreat Jezebel. His anger is terrible because thou dost make her work beyond her strength, nor give her the best food, and that thou dost punish her when she would laugh and be happy.'

'Tell her,' said the Prophet, 'that we knew not that thou were overworked and that we shall make amends. Tell her that we lovest thee and thou shalt have the best of food. Speak to her, O Jezebel, and ask if she has further commands for her poor servants.'

Jezebel looked into the eyes of the English girl, and upon her countenance rested an expression of angelic guilelessness, while from her lips issued a stream of meaningless jargon which was as unintelligible to Jezebel as to Lady Barbara or the listening villagers of the land of Midian.

'My dear child,' said Lady Barbara, when Jezebel eventually achieved a period, 'what you say is as Greek to me, but you are very beautiful and your voice is musical. I am sorry that you can understand me no better than I understand you.'

'What saith she?' demanded Abraham, the son of Abraham.

'She says that she is tired and hungry and that she wishes the offerings brought by the people to be taken to a cave – a clean cave – and that I accompany her and that she be left in peace, as she is tired and would rest; and she wishes no one but Jezebel to be with her.'

Abraham, the son of Abraham, turned to Jobab. 'Send women to make clean the cave next to mine,' he commanded, 'and have others carry the offerings to the cave, as well as clean grasses for a bed.'

'For two beds,' Jezebel corrected him.

'Yea, even for two beds,' agreed the Prophet, hastily.

And so Lady Barbara and Jezebel were installed in a well renovated cave near the bottom of the cliff, with food enough to feed a numerous company. The English girl stood at the entrance to her strange, new abode looking out across the valley as she sought to evolve some plan whereby she might get word of her predicament and her whereabouts to the outside world. In another twenty-four hours she knew the apprehension of her friends and her family would be aroused and soon many an English plane would be roaring over the Cape to Cairo route in search of her, and, as she pondered her unfortunate situation, the girl called Jezebel lay in luxurious idleness upon her bed of fresh grasses and ate from a pile of fruit near her hand, the while a happy smile of contentment illumed her lovely countenance.

The shadows of night were already falling, and Lady Barbara turned back into the cave with but a single practical idea evolved from all her thinking – that she must find the means to communicate with these people, nor could she escape the conviction that only by learning their language might this be accomplished.

As darkness came and chill night air replaced the heat of the day, Jezebel kindled a fire at the mouth of the cave. Near it the two girls sat upon a soft cushion of grass, the firelight playing upon their faces, and there the Lady Barbara commenced the long and tedious task of mastering a new language. The first step consisted in making Jezebel understand what she desired to accomplish, but she was agreeably astonished at the celerity with which the girl grasped the idea. Soon she was pointing to various objects, calling them by their English names and Jezebel was naming them in the language of the land of Midian.

Lady Barbara would repeat the word in the Midian language several times until she had mastered the pronunciation, and she noticed that, similarly, Jezebel was repeating its English equivalent. Thus was Jezebel acquiring an English vocabulary while she taught the Midian to her guest.

An hour passed while they occupied their time with their task. The village lay quiet about them. Faintly, from the distant lake, came the subdued chorus of the frogs. Occasionally a goat bleated somewhere out in the darkness. Far away, upon the opposite side of the valley, shone tiny, flickering lights – the cooking fires of another village, thought Lady Barbara.

A man, bearing a lighted torch, appeared suddenly, coming from a nearby cave. In low, monotonous tones he voiced a chant. Another man, another torch, another voice joined him. And then came others until a procession wound down toward the level ground below the caves.

Gradually the voices rose. A child screamed. Lady Barbara saw it now – a small child being dragged along by an old man.

Now the procession encircled a large boulder and halted, but the chanting did not cease, nor did the screaming of the child. Tall among the others Lady Barbara recognized the figure of the man who had last interrogated her. Abraham, the son of Abraham, the Prophet, stood behind the boulder that rose waist high in front of him. He raised his open palm and the chanting ceased. The child had ceased to scream, but its broken sobs came clearly to the ears of the two girls.

Abraham, the son of Abraham, commenced to speak, his eyes raised toward the heavens. His voice came monotonously across the little span of darkness. His grotesque features were lighted by the flickering torches that played as well upon the equally repulsive faces of his congregation.

Unaccountably, the entire scene assumed an aspect of menace in the eyes of the English girl. Apparently it was only the simple religious service of a simple people and yet, to Barbara Collis, there was something terrible about it, something that seemed fraught with horror.

She glanced at Jezebel. The girl was sitting cross legged, her elbows on her knees, her chin supported in the palms of her hands, staring straight ahead. There was no smile now upon her lips.

Suddenly the air was rent by a childish scream of fear and horror that brought the Lady Barbara's gaze back to the scene below. She saw the child, struggling and fighting, dragged to the top of the boulder; she saw Abraham, the son of Abraham, raise a hand above his head; she saw the torchlight play upon a knife; and then she turned away and hid her face in her hands.

III

The 'Gunner'

Danny 'Gunner' Patrick stretched luxuriously in his deck chair. He was at peace with the world – temporarily, at least. In his clothes were 20 G. securely hidden. Beneath his left arm pit, also securely hidden, snuggled a .45 in a specially designed holster. 'Gunner' Patrick did not expect to have to use it for a long, long time perhaps; but it was just as well to be prepared. 'Gunner' hailed from Chicago where people in his circle of society believe in preparedness.

He had never been a Big Shot, and if he had been content to remain more or less obscure he might have gone along about his business for some time until there arrived the allotted moment when, like many of his late friends and acquaintances, he should be elected to stop his quota of machine gun bullets; but Danny Patrick was ambitious. For years he had been the right hand, and that means the pistol hand, of a Big Shot. He had seen his patron grow rich – 'lousy rich,' according to Danny's notion – and he had become envious.

So Danny double-crossed the Big Shot, went over to the other side, which, incidentally, boasted a bigger and better Big Shot, and was a party to the hijacking of several truck loads of booze belonging to his former employer.

Unfortunately on the occasion of the hijacking of the last truck, one of his former pals in the service of the double-crossed recognized him; and Danny, knowing that he had been recognized, sought, quite pardonably, to eliminate this damaging evidence; but his unwilling target eluded him and before he could rectify his ballistic errors the police came.

It is true that they obligingly formed an escort to convoy the truck safely to the warehouse of the bigger and better Big Shot, but the witness to Danny's perfidy escaped.

Now Danny 'Gunner' Patrick knew the temper of his erstwhile patron – and who better? Many of the Big Shot's enemies, and several of his friends, had Danny taken for a ride. He knew the power of the Big Shot, and he feared him. Danny did not want to go for a ride himself, but he knew that if he remained in dear old Chi he would go the way of all good gunmen much too soon to suit his plans.

And so, with the 20 G. that had been the price of his perfidy, he had slipped quietly out of town; and, being wise in his day and generation, he had also slipped quietly out of the country, another thread to be woven into Fate's tapestry.

He knew that the Big Shot was slipping (that was one reason he had deserted him); and he also knew that, sooner or later, the Big Shot would have a grand funeral with truck loads of flowers and, at least, a ten thousand dollar casket. So Danny would dally in foreign climes until after the funeral.

Just where he would dally he did not know, for Danny was shy of geographic lore; but he knew he was going at least as far as England, which he also knew to be somewhere in London.

So now he lolled in the sun, at peace with the world that immediately surrounded him; or almost at peace for there rankled in his youthful breast various snubs that had been aimed in his direction by the few fellow passengers he had accosted. Danny was at a loss to understand why he was *persona non grata*. He was good looking. His clothes had been designed by one of Chicago's most exclusive tailors – they were quiet and in good taste. These things Danny knew, and he also knew that no one aboard ship had any inkling of his profession. Why then, after a few minutes conversation, did they invariably lose interest in him and thereafter look through him as though he did not exist? The 'Gunner' was both puzzled and peeved.

It was the third day out, and Danny was already fed up on ocean travel. He almost wished that he were back in Chicago where he knew he could find congenial spirits with whom to foregather, but not quite. Better a temporary isolation above ground than a permanent one below.

A young man whom he had not before noticed among the passengers came and sat down in the chair next to his. He looked over at Danny and smiled. 'Good morning,' he said. 'Lovely weather we're having.'

Danny's cold, blue eyes surveyed the stranger. 'Are we?' he replied in a tone as cold as his gaze; then he resumed his previous occupation of staring out across the rail at the illimitable expanse of rolling sea.

Lafayette Smith smiled, opened a book, settled himself more comfortably in his chair and proceeded to forget all about his discourteous neighbor.

Later that day Danny saw the young man at the swimming pool and was impressed by one of the few things that Danny could really understand – proficiency in a physical sport. The young man far outshone the other passengers both in swimming and diving, and his sun bronzed body evidenced long hours in a bathing suit.

The following morning when Danny came on deck he found that the young man had preceded him. 'Good morning,' said Danny pleasantly as he dropped into his chair. 'Nice morning.'

The young man looked up from his book. 'Is it?' he asked and let his eyes fall again to the printed page.

Danny laughed. 'Right back at me, eh?' he exclaimed. 'You see I thought youse was one of them high hat guys. Then I seen you in the tank. You sure can dive, buddy.'

Lafayette Smith, A.M., Ph.D., Sc.D., let his book drop slowly to his lap as he turned to survey his neighbor. Presently a smile stole across his face – a good natured, friendly smile. 'Thanks,' he said. 'You see it is because I like it so well. A fellow who's spent as much time at it as I have ever since I was a little shaver would have to be an awful dub not to be fairly proficient.'

'Yeah,' agreed Danny. 'It's your racket, I suppose.'

Lafayette Smith looked about the deck around his chair. He thought, at first, that Danny was referring to a tennis racquet, as that would be the thing that the word would connote to the mind of so ardent a tennis enthusiast as he. Then he caught the intended meaning and smiled. 'I am not a professional swimmer, if that is what you mean,' he said.

'Pleasure trip?' inquired Danny.

'Well, I hope it will be,' replied the other, 'but it is largely what might be called a business trip, too. Scientific investigation. I am a geologist.'

'Yeah? I never heard of that racket before.'

'It is not exactly a racket,' said Smith. 'There is not enough money in it to raise it to the importance and dignity of a racket.'

'Oh, well, I know a lot of little rackets that pay good – especially if a fellow goes it alone and doesn't have to split with a mob. Going to England?'

'I shall be in London a couple of days only,' replied Smith.

'I thought maybe you was goin' to England.'

Lafayette Smith looked puzzled. 'I am,' he said.

'Oh, you're goin' there from London?'

Was the young man trying to kid him? Very good! 'Yes,' he said, 'if I can get permission from King George to do so I shall visit England while I am in London.'

'Say, does that guy live in England? He's the fellow Big Bill was goin' to punch in the snoot. Geeze, but there is one big bag of hot wind.'

'Who, King George?'

'No, I don't know him – I mean Thompson.'

'I don't know either of them,' admitted Smith; 'but I've heard of King George.'

'You ain't never heard of Big Bill Thompson, mayor of Chicago?'

'Oh, yes; but there are so many Thompsons – I didn't know to which one you referred.'

'Do you have to get next to King George to get to England?' demanded Danny, and something in the earnestness of his tone assured Smith that the young man had not been kidding him.

'No,' he replied. 'You see, London is the capital of England. When you are in London you are, of course, in England.'

'Geeze!' exclaimed Danny. 'I sure was all wet, wasn't I; but you see,' he added confidentially, 'I ain't never been out of America before.'

'Are you making a protracted stay in England?'

'A what?'

'Are you going to remain in England for some time?'

'I'll see how I like it,' replied Danny.

'I think you'll like London,' Smith told him.

'I don't have to stay there,' Danny confided; 'I can go where I please. Where are you goin'?'

'To Africa.'

'Where the smokes come from.'

'What? Oh, yes.'

'What sort of a burgh is it? I don't think I'd like bein' bossed by a lot of smokes, though most of 'em is regular, at that. I knew some nigger cops in Chi that never looked to frame a guy.'

'You wouldn't be bothered by any policeman where I'm going,' Smith assured him; 'there are none.'

'Geeze! You don't say? But get me right, mister, I ain't worried about no cops – they ain't got nothin' on me. Though I sure would like to go somewhere where I wouldn't never see none of their ugly mugs. You know, Mister,' he added confidentially, 'I just can't like a cop.'

This young man puzzled Lafayette Smith the while he amused him. Being a scholar, and having pursued scholarly ways in a quiet university town, Smith was only aware of the strange underworld of America's great cities to such a sketchy extent as might result from a cursory and disinterested perusal of the daily press. He could not catalog his new acquaintance by any first hand knowledge. He had never talked with exactly such a type before. Outwardly the young man might be the undergraduate son of a cultured family, but when he spoke one had to revise this first impression.

'Say,' exclaimed Danny, after a short silence; 'I know about this here Africa, now. I seen a moving pitcher once – lions and elephants and a lot of foolish lookin' deer with funny monickers. So that's where you're goin'? Huntin', I suppose?'

'Not for animals, but for rocks,' explained Smith.

'Geeze! Who ain't huntin' for rocks?' demanded Danny. 'I know guys would croak their best friends for a rock.'

'Not the sort I'm going to look for,' Smith assured him.

'You don't mean diamonds then?'

'No, just rock formations that will teach me more about the structure of the earth.'

'And you can't cash in on them after you find them?'

'No.'

'Geeze, that's a funny racket. You know a lot about this here Africa, don't you?'

'Only what I've read in books,' replied Smith.

'I had a book once,' said Danny, with almost a verbal swagger.

'Yes?' said Smith politely. 'Was it about Africa?'

'I don't know. I never read it. Say, I been thinkin',' he added. 'Why don't I go to this here Africa? That pitcher I seen looked like they wasn't many people there, and I sure would like to get away from people for a while – I'm fed up on 'em. How big a place is Africa?'

'Almost four times as large as the United States.'

'Geeze! An' no cops?'

'Not where I'm going, nor very many people. Perhaps I shall see no one but the members of my safari for weeks at a time.'

'Safari?'

'My people – porters, soldiers, servants.'

'Oh, your mob.'

'It may be.'

'What say I go with you, mister? I don't understand your racket and I don't want to, but I won't demand no cut-in whatever it is. Like the old dame that attended the funeral, I just want to go along for the ride – only I'll pay my way.'

Lafayette Smith wondered. There was something about this young man he liked, and he certainly found him interesting as a type. Then, too, there was an indefinable something in his manner and in those cold, blue eyes that suggested he might be a good companion in an emergency. Furthermore, Lafayette Smith had recently been thinking that long weeks in the interior without the companionship of another white man might prove intolerable. Yet he hesitated. He knew nothing about the man. He might be a fugitive from justice. He might be anything. Well, what of it? He had about made up his mind.

'If it's expenses that's worrying you,' said Danny, noting the other's hesitation, 'forget 'em. I'll pay my share and then some, if you say so.'

'I wasn't thinking of that, though the trip will be expensive – not much more for two, though, than for one.'

'How much?'

'Frankly, I don't know, but I have been assuming that five thousand dollars should cover everything, though I may be wrong.'

Danny Patrick reached into his trousers' pocket and brought forth a great roll of bills – 50's and 100's. He counted out three thousand dollars. 'Here's three G. to bind the bargain,' he said, 'and there's more where that came from. I ain't no piker. I'll pay my share and part of yours, too.'

'No,' said Smith, motioning the proffered bills aside. 'It is not that. You see we don't know anything about each other. We might not get along together.'

'You know as much about me as I do about you,' replied Danny, 'and I'm game to take a chance. Maybe the less we know the better. Anyhow, I'm goin' to this here Africa, and if you're goin' too, we might as well go together. It'll cut down expenses, and two white fellows is got a better chance than one alone in any bunch of smokes I ever seen. Do we stick or do we split?'

Lafayette Smith laughed. Here, perhaps, was the making of an adventure, and in his scholarly heart he had long held the secret hope that some day he might go adventuring. 'We stick,' he said.

'Gimme five!' exclaimed 'Gunner' Patrick, extending his hand.

'Five what?' asked Lafayette Smith, A.M., Ph.D., Sc.D.

IV

Gathering the Strands

Weeks rolled by. Trains rattled and chugged. Steamships plowed. Black feet padded well worn trails. Three safaris, headed by white men from far separated parts of the earth, moved slowly along different trails that led toward the wild fastnesses of the Ghenzis. None knew of the presence of the others, nor were their missions in any way related.

From the West came Lafayette Smith and 'Gunner' Patrick; from the South, an English big game hunter, Lord Passmore; from the East, Leon Stabutch.

The Russian had been having trouble with his men. They had enlisted with enthusiasm, but their eagerness to proceed had waned as they penetrated more deeply into strange and unknown country. Recently they had talked with men of a village beside which they had camped, and these men had told them terrifying tales of the great band of *shiftas*, led by a white man, that was terrorizing the country toward which they were marching, killing and raping as they collected slaves to be sold in the north.

Stabutch had halted for the noonday rest upon the southern slopes of the foothills of the Ghenzis. To the north rose the lofty peaks of the main range; to the south, below them, they could see forest and jungle stretching away into the distance; about them were rolling hills, sparsely timbered, and between the hills and the forest an open, grassy plain where herds of antelope and zebra could be seen grazing.

The Russian called his headman to him. 'What's the matter with those fellows?' he asked, nodding toward the porters, who were gathered, squatting, in a circle, jabbering in low voices.

'They are afraid, Bwana,' replied the black.

'Afraid of what?' demanded Stabutch, though he well knew.

'Afraid of the *shiftas*, Bwana. Three more deserted last night.'

'We didn't need them anyway,' snapped Stabutch; 'the loads are getting lighter.'

'More will run away,' said the headman. 'They are all afraid.'

'They had better be afraid of me,' blustered Stabutch. 'If any more men desert I'll – I'll—'

'They are not afraid of you, Bwana,' the headman told him, candidly. 'They are afraid of the *shiftas* and the white man who is their chief. They do not want to be sold into slavery, far from their own country.'

'Don't tell me you believe in that cock-and-bull story, you black rascal,' snapped Stabutch. 'It's just an excuse to turn back. They want to get home so they can loaf, the lazy dogs. And I guess you're as bad as the rest of them. Who said you were a headman, anyway? If you were worth a kopeck you'd straighten those fellows out in no time; and we wouldn't have any more talk about turning back, nor any more desertions, either.'

'Yes, Bwana,' replied the black; but what he thought was his own business.

'Now, listen to me,' growled Stabutch, but that to which he would have had the headman listen was never voiced.

The interruption came from one of the porters, who leaped suddenly to his feet, voicing a low cry of warning pregnant with terror. 'Look!' he cried, pointing toward the west. 'The *shiftas*!'

Silhouetted against the sky, a group of mounted men had reined in their horses upon the summit of a low hill a mile away. The distance was too great to permit the excited watchers in the Russian's camp to distinguish details, but the very presence of a body of horsemen was all the assurance that the blacks needed to convince them that it was composed of members of the *shifta* band of which they had heard terrifying rumors that had filled their simple breasts with steadily increasing dread during the past several days. The white robes fluttering in the breeze at the summit of the distant hill, the barrels of rifles and the shafts of spears that, even at a distance, were sufficiently suggestive of their true nature to permit of no doubt, but served to definitely crystallize the conjectures of the members of Stabutch's safari and augment their panic.

They were standing now, every eye turned toward the menace of that bristling hill top. Suddenly one of the men ran toward the loads that had been discarded during the noonday halt, calling something back over his shoulder to his fellows. Instantly there was a break for the loads.

'What are they doing?' cried Stabutch. 'Stop them!'

The headman and the askaris ran quickly toward the porters, many of whom already had shouldered their loads and were starting on the back trail. The headman sought to stop them, but one, a great, burly fellow, felled him with a single blow. Then another, glancing back toward the west, voiced a shrill cry of terror. 'Look!' he cried. 'They come!'

Those who heard him turned to see the horsemen, their robes fluttering backward in the breeze, reining down the hillside toward them at a gallop.

It was enough. As one man, porters, askaris, and the headman, they turned and fled. Those who had shouldered loads threw them to the ground lest their weight retard the runner's speed.

Stabutch was alone. For an instant he hesitated on the verge of flight, but almost immediately he realized the futility of attempted escape.

With loud yells the horsemen were bearing down upon his camp; and presently, seeing him standing there alone, they drew rein before him. Hard faced, villainous appearing blacks, they presented such an appearance of evil as might have caused the stoutest heart to quail.

Their leader was addressing Stabutch in a strange tongue, but his attitude was so definitely menacing that the Russian had little need of knowledge of the other's language to interpret the threat reflected in the speaker's tones and scowling face; but he dissembled his fears and met the blacks with a cool equanimity that impressed them with the thought that the stranger must be sure of his power. Perhaps he was but the advance guard of a larger body of white men!

The *shiftas* looked about them uneasily as this thought was voiced by one of their number, for they well knew the temper and the arms of white men and feared both. Yet, notwithstanding their doubts, they could still appreciate the booty of the camp, as they cast covetous and appraising eyes upon the abandoned loads of the departed porters, most of whom were still in view as they scurried toward the jungle.

Failing to make himself understood by the white man, the leader of the *shiftas* fell into a heated argument with several of his henchmen and when one, sitting, stirrup to stirrup, beside him, raised his rifle and aimed it at Stabutch the leader struck the weapon up and berated his fellow angrily. Then he issued several orders, with the result that, while two of the band remained to guard Stabutch, the others dismounted and loaded the packs on several of the horses.

A half hour later the *shiftas* rode back in the direction from which they had come, taking with them all of the Russian's belongings and him, also, disarmed and a prisoner.

And as they rode away, keen grey eyes watched them from the concealing verdure of the jungle – eyes that had been watching every turn of events in the camp of the Russian since Stabutch had called the halt for the disastrous noonday rest.

Though considerable the distance from the jungle to the camp, nothing had escaped the keen eyes of the watcher reclining at ease in the fork of a great tree just at the edge of the plain. What his mental reactions to the happenings he had witnessed none might have guessed by any changing expression upon his stern, emotionless countenance.

He watched the retreating figures of the *shiftas* until they had disappeared from view, and then he sprang lightly to his feet and swung off through the jungle in the opposite direction – in the direction taken by the fleeing members of Stabutch's safari.

Goloba, the headman, trod fearfully the gloomy trails of the jungle; and with him were a considerable number of the other members of Stabutch's safari, all equally fearful lest the *shiftas* pursue them.

The first panic of their terror had abated; and as the minutes sped, with no sign of pursuit, they took greater heart, though there grew in the breast of Goloba another fear to replace that which was fading – it was the fear of the trusted lieutenant who has deserted his bwana. It was something that Goloba would have to explain one day, and even now he was formulating his excuse.

'They rode upon us, firing their rifles,' he said. 'There were many of them – at least a hundred.' No one disputed him. 'We fought bravely in defense of the Bwana, but we were few and could not repulse them.' He paused and looked at those walking near him. He saw that they nodded their heads in assent. 'And then I saw the Bwana fall and so, to escape being taken and sold into slavery, we ran away.'

'Yes,' said one walking at his side, 'it is all as Goloba has said. I myself—' but he got no further. The figure of a bronzed white man, naked but for a loin cloth, dropped from the foliage of the trees into the trail a dozen paces ahead of them. As one man they halted, surprise and fear writ large upon their faces.

'Which is the headman?' demanded the stranger in their own dialect, and every eye turned upon Goloba.

'I am,' replied the black leader.

'Why did you desert your bwana?'

Goloba was about to reply when the thought occurred to him that here was only a single, primitively armed white without companions, without a safari – a poor creature, indeed, in the jungle – lower than the meanest black.

'Who are you to question Goloba, the headman?' he demanded, sneeringly. 'Get out of my way,' and he started forward along the trail toward the stranger.

But the white man did not move. He merely spoke, in low, even tones. 'Goloba should know better,' he said, 'than to speak thus to any white man.'

The black hesitated. He was not quite sure of himself, but yet he ventured to hold his ground. 'Great bwanas do not go naked and alone through the forests, like the low Bagesu. Where is your safari?'

'Tarzan of the Apes needs no safari,' replied the white man.

Goloba was stunned. He had never seen Tarzan of the Apes, for he came from a country far from Tarzan's stamping ground, but he had heard tales of the great bwana – tales that had lost nothing in the telling.

'You are Tarzan?' he asked.

The white man nodded, and Goloba sank, fearfully, to his knees. 'Have mercy, great bwana!' he begged, 'Goloba did not know.'

'Now, answer my question,' said Tarzan. 'Why did you desert your bwana?'

'We were attacked by a band of *shiftas*,' replied Goloba. 'They rode upon us, firing their rifles. There were at least a hundred of them. We fought bravely—'

'Stop!' commanded Tarzan. 'I saw all that transpired. No shots were fired. You ran away before you knew whether the horsemen were enemies or friends. Speak now, but speak true words.'

'We knew that they were enemies,' said Goloba, 'for we had been warned by villagers, near whom we had camped, that these *shiftas* would attack us and sell into slavery all whom they captured.'

'What more did the villagers tell you?' asked the ape-man.

'That the *shiftas* are led by a white man.'

'That is what I wished to know,' said Tarzan.

'And now may Goloba and his people go?' asked the black. 'We fear that the *shiftas* may be pursuing us.'

'They are not,' Tarzan assured him. 'I saw them ride away toward the west, taking your bwana with them. It is of him I would know more. Who is he? What does he here?'

'He is from a country far in the north,' replied Goloba. 'He called it Russa.'

'Yes,' said Tarzan. 'I know the country. Why did he come here?'

'I do not know,' replied Goloba. 'It was not to hunt. He did not hunt, except for food.'

'Did he speak ever of Tarzan?' demanded the ape-man.

'Yes,' replied Goloba. 'Often he asked about Tarzan. At every village he asked when they had seen Tarzan and where he was; but none knew.'

'That is all,' said the ape-man. 'You may go.'

V

When the Lion Charged

Lord Passmore was camped in a natural clearing on the bank of a small river a few miles south of the jungle's northern fringe. His stalwart porters and askaris squatted over their cooking fires laughing and joking among themselves. It was two hours past sunset; and Lord Passmore, faultlessly attired in dinner clothes, was dining, his native boy, standing behind his chair, ready to anticipate his every need.

A tall, well built negro approached the fly beneath which Lord Passmore's camp table had been placed. 'You sent for me, Bwana?' he asked.

Lord Passmore glanced up into the intelligent eyes of the handsome black. There was just the faintest shadow of a smile lurking about the corners of the patrician mouth of the white man. 'Have you anything to report?' he asked.

'No, bwana,' replied the black. 'Neither to the east nor to the west were there signs of game. Perhaps the bwana had better luck.'

'Yes,' replied Passmore, 'I was more fortunate. To the north I saw signs of game. Tomorrow, perhaps, we shall have better hunting. Tomorrow I shall—' He broke off abruptly. Both men were suddenly alert, straining their ears to a faint sound that rose above the nocturnal voices of the jungle for a few brief seconds.

The black looked questioningly at his master. 'You heard it, bwana?' he asked. The white nodded. 'What was it, bwana?'

'It sounded deucedly like a machine gun,' replied Passmore. 'It came from south of us; but who the devil would be firing a machine gun here? and why at night?'

'I do not know, bwana,' replied the headman. 'Shall I go and find out?'

'No,' said the Englishman. 'Perhaps tomorrow. We shall see. Go now, and get your sleep.'

'Yes, bwana; goodnight.'

'Goodnight – and warn the askari on sentry duty to be watchful.'

'Yes, bwana.' The black bowed very low and backed from beneath the fly. Then he moved silently away, the flickering flames of the cookfires reflecting golden high lights from his smooth brown skin, beneath which played the mighty muscles of a giant.

'This,' remarked 'Gunner' Patrick, 'is the life. I ain't seen a cop for weeks.'

Lafayette Smith smiled. 'If cops are the only things you fear, Danny, your mind and your nerves can be at rest for several weeks more.'

'What give you the idea I was afraid of cops?' demanded Danny. 'I ain't never seen the cop I was afraid of. They're a bunch of punks. Anyhow, they ain't got nothin' on me. What a guy's got to look out for though is they might frame a guy. But, geeze, out here a guy don't have to worry about nothin.' He settled back easily in his camp chair and exhaled a slowly spiraling column of cigarette smoke that rose lazily in the soft night air of the jungle. 'Geeze,' he remarked after a brief silence. 'I didn't know a guy could feel so peaceful. Say, do you know this is the first time in years I ain't packed a rod?'

'A what?'

'A rod, iron, a gat – you know – a gun.'

'Why didn't you say so in the first place?' laughed Smith. 'Why don't you try talking English once in a while?'

'Geeze!' exclaimed Danny. 'You're a great guy to talk about a guy talkin' English. What's that you pulled on me the other day when we was crossin' that open rollin' country? I learned that by heart – "a country of low relief in an advanced stage of mature dissection" – an' you talk about me talkin' English! You and your thrust faults and escarpments, your calderas and solfataras – geeze!'

'Well, you're learning, Danny.'

'Learnin' what? Every racket has its own lingo. What good is your line to me? But every guy wants to know what a rod is – if he knows what's good for his health.'

'From what Ogonyo tells me it may be just as well to continue "packing your rod,"' said Smith.

'How come?'

'He says we're getting into lion country. We may even find them near here. They don't often frequent jungles, but we're only about a day's march to more open terrain.'

'Whatever that is. Talk English. Geeze! What was that?' A series of coughing grunts rose from somewhere in the solid black wall of jungle that surrounded the camp, to be followed by a thunderous roar that shook the earth.

'Simba!' cried one of the blacks, and immediately a half dozen men hastened to add fuel to the fires.

'Gunner' Patrick leaped to his feet and ran into the tent, emerging a moment later with a Thompson submachine gun. 'T'ell with a rod,' he said. 'When I get that baby on the spot I want a typewriter.'

'Are you going to take him for a ride?' inquired Lafayette Smith, whose education had progressed noticeably in the weeks he had spent in the society of Danny 'Gunner' Patrick.

'No,' admitted Danny, 'unless he tries to muscle in on my racket.'

Once again the rumbling roar of the lion shattered the quiet of the outer darkness. This time it sounded so close that both men started nervously.

'He appears to be harboring the thought,' commented Smith.

'What thought?' demanded the 'Gunner.'

'About muscling in.'

'The smokes got the same hunch,' said Danny. 'Look at 'em.'

The blacks were palpably terrified and were huddled close to the fires, the askaris fingering the triggers of their rifles. The 'Gunner' walked over to where they stood straining their eyes out into the impenetrable darkness.

'Where is he?' he asked Ogonyo, the headman. 'Have you seen him?'

'Over there,' said Ogonyo. 'It looks like something moving over there, bwana.'

Danny peered into the darkness. He could see nothing, but now he thought he heard a rustling of foliage beyond the fires. He dropped to one knee and aimed the machine gun in the direction of the sound. There was a burst of flame and the sudden rat-a-tat-tat of the weapon as he squeezed the trigger. For a moment the ringing ears of the watchers heard nothing, and then, as their auditory nerves returned to normal, to the keenest ears among them came the sound of crashing among the bushes, disminishing in the distance.

'I guess I nicked him,' said Danny to Smith, who had walked over and was standing behind him.

'You didn't kill him,' said Smith. 'You must have wounded him.'

'Simba is not wounded, bwana,' said Ogonyo.

'How do you know?' demanded Danny. 'You can't see nothin' out there.'

'If you had wounded him he would have charged,' explained the headman. 'He ran away. It was the noise that frightened him.'

'Do you think he will come back?' asked Smith.

'I do not know, bwana,' replied the negro. 'No one knows what Simba will do.'

'Of course he won't come back,' said Danny. 'The old typewriter scared him stiff. I'm going to turn in.'

Numa, the lion, was old and hungry. He had been hunting in the open country; but his muscles, while still mighty, were not what they had been in his prime. When he reared to seize Pacco, the zebra, or Wappi, the antelope, he was always just a trifle slower than he had been in the past; and his prey eluded him. So Numa, the lion, had wandered into the jungle where the scent of man had attracted him to the camp. The beast fires of the blacks blinded him; but, beyond them, his still keen scent told him there was flesh and blood, and Numa, the lion, was ravenous.

Slowly his hunger was overcoming his inherent urge to avoid the man-things; little by little it drew him closer to the hated fires. Crouched almost upon his belly he moved forward a few inches at a time. In another moment he would charge – and then came the sudden burst of flame, the shattering crash of the machine gun, the shriek of bullets above his head.

The startling suddenness with which this unexpected tumult broke the fear laden silence of the camp and the jungle snapped the taut nerves of the great cat, and his reaction was quite as natural as it was involuntary. Wheeling in his tracks, he bounded away into the forest.

The ears of Numa, the lion, were not the only jungle ears upon which the discord of 'Gunner' Patrick's typewriter impinged, for that seeming solitude of impenetrable darkness harbored a myriad life. For an instant it was motionless, startled into immobility; and then it moved on again upon the multitudinous concerns of its varied existence. Some, concerned by the strangeness of the noise, moved farther from the vicinity of the camp of the man-things; but there was at least one that curiosity attracted to closer investigation.

Gradually the camp was settling down for the night. The two bwanas had retired to the seclusion of their tent. The blacks had partially overcome their nervousness, and most of them had lain down to sleep. A few watched the beast fires near which two askaris stood on guard, one on either side of the camp.

Numa stood with low hung head out there, somewhere, in the night. The tattoo of the machine gun had not appeased his appetite, but it had added to his nervous irritability – and to his caution. No longer did he rumble forth his coughing protests against the emptiness of his belly as he watched the flames of the beast fires that now fed the flood of his anger until it submerged his fears.

And as the camp drifted gradually into sleep the tawny body of the carnivore slunk slowly closer to the dancing circle of the beast fires' light. The yellow-green eyes stared in savage fixity at an unsuspecting askari leaning sleepily upon his rifle.

The man yawned and shifted his position. He noted the condition of the fire. It needed new fuel, and the black turned to the pile of branches and dead wood behind him. As he stooped to gather what he required, his back toward the jungle, Numa charged.

The great lion wished to strike swiftly and silently; but something within him, the mark of the ages of charging forebears that had preceded him, raised a low, ominous growl in his throat.

The victim heard and so did 'Gunner' Patrick, lying sleepless on his cot. As the askari wheeled to the menace of that awesome warning, the 'Gunner' leaped to his feet, seizing the Thompson as he sprang into the open just as Numa rose, towering, above the black. A scream of terror burst from the lips of the doomed man in the instant that the lion's talons buried themselves in his shoulders. Then the giant jaws closed upon his face.

The scream, fraught with the terror of utter hopelessness, awakened the camp. Men, startled into terrified consciousness, sprang to their feet, most of them in time to see Numa, half carrying, half dragging his victim, bounding off into the darkness.

The 'Gunner' was the first to see all this and the only one to act. Without waiting to kneel he raised the machine gun to his shoulder. That his bullets must indubitably find the man if they found the lion was of no moment to Danny Patrick, intimate of sudden and violent death. He might have argued that the man was already dead, but he did not waste a thought upon a possibility which was, in any event, of no consequence, so do environment and habitude warp or dull the sensibilities of man.

The lion was still discernible in the darkness when Danny squeezed the trigger of his beloved typewriter, and this time he did not miss – perhaps unfortunately, for a wounded lion is as dangerous an engine of destruction as an all wise Providence can create.

Aroused by the deafening noise of the weapon, enraged by the wound inflicted by the single slug that entered his body, apprehending that he was to be robbed of his prey, and bent upon swift and savage reprisal, Numa dropped the askari, wheeled about, and charged straight for Danny Patrick.

The 'Gunner' was kneeling, now, to take better aim. Lafayette Smith stood just behind him, armed only with a nickel plated .32 caliber revolver that some friend had given him years before. A great tree spread above the two men – a sanctuary that Lafayette Smith, at least, should have sought, but his mind was not upon flight, for, in truth, Lafayette was assailed by no fear for his own welfare or that of his companion. He was excited, but not afraid, since he could conceive of no disaster, in the form of man or beast, overwhelming one under the protection of Danny Patrick and his submachine gun. And even in the remote contingency that they should fail, was not he, himself, adequately armed? He grasped the grip of his shiny toy more tightly and with a renewed sensation of security.

The blacks, huddled in small groups, stood wide eyed awaiting the outcome of the event, which was accomplished in a few brief seconds from the instant that one of Danny's slugs struck the fleeing carnivore.

And now as the lion came toward him, not in bounds, but rather in a low gliding rush of incredible speed, several things, surprising things, occurred almost simultaneously. And if there was the element of surprise, there was also, for Danny, at least one cause for embarrassment.

As the lion had wheeled Danny had again squeezed the trigger. The mechanism of the piece was set for a continuous discharge of bullets as long as Danny continued to squeeze and the remainder of the one hundred rounds in the drum lasted; but there was only a brief spurt of fire, and then the gun jammed.

How may one record in slow moving words the thoughts and happenings of a second and impart to the narration any suggestion of the speed and action of the instant?

Did the 'Gunner' seek, frantically, to remove the empty cartridge that had caused the jam? Did terror enter his heart, causing his fingers to tremble and bungle? What did Lafayette Smith do? Or rather what did he contemplate doing? Since he had no opportunity to do aught but stand there, a silent observer of events, I do not know.

Before either could formulate a plan wherewith to meet the emergency, a bronzed white man, naked but for a G string, dropped from the branches of the tree above them directly into the path of the charging lion. In the man's hand was a heavy spear, and as he alighted silently upon the soft mold he was already braced to receive the shock of the lion's charge upon the point of his weapon.

The impact of Numa's heavy body would have hurled a lesser man to earth; but this one kept his feet, and the well placed thrust drove into the carnivore's chest a full two feet, while in the same instant the man stepped aside. Numa, intercepted before the completion of his charge, had not yet reared to seize his intended victim. Now, surprised and thwarted by this new enemy, while the other was almost within his grasp, he was momentarily confused; and in that brief moment the strange man-thing leaped upon his back. A giant arm encircled his throat, legs of steel locked around his shrunken waist, and a stout blade was driven into his side.

Spellbound, Smith and Patrick and their blacks stood staring incredulously at the sight before them. They saw Numa turn quickly to seize his tormentor. They saw him leap and bound and throw himself to the ground in an effort to dislodge his opponent. They saw the free hand of the man repeatedly drive home the point of his knife in the tawny side of the raging lion.

From the tangled mass of man and lion there issued frightful snarls and growls, the most terrifying element of which came to the two travellers with the discovery that these bestial sounds issued not alone from the savage throat of the lion but from that of the man as well.

The battle was brief, for the already sorely wounded animal had received the spear thrust directly through its heart, only its remarkable tenacity of life having permitted it to live for the few seconds that intervened between the death blow and the collapse.

As Numa slumped suddenly to his side, the man leaped clear. For a moment he stood looking down upon the death throes of his vanquished foe, while Smith and Patrick remained in awestruck contemplation of the savage, primordial scene; and then he stepped closer; and, placing one foot upon the carcass of his kill, he raised his face to the heavens and gave tongue to a cry so hideous that the black men dropped to the ground in terror while the two whites felt the hair rise upon their scalps.

Once again upon the jungle fell the silence and the paralysis of momentary terror. Then faintly, from the far distance, came an answering challenge. Somewhere out there in the black void of night a bull ape, awakened, had answered the victory cry of his fellow. More faintly, and from a greater distance, came the rumbling roar of a lion.

The stranger stooped and seized the haft of his spear. He placed a foot against Numa's shoulder and withdrew the weapon from the carcass. Then he turned toward the two white men. It was the first intimation he had given that he had been aware of their presence.

'Geeze!' exclaimed 'Gunner' Patrick, beyond which his vocabulary failed to meet the situation.

The stranger surveyed them coolly. 'Who are you?' he asked. 'What are you doing here?'

That he spoke English was both a surprise and a relief to Lafayette Smith. Suddenly he seemed less terrifying. 'I am a geologist,' he explained. 'My name is Smith – Lafayette Smith – and my companion is Mr Patrick. I am here to conduct some field research work – purely a scientific expedition.'

The stranger pointed to the machine gun. 'Is that part of the regular field equipment of a geologist?' he asked.

'No,' replied, 'and I'm sure I don't know why Mr Patrick insisted on bringing it along.'

'I wasn't takin' no chances in a country full of strange smokes,' said the 'Gunner.' 'Say, a broad I meets on the boats tells me some of these smokes eats people.'

'It would come in handy, perhaps, for hunting,' suggested the stranger. 'A herd of antelope would make an excellent target for a weapon of that sort.'

'Geeze!' exclaimed the 'Gunner,' 'wot do you think I am, Mister, a butcher? I packs this for insurance only. It sure wasn't worth the premium this time though,' he added disgustedly; 'jammed on me right when I needed it the most. But say, you were there all right. I gotta hand it to you. You're regular, Mister, and if I can ever return the favor—' He made an expansive gesture that completed the sentence and promised all that the most exacting might demand of a reciprocatory nature.

The giant nodded. 'Don't use it for hunting,' he said, and then, turning to Smith, 'Where are you going to conduct your research?'

Suddenly a comprehending light shone in the eyes of the 'Gunner,' and a pained expression settled definitely upon his face. 'Geeze!' he exclaimed disgusted to Smith. 'I might of known it was too good to be true.'

'What?' asked Lafayette.

'What I said about there not bein' no cops here.'

'Where are you going?' asked the stranger, again.

'We are going to the Ghenzi Mountains now,' replied Smith.

'Say, who the hell are you, anyhow?' demanded the 'Gunner,' 'and what business is it of yours where we go?'

The stranger ignored him and turned again toward Smith. 'Be very careful in the Ghenzi country,' he said. 'There is a band of slave raiders working there at present, I understand. If your men learn of it they may desert you.'

'Thanks,' replied Smith. 'It is very kind of you to warn us. I should like to know to whom we are indebted,' but the stranger was gone.

As mysteriously and silently as he had appeared, he swung again into the tree above and disappeared. The two whites looked at one another in amazement.

'Geeze,' said Danny.

'I fully indorse your statement,' said Smith.

'Say, Ogonyo,' demanded the 'Gunner,' 'who was that bozo? You or any of your men know?'

'Yes, bwana,' replied the headman, 'that was Tarzan of the Apes.'

VI

The Waters of Chinnereth

Lady Barbara Collis walked slowly along the dusty path leading from the Midian village down to the lake that lay in the bottom of the ancient crater which formed the valley of the Land of Midian. At her right walked Abraham, the son of Abraham, and at her left the golden haired Jezebel. Behind them came the apostles, surrounding a young girl whose sullen countenance was enlivened occasionally by the fearful glances she cast upon the old men who formed her escort of her guard. Following the apostles marched the remainder of the villagers, headed by the elders. Other than these general divisions of the cortege, loosely observed, there was no attempt to maintain a semblance of orderly formation. They moved like sheep, now huddled together, now spewing beyond the limits of the narrow path to spread out on either side, some forging ahead for a few yards only to drop back again.

Lady Barbara was apprehensive. She had learned many things in the long weeks of her virtual captivity among this strange religious sect. Among other things she had learned their language, and the mastery of it had opened to her inquiring mind many avenues of information previously closed. And now she was learning, or she believed she was, that Abraham, the son of Abraham, was nursing in his bosom a growing scepticism of her divinity.

Her first night in Midian had witnessed her introduction to the cruel customs and rites of this degenerate descendant of the earliest Christian Church, and as she acquired a working knowledge of the language of the land and gained an appreciation of the exalted origin the leaders of the people attributed to her, and her position of spokesman for their god, she had used her influence to discourage, and even to prohibit, the more terrible and degrading practices of their religion.

While recollection of the supernatural aspects of her descent from the clouds remained clear in the weak mind of Abraham, the son of Abraham, Lady Barbara had been successful in her campaign against brutality; but daily association with this celestial visitor had tended to dissipate the awe that had at first overwhelmed the prophet of Paul, the son of Jehovah. The interdictions of his heavenly guest were all contrary to the desires of Abraham, the son of Abraham, and to the word of Jehovah as it had been interpreted by the prophets beyond the memory of man. Such were the foundations of the prophet's increasing scepticism, nor was the changing attitude of the old man toward her unrecognized by the English girl.

Today he had ignored her and was even forcing her to accompany them and witness the proof of his apostasy. What would come next? She had had not only ocular proof of the fanatical blood frenzy of the terrible old man, but she had listened for hours to detailed descriptions of orgies of frightfulness from the lips of Jezebel. Yes, Lady Barbara Collis was apprehensive, and not without reason; but she determined to make a last effort to reassert her waning authority.

'Think well Abraham, the son of Abraham,' she said to the man walking at her side, 'of the wrath of Jehovah when he sees that you have disobeyed him.'

'I walk in the path of the prophets,' replied the old man. 'Always we have punished those who defied the laws of Jehovah, and Jehovah has rewarded us. Why should he be wroth now? The girl must pay the price of her iniquity.'

'But she only smiled,' argued Lady Barbara.

'A sin in the eyes of Jehovah,' replied Abraham, the son of Abraham. 'Laughter is carnal, and smiles lead to laughter, which gives pleasure; and all pleasures are the lures of the devil. They are wicked.'

'Do not say any more,' said Jezebel, in English. 'You will only anger him, and when he is angry he is terrible.'

'What sayest thou, woman?' demanded Abraham, the son of Abraham.

'I was praying to Jehovah in the language of Heaven,' replied the girl.

The Prophet let his scowling gaze rest upon her. 'Thou doest well to pray, woman. Jehovah looks not with pleasure upon thee.'

'Then I shall continue praying,' replied the girl meekly, and to Lady Barbara, in English; 'The old devil is already planning my punishment. He has always hated me, just as they always hate us poor creatures who are not created in the same image as they.'

The remarkable difference in physical appearance and mentality that set Jezebel apart from the other Midians was an inexplicable phenomenon that had constantly puzzled Lady Barbara and would continue to puzzle her, since she could not know of the little fair haired slave girl whose virile personality still sought to express itself beyond a grave nineteen centuries old. How greatly Jezebel's mentality surpassed that of her imbecilic fellows had been demonstrated to Lady Barbara by the surprising facility with which the girl had learned to speak English while she was teaching Lady Barbara the language of the Midians. How often and how sincerely had she thanked a kindly Providence for Jezebel!

The procession had now arrived at the shore of the lake, which legend asserted to be bottomless, and had halted where a few flat lava rocks of great size overhung the waters. The apostles took their places with Abraham, the son of Abraham, upon one of the rocks, the girl in their midst; and then a half dozen younger men came forward at a signal from Jobab. One of their number carried a fibre net, and two others brought a heavy piece of lava. Quickly they threw the net over the now terrified and screaming girl and secured the lava rock to it.

Abraham, the son of Abraham, raised his hands above his head, and at the signal all knelt. He commenced to pray in that now familiar gibberish that was not Midian, nor, according to Jezebel, any language whatsoever, for she insisted that the Prophet and the Apostles, to whose sole use it was restricted, could not understand it themselves. The girl, kneeling, was weeping softly now, sometimes choking down a muffled sob, while the young men held the net securely.

Suddenly Abraham, the son of Abraham, abandoned the ecclesiastical tongue and spoke in the language of his people. 'For as she has sinned so shall she suffer,' he cried. 'It is the will of Jehovah, in his infinite mercy, that she shall not be consumed by fire, but that she shall be immersed three times in the waters of Chinnereth that her sins may be washed from her. Let us pray that they may be not too grievous, since otherwise she shall not survive.' He nodded to the six young men, who seemed well schooled in their parts.

Four of them seized the net and raised it between them, while the remaining two held the ends of long fibre ropes that were attached to it. As the four commenced to swing the body of the girl pendulum like between them, her screams and pleas for mercy rose above the silent waters of Chinnereth in a diapason of horror, mingled with which were the shrieks and groans of those who, excited beyond the capacity of their nervous systems, were falling to the ground in the throes of epileptic seizures.

To and fro, with increasing rapidity, the young men swung their terror crazed burden. Suddenly one of them collapsed to sink, writhing and foaming, to the surface of the great block of lava upon which they stood, dropping the soft body of the girl heavily to the hard rocks. As Jobab signaled to another young man to take the place of him who had fallen, an apostle screamed and dropped in his tracks.

But no one gave heed to those who had succumbed, and a moment later the girl was swinging to and fro out over the waters of Chinnereth, back over the hard face of the lava.

'In the name of Jehovah! In the name of Jehovah!' chanted Abraham, the son of Abraham, to the cadence of the swinging sack. 'In the name of Jehovah! In the name of his son—' there was a pause, and as the body of the girl swung again out over the water – 'Paul!'

It was the signal. The four young men released their holds upon the net, and the body of the girl shot downward toward the dark waters of the lake. There was a splash. The screaming ceased. The waters closed in above the victim of cruel fanaticism, leaving only a widening circle of retreating wavelets and two fibre ropes extending upward to the altar of castigation.

For a few seconds there was silence and immobility except for the groans and contortions of the now greatly increased numbers of the victims of the Nemesis of the Midians. Then Abraham, the son of Abraham, spoke again to the six executioners, who immediately laid hold of the two ropes and hauled the girl upward until she swung; dripping and choking, just above the surface of the water.

For a brief interval they held her there; and then, at a word from the Prophet, they dropped her again beneath the waters.

'You murderer!' cried Lady Barbara, no longer able to control her anger. 'Order that poor creature drawn ashore before she is drowned.'

Abraham, the son of Abraham, turned eyes upon the English girl that almost froze her with horror – the wild, staring eyes of a maniac; piercing pupils rimmed round with white. 'Silence, blasphemer!' screamed the man. 'Last night I walked with Jehovah, and He told me that you would be next.'

'Oh, please,' whispered Jezebel, tugging at Lady Barbara's sleeve. 'Do not anger him more or you are lost.'

The Prophet turned again to the six young men, and again, at his command, the victim was drawn above the surface of the lake. Fascinated by the horror of the situation, Lady Barbara had stepped to the edge of the rock, and looking down, saw the poor creature limp but still gasping in an effort to regain her breath. She was not dead, but another immersion must surely prove fatal.

'Oh, please,' she begged, turning to the Prophet, 'in the name of merciful God, do not let them lower her again!'

Without a word of reply Abraham, the son of Abraham, gave the signal; and for the third time the now unconscious girl was dropped into the lake. The English girl sank to her knees in an attitude of prayer, and raising her eyes to heaven plead fervently to her Maker to move the heart of Abraham, the son of Abraham, to compassion, or out of the fullness of His own love to save the victim of these misguided creatures from what seemed now certain death. For a full minute she prayed, and still the girl was left beneath the waters. Then the Prophet commanded that she be raised.

'If she is now pure in the eyes of Jehovah,' he cried, 'she will emerge alive. If she be dead, it is the will of Jehovah. I have but walked in the paths of the Prophets.'

The six young men raised the sagging net to the surface of the rocks where they rolled the limp form of the girl from it close to where Lady Barbara knelt in prayer. And now the Prophet appeared to notice the attitude and the pleading voice of the English girl for the first time.

'What doest thou?' he demanded.

'I pray to a God whose power and mercy are beyond your understanding,' she replied. 'I pray for the life of this poor child.'

'There is the answer to your prayer,' sneered the Prophet contemptuously, indicating the still body of the girl. 'She is dead, and Jehovah has revealed to all who may have doubted that Abraham, the son of Abraham, is His prophet and that thou are an impostor.'

'We are lost,' whispered Jezebel.

Lady Barbara thought as much herself; but she thought quickly, for the emergency was critical. Rising, she faced the Prophet. 'Yes, she is dead,' she replied, 'but Jehovah can resurrect her.'

'He can, but He will not,' said Abraham, the son of Abraham.

'Not for you, for He is angry with him who dares to call himself His prophet and yet disobeys His commands.' She stepped quickly to the side of the lifeless body. 'But for me He will resurrect her. Come Jezebel and help me!'

Now Lady Barbara, in common with most modern, athletically inclined young women, was familiar with the ordinary methods for resuscitating the drowned; and she fell to work upon the victim of the Prophet's homicidal mania with a will born not only of compassion, but of vital necessity. She issued curt orders to Jezebel from time to time, orders which broke but did not terminate a constant flow of words which she voiced in chant-like measures. She started with The Charge of the Light Brigade, but after two stanzas her memory failed and she had recourse to Mother Goose, snatches from the verse in Alice in Wonderland, Kipling, Omar Khayyam; and, as the girl after ten minutes of heartbreaking effort commenced to show signs of life, Lady Barbara closed with excerpts from Lincoln's Gettysburg Address.

Crowded about them were the Prophet, the Apostles, the Elders, and the six executioners, while beyond these the villagers pressed as close as they dared to witness the miracle – if such it were to be.

'"And that government of the people, by the people and for the people shall not perish from the earth,"' chanted Lady Barbara, rising to her feet. 'Lay the child in the net,' she commanded, turning to the wide eyed young men who had cast her into the lake, 'and carry her tenderly back to the cave of her parents. Come Jezebel!' To Abraham, the son of Abraham, she vouchsafed not even a glance.

That night the two girls sat at the entrance of their cave looking out across the uncharted valley of Midian. A full moon silvered the crest of the lofty escarpment of the crater's northern rim. In the middle distance the silent waters of Chinnereth lay like a burnished shield.

'It is beautiful,' sighed Jezebel.

'But, oh, how horrible, because of man,' replied Lady Barbara, with a shudder.

'At night, when I am alone, and can see only the beautiful things, I try to forget man,' said the golden one. 'Is there so much cruelty and wickedness in the land from which you come, Barbara?'

'There are cruelty and wickedness everywhere where the men are, but in my land it is not so bad as here where the church rules and cruelty is the sole business of the church.'

'They say the men over there are very cruel,' said Jezebel, pointing across the valley; 'but they are beautiful – not like our people.'

'You have seen them?'

'Yes. Sometimes they come searching for their strayed goats, but not often. Then they chase us into our caves, and we roll rocks down on them to keep them from coming up and killing us. They steal our goats at such times; and if they catch any of our men they kill them, too. If I were alone I would let them catch me for they are very beautiful, and I do not think they would kill me. I think they would like me.'

'I don't doubt it,' agreed Lady Barbara, 'but if I were you I would not let them catch me.'

'Why not? What have I to hope for here? Perhaps some day I shall be caught smiling or singing; and then I shall be killed, and you have not seen all of the ways in which the Prophet can destroy sinners. If I am not killed I shall certainly be taken to his cave by some horrible old man; and there, all my life, I shall be a slave to him and his other women; and the old women are more cruel to such as I than even the men. No, if I were not afraid of what lies between I should run away and go to the land of the North Midians.'

'Perhaps your life will be happier and safer here with me since we showed Abraham, the son of Abraham, that we are more powerful than he; and when the time comes that my people find me, or I discover an avenue of escape, you shall come away with me, Jezebel; though I don't know that you will be much safer in England than you are here.'

'Why?' demanded the girl.

'You are too beautiful ever to have perfect safety or perfect happiness.'

'You think I am beautiful? I always thought so, too. I saw myself when I looked into the lake or into a vessel of water; and I thought that I was beautiful, although I did not look like the other girls of the land of Midian. Yet you are beautiful and I do not look like you. Have you never been safe or happy, Barbara?'

The English girl laughed. 'I am not *too* beautiful, Jezebel,' she explained.

A footfall on the steep pathway leading to the cave caught their attention. 'Someone comes,' said Jezebel.

'It is late,' said Lady Barbara. 'No one should be coming now to our cave.'

'Perhaps it is a man from North Midian,' suggested Jezebel. 'Is my hair arranged prettily?'

'We had better be rolling a rock into position than thinking about our hair,' said Lady Barbara, with a short laugh.

'Ah, but they are such beautiful men!' sighed Jezebel.

Lady Barbara drew a small knife from one of her pockets and opened the blade. 'I do not like "beautiful" men,' she said.

The approaching footfalls were coming slowly nearer; but the two young women, sitting just within the entrance to their cave, could not see the steep pathway along with the nocturnal visitor was approaching. Presently a shadow fell across their threshold and an instant later a tall old man stepped into view. It was Abraham, the son of Abraham.

Lady Barbara rose to her feet and faced the Prophet. 'What brings you to my cave at this time of night?' she demanded. 'What is it, of such import-ance, that could not wait until morning? Why do you disturb me now?'

For a long moment the old man stood glaring at her. 'I have walked with Jehovah in the moonlight,' he said, presently; 'and Jehovah hath spoken in the ear of Abraham, the son of Abraham, Prophet of Paul, the son of Jehovah.'

'And you have come to make your peace with me as Jehovah directed?'

'Such are not the commands of Jehovah,' replied the Prophet. 'Rather He is wroth with thee who didst seek to deceive the Prophet of His son.'

'You must have been walking with someone else,' snapped Lady Barbara.

'Nay. I walked with Jehovah,' insisted Abraham, the son of Abraham. 'Thou hast deceived me. With trickery, perhaps even with sorcery, thou didst bring to life her who was dead by the will of Jehovah; and Jehovah is wroth.'

'You heard my prayers, and you witnessed the miracle of the resurrection,' Lady Barbara reminded him. 'Thinkest thou that I am more powerful than Jehovah? It was Jehovah who raised the dead child.'

'Thou speakest even as Jehovah prophesied,' said the Prophet. 'And He spoke in my ear and commanded that I should prove thee false, that all men might see thy iniquity.'

'Interesting, if true,' commented Lady Barbara; 'but not true.'

'Thou darest question the word of the Prophet?' cried the man angrily. 'But tomorrow thou shalt have the opportunity to prove they boasts. Tomor-row Jehovah shall judge thee. Tomorrow thou shalt be cast into the water of Chinnereth in a weighted net, nor will there be cords attached whereby it may be drawn above the surface.'

VII

The Slave Raider

Leon Stabutch, mounted behind one of his captors, riding to an unknown fate, was warrantably perturbed. He had been close to death at the hands of one of the band already, and from their appearance and their attitude toward him it was not difficult for him to imagine that they would require but the slightest pretext to destroy him.

What their intentions might be was highly problematical, though he could conceive of but one motive which might inspire such as they to preserve him.

But if ransom were their aim he could not conjecture any method by which these semi-savages might contact with his friends or superiors in Russia. He was forced to admit that his prospects appeared most discouraging.

The *shiftas* were forced to move slowly because of the packs some of their horses were carrying since the looting of the Russian's camp. Nor could they have ridden much more rapidly, under any circumstances, on the trail that they entered shortly following their capture of Stabutch.

Entering a narrow, rocky canyon the trail wound steeply upward to debouch at last upon a small, level mesa, at the upper end of which Stabutch saw what, at a distance, appeared to be a palisaded village nestling close beneath a rocky cliff that bounded the mesa in that direction.

This evidently was the destination of his captors, who were doubtless members of the very band the mere rumor of which had filled his men with terror. Stabutch was only sorry that the balance of the story, postulating the existence of a white leader, was evidently erroneous, since he would have anticipated less difficulty in arranging the terms and collection of a ransom with a European than with these ignorant savages.

As they neared the village Stabutch discovered that their approach had been made beneath the scrutiny of lookouts posted behind the palisade, whose heads and shoulders were now plainly visible above the crude though substantial rampart.

And presently these sentries were shouting greetings and queries to the members of the returning band as the village gate swung slowly open and the savage horsemen entered the enclosure with their captive, who was soon the center of a throng of men, women, and children, curious and questioning – a savage throng of surly blacks.

Although there was nothing actively menacing in the attitude of the savages there was a definite unfriendliness in their demeanor that cast a further gloom of apprehension upon the already depressed spirits of the Russian; and as the cavalcade entered the central compound, about which the huts were grouped, he experienced a sensation of utter hopelessness.

It was at this moment that he saw a short, bearded white man emerge from one of the squalid dwellings; and instantly the depression that had seized him was, partially at least, relieved.

The *shiftas* were dismounting, and now he was roughly dragged from the animal which had borne him from his camp and pushed unceremoniously toward the white man, who stood before the doorway from whence he had appeared surveying the prisoner sullenly, while he listened to the report of the leader of the returning band.

There was no smile upon the face of the bearded man as he addressed Stabutch after the black *shifta* had completed his report. The Russian recognized that the language employed by the stranger was Italian, a tongue which he could neither speak nor understand, and this he explained in Russian; but the bearded one only shrugged and shook his head. Then Stabutch tried English.

'That is better,' said the other brokenly. 'I understand English a little. Who are you? What was the language you first spoke to me? From what country do you come?'

'I am a scientist,' replied Stabutch. 'I spoke to you in Russian.'

'Is Russia your country?'

'Yes.'

The man eyed him intently for some time, as though attempting to read the innermost secrets of his mind, before he spoke again. Stabutch noted the squat, powerful build of the stranger, the cruel lips, only partially concealed by the heavy, black beard, and the hard, crafty eyes, and guessed that he might have fared as well at the hands of the blacks.

'You say you are a Russian,' said the man. 'Red or white?'

Stabutch wished that he might know how to answer this question. He was aware that Red Russians were not well beloved by all peoples; and that the majority of Italians were trained to hate them, and yet there was something in the personality of this stranger that suggested that he might be more favorably inclined to a Red than to a White Russian. Furthermore, to admit that he was a Red might assure the other that a ransom could be obtained more surely than from a White, whose organization was admittedly weak and poverty stricken. For these reasons Stabutch decided to tell the truth.

'I am a Red,' he said.

The other considered him intently and in silence for a moment; then he made a gesture that would have passed unnoticed by any but a Red Communist. Leon Stabutch breathed an inaudible sigh of relief, but his facial expression gave no indication of recognition of this secret sign as he answered it in accordance with the ritual of his organization, while the other watched him closely.

'Your name, comrade?' inquired the bearded one in an altered tone.

'Leon Stabutch,' replied the Russian; 'and yours, comrade?'

'Dominic Capietro. Come, we will talk inside. I have a bottle there wherewith we may toast the cause and become better acquainted.'

'Lead on, comrade,' said Stabutch; 'I feel the need of something to quiet my nerves. I have had a bad few hours.'

'I apologize for the inconvenience to which my men have put you,' replied Capietro, leading the way into the hut; 'but all shall be made right again. Be seated. As you see, I lead the simple life; but what imperial throne may compare in grandeur with the bosom of Mother Earth!'

'None, comrade,' agreed Stabutch, noting the entire absence of chairs, or even stools, that the other speech had already suggested and condoned. 'Especially,' he added, 'when enjoyed beneath a friendly roof.'

Capietro rummaged in an old duffle bag and at last withdrew a bottle which he uncorked and handed to Stabutch. 'Golden goblets are for royal tyrants, Comrade Stabutch,' he declaimed, 'but not for such as we, eh?'

Stabutch raised the bottle to his lips and took a draught of the fiery liquid, and as it burned its way to his stomach and the fumes rose to his head the last of his fears and doubts vanished. 'Tell me now,' he said, as he passed the bottle back to his host, 'why I was seized, who you are, and what is to become of me?'

'My headman told me that he found you alone, deserted by your safari, and not knowing whether you were friend or enemy he brought you here to me. You are lucky, comrade, that Dongo chanced to be in charge of the scouting party today. Another might have killed you first and inquired later. They are a pack of murderers and thieves, these good men of mine. They have been oppressed by cruel masters, they have felt the heel of the tyrant upon their necks, and their hands are against all men. You cannot blame them.

'But they are good men. They serve me well. They are the man power, I am the brains; and we divide the profits of our operations equally – half to the man power, half to the brains,' Capietro grinned.

'And your operations?' asked Stabutch.

Capietro scowled; then his face cleared. 'You are a comrade, but let me tell you that it is not always safe to be inquisitive.'

Stabutch shrugged. 'Tell me nothing,' he said. 'I do not care. It is none of my business.'

'Good,' exclaimed the Italian, 'and why you are here in Africa is none of my business, unless you care to tell me. Let us drink again.'

While the conversation that ensued, punctuated by numerous drinks, carefully eschewed personalities, the question of the other's occupation was uppermost in the mind of each; and as the natural effects of the liquor tended to disarm their suspicions and urge confidences it also stimulated the curiosity of the two, each of whom was now mellow and genial in his cups.

It was Capietro who broke first beneath the strain of an overpowering curiosity. They were sitting side by side upon a disreputably filthy rug, two empty bottles and a newly opened one before them. 'Comrade,' he cried, throwing an arm about the shoulders of the Russian affectionately, 'I like you. Dominic Capietro does not like many men. This is his motto: Like few men and love all women,' whereat he laughed loudly.

'Let us drink to that,' suggested Stabutch, joining in the laughter. '"Like few men and love all women." That is the idea!'

'I knew the minute I saw you that you were a man after my own heart, comrade,' continued Capietro, 'and why should there be secrets between comrades?'

'Certainly, why?' agreed Stabutch.

'So I shall tell you why I am here with this filthy band of thieving cutthroats. I was a soldier in the Italian army. My regiment was stationed in Eritrea. I was fomenting discord and mutiny, as a good Communist should, when some dog of a Fascist reported me to the commanding officer. I was arrested. Doubtless, I should have been shot, but I escaped and made my way into Abyssinia, where Italians are none too well liked; but when it was known that I was a deserter I was treated well.

'After a while I obtained employment with a powerful ras to train his soldiers along European lines. There I became proficient in Amharic, the official language of the country, and also learned to speak that of the Gallas, who constituted the bulk of the population of the principality of the ras for whom I worked. Naturally, being averse to any form of monarchistic government, I commenced at once to instill the glorious ideals of Communism into the breasts of the retainers of the old ras; but once again I was frustrated by an informer, and only by chance did I escape with my life.

'This time, however, I succeeded in enticing a number of men to accompany me. We stole horses and weapons from the ras and rode south where we joined a band of *shiftas*, or rather, I should say, absorbed them.

'This organized body of raiders and thieves made an excellent force with which to levy tribute upon chance travellers and caravans, but the returns were small and so we drifted down into this remote country of the Ghenzi where we can ply a lucrative trade in black ivory.'

'Black ivory? I never knew there was such a thing.'

Capietro laughed. 'Two legged ivory,' he explained.

Stabutch whistled. 'Oh,' he said, 'I think I understand. You are a slave raider; but where is there any market for slaves, other than the wage slaves of capitalistic countries?'

'You would be surprised, comrade. There are still many markets, including the mandates and protectorates of several highly civilized signatories to world court conventions aimed at the abolition of human slavery. Yes, I am a slave raider – rather a remarkable vocation for a university graduate and a former editor of a successful newspaper.'

'And you prefer this?'

'I have no alternative, and I must live. At least I think I must live – a most common form of rationalization. You see, my newspaper was anti-Fascist. And now, comrade, about yourself – what "scientific" research is the Soviet government undertaking in Africa?'

'Let us call it anthropology,' replied Stabutch. 'I am looking for a man.'

'There are many men in Africa and much nearer the coast than the Ghenzi country. You have travelled far inland looking for a man.'

'The man I look for I expected to find somewhere south of the Ghenzies,' replied Stabutch.

'Perhaps I can aid you. I know many men, at least by name and reputation, in this part of the world,' suggested the Italian.

Stabutch, had he been entirely sober, would have hesitated to give this information to a total stranger, but alcohol induces thoughtless confidences. 'I search for an Englishman known as Tarzan of the Apes,' he explained.

Capietro's eyes narrowed. 'A friend of yours?' he asked.

'I know of no one I would rather see,' replied Stabutch.

'You say he is here in the Ghenzi country?'

'I do not know. None of the natives I have questioned knew his whereabouts.'

'His country is far south of the Ghenzies,' said Capietro.

'Ah, you know of him, then?'

'Yes. Who does not? But what business have you with Tarzan of the Apes?'

'I have come from Moscow to kill him,' blurted Stabutch, and in the same instant regretted his rash admission.

Capietro relaxed. 'I am relieved,' he said.

'Why?' demanded the Russian.

'I feared he was a friend of yours,' explained the Italian. 'In which case we could not be friends; but if you have come to kill him you shall have nothing but my best wishes and heartiest support.'

Stabutch's relief was almost a thing of substance, so considerable and genuine was it. 'You, too, have a grievance against him?' he asked.

'He is a constant threat against my little operations in black ivory,' replied Capietro. 'I should feel much safer if he were out of the way.'

'Then perhaps you will help me, comrade?' inquired Stabutch eagerly.

'I have lost no ape-man,' replied Capietro, 'and if he leaves me alone I shall never look for him. That adventure, comrade, you will not have to share with me.'

'But you have taken away my means of carrying out my plans. I cannot seek Tarzan without a safari,' complained Stabutch.

'That is right,' admitted the raider; 'but perhaps the mistake of my men may be rectified. Your equipment and goods are safe. They will be returned to you, and as for men, who better could find them for you than Dominic Capietro, who deals in men?'

The safari of Lord Passmore moved northward, skirting the western foot-hills of the Ghenzi Mountains. His stalwart porters marched almost with the precision of trained soldiers, at least in that proper distances were maintained and there were no stragglers. A hundred yards in advance were three askaris and behind these came Lord Passmore, his gun bearer, and his head-man. At the head and rear of the column of porters was a detachment of askaris – well armed, efficient appearing men. The whole entourage suggested intelligent organization and experienced supervision. Evidence of willingly observed discipline was apparent, a discipline that seemed to be respected by all with the possible exception of Isaza, Lord Passmore's 'boy,' who was also his cook.

Isaza marched where his fancy dictated, laughing and joking with first one and then another of the members of the safari – the personification of the good nature that pervaded the whole party and that was constantly manifested by the laughter and singing of the men. It was evident that Lord Passmore was an experienced African traveller and that he knew what treatment to accord his followers.

How different, indeed, this well ordered safari, from another that struggled up the steep slopes of the Ghenzies a few miles to the east. Here the column was strung out for fully a mile, the askaris straggling along among the porters, while the two white men whom they accompanied forged far ahead with a single boy and a gun bearer.

'Geeze,' remarked the 'Gunner,' 'you sure picked a lousy racket! I could of stayed home and climbed up the front of the Sherman Hotel, if I had of wanted to climb, and always been within a spit of eats and drinks.'

'Oh, no you couldn't,' said Lafayette Smith.

'Why not? Who'd a stopped me?'

'Your friends, the cops.'

'That's right; but don't call 'em my friends – the lousy bums. But whereinel do you think you're going?'

'I think I perceive in this mountain range evidences of upthrust by horizontal compression,' replied Lafayette Smith, 'and I wish to examine the surface indications more closely than it is possible to do from a distance. Therefore, we must go to the mountains, since they will not come to us.'

'And what does it get you?' demanded 'Gunner' Patrick. 'Not a buck. It's a bum racket.'

Lafayette Smith laughed good naturedly. They were crossing a meadowland through which a mountain stream wound. Surrounding it was a forest. 'This would make a good camp,' he said, 'from which to work for a few days. You can hunt, and I'll have a look at the formations in the vicinity. Then we'll move on.'

'It's jake with me,' replied the 'Gunner.' 'I'm fed up on climbing.'

'Suppose you remain with the safari and get camp made,' suggested Smith. 'I'll go on up a little farther with my boy and see what I can see. It's early yet.'

'Oke,' assented the 'Gunner.' 'I'll park the mob up near them trees. Don't get lost, and, say, you better take my protection guy with you,' he added, nodding in the direction of his gun bearer.

'I'm not going to hunt,' replied Smith. 'I won't need him.'

'Then take my rod here.' The 'Gunner' started to unbuckle his pistol belt. 'You might need it.'

'Thanks, I have one,' replied Smith, tapping his .32.

'Geeze, you don't call that thing a rod, do you?' demanded the 'Gunner' contemptuously.

'It's all I need. I'm looking for rocks, not trouble. Come on Obambi,' and he motioned his boy to follow him as he started up the slope toward the higher mountains.

'Geeze,' muttered the 'Gunner,' 'I seen pipies what ain't as much of a nut as that guy; but,' he added, 'he's a regular guy at that. You can't help likin' him.' Then he turned his attention to the selection of a campsite.

Lafayette Smith entered the forest beyond the meadow-land; and here the going became more difficult, for the ground rose rapidly; and the under-brush was thick. He fought his way upward, Obambi at his heels; and at last he reached a higher elevation, where the forest growth was much thinner because of the rocky nature of the ground and the absence of top soil. Here he paused to examine the formation, but only to move on again, this time at right angles to his original direction.

Thus, stopping occasionally to investigate, he moved erratically upward until he achieved the summit of a ridge from which he had a view of miles of rugged mountains in the distance. The canyon that lay before him, separating him from the next ridge, aroused his interest. The formation of the opposite wall, he decided, would bear closer investigation.

Obambi had flung himself to the ground when Smith halted. Obambi appeared exhausted. He was not. He was merely disgusted. To him the bwana was mad, quite mad. Upon no other premises could Obambi explain this senseless climbing, with an occasional pause to examine rocks. Obambi was positive that they might have discovered plenty of rocks at the foot of the mountains had they but searched for them. And then, too, this bwana did not hunt. He supposed all bwanas came to Africa to hunt. This one, being so different, must be mad.

Smith glanced at his boy. It was too bad, he thought, to make Obambi do all this climbing unnecessarily. Certainly there was no way in which the boy might assist him, while seeing him in a constant state of exhaustion reacted unfavorably on Smith. Better by far be alone. He turned to the boy. 'Go back to camp, Obambi,' he said. 'I do not need you here.'

Obambi looked at him in surprise. Now he knew the bwana was very mad. However, it would be much more pleasant in camp than climbing about in these mountains. He rose to his feet. 'The bwana does not need me?' he asked. 'Perhaps he will need me.' Obambi's conscience was already troubling him. He knew that he should not leave his bwana alone.

'No, I shan't need you, Obambi,' Smith assured him. 'You run along back to camp. I'll come in pretty soon.'

'Yes, bwana,' and Obambi turned back down the mountain side.

Lafayette Smith clambered down into the canyon, which was deeper than he had supposed, and then worked his way up the opposite side that proved to be even more precipitous than it had appeared from the summit of the ridge. However, he found so much to interest him that he considered it well worth the effort, and so deeply absorbed was he that he gave no heed to the passage of time.

It was not until he reached the top of the far side of the canyon that he noted the diminishing light that presaged the approach of night. Even then he was not greatly concerned; but he realized that it would be quite dark before he could hope to recross the canyon, and it occurred to him that by following up the ridge on which he stood he could reach the head of the canyon where it joined the ridge from which he had descended into it, thus saving him a long, arduous climb and shortening the time, if not the distance, back to camp.

As he trudged upward along the ridge, night fell; but still he kept on, though now he could only grope his way slowly, nor did it occur to him for several hours that he was hopelessly lost.

VIII

The Baboons

A new day had dawned, and Africa greeted the age old miracle of Kudu emerging from his lair behind the eastern hills and smiled. With the exception of a few stragglers the creatures of the night had vanished, surrendering the world to their diurnal fellows.

Tongani, the baboon, perched upon his sentinel rock, surveyed the scene and, perhaps, not without appreciation of the beauties; for who are we to say that God touched so many countless of his works with beauty yet gave to but one of these the power of appreciation?

Below the sentinel fed the tribe of Zugash, the king; fierce tongani shes with their balus clinging to their backs, if very young, while others played about, imitating their elders in their constant search for food; surly, vicious bulls; old Zugash himself, the surliest and most vicious.

The keen, close-set eyes of the sentinel, constantly upon the alert downwind, perceived something moving among the little hills below. It was the top of a man's head. Presently the whole head came into view; and then the sentinel saw that it belonged to a tarmangani; but as yet he sounded no alarm, for the tarmangani was still a long way off and might not be coming in the direction of the tribe. The sentinel would watch yet a little longer and make sure, for it was senseless to interrupt the feeding of the tribe if no danger threatened.

Now the tarmangani was in full view. Tongani wished that he might have the evidence of his keen nose as well as his eyes; then there would be no doubt, for, like many animals, the tonganis preferred to submit all evidence to their sensitive nostrils before accepting the verdict of their eyes; but the wind was in the wrong direction.

Perhaps, too, Tongani was puzzled, for this was such a tarmangani as he had never before seen – a tarmangani who walked almost as naked as Tongani himself. But for the white skin he might have thought him a Gomangani. This being a tarmangani, the sentinel looked for the feared thunder stick; and because he saw none he waited before giving the alarm. But presently he saw that the creature was coming directly toward the tribe.

The tarmangani had long been aware of the presence of the baboons, being downwind from them where their strong scent was borne to his keen nostrils. Also, he had seen the sentinel at almost the same instant that the sentinel had seen him; yet he continued upward, swinging along in easy strides that suggested the power and savage independence of Numa, the lion.

Suddenly Tongani, the baboon, sprang to his feet, uttering a sharp bark, and instantly the tribe awoke to action, swarming up the low cliffs at the foot of which they had been feeding. Here they turned and faced the intruder, barking their defiance as they ran excitedly to and fro.

When they saw that the creature was alone and bore no thunder stick they were more angry than frightened, and they scolded at this interruption of their feeding. Zugash and several of the other larger bulls even clambered part way down the cliff to frighten him away; but in this they only succeeded in increasing their own anger, for the tarmangani continued upward toward them.

Zugash, the king, was now beside himself with rage. He stormed and threatened. 'Go away!' he barked. 'I am Zugash. I kill!'

. And now the stranger halted at the foot of the cliff and surveyed him. 'I am Tarzan of the Apes,' he said. 'Tarzan does not come to the stamping grounds of the tongani to kill. He comes as a friend.'

Silence fell upon the tribe of Zugash; the silence of stunning surprise. Never before had they heard either tarmangani or Gomangani speak the language of the ape-people. They had never heard of Tarzan of the Apes, whose country was far to the south; but nevertheless they were impressed by his ability to understand them and speak to them. However, he was a stranger, and so Zugash ordered him away again.

'Tarzan does not wish to remain with the tongani,' replied the ape-man; 'he desires only to pass them in peace.'

'Go away!' growled Zugash. 'I kill. I am Zugash.'

Tarzan swung up the cliff quite as easily as had the baboons. It was his answer to Zugash, the king. None was there who better knew the strength, the courage, the ferocity of the tongani than he, yet he knew, too, that he might be in this country for some time and that, if he were to survive, he must establish himself definitely in the minds of all lesser creatures as one who walked without fear and whom it was well to let alone.

Barking furiously, the baboons retreated; and Tarzan gained the summit of the cliff, where he saw that the shes and balus had scattered, many of them going farther up into the hills, while the adult bulls remained to contest the way.

As Tarzan paused, just beyond the summit of the cliff, he found himself the center of a circle of snarling bulls against the combined strength and ferocity of which he would be helpless. To another than himself his position might have appeared precarious almost to the point of hopelessness; but Tarzan knew the wild peoples of his savage world too well to expect an unprovoked attack, or a killing for the love of killing such as only man, among all the creatures of the world, habitually commits. Neither was he unaware of the danger of his position should a bull, more nervous or suspicious than his fellows, mistake Tarzan's intentions or misinterpret some trivial act or gesture as a threat against the safety of the tribe.

But he knew that only an accident might precipitate a charge and that if he gave them no cause to attack him they would gladly let him proceed upon his way unmolested. However, he had hoped to achieve friendly relations with the tongani, whose knowledge of the country and its inhabitants might prove of inestimable value to him. Better, too, that the tribe of Zugash be allies than enemies. And so he assayed once more to win their confidence.

'Tell me, Zugash,' he said, addressing the bristling king baboon, 'if there be many tarmangani in your country. Tarzan hunts for a bad tarmangani who has many Gomangani with him. They are bad men. They kill. With thunder sticks they kill. They will kill the tongani. Tarzan has come to drive them from your country.'

But Zugash only growled and placed the back of his head against the ground in challenge. The other males moved restlessly sideways, their shoulders high, their tails bent in crooked curves. Now some of the younger bulls rested the backs of their heads upon the ground, imitating the challenge of their king.

Zugash, grimacing at Tarzan, raised then lowered his brows rapidly, exposing the white skin about his eyes. Thus did the savage old king seek to turn the heart of his antagonist to water by the frightfulness of his mien; but Tarzan only shrugged indifferently and moved on again as though convinced that the baboons would not accept his overtures of friendship.

Straight toward the challenging bulls that stood in his path he walked, without haste and apparently without concern; but his eyes were narrowed and watchful, his every sense on the alert. One bull, stiff legged and arrogant, moved grudgingly aside; but another stood his ground. Here, the ape-man knew the real test would come that should decide the issue.

The two were close now, face to face, when suddenly there burst from the lips of the man-beast a savage growl, and simultaneously he charged. With an answering growl and a catlike leap the baboon bounded aside; and Tarzan passed beyond the rim of the circle, victor in the game of bluff which is played by every order of living thing sufficiently advanced in the scale of intelligence to possess an imagination.

Seeing that the man-thing did not follow upward after the shes and balus, the bulls contented themselves with barking insults after him and aiming uncomplimentary gestures at his retreating figure; but such were not the acts that menaced safety, and the ape-man ignored them.

Purposely he had turned away from the shes and their young, with the intention of passing around them, rather than precipitate a genuine attack by seeming to threaten them. And thus his way took him to the edge of a shallow ravine into which, unknown either to Tarzan or the tongani, a young mother had fled with her tiny balu.

Tarzan was still in full view of the tribe of Zugash, though he alone could see into the ravine, when suddenly three things occurred that shattered the peace that seemed again descending upon the scene. A vagrant air current wafted upward from the thick verdure below him the scent of Sheeta, the panther; a baboon voiced a scream of terror; and, looking down, the ape-man saw the young she, her balu clinging to her back, fleeing upward toward him with savage Sheeta in pursuit.

As Tarzan, reacting instantly to the necessity of the moment, leaped downward with back thrown spear hand, the bulls of Zugash raced forward in answer to the note of terror in the voice of the young mother.

From his position above the actors in this sudden tragedy of the wilds the ape-man could see the panther over the head of the baboon and realizing that the beast must reach his victim before succour could arrive he hurled his spear in the forlorn hope of stopping the carnivore, if only for a moment.

The cast was one that only a practiced hand might have dared attempt, for the danger to the baboon was almost as great as that which threatened the panther should the aim of the ape-men not be perfect.

Zugash and his bulls, bounding forward at an awkward gallop, reached the edge of the ravine just in time to see the heavy spear hurtle past the head of the she by a margin of inches only and bury itself in the breast of Sheeta. Then they were down the slope, a snarling, snapping pack, and with them went an English viscount, to fall upon a surprised, pain-maddened panther.

The baboons leaped in to snap at their hereditary foe and leaped out again, and the man-beast, as quick and agile as they, leaped and struck with his hunting knife, while the frenzied cat lunged this way and that, first at one tormentor and then at another.

Twice those powerful, raking talons reached their mark and two bulls sprawled, torn and bloody, upon the ground; but the bronzed hide of the ape-man ever eluded the rage of the wounded cat.

Short was the furious battle, ferocious the growls and snarls of the combatants, prodigious the leaps and bounds of the excited shes hovering in the background; and then Sheeta, rearing high upon his hind feet, struck savagely at Tarzan and, in the same instant, plunged to earth dead, slain by the spear point puncturing his heart.

Instantly the great tarmangani, who had once been king of the great apes, leaped close and placed a foot upon the carcass of his kill. He raised his face toward Kudu, the sun; and from his lips broke the horrid challenge of the bull ape that has killed.

For a moment silence fell upon the forest, the mountain, and jungle. Awed, the baboons ceased their restless movements and their din. Tarzan stooped and drew the spear from the quivering body of Sheeta, while the tongani watched him with a new interest.

Then Zugash approached. This time he did not rest the back of his head against the ground in challenge. 'The bulls of the tribe of Zugash are the friends of Tarzan of the Apes,' he said.

'Tarzan is the friend of the bulls of the tribe of Zugash,' responded the ape-man.

'We have seen a tarmangani,' said Zugash. 'He has many Gomangani. There are many thunder sticks among them. They are bad. Perhaps it is they whom Tarzan seeks.'

'Perhaps,' admitted the slayer of Sheeta. 'Where are they?'

'They were camped where the rocks sit upon the mountain side, as here.' He nodded toward the cliff.

'Where?' asked Tarzan again, and this time Zugash motioned along the foothills toward the south.

IX

The Great Fissure

The morning sun shone upon the bosom of Chinnereth, glancing from the breeze born ripples that moved across its surface like vast companies of soldiers passing in review with their countless spears gleaming in the sunlight – a dazzling aspect of beauty.

But to Lady Barbara Collis it connoted something quite different – a shallow splendor concealing cruel and treacherous depths, the real Chinnereth.

She shuddered as she approached its shore surrounded by the apostles, preceded by Abraham, the son of Abraham, and followed by the elders and the villagers. Among them, somewhere she knew were the six with their great net and their fibre ropes.

How alike were they all to Chinnereth, hiding their cruelty and their treachery beneath a thin veneer of godliness! But there the parallel terminated, for Chinnereth was beautiful. She glanced at the faces of the men nearest her, and again she shuddered. ' "So God created man in his own image," ' she mused. 'Who, then, created these?'

During the long weeks that fate had held her in this land of Midian she had often sought an explanation of the origin of this strange race, and the deductions of her active mind had not deviated greatly from the truth. Noting the exaggerated racial characteristics of face and form that distinguished them from other peoples she had seen, recalling their common tendency to epilepsy, she had concluded that they were the inbred descendants of a common ancestor, himself a defective and an epileptic.

This theory explained much; but it failed to explain Jezebel, who insisted that she was the child of two of these creatures and that, insofar as she knew, no new strain of blood had ever been injected into the veins of the Midian by intermating with other peoples. Yet, somehow, Lady Barbara knew that such a strain must have been introduced, though she could not guess the truth nor the antiquity of the fact that lay buried in the grave of a little slave girl.

And their religion! Again she shuddered. What a hideous travesty of the teachings of Christ! It was a confused jumble of ancient Christianity and still more ancient Judaism, handed down by word of mouth through a half imbecile people who had no written language; a people who had confused Paul the Apostle with Christ the Master and lost entirely the essence of the Master's teachings, while interpolating hideous barbarisms of their own invention. Sometimes she thought she saw in this exaggerated deviation a suggestion of parallel to other so-called Christian sects of the civilized outer world.

But now her train of thoughts was interrupted by the near approach of the procession to the shore of the lake. Here was the flat-topped lava rock of grim suggestiveness and hideous memory. How long it seemed since she had watched the six hurl their screaming victim from its well worn surface, and yet it had been but yesterday. Now it was her turn. The Prophet and the Apostles were intoning their senseless gibberish, meant to impress the villagers with their erudition and cloak the real vacuity of their minds, a practice not unknown to more civilized sects.

She was halted now upon the smooth surface of the lava, polished by soft sandals and naked feet through the countless years that these cruel rites had been enacted beside the waters of Chinnereth. Again she heard the screams of yesterday's victim. But Lady Barbara Collis had not screamed, nor would she. She would rob them of that satisfaction at least.

Abraham, the son of Abraham, motioned the six to the fore; and they came, bearing their net and their cords. At their feet lay the lava fragment that would weight the net and its contents. The Prophet raised his hands above his head and the people kneeled. In the forefront of their ranks Lady Barbara saw the golden haired Jezebel; and her heart was touched, for there was anguish in the beautiful face and tears in the lovely eyes. Here was one, at least, who could harbor love and compassion.

'I have walked with Jehovah,' cried Abraham, the son of Abraham, and Lady Barbara wondered that he did not have blisters on his feet, so often he walked with Jehovah. The levity of the conceit brought an involuntary smile to her lips, a smile that the Prophet noticed. 'You smile,' he said, angrily. 'You smile when you should scream and beg for mercy as the others do. Why do you smile?'

'Because I am not afraid,' replied Lady Barbara, though she was very much afraid.

'Why art thou not afraid, woman?' demanded the old man.

'I, too, have walked with Jehovah,' she replied, 'and He told me to fear not, because you are a false prophet, and—'

'Silence!' thundered Abraham, the son of Abraham. 'Blaspheme no more. Jehovah shall judge you in a moment.' He turned to the six. 'Into the net with her!'

Quickly they did his bidding; and as they commenced to swing her body to and fro, to gain momentum against the moment that they would release their holds and cast her into the deep lake, she heard The Prophet reciting her iniquities that Jehovah was about to judge in his own peculiar way. His speech was punctuated by the screams and groans of those of the company who were seized in the grip of the now familiar attacks to which Lady Barbara had become so accustomed as to be almost as callous to as the Midians themselves.

From her pocket the girl extracted the little pen knife that was her only weapon and held it firmly in one hand, the blade open and ready for the work she intended it to do. And what work was that? Surely, she could not hope to inflict instant death upon herself with that inadequate weapon! Yet, in the last stages of fear induced by utter helplessness and hopelessness one may attempt anything, even the impossible.

Now they were swinging her far out over Chinnereth. The Apostles and the elders were intoning their weird chant in voices excited to frenzy by the imminence of death, those who were not writhing upon the rocky face of the altar in the throes of seizures.

Suddenly came the word from Abraham, the son of Abraham. Lady

Barbara caught her breath in a last frightened gasp. The six released their holds. A loud scream arose from the huddled villagers – the scream of a woman – and as she plunged toward the dark waters Lady Barbara knew that it was the voice of Jezebel crying out in the anguish of sorrow. Then mysterious Chinnereth closed above her head.

At that very moment Lafayette Smith, A.M., Ph.D., Sc.D., was stumbling along a rocky mountain side that walled the great crater where lay the land of Midian and Chinnereth. He was no less aware of the tragedy being enacted upon the opposite side of that stupendous wall than of the fact that he was moving directly away from the camp he was seeking. Had there been anyone there to tell him, and had they told him, that he was hopelessly lost he would have been inclined to dispute the statement, so positive was he that he was taking a short cut to camp, which he imagined was but a little distance ahead.

Although he had been without supper and breakfast, hunger had not as yet caused him any annoyance, partially because of the fact that he had had some chocolate with him, which had materially assisted in allaying its pangs, and partially through his interest in the geologic formations that held the attention of his scholarly mind to the exclusion of such material considerations as hunger, thirst, and bodily comfort. Even the question of personal safety was relegated to the oblivion that usually engulfed all practical issues when Lafayette Smith was immersed in the pleasant waters of research.

Consequently he was unaware of the proximity of a tawny body, nor did the fixed and penetrating gaze of a pair of cruel yellow-green eyes penetrate the armor of his preoccupation to disturb that sixth sense that is popularly supposed to warn us of unseen danger. Yet even had any premonition of threat to his life or safety disturbed him he doubtless would have ignored it, safe in the consciousness that he was adequately protected by the possession of his .32 caliber, nickel plated pistol.

Moving northward along the lower slopes of a conical mountain, the mind of the geologist became more and more deeply engrossed in the rocky story that Nature had written upon the landscape, a story so thrilling that even thoughts of camp were forgotten; and as he made his way farther and farther from camp a great lion stalked in his wake.

What hidden urge prompted Numa thus to follow the man-thing perhaps the great cat, himself, could not have guessed. He was not hungry, for he had but recently finished a kill, nor was he a man-eater, though a properly balanced combination of circumstances might easily find the scales tipped in that direction by hunger, inevitable and oft recurring. It may have been only curiosity, or, again, some motive akin to that playfulness which is inherent in all cats.

For an hour Numa followed the man – an hour of intense interest for both of them – an hour that would have been replete with far greater interest for the man, if less pleasurable, had he shared with Numa the knowledge of their propinquity. Then the man halted before a narrow vertical cleft in the rocky escarpment towering above him. Here was an interesting entry in the book of Nature! What titanic force had thus rent the solid rock of this mighty mountain? It had its own peculiar significance, but what was it? Perhaps elsewhere on the face of the mountain, that here became precipitous, there would be other evidence to point the way to a solution. Lafayette Smith looked up at the face of the cliff towering above him, he looked ahead in the direction he had been going; and then he looked back in the direction from which he had come – and saw the lion.

For a long moment the two stared at one another. Surprise and interest were the most definitely registered of the emotions that the discovery engendered in the mind of the man. Suspicion and irritability were aroused in Numa.

'Most interesting,' thought Lafayette Smith. 'A splendid specimen;' but his interest in lions was purely academic, and his thoughts quickly reverted to the more important phenomenon of the crack in the mountain, which now, again, claimed his undivided attention. From which it may be inferred that Lafayette Smith was either an inordinately courageous man or a fool. Neither assumption, however, would be wholly correct, especially the latter. The truth of the matter is that Lafayette Smith suffered from inexperience and impracticality. While he knew that a lion was, *per se*, a threat to longevity he saw no reason why this lion should attack him. He, Lafayette Smith, had done nothing to offend this, or any other, lion; he was attending to his own affairs and, like the gentleman he was, expected others, including lions, to be equally considerate. Furthermore, he had a childlike faith in the infallibility of his nickel plated .32 should worse develop into worst. Therefore he ignored Numa and returned to contemplation of the intriguing crack.

It was several feet wide and was apparent as far up the face of the cliff as he could see. Also there was every indication that it continued far below the present surface of the ground, but had been filled by debris brought down by erosion from above. How far into the mountain it extended he could not guess; but he hoped that it ran back, and was open, for a great distance, in which event it would offer a most unique means for studying the origin of this mountain massif.

Therefore, with this thought uppermost in his mind, and the lion already crowded into the dim background of his consciousness, he entered the narrow opening to the intriguing fissure. Here he discovered that the cleft curved gradually to the left and that it extended upward to the surface, where it was considerably wider than at the bottom, thus affording both light and air for the interior.

Thrilled with excitement and glowing with pride in his discovery,

Lafayette clambered inward over the fallen rocks that littered the floor of the fissure, intent now on exploring the opening to its full extent and then working back slowly to the entrance in a more leisurely manner, at which time he would make a minute examination of whatever geological record Nature had imprinted upon the walls of this majestic corridor. Hunger, thirst, camp, and the lion were forgotten.

Numa, however, was no geologist. The great cleft aroused no palpitant enthusiasm within his broad breast. It did not cause him to forget anything, and it intrigued his interest only to the extent of causing him to speculate on why the man-thing had entered it. Having noted the indifferent attitude of the man, his lack of haste, Numa could not attribute his disappearance within the maw of the fissure to flight. All of his life things had been fleeing from him.

It had always seemed to Numa an unfair provision of Nature that things should so almost inevitably seek to escape him, especially those things he most coveted. There were, for example, Pacco, the zebra, and Wappi, the antelope, the tenderest and most delicious of his particular weaknesses, and, at the same time, the fleetest. It would have been much simpler all around had Kota the tortoise been endowed with the speed of Pacco and Pacco with the torpidity of Kota.

But in this instance there was nothing to indicate that the man-thing was fleeing him. Perhaps, then, there was treachery afoot. Numa bristled. Very cautiously he approached the fissure into which his quarry had disappeared. Numa was beginning to think of Lafayette Smith in terms of food, now, since his long stalking had commenced to arouse within his belly the first, faint suggestions of hunger. He approached the cleft and looked in. The tarmangani was not in sight. Numa was not pleased, and he evidenced his displeasure by an angry growl.

A hundred yards within the fissure Lafayette Smith heard the growl and halted abruptly. 'That damn lion!' he ejaculated. 'I had forgotten all about him.' It now occurred to him that this might be the beast's lair – a most unhappy contretemps, if true. A realization of his predicament at last supplanted the geologic reveries that had filled his mind. But what to do? Suddenly his faith in his trusty .32 faltered. As he recalled the appearance of the great beast the weapon seemed less infallible, yet it still gave him a certain sense of assurance as his fingers caressed its grip.

He determined that it would not be wise to retrace his steps toward the entrance at this time. Of course the lion might not have entered the fissure, might not even be harboring any intention of so doing. On the other hand, he might, in which event a return toward the opening could prove embarrassing, if not disastrous. Perhaps, if he waited a while, the lion would go away; and in the meantime, he decided, it would be discreet to go still farther along the cleft, as the lion, if it entered at all, might conceivably not proceed to the uttermost depths of the corridor. Further, there was the chance that he would find some sort of sanctuary farther in – a cave, a ledge to which he could climb, a miracle. Lafayette Smith was open to anything by this time.

And so he scrambled on, tearing his clothes and his flesh as well on sharp fragments of tumbled rock, going deeper into this remarkable corridor that seemed endless. In view of what might be behind him he hoped that it was endless. He had shuddered regularly to the oft recurring expectation of running into a blank wall just beyond that portion of the gently curving fissure that lay within his view ahead. He pictured the event. With his back to the rocky end of the cul-de-sac he would face back down the corridor, his pistol ready in his hand. Presently the lion would appear and discover him.

At this point he had some difficulty in constructing the scene, because he did not know just what the lion would do. Perhaps, seeing a man, cowed by the superior gaze of the human eye, he would turn in hasty retreat. And then again, perhaps he would not. Lafayette Smith was inclined to the conclusion that he would not. But then, of course, he had not had sufficient experience of wild animals to permit him to pose as an authority on the subject. To be sure, upon another occasion, while engaged in field work, he had been chased by a cow. Yet even this experience had not been conclusive – it had not served to definitely demonstrate the cow's ultimate intent – for the very excellent reason that Lafayette had attained a fence two jumps ahead of her.

Confused as the issue now seemed to be by his total ignorance of leonine psychology, he was convinced that he must attempt to visualize the expectant scene that he might be prepared for the eventuality.

Forging grimly ahead over the roughly tumbled fragments, casting an occasional glance backward, he again pictured his last stand with his back against the corridor's rocky end. The lion was creeping slowly toward him, but Lafayette was waiting until there should be no chance of a miss. He was very cool. His hand was steady as he took careful aim.

Here regrets interrupted the even tenor of his musing – regrets that he had not practiced more assiduously with his revolver. The fact that he had never discharged it troubled him, though only vaguely, since he harbored the popular subconscious conviction that if a firearm is pointed in the general direction of an animate object it becomes a deadly weapon.

However, in this mental picture he took careful aim – the fact that he was utilizing the front sight only giving him no concern. He pulled the trigger. The lion staggered and almost fell. It required a second shot to finish him, and as he sank to the ground Lafayette Smith breathed a genuine sigh of relief. He felt himself trembling slightly to the reaction of the nervous strain he had been undergoing. He stopped and, withdrawing a handkerchief from his pocket, mopped the perspiration from his forehead, smiling a little as he realized the pitch of excitement to which he had aroused himself. Doubltess the lion had already forgotten him and had gone on about his business, he soliloquized.

He was facing back in the direction from which he had come as this satisfying conclusion passed through his mind; and then, a hundred feet away, where the corridor passed from view around a curve, the lion appeared.

X

In the Clutches of the Enemy

The 'Gunner' was perturbed. It was morning, and Lafayette Smith was still missing. They had searched for him until late the previous night, and now they were setting forth again. Ogonyo, the headman, acting under instructions from the 'Gunner' had divided the party into pairs and, with the exception of four men left to guard the camp, these were to search in different directions combing the country carefully for trace of the missing man.

Danny had selected Obambi as his companion, a fact which irked the black boy considerably as he had been the target for a great deal of angry vituperation ever since Danny had discovered, the afternoon before, that he had left Smith alone in the mountains.

'It don't make no difference what he told you, you punk,' the 'Gunner' assured him, 'you didn't have no business leavin' him out there alone. Now I'm goin' to take you for a walk, and if we don't find Lafayette you ain't never comin' back.'

'Yes, bwana,' replied Obambi, who had not even a crude idea of what the white man was talking about. One thing, however, pleased him immensely and that was that the bwana insisted on carrying his own gun, leaving nothing for Obambi to carry but a light lunch and two fifty-round drums of ammunition. Not that the nine pounds and thirteen ounces of a Thompson submachine gun would have been an exceptionally heavy burden, but that Obambi was always glad to be relieved of any burden. He would have been mildly grateful for a load reduction of even thirteen ounces.

The 'Gunner,' in attempting to determine the probable route that Smith would have followed in his search for camp, reasoned in accordance with what he assumed he would have done under like circumstances; and, knowing that Smith had been last seen well above the camp and a little to the north of it, he decided to search in a northly direction along the foothills, it being obvious that a man would come downhill rather than go farther up in such an emergency.

The day was hot and by noon the 'Gunner' was tired, sweating, and disgusted. He was particularly disgusted with Africa, which, he informed Obambi, was 'a hell of a burgh.'

'Geeze,' he grumbled; 'I've walked my lousy legs off, and I ain't been no further than from The Loop to Cicero. I been six hours, and I could of done it in twenty minutes in a taxi. Of course they ain't got no cops in Africa, but they ain't got no taxis either.'

'Yes, bwana,' agreed Obambi.

'Shut up!' growled the 'Gunner.'

They were sitting beneath the shade of a tree on a hillside, resting and eating their lunch. A short distance below them the hillside dropped sheer in a fifty foot cliff, a fact that was not apparent from where they sat, any more than was the palisaded village at the cliff's base. Nor did they see the man squatting by a bush at the very brink of the cliff. His back was toward them, as from the concealment of the bush, he gazed down upon the village below.

Here, the watcher believed, was the man he sought; but he wished to make sure, which might require days of watching. Time, however, meant little or nothing to Tarzan – no more than it did to any other jungle beast. He would come back often to this vantage spot and watch. Sooner or later he would discover the truth or falsity of his suspicion that one of the white men he saw in the village below was the slave raider for whom he had come north. And so, like a great lion, the ape-man crouched, watching his quarry.

Below him Dominic Capietro and Leon Stabutch lolled in the shade of a tree outside the hut of the raider, while a half dozen slave girls waited upon them as they leisurely ate their belated breakfast.

A couple of fiery liquid bracers had stimulated their jaded spirits, which had been at low ebb after their awakening following their debauch of the previous day, though, even so, neither could have been correctly described as being in fine fettle.

Capietro, who was even more surly and quarrelsome than usual, vented his spleen upon the hapless slaves, while Stabutch ate in morose silence, which he finally broke to revert to the subject of his mission.

'I ought to get started toward the south,' he said. 'From all I can learn there's nothing to be gained looking for the ape-man in this part of the country.'

'What you in such a hurry to find him for?' demanded Capietro. 'Ain't my company good enough for you?'

'"Business before pleasure," you know, comrade,' Stabutch reminded the Italian in a conciliatory tone.

'I suppose so,' grunted Capietro.

'I should like to visit you again after I have come back from the south,' suggested Stabutch.

'You may not come back.'

'I shall. Peter Zveri must be avenged. The obstacle in the path of communism must be removed.'

'The monkey-man killed Zveri?'

'No, a woman killed him,' replied the Russian, 'but the monkey-man, as you call him, was directly responsible for the failure of all Zveri's plans and thus indirectly responsible for his death.'

'You expect to fare better than Zveri, then? Good luck to you, but I don't envy you your mission. This Tarzan is like a lion with the brain of a man. He is savage. He is terrible. In his own country he is also very powerful.'

'I shall get him, nevertheless,' said Stabutch, confidently. 'If possible I shall kill him the moment I first see him, before he has an opportunity to become suspicious; or, if I cannot do that, I shall win his confidence and his friendship and then destroy him when he least suspects his danger.'

Voices carry upward to a great distance, and so, though Stabutch spoke only in normal tones, the watcher, squatting at the cliff-top, smiled – just the faintest suggestion of a grim smile.

So that was why the man from 'Russa', of whom Goloba the headman had told him, was inquiring as to his whereabouts? Perhaps Tarzan had suspected as much, but he was glad to have definite proof.

'I shall be glad if you do kill him,' said Capietro. 'He would drive me out of business if he ever learned about me. He is a scoundrel who would prevent a man from earning an honest dollar.'

'You may put him from your mind, comrade,' Stabutch assured the raider. 'He is already as good as dead. Furnish me with men, and I shall soon be on my way toward the south.'

'My villains are already saddling to go forth and find men for your safari,' said Capietro, with a wave of his hand in the direction of the central compound, where a score of cutthroats were saddling their horses in preparation for a foray against a distant Galla village.

'May luck go with them,' said Stabutch. 'I hope – What was that?' he demanded, leaping to his feet as a sudden crash of falling rock and earth came from behind them.

Capietro was also upon his feet. 'A landslide,' he exclaimed. 'A portion of the cliff has fallen. Look! What is that?' he pointed at an object halfway up the cliff – the figure of a naked white man clinging to a tree that had found lodgment for its roots in the rocky face of the cliff. The tree, a small one, was bending beneath the weight of the man. Slowly it gave way, there was the sound of rending wood, and then the figure hurtled downward into the village where it was hidden from the sight of the two white watchers by an intervening hut.

But Stabutch had seen the giant figure of the almost naked white long enough to compare it with the description he had had of the man for whom he had come all the long way from Moscow. There could not be two such, of that he was certain. 'It is the ape-man!' he cried. 'Come, Capietro, he is ours!'

Instantly the Italian ordered several *shiftas* to advance and seize the ape-man.

Fortune is never necessarily with either the brave or the virtuous. She is, unfortunately, quite as likely to perch upon the banner of the poltroon or the blackguard. Today she deserted Tarzan completely. As he squatted upon the edge of the cliff, looking down upon the village of Dominic Capietro, he suddenly felt the earth giving beneath him. Catlike, he leaped to his feet, throwing his hands above his head, as one does, mechanically, to preserve his balance or seek support, but too late. With a small avalanche of earth and rock he slid over the edge of the cliff. The tree, growing part way down the face of the escarpment, broke his fall and for a moment, gave him hope that he might escape the greater danger of the final plunge into the village, where, if the fall did not kill him it was quite evident that his enemies would. But only for a moment were his hopes aroused. With the breaking of the bending stem hope vanished as he plunged on downward.

Danny 'Gunner' Patrick, having finished his lunch, lighted a cigarette and let his gaze wander out over the landscape that unfolded in a lovely panorama before him. City bred, he saw only a part of what there was to be seen and understood but little of that. What impressed him most was the loneliness of the prospect. 'Geeze,' he soliloquized, 'what a hideout! No one wouldn't never find a guy here.' His eyes suddenly focused upon an object in the foreground. 'Hey, smoke,' he whispered to Obambi, 'what's that?' He pointed in the direction of the thing that had aroused his curiosity.

Obambi looked and, when they found it, his keen eyes recognized it for what it was. 'It is a man, bwana,' he said. 'It is the man who killed Simba in our camp that night. It is Tarzan of the Apes.'

'How t'ell do you know?' demanded the 'Gunner.'

'There is only one Tarzan,' replied the black. 'It could be no other, as no other white man in all the jungle country or the mountain country or the plains country goes thus naked.'

The 'Gunner' rose to his feet. He was going down to have a talk with the ape-man, who, perhaps, could help him in his search for Lafayette Smith; but as he arose he saw the man below him leap to his feet and throw his arms above his head. Then he disappeared as though swallowed up by the earth. The 'Gunner,' knitted his brows.

'Geeze,' he remarked to Obambi, 'he sure screwed, didn't he?'

'What, bwana?' asked Obambi.

'Shut up,' snapped the 'Gunner.' 'That was funny,' he muttered. 'Wonder what became of him. Guess I'll give him a tail. Come on, dinge,' he concluded aloud to Obambi.

Having learned through experience (wholly the experience of others who had failed to do so) that attention to details is essential to the continued pursuit of life, liberty, and happiness, the 'Gunner' looked carefully to his Thompson as he walked rapidly but cautiously toward the spot where Tarzan had disappeared. He saw that there was a cartridge in the chamber, that the magazine drum was properly attached and that the fire control lever was set for full automatic fire.

In the village, which he could not yet see and of the presence of which he did not dream, the *shiftas* were running toward the place where they knew the body of the fallen man must lie; and in the van were Stabutch and Capietro, when suddenly there stepped from the interior of the last hut the man they sought. They did not know that he had alighted on the thatched roof of the hut from which he had just emerged, nor that, though he had broken through it to the floor below, it had so broken his fall that he had suffered no disabling injury.

To them it seemed a miracle; and to see him thus, apparently uninjured, took the two white men so by surprise that they halted in their tracks while their followers, imitating their example, clustered about them.

Stabutch was the first to regain his presence of mind. Whipping a revolver from its holster he was about to fire point blank at the ape-man, when Capietro struck his hand up. 'Wait,' growled the Italian. 'Do not be too fast. I am in command here.'

'But it is the ape-man,' cried Stabutch.

'I know that,' replied Capietro, 'and for that very reason I wish to take him alive. He is rich. He will bring a great ransom.'

'Damn the ransom,' ejaculated Stabutch. 'It is his life I want.'

'Wait until I have the ransom,' said Capietro, 'and then you can go after him.'

In the meantime Tarzan stood watching the two. He saw that his situation was fraught with exceptional danger. It was to the interest of either one of these men to kill him; and while the ransom of which one spoke might deter him temporarily he knew that but little provocation would be required to induce this one to kill him rather than to take the chance that he might escape, while it was evident that the Russian already considered that he had sufficient provocation, and Tarzan did not doubt but that he would find the means to accomplish his design even in the face of the Italian's objections.

If he could but get among them, where they could not use firearms against him, because of the danger that they might kill members of their own party, he felt that, by virtue of his superior strength, speed and agility, he might fight his way to one of the palisaded walls of the village where he would have a fair chance to escape. Once there he could scale the palisade with the speed of Manu, the monkey, and with little danger other than from the revolvers of the two whites, since he held the marksmanship of the *shiftas* in contempt.

He heard Capietro call to his men to take him alive; and then, waiting not upon them, he charged straight for the two whites, while from his throat burst the savage growl of a wild beast that had, upon more than a single occasion in the past, wrought havoc with the nerves of human antagonists.

Nor did it fail in its purpose now. Shocked and unnerved for the instant, Stabutch fell back while Capietro, who had no desire to kill the ape-man unless it became necessary, leaped to one side and urged his followers to seize him.

For a moment bedlam reigned in the village of the white raider. Yelling, cursing men milled about a white giant who fought with his bare hands, seizing an antagonist and hurling him in the faces of others, or, using the body of another like a flail, sought to mow down those who opposed him.

Among the close massed fighters, excited curs ran yelping and barking, while children and women upon the outskirts of the melee shrieked encouragement to the men.

Slowly Tarzan was gaining ground toward one of the coveted walls of the village where, as he stepped quickly backward to avoid a blow, he stumbled over a yapping cur and went down beneath a dozen men.

From the top of the cliff 'Gunner' Patrick looked down upon this scene. 'That mob has sure got him on the spot,' he said aloud. 'He's a regular guy, too. I guess here's where I step for him.'

'Yes, Bwana,' agreed the willing Obambi.

'Shut up,' said the 'Gunner,' and then he raised the butt of the Thompson to his shoulder and squeezed the trigger.

Mingled with the rapid reports of the machine gun were the screams and curses of wounded and frightened men and the shrieks of terrified women and children. Like snow before a spring shower, the pack that had surrounded Tarzan melted away as men ran for the shelter of their huts or for their saddled ponies.

Capietro and Stabutch were among the latter, and even before Tarzan could realize what had happened he saw the two racing through the open gates of the village.

The 'Gunner,' noting the satisfactory effect of his fire, had ceased, though he stood ready again to rain a hail of death down upon the village should necessity require. He had aimed only at the outskirts of the crowd surrounding the ape-man, for fear that a bullet might strike the man he was endeavoring to succour; but he was ready to risk finer shooting should any press the naked giant too closely.

He saw Tarzan standing alone in the village street like a lion at bay, and then he saw his eyes ranging about for an explanation of the burst of fire that had liberated him.

'Up here, fellar!' shouted the 'Gunner.'

The ape-man raised his eyes and located Danny instantly. 'Wait,' he called; 'I'll be up there in a moment.'

XI

The Crucifixion

As the waters of Chinnereth closed over the head of Lady Barbara, the golden haired Jezebel sprang to her feet and ran swiftly forward among the men congregated upon the great flat lava rock from which the victim of their cruel fanaticism had been hurled to her doom. She pushed apostles roughly aside as she made her way toward the brink, tears streaming from her eyes and sobs choking her throat.

Abraham, the son of Abraham, standing directly in her path, was the first to guess her purpose to throw herself into the lake and share the fate of her loved mistress. Impelled by no humanitarian urge, but rather by a selfish determination to save the girl for another fate which he already had chosen for her, the Prophet seized her as she was about to leap into the water.

Turning upon the old man like a tigress, Jezebel scratched, bit, and kicked in an effort to free herself, which she would have succeeded in doing had not the Pophet called the six executioners to his aid. Two of them seized her; and, seeing that her efforts were futile, the girl desisted; but now she turned the flood gates of her wrath upon Abraham, the son of Abraham.

'Murderer!' she cried. 'Son of Satan! May Jehovah strike thee dead for this. Curses be upon thy head and upon those of all thy kin. Damned be they and thee for the foul crime thou hast committed here this day.'

'Silence, blasphemer!' screamed Abraham, the son of Abraham. 'Make thy peace with Jehovah, for tonight thou shalt be judged by fire. Take her back to the village,' he directed the two who held her, 'and make her secure in a cave. Seest thou, too, that she escapeth not.'

'Fire or water, it be all the same to me,' cried the girl as they dragged her away, 'just so it takes me away forever from this accursed land of Midian and the mad beast who poseth as the prophet of Jehovah.'

As Jezebel moved off toward the village between her two guards the villagers fell in behind them, the women calling her foul names and otherwise reviling her, and in the rear of all came the Prophet and the Apostles, leaving a score of their fellows still lying upon the ground, where they writhed, unnoticed, in the throes of epilepsy.

The impact with the surface of the water had almost stunned Lady Barbara, but she had managed to retain her senses and control of her mental and physical powers, so that, although dazed, she was able to put into effect the plan that she had nursed from the moment that she was aware of the fate to which the Prophet had condemned her.

Being an excellent swimmer and diver the thought of being immersed below the surface of Chinnereth for a few minutes had not, in itself, caused her any great mental perturbation. Her one fear had lain in the very considerable possibility that she might be so badly injured by the impact with the water, or stunned, as to be helpless to effect her own release from the net. Her relief was great, therefore, when she discovered that she was far from helpless, nor did she delay an instant in bringing her small pocket knife to play upon the fibre strands of the net that enmeshed her.

Slashing rapidly, but yet, at the same time, in accordance with a practical plan, she severed strand after strand in a straight line, as the rock dragged her downward toward the bottom. Constantly through her mind ran a single admonition – 'Keep cool! Keep cool!' Should she permit herself to give away to hysteria, even for an instant, she knew that she must be lost. The lake seemed bottomless, the strands innumerable, while the knife grew constantly duller, and her strength appeared to be rapidly ebbing.

'Keep cool! Keep cool!' Her lungs were bursting. 'Just a moment more! Keep cool!' She felt unconsciousness creeping upon her. She struggled to drag herself through the opening she had made in the net – her senses reeled dizzily – she was almost unconscious as she shot rapidly toward the surface.

As her head rose above the surface those standing upon the rock above her had their attention riveted upon Jezebel who was engaged at that moment in kicking the prophet of Paul, the son of Jehovah, on the shins. Lady Barbara was ignorant of all this; but it was fortunate for her, perhaps, because it prevented any of the Midians from noticing her resurrection from the deep and permitted her to swim, unseen, beneath the shelter of the overhanging rock from which she had been precipitated into the lake.

She was very weak, and it was with a prayer of thanksgiving that she discovered a narrow ledge of beach at the water's edge beneath the great lava block that loomed above her. As she dragged herself wearily out upon it she heard the voices of those upon the rock overhead – the voice of Jezebel cursing the Prophet and the old man's threat against the girl.

A thrill of pride in the courage of Jezebel warmed the heart of Lady

Barbara, as did the knowledge that she had won a friend so loyal and devoted that she would put her own life in jeopardy merely for the sake of openly accusing the murderer of her friend. How magnificent she was in the primitive savagery of her denunciation! Lady Barbara could almost see her standing there defying the greatest power that her world knew, her golden hair framing her oval face, her eyes flashing, her lips curling in scorn, her lithe young body tense with emotion.

And what she had heard, and the thought of the helplessness of the young girl against the power of the vile old man, changed Lady Barbara's plans completely. She had thought to remain in hiding until night and then seek to escape this hideous valley and its mad denizens. There would be no pursuit, for they would think her dead at the bottom of Chinnereth; and thus she might seek to find her way to the outer world with no danger of interference by the people of the land of Midian.

She and Jezebel had often speculated upon the likelihood of the existence of a possible avenue of ascent of the crater wall; and from the entrance of their cave they had chosen a spot about midway of the western face of the crater, where the rim had fallen inward, as offering the best chance of escape. Tumbled masses of rock rose here from the bottom of the valley almost to the summit of the crater, and here Lady Barbara had decided to make her first bid for freedom.

But now all was changed. She could not desert Jezebel, whose life was now definitely jeopardized because of her friendship and loyalty. But what was she to do? How could she be of assistance to the girl? She did not know. Of only one thing was she certain – she must try.

She had witnessed enough horrors in the village of the South Midians to know that whatever Abraham, the son of Abraham, planned for Jezebel would doubtless be consummated after dark, the time he chose, by preference, for all the more horrible of his so-called religious rites. Only those which took them to a distance from the village, such as immersions in the waters of Chinnereth, were performed by daylight.

With these facts in mind, Lady Barbara decided that she might, with safety, wait until after dark before approaching the village. To do so earlier might only result in her own recapture, an event that would render her helpless in effecting the succour of Jezebel, while giving the Prophet two victims instead of one.

The sound of voices above her had ceased. She had heard the vituperations of the women diminishing in the distance, and by this she had known that the party had returned to the village. It was cold beneath the shadow of the rock, with her wet clothing clinging to her tired body; and so she slipped back into the water and swam along the shore a few yards until she found a spot where she could crawl out and lie in the pleasant warmth of the sun.

Here she rested again for a few minutes, and then she cautiously ascended the bank until her eyes were on a level with the ground. At a little distance she saw a woman, lying prone, who was trying to raise herself to a sitting position. She was evidently weak and dazed, and Lady Barbara realized that she was recovering from one of those horrid seizures to which nearly all the inhabitants of the village were subject. Near her were others, some lying quietly, some struggling; and in the direction of the village she saw several who had recovered sufficiently to attempt the homeward journey.

Lying very still, her forehead concealed behind a low shrub, Lady Barbara watched and waited for half an hour, until the last of the unfortunate band had regained consciousness and self-control sufficiently to permit them to depart in the direction of their squalid habitations.

She was alone now with little or no likelihood of discovery. Her clothes were still wet and exceedingly uncomfortable; so she quickly removed them and spread them in the hot sun to dry, while she luxuriated in the soothing comfort of the sun bath, alternated with an occasional dip in the waters of the lake.

Before the sun dropped to the western rim of the crater her clothing had dried; and now she sat, fully dressed again, waiting for darkness to fall. Below her lay the waters of the lake and beyond its farther shore she could dimly see the outlines of the village of the North Midians, where dwelt the mysterious 'beautiful men' of Jezebel's day dreams.

Doubtless, thought Lady Barbara, the prince charming of the golden one's imagination would prove to be a whiskered Adonis with a knotted club; but, even so, it were difficult to imagine more degraded or repulsive males than those of her own village. Almost anything – even a gorilla – might seem preferable to them.

As night approached, the girl saw little lights commence to twinkle in the northern village – the cooking fires, doubtless – and then she rose and turned her face toward the village of Abraham, the son of Abraham, of Jobab and Timothy and Jezebel, toward certain danger and possible death.

As she walked along the now familiar path toward the village, the mind of Lady Barbara Collis was vexed by the seemingly hopeless problem that confronted her, while hovering upon the verge of her consciousness was that fear of the loneliness and the darkness of an unfamiliar and inhospitable country that is inherent in most of us. Jezebel had told her that dangerous beasts were almost unknown in the land of Midian, yet her imagination conjured slinking forms in the darkness and the sound of padded feet upon the trail behind her and the breathing of savage lungs. Yet ahead of her lay a real menace more terrible, perhaps, than swiftly striking talons and powerful jaws.

She recalled that she had heard that men who had been mauled by lions, and lived to narrate their experiences, had all testified uniformly to the fact that there had been no pain and little terror during the swift moments of the experience; and she knew that there was a theory propounded by certain students of animal life that the killing of the carnivores was always swift, painless, and merciful. Why was it, she wondered, that of all created things only man was wantonly cruel and only man, and the beasts that were trained by man, killed for pleasure?

But now she was nearing the village and passing from the possibility of attack by merciful beasts to the assurance of attack by merciless men, should she be apprehended by them. To reduce this risk she skirted the village at a little distance and came to the foot of the cliff where the caves were located and where she hoped to find Jezebel and, perhaps, discover a means of liberating her.

She glanced up the face of the cliff, which seemed to be deserted, most of the villagers being congregated about a group of small cooking fires near the few huts at the foot of the cliff. They often cooked thus together, gossiping and praying and narrating experiences and revelations – they all received revelations from Jehovah when they 'walked' with Him, which was their explanation of their epileptic seizures.

The more imaginative members of the community were the recipients of the most remarkable revelations; but, as all of them were stupid, Jehovah had not, at least during Lady Barbara's sojourn among them, revealed anything of a particularly remarkable or inspiring nature. Their gossip, like their 'experiences,' was mean and narrow and sordid. Each sought constantly to discover or invent some scandal or heresy in the lives of his fellows, and if the finger pointed at one not in the good graces of the Prophet or the Apostles the victim was quite likely to make a Roman holiday.

Seeing the villagers congregated about their fires, Lady Barbara commenced the ascent of the steep path that zigzagged up the face of the cliff. She moved slowly and cautiously, stopping often to look about her, both above and below; but, notwithstanding her fears and doubts she finally reached the mouth of the cave that she and Jezebel had occupied. If she hoped to find the golden one there she was disappointed; but at least, if Jezebel were not there, it was a relief to find that no one else was; and with a sense of greater security than she had felt since the dawn of this eventful day she crawled into the interior and threw herself down upon the straw pallet that the girls had shared.

Home! This rough lair, no better than that which housed the beasts of the wilds, was home now to Lady Barbara Collis whose life had been spent within the marble halls of the Earl of Whimsey. Permeating it were memories of the strange friendship and affection that had gradually united these two girls whose origins and backgrounds could scarcely have been more dissimilar. Here each had learned the language of the other, here they had laughed and sung together, here they had exchanged confidences, and here they had planned together a future in which they would not be separated. The cold walls seemed warmer because of the love and loyalty to which they had been silent witnesses.

But now Lady Barbara was here alone. Where was Jezebel? It was the answer to that question that the English girl must find. She recalled the Prophet's threat – 'for tonight thou shalt be judged by fire.' She must hasten, then, if she were to save Jezebel. But how was she to accomplish it in the face of all the seemingly insurmountable obstacles which confronted her? – her ignorance of where Jezebel was being held, the numbers of her enemies, her lack of knowledge of the country through which they would be forced to flee should she be so fortunate as to effect the girl's escape from the village.

She roused herself. Lying here upon her pallet would accomplish nothing. She rose and looked down toward the village; and instantly she was all alertness again, for there was Jezebel. She was standing between two guards, surrounded by many villagers who maintained an open space about her. Presently the spectators separated and men appeared carrying a burden. What was it? They laid it in the center of the open space, in front of Jezebel; and then Lady Barbara saw what it was – a large wooden cross.

A man was digging a hole at the center of the circular space that had been left around the prisoner; others were bringing brush and fagots. Now the men who guarded Jezebel seized her and bore her to the ground. They laid her upon the cross and stretched her arms out upon the wooden cross arm.

Lady Barbara was horror stricken. Were they going to perpetrate the horrible atrocity of nailing her to the cross? Abraham, the son of Abraham, stood at the head of the cross, his hands in the attitude of prayer, a personification of pious hypocrisy. The girl knew that no cruelty, however atrocious, was beyond him. She knew, too, that she was powerless to prevent the consummation of this foul deed, yet she cast discretion and self interest to the winds, as, with a warning cry that shattered the silence of the night, she sped swiftly down the steep pathway toward the village – a self-sacrifice offered willingly upon the altar of friendship.

Startled by her scream, every eye was turned upward toward her. In the darkness they did not recognize her, but their stupid minds were filled with questioning and with terror as they saw something speeding down the cliff face toward them. Even before she reached the circle of firelight where they stood many had collasped in paroxysms of epilepsy induced by the nervous shock of this unexpected visitation.

When she came closer, and was recognized, others succumbed, for now indeed it appeared that a miracle had been worked and that the dead had been raised again, even as they had seen the dead girl resurrected the previous day.

Pushing aside those who did not quickly enough make way for her, Lady Barbara hastened to the center of the circle. As his eyes fell upon her, Abraham, the son of Abraham, paled and stepped back. For a moment he seemed upon the verge of a stroke.

'Who are you?' he cried. 'What are you doing here?'

'You know who I am,' replied Lady Barbara. 'Why do you tremble if you do not know that I am the messenger of Jehovah whom you reviled and sought to destroy? I am here to save the girl Jezebel from death. Later Jehovah will send His wrath upon Abraham, the son of Abraham, and upon all the people of the land of Midian for their cruelties and their sins.'

'I did not know,' cried the Prophet. 'Tell Jehovah that I did not know. Intercede for me, that Jehovah may forgive me; and anything within my power to grant shall be yours.'

So great was her surprise at the turn events had taken that Lady Barbara, who had expected only opposition and attack, was stunned for the moment. Here was an outcome so foreign to any that she had imagined that she had no response ready. She almost laughed aloud as she recalled the fears that had constantly harassed her since she had determined to attempt Jezebel's escape. And now it was all so easy.

'Liberate the girl, Jezebel,' she commanded, 'and then make food ready for her and for me.'

'Quick!' cried the Prophet. 'Raise the girl and set her free.'

'Wait!' exclaimed a thin, querulous voice behind him. 'I have walked with Jehovah.' All turned in the direction of the speaker. He was Jobab the apostle.

'Quick! Release her!' demanded Lady Barbara, who, in this interruption and in the manner and voice of the speaker, whom she knew as one of the most fanatically intolerant of the religious bigots of Midian, saw the first spark that might grow into a flame of resistance to the will of the Prophet; for she knew these people well enough to be sure that they would grasp at any excuse to thwart the abandonment of their cruel pleasure.

'Wait!' shrieked Jobab. 'I have walked with Jehovah, and He hath spoken unto me, saying: "Behold, Jobab the Apostle, a seeming miracle shall be wrought out of Chinnereth; but be not deceived, for I say unto ye that it shall be the work of Satan; and whosoever believeth in it shall perish."'

'Hallelujah!' shrieked a woman, and the cry was taken up by the others. To right and left the excited villagers were being stricken by their Nemesis. A score of writhing bodies jerked and struggled upon the ground in the throes of convulsions, the horrible choking, the frothing at the mouth, adding to the horror of the scene.

For a moment, Abraham, the son of Abraham, stood silent in thought. A cunning light flickered suddenly in his crafty eyes, and then he spoke. 'Amen!'

he said. 'Let the will of Jehovah be done as revealed to the Apostle Jobab. Let Jobab speak the work of Jehovah, and upon Jobab's head be the reward.'

'Another cross,' screamed Jobab; 'bring another cross. Let two beacon fires light the path of Jehovah in the heavens, and if either of these be His children He will not let them be consumed,' and so, as Abraham, the son of Abraham, had passed the buck to Jobab, Jobab passed it along to Jehovah, who has been the recipient of more than His share through the ages.

Futile were the threats and arguments of Lady Barbara against the blood lust of the Midians. A second cross was brought, a second hole dug, and presently both she and Jezebel were lashed to the symbols of love and raised to an upright position. The bottoms of the crosses were sunk in the holes prepared for them and earth tamped around them to hold them upright. Then willing hands brought fagots and brushwood and piled them about the bases of the two pyres.

Lady Barbara watched these preparations in silence. She looked upon the weak, degenerate faces of this degraded people; and she could not, even in the extremity of her danger, find it in her heart to condemn them too severely for doing what supposedly far more enlightened people had done, within the memory of man, in the name of religion.

She glanced at Jezebel and found the girl's eyes upon her. 'You should not have come back,' said the girl. 'You might have escaped.' Lady Barbara shook her head. 'You did it for me,' continued Jezebel. 'May Jehovah reward you, for I may only thank you.'

'You would have done the same for me at Chinnereth,' replied Lady Barbara. 'I heard you defy the Prophet there.'

Jezebel smiled. 'You are the only creature I have ever loved,' she said; 'the only one who I ever thought loved me. Of course I would die for you.'

Abraham, the son of Abraham, was praying. Young men stood ready with flaming torches, the flickering light from which danced grotesquely upon the hideous features of the audience, upon the two great crosses, and upon the beautiful faces of the victims.

'Goodbye, Jezebel,' whispered Lady Barbara.

'Goodbye,' replied the golden one.

XII

Out of the Grave

Notwithstanding the fact that Lafayette Smith had so recently visualized this very emergency and had, as it were, rehearsed his part in it, now that he stood face to face with the lion he did none of the things exactly as he had pictured. He was not at all cool when he saw the carnivore appear at the turn in the fissure; he did not face him calmly, draw a deadly bead, and fire. Nothing was in the least as he had imagined it would be. In the first place the distance between them seemed entirely inadequate and the lion much larger than he had supposed any lion could be, while his revolver seemed to shrink to proportions that represented utter futility.

All this, however, was encompassed in a single, instantaneous and overwhelming conception. No appreciable time elapsed, therefore, between the instant that he perceived the lion and that at which he commenced to jerk the trigger of his pistol, which he accomplished, without aiming, while in the act of turning to flee.

Running headlong over the jumbled rocks Lafayette Smith fled precipitately into the unknown depths of the ancient rift, at his elbow the ghastly fear that beyond each successive turn would loom the rocky terminus of his flight, while just behind him he pictured the ravenous carnivore thirsting for his blood. The fall of swiftly moving padded feet close behind him urged him to greater speed, the hot breath of the lion surged from the savage lungs to pound upon his ears like surf upon an ocean beach.

Such is the power of imagination. It is true that Numa was bounding along the bottom of the rift, but in the opposite direction to that in which Lafayette Smith bounded. Fortunately, for Lafayette, none of his wild shots had struck the lion; but the booming reverberation of the explosions in the narrow fissure had so surprised and unnerved him that he had wheeled and fled even as the man had.

Had the pursuit been as real as Lafayette imagined it, it could have urged him to no greater speed, nor could the consequent terror have nerved him to greater endurance; but physical powers have their limits, and presently the realization that his had about reached theirs forced itself upon Lafayette's consciousness and with it realization of the futility of further flight.

It was then that he turned to make his stand. He was trembling, but with fatigue rather than fear; and inwardly he was cool as he reloaded his revolver. He was surprised to discover that the lion was not on top of him, but he expected momentarily to see him appear where the fissure turned from his sight. Seating himself on a flat rock he waited the coming of the carnivore while he rested, and as the minutes passed and no lion came his wonderment increased.

Presently his scientific eye commenced to note the structure of the fissure's walls about him, and as his interest grew in the geologic facts revealed or suggested his interest in the lion waned, until, once again, the carnivore was relegated to the background of his consciousness, while in its place returned the momentarily forgotten plan to explore the rift to its farthest extent.

Recovered from the excessive fatigue of his strenuous exertion he undertook once more the exploration so rudely interrupted. Regained was the keen pleasure of discovery; forgotten, hunger, fatigue, and personal safety as he advanced along this mysterious path of adventure.

Presently the floor of the rift dropped rapidly until it was inclined at an angle that made progress difficult; and at the same time it narrowed, giving evidence that it might be rapidly pinching out. There was now barely width for him to squeeze forward between the walls when the fissure ahead of him became suddenly shrouded in gloom. Glancing up in search of an explanation of this new phenomenon Lafayette discovered that the walls far above were converging, until directly above him there was only a small streak of sky visible while ahead the rift was evidently closed entirely at the top.

As he pushed on, the going, while still difficult because of the steepness of the floor of the fissure, was improved to some extent by the absence of jumbled rocks underfoot, the closed ceiling of the corridor having offered no crumbling rim to the raging elements of the ages; but presently another handicap made itself evident – darkness, increasing steadily with each few yards until the man was groping his way blindly, though nonetheless determinedly, toward the unknown that lay ahead.

That an abyss might yawn beyond his next step may have occurred to him, but so impractical was he in all worldly matters while his scientific entity was in the ascendancy that he ignored the simplest considerations of safety. However, no abyss yawned; and presently, at a turning, daylight showed ahead. It was only a small patch of daylight; and when he reached the opening through which it shone it appeared, at first, that he had achieved the end of his quest – that he could proceed no farther.

Dropping to his hands and knees he essayed the feat of worming his way through the aperture, which he then discovered was amply large to accommodate his body; and a moment later he stood erect in astonished contemplation of the scene before him.

He found himself standing near the base of a lofty escarpment overlooking a valley that his practised eye recognized immediately as the crater of a long extinct volcano. Below him spread a panorama of rolling, tree-dotted landscape, broken by occasional huge out-croppings of weathered lava rock; and in the center a blue lake danced in the rays of an afternoon sun.

Thrilling to an identical reaction such as doubtless dominated Balboa as he stood upon the heights of Darien overlooking the broad Pacific, Lafayette Smith experienced that spiritual elation that is, perhaps, the greatest reward of the explorer. Forgotten, for the moment, was the scientific interest of the geologist, submerged by intriguing speculation upon the history of this lost valley, upon which, perhaps, the eyes of no other white man had ever gazed.

Unfortunately for the permanency of this beatific state of mind two other thoughts rudely obtruded themselves, as thoughts will. One appertained to the camp, for which he was supposed to be searching, while the other involved the lion, which was supposedly searching for him. The latter reminded him that he was standing directly in front of the mouth of the fissure, at the very spot where the lion would emerge were he following; and this suggested the impracticability of the fissure as an avenue of return to the opposite site of the crater wall.

A hundred yards away Smith espied a tree, and toward this he walked as offering the nearest sanctuary in the event the lion should reappear. Here, too, he might rest while considering plans for the future; and, that he might enjoy uninterrupted peace of mind while so engaged, he climbed up into the tree, where, straddling a limb, he leaned his back against the bole.

It was a tree of meager foliage, thus affording him an almost unobstructed view of the scene before him, and as his eyes wandered across the landscape they were arrested by something at the foot of the southern wall of the crater – something that did not perfectly harmonize with its natural surroundings. Here his gaze remained fixed as he sought to identify the thing that had attracted his attention. What it looked like he was positive that it could not be, so definite had his preconception of the inaccessibility of the valley to man impressed itself upon his mind; yet the longer he looked the more convinced he became that what he saw was a small village of thatched huts.

And what thoughts did this recognition inspire? What noble and aesthetic emotions were aroused within his breast by the sight of this lonely village in the depths of the great crater which should, by all the proofs that he had seen, have been inaccessible to man?

No, you are wrong again. What it suggested was food. For the first time since he had become lost Lafayette Smith was acutely conscious of hunger, and when he recalled that it had been more than twenty-four hours since he had eaten anything more sustantial than a few chocolates his appetite waxed ravenous. Furthermore, he suddenly realized that he was actually suffering from thirst.

At a little distance lay the lake. Glancing back toward the entrance to the fissure he discovered no lion; and so he dropped to the ground and set off in the direction of the water, laying his course so that at no time was he at any great distance from a tree.

The water was cool and refreshing; and when he had drunk his fill he became acutely conscious for the first time during the day, of an overpowering weariness. The water had temporarily relieved the pangs of hunger, and he determined to rest a few minutes before continuing on toward the distant village. Once again he assured himself that there was no pursuing lion in evidence; and then he stretched himself at full length in the deep grass that grew near the edge of the lake, and with a low tree as protection from the hot sun relaxed his tired muscles in much needed rest.

He had not intended to sleep; but his fatigue was greater than he had supposed, so that, with relaxation, unconsciousness crept upon him unawares. Insects buzzed lazily about him, a bird alighted in the tree beneath which he lay and surveyed him critically, the sun dropped lower toward the western rim, and Lafayette Smith slept on.

He dreamed that a lion was creeping toward him through high grass. He tried to rise, but he was powerless. The horror of the situation was intolerable. He tried to cry out and frighten the lion away, but no sound issued from his throat. Then he made a final supreme effort, and the shriek that resulted awakened him. He sat up, dripping with perspiration, and looked quickly and fearfully about him. There was no lion. 'Whew!' he exclaimed. 'What a relief.'

Then he glanced at the sun and realized that he had slept away the greater part of the afternoon. Now his hunger returned and with it recollection of the distant village. Rising, he drank again at the lake, and then started on his journey toward the base of the southern rim, where he hoped he would find friendly natives and food.

The way led for the greater part around the edge of the lake; and as dusk settled and then darkness it became more and more difficult to move except at a slow and cautious pace, since the ground was often strewn with fragments of lava that were not visible in the darkness.

Night brought the cheering sight of fires in the village; and these, seeming nearer than they really were, buoyed his spirits by the assurance that his journey was nearing completion. Yet, as he stumbled onward, the conviction arose that he was pursuing a will-o'-the-wisp, as the firelight appeared to retreat as rapidly as he advanced.

At last, however, the outlines of mean huts, illumined by the fires, became distinguishable and then the figures of people clustered about them. It was not until he was almost within the village that he saw with astonishment that the people were white, and then he saw something else that brought him to a sudden halt. Upon two crosses, raised above the heads of the villagers, were two girls. The firelight played upon their faces, and he saw that both were beautiful.

What weird, unholy rite was this? What strange race inhabited this lost valley? Who were the girls? That they were not of the same race as the villagers was apparent at the first casual glance at the degraded features of the latter.

Lafayette Smith hesitated. It was evident that he was witnessing some sort of religious rite or pageant; and he assumed that to interrupt it would prove far from a satisfactory introduction to these people, whose faces, which had already repelled him, impressed him so unfavorably that he questioned the friendliness of his reception even under the most favorable auspices.

And then a movement of the crowd opened for a moment an avenue to the center of the circle where the crosses stood; and the man was horrified by what was revealed for an instant to his amazed eyes, for he saw the dry brush and the fagots piled about the bottoms of the crosses and the young men with the flaming torches ready to ignite the inflammable piles.

An old man was intoning a prayer. Here and there vilagers writhed upon the ground in what Smith thought were evidences of religious ecstasy. And then the old man gave a signal, and the torch bearers applied the flames to the dry brush.

Lafayette Smith waited to see no more. Leaping forward he thrust surprised villagers from his path and sprang into the circle before the crosses. With a booted foot he kicked the already burning brush aside; and then, with his little .32 shining in his hand, he turned and faced the astonished and angry crowd.

For a moment Abraham, the son of Abraham, was paralyzed by surprise. Here was a creature beyond his experience or his ken. It might be a celestial messenger; but the old man had gone so far now, and his crazed mind was so thoroughly imbued with the lust for torture, that he might even have defied Jehovah Himself rather than forego the pleasures of the spectacle he had arranged.

At last he found his voice. 'What blasphemy is this?' he screamed. 'Set upon this infidel, and tear him limb from limb.'

'You will have to shoot, now,' said an English voice at Smith's back, 'for if you don't they will kill you.'

He realized that it was one of the girls upon the crosses – another astonishing mystery in this village of mysteries, that cool English voice. Then one of the torch bearers rushed him with a maniacal shriek, and Smith fired. With a scream the fellow clutched his chest and sprawled at the American's feet; and at the report of the pistol and the sudden collapse of their fellow the others, who had been moving forward upon the intruder, fell back, while upon all sides the overexcited creatures succumbed to the curse that had descended to them from Angustus the Ephesian, until the ground was strewn with contorted forms.

Realizing that the villagers were, for the moment at least, too disconcerted and overawed by the death of their fellow to press their attack, Smith turned his attention at once to the two girls. Replacing his pistol in its holster, he cut their bonds with his pocket knife before Abraham, the son of Abraham, could collect his scattered wits and attempt to urge his followers to a renewed attack

It was more than the work of a moment to liberate the two captives as, after he had cut the bonds that held their feet, Smith had been compelled to partially support each with one arm as he severed the fibres that secured their wrists to the cross arms, lest a bone be broken or a muscle wrenched as the full weight of the victim was thrown suddenly upon one wrist.

He had cut Lady Barbara down first; and she was assisting him with Jezebel, who, having been crucified for a longer time, was unable to stand alone, when Abraham, the son of Abraham, regained sufficient composure to permit him to think and act.

Both Lady Barbara and Smith were supporting Jezebel into whose numbed feet the blood was again beginning to circulate. Their backs were toward the Prophet; and, taking advantage of their preoccupation, the old man was creeping stealthily upon them from the rear. In his hand was a crude knife, but nonetheless formidable for its crudeness. It was the blood stained sacrificial knife of this terrible old high priest of the Midians, more terrible now because of the rage and hatred that animated the cruel, defective mind that directed the claw-like hand that wielded it.

All of his rage, all of his hatred were directed against the person of Lady Barbara, in whom he saw the author of his humiliation and his thwarted desires. Stealthily he crept upon her from behind while his followers, frozen to silence by his terrible glances, watched in breathless anticipation.

Occupied with the half-fainting Jezebel none of the three at the crosses saw the repulsive figure of the avenger as he towered suddenly behind the English girl, his right hand raised high to drive the blade deeply into her back; but they heard his sudden, shoking, gasping scream and turned in time to see the knife fall from his nerveless fingers as they clutched at his throat, and to witness his collapse.

Angustus the Ephesian had reached out of a grave digged two thousand years before, to save the life of Lady Barbara Collis – though doubtless he would have turned over in that same grave had he realized the fact.

XIII

The 'Gunner' Walks

Like a great cat, Tarzan of the Apes scaled the palisade of the raiders' village, dropped lightly to the ground upon the opposite side and ascended the cliffs a little to the south of the village where they were less precipitous. He might have taken advantage of the open gate; but the direction he chose was the shorter way; and a palisade constituted no obstacle to the foster son of Kala, the she-ape.

The 'Gunner' was waiting for him upon the summit of the cliff directly behind the village, and for the second time these strangely dissimilar men met – dissimilar, and yet, in some respects, alike. Each was ordinarily quiet to taciturnity, each was self-reliant, each was a law unto himself in his own environment; but there the similarity ceased for the extremes of environment had produced psychological extremes as remotely separated as the poles.

The ape-man had been reared amidst scenes of eternal beauty and grandeur, his associates the beasts of the jungle, savage perhaps, but devoid of avarice, petty jealousy, treachery, meanness, and intentional cruelty; while the 'Gunner' had known naught but the squalid aspects of scenery defiled by man, of horizons grotesque with screaming atrocities of architecture, of an earth hidden by concrete and asphaltum and littered with tin cans and garbage, his associates, in all walks of life, activated by grand and petty meannesses unknown to any but mankind.

'A machine gun has its possibilities,' said the ape-man, with the flicker of a smile.

'They had you in a bad spot, mister,' remarked the 'Gunner.'

'I think I should have gotten out all right,' replied Tarzan, 'but I thank you nonetheless. How did you happen to be here?'

'I been looking for my side-kick, and I happened to see you go over the edge here. Cotton ball here tipped me off that you was the guy saved me from the lion, – so I was glad to step for you.'

'You are looking for whom?'

'My side-kick, Smith.'

'Where is he?'

'I wouldn't be lookin' for him if I knew. He's went and lost himself. Been gone since yesterday afternoon.'

'Tell me the circumstances,' said Tarzan, 'perhaps I can help you.'

'That's what I was goin' to ask you,' said the 'Gunner.' 'I know my way around south of Madison Street, but out here I'm just a punk. I aint got no idea where to look for him. Geeze, take a slant at them mountains. You might as well try to meet a guy at the corner of Oak and Polk as hunt for him there. I'll tell you how it happened,' and then he briefly narrated all that was known of the disappearance of Lafayette Smith.

'Was he armed?' asked the ape-man.

'He thought he was.'

'What do you mean?'

'He packed a shiny toy pistol, what if anybody ever shot me with it, and I found it out, I'd turn him over my knee and spank him.'

'It might serve him in getting food,' said Tarzan, 'and that will be of more importance to him than anything else. He's not in much danger, except from men and starvation. Where's your camp?'

Danny nodded toward the south. 'Back there about a thousand miles,' he said.

'You'd better go to it and remain there where he can find you if he can make his way back to it, and where I can find you if I locate him.'

'I want to help you hunt for him. He's a good guy, even if he is legitimate.'

'I can move faster alone,' replied the ape-man. 'If you start out looking for him I'll probably have to find you, too.'

The 'Gunner' grinned. 'I guess you ain't so far off, at that,' he replied. 'All right, I'll beat it for camp and wait there for you. You know where our camp is at?'

'I'll find out,' replied Tarzan and turned to Obambi to whom he put a few questions in the native Bantu dialect of the black. Then he turned again to the 'Gunner.' 'I know where your camp is now. Watch out for these fellows from that village, and don't let your men wander very far from the protection of your machine gun.'

'Why,' demanded Danny, 'what are them guys?'

'They are robbers, murderers, and slave raiders,' replied Tarzan.

'Geeze,' exclaimed the 'Gunner,' 'they's rackets even in Africa, ain't they?'

'I do not know what a racket is,' replied the ape-man, 'but there is crime wherever there are men, and nowhere else.' He turned then, without word of parting, and started upward toward the mountains.

'Geeze!' muttered the 'Gunner.' 'That guy ain't so crazy about men.'

'What, bwana?' asked Obambi.

'Shut up,' admonished Danny.

The afternoon was almost spent when the 'Gunner' and Obambi approached camp. Tired and footsore as he was the white man had, nonetheless, pushed rapidly along the backtrail lest night descend upon them before they reached their destination, for Danny, in common with most city-bred humans, had discovered something peculiarly depressing and awe-inspiring

in the mysterious sounds and silences of the nocturnal wilds. He wished the
fires and companionship of men after the sun had set. And so the two covered
the distance on the return in much less time than had been consumed in
traversing it originally.

As he came in sight of the camp the brief twilight of the tropics had already
fallen, the cooking fires were burning, and to a trained eye a change would
have been apparent from the appearance of the camp when he had left it
early that morning; but Danny's eyes were trained in matters of broads, bulls,
and beer trucks and not in the concerns of camps and safaris; so, in the failing light of dusk, he did not notice that there were more men in camp than
when he had left, nor that toward the rear of it there were horses tethered
where no horses had been before.

The first intimation he had of anything unusual came from Obambi.
'White men are in the camp, bwana,' said the black – 'and many horses. Perhaps they found the mad bwana and brought him back.'

'Where do you see any white men, tar baby?' demanded the 'Gunner.'

'By the big fire in the center of camp, bwana,' replied Obambi.

'Geeze, yes, I see 'em now,' admitted Danny. 'They must have found old
Smithy all right; but I don't see him, do you?'

'No, bwana, but perhaps he is in his tent.'

The appearance of Patrick and Obambi caused a commotion in the camp
that was wholly out of proportion to its true significance. The white men
leaped to their feet and drew their revolvers while strange blacks, in response
to the commands of one of these, seized rifles and stood nervously alert.

'You don't have to throw no fit,' called Danny, 'it's only me and the smoke.'

The white men were advancing to meet him now, and the two parties
halted face to face near one of the fires. It was then that the eyes of one of the
two strange white men alighted on the Thompson sub-machine gun. Raising
his revolver he covered Danny.

'Put up your hands!' he commanded sharply.

'Wotell?' demanded the 'Gunner,' but he put them up as every sensible
man does when thus invited at the business end of a pistol.

'Where is the ape-man?' asked the stranger.

'What ape-man? What you talkin' about? What's your racket?'

'You know who I mean – Tarzan,' snapped the other.

The 'Gunner' glanced quickly about the camp. He saw his own men herded
under guard of villainous looking blacks in long robes that had once been
white; he saw the horses tethered just beyond them; he saw nothing of Lafayette Smith. The training and the ethics of gangland controlled him on the
instant. 'Don't know the guy,' he replied sullenly.

'You were with him today,' snarled the bearded white. 'You fired on my
village.'

'Who, me?' inquired the 'Gunner' innocently. 'You got me wrong, mister. I been hunting all day. I ain't seen no one. I ain't fired at nothing. Now it's my turn. What are you guys doin' here with this bunch of Ku Klux Klanners? If it's a stick up, hop to it; and get on your way. You got the drop on us, and they ain't no one to stop you. Get it over with. I'm hungry and want to feed.'

'Take the gun away from him,' said Capietro, in Galla, to one of his men, 'also his pistol,' and there was nothing for Danny 'Gunner' Patrick, with his hands above his head, to do but submit. Then they sent Obambi, under escort, to be herded with the other black prisoners and ordered the 'Gunner' to accompany them to the large fire that blazed in front of Smith's tent and his own.

'Where is your companion?' demanded Capietro.

'What companion?' inquired Danny.

'The man you have been travelling with,' snapped the Italian. 'Who else would I mean?'

'Search me,' replied the 'Gunner.'

'What you mean by that? You got something concealed upon your person?'

'If you mean money, I ain't got none.'

'You did not answer my question,' continued Capietro.

'What question?'

'Where is your companion?'

'I ain't got none.'

'Your headman told us there were two of you. What is your name?'

'Bloom,' replied Danny.

Capietro looked puzzled. 'The headman said one of you was Smith and the other Patrick.'

'Never heard of 'em,' insisted Danny. 'The smoke must of been stringin' you. I'm here alone, hunting, and my name's Bloom.'

'And you didn't see Tarzan of the Apes today?'

'Never even heard of a guy with that monacker.'

'Either he's lying to us,' said Stabutch, 'or it was the other one who fired on the village.'

'Sure, it must of been two other fellows,' Danny assured them. 'Say, when do I eat?'

'When you tell us where Tarzan is,' replied Stabutch.

'Then I guess I don't eat,' remarked Danny. 'Geeze, didn't I tell you I never heard of the guy? Do you think I know every monkey in Africa by his first name? Come on now, what's your racket? If we got anything you want, take it and screw. I'm sick lookin' at your mugs.'

'I do not understand English so well,' whispered Capietro to Stabutch. 'I do not always know what he says.'

'Neither do I,' replied the Russian; 'but I think he is lying to us. Perhaps he is trying to gain time until his companion and Tarzan arrive.'

'That is possible,' replied Capietro in his normal voice.

'Let's kill him and get out of here,' suggested Stabutch. 'We can take the prisoners and as much of the equipment as you want and be a long way from here in the morning.'

'Geeze,' exclaimed Danny, 'this reminds me of Chi. It makes me homesick.'

'How much money you pay if we don't kill you?' asked Capietro. 'How much your friends pay?'

The 'Gunner' laughed. 'Say, mister, you're giving yourself a bum steer.' He was thinking how much more one might collect for killing him, if one could make connections with certain parties on the North Side of Chicago, than for sparing his life. But here was an opportunity, perhaps, to gain time. The 'Gunner' did not wish to be killed, and so he altered his technique. 'My friends ain't rich,' he said, 'but they might come across with a few grand. How much do you want?'

Capietro considered. This must be a rich American, for only rich men could afford these African big game expeditions. 'One hundred thousand should not be excessive for a rich man like you,' he said.

'Quit your kidding,' said the 'Gunner.' 'I ain't rich.'

'What could you raise?' asked Capietro, who saw by the prisoner's expression of astonishment that the original bid was evidently out of the question.

'I might scrape up twenty grand,' suggested Danny.

'What are grand?' demanded the Italian.

'Thousand – twenty thousand,' explained the 'Gunner.'

'Poof!' cried Capietro. 'That would not pay me for the trouble of keeping you until the money could be forwarded from America. Make it fifty thousand lire and it's a bargain.'

'Fifty thousand lire? What's them?'

'A lira is an Italian coin worth about twenty cents in American money,' explained Stabutch.

Danny achieved some rapid mental calculations before he replied; and when he had digested the result he had difficulty in repressing a smile, for he discovered that his offer of twenty thousand grand was actually twice what the Italian was now demanding. Yet he hesitated to agree too willingly. 'That's ten thousand iron men,' he said. 'That's a lot of jack.'

'Iron men? Jack? I do not understand,' said Capietro.

'Smackers,' explained Danny lucidly.

'Smackers? Is there such a coin in America?' asked Capietro, turning to Stabutch.

'Doubtless a vernacularism,' said the Russian.

'Geeze, you wops is dumb,' growled the 'Gunner.' 'A smacker's a buck. Everyone knows that.'

'Perhaps if you would tell him in dollars it would be easier,' suggested Stabutch. 'We all understand the value of an American dollar.'

'That's a lot more than some Americans understand,' Danny assured him; 'but it's just what I been saying right along – ten thousand dollars – and it's too damn much.'

'That is for you to decide,' said Capietro. 'I am tired of bargaining – nobody but an American would bargain over a human life.'

'What you been doing?' demanded the 'Gunner.' 'You're the guy that started it.'

Capietro shrugged. 'It is not my life,' he said. 'You will pay me ten thousand American dollars, or you will die. Take your choice.'

'Oke,' said Danny. 'I'll pay. Now do I eat? If you don't feed me I won't be worth nothing.'

'Tie his hands,' Capietro ordered one of the *shiftas*, then he fell to discussing plans with Stabutch. The Russian finally agreed with Capietro that the palisaded village of the raider would be the best place to defend themselves in the event that Tarzan enlisted aid and attacked them in force. One of their men had seen Lord Passmore's safari; and, even if their prisoner was lying to them, there was at least another white, probably well armed, who might be considered a definite menace. Ogonyo had told them that this man was alone and probably lost, but they did not know whether or not to believe the headman. If Tarzan commandeered these forces, which Capietro knew he had the influence to do, they might expect an attack upon their village.

By the light of several fires the blacks of the captured safari were compelled to break camp and, when the loads were packed, to carry them on the difficult night march toward Capietro's village. With mounted *shiftas* in advance, upon the flanks, and bringing up the rear there was no lagging and no chance to escape.

The 'Gunner,' plodding along at the head of his own porters, viewed the prospect of that night march with unmitigated disgust. He had traversed the route twice already since sunrise; and the thought of doing it again, in the dark, with his hands tied behind him was far from cheering. To add to his discomfort he was weak from hunger and fatigue, and now the pangs of thirst were assailing him.

'Geeze,' he soliloquized, 'this ain't no way to treat a regular guy. When I took 'em for a ride I never made no guy walk, not even a rat. I'll get these damn wops yet, the lousy bums – a thinkin' they can put Danny Patrick on the spot, an' make him walk all the way!'

XIV

Flight

As the choking cry broke from the lips of Abraham, the son of Abraham, Lady Barbara and Smith wheeled to see him fall, the knife clattering to the ground from his nerveless fingers. Smith was horrified, and the girl blenched, as they realized how close death had been. She saw Jobab and the others standing there, their evil faces contorted with rage.

'We must get away from here,' he said. 'They will be upon us in a moment.'

'I'm afraid you'll have to help me support your friend,' said Smith. 'She cannot walk alone.'

'Put your left arm around her,' directed Lady Barbara. 'That will leave your right hand free for your pistol. I will support her on the other side.'

'Leave me,' begged Jezebel. 'I will only keep you from escaping.'

'Nonsense,' said Smith. 'Put your arm across my shoulders.'

'You will soon be able to walk,' Lady Barbara told her, 'when the blood gets back into your feet. Come! Let's get away from here while we can.'

Half carrying Jezebel, the two started to move toward the circle of menacing figures surrounding them. Jobab was the first to regain his wits since the Prophet had collapsed at the critical moment. 'Stop them!' he cried, as he prepared to block their way, at the same time drawing a knife from the folds of his filthy garment.

'One side, fellow!' commanded Smith, menacing Jobab with his pistol.

'The wrath of Jehovah will be upon you,' cried Lady Barbara in the Midian tongue, 'as it has been upon the others who would have harmed us, if you fail to let us pass in peace.'

'It is the work of Satan,' shrilled Timothy. 'Do not let them weaken your heart with lies, Jobab. Do not let them pass!' The elder was evidently under great mental and nervous strain. His voice shook as he spoke, and his muscles were trembling. Suddenly he, too, collapsed as had Abraham, the son of Abraham. But still Jobab stood his ground, his knife raised in a definite menace against them. All around them the circle was growing smaller and its circumference more solidly knit by the forward pressing bodies of the Midians.

'I hate to do it,' said Smith, half aloud, as he raised his pistol and aimed it at Jobab. The Apostle was directly in front of Lafayette Smith and little more than a yard distant when the American, aiming point blank at his chest, jerked the trigger and fired.

An expression of surprise mingled with that of rage which had convulsed

the unbecoming features of Jobab the Apostle. Lafayette Smith was also surprised and for the same reason – he had missed Jobab. It was incredible – there
must be something wrong with the pistol!

But Jobab's surprise, while based upon the same miracle, was of a loftier
and nobler aspect. It was clothed in the sanctity of divine revelation. It emanated from a suddenly acquired conviction that he was immune to the fire
and thunder of this strange weapon that he had seen lay Lamech low but a
few minutes earlier. Verily, Jehovah was his shield and his buckler!

For a moment, as the shot rang out, Jobab paused and then, clothed in the
fancied immunity of this sudden revelation, he leaped upon Lafayette Smith.
The sudden and unexpected impact of his body knocked the pistol from
Smith's hand and simultaneously the villagers closed in upon him. A real
menace now that they had witnessed the futility of the strange weapon.

Lafayette Smith was no weakling, and though his antagonist was inspired
by a combination of maniacal fury and religious fanaticism the outcome of
their struggle must have been a foregone conclusion had there been no outside influences to affect it. But there were. Beside the villagers, there was
Lady Barbara Collis.

With consternation she had witnessed the futility of Smith's marksmanship; and when she saw him disarmed and in the grip of Jobab, with others
of the villagers rushing to his undoing, she realized that now, indeed the lives
of all three of them were in direct jeopardy.

The pistol lay at her feet, but only for a second. Stooping, she seized it; and
then, with the blind desperation of self-preservation, she shoved the muzzle
against Jobab's side and pulled the trigger; and as he fell, a hideous shriek
upon his lips, she turned the weapon upon the advancing villagers and fired
again. It was enough. Screaming in terror, the Midians turned and fled. A
wave of nausea swept over the girl; she swayed and might have fallen had not
Smith supported her.

'I'll be all right in a moment,' she said. 'It was so horrible!'

'You were very brave,' said Lafayette Smith.

'Not as brave as you,' she replied with a weak little smile; 'but a better shot.'

'Oh,' cried Jezebel, 'I thought they would have us again. Now that they are
frightened, let us go away. It will require only a word from one of the apostles
to send them upon us again.'

'You are right,' agreed Smith. 'Have you any belongings you wish to take
with you?'

'Only what we wear,' replied Lady Barbara.

'What is the easiest way out of the valley?' asked the man, on the chance
that there might be another and nearer avenue of escape than the fissure
through which he had come.

'We know of no way out,' replied Jezebel.

'Then follow me,' directed Smith. 'I'll take you out the way I came in.'

They made their way from the village and out onto the dark plain toward Chinnereth, nor did they speak again until they had gone some distance from the fires of the Midians and felt that they were safe from pursuit. It was then that Lafayette Smith asked a question prompted by natural curiosity.

'How can it be possible that you young ladies know of no way out of this valley?' he asked. 'Why can't you go out the way you came in?'

'I could scarcely do that,' replied Jezebel; 'I was born here.'

'Born here?' exclaimed Smith. 'Then your parents must live in the valley. We can go to their home. Where is it?'

'We just came from it,' explained Lady Barbara. 'Jezebel was born in the village from which we have just escaped.'

'And those beasts killed her parents?' demanded Lafayette.

'You do not understand,' said Lady Barbara. 'Those people are her people.'

Smith was dumfounded. He almost ejaculated: 'How horrible!' but stayed the impulse. 'And you?' he asked presently. 'Are they your people, too?' There was a note of horror in his voice.

'No,' replied Lady Barbara. 'I am English.'

'And you don't know how you got into this valley?'

'Yes, I know – I came by parachute.'

Smith halted and faced her. 'You're Lady Barbara Collis!' he exclaimed.

'How did you know?' she asked. 'Have you been searching for me?'

'No, but when I passed through London the papers were full of the story of your flight and your disappearance – pictures and things, you know.'

'And you just stumbled onto me? What a coincidence! And how fortunate for me.'

'To tell you the truth, I am lost myself,' admitted Smith. 'So possibly you are about as badly off as you were before.'

'Scarcely,' she said. 'You have at least prevented my premature cremation.'

'They were really going to burn you? It doesn't seem possible in this day and age of enlightenment and civilization.'

'The Midians are two thousand years behind the times,' she told him, 'and in addition to that they are religious, as well as congenital, maniacs.'

Smith glanced in the direction of Jezebel whom he could see plainly in the light of a full moon that had but just topped the eastern rim of the crater. Perhaps Lady Barbara sensed the unspoken question that disturbed him.

'Jezebel is different,' she said. 'I cannot explain why, but she is not at all like her people. She tells me that occasionally one such as she is born among them.'

'But she speaks English,' said Smith. 'She cannot be of the same blood as the people I saw in the village, whose language is certainly not the same as hers, to say nothing of the dissimilarity of their physical appearance.'

'I taught her English,' explained Lady Barbara.

'She wants to go away and leave her parents and her people?' asked Smith.

'Of course I do,' said Jezebel. 'Why should I want to stay here and be murdered? My father, my mother, my brothers and sisters were in that crowd you saw about the crosses tonight, They hate me. They hated me from the day I was born, because I am not like them. But then there is no love in the land of Midian – only religion, which preaches love and practices hate.'

Smith fell silent as the three plodded on over the rough ground down toward the shore of Chinnereth. He was considering the responsibility that Fate had loaded upon his shoulders so unexpectedly and wondering if he were equal to the emergency, who, as he was becoming to realize, could scarcely be sure of his ability to insure his own existence in this savage and unfamiliar world.

Keenly the realization smote him that in almost thirty hours that he had been thrown exclusively upon his own resources he had discovered not a single opportunity to provide food for himself, the result of which was becoming increasingly apparent in a noticeable loss of strength and endurance. What then might he hope to accomplish with two additional mouths to feed?

And what if they encountered either savage beasts or unfriendly natives? Lafayette Smith shuddered. 'I hope they can run fast,' he murmured.

'Who?' asked Lady Barbara. 'What do you mean?'

'Oh,' stammered Lafayette. 'I – I did not know that I spoke aloud.' How could he tell her that he had lost confidence even in his .32? He could not. Never before in his life had he felt so utterly incompetent. His futility seemed to him to border on criminality. At any rate it was dishonorable, since it was deceiving these young women who had a right to expect guidance and protection from him.

He was very bitter toward himself; but that, perhaps was due partly to the nervous reaction following the rather horrible experience at the village and physical weakness that was bordering on exhaustion. He was excoriating himself for having dismissed Obambi, which act, he realized, was at the bottom of all his troubles; and then he recalled that had it not been for that there would have been no one to save these two girls from the horrible fate from which he had preserved them. This thought somewhat restored his self-esteem, for he could not escape the fact that he had, after all, saved them.

Jezebel, the circulation restored to her feet, had been walking without assistance for some time. The three had lapsed into a long silence, each occupied with his own thoughts, as Smith led the way in search of the opening into the fissure.

A full African moon lighted their way, its friendly beams lessening the difficulties of the night march. Chinnereth lay upon their right, a vision of loveliness in the moonlight, while all about them the grim mass of the crater walls seemed to have closed in upon them and to hang menacingly above their heads, for night and moonlight play strange tricks with perspective.

It was shortly after midnight that Smith first stumbled and fell. He arose quickly, berating his awkwardness; but as he proceeded, Jezebel, who was directly behind him, noticed that he walked unsteadily, stumbling more and more often. Presently he fell again, and this time it was apparent to both girls that it was only with considerable effort that he arose. The third time he fell they both helped him to his feet.

'I'm terribly clumsy,' he said. He was swaying slightly as he stood between them.

Lady Barbara observed him closely. 'You are exhausted,' she said.

'Oh, no,' insisted Smith. 'I'm all right.'

'When did you eat last?' demanded the girl.

'I had some chocolate with me,' replied Smith. 'I ate the last of it this afternoon sometime.'

'When did you eat a meal, I mean?' persisted Lady Barbara.

'Well,' he admitted, 'I had a light lunch yesterday noon, or rather day before yesterday. It must be after midnight now.'

'And you have been walking all the time since?'

'Oh, I ran part of the time,' he replied, with a weak laugh. 'That was when the lion chased me. And I slept in the afternoon before I came to the village.'

'We are going to stop right here until you are rested,' announced the English girl.

'Oh, no,' he demurred, 'we mustn't do that. I want to get you out of this valley before daylight, as they will probably pursue us as soon as the sun comes up.'

'I don't think so,' said Jezebel. 'They are too much afraid of the North Midians to come this far from the village; and, anyway, we have such a start that we can reach the cliffs, where you say the fissure is, before they could overtake us.'

'You must rest,' insisted Lady Barbara.

Reluctantly Lafayette sat down. 'I'm afraid I'm not going to be much help to you,' he said. 'You see I am not really familiar with Africa, and I fear that I am not adequately armed for your protection. I wish Danny were here.'

'Who is Danny?' asked Lady Barbara.

'He's a friend who accompanied me on this trip.'

'He's had African experience?'

'No,' admitted Lafayette, 'but one always feels safe with Danny about. He seems so familiar with firearms. You see, he is a protection guy.'

'What is a protection guy?' asked Lady Barbara.

'To be quite candid,' replied Lafayette, 'I am not at all sure that I know myself what it is. Danny is not exactly garrulous about his past; and I have hesitated to pry into his private affairs, but he did volunteer the information one day that he had been a protection guy for a Big Shot. It sounded reassuring.'

'What is a Big Shot?' inquired Jezebel.

'Perhaps a big game hunter,' suggested Lady Barbara.

'No,' said Lafayette. 'I gather from Danny's remarks that a Big Shot is a rich brewer or distiller who also assists in directing the affairs of a large city. It may be just another name for political boss.'

'Of course,' said Lady Barbara, 'it would be nice if your friend were here; but he is not, so suppose you tell us something about yourself. Do you realize that we do not even know your name?'

Smith laughed. 'That's about all there is to know about me,' he said. 'It's Lafayette Smith, and now will you introduce me to this other young lady? I already know who you are.'

'Oh, this is Jezebel,' said Lady Barbara.

There was a moment's silence. 'Is that all?' asked Smith.

Lady Barbara laughed. 'Just Jezebel,' she said. 'If we ever get out of here we'll have to find a surname for her. They don't use 'em in the land of Midian.'

Smith lay on his back looking up at the moon. Already he was commencing to feel the beneficial effects of relaxation and rest. His thoughts were toying with the events of the past thirty hours. What an adventure for a prosaic professor of geology, he thought. He had never been particularly interested in girls, although he was far from being a misogynist, and to find himself thus thrown into the intimate relationship of protector to two beautiful young women was somwehat disconcerting. And the moon had revealed that they were beautiful. Perhaps the sun might have a different story to tell. He had heard of such things and he wondered. But sunlight could not alter the cool, crisp, well bred voice of Lady Barbara Collis. He liked to hear her talk. He had always enjoyed the accent and diction of cultured English folk.

He tried to think of something to ask her that he might listen to her voice again. That raised the question of just how he should address her. His contacts with nobility had been few – in fact almost restricted to a single Russian prince who had been a door man at a restaurant he sometimes patronized, and he had never heard him addressed otherwise than as Mike. He thought Lady Barbara would be the correct formula, though that smacked a little of familiarity. Lady Collis seemed, somehow, even less appropriate. He wished he were sure. Mike would never do. Jezebel. What an archaic name! And then he fell asleep.

Lady Barbara looked down at him and raised a warning finger to her lips

407

lest Jezebel awaken him. Then she rose and walked away a short distance, beckoning the golden one to follow.

'He is about done up,' she whispered, as they seated themselves again. 'Poor chap, he has had a rough time of it. Imagine being chased by a lion with only that little pop-gun with which to defend oneself.'

'Is he from your country?' asked Jezebel.

'No, he's an American. I can tell by his accent.'

'He is very beautiful,' said Jezebel, with a sigh.

'After looking at Abraham, the son of Abraham, and Jobab, for all these weeks I could agree with you if you insisted that St Ghandi is an Adonis,' replied Lady Barbara.

'I do not know what you mean,' said Jezebel; 'but do you not think him beautiful?'

'I am less interested in his pulchritude than in his marksmanship, and that is positively beastly. He's got sand though, my word! No end. He walked right into that village and took us out from under the noses of hundreds of people with nothing but his little peashooter for protection. That, Jezebel, was top hole.'

The golden Jezebel sighed. 'He is much more beautiful than the men of the land of North Midian,' she said.

Lady Barbara looked at her companion for a long minute; then she sighed. 'If I ever get you to civilization,' she said, 'I'm afraid you are going to prove something of a problem.' Wherewith she stretched herself upon the ground and was soon asleep, for she, too, had had a strenuous day.

XV

Eshbaal, the Shepherd

The sun shining on his upturned face awakened Lafayette Smith. At first he had difficulty in collecting his thoughts. The events of the previous night appeared as a dream, but when he sat up and discovered the figures of the sleeping girls a short distance from him his mind was jerked rudely back into the world of realities. His heart sank. How was he to acquit himself creditably of such a responsibility? Frankly, he did not know.

He had no doubt but that he could find the fissure and lead his charges to the outer world, but how much better off would they be then? He had no idea now, and he realized that he never had, where his camp lay. Then there was the possibility of meeting the lion again in the fissure, and if they did not there was still the question of sustenance. What were they going to use for food, and how were they going to get it?

The thought of food awoke a gnawing hunger within him. He arose and walked to the shore of the lake where he lay on his belly and filled himself with water. When he stood up the girls were sitting up looking at him.

'Good morning,' he greeted them. 'I was just having breakfast. Will you join me?'

They returned his salutation as they arose and came toward him. Lady Barbara was smiling. 'Thank the lord, you have a sense of humor,' she said. 'I think we are going to need a lot of it before we get out of this.'

'I would much prefer ham and eggs,' he replied ruefully.

'Now I know you're an American,' she said.

'I suppose you are thinking of tea and marmalade,' he rejoined.

'I am trying not to think of food at all,' she replied.

'Have some lake,' he suggested. 'You have no idea how satisfying it is if you take enough of it.'

After the girls had drunk the three set off again, led by Smith, in search of the opening to the fissure. 'I know just where it is,' he had assured them the night before, and even now he thought that he would have little difficulty in finding it, but when they approached the base of the cliff at the point where he had expected to find it it was not there.

Along the foot of the beetling escarpment he searched, almost frantically now, but there was no sign of the opening through which he had crawled into the valley of the land of Midian. Finally, crushed, he faced Lady Barbara. 'I cannot find it,' he admitted, and there was a quality of hopelessness in his voice that touched her.

'Never mind,' she said. 'It must be somewhere. We shall just have to keep searching until we find it.'

'But it's so hard on you young ladies,' he said. 'It must be a bitter disappointment to you. You don't know how it makes me feel to realize that, with no one to depend on but me, I have failed you so miserably.'

'Don't take it that way, please,' she begged. 'Anyone might have lost his bearings in this hole. These cliffs scarcely change their appearance in miles.'

'It's kind of you to say that, but I cannot help but feel guilty. Yet I know the opening cannot be far from here. I came in on the west side of the valley, and that is where we are now. Yes, I'm sure I must find it eventually; but there is no need for all of us to search. You and Jezebel sit down here and wait while I look for it.'

'I think we should remain together,' suggested Jezebel.

'By all means,' agreed Lady Barbara.

'As you wish,' said Smith. 'We will search toward the north as far as it is possible that the opening can lie. If we don't find it we can come back here and search toward the south.'

As they moved along the base of the cliff in a northerly direction Smith became more and more convinced that he was about to discover the entrance to the fissure. He thought that he discerned something familiar in the outlook across the valley from this location, but still no opening revealed itself after they had gone a considerable distance.

Presently, as they climbed the rise and gained the summit of one of the numerous low ridges that ran, buttress-like, from the face of the cliff down into the valley, he halted in discouragement.

'What is it?' asked Jezebel.

'That forest,' he replied. 'There was no forest in sight of the opening.'

Before them spread an open forest of small trees that grew almost to the foot of the cliffs and stretched downward to the shore of the lake, forming a landscape of exceptional beauty in its park-like aspect. But Lafayette Smith saw no beauty there – he saw only another proof of his inefficiency and ignorance.

'You came through no forest on your way from the cliffs to the village?' demanded Lady Barbara.

He shook his head. 'We've got to walk all the way back now,' he said, 'and search in the other direction. It is most disheartening. I wonder if you can forgive me.'

'Don't be silly,' said Lady Barbara. 'One might think that you were a Cook's Tour courier who had got lost during a personally conducted tour of the art galleries of Paris and expected to lose his job in consequence.'

'I feel worse than that,' Smith admitted with a laugh, 'and I imagine that's saying a lot.'

'Look!' exclaimed Lady Barbara. 'There are animals of some sort down there in the forest. Don't you see them?'

'Oh, yes,' cried Jezebel, 'I see them.'

'What are they?' asked Smith. 'They look like deer.'

'They are goats,' said Jezebel. 'The North Midians have goats. They roam over this end of the valley.'

'They look like something to eat, to me,' said Lady Barbara. 'Let's go down and get one of them.'

'They will probably not let us catch them,' suggested Lafayette.

'You've a pistol,' the English girl reminded him.

'That's a fact,' he agreed. 'I can shoot one.'

'Maybe,' qualified Lady Barbara.

'I'd better go down alone,' said Smith. 'Three of us together might frighten them.'

'You'll have to be mighty careful or you'll frighten them yourself,' warned Lady Barbara. 'Have you ever stalked game?'

'No,' admitted the American, 'I never have.'

Lady Barbara moistened a finger and held it up. 'The wind is right,' she announced. 'So all you have to do is keep out of sight and make no noise.'

'How am I going to keep out of sight?' demanded Smith.

'You'll have to crawl down to them, taking advantage of trees, rocks and bushes – anything that will conceal you. Crawl forward a few feet and then stop, if they show any sign of nervousness, until they appear unconcerned again.'

'That will take a long time,' said Smith.

'It may be a long time before we find anything else to eat,' she reminded him, 'and nothing we do find is going to walk up to us and lie down and die at our feet.'

'I suppose you are right,' assented Smith. 'Here goes! Pray for me.' He dropped to his hands and knees and crawled slowly forward over the rough ground in the direction of the forest and the goats. After a few yards he turned and whispered: 'This is going to be tough on the knees.'

'Not half as hard as it's going to be on our stomachs if you don't succeed,' replied Lady Barbara.

Smith made a wry face and resumed his crawling while the two girls, laying flat now to conceal themselves from the quarry, watched his progress.

'He's not doing half badly,' commented Lady Barbara after several minutes of silent watching.

'How beautiful he is,' sighed Jezebel.

'Just at present the most beautiful things in the landscape are those goats,' said Lady Barbara. 'If he gets close enough for a shot and misses I shall die – and I know he will miss.'

'He didn't miss Lamech last night,' Jezebel reminded her.

'He must have been aiming at someone else,' commented Lady Barbara shortly.

Lafayette Smith crawled on apace. With numerous halts, as advised by Lady Barbara, he drew slowly nearer his unsuspecting quarry. The minutes seemed hours. Pounding constantly upon his brain was the consciousness that he must not fail, though not for the reason that one might naturally assume. The failure to procure food seemed a less dreadful consequence than the contempt of Lady Barbara Collis.

Now, at last, he was quite close to the nearest of the herd. Just a few more yards and he was positive that he could not miss. A low bush, growing just ahead of him, concealed his approach from the eyes of his victim. Lafayette Smith reached the bush and paused behind it. A little farther ahead he discovered another shrub still closer to the goat, a thin nanny with a large udder. She did not look very appetizing, but beneath that unprepossessing exterior Lafayette Smith knew there must be hidden juicy steaks and cutlets. He crawled on. His knees were raw and his neck ached from the unnatural position his unfamiliar method of locomotion had compelled it to assume.

He passed the bush behind which he had paused, failing to see the kid lying hidden upon its opposite side – hidden by a solicitous mamma while she fed. The kid saw Lafayette but it did not move. It would not move until its mother called it, unless actually touched by something, or terrified beyond the limit of its self-control.

It watched Lafayette crawling toward the next bush upon his itinerary – the next and last. What it thought is unrecorded, but it is doubtful that it was impressed by Lafayette's beauty.

Now the man had reached the concealment of the last bush, unseen by any other eyes than those of the kid. He drew his pistol cautiously, lest the slightest noise alarm his potential dinner. Raising himself slightly until his eyes were above the level of the bush he took careful aim. The goat was so close that a miss appeared such a remote contingency as to be of negligible consideration.

Lafayette already felt the stirring warmth of pride with which he would toss the carcass of his kill at the feet of Lady Barbara and Jezebel. Then he jerked the trigger.

Nanny leaped straight up into the air, and when she hit the ground again she was already streaking north in company with the balance of the herd. Lafayette Smith had missed again.

He had scarcely time to realize the astounding and humiliating fact as he rose to his feet when something struck him suddenly and heavily from behind – a blow that bent his knees beneath him and brought him heavily to earth in a sitting posture. No, not to earth. He was sitting on something soft that wriggled and squirmed. His startled eyes, glancing down, saw the head of a kid protruding from between his legs – little Capra hircus had been terrified beyond the limit of his self-control.

'Missed!' cried Lady Barbara Collis. 'How could he!' Tears of disappointment welled to her eyes.

Eshbaal, hunting his goats at the northern fringe of the forest cocked his ears and listened. That unfamiliar sound! And so near. From far across the valley, toward the village of the South Midians, Eshbaal had heard a similar sound, though faintly from afar, the night before. Four times it had broken the silence of the valley and no more. Eshbaal had heard it and so had his fellows in the village of Elija, the son of Noah.

Lafayette Smith seized the kid before it could wriggle free, and despite its struggles he slung it across his shoulder and started back toward the waiting girls 'He didn't miss it!' exclaimed Jezebel. 'I knew he wouldn't,' and she went down to meet him, with Lady Barbara, perplexed, following in her wake.

'Splendid!' cried the English girl as they came closer. 'You really did shoot one, didn't you? I was sure you missed.'

'I did miss,' admitted Lafayette ruefully.

'But how did you get it?'

'If I must admit it,' explained the man, 'I sat on it. As a matter of fact it got me.'

'Well, anyway, you have it,' she said.

'And it will be a whole lot better eating than the one I missed,' he assured them. 'That one was terribly thin and very old.'

'How cute it is,' said Jezebel.

'Don't,' cried Lady Barbara. 'We mustn't think of that. Just remember that we are starving.'

'Where shall we eat it?' asked Smith.

'Right here,' replied the English girl. 'There is plenty of deadwood around these trees. Have you matches?'

'Yes. Now you two look the other way while I do my duty. I wish I'd hit the old one now. This is like murdering a baby.'

Upon the opposite side of the forest Eshbaal was once again experiencing surprise, for suddenly the goats for which he had been searching came stampeding toward him.

'The strange noise frightened them,' soliloquized Eshbaal. 'Perhaps it is a miracle. The goats for which I have searched all day have been made to return unto me.'

As they dashed past, the trained eye of the shepherd took note of them. There were not many goats in the bunch that had strayed, so he had no difficulty in counting them. A kid was missing. Being a shepherd there was nothing for Eshbaal to do but set forth in search of the missing one. He advanced cautiously, alert because of the noise that he had heard.

Eshbaal was a short, stocky man with blue eyes and a wealth of blond hair and beard. His features were regular and handsome in a primitive, savage way. His single garment, fashioned from a goat skin, left his right arm entirely free, nor did it impede his legs, since it fell not to his knees. He carried a club and a rude knife.

Lady Barbara took charge of the culinary activities after Lafayette had butchered the kid and admitted that, beyond hard boiling eggs, his knowledge of cooking was too sketchy to warrant serious mention. 'And anyway,' he said, 'we haven't any eggs.'

Following the directions of the English girl, Smith cut a number of chops from the carcass; and these the three grilled on pointed sticks that Lady Barbara had had him cut from a nearby tree.

'How long will it take to cook them?' demanded Smith. 'I could eat mine raw. I could eat the whole kid raw, for that matter, in one sitting and have room left for the old nanny I missed.'

'We'll eat only enough to keep us going,' said Lady Barbara; 'then we'll wrap the rest in the skin and take it with us. If we're careful, this should keep us alive for three or four days.'

'Of course you're right,' admitted Lafayette. 'You always are.'

'You can have a big meal this time,' she told him, 'because you've been longer without food than we.'

'You have had nothing for a long time, Barbara,' said Jezebel. 'I am the one who needs the least.'

'We all need it now,' said Lafayette. 'Let's have a good meal this time, get back our strength, and then ration the balance so that it will last several days. Maybe I will sit on something else before this is gone.'

They all laughed; and presently the chops were done, and the three fell to upon them. 'Like starving Armenians,' was the simile Smith suggested.

Occupied with the delightful business of appeasing wolfish hunger, none of them saw Eshbaal halt behind a tree and observe them. Jezebel he recognized for what she was, and a sudden fire lighted his blue eyes. The others were enigmas to him – especially their strange apparel.

Of one thing Eshbaal was convinced. He had found his lost kid and there was wrath in his heart. For just a moment he watched the three; then he glided back into the forest until he was out of their sight, when he broke into a run.

The meal finished, Smith wrapped the remainder of the carcass in the skin of the kid; and the three again took up their search for the fissure.

An hour passed and then another. Still their efforts were not crowned with success. They saw no opening in the stern, forbidding face of the escarpment, nor did they see the slinking figures creeping steadily nearer and nearer – a score of stocky, yellow haired men led by Eshbaal, the Shepherd.

'We must have passed it,' said Smith at last. 'It just cannot be this far south,' yet only a hundred yards farther on lay the illusive opening into the great fissure.

'We shall have to hunt for some other way out of the valley then,' said Lady Barbara. 'There is a place farther south that Jezebel and I used to see from the mouth of our cave where the cliff looked as though it might be scaled.'

'Let's have a try at it then,' said Smith. 'Say, look there!' he pointed toward the north.

'What is it? Where?' demanded Jezebel.

'I thought I saw a man's head behind that rock,' said Smith. 'Yes, there he is again. Lord, look at 'em. They're all around.'

Eshbaal and his fellows, realizing that they were discovered, came into the open, advancing slowly toward the three.

'The men of North Midian!' exclaimed Jezebel. 'Are they not beautiful!'

'What shall we do?' demanded Lady Barbara. 'We must not let them take us.'

'We'll see what they want,' said Smith. 'They may not be unfriendly. Anyway, we couldn't escape them by running. They would overtake us in no time. Get behind me, and if they show any signs of attacking I'll shoot a few of them.'

'Perhaps you had better go out and sit on them,' suggested Lady Barbara, wearily.

'I am sorry,' said Smith, 'that my marksmanship is so poor; but, unfortunately perhaps, it never occurred to my parents to train me in the gentle art of murder. I realize now that they erred and that my education has been sadly neglected. I am only a school teacher, and in teaching the young intellect to shoot I have failed to learn to do so myself.'

'I didn't intend to be nasty,' said Lady Barbara, who detected in the irony of the man's reply a suggestion of wounded pride. 'Please forgive me.'

The North Midians were advancing cautiously, halting occasionally for brief, whispered conferences. Presently one of them spoke, addressing the three. 'Who are you?' he demanded. 'What do you in the land of Midian?'

'Can you understand him?' asked Smith, over his shoulder.

'Yes,' replied both girls simultaneously.

'He speaks the same language as Jezebel's people,' explained Lady Barbara. 'He wants to know who we are and what we are doing here.'

'You talk to him, Lady Barbara,' said Smith.

The English girl stepped forward. 'We are strangers in Midian,' she said. 'We are lost. All we wish is to get out of your country.'

'There is no way out of Midian,' replied the man. 'You have killed a kid belonging to Eshbaal. For that you must be punished. You must come with us.'

'We were starving,' explained Lady Barbara. 'If we could pay for the kid we would gladly do so. Let us go in peace.'

The Midians held another whispered conference, after which their spokesman addressed the three again. 'You must come with us,' he said, 'the women at least. If the man will go away we will not harm you, we do not want him; we want the women.'

'What did he say?' demanded Smith, and when Lady Barbara had interpreted he shook his head. 'Tell them no,' he directed. 'Also tell them that if they molest us I shall have to kill them.'

When the girls delivered this ultimatum to the Midians they laughed. 'What can one man do against twenty?' demanded their leader, then he advanced followed by his retainers. They were brandishing their clubs now, and some of them raised their voices in a savage war cry.

'You will have to shoot,' said Lady Barbara. 'There are at least twenty. You cannot miss them all.'

'You flatter me,' said smith, as he raised his .32 and levelled it at the advancing Midians.

'Go back!' shouted Jezebel, 'or you will be killed,' but the attackers only came forward the faster.

Then Smith fired. At the sharp crack of the pistol the Midians halted, surprised; but no one fell. Instead, the leader hurled his club, quickly and accurately, just as Smith was about to fire again. He dodged; but the missile struck his pistol hand a glancing blow, sending the weapon flying – then the North Midians were upon them.

XVI
Trailing

Tarzan of the Apes had made a kill. It was only a small rodent, but it would satisfy his hunger until the morrow. Darkness had fallen shortly after he had discovered the spoor of the missing American, and he was forced to abandon the search until daylight came again. The first sign of the spoor had been very faint – just the slightest imprint of one corner of a boot heel, but that had been enough for the ape-man. Clinging to a bush nearby was the scarcely perceptible scent spoor of a white man, which Tarzan might have followed even after dark; but it would have been a slow and arduous method of tracking which the ape-man did not consider the circumstances warranted. Therefore he made his kill, ate, and curled up in a patch of tall grass to sleep.

Wild beasts may not sleep with one eye open, but often it seems that they sleep with both ears cocked. The ordinary night sounds go unnoticed, while a lesser sound, portending danger or suggesting the unfamiliar, may awaken them on the instant. It was a sound falling in the latter category that awoke Tarzan shortly after midnight.

He raised his head and listened, then he lowered it and placed an ear against the ground. 'Horses and men,' he soliloquized as he rose to his feet. Standing erect, his great chest rising and falling to his breathing, he listened intently. His sensitive nostrils, seeking to confirm the testimony of his ears, dilated to receive and classify the messages that Usha, the wind, bore to them. They caught the scent of Tongani, the baboon, so strong as almost to negate the others. Tenuous, from a great distance came the scent of Sabor, the lioness, and the sweet, heavy stench of Tantor, the elephant. One by one the ape-man read these invisible messages brought by Usha, the wind; but only those interested him that spoke of horses and men.

Why did horses and men move through the night? Who and what were the men? He scarcely needed to ask himself that latter question, and only the first one interested him.

It is the business of beasts and of men to know what their enemies do. Tarzan stretched his great muscles lazily and moved down the slope of the foot hills in the direction from which had come the evidence that his enemies were afoot.

The 'Gunner' stumbled along in the darkness. Never in his twenty odd years of life had he even approximated such utter physical exhaustion. Each step he was sure must be his last. He had long since become too tired even to curse his captors as he plodded on, now almost numb to any sensation, his mind a chaos of dull misery.

But even endless journeys must ultimately end; and at last the cavalcade turned into the gateway of the village of Dominic Capietro, the raider; and the 'Gunner' was escorted to a hut where he slumped to the hard earth floor after his bonds had been removed, positive that he would never rise again.

He was asleep when they brought him food; but aroused himself long enough to eat, for his hunger was fully as great as his fatigue. Then he stretched out again and slept, while a tired and disgusted *shifta* nodded drowsily on guard outside the entrance to the hut.

Tarzan had come down to the cliff above the village as the raiders were filing through the gateway. A full moon cast her revealing beams upon the scene, lighting the figures of horses and men. The ape-man recognized Capietro and Stabutch, he saw Ogonyo, the headman of the safari of the young American geologist; and he saw the 'Gunner' stumbling painfully along in bonds.

The ape-man was an interested spectator of all that transpired in the village below. He noted particularly the location of the hut into which the white prisoner had been thrust. He watched the preparation of food, and he noted the great quantities of liquor that Capietro and Stabutch consumed while waiting for the midnight supper being prepared by slaves. The more they drank the better pleased was Tarzan.

As he watched them, he wondered how supposedly rational creatures could consider the appellation *beast* a term of reproach and *man* one of glorification. The beasts, as he knew, held an opposite conception of the relative virtues of these two orders, although they were ignorant of most of man's asininities and degredations, their minds being far too pure to understand them.

Waiting with the patience of the unspoiled primitive nervous system, Tarzan watched from the cliff top until the village below seemed to have settled down for the night. He saw the sentries in the banquette inside the palisade, but he did not see the guard squatting in the shadow of the hut where the 'Gunner' lay in heavy slumber.

Satisfied, the ape-man rose and moved along the cliff until he was beyond the village; and there, where the escarpment was less precipitous, he made his way to its base. Noiselessly and cautiously he crept to the palisade at a point that was hidden from the view of the sentries. The moon shone full upon him, but the opposite side of the palisade he knew must be in dense shadow. There he listened for a moment to assure himself that his approach had aroused no suspicion. He wished that he might see the sentries at the gate, for when he topped the palisade he would be in full view for an instant. When last he had seen them they had been squatting upon the banquette, their backs to the palisade, and apparently upon the verge of sleep. Would they remain thus?

Here, however, was a chance he must take, and so he gave the matter little thought and few regrets. What was, was; and if he could not change it he must ignore it; and so, leaping lightly upward, he seized the top of the palisade and drew himself up and over. Only a glance he threw in the direction of the sentries as he topped the barrier, a glance that told him they had not moved since he had last looked.

In the shadow of the palisade he paused to look about. There was nothing to cause him apprehension; and so he moved quickly, keeping ever in the shadows where he could, toward the hut where he expected to find the young white man. It was hidden from his view by another hut which he approached and had circled when he saw the figure of the guard sitting by the doorway, his rifle across his knees.

This was a contingency the ape-man had not anticipated, and it caused a change in his immediate plans. He drew back out of sight behind the hut he had been circling, lay down flat upon the ground, and then crawled forward again until his head protruded beyond the hut far enough to permit one eye to watch the unconscious guard. Here he lay waiting – a human beast watching its quarry.

For a long time he lay thus trusting to his knowledge of men that the moment for which he waited would arrive. Presently the chin of the *shifta* dropped to his chest; but immediately it snapped back again, erect. Then the fellow changed his position. He sat upon the ground, his legs stretched before him, and leaned his back against the hut. His rifle was still across his knees. It was a dangerous position for a man who would remain awake.

After a while his head rolled to one side. Tarzan watched him closely, as a cat watches a mouse. The head remained in the position to which it had rolled, the chin dropped, and the mouth gaped; the tempo of the breathing changed, denoting sleep.

Tarzan rose silently to his feet and as silently crept across the intervening space to the side of the unconscious man. There must be no outcry, no scuffle.

As strikes Histah, the snake, so struck Tarzan of the Apes. There was only the sound of parting vertebrae as the neck broke in the grip of those thews of steel.

The rifle Tarzan laid upon the ground; then he raised the corpse in his arms and bore it into the darkness of the hut's interior. Here he groped for a moment until he had located the body of the sleeping white, and knelt beside him. Cautiously he shook him, one hand ready to muffle any outcry the man might make, but the 'Gunner' did not awaken. Tarzan shook him again more roughly and yet without results, then he slapped him heavily across the face.

The 'Gunner' stirred. 'Geeze,' he muttered 'can't you let a guy sleep? Didn't I tell you you'd get your ransom, you damn wop?'

Tarzan permitted a faint smile to touch his lips. 'Wake up,' he whispered. 'Make no noise. I have come to take you away?'

'Who are you?'

'Tarzan of the Apes.'

'Geeze!' The 'Gunner' sat up.

'Make no noise,' cautioned the ape-man once more.

'Sure,' whispered Danny as he raised himself stiffly to his feet.

'Follow me,' said Tarzan, 'and no matter what happens stay very close to me. I am going to toss you to the top of the palisade. Try not to make any noise as you climb over, and be careful when you drop to the ground on the other side to alight with your knees flexed – it is a long drop.'

'You say you're going to toss me to the top of the palisade, guy?'

'Yes.'

'Do you know what I weigh?'

'No, and I don't care. Keep still and follow me. Don't stumble over this body.' Tarzan paused in the entrance and looked about; then he passed out, with the 'Gunner' at his heels, and crossed quickly to the palisade. Even if they discovered him now he still had time to accomplish what he had set out to do, before they could interfere, unless the sentries, firing on them, chanced to make a hit; but on that score he felt little apprehension.

As they came to the palisade the 'Gunner' glanced up, and his scepticism increased – a fat chance any guy would have to toss his one hundred and eighty pounds to the top of that!

The ape-man seized him by the collar and the seat of his breeches. 'Catch the top!' he whispered. Then he swung the 'Gunner' backward as though he had been a fifty pound sack of meal, surged forward and upward; and in the same second Danny Patrick's outstretched fingers clutched the top of the palisade.

'Geeze,' he muttered, 'if I'd missed I'd of gone clean over.'

Catlike, the ape-man ran up the barrier and dropped to the ground on the outside almost at the instant that the 'Gunner' alighted, and without a word started toward the cliff, where once again he had to assist the other to reach the summit.

Danny 'Gunner' Patrick was speechless, partly from shortness of breath following his exertions, but more, by far, from astonishment. Here was a guy! In all his experience of brawny men, and it had been considerable, he had never met, nor expected to meet, such a one as this.

'I have located the spoor of your friend,' said Tarzan.

'The what?' asked the 'Gunner.' 'Is he dead?'

'His tracks,' explained the ape-man, who was still leading the way up the slope toward the higher mountains.

'I gotcha,' said the 'Gunner.' 'But you ain't seen him?'

'No, it was too dark to follow him when I found them. We will do so in the morning.'

'If I can walk,' said the 'Gunner.'

'What's the matter with you?' demanded Tarzan. 'Injured?'

'I ain't got no legs from the knees down,' replied Danny. 'I walked my lousy dogs off yesterday.'

'I'll carry you,' suggested Tarzan.

'Nix!' exclaimed Danny. 'I can crawl, but I'll be damned if I'll let any guy carry me.'

'It will be a hard trip if you're exhausted now,' the ape-man told him. 'I could leave you somewhere near here and pick you up after I find your friend.'

'Nothing doing. I'm going to look for old Smithy if I wear 'em off to the hips.'

'I could probably travel faster alone,' suggested Tarzan.

'Go ahead,' agreed the 'Gunner' cheerfully. 'I'll tail along behind you.'

'And get lost.'

'Let me come along, mister. I'm worried about that crazy nut.'

'All right. It won't make much difference anyway. He may be a little hungrier when we find him, but he can't starve to death in a couple of days.'

'Say,' exclaimed Danny, 'how come you knew them wops had taken me for a ride?'

'I thought you walked.'

'Well, what's the difference? How did you know I was in that lousy burgh of theirs?'

'I was on the cliff when they brought you in. I waited until they were asleep. I am not ready to deal with them yet.'

'What you goin' to do to them?'

Tarzan shrugged but made no reply; and for a long time they walked on in silence through the night, the ape-man timing his speed to the physical condition of his companion, whose nerve he was constrained to admire, though his endurance and knowledge he viewed with contempt.

Far up in the hills, where he had bedded down earlier in the night, Tarzan halted and told 'Gunner' to get what rest he could before dawn.

'Geeze, them's the pleasantest words I've heard for years,' sighed Danny, as he lay down in the high grass. 'You may think you've seen a guy pound his ear, but you ain't seen nothing. Watch me,' and he was asleep almost before the words had left his mouth.

Tarzan lay down at a little distance; and he, too, was soon asleep, but at the first suggestion of dawn he was up. He saw that his companion still slept, and then he slipped silently away toward a water hole he had discovered the previous day in a rocky ravine near the cliff where he had met the tribe of Zugash, the tongani.

He kept well down the slope of the foot hills, for with the coming of dawn the wind had changed, and he wished to come upwind toward the water hole. He moved as silently as the disappearing shadows of the retreating night, his nostrils quivering to catch each vagrant scent borne upon the bosom of the early morning breeze.

There was deep mud at one edge of the water hole, where the earth had been trampled by the feet of drinking beasts; and near here he found that which he sought, the sticky sweetness of whose scent had been carried to his nostrils by Usha.

Low trees grew in the bottom of the ravine and much underbrush, for here the earth held its moisture longer than on the ridges that were more exposed to Kudu's merciless rays. It was a lovely sylvan glade, nor did its beauties escape the appreciative eyes of the ape-man, though the lure of the glade lay not this morning in its aesthetic charms, but rather in the fact that it harbored Horta, the boar.

Silently to the edge of the underbrush came the ape-man as Horta came down to the pool to drink. Upon the opposite side stood Tarzan, his bow and arrows ready in his hands; but the high brush precluded a fair shot, and so the hunter stepped out in full view of the boar. So quickly he moved that his arrow sped as Horta wheeled to run, catching the boar in the side behind the left shoulder – a vital spot.

With a snort of rage Horta turned back and charged. Straight through the pool he came for Tarzan; and as he came three more arrows, shot with unbelievable accuracy and celerity, buried themselves deep in the breast of the great beast. Bloody foam flecked his jowls and his flashing tusks, fires of hate shot from his wicked little eyes as he sought to reach the author of his hurts and wreak his vengeance before he died. •

Discarding his bow the ape-man met the mad charge of Horta with his spear, for there was no chance to elude the swift rush of that great body, hemmed, as he was, by the thick growth of underbrush. His feet braced, he dropped the point of his weapon the instant Horta was within its range, that he might have no opportunity to dodge it or strike it aside with his tusks. Straight through the great chest it drove, deep into the savage heart, yet the beast still strove to reach the man-thing that held it off with a strength almost equal to its own.

But already as good as dead on his feet was Horta, the boar. His brief, savage struggles ended; and he dropped in the shallow water at the edge of the pool. Then the ape-man placed a foot upon his vanquished foe and screamed forth the hideous challenge of his tribe.

The 'Gunner' sat suddenly erect, awakened out of a sound sleep. 'Geeze!' he exclaimed. 'What was that?' Receiving no answer he looked about. 'Wouldn't that eat you?' he murmured. 'He's went. I wonder has he run out on me? He didn't seem like that kind of a guy. But you can't never tell – I've had pals to double-cross me before this.'

In the village of Capietro a dozing sentry snapped suddenly alert, while his companion half rose to his feet. 'What was that?' demanded one.

'A hairy one has made a kill,' said the other.

Sheeta, the panther, downwind, stalking both the man and the boar, stopped in his tracks; then he turned aside and loped away in easy graceful bounds; but he had not gone far before he stopped again and raised his nose upwind. Again the scent of man; but this time a different man, nor was there any sign of the feared thunder stick that usually accompanied the scent spoor of the tarmangani. Belly low, Sheeta moved slowly up the slope toward Danny 'Gunner' Patrick.

'What to do?' mused the 'Gunner.' 'Geeze, I'm hungry! Should I wait for him or should I go on? On, where? I sure got myself in a jam all right. Where do I go? How do I eat? Hell!'

He arose and moved about, feeling out his muscles. They were lame and sore, but he realized that he was much rested. Then he scanned the distances for a sight of Tarzan, and instead, saw Sheeta, the panther, a few hundred yards away.

Danny Patrick, hoodlum, racketeer, gangster, gunman, killer, trembled in terror. Cold sweat burst from every pore, and he could feel the hair rise on his scalp. He felt a mad impulse to run; but, fortunately for Danny, his legs refused to move. He was literally, in the vernacular to which he was accustomed, scared stiff. The 'Gunner,' without a gun, was a very different man.

The panther had stopped and was surveying him. Caution and an hereditary fear of man gave the great cat pause; but he was angry because he had been frightened from his prey after hunting futilely all night, and he was very, very hungry. He growled, his face wrinkled in a hideous snarl; and Danny felt his knees giving beneath him.

Then, beyond the panther, he saw the high grass moving to the approach of another animal, which the 'Gunner' promptly assumed was the beast's mate. There was just a single, narrow strip of this high grass; and when the animal had crossed it he, too, would see Danny, who was confident that this would spell the end. One of them might hesitate to attack a man – he didn't know – but he was sure that two would not.

He dropped to his knees and did something that he had not done for many years – he prayed. And then the grasses parted; and Tarzan of the Apes stepped into view, the carcass of a boar upon one broad shoulder. Instantly the ape-man took in the scene that his nostrils had already prepared him for.

Dropping the carcass of Horta he voiced a sudden, ferocious growl that startled Sheeta no more than it did Danny Patrick. The cat wheeled, instantly on the defensive. Tarzan charged, growls rumbling from his throat; and Sheeta did exactly what he had assumed he would do – turned and fled. Then Tarzan picked up the carcass of Horta and came up the slope to Danny, who knelt opened-mouthed and petrified.

'What are you kneeling for?' asked the ape-man.

'I was just tying my boot lace,' explained the 'Gunner.'

'Here is breakfast,' said Tarzan, dropping the boar to the ground. 'Help yourself.'

'That sure looks good to me,' said Danny. 'I could eat it raw.'

'That is fine,' said Tarzan; and, squatting, he cut two strips from one of the hams. 'Here,' he said, offering one to the 'Gunner.'

'Quit your kidding,' remonstrated the latter.

Tarzan eyed him questioningly, at the same time tearing off a mouthful of the meat with his strong teeth. 'Horta is a little bit tough,' he remarked, 'but he is the best I could do without losing a great deal of time. Why don't you eat? I thought you were hungry.'

'I got to cook mine,' said the 'Gunner.'

'But you said you could eat it raw,' the ape-man reminded him.

'That's just a saying,' explained the 'Gunner.' 'I might at that, but I ain't never tried it.'

'Make a fire, then; and cook yours,' said Tarzan.

'Say,' remarked Danny a few minutes later as he squatted before his fire grilling his meat, 'did you hear that noise a little while ago?'

'What was it like?'

'I never heard nothing like it but once before – say, I just took a tumble to myself! That was you killin' the pig. I heard you yell like that the night you killed the lion in our camp.'

'We will be going as soon as you finish your meat,' said Tarzan. He was hacking off several pieces, half of which he handed to the 'Gunner' while he dropped the balance into his quiver. 'Take these,' he said. 'You may get hungry before we can make another kill.' Then he scraped a hole in the loose earth and buried the remainder of the carcass.

'What you doin' that for?' asked the 'Gunner.' 'Afraid it will smell?'

'We may come back this way,' explained Tarzan. 'If we do Horta will be less tough.'

The 'Gunner' made no comment; but he assured himself, mentally, that he 'wasn't no dog,' to bury his meat and then dig it up again after it had rotted. The idea almost made him sick.

Tarzan quickly picked up the trail of Lafayette Smith and followed it easily, though the 'Gunner' saw nothing to indicate that human foot had ever trod these hills.

'I don't see nothing,' he said.

'I have noticed that,' returned Tarzan.

'That,' thought Danny Patrick, 'sounds like a dirty crack;' but he said nothing.

'A lion picked up his trail here,' said the ape-man.

'You ain't spoofin' me are you?' demanded Danny. 'There ain't no sign of nothin' on this ground.'

'Nothing that you can see perhaps,' replied Tarzan; 'but then, though you may not know it, you so-called civilized men are almost blind and quite stone deaf.'

Soon they came to the fissure, and here Tarzan saw that the man and the lion had both gone in, the lion following the man, and that only the lion had come out.

'That looks tough for old Smithy, doesn't it?' said the 'Gunner' when Tarzan had explained the story of the spoor.

'It may,' replied the ape-man. 'I'll go on in and look for him. You can wait here or follow. You can't get lost if you stay inside this crack.'

'Go ahead,' said Danny. 'I'll follow.'

The fissure was much longer than Tarzan had imagined; but some distance from the entrance he discovered evidence that the lion had not attacked Smith, for he could see where Numa had turned about and that the man had continued on. Some recent scars on the sides of the fissure told him the rest of the story quite accurately.

'It's fortunate he didn't hit Numa,' soliloquized the ape-man.

At the end of the fissure Tarzan had some difficulty in wriggling through the aperture that opened into the valley of the land of Midian; but once through he picked up the trail of Smith again and followed it down toward the lake, while Danny, far behind him, stumbled wearily along the rough floor of the fissure.

He walked rapidly, for the spoor was plain. When he came to the shore of Chinnereth he discovered Smith's tracks intermingled with those of a woman wearing well worn European boots and another shod with sandals.

When he had first entered the valley he had seen the village of the South Midians in the distance and now he drew the false conclusion that Smith had discovered a friendly people and other whites and that he was in no danger.

His curiosity piqued by the mystery of this hidden valley, the ape-man determined to visit the village before continuing on Smith's trail. Time had never entered greatly into his calculations, trained, as he had been, by savage apes to whom time meant less than nothing; but to investigate and to know every detail of his wilderness world was as much a part of the man as is his religion to a priest.

And so he continued rapidly on toward the distant village while Danny Patrick still crawled and stumbled slowly along the rocky floor of the fissure.

Danny was tired. Momentarily he expected to meet Tarzan returning either with Smith or with word of his death; so he stopped often to rest, with the result that when he had reached the end of the fissure and crawled through to behold the mystifying sight of a strange valley spread before him, Tarzan was already out of sight.

'Geeze!' exclaimed the 'Gunner.' 'Who would have thought that hole led into a place like this? I wonder which way that Tarzan guy went?'

This thought occupied the 'Gunner' for a few minutes. He examined the ground as he had seen Tarzan do, mistook a few spots where some little rodent had scratched up the earth, or taken a dust bath, for the footprints of a man, and set forth in the wrong direction.

XVII

She is Mine!

The stocky, blond warriors of Elija, the son of Noah, quickly surrounded and seized Lafayette Smith and his two companions. Elija picked up Smith's pistol and examined it with interest; then he dropped it into a goat skin pouch that was suspended from the girdle that held his single garment about him.

'This one,' said Eshbaal, pointing to Jezebel, 'is mine.'

'Why?' asked Elija, the son of Noah.

'I saw her first,' replied Eshbaal.

'Did you hear what he said?' demanded Jezebel of Lady Barbara.

The English girl nodded apathetically. Her brain was numb with the disappointment and the horror of the situation, for in some respects their fate might be worse with these men than with those of South Midian. These were lusty, primitive warriors, not half-witted creatures whose natural passions had been weakened by generations of hereditary disease of nerve and brain.

'He wants me,' said Jezebel. 'Is he not beautiful?'

Lady Barbara turned upon the girl almost angrily, and then suddenly she remembered that Jezebel was little more than a child in experience and that she had no conception of the fate that might await her at the hands of the North Midians.

In their narrow religious fanaticism the South Midians denied even the most obvious phases of procreation. The subject was absolutely taboo and so hideous had ages of training and custom made it appear to them that mothers often killed their first born rather than exhibit these badges of sin.

'Poor little Jezebel,' said Lady Barbara.

'What do you mean, Barbara?' asked the girl. 'Are you not happy that the beautiful man wants me?'

'Listen, Jezebel,' said Lady Barbara. 'You know I am your friend, do you not?'

'My only friend,' replied the girl. 'The only person I ever loved.'

'Then believe me when I say that you must kill yourself, as I shall kill myself, if we are unable to escape from these creatures.'

'Why?' demanded Jezebel. 'Are they not more beaufitul than the South Midians?'

'Forget their fatal beauty,' replied Lady Barbara, 'but never forget what I have told you.'

'Now I am afraid,' said Jezebel.

'Thank God for that,' exclaimed the English girl.

The North Midians marched loosely and without discipline. They seemed a garrulous race, and their arguments and speeches were numerous and lengthy. Sometimes, so intent did they become on some point at argument, or in listening to a long winded oration by one of their fellows, that they quite forgot their prisoners, who were sometimes amongst them, sometimes in advance and once behind them.

It was what Lady Barbara had been awaiting and what she had to some extent engineered.

'Now!' she whispered. 'They are not looking.' She halted and turned back. They were among the trees of the forest where some concealment might be found.

Smith and Jezebel had stopped at Lady Barbara's direction; and for an instant the three paused, breathless, watching the retreating figures of their captors.

'Now run!' whispered Lady Barbara. 'We'll scatter and meet again at the foot of the cliff.'

Just what prompted Lady Barbara to suggest that they separate Lafayette Smith did not understand. To him it seemed a foolish and unnecessary decision; but as he had a great deal more confidence in Lady Barbara's judgment in practical matters than in his own he did not voice his doubts, though he accepted her plan with certain mental reservations, which guided his subsequent acts.

The English girl ran in a southeasterly direction, while Jezebel, obeying the commands of her friend, scurried off toward the southwest. Smith, glancing to the rear, discovered no indication that their captors had, as yet, missed them. For a moment he was hesitant as to what course to pusue. The conviction still gripped him that he was the natural protector of both girls, notwithstanding the unfortunate circumstances that had nullified his efforts to function successfully in that role; but he saw that it was going to be still more difficult to protect them both now that they had elected to run in different directions.

However, his decision was soon made, difficult though it was. Jezebel was in her own world; contemplation of capture by the North Midians had, so far from alarming her, appeared rather to have met with enthusiastic anticipation on her part; she could not be worse off with them than with the only other people she knew.

Lady Barbara, on the other hand, was of another world – his own world – and he had heard her say that death would be preferable to captivity among these semi-savages. His duty, therefore, was to follow and protect Lady Barbara; and so he let Jezebel take her way unprotected back toward the cliff, while he pursued the English girl in the direction of Chinnereth.

Lady Barbara Collis ran until she was out of breath. For several minutes she had distinctly heard the sounds of pursuit behind her – the heavy footfalls of a man. Frantic from hopelessness, she drew her pocket knife from a pocket of her jacket and opened the blade as she ran.

She wondered if she could destroy herself with this inadequate weapon. She was positive that she could not inflict either fatal or disabling injuries upon her pursuer with it. Yet the thought of self-destruction revolted her. The realization was upon her that she had about reached the limit of her endurance, and that the fatal decision could not be long averted, when her heritage of English fighting blood decided the question for her. There was but one thing it would permit – she must stand and defend herself. She stopped then, suddenly, and wheeled about, the little knife clutched in her right hand – a tigress at bay.

When she saw Lafayette Smith running toward her she collapsed suddenly and sank to the ground, where she sat with her back against the bole of a tree.

Lafayette Smith, breathing hard, came and sat down beside her. Neither had any breath for words.

Lady Barbara was the first to regain her power of speech. 'I thought I said we would scatter,' she reminded him.

'I couldn't leave you alone,' he replied.

'But how about Jezebel? You left her alone.'

'I couldn't go with both of you,' he reminded her, 'and you know Jezebel is really at home here. It means much more to you to escape than it means to her.'

She shook her head. 'Capture means the same thing to either of us,' she said, 'but of the two I am better able to take care of myself than Jezebel – she does not understand the nature of her danger.'

'Nevertheless,' he insisted, 'you are the more important. You have relatives and friends who care for you. Poor little Jezebel has only one friend, and that is you, unless I may consider myself a friend, as I should like to do.'

'I imagine we three have the unique distinction of being the closest corporation of friends in the world,' she replied, with a wan smile, 'and there doesn't seem to be anyone who wants to buy in.'

'The Friendless Friends Corporation, Limited,' he suggested.

'Perhaps we'd best hold a directors' meeting and decide what we should do next to conserve the interests of the stockholders.'

'I move we move,' he said.

'Seconded.' The girl rose to her feet.

'You're terribly tired, aren't you?' he asked. 'But I suppose the only thing we can do is to get as far away from the territory of the North Midians as possible. It's almost certain they will try to capture us again as soon as they discover we are missing.'

'If we can only find a place to hide until night,' she said. 'Then we can go back to the cliffs under the cover of darkness and search for Jezebel and the place that she and I thought they might be scaled.'

'This forest is so open that it doesn't afford any good hiding places, but at least we can look.'

'Perhaps we shall find a place near the lake,' said Lady Barbara. 'We ought to come to it soon.'

They walked on for a considerable distance without talking, each occupied with his own thoughts; and as no sign of pursuit developed their spirits rose.

'Do you know,' he said presently, 'that I can't help but feel that we're going to get out of this all right in the end?'

'But what a terrible experience! It doesn't seem possible that such things could have happened to me. I can't forget Jobab.' It was the first time mention had been made of the tragedy at the southern village.

'You must not give that a thought,' he said. 'You did the only thing possible under the circumstances. If you had not done what you did both you and Jezebel would have been recaptured, and you know what that would have meant.'

'But I've killed a human being,' she said. There was an awed tone in her voice.

'I killed one, too,' he reminded her, 'but I don't regret it in the least, notwithstanding the fact that I never killed anyone before. If I were not such a terrible marksman I should have killed another today, perhaps several. My regret is that I didn't.

'It's a strange world,' he continued after a moment's reflective silence. 'Now, I always considered myself rather well educated and fitted to meet the emergencies of life; and I suppose I should be, in the quiet environment of a college town; but what an awful failure I have proved to be when jolted out of my narrow little rut. I used to feel sorry for the boys who wasted their time at shooting galleries and in rabbit hunting. Men who boasted of their marksmanship merited only my contempt, yet within the last twenty-four hours I would have traded all my education along other lines for the ability to shoot straight.'

'One should know something of many things to be truly educated,' said the girl, 'but I'm afraid you exaggerate the value of marksmanship in determining one's cultural status.'

'Well, there's cooking,' he admitted. 'A person who cannot cook is not well educated. I had hoped one day to be an authority on geology; but with all I know of the subject, which of course isn't so much at that, I would probably starve to death in a land overrunning with game because I can neither shoot nor cook.'

Lady Barbara laughed. 'Don't develop an inferiority complex at this stage,' she cried. 'We need every ounce of self-assurance that we can muster. I think you are top hole. You may not be much of a marksman – that I'll have to admit, and perhaps you cannot cook; but you've one thing that covers a multitude of shortcomings in a man – you are brave.'

It was Lafayette Smith's turn to laugh. 'That's mighty nice of you,' he said. 'I'd rather you thought that of me than anything else in the world; and I'd rather you thought it than anyone else, because it would mean so much to you now; but it isn't true. I was scared stiff in that village last night and when those fellows came at us today, and that's the truth.'

'Which only the more definitely justifies my statement,' she replied.

'I don't understand.'

'Cultured and intelligent people are more ready to realize and appreciate the dangers of a critical situation than are ignorant, unimaginative types. So, when such a person stands his ground determinedly in the face of danger, or voluntarily walks into a dangerous situation from a sense of duty, as you did last night, it evidences a much higher quality of courage than that possessed by the ignorant, physical lout who hasn't brains enough to visualize the contingencies that may result from his action.'

'Be careful,' he warned her, 'or you'll make me believe all that – then I'll be unbearably egotistical. But please don't try to convince me that my inability to cook is a hallmark of virtue.'

'I – listen! What was that?' she halted and turned her eyes toward the rear.

'They have found us,' said Lafayette Smith. 'Go on – go as fast as you can! I'll try to delay them.'

'No,' she replied, 'there is no use. I'll remain with you, whatever happens.'

'Please!' he begged. 'Why should I face them if you won't take advantage of it.'

'It wouldn't do any good,' she said. 'They'd only get me later, and your sacrifice would be useless. We might as well give ourselves up in the hope that we can persuade them to free us later, or, perhaps, find the opportunity to escape after dark.'

'You had better run,' he said, 'because I am going to fight. I am not going to let them take you without raising a hand in your defense. If you get away now, perhaps I can get away later. We can meet at the foot of the cliffs – but don't wait for me if you can find a way out. Now, do as I tell you!' His tone was peremptory – commanding.

Obediently she continued on toward Chinnereth, but presently she stopped and turned. Three men were approaching Smith. Suddenly one of the three swung his club and hurled it at the American, at the same instant dashing forward with his fellows.

The club fell short of its mark, dropping at Smith's feet. She saw him stoop and seize it, and then she saw another detachment of the Midians coming through the woods in the wake of the first three.

Smith's antagonists were upon him as he straightened up with the club in his hand, and he swung it heavily upon the skull of the man who had hurled it at him and who had rushed forward in advance of his fellows with hands outstretched to seize the stranger.

Like a felled ox the man dropped; and then Lady Barbara saw Smith carry the unequal battle to the enemy, as swinging the club above his head, he rushed forward to meet them.

So unexpected was his attack that the men halted and turned to elude him, but one was too slow and the girl heard the fellow's skull crush beneath the heavy blow of the bludgeon.

Then the reinforcements, advancing at a run, surrounded and overwhelmed their lone antagonist, and Smith went down beneath them.

Lady Barbara could not bring herself to desert the man who had thus bravely, however hopelessly, sought to defend her; and when the North

Midians had disarmed and secured Smith they saw her standing where she had stood during the brief engagement.

'I couldn't run away and leave you,' she explained to Smith, as the two were being escorted toward the village of the North Midians. 'I thought they were going to kill you, and I couldn't help you – Oh, it was awful. I couldn't leave you then, could I?'

He looked at her for a moment. 'No,' he answered. '*You* couldn't.'

XVIII

A Guy and a Skirt

Danny 'Gunner' Patrick was tired and disgusted. He had walked for several hours imagining that he was following a spoor, but he had seen nothing of his erstwhile companion. He was thirsty, and so cast frequent glances in the direction of the lake.

'T'ell!' he muttered. 'I ain't goin' to tail that guy no longer till I get me a drink. My mouth feels like I'd been eating cotton for a week.'

He turned away from the cliffs and started down in the direction of the lake, the inviting waters of which sparkled alluringly in the afternoon sun; but the beauties of the scene were wasted upon the 'Gunner,' who saw only a means of quenching his thirst.

The way led through a field of scattered boulders fallen from the towering rim above. He had to pick his way carefully among the smaller ones, and his eyes were almost constantly upon the ground. Occasionally he was compelled to skirt some of the larger masses, many of which towered above his head obstructing his view ahead.

He was damning Africa in general and this section of it in particular as he rounded the corner of an usually large fragment of rock, when suddenly he stopped and his eyes went wide.

'Geeze!' he exclaimed aloud. 'A broad!'

Before him, and coming in his direction, was a golden haired girl attired in a single, scant piece of rough material. She saw him simultaneously and halted.

'Oh,' exclaimed Jezebel with a happy smile. 'Who are thou?' but as she spoke in the language of the land of Midian the 'Gunner' failed to understand her.

'Geeze,' he said. 'I knew I must of come to Africa for something, and I guess you're it. Say kid, you're about all right. I'll tell the world you *are* all right.'

'Thank you,' said Jezebel in English. 'I am so glad that you like me.'

'Geeze,' said Danny. 'You talk United States, don't you? Where you from?'

'Midian,' replied Jezebel.

'Ain't never heard of it. What you doin' here? Where're your people?'

'I am waiting for Lady Barbara,' replied the girl, 'and Smith,' she added.

'Smith! What Smith?' he demanded.

'Oh, he is beautiful,' confided Jezebel.

'Then he ain't the Smith I'm lookin' for,' said the 'Gunner.' 'What's he doin' here, and who's this Lady Barbara dame?'

'Abraham, the son of Abraham, would have killed Lady Barbara and Jezebel if Smith had not come and saved us. He is very brave.'

'Now I know it ain't my Smith,' said Danny, 'though I ain't sayin' he ain't got guts. What I mean is he wouldn't know enough to save no one – he's a geologist.'

'Who are you?' demanded Jezebel.

'Call me Danny, Kid.'

'My name is not kid,' she explained sweetly. 'It is Jezebel.'

'Jezebel! Geeze, what a monicker! You look like it ought to be Gwendolyn.'

'It is Jezebel,' she assured him. 'Do you know who I hoped you'd be?'

'No. Now just tell me, kid, who you supposed I was. Probably President Hoover or Big Bill Thompson, eh?'

'I do not know them,' said Jezebel. 'I hoped that you were the "Gunner."'

'The "Gunner"? What do you know about the "Gunner," kid?'

'My name is not kid, it is Jezebel,' she corrected him, sweetly.

'Oke, Jez,' conceded Danny, 'but tell me who wised you up to the "Gunner" bozo.'

'My name is not Jez, it is—'

'Oh, sure kid, it's Jezebel – that's oke by me; but how about the "Gunner"?'

'What about him?'

'I just been a-askin' you.'

'But I don't understand your language,' explained Jezebel. 'It sounds like English, but it is not the English Lady Barbara taught me.'

'It ain't English,' Danny assured her, seriously; 'it's United States.'

'It is quite like English though, isn't it?'

'Sure,' said the 'Gunner.' 'The only difference is we can understand English but the English don't never seem to understand all of ours. I guess they're dumb.'

'Oh, no, they're not dumb,' Jezebel assured him. 'Lady Barbara is English, and she can talk quite as well as you.'

Danny scratched his head. 'I didn't say they was dummies. I said they was dumb. Dummies can't talk only with their mitts. If a guy's dumb, he don't know nothing.'

'Oh,' said Jezebel.

'But what I asked you is, who wised you up to this "Gunner" bozo?'

'Can you say it in English, please,' asked Jezebel.

'Geeze, what could be plainer? I ask who told you about the "Gunner" and what did they tell you?' Danny was waxing impatient.

'Smith told us. He said the "Gunner" was a friend of his; and when I saw you I thought you must be Smith's friend, hunting for him.'

'Now, what do you know about that!' exclaimed Danny.

'I have just told you what I know about it,' explained the girl; 'but perhaps you did not understand me. Perhaps you are what you call dumb.'

'Are you trying to kid me, kid?' demanded the 'Gunner.'

'My name is not—'

'Oh, all right, all right. I know what your name is.'

'They why do you not call me by my name? Do you not like it?'

'Sure, kid – I mean Jezebel – sure I like it. It's a swell handle when you get used to it. But tell me, where is old Smithy?'

'I do not know such a person.'

'But you just told me you did.'

'Oh, I see,' cried Jezebel. 'Smithy is the United States for Smith. But Smith is not old. He's quite young.'

'Well, where is he?' demanded Danny, resignedly.

'We were captured by the beautiful men from North Midian,' explained Jezebel; 'but we escaped and ran away. We ran in different directions, but we are going to meet tonight farther south along the cliffs.'

'Beautiful men?' demanded the 'Gunner.' 'Did old Smithy let a bunch of fairies hoist him?'

'I do not understand,' said Jezebel.

'You wouldn't,' he assured her; 'but say, kid—'

'My name—'

'Aw, forget it – you know who I mean. As I was saying, let's me and you stick together till we find old Smithy. What say?'

'That will be nice, the "Gunner,"' she assured him.

'Say, call me Danny, k – Jezebel.'

'Yes, Danny.'

'Geeze, I never knew Danny was such a swell monicker till I heard you say it. What say we beat it for the big drink down there? I got me such a thirst my tongue's hanging out. Then we can come back to this here rock pile and look for old Smithy.'

'That will be nice,' agreed Jezebel. 'I, too, am thirsty.' She sighed. 'You can not know how happy I am, Danny.'

'Why?' he asked.

'Because you are with me.'

'Geeze, k – Jezebel, but you're sure a fast worker.'

'I do not know what you mean,' she replied, innocently.

'Well, just tell me why you're happy because I'm with you.'

'It is because I feel safe with you after what Smith told us. He said he always felt safe when you were around.'

'So that's it? All you want is a protection guy, eh? You don't like me for myself at all, eh?'

'Oh, of course I like you, Danny,' cried the girl. 'I think you are beautiful.'

'Yeah? Well, listen, sister. You may be a swell kidder – I dunno – or you may be just a dumb egg – but don't call me no names. I know what my pan looks like; and it ain't beautiful, and I ain't never wore a beret.'

Jezebel, who only caught the occasional high spots of Danny's conversation, made no reply; and they walked on in the direction of the lake, in silence, for some time. The forest was some little distance away, on their left, and they had no knowledge of what was transpiring there, nor did any sound reach their ears to acquaint them with the misfortune that was befalling Lady Barbara and Lafayette Smith.

At the lake they quenched their thirst, after which the 'Gunner' announced that he was going to rest for a while before he started back toward the cliffs. 'I wonder,' he said, 'just how far a guy can walk, because in the last two days I've walked that far and back again.'

'How far is that?' inquired Jezebel.

He looked at her a moment and then shook his head. 'It's twice as far,' he said, as he stretched himself at full length and closed his eyes. 'Geeze, but I'm about all in,' he murmured.

'In what?'

He deigned no reply and presently the girl noted from his altered breathing that he was asleep. She sat with her eyes glued upon him, and occasionally a deep sigh broke from her lips. She was comparing Danny with Abraham, the son of Abraham, with Lafayette Smith and with the beautiful men of North Midian; and the comparison was not uncomplimentary to Danny.

The hot sun was beating down upon them, for there was no shade here; and presently its effects, combined with her fatigue, made her drowsy. She lay down near the 'Gunner' and stretched luxuriously. Then she, too, fell asleep.

The 'Gunner' did not sleep very long; the sun was too hot. When he awoke he raised himself on an elbow and looked around. His eyes fell on the girl and there they rested for some time, noting the graceful contours of the lithe young body, the wealth of golden hair, and the exquisite face.

'The kid's sure some looker,' soliloquized Danny. 'I seen a lotta broads in my day, but I ain't never seen nothin' could touch her. She'd sure be a swell number dolled up in them Boul Mich rags. Geeze, wouldn't she knock their lamps out! I wonder where this Midian burgh is she says she comes from. If they's all as swell lookin' as her, that's the burgh for me.'

Jezebel stirred and he reached over and shook her on the shoulder. 'We'd better be beatin' it,' he said. 'We don't want to miss old Smithy and that dame.'

Jezebel sat up and looked about her. 'Oh,' she exclaimed, 'you frightened me. I thought something was coming.'

'Why? Been dreaming?'

'No. You said we'd have to beat something.'

'Aw, cheese it! I meant we'd have to be hittin' the trail for the big rocks.'

Jezebel looked puzzled.

'Hike back to them cliffs where you said old Smithy and that Lady Barbara dame were going to meet you.'

'Now I understand,' said Jezebel. 'All right, come on.'

But when they reached the cliffs there was no sign of Smith or Lady Barbara, and at Jezebel's suggestion they walked slowly southward in the direction of the place where she and the English girl had hoped to make a crossing to the outer world.

'How did you get into the valley, Danny?' asked the girl.

'I come through a big crack in the mountain,' he replied.

'That must be the same place Smith came though,' she said. 'Could you find it again?'

'Sure. That's where I'm headed for now.'

It was only midafternoon when Danny located the opening into the fissure. They had seen nothing of Lady Barbara and Smith, and they were in a quandary as to what was best to do.

'Maybe they come along and made their getaway while we was hittin' the hay,' suggested Danny.

'I don't know what you are talking about,' said Jezebel, 'but what I think is that they may have located the opening while we were asleep and gone out of the valley.'

'Well ain't that what I said?' demanded Danny.

'It didn't sound like it.'

'Say, you trying to high hat me?'

'High hat?'

'Aw, what's the use?' growled the 'Gunner' disgustedly. 'Let's me and you beat it out of this here dump and look for Smithy and the skirt on the other side. What say?'

'But suppose they haven't gone out?'

'Well, then we'll have to come back again; but I'm sure they must have. See this footprint?' He indicated one of his own, made earlier in the day, which pointed toward the valley. 'I guess I'm getting good,' he said. 'Pretty soon that Tarzan guy won't have no edge on me at all.'

'I'd like to see what's on the other side of the cliffs.' said Jezebel. 'I have always wanted to do that.'

'Well, you won't see nothin' much,' he assured her. 'Just some more scenery. They ain't even a hot dog stand or a single speakeasy.'

'What are those?'

'Well, you might call 'em filling stations.'

'What are filling stations?'

'Geeze, kid, what do you think I am, a college perfessor? I never saw anyone who could ask so many questions in my whole life.'

'My name—'

'Yes, I know what your name is. Now come on and we'll crawl through this hole-in-the-wall. I'll go first. You follow right behind me.'

The rough going along the rocky floor of the fissure taxed the 'Gunner's' endurance and his patience, but Jezebel was all excitement and anticipation. All her life she had dreamed of what might lie in the wonderworld beyond the cliffs.

Her people had told her that it was a flat expanse filled with sin, heresy, and iniquity, where, if one went too far he would surely fall over the edge and alight in the roaring flames of an eternal Hades; but Jezebel had been a doubter. She had preferred to picture it as a land of flowers and trees and running water, where beautiful people laughed and sang through long, sunny days. Soon she was to see for herself, and she was much excited by the prospect.

And now at last they came to the end of the great fissure and looked out across the rolling foothills toward a great forest in the distance.

Jezebel clasped her hands together in ecstacy. 'Oh, Danny,' she cried, 'how beautiful it is!'

'What?' asked the 'Gunner.'

'Oh, everything. Don't you think it is beautiful, Danny?'

'The only beautiful thing around here, k – Jezebel, is you,' said Danny.

The girl turned and looked up at him with her great blue eyes. 'Do you think I am beautiful, Danny?'

'Sure I do.'

'Do you think I am *too* beautiful?'

'There ain't no such thing,' he replied, 'but if they was you're it. What made you ask?'

'Lady Barbara said I was.'

The 'Gunner' considered this for some moments. 'I guess she's right at that, kid.'

'You like to call me Kid, don't you?' asked Jezebel.

'Well, it seems more friendly-like,' he explained, 'and it's easier to remember.'

'All right, you may call me Kid if you want to, but my name is Jezebel.'

'That's a bet,' said Danny. 'When I don't think to call you Jezebel, I'll call you kid, Sister.'

The girl laughed. 'You're a funny man, Danny. You like to say everything wrong. I'm not your sister, of course.'

'And I'm damn glad you ain't, kid.'

'Why? Don't you like me?'

Danny laughed. 'I never seen a kid like you before,' he said. 'You sure got me guessin'. But at that,' he added, a little seriously for him, 'they's one thing I ain't guessin' about and that's that you're a good little kid.'

'I don't know what you are talking about,' said Jezebel.

'And at that I'll bet you don't,' he replied; 'and now kid, let's sit down and rest. I'm tired.'

'I'm hungry,' said Jezebel.

'I ain't never see a skirt that wasn't but why did you have to bring that up? I'm so hungry I could heat hay.'

'Smith killed a kid and we ate some of that,' said Jezebel. 'He wrapped the rest up in the skin and I suppose he lost it when the North Midians attacked us. I wish—'

'Say,' exclaimed Danny, 'what a dumb-bell I am!' He reached down into one of his pockets and brought out several strips of raw meat. 'Here I been packin' this around all day and forgets all about it – and me starvin' to death.'

'What is it?' asked Jezebel, leaning closer to inspect the unsavory morsels.

'It's pig,' said Danny as he started searching for twigs and dry grass to build a fire, 'and I know where they is a lot more that I thought I couldn't never eat but I know now I could – even if I had to fight with the maggots for it.'

Jezebel helped him gather wood, which was extremely scarce, being limited to dead branches of a small variety of artemisia that grew on the mountain side; but at length they had collected quite a supply, and presently they were grilling pieces of boar meat over the flames. So preoccupied were they neither saw three horsemen draw rein at the top of a ridge a mile away and survey them.

'This is like housekeeping, ain't it?' remarked the 'Gunner.'

'What is that?' asked Jezebel.

'That's where a guy and his girlfriend get hitched and go to doin' their own cooking. Only in a way this is better – they ain't goin' to be no dishes to wash.'

'What is hitched, Danny?' asked Jezebel.

'Why – er,' Danny flushed. He had said many things to many girls in his life, many of them things that might have brought a blush to the cheek of a wooden Indian; but this was the first time, perhaps, that Danny had felt any embarrassment.

'Why – er,' he repeated, 'hitched means married.'

'Oh,' said Jezebel. She was silent for a while, watching the pork sizzling over the little flames. Then she looked up at Danny. 'I think housekeeping is fun,' she said.

'So do I,' agreed Danny; 'with you,' he added and his voice was just a trifle husky. His eyes were on her; and there was a strange light in them, that no other girl had ever seen there. 'You're a funny little kid,' he said presently. 'I never seen one like you before,' and then the neglected pork fell off the end of the sharpened twig, with which he had been holding it, and tumbled into the fire.

'Geeze!' exclaimed Danny. 'Look at that!' He fished the unsavory looking morsel from the ashes and flames and surveyed it. 'It don't look so good, but I'm goin' to fool it. I'm goin' to eat it anyway. I wouldn't care if a elephant had sat on it for a week – I'd eat it, and the elephant, too.'

'Oh, look!' cried Jezebel. 'Here come some men and they are all black. What strange beasts are they sitting on? Oh, Danny, I am afraid.'

At her first exclamation the 'Gunner' had turned and leaped to his feet. A single look told him who the strangers were – no strangers to him.

'Beat it, kid!' he cried. 'Duck back into the crack, and hit the trail for the valley. They can't follow you on gee-gees.'

The three *shiftas* were already close; and when they saw that they had been discovered they spurred forward at a gallop, and yet Jezebel stood beside the little fire, wide eyed and frightened. She had not understood the strange argot that the 'Gunner' employed in lieu of English. 'Beat it' and 'duck' and 'hit the trail' had not been included in the English idiom she had gleaned from Lady Barbara Collis. But even had she understood him it would have made no difference, for Jezebel was not of the clay that is soft in the face of danger, her little feet not of the kind that run away, leaving a companion in distress.

The 'Gunner' glanced behind him and saw her. 'For God's sake run, kid,' he cried. 'These are tough guys. I know 'em,' then the *shiftas* were upon him.

To conserve ammunition, which was always scarce and difficult to obtain, they tried to ride him down, striking at him with their rifles. He dodged the leading horseman; and as the fellow reined in to wheel his mount back to the attack, the 'Gunner' leaped to his side and dragged him from the saddle. The mount of the second *shifta* stumbled over the two men and fell unhorsing its rider.

The 'Gunner' seized the long rifle that had fallen from the hands of the man he had dragged down and scrambled to his feet. Jezebel watched him in wide eyed wonder and admiration. She saw him swing the rifle like a club and strike at the third horseman, and then she saw the one he had first grappled lunge forward and, seizing him around the legs, drag him down, while the second to be unhorsed ran in now and leaped upon him just as the remaining *shifta* struck him a heavy blow on the head.

As she saw him fall, the blood gushing from an ugly wound in his head, Jezebel ran forward to him; but the *shiftas* seized her. She was thrown to the back of a horse in front of one of them, the others mounted, and the three galloped away with their prisoner, leaving Danny 'Gunner' Patrick lying motionless in a welter of his own blood.

XIX

In the Village of Elija

As Tarzan approached the village of Abraham, the son of Abraham, he was seen by a watcher who immediately warned his fellows, with the result that when the ape-man arrived the huts were deserted, the villagers having taken refuge in the caves in the face of the towering cliff.

Abraham, the son of Abraham, from the safety of the highest cave, exhorted his people to repel the advance of this strange creature, whose partial nakedness and strange armament filled him with alarm, with the result that when Tarzan came near the base of the cliff the villagers, with much shouting, rolled rocks down the steep declivity in an effort to destroy him.

The Lord of the Jungle looked up at the howling creatures above him. Whatever his emotions his face did not reveal them. Doubtless contempt was predominant, for he read in the reception of him only fear and cowardice.

As naught but curiosity had prompted his visit to this strange village, since he knew that Smith already had quitted it, he remained only long enough for a brief survey of the people and their culture, neither of which was sufficiently attractive to detain him; and then he turned and retracted his steps toward the place on the shore of Chinnereth where he had picked up the northbound spoor of Smith and Lady Barbara and Jezebel.

He made his way in a leisurely manner, stopping beside the lake to quench his thirst and eat from his small store of boar meat; and then he lay down to rest, after the manner of beasts who have fed and are not hurried.

In the village he had quitted Abraham, the son of Abraham, gave thanks to Jehovah for their deliverance from the barbarian, though reserving proper credit to himself for his masterly defense of his flock.

And how fared it with Lady Barbara and Lafayette Smith? Following their recapture they were permitted no second opportunity to escape, as, heavily guarded, they were conducted northward toward the village of Elija, the son of Noah.

The girl was much depressed; and Smith sought to reassure her, though upon what grounds he himself could scarcely explain.

'I cannot believe that they intend to harm us,' he said. 'We have done nothing worse than kill one of their goats and that only because we were starving. I can pay them whatever price they name for the animal, and thus they will be recompensed and have no further cause for complaint against us.'

'With what will you pay them?' asked Lady Barbara.

'I have money,' replied Smith.

'Of what good would it be to them?'

'Of what good would it be to them! Why they could buy another goat if they wanted to,' he replied.

'These people know nothing of money,' she said. 'It would be worthless to them.'

'I suppose you are right,' he admitted. 'I hadn't thought of that. Well, I could give them my pistol, then.'

'They already have it.'

'But it's mine,' he exclaimed. 'They'll have to give it back to me.'

She shook her head. 'You are not dealing with civilized people guided by the codes and customs of civilization or responsible to the law-enforcing agencies with which we are familiar and which, perhaps, are all that keep us civilized.'

'We escaped once,' he ventured; 'perhaps we can escape again.'

'That, I think, is our only hope.'

The village of the North Midians, where they presently arrived, was more pretentious than that of the people at the southern end of the valley. While there were many crude huts there were also several of stone, while the entire appearance of the village was more cleanly and prosperous.

Several hundred villagers came to meet the party as soon as it was sighted, and the prisoners noted that there was no evidence of the degeneracy and disease which were such marked characteristics of the South Midians. On the contrary, these people appeared endowed with abundant health, they looked intelligent and, physically, they were a splendid race, many of them being handsome. All were golden haired and blue eyed. That they were descended from the same stock that had produced Abraham, the son of Abraham, and his degraded flock would have appeared impossible, yet such was the fact.

The women and children pushed and jostled one another and the men in their efforts to get close to the prisoners. They jabbered and laughed incessantly, the clothing of the prisoners seeming to arouse the greatest wonder and mirth.

Their language being practically the same as that of the South Midians Lady Barbara had no difficulty in understanding what they were saying, and from scraps of their conversation which she overheard she realized that her worst fears might be realized. However, the crowd offered them no personal injury; and it was apparent that in themselves they were not inherently a cruel people, though their religion and their customs evidently prescribed harsh treatment for enemies who fell into their hands.

Upon arrival in the village Lady Barbara and Smith were separated. She was taken to a hut and put in the charge of a young woman, while Smith was confined, under guard of several men, in another.

Lady Barbara's jailer, far from being ill favored, was quite beautiful, bearing a strong resemblance to Jezebel; and she proved to be quite as loquacious as the men who had captured them.

'You are the strangest looking South Midian I ever saw,' she remarked, 'and the man does not look at all like one. Your hair is neither the color of those they keep nor of those they destroy – it is just between, and your garments are such as no one ever saw before.'

'We are not Midians,' said Lady Barbara.

'But that is impossible,' cried the woman. 'There are none but Midians in the land of Midian and no way to get in or out. Some say there are people beyond the great cliffs, and some say there are only devils. If you are not a Midian perhaps you are a devil; but then, of course, you are a Midian.'

'We come from a country beyond the cliffs,' Lady Barbara told her, 'and all we want is to go back to our own country.'

'I do not think Elija will let you. He will treat you as we always treat South Midians.'

'And how is that?'

'The men are put to death because of their heresy; and the women, if they are good looking, are kept as slaves. But being a slave is not bad. I am a slave. My mother was a slave. She was a South Midian who was captured by my father who owned her. She was very beautiful. After a while the South Midians would have killed her, as you do to all your beautiful women just before their first child is born.

'But we are different. We kill the bad looking ones, both boys and girls, and also any who become subject to the strange demons which afflict the South Midians. Do you have these demons?'

'I am not a Midian, I told you,' said Lady Barbara.

The woman shook her head. 'It is true that you do not look like them, but if Elija ever believes you are not you are lost.'

'Why?' asked Lady Barbara.

'Elija is one of those who believe that the world beyond the cliffs is inhabited by demons; so, if you are not a South Midian, you must be a demon; and he would certainly destroy you as he will destroy the man; but for my part I am one of those who say they do not know. Some say that perhaps this world around Midian is inhabited by angels. Are you an angel?'

'I am not a demon,' replied Lady Barbara.

'Then you must be a South Midian or an angel.'

'I am no South Midian,' insisted the English girl.

'Then you are an angel,' reasoned the woman, 'And if you are you will have no difficulty in proving it.'

'How?'

'Just perform a miracle.'

'Oh,' said Lady Barbara.

'Is the man an angel?' demanded the woman.

'He is an American.'

'I never heard of that – is it a kind of angel?'

'Europeans do not call them that.'

'But really I think Elija will say he is a South Midian, and he will be destroyed.'

'Why do your people hate the South Midians so?' asked Lady Barbara.

'They are heretics.'

'They are very religious,' said Lady Barbara; 'they pray all the time to Jehovah and they never smile. Why do you think them heretics?'

'They insist that Paul's hair was black, while we know that it was yellow. They are very wicked, blasphemous people. Once, long before the memory of man, we were all one people; but there were many wicked heretics among us who had black hair and wished to kill all those with yellow hair; so those with yellow hair ran away and came to the north end of the valley. Ever since, the North Midians have killed all those with black hair and the South Midians all those with yellow hair. Do you think Paul had yellow hair?'

'Certainly I do,' said Lady Barbara.

'That will be a point in your favor,' said the woman.

Just then a man came to the door of the hut and summoned Lady Barbara. 'Come with me,' he commanded.

The English girl followed the messenger, and the woman who had been guarding her accompanied them. Before a large stone hut they found Elija surrounded by a number of the older men of the village, while the remainder of the population was grouped in a semi-circle facing them. Lafayette Smith stood before Elija, and Lady Barbara was conducted to the side of the American.

Elija, the Prophet, was a middle aged man of not unprepossessing appearance. He was short and stocky, extremely muscular in build, and his face was adorned with a wealth of blond whiskers. Like the other North Midians he was garbed in a single garment of goat skin, his only ornament being the pistol he had taken from Smith, which he wore on a leather thong that encircled his neck.

'This man,' said Elija, addressing Lady Barbara, 'will not talk. He makes noises, but they mean nothing. Why will he not talk?'

'He does not understand the language of the land of Midian,' replied the English girl.

'He must understand it,' insisted Elija; 'everyone understands it.'

'He is not from Midian,' said Lady Barbara.

'Then he must be a demon,' said Elija.

'Perhaps he is an angel,' suggested Lady Barbara; 'he believes that Paul's hair was yellow.'

This statement precipitated a wordy argument and so impressed Elija and his apostles that they withdrew into the interior of the hut for a secret conference.

'What's it all about, Lady Barbara?' asked Smith, who, of course, had understood nothing of what had been said.

'You believe Paul's hair was yellow, don't you?' she asked.

'I don't know what you are talking about.'

'Well, I told them you were a firm believer in the yellowness of Paul's hair.'

'Why did you tell them that?' demanded Smith.

'Because the North Midians prefer blonds,' she replied.

'But who is Paul?'

'Was, you mean. He is dead.'

'Of course I'm sorry to hear that, but who *was* he?' insisted the American.

'I am afraid you have neglected the scriptures,' she told him.

'Oh, the apostle; but what difference does it make what color his hair was?'

'It doesn't make any difference,' she explained. 'What does make a difference is that you have stated, through me, that you believe he had yellow hair; and that may be the means of saving your life.'

'What nonsense!'

'Of course – the other fellow's religion is always nonsense; but not to him. You are also suspected of being an angel. Can you imagine!'

'No! Who suspects me?'

'It was I; or at least I suggested it, and I am hoping Elija will now suspect it. If he does we are both safe, provided that, in your celestial capacity, you will intercede for me.'

'You are as good as saved then,' he said, 'for inasmuch as I cannot speak their language you can put any words you wish into my mouth without fear of being called to account.'

'That's a fact, isn't it?' she said, laughing. 'If our emergency were not so critical I could have a lot of fun, couldn't?'

'You seem to find fun in everything,' he replied, admiringly; 'even in the face of disaster.'

'Perhaps I am whistling in the dark,' she said.

They talked a great deal while they waited for Elija and the apostles to return, for it helped them to tide over the anxious minutes of nervous strain that slowly dragged into hours. They could hear the chatter and buzz of conversation within the hut, as Elija and his fellows debated, while, outside, the villagers kept up a constant babel of conversation.

'They like to talk,' commented Smith.

'And perhaps you have noticed an idiosyncrasy of the North Midians in this respect?' she asked.

'Lots of people like to talk.'

'I mean that the men gabble more than the women.'

'Perhaps in self-defense.'

'Here they come!' she exclaimed as Elija appeared in the doorway of the hut, fingering the pistol he wore as an ornament.

Darkness was already falling as the Prophet and the twelve apostles filed out to their places in the open. Elija raised his hands in a signal for silence and when quiet had been restored he spoke.

'With the aid of Jehovah,' he said, 'we have wrestled with a mighty question. There were some among us who contend that this man is a South Midian, and others that he is an angel. Mighty was the weight of the statement that he believes that Paul had yellow hair, for if such is the truth then indeed he is not a heretic; and if he is no heretic he is not a South Midian, for they, as all the world knows, are heretics. Yet again, it was brought forth that if he is a demon he might still claim that he believed in the yellowness of Paul, in order that he might deceive us.

'How were we to know? We must know lest we, through our ignorance, do sin against one of His angels and bring down the wrath of Jehovah upon our heads.

'But at last I, Elija, the son of Noah, True Prophet of Paul, the son of Jehovah, discovered the truth. The man is no angel! The revelation descended upon me in a burst of glory from Jehovah Himself – the man cannot be an angel because he has no wings!'

There was an immediate burst of 'Amens' and 'Hallelujahs' from the assembled villagers, while Lady Barbara went cold with dread.

'Therefore,' continued Elija, 'he must be either a South Midian or a demon, and in either case he must be destroyed.'

Lady Barbara turned a pale face toward Lafayette Smith – pale even through its coating of tan. Her lip trembled, just a little. It was the first indication of a weaker, feminine emotion that Smith had seen this remark-able girl display.

'What is it?' he asked. 'Are they going to harm you?'

'It is you, my dear friend,' she replied. 'You must escape.'

'But how?' he asked.

'Oh, I don't know; I don't know,' she cried, 'There is only one way. You will have to make a break for it – now. It is dark. They will not expect it. I will do something to engage their attention, and then you make a dash for the forest.'

He shook his head. 'No,' he said. 'We shall go together, or I do not go.'

'Please,' she begged, 'or it will be too late.'

Elija had been talking to one of his apostles, and now he raised his voice again so that all might hear. 'Lest we have mistaken the divine instructions of Jehovah,' he said, 'we shall place this man in the mercy of Jehovah and as Jehovah wills so shall it be. Make ready the grave. If he is indeed an angel he will arise unharmed.'

'Oh, go; please go!' cried Lady Barbara.

'What did he say?' demanded Smith.

'They are going to bury you alive,' she cried.

'And you,' he asked; 'what are they going to do to you?'

'I am to be held in slavery.'

With sharpened sticks and instruments of bone and stone a number of men were already engaged in excavating a grave in the center of the village street before the hut of Elija, who stood waiting its completion surrounded by his apostles. The Prophet was still toying with his new found ornament, concerning the purpose and mechanism of which he was wholly ignorant.

Lady Barbara was urging Smith to attempt escape while there was yet an opportunity, and the American was considering the best plan to adopt.

'You will have to come with me,' he said. 'I think if we make a sudden break right back through the village toward the cliffs we shall find our best chance for success. There are fewer people congregated on that side.'

From the darkness beyond the village on the forest side a pair of eyes watched the proceedings taking place before the hut of Elija. Slowly, silently the owner of the eyes crept closer until he stood in the shadow of a hut at the edge of the village.

Suddenly Smith, seizing Lady Barbara's hand, started at a run toward the north side of the village; and so unexpected was his break for liberty that, for a moment, no hand was raised to stay him; but an instant later, at a cry from Elija, the entire band leaped in pursuit, while from the shadow of the hut where he had stood concealed the watcher slipped forward into the village where he stood near the hut of Elija watching the pursuit of the escaped pris-oners. He was alone, for the little central compound of the village had emptied as by magic, even the women and children having joined in the chase.

Smith ran swiftly, holding tightly to the girl's hand; and close on their heels came the leaders of the pursuit. No longer did the village fires light their way; and only darkness loomed ahead, as the moon had not yet risen.

Gradually the American bore to the left, intending to swing in a half circle toward the south. There was yet a chance that they might make good their escape if they could outdistance the nearer of their pursuers until they reached the forest, for their strait gave them both speed and endurance far above normal.

But just as success seemed near they entered a patch of broken lava rock, invisible in the darkness; and Smith stumbled and fell, dragging Lady Barbara down with him. Before they could scramble to their feet the leading Midian was upon them.

The American freed himself for a moment and struggled to his feet; and again the fellow sought to seize him, but Smith swung a heavy blow to his chin and felled him.

Brief, however, was this respite, for almost immediately both the American and the English girl were overwhelmed by superior numbers and once again found themselves captives, though Smith fought until he was overpowered, knocking his antagonists to right and left.

Miserably dejected, they were dragged back to the village compound, their last hope gone; and again the Midians gathered around the open grave to witness the torture of their victim.

Smith was conducted to the edge of the excavation, where he was held by two stalwart men, while Elija raised his voice in prayer, and the remainder of the assemblage knelt, bursting forth occasionally with hallelujahs and amens.

When he had concluded his long prayer the Prophet paused. Evidently there was something on his mind which vexed him. In fact it was the pistol which dangled from the thong about his neck. He was not quite sure of its purpose, and he was about to destroy the only person who might tell him.

To Elija the pistol was quite the most remarkable possession that had ever fallen into his hands, and he was filled with a great curiosity concerning it. It might be, he argued, some magic talisman for averting evil, or, upon the other hand, it might be the charm of a demon or a sorcerer, that would work evil upon him. At that thought he quickly removed the thong from about his neck, but he still held the weapon in his hand.

'What is this?' he demanded, turning to Lady Barbara and exhibiting the pistol.

'It is a weapon,' she said. 'Be careful or it will kill someone.'

'How does it kill?' asked Elija.

'What is he saying?' demanded Smith.

'He is asking how the pistol kills,' replied the girl.

A brilliant idea occurred to the American. 'Tell him to give it to me, and I will show him,' he said.

But when she translated the offer to Elija he demurred. 'He could then kill me with it,' he said, shrewdly.

'He won't give it to you,' the girl told Smith. 'He is afraid you want to kill him.'

'I do,' replied the man.

'Tell him,' said Elija, 'to explain to me how I may kill someone with it.'

'Repeat my instructions to him very carefully,' said Smith, after Lady Barbara had translated the demand of the prophet. 'Tell him how to grasp the pistol,' and when Lady Barbara had done so and Elija held the weapon by the grip in his right hand, 'now tell him to place his index finger through the guard, but warn him not to pull the trigger.'

Elija did as he was bid. 'Now,' continued Smith, 'explain to him that in order to see how the weapon operates he should place one eye to the muzzle and look down the barrel.'

'But I can see nothing,' expostulated Elija when he had done as Lady Barbara directed. 'It is quite dark down the little hole.'

'He says it is too dark in the barrel for him to see anything,' repeated Lady Barbara ot the American.

'Explain to him that if he pulls the trigger there will be a light in the barrel,' said Smith.

'But that will be murder,' exclaimed the girl.

'It is war,' said Smith, 'and in the subsequent confusion we may escape.'

Lady Barbara steeled herself. 'You could see nothing because you did not press the little piece of metal beneath your index finger,' she explained to Elija.

'What will that do?' demanded the prophet.

'It will make a light in the little hole,' said Lady Barbara.

Elija again placed his eye against the muzzle; and this time he pulled the trigger; and as the report cracked the tense silence of the watching villagers Elija, the son of Noah, pitched forward upon his face.

Instantly Lady Barbara sprang toward Smith, who simultaneously sought to break away from the grip of the men who held him; but they, although astonished at what had occurred, were not to be caught off their guard, and though he struggled desperately they held him.

For an instant there was hushed silence; and then pandemonium broke loose as the villagers realized that their prophet was dead, slain by the wicked charm of a demon; but at the very outset of their demands for vengeance their attention was distracted by a strange and remarkable figure that sprang from the hut of Elija, stooped and picked up the pistol that had fallen from the hands of the dead man, and leaped to the side of the prisoner struggling with his guards.

This was such a man as none of them had ever seen – a giant white man with a tousled shock of black hair and with grey eyes that sent a shiver through them, so fierce and implacable were they. Naked he was but for a loin cloth of skin, and the muscles that rolled beneath his brown hide were muscles such as they never had seen before.

As the newcomer sprang toward the American one of the men guarding Smith, sensing that an attempt was being made to rescue the prisoner, swung his club in readiness to deal a blow against the strange creature advancing upon him. At the same time the other guard sought to drag Smith from the compound.

The American did not at first recognize Tarzan of the Apes, yet, though he was not aware that the stranger was bent upon his rescue, he sensed that he was an enemy of the Midians, and so struggled to prevent his guard from forcing him away.

Another Midian seized Lady Barbara with the intention of carrying her from the scene, for all the villagers believed that the strange giant was a friend of the prisoners and had come to effect their release.

Smith was successful in tearing himself free from the man who held him, and immediately sprang to the girl's assistance, felling her captor with a single blow, just as Tarzan levelled the American's pistol at the guard who was preparing to cudgel him.

The sound of this second shot and the sight of their fellow dropping to the ground, as had Elija, filled the Midians with consternation; and for a moment they fell back from the three, leaving them alone in the center of the compound.

'Quick!' called Tarzan to Smith. 'You and the girl get out of here before they recover from their surprise. I will follow you. That way,' he added, pointing toward the south.

As Lafayette Smith and Lady Barbara hurried from the village Tarzan backed slowly after them, keeping the little pistol in full view of the frightened villagers, who, having seen two of their number die beneath its terrifying magic, were loath to approach it too closely.

Until out of range of a thrown club Tarzan continued his slow retreat; then he wheeled and bounded off into the night in pursuit of Lafayette Smith and Lady Barbara Collis.

XX

The Best Three out of Five

Though Jezebel was terrified by the black faces of her captors and by the strange beasts they bestrode, the like of which she had never even imagined, her fear for herself was outweighed by her sorrow. Her one thought was to escape and return to the side of the 'Gunner', even though she believed him dead from the terrific blow that his assailant had struck him.

She struggled violently to free herself from the grasp of the man in front of whom she rode; but the fellow was far too powerful; and, though she was difficult to hold, at no time was there the slightest likelihood that she might escape. Her efforts, however, angered him and at last he struck her, bringing to the girl a realization of the futility of pitting her puny strength against his. She must wait, then, until she could accomplish by stealth what she could not effect by force.

The village of the raiders lay but a short distance from the point at which she had been captured, and but a few minutes had elapsed since that event when they rode up to its gates and into the central compound.

The shouts that greeted the arrival of a new and beautiful prisoner brought Capietro and Stabutch to the doorway of their hut.

'Now what have the black devils brought in?' exclaimed Capietro.

'It looks like a young woman,' said Stabutch.

'It is,' cried Capietro, as the *shiftas* approached the hut with their prisoner. 'We shall have company, eh, Stabutch? Who have you there, my children?' he demanded of the three who were accompanying Jezebel.

'The price of a chief's ransom, perhaps,' replied one of the blacks.

'Where did you find her?'

'Above the village a short distance, when we were returning from scouting. A man was with her. The man who escaped with the help of the ape-man.'

'Where is he! Why did you not bring him, also?' demanded Capietro.

'He fought us, and we were forced to kill him.'

'You have done well,' said Capietro. 'She is worth two of him – in many ways. Come girl, hold up your head, let us have a look at that pretty face. Come, you need not fear anything – if you are a good girl you will find Dominic Capietro a good fellow.'

'Perhaps she does not understand Italian,' suggested Stabutch.

'You are right, my friend; I shall speak to her in English.'

Jezebel had looked up at Stabutch when she heard him speak a language she understood. Perhaps this man would be a friend, she thought; but when she saw his face her heart sank.

'What a beauty!' ejaculated the Russian.

'You have fallen in love with her quickly, my friend,' commented Capietro. 'Do you want to buy her?'

'How much do you want for her?'

'Friends should not bargain,' said the Italian. 'Wait, I have it! Come, girl,' and he took Jezebel by the arm and led her into the hut, where Stabutch followed them.

'Why was I brought here?' asked Jezebel. 'I have not harmed you. Let me go back to Danny; he is hurt.'

'He is dead,' said Capietro; 'but don't you grieve, little one. You now have two friends in place of the one you have lost. Soon you will forget him; it is easy for a woman to forget.'

'I shall never forget him,' cried Jezebel. 'I want to go back to him – perhaps he is not dead.' Then she broke down and cried.

Stabutch stood eyeing the girl hungrily. Her youth and her beauty aroused a devil within him, and he made a mental vow that he would possess her. 'Do not cry,' he said, kindly. 'I am your friend. Everything will be all right.'

The new tone in his voice gave hope to Jezebel, and she looked up at him gratefully. 'If you are my friend,' she said, 'take me away from here and back to Danny.'

'After a while,' replied Stabutch, and then to Capietro, 'How much?'

'I shall not sell her to my good friend,' replied the Italian. 'Let us have a drink, and then I shall explain my plan.'

The two drank from a bottle standing on the earth floor of the hut. 'Sit down,' said Capietro, waving Jezebel to a seat on the dirty rug. Then he searched for a moment in his duffle bag and brought out a deck of soiled and grimy cards. 'Be seated, my friend,' he said to Stabutch. 'Let us have another drink, and then you shall hear my plan.'

Stabutch drank from the bottle and wiped his lips with the back of his hand. 'Well,' he said, 'what is it?'

'We shall play for her,' exclaimed the Italian, shuffling the deck, 'and whoever wins, keeps her.'

'Let us drink to that,' said Stabutch. 'Five games, eh, and the first to win three takes her?'

'Another drink to seal the bargain!' exclaimed the Italian. 'The best three out of five!'

Stabutch won the first game, while Jezebel sat looking on in ignorance of the purpose of the bits of pasteboard, and only knowing that in some way they were to decide her fate. She hoped the younger man would win, but only because he had said that he was her friend. Perhaps she could persuade him to take her back to Danny. She wondered what kind of water was in the bottle from which they drank, for she noticed that it wrought a change in them. They talked much louder now and shouted strange words when the little cards were thrown upon the rug, and then one would appear very angry while the other always laughed immoderately. Also they swayed and lurched in a peculiar manner that she had not noticed before they had drunk so much of the water from the bottle.

Capietro won the second game and the third. Stabutch was furious, but now he became very quiet. He exerted all his powers of concentration upon the game, and he seemed almost sober as the cards were dealt for the fourth game.

'She is as good as mine!' cried Capietro, as he looked at his hand.

'She will never be yours,' growled the Russian.

'What do you mean?'

'I shall win the next two games.'

The Italian laughed loudly. 'That is good!' he cried. 'We should drink to that.' He raised the bottle to his lips and then passed it to Stabutch.

'I do not want a drink,' said the Russian, in a surly tone, pushing the bottle aside.

'Ah, ha! My friend is getting nervous. He is afraid he is going to lose and so he will not drink. Sapristi! It is all the same to me. I get the brandy and the girl, too.'

'Play!' snapped Stabutch.

'You are in a hurry to lose,' taunted Capietro.

'To win,' corrected Stabutch, and he did.

Now it was the Italian's turn to curse and rage at luck, and once again the cards were dealt and the players picked up their hands.

'It is the last game,' said Stabutch.

'We have each won two,' replied Capietro. 'Let us drink to the winner – although I dislike proposing a toast to myself,' and he laughed again, but this time there was an ugly note in his laughter.

In silence, now, they resumed their play. One by one the little pasteboards fell upon the rug. The girl looked on in wondering silence. There was a tenseness in the situation that she felt, without understanding. Poor little Jezebel, she understood so little!

Suddenly, with a triumphant oath, Capietro sprang to his feet. 'I win!' he cried. 'Come, friend, drink with me to my good fortune.'

Sullenly the Russian drank, a very long draught this time. There was a sinister gleam in his eye as he handed the bottle back to Capietro. Leon Stabutch was a poor loser.

The Italian emptied the bottle and flung it to the ground. Then he turned toward Jezebel and, stooping, lifted her to her feet. 'Come, my dear,' he said, his coarse voice thick from drink, 'Give me a kiss.'

Jezebel drew back, but the Italian jerked her roughly to him and tried to draw her lips to his.

'Leave the girl alone,' growled Stabutch. 'Can't you see she is afraid of you?'

'What did I win her for?' demanded Capietro. 'To leave her alone? Mind your own business.'

'I'll make it my business,' said Stabutch. 'Take your hands off her.' He stepped forward and laid a hand on Jezebel's arm. 'She is mine by rights anyway.'

'What do you mean?'

'You cheated. I caught you at it in the last game.'

'You lie!' shouted Capietro and simultaneously he struck at Stabutch. The Russian dodged the blow and closed with the other.

Both were drunk and none too steady. It required much of their attention to keep from falling down. But as they wrestled about the interior of the hut a few blows were struck – enough to arouse their rage to fury and partially to sober them. Then the duel became deadly, as each sought the throat of the other.

Jezebel, wide eyed and terrified, had difficulty in keeping out of their way as they fought to and fro across the floor of the hut; and so centered was the attention of the two men upon one another that the girl might have escaped had she not been more afraid of the black men without than of the whites within.

Several times Stabutch released his hold with his right hand and sought for something beneath his coat and at last he found it – a slim dagger. Capietro did not see it.

They were standing in the center of the hut now, their arms locked about one another, and resting thus as though by mutual consent. They were panting heavily from their exertions, and neither seemed to have gained any material advantage.

Slowly the Russian's right hand crept up the back of his adversary. Jezebel saw, but only her eyes reflected her horror. Though she had seen many people killed she yet had a horror of killing. She saw the Russian feel for a spot on the other's back with the point of his thumb. Then she saw him turn his hand and place the dagger point where his thumb had been.

There was a smile upon Stabutch's face as he drove the blade home. Capietro stiffened, screamed, and died. As the body slumped to the ground and rolled over on its back the murderer stood over the corpse of his victim, a smile upon his lips, and his eyes upon the girl.

But suddenly the smile died as a new thought came to the cunning mind of the slayer and his eyes snapped from the face of Jezebel to the doorway of the hut where a filthy blanket answered the purpose of a door.

He had forgotten the horde of cut-throats who had called this thing upon the floor their chief! But now he recalled them and his soul was filled with terror. He did not need to ask himself what his fate would be when they discovered his crime.

'You have murdered him!' cried the girl suddenly, a note of horror in her voice.

'Be quiet!' snapped Stabutch. 'Do you want to die? They will kill us when they discover this.'

'I did not do it,' protested Jezebel.

'They will kill you just the same – afterwards. They are beasts.'

Suddenly he stooped, seized the corpse by the ankles and, dragging it to the far end of the hut, he covered it with rugs and clothing.

'Now keep quiet until I come back,' he said to Jezebel. 'If you give an alarm I'll kill you myself before they have a chance to.'

He rummaged in a dark corner of the hut and brought forth a revolver with its holster and belt, which he buckled about his hips, and a rifle which he leaned beside the doorway.

'When I return be ready to come with me,' he snapped, and raising the rug that covered the doorway, he stepped out into the village.

Quickly he made his way to where the ponies of the band were tethered. Here were several of the blacks loitering near the animals.

'Where is the headman?' he asked, but none of them understood English. He tried to tell them by means of signs, to saddle two horses, but they only shook their heads. If they understood him, as they doubtless did, they refused to take orders from him.

At this juncture the headman, attracted from a nearby hut, approached. He understood a little pidgin English, and Stabutch had no difficulty in making him understand that he wanted two horses saddled; but the headman wanted to know more. Did the chief want them?

'Yes, he wants them,' replied Stabutch. 'He sent me to get them. The chief is sick. Drink too much.' Stabutch laughed and the headman seemed to understand.

'Who go with you?' asked the headman.

Stabutch hesitated. Well, he might as well tell him – everyone would see the girl ride out with him anyway. 'The girl,' he said.

The headman's eyes narrowed. 'The Chief say?' he asked.

'Yes. The girl thinks the white man not dead. The Chief send me to look for him.'

'You take men?'

'No. Man come back with us if girl say so. Be afraid of black men. No come.'

The other nodded understandingly and ordered two horses saddled and bridled. 'Him dead,' he offered.

Stabutch shrugged. 'We see,' he replied, as he led the two animals toward the hut where Jezebel awaited him.

The headman accompanied him, and Stabutch was in terror. What if the man insisted on entering the hut to see his chief? Stabutch loosened the revolver in its holster. Now his greatest fear was that the shot might attract others to the hut. That would never do. He must find some other way. He stopped and the headman halted with him.

'Do not come to the hut yet,' said Stabutch.

'Why?' asked the headman.

'The girl is afraid. If she sees you she will think we are deceiving her, and she may refuse to show me where the man is. We promised her that no black man would come.'

The headman hesitated. Then he shrugged and turned back. 'All right,' he said.

'And tell them to leave the gates open till we have gone,' called Stabutch.

At the hut door he called to the girl. 'All ready,' he said, 'and hand me my rifle when you come out;' but she did not know what a rifle was and he had to step in and get it himself.

Jezebel looked at the horses with dismay.

At the thought of riding one of these strange beasts alone she was terrified. 'I cannot do it,' she told Stabutch.

'You will have to – or die,' he whispered. 'I'll lead the one you ride. Here, hurry.'

He lifted her into the saddle and showed her how to use the stirrups and hold the reins. Then he put a rope about the neck of her horse; and, mounting his own, he led hers out through the village gateway while half a hundred murderers watched them depart.

As they turned upward toward the higher hills the setting sun projected their shadows far ahead, and presently night descended upon them and hid their sudden change of direction from any watchers there may have been at the village gates.

XXI

An Awakening

Danny 'Gunner' Patrick opened his eyes and stared up at the blue African sky. Slowly consciousness returned and with it the realization that his head pained severely. He raised a hand and felt of it. What was that? He looked at his hand and saw that it was bloody.

'Geeze!' he muttered. 'They got me!' He tried to recall how it had happened. 'I knew the finger was on me, but how the hell did they get me? Where was I?' His thoughts were all back in Chicago, and he was puzzled. Vaguely he felt that he had made his get-away, and yet they had 'got' him. He could not figure it out.

Then he turned his head slightly and saw lofty mountains looming near. Slowly and painfully he sat up and looked around. Memory, partial and fragmentary, returned. 'I must have fell off them mountains,' he mused, 'while I was lookin' for camp.'

Gingerly he rose to his feet and was relieved to find that he was not seriously injured – at least his arms and legs were intact. 'My head never was much good. Geeze, it hurts, though.'

A single urge dominated him – he must find camp. Old Smithy would be worrying about him if he did not return. Where was Obambi? 'I wonder if the dinge fell off too,' he muttered, looking about him. But Obambi, neither dead nor alive, was in sight; and so the 'Gunner' started upon his fruitless search for camp.

At first he wandered toward the northwest, directly away from Smith's last camp. Tongani, the baboon, sitting upon his sentinel rock, saw him coming and sounded the alarm. At first Danny saw only a couple of 'monkeys' coming toward him, barking and growling. He saw them stop occasionally and place the backs of their heads against the ground and he mentally classified them as 'nutty monks;' but when their numbers were swollen to a hundred and he finally realized the potential danger lying in those powerful jaws and sharp fangs, he altered his course and turned toward the southwest.

For a short distance the tongani followed him, but when they saw that he intended them no harm they let him proceed and returned to their interrupted feeding, while the man, with a sigh of relief, continued on his way.

In a ravine Danny found water, and with the discovery came a realization of his thirst and his hunger. He drank at the same pool at which Tarzan had slain Horta, the boar; and he also washed the blood from his head and face as well as he could. Then he continued on his aimless wandering. This time he climbed higher up the slope toward the mountains, in a southeasterly direction, and was headed at last toward the location of the now abandoned camp. Chance and the tongani had set him upon the right trail.

In a short time he reached a spot that seemed familiar; and here he stopped and looked around in an effort to recall his wandering mental faculties, which he fully realized were not functioning properly.

'That bat on the bean sure knocked me cuckoo,' he remarked, half aloud. 'Geeze, what's that?' Something was moving in the tall grass through which he had just come. He watched intently and a moment later saw the head of

Sheeta, the panther, parting the grasses a short distance from him. The scene was suddenly familiar.

'I gotcha Steve!' exclaimed the 'Gunner.' 'Me and that Tarzan guy flopped here last night – now I remember.'

He also remembered how Tarzan had chased the panther away by 'running a bluff on him,' and he wondered if he could do the same thing.

'Geeze, what a ornery lookin' pan! I'll bet you got a rotten disposition – and that Tarzan guy just growled and ran at you, and you beat it. Say, I don't believe it, if I did see it myself. Whyinell don't you go on about your business, you big stiff? You give me the heeby-jeebies.' He stooped and picked up a fragment of rock. 'Beat it!' he yelled, as he hurled the missile at Sheeta.

The great cat wheeled and bounded away, disappearing in the tall grass that the 'Gunner' could now see waving along the path of the panther's retreat. 'Well, what do you know about that?' ejaculated Danny. 'I done it! Geeze, these lions ain't so much.'

His hunger now claimed his attention as his returning memory suggested a means of appeasing it. 'I wonder could I do it?' he mused, as he hunted around on the ground until he had found a thin fragment of rock, with which he commenced to scrape away the dirt from a loose heap that rose a few inches above the contour of the surrounding ground. 'I wonder could I!'

His digging soon revealed the remains of the boar Tarzan had cached against their possible return. With his pocket knife the 'Gunner' hacked off several pieces, after which he scraped the dirt back over the body and busied himself in the preparation of a fire, where he grilled the meat in a sketchy fashion that produced culinary results which ordinarily would have caused him to turn up his nose in disgust. But today he was far from particular and bolted the partially cooked and partially charred morsels like a ravenous wolf.

His memory had returned now up to the point of the meal he had eaten at this same spot with Tarzan – from there on until he had regained consciousness a short time before, it was a blank. He knew now that he could find his way back to camp from the point above the raiders' village where he and Obambi had lunched, and so he turned his footsteps in that direction.

When he had found the place, he crept on down to the edge of the cliff where it overlooked the village; and here he lay down to rest and to spy upon the raiders, for he was very tired.

'The lousy bums!' he ejaculated beneath his breath, as he saw the *shiftas* moving about the village. 'I wish I had my typewriter, I'd clean up that dump.'

He saw Stabutch emerge from a hut and walk down to the horses. He watched him while he talked to the blacks there and to the headman. Then he saw the Russian leading two saddled horses back to the hut.

'That guy don't know it,' he muttered, 'but the finger is sure on him. I'll get him on the spot some day if it takes the rest of my natural life. Geeze, glom the broad!' Stabutch had summoned Jezebel from the hut. Suddenly a strange thing happened inside the head of Danny 'Gunner' Patrick. It was as though someone had suddenly raised a window shade and let in a flood of light. He saw everything perfectly now in retrospection. With the sight of Jezebel his memory had returned!

It was with difficulty that he restrained an urge to call out and tell her that he was there; but caution stilled his tongue, and he lay watching while the two mounted and rode out of the gateway.

He rose to his feet and ran along the ridge toward the north, parallel to the course they were taking. It was already dusk. In a few minutes it would be dark. If he could only keep them in sight until he knew in what direction they finally went!

Exhaustion was forgotten as he ran through the approaching night. Dimly now he could see them. They rode for a short distance upward toward the cliffs; and then, just before the darkness swallowed them, he saw them turn and gallop away toward the northwest and the great forest that lay in that direction.

Reckless of life and limb, the 'Gunner' half stumbled, half fell down the cliffs that here had crumbled away and spilled their fragments out upon the slope below.

'I gotta catch 'em, I gotta catch 'em,' he kept repeating to himself. 'The poor kid! The poor little kid! So help me God, if I catch 'em, what I won't do to that – if he's hurt her!'

On through the night he stumbled, falling time and again only to pick himself up and continue his frantic and hopeless search for the little golden haired Jezebel who had come into his life for a few brief hours to leave a mark upon his heart that might never be erased.

Gradually the realization of it crept upon him as he groped blindly into the unknown, and it gave him strength to go on in the face of such physical exhaustion as he had never known before.

'Geeze,' he muttered, 'I sure must of fell hard for that kid.'

XXII

By a Lonely Pool

Night had fallen; and Tarzan of the Apes, leading Lady Barbara Collis and Lafayette Smith from the valley of the land of Midian, did not see the spoor of Jezebel and the 'Gunner.'

His two charges were upon the verge of exhaustion, but the ape-man led them on through the night in accordance with a plan he had decided upon. He knew that there were two more whites missing – Jezebel and Danny Patrick – and he wanted to get Lady Barbara and Smith to a place of safety that he might be free to pursue his search for these others.

To Lady Barbara and Smith the journey seemed interminable, yet they made no complaint, for the ape-man had explained the purpose of this forced march to them; and they were even more anxious than he concerning the fate of their friends.

Smith supported the girl as best he could; but his own strength was almost spent, and sometimes his desire to assist her tended more to impede than to aid her. Finally she stumbled and fell; and when Tarzan, striding in advance, heard and returned to them he found Smith vainly endeavoring to lift Lady Barbara.

This was the first intimation the ape-man had received that his charges were upon the verge of exhaustion, for neither had voiced a single complaint; and when he realized it he lifted Lady Barbara in his arms and carried her, while Smith, relieved at least of further anxiety concerning her, was able to keep going, though he moved like an automaton, apparently without conscious volition. Nor may his state be wondered at, when one considers what he had passed through during the preceding three days.

With Lady Barbara, he marvelled at the strength and endurance of the ape-man, which because of his own weakened state, seemed unbelievable even as he witnessed it.

'It is not much farther,' said Tarzan, guessing that the man needed encouragement.

'You are sure the hunter you told us of has not moved his camp?' asked Lady Barbara.

'He was there the day before yesterday,' replied the ape-man. 'I think we shall find him there tonight.'

'He will take us in?' asked Smith.

'Certainly just as you would, under similar circumstances, take in anyone who needed assistance,' replied the Lord of the Jungle. 'He is an Englishman,' he added as though that fact in itself were a sufficient answer to their doubts.

They were in a dense forest now, following an ancient game trail; and presently they saw lights flickering ahead.

'That must be the camp,' exclaimed Lady Barbara.

'Yes,' replied Tarzan, and a moment later he called out in a native dialect.

Instantly came an answering voice; and a moment later Tarzan halted upon the edge of the camp, just outside the circle of beast-fires.

Several askaris were on guard, and with them Tarzan conversed for a few moments; then he advanced and lowered Lady Barbara to her feet.

'I have told them not to disturb their bwana,' the ape-man explained. 'There is another tent that Lady Barbara may occupy, and the headman will arrange to have a shelter thrown up for Smith. You will be perfectly safe here. The men tell me their bwana is Lord Passmore. He will doubtless arrange to get you out to rail-head. In the meantime I shall try to locate your friends.'

That was all – the ape-man turned and melted into the black night before they could voice any thanks.

'Why, he's gone!' exclaimed the girl. 'I didn't even thank him.'

'I thought he would remain here until morning,' said Smith. 'He must be tired.'

'He seems tireless,' replied Lady Barbara. 'He is a superman, if ever there was one.'

'Come,' said the headman, 'your tent is over here. The boys are arranging a shelter for the bwana.'

'Goodnight, Mr Smith,' said the girl. 'I hope you sleep well.'

'Goodnight, Lady Barbara,' replied Smith. 'I hope we wake up sometime.'

And as they prepared for this welcome rest Stabutch and Jezebel were riding through the night, the man completely confused and lost.

Toward morning they drew rein at the edge of a great forest, after riding in wide circles during the greater part of the night. Stabutch was almost exhausted; and Jezebel was but little better off, but she had youth and health to give her the reserve strength that the man had undermined and wasted in dissipation.

'I've got to get some sleep,' he said, dismounting.

Jezebel needed no invitation to slip from her saddle, for she was stiff and sore from this unusual experience. Stabutch led the animals inside the forest and tied them to a tree. Then he threw himself upon the ground and was almost immediately asleep.

Jezebel sat in silence listening to the regular breathing of the man. 'Now would be the time to escape,' she thought. She rose quietly to her feet. How dark it was! Perhaps it would be better to wait until it became light enough to see. She was sure the man would sleep a long time, for it was evident that he was very tired.

She sat down again, listening to the noises of the jungle. They frightened her. Yes, she would wait until it was light; then she would untie the horses, ride one and lead the other away so that the man could not pursue her.

Slowly the minutes crept by. The sky became lighter in the east, over the distant mountains. The horses became restless. She noticed that they stood with ears pricked up and that they looked deeper into the jungle and trembled.

Suddenly there was the sound of crashing in the underbrush. The horses snorted and surged back upon their ropes, both of which broke. The noise awakened Stabutch, who sat up just as the two terrified animals wheeled and bolted. An instant later a lion leaped past the girl and the man, in pursuit of the two fleeing horses.

Stabutch sprang to his feet, his rifle in his hands. 'God!' he exclaimed. 'This is no place to sleep,' and Jezebel's opportunity had passed.

The sun was topping the eastern mountains. The day had come. Soon the searchers would be ahorse. Now that he was afoot, Stabutch knew that he must not loiter. However, they must eat, or they would have no strength to proceed; and only by his rifle could they eat.

'Climb into that tree, little one,' he said to Jezebel. 'You will be safe there while I go and shoot something for our breakfast. Watch for the lion, and if you see him returning this way shout a warning. I am going farther into the forest to look for game.'

Jezebel climbed into the tree, and Stabutch departed upon the hunt for breakfast. The girl watched for the lion, hoping it would return, for she had determined that she would give no warning to the man if it did.

She was afraid of the Russian because of things he had said to her during that long night ride. Much that he had said she had not understood at all, but she understood enough to know that he was a bad man. But the lion did not return, and presently Jezebel dozed and nearly fell out of the tree.

Stabutch, hunting in the forest, found a water hole not far from where he had left Jezebel; and here he hid behind bushes waiting for some animal to come down to drink. Nor had he long to wait before he saw a creature appear suddenly upon the opposite side of the pool. So quietly had it come that the Russian had not dreamed that a creature stirred within a mile of his post. The most surprising feature of the occurrence, however, was that the animal thus suddenly to step into view was the man.

Stabutch's evil eyes narrowed. It was *the* man – the man he had travelled all the way from Moscow to kill. What an opportunity! Fate was indeed kind to him. He would fulfill his mission without danger to himself, and then he would escape with the girl – that wondrous girl! Stabutch had never seen so beautiful a woman in his life, and now he was to possess her – she was to be his.

But first he must attend to the business of the moment. What a pleasant business it was, too. He raised his rifle very cautiously and aimed. Tarzan had halted and turned his head to one side. He could not see the rifle barrel of his enemy because of the bush behind which Stabutch hid and the fact that his eyes were centered on something in another direction.

The Russian realized that he was trembling, and he cursed himself under his breath. The nervous strain was too great. He tensed his muscles in an effort to hold his hands firm and the rifle steady and immovable upon the target. The front sight of the rifle was describing a tiny circle instead of remaining fixed upon that great chest which offered such a splendid target.

But he must fire! The man would not stand there thus forever. The thought hurried Stabutch, and as the sight passed again across the body of the ape-man the Russian squeezed the trigger.

At the sound of the shot Jezebel's eyes snapped open. 'Perhaps the lion returned,' she soliloquized, 'or maybe the man has found food. If it were the lion, I hope he missed it.'

Also, as the rifle spoke, the target leaped into the air, seized a low hung branch and disappeared amidst the foliage of the trees above. Stabutch had missed – he should have relaxed his muscles rather than tensed them.

The Russian was terrified. He felt as must one who stands upon the drop with the noose already about his neck. He turned and fled. His cunning mind suggested that he had better not return where the girl was. She was already lost to him, for he could not be burdened with her now in this flight, upon the success of which hung his very life. Accordingly he ran toward the south.

As he rushed headlong through the forest he was already out of breath when he felt a sudden sickening pain in his arm and at the same instant saw the feathered tip of an arrow waving beside him as he ran.

The shaft had pierced his forearm, its tip projecting from the opposite side. Sick with terror Stabutch increased his speed. Somewhere above him was his Nemesis, whom he could neither see nor hear. It was as though a ghostly assassin pursued him on silent wings.

Again an arrow struck him, sinking deep into the triceps of his other arm. With a scream of pain and horror Stabutch halted and, dropping upon his knees, raised his hands in supplication. 'Spare me!' he cried. 'Spare me! I have never wronged you. If you will spare—'

An arrow, speeding straight, drove through the Russian's throat. He screamed and clutched at the missile and fell forward on his face.

Jezebel, listening in the tree, heard the agonized shriek of the stricken man; and she shuddered. 'The lion got him,' she whispered. 'He was wicked. It is the will of Jehovah!'

Tarzan of the Apes dropped lightly from a tree and warily approached the dying man. Stabutch, writhing in agony and terror, rolled over on his side. He saw the ape-man approaching, his bow and arrow ready in his hand, and, dying, reached for the revolver at his hip to complete the work that he had come so far to achieve and for which he was to give his life.

No more had his hand reached the grip of his weapon than the Lord of the Jungle loosed another shaft that drove deep through the chest of the Russian, deep through his heart. Without a sound Leon Stabutch collapsed; and a moment later there rang through the jungle the fierce, uncanny victory cry of the bull ape.

As the savage notes reverberated through the forest Jezebel slid to the ground and fled in terror. She knew not where nor to what fate her flying feet led her. She obsessed by but a single idea – to escape from the terrors of that lonely spot.

XXIII

Captured

With the coming of day the 'Gunner' found himself near a forest. He had heard no sound of horses all during the night; and now that day had come, and he could see to a distance, he scanned the landscape for some sign of Stabutch and Jezebel but without success.

'Geeze,' he muttered, 'there ain't no use, I gotta rest. The poor little kid! If I only knew where the rat took her; but I don't, and I gotta rest.' He surveyed the forest. 'That looks like a swell hideout. I'll lay up there and grab off a little sleep. Geeze, I'm all in.'

As he walked toward the forest his attention was attracted to something moving a couple of miles to the north of him. He stopped short, and looked more closely as two horses, racing from the forest, dashed madly toward the foothills, pursued by a lion.

'Geeze!' exclaimed the 'Gunner,' 'those must be their horses. What if the lion got her!'

Instantly his fatigue was forgotten; and he started at a run toward the north; but he could not keep the pace up for long; and soon he was walking again, his brain a turmoil of conjecture and apprehension.

He saw the lion give up the chase and turn away almost immediately, cutting up the slope in a northeasterly direction. The 'Gunner' was glad to see him go, not for his own sake so much as for Jezebel, whom, he reasoned, the lion might not have killed after all. There was a possibility, he thought, that she might have had time to climb a tree. Otherwise, he was positive the lion must have killed her.

His knowledge of lions was slight. In common with most people, he believed that lions wandered about killing everything so unfortunate as to fall into their pathways – unless they were bluffed out as he had bluffed the panther the day before. But of course, he reasoned, Jezebel wouldn't have been able to bluff a lion.

He was walking close to the edge of the forest, making the best time that he could, when he heard a shot in the distance. It was the report of Stabutch's rifle as he fired at Tarzan. The 'Gunner' tried to increase his speed. There was too much doing there, where he thought Jezebel might be, to permit of loafing; but he was too exhausted to move rapidly.

Then, a few minutes later, the Russian's scream of agony was wafted to his ears and again he was goaded on. This was followed by the uncanny cry of the ape-man, which, for some reason, Danny did not recognize, though he had heard it twice before. Perhaps the distance and the intervening trees muffled and changed it.

On he plodded, trying occasionally to run; but his overtaxed muscles had reached their limit; and he had to give up the attempt, for already he was staggering and stumbling even at a walk.

'I ain't no good,' he muttered; 'nothing but a lousy punk. Here's a guy beatin' it with my girl, and I ain't even got the guts to work my dogs. Geeze, I'm a flop.'

A little farther on he entered the forest so that he could approach the spot, where he had seen the horses emerge, without being seen, if Stabutch were still there.

Suddenly he stopped. Something was crashing through the brush toward him. He recalled the lion and drew his pocket knife. Then he hid behind a bush and waited, nor did he have long to wait before the author of the disturbance broke into view.

'Jezebel!' he cried, stepping into her path. His voice trembled with emotion.

With a startled scream the girl halted, and then she recognized him. 'Danny!' It was the last straw – her overwrought nerves went to pieces; and she sank to the ground, sobbing hysterically.

The 'Gunner' took a step or two toward her. He staggered, his knees gave beneath him, and he sat down heavily a few yards from her; and then a strange thing happened. Tears welled to the eyes of Danny 'Gunner' Patrick; he threw himself face down on the ground; and he, too, sobbed.

For several minutes they lay there, and then Jezebel gained control of herself and sat up. 'Oh, Danny,' she cried. 'Are you hurt? Oh, your head! Don't die, Danny.'

He had quelled his emotion and was roughly wiping his eyes on his shirt sleeve. 'I ain't dyin',' he said; 'but I oughta. Someone oughta bump me off – a great big stiff like me, cryin'!'

'It's because you've been hurt, Danny,' said Jezebel.

'Naw, it ain't that. I been hurt before, but I ain't bawled since I was a little kid – when my mother died. It was something else, kid. I just blew up when I seen you, and knew that you was O.K. My nerves went blooey – just like that!' he snapped his fingers. 'You see,' he added, hesitantly, 'I guess I like you an awful lot, kid.'

'I like you, Danny,' she told him. 'You're top hole.'

'I'm what? What does that mean?'

'I don't know,' Jezebel admitted. 'It's English, and you don't understand English, do you?'

He crawled over closer to her and took her hand in his. 'Geeze,' he said, 'I thought I wasn't never goin' to see you again. Say,' he burst out violently, 'did that bum hurt you any, kid?'

'The man who took me away from the black men in the village, you mean?'

'Yes.'

'No, Danny. After he killed his friend we rode all night. He was afraid the black men would catch him.'

'What became of the rat? How did you make your getaway?'

She told him all that she knew, but they were unable to account for the sounds both had heard or to guess whether or not they had portended the death of Stabutch.

'I wouldn't be much good, if he showed up again,' said Danny. 'I gotta get my strength back some way.'

'You must rest,' she told him.

'I'll tell you what we'll do,' he said. 'We'll lay around here until we are rested up a bit; then we'll beat it back up toward the hills where I know where they's water and something to eat. It ain't very good food,' he added, 'but it's better than none. Say, I got some of it in my pocket. We'll just have a feed now.' He extracted some dirty scraps of half burned pork from one of his pockets and surveyed them ruefully.

'What is it?' asked Jezebel.

'It's pig, kid,' he explained. 'It don't look so hot, does it? Well, it don't taste no better than it looks; but it's food, and that's what we are needin' bad right now. Here, hop to it.' He extended a handful of the scraps toward her. 'Shut your eyes and hold your nose, and it ain't so bad,' he assured her. 'Just imagine you're in the old College Inn.'

Jezebel smiled and took a piece of the meat. 'United States is a funny language, isn't it, Danny?'

'Why, I don't know – is it?'

'Yes, I think so. Sometimes it sounds just like English and yet I can't understand it at all.'

'That's because you ain't used to it,' he told her; 'but I'll learn you if you want me to. Do you?'

'Oke, kid,' replied Jezebel.

'You're learnin' all right,' said Danny, admiringly.

They lay in the growing heat of the new day and talked together of many things as they rested. Jezebel told him the story of the land of Midian, of her childhood, of the eventful coming of Lady Barbara and its strange effect upon her life; and Danny told her of Chicago, but there were many things in his own life that he did not tell her – things that, for the first time, he was ashamed of. And he wondered why he was ashamed.

As they talked, Tarzan of the Apes quitted the forest and set out upon his search for them, going upward toward the hills, intending to start his search for their spoor at the mouth of the fissure. If he did not find it there he would know that they were still in the valley; if he did find it, he would follow it until he located them.

At the break of day a hundred *shiftas* rode out of their village. They had discovered the body of Capietro, and now they knew that the Russian had tricked them and fled, after killing their chief. They wanted the girl for ransom, and they wanted the life of Stabutch.

They had not ridden far when they met two riderless horses galloping back toward the village. The *shiftas* recognized them at once, and knowing that Stabutch and the girl were now afoot they anticipated little difficulty in overhauling them.

The rolling foothills were cut by swales and canyons; so that at times the vision of the riders was limited. They had been following downward along the bottom of a shallow canyon for some time, where they could neither see to a great distance nor be seen; and then their leader turned his mount toward higher ground, and as he topped the summit of a low ridge he saw a man approaching from the direction of the forest.

Tarzan saw the *shifta* simultaneously and changed his direction obliquely to the left, breaking into a trot. He knew that if that lone rider signified a force of mounted *shiftas* he would be no match for them; and, guided by the instinct of the wild beast, he sought ground where the advantage would be with him – the rough, rocky ground leading to the cliffs, where no horse could follow him.

With a yell to his followers, the *shifta* chieftain put spurs to his horse and rode at top speed to intercept the ape-man; and close behind him came his yelling, savage horde.

Tarzan quickly saw that he could not reach the cliffs ahead of them; but he maintained his steady, tireless trot that he might be that much nearer the goal when the attack came. Perhaps he could hold them off until he reached the sanctuary of the cliffs, but certainly he had no intention of giving up without exerting every effort to escape the unequal battle that must follow if they overtook him.

With savage yells the *shiftas* approached, their loose cotton garments fluttering in the wind, their rifles waving above their heads. The chief rode in the lead; and when he was near enough, the ape-man, who had been casting occasional glances rearward across a brown shoulder, stopped, wheeled and let an arrow drive at his foe; then he was away again as the shaft sank into the breast of the *shifta* chieftain.

With a scream, the fellow rolled from his saddle; and for a moment the others drew rein, but only for a moment. Here was but a single enemy, poorly armed with primitive weapons – he was no real menace to mounted riflemen.

Shouting their anger and their threats of vengeance, they spurred forward again in pursuit; but Tarzan had gained and the rocky ground was not far away.

Spreading in a great half circle, the *shiftas* sought to surround and head off their quarry, whose strategy they had guessed the moment that they had seen the course of his flight. Now another rider ventured too near, and for a brief instant Tarzan paused to loose another arrow. As this second enemy fell, mortally wounded, the ape-man continued his flight to the accompaniment of a rattle of musketry fire; but soon he was forced to halt again as several of the horsemen passed him and cut off his line of retreat.

The hail of slugs screaming past him or kicking up the dirt around him gave him slight concern, so traditionally poor was the marksmanship of these roving bands of robbers, illy equipped with ancient firearms with which, because of habitual shortage of ammunition, they had little oppor-tunity to practice.

Now they pressed closer, in a rough circle of which he was the center; and, firing across him from all sides, it seemed impossible that they should miss him; but miss him they did, though their bullets found targets among their own men and horses, until one, who had supplanted the slain chief, took command and ordered them to cease firing.

Turning again in the direction of his flight, Tarzan tried to shoot his way through the cordon of horsemen shutting off his retreat; but, though each arrow sped true to its mark, the yelling horde closed in upon him until, his last shaft spent, he was the center of a closely milling mass of shrieking enemies.

Shrilly above the pandemonium of battle rose the cries of the new leader. 'Do not kill! Do not kill!' he screamed. 'It is Tarzan of the Apes, and he is worth the ransom of a ras!'

Suddenly a giant black threw himself from his horse full upon the Lord of the Jungle, but Tarzan seized the fellow and hurled him back among the horsemen. Yet closer and closer they pressed; and now several fell upon him from their saddles, bearing him down beneath the feet of the now frantic horses.

Battling for life and liberty, the ape-man struggled against the over-powering odds that were being constantly augmented by new recruits who hurled themselves from their mounts upon the growing pile that overwhelmed him. Once he managed to struggle to his feet, shaking most of his opponents from him; but they seized him about the legs and dragged him down again; and presently succeeded in slipping nooses about his wrists and ankles, thus effectually subduing him.

Now that he was harmless many of them reviled and struck him; but there were many others who lay upon the ground, some never to rise again. The *shiftas* had captured the great Tarzan, but it had cost them dear.

Now some of them rounded up the riderless horses, while others stripped the dead of their weapons, ammunition, and any other valuables the living coveted. Tarzan was raised to an empty saddle, where he was securely bound; and four men were detailed to conduct him and the horses of the dead to the village, the wounded accompanying them, while the main body of the blacks continued the search for Stabutch and Jezebel.

XXIV

The Long Night

The sun was high in the heavens when Lady Barbara, refreshed by her long, undisturbed sleep, stepped from her tent in the camp of Lord Passmore. A smiling, handsome black boy came running toward her. 'Breakfast soon be ready,' he told her. 'Lord Passmore very sorry. He have to go hunt.'

She asked after Lafayette Smith and was told that he had just awakened, nor was it long before he joined her; and soon they were breakfasting together.

'If Jezebel and your friend were here,' she said, 'I should be very happy. I am praying that Tarzan finds them.'

'I am sure he will,' Smith assured her, 'though I am only worried about Jezebel. Danny can take care of himself.'

'Doesn't it seem heavenly to eat a meal again?' the girl remarked. 'Do you know it has been months since I have eaten anything that even vaguely approximated a civilized meal. Lord Passmore was fortunate to get such a cook for his safari. I had not such luck.'

'Have you noticed what splendid looking fellows all his men are?' asked Smith. 'They would make that aggregation of mine resemble fourth rate roustabouts with hookworm and sleeping sickness.'

'There is another very noticeable thing about them,' said Lady Barbara.

'What is that?'

'There is not a single piece of cast off European finery among them – their garb is native, pure and simple; and, while I'll have to admit there isn't much to it, it lends a dignity to them that European clothing would change to the absurd.'

'I quite agree with you,' said Smith. 'I wonder why I didn't get a safari like this.'

'Lord Passmore is evidently an African traveller and hunter of long experience. No amateur could hope to attract such men as these.'

'I shall hate to go back to my own camp, if I stay here very long,' said Smith; 'but I suppose I'll have to; and that suggests another unpleasant feature of the change.'

'And what is that?' she asked.

'I shan't see you any more,' he said with a simple directness that vouched for the sincerity of his regret.

The girl was silent for a moment, as though the suggestion had aroused a train of thought she had not before considered. 'That is true, isn't it?' she remarked, presently. 'We shan't see each other any more – but not for always. I'm sure you'll stop and visit me in London. Isn't it odd what old friends we seem? And yet we only met two days ago. Or, maybe, it doesn't seem that way to you. You see I was so long without seeing a human being of my own world that you were quite like a long lost brother, when you came along so unexpectedly.'

'I have the same feeling,' he said – 'as though I had known you forever – and –' he hesitated, ' – as though I could never get along without you in the future.' He flushed a little as he spoke those last words.

The girl looked up at him with a quick smile – a sympathetic, understanding smile. 'It was nice of you to say that,' she said. 'Why it sounded almost like a declaration,' she added, with a gay, friendly laugh.

He reached across the little camp table and laid a hand upon hers. 'Accept it as such,' he said. 'I'm not very good at saying things – like that.'

'Let's not be serious,' she begged. 'Really, we scarcely know each other, after all.'

'I have known you always,' he replied. 'I think we were amoebas together before the first Cambrian dawn.'

'Now, you've compromised me,' she cried, laughingly, 'for I'm sure there were no chaperons way back there. I hope that you were a proper amoeba. You didn't kiss me, did you?'

'Unfortunately for me amoebas have no mouths,' he said, 'but I've been profiting by several millions of years of evolution just to remedy that defect.'

'Let's be amoebas again,' she suggested.

'No,' he said, 'for then I couldn't tell you that I – I—' He choked and flushed.

'Please! Please, don't tell me,' she cried. 'We're such ripping friends – don't spoil it.'

'Would it spoil it?' he asked.

'I don't know. It might, I am afraid.'

'Can't I ever tell you?' he asked.

'Perhaps, some day,' she said.

A sudden burst of distant rifle fire interrupted them. The blacks in the camp were instantly alert. Many of them sprang to their feet, and all were listening intently to the sounds of this mysterious engagement between armed men.

The man and the girl heard the headman speaking to his fellows in some African dialect. His manner showed no excitement, his tones were low but clear. It was evident that he was issuing instructions. The men went quickly to their shelters, and a moment later Lady Barbara saw the peaceful camp transformed. Every man was armed now. As by magic a modern rifle and a bandoleer of cartridges were in the possession of each black. White feathered headdresses were being adjusted and war paint applied to glossy hides.

Smith approached the headman. 'What is the matter?' he asked. 'Is something wrong?'

'I do not know, bwana,' replied the black; 'but we prepare.'

'Is there any danger?' continued the white.

The headman straightened to his full, impressive height. 'Are we not here?' he asked.

Jezebel and the 'Gunner' were walking slowly in the direction of the distant water hole and the cached boar meat, following the bottom of a dip that was the mouth of a small canyon that led up into the hills.

They were stiff and lame and very tired; and the wound on the 'Gunner's' head pained; but, notwithstanding, they were happy as, hand in hand, they dragged their weary feet toward water and food.

'Geeze, kid,' said Danny, 'it sure is a funny world. Just think, if I hadn't met old Smithy on board that ship me and you wouldn't never have met up. It all started from that,' but then Danny knew nothing of Angustus the Ephesian.

'I got a few grand salted away, kid, and when we get out of this mess we'll go somewhere where nobody doesn't know me and I'll start over again. Get myself a garage or a filling station, and we'll have a little flat. Geeze, it's goin' to be great showin' you things. You don't know what you ain't seen – movies and railroads and boats! Geeze! You ain't seen nothin' and nobody ain't go to show you nothin', only me.'

'Yes, Danny,' said Jezebel, 'it's going to be ripping,' and she squeezed his hand.

Just then they were startled by the sound of rifle fire ahead.

'What was that?' asked Jezebel.

'It sounded like the Valentine Massacre,' said Danny, 'but I guess it's them tough smokes from the village. We better hide, kid.' He drew her toward some low bushes; and there they lay down, listening to the shouts and shots that came down to them from where Tarzan fought for his life and liberty with the odds a hundred to one against him.

After a while the din ceased, and a little later the two heard the thudding of many galloping hoofs. The sound increased in volume as it drew nearer, and Danny and Jezebel tried to make themselves as small as possible beneath the little bush in the inadequate concealment of which they were hiding.

At a thundering gallop the *shiftas* crossed the swale just above them, and all but a few had passed when one of the stragglers discovered them. His shout, which attracted the attention of others, was carried forward until it reached the new chief, and presently the entire band had circled back to learn what their fellow had discovered.

Poor 'Gunner'! Poor Jezebel! Their happiness had been short lived. Their recapture was effected with humiliating ease. Broken and dejected, they were soon on their way to the village under escort of two black ruffians.

Bound, hands and feet, they were thrown into the hut formerly occupied by Capietro and left without food or water upon the pile of dirty rugs and clothing that littered the floor.

Beside them lay the corpse of the Italian which his followers, in their haste to overtake his slayer, had not taken the time to remove. It lay upon its back, the dead eyes staring upward.

Never before in his life had the spirits of Danny Patrick sunk so low, for the very reason, perhaps, that never in his life had they risen so high as during the brief interlude of happiness he had enjoyed following his reunion with Jezebel. Now he saw no hope ahead, for, with the two white men eliminated, he feared that he might not even be able to dicker with these ignorant black men for the ransom that he would gladly pay to free Jezebel and himself.

'There goes the garage, the filling station, and the flat,' he said, lugubriously.

'Where?' asked Jezebel.

'Flooie,' explained Danny.

'But you are here with me,' said the golden one; 'so I do not care what else there is.'

'That's nice, kid; but I ain't much help, all tied up like a Christmas present. They sure picked out a swell bed for me – feels like I was lyin' on a piece of the kitchen stove.' He rolled himself to one side and nearer Jezebel. 'That's better,' he said, 'but I wonder what was that thing I was parked on.'

'Maybe your friend will come and take us away,' suggested Jezebel.

'Who, Smithy? What would he take us with – that dinky toy pistol of his?'

'I was thinking of the other that you told me about.'

'Oh, that Tarzan guy! Say kid, if he knew we was here he'd walk in and push all these nutty dumps over with one mitt and kick the smokes over the back fence. Geeze, you bet I wish he was here. There is one Big Shot, and I don't mean maybe.'

In the hut on the edge of the village was the answer to the 'Gunner's' wish, bound hand and foot, as was the 'Gunner,' and, apparently, equally helpless, constantly the ape-man was working on the thongs that confined his wrists – twisting, tugging, pulling.

The long day wore on and never did the giant captive cease his efforts to escape; but the thongs were heavy and securely tied, yet little by little he felt that they were loosening.

Towards evening the new chief returned with the party that had been searching for Stabutch. They had not found him; but scouts had located the camp of Lord Passmore, and now the *shiftas* were discussing plans for attacking it on the morrow.

They had not come sufficiently close to it to note the number of armed natives it contained; but they had glimpsed Smith and Lady Barbara; and, being sure that there were not more than two white men, they felt little hesitation in attempting the raid, since they were planning to start back for Abyssinia on the morrow.

'We will kill the white man we now have,' said the chief, 'and carry the two girls and Tarzan with us. Tarzan should bring a good ransom and the girls a good price.'

'Why not keep the girls for ourselves,' suggested another.

'We shall sell them,' said the chief.

'Who are you, to say what we shall do?' demanded the other. 'You are no chief.'

'No,' growled a villainous looking black squatting beside the first objector.

He who would be chief leaped, catlike, upon the first speaker, before any was aware of his purpose. A sword gleamed for an instant in the light of the new made cookfires and fell with terrific force upon the skull of the victim.

'Who am I?' repeated the killer, as he wiped the bloody blade upon the garment of the slain man. 'I am chief!' He looked around upon the scowling faces about him. 'Is there any who says I am not chief?' There was no demur. Ntale was chief of the *shifta* band.

Inside the dark interior of the hut where he had lain bound all day without food or water the ape-man tugged and pulled until the sweat stood in beads upon his body, but not in vain. Gradually a hand slipped through the stretched thong, and he was free. Or at least his hands were, and it took but a moment to loosen the bonds that secured his ankles.

With a low, inaudible growl he rose to his feet and stepped to the doorway.

Before him lay the village compound. He saw the *shiftas* squatting about while slaves prepared the evening meal. Nearby was the palisade. They must see him as he crossed to it, but what matter?

He would be gone before they could gather their wits. Perhaps a few stray shots would be fired; but then, had they not fired many shots at him this morning, not one of which had touched him?

He stepped out into the open, and at the same instant a burly black stepped from the next hut and saw him. With a shout of warning to his fellows the man leaped upon the escaping prisoner. Those at the fires sprang to their feet and came running toward the two.

Within their prison hut Jezebel and Danny heard the commotion and wondered.

The ape-man seized the black who would have stopped him and wheeling him about to form a shield for himself, backed quickly toward the palisade.

'Stay where you are,' he called to the advancing *shiftas*, in their own dialect. 'Stay where you are, or I will kill this man.'

'Let him kill him then,' growled Ntale. 'He is not worth the ransom we are losing,' and with a shout of encouragement to his followers he leaped quickly forward to intercept the ape-man.

Tarzan was already near the palisade as Ntale charged. He raised the struggling black above his head and hurled him upon the advancing chief, and as the two went down he wheeled and ran for the palisade.

Like Manu the monkey he scaled the high barrier. A few scattered shots followed him, but he dropped to the ground outside unscathed and disappeared in the growing gloom of the advancing night.

The long night of their captivity dragged on and still the 'Gunner' and Jezebel lay as they had been left, without food or drink, while the silent corpse of Capietro stared at the ceiling.

'I wouldn't treat nobody like this,' said the 'Gunner,' 'not even a rat.'

Jezebel raised herself to one elbow. 'Why not try it?' she whispered.

'What?' demanded Danny. 'I'd try anything once.'

'What you said about a rat made me think of it,' said Jezebel. 'We have lots of rats in the land of Midian. Sometimes we catch them – they are very good to eat. We make traps, but if we do not kill the rats soon after they are caught they gnaw their way to freedom – they gnaw the cords which bind the traps together.'

'Well, what of it?' demanded Danny. 'We ain' got no rats, and if we had – well, I won't say I wouldn't eat 'em, kid; but I don't see what it's got to do with the mess we're in.'

'We're like the rats, Danny,' she said. 'Don't you see? We're like the rats and – we can gnaw our way to freedom!'

'Well, kid,' said Danny, 'if you want to gnaw your way through the side of this hut, hop to it; but if I gets a chance to duck I'm goin' through the door.'

'You do not understand, Danny,' insisted Jezebel. 'You are an egg that cannot talk. I mean that I can gnaw the cords that fasten your wrists together.'

'Geeze, kid!' exclaimed Danny. 'Dumb ain't no name for it, and I always thought I was the bright little boy. You sure got a bean, and I don't mean maybe.'

'I wish I knew what you are talking about, Danny,' said Jezebel, 'and I wish you would let me try to gnaw the cords from your wrist. Can't you understand what I'm talking about?'

'Sure, kid, but I'll do the gnawing – my jaws are tougher. Roll over, and I'll get busy. When you're free you untie me.'

Jezebel rolled over on her stomach and Danny wriggled into position where he could reach the thongs at her wrists with his teeth. He fell to work with a will, but it was soon evident to him that the job was going to be much more difficult than he had anticipated.

He found, too, that he was very weak and soon tired; but though often he was forced to stop through exhaustion, he never gave up. Once, when he paused to rest, he kissed the little hands that he was trying to liberate. It was a gentle, reverent kiss, quite unlike the 'Gunner'; but then love is a strange force, and when it is aroused in the breast of a man by a clean and virtuous woman it makes him always a little tenderer and a little better.

Dawn was lifting the darkness with the hut, and still the 'Gunner' gnawed upon the thongs that it seemed would never part. Capietro lay staring at the ceiling, his dead eyes rolled upward, just as he had lain there staring through all the long hours of the night, unseeing.

The *shiftas* were stirring in the village, for this was to be a busy day. Slaves were preparing the loads of camp equipment and plunder that they were to carry toward the north. The fighting men were hastening their breakfasts that they might look to their weapons and their horse gear before riding out on their last raid from this village, against the camp of the English hunter.

Ntale the chief was eating beside the fire of his favorite wife. 'Make haste, woman,' he said. 'I have work to do before we ride.'

'You are chief now,' she reminded him. 'Let others work.'

'This thing I do myself,' replied the black man.

'What do you that is so important that I must hasten the preparation of the morning meal?' she demanded.

'I go to kill the white man and get the girl ready for the journey,' he replied. 'Have food prepared for her. She must eat or she will die.'

'Let her die,' replied the woman. 'I do not want her around. Kill them both.'

'Shut thy mouth!' snapped the man. 'I am chief.'

'If you do not kill her, I shall,' said the woman, 'I shall not cook for any white bitch.'

The man rose. 'I go to kill the man,' he said. 'Have breakfast for the girl when I return with her.'

XXV

The Waziri

'There!' gasped the 'Gunner.'

'I am free!' exclaimed Jezebel.

'And my jaws is wore out,' said Danny.

Quickly Jezebel turned and worked upon the thongs that confined the 'Gunner's' wrists before taking the time to loose her ankles. Her fingers were quite numb, for the cords had partially cut off the circulation from her hands; and she was slow and bungling at the work. It seemed to them both that she would never be done. Had they known that Ntale had already arisen from his breakfast fire with the announcement that he was going to kill the 'Gunner,' they would have been frantic; but they did not know it, and perhaps that were better, since to Jezebel's other handicaps was not added the nervous tension that surely would have accompanied a knowledge of the truth.

But at last the 'Gunner's' hands were free; and then both fell to work upon the cords that secured their ankles, which were less tightly fastened.

At last the 'Gunner' arose. 'The first thing I do,' he said, 'is to find out what I was lyin' on yesterday. It had a familiar feel to it; and, if I'm right – boy!'

He rummaged among the filthy rags at the end of the rut, and a moment later straightened up with a Thompson submachine gun in one hand and his revolver, belt and holster in the other – a grin on his face.

'This is the first break I've had in a long time,' he said. 'Everything's jake now, sister.'

'What are those things?' asked Jezebel.

'Them's the other half of "Gunner" Patrick,' replied Danny. 'Now, bring on your tough smokes!'

As he spoke, Ntale the chief drew aside the rug at the doorway and looked in. The interior of the hut was rather dark, and at first glance he could not make out the figures of the girl and the man standing at the far side; but, silhouetted as he was against the growing morning light beyond the doorway, he was plainly visible to his intended victim; and Danny saw that the man carried a pistol ready in his hand.

The 'Gunner' had already buckled his belt about him. Now he transferred the machine gun to his left hand and drew his revolver from its holster. He did these things quickly and silently. So quickly that, as he fired, Ntale had not realized that his prisoners were free of their bonds – a thing he never knew, as, doubtless, he never heard the report of the shot that killed him.

At the same instant that the 'Gunner' fired, the report of his revolver was drowned by yells and a shot from a sentry at the gate, to whom the coming day had revealed a hostile force creeping upon the village.

As Danny Patrick stepped over the dead body of the chief and looked out into the village he realized something of what had occurred. He saw men running hastily toward the village gates and scrambling to the banquette. He heard a fusilade of shots that spattered against the palisade, splintering the wood and tearing through to fill the village with a screaming, terror stricken mob.

His knowledge of such things told him that only high powered rifles could send their projectiles through the heavy wood of the palisade. He saw the *shiftas* on the banquette returning the fire with their antiquated muskets. He saw the slaves and prisoners cowering in a corner of the village that was freer from the fire of the attackers than other portions.

He wondered who the enemies of the *shiftas* might be, and past experience suggested only two possibilities – either a rival 'gang' or the police.

'I never thought I'd come to it, kid,' he said.

'Come to what, Danny?'

'I hate to tell you what I been hopin',' he admitted.

'Tell me, Danny,' she said. 'I won't be angry.'

'I been hopin' them guys out there was cops. Just think o' that, kid! Me, "Gunner" Patrick, a-hopin' the cops would come!'

'What are cops, Danny?'

'Laws, harness bulls – Geeze, kid, why do you ask so many questions? Cops is cops. And I'll tell you why I hope its them. If it ain't cops its a rival mob, and we'd get just as tough a break with them as with these guys.'

He stepped out into the village street. 'Well,' he said, 'here goes Danny Patrick smearin' up with the police. You stay here, kid, and lie down on your bread basket, so none of them slugs'll find you, while I go out and push the smokes around.'

Before the gate was a great crowd of *shiftas* firing through openings at the enemy beyond. The 'Gunner' knelt and raised the machine gun to his shoulder. There was the vicious b-r-r as of some titanic rattle snake; and a dozen of the massed *shiftas* collapsed, dead or screaming, to the ground.

The others turned and, seeing the 'Gunner,' realized that they were caught between two fires, for they remembered the recent occasion upon which they had witnessed the deadly effects of this terrifying weapon.

The 'Gunner' spied Ogonyo among the prisoners and slaves huddled not far from where he stood, and the sight of him suggested an idea to the white man.

'Hey! Big Smoke, you!' He waved his hand to Ogonyo. 'Come here! Bring all them guys with you. Tell 'em to grab anything they can fight with if they want to make their getaway.'

Whether or not Ogonyo understood even a small part of what the 'Gunner' said, he seemed at least to grasp the main idea; and presently the whole mob of prisoners and slaves, except the women, had placed themselves behind Danny.

The firing from the attacking force had subsided somewhat since Danny's typewriter had spoken, as though the leader of that other party had recognized its voice and guessed that white prisoners within the village might be menaced by his rifle fire. Only an occasional shot, aimed at some specific target, was coming into the village.

The *shiftas* had regained their composure to some extent and were preparing their horses and mounting, with the evident intention of executing a sortie. They were leaderless and confused, half a dozen shouting advice and instructions at the same time.

It was at this moment that Danny advanced upon them with his motley horde armed with sticks and stones, an occasional knife and a few swords hastily stolen from the huts of their captors.

As the *shiftas* realized that they were menaced thus seriously from the rear, the 'Gunner' opened fire upon them for the second time, and the confusion that followed in the village compound gave the attackers both within and without a new advantage.

The *shiftas* fought among themselves for the loose horses that were now stampeding in terror about the village; and as a number of them succeeded in mounting they rode for the village gates, overthrowing those who had remained to defend them. Some among them forced the portals open; and as the horsemen dashed out they were met by a band of black warriors, above whose heads waved white plumes, and in whose hands were modern high powered rifles.

The attacking force had been lying partially concealed behind a low ridge, and as it rose to meet the escaping *shiftas* the savage war cry of the Waziri rang above the tumult of the battle.

First to the gates was Tarzan, war chief of the Waziri, and while Muviro and a small detachment accounted for all but a few of the horsemen who had succeeded in leaving the village, the ape-man, with the remaining Waziri, charged the demoralized remnants of Capietro's band that remained within the palisade.

Surrounded by enemies, the *shiftas* threw down their rifles and begged for mercy, and soon they were herded into a corner of the village under guard of a detachment of the Waziri.

As Tarzan greeted the 'Gunner' and Jezebel he expressed his relief at finding them unharmed.

'You sure come at the right time,' Danny told him. 'This old typewriter certainly chews up the ammunition, and that last burst just about emptied the drum; but say, who are your friends? Where did you raise this mob?'

'They are my people,' replied Tarzan.

'Some gang!' ejaculated the 'Gunner,' admiringly; 'but say, have you seen anything of old Smithy?'

'He is safe at my camp.'

'And Barbara,' asked Jezebel; 'where is she?'

'She is with Smith,' replied Tarzan. 'You will see them both in a few hours. We start back as soon as I arrange for the disposal of these people.' He turned away and commenced to make inquiries among the prisoners of the *shiftas*.

'Is he not beautiful!' exclaimed Jezebel.

'Hey, sister, can that "beautiful" stuff,' warned the 'Gunner,' 'and from now on remember that I'm the only "beautiful" guy you know, no matter what my pan looks like.'

Quickly Tarzan separated the prisoners according to their tribes and villages, appointed headmen to lead them back to their homes and issued instructions to them as he explained his plans.

The weapons, ammunition, loot and belongings of the *shiftas* were divided among the prisoners, after the Waziri had been allowed to select such trifles as they desired. The captured *shiftas* were placed in charge of a large band of Gallas with orders to return them to Abyssinia and turn them over to the nearest ras.

'Why not hang them here?' asked the Galla headman. 'We shall then save all the food they would eat on the long march back to our country, besides saving us much trouble and worry in guarding them – for the ras will certainly hang them.'

'Take them back, as I tell you,' replied Tarzan. 'But if they give you trouble do with them as you see fit.'

It took little more than an hour to evacuate the village. All of Smith's loads were recovered, including Danny's precious ammunition and extra drums for his beloved Thompson; and these were assigned to Smith's porters, who were once again assembled under Ogonyo.

When the village was emptied it was fired in a dozen places; and, as the black smoke curled up toward the blue heavens, the various parties took their respective ways from the scene of their captivity, but not before the several headmen had come and knelt before the Lord of the Jungle and thanked him for the deliverance of their people.

XXVI

The Last Knot is Tied

Lafayette Smith and Lady Barbara had been mystified witnesses to the sudden transformation of the peaceful scene in the camp of Lord Passmore. All day the warriors had remained in readiness, as though expecting a summons; and when night fell they still waited.

Evidences of restlessness were apparent; and there was no singing and little laughter in the camp, as there had been before. The last that the two whites saw, as they retired for the night, were the little groups of plumed warriors squatting about their fires, their rifles ready to their hands; and they were asleep when the summons came and the sleek, black fighting men melted silently into the dark shadows of the forest, leaving only four of their number to guard the camp and the two guests.

When Lady Barbara emerged from her tent in the morning she was astonished to find the camp all but deserted. The *boy* who acted in the capacity of personal servant and cook for her and Smith was there and three other blacks. All were constantly armed; but their attitude toward her had not changed, and she felt only curiosity relative to the other altered conditions, so obvious at first glance, rather than apprehension.

When Smith joined her a few minutes later he was equally at a loss to understand the strange metamorphosis that had transformed the laughing, joking porters and askaris into painted warriors and sent them out into the night so surreptitiously, nor could they glean the slightest information from their *boy*, who, though still courteous and smiling, seemed by some strange trick of fate suddenly to have forgotten the very fair command of English that he had exhibited with evident pride on the previous day.

The long day dragged on until mid afternoon without sign of any change. Neither Lord Passmore nor the missing blacks returned, and the enigma was as baffling as before. The two whites, however, seemed to find much pleasure in one another's company; and so, perhaps, the day passed more rapidly for them than it did for the four blacks, waiting and listening through the hot, drowsy hours.

But suddenly there was a change. Lady Barbara saw her *boy* rise and stand in an attitude of eager listening. 'They come!' he said, in his own tongue, to his companions. Now they all stood and, though they may have expected only friends, their rifles were in readiness for enemies.

Gradually the sound of voices and of marching men became distinctly audible to the untrained ears of the two whites, and a little later they saw the head of a column filing through the forest toward them.

'Why there's the "Gunner"!' exclaimed Lafayette Smith. 'And Jezebel, too. How odd that they should be together.'

'With Tarzan of the Apes!' cried Lady Barbara. 'He has saved them both.'

A slow smile touched the lips of the ape-man as he witnessed the reunion of Lady Barbara and Jezebel and that between Smith and the 'Gunner'; and it broadened a little, when, after the first burst of greetings and explanations, Lady Barbara said, 'It is unfortunate that our host, Lord Passmore, isn't here.'

'He is,' said the ape-man.

'Where?' demanded Lafayette Smith, looking about the camp.

'I am "Lord Passmore,"' said Tarzan.

'You?' exclaimed Lady Barbara.

'Yes. I assumed this role when I came north to investigate the rumors I had heard concerning Capietro and his band, believing that they not only would suspect no danger, but hoping, also, that they would seek to attack and plunder my safari as they have those of others.'

'Geeze,' said the 'Gunner.' 'What a jolt they would of got!'

'That is why we never saw "Lord Passmore,"' said Lady Barbara, laughing. 'I thought him a most elusive host.'

'The first night I left you here,' explained Tarzan, 'I walked into the jungle until I was out of sight, and then I came back from another direction and entered my tent from the rear. I slept there all night. The next morning, early, I left in search of your friends and was captured myself. But everything has worked out well, and if you have no other immediate plans I hope that you will accompany me back to my home and remain a while as my guests while you recover from the rather rough experiences Africa has afforded you. Or, perhaps,' he added, 'Professor Smith and his friend wish to continue their geological investigations.'

'I, ah, well, you see,' stammered Lafayette Smith; 'I have about decided to abandon my work in Africa and devote my life to the geology of England. We, or, er – you see, Lady Barbara—'

'I am going to take him back to England and teach him to shoot before I let him return to Africa. Possibly we shall come back later, though.'

'And you Patrick,' asked Tarzan, 'are you remaining to hunt, perhaps?'

'Nix, mister,' said Danny, emphatically. 'We're goin' to California and buy a garage and filling station.'

'We?' queried Lady Barbara.

'Sure,' said the 'Gunner'; 'me and Jez.'

'Really?' exclaimed Lady Barbara. 'Is he in earnest, Jezebel?'

'Oke, kid – isn't it ripping?' replied the golden one.

TARZAN AND THE CITY OF GOLD

1

Savage Quarry

Down out of Tigre and Amhara upon Gojam and Shoa and Kaffa come the rains from June to September, carrying silt and prosperity from Abyssinia to the eastern Sudan and to Egypt, bringing muddy trails and swollen rivers and death and prosperity to Abyssinia.

Of these gifts of the rains, only the muddy trails and the swollen rivers and death interested a little band of *shiftas* that held out in the remote fastnesses of the mountains of Kaffa. Hard men were these mounted bandits, cruel criminals without even a vestige of culture such as occasionally leavens the activities of rogues, lessening their ruthlessness. Kaficho and Galla they were, the offscourings of their tribes, outlaws, men with prices upon their heads.

It was not raining now; and the rainy season was drawing to a close, for it was the middle of September; but there was still much water in the rivers, and the ground was soft after a recent rain.

The *shiftas* rode, seeking loot from wayfarer, caravan, or village; and as they rode, the unshod hoofs of their horses left a plain spoor that one night read upon the run; not that that that caused the *shiftas* any concern, because no one was looking for them. All that anyone in the district wished of the *shiftas* was to keep out of their way.

A short distance ahead of them, in the direction toward which they were riding, a hunting beast stalked its prey. The wind was blowing from it toward the approaching horsemen; and for this reason their scent spoor was not borne to its sensitive nostrils, nor did the soft ground give forth any sound beneath the feet of their walking mounts that the keen ears of the hunter might detect during the period of concentration and mild excitement attendant upon the stalk.

Though the stalker did not resemble a beast of prey, such as the term connotes to the mind of man, he was one nevertheless; for in his natural haunts he filled his belly by the chase and by the chase alone; neither did he resemble the mental picture that one might hold of a typical British lord, yet he was that too – he was Tarzan of the Apes.

All beasts of prey find hunting poor during a rain, and Tarzan was no exception to the rule. It had rained for two days, and as a result Tarzan was hungry. A small buck was drinking in a stream fringed by bushes and tall reeds, and Tarzan was worming his way upon his belly through short grass to reach a position from which he might either charge or loose an arrow or cast a spear. He was not aware that a group of horsemen had reined in upon a gentle rise a short distance behind him where they sat in silence regarding him intently.

Usha, the wind, who carries scent, also carries sound. Today, Usha carried both the scent and the sound of the *shiftas* away from the keen nostrils and the ears of the ape-man. Perhaps, endowed as he was with supersensitive perceptive faculties, Tarzan should have sensed the presence of an enemy; but 'Even the worthy Homer sometimes nods.'

However self-sufficient an animal may be it is endowed with caution, for there is none that has not its enemies. The weaker herbivora must be always on the alert for the lion, the leopard, and man; the elephant, the rhinoceros, and the lion may never relax their vigilance against man; and man must always be on guard against these and others. Yet one may not say that such caution connotes either fear or cowardice; for Tarzan, who was without fear, was the personification of caution, especially when he was far from his own stamping grounds as he was today and every creature a potential enemy.

The combination of ravenous hunger with the opportunity to satisfy it may have placed caution in abeyance as, oftentimes, a certain recklessness born of pride in his might did; but, be that as it may, the fact remains that Tarzan was wholly ignorant of the presence of that little knot of villainous bandits who were quite prepared to kill him, or anyone else, for a few poor weapons or for nothing at all.

The circumstances that brought Tarzan northward into Kaffa are not a part of this story. Perhaps they were not urgent, for the Lord of the Jungle loves to roam remote fastnesses still unspoiled by the devastating hand of civilization and needs but trifling incentive to do so. Still unsated with adventure, it may be that Abyssinia's three hundred fifty thousand square miles of semisavagery held an irresistible lure for him in their suggestion of mysterious back country and in the ethnological secrets they have guarded from time immemorial.

Wanderer, adventurer, outcast, Greek phalanx, and Roman legion, all have entered Abyssinia within times chronicled in history or legend never to reappear; and it is even believed by some that she holds the secret of the lost tribes of Israel. What wonders, then, what adventures, might not her remote corners reveal!

At the moment, however, Tarzan's mind was not occupied by thoughts of adventure; he did not know that it loomed threateningly behind him; his concern and his interest were centered upon the buck which he intended should satisfy the craving of his ravenous hunger. He crept cautiously forward. Than he, not even Sheeta, the leopard, stalks more silently or more stealthily.

From behind, the white-robed *shiftas* moved from the little rise where they had been watching him in silence, moved down toward him with spear and long-barreled matchlock. They were puzzled. Never before had they seen a white man like this one; but if curiosity were in their minds, there was only murder in their hearts.

The buck raised his head occasionally to glance about him, wary, suspicious; and when he did so, Tarzan froze into immobility. Suddenly the animal's gaze centered for an instant upon something in the direction of the ape-man; then it wheeled and bounded away. Instantly Tarzan glanced behind him, for he knew that it had not been he who had frightened his quarry but something beyond and behind him that the alert eyes of Wappi had discovered; and that quick glance revealed a half dozen horsemen moving slowly toward him, told him what they were, and explained their purpose; for, knowing that they were *shiftas*, he knew that they came only to rob and kill – knew that here were enemies more ruthless than Numa.

When they saw that he had discovered them, the horsemen broke into a gallop and bore down upon him, waving their weapons and shouting. They did not fire, evidently holding in contempt this primitively armed victim, but seemed to purpose riding him down and trampling him beneath the hoofs of their horses or impaling him upon their spears. Perhaps they thought that he would seek safety in flight, thereby giving them the added thrill of the chase; and what quarry could give the hunter greater thrills than man!

But Tarzan did not turn and run. He knew every possible avenue of escape within the radius of his vision for every danger that might reasonably be expected to confront him here, for it is the business of the creatures of the wild to know these things if they are to survive; and so he knew that there was no escape from mounted men by flight. But this knowledge threw him into no panic. Could the requirements of self-preservation have been best achieved by flight, he would have fled; but as they could not, he adopted the alternative quite as a matter of course – he stood to fight, ready to seize upon any fortuitous circumstance that might offer a chance of escape.

Tall, magnificently proportioned, muscled more like Apollo than like Hercules, garbed only in a narrow G string of lion skin with a lion's tail depending before and behind, he presented a splendid figure of primitive manhood that suggested more, perhaps, the demigod of the forest than it did man. Across his back hung his quiver of arrows and a light, short spear; the loose coils of his grass rope lay across one bronzed shoulder; at his hip swung the hunting knife of his father, the knife that had given the boy-Tarzan the first suggestion of his coming supremacy over the other beasts of the jungle on that far gone day when his youthful hand drove it into the heart of Bolgani, the gorilla; in his left hand was his bow and between the fingers four extra arrows.

As Ara, the lightning, so is Tarzan for swiftness. The instant that he had discovered and recognized the menace creeping upon him from behind and known that he had been seen by the horsemen he had leaped to his feet, and in the same instant strung his bow. Now, perhaps even before the leading *shiftas* realized the danger that confronted them, the bow was bent, the shaft sped.

Short but powerful was the bow of the ape-man; short, that it might be easily carried through the forest and the jungle; powerful, that it might send its shafts through the toughest hide to a vital organ of its prey. Such a bow was this that no ordinary man might bend it.

Straight through the heart of the leading *shifta* drove the first arrow, and as the fellow threw his arms above his head and lunged from his saddle four more arrows sped with lightning-like rapidity from the bow of the ape-man, and every arrow found a target. Another *shifta* dropped to ride no more, and three were wounded.

Only seconds had elapsed since Tarzan had discovered his danger, and already the four remaining horsemen were upon him. The three who were wounded were more interested in the feathered shafts protruding from their bodies than in the quarry they had expected so easily to overcome; but the fourth was whole, and he thundered down upon the ape-man with his spear set for the great bronzed chest.

There could be no retreat for Tarzan; there could be no sidestepping to avoid the thrust, for a step to either side would have carried him in front of one of the other horsemen. He had but a single slender hope for survival, and that hope, forlorn though it appeared, he seized upon with the celerity, strength, and agility that make Tarzan Tarzan. Slipping his bowstring about his neck after his final shot, he struck up the point of the menacing weapon of his antagonist, and grasping the man's arm swung himself to the horse's back behind the rider.

As steel-thewed fingers closed upon the *shifta's* throat he voiced a single piercing scream; then a knife drove home beneath his left shoulder blade, and Tarzan hurled the body from the saddle. The terrified horse, running free with flying reins, tore through the bushes and the reeds into the river, while the remaining *shiftas*, disabled by their wounds, were glad to abandon the chase upon the bank, though one of them, retaining more vitality than his companions, did raise his matchlock and send a parting shot after the escaping quarry.

The river was a narrow, sluggish stream but deep in the channel; and as the horse plunged into it, Tarzan saw a commotion in the water a few yards downstream and then the outline of a long, sinuous body moving swiftly toward them. It was Gimla, the crocodile. The horse saw it too and, becoming frantic, turned upstream in an effort to escape. Tarzan climbed over the high cantle of the Abyssinian saddle and unslung his spear in the rather futile hope of holding the reptile at bay until his mount could reach the safety of the opposite bank toward which he was now attempting to guide him.

Gimla is as swift as he is voracious. He was already at the horse's rump, with opened jaws, when the *shifta* at the river's edge fired wildly at the ape-man. It was well for Tarzan that the wounded man had fired hurriedly; for simultaneously with the report of the firearm, the crocodile dove; and the frenzied lashing of the water about him evidenced the fact that he had been mortally wounded.

A moment later the horse that Tarzan rode reached the opposite bank and clambered to the safety of dry land. Now he was under control again; and the ape-man wheeled him about and sent a parting arrow across the river toward the angry, cursing bandits upon the opposite side, an arrow that found its mark in the thigh of the already wounded man who had unwittingly rescued Tarzan from a serious situation with the shot that had been intended to kill him.

To the accompaniment of a few wild and scattered shots, Tarzan of the Apes galloped toward a nearby forest into which he disappeared from the sight of the angry *shiftas*.

2

The White Prisoner

Far to the south a lion rose from his kill and walked majestically to the edge of a nearby river. He cast not so much as a single glance at the circle of hyenas and jackals that had ringed him and his kill waiting for him to depart and which had broken and retreated as he rose. Nor, when the hyenas rushed in to tear at what he had left, did he appear even to see them.

There were the pride and bearing of royalty in the mien of this mighty beast; and to add to his impressiveness were his great size, his yellow, almost golden, coat, and his great black mane. When he had drunk his fill, he lifted his massive head and voiced a roar, as is the habit of lions when they have fed and drunk; and the earth shook to his thunderous voice, and a hush fell upon the jungle.

Now he should have sought his lair and slept, to go forth again at night and kill; but he did not do so. He did not do at all what might have been expected of a lion under similar circumstances. He raised his head and sniffed the air, and then he put his nose to the ground and moved to and fro like a hunting dog searching for a game scent. Finally he halted and voiced a low roar; then, with head raised, he moved off along a trail that led toward the north. The hyenas were glad to see him go; so were the jackals, who wished that the hyenas would go also. Ska, the vulture, circling above, wished that they would all leave.

At about the same time, many marches to the north, three angry, wounded *shiftas* viewed their dead comrades and cursed the fate that had led them upon the trail of the strange white giant; then they stripped the clothing and weapons from their dead fellows and rode away, loudly vowing vengeance should they ever again come upon the author of their discomfiture and secretly hoping that they never would. They hoped that they were done with him, but they were not.

Shortly after he had entered the forest, Tarzan swung to an overhanging branch beneath which his mount was passing and let the animal go its way. The ape-man was angry; the *shiftas* had frightened away his dinner. That they had sought to kill him annoyed him far less than the fact that they had spoiled his hunting. Now he must commence his search for meat all over again, but when he had filled his belly he would look into this matter of *shiftas*. Of this he was certain.

Tarzan had considered the gastronomic potentialities of the bandit's horse, but had discarded the idea. On several occasions in the past he had been forced to eat horse meat, but he had not liked it. Although he was hungry, he was far from famished; and so he preferred to hunt again until he found flesh more palatable, nor was it long before he had made his kill and eaten.

Satisfied, he lay up for a while in the crotch of a tree, but not for long. His active mind was considering the matter of the *shiftas*. Here was something that should be looked into. If the band were on the march, he need not concern himself about them; but if they were permanently located in this district, that was a different matter; for Tarzan expected to be here for some time; and it was well to know the nature, the number, and the location of all enemies. Furthermore, he felt that he could not let them escape without some additional punishment for the inconvenience they had caused him.

Returning to the river, Tarzan crossed it and took up the plain trail of the *shiftas*. It led him up and down across some low hills and then down into the narrow valley of the stream that he had crossed farther up. Here the floor of the valley was forested, the river winding through the wood. Into this wood the trail led.

It was almost dark now; the brief equatorial twilight was rapidly fading into the night; the nocturnal life of the forest and the hills was awakening; from down among the deepening shadows of the valley came the coughing grunts of a hunting lion. Tarzan sniffed the warm air rising from the valley toward the mountains; it carried with it the odors of a camp and the scent spoor of man. He raised his head, and from his deep chest rumbled a full-throated roar. Tarzan of the Apes was hunting too.

In the gathering shadows he stood then erect and silent, a lonely figure standing in solitary grandeur upon that desolate hillside. Swiftly the silent night enveloped him; his figure merged with the darkness that made hill and valley, river and forest one. Not until then did Tarzan move; then he stepped down on silent feet toward the forest. Now was every sense alert, for now the great cats would be hunting. Often his sensitive nostrils quivered as they searched the air; no slightest sound escaped his keen ears.

As he advanced, the man scent became stronger, guiding his steps. Nearer and nearer sounded the deep cough of the lion; but of Numa Tarzan had little fear at present, knowing that the great cat, being upwind, could not be aware of his presence. Doubtless Numa had heard the ape-man's roar, but he could not know that its author was approaching him.

Tarzan had estimated the lion's distance down the valley and the distance that lay between himself and the forest and had guessed that he would reach the trees before their paths crossed. He was not hunting for Numa, the lion, and with the natural caution of the wild beasts, he would avoid an encounter. It was not food either that he hunted, for his belly was full, but man, the arch-enemy of all created things.

It was difficult for Tarzan to think of himself as a man, and his psychology was more often that of the wild beast than the human, nor was he particularly proud of his species. While he appreciated the intellectual superiority of man over other creatures, he harbored contempt for him because he had wasted the greater part of his inheritance. To Tarzan, as to many other created things, contentment is the highest ultimate goal of achievement, and health and culture the principal avenues along which man may approach this goal. With scorn the ape-man viewed the overwhelming majority of mankind which was wanting in either one essential or the other, when not wanting in both. He saw the greed, the selfishness, the cowardice, and the cruelty of man; and, in view of man's vaunted mentality, he knew that these characteristics placed man upon a lower spiritual scale than the beasts, while barring him eternally from the goal of contentment.

So now, as he sought the lair of the man-things, it was not in the spirit of one who seeks his own kind but of a beast which reconnoiters the position of an enemy. The mingled odors of a camp grew stronger in his nostrils, the scents of horses and men and food and smoke. To you or to me, alone in a savage wilderness, engulfed in darkness, cognizant of the near approach of a hunting lion, these odors would have been most welcome; but Tarzan's reaction to them was that of the wild beast that knows man only as an enemy – his snarling muscles tensed as he smothered a low growl.

As Tarzan reached the edge of the forest the lion was but a short distance to his right and approaching; so the ape-man took to the trees, through which he swung silently toward the camp of the *shiftas*. Numa heard him then and roared, and the men in the camp threw more wood upon the beast fire.

To a tree overlooking the camp, Tarzan made his way. Below him he saw a band of some twenty men with their horses and equipment. A rude boma of branches and brush had been erected about the camp site as a partial protection against wild beasts, but more dependence was evidently placed upon the fire which they kept burning in the center of the camp.

In a single quick glance the ape-man took in the details of the scene below him, and then his eyes came to rest upon the only one that aroused either interest or curiosity, a white man who lay securely bound a short distance from the fire.

Ordinarily, Tarzan was no more concerned by the fate of a white man than by that of a black man or any other created thing to which he was not bound by ties of friendship; the life of a man meant less to Tarzan of the Apes than the life of an ape. But in this instance there were two factors that made the life of the captive a matter of interest to the Lord of the Jungle. First, and probably predominant, was his desire to be further avenged upon the *shiftas* for their wanton attack upon him, which had frightened away his intended kill; the second was curiosity, for the white man that lay bound below him was different from any that he had seen before, at least in so far as his apparel was concerned.

His only garment appeared to be a habergeon made up of ivory discs that partially overlay one another, unless certain ankle, wrist, neck, and head ornaments might have been considered to possess such utilitarian properties as to entitle them to a similar classification. Except for these, his arms and legs were naked. His head rested upon the ground with the face turned away from Tarzan so that the ape-man could not see his features but only that his hair was heavy and black.

As he watched the camp, seeking for some suggestion as to how he might most annoy or inconvenience the bandits, it occurred to Tarzan that a just reprisal would consist in taking from them something that they wanted, just as they had deprived him of the buck he had desired. Evidently they wished the prisoner very much or they would not have gone to the trouble of securing him so carefully; so this fact decided Tarzan to steal the white man from them. Perhaps curiosity also had a considerable part in inducing this decision, for the strange apparel of the prisoner had aroused within the ape-man a desire to know more concerning him.

To accomplish his design, he decided to wait until the camp slept; and settling himself comfortably in a crotch of the tree, he prepared to keep his vigil with the tireless patience of the hunting beast he was. As he watched, he saw several of the *shiftas* attempt to communicate with their prisoner; but it was evident that neither understood the other.

Tarzan was familiar with the language spoken by the Kafichos and Gallas, and the questions that they put to their prisoner aroused his curiosity still further. There was one question that they asked him in many different ways, in several dialects, and in signs which the captive either did not understand or pretended not to. Tarzan was inclined to believe that the latter was true, for the sign language was such that it could scarcely be misunderstood. They were asking him the way to a place where there was much ivory and gold, but they got no information from him.

'The pig understands us well enough,' growled one of the *shiftas;* 'he is just pretending that he does not.'

'If he won't tell us, what is the use of carrying him around with us and feeding him?' demanded another. 'We might as well kill him now.'

'We will let him think it over tonight,' replied one who was evidently the leader, 'and if he still refuses to speak in the morning, we will kill him then.'

This decision they attempted to transmit to the prisoner both by words and signs, and then they squatted about the fire and discussed the occurrences of the day and their plans for the future. The principal topic of their conversation was the strange white giant who had slain three of their number and escaped upon one of their horses; and after this had been debated thoroughly and in detail for some time, and the three survivors of the encounter had boasted severally of their deeds of valor, they withdrew to the rude shelters they had constructed and left the night to Tarzan, Numa, and a single sentry.

The silent watcher among the shadows of the tree waited on in patience until the camp should be sunk in deepest slumber and, waiting, planned the stroke that was to rob the *shiftas* of their prey and satisfy his own desire for revenge. As he patiently bided his time, there came strongly to his nostrils the scent spoor of Numa, the lion; and he guessed that the carnivore, attracted by the presence of the horses, was coming to investigate the camp. That he would enter it, he doubted, for the sentry was keeping the fire blazing brightly; and Numa seldom dares the fearful mystery of flames unless goaded by extreme hunger.

At last the ape-man felt that the time had come when he might translate his plan into action; all but the sentry were wrapped in slumber, and even he was dozing beside the fire. As noiselessly as the shadow of a shadow Tarzan descended from the tree, keeping well in the shadow cast by the beast fire.

For a moment he stood in silence, listening. He heard the breathing of Numa in the darkness beyond the circle of firelight, and knew that the king of beasts was near and watching. Then he looked from behind the great bole of the tree and saw that the sentry's back was still turned toward him. Silently he moved into the open; stealthily, on soundless feet, he crept toward the unsuspecting bandit. He saw the matchlock across the fellow's knees; and for it he had respect, as have all jungle animals that have been hunted.

Closer and closer he came to his prey. At last he crouched directly behind him. There must be no noise, no outcry. Tarzan waited. Beyond the rim of fire waited Numa, expectant, for he saw that very gradually the flames were diminishing. A bronzed hand shot quickly forward, fingers of steel gripped the brown throat of the sentry almost at the instant that a knife was driven from below his left shoulder blade into his heart. The sentry was dead without knowing that death threatened him, a merciful ending.

Tarzan withdrew the knife from the limp body and wiped the blade upon the once white robe of his victim; then he moved softly toward the prisoner who was lying in the open. For him, they had not bothered to build a shelter. As he made his way toward the man, Tarzan passed close to two of the shelters in which lay members of the band; but he made no noise that might awaken them. When he approached the captive more closely, he saw in the diminishing light of the fire that the man's eyes were open and that he was regarding Tarzan with level, though questioning, gaze. The ape-man put a finger to his lips to enjoin silence, and then he came and knelt beside the man and cut the thongs that secured his wrists and ankles; then he helped him to his feet, for the thongs had been drawn tightly, and his legs were numb.

For a moment he waited while the stranger tested his feet and moved them rapidly in an effort to restore circulation; then he beckoned him to follow, and all would have been well but for Numa, the lion. At this moment, either to voice his anger against the flames or to terrify the horses into a stampede, he elected to voice a thunderous roar.

So close was the lion that the sudden shattering of the deep silence of the night startled every sleeper to wakefulness. A dozen men seized their matchlocks and leaped from their shelters. In the waning light of the fire they saw no lion; but they saw their liberated captive, and they saw Tarzan of the Apes standing beside him.

Among those who ran from the shelters was the least seriously wounded of Tarzan's victims of the afternoon. Instantly recognizing the bronzed white giant, he shouted loudly to his companions, 'It is he! It is the white demon who killed our friends today.'

'Kill him!' screamed another.

'Kill them both!' cried the leader of the *shiftas*.

Completely surrounding the two white men, the *shiftas* advanced upon them; but they dared not fire because of fear that they might wound one of their own comrades. Nor could Tarzan loose an arrow nor cast a spear, for he had left all his weapons except his rope and his knife hidden in the tree above the camp that he might move with the utmost freedom and in silence while seeking to liberate the captive.

One of the bandits, more courageous, probably because less intelligent, than his fellows, rushed to close quarters with musket clubbed. It was his undoing. The man-beast crouched, growling; and, as the other was almost upon him, charged. The musket butt, hurtling through the air to strike him down, he dodged; and then he seized the weapon and wrenched it from the *shifta's* grasp as though it had been a toy in a child's hands.

Tossing the matchlock at the feet of his companion, Tarzan laid hold upon the rash Galla, spun him around, and held him as a shield against the weapons of his fellows. But despite this reverse the other *shiftas* gave no indication of giving up the battle. They saw before them two men practically defenseless, and now with redoubled shouts they pushed closer.

Two of them rushed in behind the ape-man, for it was he they feared the more; but they were to learn that their former prisoner might not be considered lightly. He had picked up the musket that Tarzan had cast aside and, grasping it close to the muzzle, was using it as a club. The heavy butt struck the foremost bandit heavily upon the side of the head, dropping him like a felled ox; and as it swung again, the second bandit leaped back barely in time to avoid a similar fate.

A quick backward glance assured Tarzan that his companion was proving himself a worthy ally, but it was evident that they could not hope to hold out long against the superior numbers pitted against them. Their only hope, he believed, lay in making a sudden, concerted rush through the thin line of foemen surrounding them, and he sought to convey his plan to the man standing back to back with him; but though he spoke to him in English and in the several continental languages with which the ape-man was familiar the only reply he received was in a language that he himself had never before heard.

What was he to do? They must go together, and both must understand the purpose animating Tarzan. But how was that possible if they could not communicate with one another? Tarzan turned and touched the other lightly on the shoulder; then he jerked his thumb in the direction he intended going and beckoned with a nod of his head.

Instantly the man nodded his understanding and wheeled about as Tarzan started to charge, still bearing the struggling *shifta* in his grasp; but the *shiftas* were determined not to let these two escape; and while they could not fire for fear of killing their comrade, they stood their ground with clubbed muskets and with spears; so that the outcome looked dark indeed for the Lord of the Jungle and his companion.

Using the man in his grasp as a flail, Tarzan sought to mow down those standing between him and liberty; but there were many of them, and presently they succeeded in dragging their comrade from the clutches of the ape-man. Now it seemed that the situation of the two whites was hopeless, for there was no longer anything to prevent the bandits using their matchlocks to advantage. The *shiftas* were in such a transport of rage that nothing less than the extermination of these two foes would satisfy them; but Tarzan and the other pressed on so closely that the muskets were useless against them for the moment; though presently some of the *shiftas* withdrew a little to one side where they might have free use of their weapons.

One fellow in particular was well placed to fire without endangering any of his fellows, and raising his matchlock to his shoulder he took careful aim at Tarzan.

3

Cats by Night

As the man raised his weapon to his shoulder to fire at Tarzan, a scream of warning burst from the lips of one of his comrades, to be drowned by the throaty roar of Numa, the lion, as the swift rush of his charge carried him over the boma into the midst of the camp.

The man who would have killed Tarzan cast a quick backward glance as the warning cry apprised him of his danger; and when he saw the lion he cast away his rifle in his excitement and terror, his terrified scream mingled with the voice of Numa, and in his anxiety to escape the fangs of the man-eater he rushed into the arms of the ape-man.

The lion, momentarily confused by the firelight and the swift movement and the shouts of the men, paused, crouching, as he looked to right and left. In that brief instant Tarzan seized the fleeing *shifta*, lifted him high above his head, and hurled him into the face of Numa; then, as the lion seized its prey and its great jaws closed upon the head and shoulder of the hapless bandit, he motioned to his companion to follow him, and, running directly past the lion, leaped the boma at the very point that Numa had leaped it. Close at his heels was the white captive of the *shiftas*, and before the bandits had recovered from the first shock and surprise of the lion's unexpected charge the two had disappeared in the shadows of the night.

Just outside the camp Tarzan left his companion for a moment while he swung into the tree where he had left his weapons and recovered them; then he led the way out of the valley up into the hills. At his elbow trotted the silent white man he had rescued from certain death at the hands of the Kafi-cho and Galla bandits.

During the brief encounter in the camp Tarzan had noted with admiration the strength, agility, and courage of the stranger who had aroused both his interest and his curiosity. Here, seemingly, was a man moulded to the dimensions of Tarzan's own standards, a quiet, resourceful, courageous fighting man. Radiating that intangible aura which we call personality, even in his silences he impressed the ape-man with a conviction that loyalty and dependability were innate characteristics of the man; so Tarzan, who ordinarily preferred to be alone, was not displeased to have the companionship of this stranger.

The moon, almost full, had risen above the black mountain mass to the east, shedding her soft light on hill and valley and forest, transforming the scene once more into that of a new world which was different from the world of daylight and from the world of moonless night, a world of strange greys and silvery greens.

Up toward a fringe of forest that clothed the upper slopes of the foothills and dipped down into canyon and ravine the two men moved as noiselessly as the passing shadow of a cloud, yet to one hidden in the dark recesses of the wood above, their approach was not unheralded, for on the breath of Usha, the wind, it was borne ahead of them to the cunning nostrils of the prince of hunters.

Sheeta, the panther, was hungry. For several days prey had been scarce and elusive. Now, in his nostrils, the scent of the man-things grew stronger as they drew nearer. It was the pure scent of man that came to him unvitiated by the hated odor of the flame-belching thunder stick that he feared and hated. Eagerly, Sheeta, the panther, awaited the coming of the men.

Within the forest, Tarzan sought a tree where they might lie up for the night. He had eaten and was not hungry. Whether or not his companion had eaten was his own concern. This was a law of the jungle from which Tarzan might deviate for a weak or wounded companion but not for a strong man able to provide for himself. Had he killed, he would have shared his kill; but he would not go forth and hunt for another.

Tarzan found a branch that forked horizontally. With his hunting knife he cut other branches and laid them across the two arms of the Y thus formed. Over this rude platform he spread leaves; and then he lay down to sleep, while from an adjacent tree upwind Sheeta watched him. Sheeta also watched the other man-thing on the ground between the two trees. The great cat did not move; he seemed scarcely to breathe. Even Tarzan was unaware of his presence, yet the ape-man was restless. A sense so delicate that he was not objectively aware of its existence seemed to warn him that all was not well. He listened intently and sniffed the air but detected nothing amiss. Below him, his companion was making his bed upon the ground in preference to risking the high-flung branches of the trees to which he was unaccustomed. It was the man upon the ground that Sheeta watched.

At last, his bed of leaves and grasses arranged to suit him, Tarzan's companion lay down. Sheeta waited. Gradually, almost imperceptibly, the sinuous muscles were drawing the hind quarters forward beneath the sleek body in preparation for the spring. Sheeta edged forward on the great limb upon which he crouched, but in doing so he caused the branch to move slightly and the leaves at its end to rustle just a little. Your ears or mine would not have been conscious of any noise, but the ears of Tarzan are not as are yours or mine.

He heard; and his eyes, turning quickly, sought and found the intruder. At the same instant Sheeta launched himself at the man lying on his rude pallet on the ground below; and as Sheeta sprang so did Tarzan. What happened happened very quickly; it was a matter of seconds only.

As the two beasts sprang, Tarzan voiced a roar that was intended both to warn his companion and to distract the attention of Sheeta from his prey. The man upon the ground leaped quickly to one side, prompted more by an instinctive reaction than by reason. The panther's body brushed him as it struck the ground, but the beast's thoughts were now upon the thing that had voiced that menacing roar rather than upon its intended prey.

Wheeling as he leaped aside, the man turned and saw the savage carnivore just as Tarzan landed full upon the beast's back. He heard the mingled growls of the two as they closed in battle, and his scalp stiffened as he realized that the sounds coming from the lips of his companion were quite as bestial as those issuing from the throat of the carnivore.

Tarzan sought a hold about the neck of the panther, while the great cat instantly attempted to roll over on its back that it might rip the body of its antagonist to shreds with the terrible talons that armed its hind feet. But this strategy the ape-man had anticipated; and rolling beneath Sheeta as Sheeta rolled, he locked his powerful legs beneath the belly of the panther; then the great cat leaped to its feet again and sought to shake the man-thing from its back; and all the while a mighty arm was tightening about its neck, closing off its wind.

With frantic leaps and bounds the panther hurled itself about in the moonlight while Tarzan's companion stood unarmed and helpless. Twice he had tried to run in and assist the ape-man, but both times the two bodies had struck him and sent him spinning across the ground. Now he saw a new factor being injected into the battle; Tarzan had succeeded in drawing his knife. Momentarily the blade flashed before his eyes; then it was buried in the body of Sheeta. The cat, screaming from pain and rage, redoubled its efforts to dislodge the creature clinging to it in the embrace of death; but again the knife fell.

Now Sheeta stood trembling upon uncertain feet as once again the knife was plunged deeply into his side; then, his great voice forever stilled, he sank lifeless to the ground as the ape-man rolled from beneath him and sprang to his feet.

The man whose life Tarzan had saved came forward and laid a hand upon the shoulder of the ape-man, speaking a few words in a low voice but in a tongue that Tarzan did not understand, though he guessed that it expressed the gratitude that the manner of the man betokened.

What thoughts were in the mind of Tarzan's companion? Twice within an hour this strange white man had saved him from death. For what reasons, the man could not guess. That sentiments of friendship and loyalty were aroused in his breast would seem only natural if he possessed either honor or gratitude, but of this we can have no knowledge until we know him better. As yet he is not even a name to us; and, following the policy of Tarzan, we shall not judge him until we know him better; then we may learn to like him, or we may have reason to despise him.

Influenced by the attack of the panther and knowing that Numa was abroad, Tarzan, by signs, persuaded the man to come up into the tree; and here the ape-man helped him construct a nest similar to his own. For the balance of the night they slept in peace, and the sun was an hour old before either stirred the following morning; then the ape-man rose and stretched himself.

Nearby, the other man sat up and looked about him. His eyes met Tarzan's, and he smiled and nodded. For the first time the ape-man had an opportunity to examine his new acquaintance by daylight. The man had removed his single garment for the night, covering himself with leaves and branches. Now as he arose, his only garment was a G string, and Tarzan saw six feet of well-muscled, well-proportioned body topped by a head that seemed to bespeak breeding and intelligence. The man's features were strong, clear cut, and harmoniously placed; the face was more noticeable for strength and rugged masculinity than for beauty.

The wild beast in Tarzan looked into the brown eyes of the stranger and was satisfied that here was one who might be trusted; the man in him noted the headband that confined the black hair, saw the strangely wrought ivory ornament in the center of the forehead, the habergeon that he was now donning, the ivory ornaments on wrists and ankles, and found his curiosity piqued.

The ivory ornament in the center of the headband was shaped like a concave, curved trowel, the point of which projected above the top of the man's head and curved forward. His wristlets and anklets were of long flat strips of ivory laid close together and fastened around the limbs by leather thongs that were laced through holes piercing the strips near their tops and bottoms. His sandals were of heavy leather, apparently elephant hide, and were supported by leather thongs fastened to the bottoms of his anklets.

On each arm below the shoulder he wore an ivory disc upon which was carved a design; about his neck was a band of smaller ivory discs elaborately carved, and from the lowest of these a strap ran down to his habergeon, which was also supported by shoulder straps. Depending from each side of his headband was another ivory disc of large size, above which was a smaller disc. The larger discs covered his ears. Heavy, curved, wedge-shaped pieces of ivory were held, one upon each shoulder, by the same straps that supported his habergeon.

That all these trappings were solely for purposes of ornamentation Tarzan did not believe. He saw that almost without exception they would serve as a protection against a cutting weapon such as a sword or battle-ax; and he could not but wonder where the stalwart warrior who wore them had had his genesis, for nowhere in the world, so far as Tarzan knew, was there a race of men wearing armor and ornaments such as these.

But speculation concerning this matter was relegated to the background of his thoughts by hunger and recollection of the remains of yesterday's kill that he had hung high in a tree of the forest farther up the river; so he dropped lightly to the ground, motioning the young warrior to follow him; and set off in the direction of his cache, keeping his keen senses always on the alert for enemies.

Cleverly hidden by leafy branches, the meat was intact when Tarzan reached it. He cut several strips and tossed them down to the warrior waiting on the ground below; then he cut some for himself and crouching in a crotch proceeded to eat it raw. His companion watched him for a moment in surprise; then he made fire with a bit of steel and flint and cooked his own portion.

As he ate, Tarzan's active mind was considering plans for the future. He had come to Abyssinia for a specific purpose, though the matter was not of such immediate importance that it demanded instant attention. In fact, in the philosophy that a lifetime of primitive environment had inspired, time was not an important consideration. The phenomenon of this ivory-armored warrior aroused questions that intrigued his interest to a far greater extent than did the problems that had brought him thus far from his own stamping grounds, and he decided that the latter should wait the solving of the riddle of this seeming anachronism that his new-made acquaintance presented.

Having no other means of communication than signs rendered an exchange of ideas between the two difficult, but when they had finished their meal and Tarzan had descended to the ground he succeeded in asking his companion in what direction he wished to go. The warrior pointed in a northeasterly direction toward the high mountains; and, as plainly as he could through the medium of signs, invited Tarzan to accompany him to his country. This invitation Tarzan accepted and motioned the other to lead the way.

For days that stretched to weeks the two men struck deeper and deeper into the heart of a stupendous mountain system. Always mentally alert and eager to learn, Tarzan took advantage of the opportunity provided by time and propinquity to learn the language of his companion, and he proved such an apt pupil that they were soon able to make themselves understood to one another.

Among the first things that Tarzan learned was that his companion's name was Valthor, while Valthor took the earliest opportunity to evince an interest in the ape-man's weapons; and as he was unarmed, Tarzan spent a day in making a spear and bow and arrows for him. Thereafter, as Valthor taught the Lord of the Jungle to speak his language, Tarzan instructed the former in the use of the bow, the spear being already a familiar weapon to the young warrior.

Thus the days and the weeks passed and the two seemed no nearer the country of Valthor than when they had started from the vicinity of the camp of the *shiftas*. Tarzan found game of certain varieties plentiful in the mountains, and it was he who kept their larder supplied. The impressive scenery that was marked by rugged grandeur held the interest of the ape-man undiminished. He hunted, and he enjoyed the beauties of unspoiled nature, practically oblivious of the passage of time.

But Valthor was less patient; and at last, late one day when they found themselves at the head of a blind canyon where stupendous cliffs barred further progress, he admitted defeat. 'I am lost,' he said simply.

'That,' remarked Tarzan, 'I could have told you many days ago.'

Valthor looked at him in surprise. 'How could you know that,' he demanded, 'when you yourself do not know in what direction my country lies?'

'I know,' replied the ape-man, 'because during the past week you have led the way toward the four points of the compass, and today we are within five miles of where we were a week ago. Across this ridge at our right, not more than five miles away, is the little stream where I killed the ibex and the gnarled old tree in which we slept that night just seven suns ago.'

Valthor scratched his head in perplexity, and then he smiled. 'I cannot dispute you,' he admitted. 'Perhaps you are right, but what are we going to do?'

'Do you know in what direction your country lies from the camp in which I found you?' asked Tarzan.

'Thenar is due east of that point,' replied Valthor; 'of that I am positive.'

'Then we are directly southwest of it now, for we have travelled a considerable distance toward the south since we entered the higher mountains. If your country lies in these mountains then it should not be difficult to find it if we can keep moving always in a northeasterly direction.'

'This jumble of mountains with their twisting canyons and gorges confuses me,' Valthor admitted. 'You see, in all my life before I have never been farther from Thenar than the valley of Onthar, and both these valleys are surrounded by landmarks with which I am so familiar that I need no other guides. It has never been necessary for me to consult the positions of the sun, the moon, nor the stars before; and so they have been of no help to me since we set out in search of Thenar. Do you believe that you could hold a course toward the northeast in this maze of mountains? If you can, then you had better lead the way rather than I.'

'I can go toward the northeast,' Tarzan assured him, 'but I cannot find your country unless it lies in my path.'

'If we reach a point within fifty or a hundred miles of it, from some high eminence we shall see Xarator,' explained Valthor; 'and then I shall know my way to Thenar, for Xarator is almost due west of Athne.'

'What are Xarator and Athne?' demanded Tarzan.

'Xarator is a great peak the center of which is filled with fire and molten rock. It lies at the north end of the valley of Onthar and belongs to the men of Cathne, the city of gold. Athne, the city of ivory, is the city from which I come. The men of Cathne, in the valley of Onthar, are the enemies of my people.'

'Tomorrow, then,' said Tarzan, 'we shall set out for the city of Athne in the valley of Thenar.'

As Tarzan and Valthor ate meat that they had cut from yesterday's kill and carried with them, many weary miles to the south a black-maned lion lashed his tail angrily and voiced a savage growl as he stood over the body of a buffalo calf he had killed and faced an angry bull pawing the earth and bellowing a few yards away.

Rare is the beast that will face Gorgo, the buffalo, when rage inflames his red-rimmed eyes; but the great lion showed no intention of leaving its prey even in the face of the bull's threatened charge. He stood his ground. The roars of the lion and the bull mingled in a savage, thunderous dissonance that shook the ground, stilling the voices of the lesser people of the jungle.

Gorgo gored the earth, working himself into a frenzy of rage. Behind him, bellowing, stood the mother of the slain calf. Perhaps she was urging her lord and master to avenge the murder. The other members of the herd had bolted into the thickest of the jungle, leaving these two to contest with Numa his right to his kill, leaving vengeance to those powerful horns backed by that massive neck.

With a celerity and agility that belied his great weight, the bull charged. That two such huge beasts could move so quickly and so lightly seemed incredible, as it seemed incredible that any creature could either withstand or avoid the menace of those mighty horns; but the lion was ready, and as the bull was almost upon him, he leaped to one side, reared upon his hind feet and with one massive, taloned paw struck the bull a terrific blow on the side of its head that wheeled it half around and sent it stumbling to its knees, half stunned and bleeding, its great jawbone crushed and splintered. And before Gorgo could regain his feet, Numa leaped full upon his back, buried his teeth in the bulging muscles of the great neck, and with one paw reached for the nose of the bellowing bull, jerking the head back with a mighty surge that snapped the vertebrae.

Instantly the lion was on his feet again facing the cow, but she did not charge. Instead, bellowing, she crashed away into the jungle, leaving the king of beasts standing with his forefeet upon his latest kill.

That night Numa fed well; yet when he had gorged himself he did not lie up as a lion should, but continued toward the north along the mysterious trail he had been following for many days.

4

Down the Flood

The new day dawned cloudy and threatening. The season of rains was over, but it appeared that a belated storm was gathering above the lofty peaks through which Tarzan and Valthor were searching for the elusive valley of Thenar. The chill of night was dissipated by no kindly warmth of sunlight. The two men shivered as they rose from their rude beds among the branches of a tree.

'We shall eat later,' announced Tarzan, 'after a little climbing has put warmth into our blood.'

'If we are lucky enough to find anything to eat,' rejoined Valthor.

'Tarzan seldom goes hungry,' replied the ape-man. 'He will not go hungry today. When Tarzan is ready to hunt, we shall eat.'

Down the box canyon they went until Tarzan found a place where they might ascend the precipitous side wall; then they toiled upward, the warrior from Athne confident that each step would be his last as he clung to the steep face of the canyon wall but too proud to reveal his fear to the agile ape-man climbing so easily above him. But he did not fall, and at last the two stood upon the summit of a mighty ridge that led upward toward lofty peaks.

Valthor's heart was pounding and he was breathing heavily, but Tarzan showed no sign of exertion. He was about to continue on up the ridge, when he glanced at his companion and saw his condition; then he squatted on the ground with a laconic 'Rest now'; and Valthor was glad to rest.

All day they moved toward the northeast. Sometimes it rained a little, and always it threatened to rain more. A great storm seemed always to be gathering, yet it never broke during the long day. Tarzan made a kill before noon, and they ate; but immediately afterward they started on again. The cold, damp, sunless air offered them no incentive for tarrying on the way.

It was late in the afternoon when they ascended out of a deep gorge and stood upon a lofty plateau. In the near foreground were no mountains, but at a distance lofty peaks were visible dimly through a light drizzle of rain. Suddenly Valthor voiced an exclamation of elation. 'We have found it!' he cried. 'There is Xarator!'

Tarzan looked in the direction that the other pointed and saw a mighty, flat-topped peak in the distance, directly above which low clouds were reflecting a dull red light. 'So that is Xarator!' he remarked. 'And Thenar is directly east of it?'

'Yes,' replied Valthor; 'which means that Onthar must be just below the edge of this plateau, almost directly in front of us. Come!'

The two walked quickly over the level, grassy ground for a mile or two to come at length to the edge of the plateau beyond which, and below them, stretched a wide valley.

'We are almost at the southern end of Onthar,' said Valthor. 'There is Cathne, the city of gold. See it – in the bend of the river at this end of that forest? It is a rich city, but its people are the enemies of my people.'

Through the rain, Tarzan saw a walled city between a forest and a river. The houses were nearly all white, and there were many domes of dull yellow. The river, which ran between them and the city, was spanned by a bridge that was also a dull yellow color in the twilight of the late afternoon storm. Tarzan saw that the river extended the full length of the valley, a distance of fourteen or fifteen miles, being fed by smaller streams coming down out of the mountains. Also extending the length of the valley was what appeared to be a well-marked road. Near the center of the valley it branched, one fork following an affluent of the main stream with which it disappeared into the mouth of a canyon on the eastern side of the valley. Directly below them and extending to the northern extremity of Onthar was a level plain dotted with trees;

across the river, a forest stretched from the farther bank to the steep hills that bounded Onthar on the east and southeast.

Tarzan's eyes wandered back to the city of Cathne. 'Why do you call it the city of gold?' he asked.

'Do you not see the golden domes and the Bridge of Gold?' demanded Valthor.

'Are they covered with gold paint?' inquired Tarzan.

'They are covered with solid gold,' replied Valthor. 'The gold on some of the domes is an inch thick, and the bridge is built of solid blocks of gold.'

Tarzan lifted his eyebrows. As he looked down upon this seemingly deserted and peaceful valley he could not but conjure another picture – a picture of what it would be if word of these vast riches were carried to the outside world, bringing the kindly beneficences of modern civilization and civilized men to Onthar. How the valley would hum and roar then with the sweet music of mill and factory! What a gorgeous spectacle would be painted against the African sky by tall chimneys spouting black smoke to hang like a sable curtain above the golden domes of Cathne!

'Where do they find their gold?' he asked.

'Their mines lie in the hills directly south of the city,' replied Valthor.

'And where is your country, Thenar?' asked the ape-man.

'Just beyond the hills east of Onthar. Do you see where the river and the road cut through the forest about five miles above the city? You can see them entering the hills just beyond the forest.'

'Yes,' replied Tarzan; 'I see.'

'The road and the river run through the Pass of the Warriors into the valley of Thenar; a little northeast of the center of the valley lies Athne, the city of ivory; there, beyond the pass, is my country.'

'How far are we from Athne?' inquired Tarzan.

'About twenty-five miles, possibly a little less,' replied Valthor.

'We might as well start now, then,' suggested the ape-man, 'for in this rain it will be more comfortable to be on the march than to lie up until morning; and in your city we can find a dry place to sleep I presume.'

'Certainly,' replied Valthor, 'but it will not be safe to attempt to cross Onthar by daylight. We should certainly be seen by the sentries on the gates of Cathne, and as these people are our enemies the chances are that we should never cross the valley without being either killed or taken prisoners. It will be bad enough at night on account of the lions, but by day it will be infinitely worse as we shall have both men and lions to contend with.'

'What lions?' demanded Tarzan.

'The men of Cathne breed lions, and there are many at large in the valley,' explained Valthor. 'That great plain that you see below us, stretching the full length of the valley on this side of the river, is called the Field of the Lions. We shall be safer if we cross it after dark.'

'Whatever you wish,' agreed Tarzan with a shrug; 'it is all the same to me if we start now or wait until dark.'

'It is not very comfortable here,' remarked the Athnean. 'The rain is cold.'

'I have been uncomfortable before,' replied Tarzan; 'rains do not last forever.'

'If we were in Athne we should be very comfortable,' sighed Valthor. 'In my father's house there are fireplaces; even now the flames are roaring about great logs, and all is warmth and comfort.'

'Above the clouds the sun is shining,' replied Tarzan, 'but we are not above the clouds; we are here where the sun is not shining and there is no fire, and we are cold.' A faint smile touched his lips. 'It does not warm me to speak of fires or the sun.'

'Nevertheless, I wish I were in Athne,' insisted Valthor. 'It is a splendid city, and Thenar is a lovely valley. In Thenar we raise goats and sheep and elephants. In Thenar there are no lions except those that stray in from Onthar; those we kill. Our farmers raise vegetables and fruits and hay; our artizans manufacture leather goods; they make cloth from the hair of goats and the wool of sheep; our carvers work in ivory and wood.

'We trade a little with the outside world, paying for what we buy with ivory and gold. Were it not for the Cathneans we should lead a happy, peaceful life without a care.'

'What do you buy from the outside world, and of whom do you buy it?' asked Tarzan.

'We buy salt, of which we have none of our own,' explained Valthor. 'We also buy steel for our weapons and black slaves and occasionally a white woman, if she be young and pretty. These things we buy from a band of *shiftas*. With this same band we have traded since before the memory of man. *Shifta* chiefs and kings of Athne have come and gone, but our relations with this band have never altered. I was searching for them when I became lost and was captured by another band.'

'Do you never trade with the people of Cathne?' asked the ape-man.

'Once each year there is a week's truce during which we trade with them in peace. They give us gold and foodstuffs and hay in exchange for the women, the salt, and the steel we buy from the *shiftas*, and the cloth, leather, and ivory that we produce.

'Besides mining gold, the Cathneans breed lions for war and sport, raise fruits, vegetables, cereals, and hay and work in gold and, to a lesser extent, in ivory. Their gold and their hay are the products most valuable to us; and of these we value the hay more, for without it we should have to decrease our elephant herds.'

'Why should two peoples so dependent upon one another fight?' asked Tarzan.

Valthor shrugged. 'I do not know; perhaps it is just a custom. Yet, though we talk much of wanting peace, we should miss the thrills and excitement that peace does not hold.' His eyes brightened. 'The raids!' he exclaimed. 'There is a sport for men! The Cathneans come with their lions to hunt our goats, our sheep, our elephants, and us. They take heads for trophies, and above all they value the head of man. They try to take our women, and when they succeed then there is war, if the family of the woman seized be of sufficient importance.

'When we wish sport we go into Onthar after gold and women or just for the sport of killing men or capturing slaves. The greatest game of all is to sell a woman to a Cathnean for much gold and then take her away from him in a raid. No, I do not think that either we or the Cathneans would care for peace.'

As Valthor talked, the invisible sun sank lower into the west; heavy clouds, dark and ominous, hid the peaks to the north, settling low over the upper end of the valley. 'I think we may start now,' he said; 'it will soon be dark.'

Downward through a gully, the sides of which hid them from the city of Cathne, the two men made their way toward the floor of the valley. From the heavy storm clouds burst a flash of lightning followed by the roar of thunder; upon the upper end of the valley the storm god loosed his wrath; water fell in a deluge of masses wiping from their sight the hills beyond the storm.

By the time they reached level ground the storm was upon them and the gully they had descended a raging mountain torrent. The swift night had fallen; utter darkness surrounded them, darkness frequently broken by vivid flashes of lightning. The pealing of the constant thunder was deafening. The rain engulfed them in solid sheets like the waves of the ocean. It was, perhaps, the most terrific storm that either of these men had ever seen.

They could not converse; only the lightning prevented their becoming separated, as it alone permitted Valthor to keep his course across the grassy floor of the valley in the direction of the city of gold where they would find the road that led to the Pass of the Warriors and on into the valley of Thenar.

Presently they came within sight of the lights of the city, a few dim lights framed by the casements of windows; and a moment later they were on the road and were moving northward against the full fury of the storm. And such a storm! As they moved toward its center it grew in intensity; against the wind that accompanied it they waged a grim battle that was sometimes to them and sometimes to the wind, for often it stopped them in their tracks and forced them back.

For miles they pitted their muscles against the Herculean strength of the storm god; and the rage of the storm god seemed to rise against them, knowing no bounds, as though he was furious that these two puny mortals should pit their strength against his. Suddenly, as though in a last titanic effort to overcome them, the lightning burst into a mighty blaze that illuminated the entire valley for seconds, the thunder crashed as it had never crashed before, and a mass of water fell that crushed the two men to earth.

As they staggered to their feet again foot-deep water swirled about their legs; they stood in a broad, racing torrent that rushed past them toward the river; but in that last effort the storm god had spent his force. The rain ceased; through a rift in the dark clouds the moon looked down, perhaps in wonder, upon a drowned world; and Valthor led the way again toward the Pass of the Warriors. The last storm of the rainy season was over.

It is seven miles from the Bridge of Gold, that is the gateway to the city of Cathne, to the ford where the road to Thenar crosses the river; and it required three hours for Valthor and Tarzan to cover the distance, two hours for the first third and one hour for the remainder; but at last they stood at the river's brink.

A boiling flood confronted them, tearing down a widened river toward the city of Cathne. Valthor hesitated. 'Ordinarily,' he said to Tarzan, 'the water is little more than a foot deep. It must be three feet deep now.'

'And it will soon be deeper,' commented the ape-man. 'Only a small portion of the storm waters have had time to reach this point from the hills and the upper valley. If we are going to cross tonight, we shall have to do it now.'

'Very well,' replied Valthor, 'but follow me; I know the ford.'

As the Athnean stepped into the water the clouds closed again beneath the moon and plunged the world once more into darkness. As Tarzan followed he could scarcely see his guide ahead of him; and as Valthor knew the ford he moved more rapidly than the ape-man with the result that presently Tarzan could not see him at all, but he felt his way toward the opposite bank without thought of disaster.

The force of the stream was mighty; but mighty, too, are the thews of Tarzan of the Apes. The water, which Valthor had thought to be three feet in depth, was soon surging to the ape-man's waist, and then he missed the ford and stepped into a hole. Instantly the current seized him and swept him away; not even the giant muscles of Tarzan could cope with the might of the flood.

The Lord of the Jungle fought the swirling waters in an effort to reach the opposite shore, but in their embrace he was powerless. Was the storm god proud or resentful to see one of his children succeed where he had failed? That is a difficult question to answer, for gods are strange creatures; they give to those who have and take from those who have not; they punish whom they love and are jealous and resentful; in which they resemble the creatures who conceived them.

Finding even his great strength powerless and weakening, Tarzan gave up the struggle to reach the opposite bank and devoted his efforts to keeping his nose above the surface of the angry flood. Even this was none too easy of accomplishment, as the rushing waters had a trick of twisting him about or turning him over. Often his head was submerged, and sometimes he floated feet first and sometimes head first; but he tried to rest his muscles as best he could against the time when some vagary of the torrent might carry him within reach of the bank upon one side or the other.

He knew that several miles below the city of Cathne the river entered a narrow gorge, for that he had seen from the edge of the plateau from which he had first viewed the valley of Onthar; and Valthor had told him that beyond the gorge it tumbled in a mighty falls a hundred feet to the bottom of a rocky canyon. Should he not succeed in escaping the clutches of the torrent before it carried him into the gorge his doom was sealed, but Tarzan felt neither fear nor panic. His life had been in jeopardy often during his savage existence, yet he still lived.

He wondered what had become of Valthor. Perhaps he, too, was being hurtled along either above or below him. But such was not the fact. Valthor had reached the opposite bank in safety and waited there for Tarzan. When the ape-man did not appear within a reasonable time, the Athnean shouted his name aloud; but though he received no answer he was still not sure that Tarzan was not upon the opposite side of the river, the loud roaring of which might have drowned the sound of the voice of either.

Then Valthor decided to wait until daylight, rather than abandon his friend in a country with which he was entirely unfamiliar. That the Athnean remained bespoke his loyalty as well as the high esteem in which he held the ape-man, for the dangers that might beset Tarzan in Onthar would prove even a greater menace to Valthor, an hereditary enemy of the Cathneans.

Through the long night he waited and, with the coming of dawn, eagerly scanned the opposite bank of the river, his slender hope for the safety of his friend dying when daylight failed to reveal any sign of him. Then, at last, he was convinced that Tarzan had been swept away to his death by the raging flood; and, with a heavy heart, he turned away from the river and resumed his interrupted journey toward the Pass of the Warriors and the Valley of Thenar.

5

The City of Gold

As Tarzan battled for his life in the swirling waters of the swollen river he lost all sense of time; the seemingly interminable struggle against death might have been enduring without beginning, might endure without end, in so far as his numbed senses were concerned. His efforts to delay the apparently inevitable end were now purely mechanical, instinctive reactions to the threat against self-preservation. The cold water had sapped the vitality of his mind as well as of his body, yet, while his heart beat, neither would admit defeat; subconsciously, without active volition, they sought to preserve him. It was well that they did.

Turnings in the river cast him occasionally against one shore and then the other. Always, then, his hands reached up in an attempt to grasp something that might stay his mad rush toward the falls and death; and at last success crowned their efforts – his fingers closed upon the stem of a heavy vine that trailed down the bank into the swirling waters, closed and held.

Instantly, almost miraculously, new life seemed to be instilled into the veins of the ape-man by the feel of that stout support in his grasp. Quickly he seized it with both hands; the river clutched at his body and tried to drag it onward toward its doom; but the vine held, and so did Tarzan.

Hand over hand the man dragged himself out of the water and onto the bank, where he lay for several minutes; then he rose slowly to his feet, shook himself like some great lion, and looked about him in the darkness, trying to penetrate the impenetrable night. Faintly, as through shrubbery, he thought that he saw a light shining dimly in the distance. Where there was a light, there should be men. Tarzan moved cautiously forward to investigate.

He knew that he had crossed the river but that he was a long distance from the point at which he had entered it. He wondered what had become of Valthor; and determined, after he had investigated the light, to start up the river in search of him; even though he feared that his companion had been swept away by the flood, as he had.

But a few steps from the river Tarzan encountered a wall, and when he was close to the wall he could no longer see the light. Reaching upward, he discovered that the top of the wall was still above the tips of his outstretched fingers; but walls which were made to keep one out also invited one to climb them. The ape-man, filled with the curiosity of the beast, desired now more than ever to investigate the light he had seen.

Stepping back a few paces, he ran toward the wall and sprang upward. His extended fingers gripped the top of the wall and clung there. Slowly he drew himself up, threw a leg across the capstones, and looked to see what might be seen upon the opposite side of the wall.

He did not see much; a square of dim light forty or fifty feet away; that was all, and it did not satisfy his curiosity. Silently he lowered himself to the ground upon the same side as the light and moved cautiously forward. Beneath his bare feet he felt stone flagging, and guessed that he was in a paved courtyard.

He had crossed about half the distance to the light when the retreating storm flashed a farewell bolt from the distance. This distant lightning but barely sufficed to momentarily relieve the darkness surrounding the ape-man, revealing a low building, a lighted window, a deeply recessed doorway in the shelter of which stood a man. It also revealed Tarzan to the man in the doorway.

Instantly the silence was shattered by the brazen clatter of a gong. The door swung open, and men bearing torches rushed out. Tarzan, impelled by the natural caution of the beast, turned to run; but as he did so, he saw other open doors upon his flanks; and armed men with torches were rushing from these as well.

Realizing that flight was useless, Tarzan stood still with folded arms as the men converged upon him from three directions. Perhaps his insatiate curiosity prompted him to await quietly the coming of the men as much as a realization of the futility of flight. Tarzan wanted to see what the men were like and what they would do. He knew that he must be in the city of gold, and his imagination was inflamed. If they threatened him, he could still fight; if they imprisoned him, he could escape; so, at least, thought Tarzan, whose self-confidence was in proportion to his great size and his giant strength.

The torches carried by some of the men showed Tarzan that he was in a paved, quadrangular courtyard enclosed by buildings upon three sides and the wall he had scaled upon the fourth. Their light also revealed the fact that he was being surrounded by some fifty men armed with spears, the points of which were directed toward him in a menacing circle.

'Who are you?' demanded one of the men as the cordon drew tightly about him. The language in which the man spoke was the same as that which Tarzan had learned from Valthor, the common language of the enemy cities of Athne and Cathne.

'I am a stranger from a country far to the south,' replied the ape-man.

'What are you doing inside the walls of the palace of Nemone?' The speaker's voice was threatening, his tone accusatory. Tarzan sensed that the presence of a stranger here was a crime in itself; but this made the situation all the more interesting; while the name, Nemone, possessed a quality that fired his interest.

'I was crossing the river far above here when the flood caught me and swept me down; it was only by chance that I finally made a landing here.'

The man who had been questioning him shrugged. 'Well,' he admitted, 'it is not for me to question you anyway. Come! You will have a chance to tell your story to an officer; but he will not believe it either.'

As the men conducted Tarzan toward one of the buildings, he thought that they seemed more curious than hostile. It was evident, however, that they were only common warriors without responsibility and that he might find the attitude of the officer class entirely different.

They conducted him into a large, low-ceilinged room which was furnished with rough benches and tables; upon the walls hung weapons, spears and swords; and there were shields of elephant hide studded with gold bosses. But there were other things in this strange room that compelled the interest of the ape-man far more than did the weapons and the shields; upon the walls were mounted the heads of animals; there were the heads of sheep and goats and lions and elephants. Among these, sinister and forbidding, were the scowling heads of men. The sight of them reminded Tarzan of the stories Valthor had told him of these men of Cathne.

Two men guarded Tarzan in one corner of the room, while another was dispatched to notify a superior of the capture; the remainder loafed about the room, talking, playing games, cleaning their weapons. The prisoner took the opportunity to examine his captors.

They were well set up men, many of them not ill-favored, though for the most part of ignorant and brutal appearance. Their helmets, habergeons, wristlets, and anklets were of elephant hide heavily embossed with gold studs. Long hair from the manes of lions fringed the tops of their anklets and wristlets and was also used for ornamental purposes along the crests of their helmets and upon some of their shields and weapons. The elephant hide that composed their habergeons was cut into discs, and the habergeon fabricated in a manner similar to that one of ivory which Valthor had worn. In the center of each shield was a heavy boss of solid gold. Upon the harnesses and weapons of these common soldiers was a fortune in the precious metal.

While Tarzan, immobile, silent, surveyed the scene with eyes that seemed scarcely to move yet missed no detail, two warriors entered the room; and the instant that they crossed the threshold silence fell upon the men congregated in the chamber; and Tarzan knew that these were officers, though their trappings would have been sufficient evidence of their superior stations in life.

Habergeons and helmets, wristlets and anklets were all of gold and ivory, as were the hilts and scabbards of their short, dagger-like swords. The two presented a gorgeous picture against the background of the grim room and the relatively somber trappings of the common soldiers.

At a word of command from one of the two, the common warriors fell back, clearing one end of the room; then the two seated themselves at a table and ordered Tarzan's guards to bring him forward. As the Lord of the Jungle halted before them both men surveyed him critically.

'Why are you in Onthar?' demanded one who was evidently the superior, since he propounded all the questions during the interview.

Tarzan answered this and other questions as he had answered similar ones at the time of his capture, but he sensed from the attitudes of the two officers that neither was impressed with the truth of his statements. They seemed to have preconceived a conviction concerning him that nothing which he might say could alter.

'He does not look much like an Athnean,' remarked the younger man.

'That proves nothing,' snapped the other. 'Naked men look like naked men. He might pass for your own cousin were he garbed as you are garbed.'

'Perhaps you are right, but why is he here? A man does not come alone from Thenar to raid in Onthar. Unless—' he hesitated; 'unless he was sent to assassinate the Queen!'

'I had thought of that,' said the older man. 'Because of what happened to the last Athnean prisoners we took, the Athneans are very angry with the Queen. Yes, they might easily attempt to assassinate her.'

'For what other reason would a stranger enter the palace grounds? He would know that he must die if he were caught.'

'Of course, and this man expected to die; but he intended killing the Queen first. He was willing to martyr himself for Athne.'

Tarzan was almost amused as he contemplated the ease with which these two convinced themselves that what they wanted to believe true, was true; but he realized that this form of one-sided trial might prove disastrous to him if his fate were to be decided by such a tribunal and so he was prompted to speak.

'I have never been in Athne,' he said quietly. 'I am from a country far to the south. An accident brought me here. I am not an enemy. I have not come to kill your Queen or any other. Until today I did not know that your city existed.' This was a long speech for Tarzan of the Apes. He was almost positive that it would not influence his captors, yet there was a chance that they might believe him. He wished to remain among these people until his curiosity concerning them had been satisfied, and he felt that he might only do this by winning their confidence; if they imprisoned him, he would see nothing while he was in prison; and when he got out of prison, he would see but little more; as he would then be concerned only with the business of escape.

Men are peculiar, and none knew this better than Tarzan, who, because he had seen rather less of men than of beasts, had been inclined to study those whom he had seen. Now he was studying the two men who were questioning him. The elder he judged to be a man accustomed to the exercise of great power; cunning, ruthless, cruel. Tarzan did not like him. His was the instinctive appraisal of the wild beast.

The younger man was of an entirely different mold. He was intelligent rather than cunning; his countenance bespoke a frank and open nature. The ape-man judged that he was both honest and courageous. It was true that he had agreed with all that the elder man had said, almost in contradiction of his own original statement that Tarzan did not resemble an Athnean; but in that the ape-man saw confirmation of his belief in the younger man's intelligence. Only a fool contradicts his superior for no good purpose.

While he was certain that the younger man had little authority, compared with that exercised by his superior, yet Tarzan thought best to address him rather than the other because he thought that he might win an ally in the younger man and was sure that he could never influence the elder unless it was very much to the latter's interests to be influenced. And so, when he spoke again, he spoke to the younger of the two officers.

'Are these men of Athne like me?' he asked.

For an instant the officer hesitated; then he said, quite frankly, 'No; they are not like you. You are unlike any man that I have seen.'

'Are their weapons like my weapons?' continued the ape-man. 'There are mine over in the corner of the room; your men took them away from me. Look at them.'

Even the elder officer seemed interested. 'Bring them here,' he ordered one of the warriors.

The man brought them and laid them on the table before the two officers; the spear, the bow, the quiver of arrows, the grass rope, and the knife. The two men picked them up one by one and examined them carefully. Both seemed interested.

'Are they like the weapons of the Athneans?' demanded Tarzan. Of course he knew that they were not, but he thought it best not to acquaint these men with the fact that he had been consorting with one of their enemies.

'They are nothing like them,' admitted the younger man. 'What do you suppose this thing is for, Tomos?' he asked his companion as he examined Tarzan's bow.

'It may be a snare of some sort,' replied Tomos; 'probably for small animals – it would be useless against anything large.'

'Let me take it,' suggested Tarzan, 'and I will show you how it is used.'

The younger man handed the bow to the ape-man.

'Be careful, Gemnon,' cautioned Tomos; 'this may be a trick, a subterfuge by which he hopes to get possession of a weapon with which to kill us.'

'He cannot kill us with that thing,' replied Gemnon. 'Let's see how he uses it. Go ahead – Let's see, what did you say your name is?'

'Tarzan,' replied the Lord of the Jungle, 'Tarzan of the Apes.'

'Well, go ahead, Tarzan; but see that you don't attempt to attack any of us.'

Tarzan stepped to the table and took an arrow from his quiver; then he glanced about the room. On the wall at the far end a lion's head with open mouth hung near the ceiling. With what appeared but a single swift motion he fitted the arrow to the bow, drew the feathered shaft to his shoulder, and released it.

Every eye in the room had been upon him, for the common warriors had been interested spectators of what had been transpiring; every eye saw the shaft quivering now where it protruded from the center of the lion's mouth; and an involuntary exclamation broke from every throat, an exclamation in which were mingled surprise and applause.

'Take the thing away from him, Gemnon,' snapped Tomos. 'It is not a safe weapon in the hands of an enemy.'

Tarzan tossed the bow to the table. 'Do the Athneans use this weapon?' he asked.

Gemnon shook his head. 'We know no men who use such a weapon,' he replied.

'Then you must know that I am no Athnean,' stated Tarzan, looking squarely at Tomos.

'It makes no difference where you are from,' snapped Tomos; 'you are an enemy.'

The ape-man shrugged but remained silent. He had accomplished all that he had hoped for. He was sure that he had convinced them both that he was not an Athnean and had aroused the interest of the younger man, Gemnon. Something might come of this; though just what, he did not know himself.

Gemnon had leaned close to Tomos and was whispering in the latter's ear, evidently urging some action upon him. Tarzan could not hear what he was saying. The elder man listened impatiently; it was clear that he was not in accord with the suggestions of his junior.

'No,' he said when the other had finished. 'I will not permit anything of the sort. The life of the Queen is too sacred to risk by permitting this fellow any freedom. We shall lock him up for the night, and tomorrow decide what shall be done with him.' He turned to a warrior who seemed to be an under-officer. 'Take this fellow to the strong house,' he said, 'and see that he does not escape.' Then he rose and strode from the room, followed by his younger companion.

When they had gone, the man in whose charge Tarzan had been left picked up the bow and examined it. 'What do you call this thing?' he demanded.

'A bow,' replied the ape-man.

'And these?'

'Arrows.'

'Will they kill a man?'

'With them I have killed men and lions and buffaloes and elephants,' replied Tarzan. 'Would you like to learn how to use them?' Perhaps, he thought, a little kindly feeling in the guardroom might be helpful to him later on. Just at present he was not thinking of escape; these people and the city of gold were far too interesting to leave until he had seen more of them.

The man fingering the bow hesitated. Tarzan guessed that he wished to try his hand with the weapon but feared to delay carrying out the order of his officer.

'It will take but a moment,' suggested Tarzan. 'See, let me show you.'

Half reluctantly the man handed him the bow and Tarzan selected another arrow.

'Hold them like this,' he directed and placed the bow and arrow correctly in the other's hands. 'Tell your men to stand aside; you may not shoot accurately at first. Aim at the lion's head, as I did. Now draw the bowstring back as far as you can.'

The man, of stocky, powerful build, tugged at the bowstring; but the bow that Tarzan bent so easily he could scarcely bend at all. When he released the arrow it flew but a few feet and dropped to the floor. 'What's wrong?' he demanded.

'It requires practice,' the ape-man told him.

'There is a trick to it,' insisted the under-officer. 'Let me see you do it again.'

The other warriors, watching with manifest interest, whispered among themselves or commented openly. 'It takes a strong man to bend that stick,' said one.

'Althides is a strong man,' retorted another.

'But he is not strong enough.'

Althides, the under-officer, watched intently while Tarzan strung the bow again and bent it; he saw how easily the stranger flexed the heavy wood, and he marvelled. The other men looked on in open admiration, and this time a shout of approval arose as Tarzan's second arrow crowded the first in the mouth of the lion. When the symbols of high authority are absent men can be human.

Althides scratched his head. 'I shall have to lock you up now,' he said, 'or old Tomos will have my head on the wall of his palace; but I shall practice with this strange weapon until I learn to use it. Are you sure that there is no trick in bending that thing you call a bow?'

'There is no trick to it,' Tarzan assured him. 'Make yourself a lighter bow and you will find it easier, or bring me the material and I will make one for you.'

'That I will do,' exclaimed Althides. 'Come now and be locked up.'

A guard accompanied Tarzan across the courtyard to another building where he was placed in a room which, in the light of the torches borne by his escort, he saw had another occupant; then they left him, locking the heavy door behind them; and Tarzan heard their footsteps dying away across the courtyard as they took themselves and their torches off, leaving him in darkness.

He could not see his companion, but he could hear his breathing. He wondered with whom fate had cast him in this remote dungeon of the city of gold.

6

The Man Who Stepped on a God

Now that the torches were gone the room was very dark, but Tarzan lost no time in starting to investigate his prison. First he groped his way to the door, which he found to be constructed of solid planking with a small, square hole cut in it about the height of his eyes. There was no sign of lock or latch upon the inside and no way of ascertaining how it was secured from the outside.

Leaving the door, Tarzan moved slowly along the walls, feeling carefully over the stone surface. He knew that the other occupant of the cell was sitting on a bench in one corner at the far end. He could still hear him breathing. As he examined the room Tarzan approached closer and closer to his fellow prisoner.

In the rear wall the ape-man discovered a window. It was small and high set. The night was so dark that he could not tell whether it opened onto the outdoors or into another apartment of the building. As an avenue of escape the window appeared quite useless, as it was much too small to accommodate the body of a man.

As Tarzan was examining the window he was close to the corner where the other man sat, and now he heard a movement there. He also noticed that the fellow's breathing had increased in rapidity, as though he were nervous or excited. At last a voice sounded through the darkness.

'What are you doing?' it demanded.

'Examining the cell,' replied Tarzan.

'It will do you no good, if you are looking for a way to escape,' said the voice. 'You won't get out of here until they take you out, no more than I shall.'

Tarzan made no reply. There seemed nothing to say; and Tarzan seldom

speaks, even when others might find much to say. He went on with his examination of the room. Passing the other occupant, he felt along the fourth and
last wall; but his search revealed nothing to repay the effort. He was in a
small, rectangular cell of stone that was furnished with a long bench at one
end and had a door and a window letting into it.

Tarzan walked to the far end of the room and sat down upon the bench.
He was cold, wet, and hungry; but he was unafraid. He was thinking of all
that had transpired since night had fallen and left him to the mercy of the
storm; he wondered what the morrow held for him. It occurred to him that
perhaps he had made a mistake in not attempting a break for liberty before
his captors had succeeded in locking him in a cell from which there seemed
little likelihood that he could escape at all, for in common with all animals he
loathed captivity. However, here he was, locked up securely; and there
seemed nothing to do but make the best of it. Some day they would take him
out or unlock his cell door; then, unless he had learned that their intentions
toward him were prompted by friendliness, he would take advantage of any
opportunity that might be offered to escape.

Presently the man in the corner of the cell addressed him. 'Who are you?'
he asked. 'When they brought you in I saw by the light of the torches that you
are neither a Cathnean nor an Athnean.' The man's voice was coarse, his
tones gruff; he demanded rather than requested. This did not please Tarzan,
so he did not reply. 'What's the matter?' growled his fellow prisoner. 'Are you
dumb?' His voice was raised angrily.

'Nor deaf,' replied the ape-man. 'You do not have to shout at me.'

The other was silent for a short time; then he spoke in an altered tone. 'We
may be locked in this hole together for a long time,' he said. 'We might as well
be friends.'

'As you will,' replied Tarzan, his involuntary shrug passing unnoticed in
the darkness of the cell.

'My name is Phobeg,' said the man; 'what is yours?'

'Tarzan,' replied the ape-man.

'Are you either Cathnean or Athnean?'

'Neither; I am from a country far to the south.'

'You would be better off had you stayed there,' offered Phobeg. 'How do
you happen to be here in Cathne?'

'I was lost,' explained the ape-man, who had no intention of telling the
entire truth and thus identifying himself as a friend of one of the Cathneans'
enemies. 'I was caught in the flood and carried down the river to your city.
Here they captured me and accused me of coming to assassinate your Queen.'

'So they think you came to assassinate Nemone! Well, whether you did
come for that purpose or not will make no difference.'

'What do you mean?' demanded Tarzan.

'I mean that in any event you will be killed in one way or another,' explained Phobeg, 'whatever way will best amuse Nemone.'

'Nemone is your Queen?' inquired the ape-man indifferently.

'By the mane of god, she is all that and more!' exclaimed Phobeg fervently. 'Such a Queen there never has been in Onthar or Thenar before nor ever will be again. By the teeth of the great one! She makes them all stand around, the priests, the captains, and the councillors.'

'But why should she have me destroyed who am only a stranger that became lost?'

'We keep no white men prisoners, only blacks as slaves. Now, were you a woman you would not be killed; and were you a very good-looking woman (not too good-looking, however) you would be assured a life of ease and luxury. But you are only a man; so you will be killed to furnish a pleasurable break in the monotony of Nemone's life.'

'And what would happen to a *too* good-looking woman?' asked Tarzan.

'Enough, if Nemone saw her,' replied Phobeg meaningly. 'To be more beautiful than the Queen is equivalent to high treason in the estimation of Nemone. Why, men hide their wives and daughters if they think that they are too beautiful; but there are few who would risk hiding an alien prisoner.

'I know a man who has a very ugly wife,' continued Phobeg, 'who never comes out of her house in the daytime. She tells her neighbors that her husband keeps her hidden for fear Nemone will see her. Then there was another who *was* too beautiful. Her husband tried to keep her hidden from Nemone, but one day the Queen saw her and ordered her nose and ears cut off. Yes, I am glad that I am an ugly man rather than a beautiful woman.'

'Is the Queen beautiful?' asked Tarzan.

'Yes, by the claws of the all-high, she is the most beautiful woman in the world.'

'Knowing her policy, as you have explained it,' remarked the ape-man, 'I can readily believe that she may be the most beautiful woman in Cathne and quite sure of remaining so as long as she lives and is Queen.'

'Do not mistake me,' said Phobeg; 'Nemone *is* beautiful; but,' and he lowered his voice to a whisper, 'she is a she-Satan. Even I who have served her faithfully may not look to her for mercy.'

'What did you do to get here?' inquired the ape-man.

'I accidentally stepped on god's tail,' replied Phobeg gloomily.

The man's strange oaths had not gone unnoticed by Tarzan, and now this latest remarkable reference to deity astounded him; but contact with strange peoples had taught him to learn certain things concerning them by observation and experience rather than by direct questioning, matters of religion being chief among these; so now he only commented, 'And therefore you are being punished.'

'Not yet,' replied Phobeg. 'The form of my punishment has not yet been decided. If Nemone has other amusements I may escape punishment, or I may come through my trial successfully and be freed; but the chances are all against me, for Nemone seldom has sufficient bloody amusement to sate her.

'Of course, if she leaves the decision of my guilt or innocence to the chances of an encounter with a single man I shall doubtless be successful in proving the latter, for I am very strong; and there is no better sword- or spear-man in Cathne; but I should have less chance against a lion, while, faced by the eternal fires of frowning Xarator, all men are guilty.'

Although the man spoke the language Valthor had taught the ape-man and he understood the words, the meaning of what he said was as Greek to Tarzan. He could not quite grasp what the amusements of the Queen had to do with the administration of justice even though the inferences to be derived from Phobeg's remarks seemed apparent; the conclusion was too sinister to be entertained by the noble mind of the Lord of the Jungle.

He was still considering the subject and wondering about the eternal fires of frowning Xarator when sleep overcame his physical discomforts and merged his speculations with his dreams; and to the south another jungle beast crouched in the shelter of a rocky ledge while the storm that had betrayed Tarzan to new enemies wasted its waning wrath and passed on into the nothingness that is the sepulcher of storms; then as the new day dawned bright and clear he arose and stepped out into the sunlight, the great lion that we have seen before, the great lion with the golden coat and the black mane.

He sniffed the morning air and stretched, yawning. His sinuous tail twitched nervously as he looked about over the vast domain that was his because he was there, as every wilderness is the domain of the king of beasts while his majesty is in residence.

From the slight elevation upon which he stood, his yellow-green eyes surveyed a broad plain, tree dotted. There was game there in plenty: wildebeest, zebra, giraffe, koodoo, and hartebeest; and the king was hungry, for the rain had prevented his making a kill the previous night. He blinked his yellow-green eyes in the new sunlight and strode majestically down toward the plain and his breakfast, as, many miles to the north, a black slave accompanied by two warriors brought breakfast to another Lord of the Jungle in a prison cell at Cathne.

At the sound of footsteps approaching his prison Tarzan awoke and arose from the cold stone floor where he had been sleeping. Phobeg sat upon the edge of the wooden bench and watched the door.

'They bring us food or death,' he said; 'one never knows.'

The ape-man made no reply. He stood there waiting until the door swung open and the slave entered with the food in a rough earthen bowl and water in a glazed jug; he looked at the two warriors standing in the open doorway and at the sunlit courtyard beyond them. What was passing in that savage mind? Perhaps the warriors would have been less at ease could they have known, but the ape-man made no move. Curiosity kept him prisoner there quite as much as armed men or sturdy door, and now he only *looked* beyond the two warriors who were eyeing him intently. They had not been on duty the night before and had not seen him, but they had heard of him. His feat with his strange weapon had been told them by their fellows.

'So this is the wild man!' exclaimed one.

'You had better be careful, Phobeg,' said the other. 'I should hate to be locked up in a cell with a wild man'; then, laughing at his joke, he slammed the door after the slave had come out; and the three went away.

Phobeg was appraising Tarzan with a new eye; his nakedness took on a new meaning in the light of that descriptive term, wild man. Phobeg noted the great height of his cell-mate, the expanse of his chest, and his narrow hips; but he greatly underestimated the strength of the symmetrical muscles that flowed so smoothly beneath the bronzed hide; then he glanced at his own gnarled and knotted muscles and was satisfied.

'So you are a wild man!' he demanded. 'How wild are you?'

Tarzan turned slowly toward the speaker. He thought that he recognized thinly veiled sarcasm in the tone of Phobeg's voice. For the first time he saw his companion in the light of day. He saw a man a few inches shorter than himself but of mighty build, a man of great girth and bulging muscles, a man who might outweigh the Lord of the Jungle by fifty pounds. He noted his prominent jaw, his receding forehead, and his small eyes. In silence Tarzan regarded Phobeg.

'Why don't you answer?' demanded the Cathnean.

'Do not be a fool,' admonished Tarzan. 'I recall that last night you said that as we might be confined here for a long time we might as well be friends. We cannot be friends by insulting one another. Food is here. Let us eat.'

Phobeg grunted and inserted one of his big paws into the pot the slave had brought. As there was no knife or fork or spoon, Tarzan had no alternative but to do likewise if he wished to eat; and so he too took food from the pot with his fingers. The food was meat; it was tough and stringy and under-cooked; had it been raw Tarzan had been better suited.

Phobeg chewed assiduously upon a mouthful of the meat until he had reduced the fibers to a pulp that would pass down his throat. 'An old lion must have died yesterday,' he remarked, 'a very old lion.'

'If we acquire the characteristics of the creatures we eat, as many men believe,' Tarzan replied, 'we should soon die of old age on this diet.'

'Yesterday I had a piece of goat's meat from Thenar,' said Phobeg. 'It was strong and none too tender, but it was better than this. I am accustomed to good food. In the temple the priests live as well as the nobles do in the palace, and so the temple guard lives well on the leavings of the priests. I was a member of the temple guard. I was the strongest man on the guard. I am the strongest man in Cathne. When raiders come from Thenar, or when I am taken there on raids the nobles marvel at my strength and bravery. I am afraid of nothing. With my bare hands I have killed men. Did you ever see a man like me?'

'No,' admitted the ape-man.

'Yes, it is well that we should be friends,' continued Phobeg, 'well for you. Everyone wants to be friends with me, for they have learned that my enemies get their necks twisted. I take them like this, by the head and the neck,' and with his great paws he went through a pantomime of seizing and twisting; 'then, crack! their spines break. What do you think of that?'

'I should think that your enemies would find that very uncomfortable,' replied Tarzan.

'Uncomfortable!' ejaculated Phobeg. 'Why, man, it kills them!'

'At least they can no longer hear,' commented the Lord of the Jungle.

'Of course they cannot hear; they are dead. I do not see what that has to do with it.'

'That does not surprise me,' Tarzan assured him.

'What does not surprise you?' demanded Phobeg. 'That they are dead? Or that they cannot hear?'

'I am not easily surprised by anything,' explained the ape-man.

Beneath his low forehead Phobeg's brows were knitted in thought. He scratched his head. 'What were we talking about?' he demanded.

'We were trying to decide which would be more terrible,' explained Tarzan patiently, 'to have you for a friend or an enemy.'

Phobeg looked at his companion for a long time. One could almost see the laborious effort of cerebration going on beneath that thick skull. Then he shook his head. 'That is not what we were talking about at all,' he grumbled. 'Now I have forgotten. I never saw anyone as stupid as you. When they called you a wild man they must have meant a crazy man. And I have got to remain locked in here with you for no one knows how long.'

'You can always get rid of me,' said Tarzan quite seriously.

'How can I get rid of you?' demanded the Cathnean.

'You can twist my neck, like this.' Tarzan mimicked the pantomime in which Phobeg had explained how he rid himself of his enemies.

'I *could* do it,' boasted Phobeg, 'but then they *would* kill me. No, I shall let you live.'

'Thanks,' said Tarzan.

'Or at least while we are locked up here together,' added Phobeg.

Experience had taught Tarzan that the more stupid or ignorant the man the more egotistical he was likely to be, but he had never before encountered such an example of crass stupidity and stupendous egotism as Phobeg presented. To be locked up at all with this brainless mass of flesh was bad enough in itself; but to be on bad terms with it at the same time would make matters infinitely less bearable, and so Tarzan determined to brook everything other than actual physical abuse that he might lighten the galling burden of incarceration.

Loss of liberty represented for Tarzan, as it does for all creatures endowed with brains, the acme of misery, more to be avoided than physical pain, yet, with stoic fortitude he accepted his fate without a murmur of protest; and while his body was confined between the narrow confines of four walls of stone his memories roved the jungle and the veldt and lived again the freedom and the experiences of the past.

He recalled the days of his childhood when fierce Kala, the she-ape that had suckled him at her hairy breast in his infancy, had protected him from the dangers of their savage life; and he recalled her gentleness and her patience with this backward child who must still be carried in her arms long after the balus of her companion shes were able to scurry through the trees seeking their own food and even able to protect themselves against their enemies by flight if nothing more.

These were his first impressions of life, dating back perhaps to his second year while he was still unable to swing through the trees or even make much progress upon the ground. After that he had developed rapidly, far more rapidly than a pampered child of civilization, for upon the quick development of his cunning and his strength depended his life.

With a faint smile he recalled the rage of old Tublat, his foster father, when Tarzan had deliberately undertaken to annoy him. Old 'Broken-nose' had always hated Tarzan because the helplessness of his long-drawn infancy had prevented Kala from bearing other apes. Tublat had argued in the meager language of the apes that Tarzan was a weakling that would never become strong enough or clever enough to be of value to the tribe. He wanted Tarzan killed; and he tried to get old Kerchak, the king, to decree his death; so when Tarzan grew old enough to understand, he hated Tublat and sought to annoy him in every way that he could.

His memories of those days brought only smiles now, save only the great tragedy of his life, the death of Kala; but that had occurred later, when he was almost a grown man. She had been saved to him while he needed her most and not taken away until after he was amply able to fend for himself and meet the other denizens of the jungle upon an equal footing. But it was not the protection of those great arms and mighty fangs that he had missed, that he still missed even today; he had missed the maternal love of that savage heart, the only mother-love that he had ever known.

And now his thoughts turned naturally to other friends of the jungle of whom Kala had been first and greatest. There were his many friends among the great apes; there was Tantor, the elephant; there was Jad-bal-ja, the Golden Lion; there was little Nkima. Poor little Nkima! Much to his disgust and amid loud howls, Nkima had been left behind this time when Tarzan set out upon his journey into the north country; but the little monkey had contracted a cold and the ape-man did not wish to expose him to the closing rains of the rainy season.

Tarzan regretted a little that he had not brought Jad-bal-ja with him, for though he could do very well for considerable periods without the companionship of man, he often missed that of the wild beasts that were his friends. Of course the Golden Lion was sometimes an embarrassing companion when one was in contact with human beings; but he was a loyal friend and good company, for only occasionally did he break the silence.

Tarzan recalled the day that he had captured the tiny cub and how he had taught the bitch, Za, to suckle it. What a cub he had been! All lion from the very first. Tarzan sighed as he thought of the days that he and the Golden Lion had hunted and fought together.

7

Nemone

Tarzan had thought, when he went without objection into the prison cell at Cathne, that the next morning he would be questioned and released, or at least be taken from the cell; and once out of the cell again, Tarzan had no intention of returning to it, the Lord of the Jungle being very certain of his own prowess.

But they had not let him out the next morning nor the next nor the next. Perhaps he might have made a break for liberty when food was brought; but each time he thought that the next day would bring his release, and waited.

Imprisonment of any nature galled him, but this experience was rendered infinitely more irksome by the presence of Phobeg. The man annoyed Tarzan; he was ignorant, a braggart, and inclined to be quarrelsome. In the interests of peace the ape-man had tolerated more from his cell-mate than he would have under ordinary circumstances; and Phobeg, being what he was, had assumed that the other's toleration was prompted by fear. Believing this, he became more arrogant and overbearing, ignorant of the fact that he was playing with death.

Phobeg had been imprisoned longer than had Tarzan, and the

confinement was making him moody. Sometimes he sat for hours staring at the floor, or, at others, he would mumble to himself, carrying on long conversations which were always acrimonious and that usually resulted in working him up into a rage; then he might seek to vent his spleen upon Tarzan. The fact that Tarzan remained silent under such provocation increased Phobeg's ire; but it also prevented an actual break between them, for it is still a fact, however trite the saying, that it takes two to make a quarrel; and Tarzan would not quarrel; at least, not yet.

'Nemone won't get much entertainment out of you,' growled Phobeg this morning after one of his tirades had elicited no response from the ape-man.

'Well, even so,' replied Tarzan, 'you should more than make up to her any amusement value that I may lack.'

'That I will,' exclaimed Phobeg. 'If it is fighting she wants, she shall see such fighting as she has never seen before when she matches Phobeg with either man or beast; but you! Bah! She will have to pit you against some half-grown child if she wishes to see any fight at all. You have no courage; your veins are filled with water. If she is wise she will dump you into Xarator. By god's tail! I should like to see you there. I'll bet my best habergeon they could hear you scream in Athne.'

The ape-man was standing gazing at the little rectangle of sky that he could see through the small, barred opening in the door. He remained silent after Phobeg had ceased speaking, totally ignoring him as though he had not spoken, as though he did not exist. Phobeg became furious. He rose from the bench upon which he had been sitting.

'Coward!' he cried. 'Why don't you answer me? By the yellow fangs of Thoos! I've a mind to beat some manners into you, so that you will know enough to answer when your betters speak.' He took a step in the direction of the ape-man.

Slowly Tarzan turned toward the angry man, his level gaze fixed upon the other's eyes, and waited. He said nothing, but his attitude was an open book that even the stupid Phobeg could read. And Phobeg hesitated.

Just what might have happened no man may know, for at that instant four warriors came and swung the door of the cell open. 'Come with us,' said one of them, 'both of you.'

Phobeg sullenly, Tarzan with the savage dignity of Numa, accompanied the four warriors across the open courtyard and through a doorway that led into a long corridor at the end of which they were ushered into a large room. Here, behind a table, sat seven warriors trapped in ivory and gold. Among them Tarzan recognized the two who had questioned him the night of his capture, old Tomos and the younger Gemnon.

'These are nobles,' whispered Phobeg to Tarzan. 'That one at the center of the table is old Tomos, the Queen's councillor. He would like to marry the

Queen, but I guess he is too old to suit her. The one on his right is Erot. He used to be a common warrior like me; but Nemone took a fancy to him, and now he is the Queen's favorite. She won't marry him though, for he is not of noble blood. The young fellow on Tomos' left is Gemnon. He is from an old and noble family. Warriors who have served him say he is a very decent sort.'

As Phobeg gossiped, the two prisoners and their guard had been standing just inside the doorway waiting to be summoned to advance, and Tarzan had had an opportunity to note the architecture and furnishings of the room. The ceiling was low and was supported by a series of engaged columns at regular intervals about the four walls. Between the columns along one side of the room behind the table at which the nobles were seated were unglazed windows, and there were three doorways: that through which Tarzan and Phobeg had been brought, which was directly opposite the windows, and one at either end of the room. The doors themselves were beautifully carved and highly polished, some of the panels containing mosaics of gold and ivory and bits of colored substances.

The floor was of stone, composed of many pieces of different shapes and sizes; but all so nicely fitted that joints were barely discernible. On the floor were a few small rugs either of the skins of lions or of a stiff and heavy wool weave. These latter contained simple designs in several colors and resembled the work of primitive people such as the Navajos of southwestern America.

Upon the walls were paintings depicting battle scenes in which lions and elephants took part with warriors, and always the warriors with the elephants appeared to be suffering defeat, while the warriors with the lions were collecting many heads from fallen foemen. Above these mural paintings was a row of mounted heads encircling the room. These were similar to those Tarzan had seen in the guardroom the night of his coming to Cathne and differed from them only in that they were better specimens and better mounted. Perhaps, too, the heads of men predominated here, scowling down upon their enemies.

But now Tarzan's examination of the room was interrupted by the voice of Tomos. 'Bring the prisoners forward,' he directed the under-officer who was one of the four warriors escorting them.

When the two men had been halted upon the opposite side of the table from the nobles, Tomos pointed at Tarzan's companion. 'Which is this one?' he demanded.

'He is called Phobeg,' replied the under-officer.

'What is the charge against him?'

'He profaned Thoos.'

'Who brought the charge?'

'The high priest.'

'It was an accident,' Phobeg hastened to explain. 'I meant no disrespect.'

'Silence!' snapped Tomos. Then he pointed at Tarzan. 'And this one?' he demanded. 'Who is he?'

'This is the one who calls himself Tarzan,' explained Gemnon. 'You will recall that you and I examined him the night he was captured.'

'Yes, yes,' said Tomos; 'I recall. He carried some sort of strange weapon.'

'Is he the man of whom you told me,' asked Erot, 'the one who came from Athne to assassinate the Queen?'

'This is the one,' replied Tomos; 'he came at night during the last storm and succeeded in making his way into the palace grounds after dark before he was discovered and arrested.'

'He does not greatly resemble an Athnean,' commented Erot.

'I am not,' said Tarzan.

'Silence!' commanded Tomos.

'Why should I be silent?' demanded Tarzan. 'There is none other to speak for me than myself; therefore I shall speak for myself. I am no enemy of your people, nor are my people at war with yours. I demand my liberty!'

'He demands his liberty,' mimicked Erot and laughed aloud as though it was a good joke; 'the slave demands his liberty!'

Tomos half rose from his seat, his face purple with rage. He banged the table with his fist. He pointed a finger at Tarzan. 'Speak when you are spoken to, slave, and not otherwise; and when Tomos, the councillor, tells you to be silent, be silent.'

'I have spoken,' said Tarzan; 'when I choose to speak again, I shall speak.'

'We have a way of silencing impudent slaves, forever,' sneered Erot.

'It is evident that he is a man from a far country,' interjected Gemnon. 'It is not strange that he neither understands our customs nor recognizes the great among us. Perhaps we should listen to him. If he is not an Athnean and no enemy, why should we imprison him or punish him?'

'He came over the palace walls at night,' retorted Tomos. 'He could have come for but one purpose, to kill our Queen; therefore he must die. The manner of his death shall be at the pleasure of Nemone, our sweet and gracious Queen.'

'He told us that the river washed him down to Cathne,' persisted Gemnon. 'It was a very dark night and he did not know where he was when he finally succeeded in crawling ashore; it was only chance that brought him to the palace.'

'A pretty story but not plausible,' countered Erot.

'Why not plausible?' demanded Gemnon. 'I think it quite plausible. We know that no man could have swum the river in the flood that was raging that night, and that this man could not have reached the spot at which he climbed the wall except by swimming the river or crossing the Bridge of Gold. We know that he did not cross the bridge, because the bridge was well guarded and no one crossed that night. Knowing therefore that he did not cross the bridge and could not have swum the river, we know that the only way he could have reached that particular spot upon the river's bank was by being swept downstream from above. I believe his story, and I believe that we should treat him as an honorable warrior from some distant kingdom until we have better reasons than we now have for believing otherwise.'

'I should not care to be the one to defend a man who came here to kill the Queen,' sneered Erot meaningly.

'Enough of this!' said Tomos curtly. 'The man shall be judged fairly and destroyed as Nemone thinks best.'

As he ceased speaking, a door at one end of the room opened and a noble resplendent in ivory and gold stepped into the chamber. Halting just within the threshold, he faced the nobles at the table.

'The Queen!' he announced in a loud voice and then stepped aside.

All eyes turned in the direction of the doorway and at the same time the nobles rose to their feet and then kneeled upon the floor, facing the doorway through which the Queen would enter. The warriors on guard, including those with Tarzan and Phobeg, did likewise, Phobeg following their example. Everyone in the room kneeled except the noble who had announced the Queen, or rather every Cathnean. Tarzan of the Apes did not kneel.

'Down, jackal!' growled one of the guards in a whisper, and then amidst deathly silence a woman stepped into view and paused, framed in the carved casing of the doorway. Regal, she stood there glancing indolently about the apartment; then her eyes met those of the ape-man and, for a moment, held there on his. A slight frown of puzzlement contracted her straight brows as she continued on into the room, approaching the table and the kneeling men.

Behind her followed a half dozen richly arrayed nobles, resplendent in burnished gold and gleaming ivory, but as they crossed the chamber Tarzan saw only the gorgeous figure of the Queen. She was clothed more simply than her escort; but that form, which her apparel revealed rather than hid, required no embellishments other than those with which nature had endowed it. She was far more beautiful than the crude Phobeg had painted her.

A narrow diadem set with red stones encircled her brow, confining her glossy black hair; upon either side of her head, covering her ears, a large golden disc depended from the diadem; while from its rear rose a slender filament of gold that curved forward, supporting a large red stone above the center of her head. About her throat was a simple golden band that held a brooch and pendant of ivory in the soft hollow of her neck. Upon her upper arms were similar golden bands supporting triangular, curved ornaments of ivory. A broad band of gold mesh supported her breasts, the band being embellished with horizontal bands of red stones, while from its upper edge depended five narrow triangles of ivory, a large one in the center and two smaller ones on either side.

A girdle about her hips was of gold mesh. It supported another ivory triangle, the slender apex of which curved slightly inward between her legs and also her scant skirt of black monkey hair that fell barely to her knees, conforming perfectly to the contours of her body.

About her wrists were numerous bracelets of ivory and gold and around her ankles were vertical strips of ivory held together by leather thongs, identical in form to those worn by Valthor and by the Cathnean men. Her feet were shod with dainty sandals; and as she moved upon them silently across the stone floor, her movements seemed to Tarzan a combination of the seductive languor of the sensualist and the sinuous grace and savage alertness of the tigress.

That she was marvellously beautiful by the standards of any land or any time grew more apparent to the Lord of the Jungle as she came nearer to him, yet her presence exhaled a subtle essence that left him wondering if her beauty were the reflection of a nature all good or all evil, for her mien and bearing suggested that there could be no compromise – Nemone, the Queen, was all one or all the other.

She kept her eyes upon him as she crossed the room slowly, and Tarzan did not drop his own from hers. There was neither boldness nor rudeness in his gaze, perhaps there was not even interest – it was the noncommittal, cautious appraisal of the wild beast that watches a creature which it neither fears nor desires.

The quizzical frown still furrowed Nemone's smooth brow as she reached the end of the table where the nobles kneeled. It was not an angry frown, and there might have been in it much of interest and something of amusement, for unusual things interested and amused Nemone, so rare were they in the monotony of her life; and it was certainly unusual to see one who did not accord her the homage due a queen.

As she halted she turned her eyes upon the kneeling nobles. 'Arise!' she commanded, and in that single word the vibrant qualities of her rich, deep voice sent a strange thrill through the ape-man. 'Who is this that does not kneel to Nemone?' she demanded, her gaze now returned to the bronzed figure standing impassively before her.

As Tarzan had been standing behind the nobles as they had turned to face Nemone when they kneeled, only two of his guards had been aware of his dereliction; but now as they arose and faced about, their countenances were filled with horror and rage when they discovered that the strange captive had so affronted their Queen.

Tomos went purple again. He spluttered with rage. 'He is an ignorant and impudent savage, my Queen,' he said; 'but as he is about to die his actions are of no consequence.'

'Why is he about to die?' demanded Nemone, 'and how is he to die?'

'He is to die because he came here in the dead of night to assassinate your majesty,' explained Tomos; 'the manner of his death rests of course in the hands of our gracious Queen.'

Nemone's dark eyes, veiled behind long lashes, appraised the ape-man, lingering upon his bronzed skin and the rolling contours of his muscles; then rising to the handsome face until her eyes met his. 'Why did you not kneel?' she asked.

'Why should I kneel to you who they have said will have me killed?' demanded Tarzan. 'Why should I kneel to you who are not my Queen? Why should I, Tarzan of the Apes, who kneels to no one, kneel to you?'

'Silence!' cried Tomos. 'Your impertinence knows no bounds. Do you not realize, ignorant slave, low savage, that you are addressing Nemone, the Queen!'

Tarzan made no reply; he did not even look at Tomos; his eyes were fixed upon Nemone. She fascinated him; but whether as a thing of beauty or a thing of evil, he did not know. He only knew that few women, other than La, the High Priestess of the Flaming God, had ever so wholly aroused his interest and his curiosity.

Tomos turned to the under-officer in command of the escort that was guarding Tarzan and Phobeg. 'Take them away!' he snapped. 'Take them back to their cell until we are ready to destroy them.'

'Wait,' said Nemone. 'I would know more of this man,' and then she turned to Tarzan. 'So you came to kill me!' Her voice was smooth, almost caressing. At the moment the woman reminded Tarzan of a cat that is playing with its victim. 'Perhaps they chose a good man for the purpose; you look as though you might be equal to any feat of arms.'

'Killing a woman is no feat of arms,' replied Tarzan. 'I do not kill women. I did not come here to kill you.'

'Then why did you come to Onthar?' inquired the Queen in her silky voice.

'That I have already explained twice to that old man with the red face,' replied Tarzan, nodding in the general direction of Tomos. 'Ask him; I am tired of explaining to people who have already decided to kill me.'

Tomos trembled with rage and half drew his slender, dagger-like sword. 'Let me destroy him, my Queen,' he cried. 'Let me wipe out the affront he has put upon my beloved ruler.'

Nemone had flushed angrily at Tarzan's words, but she did not lose control of herself. 'Sheathe your sword, Tomos,' she commanded icily; 'Nemone is competent to decide when she is affronted and what steps to take. The fellow is indeed impertinent; but it seems to me that if he affronted anyone, it was Tomos he affronted and not Nemone. However, his temerity shall not go unpunished. Who is this other?'

'He is a temple guard named Phobeg,' explained Erot. 'He profaned Thoos.'

'It would amuse us,' said Nemone, 'to see these two men fight upon the Field of the Lions. Let them fight without other weapons than those which Thoos has given them. To the victor, freedom,' she hesitated momentarily, 'freedom within limits. Take them away!'

8

Upon the Field of the Lions

Tarzan and Phobeg were back in their little stone cell; the ape-man had not escaped. He had had no opportunity to escape on the way back to his prison, for the warriors who guarded him had redoubled their vigilance, having been cautioned to do so by Erot, and the points of two spears had been kept constantly against his body.

Phobeg was moody and thoughtful. The attitude of his fellow prisoner during their examination by the nobles, his seeming indifference to the majesty and power of Nemone, had tended to alter Phobeg's former estimate of the ape-man's courage. He realized now that the fellow was either a very brave man or a very great fool; and he hoped that he was the latter, for Phobeg was to be pitted against him upon the Field of the Lions, possibly on the morrow.

Phobeg was stupid, but past experience had taught him something of the psychology of mortal combat. He knew that when a man went into battle fearing his antagonist he was already handicapped and partly defeated. Now Phobeg did not fear Tarzan; he was too stupid and too ignorant to anticipate fear. Facing probable defeat and death, he could be overcome by fear and even cowardice; but he was of too low an order, mentally, to visualize either in imagination, except in a rather vague and hazy way.

Tarzan, on the other hand, was of an entirely different temperament; and though he never knew fear it was for a very different reason. Being intelligent and imaginative, he could visualize all the possibilities of an impending encounter; but he could never know fear, because death held no terrors for him; and he had learned to suffer physical pain without the usually attendant horrors of mental anguish. Therefore, if he thought about the coming combat at all, he was not overconfident nor fearful nor nervous. Could he have known what was in the fellow's mind when he commenced to speak he would have been amused.

'It will doubtless be tomorrow,' said Phobeg grimly.

'What will be tomorrow?' inquired the ape-man.

'The combat in which I shall kill you,' explained the cheerful Phobeg.

'Oh, so you are going to kill me! Phobeg, I am surprised. I thought that you were my friend.' Tarzan's tone was serious, though a brighter man than Phobeg might have discovered in it a note of banter; but Phobeg was not bright at all, and he thought that Tarzan was already commencing to throw himself upon his mercy.

'It will soon be over,' Phobeg assured him. 'I promise that I shall not let you suffer long.'

'I suppose that you will twist my neck like this,' said Tarzan, pretending to twist something with his two hands.

'M-m-m, perhaps,' admitted Phobeg; 'but I shall have to throw you about a bit first. We must amuse Nemone, you know.'

'Surely, by all means!' assented Tarzan. 'But suppose you should not be able to throw me about? Suppose that I should throw you about? Would that amuse Nemone? Or perhaps it would amuse you!'

Phobeg laughed. 'It amuses me very much just to think about it,' he said, 'and I hope that it amuses you to think about it, for that is as near as you will ever come to throwing Phobeg about; have I not told you that I am the strongest man in Cathne?'

'Oh, of course,' admitted Tarzan. 'I had forgotten that for the moment.'

'You would do well to try to remember it,' advised Phobeg, 'or otherwise our combat will not be interesting at all.'

'And Nemone would not be amused! That would be sad. We should make it as interesting and exciting as possible, and you must not conclude it too soon.'

'You are right about that,' agreed Phobeg. 'The better it is the more generous will Nemone feel toward me when it is over; she may even give me a donation in addition to my liberty if we amuse her well.

'By the belly of Thoos!' he exclaimed, slapping his thigh. 'We must make a good fight of it and a long one. Now listen! How would this be? At first we shall pretend that you are defeating me; I shall let you throw me about a bit. You see? Then I shall get the better of it for a while, and then you. We shall take turns up to a certain point, and then, when I give you the cue, you must pretend to be frightened, and run away from me. I shall then chase you all over the arena, and that will give them a good laugh. When I catch you at last (and you must let me catch you right in front of Nemone) I shall then twist your neck and kill you, but I will do it as painlessly as possible.'

'You are very kind,' said Tarzan grimly.

'Do you like the plan?' demanded Phobeg. 'Is it not a splendid one?'

'It will certainly amuse them,' agreed Tarzan, 'if it works.'

'If it works! Why should it not work? It will, if you do your part.'

'But suppose *I* kill *you*?' inquired the Lord of the Jungle.

'There you go again!' exclaimed Phobeg. 'I must say that you are a good fellow after all, for you will have your little joke; and I can tell you that there is no one who enjoys a little joke more than Phobeg.'

'I hope that you are in the same mood tomorrow,' remarked Tarzan.

When the next day dawned the slave and the guard came with a large breakfast for the two prisoners, the best meal that had been served them since they had been imprisoned.

'Eat well,' advised one of the warriors, 'that you may have strength to fight a good fight for the entertainment of the Queen. For one of you it is the last meal; so you had both better enjoy it to the full, since there is no telling for which one of you it is the last.'

'It is the last for him,' said Phobeg, jerking a thumb in the direction of Tarzan.

'It is thus that the betting goes,' said the warrior, 'but even so one cannot always be sure. The stranger is a large man, and he looks strong.'

'There is none so strong as Phobeg,' the former temple guard reminded them.

The warrior shrugged. 'Perhaps,' he admitted, 'but I am not betting any money on either of you.'

'Twenty drachmas to ten that he runs away from me before the fight is over,' offered Phobeg.

'And if he kills you, who will pay me?' demanded the warrior. 'No, that is not a good bet,' and he went out and closed and locked the door behind him.

An hour later a large detachment of warriors came and took Tarzan and Phobeg from the prison. They led them through the palace grounds and out into an avenue bordered by old trees. It was a lovely avenue flanked by the white and gold homes of the nobles and the great two-storied palace surmounted by its golden domes.

Here were throngs of people waiting to see the start of the pageant and companies of warriors standing at ease, leaning upon their spears. It was an interesting sight to Tarzan who had been so long confined in the gloomy prison. He noted the dress of the civilians and the architecture of the splendid houses that could be glimpsed between the trees. He saw that the men wore short tunics or jerkins that were quite similar to the habergeons worn by the warriors, except that they were of a solid piece of cloth or light leather rather than of discs of elephant hide. The women wore short skirts of hair or cloth or leather, scant, clinging skirts that terminated just above the knees; a band to confine the breasts, sandals, and ornaments completed their simple attire.

Tarzan and Phobeg were escorted west along the avenue; and as they passed, the crowd commented upon them. There were many who knew Phobeg; some shouted encouragement to him; others taunted and insulted him. It appeared that Phobeg's popularity was not city wide. They discussed Tarzan freely but with no malice. He interested them, and there was much speculation as to his chances in a fight against the burly temple guard. The ape-man heard many wagers offered and taken; some were on him and some against; but it was evident that Phobeg was the favored of the bettors.

At the end of the avenue Tarzan saw the great Bridge of Gold that spanned the river. It was a splendid structure built entirely of the precious metal. Two golden lions of heroic size flanked the approach from the city, and as he was led across the bridge the ape-man saw two identical lions guarding the western end.

Out upon the plain that is called the Field of the Lions a crowd of spectators was filing toward a point about a mile from the city where many people were congregated, and toward this assemblage the detachment escorted the two gladiators. Here was a large, oval arena excavated to a depth of twenty or thirty feet in the floor of the plain. Upon the excavated earth piled symmetrically around the edges of the pit, and terraced from the plain level to the top, were arranged slabs of stone to serve as seats. At the east end of the arena was a wide ramp descending into it. Spanning the ramp was a low arch surmounted by the loges of the Queen and high nobility.

As Tarzan passed beneath the arch and descended the ramp toward the arena, he saw that nearly half the seats were already taken. The people were eating food that they had brought with them, and there was much laughter and talking. Evidently it was a gala day. He asked Phobeg.

'This is part of the celebration that annually follows the ending of the rainy season,' explained the Cathnean. 'There is entertainment of some sort here at least once a month and oftener when the weather permits. You will have an opportunity to see all the events before I kill you, as our combat will undoubtedly be the last event upon the program.'

The warriors conducted the two men to the far end of the arena where a terrace had been cut part way up the sloping side of the arena, a wooden ladder leaning against the wall giving access to it. Here, upon this terrace, Tarzan and Phobeg were installed with a few warriors to serve as guards.

Presently, from the direction of the city, Tarzan heard the music of drums and trumpets.

'Here they come!' cried Phobeg.

'Who?' asked Tarzan.

'The Queen and the lion-men,' replied his adversary.

'What are the lion-men?' inquired Tarzan.

'They are the nobles,' explained Phobeg. 'Really only the hereditary nobles are members of the clan of lions, but we usually speak of all nobles as lion-men. Erot is a noble because Nemone has created him one; but he is not a lion man, as he was not born a noble.'

'Cleave my skull! But I bet he hates that,' commented one of the guard.

'He'd give a right eye to be a lion man,' said Phobeg.

'It's too late now,' observed the warrior; 'he should have picked his parents more carefully.'

'He claims that he did pick a noble father,' explained Phobeg, 'but his mother denies it.'

Another warrior laughed. 'Son of a noble!' he scoffed. 'I know old Tibdos, the husband of Erot's mother; I know him well. He cleans the lions' cages at the breeding farm. Erot looks just like him. Son of a noble!'

'Son of a she-jackal!' growled Phobeg. 'I wish I were to fight him today instead of this poor fellow.'

'You feel sorry for him?' inquired a warrior.

'Yes, in a way,' replied Phobeg. 'He is not a half bad fellow, and I have nothing against him except that he is stupid. He cannot seem to understand the simplest things. He does not seem to realize that I am the strongest man in Cathne and that I am going to kill him this afternoon, unless they get through with the other events early and I kill him this morning.'

'How do you know that he does not realize these things?' demanded the warrior.

'Because he has never given any sign that he is very much afraid.'

'Possibly he does not believe that you can kill him,' suggested the warrior.

'Then that proves that he is very stupid; but stupid or not, I am going to kill him. I am going to twist his neck until his spine breaks. I can scarcely wait to get my hands on him; of all the things that I love there is no sensation equal to that of killing a man. I love that better than I love women.'

Tarzan glanced at the great hulk squatting beside him. 'The French have a word for that,' he remarked.

'I do not know what you are talking about,' growled Phobeg.

'I am not surprised.'

'There he goes again!' exclaimed Phobeg. 'What sense is there to that? Did I not tell you that he is stupid?'

Now the blaring of the trumpets and the beating of the drums burst with increased volume upon their ears, and Tarzan saw that the musicians were marching down the ramp into the arena at the far end of the great oval. At the same time the tumult in the stands increased as new thousands surged over the rim of the stadium and sought seats among the thousands already there.

Behind the music marched a company of warriors, and from each spear head fluttered a colored pennon. It was a stirring and colorful picture, but nothing to what followed.

A few yards in rear of the warriors came a chariot of gold drawn by four maned lions, where, half reclining upon a couch draped with furs and gaily colored cloths, rode Nemone, the Queen. Sixteen black slaves held the lions in leash; and at either side of the chariot marched six nobles resplendent in gold and ivory, while a huge black, marching behind, held a great, red parasol over the Queen. Squatting upon little seats above the rear wheels of the chariot were two small blackamoors wielding feathered fans above her.

At sight of the chariot and its royal occupant, the people in the stands arose and then kneeled down in salute to their ruler, while wave after wave of applause rolled round the amphitheater as the pageant slowly circled the arena.

Behind Nemone's chariot marched another company of warriors; these were followed by a number of gorgeously decorated wooden chariots, each drawn by two lions and driven by a noble; following these marched a company of nobles on foot, while a third company of warriors brought up the rear.

When the column had circled the arena Nemone quit her chariot and ascended to her loge above the ramp amid the continued cheering of the populace, the chariots driven by the nobles lined up in the center of the arena, the royal guard formed across the entrance to the stadium, and the nobles who had no part in the games went to their private loges.

There followed then in quick succession contests in dagger throwing and in the throwing of spears, feats of strength and skill, and foot races. Upon every event wagers were laid and the whole stadium was a bedlam of shouted wagers and odds, of curses, groans, hoots, laughter, and applause.

In the loges of Nemone and the nobles great sums changed hands upon every event. The Queen was an inveterate gambler, winning or losing a fortune upon the cast of a single dagger. When she won she smiled, and she smiled too when she lost; but men knew that contestants upon whom Nemone won regularly through the year were the recipients of royal favors, while those upon whom she consistently lost often disappeared.

When the minor sports were completed the chariot races began; and upon these the betting dwarfed all the other betting of the day, and men and women acted like maniacs as they encouraged a favorite driver, applauded a winner, or berated an unfortunate loser.

Two drivers raced in each event, the distance being always the same, one lap of the arena, for lions cannot maintain high speed for great distances. After each race the winner received a pennon from the Queen, while the loser drove up the ramp and out of the stadium amid the hoots of those who had lost money on him. Then two more raced, and when the last pair had finished the winners paired off for new events. Thus, by elimination, the contestants were eventually reduced to two, winners in each event in which they had contested. This, then, was the première racing event of the day, and the noise and the betting that it engendered surpassed all that had gone before.

The winner of this final race was acclaimed champion of the day and was presented with a golden helmet by Nemone herself, and even those who had bet upon his rival and lost their money added their voices to the ovation that the noisy throng accorded him as he drove proudly around the arena and disappeared up the ramp beneath the arch of the Queen, his golden helmet shining bravely in the sun.

'Now,' said Phobeg in a loud voice, 'the people are going to see something worthwhile. It is what they have been waiting for, and they will not be disappointed. If you have a god, fellow, pray to him, for you are about to die.'

'Are you not going to permit me to run around the arena first while you chase me?' demanded Tarzan.

9

'Death! Death!'

A score of slaves were busily cleaning up the arena following the departure of the lion-drawn chariots, the audience was standing and stretching itself, nobles were wandering from loge to loge visiting their friends, men and women were settling up past wagers and making new ones. The sounds of many voices enveloped the stadium in one mighty discord. The period was one of intermission between events.

Tarzan was annoyed. Crowds irritated his nerves. The sound of human voices was obnoxious to him. Through narrowed lids he surveyed the scene. If ever a wild beast looked upon its enemies it was then.

Phobeg was still boasting in a loud voice that was clearly audible to at least a portion of the audience sitting just above the gladiators' ledge. The attitude of the temple guard was anything but soothing to the Lord of the Jungle, but by no sign did he intimate that he heard him after his first retort.

Already the betting was running high on this last event of the day, though only a small proportion of the audience had had a fair view of the two contestants by which they might compare them. Phobeg, however, was known by reputation and was the favorite, the odds running as high as ten to one against Tarzan.

In the royal loge Nemone lay back luxuriously in the great chair that was half a throne and half a couch. She had lost heavily during the day, but she showed no ill humor. However, the nobles surrounding her were ill at ease and hoped that she would win on this last event. Each was determined to bet heavily upon the strange wild man with Nemone, so that she might win back all that she had lost to them upon earlier events, for all were assured that Nemone would back Phobeg, it being her custom to bet heavily upon all favorites.

Erot was particularly anxious that the Queen should win back what he had won from her. For some time he had been a trifle uncertain as to his position in the good graces of his sovereign; he had sensed, perhaps, that he was slipping a little; and he had had sufficient experience to know that winning money from Nemone constituted nothing less than a tremendous shove to one who had started to slip.

Therefore Erot, with the other nobles, having determined to let Nemone win their money on Phobeg sent slaves out into the audience secretly to place money enough on Phobeg to reimburse them what they lost to Nemone on Tarzan. The plan was accurately figured and neatly worked, and when the day was over Nemone would be winner and so would they, all of their losses having been more than made up by their winnings on Phobeg, which the common people would have paid.

This large volume of money going suddenly among the audience which was already favoring Phobeg and offering large odds against Tarzan found very little Tarzan money available at ten to one. The natural result was that to place their money at all they had to offer larger odds, and to reimburse themselves of their losses to Nemone, or rather their assumed losses, for no wagers had yet been laid in the royal loge, they were compelled to put up enormous sums as the odds soared upward finally until it took one hundred Phobeg drachmas to cover one of Tarzan's.

Now a trumpet sounded, and the warriors guarding Tarzan and Phobeg ordered them down into the arena and paraded them once around it that the people might compare the gladiators and choose a favorite. As they passed before the royal loge Nemone leaned forward with half-closed eyes surveying the tall stranger and the squat Cathnean.

Erot, the Queen's favorite, watched her. 'A thousand drachmas on the stranger!' he cried.

'I am betting on the stranger, too,' interjected another noble eagerly.

'So am I,' said Nemone.

Erot and the other nobles were amazed; this upset their plans completely. Of course they would win more money, but one always felt safer losing to Nemone than winning from her.

'You will lose your money,' Erot told her.

'Then why did you offer to bet on the stranger?' demanded the Queen.

'The odds were so attractive that I was tempted into taking a chance,' explained Erot quickly.

'What are the odds now?'

'One hundred to one.'

'And you think the stranger may not have even one chance in a hundred of winning?' demanded Nemone, toying idly with the hilt of her dagger.

'Phobeg is the strongest man in Cathne,' said Erot. 'I really think that the stranger has no chance at all against him; he is as good as dead already.'

'Very well then, if you feel that way about it you should bet on Phobeg,' whispered Nemone softly. 'I am going to wager 100,000 drachmas on the stranger. How much of this do you wish, my dear Erot?'

'I wish that my Queen would not risk her money on him at all,' said Erot; 'I am grieved when my beloved Queen loses.'

'You bore me, Erot.' Nemone gestured impatiently and then, turning to the other nobles, 'Is there none here who will cover my drachmas?'

Instantly they were all eager to accomodate her. To win a hundred thousand drachmas from the Queen in addition to all that they would win from the common people was too much for their cupidity; they even forgot Nemone's possible wrath in their anxiety to accommodate her now that it was certain that her decision could not be altered, and in a few minutes the bets had been recorded.

'He has a fine physique,' commented Nemone, her eyes upon the jungle lord, 'and he is taller than the other.'

'But look at Phobeg's muscles,' Erot reminded her. 'This Phobeg has killed many men; they say that he twists their necks and breaks their spines.'

'We shall see,' was the Queen's only comment.

Erot thought that he would not like to be in Phobeg's sandals, for if the stranger did not kill him Nemone most certainly would see that he did not long survive, who had robbed her of a hundred thousand drachmas.

Now the two men were posted in the arena a short distance from the royal loge, and the captain of the stadium was giving them their instructions which were extremely simple: they were to remain inside the arena and try to kill one another with their bare hands, though the use of elbows, knees, feet, or teeth was not barred; there were no other rules governing the combat. The winner was to receive his freedom, though even this had been qualified by Nemone.

'When the trumpet sounds you may attack,' said the captain of the stadium. 'And may Thoos be with you.'

Tarzan and Phobeg had been placed ten paces apart. Now they stood waiting the signal. Phobeg swelled his chest and beat upon it with his fists; he flexed his arms, swelling the great muscles of his biceps until they stood out like great knotty balls; then he hopped about, warming up his leg muscles. He was attracting all the attention, and that pleased him excessively.

Tarzan stood quietly, his arms folded loosely across his chest, his muscles relaxed. He appeared totally unconscious of the presence of the noisy multitude or even of Phobeg, but he was not unconscious of anything that was transpiring about him. His eyes and his ears were alert; it would be Tarzan who would hear the first note of the trumpet's signal; Tarzan was ready!

Tarzan cared nothing for the stupid men-things making silly noises in their throats, gathered here to see two fellow creatures that had never harmed them try to kill one another for their pleasure; he did not care what they thought about him; to him they were less than the droppings of lions that the slaves had swept up in the arena.

He did not wish to kill Phobeg, nor did he wish to be killed; but Phobeg disgusted him, and he would have liked to punish the man for his ridiculous egotism. He realized that his antagonist was a mighty man and that it might not be an easy thing to punish him without taking a great deal of punishment himself, but this risk he did not mind so that he could halt his own punishment short of crippling or death. His gaze chanced to cross the royal loge; it halted there; the eyes of Nemone met his and held them. What strange eyes were hers – so beautiful, with fires burning far beneath the surface, so mysterious!

The trumpet pealed, and Tarzan's eyes swung back to Phobeg. A strange silence fell upon the amphitheater. The two men approached one another, Phobeg strutting and confident, Tarzan with the easy, graceful stride of a lion.

'Say your prayers, fellow!' shouted the temple guard. 'I am going to kill you; but first I shall play with you for the amusement of Nemone.'

Phobeg came closer and reached for Tarzan. The ape-man let him seize him by the shoulders; then Tarzan cupped his two hands and brought the heels of them up suddenly and with great force beneath Phobeg's chin and at the same time pushed the man from him. The great head snapped back, and the fellow's huge bulk hurtled backward a dozen paces, where Phobeg sat down heavily.

A groan of surprise arose from the audience, interspersed with cheers from those who had wagered on Tarzan. Phobeg scrambled to his feet; his face was contorted with rage; in an instant he had gone berserk. With a roar, he charged the ape-man.

'No quarter!' he screamed. 'I kill you *now!*'

'Kill! Kill!' shouted the Phobeg adherents. 'Death! Death! Give us a death!'

'Don't you wish to throw me about a bit first?' asked Tarzan in a low voice, as he lightly side-stepped the other's mad charge.

'No!' screamed Phobeg, turning clumsily and charging again. 'I kill! I kill!'

Tarzan caught the outstretched hands and spread them wide; then a bronzed arm, lightninglike, clamped about Phobeg's short neck; the ape-man wheeled suddenly about, leaned forward, and hurled his antagonist over his head. Phobeg fell heavily to the sandy gravel of the arena.

Nemone leaned from the royal loge, her eyes flashing, her bosom heaving. Erot was but one of many nobles who experienced a constriction of the dia-phragm. Nemone turned to him. 'Would you like to bet a little more on the strongest man in Cathne?' she asked.

Erot smiled a sickly smile. 'The battle has only commenced,' he said.

'But already it is as good as over,' taunted Nemone.

Phobeg arose but this time more slowly, nor did he charge again but approached his antagonist warily; his tactics now were very different from what they had been. He wanted to get close enough to Tarzan to get a hold; that was all he desired, just a hold; then, he knew, he could crush the man with his great strength.

Perhaps the ape-man sensed what was in the mind of his foe, perhaps it was just chance that caused him to taunt Phobeg by holding his left wrist out to the other; but whatever it was, Phobeg seized upon the opportunity and, grasping Tarzan's wrist, sought to drag the ape-man into his embrace; then Tarzan stepped in quickly, struck Phobeg a terrific blow in the face with his right fist, seized the wrist of the hand that held his, and, again whirling quickly beneath his victim, threw him heavily once more, using Phobeg's arm as a lever and his own shoulder as a fulcrum.

This time Phobeg had difficulty in arising at all. He came up very slowly. The ape-man was standing over him. The blood froze in the veins of the Cathnean as he heard the low, beastlike growl rumbling in the throat of the stranger.

Suddenly Tarzan stooped and seized Phobeg, and, lifting him bodily, held him above his head. 'Shall I run now, Phobeg?' he growled, 'or are you too tired to chase me?' Then he hurled the man to the ground again a little nearer to the royal loge where Nemone sat, tense and thrilling.

Like a lion with its prey, the Lord of the Jungle followed the man who had taunted him and would have killed him; twice again he picked him up and hurled him closer to the end of the arena. Now the fickle crowd was scream-ing to Tarzan to kill Phobeg; Phobeg, the strongest man in Cathne; Phobeg, who twisted men's necks until their spines cracked.

Again Tarzan seized his antagonist and held him above his head. Phobeg struggled weakly, but he was quite helpless. Tarzan walked to the side of the arena near the royal loge and hurled the great body up into the audience.

'Take your strong man,' he said; 'Tarzan does not want him.' Then he walked away and stood before the ramp, waiting, as though he demanded his freedom.

Amid shrieks and howls that called to Tarzan's mind only the foulest of wild beasts, the loathsome hyena, the crowd hurled the unhappy Phobeg back into the arena. 'Kill him! Kill him!' they screamed.

Nemone leaned from her loge. 'Kill him, Tarzan!' she cried.

Tarzan shrugged with disgust and turned away.

'Kill him, slave!' commanded a noble from his luxurious loge.

'I shall not kill him,' replied the ape-man.

Nemone arose in her loge. She was flushed and excited. 'Tarzan!' she cried, and when the ape-man glanced up at her, 'why do you not kill him?'

'Why should I kill him?' demanded Tarzan. 'He cannot harm me, and I kill only in self-defense or for food; but I do not eat human flesh, so why should I kill him?'

Phobeg, bruised, battered, and helpless, arose weakly to his feet and stood reeling drunkenly. He heard the voice of the pitiless mob screaming for his death. He saw his antagonist standing a few paces away in front of the ramp, paying no attention to him, and dimly and as though from a great distance he had heard him refuse to kill him. He had heard, but he did not comprehend. He expected to be killed, for such was the custom and the law of the arena. He had sought to kill this man; he would have shown him no mercy; so he could not understand the mercy of Tarzan's indifference that had been extended to him.

Phobeg's bloodshot eyes wandered helplessly about the arena, seeking nothing or no one in particular; sympathy was not to be found there, nor mercy, nor any friend; such were not for the vanquished. The frenzied bloodlust of the mob fascinated him. A few minutes ago it had been acclaiming him; now it condemned him to death. His gaze reached the royal loge as Erot leaned far out and shouted to Tarzan standing below.

'Kill him, fellow!' he cried. 'It is the Queen's command.'

Phobeg's eyes dropped to the figure of the ape-man, and he braced himself for a final effort to delay the inevitable. He knew that he had met one mightier than himself and that he must die when the other wished; but the law of self-preservation compelled him to defend himself, however hopelessly.

The ape-man glanced up at the Queen's favorite. 'Tarzan kills only whom it pleases him to kill.' He spoke in a low voice that yet carried to the royal loge. 'I shall not kill Phobeg.'

'You fool,' cried Erot, 'do you not understand that it is the Queen's wish, that it is the Queen's command, which no one may disobey and live, that you kill the fellow?'

'If the Queen wants him killed, why doesn't she send you down to do it? She is your Queen, not mine.' There was neither awe nor respect in the voice of the ape-man.

Erot looked horrified. He glanced at the Queen. 'Shall I order the guard to destroy the impudent savage?' he asked.

Nemone shook her head. Her countenance remained inscrutable, but a strange light burned in her eyes. 'We give them both their lives,' she said. 'Set Phobeg free, and bring the other to me in the palace'; then she rose as a sign that the games were over.

Many miles to the south of the Field of the Lions in the valley of Onthar a lion moved restlessly just within the confines of a forest. He paced rapidly first in one direction and then in another; his movements were erratic; sometimes his nose was near the ground and, again, it was in the air as though he were searching for something or someone. Once he raised his head and lifted his great voice in a roar that shook the earth and sent Manu, the monkey, fleeing through the trees with his brothers and sisters. In the distance a bull elephant trumpeted, and then silence fell once more upon the jungle.

10

In the Palace of the Queen

A detachment of common warriors commanded by an under-officer had escorted Tarzan to the stadium, but he returned to the city in the company of nobles. Several of them had clustered about him immediately following the gesture of Nemone that had suggested to them that this stranger might be the recipient of further royal favors.

Congratulating him upon his victory, praising his prowess, asking innumerable questions, they followed him from the arena, and at the top of the ramp another noble accosted him. It was Gemnon.

'The Queen has commanded me to accompany you to the city and look after you,' he explained. 'This evening I am to bring you to her in the palace; but in the meantime you will want to bathe and rest, and I imagine that you might welcome some decent food after the prison fare you have been eating recently.'

'I shall be glad of a bath and good food,' replied Tarzan, 'but why should I rest? I have been doing nothing else for several days.'

'But you have just come through a terrific battle for your life!' exclaimed Gemnon. 'You must be tired.'

Tarzan shrugged his broad shoulders. 'Perhaps you had better look after Phobeg instead,' he replied. 'It is he who needs rest; I am not tired.'

Gemnon laughed. 'Phobeg should consider himself lucky to be alive. If anyone looks after him it will be himself.'

They were walking toward the city now. The other nobles had joined their own parties or had dropped behind, and Gemnon and Tarzan were alone, if two may be said to be alone who are surrounded by a chattering mob through which bodies of armed men and lion-drawn chariots are making their slow way. Those near Tarzan were discussing him animatedly, but because of the nobles they kept their distance from him. They commented upon his giant strength and the deceptive appearance of his muscular development, the flowing symmetry of which scarce proclaimed the titanic power of the steel thews of the Lord of the Jungle.

'You are popular now,' commented Gemnon.

'A few minutes ago they were screaming at Phobeg to kill me,' Tarzan reminded him.

'I am really surprised that they are so friendly,' remarked Gemnon. 'You cheated them of a death – the one thing they are all hoping and praying to see when they go to the stadium. It is for this they pay their lepta for admission. Also, most of them lost more money betting on Phobeg; but those who won on you should love you, for they won much; the odds were as high as one hundred to one against you.

'It is the nobles, though, who have the greatest grievance against you,' continued Gemnon, grinning. 'Several of them lost their entire fortunes. Those closest to Nemone always have to cover her bets; and, believing that she would bet on Phobeg, they placed large bets on him among the audience to cover their losses to Nemone; then Nemone insisted upon betting on you, and they had to bet more money on Phobeg – ten million drachmas to cover Nemone's hundred thousand. I estimate that that one small group lost close to twenty million drachmas.'

'And Nemone won ten million?' asked Tarzan.

'Yes,' replied Gemnon; 'which may account for the fact that you are alive now.'

'Why should I not be alive?'

'You flouted the Queen; before thousands of her people you refused to obey her direct command. No, not even the ten million drachmas can account for it; there is some other reason why Nemone spared you. Perhaps she is contemplating for you a death that will give her greater satisfaction. Knowing Nemone as I do, I cannot believe that she will let you live; she would not be Nemone if she forgave so serious an affront to her majesty.'

'Phobeg was going to kill me,' Tarzan reminded him.

'But Nemone is not Phobeg. Nemone is Queen, and—'

'And what?' asked the ape-man.

Gemnon shrugged. 'I was thinking aloud, which is a bad habit for one who enjoys life. Doubtless you may live long enough to know her better than you do now and then you can do your own thinking – but do not do it aloud.'

'Did you lose much on Phobeg?' inquired Tarzan.

'I won; I bet on you. I met one of Erot's slaves who was going to place some of his master's money on Phobeg; I took it all. You know I had seen a little more of you than the other nobles and I believed that you had a chance, but I was backing your intelligence and agility against Phobeg's strength, stupidity, and awkwardness; even I did not dream that you were stronger than he.'

'And the odds were good!'

Gemnon smiled. 'Too good to be overlooked; it was more than a reasonable gamble. But I cannot understand Nemone; she is a great bettor but no gambler. She always puts her money on the favorite, and may Thoos help him if he does not win.'

'A woman's intuition,' suggested the ape-man.

'I think not; Nemone is too practical and calculating to act on intuition alone; she had some other reason. What it is, none knows but Nemone. The same mysterious motivation saved your life today or, perhaps I should say, prolonged it.'

'I am going to see her this evening,' said Tarzan, 'and doubtless I shall affront her again; it seems that I have done so both times that I have seen her.'

'Do not forget that she practically sentenced you to death for the first offense,' Gemnon reminded him. 'At that time she must have been certain that Phobeg would kill you. If I were you I should not annoy her.'

When they reached the city, Gemnon took Tarzan to his own quarters in the palace. These consisted of a bedroom and bath in addition to a living room that was shared with another officer. Here Tarzan found the usual decorations of weapons, shields, and mounted heads in addition to pictures painted on leather. He saw no books, nor any other printed matter; neither was there any sign of writing materials in the rooms. He wanted to question Gemnon on this subject, but he found that he had never learned any word for writing or for a written language.

The bath interested the ape-man. The tub was a coffinlike affair made of clay and baked; the plumbing fixtures were apparently all of solid gold. While questioning Gemnon he learned that the water was brought from the mountains east of the city through clay pipes of considerable size and distributed by means of pressure tanks distributed throughout all of urban Cathne.

Gemnon summoned a slave to prepare the bath, and when Tarzan had finished, a meal was awaiting him in the living room. While he was eating, and Gemnon lounged near in conversation, another young noble entered the apartment. He had a narrow face and rather unpleasant eyes, nor was he overly cordial when Gemnon introduced him to Tarzan.

'Xerstle and I are quartered together,' Gemnon explained.

'I have orders to move out,' snapped Xerstle.

'Why is that?' asked Gemnon.

'To make room for your friend here,' replied Xerstle sourly, and then he went into his own room mumbling something about slaves and savages.

'He does not seem pleased,' remarked Tarzan.

'But I am,' replied Gemnon in a low voice. 'Xerstle and I have not gotten along well together. We have nothing in common. He is one of Erot's friends and was elevated from nothing after Erot became Nemone's favorite. He is the son of a foreman at the mines. If they had elevated his father he would have been an acquisition to the nobility, for he is a splendid man; but Xerstle is a rat – like his friend, Erot.'

'I have heard something of your nobility,' said Tarzan; 'I understand that there are two classes of nobles, and that one class rather looks upon the other with contempt even though a man of the lower class may hold a higher title than many of those in the other class.'

'We do not look upon them with contempt if they are worthy men,' replied Gemnon. 'The old nobility, the Lion-men of Cathne, is hereditary; the other is but temporary – for the lifetime of the man who has received it as a special mark of favor from the throne. In one respect at least it reflects greater glory on its possessor than does hereditary nobility, as it is often the deserved reward of merit. I am a noble by accident of birth; had I not been born a noble I might never have become one. I am a lion man because my father was; I may own lions because, beyond the memory of man, an ancient ancestor of mine led the king's lions to battle.'

'What did Erot do to win his patent of nobility?' inquired the ape-man.

Gemnon grimaced. 'Whatever services he has rendered have been personal; he has never served the state with distinction. If he owns any distinction, it is that of being the prince of flatterers, the king of sycophants.'

'Your Queen seems too intelligent a woman to be duped by flattery.'

'No one is, always.'

'There are no sycophants among the beasts,' said Tarzan.

'What do you mean by that?' demanded Gemnon. 'Erot is almost a beast.'

'You malign the beasts. Did you ever see a lion that fawned upon another creature to curry favor?'

'But beasts are different,' argued Gemnon.

'Yes; they have left all the petty meannesses to man.'

'You do not think very highly of men.'

'None does who thinks, who compares them with the beasts.'

'We are what we are born,' rejoined Gemnon; 'some are beasts, some are men, and some are men who behave like beasts.'

'But none, thank God, are beasts that behave like men,' retorted Tarzan, smiling.

Xerstle, entering from his room, interrupted their conversation. 'I have gathered my things together,' he said; 'I shall send a slave for them presently.' His manner was short and brusque. Gemnon merely nodded in assent, and Xerstle departed.

'He does not seem pleased,' commented the ape-man.

'May Xarator have him!' ejaculated Gemnon; 'though he would serve a better purpose as food for my lions,' he added as an afterthought; 'if they would eat him.'

'You own lions?' inquired Tarzan.

'Certainly,' replied Gemnon. 'I am a lion man and must own lions. It is a caste obligation. Each lion man must own lions of war to fight in the service of the Queen. I have five. In times of peace I use them for hunting and racing. Only royalty and the lion-men may own lions.'

The sun was setting behind the mountains that rimmed the western edge of the Field of the Lions as a slave entered the apartment with a lighted cresset which he hung at the end of a chain depending from the ceiling.

'It is time for the evening meal,' announced Gemnon, rising.

'I have eaten,' replied Tarzan.

'Come anyway; it may interest you to meet the other nobles of the palace.'

Tarzan arose. 'Very well,' he said and followed Gemnon from the apartment.

Forty nobles were assembled in a large dining room on the main floor of the palace as Gemnon and Tarzan entered. Tomos was there and Erot and Xerstle; several of the others Tarzan also recognized as having been seen by him before either in the council room or at the stadium. A sudden silence fell upon the assemblage as he entered, as though the men had been interrupted while discussing either him or Gemnon.

'This is Tarzan,' announced Gemnon by way of introduction as he led the ape-man to the table.

Tomos, who sat at the head of the table, did not appear pleased. Erot was scowling; it was he who spoke first. 'This table is for nobles,' he said, 'not for slaves.'

'By his own prowess and the grace of her majesty, the Queen, this man is here as my guest,' said Gemnon quietly. 'If one of my equals takes exception to his presence, I will be glad to discuss the matter with swords,' and then he turned to Tarzan. 'Because this man sits at table with nobles of my own rank I apologize for the inference he intended you to draw from his words. I hope you are not offended.'

'Does the jackal offend the lion?' asked the ape-man.

The meal was not a complete success socially. Erot and Xerstle whispered together. Tomos did not speak but applied himself assiduously to the business of eating. Several of Gemnon's friends engaged Tarzan in conversation;

and he found one or two of them agreeable, but others were inclined to be patronizing. Possibly they would have been surprised and their attitude toward him different had they known that their guest was a peer of England, but then again this might have made little impression upon them inasmuch as none of them had ever heard of England. However, Tarzan did not enlighten them. He did not care what they thought, and so the meal progressed with many silences.

When Tomos arose and the others were free to go, Gemnon conducted Tarzan to the apartments of the Queen after returning to his own apartments to don a more elaborate habergeon, helmet, and equipment.

'Do not forget to kneel when we enter the presence of Nemone,' cautioned Gemnon, 'and do not speak until she addresses you.'

A noble received them in a small anteroom where he left them while he went to announce their presence to the Queen, and as they waited Gemnon's eyes watched the tall stranger standing quietly near him.

'Have you no nerves?' he asked presently.

'What do you mean?' demanded the ape-man.

'I have seen the bravest warriors tremble who had been summoned before Nemone,' explained his companion.

'I have never trembled,' replied Tarzan. 'How is it done?'

'Perhaps Nemone will teach you to tremble.'

'Perhaps, but why should I tremble to go where a jackal does not tremble to go?'

'I do not understand what you mean by that,' said Gemnon puzzled.

'Erot is in there.'

Gemnon grinned. 'But how do you know that?' he asked.

'I know,' said Tarzan; he did not think it necessary to explain that when the noble had opened the door his sensitive nostrils had caught the scent spoor of the Queen's favorite.

'I hope not,' said Gemnon, an expression of concern upon his countenance. 'If he is there this may be a trap from which you will never come out alive.'

'One might fear the Queen,' replied Tarzan, 'but not the jackal.'

'It is the Queen of whom I was thinking.'

The noble returned to the anteroom. He nodded to Tarzan. 'Her majesty will receive you now,' he said. 'You may go, Gemnon; your attendance will not be required.' Then he turned to the ape-man once more. 'When I open the door and announce you, enter the room and kneel. Remain kneeling until the Queen tells you to arise, and do not speak until after her majesty addresses you. Do you hear?'

'I hear,' replied Tarzan. 'Open the door!'

Gemnon, just leaving the anteroom by another doorway, heard and smiled; but the noble did not smile. He frowned. The bronzed giant had spoken to him in a tone of command, but the noble did not know what to do about it; so he opened the door. But he got some revenge, or at least he thought that he did.

'The slave, Tarzan!' he announced in a loud voice.

The Lord of the Jungle stepped into the adjoining chamber, crossed to the center of it, and stood erect, silently regarding Nemone. He did not kneel. Erot was there standing at the foot of a couch upon which the Queen reclined upon fat pillows. The Queen regarded Tarzan from her deep eyes without any change of expression, but Erot scowled angrily.

'Kneel, you fool!' he commanded.

'Silence!' admonished Nemone. 'It is I who give commands.'

Erot flushed and fingered the golden hilt of his sword. Tarzan neither spoke nor moved nor took his eyes from the eyes of Nemone. Though he had thought her beautiful before, he realized now that she was even more gorgeous than he had believed it possible for any woman to be.

'I shall not need you again tonight, Erot,' said Nemone; 'you may go now.'

Now Erot paled and then turned fiery red. He started to speak but thought better of it; then he backed to the doorway, executed a bow that brought him to one knee, arose, and departed.

As Tarzan had crossed the threshold his observing eyes had noted every detail of the room's interior almost in a single, sweeping glance. The chamber was not large, but it was magnificent in its conception and its appointments. Columns of solid gold supported the ceiling, the walls were tiled with ivory, the floor a mosaic of colored stones upon which were scattered rugs of colored stuff and the skins of animals, among which was one that attracted the ape-man's instant attention – the skin of a man tanned with the head on.

On the walls were paintings, for the most part very crude, and the usual array of heads of animals and men, and at one end of the room a great lion was chained between two of the golden Doric columns. He was a very large lion with a tuft of white hair in his mane directly in the center of the back of his neck. From the instant that Tarzan entered the room the lion eyed him malevolently, and Erot had scarcely passed out and closed the door behind him when the beast sprang to his feet with a terrific roar and leaped at the ape-man. The chains stopped him and he dropped down, growling.

'Belthar does not like you,' said Nemone who had remained unmoved when the beast sprang. She noticed, too, that Tarzan had not started nor given any other indication that he had heard the lion or seen him; and she was pleased. 'He but reflects the attitude of all Cathne,' replied Tarzan.

'That is not true,' contradicted Nemone.

'No?'

'*I* like you.' Nemone's voice was low and caressing. 'You defied me before my people at the stadium today, but I did not have you destroyed. Do you suppose that I should have permitted you to live if I had not liked you? You do not kneel to me. No one else in the world has ever refused to do that and lived. I have never seen a man like you. I do not understand you. I am beginning to think that I do not understand myself. The leopard does not become a sheep in a few hours, yet it seems to me that I have changed as much as that since I first saw you; but that is not solely because I like you; I think that it is more because there is something mysterious about you that I cannot fathom. You have piqued my curiosity.'

'And when that is satisfied you will kill me, perhaps?' asked Tarzan, a half smile curving his lip.

'Perhaps,' admitted Nemone with a low laugh. 'Come here and sit down beside me; I want to talk with you; I want to know more about you.'

'I shall see that you do not learn too much,' Tarzan assured her as he crossed to the couch and seated himself facing her, while Belthar growled and strained at his chains.

'In your own country you are no slave,' said Nemone; 'but I do not need to ask that; your every act has proved it. Perhaps you are a king?'

Tarzan shook his head. 'I am Tarzan,' he said, as though that explained everything, setting him above kings.

'Are you a lion man? You *must* be,' insisted the Queen.

'It would not make me better nor worse; so what difference does it make? You might make Erot a king, but he would still be Erot.'

A sudden frown darkened Nemone's countenance. 'What do you mean by that?' she demanded. There was a suggestion of anger in her tone.

'I mean that a title of nobility does not make a man noble, that you may call a jackal a lion; but he will still be a jackal.'

'Do you not know that I am supposed to be very fond of Erot,' she demanded, 'or that you may drive my patience too far?'

Tarzan shrugged. 'You show execrable taste.'

Nemone sat up very straight. Her eyes flashed. 'I should have you killed!' she cried. Tarzan said nothing. He just kept his eyes on hers. She could not tell whether or not he was laughing at her. Finally she sank back on her pillows with a gesture of resignation. 'What is the use?' she demanded. 'You probably would not let me get any satisfaction from killing you anyway, and by this time I should be accustomed to being affronted.'

'What you are not accustomed to is hearing the truth. Everyone is afraid of you. The reason you are interested in me is because I am not. It might do you good to hear the truth more often.'

'For instance?'

'I am not going to undertake the thankless job of regenerating royalty,' Tarzan assured her with a laugh.

'Let us stop quarreling. Nemone forgives you.'

'I do not quarrel,' said Tarzan; 'only the weak and the wrong quarrel.'

'Now answer my question. Are you a lion man in your own country?'

'I am a noble,' replied the ape-man, 'but I can tell you that that means little; a ditch digger may become a noble if he control enough votes, or a rich brewer if he subscribe a large amount of money to the political party in power.'

'And which were you,' demanded Nemone, 'a ditch digger or a rich brewer?'

'Neither,' laughed Tarzan.

'Then why are you a noble?' insisted the Queen.

'For even less reason than either of those,' admitted the ape-man. 'I am a noble through no merit of my own but by an accident of birth; my family for many generations has been noble.'

'Ah!' exclaimed Nemone. 'It is just as I thought; you *are* a lion man!'

'And what of it?' demanded Tarzan.

'It simplifies matters,' she explained, but she did not amplify the explanation nor did Tarzan either understand or inquire as to its implication. As a matter of fact he was not greatly interested in the subject.

Nemone extended a hand and laid it on his, a soft, warm hand that trembled just a little. 'I am going to give you your freedom,' she said, 'but on one condition.'

'And what is that?' asked the ape-man.

'That you remain here, that you do not try to leave Onthar – or me.' Her voice was eager and just a little husky, as though she spoke under suppressed emotion.

Tarzan remained silent. He would not promise, and so he did not speak. He realized, too, how easy it would be to remain if Nemone bid one do so. She fascinated him; she seemed to exercise a subtle influence, mysterious, hypnotic; yet he was determined to make no promise.

'I will make you a noble of Cathne,' whispered Nemone. She was sitting erect now, her face close to Tarzan's. He could feel the warmth of her body close to his; the aura of some exotic scent was in his nostrils; her fingers closed upon his arm with a fierceness that hurt. 'I will have made for you helmets of gold and habergeons of ivory, the most magnificent in Cathne; I will give you lions, fifty, a hundred; you shall be the richest, the most powerful noble of my court!'

The Lord of the Jungle felt weak beneath the spell of her burning eyes. 'I do not want *such* things,' he said.

Her soft arm crept up about his neck. A tender light, that was new to them, welled in the eyes of Nemone, the Queen of Cathne. 'Tarzan!' she whispered.

And then a door at the far end of the chamber opened and a negress entered. She had been very tall, but now she was old and bent; her scraggly wool was scant and white. Her withered lips were twisted into something that might have been either a snarl or a grin, revealing her toothless gums. She stood in the doorway leaning upon a staff and shaking her head, an ancient, palsied hag.

At the interruption Nemone straightened and looked around. The expression that had transformed and softened her countenance was swept away by a sudden wave of rage, inarticulate but no less terrible.

The old hag tapped upon the floor with her staff; her head nodded ceaselessly like that of some grotesque and horrible doll, and her lips were still contorted in what Tarzan realized now was no smile but a hideous snarl. 'Come!' she cackled. 'Come! Come! Come!'

Nemone sprang to her feet and faced the woman. 'M'duze!' she screamed. 'I could kill you! I could tear you to pieces! Get out of here!'

But the old woman only tapped with her staff and cackled, 'Come! Come! Come!'

Slowly Nemone approached her. As one drawn by an invisible and irresistible power the Queen crossed the chamber, the old hag stepped aside, and the Queen passed on through the doorway into the darkness of a corridor beyond. The old woman turned her eyes upon Tarzan, and, snarling, backed through the doorway after Nemone. Noiselessly the door closed behind them.

Tarzan had arisen as Nemone arose. For an instant he hesitated and then took a step toward the doorway in pursuit of the Queen and the old hag; then he heard a door open and a step behind him, and turned to see the noble who had ushered him into Nemone's presence standing just within the threshold.

'You may return to the quarters of Gemnon,' announced the noble politely.

Tarzan shook himself as might a lion; he drew a palm across his eyes as one whose vision has been clouded by a mist; then he drew a deep sigh and moved toward the doorway as the noble stepped aside to let him pass, but whether it was a sigh of relief or regret, who may say?

As the Lord of the Jungle passed out of the chamber, Belthar sprang to the ends of his chains with a thunderous roar.

11

The Lions of Cathne

When Gemnon entered the living room of their quarters the morning after Tarzan's audience with Nemone, he found the ape-man standing by the window looking out over the palace grounds.

'I am glad to see you here this morning,' said the Cathnean.

'And surprised, perhaps,' suggested the Lord of the Jungle.

'I should not have been surprised had you never returned,' replied Gemnon. 'How did she receive you? And Erot? I suppose he was glad to have you there!'

Tarzan smiled. 'He did not appear to be, but it did not matter much as the Queen sent him away immediately.'

'And you were alone with her all evening?' Gemnon appeared incredulous.

'Belthar and I,' Tarzan corrected him. 'Belthar does not seem to like me any better than Erot does.'

'Yes, Belthar would be there,' commented Gemnon. 'She usually has him chained near her. But do not be offended if he does not like you; Belthar likes no one. Perhaps I should qualify that by saying that he likes no one alive, for he is very fond of dead men. Belthar is a man-eater. How did Nemone treat you?'

'She was gracious,' Tarzan assured him, 'and that, too, notwithstanding the fact that the first thing that I did offended her royal majesty.'

'And what was that?' demanded Gemnon.

'I remained standing when I should have kneeled,' explained Tarzan.

'But I told you to kneel,' exclaimed Gemnon.

'So did the noble at the door.'

'And you forgot?'

'No.'

'You refused to kneel? And she did not have you destroyed! It is incredible.'

'But it is true, and she offered to make me a noble and give me a hundred lions.'

Gemnon shook his head. 'What enchantment have you worked to so change Nemone?'

'None; it was I who was under a spell. I have told you these things because I do not understand them. You are the only friend I have in Cathne, and I come to you for an explanation of much that was mysterious in my visit to the Queen last night; I doubt that I or another can ever understand the woman herself. She can be tender or terrible, weak or strong within the span of a dozen seconds. One moment she is the autocrat, the next the obedient vassal of a slave.'

'Ah!' exclaimed Gemnon; 'so you saw M'duze! I'll warrant she was none too cordial.'

'No,' admitted the ape-man. 'As a matter of fact she did not pay any attention to me; she just ordered Nemone out of the room, and Nemone went. The remarkable feature of the occurrence lies in the fact that, though the Queen did not want to leave and was very angry about it, she obeyed the old black woman meekly.'

'There are many legends surrounding M'duze,' said Gemnon; 'but there is one that is whispered more often than the others, though you may rest assured that it is only whispered and, at that, only among trusted friends.

'M'duze has been a slave in the royal family since the days of Nemone's grandfather; she was only a child then, a few years older than the King's son, Nemone's father. The oldsters recall that she was a fine-looking young negress, and the legend that is only whispered is that Nemone is her daughter.

'About a year after Nemone was born, in the tenth year of her father's reign, the Queen died under peculiar and suspicious circumstances just before she was to have been confined. The child, a son, was born just before the Queen expired. He was named Alextar, and he still lives.'

'Then why is he not king?' demanded Tarzan.

'That is a long story of mystery and court intrigue and murder, perhaps, of which more is surmised than is actually known by more than two now living. Perhaps Nemone knows, but that is doubtful though she must guess close to the truth.

'Immediately following the death of the Queen the influence of M'duze increased and became more apparent. M'duze favored Tomos, a noble of little or no importance at the time; and from that day the influence and power of Tomos grew. Then, about a year after the death of the Queen, the King died. It was so obvious that he had been poisoned that a revolt of the nobles was barely averted; but Tomos, guided by M'duze, conciliated them by fixing the guilt upon a slave woman of whom M'duze was jealous and executing her.

'For ten years Tomos ruled as regent for the boy, Alextar. During this time he had, quite naturally, established his own following in important positions in the palace and in the council. Alextar was adjudged insane and imprisoned in the temple; Nemone, at the age of twelve, was crowned Queen of Cathne.

'Erot is a creature of M'duze and Tomos, a situation that has produced a *contretemps* that would be amusing were it not so tragic. Tomos wishes to marry Nemone, but M'duze will not permit it, and, if another theory is correct, her objection is well grounded. This theory is that Tomos, and not the old king, is the father of Nemone. M'duze wishes Nemone to marry Erot, but Erot is not a lion man, and, so far, the Queen has refused to break this ancient custom that requires the ruler to marry into this highest class of Cathneans.

'M'duze is insistent upon the marriage because she can control Erot; and she discourages any interest which Nemone may manifest in other men, which undoubtedly accounts for her having interrupted the Queen's visit with you.

'You may rest assured that M'duze is your enemy, and it may be of value to you to recall that whoever has stood in the old hag's path has died a violent death. Beware of M'duze and Tomos and Erot; and, as a friend, I may say to you in confidence, beware of Nemone, also. And now let us forget the cruel and sordid side of Cathne and go for that walk I promised you for this morning that you may see the beauty of the city and the riches of her citizens.'

Along avenues bordered by old trees Gemnon led Tarzan between the low white and gold homes of nobles, glimpses of which were discernible only occasionally through grilled gateways in the walls that enclosed their spacious grounds. For a mile they walked along the stone-flagged street. Passing nobles greeted Gemnon, some nodding to his companion; artizans, tradesmen, and slaves stopped to stare at the strange, bronzed giant who had overthrown the strongest man in Cathne.

Then they came to a high wall that separated this section of the city from the next. Massive gates, swung wide now and guarded by warriors, opened into a portion of the city inhabited by better class artizans and tradesmen. Their grounds were less spacious, their houses smaller and plainer; but evidences of prosperity and even affluence were apparent everywhere.

Beyond this was a meaner district, yet even here all was orderly and neat, nor was there any sign of abject poverty in either the people or their homes. Here, as in the other portions of the city, they occasionally met a tame lion either wandering about or lying before the gate of its master's grounds.

Presently the ape-man's attention was attracted by a lion a short distance ahead of them; the beast was lying on the body of a man which it was devouring.

'Your streets do not seem to be entirely safe for pedestrians,' commented the Lord of the Jungle, indicating the feeding lion with a nod of the head.

Gemnon laughed. 'You notice that the pedestrians do not seem to be much concerned,' he replied, calling attention to the people passing to and fro past the lion and its prey, merely turning aside enough to avoid them. 'The lions must eat.'

'Do they kill many of your citizens?'

'Very few. The man you see there died, and his corpse was thrown into the street for the lions. The lion did not kill him. You see he is naked; that shows that he was dead before the lion got him. When a person dies, if there be no one who can or will pay for a funeral cortege, the body is disposed of in this way if not diseased; those who die of disease and those whose relatives can afford a funeral cortege find their last resting place in Xarator, though there are also many of the latter that are thrown to the lions by preference. You know we think a great deal of lions here in Cathne, and it is no disgrace but rather the contrary to be devoured by one. You see, our god is a lion.'

'Do the lions eat human flesh exclusively?' inquired Tarzan.

'No. We hunt sheep, goats, and elephants in Thenar to provide them with food when there is not enough human flesh to keep them well fed, for we must keep them from hunger if we are to prevent them turning man-eaters.'

'Then they never kill men for food?'

'Oh, yes, occasionally; but a lion that develops that habit is destroyed; and, after all, only a few old pets are turned loose in the streets. There are about five hundred lions inside the city, and all but a few of these are kept in enclosures on their owners' property. The best racing and hunting lions are kept in private stables.

'The Queen has fully three hundred full grown males; these are the war lions. Some of the Queen's lions are trained for racing and some for hunting; she likes to hunt, and now that the rainy season is over the hunting lions of Nemone will doubtless soon be in the field.'

'Where do you get all these lions?' asked the ape-man.

'We raise them ourselves,' explained Gemnon. 'Outside the city is a breeding plant where the females are kept. It is maintained by Nemone, and each lion man who owns females pays a stipulated sum for their keep. We raise a great many lions, for there are many killed each year in hunting, during raids, and in war. You see, we hunt elephants with them; and in these hunts many lions are killed. The Atheneans also kill a number each year when we take our lions into Thenar to hunt or raid, and quite a few escape. Most of these are still running wild in the valley or in Thenar, and there are some wild lions that have come in from the mountains. All of these are very ferocious.'

As they talked they continued on toward the center of the city until they came to a large square that was bounded on all sides by shops. Here were many people. All classes from nobles to slaves mingled before the shops and in the great open square of the market place. There were lions held by slaves who were exhibiting them for sale for their noble masters who dickered with prospective purchasers, other nobles.

Near the lion market was the slave block; and as slaves, unlike lions, might be owned by anyone, there was brisk bidding on the part of many wishing to buy. A huge, black Galla was on the block as Tarzan and Gemnon paused to watch the scene. The man was entirely naked that the buyers might examine him for blemishes; his expression was one of unconcern ordinarily, though occasionally he shot a venomous glance at the owner who was expatiating upon his virtues.

'For all the interest he shows,' remarked Tarzan, 'one might think that being sold like a piece of merchandise or a bullock was a daily occurrence in his life.'

'Not quite daily,' replied Gemnon 'but no novelty. He has been sold many times. I know him well; I used to own him.'

'Look at him!' shouted the seller. 'Look at those arms; look at those legs; look at that back! He is as strong as an elephant, and not a blemish on him. Sound as a lion's tooth he is; never ill a day in his life. And docile! A child can handle him.'

'He is so refractory that no one can handle him,' commented Gemnon in a whisper to the ape-man. 'That is the reason I had to get rid of him; that is the reason he is up for sale so often.'

'There seem to be plenty of customers interested in him,' observed Tarzan.

'Do you see that slave in the red tunic?' asked Gemnon. 'He belongs to Xerstle, and he is bidding on that fellow. He knows all about him, too; he knew him when the man belonged to me.'

'Then why does he want to buy him?' asked the ape-man.

'I do not know, but there are other uses to which a slave may be put than labor. Xerstle may not care what sort of a disposition the fellow has or even whether he will work. If he owned lions I might think that he was buying the fellow for lion food as he will probably go cheap.'

It was Xerstle's slave who bought the Galla as Tarzan and Gemnon moved on to look at the goods displayed in the shops. There were many articles of leather, wood, ivory, or gold; there were dagger-swords, spears, shields, habergeons, helmets, and sandals. One shop displayed nothing but articles of apparel for women; another, perfumes and incense; there were jewelry shops, vegetable shops, and meat shops. The last displayed dried meats and fish and carcasses of goats and sheep. The fronts of these shops were heavily barred to prevent passing lions from raiding them, Gemnon explained.

Wherever Tarzan went he attracted attention; and a small crowd always followed him, for he had been recognized the moment that he had entered the market place. Boys and girls clustered about him gazing at him admiringly, and men and women who had been at the stadium the previous day told those who had not how this stranger giant had lifted Phobeg above his head and hurled him up among the audience.

'Let's get out of here,' suggested the Lord of the Jungle; 'I do not like crowds.'

'Suppose we go back to the palace and look at the Queen's lions,' said Gemnon.

'I would rather look at lions than people,' Tarzan assured him.

The war lions of Cathne were kept in stables within the royal grounds at a considerable distance from the palace. The building was of stone neatly laid and painted white; in it each lion had his separate cage; and outside were yards surrounded by high stone walls near the tops of which pointed sticks, set close together and inclined downward on the inside of the walls, kept the lions from escaping. In these yards the lions exercised themselves; there was another, larger arena where they were trained by a corps of keepers under the supervision of nobles; here the racing lions were broken to harness and the hunting lions taught to obey the commands of the hunter, to trail, to charge, to retrieve.

As Tarzan entered the stable a familiar scent spoor impinged upon his nostrils. 'Belthar is here,' he remarked to Gemnon.

'It is possible,' replied the noble, 'but I don't understand how you know it.'

As they were walking along in front of the cages inspecting the lions that were inside, Gemnon, who was in advance, suddenly halted. 'How do you do it?' he demanded. 'Last night you knew that Erot was with Nemone, though you could not see him and no one could have informed you; and now you knew that Belthar was here, and, sure enough, he is!'

Tarzan approached and stood beside Gemnon, and the instant that Belthar's eyes fell upon him the beast leaped against the bars of his cage in an effort to seize the ape-man, at the same time voicing an angry roar that shook the building.

Instantly keepers came running to the spot, certain that something had gone amiss; but Gemnon assured them that it was only Belthar exhibiting his bad temper.

'He does not like me,' said Tarzan.

'If he ever got you, he would make short work of you,' said a head keeper.

'It is evident that he would like to,' replied the ape-man.

'He is a bad one and a man-killer,' said Gemnon after the keepers had departed, 'but Nemone will not have him destroyed. Occasionally he is loosed in the palace arena with someone who has incurred Nemone's disfavor; thus she derives pleasure from the sufferings of the culprit.

'Formerly he was her best hunting lion, but the last time he was used he killed four men and nearly escaped. He has already eaten three keepers who ventured into the arena with him, and he will eat more before good fortune rids us of him.

'Nemone is supposed to entertain a superstition that in some peculiar way her life and the life of Belthar are linked by some mysterious, supernatural bond and that when one dies the other must die. Naturally, under the circumstances, it is neither politic nor safe to suggest that she destroy the old devil. It is odd that he has conceived such a violent dislike for you.'

'I have met lions before which did not like me,' said Tarzan.

'May you never meet Belthar in the open, my friend!'

12

The Man in the Lion Pit

As Tarzan and Gemnon turned away from Belthar's cage a slave approached the ape-man and addressed him. 'Nemone, the Queen, commands your presence immediately,' he said; 'you are to come to the ivory room; the noble Gemnon will wait in the anteroom. These are the commands of Nemone, the Queen.'

'What now? I wonder,' remarked Tarzan as they walked through the royal grounds toward the palace.

'No one ever knows why he is summoned to an audience with Nemone until he gets there,' commented Gemnon; 'one may be going to receive an honor or hear his death sentence. Nemone is capricious. She is always bored and always seeking relief from her boredom. Oftentimes she finds strange avenues of escape that makes one wonder if her mind – but no! Such thoughts may not even be whispered among friends.'

When Tarzan presented himself he was immediately admitted to the ivory room, where he found Nemone and Erot much as he had found them the preceding night. Nemone greeted him with a smile that was almost pathetically eager; but Erot only scowled darkly, making no effort to conceal his hatred.

'We are having a diversion this morning,' Nemone explained, 'and we summoned you and Gemnon to enjoy it with us. A party raiding in Thenar a day or so ago captured an Athnean noble; we are going to have some sport with him this morning.'

Tarzan nodded. He did not understand what she meant, and he was not particularly interested. He was thinking of M'duze and the night before; wondering what was in the mind of the strange, fascinating woman before him.

Nemone turned to Erot. 'Go and tell them we are ready,' she directed, 'and ascertain if all is in readiness for us.'

Erot flushed and backed toward the door, still scowling. 'And you need not hurry,' added the Queen; 'we are not impatient to witness the entertainment. Let them take their time, and be sure to see that all is well ordered.'

'It shall be as the Queen commands,' replied Erot in a surly tone.

When the door had closed behind him, Nemone motioned Tarzan to a seat upon the couch. 'I am afraid that Erot does not like you,' she said, smiling. 'He is furious that you do not kneel to me, and that I do not compel you to do so. I really do not know, myself, why I do not; but I guess why. Have you not, perhaps, guessed why, too?'

'There might be two reasons, either of which would be sufficient,' replied the ape-man.

'And what are they? I have been curious to know how you explained it.'

'Consideration of the customs of a stranger and courtesy to a guest,' suggested Tarzan.

Nemone considered for a moment. 'Yes,' she admitted, 'either is a fairly good reason, but neither is really in keeping with the customs of the court of Nemone. And then they are practically the same thing; so they constitute only one reason. Is there not another?'

'Yes,' replied Tarzan; 'there is an even better one; the one which probably influences you to overlook my dereliction.'

'And what is it?'

'The fact that you cannot make me kneel.'

A hard look flashed in the Queen's eyes; it was not the answer she had been hoping for. Tarzan's eyes did not leave hers; she saw amusement in them. 'Oh, why do I endure it!' she cried, and with the query her anger melted. 'You should not try to make it so hard for me to be nice to you,' she said almost appealingly. 'Why do you not meet me halfway? Why are you not nice to me, Tarzan?'

'I wish to be nice to you, Nemone,' he replied; 'but not at the price of my self-respect; but that is not the only reason why I shall never kneel to you.'

'What is the other reason?' she demanded.

'That I wish you to like me; you would not like me if I cringed to you.'

'Perhaps you are right,' she admitted musingly. 'Everyone cringes, until the sight of it disgusts me; yet I am angry when they do not cringe. Why is that?'

'You will be offended if I tell you,' warned the ape-man.

'In the past two days I have become accustomed to being offended,' she replied with a grimace of resignation; 'so you might as well tell me.'

'You are angry if they do not cringe, because you are not quite sure of yourself. You wish this outward evidence of their subservience that you may be constantly reassured that you are Queen of Cathne.'

'Who says that I am not Queen of Cathne?' she demanded, instantly on the defensive. 'Who says that will find that I am and that I have the power of life and death. If I chose, I could have you destroyed in an instant.'

'You do not impress me,' said Tarzan. 'I have not said that you are not Queen of Cathne, only that your manner may often suggest your own doubts. A queen should be so sure of herself that she can always afford to be gracious and merciful.'

For a while Nemone sat in silence, evidently pondering the thought that

Tarzan had suggested. 'They would not understand,' she said at last; 'if I were gracious and merciful they would think me weak; then they would take advantage of me; and eventually they would destroy me. You do not know them. But you are different; I can be gracious and merciful to you and you will never try to take advantage of my kindness; you will not misunderstand it.

'Oh, Tarzan, I wish that you would promise to remain in Cathne. If you will, there is nothing that you may not have from Nemone. I would build you a palace second only to my own. I would be very good to you; we – you could be very happy here.'

The ape-man shook his head. 'Tarzan can be happy in the jungle only.'

Nemone leaned close to him; she seized him fiercely by the shoulders. 'I will make you happy here,' she whispered passionately. 'You do not know Nemone. Wait! The time will come when you will want to stay – for me!'

'Erot and M'duze and Tomos may think differently,' Tarzan reminded her.

'I hate them!' cried Nemone. 'If they interfere this time, I shall kill them all; this time I shall have my own way; she shall not rob me of all happiness. But do not speak of her; never speak her name to me again. And as for Erot,' she snapped her fingers. 'I crush a worm beneath my sandal, and no one misses it. No one would miss Erot, least of all I; I have long been tired of him. He is a stupid, egotistical fool; but he is better than nothing.'

The door opened and Erot entered unceremoniously; he kneeled, but the act was nearer a gesture than an accomplished fact. Nemone flashed an angry look at him.

'Before you enter our presence,' she said coldly, 'see to it that you are properly announced and that we have expressed a desire to receive you.'

'But your majesty,' objected Erot, 'have I not been in the habit of—'

'You have gotten into bad habits,' she interrupted; 'see that you mend them. Is the diversion arranged?'

'All is in readiness, your majesty,' replied the crestfallen Erot.

'Come, then!' directed Nemone, motioning Tarzan to follow her.

In the anteroom they found Gemnon waiting, and the Queen bid him accompany them. Preceded and followed by armed guards, the three passed along several corridors and through a number of rooms, then up a stairway to the second floor of the palace. Here they were conducted to a balcony overlooking a small enclosed court. The windows opening onto this court from the first story of the building were heavily barred; and from just below the top of the parapet, behind which the Queen and her party sat, sharpened stakes protruded, giving the court the appearance of a miniature arena for wild animals.

As Tarzan looked down into the courtyard, wondering a little what the nature of the diversion was to be, a door at one end swung open and a young lion stepped out into the sunlight, blinking his eyes and looking about. When he saw those on the balcony looking down at him, he growled.

'He is going to make a good lion,' remarked Nemone. 'From a cub, he has always been vicious.'

'What is he doing in here?' asked Tarzan, 'Or what is he going to do?'

'He is going to entertain us,' replied Nemone. 'Presently an enemy of Cathne will be turned into the pit with him, the Athnean who was captured in Thenar.'

'And if he kills the lion you will give him his liberty?' demanded Tarzan.

Nemone laughed. 'I promise that I will, but he will not kill the lion.'

'He might,' said Tarzan; 'men have killed lions before.'

'With their bare hands?' asked Nemone.

'You mean the man will not be armed?' demanded Tarzan incredulously.

'Why, of course not,' exclaimed Nemone. 'He is not being put in there to kill or wound a fine young lion but to be killed.'

'And he has no chance then! That is not sport; it is murder!'

'Perhaps you would like to go down and defend him,' sneered Erot. 'The Queen would give the fellow his liberty if he had a champion who would kill the lion, for that is the custom.'

'It is a custom that is without a precedent since I have been Queen,' said Nemone. 'It is true that it is a law of the arena, but I have yet to see a champion volunteer to take the risk.'

The lion paced across the courtyard and stood directly beneath the balcony, glaring up at them. He was a splendid beast, young but full-grown.

'He is going to be a mean customer,' remarked Gemnon.

'He already is,' rejoined the Queen. 'I was going to make a racing lion of him, but after he killed a couple of trainers I decided that he would make a better hunting lion for grand hunts. There is the Athnean.' She pointed down into the courtyard. 'He is a fine-looking young fellow.'

Tarzan glanced at the stalwart figure in ivory standing upon the opposite side of the small arena bravely awaiting its fate; then the lion turned its head slowly in the direction of the prey it had not yet seen. At the same instant Tarzan seized the hilt of Erot's dagger-like sword, tore the weapon from its sheath, and, stepping to the top of the parapet, leaped for the lion below.

So quickly and so silently had he moved that none was aware of his intent until it had been accomplished. Gemnon voiced an ejaculation of astonishment; Erot, of relief; while Nemone cried out in genuine terror and alarm. Leaning over the parapet, the Queen saw the lion struggling to tear the body that had crushed it to the stone flagging or escape from beneath it. The horrid growls of the beast reverberated in the narrow confines of the pit, and mingled with them were the growls of the beast-man on its back. One bronzed arm was about the maned neck of the carnivore, two powerful legs were locked around its middle, and the sharp point of Erot's sword was awaiting the opportune instant to plunge into the savage heart. The Athnean was running toward the two embattled beasts.

'By Thoos!' exclaimed Nemone. 'If the lion kills him, I will have it torn limb from limb. It must not kill him! Go down there, Erot, and help him; go, Gemnon!'

Gemnon did not wait, but springing to the parapet, he lowered himself by the stakes and dropped into the courtyard. Erot hung back. 'Let him take care of himself,' he grumbled.

Nemone turned to the guard standing behind her. She was white with apprehension because of Tarzan and with rage and disgust at Erot. 'Throw him into the pit!' she commanded, pointing at the cringing favorite; but Erot did not wait to be thrown, and a moment later he had followed Gemnon to the stone flagging of the courtyard.

Neither Erot nor Gemnon nor the man from Athne were needed to save Tarzan from the lion, for already he had sunk the sword into the tawny side. Twice again the point drove into the wild heart before the roaring beast collapsed upon the white stones, and its great voice was stilled forever.

Then Tarzan rose to his feet. For a moment the men about him, the Queen leaning across the parapet above, the city of gold, all were forgotten. Here was no English lord but a beast of the jungle that had made its kill. With one foot upon the carcass of the lion, the ape-man raised his face toward the heavens, and from the heart of the palace of Nemone rose the hideous victory cry of the bull ape that has killed.

Gemnon and Erot shuddered, and Nemone drew back in terror; but the Athnean was unmoved; he had heard that savage challenge before. He was Valthor. And now Tarzan turned; all the savagery faded from his countenance as he stretched forth a hand and laid it on Valthor's shoulder. 'We meet again, my friend,' he said.

'And once again you save my life!' exclaimed the Athnean noble.

The two men had spoken in low tones that had not carried to the ears of Nemone or the others in the balcony; Erot, fearful that the lion might not be dead, had run to the far end of the court, where he was cowering behind a column; that Gemnon might have heard did not concern Tarzan, who trusted the young Cathnean. But those others must not know that he had known Valthor before, or immediately the old story that Tarzan had come from Athne to assassinate Nemone would be revived and then only a miracle could save either of them.

His hand still upon Valthor's shoulder, Tarzan spoke again rapidly in a whisper. 'They must not know that we are acquainted,' he said. 'They are looking for an excuse to kill me, some of them; but as far as you are concerned they do not have to look for any.'

Nemone was now calling orders rapidly to those about her. 'Go down and let Tarzan out of the arena, Tarzan and Gemnon; send them to me. Erot may go to his quarters until I give further orders; I do not wish to see him again. Take the Athnean back to his cell; later I will decide how he shall be destroyed.'

She spoke in the imperious tones of one long accustomed to absolute authority and implicit obedience, and her voice carried plainly to the ears of the men in the arena. It brought the chill of sudden fear to the heart of Erot, who saw his influence waning and recalled tales he had heard of the fate of other royal favorites who had outlived their charm. Into his cunning brain flew a score of schemes to reinstate himself, and each was based upon the elimination of the giant that had supplanted him in the affections of the Queen. He would fly to Tomos, to M'duze; neither of these could afford to see the stranger take Erot's place in the boudoir councils of Nemone and become a power behind the throne.

Tarzan heard the Queen's commands with surprise and resentment, and, wheeling, he looked up at her. 'This man is free by your own word,' he reminded her. 'If he be returned to a cell, I shall go with him, for I have told him that he would be free.'

'Do with him as you please,' cried Nemone; 'he is yours. Only come up to me, Tarzan. I thought that you would be killed, and I am still frightened.'

Erot and Gemnon heard these words with vastly different emotions; each recognized that they signalized a change in the affairs of the court of Cathne. Gemnon anticipated the effects of a better influence injected into the councils of Nemone, and was pleased. Erot saw the flimsy structure of his temporary grandeur and reflected authority crumbling to ruin. Both were astonished by this sudden revealment of a new Nemone, whom none had ever before seen bow to the authority of another than M'duze.

Accompanied by Gemnon and Valthor, Tarzan returned to the balcony where Nemone, her composure regained, awaited them. For a moment, moved by excitement and apprehension for Tarzan's safety, she had revealed a feminine side of her character that few of her intimates might even have suspected she possessed; but now she was the Queen again. She surveyed Valthor haughtily and yet with interest.

'What is your name, Athnean?' she demanded.

'Valthor,' he replied and added, 'of the house of Xanthus.'

'We know the house,' remarked Nemone; 'its head is a king's councillor; a most noble house and close to the royal line in both blood and authority.'

'My father is the head of the house of Xanthus,' said Valthor.

'Your head would have made a noble trophy for our walls,' sighed Nemone, 'but we have given our promise that you shall be freed.'

'My head would have been honored by a place among your majesty's trophies,' replied Valthor, the faintest trace of a smile upon his lips; 'but it shall have to be content to wait a more propitious event.'

'We shall look forward with keen anticipation to that moment,' rejoined Nemone graciously; 'but in the meantime we will arrange an escort to return you to Athne, and hope for better fortune the next time that you fall into our hands. Be ready then early tomorrow to return to your own country.'

'I thank your majesty,' replied Valthor; 'I shall be ready, and when I go I shall carry with me, to cherish through life, the memory of the gracious and beautiful Queen of Cathne.'

'Our noble Gemnon shall be your host until tomorrow,' announced Nemone. 'Take him with you now to your quarters, Gemnon, and let it be known that he is Nemone's guest, whom none may harm.'

Tarzan would have accompanied Gemnon and Valthor, but Nemone detained him. 'You will return to my apartments with me,' she directed; 'I wish to talk with you.'

As they walked through the palace, the Queen did not precede her companion as the etiquette of the court demanded but moved close at his side, looking up into his face as she talked. 'I was frightened, Tarzan,' she confided. 'It is not often that Nemone is frightened by the peril of another, but when I saw you leap into the arena with the lion my heart stood still. Why did you do it, Tarzan?'

'I was disgusted with what I saw,' replied the ape-man shortly.

'Disgusted! What do you mean?'

'The cowardliness of the authority that would permit an unarmed and utterly defenseless man to be forced into an arena with a lion,' explained Tarzan candidly.

Nemone flushed. 'You know that that authority is I,' she said coldly.

'Of course I know it,' replied the ape-man, 'but that only renders it the more odious.'

'What do you mean?' she snapped. 'Are you trying to drive me beyond my patience? If you knew me better you would know that that is not safe, not even for you, before whom I have already humbled myself.'

'I am not seeking to try your patience,' replied the ape-man quietly, 'for I am neither interested nor concerned in your powers of self-control. I am merely shocked that one so beautiful may at the same time be so heartless. Were you a little more human, Nemone, you would be irresistible.'

The flush faded from the Queen's face, the anger from her eyes; she moved on in silence, her mood suddenly introspective; and when they reached the anteroom leading to her private chambers, she halted at the threshold of the latter and laid a hand gently upon the arm of the man at her side.

'You are very brave,' she said. 'Only a very brave man would have leaped into the arena with the lion to save a stranger; but only the bravest of the brave could have dared to speak to Nemone as you have spoken, for the death that the lion deals may be merciful compared with that which Nemone deals when she has been affronted. Yet perhaps you knew that I would forgive you. Oh, Tarzan, what magic have you exercised to win such power over me!' She took him by the hand then and led him toward the doorway of her chambers. 'In here, alone together, you shall teach Nemone how to be human!' As the door swung open there was a new light in the eyes of the Queen of Cathne, a softer light than had ever before shone in those beautiful depths; and then it faded, to be replaced by a cold, hard glitter of bitterness and hate. Facing them, in the center of the apartment, stood M'duze.

She stood there, bent and horrible, wagging her head and tapping the stone floor with her staff. She spoke no word, but fixed them with her baleful glare. As one held in the grip of a power she is unable to resist, Nemone moved slowly toward the ancient hag, leaving Tarzan just beyond the threshold. Slowly and silently the door closed between them. Beyond it the ape-man heard, faintly, the tapping of the staff upon the colored stones of the mosaic.

13

Assassin in the Night

A great lion moved silently from the south across the border of Kaffa. If he were following a trail, the heavy rain that had terminated the wet season must have obliterated it long since; yet he moved on with a certain assurance that betokened no sign of doubt.

Why was he there? What urge had drawn him thus, contrary to the habits and customs of his kind, upon this long and arduous journey? Where was he bound? What or whom did he seek? Only he, Numa, the lion, king of beasts, knew.

In his quarters in the palace, Erot paced the floor, angry and disconsolate. Sprawled on a bench, his feet wide apart, sat Xerstle deep in thought. The two men were facing a crisis, and they were terrified. Had Erot definitely fallen from the favor of the Queen, Xerstle would be dragged down with him; of that there was no doubt.

'But there must be *something* you can do,' insisted Xerstle.

'I have seen both Tomos and M'duze,' replied Erot wearily, 'and they have promised to help. It means as much to them as it does to me. But Nemone is infatuated with this stranger. Even M'duze, who has known her all her life, has never seen her so affected by a passion as now. Even she feels that she may not be able to control the Queen in the face of her mad attachment for the naked barbarian.

'None knows Nemone better than does M'duze, and I can tell you, Xerstle, the old hag is frightened. Nemone hates her, and if the attempted thwarting of this new passion arouses her anger sufficiently it may sweep away the fear that the Queen has already held for M'duze, and she will destroy her. It is this that M'duze fears. And you can imagine how terrified old Tomos is! Without M'duze he would be lost, for Nemone tolerates him only because M'duze demands it.'

'But there must be some way,' again insisted Xerstle.

'There is no way so long as this fellow, Tarzan, is able to turn Nemone's heart to water,' answered Erot. 'Why, he does not even kneel to her; and he speaks to her as one might to a naughty slave girl. By the mane of Thoos! I believe that if he kicked her she would like it.'

'But there *is* a way!' exclaimed Xerstle in a sudden whisper. 'Listen!' and then he launched forth into a detailed explanation of his plan. Erot sat listening to his friend, an expression of rapt interest upon his face. A slave girl came from Xerstle's bedchamber, crossed the living room where the two men talked, and departed into the corridor beyond; but so engrossed were Erot and Xerstle that neither was aware that she had come or that she had gone.

In their quarters that evening Gemnon and Tarzan partook of the final meal of the day, for neither had enjoyed the prospect of again eating with the other nobles. Valthor slept in the bedroom, having asked not to be disturbed until morning.

'When you have definitely displaced Erot conditions will be different,' explained Gemnon; 'then they will fawn upon you, shower you with attentions, and wait upon your every whim.'

'That will never occur,' snapped the ape-man.

'Why not?' demanded his companion. 'Nemone is mad about you. There is nothing that she would not do for you, absolutely nothing. Why, man, you can rule Cathne if you so choose.'

'But I do not choose,' replied Tarzan. 'Nemone may be mad, but I am not; and even were I, I could never be mad enough to accept a position that had once been filled by Erot. The idea disgusts me; let us talk of something pleasant.'

'Very well,' consented Gemnon with a smile. 'Perhaps I think you are foolish, but I admit that I cannot help but admire your courage and your decency.

'And now for something more pleasant! Something very much more pleasant! I am going to take you visiting tonight. I am going to take you to see the most beautiful girl in Cathne.'

'I thought that there could be no woman in Cathne more beautiful than the Queen,' objected Tarzan.

'There would not be if Nemone knew of her,' replied Gemnon, 'but fortunately she does not know; she has never seen this girl, and may Thoos forbid that she ever does!'

'You are much interested,' remarked the ape-man, smiling.

'I am in love with her,' explained Gemnon simply.

'And Nemone has never seen her? I should think that a difficult condition to maintain, for Cathne is not large; and if the girl be of the same class as you many other nobles must know of her beauty. One would expect such news to come quickly to the ears of Nemone.'

'She is surrounded by very loyal friends, this girl of whom I speak,' replied Gemnon. 'She is Doria, the daughter of Thudos. Her father is a very powerful noble and head of the faction which wishes to place Alextar on the throne. Only Nemone's knowledge of his great power preserves his life, but owing to the strained relations that exist between Nemone and his house neither he nor members of his family are often at court. Thus it has been easier to prevent knowledge of the great beauty of Doria coming to Nemone.'

As the two men were leaving the palace a short time later they came unexpectedly upon Xerstle, who was most effusive in his greetings. 'Congratulations, Tarzan!' he exclaimed, halting the companions. 'That was a most noble feat you performed in the lion pit today. All the palace is talking about it, and let me be among the first to tell you how glad I am that you have won the confidence of our gracious and beautiful Queen by your bravery, strength, and magnanimity.'

Tarzan nodded in acknowledgment of the man's avowal and started to move on, but Xerstle held him with a gesture. 'We must see more of one another,' he continued. 'I am arranging a grand hunt, and I must have you as my guest of honor. There will be but a few of us, a most select party; and I can assure you of good sport. When all the arrangements are completed, I will let you know the day of the hunt; and now goodbye and good luck to you!'

'I care nothing about him or his grand hunt,' said Tarzan as he and Gemnon continued on toward the home of Doria.

'Perhaps it would be well to accept,' advised Gemnon. 'That fellow and his friends will bear watching, and if you are with them occasionally you can watch them that much better.'

Tarzan shrugged. 'If I am still here, I shall go with him if you think best.'

'If you are still here!' exclaimed Gemnon. 'You certainly are not expecting to get away from Cathne, are you?'

'Why, certainly,' replied Tarzan. 'I may go any day, or night; there is nothing to hold me here, and I have given no promise that I would not escape when I wished.'

Gemnon smiled a wry smile that Tarzan did not see in the semi-darkness of the ill-lit avenue through which they were passing. 'That will make it extremely interesting for me,' he remarked.

'Why?' demanded the ape-man.

'Nemone turned you over into my keeping. If you escape while I am responsible for you she will have me destroyed.'

A frown knit the brows of the Lord of the Jungle. 'I did not know that,' he said; 'but you need not worry; I shall not go until you have been relieved of responsibility.' A sudden smile lighted his countenance. 'I think I shall ask Nemone to give me over into the keeping of Erot or Xerstle.'

Gemnon chuckled. 'What a story that would make!' he cried.

An occasional torch only partially dispelled the gloom beneath the overhanging trees that bordered the avenue that led toward the palace of Thudos. At the intersection of a narrow alleyway, beneath the branches of a widespreading oak a dark figure lurked in the shadows as Tarzan and Gemnon approached. The keen eyes of the ape-man saw and recognized it as the figure of a man before they came close enough to be in danger; and Tarzan was ready even though he had no suspicion that the man's presence there was in any way concerned with him, for it is the business of the jungle bred to be always ready, whether danger threatens or not.

Just as the two came opposite the figure, Tarzan heard his name whispered in a hoarse voice. He stopped. 'Beware of Erot!' whispered the voice. 'Tonight!' Then the figure wheeled and lumbered into the denser shadows of the narrow alleyway; but in the glimpse that Tarzan got of it there was a familiar roll to the great body, just as there had been a suggestion of familiarity in the voice.

'Now who do you suppose that is?' demanded Gemnon. 'Come on! We'll capture him and find out,' and he started as though to pursue the stranger down the alley.

Tarzan laid a restraining hand upon his shoulder. 'No,' he said; 'it was someone who has tried to befriend me. If he wishes to conceal his identity, it is not for me to reveal it.'

'You are right,' assented Gemnon.

'And I think I would have learned no more by pursuing him than I already know. I recognized him by his voice and his gait, and then, as he turned to leave, a movement in the air brought his scent spoor to my nostrils. I think I would recognize that a mile away, for it is very strong; it always is in powerful men and beasts.'

'Why was he afraid of you?' asked Gemnon.

'He was not afraid of me; he was afraid of you because you are a noble.'

'He need not have been, if he is a friend of yours. I would not have betrayed him.'

'I know that, but he could not. You are a noble, and so you might be a friend of Erot. I do not mind telling you who it was, because I know you would not use the knowledge to harm him; but you will be surprised; I surely was. It was Phobeg.'

'No! Why should he befriend the man who defeated and humiliated him, and almost killed him?'

'Because he did *not* kill him. Phobeg is a simple-minded fellow, but he is the type that would not be devoid of gratitude. He is the sort that would bestow doglike devotion upon one who was more powerful than he, for he worships physical prowess.'

At the palace of Thudos the two men were ushered into a magnificent apartment by a slave after the guard at the entrance had recognized Gemnon and permitted them to pass. In the soft light of a dozen cressets they awaited the coming of the daughter of the house to whom the slave had carried Gemnon's ring to evidence the identity of her caller. The richness of the furnishings of the room were scarcely less magnificent than those Tarzan had seen in the palace of Nemone; and again, here, were the trophies of the chase prominent among the decorations upon the walls.

A human head, surmounted by a golden helmet, frowned down from sightless eyes from a place of honor above the main entrance. Though shrunken and withered in death there was still strength and majesty in its appearance; and Tarzan gazed for some moments at it, intrigued by the thought of all that had passed within that dry and ghastly skull before it found its way to grace the trophies upon the palace walls of the noble Thudos. What fierce or kindly thoughts, what hates, what loves, what rages had been born and lived and died behind that parchment forehead? What tales those dried and shrivelled lips might tell could the hot blood of the fighting man give them life once more!

'A splendid trophy,' commented Gemnon, attracted by his companion's evident interest in the head. 'It is the most valuable trophy in Cathne; there is no other to equal it, and there may never be another. That head belonged to a king of Athne. Thudos took it himself in battle as a young man.'

'I rather like the idea,' said Tarzan thoughtfully. 'In the world from which I come men fill their trophy rooms with the heads of creatures who are not their enemies, who would be their friends if man would let them. Your most valued trophies are the heads of your enemies who have had an equal opportunity to take your head. Yes, it is a splendid idea!'

The light fall of soft sandals upon stone announced the coming of their hostess, and both men turned toward the doorway leading into a small open garden from which she was coming. Tarzan saw a girl of exquisite beauty; but whether she were more beautiful than Nemone he could not say, there are so many things that enter into the making of a beautiful countenance; yet he acknowledged to himself that Thudos was wise in keeping her hidden from the Queen.

She greeted Gemnon with the sweet familiarity of an old friend, and when Tarzan was presented her manner was cordial and unaffected, yet always the fact that she was the daughter of Thudos seemed a part of her.

'I saw you in the stadium,' she said, and then, with a laugh, 'I lost many drachmas because of you.'

'I am sorry,' said Tarzan. 'Perhaps had I known that you were betting on Phobeg I should have let him kill me.'

'That is an idea,' exclaimed Doria, laughing. 'If you fight in the stadium again I shall tell you beforehand which man I am placing my money on, and then I shall be sure to win.'

'I see that I must make you like me so well that you will not want to bet on my opponent.'

'From what I have seen of him,' interjected Gemnon, 'I think Tarzan will always be a safe bet – in an arena.'

'What do you mean?' demanded the girl. 'There is the suggestion of another significance in your words.'

'I am afraid my friend will not be so safe in a boudoir,' laughed the young noble.

'We have already heard that he has been more than successful,' said Doria with just the faintest note of something that might have been disgust.

'Do not judge him too harshly,' pleaded Gemnon; 'he is still doing his best to get himself destroyed.'

'That should not be difficult in the palace of Nemone, though we have already heard startling tales of his refusal to kneel before the Queen. One who has survived that may not have as much to fear as we have imagined,' returned Doria.

'Your Queen understands why I do not kneel,' explained Tarzan. 'It is through no disrespect nor boorish bravado, but because of the habits of a lifetime and the exigencies of my existence. Had I not been commanded to kneel, I might have knelt. I am afraid that I cannot explain the psychology of my position so that another may understand it; but it is plain to me that I must not bow to any authority against my will, unless I am compelled to do so by force.'

The three had spent the evening in pleasant conversation, and Gemnon and Tarzan were about to leave, when a middle-aged man entered the room. It was Thudos, the father of Doria. He greeted Gemnon cordially and seemed pleased to meet Tarzan whom he immediately commenced to question relative to the world outside the valleys of Onthar and Thenar.

Thudos was a strikingly handsome man, with strong features, an athletic build, and eyes that were serious and stern that yet had wrinkles at their corners that betokened much laughter. His was a face that one might trust, for integrity, loyalty, and courage had left their imprints plainly upon it, at least for eyes as observant as those of the Lord of the Jungle.

When the two guests rose to leave again, Thudos seemed satisfied with his appraisal of the stranger. 'I am glad that Gemnon brought you,' he said. 'The very fact that he did convinces me that he has confidence in your friendship and loyalty, for, as you may already know, the position of my house at the court of Nemone is such that we receive only assured friends within our walls.'

'I understand,' replied the ape-man. He made no other reply, but both Thudos and Doria felt that here was a man who might be trusted.

As the two men entered the avenue in front of the palace of their host, a figure slunk into the shadow of a tree a few paces from them; and neither saw it. Then they walked leisurely toward their apartments in the palace, discussing the noble Thudos and his matchless daughter.

'I have been curious to ask you,' said Tarzan, 'how Doria dared come to the stadium when her life is constantly in danger should her beauty become known to the Queen?'

'She is always disguised when she goes abroad,' replied Gemnon. 'A few touches by an expert hand and hollows appear in her cheeks and beneath her eyes, her brow is wrinkled; and behold! She is no longer the most beautiful woman in the world. Nemone would not give her a second thought if she saw her, but still care is taken to see that Nemone does not see her too closely even then. It is informers we fear the most. Thudos never sells a slave who has seen Doria, and once a new slave enters the palace walls he never leaves them again until long years of service have proved him, and his loyalty is unquestioned.

'It is a monotonous life for Doria, the penalty she pays for beauty; but all that we can do is hope and pray that relief will come some day in the death of Nemone or the elevation of Alextar to the throne.'

Valthor was asleep on Tarzan's couch when the ape-man entered his bedroom. He had had little rest since his capture, and, in addition, he was suffering from a slight wound; so Tarzan moved softly that he might not disturb him and made no light in the room, the darkness of which was partially dispelled by the moonlight.

Spreading some skins on the floor against the wall opposite the window, the ape-man lay down and was soon asleep, while in the apartment above him two men crouched in the dark beside the window that was directly above that in Tarzan's bedroom.

For a long time they crouched there in silence. One was a large, powerful man; the other smaller and lighter. Fully an hour passed before either moved other than to change a cramped position for one more comfortable; then the smaller man arose. One end of a long rope was knotted about his body beneath his armpits; in his right hand he carried a slim dagger-sword.

Cautiously and silently he went to the window and looked out, his careful gaze searching the grounds below; then he sat on the sill and swung his legs through the window. The larger man, holding the rope firmly with both hands, braced himself. The smaller turned over on his belly and slid out of the window. Hand over hand, the other lowered him; his head disappeared below the sill.

Very carefully, so as to make no noise, the larger man lowered the smaller until the feet of the latter rested on the sill of Tarzan's bedroom window. Here the man reached in and took hold of the casing; then he jerked twice upon the rope to acquaint his fellow with the fact that he had reached his destination safely and the other let the rope slip through his fingers loosely as the movements of the man below dragged it slowly out.

The smaller man stepped gingerly to the floor inside the room. Without hesitation he moved toward the bed, his weapon raised and ready in his hand. He made no haste; his one purpose for the present appeared to be the achievement of absolute silence. It was evident that he feared to awaken the sleeper. Even when he reached the bed he stood there for a long time searching with his eyes for the right spot to strike that the blow might bring instant death. The assassin knew that Gemnon slept in another bedroom across the living room; what he did not know was that Valthor, the Athnean, lay stretched on the bed beneath his keen weapon.

As the assassin hesitated, Tarzan of the Apes opened his eyes. Though the intruder had made no sound his mere presence in the room had aroused the ape-man; perhaps the effluvium from his body, impinging upon the sensitive nostrils of the sleeping beast-man, carried the same message to the alert brain that sound would have carried.

It is said that a sleeping dog awakened by the touch of a cart wheel reacts so quickly that he can escape harm by leaping aside before the wheel crushes him. I do not believe this; but I am convinced that the so-called lower animals awaken in full and complete possession of all their faculties; not slowly, faculty by faculty, as is the case with man. Thus awoke Tarzan, master of all his powers.

At the instant that he opened his eyes he saw the stranger in the room, saw the dagger raised above the form of the sleeping Valthor, read the whole story in a single glance, and in the same moment arose and leaped upon the unsuspecting murderer who was dragged back from his victim at the very instant that his weapon was descending.

As the two men crashed to the floor, Valthor awoke and sprang from his cot; but by the time he had discovered what was transpiring the would-be assassin lay dead upon the floor, and Tarzan of the Apes stood with one foot upon the body of his kill. For an instant the ape-man hesitated, his face upturned as the weird scream of the victorious bull ape trembled on his lips; but then he shook his head, and only a low growl rumbled upward from the deep chest.

Valthor had heard these growls before and was neither surprised nor shocked. The man in the room above had heard only beasts growl, and the sound made him hesitate and wonder. He had heard, too, the crash of the two bodies as Tarzan had hurled the other to the floor, and while he had not interpreted that correctly it had suggested resistance and put him on his guard. Cautiously he stepped closer to the window and looked out, listening.

In the room below, Tarzan of the Apes seized the corpse of the man who had come to kill him and hurled it through the window into the grounds beneath. The man above saw and, turning, slunk from the room and vanished among the dark shadows of the palace corridors.

14

The Grand Hunt

With the breaking of dawn Tarzan and Valthor arose, for the latter was to set out upon his journey to Athne early. The previous evening a slave had been directed to serve breakfast at daybreak, and the two men now heard him arranging the table in the adjoining room.

'We have met again, and again we part,' commented Valthor as he fastened his sandal straps to the ivory guards that encircled his ankles. 'I wish that you were going with me to Athne, my friend.'

'I would go with you were it not for the fact that Gemnon's life would be forfeited should I leave Cathne while he is responsible for me,' replied the ape-man, 'but you may rest assured that some day I shall pay you a visit in Athne.'

'I never expected to see you alive again after we were separated by the flood,' continued Valthor, 'and when I recognized you in the lion pit I could not believe my own eyes. Four times at least have you saved my life, Tarzan; and you may be assured of a warm welcome in the house of my father at Athne whenever you come.'

'The debt, if you feel that there was one, is wiped out,' Tarzan assured him, 'since you saved my life last night.'

'I saved your life! What are you talking about?' demanded Valthor. 'How did I save your life?'

'By sleeping in my bed,' explained the Lord of the Jungle.

Valthor laughed. 'A courageous, a heroic act!' he mocked.

'But nevertheless it saved my life,' insisted the ape-man 'What saved whose life?' demanded a voice at the door.

'Good morning, Gemnon!' greeted Tarzan. 'My compliments and congratulations!'

'Thanks! But what about?' demanded the Cathnean.

'Upon your notable ability as a sound sleeper,' explained Tarzan, smiling.

Gemnon shook his head dubiously. 'Your words are beyond me. What are you talking about?'

'You slept last night through an attempted assassination, the killing of the culprit, and the disposition of his body. Phobeg's warning was no idle gossip.'

'You mean that someone came here last night to kill you?'

'And almost killed Valthor instead,' and then Tarzan briefly narrated the events of the attempt upon his life.

'Had you ever seen the man before?' asked Gemnon. 'Did you recognize him?'

'I paid little attention to him,' admitted Tarzan; 'I threw him out of the window; but I do not recall having seen him before.'

'Was he a noble?'

'No, he was a common warrior. Perhaps you will recognize him when you see him.'

'I shall have to have a look at him and report the matter at once,' said Gemnon. 'Nemone is going to be furious when she hears this.'

'She may have instigated it herself,' suggested Tarzan; 'she is half mad.'

'Hush!' cautioned Gemnon. 'It is death even to whisper that thought. No, I do not believe it was Nemone; but were you to accuse Erot, M'duze, or Tomos I could easily agree to that. I must go now, and if I do not return before you leave, Valthor, be assured that I have enjoyed entertaining you. It is unfortunate that we are enemies and that the next time we meet we shall have to endeavor to take one another's head.'

'It is unfortunate and foolish,' replied Valthor.

'But it is the custom,' Gemnon reminded him.

'Then may we never meet, for I could never take pleasure in killing you.'

'Here's to it, then,' cried Gemnon, raising his hand as though it held a drinking horn. 'May we never meet again!' and with that he turned and left them.

Tarzan and Valthor had but scarcely finished their meal when a noble arrived to tell them that Valthor's escort was ready to depart, and a moment later, with a brief farewell, the Athnean left.

Tarzan's liking for Valthor, combined with his curiosity to see the city of ivory, determined him to visit the valley of Thenar before he returned to his own country; but that is a matter apart, having nothing to do with this story, which has seen the last of the likable young noble of Athne.

By Nemone's command the ape-man's weapons had been returned to him, and he was engaged in inspecting them, looking to the points and feathers of his arrows, his bowstring, and his grass rope, when Gemnon returned. The Cathnean was quite evidently angry and not a little excited. This was one of the few occasions upon which Tarzan had seen his warder other than smiling and affable.

'I have had a bad half hour with the Queen,' explained Gemnon. 'I was lucky to get away with my life. She is furious over this attempt upon your life and blames me for neglect of duty. What am I to do? Sit on your window sill all night?'

Tarzan laughed. 'I am an embarrassment,' he said lightly, 'and I am sorry; but how can I help it? It was an accident that brought me here; it is perversity that keeps me, the perversity of a spoiled woman.'

'You had better not tell her that, nor let another than me hear you say it,' Gemnon cautioned him.

'I may tell her,' laughed Tarzan; 'I am afraid I have never acquired that entirely human accomplishment called diplomacy.'

'She has sent me to summon you; and I warn you to exercise a little judgment, even though you have no diplomacy. She is like a raging lion, and whoever arouses her further will be in for a mauling.'

'What does she want of me?' demanded Tarzan. 'Am I to remain in this house, caged up like a pet dog, to run at the beck of a woman?'

'She is investigating this attempt upon your life and has summoned others to be questioned,' Gemnon explained.

Gemnon led the way to a large audience chamber where the nobles of the court were congregated before a massive throne on which the Queen sat, her beautiful brows contracted in a frown. As Tarzan and Gemnon entered the room, she looked up; but she did not smile. A noble advanced and led the two men to seats near the foot of the throne.

As Tarzan glanced about the faces of those near him, he saw Tomos, and Erot, and Xerstle. Erot was nervous; he fidgeted constantly upon his bench; he played with his fingers and with the hilt of his sword; occasionally he glanced appealingly up at Nemone, but if she recognized that he was there, her expression did not acknowledge it.

'We have been awaiting you,' said the Queen as Tarzan took his seat. 'It appears that you did not exert yourself to hasten in response to our command.'

Tarzan looked up at her with an amused smile. 'On the contrary, your majesty, I returned at once with the noble Gemnon,' he explained respectfully.

'We have summoned you to tell the story of what happened in your apartment last night that resulted in the killing of a warrior.' She then turned to a noble standing at her side and whispered a few words in his ear, whereupon the man quit the room. 'You may proceed,' she said, turning again to Tarzan.

'There is little to tell,' replied the ape-man, rising. 'A man came to my room to kill me, but I killed him instead.'

'How did he enter your room?' demanded Nemone. 'Where was Gemnon? Did he admit the fellow?'

'Of course not,' replied Tarzan. 'Gemnon was asleep in his own room; the man who would have killed me was lowered from the window of the apartment above mine and entered through my window; there was a long rope tied about his body.'

'How did you know he came to kill you? Did he attack you?'

'Valthor, the Athnean, was sleeping in my bed; I was sleeping on the floor. The man did not see me, for the room was dark. He went to the bed where he thought I was sleeping. I awoke as he stood over Valthor, his sword raised in his hand ready to strike. Then I killed him and threw his body out of the window.'

'Did you recognize him? Had you ever seen him before?' asked the Queen.

'I did not recognize him.'

There was a noise at the entrance to the audience chamber that caused Nemone to glance up. Four slaves bore a stretcher into the room and laid it at the foot of the throne; on it was the corpse of a man.

'Is this the fellow who attempted your life?' demanded Nemone.

'It is,' replied Tarzan.

She turned suddenly upon Erot. 'Did you ever see this man before?' she demanded.

Erot arose. He was white and trembled a little. 'But your majesty, he is only a common warrior,' he countered; 'I may have seen him often, yet have forgotten him; that would not be strange, I see so many of them.'

'And you,' the Queen addressed a young noble standing near, 'have you ever seen this man before?'

'Often,' replied the noble; 'he was a member of the palace guard and in my company.'

'How long has he been attached to the palace?' demanded Nemone.

'Not a month, your majesty.'

'And before that? Do you know anything about his prior service?'

'He was attached to the retinue of a noble, your majesty,' replied the young officer hesitantly.

'What noble?' demanded Nemone.

'Erot,' replied the witness in a low voice.

The Queen looked long and searchingly at Erot. 'You have a short memory,' she said presently, an undisguised sneer in her voice, 'or perhaps you have so many warriors in your retinue that you cannot recall one who has been out of your service for a month!'

Erot was pale and shaken. He looked long at the face of the dead man before he spoke again. 'I do recall him now, your majesty, but he does not look the same. Death has changed him; that is why I did not recognize him immediately.'

'You are lying,' snapped Nemone. 'There are some things about this affair that I do not understand; what part you have had in it, I do not know; but I am sure that you had some part, and I am going to find out what. In the meantime you are banished from the palace; there may be others,' she looked meaningly at Tomos, 'but I shall find them all out, and when I do it will be the lion pit for the lot!'

Rising, she descended from the throne, and all knelt save Tarzan. As she passed him on her way from the chamber, she paused and looked long and searchingly into his eyes. 'Be careful,' she whispered; 'your life is in danger. I dare not see you for a while, for there is one so desperate that not even I could protect you should you visit my apartments again. Tell Gemnon to quit the palace and take you to his father's house. You will be safer there, but even then far from safe. In a few days I shall have removed the obstacles that stand between us; until then, Tarzan, goodbye!'

The ape-man bowed, and the Queen of Cathne passed on out of the audience chamber. The nobles rose. They drew away from Erot and clustered about Tarzan. In disgust the ape-man drew away. 'Come, Gemnon,' he said; 'there is nothing to keep us here longer.'

Xerstle blocked their way as they were leaving the chamber. 'Everything is ready for the grand hunt,' he exclaimed, rubbing his palms together genially. 'I thought this tiresome audience would prevent our starting today, but it is still early. The lions and the quarry are awaiting us at the edge of the forest. Get your weapons and join me in the avenue.'

Gemnon hesitated. 'Who are hunting with you?' he asked.

'Just you and Tarzan and Pindes,' explained Xerstle; 'a small and select company that ensures a good hunt.'

'We will come,' said the ape-man.

As the two returned to their quarters to get their weapons Gemnon appeared worried. 'I am not sure that it is wise to go,' he said.

'And why not?' inquired Tarzan.

'This may be another trap for you.'

The ape-man shrugged. 'It is quite possible, but I cannot remain cooped up in hiding. I should like to see what a grand hunt is; I have heard the term so often since I came to Cathne. Who is Pindes? I do not recall him.'

'He was an officer of the guard when Erot became the Queen's favorite, but through Erot he was dismissed. He is not a bad fellow but weak and easily influenced; however, he must hate Erot, and so I think you have nothing to fear from him.'

'I have nothing to fear from anyone,' Tarzan assured him.

'Perhaps you think not, but be on guard.'

'I am always on guard; had I not been I should have been dead long ago.'

'Your self-complacency may be your undoing,' growled Gemnon testily.

Tarzan laughed. 'I appreciate both danger and my own limitations, but I cannot let fear rob me of my liberty and the pleasures of life; fear is to be more dreaded than death. You are afraid, Erot is afraid, Nemone is afraid; and you are all unhappy. Were I afraid, I should be unhappy but no safer. I prefer to be simply cautious. And by the way, speaking of caution, Nemone instructed me to tell you to take me from the palace and keep me in your father's house. She says the palace is no safe place for me. I really think that it is M'duze who is after me.'

'M'duze and Erot and Tomos,' said Gemnon; 'there is a triumvirate of greed and malice and duplicity that I should hate to have upon my trail.'

At his quarters, Gemnon gave orders that his and Tarzan's belongings be moved to the house of his father while the two men were hunting; then they went to the avenue where they found Xerstle and Pindes awaiting them. The latter was a man of about thirty, rather good looking but with a weak face and eyes that invariably dropped from a direct gaze. He met Tarzan with great cordiality, and as the four men walked along the main avenue of the city toward the eastern gate he was most affable.

'You have never been on a grand hunt?' he asked Tarzan.

'No; I have no idea what the term means,' replied the ape-man.

'We shall not tell you then, but shall let you see for yourself; then you will enjoy it the more. Of course you hunt much in your own country, I presume.'

'I hunt for food only or for my enemies,' replied the ape-man.

'You never hunt for pleasure?' demanded Pindes.

'I take no pleasure in killing.'

'Well, you won't have to kill today,' Pindes assured him; 'the lions will do our killing; and I can promise you that you will enjoy the thrill of the chase, that reaches its highest point in the grand hunt.'

Beyond the eastern gate an open, parklike plain stretched for a short distance to the forest. Near the gate four stalwart slaves held two lions in leash, while a fifth man, naked but for a dirty loin cloth, squatted upon the ground a short distance away.

As the four hunters approached the party Xerstle explained to Tarzan that the leashed beasts were his hunting lions, and as the ape-man's observant eyes ran over the five men who were to accompany them on the hunt he recognized the stalwart black seated upon the ground apart as the man he had seen upon the auction block in the market place; then Xerstle approached the fellow and spoke briefly with him, evidently giving him orders. When Xerstle had finished, the native started off at a trot across the plain in the direction of the forest. Everyone watched his progress.

'Why is he running ahead?' asked Tarzan. 'He will frighten away the quarry.'

Pindes laughed. 'He is the quarry.'

'You mean—' demanded Tarzan with a scowl.

'That this is a grand hunt,' cried Xerstle, 'where we hunt man, the grandest quarry.'

The ape-man's eyes narrowed. 'I see,' he said; 'you are cannibals; you eat the flesh of men.'

Gemnon turned away to hide a smile.

'No!' shouted Pindes and Xerstle in unison. 'Of course not.'

'Then why do you hunt him, if not to eat him?'

'For pleasure,' explained Xerstle.

'Oh, yes; I forgot. And what happens if you do not get him? Is he free then?'

'I should say not; not if we can capture him again,' cried Xerstle. 'Slaves cost too much money to be lightly thrown away like that.'

'Tell me more of the grand hunt,' insisted Tarzan. 'I think I am going to get much satisfaction from this one.'

'I hope so,' replied Xerstle. 'When the quarry reaches the forest we loose the lions; then the sport commences.'

'If the fellow takes to the trees,' explained Pindes, 'we leash the lions and drive him out with sticks and stones or with our spears; then we give him a little start and loose the lions again. Pretty soon they catch him; and it is the aim of the hunters to be in at the kill, for there is where the real thrills come. Have you ever seen two lions kill a man?'

When the black reached the forest, Xerstle spoke a word of command to the keepers and they unleashed the two great beasts. From their actions it was evident that they were trained to the sport. From the moment the native had started out toward the forest the lions had strained and tugged upon their leashes, so that it was only by the use of their spears that the keepers restrained the beasts from dragging them across the plain; and when they were at last set free they bounded away in pursuit of the unfortunate creature who had been chosen to give Xerstle and his guests a few hours of entertainment.

Halfway to the forest the lions settled down to a much slower gait, and the hunters commenced gradually to overhaul them. Xerstle and Pindes appeared excited, far more excited than the circumstances of the hunt warranted; Gemnon was silent and thoughtful; Tarzan was disgusted and bored. But before they reached the forest his interest was aroused, for a plan had occurred to him whereby he might derive some pleasure from the day's sport.

The wood, which the hunters presently entered a short distance behind the lions, was of extraordinary beauty; the trees were very old and gave evidence of having received the intelligent care of man, as did the floor of the forest. There was little or no deadwood in the trees and only occasional clumps of underbrush upon the ground between them. As far as Tarzan could see among the boles of the trees the aspect was that of a well-kept park rather than of a natural wood, and in answer to a comment he made upon this fact Gemnon explained that for ages his people had given regular attention to the conservation of this forest from the city of gold to the Pass of the Warriors.

Heavy lianas swung in graceful loops from tree to tree; higher up toward the sunlight Tarzan caught glimpses of brilliant tropical blooms; there were monkeys in the trees and gaudy, screaming birds. The scene filled the ape-man with such a longing for the freedom that was his life that, for the moment, he almost forgot that Gemnon's life hinged upon his abandoning all thought of escape while the young noble was responsible to the Queen for his safekeeping.

Once within the forest Tarzan dropped gradually to the rear of the party, and then, when none was looking, swung to the branches of a tree. Plain to his nostrils had been the scent spoor of the quarry from the beginning of the chase, and now the ape-man knew, possibly even better than the lions, the direction of the hopeless flight of the doomed black.

Swinging through the trees in a slight detour that carried him around and beyond the hunters without revealing his desertion to them, Tarzan sped through the middle terraces of the forest as only the Lord of the Jungle can.

Stronger and stronger in his nostrils waxed the scent of the quarry; behind him came the lions and the hunters; and he knew that he must act quickly, for they were no great distance in his rear. A grim smile lighted his grey eyes as he considered the *dénouement* of the project he had undertaken.

Presently he saw the black running through the forest just ahead of him. The fellow was moving at a dogged trot, casting an occasional glance behind him. He was a splendidly muscled Galla, a perfect type of primitive manhood, who seemed bent upon giving the best account of himself that he might against the hopeless odds that must eventually win the game in which his life was the stake. There was neither fear nor panic in his flight, merely inflexible determination to surrender to the inevitable only as a last resort.

Tarzan was directly above the man now, and he spoke to him in the language of his people. 'Take to the trees,' he called down.

The native looked up, but he did not stop. 'Who are you?' he demanded.

'An enemy of your master, who would help you escape,' replied the ape-man.

'There is no escape; if I take to the trees they will stone me down.'

'They will not find you; I will see to that.'

'Why should you help me?' demanded the native, but he stopped now and looked up again, searching for the man whose voice came down to him in a tongue that gave him confidence in the speaker.

'I have told you that I am an enemy of your master.'

Now the black saw the bronzed figure of the giant above him. 'You are a white man!' he exclaimed. 'You are trying to trick me. Why should a white man help me?'

'Hurry!' admonished Tarzan, 'or it will be too late, and no one can help you.'

For just an instant longer the African hesitated; then he leaped for a low-hanging branch and swung himself up into the tree as Tarzan came down to meet him.

'They will come soon and stone us both down,' he said. There was no hope in his voice nor any fear, only dumb apathy.

15

The Plot that Failed

Through the trees toward the east the ape-man carried the Galla slave who was to have been the victim of Xerstle's day of sport. At first the man had demurred; but as the growling of the hunting lions had increased in volume, denoting their close approach, he had resigned himself to what he may have considered the lesser of two evils.

Swiftly, the giant of the jungle bore the Galla toward the east where, beyond the forest, loomed the mountains that hemmed Onthar upon that side. For a mile he carried him through the trees and then swung lightly to the ground.

'If the lions ever pick up your trail now,' he said, 'it will not be until long after you have reached the mountains and safety. But do not delay – go now.'

The native fell upon his knees and took the hand of his savior in his own. 'I am Hafim,' he said. 'If I could serve you, I would die for you. Who are you?'

'I am Tarzan of the Apes. Now go your way and lose no time.'

'One more favor,' begged the black.

'What?'

'I have a brother. He, too, was captured by these people when they captured me. He is a slave in the gold mines south of Cathne. His name is Niaka. If you should ever go to the gold mines, tell him that Hafim has escaped. It will make him happier, and perhaps then he will try to escape.'

'I shall tell him. Now go.'

Silently the African disappeared among the boles of the forest trees, and Tarzan sprang again into the branches and swung rapidly back in the direction of the hunters. When he reached them, dropping to the ground and approaching them from behind, they were clustered near the spot at which Hafim had taken to the trees.

'Where have you been?' asked Xerstle. 'We thought that you had become lost.'

'I dropped behind,' replied the ape-man; 'but where is your quarry? I thought that you would have had him by this time.'

'We cannot understand it,' admitted Xerstle. 'It is evident that he climbed this tree, because the lions followed him to this very spot, where they stood looking up into the tree; but they did not growl as though they saw the man. Then we leashed them again and sent one of the keepers into the tree, but he saw no sign of the quarry.'

'It is a mystery!' exclaimed Pindes.

'It is indeed,' agreed Tarzan; 'at least for those who do not know the secret.'

'Who does know the secret?' demanded Xerstle.

'The black slave who has escaped you must know, if no other.'

'He has not escaped me,' snapped Xerstle. 'He has but prolonged the hunt and increased its interest.'

'It would add to the excitement of the day to lay some bets on that,' said the ape-man. 'I do not believe that your lions can again pick up the trail in time to bring down the quarry before dark.'

'A thousand drachmas that they do!' cried Xerstle.

'Being a stranger who came naked into your country, I have no thousand drachmas,' said Tarzan; 'but perhaps Gemnon will cover your bet.' He turned his face away from Xerstle and Pindes and, looking at Gemnon, slowly closed one eye.

'Done!' exclaimed Gemnon to Xerstle.

'I only demand the right to conduct the hunt in my own way,' said the latter.

'Of course,' agreed Gemnon, and Xerstle turned his face toward Pindes and slowly closed one eye.

'We shall separate, then,' explained Xerstle, 'and as you and Tarzan are betting against me, one of you must accompany me and the other go with Pindes so that all may be sure that the hunt is prosecuted with fairness and determination.'

'Agreed,' said Tarzan.

'But I am responsible to the Queen for the safe return of Tarzan,' demurred Gemnon; 'I do not like to have him out of my sight even for a short time.'

'I promise that I shall not try to escape,' the ape-man assured him.

'It was not that alone of which I was thinking,' explained Gemnon.

'And I can assure you that I can take care of myself, if you feel fears for my safety,' added Tarzan.

'Come, let us go,' urged Xerstle. 'I shall hunt with Gemnon and Pindes with Tarzan. We shall take one lion, they the other.'

Reluctantly Gemnon assented to the arrangement, and presently the two parties separated, Xerstle and Gemnon going toward the northwest while Pindes and Tarzan took an easterly direction. The latter had proceeded but a short distance, the lion still upon its leash, when Pindes suggested that they separate, spreading out through the forest, and thus combing it more carefully.

'You go straight east,' he said to Tarzan, 'the keepers and the lion will go northeast, and I will go north. If any comes upon the trail he may shout to attract the others to his position. If we have not located the quarry in an hour let us all converge toward the mountains at the eastern side of the forest.'

The ape-man nodded and started off in the direction assigned him, soon disappearing among the trees; but neither Pindes nor the keepers moved from where he had left them, the keepers held by a whispered word from Pindes. The leashed lion looked after the departing ape-man, and Pindes smiled. The keepers looked at him questioningly.

'Such sad accidents have happened many times before,' said Pindes.

Tarzan moved steadily toward the east. He knew that he would not find the Negro and so he did not look for him. The forest interested him but not to the exclusion of all else; his keen faculties were always upon the alert. Presently he heard a noise behind him and glancing back was not surprised by what he saw. A lion was stalking him, a lion wearing the harness of a hunting lion of Cathne. It was one of Xerstle's lions; it was the same lion that had accompanied Pindes and Tarzan.

Instantly the ape-man guessed the truth, and a grim light glinted in his eyes; it was no light of anger, but there was disgust in it and the shadowy suggestion of a savage smile. The lion, realizing that its quarry had discovered it, began to roar. In the distance Pindes heard and smiled.

'Let us go now,' he said to the keepers; 'we must not find the remains too quickly; that might not look well.' The three men moved slowly off toward the north.

From a distance Gemnon and Xerstle heard the roar of the hunting lion. 'They have picked up the trail,' said Gemnon, halting; 'we had best join them.'

'Not yet,' demurred Xerstle. 'It may be a false trail. The animal with them is not so good a hunter as ours; he is not so well trained. We will wait until we hear the hunters call.' But Gemnon was troubled.

Tarzan stood waiting the coming of the lion. He could have taken to the trees and escaped, but a spirit of bravado prompted him to remain. He hated treachery, and exposing it gave him pleasure. He carried a Cathnean spear and his own hunting knife; his bow and arrows he had left behind.

The lion came nearer; it seemed vaguely disturbed. Perhaps it did not understand why the quarry stood and faced it instead of running away. Its tail twitched; its head was flattened; slowly it came on again, its wicked eyes gleaming angrily.

Tarzan waited. In his right hand was the sturdy Cathnean spear, in his left the hunting knife of the father he had never known. He measured the distance with a trained eye as the lion started its swift, level charge; then, when it was coming at full speed, his spear hand flew back and he launched the heavy weapon.

Deep beneath the left shoulder it drove, deep into the savage heart; but it checked the beast's charge for but an instant. Infuriated now, the carnivore rose upon its hind legs above the ape-man, its great, taloned paws reaching to drag him to the slavering jowls; but Tarzan, swift as Ara, the lightning, stooped and sprang beneath them, sprang to one side and then in again, closing with the lion, leaping upon its back.

With a hideous roar, the animal wheeled and sought to bury its great fangs in the bronzed body or reach it with those raking talons. It threw itself to right and left as the creature clinging to it drove a steel blade repeatedly into the already torn and bleeding heart.

The vitality and life tenacity of a lion are astounding; but even that mighty frame could not for long withstand the lethal wounds its adversary had inflicted, and presently it slumped to earth and, with a little quiver, died. Then the ape-man leaped to his feet. With one foot upon the carcass of his kill, Tarzan of the Apes raised his face to the leafy canopy of the Cathnean forest and from his great chest rolled the hideous victory cry of the bull ape which has killed.

As the uncanny challenge reverberated down the forest aisles, Pindes and the two keepers looked questioningly at one another and laid their hands upon their sword hilts.

'In the name of Thoos! What was that?' demanded one of the keepers.

'By the name of Thoos! I never heard a sound so horrible before,' answered his companion, looking fearfully in the direction from which those weird notes had come.

'Silence!' admonished Pindes. 'Do you want the thing to creep upon us unheard because of your jabbering!'

'What was it, master?' asked one of the men in a whisper.

'It may have been the death cry of the stranger,' suggested Pindes, voicing the hope that was in his heart.

'It sounded not like a death cry, master,' replied the black; 'there was a note of strength and elation in it and none of weakness and defeat.'

'Silence, fool!' grumbled Pindes.

At a little distance, Gemnon and Xerstle heard, too. 'What was that?' demanded the latter.

Gemnon shook his head. 'I do not know, but we had better go and find out. I did not like the sound of it.'

Xerstle appeared nervous. 'It was nothing, perhaps, but the wind in the trees; let us go on with our hunting.'

'There is no wind,' demurred Gemnon. 'I am going to investigate. I am responsible for the safety of the stranger; but, even of more importance than that, I like him.'

'Oh, so do I!' exclaimed Xerstle eagerly. 'But nothing could have happened to him; Pindes is with him.'

'That is precisely what I was thinking,' observed Gemnon.

'That nothing could have happened to him?'

'That Pindes is with him!'

Xerstle shot a quick, suspicious look at the other, motioned to the keepers to follow with the leashed lion, and fell in behind Gemnon who had already started back toward the point at which they had separated from their companions.

In the meantime Pindes, unable to curb his curiosity, overcame his fears and started after Tarzan for the purpose of ascertaining what had befallen him as well as tracing the origin of the mysterious cry that had so filled him and his servants with wondering awe. Rather nervously, the two lion keepers followed him through the brooding silence of the forest, all three men keeping a careful lookout ahead and upon every side.

They had not gone far when Pindes, who was in the lead, halted suddenly and pointed straight ahead. 'What is that?' he demanded.

The keepers pressed forward. 'Mane of Thoos!' cried one, 'It is the lion!'

They advanced slowly, watching the lion, looking to right and left. 'It is dead!' exclaimed Pindes.

The three men examined the body of the dead beast, turning it over. 'It has been stabbed to death,' announced one of the keepers.

'The Galla slave had no weapon,' said Pindes thoughtfully.

'The stranger carried a knife,' a keeper reminded him.

'Whoever killed the lion must have fought it hand-to-hand,' reflected Pindes aloud.

'Then he must be lying nearby dead or wounded, master.'

'Search for him!' directed Pindes.

'He could have killed Phobeg with his bare hands that day that he threw him into the audience at the stadium,' a keeper reminded the noble. 'He carried him around as though Phobeg were a babe. He is very strong.'

'What has that to do with the matter?' demanded Pindes irritably.

'I do not know, master; I was only thinking.'

'I did not tell you to think,' snapped Pindes; 'I told you to hunt for the man that killed the lion; he must be dying or dead nearby.'

While they hunted, Xerstle and Gemnon were drawing nearer. The latter was much concerned about the welfare of his charge. He trusted neither Xerstle nor Pindes, and now he commenced to suspect that he and Tarzan had been deliberately separated for sinister purposes. He was walking a little behind Xerstle at the time; the keepers, with the lion, were just ahead of them. He felt a hand upon his shoulder and wheeled about; there stood Tarzan, a smile upon his lips.

'Where did you drop from?' demanded Gemnon.

'We separated to search for the Galla, Pindes and I,' explained the ape-man as Xerstle turned at the sound of Gemnon's voice and discovered him.

'Did you hear that terrible scream a while ago?' demanded Xerstle. 'We thought it possible that one of you was hurt, and we were hurrying to investigate.'

'Did someone scream?' inquired Tarzan innocently. 'Perhaps it was Pindes, for I am not hurt.'

Shortly after Tarzan had rejoined them Xerstle and Gemnon came upon Pindes and his two lion keepers searching the underbrush and the surrounding forest. As his eyes fell upon Tarzan, Pindes' eyes went wide in astonishment, and he paled a little.

'What has happened?' demanded Xerstle. 'What are you looking for? Where is your lion?'

'He is dead,' explained Pindes. 'Someone or something stabbed him to death.' He did not look at Tarzan; he feared to do so. 'We have been looking for the man who did it, thinking that he must have been badly mauled and, doubtless, killed.'

'Have you found him?' asked Tarzan.

'No.'

'Shall I help you search for him? Suppose you and I, Pindes, go away alone and look for him!' suggested the ape-man.

For a moment Pindes seemed choking as he sought for a reply. 'No!' he exclaimed presently. 'It would be useless; we have searched carefully; there is not even a sign of blood to indicate that he was wounded.'

'And you found no trace of the quarry?' asked Xerstle.

'None,' replied Pindes. 'He has escaped, and we might as well return to the city. I have had enough hunting for today.'

Xerstle grumbled. It was getting late; he had lost his quarry and one of his lions; but there seemed no reason to continue the hunt, and so he grudgingly acquiesced.

'So this is a grand hunt?' remarked Tarzan meditatively. 'Perhaps it has not been thrilling; but I have enjoyed it greatly. However, Gemnon appears to be the only one who has profited by it; he has won a thousand drachmas.'

Xerstle only grunted and strode on moodily toward the city. When the party separated before the house of Gemnon's father Tarzan stood close to Xerstle and whispered in a low voice. 'My compliments to Erot, and may he have better luck next time!'

16

In the Temple of Thoos

As Tarzan sat with Gemnon and the latter's father and mother at dinner that evening a slave entered the room to announce that a messenger had come from the house of Thudos, the father of Doria, with an important communication for Gemnon.

'Fetch him here,' directed the young noble, and a moment later a tall Negro was ushered into the apartment.

'Ah, Gemba!' exclaimed Gemnon in a kindly tone, 'you have a message for me?'

'Yes, master,' replied the slave, 'but it is important – and secret.'

'You may speak before these others, Gemba,' replied Gemnon. 'What is it?'

'Doria, the daughter of Thudos, my master, has sent me to tell you that by a ruse the noble Erot gained entrance to her father's house and spoke with her today. What he said to her was of no importance; only the fact that he saw her is important.'

'The jackal!' exclaimed Gemnon's father.

Gemnon paled. 'That is all?' he inquired.

'That is all, master,' replied Gemba.

Gemnon took a gold coin from his pocket pouch and handed it to the slave. 'Return to your mistress, and tell her that I shall come and speak with her father tomorrow.'

After the slave had withdrawn Gemnon looked hopelessly at his father. 'What can I do?' he asked. 'What can Thudos do? What can anyone do? We are helpless.'

'Perhaps I can do something,' suggested Tarzan. 'For the moment I seem to hold the confidence of your Queen; when I see her I shall question her, and if it is necessary I shall intercede on your behalf.'

A new hope sprang to Gemnon's eyes. 'If you will!' he cried. 'She will listen to you. I believe that you alone might save Doria; but remember that the Queen must not see her, for should she, nothing can save her – she will be either disfigured or killed.'

Early the next morning a messenger from the palace brought a command to Tarzan to visit the Queen at noon, with instructions to Gemnon to accompany Tarzan with a strong guard as she feared treachery on the part of Tarzan's enemies.

'They must be powerful enemies that dare attempt to thwart the wishes of Nemone,' commented Gemnon's father.

'There is only one in all Cathne who dares do that,' replied Gemnon.

The older man nodded. 'The old she-devil! Would but that Thoos destroyed her! How shameful it is that Cathne should be ruled by a slave woman!'

'I have seen Nemone look at her as though she wished to kill her,' said Tarzan.

'Yes, but she will never dare,' prophesied Gemnon's father. 'Between the old witch and Tomos a threat of some sort is held over the Queen's head so that she dares not destroy either one of them, yet I am sure she hates them both; and it is seldom that she permits one to live whom she hates.'

'It is thought that they hold the secret of her birth, a secret that would destroy her if it were announced to the people,' explained Gemnon; 'but come, we have the morning to ourselves; I shall not visit Thudos until after you have talked with Nemone; what shall we do in the meantime?'

'I should like to visit the mines of Cathne,' replied Tarzan; 'shall we have time?'

'Yes, we shall,' replied Gemnon; 'the Mine of the Rising Sun is not far; and as there is little to see after you get there, the trip will not take long.'

On the road from Cathne to the nearer mine, Gemnon pointed out the breeding plant where the war and hunting lions of Cathne are bred; but they did not stop to visit the place, and presently they were winding up the short mountain road to the Gold Mine of the Rising Sun.

As Gemnon had warned him, there was little of interest for Tarzan to see.

The workings were open, the mother lode lying practically upon the surface of the ground; and so rich was it that only a few slaves working with crude picks and bars were needed to supply the coffers of Cathne with vast quantities of the precious metal. But it was not the mines nor gold that had caused Tarzan to wish to visit the diggings. He had promised Hafim that he would carry a message to his brother, Niaka; and it was for this purpose that he had suggested the visit.

As he moved about among the slaves, ostensibly inspecting the lode, he finally succeeded in separating himself sufficiently from Gemnon and the warriors who guarded the workers to permit him to speak unnoticed to one of the slaves.

'Which is Niaka?' he asked in Galla, lowering his voice to a whisper.

The black looked up in surprise, but at a warning gesture from Tarzan bent his head again and answered in a whisper, 'Niaka is the big man at my right. He is headman; you see that he does not work.'

Tarzan moved then in the direction of Niaka, and when he was close stopped beside him and leaned as though inspecting the lode that was uncovered at his feet. 'Listen,' he whispered. 'I bring you a message, but let no one know that I am talking to you. It is from your brother, Hafim. He has escaped.'

'How?' whispered Niaka.

Briefly, Tarzan explained.

'It was you, then, who saved him?'

The ape-man nodded.

'I am only a poor slave,' said Niaka, 'and you are a powerful noble, no doubt; so I can never repay you. But should you ever need any service that Niaka can render, you have but to command; with my life I would serve you. In that little hut below the diggings I live with my woman; because I am headman I am trusted and live thus alone. If you ever want me you will find me there.'

'I ask no return for what I did,' replied Tarzan, 'but I shall remember where you live; one never knows what the future holds.'

He moved away then and joined Gemnon; and presently the two turned back toward the city, while in the palace of the Queen Tomos entered the apartment of Nemone and knelt.

'What now?' she demanded. 'Is the affair so urgent that I must be interrupted at my toilet?'

'It is, majesty,' replied the councillor, 'and I beg that you send your slaves away. What I have to say is for your ears alone.'

There were four Negro girls working on Nemone's nails, one at each foot and one at each hand, and a white girl arranging her hair. To the last the

Queen spoke, 'Take the slaves away, Maluma, and send them to their quarters; you may wait in the adjoining room.'

Then she turned to the councillor, who had arisen. 'Well, what is it?'

'Your majesty has long had reason to suspect the loyalty of Thudos,' Tomos reminded her, 'and in the interest of your majesty's welfare and the safety of the throne, I am constantly watchful of the activities of this powerful enemy. Spurred on by love and loyalty, the noble Erot has been my most faithful agent and ally; and it is really to him that we owe the information that I bring you.'

Nemone tapped her sandalled foot impatiently upon the mosaic floor. 'Have done with the self-serving preamble, and tell me what you have to tell me,' she snapped, for she did not like Tomos and made no effort to hide her feelings.

'Briefly, then, it is this; Gemnon conspires also with Thudos, hoping, doubtless, that his reward will be the beautiful daughter of his chief.'

'That hollow-checked strumpet!' exclaimed Nemone. 'Who said she was beautiful?'

'Erot tells me that Gemnon and Thudos believe her the most beautiful woman in the world,' replied Tomos.

'Impossible! Did Erot see her?'

'Yes, majesty, he saw her.'

'What does Erot say?' demanded the Queen.

'That she is indeed beautiful,' replied the councillor. 'There are others who think so too,' he added.

'What others?'

'One who has been drawn into the conspiracy with Gemnon and Thudos by the beauty of Doria, the daughter of Thudos.'

'Whom do you mean? Speak out! I know you have something unpleasant in your mind that you are suffering to tell me, hoping that it will make me unhappy.'

'Oh, majesty, you wrong me!' cried Tomos. 'My only thoughts are for the happiness of my beloved Queen.'

'Your words stink with falseness,' sneered Nemone. 'But get to the point; I have other matters to occupy my time.'

'I but hesitated to name the other for fear of wounding your majesty,' said Tomos oilily; 'but if you insist, it is the stranger called Tarzan.'

Nemone sat up very straight. 'What fabric of lies is this you and M'duze are weaving?' she demanded.

'It is no lie, majesty. Tarzan and Gemnon were seen coming from the house of Thudos late at night. Erot had followed them there; he saw them go in; they were there a long while; hiding in the shadows across the avenue, he saw them come out. He says that they were quarrelling over Doria, and he believes that it was Gemnon who sought the life of Tarzan because of jealousy.'

Nemone sat straight and stiff upon her couch; her face was pale and tense with fury. 'Someone shall die for this,' she said in a low voice. 'Go!'

Tomos backed from the room. He was elated until he had time to reflect more fully upon her words; then he reflected that Nemone had not stated explicitly who should die. He had assumed that she meant Tarzan, because it was Tarzan whom he wished to die; but it presently occurred to him that she might have meant another, and he was less elated. It was almost noon when Tarzan and Gemnon returned to the city, and time for the latter to conduct Tarzan to his audience with Nemone. With a guard of warriors they went to the palace, where the ape-man was immediately admitted alone into the presence of the Queen.

'Where have you been?' she demanded.

Tarzan looked at her in surprise; then he smiled. 'I visited the Mine of the Rising Sun.'

'Where were you last night?'

'At the house of Gemnon,' he replied.

'You were with Doria!' accused Nemone.

'No,' said the ape-man; 'that was the night before.'

He had been surprised by the accusation and the knowledge that it connoted, but he did not let her see that he was surprised. He was not thinking of himself but of Doria and Gemnon, seeking a plan whereby he might protect them. It was evident that some enemy had turned informer and that Nemone already knew of the visit to the house of Thudos; therefore he felt that it would but have aroused the Queen's suspicions to have denied it; to admit it freely, to show that he sought to conceal nothing, would allay them. As a matter of fact Tarzan's frank and ready reply left Nemone rather flat.

'Why did you go to the house of Thudos?' she asked, but this time her tone was not accusing.

'You see, Gemnon does not dare to leave me alone for fear that I shall escape or that something may befall me; and so he is forced to take me wherever he goes. It is rather hard on him, Nemone, and I have been intending to ask you to make someone else responsible for me for at least a part of the time.'

'We will speak of that later,' replied the Queen. 'Why does Gemnon got to the house of Thudos?' Nemone's eyes narrowed suspiciously.

The ape-man smiled. 'What a foolish question for a woman to ask!' he exclaimed. 'Gemnon is in love with Doria. I thought all Cathne knew that; he certainly takes enough pains to tell all his acquaintances.'

'You are sure that it is not you who are in love with her?' demanded Nemone.

Tarzan looked at her with disgust he made no effort to conceal. 'Do not be a fool, Nemone,' he said. 'I do not like foolish women.'

The jaw of the Queen of Cathne dropped. In all her life no one had ever addressed her in words or tones like these. For a moment they left her speechless, but in that moment of speechlessness there came the sudden realization that the very things that shocked her also relieved her mind of gnawing suspicion and of jealousy – Tarzan did not love Doria. And, too, she was compelled to admit that his indifference to her position or her anger increased her respect for him and made him still more desirable in her eyes. She had never known such a man before; none had ever ruled her. Here was one who might if he wished, but she was troubled by the fear that he did not care enough about her to wish to rule her.

When she spoke again, she had regained her calm. 'I was told that you loved her,' she explained, 'but I did not believe it. Is she very beautiful? I have heard that she is considered the most beautiful woman in Cathne.'

'Perhaps Gemnon thinks so,' replied Tarzan with a laugh, 'but you know what love does to the eyes of youth.'

'What do you think of her?' demanded the Queen.

The ape-man shrugged. 'She is not bad looking,' he said.

'Is she as beautiful as Nemone?' demanded the Queen.

'As the brilliance of a far star is to the brilliance of the sun.'

The reply appeared to please Nemone. She arose and came closer to Tarzan. 'You think me beautiful?' she asked in soft, insinuating tones.

'You are very beautiful, Nemone,' he answered truthfully.

She pressed against him, caressing his shoulder with a smooth, warm palm. 'Love me, Tarzan,' she whispered, her voice husky with emotion.

There was a rattling of chains at the far end of the room, followed by a terrific roar as Belthar sprang to his feet. Nemone shrank suddenly away from the ape-man; a shudder ran through her body, and an expression, half fright, half anger, suffused her face.

'It is always something,' she said irritably, trembling a little. 'Belthar is jealous. There is a strange bond linking the life of that beast to my life. I do not know what it is; I wish I did.' A light, almost of madness, glittered in her eyes. 'I wish I knew! Sometimes I think he is the mate that Thoos intended for me; sometimes I think he is myself in another form; but this I know: when Belthar dies, I die!'

She looked up rather sadly at Tarzan as again her mood changed. 'Come, my friend,' she said; 'we shall go to the temple together and perhaps Thoos may answer the questions that are in the heart of Nemone.' She struck a bronze disc that depended from the ceiling, and as the brazen notes reverberated in the room a door opened and a noble bowed low upon the threshold.

'The guard!' commanded the Queen. 'We are visiting Thoos in his temple.'

The progress to the temple was in the nature of a pageant – marching warriors with pennons streaming from spear tips, nobles resplendent in gorgeous trappings, the Queen in a golden chariot drawn by lions. Tomos walked upon one side of the glittering car, Tarzan upon the other where Erot had previously walked.

The ape-man was as uneasy as a forest lion as he strode between the lines of gaping citizenry. Crowds annoyed and irritated him; formalities irked him; his thoughts were far away in the distant jungle that he loved. He knew that Gemnon was nearby watching him; but whether he were nearby or not, Tarzan would not attempt to escape while this friend was responsible for him. His mind occupied with such thoughts, he spoke to the Queen.

'At the palace,' he reminded her, 'I spoke to you concerning the matter of relieving Gemnon of the irksome job of watching me.'

'Gemnon has acquitted himself well,' she replied. 'I see no reason for changing.'

'Relieve him then occasionally,' suggested Tarzan. 'Let Erot take his place.'

Nemone looked at him in astonishment. 'But Erot hates you!' she exclaimed.

'All the more reason that he would watch me carefully,' argued Tarzan.

'He would probably kill you.'

'He would not dare if he knew that he must pay for my death or escape with his own life,' suggested Tarzan.

'You like Gemnon, do you not?' inquired Nemone innocently.

'Very much,' the ape-man assured her.

'Then he is the man to watch you, for you would not imperil his life by escaping while he is responsible.'

Tarzan smiled inwardly and said no more; it was evident that Nemone was no fool. He would have to devise some other plan of escape that would not jeopardize the safety of his friend.

They were approaching the temple now and his attention was distracted by the approach of a number of priests leading a slave girl in chains. They brought her to the chariot of Nemone, and while the procession halted the priests chanted in a strange gibberish that Tarzan could not understand. Later he learned that no one understood it, not even the priests; but when he asked why they recited something that they could not understand no one could tell him.

Gemnon thought that once the words had meant something, but they had been repeated mechanically for so many ages that at length the original pronunciation had been lost and the meaning of the words forgotten.

When the chant was completed the priests chained the girl to the rear of the Queen's chariot; and the march was resumed, the priests following behind the girl.

At the entrance to the temple Phobeg was on guard as a girl entered to worship. Recognizing the warrior, she greeted him and paused for a moment's conversation, the royal party having not yet entered the temple square.

'I have not seen you to talk with for a long time, Phobeg,' she said. 'I am glad that you are back again on the temple guard.'

'Thanks to the stranger called Tarzan I am alive and here,' replied Phobeg.

'I should think that you would hate him,' exclaimed the girl.

'Not I,' cried Phobeg. 'I know a better man when I see one. I admire him. And did he not grant me my life when the crowd screamed for my death?'

'That is true,' admitted the girl. 'And now *he* needs a friend.'

'What do you mean, Maluma?' demanded the warrior.

'I was in an adjoining room when Tomos visited the Queen this morning,' explained the girl, 'and I overheard him tell her that Thudos and Gemnon and Tarzan were conspiring against her and that Tarzan loved Doria, the daughter of Thudos.'

'How did Tomos know these things?' asked Phobeg. 'Did he offer proof?'

'He said that Erot had watched and had seen Gemnon and Tarzan visit the house of Thudos,' explained Maluma. 'He also told her that Erot had seen Doria and had reported that she was very beautiful.'

Phobeg whistled. 'That will be the end of the daughter of Thudos,' he said.

'It will be the end of the stranger, too,' phophesied Maluma; 'and I am sorry, for I like him. He is not like the jackal, Erot, whom everyone hates.'

'Here comes the Queen!' exclaimed Phobeg as the head of the procession debouched into the temple square. 'Run along now and get a good place, for there will be something to see today; there always is when the Queen comes to worship god.'

Before the temple, Nemone alighted from her chariot and walked up the broad stairway to the ornate entrance. Behind her were the priests with the slave girl, a frightened, wide-eyed girl with tears upon her cheeks. Following them came the nobles of the court, the warriors of the guard remaining in the temple square before the entrance.

The temple was a large three-storied building with a great central dome about the interior of which ran galleries at the second and third stories. The interior of the dome was of gold as were the pillars that supported the galleries, while the walls of the building were embellished with colorful mosaics. Directly opposite the main entrance, on a level with a raised dais, a great cage was built into a niche, and on either side of the cage was an altar supporting a lion carved from solid gold. Before the dais was a stone railing inside of which was a throne and a row of stone benches facing the cage in the niche.

Nemone advanced and seated herself upon the throne, while the nobles took their places upon the benches. No one paid any attention to Tarzan; so he remained outside the railing, a mildly interested spectator.

He had noticed a change come over Nemone the instant that she had entered the temple. She had shown signs of extreme nervousness, the expression of her face had changed; it was tense and eager; there was a light in her eyes that was like the mad light he had seen there occasionally before, yet different – the light of religious fanaticism.

Tarzan saw the priests lead the girl up onto the dais and then, beyond them, he saw something rise up in the cage. It was an old and mangy lion. The high priest began a meaningless, singsong chant, in which the others joined occasionally as though making responses. Nemone leaned forward eagerly; her eyes were fastened upon the old lion. Her breasts rose and fell to her excited breathing.

Suddenly the chanting ceased and the Queen arose. 'O Thoos!' she cried, her hands outstretched toward the mangy old carnivore. 'Nemone brings you greetings and an offering. Receive them from Nemone and bless her. Give her life and health and happiness; most of all Nemone prays for happiness. Preserve her friends and destroy her enemies. And, O Thoos, give her the one thing that she most desires – love, the love of the one man in all the world that Nemone has ever loved!' And the lion glared at her through the bars.

She spoke as though in a trance, as though oblivious to all else around her save the god to which she prayed. There were pathos and tragedy in her voice, and a great pity rose in the breast of the ape-man for this poor Queen who had never known love and who never might because of the warped brain that mistook passion for affection and lust for love.

As she sat down weakly upon her golden throne, the priests led the slave girl away through a doorway at one side of the cage; and, as she passed, the lion leaped for her, striking heavily against the bars that restrained him. His growls rolled through the temple, filling the chamber with thunderous sound, echoing and reechoing from the golden dome.

Nemone sat, silent and rigid, upon her throne staring straight ahead at the lion in the cage; the priests and many of the nobles were reciting prayers in monotones. It was evident to Tarzan that they were praying to the lion, for every eye was upon the repulsive beast; and some of the questions that had puzzled him when he had first come to Cathne were answered. He understood now the strange oaths of Phobeg and his statement that he had stepped upon the tail of god.

Suddenly a beam of light shone down directly into the cage from above, flooding the beast-god with its golden rays. The lion, which had been pacing restlessly to and fro, stopped and looked up, his jaws parted, saliva dripping from his jowls. The audience burst in unison into a singsong chant. Tarzan, half guessing what was about to occur, arose from the rail upon which he had been sitting, and started forward.

But whatever his intention may have been, he was too late to prevent the tragedy that followed instantly. Even as he arose the body of the slave girl dropped from above into the clutches of the waiting lion. A single piercing scream mingled with the horrid roars of the man-eater and then died as its author died.

Tarzan turned away in disgust and anger and walked from the temple out into the fresh air and the sunlight, and as he did so a warrior at the entrance hailed him by name in a whisper. There was a cautionary warning in the voice that prompted the ape-man to give no apparent sign of having heard as he turned his eyes casually in the direction from which the words had come, nor did he betray his interest when he discovered that it was Phobeg who had addressed him.

Turning slowly, so that his back was toward the warrior, Tarzan looked back into the temple as though expecting the return of the royal party; then he backed to the side of the entrance as one might who waits and stood so close to Phobeg that the latter might have touched him by moving his spear hand a couple of inches; but neither gave any sign of being aware of the identity or presence of the other.

In a low whisper, through lips that scarcely moved, Phobeg spoke. 'I must speak to you! Come to the rear of the temple two hours after the sun has set. Do not answer, but if you hear and will come, turn your head to the right.'

As Tarzan gave the assenting signal the royal party commenced to file from the temple, and he fell in behind Nemone. The Queen was quiet and moody, as she always was after the sight of torture and blood at the temple had aroused her to religious frenzy; the reaction left her weak and indifferent. At the palace, she dismissed her following, including Tarzan, and withdrew to the seclusion of her apartments.

17

The Secret of the Temple

After the royal party left the temple Maluma came out and paused again to gossip with Phobeg. For some time they talked before she bid him goodbye and started back toward the palace. They spoke of many things – of the man in the secret prison behind a heavy golden door beneath the temple floor, of Erot and Tomos, of Nemone and Tarzan, of Gemnon and Doria, and of themselves. Being human, they talked mostly of themselves. It was late when Maluma returned to the palace. It was already the evening meal hour.

In the home of his father, Gemnon paced the floor of the patio as he awaited the summons to the evening meal. Tarzan half sat, half reclined upon a stone bench. He saw that his friend was worried; and it troubled him, troubled him most perhaps because he knew that there were grave causes for apprehension; and he was not certain that he could avert the disaster that threatened.

Seeking to divert Gemnon's mind from his troubles, Tarzan spoke of the ceremony at the temple, but principally of the temple itself, praising its beauty, commenting upon its magnificence. 'It is splendid,' he commented; 'too splendid for the cruel rites we witnessed there today.'

'The girl was only a slave,' replied Gemnon, 'and god must eat. It is no wrong to make offerings to Thoos; but the temple *does* hide a real wrong. Somewhere within it is hidden Alextar, the brother of Nemone; and while he rots there the corrupt Tomos and the cruel M'duze rule Cathne through the mad Nemone.

'There are many who would have a change and place Alextar on the throne, but they fear the wrath of the terrible triumvirate. So we go on, and nothing is done. Victim after victim succumbs to the malignant jealousy and fear that constantly animate the throne.

'We have little hope today; we shall have no hope if the Queen carries out the plan she is believed to be contemplating and destroys Alextar. There are reasons why it would be to her advantage to do so, the most important being the right of Alextar to proclaim himself king should he ever succeed in reaching the palace.

'If Nemone should die Alextar would become king, and the populace would insist that he take his rightful place. For this reason Tomos and M'duze are anxious to destroy him. It is to Nemone's credit that she has withstood their importunities for all these years, steadfastly refusing to destroy Alextar; but if ever he seriously threatens her power, he is lost; and rumors that have reached her ears that a plot has been perfected to place him on the throne may already have sealed his doom.'

During the meal that evening Tarzan considered plans for visiting Phobeg at the temple. He wished to go alone but knew that he would place Gemnon in an embarrassing position should he suggest such a plan, while to permit the noble to accompany him might not only seal Phobeg's lips but jeopardize his safety as well; therefore he decided to go secretly.

Following the stratagem he had adopted, he remained in conversation with Gemnon and his parents until almost two hours after the sun had set; then he excused himself, saying that he was tired, and went to the room that had been assigned him. But he did not tarry there. Instead, he merely crossed the room from the door to the window and stepped out into the patio upon which it faced. Here, as throughout the gardens and avenues of the section of the city occupied by the nobility, grew large, old trees; and a moment later the Lord of the Jungle was swinging through his native element toward the golden temple of Thoos.

He stopped at last in a tree near the rear of the temple where he saw the huge and familiar figure of Phobeg waiting in the shadows below. Soundlessly, the ape-man dropped to the ground in front of the astonished warrior.

'By the great fangs of Thoos!' ejaculated Phobeg, 'but you gave me a start.'

'You expected me,' was Tarzan's only comment.

'But not from the skies,' retorted Phobeg. 'However, you are here and it is well; I have much more to tell you than when I asked you to come. I have learned more since.'

'I am listening,' said Tarzan.

'A girl in the service of the Queen overheard a conversation between Nemone and Tomos,' commenced Phobeg. 'Tomos accused you and Gemnon and Thudos of conspiring against her. Erot spied upon you and knew of your long visit at the home of Thudos a few nights since; he also managed to enter the house on some pretext the following night and saw Doria, the daughter of Thudos. Tomos told Nemone that Doria was very beautiful and that you were in love with her.

'Nemone is not yet convinced that you love Doria, but to be on the safe side she has ordered Tomos to have the girl abducted and brought to the temple where she will be imprisoned until Nemone decides upon her fate. She may destroy her, or she may be content to have her beauty disfigured.

'But what you must know is this: If you give Nemone the slightest reason to believe that you are conspiring against her or that you are fond of Doria she will have you killed. All that I can do is warn you.'

'You warned me once before, did you not?' asked Tarzan, 'The night that Gemnon and I went to the house of Thudos.'

'Yes, that was I,' replied Phobeg.

'Why have you done these things?' asked the ape-man.

'Because I owe my life to you,' replied the warrior, 'and because I know a man when I see one. If a man can pick Phobeg up and toss him around as though he were a baby, Phobeg is willing to be his slave.'

'I can only thank you for what you have told me, Phobeg,' said Tarzan. 'Now tell me more. If Doria is brought to the temple where will she be imprisoned?'

'That is hard to say. Alextar is kept in rooms beneath the floor of the temple, but there are rooms upon the second and third floors where a prisoner might be safely confined, especially a woman.'

'Could you get word to me if she is arrested?'

'I could try,' replied Phobeg.

'Good! Is there anything further?'

'No.'

'Then I shall return to Gemnon and warn him. Perhaps we shall find a way to pacify Nemone or outwit her.'

'Either would be difficult,' commented Phobeg, 'but goodbye and good luck!'

Tarzan swung into the tree above the warrior's head and disappeared among the shadows of the night, while Phobeg shook his head in wonderment and returned to his quarters in the temple.

The ape-man made his way to his room by the same avenue he had left it and went immediately to the common living room where the family ordinarily congregated for the evenings. Here he found Gemnon's father and mother, but Gemnon was not there.

'You could not sleep?' inquired the mother.

'No,' replied the ape-man. 'Where is Gemnon?'

'He was summoned to the palace a short time after you went to your room,' explained Gemnon's father.

Announcing that he would wait up until the son returned, Tarzan remained in the living room in conversation with the parents. He wondered a little that Gemnon should have been summoned to the palace at such an hour; and the things that Phobeg had told him made him a little apprehensive, but he kept his own council rather than frighten his host and hostess.

Scarcely an hour had passed when they heard a summons at the outer gate, and presently a slave came to announce that a warrior wished to speak to Tarzan upon a matter of urgent necessity.

The ape-man arose. 'I will go outside and see him,' he said.

'Be careful,' cautioned Gemnon's father. 'You have bitter enemies who would be glad to see you destroyed.'

'I shall be careful,' Tarzan assured him as he left the room behind the slave.

At the gate two warriors connected with the house were detaining a huge man whom Tarzan recognized even from a distance as Phobeg. 'I must speak with you at once and alone,' said the latter.

'This man is all right,' Tarzan told the guards. 'Let him enter and I will talk with him in the garden.'

When they had walked a short distance from the guards Tarzan paused and faced his visitor. 'What is it?' he asked. 'You have brought me bad news?'

'Very bad,' replied Phobeg. 'Gemnon, Thudos, and many of their friends have been arrested and are now in the palace dungeons. Doria has been taken and is imprisoned in the temple. I did not expect to find you at liberty, but took the chance that Nemone's interest in you might have saved you temporarily. If you can escape from Cathne, do so at once; her mood may change at any moment; she is as mad as a monkey.'

'Thank you, Phobeg,' said the ape-man. 'Now get back to your quarters before you become embroiled in this affair.'

'And you will escape?' asked the warrior.

'I owe something to Gemnon,' replied Tarzan, 'for his kindness and his friendship; so I shall not go until I have done what I can to help him.'

'No one can help him,' stated Phobeg emphatically. 'All that you will do is get yourself in trouble.'

'I shall have to chance it, and now goodbye, my friend; but before you go tell me where Doria is imprisoned.'

'On the third floor of the temple at the rear of the building just above the doorway where I awaited you this evening.'

Tarzan accompanied Phobeg to the gate and out into the avenue. 'Where are you going?' demanded the latter.

'To the palace.'

'You, too, are mad,' protested Phobeg, but already the ape-man had left him and was walking rapidly along the avenue in the direction of the palace.

It was late; but Tarzan was now a familiar figure to the palace guards; and when he told them that Nemone had summoned him they let him enter, nor was he stopped until he had reached the anteroom outside the Queen's apartments. Here a noble on guard protested that the hour was late and that the Queen had retired, but Tarzan insisted upon seeing her.

'Tell her it is Tarzan,' he said.

'I do not dare disturb her,' explained the noble nervously, fearful of Nemone's wrath should she be disturbed and almost equally fearful of it should he refuse to announce this new favorite who had replaced Erot.

'I dare,' said Tarzan and stepped to the door leading to the ivory room where Nemone had been accustomed to receive him. The noble sought to interfere but the ape-man pushed him aside and attempted to open the door only to find it securely bolted upon the opposite side; then with his clenched fist he pounded loudly upon its carved surface.

Instantly from beyond it came the savage growls of Belthar and a moment later the frightened voice of a woman. 'Who is there?' she demanded. 'The Queen sleeps. Who dares disturb her?'

'Go and awaken her,' shouted Tarzan through the door. 'Tell her that Tarzan is here and wishes to see her at once.'

'I am afraid,' replied the girl. 'The Queen will be angry. Go away, and come in the morning.'

Then Tarzan heard another voice beyond the door demanding, 'Who is it comes pounding on Nemone's door at such an hour?' and recognized it as the Queen's.

'It is the noble Tarzan,' replied the slave girl.

'Draw the bolts and admit him,' commanded Nemone, and as the door swung open Tarzan stepped into the ivory room, now so familiar to him.

The Queen stood halfway across the apartment, facing him. Her hair was dishevelled, her face slightly flushed. She had evidently arisen from her bed in an adjoining room and thrown a light scarf about her before stepping into the ivory room. She was very beautiful. There was an eager, questioning light in her eyes. She directed the slave to rebolt the door and leave the apartment; then she turned and, walking to the couch, motioned Tarzan to approach. As she sank among the soft cushions she motioned Tarzan to her side.

'I am glad you came,' she said. 'I could not sleep. I have been thinking of you. But tell me! Why did you come? Had you been thinking of me?'

'I have been thinking of you, Nemone,' replied the ape-man; 'I have been thinking that perhaps you will help me; that you can help me, I know.'

'You have only to ask,' replied the Queen softly. 'There is no favor that you may not have from Nemone for the asking.'

A single cresset shed a soft, flickering light that scarcely dispelled the darkness of the room, at the far end of which the yellow-green eyes of Belthar blazed like twin lamps of Hell. Mingling with the acrid scent of the carnivore and the languorous fumes of incense was the seductive aura of the scented body of the woman. Her warm breath was on Tarzan's cheek as she drew him down beside her.

'At last you have come to me of your own volition,' she whispered. 'Ah, Thoos! How I have hungered for this moment!'

Her soft, bare arms slipped quickly about his neck and drew him close. 'Tarzan! My Tarzan!' she almost sobbed, and then that same fatal door at the far end of the apartment opened and the tapping of a metal-shod staff upon the stone floor brought them both erect to gaze into the snarling face of M'duze.

'You fool!' cried the old hag in a shrill falsetto. 'Send the man away! Unless you would see him killed here before your eyes. Send him away at once!'

Nemone sprang to her feet and faced the old woman who was now trembling with rage. 'You have gone too far, M'duze,' she said in a cold and level voice. 'Go to your room, and remember that I am Queen.'

'Queen! Queen!' cackled the hideous creature with a sharp, sarcastic laugh. 'Send your lover away, or I'll tell him who and what you are.'

Nemone glided quickly toward her, and as she passed a low stand she stooped and seized something that lay there. Suddenly the slave woman shrieked and shrank away, but before she could turn and flee Nemone was upon her and had seized her by the hair. M'duze raised her staff and struck at the Queen, but the blow only aroused the frenzied woman to still greater fury.

'Always you have ruined my life,' cried Nemone, 'you and your foul paramour, Tomos. You have robbed me of happiness, and for that, *this!*' and she drove the gleaming blade of a knife into the withered breast of the screaming woman, 'and this, and this, and this!' and each time the blade sank deep to emphasize the venom in the words and the heart of Nemone, the queen.

Presently M'duze ceased shrieking and sank to the floor. Someone was pounding upon the door to the anteroom, and the terrified voices of nobles and guardsmen could be heard demanding entrance. In his corner Belthar tugged at his chains and roared. Nemone stood looking down upon the death struggles of M'duze with blazing eyes and snarling lip. 'Curses upon your black soul!' she cried, and then she turned slowly toward the door upon which the pounding of her retainers' fists resounded. 'Have done!' she called imperiously. 'I, Nemone, the Queen, am safe. The screams that you heard were those of an impudent slave whom Nemone was correcting.'

The voices beyond the door died away as the guardsmen returned to their posts; then Nemone faced Tarzan. She looked suddenly worn and very tired. 'That favor,' she said, 'ask it another time; Nemone is unstrung.'

'I must ask it now,' replied Tarzan; 'tomorrow may be too late.'

'Very well,' she said; 'I am listening. What is it?'

'There is a noble in your court who has been very kind to me since I have been in Cathne,' commenced Tarzan. 'Now he is in trouble, and I have come to ask you to save him.'

Nemone's brow clouded. 'Who is he?' she demanded.

'Gemnon,' replied the ape-man. 'He has been arrested with Thudos and the daughter of Thudos and several of their friends. It is only a plot to destroy me.'

'You dare come to me to intercede for traitors!' cried the Queen, blazing with sudden fury. 'But I know the reason; you love Doria!'

'I do not love her; I have seen her but once. Gemnon loves her. Let them be happy, Nemone.'

'I am not happy,' she replied; 'why should they be happy? Tell me that you love me, Tarzan, and I shall be happy!' Her voice was vibrant with appeal. For a moment she forgot that she was queen.

'A flower does not bloom in the seed,' he replied; 'it grows gradually, and thus love grows. The other, that bursts forth spontaneously from its own heat, is not love; it is passion. I have not known you either long or well, Nemone; that is my answer.'

She turned away and buried her face in her arms as she sank to the couch; he saw her shoulders shaken by sobs, and pity filled his heart. He drew nearer to console her, but he had no chance to speak before she wheeled upon him, her eyes flashing through tears. 'The girl, Doria, dies!' she cried. 'Xarator shall have her tomorrow!'

Tarzan shook his head sadly. 'You have asked me to love you,' he said. 'Do you expect me to love one who ruthlessly destroys my friends?'

'If I save them will you love me?' demanded Nemone.

'That is a question that I cannot answer. The best that I may say is that I may then respect and admire you; whereas, if you kill them without reason there can be no chance that I shall ever love you.'

She looked at him now out of dull, lowering eyes. 'What difference does it make?' she almost growled. 'No one loves me. Tomos wanted to be king, Erot wished riches and power, M'duze wished to exercise the majesty that she could never possess; if one of them felt any affection for me it was M'duze, and I have killed her.' She paused, a wild light flamed in her eyes. 'I hate them!' she screamed. 'I hate them all! I shall kill them! I shall kill everyone! I shall kill you!' Then, as swiftly, her mood changed. 'Oh, what am I saying?' she cried. She put her palms to her temples. 'My head! It hurts.'

'And my friends!' asked Tarzan; 'You will not harm them?'

'Perhaps not,' she replied indifferently, and then, as quickly changing again, 'The girl dies! If you intercede for her again her sufferings shall be greater; Xarator is merciful – more merciful than Nemone.'

'When will she die?' asked Tarzan.

'She will be sewn into hides tonight and carried to Xarator tomorrow. You shall accompany us; do you understand?'

The ape-man nodded. 'And my other friends?' he asked, 'They will be saved?'

'You shall come to me tomorrow night,' replied Nemone. 'We shall see then how you have decided to treat Nemone; then she will know how to treat your friends.'

18

Flaming Xarator

Her wrists and ankles bound, Doria, the daughter of Thudos, lay on a pile of skins in a room upon the third floor of the Temple of Thoos. Diffused moonlight entered the single window, relieving the darkness of the interior of her prison. She had seen her father seized and dragged away; she was in the power of one so ruthless that she knew she could expect no mercy and that either death or cruel disfigurement awaited her, yet she did not weep. Above her grief rose the pride of the noble blood of the house of Thudos, the courage of a line of warriors that stretched back into the forgotten ages; and she was brave.

She thought of Gemnon; and then the tears almost came, not for herself but for him because of the grief that would be his when he learned of her fate. She did not know that he too had fallen into the clutches of the enemies of her father.

Presently she heard the sound of footsteps approaching along the corridor, heard them stop before the door behind which she was locked. The door swung open and the room was illuminated by the light of a torch held in the hand of a man who entered and closed the door behind him.

The girl lying upon the pile of skins recognized Erot. She saw him place the blazing torch in a wall socket designed for the purpose and turn toward her.

'Ah, the lovely Doria!' he exclaimed. 'What ill fate has brought you here?'

'Doubtless the noble Erot could answer that question better than I,' she replied.

'Yes, I believe that he could; in fact I know it. It was I who caused you to be brought here; it was I who caused your father to be imprisoned; it was I who sent Gemnon to the same cell with the noble Thudos.'

'Gemnon imprisoned!' cried the girl.

'Yes, with many other conspirators against the throne. Behind his back they used to sneer at Erot because he was not a lion man; they will not sneer for long. Erot has answered them; now they know that Erot is more powerful than they.'

'And what is to be done with me?' asked the girl.

'Nemone has decreed Xarator for you,' replied Erot. 'You are even now lying upon the skins in which you are to be sewn. It is for that purpose that I am here. My good friend Tomos, the councillor, sent me to sew you into the bag; but first let us enjoy together your last night on earth. Be generous, and perhaps I can avert the doom that Nemone will doubtless decree for your father and your lover. She is permitting them to live through tomorrow at least, that they may witness your destruction, for thus runs the kindly mind of sweet Nemone.' He laughed harshly. 'The hell-cat! May the devil get her in the end!'

'You have not even the decency of gratitude,' said Doria contemptuously. 'The Queen has lavished favors upon you, given you power and riches; it is inconceivable that one can be so vile an ingrate as you.'

Erot laughed. 'Tomorrow you will be dead,' he said; 'so what difference does it make what you think of me? Tonight you shall give me love, though your heart be filled with hate. There is nothing in the world but love and hate, the two most pleasurable emotions that great Thoos has given us; let us enjoy them to the full!' He came and kneeled at her side and took her in his arms, covering her face and lips with kisses. She struggled to repulse him, but in her bonds she was helpless to protect herself.

He was panting with passion as he untied the thongs that secured her ankles. 'You are more beautiful than Nemone,' he cried huskily as he strained her to him.

A low growl sounded from the direction of the window. Erot raised his face from the soft neck of Doria and looked. He went ashy white as he leaped to his feet and fled toward the door upon the opposite side of the room, his craven heart pounding in terror.

It was early in the morning as the *cortège* formed that was to accompany the doomed Doria to Xarator, for Xarator lies sixteen miles from the city of Cathne in the mountains at the far end of the valley of Onthar; and the procession could move no faster than the lions drawing the chariot of the Queen would walk, which was not fast. Bred for generations for this purpose, the lions of Cathne had far greater endurance than forest-bred lions, yet it would be well into the night before it could be hoped to make the long journey to Xarator and return; therefore hundreds of slaves bore torches with which to light the homeward journey after night had fallen.

Nemone entered her chariot. She was wrapped in woolen robes and the skins of animals, for the morning air was still chill. At her side walked Tomos, nervous and ill at ease. He knew that M'duze was dead and wondered if he would be next. The Queen's manner was curt and abrupt, filling him with dread, for now there was no M'duze to protect him from the easily aroused wrath of Nemone.

'Where is Tarzan?' she demanded.

'I do not know, majesty,' replied Tomos. 'I have not seen him.'

She looked at him sharply. 'Don't lie to me!' she snapped. 'You do know where he is; and if any harm has befallen him, you go to the lion pit.'

'But, majesty,' cried Tomos, 'I know nothing about him. I have not seen him since we left the temple yesterday.'

'Produce him,' commanded Nemone sullenly. 'It grows late, and Nemone is not accustomed to wait upon any.'

'But, majesty—' began Tomos again.

'Produce him!' interrupted Nemone.

'But ...'

'Here he comes now!' exclaimed Nemone as Tarzan strode up the avenue toward her.

Tomos breathed a sigh of relief and wiped the perspiration from his forehead. He did not like Tarzan, yet in all his life he had never before been so glad to see anyone alive and well.

'You are late,' said Nemone as Tarzan stopped beside her chariot.

The Lord of the Jungle made no reply.

'We are not accustomed to being delayed,' she continued a little sharply.

'Perhaps if you placed me in the custody of Erot, as I suggested, he would deliver me on time in future.'

Nemone ignored this and turned to Tomos. 'We are ready,' she said.

At a word from the councillor a trumpeter at his side raised his instrument to his lips and sounded a call. Slowly the long procession began to move, and like a huge serpent crawled toward the Bridge of Gold. The citizens lining the avenue moved with it, men, women, and children. The women and children carried packages in which food was wrapped, the men bore arms. A journey to Xarator was an event; it took them the length of Onthar where wild lions roamed and where Athnean raiders might set upon them at any moment of the day or night, especially of the night; so the march took on something of the aspects of both a pageant and a military excursion.

Behind the golden chariot of the Queen rolled a second chariot on the floor of which lay a bundle sewn in the skins of lions. Chained to this chariot were Thudos and Gemnon. Following were a hundred chariots driven by nobles in gold and ivory, while other nobles on foot entirely surrounded the chariot of the Queen.

There were columns of marching warriors in the lead; and in the rear were the war lions of Cathne, the royal fighting lions of the Queen. Keepers held them on leashes of gold, and proud nobles of ancient families marched beside them – the lion-men of Cathne.

The barbaric splendor of the scene impressed even the ape-man who cared little for display, though he gave no outward sign of interest as he strode at the wheel of Nemone's chariot drawn by its eight great lions held in leash by twenty-four powerful blacks in tunics of red and gold.

The comments of the crowd came to the ears of Tarzan as they marched through the city and out across the Bridge of Gold onto the road that runs north through the Field of the Lions. 'There is the stranger who defeated Phobeg.' 'Yes, he has taken Erot's place in the council.' 'He is the Queen's favorite now.' 'Where is Erot?' 'I hope he is dead; this other is better.' 'He will soon be as bad; they all get alike when they get rich and powerful.' 'Had you heard the rumor that M'duze is dead?' 'She *is* dead; my cousin's husband is a palace guard. He told my cousin.' 'What is that?' 'M'duze is dead!' 'May Thoos be praised!' 'Have you heard? M'duze is dead!' and so it ran through the two streams of citizens that hemmed the royal pageant on either side, and always above the other comment rose the half exultant cry, 'M'duze is dead!'

Nemone appeared preoccupied; she sat staring straight ahead; if she heard the comments of her people she gave no sign. What was passing behind that beautiful mask that was her face? Chained to the chariot behind her were two enemies; others were in her prisons. A girl who dared vie with her in beauty lay insensible in a sack of skins jolting over the rough road in the dust of the Queen's chariot. Her Nemesis was dead. The man she loved walked at her side. Nemone should have been happy; but she was not.

The sun, climbing into the heavens, was bringing heat. Slaves carrying an umbrella over the Queen adjusted it to fend the hot rays from her; others waved lions' tails attached to the ends of long poles to and fro about her to drive the insects away; a gentle breeze carried the dust of the long column lazily toward the west.

Nemone sighed and turned to Tarzan. 'Why were you late?' she asked.

'Would it be strange that I overslept?' he asked. 'It was late when I left the palace, and there was no keeper to awaken me since you took Gemnon away.'

'Had you wished to see me again as badly as I wished to see you, you would not have been late.'

'I was as anxious to be here as you,' he replied.

'You have never seen Xarator?' she asked.

'No.'

'It is a holy mountain, created by Thoos for the enemies of the kings and queens of Cathne; in all the world there is nothing like it.'

'I am going to enjoy seeing it,' replied the ape-man grimly.

They were approaching a fork in the road. 'That road leading to the right runs through the Pass of the Warriors into the valley of Thenar,' she explained. 'Some day I shall send you on a raid to Thenar, and you shall bring me back the head of one of Athne's greatest warriors.'

Tarzan thought of Valthor and wondered if he had reached Athne in safety. He glanced back at Thudos and Gemnon. He had not spoken to them, but it was because of them that he was here. He might easily have escaped had he not determined to remain until he was certain that he could not aid these friends. Their case appeared hopeless, yet the ape-man had not given up hope.

At noon the procession stopped for lunch. The populace scattered about seeking the shade of the trees that dotted the plain and that had not already been selected by the Queen and the nobles. The lions were led into shade, where they lay down to rest. Warriors, always on the lookout for danger, stood guard about the temporary encampment. There was always danger on the Field of the Lions.

The halt was brief; in half an hour the cavalcade was on the march again. There was less talking now; silence and the great heat hung over the dusty column. The hills that bounded the valley upon the north were close, and soon they entered them, following a canyon upward to a winding mountain road that led into the hills above.

Presently the smell of sulphur fumes came plainly to the nostrils of the ape-man, and a little later the column turned the shoulder of a great mass of volcanic rock and came upon the edge of a huge crater. Far below, molten rock bubbled, sending up spurts of flame, geysers of steam, and columns of yellow smoke. The scene was impressive and awe-inspiring. Before Cathne, before Rome, before Athens, before Babylon, before Egypt Xarator had towered in lonely majesty above the lesser peaks. Beside that mighty cauldron queen and noble shrank to pitiful insignificance though perhaps there was but one in that great throng that realized this. Tarzan stood with folded arms and bent head gazing down into the seething inferno until the Queen touched him on the shoulder. 'What do you think of Xarator?' she asked.

He shook his head. 'There are some emotions,' he answered slowly, 'for which no words have yet been coined.'

'It was created by Thoos for the kings of Cathne,' she explained proudly.

Tarzan made no reply; perhaps he was thinking that here again the lexicographers had failed to furnish words adequate to the occasion.

On either side of the royal party the people crowded close to the edge of the crater that they might miss nothing of what was about to transpire. The children laughed and played, or teased their mothers for the food that was being saved for the evening meal upon the return journey to Cathne.

Tarzan saw Thudos and Gemnon standing beside the chariot in which lay the still form of the victim. Of what emotions were passing within their minds none appeared through the masks of stern pride that sat upon their countenances, yet Tarzan well knew the suffering of their torn and bleeding hearts. He had not spoken to them once this day, for he had not had an opportunity to speak to them except in the presence of others; and whatever he might have to say to them must be for their ears only. He had not given up the hope of helping them, but he could not conceive that open and unnecessary familiarity with them at this time might accomplish anything more than to still further arouse the suspicions of Nemone and increase the watchfulness of all their enemies.

If Gemnon or Thudos noticed the neglect of their former friend and guest they gave no sign, for neither gave him any greater attention as he walked beside the chariot of the Queen a few paces in advance of them than they gave to the lions drawing the car to which they were secured. Their thoughts were upon the poor, dumb thing jolting upon the hard planks that formed the floor of the springless chariot bearing it to its doom. Not once had they seen the girl move, not once had she uttered a sound; and they hoped that she was either insensible or dead, for thus would she be saved the anguish of these last moments and Nemone be robbed of the essence of her triumph.

The ceremony at Xarator, though it bore the authority of so-called justice, was of a semi-religious nature that required the presence and active participation of priests, two of whom lifted the sack containing the victim from the chariot and placed it at the edge of the crater at the feet of the Queen.

About it, then, gathered a dozen priests, some of whom carried musical instruments; and as they chanted in unison, the beating of their drums rose and fell while the wailing notes of their wind instruments floated out across the inferno of the seething pit like the plaint of a lost soul.

Thudos and Gemnon had been brought nearer the spot that Nemone might enjoy their agony to the full, for this was not only a part of their punishment but a considerable portion of the pleasure of the Queen.

She saw that they were giving no evidences of grief, thus robbing her of much of the satisfaction she had hoped to derive from the destruction of the daughter of one, the sweetheart of the other; and she was vexed. But she was not entirely discouraged; a new plan to further try their fortitude had occurred to her.

As two of the priests lifted the body from the ground and were about to hurl it into the crater, she stopped them with a curt command. 'Wait!' she cried. 'We would look upon the too great beauty of Doria, the daughter of Thudos, the traitor; we would permit her father and her lover to see her once again that they may better visualize her anguish and appreciate their own; that all may long remember that it is not well to conspire against Nemone. Cut the bag, and expose the body of the sacrifice!'

All eyes were upon the priest who drew his dagger and ripped open the bag along one loosely sewn seam. The eyes of Thudos and Gemnon were fixed upon the still figure outlined beneath the tawny skins of lions; beads of perspiration stood upon their foreheads; their jaws and their fists were clenched. The eyes of Tarzan turned from the activities of the priest to the face of the Queen; between narrowed lids, from beneath stern brows they watched her.

The priests, gathering the bag by one side, raised it and let the body roll out upon the ground where all could see it. There was a gasp of astonishment. Nemone cried out in a sudden fit of rage. The body was that of Erot, and he was dead!

19

The Queen's Quarry

After the first involuntary cries of surprise and rage an ominous silence fell upon the barbaric scene. Now all eyes were centered upon the Queen, whose ordinarily beautiful countenance was almost hideous from rage, a rage which, after her single angry cry, choked further utterance for the moment. But at length she found her voice and turned furiously upon Tomos.

'What means this?' she demanded, her voice now controlled and as cold as the steel in the sheath at her side.

Tomos, who was as much astounded as she, stammered as he trembled in his sandals of elephant hide. 'There are traitors even in the temple of Thoos!' he cried. 'I chose Erot to prepare the girl for the embraces of Xarator because I knew that his loyalty to his Queen would insure the work being well done. I did not know, O gracious Nemone, that this vile crime had been committed or that the body of Erot had been substituted for that of the daughter of Thudos until this very instant.'

With an expression of disgust the Queen commanded the priests to hurl the body of Erot into the crater, and as it was swallowed by the fiery pit she ordered an immediate return to Cathne.

In morose and gloomy silence she rode down the winding mountain trail and out onto the Field of the Lions, and often her eyes were upon the bronzed giant striding beside her chariot.

At last she broke her silence. 'Two of your enemies are gone now,' she said. 'I destroyed one; whom do you think destroyed the other?'

'Perhaps I did,' suggested Tarzan with a smile.

'I had been thinking of that possibility,' replied Nemone, but she did not smile.

'Whoever did it performed a service for Cathne.'

'Perhaps,' she half agreed, 'but it is not the killing of Erot that annoys me; it is the effrontery that dared interfere with the plans of Nemone. Whoever did it has spoiled for me what would otherwise have been a happy day; nor have they accomplished anything in the interest of Thudos or his daughter or Gemnon. I shall find the girl, and her passing will be far more bitter than that from which she was saved today; she cannot escape me. Thudos and Gemnon will also pay more heavily because someone dared flout the Queen.'

Tarzan shrugged his broad shoulders, but remained silent.

'Why do you not speak?' demanded the Queen.

'There is nothing to say,' he replied; 'I can only disagree with you without convincing you; I should only make you more angry than you are. I find no pleasure in making people angry or unhappy unless it is for some good purpose.'

'You mean that I do?' she demanded.

'Obviously.'

She shook her head angrily. 'Why do I abide you!' she exclaimed.

'Possibly as a counterirritant to relieve other irritations,' he suggested.

'Some day I shall lose my patience and have you thrown to the lions,' she ejaculated sharply. 'What will you do then?'

'Kill the lion,' replied the ape-man.

'Not the lion that I shall throw you to,' Nemone assured him.

The tedious journey back to Cathne ended at last, and with flaring torches lighting the way the Queen's *cortège* crossed the Bridge of Gold and entered the city. Here she immediately ordered a thorough search to be made for Doria.

Thudos and Gemnon, happy but mystified, were returned to their cell to await the new doom that Nemone would fix for them when the mood again seized her to be entertained. Tarzan was commanded to accompany Nemone into the palace and dine with her. Tomos had been dismissed with a curt injunction to find Doria or prepare for the worst!

Tarzan and the Queen ate alone in a small dining room attended only by slaves, and when the meal was over Nemone conducted him to the now all too familiar ivory room, where he was greeted by the angry growls of Belthar.

'Erot and M'duze are dead,' said the Queen, 'and I have sent Tomos away; there will be none to disturb us tonight.' Again her voice was soft, her manner gentle.

The ape-man sat with his eyes fixed upon her, studying her. It seemed incredible that this sweet and lovely woman could be the cruel tyrant that was Nemone, the Queen. Every soft line and curving contour spoke of femininity and gentleness and love; and in those glorious eyes smoldered a dreamy light that exercised a strange hypnotic influence upon him, gently pushing the memories of her ruthlessness into the oblivion of forgetfulness.

She leaned closer to him. 'Touch me, Tarzan,' she whispered softly.

Drawn by a power that is greater than the will of man he placed a hand upon hers. She breathed a deep sigh of contentment and leaned her cheek against his breast; her warm breath caressed his naked skin; the perfume of her hair was in his nostrils. She spoke, but so low that he could not catch her words.

'What did you say?' he asked.

'Take me in your arms,' she breathed faintly.

He passed a palm across his eyes as though to wipe away a mist, and in the moment of his hesitation she threw her arms about his neck and covered his face and lips with hot kisses.

'Love me, Tarzan!' she cried passionately. 'Love me! Love me! Love me!'

She slipped to the floor until she knelt at his feet. 'Oh, Thoos, god of gods!' she murmured, 'How I love you!'

The Lord of the Jungle looked down at her, at a queen grovelling at his feet, and the spell that had held him vanished; beneath the beautiful exterior he saw the crazed mind of a mad woman; he saw the creature that cast defenseless men to wild beasts, that disfigured or destroyed women who might be more beautiful than she; and all that was fine in him revolted.

With a half growl he arose to his feet, and as he did so Nemone slipped to the floor and lay there silent and rigid. He started toward the door, and then turned and coming back lifted her to the couch. As he did so, Belthar strained at his chains and the chamber shook to his roars.

Nemone opened her eyes and for a moment gazed questioningly at the man above her; then she seemed to realize what had happened, and the mad, cruel light of rage blazed in her eyes. Leaping to her feet she stood trembling before him.

'You refuse my love!' she screamed. 'You spurn me? You dare spurn the love of a Queen! Thoos! And I knelt at your feet!' She sprang to one side of the room where a metal gong depended from the ceiling and seizing the striker smote it three times. The brazen notes rang through the chamber mingling with the roars of the infuriated lion.

Tarzan stood watching her; she seemed wholly irresponsible, quite mad. It would be useless to attempt to reason with her. He moved slowly toward the door; but before he reached it it swung open, and a score of warriors accompanied by two nobles rushed in.

'Take this man!' ordered Nemone. 'Throw him into the cell with the other enemies of the Queen!'

Tarzan was unarmed. He had worn only a sword when he entered the ivory room and that he had unbuckled and laid upon a stand near the doorway. There were twenty spears levelled at him, twenty spears that entirely encircled him. With a shrug he surrendered. It was that or death. In prison he might find the means to escape; at least he would see Gemnon again, and there was something that he very much wished to tell Gemnon and Thudos.

As the soldiers conducted him from the room and the door closed behind them, Nemone threw herself among the cushions of her couch, her body wracked by choking sobs. The great lion grumbled in the dusky corner of the room. Suddenly Nemone sat erect and her eyes blazed into the blazing eyes of the lion. For a moment she sat there thus, and then she arose and a peal of maniacal laughter broke from her lips. Still laughing, she crossed the room and passed through the doorway that led to her bedchamber.

Thudos and Gemnon sitting in their cell heard the tramp of marching men approaching the prison in which they were confined. 'Evidently Nemone cannot wait until tomorrow,' said Thudos.

'You think she is sending for us now?' asked Gemnon.

'What else?' demanded the older man. 'The lion pit can be illuminated.'

As they waited and listened the steps stopped outside their cell, the door was pushed open, and a man entered. The warriors had carried no torches and neither Thudos nor Gemnon could discern the features of the newcomer, though in the diffused light that filtered in through the small window and the aperture in the door they noted that he was a large man.

None of them spoke until the guard had departed out of earshot. 'Greetings, Thudos and Gemnon!' exclaimed the new prisoner cheerily.

'Tarzan!' exclaimed Gemnon.

'None other,' admitted the ape-man.

'What brings you here?' demanded Thudos.

'Twenty warriors and the whim of a woman, an insane woman,' replied Tarzan.

'So you have fallen from favor!' exclaimed Gemnon. 'I am sorry.'

'It was inevitable,' said Tarzan.

'And what will your punishment be?'

'I do not know, but I suspect that it will be quite sufficient. However, that is something that need not concern any of us until it happens; maybe it won't happen.'

'There is no room in the dungeon of Nemone for optimism,' remarked Thudos with a grim laugh.

'Perhaps not,' agreed the ape-man, 'but I shall continue to indulge myself. Doubtless Doria felt hopeless in her prison in the temple last night, yet she escaped Xarator.'

'That is a miracle that I cannot fathom,' said Gemnon.

'It was quite simple,' Tarzan assured him. 'A loyal friend, whose identity you may guess, came and told me that she was a prisoner in the temple. I went at once to find her. Fortunately the trees of Cathne are old and large and numerous; one of them grows close to the rear of the temple, its branches almost brushing the window of the room in which Doria was confined. When I arrived there, I found Erot annoying Doria; I also found the sack in which he had purposed tying her for the journey to Xarator. What was simpler? I let Erot take the ride that had been planned for Doria.'

'You saved her! Where is she?' cried Thudos, his voice breaking in the first emotion he had displayed since he had learned of his daughter's plight.

'Come close,' cautioned Tarzan, 'lest the walls themselves be enemies.' The two men pressed close to the speaker who continued in a low whisper, 'Do you recall, Gemnon, that when we were at the gold mine I spoke aside to one of the slaves there?'

'I believe that I did notice it,' replied Gemnon; 'I thought you were asking questions about the operation of the mine.'

'No; I was delivering a message from his brother, and so grateful was he that he begged that he be permitted to serve me if the opportunity arose. It was to arise much sooner than either of us could have expected; and so, when it was necessary to find a hiding place for Doria, I thought immediately of the isolated hut of Niaka, the headman of the black slaves at the gold mine.

'She is there now, and the man will protect her as long as is necessary. He has promised me that if he hears nothing from me for half a moon he is to understand that none of us three can come to her aid, and that then he will get word to the faithful slaves of the house of Thudos. He says that that will be difficult but not impossible.'

'Doria safe!' whispered Gemnon. 'Thudos and I may now die happy.'

Thudos extended his hand through the darkness and laid it on the ape-man's shoulder. 'There is no way in which I can express my gratitude,' he said, 'for there are no words in which to couch it.'

For some time the three men sat in silence that was broken at last by Gemnon. 'How did it happen that you knew the brother of a slave well enough to carry a message from one to the other?' he asked, a note of puzzlement in his voice.

'Do you recall Xerstle's grand hunt?' asked Tarzan with a laugh.

'Of course, but what has that to do with it?' demanded Gemnon.

'Do you remember the quarry, the man we saw on the slave block in the market place?'

'Yes.'

'He is the brother of Niaka,' explained Tarzan.

'But you never had an opportunity to speak to him,' objected the young noble.

'Oh, but I did. It was I who helped him escape. That was why his brother was so grateful to me.'

'I still do not understand,' said Gemnon.

'There is probably much connected with Xerstle's grand hunt that you do not understand,' suggested Tarzan. 'In the first place, the purpose of the hunt was, primarily, to destroy me rather than the nominal quarry; the scheme was probably hatched between Xerstle and Erot. In the second place, I didn't approve of the ethics of the hunters; the poor devil they were chasing had no chance. I went ahead, therefore, through the trees until I overtook the black; then I carried him for a mile to throw the lions off the scent. You know how well the plan succeeded.

'When I came back and we laid the wager, that gave Xerstle and Pindes the opening they wished but which they would have found by some other means before the day was over; so Pindes took me with him; and after we were far enough away from you he suggested that we separate, whereupon he loosed his lion upon me.'

'And it was you who killed the lion?'

'I should have much preferred to have killed Pindes and Xerstle, but I felt that the time was not yet ripe. Now, perhaps, I shall never have the opportunity to kill them,' he added regretfully.

'Now I am doubly sorry that I must die,' said Gemnon.

'Why more so than before?' asked Thudos.

'I shall never have the opportunity to tell the story of Xerstle's grand hunt,' he explained. 'What a story *that* would make!'

The morning dawned bright and beautiful, just as though there was no misery or sorrow or cruelty in the world; but it did not change matters at all, other than to make the cell in which the three men were confined uncomfortably warm as the day progressed.

Shortly after noon a guard came and took Tarzan away. All three of the prisoners were acquainted with the officer who commanded it, a decent fellow who spoke sympathetically to them.

'Is he coming back?' asked Thudos, nodding toward Tarzan.

The officer shook his head. 'No; the Queen hunts today.'

Thudos and Gemnon pressed the ape-man's shoulder. No word was spoken, but that wordless farewell was more eloquent than words. They saw him go out, saw the door close behind him; but neither spoke, and so they sat for a long hour in silence.

In the guardroom, to which he had been conducted from his cell, Tarzan was heavily chained; a golden collar was placed about his neck, and a chain reaching from each side of it was held in the hands of a warrior.

'Why all the precautions?' demanded the ape-man.

'It is merely a custom,' explained the officer; 'it is always thus that the Queen's quarry is led to the Field of the Lions.'

Once again Tarzan of the Apes walked near the chariot of the Queen of Cathne; but this time he walked behind it, a chained prisoner between two stalwart warriors and surrounded by a score of others. Once again he crossed the Bridge of Gold out onto the Field of the Lions in the valley of Onthar.

The procession did not go far, scarcely more than a mile from the city. A great concourse of people accompanied it, for Nemone had invited the entire city to witness the degradation and death of the man who had spurned her love. She was about to be avenged, but she was not happy. With scowling brows she sat brooding in her chariot as it stopped at last at the point she had selected for the start of the hunt. Not once had she turned to look at the chained man behind her. Perhaps she had been certain that she would have been rewarded by no indication of terror in his mien, or perhaps she did not dare to look at the man she had loved for fear that her determination might weaken.

But now that the time had come she cast her indecision aside, if any had been annoying her, and ordered the guard to fetch the prisoner to her. She was looking straight ahead as the ape-man halted by the wheel of her chariot.

'Send all away except the two warriors who hold him,' commanded Nemone.

'You may send them, too, if you wish,' said Tarzan; 'I give you my word not to harm you or try to escape while they are away.'

Nemone, still looking straight ahead, was silent for a moment; then, 'You may all go; I would speak with the prisoner alone.'

When the guard had departed a number of paces, the Queen turned her eyes toward Tarzan and found his smiling into her own. 'You are going to be very happy, Nemone,' he said in an easy, friendly voice.

'What do you mean?' she asked. 'How am I going to be happy?'

'You are going to see me die; that is if the lion catches me,' he laughed, 'and you like to see people die.'

'You think that will give me pleasure? Well, I thought so myself; but now I am wondering if it will. I never get quite the pleasure from death that I anticipate I shall; nothing in life is ever what I hope for.'

'Possibly you don't hope for the right things,' he suggested. 'Did you ever try hoping for something that would bring pleasure and happiness to someone beside yourself?'

'Why should I?' she asked. 'I hope for my own happiness; let others do the same. I strive for my own happiness—'

'And never have any,' interrupted the ape-man good-naturedly.

'Probably I should have less if I strove only for the happiness of others,' she insisted.

'There are people like that,' he assented; 'perhaps you are one of them; so you might as well go on striving for happiness in your own way. Of course you won't get it, but you will at least have the pleasures of anticipation, and that is something.'

'I think I know myself and my own affairs well enough to determine for myself how to conduct my life,' she said with a note of asperity in her voice.

Tarzan shrugged. 'It was not in my thoughts to interfere,' he said. 'If you are determined to kill me and are quite sure that you will derive pleasure from it, why, I should be the last in the world to suggest that you abandon the idea.'

'You do not amuse me,' said Nemone haughtily; 'I do not care for irony that is aimed at myself.' She turned fiercely on him. 'Men have died for less!' she cried, and the Lord of the Jungle laughed in her face.

'How many times?' he asked.

'A moment ago,' said Nemone, 'I was beginning to regret the thing that is about to happen. Had you been different, had you sought to conciliate me, I might have relented and returned you to favor; but you do everything to antagonize me. You affront me, you insult me, you laugh at me.' Her voice was rising, a barometric indication, Tarzan had learned, of her mental state.

'And yet, Nemone, I am drawn to you,' admitted the ape-man. 'I cannot understand it. You are attracted to me in spite of wounded pride and lacerated dignity; and I to you though I hold in contempt your principles, your ideals, and your methods. It is strange, isn't it?'

The woman nodded. 'It is strange,' she mused. 'I never loved one as I loved you, and yet I am going to kill you notwithstanding the fact that I still love you.'

'And you will go on killing people and being unhappy until it is your turn to be killed,' he said sadly.

She shuddered. 'Killed!' she repeated. 'Yes, they are all killed, the kings and queens of Cathne; but it is not my turn yet. While Belthar lives Nemone lives.' She was silent for a moment. 'You may live too, Tarzan; there is something that I would rather see you do than see you die.' She paused as though expecting him to ask her what it was, but he manifested no interest, and she continued, 'Last night I knelt at your feet and begged for your love. Kneel here, before my people, kneel at my feet and beg for mercy, and you may live.'

'Bring on your lion,' said Tarzan; 'his mercy might be kinder than Nemone's.'

'You refuse?' she demanded angrily.

'You would kill me eventually,' he replied; 'there is a chance that the lion may not be able to.'

'Not a chance!' she said. 'Have you seen the lion?'

'No.'

She turned and called a noble, 'Have the hunting lion brought to scent the quarry!'

Behind them there was a scattering of troops and nobles as they made an avenue for the hunting lion and his keepers, and along the avenue Tarzan saw a great lion straining at the golden leashes to which eight men clung. Growling and roaring, the beast sprang from side to side in an effort to seize a keeper or lay hold upon one of the warriors or nobles that lined the way; so that it was all that four stalwart men on either side of him could do to prevent his accomplishing his design.

A flaming-eyed devil, he came toward the chariot of Nemone, but he was still afar when Tarzan saw the tuft of white hair in the center of his mane between his ears. It was Belthar!

Nemone was eyeing the man at her side as a cat might eye a mouse, but though the lion was close now she saw no change in the expression on Tarzan's face. 'Do you not recognize him?' she demanded.

'Of course I do,' he replied.

'And you are not afraid?'

'Of what?' he asked, looking at her wonderingly.

She stamped her foot in anger, thinking that he was trying to rob her of the satisfaction of witnessing his terror; for how could she know that Tarzan of the Apes could not understand the meaning of *fear?* 'Prepare for the grand hunt!' she commanded, turning to a noble standing with the guard that had waited just out of earshot of her conversation with the quarry.

The warriors who had held Tarzan in leash ran forward and picked up the golden chains that were attached to the golden collar about his neck, the guard took posts about the chariot of the Queen, and Tarzan was led a few yards in advance of it. Then the keepers brought Belthar closer to him, holding him just out of reach but only with difficulty, for when the irascible beast recognized the ape-man he flew into a frenzy of rage that taxed the eight men to hold him at all.

Warriors were deploying on either side of a wide lane leading toward the north from the chariot of Nemone. In solid ranks they formed on either side of this avenue, facing toward its center, their spear points dropped to form a wall of steel against the lion should he desert the chase and break to right or left. Behind them, craning necks to see above the shoulders of the fighting men, the populace pushed and shoved for advantageous points from which to view the spectacle.

A noble approached Tarzan. He was Phordos, the father of Gemnon, hereditary captain of the hunt for the rulers of Cathne. He came quite close to Tarzan and spoke to him in a low whisper, 'I am sorry that I must have a part in this,' he said, 'but my office requires it,' and then aloud, 'In the name of the Queen, silence! These are the rules of the grand hunt of Nemone, Queen of Cathne: The quarry shall move north down the center of the lane of warriors; when he has proceeded a hundred paces the keepers shall unleash the hunting lion, Belthar; let no man distract the lion from the chase or aid the quarry, under penalty of death. When the lion has killed and while he is feeding let the keepers, guarded by warriors, retake him.'

Then he turned to Tarzan. 'You will run straight north until Belthar overtakes you,' he said.

'What if I elude him and escape?' demanded the ape-man. 'Shall I have my freedom then?'

Phordos shook his head sadly. 'You will not escape him,' he said. Then he turned toward the Queen and knelt. 'All is in readiness, your majesty. Shall the hunt commence?'

Nemone looked quickly about her. She saw that the guards were so disposed that she might be protected in the event that the lion turned back; she saw that slaves from her stables carried great nets with which Belthar was to be retaken after the hunt. She knew and they knew that not all of them would return alive to Cathne, but that would but add to the interest and excitement of the day. She nodded her head to Phordos. 'Let the lion scent the quarry once more; then the hunt may start,' she directed.

The keepers let Belthar move a little closer to the ape-man, but not before they had enlisted the aid of a dozen additional men to prevent his dragging the original eight until he was within reach of the quarry.

Nemone leaned forward eagerly, her eyes upon the savage beast that was the pride of her stable; the light of insanity gleamed in them now. 'It is enough!' she cried. 'Belthar knows him now, nor will he ever leave his trail until he has tracked him down and killed him, until he has reaped his reward and filled his belly with the flesh of his kill, for there is no better hunting lion in all Cathne than Belthar.'

Along the gauntlet of warriors that the quarry and the lion were to run spears had been stuck into the ground at intervals, and floating from the hafts of these were different colored pennons. The populace, the nobles, and the Queen had laid wagers upon the color of the pennon nearest which they thought the kill would occur, and they were still betting when Phordos slipped the collar from Tarzan's neck.

In a hollow near the river that runs past Cathne a lion lay asleep in dense brush, a mighty beast with a yellow coat and a great black mane. Strange sounds coming to him from the plain disturbed him, and he rumbled complainingly in his throat; but as yet he seemed only half awake. His eyes were closed, but his half wakefulness was only seeming. Numa was awake, but he wanted to sleep and was angry with the men-things that were disturbing him. They were not too close as yet; but he knew that if they came closer he would have to get up and investigate, and that he did not want to do; he felt very lazy.

Out on the field Tarzan was striding along the spear-bound lane. He counted his steps, knowing that at the hundredth Belthar would be loosed upon him. The ape-man had a plan. Across the river to the east was the forest in which he had hunted with Xerstle and Pindes and Gemnon; could he reach it, he would be safe. No lion or no man could hope ever to overtake the Lord of the Jungle once he swung to the branches of those trees.

But could he reach the wood before Belthar overtook him? Tarzan was swift, but there are few creatures as swift as Numa at the height of his charge. With a start of a hundred paces, the ape-man felt that he might outdistance an ordinary lion; but Belthar was no ordinary lion. He was the result of generations of breeding that had resulted in the power of sustaining great speed for a much longer time than would have been possible for a wild lion, and of all the hunting lions of Cathne Belthar was the best.

At the hundredth pace Tarzan leaped forward at top speed. Behind him he heard the frenzied roar of the hunting lion as his leashes were slipped and, mingling with it, the roar of the crowd.

Smoothly and low ran Belthar, the hunting lion, swiftly closing up the distance that separated him from the quarry. He looked neither to right nor to left; his fierce, blazing eyes remained fixed upon the fleeing man ahead.

Behind him rolled the chariot of the Queen, the drivers goading their lions to greater speed that Nemone might be in at the kill, yet Belthar outdistanced them as though they were rooted to the ground. The Queen, in her excitement, was standing erect, screaming encouragement to Belthar. Her eyes blazed scarcely less fiercely than those of the savage carnivore she cheered on; her bosoms rose and fell to her excited breathing; her heart raced with the racing death ahead. The Queen of Cathne was consumed by the passion of love turned to hate.

The nobles, the warriors, and the crowd were streaming after the chariot of the Queen. Belthar was gaining on the quarry when Tarzan turned suddenly to the east toward the river after he had passed the end of the gauntlet that had held him to a straight path at the beginning of his flight.

A scream of rage burst from the lips of Nemone as she saw and realized the purpose of the quarry. A sullen roar rose from the pursuing crowd. They had not thought that the hunted man had a chance, but now they understood that he might yet reach the river and the forest. This, of course, did not mean to them he would then escape, for they well knew that Belthar would pursue him across the river; what they feared was that they might be robbed of the thrills of witnessing the kill.

But presently their anger turned to relief as they saw that Belthar was gaining on the man so rapidly that there was no chance that the latter might reach the river before he was overhauled and dragged down.

Tarzan, too, glancing back over a bronzed shoulder, realized that the end was near. The river was still two hundred yards away and the lion, steadily gaining on him, but fifty.

Then the ape-man turned and waited. He stood at ease, his arms hanging at his side; but he was alert and ready. He knew precisely what Belthar would do, and he knew what he would do. No amount of training would have changed the lion's instinctive method of attack; he would rush at Tarzan, rear upon his hind feet when close, seize him with his taloned paws and drive his great fangs through his head or neck or shoulder; then he would drag him down and devour him.

But Tarzan had met the charge of lions before. It would not be quite so easy for Belthar as Belthar and the screaming audience believed, yet the ape-man guessed that, without a knife, he could do no more than delay the inevitable. He would die fighting, however; and now, as Belthar charged growling upon him, he crouched slightly and answered the roaring challenge of the carnivore with a roar as savage as the lion's.

Suddenly he detected a new note in the voice of the crowd, a note of surprise and consternation. Belthar was almost upon him as a tawny body streaked past the ape-man, brushing his leg as it came from behind him; and as Belthar rose upon his hind feet fell upon him, a fury of talons and gleaming fangs, a great lion with a golden coat and a black mane – a mighty engine of rage and destruction.

Roaring and growling, the two great beasts rolled upon the ground as they tore at one another with teeth and claws while the astounded ape-man looked on and the chariot of the Queen approached, and the breathless crowd pressed forward.

The strange lion was larger than Belthar and more powerful, a giant of a lion in the full prime of his strength and ferocity; and he fought as one inspired by all the demons of Hell. Presently Belthar gave him an opening; and his great jaws closed upon the throat of the hunting lion of Nemone, jaws that drove mighty fangs through the thick mane of his adversary, through hide and flesh deep into the jugular of Belthar; then he braced his feet and shook Belthar as a cat might shake a mouse, breaking his neck.

Dropping the carcass to the ground, the victor faced the astonished Cathneans with snarling face; then he slowly backed to where the ape-man stood and stopped beside him, and Tarzan laid his hand upon the black mane of Jad-bal-ja, the Golden Lion.

For a long moment there was unbroken silence as the two faced the enemies of the Lord of the Jungle, and the awed Cathneans only stood and stared; then a woman's voice rose in a weird scream. It was Nemone. Slowly she stepped from her golden car and amidst utter silence walked toward the carcass of the dead Belthar while her people watched her, motionless and wondering.

She stopped with her sandalled feet touching the bloody mane of the hunting lion and gazed down upon the dead carnivore. She might have been in silent prayer for the minute that she stood there; then she raised her head suddenly and looked about her. There was a wild gleam in her eyes and she was very white, white as the ivory ornament in the hollow of her throat.

'Belthar is dead!' she screamed, and whipping her dagger from its sheath drove its glittering point deep into her own heart. Without a sound she sank to her knees and toppled forward across the body of the dead Belthar.

As the moon rose, Tarzan placed a final rock upon a mound of earth beside the river that runs to Cathne through the valley of Onthar.

The warriors and the nobles and the people had followed Phordos to the city to empty the dungeons of Nemone and proclaim Alextar King, leaving their dead Queen lying at the edge of the Field of the Lions with the dead Belthar.

The human service they had neglected the beast-man had performed, and now beneath the soft radiance of an African moon he stood with bowed head beside the grave of a woman who had found happiness at last.

TARZAN AND THE LION MAN

CHAPTER ONE

In Conference

Mr Milton Smith, Executive Vice President in Charge of Production, was in conference. A half dozen men lounged comfortably in deep, soft chairs and divans about his large, well-appointed office in the B.O. studio. Mr Smith had a chair behind a big desk, but he seldom occupied it. He was an imaginative, dramatic, dynamic person. He required freedom and space in which to express himself. His large chair was too small; so he paced about the office more often than he occupied his chair, and his hands interpreted his thoughts quite as fluently as did his tongue.

'It's bound to be a knock-out,' he assured his listeners; 'no synthetic jungle, no faked sound effects, no toothless old lions that every picture fan in the U.S. knows by their first names. No, sir! This will be the real thing.'

A secretary entered the room and closed the door behind her. 'Mr Orman is here,' she said.

'Good! Ask him to come in, please.' Mr Smith rubbed his palms together and turned to the others. 'Thinking of Orman was nothing less than an inspiration,' he exclaimed. 'He's just the man to make this picture.'

'Just another of your inspirations, Chief,' remarked one of the men. 'They've got to hand it to you.'

Another, sitting next to the speaker, leaned closer to him. 'I thought you suggested Orman the other day,' he whispered.

'I did,' said the first man out of the corner of his mouth.

Again the door opened, and the secretary ushered in a stocky, bronzed man who was greeted familiarly by all in the room. Smith advanced and shook hands with him.

'Glad to see you, Tom,' he said. 'Haven't seen you since you got back from Borneo. Great stuff you got down there. But I've got something bigger still on the fire for you. You know the clean-up Superlative Pictures made with their last jungle picture?'

'How could I help it; it's all I've heard since I got back. Now I suppose everybody's goin' to make jungle pictures.'

'Well, there are jungle pictures and jungle pictures. We're going to make a real one. Every scene in that Superlative picture was shot inside a radius of twenty-five miles from Hollywood except a few African stock shots, and the sound effects – lousy!' Smith grimaced his contempt.

'And where are we goin' to shoot?' inquired Orman; 'Fifty miles from Hollywood?'

'No, sir! We're goin' to send a company right to the heart of Africa, right to the – ah – er – what's the name of that forest, Joe?'

'The Ituri Forest.'

'Yes, right to the Ituri Forest with sound equipment and everything. Think of it, Tom! You get the real stuff, the real natives, the jungle, the animals, the sounds. You "shoot" a giraffe, and at the same time you record the actual sound of his voice.'

'You won't need much sound equipment for that, Milt.'

'Why?'

'Giraffes don't make any sounds; they're supposed not to have any vocal organs.'

'Well, what of it? That was just an illustration. But take the other animals for instance; lions, elephants, tigers – Joe's written in a great tiger sequence. It's goin' to yank 'em right out of their seats.'

'There ain't any tigers in Africa, Milt,' explained the director.

'Who says there ain't?'

'I do,' replied Orman, grinning.

'How about it, Joe?' Smith turned toward the scenarist.

'Well, Chief, you said you wanted a tiger sequence.'

'Oh, what's the difference? We'll make it a crocodile sequence.'

'And you want me to direct the picture?' asked Orman.

'Yes, and it will make you famous.'

'I don't know about that, but I'm game – I ain't ever been to Africa. Is it feasible to get sound trucks into Central Africa?'

'We're just having a conference to discuss the whole matter,' replied Smith. 'We've asked Major White to sit in. I guess you men haven't met – Mr Orman, Major White,' and as the two men shook hands Smith continued. 'The major's a famous big game hunter, knows Africa like a book. He's to be technical advisor and go along with you.'

'What do you think, Major, about our being able to get sound trucks into the Ituri Forest?' asked Orman.

'What'll they weigh? I doubt that you can get anything across Africa that weighs over a ton and a half.'

'Ouch!' exclaimed Clarence Noice, the sound director. 'Our sound trucks weigh seven tons, and we're planning on taking two of them.'

'It just can't be done,' said the major.

'And how about the generator truck?' demanded Noice. 'It weighs nine tons.'

The major threw up his hands. 'Really, gentlemen, it's preposterous.'

'Can you do it, Tom?' demanded Smith, and without waiting for a reply, 'You've got to do it.'

'Sure I'll do it – if you want to foot the bills.'

'Good!' exclaimed Smith. 'Now that's settled let me tell you something about the story. Joe's written a great story – it's goin' to be a knock-out. You see this fellow's born in the jungle and brought up by a lioness. He pals around with the lions all his life – doesn't know any other friends. The lion is king of beasts; when the boy grows up he's king of the lions; so he bosses the whole menagerie. See? Big shot of the jungle.'

'Sounds familiar,' commented Orman.

'And then the girl comes in, and here's a great shot! She doesn't know anyone's around, and she's bathing in a jungle pool. Along comes the Lion Man. He ain't ever seen a woman before. Can't you see the possibilities, Tom? It's goin' to knock 'em cold.' Smith was walking around the room, acting out the scene. He was the girl bathing in the pool in one corner of the room, and then he went to the opposite corner and was the Lion Man. 'Great, isn't it?' he demanded. 'You've got to hand it to Joe.'

'Joe always was an original guy,' said Orman. 'Say, who you got to play this Lion Man that's goin' to pal around with the lions? I hope he's got the guts.'

'Best ever, a regular find. He's got a physique that's goin' to have all the girls goofy.'

'Yes, them and their grandmothers,' offered another conferee.

'Who is he?'

'He's the world's champion marathoner.'

'Marathon dancer?'

'No, marathon runner.'

'If I was playin' that part I'd rather be a sprinter than a distance runner. What's his name?'

'Stanley Obroski.'

'Stanley Obroski? Never heard of him.'

'Well, he's famous nevertheless; and wait till you see him! He's sure got "It," and I don't mean maybe.'

'Can he act?' asked Orman.

'He don't have to act, but he looks great stripped – I'll run his tests for you.'

'Who else is in the cast?'

'The Madison's cast for lead opposite Obroski and—'

'M-m-m, Naomi's plenty hot at 34 north; she'll probably melt at the Equator.'

'And Gordon Z. Marcus goes along as her father; he's a white trader.'

'Think Marcus can stand it? He's getting along in years.'

'Oh, he's r'arin' to go. Major White, here, is taking the part of a white hunter.'

'I'm afraid,' remarked the major, 'that as an actor I'll prove to be an excellent hunter.'

'Oh, all you got to do is act natural. Don't worry.'

'No, let the director worry,' said the scenarist; 'that's what he's paid for.'

'And rewritin' bum continuity,' retorted Orman. 'But say, Milt, gettin' back to Naomi. She's great in cabaret scenes and flaming youth pictures, but when it comes to steppin' out with lions and elephants – I don't know.'

'We're sendin' Rhonda Terry along to double for her.'

'Good! Rhonda'd go up and bite a lion on the wrist if a director told her to; and she does look a lot like the Madison, come to think of it.'

'Which is flatterin' the Madison, if anyone asks me,' commented the scenarist.

'Which no one did,' retorted Smith.

'And again, if anyone asks me,' continued Joe, 'Rhonda can act circles all around Madison. How some of these punks get where they are beats me.'

'And you hangin' around studios for the last ten years!' scoffed Orman. 'You must be dumb.'

'He wouldn't be an author if he wasn't,' gibed another conferee.

'Well,' asked Orman, 'who else am I takin'? Who's my chief cameraman?'

'Bill West.'

'Fine.'

'What with your staff, the cast, and drivers you'll have between thirty-five and forty whites. Besides the generator truck and the two sound trucks, you'll have twenty five-ton trucks and five passenger cars. We're picking technicians and mechanics who can drive trucks so as to cut down the size of the company as much as possible. I'm sorry you weren't in town to pick your own company, but we had to rush things. Everyone's signed up but the assistant director. You can take anyone along you please.'

'When do we leave?'

'In about ten days.'

'It's a great life,' sighed Orman. 'Six months in Borneo, ten days in Hollywood, and then another six months in Africa! You guys give a fellow just about time to get a shave between trips.'

'Between drinks, did you say?' inquired Joe.

'Between drinks!' offered another. 'There isn't any between drinks in Tom's young life.'

CHAPTER TWO
Mud

Sheykh Ab el-Ghrennem and his swarthy followers sat in silence on their ponies and watched the mad Nasara sweating and cursing as they urged on two hundred blacks in an effort to drag a nine-ton generator truck through the muddy bottom of a small stream.

Nearby, Jerrold Baine leaned against the door of a muddy touring car in conversation with the two girls who occupied the back seat.

'How you feeling, Naomi?' he inquired.

'Rotten.'

'Touch of fever again?'

'Nothing but since we left Jinja. I wish I was back in Hollywood; but I won't ever see Hollywood again. I'm going to die here.'

'Aw, shucks! You're just blue. You'll be all right.'

'She had a dream last night,' said the other girl. 'Naomi believes in dreams.'

'Shut up,' snapped Miss Madison.

Rhonda Terry nodded. 'I guess I'm just lucky.'

'You'd better touch wood,' advised the Madison; then she added, 'Rhonda's physical, purely physical. No one knows what we artistes suffer, with our high-strung, complex, nervous organizations.'

'Better be a happy cow than a miserable artiste,' laughed Rhonda.

'Beside that, Rhonda gets all the breaks,' complained Naomi. 'Yesterday they shoot the first scene in which I appear, and where was I? Flat on my back with an attack of fever, and Rhonda has to double for me – even in the close-ups.'

'It's a good thing you look so much alike,' said Baine. 'Why, knowing you both as well as I do, I can scarcely tell you apart.'

'That's the trouble,' grumbled Naomi. 'People'll see her and think it's me.'

'Well, what of it?' demanded Rhonda. 'You'll get the credit.'

'Credit!' exclaimed Naomi. 'Why, my dear, it will ruin my reputation. You are a sweet girl and all that, Rhonda; but remember, I am Naomi Madison. My public expects superb acting. They will be disappointed, and they will blame me.'

Rhonda laughed good-naturedly. 'I'll do my best not to entirely ruin your reputation, Naomi,' she promised.

'Oh, it isn't your fault,' exclaimed the other. 'I don't blame you. One is born with the divine afflatus, or one is not. That is all there is to it. It is no more your fault that you can't act than it is the fault of that sheik over there that he was not born a white man.'

'What a disillusionment that sheik was!' exclaimed Rhonda.

'How so?' asked Baine.

'When I was a little girl I saw Rudolph Valentino on the screen; and, ah, brothers, sheiks was sheiks in them days!'

'This bird sure doesn't look much like Valentino,' agreed Baine.

'Imagine being carried off into the desert by that bunch of whiskers and dirt! And here I've just been waiting all these years to be carried off.'

'I'll speak to Bill about it,' said Baine.

The girl sniffed. 'Bill West's a good cameraman, but he's no sheik. He's just about as romantic as his camera.'

'He's a swell guy,' insisted Baine.

'Of course he is; I'm crazy about him. He'd make a great brother.'

'How much longer we got to sit here?' demanded Naomi, peevishly.

'Until they get the generator truck and twenty-two other trucks through that mud hole.'

'I don't see why we can't go on. I don't see why we have to sit here and fight flies and bugs.'

'We might as well fight 'em here as somewhere else,' said Rhonda.

'Orman's afraid to separate the safari,' explained Baine. 'This is a bad piece of country. He was warned against bringing the company here. The natives never have been completely subdued, and they've been acting up lately.'

They were silent for a while, brushing away insects and watching the heavy truck being dragged slowly up the muddy bank. The ponies of the Arabs stood switching their tails and biting at the stinging pests that constantly annoyed them.

Sheykh Ab el-Ghrennem spoke to one at his side, a swarthy man with evil eyes. 'Which of the *benat*, Atewy, is she who holds the secret of the valley of diamonds?'

'*Billah!*' exclaimed Atewy, spitting. 'They are as alike as two pieces of *jella*. I cannot be sure which is which.'

'But one of them hath the paper? You are sure?'

'Yes. The old *Nasrany*, who is the father of one of them, had it; but she took it from him. The young man leaning against that invention of *Sheytan*, talking to them now, plotted to take the life of the old man that he might steal the paper; but the girl, his daughter, learned of the plot and took the paper herself. The old man and the young man both believe that the paper is lost.'

'But the *bint* talks to the young man who would have killed her father,' said the sheykh. 'She seems friendly with him. I do not understand these Christian dogs.'

'Nor I,' admitted Atewy. 'They are all mad. They quarrel and fight, and then immediately they sit down together, laughing and talking. They do things in great secrecy while everyone is looking on. I saw the *bint* take the paper while the young man was looking on, and yet he seems to know nothing of it. He went soon after to her father and asked to see it. It was then the old man searched for it and could not find it. He said that it was lost, and he was heartbroken.'

'It is all very strange,' murmured Sheykh Ab el-Ghrennem. 'Are you sure that you understand their accursed tongue and know that which they say, Atewy?'

'Did I not work for more than a year with a mad old *Nasrany* who dug in the sands at *Kheybar*? If he found only a piece of a broken pot be would he happy all the rest of the day. From him I learned the language of *el-Engleys*.'

'*Wellah!*' sighed the sheykh; 'It must be a great treasure indeed, greater than those of Howara and Geryeh combined; or they would not have brought so many carriages to transport it.' He gazed with brooding eyes at the many trucks parked upon the opposite bank of the stream waiting to cross.

'When shall I take the *bint* who hath the paper?' demanded Atewy after a moment's silence.

'Let us bide our time,' replied the sheykh. 'There be no hurry, since they be leading us always nearer to the treasure and feeding us well into the bargain. The *Nasrany* are fools. They thought to fool the *Bedauwy* with their picture taking as they fooled *el-Engleys*, but we are brighter than they. We know the picture making is only a blind to hide the real purpose of their safari.'

Sweating, mud covered, Mr Thomas Orman stood near the line of blacks straining on the ropes attached to a heavy truck. In one hand he carried a long whip. At his elbow stood a bearer, but in lieu of a rifle he carried a bottle of Scotch.

By nature Orman was neither a harsh nor cruel taskmaster. Ordinarily, both his inclinations and his judgment would have warned him against using the lash. The sullen silence of the blacks which should have counselled him to forbearance only irritated him still further.

He was three months out of Hollywood and already almost two months behind schedule, with the probability staring him in the face that it would be another month before they could reach the location where the major part of the picture could be shot. His leading woman had a touch of fever that might easily develop into something that would keep her out of the picture entirely. He had already been down twice with fever, and that had had its effects upon his disposition. It seemed to him that everything had gone wrong, that every-thing had conspired against him. And now these damn niggers, as he thought of them, were lying down on the job.

'Lay into it, you lazy bums!' he yelled, and the long lash reached out and wrapped around the shoulders of a black.

A young man in khaki shirt and shorts turned away in disgust and walked toward the car where Baine was talking to the two girls. He paused in the shade of a tree; and, removing his sun helmet, wiped the perspiration from his forehead and the inside of the hat band; then he moved on again and joined them.

Baine moved over to make room for him by the rear door of the car. 'You look sore, Bill,' he remarked.

West swore softly. 'Orman's gone nuts. If he doesn't throw that whip away and leave the booze alone we're headed for a lot of grief.'

'It's in the air,' said Rhonda. 'The men don't laugh and sing the way they used to.'

'I saw Kwamudi looking at him a few minutes ago,' continued West. 'There was hate in his eyes all right, and there was something worse.'

'Oh, well,' said Baine, 'you got to treat those niggers rough; and as for Kwamudi, Tom can tie a can to him and appoint someone else headman.'

'Those slave driving days are over, Baine; and the blacks know it. Orman'll get in plenty of trouble for this if the blacks report it, and don't fool yourself about Kwamudi. He's no ordinary headman; he's a big chief in his own country, and most of our blacks are from his own tribe. If he says quit, they'll quit; and don't you forget it. We'd be in a pretty mess if those fellows quit on us.'

'Well, what are we goin' to do about it? Tom ain't asking our advice that I've ever noticed.'

'You could do something, Naomi,' said West, turning to the girl.

'Who, me? What could I do?'

'Well, Tom likes you a lot. He'd listen to you.'

'Oh, nerts! It's his own funeral. I got troubles of my own.'

'It may be your funeral, too,' said West.

'Blah!' said the girl. 'All I want to do is get out of here. How much longer I got to sit here and fight flies? Say, where's Stanley? I haven't seen him all day.'

'The Lion Man is probably asleep in the back of his car,' suggested Baine. 'Say, have you heard what Old Man Marcus calls him?'

'What does he call him?' demanded Naomi.

'Sleeping Sickness.'

'Aw, you're all sore at him,' snapped Naomi, 'because he steps right into a starring part while you poor dubs have been working all your lives and are still doin' bits. Mr Obroski is a real artiste.'

'Say, we're going to start!' cried Rhonda. 'There's the signal.'

At last the long motorcade was underway. In the leading cars was a portion of the armed guards, the askaris; and another detachment brought up the rear. To the running boards of a number of the trucks clung some of the blacks, but most of them followed the last truck afoot. Pat O'Grady, the assistant director, was in charge of these.

O'Grady carried no long whip. He whistled a great deal, always the same tune; and he joshed his charges unmercifully, wholly ignoring the fact that they understood nothing that he said. But they reacted to his manner and his smile, and slowly their tenseness relaxed. Their sullen silence broke a little, and they talked among themselves. But still they did not sing, and there was no laughter.

'It would be better,' remarked Major White, walking at O'Grady's side, 'if you were in full charge of these men at all times. Mr Orman is temperamentally unsuited to handle them.'

O'Grady shrugged. 'Well, what is there to do about it?'

'He won't listen to me,' said the major. 'He resents every suggestion that I make. I might as well have remained in Hollywood.'

'I don't know what's got into Tom. He's a mighty good sort. I never saw him like this before.' O'Grady shook his head.

'Well, for one thing there's too much Scotch got into him,' observed White.

'I think it's the fever and the worry.' The assistant director was loyal to his chief.

'Whatever it is we're in for a bad mess if there isn't a change,' the Englishman prophesied. His manner was serious, and it was evident that he was worried.

'Perhaps you're—' O'Grady started to reply, but his words were interrupted by a sudden rattle of rifle fire coming, apparently, from the direction of the head of the column.

'My lord! What now?' exclaimed White, as, leaving O'Grady, he hurried toward the sound of the firing.

CHAPTER THREE

Poisoned Arrows

The ears of man are dull. Even on the open veldt they do not record the sound of a shot at any great distance. But the ears of hunting beasts are not as the ears of man; so hunting beasts at great distances paused when they heard the rifle fire that had startled O'Grady and White. Most of them slunk farther away from the dread sound.

Not so two lying in the shade of a tree. One was a great black-maned golden lion; the other was a man. He lay upon his back, and the lion lay beside him with one huge paw upon his chest.

'Tarmangani!' murmured the man.

A low growl rumbled in the cavernous chest of the carnivore.

'I shall have to look into this matter,' said the man, 'perhaps tonight, perhaps tomorrow.' He closed his eyes and fell asleep again, the sleep from which the shots had aroused him.

The lion blinked his yellow-green eyes and yawned; then he lowered his great head, and he too slept.

Near them lay the partially devoured carcass of a zebra, the kill that they had made at dawn. Neither Ungo, the jackal, nor Dango, the hyena, had as yet scented the feast; so quiet prevailed, broken only by the buzzing of insects and the occasional call of a bird.

Before Major White reached the head of the column the firing had ceased, and when he arrived he found the askaris and the white men crouching behind trees gazing into the dark forest before them, their rifles ready. Two black soldiers lay upon the ground, their bodies pierced by arrows. Already their forms were convulsed by the last throes of dissolution. Naomi Madison crouched upon the floor of her car. Rhonda Terry stood with one foot on the running board, a pistol in her hand.

White ran to Orman who stood with rifle in hand peering into the forest. 'What happened, Mr Orman?' he asked.

'An ambush,' replied Orman. 'The devils just fired a volley of arrows at us and then beat it. We scarcely caught a glimpse of them.'

'The Bansutos,' said White.

Orman nodded. 'I suppose so. They think they can frighten me with a few arrows, but I'll show the dirty niggers.'

'This was just a warning, Orman. They don't want us in their country.'

'I don't care what they want; I'm going in. They can't bluff me.'

'Don't forget, Mr Orman, that you have a lot of people here for whose lives you are responsible, including two white women, and that you were warned not to come through the Bansuto country.'

'I'll get my people through all right; the responsibility is mine, not yours.' Orman's tone was sullen, his manner that of a man who knows that he is wrong but is constrained by stubborness from admitting it.

'I cannot but feel a certain responsibility myself,' replied White. 'You know I was sent with you in an advisory capacity.'

'I'll ask for your advice when I want it.'

'You need it now. You know nothing about these people or what to expect from them.'

'The fact that we were ready and sent a volley into them the moment that they attacked has taught 'em a good lesson,' blustered Orman. 'You can be sure they won't bother us again.'

'I wish that I could be sure of that, but I can't. We haven't seen the last of those beggars. What you have seen is just a sample of their regular strategy of warfare. They'll never attack in force or in the open – just pick us off two or three at a time; and perhaps we'll never see one of them.'

'Well, if you're afraid, go back,' snapped Orman. 'I'll give you porters and a guard.'

White smiled. 'I'll remain with the company, of course.' Then he turned back to where Rhonda Terry still stood, a trifle pale, her pistol ready in her hand.

'You'd best remain in the car, Miss Terry,' he said. 'It will afford you some protection from arrows. You shouldn't expose yourself as you have.'

'I couldn't help but overhear what you said to Mr Orman,' said the girl. 'Do you really think they will keep on picking us off like this?'

'I am afraid so; it is the way they fight. I don't wish to frighten you unnecessarily, but you must be careful.'

She glanced at the two bodies that lay quiet now in the grotesque and horrible postures of death. 'I had no idea that arrows could kill so quickly.' A little shudder accompanied her words.

'They were poisoned,' explained the major.

'Poisoned!' There was a world of horror in the single word.

White glanced into the tonneau of the car. 'I think Miss Madison has fainted,' he said.

'She would!' exclaimed Rhonda, turning toward the unconscious girl.

Together they lifted her to her seat, and Rhonda applied restoratives; and, as they worked, Orman was organizing a stronger advance guard and giving orders to the white men clustered about him.

'Keep your rifles ready beside you all the time. I'll try to put an extra armed man on every truck. Keep your eyes open, and at the first sight of anything suspicious, shoot.

'Bill, you and Baine ride with the girls; I'll put an askari on each running board of their car. Clarence, you go to the rear of the column and tell Pat what has happened. Tell him to strengthen the rear guard, and you stay back there and help him.

'And Major White!' The Englishman came forward. 'I wish you'd see old el-Ghrennem and ask him to send half his force to the rear and the other half up with us. We can use 'em to send messages up and down the column, if necessary.

'Mr Marcus,' he turned to the old character man, 'you and Obroski ride near the middle of the column.' He looked about him suddenly. 'Where is Obroski?'

No one had seen him since the attack. 'He was in the car when I left it,' said Marcus. 'Perchance he has fallen asleep again.' There was a sly twinkle in the old eyes.

'Here he comes now,' said Clarence Noice.

A tall, handsome youth with a shock of black hair was approaching from down the line of cars. He wore a six-shooter strapped about his hips and carried a rifle. When he saw them looking toward him he commenced to run in their direction.

'Where are they?' he called. 'Where did they go?'

'Where you been?' demanded Orman.

'I been looking for them. I thought they were back there'

Bill West turned toward Gordon Z. Marcus and winked a slow wink.

Presently the column moved forward again. Orman was with the advance guard, the most dangerous post; and White remained with him.

Like a great snake the safari wound its way into the forest, the creaking of springs, the sound of the tires, the muffled exhausts its only accompaniment. There was no conversation – only tense, fearful expectancy.

There were many stops while a crew of blacks with knives and axes hewed a passage for the great trucks. Then on again into the shadows of the primitive wilderness. Their progress was slow, monotonous, heartbreaking.

At last they came to a river. 'We'll camp here,' said Orman.

White nodded. To him had been delegated the duty of making and breaking camp. In a quiet voice he directed the parking of the cars and trucks as they moved slowly into the little clearing along the river bank.

As he was thus engaged, those who had been passengers climbed to the ground and stretched their legs. Orman sat on the running board of a car and took a drink of Scotch. Naomi Madison sat down beside him and lighted a cigarette. She darted fearful glances into the forest around them and across the river into the still more mysterious wood beyond.

'I wish we were out of here, Tom,' she said. 'Let's go back before we're all killed.'

'That ain't what I was sent out here for. I was sent to make a picture, and I'm goin' to make it in spite of hell and high water.'

She moved closer and leaned her lithe body against him. 'Aw, Tom, if you loved me you'd take me out of here. I'm scared. I know I'm going to die. If it isn't fever it'll be those poisoned arrows.'

'Go tell your troubles to your Lion Man,' growled Orman, taking another drink.

'Don't be an old meany, Tom. You know I don't care anything about him. There isn't anyone but you.'

'Yes, I know it – except when you think I'm not looking. You don't think I'm blind, do you?'

'You may not be blind, but you're all wet,' she snapped angrily. 'I—'

A shot from the rear of the column halted her in mid-speech. Then came another and another in quick succession, followed by a fusillade.

Orman leaped to his feet. Men started to run toward the rear. He called them back. 'Stay here!' he cried. 'They may attack here, too – if that's who it is back again. Major White! Tell the sheik to send a horseman back there *pronto* to see what's happened.'

Naomi Madison fainted. No one paid any attention to her. They left her lying where she had fallen. The black askaris and the white men of the company stood with rifles in tense fingers, straining their eyes into the woods about them.

The firing at the rear ceased as suddenly as it had begun. The ensuing silence seemed a thing of substance. It was broken by a weird, blood-curdling scream from the dark wood on the opposite bank of the river.

'Gad!' exclaimed Baine. 'What was that?'

'I think the bounders are just trying to frighten us,' said White.

'Insofar as I am concerned they have succeeded admirably,' admitted Marcus. 'If one could be scared out of seven years growth retroactively, I would soon be a child again.'

Bill West threw a protective arm about Rhonda Terry. 'Lie down and roll under the car,' he said. 'You'll be safe from arrows there.'

'And get grease in my eyes? No, thanks.'

'Here comes the sheik's man now,' said Baine. 'There's somebody behind him on the horse – a white man.'

'It's Clarence,' said West.

As the Arab reined his pony in near Orman, Noice slipped to the ground.

'Well, what was it?' demanded the director.

'Same thing that happened up in front back there,' replied Noice. 'There was a volley of arrows without any warning, two men killed; then we turned and fired; but we didn't see anyone, not a soul. It's uncanny. Say, those blacks of ours are all shot. Can't see anything but the whites of their eyes, and they're shaking so their teeth rattle.'

'Is Pat hurryin' the rest of the safari into camp?' asked Orman.

Noice grinned. 'They don't need any hurryin'. They're comin' so fast that they'll probably go right through without seein' it.'

A scream burst in their midst, so close to them that even the stolid Major White jumped. All wheeled about with rifles ready.

Naomi Madison had raised herself to a sitting position. Her hair was dishevelled, her eyes wild. She screamed a second time and then fainted again.

'Shut up!' yelled Orman, frantically, his nerves on edge; but she did not hear him.

'If you'll have our tent set up, I'll get her to bed,' suggested Rhonda.

Cars, horsemen, black men afoot were crowding into the clearing. No one wished to be left back there in the forest. All was confusion.

Major White, with the assistance of Bill West, tried to restore order from chaos; and when Pat O'Grady came in, he helped.

At last camp was made. Blacks, whites, and horses were crowded close together, the blacks on one side, the whites on the other.

'If the wind changes,' remarked Rhonda Terry, 'we're sunk.'

'What a mess,' groaned Baine, 'and I thought this was going to be a lovely outing. I was so afraid I wasn't going to get the part that I was almost sick.'

'Now you're sick because you did get it.'

'I'll tell the world I am.'

'You're goin' to be a whole lot sicker before we get out of this Bansuto country,' remarked Bill West.

'You're telling me!'

'How's the Madison, Rhonda?' inquired West.

The girl shrugged. 'If she wasn't so darned scared she wouldn't be in such a bad way. That last touch of fever's about passed, but she just lies there and shakes – scared stiff.'

'You're a wonder, Rhonda. You don't seem to be afraid of anything.'

'Well, I'll be seein' yuh,' remarked Baine as he walked toward his own tent.

'Afraid!' exclaimed the girl. 'Bill, I never knew what it was to be afraid before. Why, I've got goose-pimples inside.'

West shook his head. 'You're sure a game kid. No one would ever know you were afraid – you don't show it.'

'Perhaps I've just enough brains to know that it wouldn't get me anything. It doesn't even get her sympathy.' She nodded her head toward the tent.

West grimaced. 'She's a—' he hesitated, searching for adequate invective.

The girl placed her fingers against his lips and shook her head. 'Don't say it,' she admonished. 'She can't help it. I'm really sorry for her.'

'You're a wonder! And she treats you like scum. Gee, kid, but you've got a great disposition. I don't see how you can be decent to her. It's that dog-gone patronizing air of hers toward you that gets my nanny. The great artiste! Why, you can act circles all around her, kid; and as for looks! You got her backed off the boards.'

Rhonda laughed. 'That's why she's a famous star and I'm a double. Quit your kidding.'

'I'm not kidding. The company's all talking about it. You stole the scenes we shot while she was laid up. Even Orman knows it, and he's got a crush on her.'

'You're prejudiced – you don't like her.'

'She's nothing in my young life, one way or another. But I do like you, Rhonda. I like you a lot. I – oh, pshaw – you know what I mean.'

'What are you doing, Bill – making love to me?'

'I'm trying to.'

'Well, as a lover you're a great cameraman – and you'd better stick to your camera. This is not exactly the ideal setting for a love scene. I am surprised that a great cameraman like you should have failed to appreciate that. You'd never shoot a love scene against this background.'

'I'm shootin' one now, Rhonda. I love you.'

'Cut!' laughed the girl.

CHAPTER FOUR

Dissension

Kwamudi, the black headman, stood before Orman. 'My people go back,' he said; 'not stay in Bansuto country and be killed.'

'You can't go back,' growled Orman. 'You signed up for the whole trip. You tell 'em they got to stay; or, by George, I'll—'

'We not sign up to go Bansuto country; we not sign up be killed. You go back, we come along. You stay, we go back. We go daylight.' He turned and walked away.

Orman started up angrily from his camp chair, seizing his ever ready whip. 'I'll teach you, you black—!' he yelled.

White, who had been standing beside him, seized him by the shoulder. 'Stop!' His voice was low but his tone peremptory. 'You can't do that! I haven't interfered before, but now you've got to listen to me. The lives of all of us are at stake.'

'Don't you interfere, you meddlin' old fool,' snapped Orman. 'This is my show, and I'll run it my way.'

'You'd better go soak your head, Tom,' said O'Grady; 'you're full of hootch. The major's right. We're in a tight hole, and we won't ever get out of it on Scotch.' He turned to the Englishman. 'You handle things, Major. Don't pay any attention to Tom; he's drunk. Tomorrow he'll be sorry – if he sobers up. We're all back of you. Get us out of the mess if you can. How long would it take to get out of this Bansuto country if we kept on in the direction we want to go?'

Orman appeared stunned by this sudden defection of his assistant. It left him speechless.

White considered O'Grady's question. 'If we were not too greatly delayed by the trucks, we could make it in two days,' he decided finally.

'And how long would it take us to reach the location we're headed for if we have to go back and go around the Bansuto country?' continued O'Grady.

'We couldn't do it under two weeks,' replied the major. 'We'd be lucky if we made it in that time. We'd have to go way to the south through a beastly rough country.'

'The studio's put a lot of money into this already,' said O'Grady, 'and we haven't got much of anything to show for it. We'd like to get onto location as quick as possible. Don't you suppose you could persuade Kwamudi to go on? If we turn back, we'll have those beggars on our neck for a day at least. If we go ahead, it will only mean one extra day of them. Offer Kwamudi's bunch extra pay if they'll stick – it'll be a whole lot cheaper for us than wastin' another two weeks.'

'Will Mr Orman authorize the bonus?' asked White.

'He'll do whatever I tell him, or I'll punch his fool head,' O'Grady assured him.

Orman had sunk back into his camp chair and was staring at the ground. He made no comment.

'Very well,' said White. 'I'll see what I can do. I'll talk to Kwamudi over at my tent, if you'll send one of the boys after him.'

White walked over to his tent, and O'Grady sent a black boy to summon the headman; then he turned to Orman. 'Go to bed, Tom,' he ordered, 'and lay off that hootch.'

Without a word, Orman got up and went into his tent.

'You put the kibosh on him all right, Pat,' remarked Noice, with a grin. 'How do you get away with it?'

O'Grady did not reply. His eyes were wandering over the camp, and there was a troubled expression on his usually smiling face. He noted the air of constraint, the tenseness; as though all were waiting for something to happen, they knew not what.

He saw his messenger overhaul Kwamudi and the headman turn back toward White's tent. He saw the blacks silently making their little cooking fires. They did not sing or laugh, and when they spoke they spoke in whispers.

The Arabs were squatting in the *mukaad* of the sheykh's *beyt*. They were a dour lot at best; and their appearance was little different tonight than ordinarily, yet he sensed a difference.

Even the whites spoke in lower tones than usual and there was less chaffing. And from all the groups constant glances were cast toward the surrounding forest.

Presently he saw Kwamudi leave White and return to his fellows; then O'Grady walked over to where the Englishman was sitting in a camp chair, puffing on a squat briar. 'What luck?' he asked.

'The bonus got him,' replied White. 'They will go on, but on one other condition.'

'What is that?'

'His men are not to be whipped.'

'That's fair enough,' said O'Grady.

'But how are you going to prevent it?'

'For one thing, I'll throw the whip away; for another, I'll tell Orman we'll all quit him if he doesn't lay off. I can't understand him; he never was like this before. I've worked with him a lot during the last five years.'

'Too much liquor,' said White; 'it's finally got him.'

'He'll be all right when we get on location and get to work. He's been worrying too much. Once we get through this Bansuto country everything'll be jake.'

'We're not through it yet, Pat. They'll get some more of us tomorrow and some more the next day. I don't know how the blacks will stand it. It's a bad business. We really ought to turn around and go back. It would be better to lose two weeks time than to lose everything, as we may easily do if the blacks quit us. You know we couldn't move through this country without them.'

'We'll pull through somehow,' O'Grady assured him. 'We always do. Well, I'm goin' to turn in. Goodnight, Major.'

The brief equatorial twilight had ushered in the night. The moon had not risen. The forest was blotted out by a pall of darkness. The universe had shrunk to a few tiny earth fires surrounded by the huddled forms of men and, far above, a few stars.

Obroski paused in front of the girls' tent and scratched on the flap. 'Who is it?' demanded Naomi Madison from within.

'It's me, Stanley.'

She bade him enter; and he came in to find her lying on her cot beneath a mosquito bar, a lantern burning on a box beside her.

'Well,' she said peevishly, 'it's a wonder anyone came. I might lie here and die for all anyone cares.'

'I'd have come sooner, but I thought of course Orman was here.'

'He's probably in his tent soused.'

'Yes, he is. When I found that out I came right over.'

'I shouldn't think you'd be afraid of him. I shouldn't think *you'd* be afraid of anything.' She gazed admiringly on his splendid physique, his handsome face.

'Me afraid of that big stiff!' he scoffed. 'I'm not afraid of anything, but you said yourself that we ought not to let Orman know about – about you and me.'

'No,' the acquiesced thoughtfully, 'that wouldn't be so good. He's got a nasty temper, and there's lots of things a director can do if he gets sore.'

'In a picture like this he could get a guy killed and make it look like an accident,' said Obroski.

She nodded. 'Yes. I saw it done once. The director and the leading man were both stuck on the same girl. The director had the wrong command given to a trained elephant.'

Obroski looked uncomfortable. 'Do you suppose there's any chance of his coming over?'

'Not now. He'll be dead to the world 'til morning.'

'Where's Rhonda?'

'Oh, she's probably playing contract with Bill West and Baine and old man Marcus. She'd play contract and let me lie here and die all alone.'

'Is she all right?'

'What do you mean, all right?'

'She wouldn't tell Orman about us – about my being over here – would she?'

'No, she wouldn't do that – she ain't that kind.'

Obroski breathed a sigh of relief. 'She knows about us, don't she?'

'She ain't very bright; but she ain't a fool, either. The only trouble with Rhonda is, she's got it in her head she can act since she doubled for me while I was down with the fever. Someone handed her some applesauce, and now she thinks she's some pumpkin. She had the nerve to tell me that I'd get credit for what she did. Believe me, she won't get past the cutting room when I get back to Hollywood – not if I know my groceries and Milt Smith.'

'There couldn't anybody act like you, Naomi,' said Obroski. 'Why, before I ever dreamed I'd be in pictures I used to go see everything you were in. I got an album full of your pictures I cut out of movie magazines and newspapers. And now to think that I'm playin' in the same company with you, and that' – he lowered his voice – 'you love me! You do love me, don't you?'

'Of course. I do.'

'Then I don't see why you have to act so sweet on Orman.'

'I got to be diplomatic – I got to think of my career.'

'Well, sometimes you act like you were in love with him,' he said, petulantly.

'That answer to a bootlegger's dream! Say, if he wasn't a big director I couldn't see him with a hundred-inch telescope.'

In the far distance a wailing scream echoed through the blackness of the night, a lion rumbled forth a thunderous answer, the hideous, mocking voice of a hyena joined the chorus.

The girl shuddered. 'God! I'd give a million dollars to be back in Hollywood.'

'They sound like lost souls out there in the night,' whispered Obroski.

'And they're calling to us. They're waiting for us. They know that we'll come, and then they'll get us.'

The flap of the tent moved, and Obroski jumped to his feet with a nervous start. The girl sat straight up on her cot, wide eyed. The flap was pulled back, and Rhonda Terry stepped into the light of the lone lantern.

'Hello, there!' she exclaimed cheerily.

'I wish you'd scratch before you come in,' snapped Naomi. 'You gave me a start.'

'If we have to camp this close to the black belt every night we'll all be scratching.' She turned to Obroski. 'Run along home now; it's time all little Lion-men were in bed.'

'I was just going,' said Obroski. 'I—'

'You'd better. I just saw Tom Orman reeling in this direction.'

Obroski paled. 'Well, I'll be running along,' he said hurriedly, while making a quick exit.

Naomi Madison looked distinctly worried. 'Did you really see Tom out there?' she demanded.

'Sure. He was wallowing around like the Avalon in a heavy sea.'

'But they said he went to bed.'

'If he did, he took his bottle to bed with him.'

Orman's voice came to them from outside. 'Hey, you! Come back here!'

'Is that you, Mr Orman?' Obroski's voice quavered noticeably.

'Yes, it's me. What you doin' in the girls' tent? Didn't I give orders that none of you guys was to go into that tent?'

'I was just lookin' for Rhonda. I wanted to ask her something.'

'You're a liar. Rhonda wasn't there. I just saw her go in. You been in there with Naomi. I've got a good mind to bust your jaw.'

'Honestly, Mr Orman, I was just in there a minute. When I found Rhonda wasn't there I came right out.'

'You came right out after Rhonda went in, you dirty, sneakin' skunk; and now you listen to me. You lay off Naomi. She's my girl. If I ever find you monkeyin' around her again I'll kill you. Do you get that?'

'Yes, sir.'

Rhonda looked at Naomi and winked. 'Papa cross; papa spank,' she said.

'My God! He'll kill me,' shuddered Naomi.

The flap of the tent was thrust violently aside, and Orman burst into the tent. Rhonda wheeled and faced him.

'What do you mean by coming into our tent?' she demanded. 'Get out of here!'

Orman's jaw dropped. He was not accustomed to being talked to like that, and it took him off his feet. He was as surprised as might be a pit bull slapped in the face by a rabbit. He stood swaying at the entrance for a moment, staring at Rhonda as though he had discovered a new species of animal.

'I just wanted to speak to Naomi,' he said. 'I didn't know you were here.'

'You can speak to Naomi in the morning. And you did know that I was here; I heard you tell Stanley.'

At the mention of Obroski's name Orman's anger welled up again. 'That's what I'm goin' to talk to her about.' He took a step in the direction of Naomi's cot. 'Now look here, you dirty little tramp,' he yelled, 'you can't make a monkey of me. If I ever catch you playin' around with that Polack again I'll beat you into a pulp.'

Naomi shrank back, whimpering. 'Don't touch me! I didn't do anything. You got it all wrong, Tom. He didn't come here to see me; he came to see Rhonda. Don't let him get me, Rhonda; for God's sake, don't let him get me.'

Orman hesitated and looked at Rhonda. 'Is that on the level?' he asked.

'Sure,' she replied; 'he came to see me. I asked him to come.'

'Then why didn't he stay after you came in?' Orman thought he had her there.

'I saw you coming, and I told him to beat it.'

'Well, you got to cut it out,' snapped Orman. 'There's to be no more men in this tent – do your visiting outside.'

'That suits me,' said Rhonda. 'Goodnight.'

As Orman departed, the Madison sank back on her cot trembling. 'Phew!' she whispered after she thought the man was out of hearing; 'That was a close shave.' She did not thank Rhonda. Her selfish egotism accepted any service as her rightful due.

'Listen.' said the other girl. 'I'm hired to double for you in pictures, not in your love affairs. After this, watch your step.'

Orman saw a light in the tent occupied by West and one of the other cameramen. He walked over to it and went in. West was undressing. 'Hello, Tom!' he said. 'What brings you around? Anything wrong?'

'There ain't now, but there was. I just run that dirty Polack out of the girls' tent. He was over there with Rhonda.'

West paled. 'I don't believe it.'

'You callin' me a liar?' demanded Orman.

'Yes, you and anyone else who says that.'

Orman shrugged. 'Well, she told me so herself – said she asked him over and made him scram when she saw me coming. That stuff's got to stop, and I told her so. I told the Polack too, the damn pansy;' then he lurched out and headed for his own tent.

Bill West lay awake until almost morning.

CHAPTER FIVE

Death

While the camp slept, a bronzed white giant, naked but for a loin cloth, surveyed it – sometimes from the branches of overhanging trees, again from the ground inside the circle of the sentries. Then, he moved among the tents of the whites and the shelters of the blacks as soundlessly as a shadow. He saw everything, he heard much. With the coming of dawn he melted away into the mist that enveloped the forest.

It was long before dawn that the camp commenced to stir. Major White had snatched a few hours sleep after midnight. He was up early routing out the cooks, getting the whites up so that their tents could be struck for an early start, directing the packing and loading by Kwamudi's men. It was then that he learned that fully twenty-five of the porters had deserted during the night.

He questioned the sentries, but none had seen anyone leave the camp during the night. He knew that some of them lied. When Orman came out of his tent he told him what had happened.

The director shrugged. 'We still got more niggers than we need anyway.'

'If we have any more trouble with the Bansutos today, we'll have more desertions tonight.' White warned. 'They may all leave in spite of Kwamudi, and if we're left in this country without porters I wouldn't give a fig for our chances of ever getting out.

'I still think, Mr Orman, that the sensible thing would be to turn back and make a detour. Our situation is extremely grave.'

'Well, turn back if you want to, and take the niggers with you,' growled Orman. 'I'm going on with the trucks and the company.' He turned and walked away.

The whites were gathering at the mess table – a long table that accommodated them all. In the dim light of the coming dawn and the mist rising from the ground figures at a little distance appeared spectral, and the illusion was accentuated by the silence of the company. Everyone was cold and sleepy. They were apprehensive too of what the day held for them. Memory of the black soldiers, pierced by poisoned arrows, writhing on the ground was too starkly present in every mind.

Hot coffee finally thawed them out a bit. It was Pat O'Grady who thawed first. 'Good morning, dear teacher, good morning to you,' he sang in an attempt to reach a childish treble.

'Ain't we got fun!' exclaimed Rhonda Terry. She glanced down the table and saw Bill West. She wondered a little, because he had always sat beside her before. She tried to catch his eye and smile at him, but he did not look in her direction – he seemed to be trying to avoid her glance.

'Let us eat and drink and be merry; for tomorrow we die,' misquoted Gordon Z. Marcus.

'That's not funny,' said Baine.

'On second thought I quite agree with you,' said Marcus. 'I loosed a careless shaft at humor and hit truth—'

'Right between the eyes,' said Clarence Noice.

'Some of us may not have to wait until tomorrow,' offered Obroski; 'some of us may get it today.' His voice sounded husky.

'Can that line of chatter!' snapped Orman. 'If you're scared, keep it to yourself.'

'I'm not scared,' said Obroski.

'The Lion Man scared? Don't be foolish.' Baine winked at Marcus. 'I tell you, Tom, what we ought to do now that we're in this bad country. It's funny no one thought of it before.'

'What's that?' asked Orman.

'We ought to send the Lion Man out ahead to clear the way for the rest of us; he'd just grab these Bansutos and break 'em in two if they got funny.'

'That's not a bad idea,' replied Orman grimly. 'How about it, Obroski?'

Obroski grinned weakly. 'I'd like to have the author of that story here and send him out,' he said.

'Some of those smokes had good sense anyway,' volunteered a truck driver at the foot of the table.

'How come?' asked a neighbor.

'Hadn't you heard? About twenty-five or thirty of 'em pulled their freight out of here – they beat it back for home.'

'Those bimbos must know,' said another; 'this is their country.'

'That's what we ought to do,' growled another – 'get out of here and go back.'

'Shut up!' snapped Orman. 'You guys make me sick. Who ever picked this outfit for me must have done it in a pansy bed.'

Naomi Madison was sitting next to him. She turned her frightened eyes up to him. 'Did some of the blacks really run away last night?' she asked.

'For Pete's sake! Don't you start in too,' he exclaimed; then he got up and stamped away from the table.

At the foot of the table someone muttered something that sounded like that epithet which should always be accompanied with a smile; but it was not.

By ones and twos they finished their breakfasts and went about their duties. They went in silence without the customary joking that had marked the earlier days of the expedition.

Rhonda and Naomi gathered up the hand baggage that they always took in the car with them and walked over to the machine. Baine was at the wheel warming up the motor. Gordon Z. Marcus was stowing a make-up case in the front of the car.

'Where's Bill?' asked Rhonda.

'He's going with the camera truck today,' explained Baine.

'That's funny,' commented Rhonda. It suddenly occurred to her that he was avoiding her, and she wondered why. She tried to recall anything that she had said or done that might have offended him, but she could not. She felt strangely sad.

Some of the trucks had commenced to move toward the river. The Arabs and a detachment of askaris had already crossed to guard the passage of the trucks.

'They're going to send the generator truck across first,' explained Baine. 'if they get her across the rest will be easy. If they don't, we'll have to turn back.'

'I hope it gets stuck so fast they never get it out,' said the Madison.

The crossing of the river, which Major White had anticipated with many misgivings, was accomplished with ease; for the bottom was rocky and the banks sloping and firm. There was no sign of the Bansutos, and no attack was made on the column as it wound its way into the forest ahead.

All morning they moved on with comparative ease, retarded only by the ordinary delays consequent upon clearing a road for the big trucks where trees had to be thinned. The underbrush they bore down beneath them, flattening it out into a good road for the lighter cars that followed.

Spirits became lighter as the day progressed without revealing any sign of the Bansutos. There was a noticeable relaxation. Conversation increased and occasionally a laugh was heard. Even the blacks seemed to be returning to normal. Perhaps they had noticed that Orman no longer carried his whip, nor did he take any part in the direction of the march.

He and White were on foot with the advance guard, both men constantly alert for any sign of danger. There was still considerable constraint in their manner, and they spoke to one another only as necessity required.

The noonday stop for lunch passed and the column took up its snakelike way through the forest once more. The ring of axes against wood ahead was accompanied by song and laughter. Already the primitive minds of the blacks had cast off the fears that had assailed them earlier in the day.

Suddenly, without warning, a dozen feathered missiles sped from the apparently deserted forest around them. Two blacks fell. Major White, walking beside Orman, clutched at a feathered shaft protruding from his breast and fell at Orman's feet. The askaris and the Arabs fired blindly into the forest. The column came to a sudden halt.

'Again!' whispered Rhonda Terry.

Naomi Madison screamed and slipped to the floor of the car. Rhonda opened the door and stepped out onto the ground.

'Get back in, Rhonda!' cried Baine. 'Get under cover.'

The girl shook her head as though the suggestion irritated her. 'Where is Bill?' she asked. 'Is he up in front?'

'Not way up,' replied Baine; 'only a few cars ahead of us.'

The men all along the line of cars slipped to the ground with their rifles and stood searching the forest to right and left for some sign of an enemy.

A man was crawling under a truck.

'What the hell are you doing, Obroski?' demanded Noice.

'I – I'm going to lie in the shade until we start again.'

Noice made a vulgar sound with his lips and tongue.

In the rear of the column Pat O'Grady stopped whistling. He dropped back with the askaris guarding the rear. They had faced about and were nervously peering into the forest. A man from the last truck joined them and stood beside O'Grady.

'Wish we could get a look at 'em once,' he said.

'It's tough tryin' to fight a bunch of guys you don't ever see,' said O'Grady.

'It sort of gets a guy's nanny,' offered the other. 'I wonder who they got up in front this time.'

O'Grady shook his head.

'It'll be our turn next; it was yesterday,' said the man.

O'Grady looked at him. He saw that he was not afraid – he was merely stating what he believed to be a fact. 'Can't ever tell,' he said. 'If it's a guy's time, he'll get it; if it isn't, he won't.'

'Do you believe that? I wish I did.'

'Sure – why not? It's pleasanter. I don't like worryin.''

'I don't know,' said the other dubiously. 'I ain't superstitious.' He paused and lighted a cigarette.

'Neither am I,' said O'Grady.

'I got one of my socks on wrong side out this morning,' the man volunteered thoughtfully.

'You didn't take it off again, did you?' inquired O'Grady.

'No.'

'That's right; you shouldn't.'

Word was passed back along the line that Major White and two askaris had been killed. O'Grady cursed. 'The major was a swell guy,' he said. 'He was worth all the lousy coons in Africa. I hope I get a chance to get some of 'em for this.'

The porters were nervous, frightened, sullen. Kwamudi came up to O'Grady. 'Black boys not go on,' he said. 'They turn back – go home.'

'They better stick with us,' O'Grady told him. 'If they turn back they'll all be killed; they won't have a lot of us guys with rifles to fight for 'em. Tomorrow we ought to be out of this Bansuto country. You better advise 'em to stick, Kwamudi.'

Kwamudi grumbled and walked away.

'That was just a bluff,' O'Grady confided to the other white. 'I don't believe they'd turn back through this Bansuto country alone.'

Presently the column got underway again, and Kwamudi and his men marched with it.

Up in front they had laid the bodies of Major White and the two blacks on top of one of the loads to give them decent burial at the next camp. Orman marched well in advance with set, haggard face. The askaris were nervous and held back. The party of blacks clearing the road for the leading truck was on the verge of mutiny. The Arabs lagged behind. They had all had confidence in White, and his death had taken the heart out of them. They remembered Orman's lash and his cursing tongue; they would not have followed him at all had it not been for his courage. That was so evident that it commanded their respect.

He didn't curse them now. He talked to them as he should have from the first. 'We've got to go on,' he said. 'If we turn back we'll be worse off. Tomorrow we ought to be out of this.'

He used violence only when persuasion failed. An axe man refused to work and started for the rear. Orman knocked him down and then kicked him back onto the job. That was something they could all understand. It was right because it was just. Orman knew that the lives of two hundred people depended upon every man sticking to his job, and he meant to see that they stuck.

The rear of the column was not attacked that day, but just before they reached a camping place another volley of arrows took its toll from the head of the column. This time three men died, and an arrow knocked Orman's sun helmet from his head.

It was a gloomy company that made camp late that afternoon. The death of Major White had brought their own personal danger closer to the white members of the party. Before this they had felt a certain subconscious sense of immunity, as though poisoned arrows of the Bansutos could deal death only to black men. Now they were quick to the horror of their own situation. Who would be next? How many of them were asking themselves this question!

CHAPTER SIX

Remorse

Atewy, the arab, taking advantage of his knowledge of English, often circulated among the Americans, asking questions, gossiping. They had become so accustomed to him that they thought nothing of his presence among them; nor did his awkward attempts at joviality suggest to them that he might be playing a part for the purpose of concealing ulterior motives, though it must have been apparent to the least observing that by nature Atewy was far from jovial.

He was, however, cunning; so he hid the fact that his greatest interest lay in the two girl members of the company. Nor did he ever approach them unless men of their own race were with them.

This afternoon Rhonda Terry was writing at a little camp table in front of her tent, for it was not yet dark. Gordon Z. Marcus had stopped to chat with her. Atewy from the corners of his eyes noted this and strolled casually closer.

'Turning literary, Rhonda?' inquired Marcus.

The girl looked up and smiled. 'Trying to bring my diary up to date.'

'I fear that it will prove a most lugubrious document.'

'Whatever that is. Oh, by the way!' She picked up a folded paper. 'I just found this map in my portfolio. In the last scene we shot they were taking close-ups of me examining it. I wonder if they want it again – I'd like to swipe it for a souvenir.'

As she unfolded the paper Atewy moved closer, a new light burning in his eyes.

'Keep it,' suggested Marcus, 'until they ask you for it. Perhaps they're through with it. It's a most authentic looking thing, isn't it? I wonder if they made it in the studio.'

'No. Bill says that Joe found it between the leaves of a book he bought in a secondhand book store. When he was commissioned to write this story it occurred to him to write it around this old map. It *is* intriguing, isn't it? Almost makes one believe that it would be easy to find a valley of diamonds.' She folded the map and replaced it in her portfolio. Hawklike, the swarthy Atewy watched her.

Marcus regarded her with his kindly eyes. 'You were speaking of Bill,' he said. 'What's wrong with you two children? He used to be with you so much.'

With a gesture Rhonda signified her inability to explain. 'I haven't the remotest idea,' she said. 'He just avoids me as though I were some particular variety of pollen to which he reacted. Do I give you hives or hay fever?'

Marcus laughed. 'I can imagine, Rhonda, that you might induce high temperatures in the male of the species; but to suggest hives or hay fever – that would be sacrilege.'

Naomi Madison came from the tent. Her face was white and drawn. 'My God!' she exclaimed. 'How can you people joke at such a time? Why, any minute any of us may be killed!'

'We must keep up our courage,' said Marcus. 'We cannot do it by brooding over our troubles and giving way to our sorrows.'

'Pulling a long face isn't going to bring back Major White or those other poor fellows,' said Rhonda. 'Everyone knows how sorry everyone feels about it; we don't have to wear crêpe to prove that.'

'Well, we might be respectful until after the funeral anyway,' snapped Naomi.

'Don't be stupid,' said Rhonda, a little tartly.

'When are they going to bury them, Mr Marcus?' asked Naomi.

'Not until after dark. They don't want the Bansutos to see where they're buried.'

The girl shuddered. 'What a horrible country! I feel that I shall never leave it – alive.'

'You certainly won't leave it dead.' Rhonda, who seldom revealed her emotions, evinced a trace of exasperation.

The Madison sniffed. 'They would never bury *me* here. My public would never stand for that. I shall lie in statè in Hollywood.'

'Come, come!' exclaimed Marcus. 'You girls must not dwell on such morbid, depressing subjects. We must all keep our minds from such thoughts. How about a rubber of contract before supper? We'll just about have time.'

'I'm for it,' agreed Rhonda.

'You would be,' sneered the Madison; 'you have no nerves. But no bridge for me at such a time. I am too highly organized, too temperamental. I think that is the way with all true artistes, don't you, Mr Marcus? We are like highstrung thoroughbreds.'

'Well,' laughed Rhonda, running her arm through Marcus', 'I guess we'll have to go and dig up a couple more skates if we want a rubber before supper. Perhaps we could get Bill and Jerrold. Neither of them would ever take any prizes in a horse show.'

They found Bill West pottering around his cameras. He declined their invitation glumly. 'You might get Obroski,' he suggested, 'if you can wake him up.'

Rhonda shot a quick glance at him through narrowed lids. 'Another thoroughbred,' she said, as she walked away. And to herself she thought, 'That's the second crack he's made about Obroski. All right, I'll show him!'

'Where to now, Rhonda?' inquired Marcus.

'You dig up Jerrold; I'm going to find Obroski. We'll have a game yet.'

They did, and it so happened that their table was set where Bill West could not but see them. It seemed to Marcus that Rhonda laughed a little more than was usual and a little more than was necessary.

That night white men and black carried each their own dead into the outer darkness beyond the range of the campfires and buried them. The graves were smoothed over and sprinkled with leaves and branches, and the excess dirt was carried to the opposite side of the camp where it was formed in little mounds that looked like graves.

The true graves lay directly in the line of march of the morrow. The twenty-three trucks and the five passenger cars would obliterate the last trace of the new-made graves.

The silent men working in the dark hoped that they were unseen by prying eyes; but long into the night a figure lay above the edge of the camp, hidden by the concealing foliage of a great tree, and observed all that took place below. Then, when the last of the white men had gone to bed, it melted silently into the somber depths of the forest.

Toward morning Orman lay sleepless on his army cot. He had tried to read to divert his mind from the ghastly procession of thoughts that persisted despite his every effort to sleep or to think of other things. In the light of the lantern that he had placed near his head harsh shadows lined his face as a drawn and haggard mask.

From his cot on the opposite side of the tent Pat O'Grady opened his eyes and surveyed his chief. 'Hell, Tom,' he said, 'you better get some sleep or you'll go nuts.'

'I can't sleep.' replied Orman wearily. 'I keep seein' White. I killed him. I killed all those blacks.'

'Hooey!' scoffed O'Grady. 'It wasn't any more your fault than it was the studio's. They sent you out here to make a picture, and you did what you thought was the right thing. There can't nobody blame you.'

'It was my fault all right. White warned me not to come this way. He was right; and I knew he was right, but I was too damn pig-headed to admit it.'

'What you need is a drink. It'll brace you up and put you to sleep.'

'I've quit.'

'It's all right to quit; but don't quit so sudden – taper off.'

Orman shook his head. 'I ain't blamin' it on the booze,' he said; 'there's no one nor nothing to blame but me – but if I hadn't been drinkin' this would never have happened, and White and those other poor devils would have been alive now.'

'One won't hurt, Tom; you need it.'

Orman lay silent in thought for a moment; then he threw aside the mosquito bar and stood up. 'Perhaps you're right, Pat,' he said.

He stepped to a heavy, well-worn pigskin bag that stood at the foot of his cot and, stooping, took out a fat bottle and a tumbler. He shook a little as he filled the latter to the brim.

O'Grady grinned. 'I said one drink, not four.'

Slowly Orman raised the tumbler toward his lips. He held it there for a moment looking at it; then his vision seemed to pass beyond it, pass through the canvas wall of the tent out into the night toward the new-made graves.

With an oath, he hurled the full tumbler to the ground; the bottle followed it, breaking into a thousand pieces.

'That's goin' to be hell on bare feet,' remarked O'Grady.

'I'm sorry, Pat,' said Orman; then he sat down wearily on the edge of his cot and buried his face in his hands.

O'Grady sat up, slipped his bare feet into a pair of shoes, and crossed the tent. He sat down beside his friend and threw an arm about his shoulders.

'Buck up, Tom!' That was all he said, but the pressure of the friendly arm was more strengthening than many words or many drinks.

From somewhere out in the night came the roar of a lion and a moment later a blood-curdling cry that seemed neither that of beast nor man.

'Sufferin' cats!' ejaculated O'Grady. 'What was that?'

Orman had raised his head and was listening. 'Probably some more grief for us,' he replied forebodingly.

They sat silent for a moment then, listening.

'I wonder what could make such a noise.' O'Grady spoke in hushed tones.

'Pat,' Orman's tone was serious, 'do you believe in ghosts?'

O'Grady hesitated before he replied. 'I don't know – but I've seen some funny things in my time.'

'So have I,' said Orman.

But perhaps of all that they could conjure to their minds nothing so strange as the reality; for how could they know that they had heard the victory cry of an English lord and a great lion who had just made their kill together?

CHAPTER SEVEN

Disaster

The cold and gloomy dawn but reflected the spirits of the company as the white men dragged themselves lethargically from their blankets. But the first to view the camp in the swiftly coming daylight were galvanized into instant wakefulness by what it revealed.

Bill West was the first to suspect what had happened. He looked wonderingly about for a moment and then started, almost at a run, for the crude shelters thrown up by the blacks the previous evening.

He called aloud to Kwamudi and several others whose names he knew, but there was no response. He looked into shelter after shelter, and always the results were the same. Then he hurried over to Orman's tent. The director was just coming out as West ran up. O'Grady was directly behind him.

'What's the matter with breakfast?' demanded the latter. 'I don't see a sign of the cooks.'

'And you won't,' said West; 'they've gone, ducked, vamoosed. If you want breakfast, you'll cook it yourself.'

'What do you mean gone, Bill?' asked Orman.

'The whole kit and caboodle of 'em have run out on us,' explained the cameraman. 'There's not a smoke in camp. Even the askaris have beat it. The camp's unguarded, and God only knows how long it has been.'

'Gone!' Orman's inflection registered incredulity. 'But they couldn't! Where have they gone?'

'Search me,' replied West. 'They've taken a lot of our supplies with 'em too. From what little I saw I guess they outfitted themselves to the queen's taste. I noticed a couple of trucks that looked like they'd been rifled.'

Orman swore softly beneath his breath; but he squared his shoulders, and the haggard, hang-dog expression he had worn vanished from his face. O'Grady had been looking at him with a worried furrow in his brow; now he gave a sigh of relief and grinned – the Chief was himself again.

'Rout everyone out,' Orman directed. 'Have the drivers check their loads. You attend to that, Bill, while Pat posts a guard around the camp. I see old el-Gran'ma'am and his bunch are still with us. You better put them on guard duty, Pat. Then round up everyone else at the mess tables for a palaver.'

While his orders were being carried out Orman walked about the camp making a hurried survey. His brain was clear. Even the effects of a sleepless night seemed to have been erased by this sudden emergency call upon his resources. He no longer wasted his nervous energy upon vain regrets, though he was still fully conscious of the fact that this serious predicament was of his own making.

When he approached the mess table five minutes later the entire company was assembled there talking excitedly about the defection of the blacks and offering various prophecies as to the future, none of which were particularly roseate.

Orman overheard one remark. 'It took a case of Scotch to get us into this mess, but Scotch won't ever get us out of it.'

'You all know what has happened,' Orman commenced; 'and I guess you all know why it happened, but criminations won't help matters. Our situation really isn't so hopeless. We have men, provisions, arms, and transportation. Because the coons deserted us doesn't mean that we've got to sit down here and kiss ourselves goodbye.

'Nor is there any use in turning around now and going back – the shortest way out of Bansuto country is straight ahead. When we get out of it we can recruit more blacks from friendly tribes and go ahead with the picture.

'In the meantime everyone has got to work and work hard. We have got to do the work the blacks did before – make camp, strike camp, unload and load, cook, cut trail, drag trucks through mud holes, stand guard on the march and in camp. That part and trail cutting will be dangerous, but everyone will have to take his turn at it – everyone except the girls and the cooks; they're the most important members of the safari.' A hint of one of Orman's old smiles touched his lips and eyes.

'Now,' he continued, 'the first thing to do is eat. Who can cook?'

'I can like nobody's business,' said Rhonda Terry.

'I'll vouch for that,' said Marcus. 'I've eaten a chicken dinner with all the trimmings at Rhonda's apartment.'

'I can cook,' spoke up a male voice.

Everyone turned to see who had spoken; he was the only man who had volunteered for the only safe assignment.

'When did you learn to cook, Obroski?' demanded Noice. 'I went camping with you once; and you couldn't even build a fire, let alone cook on one after someone else had built it.'

Obroski flushed. 'Well, someone's got to help Rhonda,' he said lamely, 'and no one else offered to.'

'Jimmy, here, can cook,' offered an electrician. 'He used to be assistant chef in a cafeteria in L. A.'

'I don't want to cook,' said Jimmy. 'I don't want no cinch job. I served in the Marines in Nicaragua. Gimme a gun, and let me do guard duty.'

'Who else can cook?' demanded Orman. 'We need three.'

'Shorty can cook,' said a voice from the rear. 'He used to run a hot-dog stand on Ventura Boulevard.'

'O.K.!' said Orman. 'Miss Terry is chief cook; Jimmy and Shorty will help her; Pat will detail three more for K.P. every day. Now get busy. While the cooks are rustling some grub the rest of you strike the tents and load the trucks.'

'Oh, Tom,' said Naomi Madison at his elbow, 'my personal boy has run away with the others. I wish you would detail one of the men to take his place.'

Orman wheeled and looked at her in astonishment. 'I'd forgotten all about you, Naomi. I'm glad you reminded me. If you can't cook, and I don't suppose you can, you'll peel spuds, wait on the tables, and help wash dishes.'

For a moment the Madison looked aghast; then she smiled icily. 'I suppose you think you are funny,' she said, 'but really this is no time for joking.'

'I'm not joking, Naomi.' His tone was serious, his face unsmiling.

'Do you mean to say that you expect me, Naomi Madison, to peel potatoes, wait on table, and wash dishes! Don't be ridiculous – I shall do nothing of the kind.'

'Be yourself, Naomi! Before Milt Smith discovered you you were slinging hash in a joint on Main Street; and you'll do it again here, or you won't eat.' He turned and walked away.

During breakfast Naomi Madison sat in haughty aloofness in the back seat of an automobile. She did not wait on table, nor did she eat.

Americans and Arabs formed the advance and rear guards when the safari finally got underway; but the crew that cut trail was wholly

American – the Arabs would fight, but they would not work; that was beneath their dignity.

Not until the last kitchen utensil was washed, packed, and loaded did Rhonda Terry go to the car in which she and Naomi Madison rode. She was flushed and a little tired as she entered the car.

Naomi eyed her with compressed lips. 'You're a fool, Rhonda,' she snapped. 'You shouldn't have lowered yourself by doing that menial work. We were not employed to be scullery maids.'

Rhonda nodded toward the head of the column. 'There probably isn't anything in those boys' contracts about chopping down trees or fighting cannibals.' She took a paper-wrapped parcel from her bag. 'I brought you some sandwiches. I thought you might be hungry.'

The Madison ate in silence, and for a long time thereafter she seemed to be immersed in thought.

The column moved slowly. The axe men were not accustomed to the sort of work they were doing, and in the heat of the equatorial forest they tired quickly. The trail opened with exasperating slowness as though the forest begrudged every foot of progress that they made.

Orman worked with his men, wielding an axe when trees were to be felled, marching with the advance guard when the trail was opened.

'Tough goin',' remarked Bill West, leaning his axe handle against his hip and wiping the perspiration from his eyes.

'This isn't the toughest part of it,' replied Orman.

'How come?'

'Since the guides scrammed we don't know where we're goin'.'

West whistled. 'I hadn't thought of that.'

As they trudged on an opening in the forest appeared ahead of them shortly after noon. It was almost treeless and covered with a thick growth of tall grass higher than a man's head.

'That certainly looks good,' remarked Orman. 'We ought to make a little time for a few minutes.'

The leading truck forged into the open, flattening the grass beneath its great tires.

'Hop aboard the trucks!' Orman shouted to the advance guard and the axe men. 'Those beggars won't bother us here; there are no trees to hide them.'

Out into the open moved the long column of cars. A sense of relief from the oppressive closeness of the forest animated the entire company.

And then, as the rearmost truck bumped into the clearing, a shower of arrows whirred from the tall grasses all along the line. Savage war cries filled the air; and for the first time the Bansutos showed themselves, as their spearmen rushed forward with screams of hate and blood lust.

A driver near the head of the column toppled from his seat with an arrow through his heart. His truck veered to the left and went careering off into the midst of the savages.

Rifles cracked, men shouted and cursed, the wounded screamed. The column stopped, that every man might use his rifle. Naomi Madison slipped to the floor of the car. Rhonda drew her revolver and fired into the faces of the onrushing blacks. A dozen men hurried to the defense of the car that carried the two girls.

Someone shouted, 'Look out! They're on the other side too.' Rifles were turned in the direction of the new threat. The fire was continuous and deadly. The Bansutos, almost upon them, wavered and fell back. A fusillade of shots followed them as they disappeared into the dense grass, followed and found many of them.

It was soon over; perhaps the whole affair had not lasted two minutes. But it had wrought havoc with the company. A dozen men were dead or dying, a truck was wrecked, the morale of the little force was shattered.

Orman turned the command of the advance guard over to West and hurried back down the line to check up on casualties. O'Grady was running forward to meet him.

'We'd better get out of here, Tom,' he cried; 'those devils may fire the grass.'

Orman paled. He had not thought of that. 'Load the dead and wounded onto the nearest cars, and get going!' he ordered. 'We'll have to check up later.'

The relief that the party had felt when they entered the grassy clearing was only equalled by that which they experienced when they left it to pull into the dense, soggy forest where the menace of fire, at least, was reduced to a minimum.

Then O'Grady went along the line with his roster of the company checking the living and the dead. The bodies of Noice, Baine, seven other Americans and three Arabs were on the trucks.

'Obroski!' shouted O'Grady. 'Obroski! Has anyone seen Obroski!'

'Bless my soul!' exclaimed Gordon Z. Marcus. 'I saw him. I remember now. When those devils came up on our left, he jumped out of the other side of the car and ran off into that tall grass.'

Orman started back toward the rear of the column. 'Where you goin', Tom?' demanded West.

'To look for Obroski.'

'Yon can't go alone. I'll go with you.'

Half a dozen others accompanied them, but though they searched for the better part of an hour they found no sign of Obroski either dead or alive.

Silent, sad, and gloomy, the company found a poor camping site late in the afternoon. When they spoke, they spoke in subdued tones, and there was no joking or laughing. Glumly they sat at table when supper was announced, and few appeared to notice and none commented upon the fact that the famous Naomi Madison waited on them.

CHAPTER EIGHT
The Coward

We are all either the victims or the beneficiaries of heredity and environment. Stanley Obroski was one of the victims. Heredity had given him a mighty physique, a noble bearing, and a handsome face. Environment had sheltered and protected him throughout his life. Also, everyone with whom he had come in contact had admired his great strength and attributed to him courage commensurate to it.

Never until the past few days had Obroski been confronted by an emergency that might test his courage, and so all his life he had been wondering if his courage would measure up to what was expected of it when the emergency developed.

He had given the matter far more thought than does the man of ordinary physique because he knew that so much more was expected of him than of the ordinary man. It had become an obsession together with the fear that he might not live up to the expectations of his admirers. And finally he became afraid – afraid of being afraid.

It is a failing of nearly all large men to be keenly affected by ridicule. It was the fear of ridicule, should he show fear, rather than fear of physical suffering, that Obroski shrank from; though perhaps he did not realise this. It was a psyche far too complex for easy analysis.

But the results were disastrous. They induced a subconscious urge to avoid danger rather than risk showing fear and thus inducing ridicule.

And when the first shower of arrows fell among the cars of the safari Obroski leaped from the opposite side of the automobile in which he was riding and disappeared among the tall grasses that hemmed them in on both sides. His reaction to danger had been entirely spontaneous – a thing beyond his will.

As he pushed blindly forward he was as unthinking as a terrified animal bent only upon escape. But he had covered only a few yards when he ran directly into the arms of a giant black warrior.

Here indeed was an emergency. The black was as surprised as Obroski. He probably thought that all the whites were charging to the attack; he was terrified. He wanted to flee, but the white was too close; so he leaped for him, calling loudly for his fellows as he did so.

It was too late for Obroski to escape the clutching fingers of the black. If he didn't do something the man would kill him! If he could get rid of the fellow he could run back to the safari. He *must* get rid of him!

The black had seized him by the clothes, and now Obroski saw a knife in the fellow's free hand. Death stared him in the face! Heretofore Obroski's dangers had always been more or less imaginary; now he was faced with a stark reality.

Terror galvanized his mind and his giant muscles into instant action. He seized the black and lifted him above his head; then he hurled him heavily to the ground.

The black, fearful of his life, started to rise; and Obroski, equally fearful of his own, lifted him again high overhead and again cast him down. As he did so a half dozen blacks closed upon him from the tall surrounding grasses and bore him to the earth.

His mind half numb with terror, Obroski fought like a cornered rat. The blacks were no match for his great muscles. He seized them and tossed them aside; then he turned to run. But the black he had first hurled to the ground reached out and seized him by an ankle, tripping him; then the others were upon him again and more came to their assistance. They held him by force of numbers and bound his hands behind him.

In all his life Stanley Obroski had never fought before. A good disposition and his strange complex had prevented him from seeking trouble, and his great size and strength had deterred others from picking quarrels with him. He had never realized his own strength; and now, his mental faculties cloyed by terror, he only partly appreciated it. All he could think of was that they had bound his hands and he was helpless; that they would kill him.

At last they dragged him to his feet. Why they did not kill him he could not guess – then. They seemed a little awed by his great size and strength. They jabbered much among themselves as they led him away toward the forest.

Obroski heard the savage war cries of the main body as it attacked the safari and the crack of rifles that told that his fellows were putting up a spirited defense. A few bullets whirred close, and one of his captors lunged forward with a slug in his heart.

They took him into the forest and along a winding trail where presently they were overtaken by other members of the tribe, and with the arrival of each new contingent he was surrounded by jabbering savages who punched him and poked him, feeling of his great muscles, comparing his height with theirs.

Bloodshot eyes glared from hideous, painted faces – glared in hatred that required no knowledge of their language to interpret. Some threatened him with spears and knives, but the party that had captured him preserved him from these.

Stanley Obroski was so terrified that he walked as one in a trance, giving no outward sign of any emotion; but the blacks thought that his manner was indicative of the indifference of great bravery.

At last a very large warrior overtook them. He was resplendent in paint and feathers, in many necklaces and armlets and anklets. He bore an ornate shield, and his spear and his bow and the quiver for his arrows were more gorgeously decorated than those of his fellows.

But it was his commanding presence and his air of authority more than these that led Obroski to infer that he was a chief. As he listened to the words of those who had made the capture, he examined the prisoner with savage disdain; then he spoke commandingly to those about him and strode on. The others followed, and afterward none threatened to harm the white man.

All afternoon they marched, deeper and deeper into the gloomy forest. The cords about Obroski's wrists cut into the flesh and hurt him; another cord about his neck, by which a savage led him, was far too tight for comfort; and when the savage jerked it, as he occasionally did, Obroski was half choked.

He was very miserable, but he was so numb with terror that he made no outcry nor any complaint. Perhaps he felt that it would be useless, and that the less he caused them annoyance or called attention to himself the better off he would be.

The result of this strategy, if such it were, he could not have guessed; for he could not understand their words when they spoke among themselves of the bravery of the white man who showed no fear.

During the long march his thoughts were often of the members of the company he had deserted. He wondered how they had fared in the fight and if any had been killed. He knew that many of the men had held him in contempt before. What would they think of him now! Marcus must have seen him run away at the first threat of danger. Obroski winced, the old terrifying fear of ridicule swept over him; but it was nothing compared to the acute terror he suffered as he shot quick glances about him at the savage faces of his captors and recalled the stories he had heard of torture and death at the hands of such as these.

He heard shouting ahead, and a moment later the trail debouched onto a clearing in the center of which was a palisaded village of conical, straw-thatched huts. It was late in the afternoon, and Obroski knew that they must have covered considerable distance since his capture. He wondered, in the event that he escaped or they released him, if he could find his way back to the trail of the safari. He had his doubts.

As they entered the village, women and children pressed forward to see him. They shouted at him. From the expressions of the faces of many of the women he judged that they were reviling and cursing him. A few struck or clawed him. The children threw stones and refuse at him.

The warriors guarding him beat his assailants off, as they conducted him down the single street of the village to a hut near the far end. Here they motioned him to enter; but the doorway was so low that one might only pass through it on hands and knees, and as his hands were fastened behind his back that was out of the question for him. So they threw him down and dragged him in. Then they bound his ankles and left him.

The interior of the hut was dark, but as his eyes became accustomed to the change from daylight he was able to see his surroundings dimly. It was then that he became aware that he was not alone in the hut. Within the range of his vision he saw three figures, evidently men. One was stretched out upon the packed earth floor, the other two sat hunched forward over their updrawn knees. He felt the eyes of the latter upon him. He wondered what they were doing there – if they, too, were prisoners.

Presently one of them spoke. 'How the Bansuto get you, Bwana Simba?' It was the name the blacks of the safari had given him because of the part that he was to take in the picture, that of the Lion Man.

'Who the devil are you?' demanded Obroski.

'Kwamudi,' replied the speaker.

'Kwamudi! Well, it didn't do you much good to run away—' He almost added 'either' but stopped himself in time. 'They attacked the safari shortly after noon. I was taken prisoner then. How did they get you?'

'Early this morning. I had followed my people, trying to get them to return to the safari.' Obroski guessed that Kwamudi was lying. 'We ran into a party of warriors coming from a distant village to join the main tribe. They killed many of my people. Some escaped. They took some prisoners. Of these they killed all but Kwamudi and these two. They brought us here.'

'What are they going to do with you? Why didn't they kill you when they killed the others?'

'They not kill you, they not kill Kwamudi, they not kill these others – yet – all for same reason. Kill by and by.'

'Why? What do they want to kill us for?'

'They eat.'

'Eh? You don't mean to say they're cannibals!'

'Not like some. Bansuto not eat men all time; not eat all men. Only chiefs, brave men, strong men. Eat brave men, make them brave; eat strong men, make them strong; eat chiefs, make them wise.'

'How horrible!' muttered Obroski. 'But they can't eat me – I am not a chief – I am not brave – I am a coward,' he mumbled.

'What, Bwana'?'

'Oh, nothing. When do you suppose they'll do it? Right away?'

Kwamudi shook his head. 'Maybe. Maybe not for long time. Witch doctor make medicine, talk to spirits, talk to moon. They tell him when. Maybe soon, maybe long time.'

'And will they keep us tied up this way until they kill us? It's mighty uncomfortable. But then, you aren't tied, are you?'

'Yes, Kwamudi tied – hands and feet. That why he lean forward across his knees.'

'Can you talk their language, Kwamudi?'

'A little.'

'Ask them to free our hands, and our feet too if they will.'

'No good. Waste talk.'

'Listen, Kwamudi! They want us to be strong when they eat us, don't they?'

'Yes, Bwana.'

'Very well; then get hold of the chief and tell him that if he keeps us tied up like this we'll get weak. He's certainly got brains enough to know that that's true. He's got plenty of warriors to guard us, and I don't see how we could get out of this village anyhow – not with all those harpies and brats hanging around.'

Kwamudi understood enough of what the white man had said to get the main idea. 'First time I get a chance, I tell him,' he said.

Darkness fell. The light from the cooking fires was visible through the low doorway of the prison hut. Women were screaming and wailing for the warriors who had fallen in battle that day. Many had painted their bodies from head to feet with ashes, rendering them even more hideous than nature had fashioned them. Others laughed and gossiped.

Obroski was thirsty and hungry, but they brought him neither water nor food. The hours dragged on. The warriors commenced to dance in celebration of their victory. Tom-toms boomed dismally through the night. The wails of the mourners, the screams and war cries of the dancers rose and fell in savage consonance with the savage scene, adding to the depression of the prisoners.

'This is no way to treat people you're going to eat,' grumbled Obroski. 'You ought to get 'em fat, not starve 'em thin.'

'Bansuto do not care about our fat,' observed Kwamudi. 'They eat our hearts, the palms of our hands, the soles of our feet. They eat the muscles from your arms and legs. They eat my brains.'

'You're not very cheering, and you're not very complimentary,' said Obroski with a wry smile. 'But at that there isn't much to choose between our brains, for they've ended up by getting us both into the same hole.'

CHAPTER NINE

Treachery

Orman and Bill West entered the cook tent after supper. 'We're going to do the dishes, Rhonda,' said the director. 'We're so short-handed now we got to take the K.P.'s off and give 'em to Pat for guard duty. Jimmy and Shorty will stay on cooking and help with the other work.'

Rhonda demurred with a shake of her head. 'You boys have had a tough day. All we've done is sit in an automobile. Sit down here and smoke and talk to us – we need cheering up. The four of us can take care of the dishes. Isn't that right?' She turned toward Jimmy, Shorty, and Naomi.

'Sure!' said Jimmy and Shorty in unison.

Naomi nodded. 'I've washed dishes till after midnight for a lot of Main Street bums many a time. I guess I can wash 'em for you bums, too,' she added with a laugh. 'But for the love o' Mike, do as Rhonda said – sit down and talk to us, and *say something funny*. I'm nearly nuts.'

There was a moment's awkward silence. They could have been only a little more surprised had they seen Queen Mary turn handsprings across Trafalgar Square.

Then Tom Orman laughed and slapped Naomi on the back. 'Atta girl!' he exclaimed.

Here was a new Madison; they were all sure that they were going to like her better than the old.

'I don't mind sitting down,' admitted West. 'And I don't mind talking, but I'm damned if I can be funny – I can't forget Clarence and Jerrold and the rest of them.'

'Poor Stanley,' said Rhonda. 'He won't even get a decent burial.'

'He don't deserve one,' growled Jimmy, who had served with the Marines; 'he deserted under fire.'

'Let's not be too hard on him,' begged Rhonda. 'No one is a coward because he wants to be. It's something one can't help. We ought to pity him.' Jimmy grumbled in dissent.

Bill West grunted. 'Perhaps we would, if we were all stuck on him.'

Rhonda turned and eyed him coolly. 'He may have had his faults,' she said, 'but at least I never heard him say an unkind thing about anyone.'

'He was never awake long enough,' said Jimmy contemptuously.

'I don't know what I'm goin' to do without him,' observed Orman. 'There isn't anybody in the company I can double for him.'

'You don't think you're going on with the picture after what's happened, do you?' asked Naomi.

'That's what we came over here for, and that's what were goin' to do if it takes a leg,' replied Orman.

'But you've lost your leading man and your heavy and your sound man and a lot more, and you haven't any guides, and you haven't any porters. If you think you can go on with a picture like that, you're just plain cuckoo, Tom.'

'I never saw a good director who wasn't cuckoo,' said Bill West.

Pat O'Grady stuck his head inside the tent. 'The Chief here?' he asked. 'Oh, there you are! Say, Tom, Atewy says old Ghrennem will stand all the guard with his men from 12 to 6 if we'll take care of it from now to midnight. He wants to know if that's all right with you. Atewy says the Arabs can do better together than workin' with Americans that they can't understand.'

'OK.' replied Orman. 'That's sort of decent of 'em takin' that shift. It'll give our boys a chance to rest up before we shove off in the morning, and God knows they need it. Tell 'em we'll call 'em at midnight.'

Exhausted by the physical and nervous strains of the day, those members of the company that were not on guard were soon asleep. For the latter it was a long stretch to midnight, a tour of duty rendered still more trying by the deadly monotony of the almost unbroken silence of the jungle. Only faintly from great distances came the usual sounds to which they had become accustomed. It was as though they had been abandoned by even the beasts of the forest. But at last midnight came, and O'Grady awoke the Arabs. Tired men stumbled through the darkness to their blankets, and within fifteen minutes every American in the camp was deep in the sleep of utter exhaustion.

Even the unwonted activity of the Arabs could not arouse them; though, to be sure, the swart sons of the desert moved as silently as the work they were engaged upon permitted – rather unusual work it seemed for those whose sole duty it was to guard the camp.

It was full daylight before an American stirred – several hours later than it was customary for the life of the camp to begin.

Gordon Z. Marcus was the first to be up, for old age is prone to awaken earlier than youth. He had dressed hurriedly, for he had noted the daylight and the silence of the camp. Even before he came into the open he sensed that something was amiss. He looked quickly about. The camp seemed deserted. The fires had died to smoldering embers. No sentry stood on guard.

Marcus hastened to the tent occupied by Orman and O'Grady, and without formality burst into the interior. 'Mr Orman! Mr Orman!' he shouted.

Orman and O'Grady, startled out of deep sleep by the excited voice of the old character man, threw aside their mosquito bars and leaped from their cots.

'What's wrong?' demanded Orman.

'The Arabs!' exclaimed Marcus. 'They've gone! Their tents, their horses, everything!'

Neither of the other men spoke as they quickly slipped into their clothes and stepped out into the open. Orman looked quickly about the camp.

'They must have been gone for hours,' he said; 'the fires are out.' Then he shrugged. 'We'll have to get along without them, but that doesn't mean that we got to stop eating. Where are the cooks? Wake the girls, Marcus, please, and rout out Jimmy and Shorty.'

'I thought those fellows were getting mighty considerate all of a sudden when they offered to stand guard after midnight last night,' remarked O'Grady.

'I might have known there was something phoney about it,' growled Orman. 'They played me for a sucker. I'm nothin' but a damn boob.'

'Here comes Marcus again,' said O'Grady. 'I wonder what's eatin' him now – he looks fussed.'

And Gordon Z. Marcus was fussed. Before he reached the two men he called aloud to them. 'The girls aren't there,' he shouted, 'and their tent's a mess.'

Orman turned and started on a run for the cook tent. 'They're probably getting breakfast,' he explained. But there was no one in the cook tent.

Everyone was astir now; and a thorough search of the camp was made, but there was no sign of either Naomi Madison or Rhonda Terry. Bill West searched the same places again and again, unwilling to believe the abhorrent evidence of his own eyes. Orman was making a small pack of food, blankets, and ammunition.

'Why do you suppose they took them?' asked Marcus.

'For ransom, most likely,' suggested O'Grady.

'I wish I was sure of that,' said Orman; 'but there is still a safe market for girls in Africa and Asia.'

'I wonder why they tore everything to pieces so in the tent,' mused Marcus. 'It looks like a cyclone had struck it.'

'There wasn't any fight,' said O'Grady. 'It would have waked some of us up if there had been.'

'The Arabs were probably looking for loot,' suggested Jimmy.

Bill West had been watching Orman. Now he too was making a pack. The director noticed it.

'What do you think you're goin' to do?' he asked.

'I'm goin' with you,' replied West.

Orman shook his head. 'Nothing doing! This is my funeral.'

West continued his preparations without reply.

'If you fellows are going out to look for the girls, I'm goin' with you,' announced O'Grady.

'Same here,' said another.

The whole company volunteered.

'I'm goin' alone,' announced Orman. 'One man on foot can travel faster than this motorcade and faster than men on horseback who will have to stop and cut trail in places.'

'But what in hell can one man do after he catches up with those rats?' demanded O'Grady. 'He'll just get himself killed. He can't fight 'em all.'

'I don't intend to fight,' replied Orman. 'I got the girls into this mess by not using my head; I'm going to use it to get them out. Those Arabs will do any-thing for money, and I can offer them more for the girls than they can hope to get from anyone else.'

O'Grady scratched his head. 'I guess you're right, Tom.'

'Sure I'm right. You are in charge of the outfit while I'm away. Get it to the Omwamwi Falls, and wait there for me. You'll be able to hire natives there. Send a runner back to Jinja by the southern route with a message for the stu-dio telling what's happened and asking for orders if I don't show up again in thirty days.'

'You're not going without breakfast!' demanded Marcus.

'No; I'll eat first,' replied Orman.

'How about grub?' shouted O'Grady.

'Comin' right up!' yelled back Shorty from the cook tent.

Orman ate hurriedly, giving final instructions to O'Grady between mouth-fuls. When he had finished he got up, shouldered his pack, and picked up his rifle.

'So long, boys!' he said.

They crowded up to shake his hand and wish him luck. Bill West was adjusting the straps of a pack that he had slung to his back. Orman eyed him.

'You can't come, Bill,' he said. 'This is my job.'

'I'm coming along,' replied West.

'I won't let you.'

'You and who else?' demanded West, and then added in a voice that he tried hard to control, 'Rhonda's out there somewhere.'

The hard lines of grim stubbornness on Orman's face softened. 'Come on then,' he said; 'I hadn't thought of it that way, Bill.'

The two men crossed the camp and picked up the plain trail of the horse-men moving northward.

CHAPTER TEN

Torture

Stanley Obroski had never before welcomed a dawn with such enthusiasm. The new day might bring him death, but almost anything would be preferable to the hideous discomforts of the long night that had finally dragged its pain-racked length into the past.

His bonds had hurt him; his joints ached from long inaction and from cold; he was hungry, but he suffered more from thirst; vermin crawled over him at will and bit him; they and the cold and the hideous noises of the mourners and the dancers and the drums had combined to deny him sleep.

All these things had sapped his strength, both physical and nervous, leaving him exhausted. He felt like a little child who was afraid and wanted to cry. The urge to cry was almost irresistible. It seemed to offer relief from the maddening tension.

A vague half-conviction forced its way into the muddy chaos of his numb brain – crying would be a sign of fear, and fear meant cowardice! Obroski did not cry. Instead, he found partial relief in swearing. He had never been given to profanity, but even though he lacked practice he acquitted himself nobly.

His efforts awoke Kwamudi who had slept peacefully in this familiar environment. The two men conversed haltingly – mostly about their hunger and thirst.

'Yell for water and food,' suggested Obroski, 'and keep on yelling until they bring it.'

Kwamudi thought that might be a good plan, and put it into execution. After five minutes it brought results. One of the guards outside the hut was awakened. He came in saying things.

In the meantime both the other prisoners had awakened and were sitting up. One of these was nearer the hut doorway than his fellows. He therefore chanced to be the first in the path of the guard, who commenced to belabor him over the head and shoulders with the haft of his spear.

'If you make any more noise like that,' said the guard, 'I'll cut out the tongues of all of you.' Then he went outside and fell asleep again.

'That idea,' observed Obroski, 'was not so hot.'

'What, Bwana?' inquired Kwamudi.

The morning dragged on until almost noon, and still the village slept. It was sleeping off the effects of the previous night's orgy. But at last the women commenced to move about, making preparations for breakfast.

Fully an hour later warriors came to the hut. They dragged and kicked the prisoners into the open and jerked them to their feet after removing the bonds from their ankles; then they led them to a large hut near the center of the village. It was the hut of Rungula, chief of the Bansutos.

Rungula sat on a low stool before the doorway. Behind him were ranged the more important sub-chiefs; and on the flanks, forming a wide semicircle, were grouped the remainder of the warriors – a thousand savage fighting men from many a far-flung Bansuto village.

From the doorway of the chief's hut several of his wives watched the proceedings, while a brood of children spewed out between their feet into the open sunshine.

Rungula eyed the white prisoner with scowling brows; then he spoke to him.

'What is he saying, Kwamudi?' asked Obroski.

'He is asking what you were doing in his country.'

'Tell him that we were only passing through – that we are friends – that he must let us go.'

When Kwamudi interpreted Obroski's speech Rungula laughed. 'Tell the white man that only a chief who is greater than Rungula can say *must* to Rungula and that there is no chief greater than Rungula.

'The white man will be killed and so will all his people. He would have been killed yesterday had he not been so big and strong.'

'He will not stay strong if he does not have food and water,' replied Kwamudi. 'None of us will do you any good if you starve us and keep us tied up.'

Rungula thought this over and discussed it with some of his lieutenants; then he stood up and approached Obroski. He fingered the white man's shirt, jabbering incessantly. He appeared much impressed also by Obroski's breeches and boots.

'He says for you to take off your clothes, Bwana,' said Kwamudi; 'he wants them.'

'All of them?' inquired Obroski.

'All of them, Bwana.'

Exhausted by sleeplessness, discomfort, and terror, Obroski had felt that nothing but torture and death could add to his misery, but now the thought of nakedness awoke him to new horrors. To the civilized man clothing imparts a self-confidence that is stripped away with his garments. But Obroski dared not refuse.

'Tell him I can't take my clothes off with my hands tied behind my back.'

When Kwamudi had interpreted this last, Rungula directed that Obroski's hands be released.

The white man removed his shirt and tossed it to Rungula. Then the chief pointed at his boots. Slowly Obroski unlaced and removed them, sitting on the ground to do so. Rungula became intrigued by the white man's socks and jerked these off himself.

Obroski rose and waited. Rungula felt of his great muscles and jabbered some more with his fellows. Then he called his tallest warrior and stood him beside the prisoner. Obroski towered above the man. The blacks jabbered excitedly.

Rungula touched Obroski's breeches and grunted.

'He want them,' said Kwamudi.

'Oh, for Pete's sake, tell him to have a heart,' exclaimed Obroski. 'Tell him I got to have something to wear.'

Kwamudi and the chief spoke together briefly, with many gesticulations.

'Take them off, Bwana,' said the former. 'There is nothing else you can do. He says he will give you something to wear.'

As he unbuttoned his breeches and slipped them off, Obroski was painfully aware of giggling girls and women in the background. But the worst was yet to come – Rungula was greatly delighted by the gay silk shorts that the removal of the breeches revealed.

When these had passed to the ownership of Rungula, Obroski could feel the hot flush beneath the heavy coat of tan he had acquired on the beach at Malibu.

'Tell him to give me something to wear,' he begged.

Rungula laughed uproariously when the demand was made known to him; but he turned and called something to the women in his hut, and a moment later a little pickaninny came running out with a very dirty G string which he threw at Obroski's feet.

Shortly after, the prisoners were returned to their hut; but their ankles were not bound again, nor were Obroski's wrists. While he was removing the bonds from the wrists of his fellow prisoners a woman came with food and water for them. Thereafter they were fed with reasonable regularity.

Monotonously the days dragged. Each slow, hideous night seemed an eternity to the white prisoner. He shivered in his nakedness and sought warmth by huddling close between the bodies of two of the blacks. All of them were alive with vermin.

A week passed, and then one night some warriors came and took one of the black prisoners away. Obroski and the others watched through the doorway. The man disappeared around the corner of a hut near the chief's. They never saw him again.

The tom-toms commenced their slow thrumming; the voices of men rose in a weird chant; occasionally the watchers caught a glimpse of savage dancers as their steps led them from behind the corner of a hut that hid the remainder of the scene.

Suddenly a horrid scream of agony rose above the voices of the dancers.

For a half hour occasional groans punctuated the savage cries of the warriors, but at last even these ceased.

'He is gone, Bwana,' whispered Kwamudi.

'Yes, thank God!' muttered the white man. 'What agony he must have suffered!'

The following night warriors came and took away the second black prisoner. Obroski tried to stop his ears against the sounds of the man's passing. That night he was very cold, for there was only Kwamudi to warm him on one side.

'Tomorrow night, Bwana,' said the black, 'you will sleep alone.'

'And the next night—?'

'There will be none, Bwana – for you.'

During the cold, sleepless hours Obroski's thoughts wandered back through the past, the near past particularly. He thought of Naomi Madison, and wondered if she were grieving much over his disappearance. Something told him she was not.

Most of the other figures were pale in his thoughts – he neither liked nor disliked them; but there was one who stood out even more clearly than the memory picture of Naomi. It was Orman. His hatred of Orman rose above all his other passions – it was greater than his love for Naomi, greater than his fear of torture and death. He hugged it to his breast now and nursed it and thanked God for it, because it made him forget the lice and the cold and the things that were to happen to him on the next night or the next.

The hours dragged on; day came and went, and night came again. Obroski and Kwamudi, watching, saw warriors approaching the hut.

'They come, Bwana,' said the black. 'Goodbye!'

But this time they took them both. They took them to the open space before the hut of Rungula, chief of the Bansutos, and tied them flat against the boles of two trees, facing one another.

Here Obroski watched them work upon Kwamudi. He saw tortures so fiendish, so horrible, so obscene that he feared for his reason, thinking that these visions must be the figments of a mad brain. He tried to look away, but the horror of it fascinated him. And so he saw Kwamudi die.

Afterward he saw even more disgusting sights, sights that nauseated him. He wondered when they would commence on him, and prayed that it would be soon and soon over. He tried to steel himself against fear, but he knew that he was afraid. By every means within the power of his will he sought to bolster a determination not to give them the satisfaction of knowing that he suffered when his turn came; for he had seen that they gloated over the agonies of Kwamudi.

It was almost morning when they removed the thongs that bound him to the tree and led him back to the hut. Then it became evident that they were not going to kill him – this night. It meant that his agony was to be prolonged.

In the cold of the coming dawn he huddled alone on the filthy floor of his prison, sleepless and shivering; and the lice swarmed over his body unmolested. He had plumbed the nadir of misery and hopelessness and found there a dull apathy that preserved his reason.

Finally he slept, nor did he awaken until midafternoon. He was warm then; and new life seemed to course through his veins, bringing new hope. Now he commenced to plan. He would not die as the others had died, like sheep led to the slaughter. The longer he considered his plan the more anxious he became to put it into execution, awaiting impatiently those who were to lead him to torture.

His plan did not include escape; for that he was sure was impossible, but it did include a certain measure of revenge and death without torture. Obroski's reason was tottering.

When he saw the warriors coming to get him he came out of the hut and met them, a smile upon his lips.

Then they led him away as they had led the three blacks before him.

CHAPTER ELEVEN

The Last Victim

Tarzan of the Apes was ranging a district that was new to him, and with the keen alertness of the wild creature he was alive to all that was strange or unusual. Upon the range of his knowledge depended his ability to cope with the emergencies of an unaccustomed environment. Nothing was so trivial that it did not require investigation; and already, in certain matters concerning the haunts and habits of game both large and small, he knew quite as much if not more than many creatures that had been born here.

For three nights he had heard the almost continuous booming of tom-toms, faintly from afar; and during the day following the third night he had drifted slowly in his hunting in the direction from which the sounds had come.

He had seen something of the natives who inhabited this region. He had witnessed their methods of warfare against the whites who had invaded their territory. His sympathies had been neither with one side nor the other. He had seen Orman, drunk, lashing his black porters; and he had felt that whatever misfortunes overtook him he deserved them.

Tarzan did not know these Tarmangani; and so they were even less to him than the other beasts that they would have described as lower orders but which Tarzan, who knew all orders well, considered their superiors in many aspects of heart and mind.

Some passing whim, some slight incitement, might have caused him to befriend them actively, as he had often befriended Numa and Sabor and Sheeta, who were by nature his hereditary enemies. But no such whim had seized him, no such incitement had occurred; and he had seen them go upon their way and had scarcely given them a thought since the last night that he had entered their camp.

He had heard the fusillade of shots that had followed the attack of the Bansutos upon the safari; but he had been far away, and as he had already witnessed similar attacks during the preceding days his curiosity was not aroused; and he had not investigated.

The doings of the Bansutos interested him far more. The Tarmangani would soon be gone – either dead or departed – but the Gomangani would be here always; and he must know much about them if he were to remain in their country.

Lazily he swung through the trees in the direction of their village. He was alone now; for the great golden lion. Jad-bal-ja, was hunting elsewhere, hunting trouble, Tarzan thought with a half smile as he recalled the sleek young lioness that the great beast had followed off into the forest fastness.

It was dark before the ape-man reached the village of Rungula. The rhythm of the tom-toms blended with a low, mournful chant. A few warriors were dancing listlessly – a tentative excursion into the borderland of savage ecstacy into which they would later hurl themselves as their numbers increased with the increasing tempo of the dance.

Tarzan watched from the concealment of the foliage of a tree at the edge of the clearing that encircled the village. He was not greatly interested; the savage orgies of the blacks were an old story to him. Apparently there was nothing here to hold his attention, and he was about to turn away when his eyes were attracted to the figure of a man who contrasted strangely with the savage black warriors of the village.

He was entering the open space where the dancers were holding forth – a tall, bronzed, almost naked white man surrounded by a group of warriors. He was evidently a prisoner.

The ape-man's curiosity was aroused. Silently he dropped to the ground, and keeping in the dense shadows of the forest well out of the moonlight he circled to the back of the village. Here there was no life, the interest of the villagers being centered upon the activities near the chief's hut.

Cautiously but quickly Tarzan crossed the strip of moonlit ground between the forest and the palisade. The latter was built of poles sunk into the ground close together and lashed with pliant creepers. It was about ten feet high.

A few quick steps, a running jump, and Tarzan's fingers closed upon the top of the barrier. Drawing himself cautiously up, he looked over into the village. In silence he listened, sniffing the air. Satisfied, he threw a leg over the top of the palisade; and a moment later dropped lightly to the ground inside the village of Rungula, the Bansuto.

When the ground had been cleared for the village a number of trees had been left standing within the palisade to afford shelter from the equatorial sun. One of these overhung Rungula's hut, as Tarzan had noticed from the forest; and it was this tree that he chose from which to examine the white prisoner more closely.

Keeping well in the rear of the chief's hut and moving cautiously from the shadow of one hut to that of the next, the ape-man approached his goal. Had he moved noisily the sound of his coming would have been drowned by the tom-toms and the singing; but he moved without sound, as was second nature to him.

The chance of discovery lay in the possibility that some native might not have yet left his hut to join the throng around the dancers and that such a belated one would see the strange white giant and raise an alarm. But Tarzan came to the rear of Rungula's hut unseen.

Here fortune again favored him; for while the stem of the tree he wished to enter stood in front of the hut in plain view of the entire tribe another, smaller tree, grew at the rear of the hut; and, above it, mingled its branches with its fellow.

As the ape-man moved stealthily into the trees and out upon a great branch that would hold his weight without bending, the savage scene below unfolded itself before him. The tempo of the dance had increased. Painted warriors were leaping and stamping around a small group that surrounded the prisoner, and as Tarzan's gaze fell upon the man he experienced something in the nature of a shock. It was as though his disembodied spirit hovered above and looked down upon himself, so startling was the likeness of this man to the Lord of the Jungle.

In stature, in coloring, even in the molding of his features he was a replica of Tarzan of the Apes; and Tarzan realized it instantly although it is not always that we can see our own likeness in another even when it exists.

Now indeed was the ape-man's interest aroused. He wondered who the man was and where he had come from. By the merest accident of chance he had not seen him when he had visited the camp of the picture company, and so he did not connect him with these people. His failure to do so might have been still further explained by the man's nakedness. The clothing that had been stripped from him might, had he still worn it, have served to place him definitely; but his nakedness gave him only fellowship with the beasts. Perhaps that is why Tarzan was inclined to be favorably impressed with him at first sight.

Obroski, unconscious that other eyes than those of black enemies were upon him, gazed from sullen eyes upon the scene around him. Here, at the hands of these people, his three fellow prisoners had met hideous torture and death; but Obroski was in no mind to follow docilely in their footsteps. He had a plan.

He expected to die. He could find no slenderest hope for any other outcome, but he did not intend to submit supinely to torture. He had a plan.

Rungula squatted upon a stool eyeing the scene from bloodshot eyes beneath scowling brows. Presently he shouted directions to the warriors guarding Obroski, and they led him toward the tree on the opposite side of the open space. With thongs they prepared to bind him to the bole of the tree, and then it was that the prisoner put his plan into action; the plan of a fear-maddened brain.

Seizing the warrior nearest him he raised the man above his head as though he had been but a little child and hurled him into the faces of the others, knocking several of them to the ground. He sprang forward and laid hold upon a dancing buck, and him he flung to earth so heavily that he lay still as though dead.

So sudden, so unexpected had been his attack that it left the Bansutos momentarily stunned; then Rungula leaped to his feet. 'Seize him!' he cried; 'But do not harm him.' Rungula wished the mighty stranger to die after the manner of Rungula's own choosing, not the swift death that Obroski had hoped to win by his single-handed attack upon a thousand armed warriors.

As they closed upon him. Obroski felled them to right and left with mighty blows rendered even more terrific by the fear-maddened brain that directed them. Terror had driven him berserk.

The cries of the warriors, the screams of the women and children formed a horrid cacophony in his ears that incited him to madder outbursts of fury. The arms that reached out to seize him he seized and broke like pipe stems.

He wanted to scream and curse, yet he fought in silence. He wanted to cry out against the terror that engulfed him, but he made no sound. And so, in terror, he fought a thousand men.

But this one-sided battle could not go on for long. Slowly, by force of numbers, they closed upon him; they seized his ankles and his legs. With heavy fists he struck men unconscious with a single blow; but at last they dragged him down.

And then—

CHAPTER TWELVE
The Map

'Weyley!' sighed Eyad, dolorously. 'Methinks the sheykh hath done wrong to bring these *benat* with us. Now will the *Nasara* follow us with many guns; they will never cease until they have destroyed us and taken the *benat* back for themselves – I know *el-Engleys*.'

'*Ullah yelbisak berneta!*' scoffed Atewy.

'Thou foundest the map; was not that enough? They would not have followed and killed us for the map, but when you take away men's women they follow and kill – yes! Be they Arab, English, or Negro.' Eyad spat a period.

'I will tell thee, fool, why we brought the two girls,' said Atewy. 'There may be no valley of diamonds, or we may not find it. Should we therefore, after much effort, return to our own country empty-handed? These girls are not ill-favored. They will bring money at several places of which I know, or it may be that the mad *Nasara* will pay a large ransom for their return. But in the end we shall profit if they be not harmed by us; which reminds me, Eyad, that I have seen thee cast evil eyes upon them. *Wellah!* If one harms them the sheykh will kill him; and if the sheykh doth not, I will.'

'They will bring us nothing but trouble,' insisted Eyad. 'I wish that we were rid of them.'

'And there is still another reason why we brought them,' continued Atewy. 'The map is written in the language of *el-Engleys*, which I can speak but cannot read; the *benat* will read it to me. Thus it is well to keep them.'

But still Eyad grumbled. He was a dour young *Beduwy* with sinister eyes and a too full lower lip. Also, he did not speak what was in his thoughts; for the truth was not in him.

Since very early in the morning the horsemen had been pushing northward with the two girls. They had found and followed an open trail, and so had suffered no delays. Near the center of the little column rode the prisoners, often side by side; for much of the way the trail had been wide. It had been a trying day for them, not alone because of the fatigue of the hard ride, but from the nervous shock that the whole misadventure had entailed since Atewy and two others had crept into their tent scarcely more than an hour after midnight, silenced them with threats of death, and, after ransacking the tent, carried them away into the night.

All day long they had waited expectantly for signs of rescue, though realizing that they were awaiting the impossible. Men on foot could not have overtaken the horsemen, and no motor could traverse the trail they had followed without long delays for clearing trail in many places.

'I can't stand much more,' said Naomi. 'I'm about through.'

Rhonda reined closer to her. 'If you feel like falling, take hold of me.' she said. 'It can't last much longer today. They'll be making camp soon. It sure has been a tough ride – not much like following Ernie Vogt up Coldwater Canyon; and I used to come home from one of those rides and think I'd done something. Whew! They must have paved this saddle with bricks.'

'I don't see how you can stay so cheerful.'

'Cheerful! I'm about as cheerful as a Baby Star whose option hasn't been renewed.'

'Do you think they're going to kill us, Rhonda?'

'They wouldn't have bothered to bring us all this way to kill us. They're probably after a ransom.'

'I hope you're right. Tom'll pay 'em anything to get us back. But suppose they're going to sell us! I've heard that they sell white girls to black sultans in Africa.'

'The black sultan that gets me is goin' to be out of luck.'

The sun was low in the west when the Arabs made camp that night. Sheykh Ab el-Ghrennem had no doubt but that angry and determined men were pursuing him, but he felt quite certain that now they could not overtake him.

His first thought had been to put distance between himself and the *Nasara* he had betrayed – now he could look into the matter of the map of which Atewy had told him, possession of which had been the principal incentive of his knavery.

Supper over, he squatted where the light of the fire fell upon the precious document; and Atewy leaning over his shoulder scanned it with him.

'I can make nothing of it,' growled the sheykh. 'Fetch the *bint* from whom you took it.'

'I shall have to fetch them both,' replied Atewy, 'since I cannot tell them apart.'

'Fetch them both then,' commanded el-Ghrennem; and while he waited he puffed meditatively upon his *nargily*, thinking of a valley filled with diamonds and of the many riding camels and mares that they would buy; so that he was in a mellow humor when Atewy returned with the prisoners.

Rhonda walked with her chin up and the glint of battle in her eye, but Naomi revealed her fear in her white face and trembling limbs.

Sheykh Ab el-Ghrennem looked at her and smiled. '*Ma aleyk*,' he said in what were meant to be reassuring tones.

'He says,' interpreted Atewy, 'that thou hast nothing to fear – that there shall no evil befall thee.'

'You tell him,' replied Rhonda, 'that it will be just too bad for him if any evil does befall us and that if he wants to save his skin he had better return us to our people *pronto*.'

'The *Bedauwy* are not afraid of your people,' replied Atewy, 'but if you do what the sheykh asks no harm will come to you.'

'What does he want?' demanded Rhonda.

'He wishes you to help us to find the valley of diamonds,' replied Atewy.

'What valley of diamonds?'

'It is on this map which we cannot read because we cannot read the language of *el-Engleys*.' He pointed at the map the sheykh was holding.

Rhonda glanced at the paper and broke into laughter. 'You don't mean to tell me that you dumb bunnies kidnapped us because you believe that there *is* a valley of diamonds! Why, that's just a prop map.'

'Dumb bunnies! Prop! I do not understand.'

'I am trying to tell you that that map doesn't mean a thing. It was just for use in the picture we are making. You might as well return us to our people, for there isn't any valley of diamonds.'

Atewy and the sheykh jabbered excitedly to one another for a few moments, and then the former turned again to the girl. 'You cannot make fools of the *Bedauwy*,' he said. 'We are smarter than you. We knew that you would say that there is no valley of diamonds, because you want to save it all for your father. If you know what is well for you you will read this map for us and help us find the valley. Otherwise—' he scowled horridly and drew a forefinger across his throat.

Naomi shuddered; but Rhonda was not impressed – she knew that while they'd ransom or sale value the Arabs would not destroy them except as a last resort for self-protection.

'You are not going to kill us, Atewy,' she said, 'even if I do not read the map to you; but there is no reason why I should not read it. I am perfectly willing to; only don't blame us if there is no valley of diamonds.'

'Come here and sit beside Ab el-Ghrennem and read the map to us,' ordered Atewy.

Rhonda kneeled beside the sheykh and looked over his shoulder at the yellowed, time worn map. With a slender finger she pointed at the top of the map. 'This is north,' she said, 'and up here – this is the valley of diamonds. You see this little irregular thing directly west of the valley and close to it? It has an arrow pointing to it and a caption that says, "*Monolithic column: Red granite outcropping near only opening into valley*." And right north of it this arrow points to "*Entrance to valley*."

'Now here, at the south end of the valley, is the word "*Falls*" and below the falls a river that runs south and then southwest.'

'Ask her what this is,' the sheykh instructed Atewy, pointing to characters at the eastern edge of the map southeast of the falls.

'That says "*Cannibal village*"; explained the girl. 'And all across the map down there it says, "*Forest!*" See this river that rises at the southeast edge of the valley, flows east, southeast, and then west in a big loop before it enters the "*Big river*" here. Inside this loop it says, "*Open country*," and near the west end of the loop is a "*Barren, cone shaped hill – volcanic*." Then here is another river that rises in the southeast part of the map and flows northwest, empty-ing into the second river just before the latter joins the big river.'

Sheykh Ab el-Ghrennem ran his fingers through his beard as he sat in thoughtful contemplation of the map. At last he placed a finger on the falls.

'*Shuf*, Atewy!' he exclaimed. 'This should be the Omwamwi Falls, and over here the village of the Bansuto. We are here.' He pointed at a spot near the junction of the second and third rivers. 'Tomorrow we should cross this other river and come into open country. There we shall find a barren hill.'

'*Billah!*' exclaimed Atewy. 'If we do we shall soon be in the valley of dia-monds, for the rest of the way is plain.'

'What did the sheik say?' asked Rhonda.

Atewy told her, adding, 'We shall all be very rich; then I shall buy you from the sheykh and take you back to my *ashirat*.'

'You and who else?' scoffed Rhonda.

'*Billah!* No one else. I shall buy you for myself alone.'

'*Caveat emptor*,' advised the girl.

'I do not understand, *bint*,' said Atewy.

'You will if you ever buy *me*. And when you call me *bint*, smile. It doesn't sound like a nice word.'

Atewy grinned. He translated what she had said to the sheykh, and they both laughed. 'The *Narrawia* would be good to have in the beyt of Ab el-Ghrennem,' said the sheykh, who had understood nothing of what Atewy had said to Rhonda. 'When we are through with this expedition, I think that I shall keep them both; for I shall be so rich that I shall not have to sell them. This one will amuse me; she hath a quick tongue that is like *aud* in tasteless food.'

Atewy was not pleased. He wanted Rhonda for himself; and he was deter-mined to have her, sheykh or no sheykh. It was then that plans commenced to formulate in the mind of Atewy that would have caused Sheykh Ab el-Ghrennem's blood pressure to rise had he known of them.

The Arabs spread blankets on the ground near the fire for the two girls; and the sentry who watched the camp was posted near, that they might have no opportunity to escape.

'We've got to get away from these highbinders, Naomi,' said Rhonda as the girls lay close together beneath their blankets. 'When they find out that the valley of diamonds isn't just around the corner, they're going to be sore. The poor saps really believe that the map is genuine – they expect to find that barren, volcanic hill tomorrow. When they don't find it tomorrow, nor next week nor next, they'll just naturally sell us "down river"; and by that time we'll be so far from the outfit that we won't have a Chinaman's chance ever to find it.'

'You mean to go out alone into this forest at night!' whispered Naomi, aghast. 'Think of the lions!'

'I am thinking of them; but I'm thinking of some fat, greasy, black sultan too. I'd rather take a chance with the lion – he'd be sporting at least.'

'It's all so horrible! Oh, why did I ever leave Hollywood!'

'D'you know it's a funny thing, Naomi, that a woman has to fear her own kind more than she does the beasts of the jungle. It sort o' makes one wonder if there isn't something wrong somewhere – it's hard to believe that a divine intelligence would create something in His own image that was more brutal and cruel than anything else that He created. It kind of explains why some of the ancients worshipped snakes and bulls and birds. I guess they had more sense than we have.'

At the edge of the camp Atewy squatted beside Eyad. 'You would like one of the white *benat*, Eyad,' whispered Atewy. 'I have seen it in your eyes.'

Eyad eyed the other through narrowed lids. 'Who would not?' he demanded. 'Am I not a man?'

'But you will not get one, for the sheykh is going to keep them both. You will not get one – unless—'

'Unless what?' inquired Eyad.

'Unless an accident should befall Ab el-Ghrennem. Nor will you get so many diamonds, for the sheykh's share of the booty is one fourth. If there were no sheykh we should divide more between us.'

'Thou art *hatab lil nar*,' ejaculated Eyad.

'Perhaps I *am* fuel for hell-fire,' admitted Atewy, 'but I shall burn hot while I burn.'

'What dost *thou* get out of it?' inquired Eyad after a short silence.

Atewy breathed an inaudible sigh of relief. Eyad was coming around! 'The same as thou,' he replied, 'my full share of the diamonds and one of the *benat*.'

'Accidents befall sheykhs even as they befall other men,' philosophized Eyad as he rolled himself in his blanket and prepared to sleep.

Quiet fell upon the camp of the Arabs. A single sentry squatted by the fire, half-dozing. The other Arabs slept.

Not Rhonda Terry. She lay listening to the diminishing sounds of the camp, she heard the breathing of sleeping men, she watched the sentry, whose back was toward her.

She placed her lips close to one of Naomi Madison's beautiful ears. 'Listen!' she whispered, 'but don't move nor make a sound. When I get up, follow me. That is all you have to do. Don't make any noise.'

'What are you going to do?' The Madison's voice was quavering.

'Shut up, and do as I tell you.'

Rhonda Terry had been planning ahead. Mentally she had rehearsed every smallest piece of business in the drama that was to be enacted. There were no lines – at least she hoped there would be none. If there were the tag might be very different from that which she hoped for.

She reached out and grasped a short, stout piece of wood that had been gathered for the fire. Slowly, stealthily, cat-like, she drew herself from her blankets. Trembling, Naomi Madison followed her.

Rhonda rose, the piece of firewood in her hand. She crept toward the back of the unsuspecting sentry. She lifted the stick above the head of the Arab. She swung it far back, and then—

CHAPTER THIRTEEN

A Ghost

Orman and Bill West tramped on through the interminable forest. Day after day they followed the plain trail of the horsemen, but then there came a day that they lost it. Neither was an experienced tracker. The trail had entered a small stream, but it had not emerged again directly upon the opposite bank.

Assuming that the Arabs had ridden in the stream bed for some distance either up or down before coming out on the other side, they had crossed and searched up and down the little river but without success. It did not occur to either of them that their quarry had come out upon the same side that they had entered, and so they did not search upon that side at all. Perhaps it was only natural that they should assume that when one entered a river it was for the purpose of crossing it.

The meager food supply that they had brought from camp was exhausted, and they had had little luck in finding game. A few monkeys and some rodents had fallen to their rifles, temporarily averting starvation; but the future looked none too bright. Eleven days had passed, and they had accomplished nothing.

'And the worst of this mess,' said Orman, 'is that we're lost. We've wandered so far from that stream where we lost the trail that we can't find our back track.'

'I don't want to find any back track,' said West. 'Until I find Rhonda I'll never turn back.'

'I'm afraid we're too late to do 'em much good now, Bill.'

'We could take a few pot shots at those lousy Arabs.'

'Yes, I'd like to do that; but I got to think of the rest of the company. I got to get 'em out of this country. I thought we'd overtake el-Ghrennem the first day and be back in camp the next. I've sure made a mess of everything. Those two cases of Scotch will have cost close to a million dollars and God knows how many more lives before any of the company sees Hollywood again.

'Think of it, Bill – Major White, Noice. Baine, Obroski, and seven others killed, to say nothing of the Arabs and blacks – and the girls gone. Sometimes I think I'll go nuts, just thinking about them.'

West said nothing. He had been thinking about it a great deal, and thinking too of the day when Orman must face the wives and sweethearts of those men back in Hollywood. No matter what Orman's responsibility, West pitied him.

When Orman spoke again it was as though he had read the other's mind. 'If it wasn't so damn yellow.' he said, 'I'd bump myself off; it would be a lot easier than what I've got before me back home.'

As the two men talked they were walking slowly along a game trail that wandered out of one unknown into another. For long they had realized that they were hopelessly lost.

'I don't know why we keep on,' remarked West. 'We don't know where we're headed.'

'We won't find out by sitting down, and maybe we'll find something or someone if we keep going long enough.'

West glanced suddenly behind him. 'I thought so,' he said in a low tone. 'I thought I'd been hearing something.'

Orman's gaze followed that of his companion. 'Anyway we got a good reason now for not sitting down or turning back,' he said.

'He's been following us for a long time,' observed West. 'I heard him quite a way back, now that I think of it.'

'I hope we're not detaining him.'

'Why do you suppose he's following us?' asked West.

'Perhaps he's lonesome.'

'Or hungry.'

'Now that you mention it, he does look hungry,' agreed Orman.

'This is a nasty place to be caught too. The trail's so narrow and with this thick undergrowth on both sides we couldn't get out of the way of a charge. And right here the trees are all too big to climb.'

'We might shoot him,' suggested Orman, 'but I'm leary of these rifles. White said they were a little too light to stop big game, and if we don't stop him it'll be curtains for one of us.'

'I'm a bum shot,' admitted West. 'I probably wouldn't even hit him.'

'Well, he isn't coming any closer. Let's keep on going and see what happens.'

The men continued along the trail, continually casting glances rearward. They held their rifles in readiness. Often, turns in the trail hid from their view momentarily the grim stalker following in their tracks.

'They look different out here, don't they?' remarked West. 'Fiercer and sort of – inevitable, if you know what I mean – like death and taxes.'

'Especially death. And they take all the wind out of a superiority complex. Sometimes when I've been directing I've thought that trainers were a nuisance, but I'd sure like to see Charlie Gay step out of the underbrush and say, "Down, Slats!"'

'Say, do you know this fellow looks something like Slats – got the same mean eye?'

As they talked, the trail debouched into a small opening where there was little underbrush and the trees grew farther apart. They had advanced only a short distance into it when the stalking beast dogging their footsteps rounded the last turn in the trail and entered the clearing.

He paused a moment in the mouth of the trail, his tail twitching, his great jowls dripping saliva. With lowered head he surveyed them from yellow-green eyes, menacingly. Then he crouched and crept toward them.

'We've got to shoot, Bill,' said Orman; 'he's going to charge.'

The director shot first, his bullet creasing the lion's scalp. West fired and missed. With a roar, the carnivore charged. The empty shell jammed in the breech of West's rifle. Orman fired again when the lion was but a few paces from him; then he clubbed his rifle as the beast rose to seize him. A great paw sent the rifle hurtling aside, spinning Orman dizzily after it.

West stood paralyzed, his useless weapon clutched in his hands. He saw the lion wheel to spring upon Orman; then he saw something that left him stunned, aghast. He saw an almost naked man drop from the tree above them full upon the lion's back.

A great arm encircled the beast's neck as it reared and turned to rend this new assailant. Bronzed legs locked quickly beneath its belly. A knife flashed as great muscles drove the blade into the carnivore's side again and again. The lion hurled itself from side to side as it sought to shake the man from it. Its mighty roars thundered in the quiet glade, shaking the earth.

Orman, uninjured, had scrambled to his feet. Both men, spellbound, were watching this primitive battle of Titans. They heard the roars of the man mingle with those of the lion, and they felt their flesh creep.

Presently the lion leaped high in the air, and when he crashed to earth he did not rise again. The man upon him leaped to his feet. For an instant he surveyed the carcass; then he placed a foot upon it, and raising his face toward the sky voiced a weird cry that sent cold shivers down the spines of the two Americans.

As the last notes of that inhuman scream reverberated throughout the forest, the stranger, without a glance at the two he had saved, leaped for an overhanging branch, drew himself up into the tree, and disappeared amidst the foliage above.

Orman, pale beneath his tan, turned toward West. 'Did you see what I saw, Bill?' he asked, his voice shaking.

'I don't know what you saw, but I know what I *thought* I saw – but I *couldn't* have seen it.'

'Do you believe in ghosts, Bill?'

'I – I don't know – you don't think?'

'You know as well as I do that that couldn't have been him; so it must have been his ghost.'

'But we never knew for sure that Obroski was dead, Tom.'

'We know it now.'

CHAPTER FOURTEEN
A Madman

As Stanley Obroski was dragged to earth in the village of Rungula, the Bansuto, a white man, naked but for a G string, looked down from the foliage of an overhanging tree upon the scene below and upon the bulk of the giant chieftain standing beneath him.

The pliant strands of a strong rope braided from jungle grasses swung in his powerful hands, the shadow of a grim smile played about his mouth.

Suddenly the rope shot downward; a running noose in its lower end settled about Rungula's body, pinning his arms at his sides. A cry of surprise and terror burst from the chief's lips as he felt himself pinioned; and as those near him turned, attracted by his cry, they saw him raised quickly from the ground to disappear in the foliage of the tree above as though hoisted by some supernatural power.

Rungula felt himself dragged to a sturdy branch, and then a mighty hand seized and steadied him. He was terrified, for he thought his end had come. Below him a terrified silence had fallen upon the village. Even the prisoner was forgotten in the excitement and fright that followed the mysterious disappearance of the chief.

Obroski stood looking about him in amazement. Surrounded by struggling warriors as he had been he had not seen the miracle of Rungula's ascension. Now he saw every eye turned upward at the tree that towered above the chief's hut. He wondered what they were looking at. He could see nothing unusual. All that lingered in his memory to give him a clue was the sudden, affrighted cry of Rungula as the noose had tightened about him.

Rungula heard a voice speaking, speaking his own language. 'Look at me!' it commanded.

Rungula turned his eyes toward the thing that held him. The light from the village fires filtered through the foliage to dimly reveal the features of a white man bending above him. Rungula gasped and shrank back. '*Walumbe!*' he muttered in terror.

'I am not the god of death,' replied Tarzan; 'I am not Walumbe. But I can bring death just as quickly, for I am greater than Walumbe. I am Tarzan of the Apes!'

'What do you want?' asked Rungula through chattering teeth. 'What are you going to do to me?'

'I tested you to see if you were a good man and your people good people. I made myself into two men, and one I sent where your warriors could capture him. I wanted to see what you would do to a stranger who had not harmed you. Now I know. For what you have done you should die. What have you to say?'

'You are here,' said Rungula, 'and you are also down there.' He nodded toward the figure of Obroski standing in surprised silence amidst the warriors. 'Therefore you must be a demon. What can I say to a demon? I can give you food and drink and weapons. I can give you girls who can cook and draw water and fetch wood and work all day in the fields – girls with broad hips and strong backs. All these things will I give you if you will not kill me – if you will just go away and leave us alone.'

'I do not want your food nor your weapons, nor your women. I want but one thing from you. Rungula, as the price of your life.'

'What is that, Master?'

'Your promise that you will never again make war upon white men, and that when they come through your country you will help them instead of killing them.'

'I promise, Master.'

'Then call down to your people, and tell them to open the gates and let the prisoner go out into the forest.'

Rungula spoke in a loud voice to his people, and they fell away from Obroski, leaving him standing alone; then warriors went to the village gates and swung them open.

Obroski heard the voice of the chief coming from high in a tree, and he was mystified. He also wondered at the strange action of the natives and suspected treachery. Why should they fall back and leave him standing alone when a few moments before they were trying to seize him and bind him to a tree? Why should they throw the gates wide open? He did not move. He waited, believing that he was being baited into an attempt at escape for some ulterior purpose.

Presently another voice came from the tree above the chief's hut, addressing him in English. 'Go out of the village into the forest,' it said. 'They will not harm you now. I will join you in the forest.'

Obroski was mystified; but the quiet English voice reassured him, and he turned and walked down the village street toward the gateway.

Tarzan removed the rope from about Rungula, ran lightly through the tree to the rear of the hut and dropped to the ground. Keeping the huts between himself and the villagers, he moved swiftly to the opposite end of the village, scaled the palisade, and dropped into the clearing beyond. A moment later he was in the forest and circling back toward the point where Obroski was entering it.

The latter heard no slightest noise of his approach, for there was none. One instant he was entirely alone, and the next a voice spoke close behind him. 'Follow me,' it said.

Obroski wheeled. In the darkness of the forest night he saw dimly only the figure of a man about his own height. 'Who are you?' he asked.

'I am Tarzan of the Apes.'

Obroski was silent, astonished. He had heard of Tarzan of the Apes, but he had thought that it was no more than a legendary character – a fiction of the folklore of Africa. He wondered if this were some demented creature who imagined that it was Tarzan of the Apes. He wished that he could see the fellow's face; that might give him a clue to the sanity of the man. He wondered what the stranger's intentions might be.

Tarzan of the Apes was moving away into the forest. He turned once and repeated his command, 'Follow me!'

'I haven't thanked you yet for getting me out of that mess.' said Obroski as he moved after the retreating figure of the stranger. 'It was certainly decent of you. I'd have been dead by now if it hadn't been for you.'

The ape-man moved on in silence, and Obroski followed him. The silence preyed a little upon his nerves. It seemed to bear out his deduction that the man was not quite normal, not as other men. A normal man would have been asking and answering innumerable questions had he met a stranger for the first time under such exciting circumstances.

And Obroski's deductions were not wholly inaccurate – Tarzan is not as other men; the training and the instincts of the wild beast have given him standards of behaviour and a code of ethics peculiarly his own. For Tarzan there are times for silence and times for speech. The depths of the night, when hunting beasts are abroad, is no time to go gabbling through the jungle; nor did he ever care much for speech with strangers unless he could watch their eyes and the changing expressions upon their faces, which often told him more than their words were intended to convey.

So in silence they moved through the forest, Obroski keeping close behind the ape-man lest he lose sight of him in the darkness. Ahead of them a lion roared; and the American wondered if his companion would change his course or take refuge in a tree, but he did neither. He kept on in the direction they had been going.

Occasionally the voice of the lion sounded ahead of them, always closer. Obroski, unarmed and practically naked, felt utterly helpless and, not unaccountably, nervous. Nor was his nervousness allayed when a cry, half roar and half weird scream, burst from the throat of his companion.

After that he heard nothing from the lion for some time; then, seemingly just ahead of them, he heard throaty, coughing grunts. The lion! Obroski could scarcely restrain a violent urge to scale a tree, but he steeled himself and kept on after his guide.

Presently they came to an opening in the forest beside a river. The moon had risen. Its mellow light flooded the scene, casting deep shadows where tree and shrub dotted the grass carpeted clearing, dancing on the swirling ripples of the river.

But the beauty of the scene held his eye for but a brief instant as through the shutter of a camera; then it was erased from his consciousness by a figure looming large ahead of them in the full light of the African moon. A great lion stood in the open watching them as they approached. Obroski saw the black mane ripple in the night wind, the sheen of the yellow body in the moonlight. Now, beyond him, rose a lioness. She growled.

The stranger turned to Obroski. 'Stay where you are,' he said. 'I do not know this Sabor; she may be vicious.'

Obroski stopped, gladly. He was relieved to discover that he had stopped near a tree. He wished that he had a rifle, so that he might save the life of the madman walking unconcernedly toward his doom.

Now he heard the voice of the man who called himself Tarzan of the Apes, but he understood no word that the man spoke: 'Tarmangani yo, Jad-bal-ja tand bundolo. Savor tand bundolo.'

The madman was talking to the great lion! Obroski trembled for him as he saw him drawing nearer and nearer to the beast.

The lioness rose and slunk forward. 'Kreeg-ah Sabor!' exclaimed the man.

The lion turned and rushed upon the lioness, snarling; she crouched and leaped away. He stood over her growling for a moment; then he turned and walked forward to meet the man. Obroski's heart stood still.

He saw the man lay a hand upon the head of the huge carnivore and then turn and look back at him. 'You may come up now,' he said, 'that Jad-bal-ja may get your scent and know that you are a friend. Afterward he will never harm you – unless I tell him to.'

Obroski was terrified. He wanted to run, to climb the tree beside which he stood, to do anything that would get him away from the lion and the lioness: but he feared still more to leave the man who had befriended him. Paralyzed by fright, he advanced; and Tarzan of the Apes, believing him courageous, was pleased.

Jad-bal-ja was growling in his throat. Tarzan spoke to him in a low voice, and he stopped. Obroski came and stood close to him, and the lion sniffed at his legs and body. Obroski felt the hot breath of the flesh eater on his skin.

'Put your hand on his head,' said Tarzan. 'If you are afraid do not show it.'

The American did as he was bid. Presently Jad-bal-ja rubbed his head against the body of the man; then Tarzan spoke again, and the lion turned and walked away toward the lioness, lying down beside her.

Now, for the first time, Obroski looked at his strange companion under the light of the full moon. He voiced an exclamation of amazement – he might have been looking into a mirror.

Tarzan smiled – one of his rare smiles. 'Remarkable, isn't it?' he said.

'It's uncanny,' replied Obroski.

'I think that is why I saved you from the Bansutos – it was too much like seeing myself killed.'

'I'm sure you would have saved me anyway.'

The ape-man shrugged. 'Why should I have? I did not know you.' Tarzan stretched his body upon the soft grasses. 'We shall lie up here for the night,' he said.

Obroski shot a quick glance in the direction of the two lions lying a few yards away, and Tarzan interpreted his thoughts.

'Don't worry about them,' he said. 'Jad-bal-ja will see that nothing harms you, but look out for the lioness when he is not around. He just picked her up the other day. She hasn't made friends with me yet, and she probably never will. Now, if you care to, tell me what you are doing in this country.'

Briefly Obroski explained, and Tarzan listened until he had finished.

'If I had known you were one of that safari I probably would have let the Bansutos kill you.'

'Why? What have you got against us?'

'I saw your leader whipping his blacks,' replied Tarzan.

Obroski was silent for a time. He had come to realize that this man who called himself Tarzan of the Apes was a most remarkable man, and that his power for good or evil in this savage country might easily be considerable. He would be a good friend to have, and his enmity might prove fatal. He could ruin their chances of making a successful picture – he could ruin Orman.

Obroski did not like Orman. He had good reasons not to like him. Naomi Madison was one of these reasons. But there were other things to consider than a personal grudge. There was the money invested by the studio, the careers of his fellow players, and even Orman – Orman was a great director.

He explained all this to Tarzan – all except his hatred of Orman. 'Orman,' he concluded. 'was drunk when he whipped the blacks, he had been down with fever, he was terribly worried. Those who knew him best said it was most unlike him.'

Tarzan made no comment, and Obroski said no more. He lay looking up at the great full moon, thinking. He thought of Naomi and wondered. What was there about her that he loved? She was petty, inconsiderate, arrogant, spoiled. Her character could not compare with that of Rhonda Terry, for instance; and Rhonda was fully as beautiful.

At last he decided that it was the glamour of the Madison's name and fame that had attracted him – stripped of these, there was little about her to inspire anything greater than an infatuation such as a man might feel for any beautiful face and perfect body.

He thought of his companions of the safari, and wondered what they would think if they could see him now lying down to sleep with a wild man and two savage African lions. Smiling, he dozed and fell asleep. He did not see the lioness rise and cross the clearing with Jad-bal-ja pacing majestically behind her as they set forth upon the grim business of the hunt.

CHAPTER FIFTEEN

Terror

As Rhonda Terry stood with her weapon poised above the head of the squatting sentry, the man turned his eyes quickly in her direction. Instantly he realized his danger and started to rise as the stick descended; thus the blow had far more force than it otherwise would have, and he sank senseless to the ground without uttering a sound.

The girl looked quickly about upon the sleeping camp. No one stirred. She beckoned the trembling Naomi to follow her and stepped quickly to where some horse trappings lay upon the ground. She handed a saddle and bridle to the Madison and took others for herself.

Half dragging, half carrying their burdens they crept to the tethered ponies. Here, the Madison was almost helpless; and Rhonda had to saddle and bridle both animals, giving thanks for the curiosity that had prompted her days before to examine the Arab tack and learn the method of its adjustment.

Naomi mounted, and Rhonda passed the bridle reins of her own pony to her companion. 'Hold him,' she whispered, 'and hold him tight.'

She went quickly then to the other ponies, turning them loose one after another. Often she glanced toward the sleeping men. If one of them should awaken, they would be recaptured. But if she could carry out her plan they would be safe from pursuit. She felt that it was worth the risk.

Finally the last pony was loose. Already, cognizant of their freedom, some of them had commenced to move about. Herein had lain one of the principal dangers of the girl's plan, for free horses moving about a camp must quickly awaken such horsemen as the Beduins.

She ran quickly to her own pony and mounted. 'We are going to try to drive them ahead of us for a little way,' she whispered. 'If we can do that we shall be safe – as far as Arabs are concerned.'

As quietly as they could, the girls reined their ponies behind the loose stock and urged them away from camp. It seemed incredible to Rhonda that the noise did not awaken the Arabs.

The ponies had been tethered upon the north side of the camp, and so it was toward the north that they drove them. This was not the direction in which their own safari lay, but Rhonda planned to circle back around the Arabs after she had succeeded in driving off their mounts.

Slowly the unwilling ponies moved toward the black shadows of the forest beyond the little opening in which the camp had been pitched – a hundred feet, two hundred, three hundred. They were almost at the edge of the forest when a cry arose from behind them. Then the angry voices of many men came to them in a babel of strange words and stranger Arab oaths.

It was a bright, starlit night. Rhonda knew that the Arabs could see them. She turned in her saddle and saw them running swiftly in pursuit. With a cowboy yell and a kick of her heels she urged her pony onto the heels of those ahead. Startled, they broke into a trot.

'Yell, Naomi!' cried the girl. 'Do anything to frighten them and make them run.'

The Madison did her best, and the yells of the running men approaching added to the nervousness of the ponies. Then one of the Arabs fired his musket; and as the bullet whistled above their heads the ponies broke into a run, and, followed by the two girls, disappeared into the forest.

The leading pony had either seen or stumbled upon a trail, and down this they galloped. Every step was fraught with danger for the two fugitives. A low hanging branch or a misstep by one of their mounts would spell disaster, yet neither sought to slacken the speed. Perhaps they both felt that anything would be preferable to falling again into the hands of old Ab el-Ghrennem.

It was not until the voices of the men behind them were lost in the distance that Rhonda reined her pony to a walk. 'Well, we made it!' she cried exultantly. 'I'll bet old Apple Gran'ma'am is chewing his whiskers. How do you feel – tired?'

The Madison made no reply; then Rhonda heard her sobbing. 'What's the matter?' she demanded. 'You haven't been hurt, have you?' Her tone was worried and solicitous.

'I – I'm – so frightened. Oh, I – never was so frightened in all my life,' sobbed the Madison.

'Oh, buck up, Naomi; neither was I; but weeping and wailing and gnashing our teeth won't do us any good. We got away from them, and a few hours ago that seemed impossible. Now all we have to do is ride back to the safari, and the chances are we'll meet some of the boys looking for us.'

'I'll never see any of them again. I've known all along that I'd die in this awful country,' and she commenced to sob again hysterically.

Rhonda reined close to her side and put an arm around her.

'It *is* terrible, dear,' she said; 'but we'll pull through. I'll get you out of this, and some day we'll lie on the sand at Malibu again and laugh about it.'

For a time neither of them spoke. The ponies moved on through the dark forest at a walk. Ahead of them the loose animals followed the trail that human eyes could not see. Occasionally one of them would pause, snorting, sensing something that the girls could neither see nor hear; then Rhonda would urge them on again, and so the long hours dragged out toward a new day.

After a long silence, Naomi spoke. 'Rhonda,' she said, 'I don't see how you can be so decent to me. I used to treat you so rotten. I acted like a dirty little cat. I can see it now. The last few days have done something to me – opened my eyes, I guess. Don't say anything – I just want you to know – that's all.'

'I understand,' said Rhonda softly. 'It's Hollywood – we all try to be something we're not, and most of us succeed only in being something we ought not to be.'

Ahead of them the trail suddenly widened, and the loose horses came to a stop. Rhonda tried to urge them on, but they only milled about and would not advance.

'I wonder what's wrong,' she said and urged her pony forward to find a river barring their path. It was not a very large river; and she decided to drive the ponies into it, but they would not go.

'What are we to do?' asked Naomi.

'We can't stay here,' replied Rhonda. 'We've got to keep on going for a while. If we turn back now we'll run into the shieks.'

'But we can't cross this river.'

'I don't know about that. There must be a ford here – this trail runs right to the river, right into it. You can see how it's worn down the bank right into the water. I'm going to try it.'

'Oh, Rhonda, we'll drown!'

'They say it's an easy death. Come on!' She urged her pony down the bank into the water. 'I hate to leave these other ponies,' she said. 'The sheiks'll find them and follow us, but if we can't drive them across there's nothing else to be done.'

Her pony balked a little at the edge of the water, but at last he stepped in, snorting. 'Keep close to me, Naomi. I have an idea two horses will cross better together than one alone. If we get into deep water try to keep your horse's head pointed toward the opposite bank.'

Gingerly the two ponies waded out into the stream. It was neither deep nor swift, and they soon gained confidence. On the bank behind them the other ponies gathered, nickering to their companions.

As they approached the opposite shore Rhonda heard a splashing in the water behind her. Turning her head, she saw the loose ponies following them across; and she laughed. 'Now I've learned something,' she said. 'Here we've been driving them all night, and if we'd left 'em alone they'd have followed us.'

Dawn broke shortly after they had made the crossing, and the light of the new day revealed an open country dotted with trees and clumps of brush. In the northwest loomed a range of mountains. It was very different country from any they had seen for a long time.

'How lovely!' exclaimed Rhonda.

'Anything would be lovely after that forest,' replied Naomi. 'I got so that I hated it.'

Suddenly Rhonda drew rein and pointed. 'Do you see what I see?' she demanded.

'That hill?'

'Do you realize that we have just crossed a river out of a forest and come into open country and that there is a "barren, cone-shaped hill – volcanic"?'

'You don't mean—!'

'The map! And there, to the northwest, are the mountains. If it's a mere coincidence it's a mighty uncanny one.'

Naomi was about to reply when both their ponies halted, trembling. With dilated nostrils and up-pricked ears they stared at a patch of brush close upon their right and just ahead. Both girls looked in the same direction.

Suddenly a tawny figure broke from the brush with a terrific roar. The ponies turned and bolted. Rhonda's was to the right of Naomi's and half a neck in advance. The lion was coming from Rhonda's side. Both ponies were uncontrollable. The loose horses were bolting like frightened antelopes.

Naomi, fascinated, kept her eyes upon the lion. It moved with incredible speed. She saw it leap and seize the rump of Rhonda's pony with fangs and talons. Its hindquarters swung down under the pony's belly. The frightened creature kicked and lunged, hurling Rhonda from the saddle; and then the lion dragged it down before the eyes of the terrified Madison.

Naomi's pony carried her from the frightful scene. Once she looked back. She saw the lion standing with its forepaws on the carcass of the pony. Only a few feet away Rhonda's body lay motionless.

The frightened ponies raced back along the trail they had come. Naomi was utterly powerless to check or guide the terrified creature that carried her swiftly in the wake of its fellows. The distance they had covered in the last hour was traversed in minutes as the frightened animals drew new terror from the galloping hoofs of their comrades.

The river that they had feared to cross before did not check them now. Lunging across, they threw water high in air, waking the echoes of the forest with their splashing.

Heartsick, terrified, hopeless, the girl clung to her mount; but for once in her life the thoughts of the Madison were not of herself. The memory of that still figure lying close to the dread carnivore crowded thoughts of self from her mind – her terror and her hopelessness and her heartsickness were for Rhonda Terry.

CHAPTER SIXTEEN

Eyad

Long day had followed long day as Orman and West searched vainly through dense forest and jungle for the trail they had lost. Nearly two weeks had passed since they had left camp in search of the girls when their encounter with the lion and the 'ghost' of Obroski took place.

The encounter left them unnerved, for both were weak from lack of food and their nerves harassed by what they had passed through and by worry over the fate of Naomi and Rhonda.

They stood for some time by the carcass of the lion, looking and listening for a return of the apparition.

'Do you suppose,' suggested West, 'that hunger and worry could have affected us so much that we imagined we saw – what we think we saw?'

Orman pointed at the dead lion. 'Are we imagining *that?*' he demanded. 'Could we both have the same hallucination at the same instant? No! We saw what we saw. I don't believe in ghosts – or I never did before – but if that wasn't Obroski's ghost it was Obroski; and you know as well as I that Obroski would never have had the guts to tackle a lion even if he could have gotten away with it.'

West rubbed his chin meditatively. 'You know, another explanation has occurred to me. Obroski was the world's prize coward. He may have escaped the Bansutos and got lost in the jungle. If he did, he would have been scared stiff every minute of the days and nights. Terror might have driven him crazy. He may be a madman now, and you know maniacs are supposed to be ten times as strong as ordinary men.'

'I don't know about maniacs being any stronger,' said Orman; 'that's a popular theory, and popular theories are always wrong; but everyone knows that when a man's crazy he does things that he wouldn't do when he's sane. So perhaps you're right – perhaps that was Obroski gone nuts. No one but a nut would jump a lion; and Obroski certainly wouldn't have saved my life if he'd been sane – he didn't have any reason to be very fond of me.'

'Well, whatever prompted him, he did us a good turn in more ways than one – he left us something to eat.' West nodded toward the carcass of the lion.

'I hope we can keep him down,' said Orman; 'he looks mangy.'

'I don't fancy cat meat myself,' admitted West, 'but I could eat a pet dog right now.'

After they had eaten and cut off pieces of the meat to carry with them they set out again upon their seemingly fruitless search. The food gave them new strength; but it did little to raise their spirits, and they plodded on as dejected as before.

Toward evening West, who was in the lead, stopped suddenly and drew back, cautioning Orman to silence. The latter advanced cautiously to where West stood pointing ahead at a lone figure squatting over a small fire near the bank of a stream.

'It's one of el-Ghrennem's men,' said West.

'It's Eyad,' replied Orman. 'Do you see anyone with him?'

'No. What do you suppose he is doing here alone?'

'We'll find out. Be ready to shoot if he tries any funny business or if any more of them show up.'

Orman advanced upon the lone figure, his rifle ready; and West followed at his elbow. They had covered only a few yards when Eyad looked up and discovered them. Seizing his musket, he leaped to his feet; but Orman covered him.

'Drop that gun!' ordered the director.

Eyad understood no English, but he made a shrewd guess at the meaning of the words, doubtless from the peremptory tone of the American's voice, and lowered the butt of his musket to the ground.

The two approached him. 'Where is el-Ghrennem?' demanded Orman. 'Where are Miss Madison and Miss Terry?'

Eyad recognized the names and the interrogatory inflection. Pointing toward the north he spoke volubly in Arabic. Neither Orman nor West understood what he said, but they saw that he was much excited. They saw too that he was emaciated, his garments in rags, and his face and body covered with wounds. It was evident that he had been through some rough experiences.

When Eyad realized that the Americans could not understand him he resorted to pantomime, though he continued to jabber in Arabic.

'Can you make out what he's driving at, Tom?' asked West.

'I picked up a few words from Atewy but not many. Something terrible seems to have happened to all the rest of the party – this bird is scared stiff. I get *sheykh* and *el-Beduw* and *benat*; he's talking about el-Ghrennem, the other Beduins, and the girls – *benat* is the plural of *bint*, girl. One of the girls has been killed by some animal – from the way he growled and roared when he was explaining it, I guess it must have been pretty awful.'

West paled. 'Does he know which girl was killed?' he asked.

'I can't make out which one – perhaps both are dead.'

'We've got to find out. We've got to go after them. Can he tell us where they were when this thing happened?'

'I'm going to make him guide us,' replied Orman. 'There's no use going on tonight – it's too late. In the morning we'll start.'

They made a poor camp and cooked some of their lion meat. Eyad ate ravenously. It was evident that he had been some time without food. Then they lay down and tried to sleep, but futile worry kept the two Americans awake until late into the night.

To the south of them, several miles away, Stanley Obroski crouched in the fork of a tree and shivered from cold and fear. Below him a lion and a lioness fed upon the carcass of a buck. Hyenas, mouthing their uncanny cries, slunk in a wide circle about them. Obroski saw one, spurred by hunger to greater courage, slink in to seize a mouthful of the kill. The great lion, turning his head, saw the thief and charged him, growling savagely. The hyena retreated but not quickly enough. A mighty, raking paw flung it bleeding and lifeless among its fellows. Obroski shuddered and clung more tightly to the tree. A full moon looked down upon the savage scene.

Presently the figure of a man strode silently into the clearing. The lion looked up and growled and an answering growl came from the throat of the man. Then a hyena charged him, and Obroski gasped in dismay. What would become of him if this man were killed! He feared him, but he feared him least of all the other horrid creatures of the jungle.

He saw the man side-step the charge, then stoop quickly and seize the unclean beast by the scruff of its neck. He shook it once, then hurled it onto the kill where the two lions fed. The lioness closed her great jaws upon it once and then cast it aside. The other hyenas laughed hideously.

Tarzan looked about him. 'Obroski!' he called.

'I'm up here,' replied the American.

Tarzan swung lightly into the tree beside him. 'I saw two of your people today,' he said – 'Orman and West.'

'Where are they? What did they say?'

'I did not talk with them. They are a few miles north of us. I think they are lost.'

'Who was with them?'

'They were alone. I looked for their safari, but it was nowhere near. Farther north I saw an Arab from your safari. He was lost and starving.'

'The safari must be broken up and scattered,' said Obroski. 'What could have happened? What could have become of the girls?'

'Tomorrow we'll start after Orman,' said Tarzan. 'Perhaps he can answer your questions.'

CHAPTER SEVENTEEN
Alone

For several moments Rhonda Terry lay quietly where she had been hurled by her terrified horse. The lion stood with his forefeet on the carcass of his kill, growling angrily after the fleeing animal that was carrying Naomi Madison back toward the forest.

As Rhonda Terry gained consciousness the first thing that she saw as she opened her eyes was the figure of the lion standing with its back toward her, and instantly she recalled all that had transpired. She tried to find Naomi without moving her head, for she did not wish to attract the attention of the lion; but she could see nothing of the Madison.

The lion sniffed at his kill; then he turned and looked about. His eyes fell on the girl, and a low growl rumbled in his throat. Rhonda froze in terror. She wanted to close her eyes to shut out the hideous snarling face, but she feared that even this slight movement would bring the beast upon her. She recalled having heard that if animals thought a person dead they would not molest the body. It also occurred to her that this might not hold true in respect to meat eaters.

So terrified was she that it was with the utmost difficulty that she curbed an urge to leap to her feet and run, although she knew that such an act would prove instantly fatal. The great cat could have overtaken her with a single bound.

The lion wheeled slowly about and approached her, and all the while that low growl rumbled in his throat. He came close and sniffed at her body. She felt his hot breath against her face, and its odor sickened her.

The beast seemed nervous and uncertain. Suddenly he lowered his face close to hers and growled ferociously, his eyes blazed into hers. She thought that the end had come. The brute raised a paw and seized her shoulder. He turned her over on her face. She heard him sniffing and growling above her. For what seemed an eternity to the frightened girl he stood there; then she realized that he had walked away.

From her one unobscured eye she watched him after a brief instant that she had become very dizzy and almost swooned. He returned to the body of the horse and worried it for a moment; then he seized it and dragged it toward the bushes from which he had leaped to the attack.

The girl marvelled at the mighty strength of the beast, as it dragged the carcass without seeming effort and disappeared in the thicket. Now she commenced to wonder if she had been miraculously spared or if the lion, having hidden the body of the horse, would return for her.

She raised her head a little and looked around. About twenty feet away grew a small tree. She lay between it and the thicket where she could hear the lion growling.

Cautiously she commenced to drag her body toward the tree, glancing constantly behind in the direction of the thicket. Inch by inch, foot by foot she made her slow way. Five feet, ten, fifteen! She glanced back and saw the lion's head and forequarters emerge from the brush.

No longer was there place for stealth. Leaping to her feet she raced for the tree. Behind, she heard the angry roar of the lion as it charged.

She sprang for a low branch and scrambled upward. Terror gave her an agility and a strength far beyond her normal powers. As she climbed frantically upward among the branches she felt the tree tremble to the impact of the lion's body as it hurtled against the bole, and the raking talons of one great paw swept just beneath her foot.

Rhonda Terry did not stop climbing until she had reached a point beyond which she dared not go; then, clinging to the now slender stem, she looked down.

The lion stood glaring up at her. For a few minutes he paced about the tree; and then, with an angry growl, he strode majestically back to his thicket.

It was not until then that the girl descended to a more secure and comfortable perch, where she sat trembling for a long time as she sought to compose herself.

She had escaped the lion, at least temporarily; but what lay in the future for her? Alone, unarmed, lost in a savage wilderness, upon what thin thread could she hang even the slightest vestige of a hope!

She wondered what had become of Naomi. She almost wished that they had never attempted to escape from the Arabs. If Tom Orman and Bill West and the others were looking for them they might have had a chance to find them had they remained the captives of old Sheik Ab el-Ghrennem, but now could anyone ever find them?

From her tree sanctuary she could see quite a distance in all directions. A tree dotted plain extended northwest toward a range of mountains. Close to the northeast of her rose the volcanic, cone-shaped hill that she had been pointing out to Naomi when the lion charged.

All these landmarks, following so closely the description on the map, intrigued her curiosity and started her to wondering and dreaming about the valley of diamonds. Suddenly she recalled something that Atewy had told her – that the falls at the foot of the valley of diamonds must be the Omwamwi Falls toward which the safari had been moving.

If that were true she would stand a better chance of rejoining the company were she to make her way to the falls and await them there than to return to the forest where she was certain to become lost.

She found it a little amusing that she should suddenly be pinning her faith to a property map, but her situation was such that she must grasp at any straw.

The mountains did not seem very far away, but she knew that distances were usually deceiving. She thought that she might reach them in a day, and believed that she might hold out without food or water until she reached the river that she prayed might be there.

Every minute was precious now, but she could not start while the lion lay up in the nearby thicket. She could hear him growling as he tore at the carcass of the horse.

An hour passed, and then she saw the lion emerge from his lair. He did not even glance toward her, but moved off in a southerly direction toward the river that she and Naomi had crossed a few hours before.

The girl watched the beast until it disappeared in the brush that grew near the river; then she slipped from the tree and started toward the northwest and the mountains.

The day was still young, the terrain not too difficult, and Rhonda felt comparatively fresh and strong despite her night ride and the harrowing experiences of the last few hours – a combination of circumstances that buoyed her with hope.

The plain was dotted with trees, and the girl directed her steps so that she might at all times be as near as possible to one of these. Sometimes this required a zigzag course that lengthened the distance, but after her experience with the lion she did not dare be far from sanctuary at any time.

She turned often to look back in the direction she had come, lest the lion follow and surprise her. As the hours passed the sun shone down hotter and hotter. Rhonda commenced to suffer from hunger and thirst; her steps were dragging; her feet seemed weighted with lead. More and more often she stopped beneath the shade of a tree to rest. The mountains seemed as far away as ever. Doubts assailed her.

A shadow moved across the ground before her. She looked up. Circling above was a vulture. She shuddered. 'I wonder if he only hopes,' she said aloud, 'or if he *knows.*'

But she kept doggedly on. She would not give up – not until she dropped in her tracks. She wondered how long it would be before that happened.

Once as she was approaching a large black rock that lay across her path it moved and stood up, and she saw that it was a rhinoceros. The beast ran around foolishly for a moment, its nose in the air; then it charged. Rhonda clambered into a tree, and the great beast tore by like a steam locomotive gone mad.

As it raced off with its silly little tail in the air the girl smiled. She realized that she had forgotten her exhaustion under the stress of emergency, as bedridden cripples sometimes forget their affliction when the house catches fire.

The adventure renewed her belief in her ability to reach the river, and she moved on again in a more hopeful frame of mind. But as hot and dusty hour followed hot and dusty hour and the pangs of thirst assailed her with increasing violence, her courage faltered again in the face of the weariness that seemed to penetrate to the very marrow of her bones.

For a long time she had been walking in a depression of the rolling plain, her view circumscribed by the higher ground around her. The day was drawing to a close. Her lengthening shadow fell away behind her. The low sun was in her eyes.

She wanted to sit down and rest, but she was afraid that she would never get up again. More than that, she wanted to see what lay beyond the next rise in the ground. It is always the next summit that lures the traveller on even though experience may have taught him that he need expect nothing more than another rise of ground farther on.

The climb ahead of her was steeper than she had anticipated, and it required all her strength and courage to reach the top of what she guessed might have been an ancient river bank or, perhaps, a lateral moraine; but the view that was revealed rewarded her for the great effort.

Below her was a fringe of wood through which she could see a broad river, and to her right the mountains seemed very close now.

Forgetful of lurking beast or savage man, the thirst tortured girl hurried down toward the tempting water of the river. As she neared the bank she saw a dozen great forms floating on the surface of the water. A huge head was raised with wide distended jaws revealing a cavernous maw, but Rhonda did not pause. She rushed to the bank of the river and threw herself face down and drank while the hippopotamuses, snorting and grunting, viewed her with disapproval.

That night she slept in a tree, dozing fitfully and awakening to every sudden jungle noise. From the plain came the roar of the hunting lions. Below her a great herd of hippopotamuses came out of the river to feed on land, their grunting and snorting dispelling all thoughts of sleep. In the distance she heard the yelp of the jackal and the weird cry of the hyena, and there were other strange and terrifying noises that she could not classify. It was not a pleasant night.

Morning found her weak from loss of sleep, fatigue, and hunger. She knew that she must get food, but she did not know how to get it. She thought that perhaps the safari had reached the falls by now, and she determined to go up river in search of the falls in the hope that she might find her people – a vague hope in the realization of which she had little faith.

She discovered a fairly good game trail paralleling the river, and this she followed upstream. As she stumbled on she became conscious of an insistent, muffled roaring in the distance. It grew louder as she advanced, and she guessed that she was approaching the falls.

Toward noon she reached them – an imposing sight much of the grandeur of which was lost on her fatigue benumbed sensibilities. The great river poured over the rim of a mighty escarpment that towered far above her. A smother of white water and spume filled the gorge at the foot of the falls. The thunderous roar of the falling water was deafening.

Slowly the grandeur and the solitude of the scene gripped her. She felt as might one who stood alone, the sole inhabitant of a world, and looked upon an eternal scene that no human eye had ever scanned before.

But she was not alone. Far up, near the top of the escarpment, on a narrow ledge a shaggy creature looked down upon her from beneath beetling brows. It nudged another like it and pointed.

For a while the two watched the girl; then they started down the escarpment. Like flies they clung to the dizzy cliff, and when the ledge ended they swung to sturdy trees that clung to the rocky face of the great wall.

Down, down they came, two great first-men, shaggy, powerful, menacing. They dropped quickly, and always they sought to hide their approach from the eyes of the girl.

The great falls, the noise, the boiling river left Rhonda Terry stunned and helpless. There was no sign of her people, and if they were camped on the opposite side of the river she felt that they might as well be in another world, so impassable seemed the barrier that confronted her.

She felt very small and alone and tired. With a sigh she sat down on a rounded boulder and leaned against another piled behind it. All her remaining strength seemed to have gone from her. She closed her eyes wearily, and two tears rolled down her cheeks. Perhaps she dozed, but she was startled into wakefulness by a voice speaking near her. At first she thought she was dreaming and did not open her eyes.

'She is alone,' the voice said. 'We will take her to God – he will be pleased.'

It was an English voice, or at least the accent was English; but the tones were gruff and deep and guttural. The strange words convinced her she was dreaming. She opened her eyes, and shrank back with a little scream of terror. Standing close to her were two gorillas, or such she thought them to be until one of them opened its mouth and spoke.

'Come with us,' it said; 'we are going to take you to God;' then it reached out a mighty, hairy hand and seized her.

CHAPTER EIGHTEEN

Gorilla King

Rhonda Terry fought to escape the clutches of the great beast thing that held her, but she was helpless in the grasp of those giant muscles. The creature lifted her easily and tucked her under one arm.

'Be quiet,' it said, 'or I'll wring your neck.'

'You had better not,' cautioned his companion. 'God will be angry if you do not bring this one to him alive and unharmed. He has been hoping for such a she as this for a long time.'

'What does *he* want of her? He is so old now that he can scarcely chew his food.'

'He will probably give her to Henry the Eighth.'

'He already has seven wives. I think that I shall hide her and keep her for myself.'

'You will take her to God,' said the other. 'If you don't, I will.'

'We'll see about that!' cried the creature that held the girl.

He dropped her and sprang, growling, upon his fellow. As they closed, great fangs snapping, Rhonda leaped to her feet and sought to escape.

The whole thing seemed a hideous and grotesque nightmare, yet it was so real that she could not know whether or not she were dreaming.

As she bolted, the two ceased their quarrelling and pursued her. They easily overtook her, and once again she was a captive.

'You see what will happen,' said the beast that had wished to take her to God, 'if we waste time quarrelling over her. I will not let you have her unless God gives her to you.'

The other grumbled and tucked the girl under his arm again. 'Very well,' he said, 'but Henry the Eighth won't get her. I'm sick of that fellow. He thinks he is greater than God.'

With the agility of monkeys the two climbed up the tall trees and precarious ledges they had descended while Rhonda Terry closed her eyes to shut out the terror of the dizzy heights and sought to convince herself that she was dreaming.

But the reality was too poignant. Even the crass absurdity of the situation failed to convince her. She knew that she was not dreaming and that she was really in the power of two huge gorillas who spoke English with a marked insular accent. It was preposterous, but she knew that it was true.

To what fate were they bearing her? From their conversation she had an inkling of what lay in store for her. But who was Henry the Eighth? And who was God?

Up and up the beast bore her until at last they stood upon the summit of the escarpment. Below them, to the south, the river plunged over the edge of the escarpment to form Omwamwi Falls; to the north stretched a valley hemmed in by mountains – the valley of diamonds, perhaps.

The surprise, amounting almost to revulsion, that she had experienced when she first heard the two beasts speak a human language had had a strange effect upon her in that while she understood that they were speaking English it had not occurred to her that she could communicate with them in the same language – the adventure seemed so improbable that perhaps she still doubted her own senses.

The first shock of capture had been neutralized by the harrowing ascent of the escarpment and the relief at gaining the top in safety. Now she had an instant in which to think clearly, and with it came the realization that she had the means of communicating with her captors.

'Who are you?' she demanded, 'And why have you made me prisoner?'

The two turned suddenly upon her. She thought that their faces denoted surprise.

'She speaks English!' exclaimed one of them.

'Of course I speak English. But tell me what you want of me. You have no right to take me with you. I have not harmed you. I was only waiting for my own people. Let me go!'

'This will please God.' said one of her captors. 'He has always said that if he could get hold of an English woman he could do much for the race.'

'Who is this thing you call God?' she demanded.

'He is not a thing – he is a man.' replied the one who had carried her up the escarpment. 'He is very old – he is the oldest creature in the world and the wisest. He created us. But some day he will die, and then we shall have no god.'

'Henry the Eighth would like to be God,' said the other.

'He never will while Wolsey lives – Wolsey would make a far better god than he.'

'Henry the Eighth will see that he doesn't live.'

Rhonda Terry closed her eyes and pinched herself. She must be dreaming! Henry the Eighth! Thomas Wolsey! How preposterous seemed these familiar allusions to sixteenth century characters from the mouths of hairy gorillas.

The two brutes had not paused at the summit of the escarpment, but had immediately commenced the descent into the valley. Neither of them, not even the one that had carried her up the steep ascent, showed the slightest sign of fatigue even by accelerated breathing.

The girl was walking now, though one of the brutes held her arm and jerked her roughly forward when her steps lagged.

'I cannot walk so fast,' she said finally. 'I have not eaten for a long time, and I am weak.'

Without a word the creature gathered her under one arm and continued on down into the valley. Her position was uncomfortable, she was weak and frightened. Several times she lost consciousness.

How long that journey lasted she did not know. When she was conscious her mind was occupied by futile speculation as to the fate that lay ahead of her. She tried to visualize the *God* of these brutal creatures. What mercy, what pity might she expect at the hands of such a thing? – if, indeed, their god existed other than in their imaginations.

After what seemed a very long time the girl heard voices in the distance, growing louder as they proceeded; and soon after he who carried her set her upon her feet.

As she looked about her she saw that she stood at the bottom of a cliff before a city that was built partially at the foot of the cliff and partially carved from its face.

The approach to the city was bordered by great fields of bamboo, celery, fruits, and berries in which many gorillas were working with crude, hand-made implements.

As they caught sight of the captive these workers left their fields and clustered about asking many questions and examining the girl with every indication of intelligent interest, but her captors hurried her along into the city.

Here again they were surrounded by curious crowds; but nowhere was any violence offered the captive, the attitude of the gorillas appearing far more friendly than that which she might have expected from human natives of this untracked wilderness.

That portion of the city that was built upon the level ground at the foot of the cliff consisted of circular huts of bamboo with thatched conical roofs, of rectangular buildings of sun dried bricks, and others of stone.

Near the foot of the cliff was a three-story building with towers and ramparts, roughly suggestive of medieval England; and farther up the cliff, upon a broad ledge, was another even larger structure of similar architecture.

Rhonda's captors led her directly to the former building, before the door of which squatted two enormous gorillas armed with crude weapons that resembled battle axes; and here they were stopped while the two guards examined Rhonda and questioned her captors.

Again and again the girl tried to convince herself that she was dreaming. All her past experience, all her acquired knowledge stipulated the utter absurdity of the fantastic experiences of the past few hours. There could be no such things as gorillas that spoke English, tilled fields, and lived in stone castles. And yet here were all these impossibilities before her eyes as concrete evidence of their existence.

She listened as one in a dream while her captors demanded entrance that they might take their prisoner before the king; she heard the guard demur, saying that the king could not be disturbed as he was engaged with the Privy Council.

'Then we'll take her to God.' threatened one of her captors. 'and when the king finds out what you have done you'll he working in the quarry instead of sitting here in the shade.'

Finally a young gorilla was summoned and sent into the palace with a message. When he returned it was with the word that the king wished to have the prisoner brought before him at once.

Rhonda was conducted into a large room the floor of which was covered with dried grass. On a dais at one end of the room an enormous gorilla paced to and fro while a half dozen other gorillas squatted in the grass at the foot of the dais – enormous, shaggy beasts, all.

There were no chairs nor tables nor benches in the room, but from the center of the dais rose the bare trunk and leafless branches of a tree.

As the girl was brought into the room the gorilla on the dais stopped his restless pacing and scrutinized her. 'Where did you find her, Buckingham?' he demanded.

'At the foot of the falls, Sire,' replied the beast that had captured her.

'What was she doing there?'

'She said that she was looking for her friends, who were to meet her at the falls.'

'She *said!* You mean that she speaks English?' demanded the king.

'Yes, I speak English.' said Rhonda; 'and if I am not dreaming, and you are the king, I demand that you send me back to the falls, so that I may find my people.'

'Dreaming? What put that into your head? You are not asleep, are you?'

'I do not know,' replied Rhonda. 'Sometimes I am sure that I must be.'

'Well, you are not,' snapped the king. 'And who put it into your head that there might be any doubt that I am king? That sounds like Buckingham.'

'Your majesty wrongs me,' said Buckingham stiffly. 'It was I who insisted on bringing her to the king.'

'It is well you did; the wench pleases us. We will keep her.'

'But, your majesty,' exclaimed the other of Rhonda's two captors, 'it is our duty to take her to God. We brought her here first that your majesty might see her; but we must take her on to God, who has been hoping for such a woman for years.'

'What, Cranmer! Are you turning against me too?'

'Cranmer is right,' said one of the great bulls squatting on the floor. 'This woman should be taken to God. Do not forget, Sire, that you already have seven wives.'

'That is just like you, Wolsey,' snapped the king peevishly. 'You are always taking the part of God.'

'We must all remember,' said Wolsey. 'that we owe everything to God. It was he who created us. He made us what we are. It is he who can destroy us.'

The king was pacing up and down the straw covered dais rapidly. His eyes were blazing, his lips drawn back in a snarl. Suddenly he stopped by the tree and shook it angrily as though he would tear it from the masonry in which it was set. Then he climbed quickly up into a fork and glared down at them. For a moment he perched there, but only for a moment. With the agility of a small monkey he leaped to the floor of the dais. With his great fists he beat upon his hairy breast, and from his cavernous lungs rose a terrific roar that shook the building.

'I am king!' he screamed. 'My word is law. Take the wench to the women's quarters!'

The beast the king had addressed as Wolsey now leaped to his feet and commenced to beat his breast and scream. 'This is sacrilege,' he cried. 'He who defies God shall die. That is the law. Repent, and send the girl to God!'

'Never!' shrieked the king. 'She is mine.'

Both brutes were now beating their breasts and roaring so loudly that their words could scarcely be distinguished; and the other bulls were moving restlessly, their hair bristling, their fangs bared.

Then Wolsey played his ace. 'Send the girl to God,' he bellowed, 'or suffer excommunication!'

But the king had now worked himself to such a frenzy that he was beyond reason. 'The guard! The guard!' he screamed. 'Suffolk, call the guard, and take Cardinal Wolsey to the tower! Buckingham, take the girl to the women's quarters or off goes your head.'

The two bulls were still beating their breasts and screaming at one another as Rhonda Terry was dragged from the apartment by the shaggy Buckingham.

Up a circular stone stairway the brute dragged her and along a corridor to a room at the rear of the second floor. It was a large room in the corner of the buildings, and about its grass strewn floor squatted or lay a number of adult gorillas, while young ones of all ages played about or suckled at their mothers' breasts.

Many of the beasts were slowly eating celery stalks, tender bamboo tips, or fruit; but all activity ceased as Buckingham dragged the American girl into their midst.

'What have you there, Buckingham?' growled an old she.

'A girl we captured at the falls,' replied Buckingham. 'The king commanded that she be brought here, your majesty.' Then he turned to his captive. 'This is Queen Catherine,' he said, 'Catherine of Aragon.'

'What does he want of her?' demanded Catherine peevishly.

Buckingham shrugged his broad shoulders and glanced about the room at the six adult females. 'Your majesties should well be able to guess.'

'Is he thinking of taking that puny, hairless thing for a wife?' demanded another, sitting at a little distance from Catherine of Aragon.

'Of course that's what he's thinking of, Anne Boleyn,' snapped Catherine; 'or he wouldn't have sent her here.'

'Hasn't he got enough wives already?' demanded another.

'That is for the king to decide,' said Buckingham as he quitted the room.

Now the great shes commenced to gather closer to the girl. They sniffed at her and felt of her clothing. The younger ones crowded in, pulling at her skirt. One, larger than the rest, grabbed her by the ankles and pulled her feet from under her; and, as she fell, it danced about the room, grimacing and screaming.

As she tried to rise it rushed toward her; and she struck it in the face, thinking it meant to injure her. Whereupon it ran screaming to Catherine of Aragon, and one of the other shes seized Rhonda by the shoulder and pushed her so violently that she was hurled against the wall.

'How dare you lay hands on the Prince of Wales!' cried the beast that had pushed her.

The Prince of Wales, Catherine of Aragon. Anne Boleyn! If not asleep, Rhonda Terry was by this time positive that she had gone mad. What possible explanation could there be for such a mad burlesque in which gorillas acted the parts and spoke with the tongues of men? – what other than the fantasy of sleep or insanity? None.

She sat huddled against the wall where she had fallen and buried her face in her arms.

CHAPTER NINETEEN

Despair

The frightened pony carried Naomi Madison in the wake of its fellows. She could only cling frantically to the saddle, constantly fearful of being brushed to the ground.

Presently, where the trail widened into a natural clearing, the horses in front of her stopped suddenly; and the one she rode ran in among them before it stopped too.

Then she saw the reason – Sheykh Ab el-Ghrennem and his followers. She tried to rein her horse around and escape; but he was wedged in among the other horses, and a moment later the little herd was surrounded. Once more she was a prisoner.

The sheykh was so glad to get his horses back that he almost forgot to be angry over the trick that had robbed him of them temporarily. He was glad, too, to have one of his prisoners. She could read the map to them and be useful in other ways if he decided not to sell her.

'Where is the other one?' demanded Atewy.

'She was killed by a lion,' replied Naomi.

Atewy shrugged. 'Well, we still have you; and we have the map. We shall not fare so ill.'

Naomi recalled the cone shaped volcanic hill and the mountains in the distance. 'If I lead you to the valley of diamonds will you return me to my people?' she asked.

Atewy translated to el-Ghrennem. The old sheykh nodded. 'Tell her we will do that if she leads us to the valley of diamonds,' he said. '*Wellah!* yes; tell her that; but after we find the valley of diamonds we may forget what we have promised. But do not tell her *that.*'

Atewy grinned. 'Lead us to the valley of diamonds,' he said to Naomi, 'and all that you wish will be done.'

Unaccustomed to the strenuous labor of pushing through the jungle on foot that the pursuit of the white girls and their ponies had necessitated, the Arabs made camp as soon as they reached the river.

The following day they crossed to the open plain; and when Naomi called their attention to the volcanic hill and the location of the mountains to the northwest, and they had compared these landmarks with the map, they were greatly elated.

But when they reached the river below the falls the broad and turbulent stream seemed impassable and the cliffs before them unscalable.

They camped that night on the east side of the river; and late into the night discussed plans for crossing to the west side, for the map clearly indicated but a single entrance to the valley of diamonds, and that was several miles northwest of them.

In the morning they started downstream in search of a crossing, but it was two days before they found a place where they dared make the attempt. Even here they had the utmost difficulty in negotiating the river, and consumed most of the day in vain attempts before they finally succeeded in winning to the opposite shore with the loss of two men and their mounts.

The Madison had been almost paralyzed by terror, not alone by the natural hazards of the swift current but by the constant menace of the crocodiles with which the stream seemed alive. Wet to the skin, she huddled close to the fire; and finally, hungry and miserable, dropped into a sleep of exhaustion.

What provisions the Arabs had had with them had been lost or ruined in the crossing, and so much time had been consumed in reaching the west bank that they had been unable to hunt for game before dark. But they were accustomed to a life of privation and hardship, and their spirits were buoyed by the certainty that all felt that within a few days they would be scooping up diamonds by the handfuls from the floor of the fabulous valley that now lay but a short distance to the north.

Coming down the east bank of the river they had consumed much time in unsuccessful attempts to cross the stream, and they had been further retarded by the absence of a good trail. But on the west side of the river they found a wide and well beaten track along which they moved rapidly.

Toward the middle of the afternoon of the first day after crossing the river Naomi called to Atewy who rode near her.

'Look!' she said, pointing ahead. 'There is the red granite column shown on the map. Directly east of it is the entrance to the valley.'

Atewy, much excited, transmitted the information to el-Ghrennem and the others; and broad grins wreathed their usually saturnine countenances.

'And now,' said Naomi, 'that I have led you to the valley, keep your promise to me and send me back to my people.'

'Wait a bit,' replied Atewy. 'We are not in the valley yet. We must be sure that this is indeed the valley of diamonds. You must come with us yet a little farther.'

'But that was not the agreement,' insisted the girl. 'I was to lead you to the valley, and that I have done. I am going back to look for my people now whether you send anyone with me or not.'

She wheeled her pony to turn back along the trail they had come. She did not know where her people were; but she had heard the Arabs say that the falls they had passed were the Omwamwi Falls, and she knew that the safari had been marching for this destination when she had been stolen more than a week before. They must be close to them by this time.

But she was not destined to carry her scheme into execution, for as she wheeled her mount Atewy spurred to her side, grasped her bridle rein, and, with an oath, struck her across the face.

'The next time you try that you'll get something worse,' he threatened.

Suffering from the blow, helpless, hopeless, the girl broke into tears. She thought that she had plumbed the uttermost depths of terror and despair, but she did not know what the near future held in store for her.

That night the Arabs camped just east of the red granite monolith that they believed marked the entrance to the valley of diamonds, at the mouth of a narrow canyon.

Early the following morning they started up the canyon on the march that they believed would lead them to a country of fabulous wealth. From far above them savage eyes looked down from scowling black faces, watching their progress.

CHAPTER TWENTY

'Come with Me!'

In the light of a new day Tarzan of the Apes stood looking down upon the man who resembled him so closely that the ape-man experienced the uncanny sensation of standing apart, like a disembodied spirit, viewing his corporeal self.

It was the morning that they were to have set off in search of Orman and West, but Tarzan saw that it would be some time before Obroski would travel again on his own legs.

With all the suddenness with which it sometimes strikes, fever had seized the American. His delirious ravings had awakened Tarzan, but now he lay in a coma.

The Lord of the Jungle considered the matter briefly. He neither wished to leave the man alone to the scant mercy of the jungle, nor did he wish to remain with him. His conversations with Obroski had convinced him that no matter what his inclinations might be the dictates of simplest humanity required that he do what he might to succour the innocent members of Orman's party. The plight of the two girls appealed especially to his sense of chivalry, and it was with his usual celerity that he reached a decision.

Lifting the unconscious Obroski in his arms he threw him across one of his broad shoulders and swung off through the jungle toward the south.

All day he travelled, stopping briefly once for water, eating no food. Sometimes the American lay unconscious, sometimes he struggled and raved in delirium; or, again, consciousness returning, he begged the ape-man to stop and let him rest. But Tarzan ignored his pleas, and moved on toward the south.

Toward evening the two came to a native village beyond the Bansuto country. It was the village of the chief, Mpugu, whom Tarzan knew to be friendly to whites as well as under obligations to the Lord of the Jungle who had once saved his life.

Obroski was unconscious when they arrived in the village, and Tarzan placed him in a hut which Mpugu placed at his disposal.

'When he is well, take him to Jinja.' Tarzan instructed Mpugu, 'and ask the commissioner to send him on to the coast.'

The ape-man remained in the village only long enough to fill his empty belly; then he swung off again through the gathering dusk toward the north, while far away, in the city of the gorilla king, Rhonda Terry crouched in the dry grass that littered the floor of the quarters of the king's wives and dreamed of the horrid fate that awaited her.

A week had passed since she had been thrust into this room with its fierce denizens. She had learned much concerning them since then, but not the secret of their origin. Most of them were far from friendly, though none offered her any serious harm. Only one of them paid much attention to her, and from this one and the conversations she had overheard she had gained what meager information she had concerning them.

The six adult females were the wives of the king, Henry the Eighth; and they bore the historic names of that much married English king. There were Catherine of Aragon, Anne Boleyn, Jane Seymour, Anne of Cleves, Catherine Howard, and Catherine Parr.

It was Catherine Parr, the youngest, who had been the least unfriendly; and that, perhaps, because she had suffered at the hands of the others and hated them.

Rhonda told her that there had been a king in a far country four hundred years before who had been called Henry the Eighth and who had had six wives of the same names as theirs and that such an exact parallel seemed beyond the realms of possibility – that in this far off valley their king should have found six women that he wished to marry who bore those identical names.

'Those were not our names before we became the wives of the king.' explained Catherine Parr. 'When we were married to the king we were given these names.'

'By the king?'

'No – by God.'

'What is your god like?' asked Rhonda.

'He is very old. No one knows how old he is. He has been here in England always. He is the god of England. He knows everything and is very powerful.'

'Have you ever seen him?'

'No. He has not come out of his castle for many years. Now, he and the king are quarrelling. That is why the king has not been here since you came. God has threatened to kill him if he takes another wife.'

'Why?' asked Rhonda.

'God says Henry the Eighth may have only six wives – there are no names for more.'

'There doesn't seem much sense in that.' commented the girl.

'We may not question God's reasons. He created us, and he is all-wise. We must have faith; otherwise he will destroy us.'

'Where does your god live?'

'In the great castle on the ledge above the city. It is called The Golden Gates. Through it we enter into heaven after we die – if we have believed in God and served him well.'

'What is the castle like inside?' asked Rhonda, 'this castle of God?'

'I have never been in it. Only the king and a few of his nobles, the cardinal, the archbishop, and the priests have ever entered The Golden Gates and come out again. The spirits of the dead enter, but, of course, they never come back. And occasionally God sends for a young man or a young woman. What happens to them no one knows, but they never come back either. It is said—' she hesitated.

'What is said?' Rhonda found herself becoming intrigued by the mystery surrounding this strange god that guarded the entrance to heaven.

'Oh, terrible things are said; but I dare not even whisper them. I must not think them. God can read our thoughts. Do not ask me any more questions. You have been sent by the devil to lure me to destruction,' and that was the last that Rhonda could get out of Catherine Parr.

Early the next day the American girl was awakened by horrid growls and roars that seemed to come not only from outside the palace but from the interior as well.

The she gorillas penned in the quarters with her were restless. They

growled as they crowded to the windows and looked down into the courtyard and the streets beyond.

Rhonda came and stood behind them and looked over their shoulders.
She saw shaggy beasts struggling and fighting at the gate leading through the
outer wall, surging through the courtyard below, and battling before the
entrance to the palace. They fought with clubs and battle axes, talons and
fangs.

'They have freed Wolsey from the tower,' she heard Jane Seymour say, 'and
he is leading God's party against the king.'

Catherine of Aragon squatted in the dry grass and commenced to peel a
banana. 'Henry and God are always quarrelling,' she said wearily – 'and nothing ever comes of it. Every time Henry wants a new wife they quarrel.'

'But I notice he always gets his wife,' said Catherine Howard.

'He has had Wolsey on his side before – this time it may be different. I have
heard that God wants this hairless she for himself. If he gets her that will be
the last anyone will ever see of her – which suits me.' Catherine of Aragon
bared her fangs at the American girl, and then returned her attention to the
banana.

The sound of fighting surged upward from the floor below until they heard
it plainly in the corridor outside the closed door of their quarters. Suddenly
the door was thrown open, and several bulls burst into the room.

'Where is the hairless one?' demanded the leading bull. 'Ah, there she is!'

He crossed the room and seized Rhonda roughly by the wrist.

'Come with me!' he ordered. 'God has sent for you.'

CHAPTER TWENTY-ONE
Abducted

The Arabs made their way up the narrow canyon toward the summit of the
pass that led into the valley of diamonds. From above, fierce, cruel eyes
looked down. Ab el-Ghrennem gloated exultantly. He had visions of the rich
treasure that was soon to give him wealth beyond his previous wildest dreams
of avarice. Atewy rode close to Naomi Madison to prevent her from
escaping.

At last they came to a precipitous wall that no horse could scale. The perpendicular sides of the rocky canyon had drawn close together.

'The horses can go no farther.' announced Ab el-Ghrennem. 'Eyad, thou
shalt remain with them. The rest of us will continue on foot.'

'And the girl?' asked Atewy.

'Bring her with us, lest she escape Eyad while he is guarding the horses,' replied the sheykh. 'I would not lose her.'

They scrambled up the rocky escarpment, dragging Naomi Madison with them, to find more level ground above. The rocky barrier had not been high, but sufficient to bar the progress of a horse.

Sitting in his saddle, Eyad could see above it and watch his fellows continuing on up the canyon, which was now broader with more sloping walls upon which timber grew as it did upon the summit.

They had proceeded but a short distance when Eyad saw a black, shaggy, manlike figure emerge from a bamboo thicket above and behind the sheykh's party. Then another and another followed the first. They carried clubs or axes with long handles.

Eyad shouted a warning to his comrades. It brought them to a sudden halt, but it also brought a swarm of the hairy creatures pouring down the canyon sides upon them.

Roaring and snarling, the beasts closed in upon the men. The matchlocks of the Arabs roared, filling the canyon with thundering reverberations, adding to the bedlam.

A few of the gorillas were hit. Some fell; but the others, goaded to a frightful rage by their wounds, charged to close quarters. They tore the weapons from the hands of the Arabs and cast them aside. Seizing the men in their powerful hands, they sank great fangs into the throats of their adversaries. Others wielded club or battle axe.

Screaming and cursing, the Arabs sought now only to escape. Eyad was filled with terror as he saw the bloody havoc being wrought upon his fellows. He saw a great bull gather the girl into his arms and start up the slope of the canyon wall toward the wooded summit. He saw two mighty bulls descending the canyon toward him. Then Eyad wheeled and put spurs to his horse. Clattering down the canyon, he heard the sounds of conflict growing dimmer and dimmer until at last he could hear them no longer.

And as Eyad disappeared in the lower reaches of the canyon, Buckingham carried Naomi Madison into the forest above the strange city of the gorilla king.

Buckingham was mystified. He thought that this hairless she was the same creature he had captured many days before below the great falls that he knew as Victoria Falls. Yet only this very morning he had seen her taken by Wolsey to the castle of God.

He paused beyond the summit at a point where the city of gorillas could be seen below them. He was in a quandary. He very much wanted this she for himself, but then both God and the king wanted her. He stood scratching his head as he sought to evolve a plan whereby he might possess her without incurring the wrath of two such powerful personages.

Naomi, hanging in the crook of his arm, was frozen with horror. The Arabs had seemed bad enough, but this horrid brute! She wondered when he would kill her and how.

Presently he stood her on her feet and looked at her. 'How did you escape from God?' he demanded.

Naomi Madison gasped in astonishment, and her eyes went wide. A great fear crept over her, a fear greater than the physical terror that the brute itself aroused – she feared that she was losing her reason. She stood with wild, staring eyes gazing at the beast. Then, suddenly, she burst into wild laughter.

'What are you laughing at?' growled Buckingham.

'At you,' she cried. 'You think you can fool me, but you can't. I know that I am just dreaming. In a moment I'll be awake, and I'll see the sun coming in my bedroom window. I'll see the orange tree and the loquat in my patio. I'll see Hollywood stretching below me with its red roofs and its green trees.'

'I don't know what you are talking about.' said Buckingham. 'You are not asleep. You are awake. Look down there, and you will see London and the Thames.'

Naomi looked where he indicated. She saw a strange city on the banks of a small river. She pinched herself; and it hurt, but she did not awake. Slowly she realized that she was not dreaming, that the terrible unrealities she had passed through were real.

'Who are you? What are you?' she asked.

'Answer my question,' commanded Buckingham. 'How did you escape from God?'

'I don't know what you mean. The Arabs captured me. I escaped from them once, but they got me again.'

'Was that before I captured you several days ago?'

'I never saw you before.'

Buckingham scratched his head again. 'Are there two of you?' he demanded. 'I certainly caught you or another just like you at the falls over a week ago.'

Suddenly Naomi thought that she comprehended. 'You caught a girl like me?' she demanded.

'Yes.'

'Did she wear a red handkerchief around her neck?'

'Yes.'

'Where is she?'

'If you are not she, she is with God in his castle – down there.' He leaned out over the edge of the cliff and pointed to a stone castle on a ledge far below. He turned toward her as a new idea took form in his mind. 'If you are not she,' he said, 'then God has the other one – and I can have you!'

'No! No!' cried the girl. 'Let me go! Let me go back to my people.'

Buckingham seized her and tucked her under one of his huge arms. 'Neither God nor Henry the Eighth shall ever see you,' he growled. 'I'll take you away where they can't find you – they shan't rob me of you as they robbed me of he other. I'll take you to a place where there is food and water. I'll build a shelter among the trees. We'll be safe there from both God and the king.'

Naomi struggled and struck at him; but he paid no attention to her, as he swung off to the south toward the lower end of the valley.

CHAPTER TWENTY-TWO
The Imposter

The Lord of the Jungle awoke and stretched. A new day was dawning. He had travelled far from Mpugu's village the previous night before he lay up to rest. Now, refreshed, he swung on toward the north. He would make a kill and eat on the way, or he would go hungry – it depended upon the fortunes of the trail. Tarzan could go for long periods without food with little inconvenience. He was no such creature of habit as are the poor slaves of civilization.

He had gone but a short distance when he caught the scent spoor of men – tarmangani – white men. And before he saw them he had recognized them by their scent.

He paused in a tree above them and looked down upon them. There were three of them – two whites and an Arab. They had made a poor camp the night before. Tarzan saw no sign of food. The men looked haggard, almost exhausted. Not far from them was a buck, but the starving men did not know it. Tarzan knew it because Usha, the wind, was carrying the scent of the buck to his keen nostrils.

Seeing their dire need and fearing that they might frighten the animal away before he could kill it, Tarzan passed around them unseen and swung silently on through the trees.

Wappi, the antelope, browsed on the tender grasses of a little clearing. He would take a few mouthfuls; then raise his head, looking and listening – always alert. But he was not sufficiently alert to detect the presence of the noiseless stalker creeping upon him.

Suddenly the antelope started! He had heard, but it was too late. A beast of prey had launched itself upon him from the branches of a tree.

A quarter of a mile away Orman had risen to his feet. 'We might as well get going, Bill,' he said.

'Can't we make this bird understand that we want him to guide us to the point where he last saw one of the girls?'

'I've tried. You've heard me threaten to kill him if he doesn't, but he either can't or won't understand.'

'If we don't get something to eat pretty soon we won't ever find anybody. If—' The incompleted sentence died in a short gasp.

An uncanny cry had come rolling out of the mysterious jungle fastness, freezing the blood in the veins of all three men.

'The ghost!' said Orman in a whisper.

An involuntary shudder ran through West's frame. 'You know that's all hooey. Tom,' he said.

'Yes, I know it,' admitted Orman; 'but—'

'That probably wasn't – Obroski at all. It must have been some animal,' insisted West.

'Look!' exclaimed Orman, pointing beyond West.

As the cameraman wheeled he saw an almost naked white man walking toward them, the carcass of a buck across on broad shoulder.

'Obroski!' exclaimed West.

Tarzan saw the two men gazing at him in astonishment he heard West's ejaculation, and he recalled the striking resemblance that he and Obroski bore to one another. If the shadow of a smile was momentarily reflected by his grey eyes it was gone when he stopped before the two men and tossed the carcass of the buck at their feet.

'I thought you might be hungry,' he said. 'You look hungry.'

'Obroski!' muttered Orman. 'Is it really you?' He stepped closer to Tarzan and touched his shoulder.

'What did you think I was – a ghost?' asked the ape-man.

Orman laughed – an apologetic, embarrassed laugh. 'I – well – we thought you were dead. It was so surprising to see you – and then the way that you killed the lion the other day – you did kill the lion, didn't you?'

'He seemed to be dead,' replied the ape-man.

'Yes, of course; but then it didn't seem exactly like you, Obroski – we didn't know that you could do anything like that.'

'There are probably a number of things about me that you don't know. But never mind about that. I've come to find out what you know about the girls. Are they safe? And how about the rest of the safari?'

'The girls were stolen by the Arabs almost two weeks ago. Bill and I have been looking for them. I don't know where the rest of the outfit are. I told Pat to try to get everything to Omwamwi Falls and wait for me there if I didn't show up before. We captured this Arab. It's Eyad – you probably remember him. Of course we can't understand his lingo; but from what we can make out one of the girls has been killed by a wild beast, and something terrible has happened to the other girl and the rest of the Arabs.'

Tarzan turned to Eyad; and, much to the Arab's surprise, questioned him in his own tongue while Orman and West looked on in astonishment. The two spoke rapidly for a few minutes; then Tarzan handed Eyad an arrow, and the man, squatting on his haunches, smoothed a little area of ground with the palm of his hand and commenced to draw something with the point of the arrow.

'What's he doing?' asked West. 'What did he say?'

'He's drawing a map to show me where this fight took place between the Arabs and the gorillas.'

'Gorillas! What did he say about the girls?'

'One of them was killed by a lion a week or more ago, and the last he saw of the other she was being carried off by a big bull gorilla.'

'Which one is dead?' asked West. 'Did he say?'

Tarzan questioned Eyad, and then turned to the American. 'He does not know. He says that he could never tell the two girls apart.'

Eyad had finished his map and was pointing out the different landmarks to the ape-man. Orman and West were also scrutinizing the crude tracing.

The director gave a short laugh. 'This bird's stringin' you, Obroski,' he said. 'That's a copy of a fake map we had for use in the picture.'

Tarzan questioned Eyad rapidly in Arabic; then he turned again to Orman. 'I think he is telling the truth,' he said. 'Anyway, I'll soon know. I am going up to this valley and look around. You and West follow on up to the falls. Eyad can guide you. This buck will last you until you get there.' Then he turned and swung into the trees.

The three men stood staring at the spot for a moment. Finally Orman shook his head. 'I never was so fooled in anyone before in my life.' he said. 'I had Obroski all wrong – we all did. By golly. I never saw such a change in a man before in my whole life.'

'Even his voice has changed,' said West.

'He certainly was a secretive son-of-a-gun,' said Orman. 'I never had the slightest idea that he could speak Arabic.'

'I think he mentioned that there were several things about him that you did not know.'

'If I wasn't so familiar with that noble mug of his and that godlike physique I'd swear that this guy isn't Obroski at all.'

'Not a chance,' said West. 'I'd know him in a million.'

CHAPTER TWENTY-THREE
Man and Beast

The great bull gorilla carried Naomi Madison south along the wooded crest of the mountains toward the southern end of the valley. When they came to open spaces he scurried quickly across them, and he looked behind him often as though fearing pursuit.

The girl's first terror had subsided, to be replaced by a strange apathy that she could not understand. It was as though her nervous system was under the effects of an anesthetic that deadened her susceptibility to fear but left all her other faculties unimpaired. Perhaps she had undergone so much that she no longer cared what befell her.

That she could converse in English with this brutal beast lent an unreality to the adventure that probably played a part in inducing the mental state in which she found herself. After this, anything might be, anything might happen.

The uncomfortable position in which she was being carried and her hunger presently became matters of the most outstanding importance, relegating danger to the background.

'Let me walk,' she said.

Buckingham grunted and lowered her to her feet. 'Do not try to run away from me,' he warned.

They continued on through the woods toward the south, the beast sometimes stopping to look back and listen. He was moving into the wind; so his nose was useless in apprehending danger from the rear.

During one of these stops Naomi saw fruit growing upon a tree. 'I am hungry,' she said. 'Is this fruit good to eat?'

'Yes,' he replied and permitted her to gather some; then he pushed on again.

They had come almost to the end of the valley and were crossing a space almost devoid of trees at a point where the mountains fell in a series of precipitous cliffs down to the floor of the valley when the gorilla paused as usual under such circumstances to glance back.

The girl, thinking he feared pursuit by the Arabs, always looked hopefully back at such times. Even the leering countenance of Atewy would have been a welcome sight under such circumstances. Heretofore they had seen no sign of pursuit, but this time a figure emerged from the patch of wood they had just quitted – it was the lumbering figure of a bull gorilla.

With a snarl, Buckingham lifted the girl from her feet and broke into a lumbering run. A short distance within the forest beyond the clearing he turned abruptly toward the cliff; and when he reached the edge he swung the girl to his back, telling her to put her arms about his neck and hang on.

Naomi Madison glanced once into the abyss below; then she shut her eyes and prayed for strength to hang onto the hairy creature making its way down the sheer face of the rocky escarpment.

What he found to cling to she did not know, for she did not open her eyes until he loosed her hands by main strength and let her drop to her feet behind him.

'I'll come back for you when I have thrown Suffolk off the trail,' said the beast and was gone.

Then Madison found herself in a small natural cave in the face of the cliff. A tiny stream of water trickled from a hidden spring, formed a little pool at the front of the cave, and ran over the edge down the face of the cliff. A part of the floor of the cave was dry; but there was no covering upon it, only the bare rock.

The girl approached the ledge and looked down. The great height of the seemingly bare cliff face made her shrink back, giddy. Then she tried it again and looked up. There seemed scarcely a hand or foothold in any direction. She marvelled that the heavy gorilla had been able to make his way to the cave safely, burdened by her weight.

As she examined her situation, Buckingham clambered quickly to the summit of the cliff and continued on toward the south. He moved slowly, and it was not long before the pursuing beast overtook him.

The creature upon his trail hailed him. 'Where is the hairless she?' he demanded.

'I do not know,' replied the other. 'She has run away from me. I am looking for her.'

'Why did you run away from me, Buckingham?'

'I did not know it was you, Suffolk. I thought you were one of Wolsey's men trying to rob me of the she so that I could not take her to the king.'

Suffolk grunted. 'We had better find her. The king is not in a good humor. How do you suppose she escaped from God?'

'She did not escape from God – this is a different she, though they look much alike.' The two passed on through the forest, searching for the Madison.

For two nights and two days the girl lay alone in the rocky cave. She could neither ascend nor descend the vertical cliff. If the beast did not return for her, she must starve. This she knew, yet she hoped that it would not return.

The third night fell. Naomi was suffering from hunger. Fortunately the little trickle of water through the cave saved her from suffering from thirst also. She heard the savage sounds of the night life of the wilderness, but she was not afraid. The cave had at least that advantage. If she had food she could live there in safety indefinitely, but she had no food.

The first pangs of hunger had passed. She did not suffer. She only knew that she was growing weaker. It seemed strange to her that she, Naomi Madison, should be dying of hunger – and alone! Why, in all the world the only creature that could save her from starvation, the only creature that knew where she was was a great, savage gorilla – she who numbered her admirers by the millions, whose whereabouts, whose every act was chronicled in a hundred newspapers and magazines. She felt very small and insignificant now. Here was no room for arrogant egotism.

During the long hours she had had more opportunity for self-scrutiny than ever before, and what she discovered was not very flattering. She realized that she had already changed much during the past two weeks – she had learned much from the attitude of the other members of the safari toward her but most of all from the example that Rhonda Terry had set her. If she were to have the chance, she knew that she would be a very different woman; but she did not expect the chance. She did not want life at the price she would have to pay. She prayed that she might die before the gorilla returned to claim his prize.

She slept fitfully through her third night – the rocky floor that was her bed was torture to her soft flesh. The morning sun, shining full into the mouth of her cave, gave her renewed hope even though her judgment told her that there was no hope.

She drank, and bathed her hands and face; then she sat and looked out over the valley of diamonds. She should have hated it, for it had aroused the avarice that had brought her to this sorry pass; but she did not – it was too beautiful.

Presently her attention was attracted by a scraping sound outside the cave and above it. She listened intently. What could it be?

A moment later a black, hairy leg appeared below the top of the mouth of the cave; and then the gorilla dropped to the narrow ledge before it. The thing had returned! The girl crouched against the back wall, shuddering.

The brute stooped and peered into the gloomy cavern. 'Come here!' it commanded. 'I see you. Hurry – we have no time to waste. They may have followed me. Suffolk has had me watched for two days. He did not believe that you had run away. He guessed that I had hidden you. Come! Hurry!'

'Go away and leave me,' she begged. 'I would rather stay here and die.'

He made no answer at once, but stooped and came toward her. Seizing her roughly by the arm he dragged her to the mouth of the cave. 'So I'm not good enough for you?' he growled. 'Don't you know that I am the Duke of Buckingham? Get on my back, and hold tight.'

He swung her up into position, and she clung about his neck. She wanted to hurl herself over the edge of the cliff, but she could not raise her courage to the point. Against her will she clung to the shaggy brute as he climbed the sheer face of the cliff toward the summit. She did not dare even to look down.

At the top he lowered her to her feet and started on southward toward the lower end of the valley, dragging her after him.

She was weak; and she staggered, stumbling often. Then he would jerk her roughly to her feet and growl at her, using strange, medieval oaths.

'I can't go on.' she said. 'I am weak. I have had nothing to eat for two days.'

'You are just trying to delay me so that Suffolk can overtake us. You would rather belong to the king, but you won't. You'll never see the king. He is just waiting for an excuse to have my head, but he won't ever get it. We're never going back to London, you and I. We'll go out of the valley and find a place below the falls.'

Again she stumbled and fell. The beast became enraged. He kicked her as she lay on the ground; then he seized her by the hair and dragged her after him.

But he did not go far thus. He had taken but a few steps when he came to a sudden halt. With a savage growl and upturned lips baring powerful yellow fangs he faced a figure that had dropped from a tree directly in his path.

The girl saw too, and her eyes went wide. 'Stanley!' she cried. 'Oh, Stanley, save me, save me!'

It was the startled cry of a forlorn hope, but in the instant of voicing it she knew that she could expect no help from Stanley Obroski, the coward. Her heart sank, and the horror of her position seemed suddenly more acute because of this brief instant of false reprieve.

The gorilla released his hold upon her hair and dropped her to the ground, where she lay too weak to rise, watching the great beast at her side and the bronzed white giant facing it.

'Go away, Bolgani!' commanded Tarzan in the language of the great apes. 'The she is mine. Go away, or I kill!'

Buckingham did not understand the tongue of this stranger, but he understood the menace of his attitude. 'Go away!' he cried in English. 'Go away, or I will kill you!' Thus a beast spoke in English to an Englishman who spoke the language of the beasts!

Tarzan of the Apes is not easily astonished; but when he heard Bolgani, the gorilla, speak to him in English he at first questioned his sanity. But whatever the condition of either it could not conceal the evident intent of the bull gorilla advancing menacingly toward him as it beat its breast and screamed its threats.

Naomi Madison watched with horror-wide, fascinated eyes. She saw the man she thought to be Stanley Obroski crouch slightly as though waiting to receive the charge. She wondered why he did not turn and run – that was what all who knew him, including herself, would have expected of Stanley Obroski.

Suddenly the gorilla charged, and still the man held his ground. Great hairy paws reached out to seize him; but he eluded them with quick, panther-like movements. Stooping, he sprang beneath a swinging arm; and before the beast could turn leaped upon its back. A bronzed arm encircled the squat neck of the hairy Buckingham. In a frenzy of rage the beast swung around, clawing futilely to rid himself of his antagonist.

He felt the steel thews of the ape-man's arm tightening, and realized that he was coping with muscles far beyond what he had expected. He threw himself to the ground in an effort to crush his foe with his great weight, but Tarzan broke the fall with his feet and slipped partially from beneath the hairy body.

Then Buckingham felt powerful jaws close upon his neck near the jugular, he heard savage growls mingling with his own. Naomi Madison heard too, and a new horror filled her soul. Now she knew why Stanley Obroski had not fled in terror – he had gone mad! Fear and suffering had transformed him into a maniac.

She shuddered at the thought, she shrank within herself as she saw his strong white teeth sink into the black hide of the gorilla and heard the bestial growls rumbling from that handsome mouth.

The two beasts rolled over and over upon the ground, the roars of the gorilla mingling with the growls of the man; and the girl, leaning upon her hands, watched through fascinated, horror stricken eyes.

She knew that there could be but one outcome – even though the man appeared to have a slight initial advantage, the giant strength of the mighty bull must prevail in the end. Then she saw a knife flash, reflecting the rays of the morning sun. She saw it driven into the great bull's side. She heard his agonized shriek of pain and rage. She saw him redouble his efforts to dislodge the creature clinging to his back.

Again and again the knife was driven home. Suddenly the maddened struggles of the bull grew weaker; then they ceased and with a convulsive shudder the great form relaxed and lay inert.

The man leaped erect; he paid no attention to the girl; upon his face was the savage snarl of a wild beast. Naomi was terrified; she tried to crawl away and hide from him, but she was too weak. He placed a foot upon the carcass of the dead bull and threw back his head; then from his parted lips burst a cry that made her flesh creep. It was the victory cry of the bull ape, and as its echoes died away in the distance the man turned toward her.

All the savagery had vanished from his face; his gaze was intent and earnest. She looked for a maniacal light in his eyes, but they seemed sane and normal.

'Are your injured?' he asked.

'No.' she said and tried to rise, but she had not the strength.

He came and lifted her to her feet. He was so strong! A sense of security swept over her and unnerved her. She threw her arms about his neck and commenced to sob.

'Oh, Stanley! Stanley!' she gasped. She tried to say more, but her sobs choked her.

Obroski had told Tarzan a great deal about the members of the company. He knew the names of all of them, and had identified most of them from having seen them while he had watched the safari in the past. He knew of the budding affair between Obroski and Naomi Madison, and he guessed now from the girl's manner that she must be Naomi. It suited him that these people should think him Stanley Obroski, for the sometimes grim and terrible life that he led required the antidote of occasional humor.

He lifted her in his arms. 'Why are you so weak?' he asked. 'Is it from hunger?'

She sobbed a scarcely audible 'Yes,' and buried her face in the hollow of his neck. She was still half afraid of him. It was true that he did not act like a madman, but what else could account for the remarkable accession of courage and strength that had transformed him in the short time since she had last seen him.

She had known that he was muscular; but she had never attributed to him such superhuman strength as that which he had displayed during his duel with the gorilla, and she had known that he was a coward. But this man was no coward.

He carried her for a short distance, and then put her down on a bed of soft grasses. 'I will get you something to eat,' he said.

She saw him swing lightly into the trees and disappear, and again she was afraid. What a difference it made when he was near her! She puckered her brows to a sudden thought. Why did she feel so safe with Stanley Obroski now? She had never looked upon him as a protector or as able to protect. Everyone had considered him a coward. Whatever metamorphosis had occurred had been sufficiently deeprooted to carry its impression to her subconscious mind imparting this new feeling of confidence.

He was gone but a short time, returning with some nuts and fruit. He came and squatted beside her. 'Eat a little at a time,' he cautioned. 'After a while I will get flesh for you; that will bring back your strength.'

As she ate she studied him. 'You have changed, Stanley,' she said.

'Yes?'

'But I like you better. To think that you killed that terrible creature singlehanded! It was marvellous.'

'What sort of a beast was it?' he asked. 'It spoke English.'

'It is a mystery to me. It called itself an Englishman and said that it was the Duke of Buckingham. Another one pursued it whom it called Suffolk. A great number of them attacked us at the time that this one took me from the Arabs. They live in a city called London – he pointed it out to me. And Rhonda is a captive there in a castle on a ledge a little above the main part of the city – he said that she was with God in his castle.'

'I thought Rhonda had been killed by a lion,' said Tarzan.

'So did I until that creature told me differently. Oh, the poor dear! Perhaps it would have been better had the lion killed her. Think of being in the power of those frightful half-men!'

'Where is this city?' asked Tarzan.

'It is back there a way at the foot of the cliff – one can see it plainly from the summit.'

The man rose and lifted the girl into his arms again. 'Where are you going?' she asked.

'I am going to take you to Orman and West. They should be at the falls before night.'

'Oh! They are alive?'

'They were looking for you, and they got lost. They have been hungry, but otherwise they have gotten along all right. They will he glad to see you.'

'And then we can get out of this awful country?' she asked.

'First we must find out what became of the others and save Rhonda,' he replied.

'Oh, but she can't be saved!' exclaimed the girl. 'You should see how those devils fight – the Arabs, even with their guns, were helpless against them. There isn't a chance in the world of saving poor Rhonda, even if she is alive – which doubt.'

'We must try – and, anyway. I wish to see this gorilla city of London.'

'You mean you would go there!'

'How else can I see it?'

'Oh, Stanley, please don't go back there!'

'I came here for you.'

'Well, then, let Bill West go after Rhonda.'

'Do you think he could get her?'

'I don't think anyone can get her.'

'Perhaps not,' he said, 'but at least I shall see the city and possibly learn something about these gorillas that talk English. There is a mystery worth solving.'

They had reached the south end of the valley where the hills drop down almost to the level of the river. The current here, above the falls, was not swift; and Tarzan waded in with the girl still in his arms.

'Where are you going?' she cried, frightened.

'We have got to cross the river, and it is easier to cross here than below the falls. There the current is much swifter, and there are hippopotamuses and crocodiles. Take hold of my shoulders and hold tight.'

He plunged in and struck for the opposite shore, while the terrified girl clung to him in desperation. The farther bank looked far away indeed. Below she could hear the roar of the falls. They seemed to be drifting down toward them.

But presently the strong, even strokes of the swimmer reassured her. He seemed unhurried and unexcited, and gradually she relaxed as though she had absorbed a portion of his confidence. But she sighed in relief as he clambered out on solid ground.

Her terror at the river crossing was nothing to that which she experienced in the descent of the escarpment to the foot of the falls – it froze her to silent horror.

The man descended as nimbly as a monkey; the burden of her weight seemed nothing to him. Where had Stanley Obroski acquired the facility that almost put to shame the mountain goat and the monkey?

Halfway down he called her attention to three figures near the foot of the cliff. 'There are Orman and West and the Arab,' he said, but she did not dare look down.

The three men below them were watching in astonishment – they had just recognized that of the two descending toward them one was Obroski and the other a girl, but whether Naomi or Rhonda they could not be sure.

Orman and West ran forward to meet them as they neared the foot of the cliff. Tears came to Orman's eyes as he took Naomi in his arms; and West was glad to see her too, but he was saddened when he discovered that it was not Rhonda.

'Poor girl!' he muttered as they walked back to their little camp. 'Poor Rhonda! What an awful death!'

'But she is not dead,' said Naomi.

'Not dead! How do you know?'

'She is worse than dead, Bill,' and then Naomi told all she knew of Rhonda's fate.

When she was through, Tarzan rose. 'You have enough of that buck left to last until you can make a kill?' he asked.

'Yes,' replied Orman.

'Then I'll be going,' said the ape-man.

'Where?' asked the director.

'To find Rhonda.'

West leaped to his feet. 'I'll go with you, Stanley,' he cried.

'But, my God, man! you can't save her now. After what Eyad has told us of those beasts and Naomi's experience with them you must know that you haven't a chance.' Orman spoke with great seriousness.

'It is my duty to go anyway,' said West, 'not Stanley's; and I'm going.'

'You'd better stay here,' advised Tarzan. 'You wouldn't have a chance.'

'Why wouldn't I have as good a chance as you?' demanded West.

'Perhaps you would, but you would delay me.' Tarzan turned away and walked toward the foot of the escarpment.

Naomi Madison watched him through half closed eyes. 'Goodbye, Stanley!' she called.

'Oh, goodbye!' replied the ape-man and continued on.

They saw him seize a trailing liana and climb to another handhold; the quick equatorial night engulfed him before he reached the top.

West had stood silently watching him, stunned by his grief. 'I'm going with him,' he said finally and started for the escarpment.

'Why, you couldn't climb that place in the daytime, let alone after dark,' warned Orman.

'Don't be foolish, Bill,' counselled Naomi. 'We know how you feel, but there's no sense throwing away another life uselessly. Even Stanley'll never come back.' She commenced to sob.

'Then I won't either,' said West; 'but I'm goin.'

CHAPTER TWENTY-FOUR

God

Beyond the summit of the escarpment the ape-man moved silently through the night. He heard familiar noises, and his nostrils caught familiar scents that told him that the great cats roamed this strange valley of the gorillas.

He crossed the river farther up than he had swum it with Naomi, and he kept to the floor of the valley as he sought the mysterious city. He had no plan, for he knew nothing of what lay ahead of him – his planning must await the result of his reconnaissance.

He moved swiftly, often at a trot that covered much ground; and presently he saw dim lights ahead. That must be the city! He left the river and moved in a straight line toward the lights, cutting across a bend in the river which again swung back into his path just before he reached the shadowy mass of many buildings.

The city was walled, probably, he thought, against lions; but Tarzan was not greatly concerned – he had scaled walls before. When he reached this one he discovered that it was not high – perhaps ten feet – but sharpened stakes, pointing downward, had been set at close intervals just below the capstones, providing an adequate defense against the great cats.

The ape-man followed the wall back toward the cliff, where it joined the rocky, precipitous face of the escarpment. He listened, scenting the air with his delicate nostrils, seeking to assure himself that nothing was near on the opposite side of the wall.

Satisfied, he leaped for the stakes. His hands closed upon two of them; then he drew himself up slowly until his hips were on a level with his hands, his arms straight at his sides. Leaning forward, he let his body drop slowly forward until it rested on the stakes and the top of the wall.

Now he could look down into the narrow alleyway beyond the barrier. There was no sign of life as far as he could see in either direction – just a dark, shadowy, deserted alleyway. It required but a moment now to draw his body to the wall top and drop to the ground inside the city of the gorillas.

From the vantage point of the wall he had seen lights a short distance above the level of the main part of the city and what seemed to be the shadowy outlines of a large building. That, he conjectured, must be the castle of God, of which Naomi Madison had spoken.

If he were right, that would be his goal; for there the other girl was supposed to be imprisoned. He moved along the face of the cliff in a narrow, winding alley that followed generally the contour of the base of the mountain, though sometimes it wound around buildings that had been built against the cliff.

He hoped that he would meet none of the denizens of the city, for the passage was so narrow that he could not avoid detection; and it was so winding that an enemy might be upon him before he could find concealment in a shadowy doorway or upon a rooftop, which latter he had decided would make the safest hiding place and easy of access, since many of the buildings were low.

He heard voices and saw the dim glow of lights in another part of the city, and presently there rose above the strange city the booming of drums.

Shortly thereafter Tarzan came to a flight of steps cut from the living rock of the cliff. They led upward, disappearing in the gloom above; but they pointed in the general direction of the building he wished to reach. Pausing only long enough to reconnoiter with his ears, the ape-man started the ascent.

He had climbed but a short distance when he turned to see the city spread out below him. Not far from the foot of the cliff rose the towers and battlements of what appeared to he a medieval castle. From within its outer walls came the light that he had seen dimly from another part of the city; from here too came the sound of drumming. It was reminiscent of another day, another scene. In retrospection it all came vividly before him now.

He saw the shaggy figures of the great apes of the tribe of Kerchak. He saw an earthen drum. About it the apes were forming a great circle. The females and the young squatted in a thin line at its periphery, while just in front of them ranged the adult males. Before the drum sat three old females, each armed with a knotted branch fifteen or eighteen inches in length.

Slowly and softly they began tapping upon the resounding surface of the drum as the first, faint rays of the ascending moon silvered the encircling treetops. Then, as the light in the amphitheater increased, the females augmented the frequency and force of their blows until presently a wild, rhythmic din pervaded the great jungle for miles in every direction.

As the din of the drum rose to almost deafening volume Kerchak sprang into the open space between the squatting males and the drummers. Standing erect he threw his head far back and looking full into the eyes of the rising moon he beat upon his breast with his great hairy paws and emitted a fearful, roaring shriek.

Then, crouching, Kerchak slunk noiselessly around the open circle, veering away from a dead body that lay before the altar-drum; but, as he passed, keeping his fierce, wicked eyes upon the corpse.

Another male then sprang into the arena and, repeating the horrid cries of his king, followed stealthily in his wake. Another and another followed in quick succession until the jungle reverberated with the now almost ceaseless notes of their bloodthirsty screams. It was the challenge and the hunt.

How plainly it all came back to the ape-man now as he heard the familiar beating of the drums in this far-off city!

As he ascended the steps farther he could see over the top of the castle wall below into the courtyard beyond. He saw a number of gorillas dancing to the booming of the drums. The scene was lit by torches, and as he watched, a fire was lighted near the dancers. The dry material of which it was built ignited quickly and blazed high, revealing the scene in the courtyard like daylight and illuminating the face of the cliff and the stairway that Tarzan was ascending; then it died down as quickly as it had arisen.

The ape-man hastened up the stone stairway that wound and zigzagged up the cliff face, hoping that no eye had discerned him during the brief illumination of the cliff. There was no indication that he had been discovered as he approached the grim pile now towering close above him, because the strange figure gazing down upon him from the ramparts of the castle gave no sign that might apprise the ape-man of its presence. Chuckling, it turned away and disappeared through an embrasure in a turret.

At the top of the stairway Tarzan found himself upon a broad terrace, the forepart of the great ledge upon which the castle was built. Before him rose the grim edifice without wall or moat looming menacingly in the darkness.

The only opening on the level of the ledge was a large double doorway, one of the doors of which stood slightly ajar. Perhaps the Lord of the Jungle should have been warned by this easy accessibility. Perhaps it did arouse his suspicions – the natural suspicion of the wild thing for a trap – but he had come here for the purpose of entering this building; and he could not ignore such a God-given opportunity.

Cautiously he approached the doorway. Beyond was only darkness. He pushed against the great door, and it swung silently inward. He was glad that the hinges had not creaked. He paused a moment in the opening, listening. From within came the scent of gorillas and a strange man-like scent that intrigued and troubled him, but he neither heard nor saw signs of life beyond the doorway.

As his eyes became accustomed to the gloom of the interior he saw that he was in a semi-circular foyer in the posterior wall of which were set several doors. Approaching the door farthest to the left he tried it; but it was locked, nor could he open the second. The third, however, swung in as he pushed upon it, revealing a descending staircase.

He listened intently but heard nothing; then he tried the fourth door. It too was locked. So were the fifth and sixth. This was the last door and he returned to the third. Passing through it he descended the stairway, feeling his way through the darkness.

Still all was silence. Not a sound had come to his ears since he had entered the building to suggest that there was another within it than himself; yet he knew that there were living creatures there. His sensitive nostrils had told him that and the strange, uncanny instinct of the jungle beast.

At the foot of the stairs he groped with his hands, finding a door. He felt for and found a latch. Lifting it, he pushed upon the door; and it opened. There came strongly to his nostrils the scent of a woman – a white woman! Had he found her? Had he found the one he sought?

The room was utterly dark. He stepped into it, and as he released the door he heard it close behind him with a gentle click. With the quick intuition of the wild beast, he guessed that he was trapped. He sprang back to the door, seeking to open it; but his fingers found only a smooth surface.

He stood in silence, listening, waiting. He heard rapid breathing at a little distance from him. Insistent in his nostrils was the scent of the woman. He guessed that the breathing he heard was hers; its tempo connoted fear. Cautiously he approached the sound.

He was quite close when a noise ahead of him brought him to a sudden halt. It sounded like the creaking of rusty hinges. Then a light appeared revealing the whole scene.

Directly before him on a pallet of straw sat a white woman. Beyond her was a door constructed of iron bars through which he saw another chamber. At the far side of this second chamber was a doorway in which stood a strange creature holding a lighted torch in one hand. Tarzan could not tell if it were human or gorilla.

It approached the barred doorway, chuckling softly to itself. The woman had turned her face away from Tarzan and was looking at the thing in horror. Now she turned a quick glance toward the ape-man. He saw that she was quite like the girl, Naomi, and very beautiful.

As her eyes fell upon him, revealed by the flickering light of the torch, she gasped in astonishment. 'Stanley Obroski!' she ejaculated. 'Are you a prisoner, too?'

'I guess I am,' replied the ape-man.

'What were you doing here? How did they get you here? I thought you were dead.'

'I came here to find you,' he replied.

'You!' Her tone was incredulous.

The creature in the next room had approached the bars, and stood there chuckling softly. Tarzan looked up at it. It had the face of a man, but its skin was black like that of a gorilla. Its grinning lips revealed the heavy fangs of the anthropoid. Scant black hair covered those portions of its body that an open shirt and a loin cloth revealed. The skin of the body, arms, and legs was black with large patches of white. The bare feet were the feet of a man; the hands were black and hairy and wrinkled, with long, curved claws; the eyes were the sunken eyes of an old man – a very old man.

'So you are acquainted?' he said. 'How interesting! And you came to get her, did you? I thought that you had come to call on me. Of course it is not quite the proper thing for a stranger to come by night without an invitation – and by stealth.

'It was just by the merest chance that I learned of your coming. I have Henry to thank for that. Had he not been staging a dance I should not have known, and thus I should have been denied the pleasure of receiving you as I have.

'You see, I was looking down from my castle into the courtyard of Henry's palace when his bonfire flared up and lighted the Holy Stairs – and there you were!'

The creature's voice was well modulated, its diction that of a cultivated Englishman. The incongruity between its speech and its appearance rendered the latter all the more repulsive and appalling by contrast.

'Yes, I came for this girl,' said the ape-man.

'And now you are a prisoner too.' The creature chuckled.

'What do you want of us?' demanded Tarzan. 'We are not enemies; we have not harmed you.'

'What do I want of you! That is a long story. But perhaps you two would understand and appreciate it. The beasts with which I am surrounded hear, but they do not understand. Before you serve my final purpose I shall keep you for a while for the pleasure of conversing with rational human beings.

'I have not seen any for a long time, a long, long time. Of course I hate them nonetheless, but I must admit that I shall find pleasure in their companionship for a short time. You are both very good-looking too. That will make it all the more pleasant, just as it increases your value for the purpose for which I intend you – the final purpose, you understand. I am particularly pleased that the girl is so beautiful. I always did have a fondness for blonds. Were I not already engaged along other lines of research, and were it possible, I should like nothing better than to conduct a scientific investigation to determine the biological or psychological explanation of the profound attraction that the blond female has for the male of all races.'

From the pocket of his shirt he extracted a couple of crudely fashioned cheroots, one of which he proferred through the bars to Tarzan. 'Will you not smoke, Mr – ah – er – Obroski I believe the young lady called you. Stanley Obroski! That would be a Polish name, I believe; but you do not resemble a Pole. You look quite English – quite as English as I.'

'I do not smoke,' said Tarzan, and then added, 'thank you.'

'You do not know what you miss – tobacco is such a boon to tired nerves.'

'My nerves are never tired.'

'Fortunate man! And fortunate for me too, I could not ask for anything better than a combination of youth with a healthy body and a healthy nervous system – to say nothing of your unquestionable masculine beauty. I shall be wholly regenerated.'

'I do not know what you are talking about,' said Tarzan.

'No, of course not. How could one expect that you would understand what I alone in all the world know! But some other time I shall be delighted to explain. Right now I must go up and have a look down into the king's courtyard. I find that I must keep an eye on Henry the Eighth. He has been grossly misbehaving himself of late – he and Suffolk and Howard. I shall leave this torch burning for you – it will make it much more pleasant; and I want you to enjoy yourselves as much as possible before the – ah – er – well, *au revoir!* Make yourselves quite at home.' He turned and crossed toward a door at the opposite side of the room, chuckling as he went.

Tarzan stepped quickly to the bars separating the two rooms. 'Come back here!' he commanded. 'Either let us out of this hole or tell us why you are holding us – what you intend doing with us.'

The creature wheeled suddenly, its expression transformed by a hideous snarl. 'You dare issue orders to me!' it screamed.

'And why not?' demanded the ape-man. 'Who are you?'

The creature took a step nearer the bars and tapped its hairy chest with a horny talon. 'I am God!' it cried.

CHAPTER TWENTY-FIVE

'Before I Eat You!'

As the thing that called itself God departed from the other chamber, closing the door after it, Tarzan turned toward the girl sitting on the straw of their prison cell.

'I have seen many strange things in my life.' he said. 'but this is by far the strangest. Sometimes I think that I must be dreaming.'

'That is what I thought at first.' replied the girl; 'but this is no dream – it is a terrible, a frightful reality.'

'Including God?' he asked.

'Yes; even God is a reality. That thing is the god of these gorillas. They all fear him and most of them worship him. They say that he created them. I do not understand it – it is all like a hideous chimera.'

'What do you suppose he intends to do with us?'

'Oh, I don't know; but it is something horrible,' she replied. 'Down in the city they venture hideous guesses, but even they do not know. He brings young gorillas here, and they are never seen again.'

'How long have you been here?'

'I have been in God's castle since yesterday, but I was in the palace of Henry the Eighth for more than a week. Don't those names sound incongruous when applied to beasts?'

'I thought that nothing more could ever sound strange to me after I met *Buckingham* this morning and heard him speak English – a bull gorilla!'

'You met Buckingham? It was he who captured me and brought me to this city. Did he capture you too?'

Tarzan shook his head. 'No. He had captured Naomi Madison.'

'Naomi! What became of her?'

'She is with Orman and West and one of the Arabs at the foot of the falls. I came here to find you and take you to them; but it is commencing to look as though I had made a mess of it – getting captured myself.'

'But how did Naomi get away from Buckingham?' demanded the girl.

'I killed him.'

'*You* killed *Buckingham!*' She looked at him with wide, unbelieving eyes.

From the reactions of the others toward his various exploits Tarzan had already come to understand that Obroski's friends had not held his courage in very high esteem, and so it amused him all the more that they should mistake him for this unquestioned coward.

The girl surveyed him in silence through level eyes for several moments as though she were trying to read his soul and learn the measure of his imposture; then she shook her head.

'You're not a bad kid, Stanley,' she said; 'but you mustn't tell naughty stories to your Aunt Rhonda.'

One of the ape-man's rare smiles bared his strong, white teeth. 'No one can fool you, can they?' he asked admiringly.

'Well, I'll admit that they'd have to get up pretty early in the morning to put anything over on Rhonda Terry. But what I can't understand is that make-up of yours – the scenery – where did you get it and why? I should think you'd freeze.'

'You will have to ask Rungula, chief of the Bansutos,' replied Tarzan.

'What has he to do with it?'

'He appropriated the Obroski wardrobe.'

'I commence to see the light. But if you were captured by the Bansutos, how did you escape?'

'If I told you you would not believe me. You do not believe that I killed Buckingham.'

'How could I, unless you sneaked up on him while he was asleep? It just isn't in the cards, Stanley, for any man to have killed that big gorilla unless he had a rifle – that's it! You shot him.'

'And then threw my rifle away?' inquired the ape-man.

'M-m-m, that doesn't sound reasonable, does it? No, I guess you're just a plain damn liar, Stanley.'

'Thank you.'

'Don't get sore. I really like you and always have; but I have seen too much of life to believe in miracles, and the idea of you killing Buckingham single-handed would be nothing short of a miracle.'

Tarzan turned away and commenced to examine the room in which they were confined. The flickering light of the torch in the adjoining room lighted it dimly. He found a square chamber, the walls of which were faced with roughly hewn stone. The ceiling was of planking supported by huge beams. The far end of the room was so dark that he could not see the ceiling at that point; the last beam cast a heavy shadow there upon the ceiling. He thought he detected a steady current of air moving from the barred doorway of the other room to this far corner of their cell, suggesting an opening there; but he could find none, and abandoned the idea.

Having finished his inspection he came and sat down on the straw beside Rhonda. 'You say you have been here a week?' he inquired.

'In the city – not right here,' she replied. 'Why?'

'I was thinking – they must feed you, then?' he inquired.

'Yes; celery, bamboo tips, fruit, and nuts – it gets monotonous.'

'I was not thinking of *what* they fed you but of how. How is your food brought to you and when? I mean since you have been in this room.'

'When they brought me here yesterday they gave me enough food for the day; this morning they brought me another day's supply. They bring it into that next room and shove it through the bars – no dishes or anything like that – they just shove it through onto the floor with their dirty, bare hands, or paws. All except the water – they bring water in that gourd there in the corner.'

'They don't open the door, then, and come into the room?'

'No.'

'That is too bad.'

'Why?'

'If they opened the door we might have a chance to escape,' explained the ape-man.

'Not a chance – the food is brought by a big bull gorilla. Oh, I forgot!' she exclaimed, laughing. 'You'd probably break him in two and throw him in the waste basket like you did Buckingham.'

Tarzan laughed with her. 'I keep forgetting that I am a coward,' he said. 'You must be sure to remind me if any danger threatens us.'

'I guess you won't have to be reminded, Stanley.' She was looking at him again closely. 'But you have changed in some way,' she ventured finally. 'I don't know just how to explain it, but you seem to have more assurance. And you sure put up a good front when you were talking to God. Say! Do you suppose what you've been through the past few weeks has affected your mind?'

Further conversation was interrupted by the return of God. He pulled a chair up in front of the barred door and sat down.

'Henry is a fool,' he announced. 'He's trying to work his followers up to a pitch that will make it possible for him to induce them to attack heaven and kill God. Henry wants to be God. I made him a king, and now he wants to be God. But he gave them too much to drink; and now most of them are asleep in the palace courtyard, including Henry. They won't bother me tonight; so I thought I'd come down and have a pleasant visit with you. There won't be many more opportunities, for you will have to serve your purpose before something happens to prevent. I can't take any chances.'

'What is this strange purpose we are to serve?' asked Rhonda.

'It is purely scientific; but it is a long story and I shall have to start at the beginning,' explained God.

'The beginning!' he repeated dreamily. 'How long ago it was! It was while I was still an undergraduate at Oxford that I first had a glimmering of the light that finally dawned. Let me see – that must have been about 1855. No, it was before that – I graduated in '55. That's right, I was born in '33 and I was twenty-two when I graduated.

'I had always been intrigued by Lamarck's investigations and later by Darwin's. They were on the right track, but they did not go far enough; then, shortly after my graduation, I was travelling in Austria when I met a priest at Brunn who was working along lines similar to mine. His name was Mendel. We exchanged ideas. He was the only man in the world who could appreciate me, but he could not go all the way with me. I got some help from him; but, doubtless, he got more from me; though I never heard anything more about him before I left England.

'In 1857 I felt that I had practically solved the mystery of heredity, and in that year I published a monograph on the subject. I will explain the essence of my discoveries in as simple language as possible, so that you may understand the purpose you are to serve.

'Briefly, there are two types of cells that we inherit from our parents – body cells and germ cells. These cells are composed of chromosomes containing genes – a separate gene for each mental and physical characteristic. The body cells, dividing, multiplying, changing, growing, determine the sort of individual we are to be; the germ cells, remaining practically unchanged from our conception, determine what characteristics our progeny will inherit, through us, from our progenitors and from us.

'I determined that heredity could be controlled through the transference of these genes from one individual to another. I learned that the genes never die; they are absolutely indestructible – the basis of all life on earth, the promise of immortality throughout all eternity.

'I was certain of all this, but I could carry on no experiments. Scientists scoffed at me, the public laughed at me, the authorities threatened to lock me up in a madhouse. The church wished to crucify me.

'I hid, and carried on my research in secret. I obtained genes from living subjects – young men and women whom I enticed to my laboratory on various pretexts. I drugged them and extracted germ cells from them. I had not discovered at that time, or, I should say, I had not perfected the technic of recovering body cells.

'In 1858 I managed, through bribery, to gain access to a number of tombs in Westminster Abbey; and from the corpses of former kings and queens of England and many a noble lord and lady I extracted the deathless genes.

'It was the rape of Henry the Eighth that caused my undoing. I was discovered in the act by one who had not been bribed. He did not turn me over to the authorities, but he commenced to blackmail me. Because of him I faced either financial ruin or a long term in prison.

'My fellow scientists had flouted me; the government would punish me; I saw that my only rewards for my labors for mankind were to be ingratitude and persecution. I grew to hate man, with his bigotry, his hypocrisy, and his ignorance. I still hate him.

'I fled England. My plans were already made. I came to Africa and employed a white guide to lead me to gorilla country. He brought me here; then I killed him, so that no one might learn of my whereabouts.

'There were hundreds of gorillas here, yes, thousands. I poisoned their food, I shot them with poisoned arrows; but I used a poison that only anesthetized them. Then I removed their germ cells and substituted human cells that I had brought with me from England in a culture medium that encouraged their multiplication.'

The strange creature seemed warmed by some mysterious inner fire as he discoursed on this, his favorite subject. The man and the girl listening to him almost forgot the incongruity of his cultured English diction and his hideous, repulsive appearance – far more hideous and repulsive than that of the gorillas; for he seemed neither beast nor man but rather some horrid hybrid born of an unholy union. Yet the mind within that repellant skull held them fascinated.

'For years I watched them,' he continued, 'with increasing disappointment. From generation to generation I could note no outward indication that the human germ cells had exerted the slightest influence upon the anthropoids; then I commenced to note indications of greater intelligence among them. Also, they quarrelled more, were more avaricious, more vindictive – they were revealing more and more the traits of man. I felt that I was approaching my goal.

'I captured some of the young and started to train them. Very shortly after this training commenced I heard them repeating English words among themselves – words that they had heard me speak. Of course they did not know the meaning of the words; but that was immaterial – they had revealed the truth to me. My gorillas had inherited the minds and vocal organs of their synthetic human progenitors.

'The exact reason why they inherited these human attributes and not others is still a mystery that I have not solved. But I had proved the correctness of my theory. Now I set to work to educate my wards. It was not difficult. I sent these first out as missionaries and teachers.

'As the gorillas learned and came to me for further instruction, I taught them agriculture, architecture, and building – among other things. Under my direction they built this city, which I named London, upon the river that I have called Thames. We English always take England wherever we go.

'I gave them laws, I became their god, I gave them a royal family and a nobility. They owe everything to me, and now some of them want to turn upon me and destroy me – yes, they have become very human. They have become ambitious, treacherous, cruel – they are almost men.'

'But you?' asked the girl. 'You are not human. You are part gorilla. How could you have been an Englishman?'

'I am an Englishman, nevertheless,' replied the creature. 'Once I was a very handsome Englishman. But old age overtook me. I felt my powers failing. I saw the grave beckoning. I did not wish to die, for I felt that I had only commenced to learn the secrets of life.

'I sought some means to prolong my own and to bring back youth. At last I was successful. I discovered how to segregate body cells and transfer them from one individual to another. I used young gorillas of both sexes and transplanted their virile, youthful body cells to my own body.

'I achieved success in so far as staying the ravages of old age is concerned and renewing youth, but as the body cells of the gorillas multiplied within me I began to acquire the physical characteristics of gorillas. My skin turned black, hair grew upon all parts of my body, my hands changed, my teeth; some day I shall be, to all intents and purpose, a gorilla. Or rather I should have been had it not been for the fortunate circumstance that brought you to me.'

'I do not understand,' said Rhonda.

'You will. With the body cells from you and this young man I shall not only insure my youth, but I shall again take on the semblance of man.' His eyes burned with a mad fire.

The girl shuddered. 'It is horrible!' she exclaimed.

The creature chuckled. 'You will be serving a noble purpose – a far more noble purpose than as though you had merely fulfilled the prosaic biological destiny for which you were born.'

'But you will not have to kill us!' she exclaimed. 'You take the germ cells from gorillas without killing them. When you have taken some from us, you will let us go?'

The creature rose and came close to the bars. His yellow fangs were bared in a fiendish grin. 'You do not know all,' he said. A mad light shone in his blazing eyes. 'I have not told you all that I have learned about rejuvenation. The new body cells are potent, but they work slowly. I have found that by eating the flesh and the glands of youth the speed of the metamorphosis is accelerated.

'I leave you now to meditate upon the great service that you are to render science!' He backed toward the far door of the other apartment. 'But I will return. Later I shall eat you – eat you both. I shall eat the man first; and then, my beauty, I shall eat you! But before I eat you – ah, before I eat you!'

Chuckling, he backed through the doorway and closed the door after him.

CHAPTER TWENTY-SIX
Trapped

'It looks like curtain,' said the girl.

'Curtain?'

'The end of the show.'

Tarzan smiled. 'I suppose you mean that there is no hope for us – that we are doomed.'

'It looks like it, and I am afraid. Aren't you afraid?'

'I presume that I am supposed to be, eh?'

She surveyed him from beneath puckered brows. 'I cannot understand you, Stanley,' she said. 'You do not seem to be afraid now, but you used to be afraid of everything. Aren't you really afraid, or are you just posing – the actor, you know?'

'Perhaps I feel that what is about to happen is about to happen and that being afraid won't help any. Fear will never get us out of here alive, and I certainly don't intend to stay here and die if I can help it.'

'I don't see how we are going to get out,' said Rhonda.

'We are nine tenths out now.'

'What do you mean?'

'We are still alive,' he laughed, 'and that is fully nine tenths of safety. If we were dead we would be a hundred per cent, lost; so alive we should certainly be at least ninety per cent, saved.'

Rhonda laughed. 'I didn't know you were such an optimist,' she declared.

'Perhaps I have something to be optimistic about,' he replied. 'Do you feel that draught on the floor?'

She looked up at him quickly. There was a troubled expression in her eyes as she scrutinized his. 'Perhaps you had better lie down and try to sleep,' she suggested. 'You are overwrought.'

It was his turn to eye her. 'What do you mean?' he asked. 'Do I seem exhausted?'

'No, but – but I just thought the strain might have been too great on you.'

'What strain?' he inquired.

'What strain!' she exclaimed. 'Stanley Obroski, you come and lie down here and let me rub your head – perhaps it will put you to sleep.'

'I'm not sleepy. Don't you want to get out of here?'

'Of course I do, but we can't.'

'Perhaps not, but we can try. I asked you if you felt the draught on the floor.'

'Of course I feel it, but what has that to do with anything. I'm not cold.'

'It may not have anything to do with anything,' Tarzan admitted, 'but it suggests possibilities.'

'What possibilities?' she demanded.

'A way out. The fresh air comes in from that other room through the bars of that door; it has to go out somewhere. The draught is so strong that it suggests a rather large opening. Do you see any large opening in this room through which the air could escape.'

The girl rose to her feet. She was commencing to understand the drift of his remarks. 'No,' she said, 'I see no opening.'

'Neither do I; but there must be one, and we know that it must be some place that we cannot see.' He spoke in a whisper.

'Yes, that is right.'

'And the only part of this room that we can't see plainly is among the dark shadows on the ceiling over in that far corner. Also, I have felt the air current moving in that direction.'

He walked over to the part of the room he had indicated and looked up into the darkness. The girl came and stood beside him, also peering upward.

'Do you see anything?' she asked, her voice barely audible.

'It is very dark,' he replied, 'but I think that I do see something – a little patch that appears darker than the rest, as though it had depth.'

'Your eyes are better than mine.' she said. 'I see nothing.'

From somewhere apparently directly above them, but at a distance, sounded a hollow chuckle, weird, uncanny.

Rhonda laid her hand impulsively on Tarzan's arm. 'You are right,' she whispered. 'There is an opening above us – that sound came down through it.'

'We must be very careful what we say above a whisper,' he cautioned.

The opening in the ceiling, if such it were, appeared to be directly in the corner of the room. Tarzan examined the walls carefully, feeling every square foot of them as high as he could reach; but he found nothing that would give him a handhold. Then he sprang upward with outstretched hand – and felt an edge of an opening in the ceiling.

'It is there,' he whispered.

'But what good will it do us? We can't reach it.'

'We can try,' he said; then he stooped down close to the wall in the corner of the room. 'Get on my shoulders,' he directed – 'stand on them. Support yourself with your hands against the wall.'

Rhonda climbed to his broad shoulders. Grasping her legs to steady her, he rose slowly until he stood erect.

'Feel carefully in all directions.' he whispered. 'Estimate the size of the opening; search for a handhold.'

For some time the girl was silent. He could tell by the shifting of her weight from one foot to the other and by the stretching of her leg muscles that she was examining the opening in every direction as far as she could reach.

Presently she spoke to him. 'Let me down,' she said.

He lowered her to the floor. 'What did you discover?' he asked.

'The opening is about two feet by three. It seems to extend inward over the top of the wall at one side – I could distinctly feel a ledge there. If I could get on it I could explore higher.'

'We'll try again,' said Tarzan. 'Put your hands on my shoulders.' They stood facing one another. 'Now place your left foot in my right hand. That's it! Straighten up and put your other foot in my left hand. Now keep your legs and body rigid, steady yourself with your hands against the wall; and I'll lift you up again – probably a foot and a half higher than you were before.'

'All right,' she whispered. 'Lift!'

He raised her easily but slowly to the full extent of his arms. For a moment he held her thus; then, first from one hand and then from the other, her weight was lifted from him.

He waited, listening. A long minute of silence ensued; then, from above him, came a surprised 'Ouch!'

Tarzan made no sound, he asked no question – he waited. He could hear her breathing, and knew that nothing very serious had surprised that exclamation from her. Presently he caught a low whisper from above.

'Toss me your rope!'

He lifted the grass rope from where it lay coiled across one shoulder and threw a loop upward into the darkness toward the girl above. The first time, she missed it and it fell back; but the next, she caught it. He heard her working with it in the darkness above.

'Try it,' she whispered presently.

He seized the rope above his head and raised his feet from the ground so that it supported all his weight. It held without slipping; then, hand over hand, he climbed. He felt the girl reach out and touch his body; then she guided one of his feet to the ledge where she stood – a moment later he was standing by her side.

'What have you found?' he asked, straining his eyes through the darkness.

'I found a wooden beam,' she replied. 'I bumped my head on it.'

He understood now the origin of the exclamation he had heard, and reaching out felt a heavy beam opposite his shoulders. The rope was fastened around it. The ledge they were standing on was evidently the top of the wall of the room below. The shaft that ran upward was, as the girl had said, about two feet by three. The beam bisected its longer axis, leaving a space on each side large enough to permit a man's body to pass.

Tarzan wedged himself through, and clambered to the top of the beam.

Above him, the shaft rose as far as he could reach without handhold or foothold.

He leaned down toward the girl. 'Give me your hand,' he said, and lifted her to the beam. 'We've got to do a little more exploring,' he whispered. 'I'll lift you as I did before.'

'I hope you can keep your balance on this beam,' she said, but she did not hesitate to step into his cupped hands.

'I hope so,' he replied laconically.

For a moment she groped about above her; then she whispered, 'Let me down.'

He lowered her to his side, holding her so that she would not lose her balance and fall.

'Well?' he asked.

'I found another beam,' she said, 'but the top of it is just out of my reach. I could feel the bottom and a part of each side, but I was just a few inches too short to reach the top. What are we to do? It is just like a nightmare – straining here in the darkness, with some horrible menace lurking ready to seize one, and not being quite able to reach the sole means of safety.'

Tarzan stooped and untied the rope that was still fastened around the beam upon which they stood.

'The tarmangani have a number of foolish sayings.' he remarked. 'One of them is that there are more ways than one of skinning a cat.'

'Who are the tarmangani?' she asked.

Tarzan grinned in the safety of the concealing darkness. For a moment he had forgotten that he was playing a part. 'Oh, just a silly tribe,' he replied.

'That is an old saying in America. I have heard my grandfather use it. It is strange that an African tribe should have an identical proverb.'

He did not tell her that in his mother tongue, the first language of the great apes, tarmangani meant any or all white men.

He coiled the rope; and, holding one end, tossed the coils into the darkness of the shaft above him. They fell back on top of them. Again he coiled and threw – again with the same result. Twice more he failed, and then the end of the rope that he held in his hand remained stretching up into the darkness while the opposite end dropped to swing against them. With the free end that he had thrown over the beam he bent a noose around the length that depended from the opposite side of the beam, making it fast with a bowline knot; then he pulled the noose up tight against the beam above.

'Do you think you can climb it?' he asked the girl.

'I don't know,' she said, 'but I can try.'

'You might fall,' he warned. 'I'll carry you.' He swung her lightly to his back before she realized what he purposed. 'Hold tight!' he admonished; then he swarmed up the rope like a monkey.

At the top he seized the beam and drew himself and the girl onto it; and here they repeated what they had done before, searching for and finding another beam above the one upon which they stood.

As the ape-man drew himself to the third beam he saw an opening directly before his face, and through the opening a star. Now the darkness was relieved. The faint light of a partially cloudy night revealed a little section of flat roof bounded by a parapet, and when Tarzan reconnoitered further he discovered that they had ascended into one of the small towers that surmounted the castle.

As he was about to step from the tower onto the roof he heard the uncanny chuckle with which they were now so familiar, and drew back into the darkness of the interior. Silent and motionless the two stood there waiting, listening.

The chuckling was repeated, this time nearer; and to the keen ears of Tarzan came the sound of naked feet approaching. His ears told him more than this; they told him that the thing that walked did not walk alone – there was another with it.

Presently they came in sight, walking slowly. One of them, as the ape-man had guessed, was the creature that called itself God; the other was a large bull gorilla.

As they came opposite the two fugitives they stopped and leaned upon the parapet, looking down into the city.

'Henry should not have caroused tonight, Cranmer,' remarked the creature called God. 'He has a hard day before him tomorrow.'

'How is that, My Lord God?' inquired the other.

'Have you forgotten that this is the anniversary of the completion of the Holy Stairway to Heaven?'

''Sblood! So it is, and Henry has to walk up it on his hands to worship at the feet of his God.'

'And Henry is getting old and much too fat. The sun will be hot too. But – it humbleth the pride of kings and teacheth humility to the common people.'

'Let none forget that thou art the Lord our God, O Father!' said Cranmer piously.

'And what a surprise I'll have for Henry when he reaches the top of the stairs! There I'll stand with this English girl I stole from him kneeling at my feet. You sent for her, didn't you, Cranmer?'

'Yes, My Lord, I sent one of the lesser priests to fetch her. They should be here any minute now. But, My Lord, do you think that it will be wise to anger Henry further? You know that many of the nobles are on his side and are plotting against you.'

A horrid chuckle broke from the lips of the gorilla-man. 'You forget that I am God,' he said. 'You must never forget that fact, Cranmer. Henry is forgetting it, and his poor memory will prove his undoing.' The creature straightened up to its full height. An ugly growl supplanted the chuckle of a moment before. 'You all forget,' he cried, 'that it was I who created you; it is I who can destroy you! First I shall make Henry mad, and then I shall crush him. That is the kind of god that humans like – it is the only kind they can understand. Because they are jealous and cruel and vindictive they have to have a jealous, cruel, vindictive god. I was able to give you only the minds of humans; so I have to be a god that such minds can appreciate. Tomorrow Henry shall appreciate me to the full!'

'What do you mean, My Lord?'

The gorilla god chuckled again. 'When he reaches the top of the stairs I am going to blast him; I am going to destroy him.'

'You are going to kill the king! But, My Lord, the Prince of Wales is too young to be king.'

'He will not be king – I am tired of kings. We shall pass over Edward VI and Mary. That is one of the advantages of having God on your side, Cranmer – we shall skip eleven years and save you from burning at the stake. The next sovereign of England will be Queen Elizabeth.'

'Henry has many daughters from which to choose, My Lord,' said Cranmer.

'I shall choose none of them. I have just had an inspiration, Cranmer.'

'From whence, My Lord God?'

'From myself, of course, you fool! It is perfect. It is ideal.' He chuckled appreciatively. 'I am going to make this English girl queen of England – Queen Elizabeth! She will be tractable – she will do as I tell her; and she will serve all my other purposes as well. Or almost all. Of course I cannot eat her, Cranmer. One cannot eat his queen and have her too.'

'Here comes the under priest, My Lord,' interrupted Cranmer.

'He is alone,' exclaimed God. 'He has not brought the girl.'

An old gorilla lumbered up to the two. He appeared excited.

'Where is the girl?' demanded God.

'She was not there, My Lord. She is gone, and the man too.'

'Gone! But that is impossible.'

'The room is empty.'

'And the doors! Had they been unlocked – either of them?'

'No, My Lord; they were both locked,' replied the under priest.

The gorilla god went suddenly silent. For a few moments he remained in thought; then he spoke in very low tones to his two companions.

Tarzan and the girl watched them from their place of concealment in the tower. The ape-man was restless. He wished that they would go away so that he could search for some avenue of escape from the castle. Alone, he might have faced them and relied on his strength and agility to win his freedom;

but he could not hope to make good the escape of the girl and himself both in the face of their ignorance of a way out of the castle and the numbers which he was sure the gorilla god could call to his assistance in case of need.

He saw the priest turn and hurry away. The other two walked a short distance from the tower, turned so that they faced it, leaned against the parapet, and continued their conversation; though now Tarzan could no longer overhear their exact words. The position of the two was such that the fugitives could not have left the tower without being seen by them.

The ape-man became apprehensive. The abnormal sensibility of the hunted beast warned him of impending danger; but he did not know where to look for it, nor in what form to expect it.

Presently he saw a bull gorilla roll within the range of his vision. The beast carried a pike. Behind him came another similarly armed, and another and another and another until twenty of the great anthropoids were gathered on the castle roof.

They clustered about Cranmer and the gorilla god for a minute or two. The latter was talking to them. Tarzan could recognize the tones if not the words. Then the twenty approached the tower and grouped themselves in a semi-circle before the low aperture leading into it.

Both Rhonda Terry and the Lord of the Jungle were assured that their hiding place was guessed if not known, yet they could not be certain. They would wait. That was all they could do. However, it was an easy place to defend; and they might remain there awaiting some happy circumstance that would give them a better chance of escape than was presented to them at the moment.

The gorillas on the roof seemed only to be waiting. They did not appear to be contemplating an investigation of the interior of the tower. Perhaps, thought Tarzan, they were there for some other purpose than that which he had imagined. They might have been gathered in preparation for the coming of the king to his death in the morning.

By the parapet stood the gorilla god with the bull called Cranmer. The weird chuckle of the former was the only sound that broke the silence of the night. The ape-man wondered why the thing was chuckling.

A sudden upward draught from the shaft below them brought a puff of acrid smoke and a wave of heat. Tarzan felt the girl clutch his arm. Now he knew why the gorillas waited so patiently before the entrance to the tower. Now he knew why the gorilla god chuckled.

CHAPTER TWENTY-SEVEN
Holocaust

Tarzan considered the problem that confronted him. It was evident that they could not long endure the stifling, blinding smoke. To make a sudden attack upon the gorillas would be but to jeopardize the life of his companion without offering her any hope of escape. Had he been alone it would have been different, but now there seemed no alternative to coming quietly out and giving themselves up.

On the other hand he knew that the gorilla god purposed death for him and either death or a worse fate for the girl. Whatever course he pursued, then, would evidently prove disastrous. The ape-man, seldom hesitant in reaching a decision, was frankly in a quandary.

Briefly he explained his doubts to Rhonda. 'I think I'll rush them,' he concluded. 'At least there will be some satisfaction in that.'

'They'd only kill you, Stanley,' she said. 'Oh, I wish you hadn't come. It was brave, but you have just thrown away your life. I can never—' The stifling smoke terminated her words in a fit of coughing.

'We can't stand this any longer,' he muttered. 'I'm going out. Follow me, and watch for a chance to escape.'

Stooping low, the ape-man sprang from the tower. A savage growl rumbled from his deep chest. The girl, following directly behind him, heard and was horrified. She thought only of the man with her as Stanley Obroski, the coward; and she believed that his mind must have been deranged by the hopelessness of his situation.

The gorillas leaped forward to seize him. 'Capture him!' cried the gorilla god. 'But do not kill him.'

Tarzan leaped at the nearest beast. His knife flashed in the light of the torches that some of the creatures carried. It sank deep into the chest of the victim that chance had placed in the path of the Lord of the Jungle. The brute screamed, clutched at the ape-man only to collapse at his feet.

But others closed upon the bronzed giant; then another and another tasted the steel of that swift blade. The gorilla god was beside himself with rage and excitement. 'Seize him! Seize him!' he screamed. 'Do not kill him! He is mine!'

During the excitement Rhonda sought an avenue of escape. She slunk behind the battling beasts to search for a stairway leading from the roof. Every eye, every thought was on the battle being waged before the tower. No one noticed the girl. She came to a doorway in another tower. Before her she saw the top of a flight of stairs. They were illuminated by the flickering light of torches.

At a run she started down. Below her, smoke was billowing, shutting off her view. It was evident, she guessed, that the smoke from the fire that had been lighted to dislodge Obroski and herself from the tower had drifted to other parts of the castle.

At a turn in the stairs she ran directly into the arms of a gorilla leaping upward. Behind him were two others. The first seized her and whirled her back to the others. 'She must be trying to escape,' said her captor. 'Bring her along to God;' then he leaped swiftly on up the stairs.

Three gorillas had fallen before Tarzan's knife, but the fourth seized his wrist and struck at him with the haft of his pike. The ape-man closed; his teeth sought the jugular of his antagonist and fastened there. The brute screamed and sought to tear himself free; then one of his companions stepped in and struck Tarzan heavily across one temple with the butt of a battle axe.

The Lord of the Jungle sank senseless to the roof amid the victorious shouts of his foemen. The gorilla god pushed forward.

'Do not kill him!' he screamed again.

'He is already dead, My Lord,' said one of the gorillas.

The god trembled with disappointment and rage, and was about to speak when the gorilla that had recaptured Rhonda forced its way through the crowd.

'The castle is afire, My Lord!' he cried. 'The smudge that was built to smoke out the prisoners spread to the dry grass on the floor of their cell, and now the beams and floor above are all ablaze – the first floor of the castle is a roaring furnace. If you are not to be trapped, My Lord, you must escape at once.'

Those who heard him looked quickly about. A dense volume of smoke was pouring from the tower from which Tarzan and Rhonda had come; smoke was coming from other towers nearby; it was rising from beyond the parapet, evidently coming from the windows of the lower floors.

There was instant uneasiness. The gorillas rushed uncertainly this way and that. All beasts are terrified by fire, and the instincts of beasts dominated these aberrant creatures. Presently, realizing that they might be cut off from all escape, panic seized them.

Screaming and roaring, they bolted for safety, deserting their prisoners and their god. Some rushed headlong down blazing stairways to death, others leaped the parapet to an end less horrible, perhaps, but equally certain.

Their piercing shrieks, their terrified roars rose above the crackling and the roaring of the flames, above the screamed commands of their gorilla god, who, seeing himself deserted by his creatures, completely lost his head and joined in the mad rush for safety.

Fortunately for Rhonda, the two who had her in their charge ignored the instructions of their fellow to bring her before their god; but, instead, turned and fled down the stairway before retreat was cut off by the hungry flames licking their upward way from the pits beneath the castle.

Fighting their way through blinding smoke, their shaggy coats at one time seared by a sudden burst of flame, the maddened brutes forgot their prisoner, forgot everything but their fear of the roaring flames. Even when they won to the comparative safety of a courtyard they did not stop, but ran on until they had swung open an outer gate and rushed headlong from the vicinity of the castle.

Rhonda, almost equally terrified but retaining control of her wits, took advantage of this opportunity to escape. Following the two gorillas, she came out upon the great ledge upon which the castle stood. The rising flames now illuminated the scene, and she saw behind her a towering cliff, seemingly unscalable. Below her lay the city, dark but for a few flickering torches that spotted the blackness of the night with their feeble rays.

To her right she saw the stairway leading from the castle ledge to the city below – the only avenue of escape that she could discern. If she could reach the city, with its winding, narrow alleyways, she might make her way unseen across the wall and out into the valley beyond.

The river would lead her down the valley to the brink of the escarpment at the foot of which she knew that Orman and West and Naomi were camped. She shuddered at the thought of descending that sheer cliff, but she knew that she would risk much more than this to escape the horrors of the valley of diamonds.

Running quickly along the ledge to the head of the stairway, she started downward toward the dark city. She ran swiftly, risking a fall in her anxiety to escape. Behind her rose the roaring and the crackling of the flames gutting the castle of God, rose the light of the fire casting her dancing shadow grotesquely before her, illuminating the stairway; and then, to her horror, a horde of gorillas rushing up to the doomed building.

She stopped, but she could not go back. There was no escape to the right nor to the left. Her only chance lay in the possibility that they might ignore her in their excitement. Then the leader saw her.

'The girl!' they cried. 'The hairless one! Catch her! Take her to the king!'

Hairy hands seized her. They passed her back to those behind. 'Take her to the king!' And again she was hustled and pushed on to others behind. 'Take her to the king! Take her to the king!' And so, pulled and hauled and dragged, she was borne down to the city and to the palace of the king.

Once again she found herself with the shes of Henry's harem. They cuffed her and growled at her, for most of them did not wish her back. Catherine of Aragon was the most vindictive. She would have torn the girl to pieces had not Catherine Parr intervened.

'Leave her alone,' she warned; 'or Henry will have us all beaten, and some of us will lose our heads. All he needs is an excuse to get yours, Catherine,' she told the old queen.

At last they ceased abusing her; and, crouching in a corner, she had an opportunity to think for the first time since she had followed Tarzan from the tower. She thought of the man who had risked his life to save hers. It seemed incredible that all of them had so misunderstood Stanley Obroski. Strength and courage seemed so much a part of him now that it was unbelievable that not one of them had ever discerned it. She saw him now through new eyes with a vision that revealed qualities such as women most admire in men and invoked a tenderness that brought a sob to her throat.

Where was he now? Had he escaped? Had they recaptured him? Was he a victim of the flames that she could see billowing from the windows of the great castle on the ledge? Had he died for her?

Suddenly she sat up very straight, her fists clenched until her nails bit into her flesh. A new truth had dawned upon her. This man whom yesterday she had considered with nothing but contempt had aroused within her bosom an emotion that she had never felt for any other man. Was it love? Did she love Stanley Obroski?

She shook her head as though to rid herself of an obsession. No, it could not be that. It must be gratitude and sorrow that she felt – nothing more. Yet the thought persisted. The memory of no other man impinged upon her thoughts in this moment of her extremity before, exhausted by fatigue and excitement, she finally sank into restless slumber.

And while she slept the castle on the ledge burned itself out, the magnificent funeral pyre of those who had been trapped within it.

CHAPTER TWENTY-EIGHT

Through Smoke and Flame

As the terrified horde fought for safety and leaped to death from the roof of the castle of God, the gorilla god himself scurried for a secret stairway that led to the courtyard of the castle.

Cranmer and some of the priests knew also of this stairway; and they, too, bolted for it. Several members of the gorilla guard, maddened by terror, followed them; and when they saw the entrance to the stairway fought to be the first to avail themselves of its offer of safety.

Through this fighting, screaming pack the gorilla god sought to force his way. He was weaker than his creatures, and they elbowed him aside.

Screaming commands and curses which all ignored, he pawed and clawed in vain endeavor to reach the entrance to the stairs; but always they beat him back.

Suddenly terror and rage drove him mad. Foaming at the mouth, gibbering like a maniac, he threw himself upon the back of a great bull whose bulk barred his way. He beat the creature about the head and shoulders, but the terrified brute paid no attention to him until he sank his fangs deep in its neck; then with a frightful scream it turned upon him. With its mighty paws it tore him from his hold; then, lifting him above its head, the creature hurled him from it. The gorilla god fell heavily to the roof and lay still, stunned.

The crazed beasts at the stairway fought and tore at one another, jamming and wedging themselves into the entrance until they clogged it; then those that remained outside ran toward other stairways, but now it was too late. Smoke and flame roared from every turret and tower. They were trapped!

By ones and twos, with awful shrieks, they hurled themselves over the parapet, leaving the roof to the bodies of the gorilla god and his erstwhile captive.

The flames roared up through the narrow shafts of the towers, transforming them into giant torches, illuminating the face of the cliff towering above, shedding weird lights and shadows on the city and the valley. They ate through the roof at the north end of the castle, and the liberated gases shot smoke and flame high into the night. They gnawed through a great roof beam, and a section of the roof fell into the fiery furnace below showering the city with sparks. Slowly they crept toward the bodies of the ape-man and the gorilla god.

Before the castle, the Holy Stairway and the ledge were packed with the horde that had come up from the city to watch the holocaust. They were awed to silence. Somewhere in that grim pile was their god. They knew nothing of immortality, for he had not taught them that. They thought that their god was dead, and they were afraid. These were the lowly ones. The creatures of the king rejoiced; for they envisaged the power of the god descending upon the shoulders of their leader, conferring more power upon themselves. They were gorillas contaminated by the lusts and greed of men.

On the roof one of the bodies stirred. The eyes opened. It was a moment before the light of consciousness quickened them; then the man sat up. It was Tarzan. He leaped to his feet. All about him was the roaring and crackling of the flames. The heat was intense, almost unbearable.

He saw the body of the gorilla god lying near him. He saw it move. Then the creature sat up quickly and looked about. It saw Tarzan. It saw the flames licking and leaping on all sides, dancing the dance of death – its death.

Tarzan gave it but a single glance and walked away. That part of the roof closest to the cliff was freest of flames, and toward the parapet there he made his way.

The gorilla god followed him 'We are lost,' he said. 'Every avenue of escape is cut off.'

The ape-man shrugged and looked over the edge of the parapet down the side of the castle wall. Twenty feet below was the roof of a section of the building that rose only one story. It was too far to jump. Flames were coming from the windows on that side, flames and smoke, but not in the volumes that were pouring from the openings on the opposite side.

Tarzan tested the strength of one of the merlons of the battlemented parapet. It was strong. The stones were set in good mortar. He uncoiled his rope, and passed it about the merlon.

The gorilla god had followed him and was watching. 'You are going to escape!' he cried. 'Oh, save me too.'

'So that you can kill and eat me later?' asked the apeman.

'No, no! I will not harm you. For God's sake save me!'

'I thought you were God. Save yourself.'

'You can't desert me. I'm an Englishman. Blood is thicker than water – you wouldn't see an Englishman die when you can save him!'

'I am an Englishman.' replied the ape-man, 'but you would have killed me and eaten me into the bargain.'

'Forgive me that. I was mad to regain my human form, and you offered the only chance that I may ever have. Save me, and I will give you wealth beyond man's wildest dreams of avarice.'

'I have all I need,' replied Tarzan.

'You don't know what you are talking about. I can lead you to diamonds. Diamonds! Diamonds! You can scoop them up by the handful.'

'I care nothing for your diamonds,' replied the ape-man, 'but I will save you on one condition.'

'What is that?'

'That you help me save the girl, if she still lives, and get her out of this valley.'

'I promise. But hurry – soon it will be too late.'

Tarzan had looped the center of his rope about the merlon; the loose ends dangled a few feet above the roof below. He saw that the rope hung between windows where the flames could not reach it.

'I will go first,' he said, 'to be sure that you do not run away and forget your promise.'

'You do not trust me!' exclaimed the gorilla god.

'Of course not – you are a man.'

He lowered his body over the parapet, hung by one hand, and seized both strands of the rope in the other.

The gorilla god shuddered. 'I could never do that,' he cried. 'I should fall. It is awful!' He covered his eyes with his hands.

'Climb over the parapet and get on my back, then,' directed the ape-man. 'Here, I will steady you.' He reached up a powerful hand.

'Will the rope hold us both?'

'I don't know. Hurry, or I'll have to go without you. The heat is getting worse.'

Trembling, the gorilla god climbed over the parapet; and, steadied and assisted by Tarzan, slid to the ape-man's back where he clung with a deathlike grip about the bronzed neck.

Slowly and carefully Tarzan descended. He had no doubt as to the strength of the rope on a straight pull, but feared that the rough edges of the merlon might cut it.

The heat was terrific. Flames leaped out of the openings on each side of them. Acrid, stifling smoke enveloped them. Where the descent at this point had seemed reasonably safe a moment before, it was now fraught with dangers that made the outcome of their venture appear more than doubtful. It was as though the fire demon had discovered their attempt to escape his clutches and had marshalled all his forces to defeat it and add them to his list of victims.

With grim persistence Tarzan continued his slow descent. The creature clinging to his back punctuated paroxysms of coughing and choking with piercing screams of terror. The ape-man kept his eyes closed and tried not to breathe in the thick smoke that enveloped them.

His lungs seemed upon the point of bursting when, to his relief, his feet touched solid footing. Instantly he threw himself upon his face and breathed. The rising smoke, ascending with the heat of flames, drew fresh air along the roof on which the two lay; and they filled their lungs with it.

Only for a moment did Tarzan lie thus; then he rolled over on his back and pulled rapidly upon one end of the rope until the other had passed about the merlon above and fell to the roof beside him.

This lower roof on which they were was but ten feet above the level of the ground; and, using the rope again, it was only a matter of seconds before the two stood in comparative safety between the castle and the towering cliff.

'Come now,' said the ape-man; 'we will go around to the front of the castle and find out if the girl escaped.'

'We shall have to be careful,' cautioned the gorilla god. 'This fire will have attracted a crowd from the city. I have many enemies in the palace of the king who would be glad to capture us both. Then we should be killed and the girl lost – if she is not already dead.'

'What do you suggest, then?' Tarzan was suspicious. He saw a trap, he saw duplicity in everything conceived by the mind of man.

'The fire has not reached this low wing yet,' explained the other. 'It is the entrance to a shaft leading down to the quarters of a faithful priest who dwells in a cave at the foot of the cliff on a level with the city. If we can reach him we shall be safe. He will hide us and do my bidding.'

Tarzan scowled. He had the wild beast's aversion to entering an unfamiliar enclosure, but he had overheard enough of the conversation between the gorilla god and Cranmer to know that the former's statement was at least partially true – his enemies in the palace might gladly embrace an opportunity to imprison or destroy him.

'Very well,' he assented; 'but I am going to tie this rope around your neck so that you may not escape me, and remind you that I still have the knife with which I killed several of your gorillas. I and the knife will always be near you.'

The gorilla god made no reply; but he submitted to being secured, and then led the way into the building and to a cleverly concealed trap opening into the top of a shaft descending into darkness.

Here a ladder led downward, and Tarzan let his companion precede him into the Stygian blackness of the shaft. They descended for a short distance to a horizontal corridor which terminated at another vertical shaft. These shafts and corridors alternated until the gorilla god finally announced that they had reached the bottom of the cliff.

Here they proceeded along a corridor until a heavy wooden door blocked their progress. The gorilla god listened intently for a moment, his ear close to the planking of the door. Finally he raised the latch and pushed the door silently ajar. Through the crack the ape-man saw a rough cave lighted by a single smoky torch.

'He is not here,' said the gorilla god as he pushed the door open and entered. 'He has probably gone with the others to see the fire.'

Tarzan looked about the interior. He saw a smoke blackened cave, the floor littered with dirty straw. Opposite the doorway through which they had entered was another probably leading into the open. It was closed with a massive wooden door. Near the door was a single small window. Some sacks made of the skins of animals hung from pegs driven into the walls. A large jar sitting on the floor held water.

'We shall have to await his return,' said the gorilla god. 'In the meantime let us eat.'

He crossed to the bags hanging on the wall and examined their contents, finding celery, bamboo tips, fruit, and nuts. He selected what he wished and sat down on the floor. 'Help yourself,' he invited with a wave of a hand toward the sacks.

'I have eaten,' said Tarzan and sat down near the gorilla god where he could watch both him and the doorway.

His companion ate in silence for a few minutes; then he looked up at the ape-man. 'You said that you did not want diamonds.' His tone was sceptical. 'Then why did you come here?'

'Not for diamonds.'

The gorilla god chuckled. 'My people killed some of your party as they were about to enter the valley. On the body of one of them was a map of this valley – the valley of diamonds. Are you surprised that I assume that you came for the diamonds?'

'I knew nothing of the map. How could we have had a map of this valley which, until we came, was absolutely unknown to white men?'

'You had a map.'

'But who could have made it?'

'I made it.'

'You! How could we have a map that you made? Have you returned to England since you first came here?'

'No – but I made that map.'

'You came here because you hated men and to escape them. It is not reasonable that you should have made a map to invite men here, and if you did make it how did you get it to America or to England or wherever it was that these – my people got it?' demanded Tarzan.

'I will tell you. I loved a girl. She was not interested in a poor scientist with no financial future ahead of him. She wanted wealth and luxuries. She wanted a rich husband.

'When I came to this valley and found the diamonds I thought of her. I cannot say that I still loved her, but I wanted her. I should have liked to be revenged upon her for the suffering that she had caused me. I thought what a fine revenge it would be to get her here and keep her here as long as she lived. I would give her wealth – more wealth than any other creature in the world possessed; but she would be unable to buy anything with it.' He chuckled as he recalled his plan.

'So I made the map, and I wrote her a letter. I told her to tell no one but to come here alone; so that no one else would know about our treasure and steal it from us. I told her just what to do, where to land, and how to form her safari. Then I waited. I have been waiting for seventy-four years, but she has never come.

'I had gone to considerable effort to get the letter to her. It had been necessary for me to go a long way from the valley to find a friendly tribe of natives and employ one of them as a runner to take my letter to the coast. I never knew whether or not the letter reached the coast. The runner might have been killed. Many things might have happened. I often wondered what became of the map. Now it has come back to me – after seventy-four years.' Again he chuckled. 'And brought another girl – a very much prettier girl. Mine would be – let's see – ninety-four years old, a toothless hag.' He sighed. 'But now I suppose that I shall not have either of them.'

There was a sound at the outer door. Tarzan sprang to his feet. The door opened, and an old gorilla started to enter. At sight of the ape-man he bared his fangs and paused.

'It is all right, Father Tobin,' said the gorilla god, 'Come in and close the door.'

'My Lord!' exclaimed the old gorilla as he closed the door behind him and threw himself upon his knees. 'We thought that you had perished in the flames. Praises be to heaven that you have been spared to us.'

'Blessing be upon you, my son,' replied the gorilla god. 'And now tell me what has happened in the city.'

'The castle is destroyed.'

'Yes, I knew that; but what of the king? Does he think me dead?'

'All think so; and, may curses descend upon him, Henry is pleased. They say that he will proclaim himself God.'

'Do you know aught of the fate of the girl Wolsey rescued from Henry's clutches and brought to my castle? Did she die in the fire?' asked the gorilla god.

'She escaped, My Lord. I saw her.'

'Where is she?' demanded Tarzan.

'The king's men recaptured her and took her to the palace.'

'That will be the end of her,' announced the gorilla god. 'for if Henry insists on marrying her, as he certainly will, Catherine of Aragon will tear her to pieces.'

'We must get her away from him at once,' said Tarzan.

The gorilla god shrugged. 'I doubt if that can be done.'

'You have said that someone did it before – Wolsey I think you called him.'

'But Wolsey had a strong incentive.'

'No stronger than the one you have,' said the ape-man quietly, but he jerked a little on the rope about God's neck and fingered the hilt of his hunting knife.

'But how can I do it?' demanded the gorilla god. 'Henry has many soldiers. The people think that I am dead, and now they will be more afraid of the king than ever.'

'You have many faithful followers, haven't you?' inquired Tarzan.

'Yes.'

'Then send this priest to gather them. Tell them to meet outside this cave with whatever weapons they can obtain.'

The priest was looking in astonishment from his god to the stranger who spoke to him with so little reverence and who held an end of the rope tied about the god's neck. With horror, he had even seen the creature jerk the rope.

'Go. Father Tobin,' said the gorilla god, 'and gather the faithful.'

'And see that there is no treachery,' snapped Tarzan. 'I have your god's promise to help me save that girl. You see this rope about his neck? You see this knife at my side?'

The priest nodded.

'If you both do not do all within your power to help me your god dies.'
There was no mistaking the sincerity of that statement.

'Go, Father Tobin,' said the gorilla god.

'And hurry,' added Tarzan.

'I go, My Lord,' cried the priest; 'but I hate to leave you in the clutches of
this creature.'

'He will be safe enough if you do your part,' Tarzan assured him.

The priest knelt again, crossed himself, and departed. As the door closed
after him, Tarzan turned to his companion. 'How is it,' he asked, 'that you
have been able to transmit the power to speak and perhaps to reason to these
brutes, yet they have not taken on any of the outward physical attributes of
man?'

'That is due to no fault of mine,' replied the gorilla god, 'but rather to an
instinct of the beasts themselves more powerful than their newly acquired
reasoning faculties. Transmitting human germ cells from generation to generation, as they now do, it is not strange that there are often born to them
children with the physical attributes of human beings. But in spite of all I can
do these sports have invariably been destroyed at birth.

'In the few cases where they have been spared they have developed into
monsters that seem neither beast nor human – manlike creatures with all the
worst qualities of man and beast. Some of these have either been driven out
of the city or have escaped, and there is known to be a tribe of them living in
caves on the far side of the valley.

'I know of two instances where the mutants were absolutely perfect in
human form and figure but possessed the minds of gorillas; the majority,
however, have the appearance of grotesque hybrids.

'Of these two, one was a very beautiful girl when last I saw her but with the
temper of a savage lioness; the other was a young man with the carriage and
the countenance of an aristocrat and the sweet amiability of a Jack the
Ripper.

'And now, young man,' continued the gorilla god, 'when my followers have
gathered here, what do you purpose doing?'

'Led by us,' replied Tarzan, 'they will storm the palace of the king and take
the girl from him.'

CHAPTER TWENTY-NINE
Death at Dawn

Rhonda Terry awoke with a start. She heard shouting and growls and screams and roars that sounded very close indeed. She saw the shes of Henry's harem moving about restlessly. Some of them uttered low growls like nervous, half frightened beasts; but it was not these sounds that had awakened her – they came through the unglazed windows of the apartment, loud, menacing.

She rose and approached a window. Catherine of Aragon saw her and bared her fangs in a vicious snarl.

'It is the she they want.' growled the old queen.

From the window Rhonda saw in the light of torches a mass of hairy forms battling to the death. She gasped and pressed a hand to her heart, for among them she saw Stanley Obroski fighting his way toward an entrance to the palace.

At first it seemed to her that he was fighting alone against that horde of beasts, but presently she realized that many of them were his allies. She saw the gorilla god close to Obroski; she even saw the grass rope about the creature's neck. Now her only thought was of the safety of Obroski.

Vaguely she heard voices raised about her in anger; then she became conscious of the words of the old queen. 'She has caused all this trouble.' Catherine of Aragon was saying. 'If she were dead we should have peace.'

'Kill her, then,' said Anne of Cleves.

'Kill her!' screamed Anne Boleyn.

The girl turned from the window to see the savage beasts advancing upon her – great hairy brutes that could tear her to pieces. The incongruity of their human speech and their bestial appearance seemed suddenly more shocking and monstrous than ever before.

One of them stepped forward from her side and stood in front of her, facing the others. It was Catherine Parr. 'Leave her alone,' she said. 'It is not her fault that she is here.'

'Kill them both! Kill Parr too!' screamed Catherine Howard.

The others took up the refrain. 'Kill them both!' The Howard leaped upon the Parr; and with hideous growls the two sought each other's throat with great, yellow fangs. Then the others rushed upon Rhonda Terry.

There was no escape. They were between her and the door; the windows were barred. Her eyes searched vainly for something with which to beat them off, but there was nothing. She backed away from them, but all the time she knew that there was no hope.

Then the door was suddenly thrown open, and three great bulls stepped into the apartment. 'His Majesty, the King!' cried one of them, and the shes quieted their tongues and fell away from Rhonda. Only the two battling on the floor did not hear.

The great bull gorilla that was Henry the Eighth rolled into the room. 'Silence!' he bellowed, and crossing to the embattled pair he kicked and cuffed them until they desisted. 'Where is the fair, hairless one?' he demanded, and then his eyes alighted upon Rhonda where she stood almost hidden by the great bulks of his wives.

'Come here!' he commanded. 'God has come for you, but he'll never get you. You belong to me.'

'Let him have her, Henry,' cried Catherine of Aragon; 'she has caused nothing but trouble.'

'Silence, woman!' screamed the king; 'or you'll go to the Tower and the block.'

He stepped forward and seized Rhonda, throwing her across one shoulder as though she had no weight whatever; then he crossed quickly to the door. 'Stand in the corridor here, Suffolk and Howard, and, if God's men reach this floor, hold them off until I have time to get safely away.'

'Let us go with you, Sire,' begged one of them.

'No; remain here until you have news for me; then follow me to the north end of the valley, to the canyon where the east branch of the Thames rises.' He turned then and hurried down the corridor.

At the far end he turned into a small room, crossed to a closet, and raised a trap door. 'They'll never follow us here, my beauty,' he said. 'I got this idea from God, but he doesn't know that I made use of it.'

Like a huge monkey he descended a pole that led downward into the darkness, and after they reached the bottom Rhonda became aware that they were traversing a subterranean corridor. It was very long and very dark. The gorilla king moved slowly, feeling his way; but at last they came out into the open.

He had set Rhonda down upon the floor of the corridor, and she had been aware by the noises that she heard that he was moving some heavy object. Then she had felt the soft night air and had seen stars above them. A moment later they stood upon the bank of a river at the foot of a low cliff while Henry replaced a large, flat stone over the dark entrance to the tunnel they had just quitted.

Then commenced a trek of terror for Rhonda. Following the river, they hurried along through the night toward the upper end of the valley. The great brute no longer carried her but dragged her along by one wrist. He seemed nervous and fearful, occasionally stopping to sniff the air or listen. He moved almost silently, and once or twice he cautioned her to silence.

After a while they crossed the river toward the east where the water, though swift, was only up to their knees; then they continued in a northeasterly direction. There was no sound of pursuit, yet the gorilla's nervousness increased. Presently Rhonda guessed the reason for it – from the north came the deep throated roar of a lion.

The gorilla king growled deep in his chest and quickened his pace. A suggestion of dawn was tinging the eastern horizon. A cold mist enveloped the valley. Rhonda was very tired. Every muscle in her body ached and cried out for rest, but still her captor dragged her relentlessly onward.

Now the voice of the lion sounded again, shattering the silence of the night, making the earth tremble. It was much closer than before – it seemed very near. The gorilla broke into a lumbering run. Dawn was coming. Nearby objects became visible.

Rhonda saw a lion ahead of them and a little to their left. The gorilla king saw it too, and changed his direction toward the east and a fringe of trees that were visible now about a hundred yards ahead of them.

The lion was approaching them at an easy, swinging walk. Now he too changed his direction and broke into a trot with the evident intention of heading them off before they reached the trees.

Rhonda noticed how his flat belly swung from side to side to the motion of his gait. It is strange how such trivialities often impress one at critical moments of extreme danger. He looked lean and hungry. He was roaring almost continuously now as though he were attempting to lash himself into a rage. He commenced to gallop.

Now it became obvious that they could never reach the trees ahead of him. The gorilla paused, growling. Instantly the lion changed its course again and came straight for them. The gorilla hesitated; then he lifted the girl in his powerful paws and hurled her into the path of the lion, at the same time turning and running at full speed back in the direction from which they had come. His prize had become the offering which he hoped would save his life.

But he reckoned without sufficient knowledge of lion psychology. Rhonda fell face downward. She knew that the lion was only a few yards away and coming toward her, that she could not escape him; but she recalled her other experience with a lion, and so she lay very still. After she fell she did not move a muscle.

It is the running creature that attracts the beast of prey. You have seen that exemplified by your own dog, which is a descendant of beasts of prey. Whatever runs he must chase. He cannot help it. Provided it is running away from him he has to chase it because he is the helpless pawn of a natural law a million years older than the first dog.

If Henry the Eighth had ever known this he must have forgotten it; otherwise he would have made the girl run while he lay down and remained very quiet. But he did not, and the inevitable happened. The lion ignored the still figure of the girl and pursued the fleeing gorilla.

Rhonda felt the lion pass swiftly, close to her; then she raised her head and looked. The gorilla was moving much more swiftly than she had guessed possible, but not swiftly enough. In a moment the lion would overhaul it. They would be some distance from Rhonda when this happened, and the lion would certainly be occupied for a few moments with the killing of its prey. It seemed incredible that the huge ape, armed as it was with powerful jaws and mighty fighting fangs, would not fight savagely for self-preservation.

The girl leaped to her feet, and without a backward glance raced for the trees. She had covered but a few yards when she heard terrific roars and growls and screams that told her that the lion had overtaken the gorilla and that the two beasts were already tearing at one another. As long as these sounds lasted she knew that her flight would not be noticed by the lion.

When, breathless, she reached the trees she stopped and looked back. The lion was dragging the gorilla down, the great jaws closed upon its head, there was a vicious shake; and the ape went limp. Thus died Henry the Eighth.

The carnivore did not even look back in her direction but immediately crouched upon the body of its kill and commenced to feed. He was very hungry.

The girl slipped silently into the wood. A few steps brought her to the bank of a river. It was the east fork of the Thames, the wood a fringe of trees on either side. Thinking to throw the lion off her trail should it decide to follow her, as well as to put the barrier of the river between them, she entered it and swam to the opposite shore.

Now, for the first time in many a long day, she was inspired by hope. She was free! Also, she knew where her friends were; and that by following the river down to the escarpment that formed the Omwamwi Falls she could find them. What dangers beset her path she did not know, but it seemed that they must be trivial by comparison with those she had already escaped. The trees that lined the river bank would give her concealment and protection, and before the day was over she would be at the escarpment. How she was to descend it she would leave until faced by the necessity.

She was tired, but she did not stop to rest – there could be no rest for her until she had found safety. Following the river, she moved southward. The sun had risen above the mountains that hemmed the valley on the east. Her body was grateful for the warmth that dispelled the cold night mists.

Presently the river turned in a great loop toward the east, and though she knew that following the meanderings of the river would greatly increase the distance that she must travel there was no alternative – she did not dare leave the comparative safety of the wood nor abandon this unfailing guide that would lead her surely to her destination.

On and on she plodded in what approximated a lethargy of fatigue, dragging one foot painfully after another. Her physical exhaustion was reflected in her reactions. They were dull and slow. Her senses were less acute. She either failed to hear unusual sounds or interpret them as subjects worthy of careful investigation. It was this that brought disaster.

When she became aware of danger it was too late. A hideous creature, half man, half gorilla, dropped from a tree directly in her path. It had the face of a man, the ears and body of an ape.

The girl turned to run toward the river, thinking to plunge in and escape by swimming; but as she turned another fearsome thing dropped from the trees to confront her; then, growling and snarling, the two leaped forward and seized her. Each grasped her by an arm, and one pulled in one direction while the other pulled in the opposite. They screamed and gibbered at one another.

She thought that they must wrench her arms from their sockets. She had given up hope when a naked white man dropped from an overhanging branch. He carried a club in his hand, and with it belabored first one and then the other of her assailants until they relinquished their holds upon her. But to her horror she saw that her rescuer gibbered and roared just as the others had.

Now the man seized her and stood snarling like a wild beast as a score of terrible beast-men swung from the trees and surrounded them. The man who held her was handsome and well formed; his skin was tanned to a rich bronze; a head of heavy blond hair fell from his shoulders like the mane of a lion.

The creatures that surrounded them were hybrids of all degrees of repulsiveness; yet he seemed one of them, for he made the same noises that they made. Also, it was evident that he had been in the trees with them. The others seemed to stand a little in awe of him or of his club; for, while they evidently wanted to come and lay hands upon the girl, they kept their distance, out of range of the man's weapon.

The man started to move away with his captive, to withdraw from the circle surrounding them; then, above the scolding of the others, a savage scream sounded from the foliage overhead.

The man and the beasts glanced nervously aloft. Rhonda let her eyes follow in the direction in which they were looking. Involuntarily she voiced a gasp of astonishment at what she beheld. Swinging downward toward them with the speed and agility of a monkey was a naked white girl, her golden hair streaming out behind her. From between her perfect lips issued the horrid screams of a beast.

As she touched the ground she ran toward them. Her face, even though reflecting savage rage, was beautiful; her youthful body was flawless in its perfection. But her disposition was evidently something else.

As she approached, the beasts surrounding Rhonda and the man edged away, making a path for her, though they growled and bared their teeth at her. She paid no attention to them, but came straight for Rhonda.

The man screamed at her, backing away; then he whirled Rhonda to a shoulder, turned, and bolted. Even burdened with the weight of his captive he ran with great speed. Behind him, raging and screaming, the beautiful she-devil pursued.

CHAPTER THIRTY
The Wild-Girl

The Palace Guard gave way before the multitude of faithful that battered at the doors of the king's house at the behest of their god. The god was pleased. He wished to punish Henry, but he had never before quite dared to assault the palace. Now he was victorious; and in victory one is often generous, especially to him who made victory possible.

Previously he had fully intended to break his promise to Tarzan and revenge himself for the affront that had been put upon his godhood, but now he was determined to set both the man and the girl free.

Tarzan cared nothing for the political aspects of the night's adventure. He thought only of Rhonda. 'We must find the girl,' he said to the gorilla god the moment that they had gained entrance to the palace. 'Where could she be?'

'She is probably with the other women. Come with me – they are upstairs.'

At the top of the stairs stood Howard and Suffolk to do the bidding of their king; but when they saw their god ascending toward them and the lower hall and the stairs behind him filled with his followers and recalled that the king had fled, they experienced a change of heart. They received God on bended knee and assured him that they had driven Henry out of the palace and were just on their way downstairs to fall tooth and nail upon God's enemies; and God knew that they lied, for it was he himself who had implanted the minds of men in their gorilla skulls.

'Where is the hairless she?' demanded the gorilla god.

'Henry took her with him,' replied Suffolk.

'Where did he go?'

'I do not know. He ran to the end of the corridor and disappeared.'

'Someone must know,' snapped Tarzan.

'Perhaps Catherine of Aragon knows,' suggested Howard.

'Where is she?' demanded the ape-man.

They led the way to the door of the harem. Suffolk swung the door open. 'My Lord God!' he announced.

The shes, nervous and frightened, had been expecting to be dragged to their death by the mob. When they saw the gorilla god they fell on their knees before him.

'Have mercy, My Lord God!' cried Catherine of Aragon. 'I am your faithful servant.'

'Then tell me where Henry is,' demanded the god.

'He fled with the hairless she,' replied the old queen.

'Where?'

The rage of a jealous female showed Catherine of Aragon how to have her revenge. 'Come with me,' she said.

They followed her down the corridor to the room at the end and into the closet there. Then she lifted the trap door. 'This shaft leads to a tunnel that runs under the city to the bank of the river beyond the wall – he and that hairless thing went this way.'

The keen scent of the ape-man detected the delicate aroma of the white girl. He knew that the king gorilla had carried her into this dark hole. Perhaps they were down there now, the king hiding from his enemies until it would be safe for him to return; or perhaps there was a tunnel running beyond the city as the old she had said, and the gorilla had carried his captive off to some fastness in the mountains surrounding the valley.

But in any event the ape-man must go on now alone – he could trust none of the creatures about him to aid him in the pursuit and capture of one of their own kind. He had already removed his rope from around the neck of the gorilla god; now it lay coiled across one shoulder; at his hip swung his hunting knife. Tarzan of the Apes was prepared for any emergency.

Without a word, he swung down the pole into the black abyss below. The gorilla god breathed a sigh of relief when he had departed.

Following the scent spoor of those he sought, Tarzan traversed the tunnel that led from the bottom of the shaft to the river bank. He pushed the great stone away from the entrance and stepped out into the night. He stood erect, listening and sniffing the air. A scarcely perceptible air current was moving up toward the head of the valley. It bore no suspicion of the scent he had been following. All that this indicated was that his quarry was not directly south of him. The gorilla king might have gone to the east or the west or the north; but the river flowed deep and swift on the east, and only the north and west were left.

Tarzan bent close to the ground. Partly by scent, partly by touch he found the trail leading toward the north; or, more accurately, toward the northeast between the river and the cliffs. He moved off upon it; but the necessity for stopping often to verify the trail delayed him, so that he did not move quite as rapidly as the beast he pursued.

He was delayed again at the crossing of the river, for he passed the place at which the trail turned sharply to the right into the stream. He had to retrace his steps, searching carefully until he found it again. Had the wind been right, had the gorilla been moving directly upwind, Tarzan could have trailed him at a run.

The enforced delays caused no irritation or nervousness such as they would have in the ordinary man, for the patience of the hunting beast is infinite. Tarzan knew that eventually he would overhaul his quarry, and that while they were on the move the girl was comparatively safe.

Dawn broke as he crossed the river. Far ahead he heard the roaring of a hunting lion, and presently with it were mingled the snarls and screams of another beast – a gorilla. And the ape-man knew that Numa had attacked one of the great apes. He guessed that it was the gorilla king. But what of the girl? He heard no human voice mingling its screams with that of the anthropoid. He broke into a run.

Presently, from a little rise of rolling ground, he saw Numa crouching upon his kill. It was light enough now for him to see that the lion was feeding upon the body of a gorilla. The girl was nowhere in sight.

Tarzan made a detour to avoid the feeding carnivore. He had no intention of risking an encounter with the king of beasts – an encounter that would certainly delay him and possibly end in death.

He passed at a considerable distance upwind from the lion; and when the beast caught his scent it turned its head in his direction and growled, but it did not rise from its kill.

Beyond the lion, near the edge of the wood, Tarzan picked up the trail of the girl again. He followed it across the second river. It turned south here, upwind; and now he was below her and could follow her scent spoor easily. At a trot he pressed on.

Now other scent spoor impinged upon his nostrils, mingling with those of the girl. They were strange scents – a mixture of mangani and tarmangani, of great ape and white man, of male and of female.

Tarzan increased his gait. That strange instinct that he shared with the other beasts of the forest warned him that danger lay ahead – danger for the girl and perhaps for himself. He moved swiftly and silently through the fringe of forest that bordered the river.

The strange scents became stronger in his nostrils. A babel of angry voices arose in the distance ahead. He was nearing them. He took to the trees now, to his native element; and he felt at once the sense of security and power that the trees always imparted to him. Here, as nowhere else quite in the same measure, was he indeed Lord of the Jungle.

Now he heard the angry, raging voice of a female. It was almost human, yet the beast notes predominated; and he could recognize words spoken in the language of the great apes. Tarzan was mystified.

He was almost upon them now, and a moment later he looked down upon a strange scene. There were a score of monstrous creatures – part human, part gorilla. And there was a naked white man just disappearing among the trees with the girl he sought across one shoulder. Pursuing them was a white girl with golden hair streaming behind her. She was as naked as the other beasts gibbering and screaming in her wake.

The man bearing Rhonda Terry ran swiftly, gaining upon the golden haired devil behind him. They both out-stripped the other creatures that had started in pursuit, and presently these desisted and gave up the chase.

Tarzan, swinging through the trees, gained slowly on the strange pair; and so engrossed were they in the business of escape and pursuit that they did not glance up and discover him.

Now the ape-man caught up with the running girl and passed her. Her burst of speed had taken toll of her strength, and she was slowing down. The man had gained on her, too; and now considerable distance separated them.

Through the trees ahead of him Tarzan saw a stretch of open ground, beyond which rose rocky cliffs; then the forest ended. Swinging down to earth, he continued the pursuit; but he had lost a little distance now, and though he started to gain gradually on the fleeing man, he realized that the other would reach the cliffs ahead of him. He could hear the pursuing girl panting a short distance behind him.

Since he had first seen the naked man and woman and the grotesque monsters that they had left behind in the forest, Tarzan had recalled the story that the gorilla god had told him of the mutants that had escaped destruction and formed a tribe upon this side of the valley. These, then, were the terrible fruits of the old biologist's profane experiment – children of the unnatural union of nature and science.

It was only the passing consciousness of a fact to which the ape-man now had no time to give thought. His every faculty was bent upon the effort of the moment – the overtaking of the man who carried Rhonda Terry. Tarzan marvelled at the man's speed burdened as he was by the weight of his captive.

The cliffs were only a short distance ahead of him now. At their base were piled a tumbled mass of fragments that had fallen from above during times past. The cliffs themselves presented a series of irregular, broken ledges; and their face was pitted with the mouths of innumerable caves.

As the man reached the rubble at the foot of the cliffs, he leaped from rock to rock like a human chamois; and after him came the ape-man, but slower; for he was unaccustomed to such terrain – and behind him, the savage she.

Clambering from ledge to ledge the creature bore Rhonda Terry aloft; and Tarzan followed, and the golden haired girl came after. Far up the cliff face the man pushed Rhonda roughly into a cave mouth and turned to face his pursuer.

Tarzan of the Apes turned abruptly to the right then and ran along a narrow ascending ledge with the intention of gaining the ledge upon which the other stood without having to ascend directly into the face of his antagonist. The man guessed his purpose and started along his own ledge to circumvent him. Below them the girl was clambering upward.

'Go back!' shouted the man in the language of the great apes. 'Go back! I kill!'

'Rhonda!' called the ape-man.

The girl crawled from the cave out onto the ledge. 'Stanley!' she cried in astonishment.

'Climb up the cliff,' Tarzan directed. 'You can follow the ledges up. I can keep him occupied until you get to the top. Then go south toward the lower end of the valley.'

'I'll try,' she replied and started to climb from ledge to ledge.

The girl ascending from below saw her and shouted to the man. 'Kreegah!' she screamed. 'The she is escaping!'

Now the man turned away from Tarzan and started in pursuit of Rhonda; and the ape-man, instead of following directly after him, clambered to a higher ledge, moving diagonally in the direction of the American girl.

Rhonda, spurred on by terror, was climbing much more rapidly than she herself could have conceived possible. The narrow ledges, the precarious footing would have appalled her at any other time; but now she ignored all danger and thought only of reaching the summit of the cliff before the strange white man overtook her.

And so it was that by a combination of her speed and Tarzan's strategy the ape-man was able to head off her pursuer before he overtook her.

When the man realized that he had been intercepted he turned upon Tarzan with a savage, snarling growl, his handsome face transformed into that of a wild beast.

The ledge was narrow. It was obvious to Tarzan that the two could not do battle upon it without falling; and while at this point there was another ledge only a few feet below, it could only momentarily stay their descent – while they fought they must roll from ledge to ledge until one or both of them were badly injured or killed.

A quick glance showed him that the wild-girl was ascending toward them. Below and beyond her appeared a number of the grotesque hybrids that had again taken up the chase. Even if the ape-man were the one to survive the duel, all these creatures might easily be upon him before it was concluded.

Reason dictated that he should attempt to avoid so useless an encounter in which he would presumably lose his life either in victory or defeat. These observations and deductions registered upon his brain with the speed of a camera shutter flashing one exposure rapidly after another. Then the decision was taken from him – the man-beast charged. With a bestial roar he charged.

The girl, ascending, screamed savage encouragement; the horrid mutants gibbered and shrieked. Above them all, Rhonda turned at the savage sounds and looked down. With parted lips, her hand pressed to her heart, she watched with dismay and horror.

Crouching, Tarzan met the charge. The man-beast fought without science but with great strength and ferocity. Whatever thin veneer of civilization his contacts with men had imparted to the ape-man vanished now. Here was a beast meeting a beast.

A low growl rumbled from the throat of the Lord of the Jungle, snarling-muscles drew back his lip to expose strong, white teeth, the primitive weapons of the first-man.

Like charging bulls they came together, and like mad panthers each sought the other's throat. Locked in feral embrace they swayed a moment upon the ledge; then they toppled over the brink.

At that moment Rhonda Terry surrendered the last vestige of hope. She had ascended the cliff to a point beyond which she could discover no foothold for further progress. The man whom she believed to be Stanley Obroski, whose newly discovered valor had become the sole support of whatever hope of escape she might have entertained, was already as good as dead; for if the fall did not kill him the creatures swarming up the cliff toward him would. Yet self-pity was submerged in the grief she felt for the fate of the man. Her original feeling of contempt for him had changed to one of admiration, and this had grown into an emotion that she could scarcely have analysed herself. It was something stronger than friendship; perhaps it was love. She did not want to see him die; yet, fascinated, her eyes clung to the scene below.

But Tarzan had no mind to die now. In ferocity, in strength, he was equal to his antagonist; in courage and intellect, he was his superior. It was by his own intelligent effort that the two had so quickly plunged from the ledge to another a few feet below; and as he had directed the fall, so he directed the manner of their alighting. The man-beast was underneath; Tarzan was on top.

The former struck upon the back of his head, as Tarzan had intended that he should; and one of the ape-man's knees was at his stomach; so not only was he stunned into insensibility, but the wind was knocked out of him. He would not fight again for some considerable time.

Scarcely had they struck the lower ledge than Tarzan was upon his feet. He saw the monsters scrambling quickly toward him; he saw the wild-girl already reaching out to clutch him, and in the instant his plan was formed.

The girl was on the ledge below, reaching for one of his ankles to drag him down. He stooped quickly and seized her by the hair; then he swung her, shrieking and screaming, to his shoulder.

She kicked and scratched and tried to bite him; but he held her until he had carried her to a higher ledge; then he threw her down and made his rope fast about her body. She fought viciously, but her strength was no match for that of the ape-man.

The creatures scaling the cliff were almost upon them by the time that Tarzan had made the rope secure; then he ran nimbly upward from ledge to ledge dragging the girl after him; and in this way he was out of her reach, and she could not hinder him.

The highest ledge, that from which Rhonda watched wide-eyed the changing scenes of the drama being enacted below her, was quite the widest of all. Opening on to it was the mouth of a cave. Above it the cliff rose, unscalable, to the summit.

To this ledge Tarzan dragged the now strangely silent wild-girl; and here he and Rhonda were cornered, their backs against a wall, with no avenue of escape in any direction.

The girl clambered the last few feet to the ledge; and when she stood erect, facing Tarzan, she no longer fought. The savage snarl had left her face. She smiled into the eyes of the ape-man, and she was very beautiful; but the man's attention was now upon the snarling pack, the leaders of which were mounting rapidly toward this last ledge.

'Go back,' shouted Tarzan, 'or I kill your she!'

This was the plan that he had conceived to hold them off, using the girl as a hostage. It was a good plan; but, like many another good plan, it failed to function properly.

'They will not stop,' said the girl. 'They do not care if you kill me. You have taken me. I belong to you. They will kill us all and eat us – if they can. Throw rocks down on them; drive them back; then I will show you how we can get away from them.'

Following her own advice, she picked up a bit of loose rock and hurled it at the nearest of the creatures. It struck him on the head, and he tumbled backward to a lower ledge. The girl laughed and screamed taunts and insults at her former companions.

Tarzan, realizing the efficacy of this mode of defense, gathered fragments of rock and threw them at the approaching monsters; then Rhonda joined in the barrage, and the three rained down a hail of missiles that drove their enemies to the shelter of the caves below.

'They won't eat us for a while.' laughed the girl.

'You eat human flesh?' asked Tarzan.

'Not Malb'yat nor I,' she replied; 'but they do – they eat anything.'

'Who is Malb'yat?'

'My he – you fought with him and took me from him. Now I am yours. I will fight for you. No one else shall have you!' She turned upon Rhonda with a snarl, and would have attacked her had not Tarzan seized her.

'Leave her alone,' he warned.

'You shall have no other she but me,' said the wild-girl.

'She is not mine,' explained the ape-man; 'you must not harm her.'

The girl continued to scowl at Rhonda, but she quit her efforts to reach her. 'I shall watch,' she said. 'What is her name?'

'Rhonda.'

'And what is yours?' she demanded.

'You may call me Stanley,' said Tarzan. He was amused, but not at all disconcerted, by the strange turn events had taken. He realized that their only chance of escape might be through this strange, beautiful, little savage, and he could not afford to antagonize her.

'Stanley,' she repeated, stumbling a little over the strange word. 'My name is Balza.'

Tarzan thought that it fitted her well, for in the language of the great apes it meant golden girl. Ape names are always descriptive. His own meant white skin. Malb'yat was yellow head.

Balza stooped quickly and picked up a rock which she hurled at a head that had been cautiously poked from a cave mouth below them. She scored another hit and laughed gaily.

'We will keep them away until night,' she said; 'then we will go. They will not follow us at night. They are afraid of the dark. If we went now they would follow us, and there are so many of them that we should all be killed.'

The girl interested Tarzan. Remembering what the gorilla god had told him of these mutants, he had assumed that her perfect human body was dominated by the brain of a gorilla; but he had not failed to note that she had repeated the name he had given her – something no gorilla could have done.

'Do you speak English?' he asked in that language.

She looked at him in surprise. 'Yes,' she replied; 'but I didn't imagine that you did.'

'Where did you learn it?' he asked.

'In London – before they drove me out.'

'Why did they drive you out?'

'Because I was not like them. My mother kept me hidden for years, but at last they found me out. They would have killed me had I remained.'

'And Malb'yat is like you?'

'No, Malb'yat is like the others. He cannot learn a single English word. I like you much better. I hope that you killed Malb'yat.'

'I didn't, though,' said the ape-man. 'I see him moving on the ledge down there where he has been lying.'

The girl looked; then she picked up a rock and flung it at the unfortunate Malb'yat. It missed him, and he crawled to shelter. 'If he gets me back he'll beat me,' she remarked.

'I should think he'd kill you,' said Tarzan.

'No – there is no one else like me. The others are ugly – I am beautiful. No, he will never kill me, but the shes would all like to.' She laughed gaily. 'I suppose this one would like to kill me.' She nodded toward Rhonda.

The American girl had been a surprised and interested listener to that part of the conversation that had been carried on in English, but she had not spoken.

'I do not want to kill you,' she said. 'There is no reason why we should not be friends.'

Balza looked at her in surprise; then she studied her carefully.

'Is she speaking the truth?' she asked Tarzan.

The ape-man nodded. 'Yes.'

'Then we are friends,' said Balza to Rhonda. Her decisions in matters of love, friendship, or murder were equally impulsive.

For hours the three kept vigil upon the ledge, but only occasionally was it necessary to remind the monsters below them to keep their distance.

CHAPTER THIRTY-ONE

Diamonds!

At last the long day drew to a close. All were hungry and thirsty. All were anxious to leave the hard, uncomfortable ledge where they had been exposed to the hot African sun since morning.

Tarzan and Rhonda had been entertained and amused by the savage little wild-girl. She was wholly unspoiled and without inhibitions of any nature. She said or did whatever she wished to say or do with a total lack of self-consciousness that was disarming and, often, not a little embarrassing.

As the sun was dropping behind the western hills across the valley, she rose to her feet. 'Come,' she said; 'we can go now. They will not follow, for it will soon be night.'

She led the way into the interior of the cave that opened upon the ledge.

The cave was narrow but quite straight. The girl led them to the back of the cave to the bottom of a natural chimney formed by a cleft in the rocky hill. The twilight sky was visible above them, the light revealing the rough surface of the interior of the chimney to its top a few yards up.

Tarzan took in the situation at a glance. He saw that by bracing their backs against one side of the chimney, their feet against the other, they could work themselves to the top; but he also realized that the rough surface would scratch and tear the flesh of the girls' backs.

'I'll go first,' he said. 'Wait here, and I'll drop a rope for you. It's strange, Balza, that your people didn't come to the cliff top and get us from above – they could have come down this chimney and taken us by surprise.'

'They are too stupid,' replied the girl. 'They have brains enough only to follow us; they would never think of going around us and heading us off.'

'Which is fortunate for us and some of them,' remarked the ape-man as he started the ascent of the chimney.

Reaching the top, he lowered his rope and raised the two girls easily to his side, where they found themselves in a small, bowl shaped gully the floor of which was covered with rough, crystallized pebbles that gave back the light of the dying day, transforming the gully into a well of soft luminance.

The moment that her eyes fell upon the scene, Rhonda voiced an exclamation of surprised incredulity. 'Diamonds!' she gasped. 'The valley of diamonds!'

She stooped and gathered some of the precious stones in her hands. Balza looked at her in surprise; the gems meant nothing to her. Tarzan, more sophisticated, gathered several of the larger specimens.

'May I take some with me?' asked Rhonda.

'Why not?' inquired the ape-man. 'Take what you can carry comfortably.'

'We shall all be rich!' exclaimed the American girl. 'We can bring the whole company here and take truck loads of these stones back with us – why, there must be tons of them here!'

'And then do you know what will happen?' asked Tarzan.

'Yes,' she replied. 'I shall have a villa on the Riviera, a town house in Beverly Hills, a hundred and fifty thousand dollar cottage at Malibu, a place at Palm Beach, a penthouse in New York, a—'

'You will have no more than you have always had,' the ape-man interrupted, 'for if you took all these diamonds back to civilization the market would be glutted; and diamonds would be as cheap as glass. If you are wise, you will take just a few for yourself and your friends; and then tell nobody how they may reach the valley of diamonds.'

Rhonda pondered this for a moment. 'You are right,' she admitted. 'From this moment, as far as I am concerned, there is no valley of diamonds.'

During the brief twilight Balza guided them to a trail that led down into the valley some distance below the cave dwellings of the tribe of mutants, and all during the night they moved southward toward the escarpment and Omwamwi Falls.

The way was new to all of them, for Balza had never been far south of the cave village; and this, combined with the darkness, retarded them, so that it was almost dawn when they reached the escarpment.

For much of the way Tarzan carried Rhonda, who was almost exhausted by all that she had passed through, and only thus were they able to progress at all. But Balza was tireless, moving silently in the footsteps of her man, as she now considered Tarzan. She did not speak, for experience and instinct both had trained her to the necessity for stealth if one would pass through savage nights alive. Every sense must be alert, concentrated upon the business of self-preservation. But who may know what passed in that savage little brain as the beautiful creature followed her new lord and master out into a strange world?

In the early dawn the scene from the top of the escarpment looked weird and forbidding to Rhonda Terry. The base was mist hidden. Only the roar of the falls, rising sepulchral, like the voices of ghostly Titans from the tomb, belied the suggestion of bottomless depth. She seemed to be gazing down into another world, a world she would never reach alive.

Strong in her memory was that other experience when the giant gorilla had carried her up this dizzy height. She knew that she could never descend it safely alone. She knew that Stanley Obroski could not carry her down. She had learned that he could do many things with the possibility of which none might ever have credited him a few weeks before, but here was something that no man might do. She even doubted his ability to descend alone.

Even as these thoughts passed quickly through her mind the man swung her across one broad shoulder and started the descent. Rhonda gasped, but she clenched her teeth and made no outcry. Seemingly with all the strength of the bull gorilla and with far greater agility he swung down into the terrifying abyss, finding foothold and handhold with unerring accuracy; and after him came Balza, the wild-girl, as sure of herself as any monkey.

And at last the impossible was achieved – the three stood safely at the foot of the escarpment. The sun had risen, and before it the mist was disappearing. New hope rose in the breast of the American girl, and new strength animated her body.

'Let me down. Stanley,' she said, 'I am sure I can walk all right now. I feel stronger.'

He lowered her to the ground. 'It is not a great way to the camp where I left Orman and the others,' he said.

Rhonda glanced at Balza and cleared her throat. 'Of course we're all from Hollywood,' she said. 'but don't you think we ought to rig some sort of skirt for Balza before we take her into camp?'

Tarzan laughed. 'Poor Balza,' he said; 'she will have to eat of the apple soon enough now that she is coming into contact with civilized man. Let her keep her naturalness and her purity of mind as long as she may.'

'But I was thinking of her,' remonstrated Rhonda.

'She won't be embarrassed,' Tarzan assured her. 'A skirt would probably embarrass her far more.'

Rhonda shrugged. 'O.K.' she said. 'And Tom and Bill forgot how to blush years ago, anyway.'

They had proceeded but a short distance down the river when Tarzan stopped and pointed. 'There is where they were camped,' he said, 'but they are gone.'

'What could have happened to them? Weren't they going to wait for you?'

The ape-man stood listening and sniffing the air. 'They are farther down the river,' he announced presently, 'and they are not alone – there are many with them.'

They continued on for over a mile when they suddenly came in sight of a large camp. There were many tents and motor trucks.

'The safari!' exclaimed Rhonda. 'Pat got through!'

As they approached the camp someone saw them and commenced to shout; then there was a stampede to meet them. Everyone kissed Rhonda, and Naomi Madison kissed Tarzan; whereat, with a growl, Balza leaped for her. The ape-man caught the wild-girl around the waist and held her, while Naomi shrank back, terrified.

'Hands off Stanley.' warned Rhonda with a laugh. 'The young lady has annexed him.'

Tarzan took Balza by the shoulders and wheeled her about until she faced him. 'These are my people,' he said. 'Their ways are not as your ways. If you quarrel with them I shall send you away. These shes are your friends.'

Everyone was staring at Balza with open admiration, Orman with the eye of a director discovering a type, Pat O'Grady with the eye of an assistant director – which is something else again.

'Balza,' continued the ape-man, 'go with these shes. Do as they tell you. They will cover your beautiful body with uncomfortable clothing, but you will have to wear it. In a month you will be smoking cigarettes and drinking high balls; then you will be civilized. Now you are only a barbarian. Go with them and be unhappy.'

Everyone laughed except Balza. She did not know what it was all about; but her god had spoken, and she obeyed. She went with Rhonda and Naomi to their tent.

Tarzan talked with Orman, Bill West, and O'Grady. They all thought that he was Stanley Obroski, and he did not attempt to undeceive them. They told him that Bill West had spent half the previous night trying to scale the escarpment. He had ascended far enough to see the campfires of the safari and the headlights of some of the trucks; then, forced to abandon his attempt to reach the summit, he had returned and led the others to the main camp.

Orman was now enthusiastic to go ahead with the picture. He had his star back again, his leading woman, and practically all the other important members of his cast. He decided to play the heavy himself and cast Pat O'Grady in Major White's part, and he had already created a part for Balza. 'She'll knock 'em cold,' he prophesied.

CHAPTER THIRTY-TWO
Goodbye, Africa!

For two weeks Orman shot scene after scene against the gorgeous background of the splendid river and the magnificent falls. Tarzan departed for two days and returned with a tribe of friendly natives to replace those that had departed. He led the cameramen to lions, to elephants, to every form of wildlife that the district afforded; and all marvelled at the knowledge, the power, and the courage of Stanley Obroski.

Then came a sad blow. A runner arrived bringing a cable-gram to Orman. It was from the studio; and it ordered him to return at once to Hollywood, bringing the company and equipment with him.

Everyone except Orman was delighted. 'Hollywood!' exclaimed Naomi Madison. 'Oh, Stanley, just think of it! Aren't you crazy to get to Hollywood?'

'Perhaps that's the right word,' he mused.

The company danced and sang like children watching the school house burn, and Tarzan watched them and wondered. He wondered what this Hollywood was like that it held such an appeal to these men and women. He thought that some day he might go and see for himself.

Over broken trails the return journey was made with ease and speed. Tarzan accompanied the safari through the Bansuto country, assuring them that they would have no trouble. 'I arranged that with Rungula before I left his village,' he explained.

Then he left them, saying that he was going on ahead to Jinja. He hastened to the village of Mpugu, where he had left Obroski. Mpugu met him with a long face. 'White bwana die seven days ago,' announced the chief. 'We take his body to Jinja so that the white men know that we did not kill him.'

Tarzan whistled. It was too bad, but there was nothing to do about it. He had done the best that he could for Obroski.

Two days later the Lord of the Jungle and Jad-bal-ja, the Golden Lion, stood on a low eminence and watched the long caravan of trucks wind toward Jinja.

In command of the rear guard walked Pat O'Grady. At his side was Balza. Each had an arm around the other, and Balza puffed on a cigarette.

CHAPTER THIRTY-THREE

Hello, Hollywood!

A year had passed.

A tall, bronzed man alighted from The Chief in the railroad station at Los Angeles. The easy, majestic grace of his carriage; his tread, at once silent and bold; his flowing muscles; the dignity of his mien; all suggested the leonine, as though he were, indeed, a personification of Numa, the lion.

A great throng of people crowded about the train. A cordon of good natured policemen held them back, keeping an aisle clear for the alighting passengers and for the great celebrity that all waited with such eagerness.

Cameras clicked and whirred for local papers, for news syndicates, for news reels; eager reporters, special correspondents, and sob-sisters pressed forward.

At last the crowd glimpsed the celebrity, and a great roar of welcome billowed into the microphones strategically placed by Freeman Lang.

A slip of a girl with green hair had alighted from The Chief; her publicity agent preceded her, while directly behind her were her three secretaries, who were followed by a maid leading a gorilla.

Instantly she was engulfed by the reporters. Freeman forced his way to her side. 'Won't you say just a word to all your friends of the air?' he asked, taking her by the arm. 'Right over here, please, dear.'

She stepped to the microphone. 'Hello, everybody! I wish you were all here. It's simply mahvellous. I'm so happy to be back in Hollywood.'

Freeman Lang took the microphone. 'Ladies and gentlemen,' he announced, 'you have just heard the voice of the most beautiful and most popular little lady in motion pictures today. You should see the crowds down here at the station to welcome her back to Hollywood. I've seen lots of these homecomings, but honestly folks I never saw anything like this before – all Los Angeles has turned out to greet B.O.'s beautiful star – the glorious Balza.'

There was a suspicion of a smile in the eyes of the bronzed stranger as he succeeded at last in making his way through the crowd to the street, where he hailed a taxi and asked to be driven to a hotel in Hollywood.

As he was registering at The Roosevelt, a young man leaning against the desk covertly noted his entry, John Clayton, London; and as Clayton followed the bell boy toward the elevator, the young man watched him, noting the tall figure, the broad shoulders, and the free, yet cat-like stride.

From the windows of his room Clayton looked down upon Hollywood Boulevard, upon the interminable cars gliding noiselessly east and west. He caught glimpses of tiny trees and little patches of lawn where the encroachment of shops had not obliterated them, and he sighed.

He saw many people riding in cars or walking on the cement sidewalks and the suggestion of innumerable people in the crowded, close built shops and residences; and he felt more alone than he ever had before in all his life.

The confining walls of the hotel room oppressed him; and he took the elevator to the lobby, thinking to go into the hills that he had seen billowing so close, to the north.

In the lobby a young man accosted him. 'Aren't you Mr Clayton?' he asked.

Clayton eyed the stranger closely for a moment before he replied. 'Yes, but I do not know you.'

'You have probably forgotten, but I met you in London.'

Clayton shook his head. 'I never forget.'

The young man shrugged and smiled. 'Pardon me, but nevertheless I recognized you. Here on business?' He was unembarrassed and unabashed.

'Merely to see Hollywood,' replied Clayton. 'I have heard so much about it that I wished to see it.'

'Got a lot of friends here, I suppose.'

'No one knows me here.'

'Perhaps I can be of service to you,' suggested the young man. 'I am an old timer here – been here two years. Nothing to do – glad to show you around. My name is Reece.'

Clayton considered for a moment. He had come to see Hollywood. A guide might be helpful. Why not this young man as well as someone else? 'It is kind of you,' he said.

'Well, then, how about a little lunch? I suppose you would like to see some of the motion picture celebrities – they all do.'

'Naturally!' admitted Clayton. 'They are the most interesting denizens of Hollywood.'

'Very well! We'll go to the Brown Derby. You'll see a lot of them there.'

As they alighted from a taxi in front of the Brown Derby, Clayton saw a crowd of people lined up on each side of the entrance. It reminded him of the crowds he had seen at the station welcoming the famous Balza.

'They must be expecting a very important personage,' he said to Reece.

'Oh, these boobs are here every day,' replied the young man.

The Brown Derby was crowded – well groomed men, beautifully gowned girls. There was something odd in the apparel, the ornaments, or the hair dressing of each, as though each was trying to out-do the others in attracting attention to himself. There was a great deal of chattering and calling back and forth between tables: 'How ah you?' 'How mahvellous you look!' 'How ah you?' 'See you at the Chinese tonight?' 'How ah you?'

Reece pointed out the celebrities to Clayton. One or two of the names were familiar to the stranger, but they all looked so much alike and talked so much alike, and said nothing when they did talk, that Clayton was soon bored. He was glad when the meal was over. He paid the check, and they went out.

'Doing anything this evening?' asked Reece.

'I have nothing planned.'

'Suppose we go to the première of Balza's latest picture, Soft Shoulders, at the Chinese. I have a ticket; and I know a fellow who can get you one, but it will probably cost you twenty-five smackers.' He eyed Clayton questioningly.

'Is it something that I ought to see if I am to see Hollywood?'

'Absolutely!'

A glare of lights illuminated the front of Grauman's Chinese Theater and the sky above, twenty thousand people milled and pushed and elbowed in Hollywood Boulevard, filling the street from building line to building line, a solid mass of humanity blocking all traffic. Policemen shouldered and sweated. Street cars were at a standstill. Clayton and Reece walked from The Roosevelt through the surging crowd.

As they approached the theater Clayton heard loud speakers broadcasting the arrival of celebrities who had left their cars two or three blocks away and forced their way through the mob to the forecourt of the theater.

The forecourt of the theater was jammed with spectators and autograph seekers. Several of the former had brought chairs; many had been sitting or standing there since morning that they might be assured of choice vantage spots from which to view the great ones of filmdom's capital.

As Clayton entered the forecourt, the voice of Freeman Lang was filling the boulevard from the loud speakers. 'The celebrities are coming thick and fast now. Naomi Madison is just getting out of her car – and there's her new husband with her, the Prince Mudini. And here comes the sweetest little girl, just coming into the forecourt now. It's Balza herself! I'll try to get her to say something to you. Oh, Sweetheart, come over here. My, how gorgeous you're looking tonight. Won't you say just a word to all your friends of the air? Right over here, please, dear.'

A dozen autograph pests were poking pencils and books toward Balza, but she quieted them with her most seductive smile and approached the microphone.

'Hello, everybody!' she lisped. 'I wish you were all here. It's simply mahvellous. I'm so happy to be back in Hollywood.'

Clayton smiled enigmatically, the crowd in the street roared its applause, and Freeman turned to greet the next celebrity. 'And here comes – well, he can't get through the crowd. Honestly, folks, this crowd is simply tremendous. We've officiated at a lot of premières, but we've never seen anything like this. The police can't hold 'em back. They're crowding right up here on top of the microphone. Yes, here he comes! Hello, there, Jimmie! Right over here. The folks want to hear from you. This is Jimmie Stone, second assistant production manager of the B.O. Studio, whose super feature, Soft Shoulders, is being premièred here tonight in Grauman's Chinese Theater.'

'Hello, efferybody. I wish you was all here. It's simply marvellous. Hello, Momma!'

'Let's go inside,' suggested Clayton.

'Well, Clayton, how did you like the picture?' asked Reece.

'The acrobats in the prologue were splendid,' replied the Englishman.

Reece looked a little crestfallen. Presently he brightened. 'I'll tell you what we'll do,' he announced. 'I'll get hold of a couple more fellows and we'll go to a party.'

'At this time of night?'

'Oh, it's early. There's Billy Brouke now. Hi, there, Billy! Say, I want you to meet Mr Clayton, an old friend of mine from London. Mr Clayton, this is Billy Brouke. How about a little party, Billy?'

'O.K. by me! We'll go in my car; it's parked around the corner.'

On a side street near Franklin they climbed into a flashy roadster. Brouke drove west a few blocks on Franklin and then turned up a narrow street that wound into the hills.

Clayton was troubled. 'Perhaps your friends may not be pleased if you bring a stranger,' he suggested.

Reece laughed. 'Don't worry,' he admonished; 'they'll be as glad to see you as they will be to see us.'

That made Brouke laugh, too. 'I'll say they will,' he commented.

Presently they came to the end of the street. 'Hell!' muttered Brouke and turned the car around. He turned into another street and followed that for a few blocks; then he turned back toward Franklin.

'Forgotten where your friends live?' asked Clayton.

On a side street in an otherwise quiet neighbourhood they sighted a brilliantly lighted house in front of which several cars were parked; laughter and the sounds of radio music were coming from an open window.

'This looks like the place,' said Reece.

'It is,' said Brouke with a grin, and drew up at the curb.

A Filipino opened the door in answer to their ring. Reece brushed in past him, and the others followed. A man and a girl were sitting on the stairs leading to the upper floor. They were attempting to kiss one another ardently without spilling the contents of the cocktail glasses they held. They succeeded in kissing one another, paying no attention to the newcomers.

To the right of the reception hall was a large living room in which several couples were dancing to the radio music; others were sprawled about on chairs and divans; all were drinking. There was a great deal of laughter.

'The party's getting good,' commented Brouke, as he led the way into the living room. 'Hello, everybody!' he cried. 'Where's the drinks? Come on, boys!' and he started for the back of the house, doing a little dance step on the way.

A middle-aged man, greying at the temples, rose from a divan and approached Reece. There was a puzzled expression on his face. 'I don't believe—' he started, but Brouke interrupted him.

'It's all right, old man!' he exclaimed. 'Sorry to be late. Shake hands with Mr Reece and Mr Clayton of London. How about a little drink?' and without waiting for an answer he headed for the kitchen. Reece and the host followed him, but Clayton hesitated. He had failed to note any exuberant enthusiasm in the attitude of the greying man whom he assumed to be the master of the house.

A tall blond, swaying a little, approached him. 'Haven't I met you somewhere before, Mr – ah—'

'Clayton,' he came to her rescue.

'How about a little dance?' she demanded. 'My boy friend,' she confided, as they swung into the rhythm of the music, 'passed out, and they had to put him to bed.'

She talked incessantly, but Clayton managed to ask her if she knew Rhonda Terry.

'Know Rhonda Terry! I should say I do. She's in Samoa now starring in her husband's new picture.'

'Her husband! Is she married?'

'Yes, she's married to Tom Orman, the director. Do you know her?'

'I met her once,' replied Clayton.

'She was all broken up over Stanley Obroski's death, but she finally snapped out of it and married Tom. Obroski sure made a name for himself in Africa. Say, that bunch is still talking about the way he killed lions and gorillas with one hand tied behind him.'

Clayton smiled politely.

After the dance she drew him over to a sofa on which two men were sitting. 'Abe,' she said to one of the men, 'here's a find for you. This is Mr Potkin, Mr Clayton, Abe Potkin, you know; and this is Mr Puant, Dan Puant, the famous scenarist.'

'We've been watching Mr Clayton,' replied Potkin.

'You'd better grab him,' advised the girl; 'you'll never find a better Tarzan.'

'He isn't exactly the type, but he might answer; I've been noticing him,' said Potkin. 'What do you think, Dan?'

'He's not my idea of Tarzan, but he might do.'

'Of course his face doesn't look like Tarzan; but he's big, and that's what I want,' replied Potkin.

'He hasn't a name; nobody ever heard of him, and you said you wanted a big name,' argued Puant.

'We'll use that platinum blond, Era Dessent, opposite him; she's got a lot of sex appeal and a big name.'

'I got an idea!' exclaimed Puant. 'I'll write the story around Dessent and some good looking juvenile, bring in another fem with "It" and a heavy with a big name; and we can use Clayton in long shots with apes for atmosphere.'

'That's a swell idea, Dan; get in a lot of sex stuff and a triangle and a ball-room or cabaret scene – a big one with a jazz orchestra. What we want is something different.'

'That ought to fix it so that we can use this fellow,' said Puant, 'for it won't make much difference who takes the part of Tarzan.'

'How about it, Mr Clayton?' inquired Potkin with an ingratiating smile.

At this juncture Reece and Brouke romped in from the kitchen, each with a bottle. The host was following, expostulating.

'Have a drink, everybody!' cried Brouke. 'The party's goin' stale.'

They passed about the room filling up glasses with neat bourbon or gin; sometimes they mixed them. They paused occasionally to take a drink themselves. Finally they disappeared into the hallway looking for other empty glasses.

'Well.' demanded Potkin, after the interruption had passed, 'how about it?'

Clayton eyed him questioningly. 'How about what?'

'I'm going to make a jungle picture,' explained Potkin. 'I got a contract for a Tarzan picture, and I want a Tarzan. I'll make a test of you tomorrow morning.'

'You think I might fill the rôle Tarzan of the Apes?' inquired Clayton, as a faint smile touched his lips.

'You ain't just what I want, but you might do. You see, Mr Puant, here, can write a swell Tarzan story even if we ain't got no Tarzan at all. And, say! It will make you. You ought almost to pay me for such a chance. But I tell you what I do; I like you, Mr Clayton; I give you fifty dollars a week, and look at all the publicity you get that it don't cost you nothing. You be over at the studio in the morning; and I make a test of you, eh?'

Clayton stood up. 'I'll think it over,' he said and started across the room.

A good-looking young woman came running in from the reception hall, Brouke was pursuing her. 'Leave me alone, you cad!' she cried.

The greying host was close behind Brouke. 'Leave my wife alone,' he shouted, 'and get out of here!'

Brouke gave the man a push that sent him staggering back against a chair, over which he fell in a heap next to the wall; then he seized the woman, lifted her in his arms, and ran out into the hall.

Clayton looked on in amazement. He turned and saw the girl, Maya, at his elbow. 'Your friend is getting a little rough,' she said.

'He is not my friend,' replied Clayton. 'I just met him this evening. He invited me to come to this party that is being given by a friend of his.'

The girl laughed. 'Friend of his!' she mimicked. 'Joe never saw any of you guys before. You—' she looked at him closely – 'you don't mean to say you didn't know you were crashing a party in a stranger's house!'

Clayton looked bewildered. 'They were not friends of these people?' he demanded. 'Why didn't they order us out? Why didn't they call the police?'

'And have the police find a kitchen full of booze? Quit your kidding, Big Boy.'

A woman's scream was wafted down from the upper floor. The host was staggering to his feet. 'My God, my wife!' he cried.

Clayton sprang into the hall and leaped up the stairs. He heard cries coming from behind a closed door; it was locked; he put his shoulder to it, and it flew open with a crash.

Inside the room a woman was struggling in the clutches of the drunken Brouke. Clayton seized the man by the scruff of the neck and tore him away. Brouke voiced a scream of pain and rage; then he turned upon Clayton, but he was helpless in the giant grip of those mighty muscles.

A police siren wailed in the distance. That seemed to sober Brouke. 'Drop me, you damn fool,' he cried; 'here come the police!'

Clayton carried the struggling man to the head of the stairs and pitched him down; then he turned back to the room where the woman lay on the floor where she had fallen. He raised her to her feet.

'Are you hurt?' he asked.

'No, just frightened. He was trying to make me tell him where I kept my jewels.'

The police siren sounded again, much closer now. 'You better get out. Joe's awful sore. He'll have all three of you arrested.'

Clayton glanced toward an open window, near which the branches of a great oak shone in the light from the street lamps in front of the house. He placed a foot upon the sill and leaped into the darkness. The woman screamed.

In the morning Clayton found Reece waiting for him in the lobby of the hotel. 'Great little party, eh, what?' demanded the young man.

'I thought you would be in jail,' said Clayton.

'Not a chance. Billy Brouke has a courtesy card from one of the Big Shots. Say, I see you're going to work for Abe Potkin, doing Tarzan.'

'Who told you that?'

'It's in Louella Parsons' column in the *Examiner*.'

'I'm not.'

'You're wise. But I'll tell you a good bet, if you are thinking of getting into movies. Prominent Pictures is casting a new Tarzan picture, and—'

A bell boy approached them. 'Telephone call for you, Mr Clayton,' he said.

Clayton stepped to the booth and picked up the receiver.

'This is Clayton.' he said.

'This is the casting office of Prominent Pictures. Can you come right over for an interview?'

'I'll think about it,' replied Clayton, and hung up.

'That was Prominent Pictures calling me,' he said as he rejoined Reece. 'They want me to come over for an interview.'

'You'd better go; if you get in with Prominent, you're made.'

'It might be interesting.'

'Think you could do Tarzan?'

'I might.'

'Dangerous part. I wouldn't want any of it in mine.'

'I think I'll go over.' He turned toward the street.

'Say, old man,' said Reece, 'could you let me have ten until Saturday?'

The casting director sized Clayton up. 'You look all right to me; I'll take you up to Mr Goldeen; he's production manager. Had any experience?'

'As Tarzan?'

The casting director laughed. 'I mean in pictures.'

'No.'

'Well, you might be all right at that. You don't have to be a Barrymore to play Tarzan. Come on, we'll go up to Mr Goldeen's office.'

They had to wait a few minutes in the outer office, and then a secretary ushered them in.

'Hello, Ben!' the casting director greeted Goldeen. 'think I've got just the man for you. This is Mr Clayton, Mr Goldeen.'

'For what?'

'For Tarzan.'

'Oh; m-m-m.'

Goldeen's eyes surveyed Clayton critically for an instant then the production manager made a gesture with his palm as though waving them away. He shook his head. 'Not the type,' he snapped. 'Not the type, at all.'

As Clayton followed the casting director from the room the shadow of a smile touched his lips.

'I'll tell you what,' said the casting director; 'there may be a minor part in it for you; I'll keep you in mind. If anything turns up, I'll give you a ring. Goodbye!'

Later in the day as Clayton was looking through an afternoon paper he saw a banner spread across the top of the theatrical page: CYRIL WAYNE TO DO TARZAN. FAMOUS ADAGIO DANCER SIGNED BY PROMINENT PICTURES FOR STELLAR ROLE IN FORTHCOMING PRODUCTION.

A week passed. Clayton was preparing to leave California and return home. The telephone in his room rang. It was the casting director at Prominent Pictures. 'Got a bit for you in the Tarzan picture,' he announced. 'Be at the studio at seven-thirty tomorrow morning.'

Clayton thought a moment. 'All right,' he said; 'seven-thirty.'

He felt that it might be an interesting experience that would round out his stay in Hollywood.

'Say, you,' shouted the assistant director, 'what's *your* name?'

'Clayton.'

'Oh, you're the guy that takes the part of the white hunter that Tarzan rescues from the lion.'

Cyril Wayne, garbed in a loin cloth, his body covered with brown make-up, was eyeing Clayton and whispering to the director, who now also turned and looked.

'Geeze!' exclaimed the director, 'He'll steal the picture. What dumb-egg ever cast him?'

'Can't you fake it?' asked Wayne.

'Sure, just a flash of him. We won't show his face at all. Let's get busy and rehearse the scene. Here, you, come over here. What's your name?'

'Clayton.'

'Listen, Clayton. You're supposed to be comin' straight toward the camera through this jungle in the first shot. You're scared stiff; you keep lookin' behind you. You're about all in, too; you stagger like you was about ready to fall down. You see, you're lost in the jungle. There's a lion stalkin' you. We'll cut the lion shots in. Then in the last scene the lion is right behind you – and the lion's really in this scene with you, but you needn't be scared; he won't hurt you. He's perfectly tame and gentle. You scream. You draw your knife. Your knees shake. Tarzan hears you and comes swinging through the trees. Say, is that double here that's goin' to swing through the trees for Cyril?' he interrupted himself to address his assistant. Assured that the double was on the set, he continued, 'The lion charges; Tarzan swings down between you and the lion. We get a close up of you there; keep your back to the camera. Then Tarzan leaps on the lion and kills it. Say, Eddie, has that lion tamer that's doublin' for Cyril in the kill got his make-up on even? He looked lousy in the rushes yesterday.'

'Everything's all O.K., Chief,' replied the assistant.

'All ready then – everybody!' yelled the director. 'Get in there, Clayton, and remember there's a lion behind you and you're scared stiff.'

The rehearsal was satisfactory and the first shots pleased the director; then came the big scene in which Wayne and Clayton and the lion appeared. The lion was large and handsome. Clayton admired him. The trainer cautioned them all that if anything went wrong they were to stand perfectly still, and under no circumstances was anyone to touch Leo.

The cameras were grinding; Clayton staggered and half fell. He looked fearfully behind him and uttered a scream of terror. Cyril Wayne dropped from the branch of a low tree just as the lion emerged from the jungle behind Clayton. And then something went wrong.

The lion voiced an ugly roar and crouched. Wayne, sensing danger and losing his head, bolted past Clayton; the lion charged. Leo would have passed Clayton, who had remained perfectly still, and pursued the fleeing Wayne; but then something else happened.

Clayton, realizing more than any of the others the danger that menaced the actor, sprang for the beast and leaped upon its back. A powerful arm encircled the lion's neck. The beast wheeled and struck at the man-thing clinging to it, but the terrible talons missed their mark. Clayton locked his legs beneath the sunken belly of the carnivore. The lion threw itself to the ground and lashed about in a frenzy of rage.

With his hideous growls mingled equally bestial growls from the throat of the man. The lion regained its feet and reared upon its hind legs. The knife that they had given Clayton flashed in the air. Once, twice, three times it was driven deep into the side of the frenzied beast; then Leo slumped to the ground, shuddered convulsively and lay still.

Clayton leaped erect; he placed one foot upon his kill and raised his face to the heavens; then he checked himself and that same slow smile touched his lips.

An excited man rushed onto the set. It was Benny Goldeen, the production manager.

'My God!' he cried. 'You've killed our best lion. He was worth ten thousand dollars if he was worth a cent. You're afired!'

The clerk at The Roosevelt looked up. 'Leaving us, Mr Clayton?' he asked politely. 'I hope you have enjoyed Hollywood.'

'Very much indeed,' replied Clayton; 'but I wonder if you could give me some information?'

'Certainly; what is it?'

'What is the shortest route to Africa?'

THE END

TARZAN AND THE LEOPARD MEN

CHAPTER ONE

Storm

The girl turned uneasily upon her cot. The fly, bellying in the rising wind, beat noisily against the roof of the tent. The guy ropes creaked as they tugged against their stakes. The unfastened flaps of the tent whipped angrily. Yet, in the midst of this growing pandemonium, the sleeper did not fully awaken. The day had been a trying one. The long, monotonous march through the sweltering jungle had left her exhausted, as had each of the weary marches that had preceded it through the terrible, gruelling days since she had left rail-head in that dim past that seemed now a dull eternity of suffering.

Perhaps she was less exhausted physically than before, as she was gradually becoming inured to the hardships; but the nervous strain of the past few days had taken its toll of energy since she had become aware of the growing insubordination of the black men who were her only companions on this rashly conceived and ill ordered safari.

Young, slight of build, accustomed to no sustained physical effort more gruelling than a round of golf, a few sets of tennis, or a morning canter on the back of a well-mannered mount, she had embarked upon this mad adventure without the slightest conception of the hardships and dangers that it would impose. Convinced almost from the first day that her endurance might not be equal to the heavy tax placed upon it, urged by her better judgment to turn back before it became too late, she had sturdily, and perhaps stubbornly, pushed on deeper and deeper into the grim jungle from which she had long since practically given up hope of extricating herself. Physically frail she might be for such an adventure, but no paladin of the Round Table could have boasted a sturdier will.

How compelling must be the exigency that urged her on! What necessity drove her from the paths of luxury and ease into the primeval forest and this unaccustomed life of danger, exposure, and fatigue? What ungovernable urge denied her the right of self-preservation now that she was convinced that her only chance of survival lay in turning back? Why had she come? Not to hunt; she had killed only under the pressure of necessity for food. Not to photograph the wildlife of the African hinterland; she possessed no camera. Not in the interests of scientific research; if she had ever had any scientific interest it had been directed principally upon the field of cosmetics, but even that had languished and expired in the face of the fierce equatorial sun and before an audience consisting exclusively of low browed, West African blacks. The riddle, then, remains a riddle as unfathomable and inscrutable as the level gaze of her brave grey eyes.

The forest bent beneath the heavy hand of Usha, the wind. Dark clouds obscured the heavens. The voices of the jungle were silenced. Not even the greatest of the savage beasts risked calling the attention of the mighty forces of Nature to their presence. Only the sudden flares of the windswept beast-fires illumined the camp in fitful bursts that wrought grotesquely dancing shadow-shapes from the prosaic impedimenta of the safari, scattered upon the ground.

A lone and sleepy askari, bracing his back against the growing gale, stood careless guard. The camp slept, except for him and one other; a great hulking black, who crept stealthily toward the tent of the sleeping girl.

Then the fury of the storm broke upon the crouching forest. Lightning flashed. Thunder boomed, and rolled, and boomed again. Rain fell. At first in great drops and then in solid, wind-sped sheets it enveloped the camp.

Even the sleep of utter exhaustion could not withstand this final assault of Nature. The girl awoke. In the vivid and almost incessant flashes of lightning she saw a man entering the tent. Instantly she recognised him. The great, hulking figure of Golato the headman might not easily be mistaken for another. The girl raised herself upon an elbow.

'Is there something wrong, Golato?' she asked. 'What do you want?'

'You, Kali Bwana,' answered the man huskily.

So it had come at last! For two days she had been dreading it, her fears aroused by the changed attitude of the man toward her; a change that was reflected in the thinly veiled contempt of the other members of her party for her orders, in the growing familiarities of their speech and actions. She had seen it in the man's eyes.

From a holster at the side of her cot she drew a revolver. 'Get out of here,' she said, 'or I'll kill you.'

For answer the man leaped toward her. Then she fired.

Moving from west to east, the storm cut in a swathe through the forest. In its wake lay a trail of torn and twisted branches, here and there an uprooted tree. It sped on, leaving the camp of the girl far behind.

In the dark a man crouched in the shelter of a great tree, protected from the full fury of the wind by its hoary bole. In the hollow of one of his arms something cuddled close to his naked hide for warmth. Occasionally he spoke to it and caressed it with his free hand. His gentle solicitude for it suggested that it might be a child, but it was not. It was a small, terrified, wholly miserable little monkey. Born into a world peopled by large, savage creatures with a predilection for tender monkey meat he had early developed, perhaps inherited, an inferiority feeling that had reduced his activities to a series of screaming flights from dangers either real or imaginary.

His agility, however, often imparted a certain appearance of reckless bravado in the presence of corporeal enemies from whom experience had taught him he could easily escape; but in the face of Usha, the wind, Ara, the lightning, and Pand, the thunder, from whom none might escape, he was reduced to the nadir of trembling hopelessness. Not even the sanctuary of the mighty arms of his master, from whose safe embrace he had often thrown insults into the face of Numa, the lion, could impart more than a fleeting sense of security.

He cowered and whimpered to each new gust of wind, each flash of lightning, each stunning burst of thunder. Suddenly the fury of the storm rose to the pinnacle of its Titanic might; there was the sound of rending wood from the ancient fibres of the jungle patriarch at whose foot the two had sought shelter. Catlike, from his squatting position, the man leaped to one side even as the great tree crashed to earth, carrying a half dozen of its neighbours with it. As he jumped he tossed the monkey from him, free of the branches of the fallen monarch. He, himself, was less fortunate. A far spreading limb struck him heavily upon the head and, as he fell, pinned him to the ground.

Whimpering, the little monkey crouched in an agony of terror while the tornado, seemingly having wrought its worst, trailed off toward the east and new conquests. Presently, sensing the departure of the storm, he crept fearfully in search of his master, calling to him plaintively from time to time. It was dark. He could see nothing beyond a few feet from the end of his generous, sensitive nose. His master did not answer and that filled the little monkey with dire forebodings; but presently he found him beneath the fallen tree, silent and lifeless.

Nyamwegi had been the life of the party in the little thatched village of Kibbu, where he had gone from his own village of Tumbai to court a dusky belle. His vanity flattered by the apparent progress of his suit and by the very evident impression that his wit and personality had made upon the company of young people before whom he had capered and boasted, he had ignored the passage of time until the sudden fall of the equatorial night had warned him that he had long overstayed the time allowed him by considerations of personal safety.

Several miles of grim and forbidding forest separated the villages of Kibbu and Tumbai. They were miles fraught by night with many dangers, not the least of which to Nyamwegi were the most unreal, including, as they did, the ghosts of departed enemies and the countless demons that direct the destinies of human life, usually with malign intent.

He would have preferred to remain the night in Kibbu as had been suggested by his inamorata; but there was a most excellent reason why he could not, a reason that transcended in potency even the soft blandishments of a sweetheart or the terrors of the jungle night. It was a tabu that had been placed upon him by the witch-doctor of Tumbai for some slight transgression when the latter had discovered that, above all things, Nyamwegi would doubtless wish to spend many nights in Kibbu village. For a price the tabu might be lifted, a fact which doubtless had more to do with its imposition than the sin it purported to punish; but then, of course, the church must live – in Africa as elsewhere. The tragedy lay in the fact that Nyamwegi did not have the price; and tragedy indeed it proved for poor Nyamwegi.

On silent feet the young warrior followed the familiar trail toward Tumbai. Lightly he carried his spear and shield, at his hip swung a heavy knife; but of what potency were such weapons against the demons of the night? Much more efficacious was the amulet suspended about his neck, which he fingered often as he mumbled prayers to his 'muzimo,' the protecting spirit of the ancestor for whom he had been named.

He wondered if the girl were worth the risk, and decided that she was not.

Kibbu village lay a mile behind when the storm overtook Nyamwegi. At first his anxiety to reach Tumbai and his fear of the night urged him on despite the buffetings of the gale; but at last he was forced to seek what shelter he could beneath a giant tree, where he remained until the greatest fury of the elements had subsided, though the lightning was still illuminating the forest as he pushed on. Thus the storm became his undoing, for where he might have passed unnoticed in the darkness the lightning revealed his presence to whatever enemy might be lurking along the trail.

He was already congratulating himself that half the journey had been accomplished when, without warning, he was seized from behind. He felt sharp talons sink into his flesh. With a scream of pain and terror he wheeled to extricate himself from the clutches of the thing that had seized him, the terrifying, voiceless thing that made no sound. For an instant he succeeded in breaking the hold upon his shoulders and as he turned, reaching for his knife, the lightning flashed, revealing to his horrified eyes a hideous human face surmounted by the head of a leopard.

Nyamwegi struck out blindly with his knife in the ensuing darkness, and simultaneously he was seized again from behind by rending talons that sank into his chest and abdomen as the creature encircled him with hairy arms. Again vivid lightning brought into high relief the tragic scene. Nyamwegi could not see the creature that gripped him from behind; but he saw three others menacing him in front and on either side, and he abandoned hope as he recognised his assailants, from their leopard skins and masks, as members of the feared secret order of Leopard Men.

Thus died Nyamwegi the Utenga.

CHAPTER TWO
The Hunter

The dawn-light danced among the tree tops above the grass-thatched huts of the village of Tumbai as the chief's son, Orando, arose from his crude pallet of straw and stepped out into the village street to make an offering to his 'muzimo,' the spirit of the long dead ancestor for whom he had been named, preparatory to setting out upon a day of hunting. In his outstretched palm he held an offering of fine meal as he stood like an ebony statue, his face upturned toward the heavens.

'My namesake, let us go to the hunt together.' He spoke as one might who addresses a familiar but highly revered friend. 'Bring the animals near to me and ward off from me all danger. Give me meat today, oh, hunter!'

The trail that Orando followed as he set forth alone to hunt was for a couple of miles the same that led to Kibbu village. It was an old, familiar trail; but the storm of the preceding night had wrought such havoc with it that in many places it was as unrecognisable as it was impassable. Several times fallen trees forced him to make detours into the heavy underbrush that often bordered the trail upon each side. It was upon such an occasion that his attention was caught by the sight of a human leg protruding from beneath the foliage of a newly uprooted tree.

Orando halted in his tracks and drew back. There was a movement of the foliage where the man lay. The warrior poised his light hunting spear, yet at the same time he was ready for instant flight. He had recognised the bronzed flesh as that of a white man and Orando, the son of Lobongo, the chief, knew no white man as friend. Again the foliage moved, and the head of a diminutive monkey was thrust through the tangled verdure.

As its frightened eyes discovered the black man the little creature voiced a scream of fright and disappeared beneath the foliage of the fallen tree, only to reappear again a moment later upon the opposite side where it climbed up into the branches of a jungle giant that had successfully withstood the onslaughts of the storm. Here, far above the ground, in fancied security, the small one perched upon a swaying limb and loosed the vials of its wrath upon Orando.

But the hunter accorded it no further attention. Today he was not hunting little monkeys, and for the moment his interest was focussed upon the suggestion of tragedy contained in that single, bronzed leg. Creeping cautiously forward, Orando stooped to look beneath the great mass of limbs and leaves that concealed the rest of the body from his view, for he must satisfy his curiosity.

He saw a giant white man, naked but for a loin cloth of leopard skin, pinned to the ground by one of the branches of the fallen tree. From the face turned toward him two grey eyes surveyed him; the man was not dead.

Orando had seen but few white men; and those that he had seen had worn strange, distinctive apparel. They had carried weapons that vomited smoke, and flame, and metal. This one was clothed as any native warrior might have been, nor was there visible any of those weapons that Orando hated and feared.

Nevertheless the stranger was white and, therefore, an enemy. It was possible that he might extricate himself from his predicament and, if he did, become a menace to the village of Tumbai. Naturally, therefore, there was but one thing for a warrior and the son of a chief to do. Orando fitted an arrow to his bow. The killing of this man meant no more to him than would have the killing of the little monkey.

'Come round to the other side,' said the stranger; 'your arrow cannot reach my heart from that position.'

Orando dropped the point of his missile and surveyed the speaker in surprise, which was engendered, not so much by the nature of his command, as by the fact that he had spoken in the dialect of Orando's own people.

'You need not fear me,' continued the white, noticing Orando's hesitation, 'I am held fast by this branch and cannot harm you.'

What sort of man was this? Had he no fear of death? Most men would have begged for their lives. Perhaps this one sought death.

'Are you badly injured?' demanded Orando.

'I think not. I feel no pain.'

'Then why do you wish to die?'

'I do not wish to die.'

'But you told me to come around and shoot you in the heart. Why did you say that if you do not wish to die?'

'I know that you are going to kill me. I asked you to make sure that your first arrow enters my heart. Why should I suffer pain needlessly?'

'And you are not afraid to die?'

'I do not know what you mean.'

'You do not know what fear is?'

'I know the word, but what has it to do with death? All things die. Were you to tell me that I must live forever, then I might feel fear.'

'How it is that you speak the language of the Utengas?' demanded Orando. The man shook his head. 'I do not know.'

'Who are you?' Orando's perplexity was gradually becoming tinged with awe. 'I do not know,' replied the stranger.

'From what country do you come?'

Again the man shook his head. 'I do not know.'

'What will you do if I release you?'

'And do not kill me?' queried the white.

'No, not kill you.'

The man shrugged. 'What is there to do? I shall hunt for food because I am hungry. Then I shall find a place to lie up and sleep.'

'You will not kill me?'

'Why should I? If you do not try to kill me I shall not try to kill you.'

The black warrior wormed his way through the tangled branches of the fallen tree to the side of the pinioned white man, where he found that a single branch resting across the latter's body prevented the prisoner from getting his arms, equipped with giant muscles, into any position where he might use them effectively for his release. It proved, however, a comparatively easy matter for Orando to raise the limb the few inches necessary to permit the stranger to worm his body from beneath it, and a moment later the two men faced one another beside the fallen tree while a little monkey chattered and grimaced from the safety of the foliage above them.

Orando felt some doubt as to the wisdom of his rash act. He could not satisfactorily explain what had prompted him to such humane treatment of a stranger, yet despite his doubts something seemed to assure him that he had acted wisely. However, he held his spear in readiness and watched the white giant before him with a cautious eye.

From beneath the tree that had held him prisoner the man recovered his weapons, a bow and spear. Over one shoulder hung a quiver of arrows; across the other was coiled a long, fibre rope. A knife swung in a sheath at his hip. His belongings recovered, he turned to Orando.

'Now we hunt,' agreed Orando.

'Where?'

'I know where the pigs feed in the morning and where they lie up in the heat of the day,' said Orando.

As they spoke Orando had been appraising the stranger. He noted the clean-cut features, the magnificent physique. The flowing muscles that rolled beneath a skin sun-tanned almost to the hue of his own impressed him by their suggestion of agility and speed combined with great strength. A shock of black hair partially framed a face of rugged, masculine beauty from which two steady, grey eyes surveyed the world fearlessly. Over the left temple was a raw gash (legacy of the storm's fury) from which blood had flowed, and dried in the man's hair and upon his cheek. In moments of silence his brows were often drawn together in thought, and there was a puzzled expression in his eyes. At such times he impressed Orando as one who sought to recall something he had forgotten; but what it was, the man did not divulge.

Orando led the way along the trail that still ran in the direction of Kibbu village. Behind him came his strange companion upon feet so silent that the black occasionally cast a backward glance to assure himself that the white man had not deserted him. Close above them the little monkey swung through the trees, chattering and jabbering.

Presently Orando heard another voice directly behind him that sounded like another monkey speaking in lower tones than those of the little fellow above them. He turned his head to see where the other monkey, sounding so close, could be. To his astonishment he saw that the sounds issued from the throat of the man behind him. Orando laughed aloud. Never before had he seen a man who could mimic the chattering of monkeys so perfectly. Here, indeed, was an accomplished entertainer.

But Orando's hilarity was short-lived. It died when he saw the little monkey leap nimbly from an over-hanging branch to the shoulder of the white man and heard the two chattering to one another, obviously carrying on a conversation.

What sort of man was this, who knew no fear, who could speak the language of the monkeys, who did not know who he was, nor where he came from? This question, which he could not answer, suggested another equally unanswerable, the mere consideration of which induced within Orando qualms of uneasiness. 'Was this creature a mortal man at all?'

This world into which Orando had been born was peopled by many creatures, not the least important and powerful of which were those that no man ever saw, but which exercised the greatest influence upon those one might see. There were demons so numerous that one might not count them all, and the spirits of the dead who more often than not were directed by demons whose purposes, always malign, they carried out. These demons and sometimes the spirits of the dead occasionally took possession of the body of a living creature, controlling its thoughts, its actions and its speech. Why, right in the river that flowed past the village of Tumbai dwelt a demon to which the villagers had made offerings of food for many years. It had assumed the likeness of a crocodile, but it had deceived no one; least of all the old witch-doctor who had recognised it immediately for what it was after the chief had threatened him with death when his charms had failed to frighten it away or his amulets to save villagers from its voracious jaws. It was easy, therefore, for Orando to harbour suspicions concerning the creature moving noiselessly at his heels.

A feeling of uneasiness pervaded the son of the chief. This was somewhat mitigated by the consciousness that he had treated the creature in a friendly way and, perhaps, earned its approbation. How fortunate it was that he had reconsidered his first intention of loosing an arrow into its body! That would have been fatal; not for the creature but for Orando. It was quite obvious now why the stranger had not feared death, knowing that, being a demon, it could not die. Slowly it was all becoming quite clear to the black hunter, but he did not know whether to be elated or terrified. To be the associate of a demon might be a distinction, but it also had its distressing aspects. One never knew what a demon might be contemplating, though it was reasonably certain to be nothing good.

Orando's further speculations along this line were rudely interrupted by a sight that met his horrified gaze at a turning of the trail. Before his eyes lay the dead and mutilated body of a warrior. The hunter required no second glance to recognise in the upturned face the features of his friend and comrade, Nyamwegi. But how had he come to his death?

The stranger came and stood at Orando's side, the little monkey perched upon his shoulder. He stooped and examined the body of Nyamwegi, turning the corpse over upon its face, revealing the cruel marks of steel claws.

'The Leopard Men,' he remarked briefly and without emotion, as one might utter the most ordinary commonplace.

But Orando was bursting with emotion. Immediately when he had seen the body of his friend he had thought of the Leopard Men, though he had scarcely dared to acknowledge his own thought, so fraught with terror was the very suggestion. Deeply implanted in his mind was fear of this dread secret society, the weird cannibalistic rites of which seemed doubly horrible because they could only be guessed at, no man outside their order ever having witnessed them and lived.

He saw the characteristic mutilation of the corpse, the parts cut away for the cannibalistic orgy of which they would be the 'piece de resistance.' Orando saw and shuddered; but, though he shuddered, in his heart was more of rage than of fear. Nyamwegi had been his friend. From infancy they had grown to manhood together. Orando's soul cried out for vengeance against the fiends who had perpetrated this vile outrage, but what could one man do alone against many? The maze of footsteps in the soft earth about the corpse indicated that Nyamwegi had been overcome by numbers.

The stranger, leaning on his spear, had been silently watching the black warrior, noting the signs of grief and rage reflected in the mobile features.

'You knew him?' he asked.

'He was my friend.'

The stranger made no comment, but turned and followed a trail that ran toward the south Orando hesitated. Perhaps the demon was leaving him. Well, in a way that would be a relief; but, after all, he had not been a bad demon, and certainly there was something about him that inspired confidence and a sense of security. Then, too, it was something to be able to fraternise with a demon and, perhaps, to show him off in the village. Orando followed.

'Where are you going?' he called after the retreating figure of the giant white.

'To punish those who killed your friend.'

'But they are many,' remonstrated Orando. 'They will kill us.'

'They are four,' replied the stranger. 'I kill.'

'How do you know there are but four?' demanded the black.

The other pointed to the trail at his feet. 'One is old and limps,' he said; 'One is tall and thin; the other two are young warriors. They step lightly, although one of them is a large man.'

'You have seen them?'

'I have seen their spoor; that is enough.'

Orando was impressed. Here, indeed, was a tracker of the first order; but perhaps he possessed something of a higher order than human skill. The thought thrilled Orando; but if it caused him a little fear, too, he no longer hesitated. He had cast his lot, and he would not turn back now.

'At least we can see where they go,' he said. 'We can follow them to their village, and afterward we can return to Tumbai, where my father, the chief, lives. He will send runners through the Watenga country; and the war drums will boom, summoning the Utenga warriors. Then will we go and make war upon the village of the Leopard Men, that Nyamwegi may be avenged in blood.'

The stranger only grunted and trotted on. Sometimes Orando, who was rated a good tracker by his fellows, saw no spoor at all; but the white demon never paused, never hesitated. The black marvelled and his admiration grew; likewise his awe. He had leisure to think now, and the more he thought the more convinced he was that this was no mortal who guided him through the jungle upon the trail of the Leopard Men. If it were, indeed, a demon, then it was a most remarkable demon, for by no word or sign had it indicated any malign purpose. It was then, engendered by this line of reasoning, that a new and brilliant thought illuminated the mind of Orando like a bright light bursting suddenly through darkness. This creature, being nothing mortal, must be the protecting spirit of that departed ancestor for whom Orando had been named – his 'muzimo.'

Instantly all fear left the black warrior. Here was a friend and a protector. Here was the very 'namesake' whose aid he had invoked before setting out upon the hunt, he whom he had propitiated with a handful of meal. Suddenly Orando regretted that the offering had not been larger. A handful of meal seemed quite inadequate to appease the hunger of the powerful creature trotting tirelessly ahead of him, but perhaps 'muzimos' required less food than mortals. That seemed quite reasonable, since they were but spirits. Yet Orando distinctly recalled that before he had released the creature from beneath the tree it had stated that it wished to hunt for food as it was hungry.

Oh, well, perhaps there were many things concerning 'muzimos' that Orando did not know; so why trouble his head about details? It was enough that this must be his 'muzimo.' He wondered if the little monkey perched upon his 'muzimo's' shoulder was also a spirit. Perhaps it was Nyamwegi's ghost. Were not the two very friendly, as he and Nyamwegi had been throughout their lives? The thought appealed to Orando, and henceforth he thought of the little monkey as Nyamwegi. Now it occurred to him to test his theory concerning the white giant.

'Muzimo!' he called.

The stranger turned his head and looked about. 'Why did you call "muzimo"?' he demanded.

'I was calling you, Muzimo,' replied Orando.

'Is that what you call me?'

'Yes.'

'What do you want?'

Now Orando was convinced that he had made no mistake. What a fortunate man he was! How his fellows would envy him!

'Why did you call to me?' insisted the other.

'Do you think we are close to the Leopard Men, Muzimo?' inquired Orando, for want of any better question to ask.

'We are gaining on them, but the wind is in the wrong direction. I do not like to track with the wind at my back, for then Usha can run ahead and tell those I am tracking that I am on their trail.'

'What can we do about it?' demanded Orando. 'The wind will not change for me, but perhaps you can make it blow in a different direction.'

'No,' replied the other, 'but I can fool Usha, the wind. That I often do. When I am hunting upwind I can remain on the ground in safety, for then Usha can only carry tales to those behind me, for whom I care nothing; but when I hunt downwind I travel through the trees, and Usha carries my scent spoor above the head of my quarry. Or sometimes I move swiftly and circle the hunted one, and then Usha comes down to my nostrils and tells me where it is. Come!' The stranger swung lightly to the low-hanging branch of a great tree.

'Wait!' cried Orando. 'I cannot travel through the trees.'

'Go upon the ground, then. I will go ahead through the trees and find the Leopard Men.'

Orando would have argued the wisdom of this plan; but the white disappeared amidst the foliage, the little monkey clinging tightly to its perch upon his shoulder.

'That,' thought Orando, 'is the last that I shall see of my "muzimo." When I tell this in the village they will not believe me. They will say that Orando is a great liar.'

Plain before him now lay the trail of the Leopard Men. It would be easy to follow; but, again, what could one man hope to accomplish against four, other than his own death? Yet Orando did not think of turning back. Perhaps he could not, alone, wreak his vengeance upon the slayers of Nyamwegi; but he could, at least, track them to their village, and later lead the warriors of Lobongo, the chief, his father, in battle against it.

The black warrior moved tirelessly in a rhythmic trot that consumed the miles with stubborn certainty, relieving the monotony by reviewing the adventures of the morning. Thoughts of his 'muzimo' occupied his mind almost to the exclusion of other subjects. Such an adventure was without parallel in the experience of Orando, and he enjoyed dwelling upon every phase of it. He recalled, almost with the pride of personal possession, the prowess of this other self of his from the spirit world. Its every mannerism and expression was photographed indelibly upon his memory; but that which impressed him most was an indefinable something in the steel-grey eyes, a haunting yearning that suggested a constant effort to recall an illusive memory.

What was his 'muzimo' trying to recall? Perhaps it was the details of his earthly existence. Perchance he sought to conjure once again the reactions of the flesh to worldly stimuli. Doubtless he regretted his spirit state and longed to live again – to live and fight and love.

With such thoughts as their accompaniment the miles retreated beneath his pounding feet. With such thoughts his mind was occupied to the exclusion of matters which should have concerned him more. For instance, he did not note how fresh the spoor of his quarry had become. In puddles left by the rain of the previous night and roiled by the passage of feet the mud had not yet settled when Orando passed; in places the earth at the edges of footprints was still falling back into the depressions but these things Orando failed to note, though he was accounted a good tracker. It is well that a man should keep his mind concentrated upon a single thing at a time unless he has a far more elastic mind than Orando. One may not dream too long in the savage jungle.

When Orando came suddenly into a small, natural clearing he failed to notice a slight movement of the surrounding jungle foliage. Had he, he would have gone more cautiously; and doubtless his jungle-craft would have suggested the truth, even though he could not have seen the four pairs of greedy, malevolent eyes that watched him from behind the concealing verdure; but when he reached the centre of the clearing he saw all that he should have guessed before, as, with savage cries, four hideously caparisoned warriors leaped into the open and sprang toward him.

Never before had Orando, the son of Lobongo, seen one of the feared and hated members of the dread society of Leopard Men; but as his eyes fell upon these four there was no room for doubt as to their identity. And then they closed upon him.

CHAPTER THREE
Dead Men who Spoke

As the girl fired, Golato voiced a cry of pain, wheeled and dashed from the tent, his left hand grasping his right arm above the elbow. Then Kali Bwana arose and dressed, strapping a cartridge belt, with its holster and gun, about her hips. There could be no more thought of sleep that night, for even though Golato might be 'hors de combat' there were others to be feared almost as much as he.

She lighted a lantern and, seated in a camp-chair with her rifle across her knees, prepared to spend the remainder of the night in wakeful watching; but if she anticipated any further molestation she was agreeably disappointed. The night dragged its interminable length until outraged Nature could be no longer denied, and presently the girl dozed in her chair

When she awoke the new sun was an hour old. The storm had passed leaving only mud and soggy canvas in its wake to mark its passage across the camp. The girl stepped to the flap of her tent and called to her 'boy' to prepare her bath and her breakfast. She saw the porters preparing the loads. She saw Golato, his arm roughly bandaged and supported in a crude sling. She saw her 'boy' and called to him again, this time peremptorily: but he ignored her summons and went on with the roping of a pack. Then she crossed over to him, her eyes flashing.

'You heard me call you, Imba,' she said. 'Why did you not come and prepare my bath and my breakfast?'

The fellow, a middle-aged man of sullen demeanour, scowled and hung his head. Golato, surly and glowering, looked on. The other members of the safari had stopped their work and were watching, and among them all there was not a friendly eye.

'Answer me, Imba,' commanded the girl. 'Why do you refuse to obey me?'

'Golato is headman,' was the surly rejoinder. 'He gives orders. Imba obey Golato.'

'Imba obeys me,' snapped Kali Bwana. 'Golato is no longer headman.' She drew her gun from its holster and let the muzzle drop on Imba. 'Get my bath ready. Last night it was dark. I could not see well, so I only shot Golato in the arm. This morning, I can see to shoot straighter. Now move!'

Imba cast an imploring glance in the direction of Golato, but the ex-headman gave him no encouragement. Here was a new Kali Bwana, bringing new conditions, to which Golato's slow mind had not yet adapted itself. Imba moved sheepishly toward the tent of his mistress. The other blacks muttered in low tones among themselves.

Kali Bwana had found herself, but it was too late. The seeds of discontent and mutiny were too deeply sown; they had already germinated, and although she might wrest a fleeting victory the end could bring only defeat. She had the satisfaction, however, of seeing Imba prepare her bath and, later, her breakfast; but while she was eating the latter she saw her porters up-loading, preparatory to departure, although her own tent had not been struck, nor had she given any orders for marching.

'What is the meaning of this?' she demanded, walking quickly to where the men were gathered. She did not address Golato, but another who had been his lieutenant and whom she had intended appointing headman in his place.

'We are going back,' replied the man.

'You cannot go back and leave me alone,' she insisted.

'You may come with us,' said the black. 'But you will have to look after yourself,' he added.

'You shall not do anything of the sort,' cried the girl, thoroughly exasperated. 'You agreed to accompany me wherever I went. Put down your loads, and wait until you get marching orders from me.'

As the men hesitated she drew her revolver. It was then that Golato interfered. He approached her with the askaris, their rifles ready. 'Shut up, white woman,' he snarled, 'and get back to your tent. We are going back to our own country. If you had been good to Golato this would not have happened; but you were not, and this is your punishment. If you try to stop us these men will kill you. You may come with us, but you will give no orders. Golato is master now.'

'I shall not go with you, and if you desert me here you know what your punishment will be when I get back to rail-head and report the matter to the commissioner.'

'You will never get back,' replied Golato sullenly. Then he turned to the waiting porters and gave the command to march.

It was with sinking heart that the girl saw the party file from camp and disappear in the forest. She might have followed, but pride had a great deal to do with crystalising her decision not to. Likewise, her judgment assured her that she would be far from safe with this sullen, mutinous band at whose head was as great a menace to her personal safety as she might find in all Africa. Again, there was the pertinacity of purpose that had kept her forging ahead upon her hopeless mission long after mature judgment had convinced her of its futility. Perhaps it was no more than ordinary stubbornness; but whatever it was it held her to what she conceived to be her duty, even though it led to what she now knew must be almost certain death.

Wearily she turned back toward her tent and the single load of provisions they had left behind for her sustenance. What was she to do? She could not go on, and she would not go back. There was but a single alternative. She must remain here, establishing a permanent camp as best she could, and await the remotely possible relief party that might come after long, long months.

She was confident that her safari could not return to civilisation without her and not arouse comment and investigation; and when investigation was made someone at least among all those ignorant, black porters would divulge the truth. Then there would be a searching party organised unless Golato succeeded with his lying tongue in convincing them that she was already dead. There was a faint hope, however, and to that she would cling. If, perchance, she could cling to life also during the long wait she might be saved at the last.

Taking stock of the provisions that the men had left behind for her, she found that she had enough upon which to subsist for a month, provided that she exercised scrupulous economy in their use. If game proved plentiful and her hunting was successful, this time might be indefinitely prolonged. Starvation, however, was not the only menace that she apprehended nor the most dreaded. There were prowling carnivores against which she had little defence to offer. There was the possibility of discovery by unfriendly blacks. There was always the danger (and this she dreaded most) of being stricken by one of the deadly jungle fevers.

She tried to put such thoughts from her mind, and to do so she occupied herself putting her camp in order, dragging everything perishable into her tent and finally, commencing the construction of a crude 'boma' as a protection against the prowlers of the night. The work was fatiguing, necessitating frequent rests, during which she wrote in her diary, to which she confided nothing of the fears that assailed her, fears that she dreaded admitting, even to herself. Instead, she confined herself to a narration of the events of the past few days since she had last written. Thus she occupied her time as Fate marshalled the forces that were presently to drag her into a situation more horrible than any that she could possibly have conceived.

As the four, clothed in the leopard skins of their order, closed upon Orando there flashed to the mind of the son of the chief a vision of the mutilated corpse of his murdered friend; and in that mental picture he saw a prophecy of his own fate; but he did not flinch. He was a warrior, with a duty to perform. These were the murderers of his comrade, the enemies of his people. He would die, of that he was certain; but first he would avenge Nyamwegi. The enemy should feel the weight of the wrath of a Utenga fighting-man.

The four Leopard Men were almost upon him as he launched his spear. With a scream one of the foemen dropped, pierced by the sharp tip of the

Utenga's weapon. Fortunate it was for Orando that the methods of the Leopard Men prescribed the use of their improvised steel claws as weapons in preference to spears or arrows, which they resorted to only in extremities or when faced by superior numbers. The flesh for their unholy rites must die beneath their leopard claws, or it was useless for religious purposes. Maddened by fanaticism, they risked death to secure the coveted trophies. To this Orando owed the slender chance he had to overcome his antagonists. But at best the respite from death could be but brief.

The remaining three pressed closer, preparing for the lethal charge in simulation of the carnivore they personified. Silence enveloped the jungle, as though Nature awaited with bated breath the consummation of this savage tragedy. Suddenly the quiet was shattered by the scream of a monkey in a tree overhanging the clearing. The sound came from behind Orando. He saw the two opponents who were facing him dart startled glances beyond him. He heard a scream that forced his attention rearward in a brief glance, and what he saw brought the sudden joy of an unexpected reprieve from death. In the grasp of his 'muzimo', the third of the surviving Leopard Men was struggling impotently against death.

Then Orando wheeled again to face his remaining enemies, while, from behind him, came savage growls that stiffened the hairs upon his scalp. What new force had been thus suddenly injected into the grim scene? He could not guess, nor could he again risk even a brief backward glance. His whole attention was now required by the hideous creatures sneaking toward him, their curved, steel talons opened, claw-like, to seize him.

The action that is so long in the telling occupied but a few seconds of actual time. A shriek mingled with the growls that Orando had heard. The Leopard Men leaped swiftly toward him. A figure brushed past him from the rear and, with a savage growl, leaped upon the foremost Leopard Man. It was Orando's 'muzimo'. The heart of the black warrior missed a beat as he realised that those beast-like sounds had issued from the throat of his 'namesake'. But if the fact perturbed Orando it utterly demoralised the fourth antagonist who had been advancing upon him, with the result that the fellow wheeled and bolted for the jungle, leaving the sole survivor of his companions to his fate.

Orando was free now to come to the aid of his 'muzimo', who was engaged with the larger of the two younger Leopard Men; but he quickly realised that his 'muzimo' required no aid. In a grip of steel he held the two clawed hands, while his free hand grasped the throat of his antagonist. Slowly but as inexorably as Fate he was choking the life from the struggling blackman. Gradually his victim's efforts grew weaker, until suddenly, with a convulsive shudder, the body went limp. Then the white cast it aside. For a moment he stood gazing at it, a puzzled expression upon his face; and then, apparently mechanically, he advanced slowly to its side and placed a foot upon it. The reaction was instantaneous and remarkable. Doubt and hesitation were suddenly swept from the noble features of the giant to be replaced by an expression of savage exultation as he lifted his face to the heavens and gave voice to a cry so awesome that Orando felt his knees tremble beneath him.

The Utenga had heard that cry before, far in the depths of the forest, and knew it for what it was; the victory cry of the bull ape. But why was his 'muzimo' voicing the cry of a beast? Here was something that puzzled Orando quite as much as had the materialisation of this ancestral spirit. There had never been any doubt in his mind as to the existence of 'muzimos.' Everyone possessed a 'muzimo,' but there were certain attributes that all men attributed to 'muzimos,' and all these were human attributes. Never in his life had Orando heard it even vaguely hinted that 'muzimos' growled like Simba, the lion, or screamed as the bull apes scream when they have made a kill. He was troubled and puzzled. Could it be that his 'muzimo' was also the 'muzimo' of some dead lion and departed ape? And if such were the case might it not be possible that, when actuated by the spirit of the lion or the ape, instead of by that of Orando's ancestor, he would become a menace instead of a blessing?

Suspiciously, now, Orando watched his companion, noting with relief the transition of the savage facial expression to that of quiet dignity that normally marked his mien. He saw the little monkey that had fled to the trees during the battle return to the shoulder of the 'muzimo,' and considering this an accurate gauge of the latter's temper he approached, though with some trepidation.

'Muzimo,' he ventured timidly, 'you came in time and saved the life of Orando. It is yours.'

The white was silent. He seemed to be considering this statement. The strange, half bewildered expression returned to his eyes.

'Now I remember,' he said presently. 'You saved my life. That was a long time ago.'

'It was this morning, Muzimo.'

The white man shook his head and passed a palm across his brow.

'This morning,' he repeated thoughtfully. 'Yes, and we were going to hunt. I am hungry. Let us hunt.'

'Shall we not follow the one who escaped?' demanded Orando. 'We were going to track the Leopard Men to their village, that my father, the chief, might lead the Utengas against it.'

'First let us speak with the dead men,' said Muzimo. 'We shall see what they have to tell us.'

'You can speak with the dead?' Orando's voice trembled at the suggestion.

'The dead do not speak with words,' explained Muzimo; 'but nevertheless they often have stories to tell. We shall see. This one,' he continued, after a brief inspection of the corpse of the man he had killed last, 'is the larger of the two young men. There lies the tall thin man, and yonder, with your spear through his heart, is he who limped, an old man with a crippled leg. These three, then, have told us that he who escaped is the smaller of the two young men.'

Now, more carefully, he examined each of the corpses, noting their weapons and their ornaments, dumping the contents of their pouches upon the ground. These he scanned carefully, paying particular attention to the amulets of the dead men. In a large package carried by the crippled old man, he found parts of a human body.

'There is no doubt now but that these were the killers of Nyamwegi,' said Orando; 'for these are the same parts that were removed from his body.'

'There was never any doubt,' asserted Muzimo confidently. 'The dead men did not have to tell me that.'

'What have they told you, Muzimo?'

'Their filed teeth have told me that they are eaters of men; their amulets and the contents of their pouches have told me that their village lies upon the banks of a large river. They are fishermen; and they fear Gimla, the crocodile, more than they fear aught else. The hooks in their pouches tell me the one and their amulets the other. From their ornaments and weapons, by the cicatrices upon their foreheads and chins I know their tribe and the country it inhabits. I do not need to follow the young warrior; his friends have told me where he is going. Now we may hunt. Later we can go to the village of the Leopard Men.'

'Even as I prayed today before setting out from the village, you have protected me from danger,' observed Orando, 'and now, if you bring the animals near to me and give me meat, all of my prayers will have been fulfilled.'

'The animals go where they will,' responded Muzimo. 'I cannot lead them to you, but I can lead you to them; and when you are near, then, perhaps, I can frighten them toward you. Come.'

He turned backward along the trail down which they had followed the Leopard Men and fell into an easy trot, while Orando followed, his eyes upon the broad shoulders of his 'muzimo' and the spirit of Nyamwegi, perched upon one of them. Thus they continued silently for a half hour, when Muzimo halted.

'Move forward slowly and cautiously,' he directed. 'The scent spoor of Wappi, the antelope, has grown strong in my nostrils. I go ahead through the trees to get upon the other side of him. When he catches my scent he will move away from me toward you. Be ready.'

Scarcely had Muzimo ceased speaking before he disappeared amidst the overhanging foliage of the forest, leaving Orando filled with wonder and admiration, with which was combined overweening pride in his possession of a 'muzimo' such as no other man might boast. He hoped that the hunting would be quickly concluded that he might return to the village of Tumbai and bask in the admiration and envy of his fellows as he nonchalantly paraded his new and wondrous acquisition before their eyes. It was something, of course, to be a chief's son, just as it was something to be a chief or a witch-doctor; but to possess a 'muzimo' that one might see and talk to and hunt with – ah, that was glory transcending any that might befall mortal man.

Suddenly Orando's gloating thoughts were interrupted by a slight sound of something approaching along the trail from the direction in which he was moving. Just the suggestion of a sound it was, but to the ears of the jungle hunter it was sufficient. You or I could not have heard it; nor, hearing it, could we have interpreted it; but to Orando it bore a message as clear to his ears as is the message of a printed page to our eyes. It told him that a hoofed animal was approaching him, walking quickly, though not yet in full flight. A turn in the trail just ahead of him concealed him from the view of the approaching animal. Orando grasped his spear more firmly, and stepped behind the bole of a small tree that partially hid him from the sight of any creature coming toward him. There he stood, motionless as a bronze statue, knowing that motion and scent are the two most potent stimuli to fear in the lower orders. What wind there was moved from the unseen animal toward the man, precluding the possibility of his scent reaching the nostrils of the hunted; and as long as Orando did not move, the animal, he knew, would come fearlessly until it was close enough to catch his scent, which would be well within spear range.

A moment later there came into view one of those rarest of African animals, an okapi. Orando had never before seen one of them, for they ranged much farther to the west than the Watenga country. He noted the giraffe-like markings on the hind quarters and forelegs; but the short neck deceived him, and he still thought that it was an antelope. He was all excitement now, for here was real meat and plenty of it, the animal being larger than an ordinary cow. The blood raced through the hunter's veins, but outwardly he was calm. There must be no bungling now; every movement must be perfectly timed – a step out into the trail and, simultaneously, the casting of the spear, the two motions blending into each other as though there was but one.

At that instant the okapi wheeled to flee. Orando had not moved, there had been no disturbing sound audible to the ears of the man; yet something had frightened the quarry just a fraction of a second too soon. Orando was disgusted. He leaped into the trail to cast his spear, in the futile hope that it might yet bring down his prey; and as he raised his arm he witnessed a scene that left him gaping in astonishment.

From the trees above the okapi, a creature launched itself onto the back of the terrified animal. It was Muzimo. From his throat rumbled a low growl. Orando stood spellbound. He saw the okapi stumble and falter beneath the weight of the savage man-beast. Before it could recover itself a hand shot out and grasped it by the muzzle. Then steel thews wrenched the head suddenly about, so that the vertebrae of the neck snapped. An instant later a keen knife had severed the jugular, and as the blood gushed from the carcass Orando heard again the victory cry of the bull-ape. Faintly, from afar, came the answering challenge of a lion.

'Let us eat,' said Muzimo, as he carved generous portions from the quivering carcass of his kill.

'Yes, let us eat,' agreed Orando.

Muzimo grunted as he tossed a piece of the meat to the black. Then he squatted on his haunches and tore at his portion with his strong, white teeth. Cooking fires were for the effete, not for this savage jungle god whose 'mores' harked back through the ages to the days before men had mastered the art of making fire.

Orando hesitated. He preferred his meat cooked, but he dreaded losing face in the presence of his 'muzimo.' He deliberated for but a second; then he approached Muzimo with the intention of squatting down beside him to eat. The forest god looked up, his teeth buried in the flesh from which he was tearing a piece. A sudden, savage light blazed in his eyes. A low growl rumbled warningly in his throat. Orando had seen lions disturbed at their kills. The analogy was perfect. The black withdrew and squatted at a distance. Thus the two finished their meal in a silence broken only by the occasional low growls of the white.

CHAPTER FOUR

Sobito, the Witch-Doctor

Two white men sat before a much patched, weatherworn tent. They sat upon the ground, for they had no chairs. Their clothing was, if possible, more patched and weatherworn than their tent. Five blacks squatted about a cookfire at a little distance from them. Another black was preparing food for the white men at a small fire near the tent.

'I'm sure fed up on this,' remarked the older man.

'Then why don't you beat it?' demanded the other, a young man of twenty-one or twenty-two.

His companion shrugged. 'Where? I'd be just another dirty bum, back in the States. Here, I at least have the satisfaction of servants, even though I know damn well they don't respect me. It gives me a certain sense of "class" to be waited upon. There, I'd have to wait on somebody else. But you – I can't see why you want to hang around this lousy Godforsaken country, fighting bugs and fever. You're young. You've got your whole life ahead of you and the whole world to carve it out of any way you want.'

'Hell!' exclaimed the younger man. 'You talk as though you were a hundred. You aren't thirty yet. You told me your age, you know, right after we threw in together.'

'Thirty's old,' observed the other. 'A guy's got to get a start long before thirty. Why, I know fellows who made theirs and retired by the time they were thirty. Take my dad for instance—' He went silent then, quite suddenly. The other urged no confidences.

'I guess we'd be a couple of bums back there,' he remarked laughing.

'You wouldn't be a bum anywhere, Kid,' remonstrated his companion. He broke into sudden laughter.

'What are you laughing about?'

'I was thinking about the time we met; it's just about a year now. You tried to make me think you were a tough guy from the slums. You were a pretty good actor – while you were thinking about it.'

The Kid grinned. 'It was a hell of a strain on my histrionic abilities,' he admitted; 'but, say, Old Timer, you didn't fool anybody much, yourself. To listen to you talk one would have imagined that you were born in the jungle and brought up by apes, but I tumbled to you in a hurry. I said to myself, "Kid, it's either Yale or Princeton; more likely Yale."'

'But you didn't ask any questions. That's what I liked about you.'

'And you didn't ask any. Perhaps that's why we've got along together so well. People who ask questions should be taken gently, but firmly, by the hand, led out behind the barn and shot. It would be a better world to live in.'

'Oke, Kid; but still it's rather odd, at that, that two fellows should pal together for a year, as we have, and not know the first damn thing about one another – as though neither trusted the other.'

'It isn't that with me,' said the Kid; 'but there are some things that a fellow just can't talk about – to anyone.'

'I know,' agreed Old Timer. 'The thing each of us can't talk about probably explains why he is here. It was a woman with me; that's why I hate 'em. These native Shebas fulfil all my requirements as far as women are concerned, but they offend my olfactories.'

'Simple, wholesome, outdoor girls with cow dung and lice in their hair,' supplemented the Kid. 'Just lookin' at 'em would be enough to make me fall in love with the first white woman I saw; let alone smellin' 'em.'

'Not me,' said Old Timer. 'I hate the sight of a white woman. I hope to God I never see another one as long as I live.'

'Hooey!' scoffed the younger man. 'I'd bet you fall for the first skirt you see – if I had anything to bet.'

'We won't have anything to eat or anyone to cook it for us if we don't have a little luck pronto,' observed the other. 'It commences to look as though all the elephants in Africa had beat it for parts unknown.'

'Old Bobolo swore we'd find 'em here, but I think old Bobolo is a liar.'

'I have suspected that for some time,' admitted Old Timer.

The Kid rolled a cigarette. 'All he wanted was to get rid of us, or, to state the matter more accurately, to get rid of you.'

'Why me?'

'He didn't like the goo-goo eyes his lovely daughter was making at you. You've sure got a way with the women, Old Timer.'

'It's because I haven't that I'm here,' the older man assured him.

'Says you.'

'Kid, I think you are the one who is girl-crazy. You can't get your mind off the subject. Forget 'em for a while, and let's get down to business. I tell you we've got to do something and do it damn sudden. If these loyal retainers of ours don't see a little ivory around the diggings pretty soon they'll quit us. They know as well as we do that it's a case of no ivory, no pay.'

'Well, what are we going to do about it; manufacture elephants?'

'Go out and find 'em. Thar's elephants in them thar hills, men; but they aren't going to come trotting into camp to be shot. The natives won't help us; so we've got to get out and scout for them ourselves. We'll each take a couple of men and a few days' rations; then we'll head in different directions, and if one of us doesn't find elephant tracks I'm a zebra.'

'How much longer do you suppose we'll be able to work this racket without getting caught?' demanded The Kid.

'I've been working it for two years, and I haven't been nabbed yet,' replied Old Timer; 'and believe me, I don't want to be nabbed. Have you ever seen their lousy jail?'

'They wouldn't put white men in that, would they?' The Kid looked worried.

'They might. Ivory poachin' makes 'em sorer than Billy Hell.'

'I don't blame 'em,' said The Kid. 'It's a lousy racket.'

'Don't I know it?' Old Timer spat vehemently. 'But a man's got to eat, hasn't he? If I knew a better way to eat I wouldn't be an ivory poacher. Don't think for a minute that I'm stuck on the job or proud of myself. I'm not. I just try not to think of the ethics of the thing, just like I try to forget that I was ever decent. I'm a bum, I tell you, a dirty, lowdown bum; but even bums cling to life – though God only knows why. I've never dodged the chance of kicking off, but somehow I always manage to wiggle through. If I'd been any good on earth; or if anyone had cared whether I croaked or not, I'd have been dead long ago. It seems as though the Devil watches over things like me and protects them, so that they can suffer as long as possible in this life before he forks them into eternal hell-fire and brimstone in the next.'

'Don't brag,' advised The Kid. 'I'm just as big a bum as you. Likewise, I have to eat. Let's forget ethics and get busy.'

'We'll start tomorrow,' agreed Old Timer.

Muzimo stood silent with folded arms, the centre of a chattering horde of natives in the village of Tumbai. Upon his shoulders squatted The Spirit of Nyamwegi. He, too, chattered. It was fortunate, perhaps, that the villagers of Tumbai could not understand what The Spirit of Nyamwegi said. He was hurling the vilest of jungle invective at them, nor was there in all the jungle another such master of diatribe. Also, from the safety of Muzimo's shoulder, he challenged them to battle, telling them what he would do to them if he ever got hold of them. He challenged them singly and 'en masse.' It made no difference to The Spirit of Nyamwegi how they came, just so they came.

If the villagers were not impressed by The Spirit of Nyamwegi, the same is not true of the effect that the presence of Muzimo had upon them after they had heard Orando's story, even after the first telling. By the seventh or eighth telling their awe was prodigious. It kept them at a safe distance from this mysterious creature of another world.

There was one sceptic, however. It was the village witch-doctor, who doubtless felt that it was not good business to admit too much credence in a miracle not of his own making. Whatever he felt, and it is quite possible that he was as much in awe as the others, he hid it under a mask of indifference, for he must always impress the laity with his own importance.

The attention bestowed upon this stranger irked him; it also pushed him entirely out of the limelight. This nettled him greatly. Therefore, to call attention to himself, as well as to re-establish his importance, he strode boldly up to Muzimo. Whereupon The Spirit of Nyamwegi screamed shrilly and took refuge behind the back of his patron. The attention of the villagers was now attracted to the witch-doctor, which was precisely what *he* desired. The chattering ceased. All eyes were on the two. This was the moment the witch-doctor had awaited. He puffed himself to his full height and girth. He swaggered before the spirit of Orando's ancestor. Then he addressed him in a loud tone.

'You say that you are the "muzimo" of Orando, the son of Lobongo; but how do we know that your words are true words? You say that the little monkey is the ghost of Nyamwegi. How do we know that, either?'

'Who are you, old man, who asks me these questions?' demanded Muzimo.

'I am Sobito, the witch-doctor.'

'You say that you are Sobito, the witch-doctor; but how do I know that your words are true words?'

'Everyone knows that I am Sobito, the witch-doctor.' The old man was becoming excited. He discovered that he had been suddenly put upon the defensive, which was not at all what he had intended. 'Ask anyone. They all know me.'

'Very well, then,' said Muzimo; 'ask Orando who I am. He, alone, knows me. I have not said that I am his "muzimo." I have not said that the little monkey is the ghost of Nyamwegi. I have not said who I am. I have not said anything. It does not make any difference to me who you think I am; but if it makes a difference to you, ask Orando,' whereupon he turned about and walked away, leaving Sobito to feel that he had been made to appear ridiculous in the eyes of his clansmen.

Fanatical, egotistical, and unscrupulous, the old witch-doctor was a power in the village of Tumbai. For years he had exercised his influence, sometimes for good and sometimes for evil, upon the villagers. Even Lobongo, the chief, was not as powerful as Sobito, who played upon the superstitions and fears of his ignorant followers until they dared not disobey his slightest wish.

Tradition and affection bound them to Lobongo, their hereditary chief; fear held them in the power of Sobito, whom they hated. Inwardly they were pleased that Orando's 'muzimo' had flaunted him; but, when the witch-doctor came among them and spoke disparagingly of the 'muzimo' they only listened in sullen silence, daring not to express their belief in him.

Later, the warriors gathered before the hut of Lobongo to listen to the formal telling of the story of Orando. It was immaterial that they had heard it several times already. It must be told again in elaborate detail before a council of the chief and his warriors; and so once more Orando retold the oft-told tale, nor did it lose anything in the telling. More and more courageous became the deeds of Orando, more and more miraculous those of Muzimo; and when he closed his oration it was with an appeal to the chief and his warriors to gather the Utengas from all the villages of the tribe and go forth to avenge Nyamwegi. Muzimo, he told them, would lead them to the village of the Leopard Men.

There were shouts of approval from the younger men, but the majority of the older men sat in silence. It is always thus; the younger men for war, the older men for peace. Lobongo was an old man. He was proud that his son should be war-like. That was the reaction of the father, but the reaction of age was all against war. So he, too, remained silent. Not so, Sobito. To his personal grievance against Muzimo were added other considerations that inclined him against this contemplated foray; at least one of which (and the most potent) was a secret he might not divulge with impunity. Scowling forbiddingly he leaped to his feet.

'Who makes this foolish talk of war?' he demanded. 'Young men. What do young men know of war? They think only of victory. They forget defeat. They forget that if they make war upon a village the warriors of that village will come some day and make war upon us. What is to be gained by making war upon the Leopard Men? Who knows where their village lies? It must be very far away. Why should our warriors go far from their own country to make war upon the Leopard Men? Because Nyamwegi has been killed? Nyamwegi has already been avenged. This is foolish talk, this war-talk. Who started it? Perhaps it is a stranger among us who wishes to make trouble for us.' He looked at Muzimo. 'Who knows why? Perhaps the Leopard Men have sent one of their own people to lure us into making war upon them. Then all our warriors will be ambushed and killed. That is what will happen. Make no foolish talk about war.'

As Sobito concluded his harangue and again squatted upon his heels Orando arose. He was disturbed by what the old witch-doctor had said; and he was angry, too; angry because Sobito had impugned the integrity of his 'muzimo.' But his anger was leashed by his fear of the powerful old man; for who dares openly oppose one in league with the forces of darkness, one whose enmity can spell disaster and death? Yet Orando was a brave warrior and a loyal friend, as befitted one in whose veins flowed the blood of hereditary chieftanship; and so he could not permit the innuendoes of Sobito to go entirely unchallenged.

'Sobito has spoken against war,' he began. 'Old men always speak against war, which is right if one is an old man. Orando is a young man, yet he, too, would speak against war if it were only the foolish talk of young men who wished to appear brave in the eyes of women; but now there is a reason for war. Nyamwegi has been killed. He was a brave warrior. He was a good friend. Because we have killed three of those who killed Nyamwegi we cannot say that he is avenged. We must go and make war upon the chief who sent these murderers into the Watenga country, or he will think that the Utengas are all old women. He will think that whenever his people wish to eat the flesh of man they have only to come to the Watenga country to get it.

'Sobito has said that perhaps the Leopard Men sent a stranger among us to lure us into ambush. There is only one stranger among us – Muzimo. But Muzimo cannot be a friend of the Leopard Men. With his own eyes Orando saw him kill two of the Leopard Men; he saw the fourth run away very fast when his eyes discovered the might of Muzimo. Had Muzimo been his friend he would not have run away.

'I am Orando, the son of Lobongo. Some day I shall be chief. I would not lead the warriors of Lobongo into a foolish war. I am going to the village of the Leopard Men and make war upon them, that they may know that not all the Utenga warriors are old women. Muzimo is going with me. Perhaps there are a few brave men who will accompany us. I have spoken.'

Several of the younger warriors leaped from their haunches and stamped their feet in approval. They raised their voices in the war-cry of their clan and brandished their spears. One of them danced in a circle, leaping high and jabbing with his spear.

'Thus will I kill the Leopard Men!' he cried.

Another leaped about, slashing with his knife. 'I cut the heart from the chief of the Leopard Men!' He pretended to tear at something with his teeth, while he held it tightly in his hands. 'I eat the heart of the chief of the Leopard Men!'

'War! War!' cried others, until there were a dozen howling savages dancing in the sunlight, their sleek hides glistening with sweat, their features contorted by hideous grimaces.

Then Lobongo arose. His deep voice boomed above the howling of the dancers as he commanded them to silence. One by one they ceased their howling, but they gathered together in a little knot behind Orando.

'A few of the young men have spoken for war,' he announced, 'but we do not make war lightly because a few young men wish to fight. There are times for war and times for peace. We must find out if this is the time for war; otherwise we shall find only defeat and death at the end of the war-trail. Before undertaking war we must consult the ghosts of our dead chiefs.'

'They are waiting to speak to us,' cried Sobito. 'Let there be silence while I speak with the spirits of the chiefs who are gone.'

As he spoke there was the gradual beginning of a movement among the tribesmen that presently formed a circle in the centre of which squatted the witch-doctor. From a pouch he withdrew a number of articles which he spread upon the ground before him. Then he called for some dry twigs and fresh leaves, and when these were brought he built a tiny fire. With the fresh leaves he partially smothered it, so that it threw off a quantity of smoke. Stooping, half doubled, the witch-doctor moved cautiously around the fire, describing a small circle, his eyes constantly fixed upon the thin column of smoke spiralling upward in the quiet air of the drowsy afternoon. In one hand Sobito held a small pouch made of the skin of a rodent, in the other the tail of a hyena, the root bound with copper wire to form a handle.

Gradually the old man increased his pace until, at last, he was circling the fire rapidly in prodigious leaps and bounds; but always his eyes remained fixed upon the spiralling smoke column. As he danced he intoned a weird jargon, a combination of meaningless syllables interspersed with an occasional shrill scream that brought terror to the eyes of his spellbound audience.

Suddenly he halted, and stooping low tossed some powder from his pouch upon the fire; then with the root of the hyena tail he drew a rude geometric figure in the dust before the blaze. Stiffening, he closed his eyes and appeared to be listening intently, his face turned partially upward.

In awestruck silence the warriors leaned forward waiting. It was a tense moment and quite effective. Sobito prolonged it to the utmost. At last he opened his eyes and let them move solemnly about the circle of expectant faces, waiting again before he spoke.

'There are many ghosts about us,' he announced. 'They all speak against war. Those who go to battle with the Leopard Men will die. None will return. The ghosts are angry with Orando. The true "muzimo" of Orando spoke to me; it is very angry with Orando. Let Orando beware. That is all; the young men will not go to war against the Leopard Men.'

The warriors gathered behind Orando looked questioningly at him and at Muzimo. Doubt was written plainly upon every face. Gradually they began to move, drifting imperceptibly away from Orando. Then the son of the chief looked at Muzimo questioningly. 'If Sobito has spoken true words,' he said, 'you are not my "muzimo."' The words seemed a challenge.

'What does Sobito know about it?' demanded Muzimo. 'I could build a fire and wave the tail of Dango. I could make marks in the dirt and throw powders on the fire. Then I could tell you whatever I wanted to tell you, just as Sobito has told you what he wanted you to believe; but such things prove nothing. The only way you can know if a war against the Leopard Men will succeed is to send warriors to fight them. Sobito knows nothing about it.'

The witch-doctor trembled from anger. Never before had a creature dared voice a doubt as to his powers. So abjectly had the members of his clan acknowledged his infallibility that he had almost come to believe in it himself. He shook a withered finger at Muzimo.

'You speak with a lying tongue,' he cried. 'You have angered my fetish. Nothing can save you. You are lost. You will die.' He paused as a new idea was born in his cunning brain. 'Unless,' he added, 'you go away, and do not come back.'

Having no idea as to his true identity, Muzimo had had to accept Orando's word that he was the ancestral spirit of the chief's son; and having heard himself described as such innumerable times he had come to accept it as fact. He felt no fear of Sobito, the man, and when Sobito, the witch-doctor, threatened him he recalled that he was a 'muzimo' and, as such, immortal. How, therefore, he reasoned, could the fetish of Sobito kill him? Nothing could kill a spirit.

'I shall not go away,' he announced. 'I am not afraid of Sobito.'

The villagers were aghast. Never had they heard a witch-doctor flouted and defied as Muzimo had flouted and defied Sobito. They expected to see the rash creature destroyed before their eyes, but nothing happened. They looked at Sobito, questioningly, and that wily old fraud, sensing the critical turn of the event and fearing for his prestige, overcame his physical fear of the strange, white giant in the hope of regaining his dignity by a single bold stroke.

Brandishing his hyena tail, he leaped toward Muzimo. 'Die!' he screamed. 'Nothing can save you now. Before the moon has risen the third time you will be dead. My fetish has spoken!' He waved the hyena tail in the face of Muzimo.

The white man stood with folded arms, a sneer upon his lips. 'I am Muzimo,' he said; 'I am the spirit of the ancestor of Orando. Sobito is only a man; his fetish is only the tail of Dango.' As he ceased speaking his hand shot out and snatched the fetish from the grasp of the witch doctor. 'Thus does Muzimo with the fetish of Sobito!' he cried, tossing the tail into the fire to the consternation of the astonished villagers.

Seized by the unreasoning rage of fanaticism Sobito threw caution to the winds and leaped for Muzimo, a naked blade in his upraised hand. There was the froth of madness upon his bared lips. His yellow fangs gleamed in a hideous snarl. He was the personification of hatred and maniacal fury. But swift and vicious as was his attack it did not find Muzimo unprepared. A bronzed hand seized the black wrist of the witch doctor in a grip of steel; another tore the knife from his grasp. Then Muzimo picked him up and held him high above his head as though Sobito were some incorporeal thing without substance or weight.

Terror was writ large upon the countenances of the astounded onlookers; an idol was in the clutches of an iconoclast. The situation had passed beyond the scope of their simple minds, leaving them dazed. Perhaps it was well for Muzimo that Sobito was far from being a beloved idol.

Muzimo looked at Orando. 'Shall I kill him?' he asked, almost casually.

Orando was as shocked and terrified as his fellows. A lifetime of unquestioning belief in the supernatural powers of witch-doctors could not be overcome in an instant. Yet there was another force working upon the son of the chief. He was only human. Muzimo was his 'muzimo,' and being very human he could not but feel a certain justifiable pride in the fearlessness and prowess of this splendid enigma whom he had enthusiastically accepted as the spirit of his dead ancestor. However, witch-doctors were witch-doctors. Their powers were well known to all men. There was, therefore, no wisdom in tempting fate too far.

Orando ran forward. 'No!' he cried. 'Do not kill him.'

Upon the branch of a tree a little monkey danced, screaming and scolding.

'Kill him!' he shrieked. 'Kill him!' He was a very bloodthirsty little monkey was The Spirit of Nyamwegi. Muzimo tossed Sobito to the ground in an ignominious heap.

'He is no good,' he announced. 'No witch-doctor is any good. His fetish was no good. If it had been, why did it not protect Sobito? Sobito did not know what he was talking about. If there are any brave warriors among the Utengas they will come with Orando and Muzimo and make war on the Leopard Men.'

A low cry, growing in volume, rose among the younger warriors; and in the momentary confusion Sobito crawled to his feet and sneaked away toward his hut. When he was safety out of reach of Muzimo he halted and faced about. 'I go,' he called back, 'to make powerful medicine. Tonight the white man who calls himself Muzimo dies.'

The white giant took a few steps in the direction of Sobito, and the witch-doctor turned and fled. The young men, seeing the waning of Sobito's power, talked loudly now of war. The older men talked no more of peace. One and all, they feared and hated Sobito. They were relieved to see his power broken. Tomorrow they might be afraid again, but today they were free from the domination of a witch-doctor for the first time in their lives.

Lobongo, the chief, would not sanction war; but influenced by the demands of Orando and other young men, he at last grudgingly gave his approval to the formation of a small raiding party. Immediately runners were dispatched to other villages to seek recruits, and preparations were begun for a dance to be held that night.

Because of Lobongo's refusal to make general war against the Leopard Men there was no booming of war-drums; but news travels fast in the jungle; and night had scarcely closed down upon the village of Tumbai before warriors from the nearer villages commenced coming in to Tumbai by ones and twos to join the twenty volunteers from Lobongo's village, who swaggered and strutted before the admiring eyes of the dusky belles preparing the food and native beer that would form an important part of the night's festivities.

From Kibbu came ten young warriors, among them the brother of the girl Nyamwegi had been courting and one Lupingu, from whom the murdered warrior had stolen her heart. That Lupingu should volunteer to risk his life for the purpose of avenging Nyamwegi passed unnoticed, since already thoughts of vengeance had been submerged by lust for glory and poor Nyamwegi practically forgotten by all but Orando.

There was much talk of war and of brave deeds that would be accomplished; but the discomfiture of Sobito, being still fresh in every mind, also had an important part in the conversations. The village gossips found it a choice morsel with which to regale the warriors from other villages, with the result that Muzimo became an outstanding figure that reflected more glory upon the village of Tumbai than ever Sobito had. The visiting warriors regarded him with awe and some misgivings. They were accustomed to spirits that no one ever saw; the air was full of them. It was quite another matter to behold one standing in their midst.

Lupingu, espeially, was perturbed. Recently he had purchased a love charm from Sobito. He was wondering now if he had thrown away, uselessly, the little treasure he had paid for it. He decided to seek out the witch-doctor and make inquiries; perhaps there was not so much truth in what he had heard. There was also another reason why he wished to consult Sobito, a reason of far greater importance than a love charm.

When he could do so unnoticed, Lupingu withdrew from the crowd milling in the village street and sneaked away to Sobito's hut. Here he found the old witch-doctor squatting upon the floor surrounded by charms and fetishes. A small fire burning beneath a pot fitfully lighted his sinister features, which were contorted by so hideous a scowl that Lupingu almost turned and fled before the old man looked up and recognised him.

For a long time Lupingu sat in the hut of the witch-doctor. They spoke in whispers, their heads close together. When Lupingu left he carried with him an amulet of such prodigious potency that no enemy weapon could inflict injury upon him, and in his head he carried a plan that caused him both elation and terror.

CHAPTER FIVE
'Unspeakable Boor!'

Long days of loneliness. Long nights of terror. Hopelessness and vain regrets so keen that they pained as might physical hurts. Only a brave heart had kept the girl from going mad since her men had deserted her. That seemed an eternity ago; days were ages.

Today she had hunted. A small boar had fallen to her rifle. At the sound of the shot, coming faintly to his ears, a white man had halted, scowling. His three black companions jabbered excitedly.

With difficulty the girl had removed the viscera of the boar, thus reducing its weight sufficiently so that she could drag it to her camp; but it had been an ordeal that had taxed her strength and endurance to their limits. The meat was too precious, however, to be wasted; and she had struggled for hours, stopping often to rest, until at last, exhausted, she had sunk beside her prize before the entrance of her tent.

It was not encouraging to consider the vast amount of labour that still confronted her before the meat would be safe for future use. There was the butchering. The mere thought of it appalled her. She had never seen an animal butchered until after she had set out upon this disastrous safari. In all her life she had never even so much as cut a piece of raw meat. Her preparation, therefore, was most inadequate; but necessity overcomes obstacles, as it mothers inventions. She knew that the boar must be butchered, and the flesh cut into strips and that these strips must be smoked. Even then they would not keep long, but she knew no better way.

With her limited knowledge of practical matters, with the means at hand, she must put up the best fight for life of which she was capable. She was weak and inexperienced and afraid; but nonetheless it was a courageous heart that beat beneath her once chic but now soiled and disreputable flannel shirt. She was without hope, yet she would not give up.

Wearily, she had commenced to skin the boar, when a movement at the edge of the clearing in which her camp had been pitched attracted her attention. As she looked up she saw four men standing silently, regarding her. One was a white man. The other three were blacks. As she sprang to her feet hope welled so strongly within her that she reeled slightly with dizziness; but instantly she regained control of herself and surveyed the four, who were now advancing, the white man in the lead. Then, when closer scrutiny was possible, hope waned. Never in her life had she seen so disreputable appearing a white man. His filthy clothing was a motley of rags and patches; his face was unshaven; his hat was a nondescript wreck that might only be distinguished as a hat by the fact that it surmounted his head; his face was stern and forbidding. His eyes wandered suspiciously about her camp; and when he halted a few paces from her, scowling, there was no greeting on his lips.

'Who are you?' he demanded. 'What are you doing here?'

His tone and words antagonised her. Never before had any white man addressed her in so cavalier a manner. In a proud and spirited girl the reaction was inevitable. Her chin went up; she eyed him coldly; the suggestion of a supercilious sneer curved her short upper lip; her eyes evaluated him disdainfully from his run-down boots to the battered thing that covered his dishevelled hair. Had his manner and address been different she might have been afraid of him, but now for the moment at least she was too angry to be afraid.

'I cannot conceive that either matter concerns you,' she said, and turned her back on him

The scowl deepened on the man's face, and angry words leaped to his tongue; but he controlled himself, regarding her silently. Had he not already seen her face he would have guessed from the lines of her haughty little back that she was young. Having seen her face he knew that she was beautiful. She was dirty, hot, perspiring, and covered with blood; but she was still beautiful. How beautiful she must be when properly garbed and groomed he dared not even imagine. He had noticed her blue-grey eyes and long lashes; they alone would have made any face beautiful. Now he was appraising her hair, confined in a loose knot at the nape of her neck; it had that peculiar quality of blondness that is described, today, as platinum.

It had been two years since Old Timer had seen a white woman. Perhaps if this one had been old and scrawny, or had buckteeth and a squint, he might have regarded her with less disapprobation and addressed her more courteously. But the moment that his eyes had beheld her, her beauty had recalled all the anguish and misery that another beautiful girl had caused him, arousing within him the hatred of woman that he had nursed and cherished for two long years.

He stood in silence for a moment; and he was glad that he had; for it permitted him to quell the angry, bitter words that he might otherwise have spoken. It was not that he liked women any better, but that he realised and admired the courageousness of her reply.

'It may not be any of my business,' he said presently, 'but perhaps I shall have to make it so. It is rather unusual to see a white woman alone in this country. You are alone?' There was a faint note of concern in the tone of his question.

'I was quite alone,' she snapped, 'and I should prefer being so again.'

'You mean that you are without porters or white companions?'

'Quite.'

As her back was toward him she did not see the expression of relief that crossed his face at her admission. Had she, she might have felt greater concern for her safety, though his relief had no bearing upon her welfare; his anxiety as to the presence of white men was simply that of the elephant poacher.

'And you have no means of transportation?' he queried.

'None.'

'You certainly did not come this far into the interior alone. What became of the other members of your party?'

'They deserted me.'

'But your white companions – what of them?'

'I had none.' She had faced him by now, but her attitude was still unfriendly.

'You came into the interior without any white men?' There was scepticism in his tone.

'I did.'

'When did your men desert you?'

'Three days ago.'

'What do you intend doing? You can't stay here alone, and I don't see how you can expect to go on without porters.'

'I have stayed here three days alone; I can continue to do so until—'

'Until what?'

'I don't know.'

'Look here,' he demanded; 'what in the world are you doing here, anyway?'

A sudden hope seemed to flash to her brain. 'I am looking for a man,' she said. 'Perhaps you have heard of him; perhaps you know where he is.' Her voice was vibrant with eagerness.

'What's his name?' asked Old Timer.

'Jerry Jerome.' She looked up into his face hopefully.

He shook his head. 'Never heard of him.'

The hope in her eyes died out, suffused by the faintest suggestion of tears. Old Timer saw the moisture of her eyes, and it annoyed him. Why did women always have to cry? He steeled his heart against the weakness that was sympathy and spoke brusquely. 'What do you think you're going to do with that meat?' he demanded.

Her eyes widened in surprise. There were no tears in them now, but a glint of anger. 'You are impossible. I wish you would get out of my camp and leave me alone.'

'I shall do nothing of the kind,' he replied. Then he spoke rapidly to his three followers in their native dialect, whereupon the three advanced and took possession of the carcass of the boar.

The girl looked on in angry surprise. She recalled the heart-breaking labour of dragging the carcass to camp. Now it was being taken from her. The thought enraged her. She drew her revolver from its holster. 'Tell them to leave that alone,' she cried, 'or I'll shoot them. It's mine.'

'They're only going to butcher it for you,' explained Old Timer. 'That's what you wanted, isn't it? Or were you going to frame it?'

His sarcasm nettled her, but she realised that she had misunderstood their purpose. 'Why didn't you say so?' she demanded. 'I was going to smoke it. I may not always be able to get food easily.'

'You won't have to,' he told her; 'we'll look after that.'

'What do you mean?'

'I mean that as soon as I'm through here you're going back to my camp with me. It ain't my fault that you're here; and you're a damn useless nuisance, like all other women; but I couldn't leave a white rat here alone in the jungle, much less a white woman.'

'What if I don't care to go with you?' she inquired haughtily.

'I don't give a damn what you think about it,' he snapped; 'you're going with me. If you had any brains you'd be grateful. It's too much to expect you to have a heart. You're like all the rest – selfish, inconsiderate, ungrateful.'

'Anything else?' she inquired.

'Yes. Cold, calculating, hard.'

'You do not think much of women, do you?'

'You are quite discerning.'

'And just what do you purpose doing with me when we get to your camp?' she asked.

'If we can scrape up a new safari for you I'll get you out of Africa as quickly as I can,' he replied.

'But I do not wish to get out of Africa. You have no right to dictate to me. I came here for a purpose, and I shall not leave until that purpose is fulfilled.'

'If you came here to find that Jerome fellow it is my duty to a fellow man to chase you out before you can find him.'

Her level gaze rested upon him for several moments before she replied. She had never before seen a man like this. Such candour was unnatural. She decided that he was mentally unbalanced; and having heard that the insane should be humoured, lest they became violent, she determined to alter her attitude toward him.

'Perhaps you are right,' she admitted. 'I will go with you.'

'That's better,' he commented. 'Now that that's settled let's have everything else clear. We're starting back to my camp as soon as I get through with my business here. That may be tomorrow or next day. You're coming along. One of my boys will look after you – cooking and all that sort of stuff. But I don't want to be bothered with any women. You leave me alone, and I'll leave you alone. I don't even want to talk to you.'

'That will be mutually agreeable,' she assured him, not without some asperity. Since she was a woman and had been for as long as she could recall the object of masculine adulation, such a speech, even from the lips of a disreputable ragamuffin whose sanity she questioned, could not but induce a certain pique.

'One more thing,' he added. 'My camp is in Chief Bobolo's country. If anything happens to me have my boys take you back there to my camp. My partner will look after you. Just tell him that I promised to get you back to the coast.' He left her then and busied himself with the simple preparation of his modest camp, calling one of the men from the butchering to pitch his small tent and prepare his evening meal, for it was now late in the afternoon. Another of the boys was detailed to serve the girl.

From her tent that evening she could see him sprawled before a fire, smoking his pipe. From a distance she gazed at him contemptuously, convinced that he was the most disagreeable person she had ever encountered, yet forced to admit that his presence gave her a feeling of security she had not enjoyed since she had entered Africa. She concluded that even a crazy white man was better than none. But was he crazy? He seemed quite normal and sane in all respects other than his churlish attitude toward her. Perhaps he was just an ill-bred boor with some fancied grievance against women. Be that as it might he was an enigma, and unsolved enigmas have a way of occupying one's thoughts. So, notwithstanding her contempt for him, he filled her reveries quite to the exclusion of all else until sleep claimed her.

Doubtless she would have been surprised to know that similarly the man's mind was occupied with thoughts of her, thoughts that hung on with bulldog tenacity despite his every effort to shake them loose. In the smoke of his pipe he saw her, unquestionably beautiful beyond comparison. He saw the long lashes shading the depths of her blue-grey eyes; her lips, curved deliciously; the alluring sheen of her wavy blonde hair; the perfection of her girlish figure.

'Damn!' muttered Old Timer. 'Why in hell did I have to run into her?'

The following morning he left camp early, taking two of the boys with him; leaving the third, armed with an old rifle, to protect the girl and attend to her wants. She was already up when he departed, but he did not look in her direction as he strode out of camp, though she furtively watched him go, feeding her contempt on a final disparaging appraisement of his rags and tatters.

'Unspeakable boor!' she whispered venomously as a partial outlet for her pent up hatred of the man.

Old Timer had a long, hard day. No sign of elephant rewarded his search, nor did he contact a single native from whom he might obtain information as to the whereabouts of the great herd that rumour and hope had located in this vicinity.

Not only was the day one of physical hardship, but it had been mentally trying as well. He had been disappointed in not locating the ivory they needed so sorely, but this had been the least of his mental perturbation. He had been haunted by thoughts of the girl. All day he had tried to rid his mind of recollection of that lovely face and the contours of her perfect body, but they persisted in haunting him. At first they had aroused other memories, painful memories of another girl. But gradually the vision of that other girl had faded until only the blue-grey eyes and blonde hair of the girl in the lonely camp persisted in his thoughts.

When he turned back toward camp at the end of his fruitless search for elephant signs a new determination filled him with disquieting thoughts and spurred him rapidly upon the back-trail. It had been two years since he had seen a white woman, and then Fate had thrown this lovely creature across his path. What had women ever done for him? 'Made a bum of me,' he soliloquized; 'ruined my life. This girl would have been lost but for me. She owes me something. All women owe me something for what one woman did to me. This girl is going to pay the debt.

'God, but she's beautiful! And she belongs to me. I found her, and I am going to keep her until I am tired of her. Then I'll throw her over the way I was thrown over. See how the woman will like it! Gad, what lips! Tonight they will be mine. She'll be all mine, and I'll make her like it. It's only fair. I've got something coming to me in this world. I'm entitled to a little happiness; and, by God, I'm going to have it.'

The great sun hung low in the west as the man came in sight of the clearing. The tent of the girl was the first thing that greeted his eyes. The soiled canvas suggested an intimacy that was provocative; it had sheltered and protected her; it had shared the most intimate secrets of her alluring charm. Like all inanimate objects that have been closely associated with an individual the tent reflected something of the personality of the girl. The mere sight of it stirred the man deeply. His passions, aroused by hours of anticipation, surged through his head like wine. He quickened his pace in his eagerness to take the girl in his arms.

Then he saw an object lying just beyond her tent that turned him cold with apprehension. Springing forward at a run, closely followed by his two retainers, he came to a halt beside the grisly thing that had attracted his horrified attention and turned the hot wave of his desire to cold dread. It was the dead and horribly mutilated body of the black he had left to guard the girl. Cruel talons had lacerated the flesh with deep wounds that might have been inflicted by one of the great carnivores, but the further mutilation of the corpse had been the work of man.

Stooping over the body of their fellow the two blacks muttered angrily in their native tongue; then one of them turned to Old Timer. 'The Leopard Men, Bwana,' he said.

Fearfully, the white man approached the tent of the girl, dreading what he might find there, dreading even more that he might find nothing. As he threw aside the flap and looked in, his worst fears were realised; the girl was not there. His first impulse was to call aloud to her as though she might be somewhere near in the forest; but as he turned to do so he suddenly realised that he did not know her name, and in the brief pause that this realisation gave him the futility of the act was borne in upon him. If she still lived she was far away by now in the clutches of the black fiends who had slain her protector.

A sudden wave of rage overwhelmed the white man, his hot desire for the girl transmuted to almost maniacal anger toward her abductors. He forgot that he himself would have wronged her. Perhaps he thought only of his own frustrated hopes; but he believed that he was thinking only of the girl's helplessness, of the hideousness of her situation. Ideas of rescue and vengeance filled his whole being, banishing the fatigue of the long, arduous day.

It was already late in the afternoon, but he determined upon immediate pursuit. Following his orders the two blacks hastily buried their dead comrade, made up two packs with such provisions and camp necessities as the marauders had not filched, and with the sun but an hour high followed their mad master upon the fresh trail of the Leopard Men.

CHAPTER SIX

The Traitor

The warriors of Watenga had not responded with great enthusiasm to the call to arms borne by the messengers of Orando. There were wars, and wars. One directed against the feared secret order of the Leopard Men did not appear to be highly popular. There were excellent reasons for this. In the first place the very name of Leopard Man was sufficient to arouse terror in the breast of the bravest, the gruesome methods of the Leopard Men being what they were. There was also the well known fact that, being a secret order recruited among unrelated clans, some of one's own friends might be members, in which event an active enemy of the order could easily be marked for death. And such a death!

It is little wonder, then, that from thousands of potential crusaders Orando discovered but a scant hundred awaiting the call to arms the morning following the celebration and war dance at Tumbai. Even among the hundred there were several whose martial spirit had suffered eclipse overnight. Perhaps this was largely due to the after effects of an overdose of native beer. It is not pleasant to set out for war with a headache.

Orando was moving about among the warriors squatting near the numerous cooking fires. There was not much talk this morning and less laughter; the boasting of yester eve was stilled. Today war seemed a serious business; yet, their bellies once filled with warm food, they would go forth presently with loud yells, with laughter, and with song.

Orando made inquiries. 'Where is Muzimo?' he asked, but no one had seen Muzimo. He and The Spirit of Nyamwegi had disappeared. This seemed an ill omen. Someone suggested that possibly Sobito had been right; Muzimo might be in league with the Leopard Men. This aroused inquiry as to the whereabouts of Sobito. No one had seen him either; which was strange, since Sobito was an early riser and not one to be missing when the cookpots were a-boil. An old man went to his hut and questioned one of the witch-doctor's wives. Sobito was gone! When this fact was reported conversation waxed. The enmity between Muzimo and Sobito was recalled, as was the latter's threat that Muzimo would die before morning. There were those who suggested that perhaps it was Sobito who was dead, while others recalled the fact that there was nothing unusual in his disappearance. He had disappeared before. In fact, it was nothing unusual for him to absent himself mysteriously from the village for days at a time. Upon his return after such absences he had darkly hinted that he had been sitting in council with the spirits and demons of another world, from whom he derived his supernatural powers.

Lupingu of Tibbu thought that they should not set out upon the war trail in the face of such dire omens. He went quietly among the warriors seeking adherents to his suggestion that they disband and return to their own villages, but Orando shamed them out of desertion. The old men and the women would laugh at them, he told them. They had much too much talk about war; they had boasted too much. They would lose face forever if they failed to go through with it now.

'But who will guide us to the village of the Leopard Men now that your "muzimo" has deserted you?' demanded Lupingu.

'I do not believe that he has deserted me,' maintained Orando stoutly. 'Doubtless he, too, has gone to take council with the spirits. He will return and lead us.'

As though in answer to his statement, which was also a prayer, a giant figure dropped lightly from the branches of a nearby tree and strode toward him. It was Muzimo. Across one of his broad shoulders rested the carcass of a buck. On top of the buck sat The Spirit of Nyamwegi, screaming shrilly to attract attention to his prowess. 'We are mighty hunters,' he cried. 'See what we have killed.' No one but Muzimo understood him, but that made no difference to The Spirit of Nyamwegi because he did not know that they could not understand him. He thought that he was making a fine impression, and he was quite proud of himself.

'Where have you been, Muzimo?' asked Orando. 'Some said that Sobito had slain you.'

Muzimo shrugged. 'Words do not kill. Sobito is full of words.'

'Have you killed Sobito?' demanded an old man.

'I have not seen Sobito since before Kudu, the sun, went to his lair last night,' replied Muzimo.

'He is gone from the village,' explained Orando. 'It was thought that maybe—'

'I went to hunt. Your food is no good; you spoil it with fire.' He squatted down at the bole of a tree and cut meat from his kill, which he ate, growling. The blacks looked on terrified, giving him a wide berth.

When he had finished his meal he arose and stretched his great frame, and the action reminded them of Simba, the lion. 'Muzimo is ready,' he announced. 'If the Utengas are ready let us go.'

Orando gathered his warriors. He selected his captains and gave the necessary orders for the conduct of the march. This all required time, as no point could be decided without a general argument in which all participated whether the matter concerned them or not.

Muzimo stood silently aside. He was wondering about these people. He was wondering about himself. Physically he and they were much alike; yet in addition to the difference in coloration there were other differences, those he could see and those he could not see but sensed. The Spirit of Nyamwegi was like them and like him, too; yet here again was a vast difference. Muzimo knit his brows in perplexity. Vaguely, he almost recalled a fleeting memory that seemed the key to the riddle; but it eluded him. He felt dimly that he had had a past, but he could not recall it. He recalled only the things that he had seen and the experiences that had come to him since Orando had freed him from the great tree that had fallen on him; yet he appreciated the fact that when he had seen each seemingly new thing he had instantly recognised it for what it was – man, the okapi, the buck, each and every animal and bird that had come within the range of his vision or his sensitive ears or nostrils. Nor had he been at a loss to meet each new emergency of life as it confronted him.

He had thought much upon this subject (so much that at times the effort of sustained thought tired him), and he had come to the conclusion that somewhere, sometime he must have experienced many things. He had questioned Orando casually as to the young black's past, and learned that he could recall events in clear detail as far back as his early childhood. Muzimo could recall but a couple of yesterdays. Finally he came to the conclusion that his mental state must be the natural state of spirits, and because it was so different from that of man he found in it almost irrefutable proof of his spirithood. With a feeling of detachment he viewed the antics of man, viewed them contemptuously. With folded arms he stood apart in silence, apparently as oblivious to the noisy bickerings of the blacks as to the chattering and scolding of The Spirit of Nyamwegi perched upon his shoulder.

But at last the noisy horde was herded into something approximating order; and, followed by laughing, screaming women and children, started upon its march toward high adventure. Not, however, until the latter turned back did the men settle down to serious marching, though Lupingu's croakings of eventual disaster had never permitted them to forget the seriousness of their undertaking.

For three days they marched, led by Orando and guided by Muzimo. The spirits of the warriors were high as they approached their goal. Lupingu had been silenced by ridicule. All seemed well. Muzimo had told them that the village of the Leopard Men lay near at hand and that upon the following morning he would go ahead alone and reconnoitre.

With the dawning of the fourth day all were eager, for Orando had never ceased to incite them to anger against the murderers of Nyamwegi. Constantly he had impressed them with the fact that The Spirit of Nyamwegi was with them to watch over and protect them, that his own 'muzimo' was there to insure them victory.

It was while they were squatting about their breakfast fires that someone discovered that Lupingu was missing. A careful search of the camp failed to locate him; and it was at once assumed that, nearing the enemy, he had deserted through fear. Loud was the condemnation, bitter the scorn that this cowardly defection aroused. It was still the topic of angry discussion as Muzimo and The Spirit of Nyamwegi slipped silently away through the trees toward the village of the Leopard Men.

A fibre rope about her neck, the girl was being half led, half dragged through the jungle. A powerful young black walking ahead of her held the free end of the rope; ahead of him an old man led the way; behind her was a second young man. All three were strangely garbed in leopard skins. The heads of leopards, cunningly mounted, fitted snugly over their woolly pates. Curved steel talons were fitted to their fingers. Their teeth were filed, their faces hideously painted. Of the three, the old man was the most terrifying. He was the leader. The others cringed servilely when he gave commands.

The girl could understand little that they said. She had no idea as to the fate that was destined for her. As yet they had not injured her, but she could anticipate nothing other than a horrible termination of this hideous adventure. The young man who led her was occasionally rough when she stumbled or faltered, but he had not been actually brutal. Their appearance, however, was sufficient to arouse the direst forebodings in her mind; and she had always the recollection of the horrid butchery of the faithful black man who had been left to guard her.

Thoughts of him reminded her of the white man who had left him to protect her. She had feared and mistrusted him; she had wanted to be rid of him. Now she wished that she were back in his camp. She did not admire him any more than she had. It was merely that she considered him the lesser of two evils. As she recalled him she thought of him only as an ill-mannered boor, as quite the most disagreeable person she had ever seen. Yet there was that about him which aroused her curiosity. His English suggested anything other than illiteracy. His clothes and his attitude toward her placed him upon the lowest rung of the social scale. He occupied her thoughts to a considerable extent, but he still remained an inexplicable enigma.

For two days her captors followed obscure trails. They passed no villages, saw no other human beings than themselves. Then, toward the close of the second day they came suddenly upon a large, palisaded village beside a river. The heavy gates that barred the entrance were closed, although the sun had not yet set, but when they had approached closely enough to be recognised they were admitted following a short parley between the old man and the keepers of the gate.

The stronghold of the Leopard Men was the village of Gato Mgungu, chief of a once powerful tribe that had dwindled in numbers until now it boasted but this single village. But Gato Mgungo was also chief of the Leopard Men, a position which carried with it a sinister power far above that of many a chief whose villages were more numerous and whose tribes were numerically far stronger. This was true largely because of the fact that the secret order whose affairs he administered was recruited from unrelated clans and villages; and, because of the allegiance enforced by its strict and merciless code, Gato Mgungu demanded the first loyalty of its members, even above their loyalty to their own tribes or families. Thus, in nearly every village within a radius of a hundred miles Gato Mgungu had followers who kept him informed as to the plans of other chiefs, followers who must even slay their own kin if the chief of the Leopard Men so decreed.

In the village of Gato Mgungu alone were all the inhabitants members of the secret order; in the other villages his adherents were unknown, or, at most, only suspected of membership in the feared and hated order. To be positively identified as a Leopard Man, in most villages, would have been to meet sudden, mysterious death; for so loathed were they a son would kill his own father if he knew that he was a member of the sect, and so feared that no man dared destroy one except in secret lest the wrath and the terrible vengeance of the order fall upon him.

In secret places, deep hidden in impenetrable jungle, the Leopard Men of outlying districts performed the abhorrent rites of the order except upon those occasions when they gathered at the village of Gato Mgungu, near which was located their temple. Such was the reason for the gathering that now filled the village with warriors and for the relatively small number of women and children that the girl noticed as she was dragged through the gateway into the main street.

Here the women, degraded, hideous, filed-tooth harpies, would have set upon her and torn her to pieces but for the interference of her captors, who laid about them with the hafts of their spears, driving the creatures off until the old man could make himself heard. He spoke angrily with a voice of authority; and immediately the women withdrew, though they cast angry, venomous glances at the captive that boded no good for her should she fall into their hands.

Guarding her closely, her three captors led her through a horde of milling warriors to a large hut before which was seated an old, wrinkled black with a huge belly. This was Gato Mgungu, chief of the Leopard Men. As the four approached he looked up, and at sight of the white girl a sudden interest momentarily lighted his blood-shot eyes that ordinarily gazed dully from between red and swollen lids. Then he recognised the old man and addressed him.

'You have brought me a present, Lulimi?' he demanded.

'Lulimi has brought a present,' replied the old man, 'but not for Gato Mgungu alone.'

'What do you mean?' The chief scowled now.

'I have brought a present for the whole clan and for the Leopard God.'

'Gato Mgungu does not share his slaves with others,' the chief growled.

'I have brought no slave,' snapped Lulimi. It was evident that he did not greatly fear Gato Mgungu. And why should he, who was high in the priesthood of the Leopard Clan?

'Then why have you brought this white woman to my village?'

By now there was a dense half-circle of interested auditors craning their necks to view the prisoner and straining their ears to catch all that was passing between these two great men of their little world. For this audience Lulimi was grateful, for he was never so happy as when he held the centre of the stage, surrounded by credulous and ignorant listeners. Lulimi was a priest.

'Three nights ago we lay in the forest far from the village of Gato Mgungu, far from the temple of the Leopard God.' Already he could see his auditors pricking up their ears. 'It was a dark night. The lion was abroad and the leopard. We kept a large fire burning to frighten them away. It was my turn to watch. The others slept. Suddenly I saw two green eyes shining just beyond the fire. They blazed like living coals. They came closer, and I was afraid; but I could not move. I could not call out. My tongue stuck to the roof of my mouth. My jaws would not open. Closer and closer they came, those terrible eyes, until, just beyond the fire, I saw a great leopard, the largest leopard that I have ever seen. I thought that the end of my days had come and that I was about to die.

'I waited for him to spring upon me, but he did not spring. Instead, he opened his mouth and spoke to me.' Gasps of astonishment greeted this statement while Lulimi paused for effect.

'What did he say to you?' demanded Gato Mgungu.

'He said, "I am the brother of the Leopard God. He sent me to find Lulimi, because he trusts Lulimi. Lulimi is a great man. He is very brave and wise. There is no one knows as much as Lulimi."'

Gato Mgungu looked bored. 'Did the Leopard God send his brother three marches to tell you that?'

'He told me other things, many things. Some of them I can repeat, but others I may never speak of. Only the Leopard God, and his brother, and Lulimi know these things.'

'What has all this to do with the white woman?' demanded Gato Mgungu.

'I am getting to that,' replied Lulimi sourly. He did not relish these interruptions. 'Then, when the brother of the Leopard God had asked after my health, he told me that I was to go to a certain place the next day and that there I should find a white woman. She would be alone in the jungle with one black man. He commanded me to kill the black man and bring the woman to his temple to be high priestess of the Leopard Clan. This Lulimi will do. Tonight Lulimi takes the white high priestess to the great temple. I have spoken.'

For a moment there was awed silence. Gato Mgungu did not seem pleased; but Lulimi was a powerful priest to whom the rank and file looked up, and he had greatly increased his prestige by this weird tale. Gato Mgungu was sufficiently a judge of men to know that. Furthermore, he was an astute old politician, with an eye to the future. He knew that Imigeg, the high priest, was a very old man who could not live much longer and that Lulimi, who had been laying his plans to that end for years, would doubtless succeed him.

Now a high priest friendly to Gato Mgungu could do much to increase the power and prestige of the chief and, incidentally, his revenues; while one who was inimical might threaten his ascendancy. Therefore, reading thus plainly the handwriting on the wall, Gato Mgungu seized this opportunity to lay the foundations of future friendship and understanding between them though he knew that Lulimi was an old fraud and his story doubtless a canard.

Many of the warriors, having sensed in the chief's former attitude a certain antagonism to Lulimi, were evidently waiting a cue from their leader. As Gato Mgungu jumped, so would the majority of the fighting men; but when the day came that a successor to Imigeg must be chosen it would be the priests who would make the selection, and Gato Mgungu knew that Lulimi had a long memory.

All eyes were upon the chief as he cleared his royal throat. 'We have heard the story of Lulimi,' he said. 'We all know Lulimi. In his own village he is a great witch-doctor. In the temple of the Leopard God there is no greater priest after Imigeg. It is not strange that the brother of the Leopard God should speak to Lulimi. Gato Mgungu is only a fighting man. He does not talk with gods and demons. This is not a matter for warriors. It is a matter for priests. All that Lulimi has said we believe, but let us take the white woman to the temple. The Leopard God and Imigeg will know whether the jungle leopard spoke true words to Lulimi or not. Has not my tongue spoken wise words, Lulimi?'

'The tongue of Gato Mgungu, the chief, always speaks wise words,' replied the priest, who was inwardly delighted that the chief's attitude had not been, as he had feared, antagonistic. And thus the girl's fate was decided by the greed of corrupt politicians, temporal and ecclesiastical, suggesting that the benighted blacks of Central Africa are in some respects quite as civilised as we.

As preparations were being made to conduct the girl to the temple, a lone warrior, sweat-streaked and breathless, approached the gates of the village. Here he was halted, but when he had given the secret sign of the Leopard Clan he was admitted. There was much excited jabbering at the gateway; but to all questions the newcomer insisted that he must speak to Gato Mgungu immediately upon a matter of urgent importance, and presently he was brought before the chief.

Again he gave the secret sign of the Leopard Clan as he faced Gato Mgungu.

'What message do you bring?' demanded the chief.

'A few hours' march from here a hundred Utenga warriors led by Orando, the son of Lobongo, the chief, are waiting to attack your village. They come to avenge Nyamwegi of Kibbu, who was killed by members of the clan. If you send warriors at once to hide beside the trail they can ambush the Utengas and kill them all.'

'Where lies their camp?'

The messenger described the location minutely; and when he had finished, Gato Mgungu ordered a sub-chief to gather three hundred warriors and march against the invaders; then he turned to the messenger. 'We shall feast tonight upon our enemies,' he growled, 'and you shall sit beside Gato Mgungu and have the choicest morsels.'

'I may not remain,' replied the messenger. 'I must return from whence I came lest I be suspected of carrying word to you.'

'Who are you?' demanded Gato Mgungu.

'I am Lupingu of Kibbu, in the Watenga country,' replied the messenger.

CHAPTER SEVEN

The Captive

Knowing nothing of the meaning of what was transpiring around her, the girl sensed in the excitement and activity following the coming of the messenger something of the cause that underlay them. She saw fighting men hurriedly arming themselves; she saw them depart from the village. In her heart was a hope that perhaps the enemy they went to meet might be a succouring party is search of her. Reason argued to the contrary; but hope catches at straws, unreasoning.

When the war party had departed, attention was again focused upon the girl. Lulimi waxed important. He ordered people about right and left. Twenty men armed with spears and shields and carrying paddles formed about her as an escort. Led by Lulimi, they marched through the gateway of the village down to the river. Here they placed her in a large canoe which they launched in silence, knowing that enemies were not far distant. There was no singing or shouting as there would have been upon a similar occasion under ordinary circumstances. In silence they dipped their paddles into the swift stream; silently they sped with the current down the broad river, keeping close to the river bank upon the same side as that upon which they had launched the craft by the village of Gato Mgungu.

Poor little Kali Bwana! They had taken the rope from about her neck; they treated her now with a certain respect, tinged with awe, for was she not to be the high priestess of the Leopard God? But of that she knew nothing. She could only wonder, as numb with hopelessness she watched the green verdure of the river bank move swiftly past. Where were they taking her? To what horrid fate? She noted the silence and the haste of her escort; she recalled the excitement following the coming of the messenger to the village and the hasty exodus of the war party.

All these facts combined to suggest that her captors were hurrying her away from a rescuing party. But who could have organised such an expedition? Who knew of her plight? Only the bitter man of rags and patches. But what could he do to effect her rescue, even if he cared to do so? It had been evident to her that he was a poor and worthless vagabond. His force consisted now of but two natives. His camp, he had told her, was several marches from where he had found her. He could not possibly have obtained reinforcements from that source in the time that had elapsed since her capture, even if they existed, which she doubted. She could not imagine that such a sorry specimen of poverty commanded any resources whatever. Thus she was compelled to abandon hope of succour from this source; yet hope did not die. In the last extremity one may always expect a miracle.

For a mile or two the canoe sped down the river, the paddles rising and falling with clock-like regularity and almost in silence; then suddenly the speed of the craft was checked, and its nose turned toward the bank. Ahead of them the girl saw the mouth of a small affluent of the main river, and presently the canoe slid into its sluggish waters.

Great trees arched above the narrow, winding stream; dense underbrush choked the ground between their boles; matted vines and creepers clung to their mossy branches, or hung motionless in the breathless air, trailing almost to the surface of the water; gorgeous blooms shot the green with vivid colour. It was a scene of beauty, yet there hung about it an air of mystery and death like a noxious miasma. It reminded the girl of the face of a lovely woman behind whose mask of beauty hid a vicious soul. The silence, the scent of rotting things in the heavy air oppressed her.

Just ahead a great, slimy body slid from a rotting log into the slow moving waters. It was a crocodile. As the canoe glided silently through the semi-darkness the girl saw that the river was fairly alive with these hideous reptiles whose presence served but to add to the depression that already weighed so heavily upon her.

She sought to arouse her drooping spirits by recalling the faint hope of rescue that she had entertained and clung to ever since she had been so hurriedly removed from the village. Fortunately for her peace of mind she did not know her destination, nor that the only avenue to it lay along this crocodile-infested stream. No other path led through the matted jungle to the cleverly hidden temple of the Leopard Men. No other avenue than this fetid river gave ingress to it, and this was known to no human being who was not a Leopard Man.

The canoe had proceeded up the stream for a couple of miles when the girl saw upon the right bank just ahead of them a large, grass-thatched building. Unaccustomed as she had been during the past few months to seeing any structure larger than the ordinary native huts, the size of this building filled her with astonishment. It was quite two hundred feet long and fifty wide, nor less than fifty feet in height. It lay parallel to the river, its main entrance being in the end they were approaching. A wide verandah extended across the front of the building along the side facing the river. The entire structure was elevated on piles to a height of about ten feet above the ground. She did not know it, but this was the temple of the Leopard God, whose high priestess she was destined to be.

As the canoe drew closer to the building a number of men emerged from its interior. Lulimi rose from the bottom of the craft where he had been squatting and shouted a few words to the men on the temple porch. They were the secret passwords of the order, to which one of the guardians of the temple replied, whereupon the canoe drew in to the shore.

A few curious priests surrounded Lulimi and the girl as the old man escorted her up the temple steps to the great entrance flanked by grotesquely carved images and into the half-light of the interior. Here she found herself in an enormous room open to the rafters far above her head. Hideous masks hung upon the supporting columns with shields, and spears, and knives, and human skulls. Idols, crudely carved, stood about the floor. Many of these represented a human body with the head of an animal, though so rude was the craftsmanship that the girl could not be certain what animal they were intended to represent. It might be a leopard, she thought.

At the far end of the room, which they were approaching, she discerned a raised dais. It was, in reality, a large platform paved with clay. Upon it, elevated a couple of feet, was a smaller dais about five feet wide and twice as long, which was covered with the skins of animals. A heavy post supporting a human skull was set in the centre of the long dimension of the smaller dais close to its rear edge. These details she noted only casually at the time. She was to have reason to remember them vividly later.

As Lulimi led her toward the dais a very old man emerged from an opening in the wall at its back and came toward them. He had a particularly repellent visage, the ugliness of which was accentuated by the glowering scowl with which he regarded her.

As his old eyes fell upon Lulimi they were lighted dimly by a feeble ray of recognition. 'It is you?' he mumbled. 'But why do you bring this white woman? Who is she? A sacrifice?'

'Listen, Imigeg,' whispered Lulimi, 'and think well. Remember your prophecy.'

'What prophecy?' demanded the high priest querulously. He was very old; and his memory sometimes played him tricks, though he did not like to admit it.

'Long ago you said that some day a white priestess would sit with you and the Leopard God, here on the great throne of the temple. Now your prophecy shall be fulfilled. Here is the white priestess, brought by Lulimi, just as you prophesied.'

Now Imigeg did not recall having made any such prophecy, for the very excellent reason that he never had done so; but Lulimi was a wily old person who knew Imigeg better than Imigeg knew himself. He knew that the old high priest was rapidly losing his memory; and he knew, too, that he was very sensitive on the subject, so sensitive that he would not dare deny having made such a prophecy as Lulimi imputed to him.

For reasons of his own Lulimi desired a white priestess. Just how it might redound to his benefit is not entirely clear, but the mental processes of priests are often beyond the ken of lay minds. Perhaps his reasons might have been obvious to a Hollywood publicity agent; but however that may be, the method he had adopted to ensure the acceptance of his priestess was entirely successful.

Imigeg swallowed the bait, hook, line, and sinker. He swelled with importance. 'Imigeg talks with the demons and the spirits,' he said; 'they tell him everything. When we have human flesh for the Leopard God and his priests, the white woman shall be made high priestess of the order.'

'That should be soon then,' announced Lulimi.

'How do you know that?' demanded Imigeg.

'My "muzimo" came to me and told me that the warriors now in the village of Gato Mgungu would march forth today, returning with food enough for all.'

'Good,' exclaimed Imigeg quickly; 'it is just as I prophesied yesterday to the lesser priests.'

'Tonight then,' said Lulimi. 'Now you will want to have the white woman prepared.'

At the suggestion Imigeg clapped his hands, whereupon several of the lesser priests advanced. 'Take the woman,' he instructed one of them to the quarters of the priestesses. 'She is to be high priestesses of the order. Tell them this and that they shall prepare her. Tell them, also, that Imigeg holds them responsible for her safety.'

The lesser priest led the girl through the opening at the rear of the dais, where she discovered herself in a corridor flanked on either side by rooms. To the door of one of these the man conducted her and, pushing her ahead, entered. It was a large room in which were a dozen women, naked but for tiny G strings. Nearly all of them were young; but there was one toothless old hag, and it was she whom the man addressed.

The angry and resentful movement of the women toward the white girl at the instant that she entered the room was halted at the first words of her escort. 'This is the new high priestess of the Leopard God,' he announced. 'Imigeg sends orders that you are to prepare her for the rites to be held tonight. If any harm befalls her you will be held accountable, and you all know the anger of Imigeg.'

'Leave her with me,' mumbled the old woman. 'I have served in the temple through many rains, and I have not filled the belly of the Leopard God yet.'

'You are too old and tough,' snarled one of the younger women.

'You are not,' snapped the old hag. 'All the more reason that you should be careful not to make Imigeg angry, or Mumga, either. Go,' she directed the priest. 'The white woman will be safe with old Mumga.'

As the man left the room the women gathered about the girl. Hatred distorted their features. The younger women tore at her clothing. They pushed and pulled her about, all the while jabbering excitedly; but they did not injure her aside from a few scratches from claw-like nails.

The reason for bringing her here at all was unknown to Kali Bwana; the intentions of the women were, similarly, a mystery. Their demeanour boded her no good, and she believed that eventually they would kill her. Their degraded faces, their sharp-filed, yellow fangs, their angry voices and glances left no doubt in her mind as to the seriousness of her situation or the desires of the harpies. That a power which they feared restrained them she did not know. She saw only the menace of their attitude toward her and their rough and brutal handling of her.

One by one they stripped her garments from her until she stood even more naked than they, and then she was accorded a respite as they fell to fighting among themselves for her clothing. For the first time she had an opportunity to note her surroundings. She saw that the room was the common sleeping and eating apartment of the women. Straw mats were stretched across one of its sides. There was a clay hearth at one end directly below a hole in the roof, through which some of the smoke from a still smouldering fire was finding its way into the open air, though most of it hung among the rafters of the high ceiling, from whence it settled down to fill the apartment with acrid fumes. A few cooking pots stood on or beside the hearth. There were earthen jars and wooden boxes, fibre baskets and pouches of skin strewn upon the floor along the walls, many near the sleeping mats. From pegs stuck in the walls depended an array of ornaments and finery: strings of beads, necklaces of human teeth and of the teeth of leopards, bracelets of copper and iron and anklets of the same metals, feather head-dresses and breastplates of metal and of hide, and innumerable garments fashioned from the black-spotted, yellow skins of leopards. Everything in the apartment bespoke primitive savagery in keeping with its wild and savage inmates.

When the final battle for the last vestige of her apparel had terminated the women again turned their attention to the girl. Old Mumga addressed her at considerable length, but Kali Bwana only shook her head to indicate that she could understand nothing that was said to her. Then at a word from the old woman they laid hold of her again, none too gently. She was thrown upon one of the filthy sleeping mats, an earthen jar was dragged to the side of the mat, and two young women proceeded to anoint her with a vile smelling oil, the base of which might have been rancid butter. This was rubbed in by rough hands until her flesh was almost raw; then a greenish liquid, which smelled of bay leaves and stung like fire, was poured over her; and again she was rubbed until the liquid had evaporated.

When this ordeal had been concluded, leaving her weak and sick from its effects, she was clothed. Much discussion accompanied this ceremony, and several times women were sent to consult Imigeg and to fetch apparel from other parts of the temple. Finally they seemed satisfied with their handiwork, and Kali Bwana, who had worn some of the most ridiculous creations of the most famous couturiers of Paris, stood clothed as she had never been clothed before.

First they had adjusted about her slim, fair waist a loin cloth made from the skins of unborn leopard cubs; and then, over one shoulder, had been draped a gorgeous hide of vivid yellow, spotted with glossy black. This garment hung in graceful folds almost to her knee on one side, being shorter on the other. A rope of leopard tails gathered it loosely about her hips. About her throat was a necklace of human teeth; upon her wrists and arms were heavy bracelets, at least two of which she recognised as gold. In similar fashion were her ankles adorned, and then more necklaces were hung about her neck. Her head-dress consisted of a diadem of leopard skin supporting a variety of plumes and feathers which entirely encircled her head. But the finishing touch brought a chill of horror to her; long, curved talons of gold were affixed to her fingers and thumbs, recalling the cruel death of the black who had striven so bravely and so futilely to protect her.

Thus was Kali Bwana prepared for the hideous rites of the Leopard Men that would make her high priestess of their savage god.

CHAPTER EIGHT

Treason Unmasked

Muzimo loafed through the forest. He was glad to be alone, away from the noisy, boasting creatures that were men. True, The Spirit of Nyamwegi was given to boasting; but Muzimo never paid much attention to him. Sometimes he chided him for behaving so much like men; and as long as The Spirit of Nyamwegi could remember, he was quiet; but his memory was short. Only when a certain stern expression entered the eyes of Muzimo and he spoke in a low voice that was half growl, was The Spirit of Nyamwegi quiet for long; but that occurred only when there was important need for silence.

Muzimo and The Spirit of Nyamwegi had departed early from the camp of the Utengas for the purpose of locating and spying upon the village of the Leopard Men, but time meant nothing to Muzimo. This thing that he had set out to do, he would do when he was ready. So it was that the morning was all but spent before Muzimo caught sight of the village.

The warriors had already departed in search of the enemies from Watenga, and Muzimo had not seen them because he had taken a circuitous route from the camp to the village. The girl had also been taken away to the temple, though even had she still been there her presence would have meant nothing to the ancestral spirit of Orando, who was no more concerned with the fate of whites than he was with the fate of blacks.

The village upon which he looked from the concealing verdure of a nearby tree differed little from the quiet native village of Tumbai except that its palisade was taller and stronger. There were a few men and women in its single main street, the former lolling in the shade of trees, the latter busy with the endless duties of their sex, which they lightened by the worldwide medium of gossip.

Muzimo was not much interested in what he saw, at least at first. There was no great concourse of warriors. A hundred Utengas, if they could surprise the village, could wreak vengeance upon it easily. He noted, however, that the gates were thick and high, that they were closed, and that a guard of warriors squatted near them in the shade of the palisade. Perhaps, he thought, it would be better to take the place by night when a few agile men might scale the palisade undetected and open the gates for their fellows. He finally decided that he would do that himself without assistance. For Muzimo it would be a simple matter to enter the village undetected.

Suddenly his eyes were arrested by a group before a large hut. There was a large man, whom he intuitively knew to be the chief, and there were several others with whom he was conversing; but it was not the chief who arrested his attention. It was one of the others. Instantly Muzimo recognised him, and his grey eyes narrowed. What was Lupingu doing in the village of the Leopard Men? It was evident that he was not a prisoner, for it was plainly to be seen that the conversation between the men was amicable.

Muzimo waited. Presently he saw Lupingu leave the party before the chief's hut and approach the gates. He saw the warriors on guard open them, and he saw Lupingu pass through them and disappear into the forest in the direction of the camp of the Utengas. Muzimo was puzzled. What was Lupingu going to do? What had he already done? Perhaps he had gone to spy upon the Leopard Men and was returning with information for Orando.

Silently Muzimo slipped from the tree in which he had been hiding, and swung through the trees upon the trail of Lupingu, who, ignorant of the presence of the Nemesis hovering above him, trotted briskly in the direction of the camp of the tribesmen he had betrayed.

Presently from a distance, far ahead, Muzimo heard sounds, sounds that the ears of Lupingu could not hear. They told him that many people were coming through the forest in his direction. Later he interpreted them as the sounds made by warriors marching hurriedly. They were almost upon him before Lupingu heard them. When he did he went off from the trail a short distance and hid in the underbrush.

Muzimo waited among the foliage above the trees. He had caught the scent of the oncoming men and had recognised none that was familiar to him. It was the scent of black warriors, and mixed with it was the scent of fresh blood. Some of them were wounded. They had been in battle.

Presently they came in sight; and he saw that they were not the Utengas, as his nostrils had already told him. He guessed that they were from the village of the Leopard Men, and that they were returning to it. This accounted for the small number of warriors that he had seen in the village. Where had they been? Had they been in battle with Orando's little force?

He counted them, roughly, as they passed below him. There were nearly three hundred of them, and Orando had but a hundred warriors. Yet he was sure that Orando had not been badly defeated, for he saw no prisoners nor were they bringing any dead warriors with them, not even their own dead, as they would have, if they were Leopard Men and had been victorious.

Evidently, whoever they had fought, and it must have been Orando, had repulsed them; but how had the Utengas fared? Their losses must have been great in battle with a force that so greatly outnumbered them. But all this was only surmise. Presently he would find the Utengas and learn the truth. In the meantime he must keep an eye on Lupingu who was still hiding at one side of the trail.

When the Leopard Men had passed, Lupingu came from his concealment, and continued on in the direction he had been going, while above him and a little in his rear swung Muzimo and The Spirit of Nyamwegi.

When they came at last to the place where the Utengas had camped, they found only grim reminders of the recent battle; the Utengas were not there. Lupingu looked about him, a pleased smile on his crafty face. His efforts had not been in vain; the Leopard Men had at least driven the Utengas away, even though it had been as evident to him as it had been to Muzimo that their victory had been far from decisive.

For a moment he hesitated, of two minds as to whether to follow his former companions, or return to the village and take part in the ceremonies at the temple at the installation of the white priestess; but at last he decided that the safer plan was to rejoin the Utengas, lest a prolonged absence should arouse their suspicions as to his loyalty. He did not know that the matter was not in his hands at all, or that a power far greater than his own lurked above him, all but reading his mind, a power that would have frustrated an attempt to return to the village of Gato Mgungu and carried him by force to the new camp of Orando.

Lupingu had jogged on along the plain trail of the retreating Utengas for a couple of miles when he was halted by a sentry whom he recognised at once as the brother of the girl whose affections Nyamwegi had stolen from him. When the sentry saw that it was Lupingu, the traitor was permitted to pass; and a moment later he entered the camp, which he found bristling with spears, the nerve-shaken warriors having leaped to arms at the challenge of the sentry.

There were wounded men groaning upon the ground, and ten of the Utenga dead were stretched out at one side of the camp, where a burial party was digging a shallow trench in which to inter them.

A volley of questions was hurled at Lupingu as he sought out Orando, and the angry or suspicious looks that accompanied them warned him that his story must be a most convincing one if it were to avail him.

Orando greeted him with a questioning scowl. 'Where have you been, Lupingu, while we were fighting?' he demanded.

'I, too, have been fighting,' replied Lupingu glibly.

'I did not see you,' countered Orando. 'You were not there. You were not in camp this morning. Where were you? See that your tongue speaks no lies.'

'My tongue speaks only true words,' insisted Lupingu. 'Last night I said to myself: "Orando does not like Lupingu. There are many who do not like Lupingu. Because he advised them not to make war against the Leopard Men they do not like him. Now he must do something to show them that he is a brave warrior. He must do something to save them from the Leopard Men."

'And so I went out from camp while it was still dark to search for the village of the Leopard Men, that I might spy upon them and bring word to Orando. But I did not find the village. I became lost, and while I was searching for it I met many warriors. I did not run. I stood and fought with them until I had killed three. Then some came from behind and seized me. They made me prisoner, and I learned that I was in the hands of the Leopard Men.

'Later they fought with you. I could not see the battle, as their guards held me far behind the fighting men; but after a while the Leopard Men ran away, and I knew that the Utengas had been victorious. In the excitement I escaped and hid. When they had all gone I came at once to the camp of Orando.'

The son of Lobongo, the chief, was no fool. He did not believe Lupingu's story, but he did not guess the truth. The worst interpretation that he put on Lupingu's desertion was cowardice in the face of an impending battle; but that was something to be punished by the contempt of his fellow warriors and the ridicule of the women of his village when he returned to Kibbu.

Orando shrugged. He had other, more important matters to occupy his thoughts. 'If you want to win the praise of warriors,' he advised, 'remain and fight beside them.' Then he turned away.

With startling suddenness that shocked the frayed nerves of the Utengas, Muzimo and The Spirit of Nyamwegi dropped unexpectedly into their midst from the overhanging branches of a tree. Once again three score spears danced nervously, their owners ready to fight or fly as the first man set the example; but when they saw who it was their fears were calmed; and perhaps they felt a little more confidence, for the presence of two friendly spirits is most reassuring to a body of half defeated warriors fearful of the return of the enemy.

'You have had a battle,' said Muzimo to Orando. 'I saw the Leopard Men running away; but your men act as though they, too, had been defeated. I do not understand.'

'They came to our camp and fell upon us while we were unprepared,' explained Orando. 'Many of our men were killed or wounded in their first charge, but the Utengas were brave. They rallied and fought the Leopard Men off, killing many, wounding many; then the Leopard Men ran away, for we were fighting more bravely than they.

'We did not pursue them, because they greatly outnumbered us. After the battle my men were afraid they might return in still greater numbers. They did not wish to fight any more. They said that we had won, and that now Nyamwegi was fully avenged. They want to go home. Therefore we fell back to this new camp. Here we bury our dead. Tomorrow we do what the gods decide. I do not know.

'What I should like to know, though, is how the Leopard Men knew we were here. They shouted to us and told us that the god of the Leopard Men had sent them to our camp to get much flesh for a great feast. They said that tonight they would eat us all. It was those words that frightened the Utengas and made them want to go home.'

'Would you like to know who told the Leopard Men that you were coming and where our camp was?' asked Muzimo.

Lupingu's eyes reflected a sudden fear. He edged off toward the jungle. 'Watch Lupingu,' directed Muzimo, 'lest he go again to "spy upon the Leopard Men."' The words were scarcely uttered before Lupingu bolted; but a dozen warriors blocked his way; and presently he was dragged back, struggling and protesting. 'It was not a god that told the Leopard Men that the Utengas were coming,' continued Muzimo. 'I crouched in a tree above their village, and saw the one who told them talking to their chief. Very friendly were they, as though both were Leopard Men. I followed him when he left the village. I saw him hide when the retreating warriors passed in the jungle. I followed him to the camp of the Utengas. I heard his tongue speak lies to Orando. I am Muzimo. I have spoken.'

Instantly hoarse cries for vengeance arose. Men fell upon Lupingu and knocked him about. He would have been killed at once had not Muzimo interfered. He seized the wretched man and shielded him with his great body, while The Spirit of Nyamwegi fled to the branches of a tree and screamed excitedly as he danced up and down in a perfect frenzy of rage, though what it was all about he did not know.

'Do not kill him,' commanded Muzimo, sternly. 'Leave him to me.'

'The traitor must die,' shouted a warrior.

'Leave him to me,' reiterated Muzimo.

'Leave him to Muzimo,' commanded Orando; and at last, disgruntled, the warriors desisted from their attempts to lay hands upon the wretch.

'Bring ropes,' directed Muzimo, 'and bind his wrists and ankles.'

When eager hands had done as Muzimo bid, the warriors formed a half circle before him and Lupingu, waiting expectantly to witness the death of the prisoner, which they believed would take the form of some supernatural and particularly atrocious manifestation.

They saw Muzimo lift the man to one broad shoulder. They saw him take a few running steps, leap as lightly into the air as though he bore no burden whatsoever, seize a low-hanging limb as he swung himself upward, and disappear amidst the foliage above, melting into the shadows of the coming dusk.

CHAPTER NINE

The Leopard God

Night was approaching. The sun, half hidden by the tops of forest trees, swung downward into the west. Its departing rays turned the muddy waters of a broad river to the semblance of molten gold. A ragged white man emerged from a forest trail upon the outskirts of a broad field of manioc, at the far side of which a palisaded village cast long shadows back to meet the shadows of the forest where he stood with is two black companions. To his right the forest hemmed the field and came down to overhang the palisade at the rear of the village.

'Do not go on, Bwana,' urged one of the blacks. 'It is the village of the Leopard Men.'

'It is the village of old Gato Mgungu,' retorted Old Timer. 'I have traded with him in the past.'

'Then you came with many followers and with guns; then Gato Mgungu was a trader. Today you come with only two boys; today you will find that old Gato Mgungu is a Leopard Man.'

'Bosh!' exclaimed the white man. 'He would not dare harm a white.'

'You do not know them,' insisted the black. 'They would kill their own mothers for flesh if there was no one to see them do it.'

'Every sign that we have seen indicates that the girl was brought here,' argued Old Timer. 'Leopard Men or no Leopard Men, I am going into the village.'

'I do not wish to die,' said the black.

'Nor do I,' agreed his fellow.

'Then wait for me in the forest. Wait until the shadow of the forest has left the palisade in the morning. If I have not returned then, go back to the camp where the young bwana waits and tell him that I am dead.'

The blacks shook their heads. 'Do not go, Bwana. The white woman was not your wife, neither was she your mother nor your sister. Why should you die for a woman who was nothing to you?'

Old Timer shook his head. 'You would not understand.' He wondered if he himself understood. Vaguely he realised that the force that was driving him on was not governed by reason; back of it was something inherent, bred into his fibre through countless generations of his kind. Its name was duty. If there was another more powerful force actuating him he was not conscious of it. Perhaps there was no other. There were lesser forces, though, and one of them was anger and another, desire for revenge. But two days of tracking through the jungle had cooled these to the point where he would no longer have risked his life to gratify them. It was the less obvious but more powerful urge that drove him on.

'Perhaps I shall return in a few minutes,' he said, 'but if not, then until tomorrow morning!' He shook their hands in parting.

'Good luck, Bwana!'

'May the good spirits watch over you, Bwana!'

He strode confidently along the path that skirted the manioc field toward the gates set in the palisade. Savage eyes watched his approach. Behind him the eyes of his servitors filled with tears. Inside the palisade a warrior ran to the hut of Gato Mgungu.

'A white man is coming,' he reported. 'He is alone.'

'Let him enter, and bring him to me,' ordered the chief.

As Old Timer came close to the gates one of them swung open. He saw a few warriors surveying him more or less apathetically. There was nothing in their demeanour to suggest antagonism, neither was their greeting in any way friendly. Their manner was wholly perfunctory. He made the sign of peace, which they ignored; but that did not trouble him. He was not concerned with the attitude of warriors, only with that of Gato Mgungu, the chief. As he was, so would they be.

'I have come to visit my friend, Gato Mgungu,' he announced.

'He is waiting for you,' replied the warrior who had taken word of his coming to the chief. 'Come with me.'

Old Timer noted the great number of warriors in the village. Among them he saw wounded men and knew that there had been a battle. He hoped that they had been victorious. Gato Mgungu would be in better humour were such the case. The scowling, unfriendly glances of the villagers did not escape him as he followed his guide toward the hut of the chief. On the whole, the atmosphere of the village was far from reassuring; but he had gone too far to turn back, even had he been of a mind to do so.

Gato Mgungu received him with a surly nod. He was sitting on a stool in front of his hut surrounded by a number of his principal followers. There was no answering smile or pleasant word to Old Timer's friendly greeting. The aspect of the situation appeared far from roseate.

'What are you doing here?' demanded Gato Mgungu.

The smile had faded from the white man's face. He knew that this was no time for soft words. There was danger in the very air. He sensed it without knowing the reason for it; and he knew that a bold front, alone, might release him from a serious situation.

'I have come for the white girl,' he said.

Gato Mgungu's eyes shifted. 'What white girl?' he demanded.

'Do not lie to me with questions,' snapped Old Timer. 'The white girl is here. For two days I have followed those who stole her from my camp. Give her to me. I wish to return to my people who wait for me in the forest.'

'There is no white girl in my village,' growled Gato Mgungu, 'nor do I take orders from white men. I am Gato Mgungu, the chief. I give orders.'

'You'll take orders from me, you old scoundrel,' threatened the other, 'or I'll have a force down on your village that'll wipe it off the map.'

Gato Mgungu sneered. 'I know you, white man. There are two of you and six black men in your safari. You have few guns. You are poor. You steal ivory. You do not dare go where the white rulers are. They would put you in jail. You come with big words, but big words do not frighten Gato Mgungu; and now you are my prisoner.'

'Well, what of it?' demanded Old Timer. 'What do you think you're going to do with me?'

'Kill you,' replied Gato Mgungu.

The white man laughed. 'No you won't; not if you know what's good for you. The government would burn your village and hang you when they found it out.'

'They will not find it out,' retorted the chief. 'Take him away. See that he does not escape.'

Old Timer looked quickly around at the evil, scowling faces surrounding him. It was then that he recognised the chief, Bobolo, with whom he had long been upon good terms. Two warriors laid heavy hands upon him to drag him away. 'Wait!' he exclaimed, thrusting them aside. 'Let me speak to Bobolo. He certainly has sense enough to stop this foolishness.'

'Take him away!' shouted Gato Mgungu.

Again the warriors seized him, and as Bobolo made no move to intercede on his behalf the white man accompanied his guard without further demonstration. After disarming him they took him to a small hut, filthy beyond description, and, tying him securely, left him under guard of a single sentry who squatted on the ground outside the low doorway; but they neglected to remove the pocket knife from a pocket in his breeches.

Old Timer was very uncomfortable. His bonds hurt his wrists and ankles. The dirt floor of the hut was uneven and hard. The place was alive with crawling, biting things. It was putrid with foul stenches. In addition to these physical discomforts the outlook was mentally depressing. He began to question the wisdom of his quixotic venture and to upbraid himself for not listening to the council of his two followers.

But presently thoughts of the girl and the horrid situation in which she must be, if she still lived, convinced him that even though he had failed he could not have done otherwise than he had. He recalled to his mind a vivid picture of her as he had last seen her, he recounted her perfections of face and figure, and he knew that if chance permitted him to escape from the village of Gato Mgungu he would face even greater perils to effect her rescue.

His mind was still occupied with thoughts of her when he heard someone in conversation with his guard, and a moment later a figure entered the hut. It was now night; the only light was that reflected from the cooking fires burning about the village and a few torches set in the ground before the hut of the chief. The interior of his prison was in almost total darkness. The features of his visitor were quite invisible. He wondered if he might be the executioner, come to inflict the death penalty pronounced by the chief; but at the first words he recognised the voice of Bobolo.

'Perhaps I can help you,' said his visitor. 'You would like to get out of here?'

'Of course. Old Mgungu must have gone crazy. What's the matter with the old fool, anyway?'

'He does not like white men. I am their friend. I will help you.'

'Good for you Bobolo,' exclaimed Old Timer. 'You'll never regret it.'

'It cannot be done for nothing,' suggested Bobolo.

'Name your price.'

'It is not my price,' the black hastened to assure him; 'it is what I shall have to pay to others.'

'Well, how much?'

'Ten tusks of ivory.'

Old Timer whistled. 'Wouldn't you like a steam yacht and a Rolls Royce, too?'

'Yes,' agreed Bobolo, willing to accept anything whether or not he knew what it was.

'Well, you don't get them; and, furthermore, ten tusks are too many.'

Bobolo shrugged. 'You know best, white man, what your life is worth.' He arose to go.

'Wait!' exclaimed Old Timer. 'You know it is hard to get any ivory these days.'

'I should have asked for a hundred tusks; but you are a friend, and so I asked only ten.'

'Get me out of here and I will bring the tusks to you when I get them. It may take time, but I will bring them.'

Bobolo shook his head. 'I must have the tusks first. Send word to your white friend to send me the tusks; then you will be freed.'

'How can I send word to him? My men are not here.'

'I will send a messenger.'

'All right, you old horse-thief,' consented the white. 'Untie my wrists and I'll write a note to him.'

'That will not do. I would not know what the paper that talks said. It might say things that would bring trouble to Bobolo.'

'You're darn right it would,' soliloquized Old Timer. 'If I could get the notebook and pencil out of my pocket The Kid would get a message that would land you in jail and hang Gato Mgungu into the bargain.' But aloud he said, 'How will he know that the message is from me?'

'Send something by the messenger that he will know is yours. You are wearing a ring. I saw it today.'

'How do I know you will send the right message?' demurred Old Timer. 'You might demand a hundred tusks.'

'I am your friend. I am very honest. Also, there is no other way. Shall I take the ring?'

'Very well; take it.'

The black stepped behind Old Timer and removed the ring from his finger. 'When the ivory comes you will be set free,' he said as he stooped, and passed out of the hut.

'I don't take any stock in the old fraud,' thought the white man, 'but a drowning man clutches at a straw.'

Bobolo grinned as he examined the ring by the light of a fire. 'I am a bright man,' he muttered to himself. 'I shall have a ring as well as the ivory.' As for freeing Old Timer, that was beyond his power; nor had he any intention of even attempting it. He was well contented with himself when he joined the other chiefs who were sitting in council with Gato Mgungu.

They were discussing, among other things, the method of dispatching the white prisoner. Some wished to have him slain and butchered in the village that they might not have to divide the flesh with the priests and the Leopard God at the temple. Others insisted that he be taken forthwith to the high priest that his flesh might be utilised in the ceremonies accompanying the induction of the new white high priestess. There was a great deal of oratory, most of which was inapropos; but that is ever the way of men in conferences. Black or white, they like to hear their own voices.

Gato Mgungu was in the midst of a description of heroic acts that he had performed in a battle that had been fought twenty years previously when he was silenced by a terrifying interruption. There was a rustling of the leaves in the tree that overhung his hut; a heavy object hurtled down into the centre of the circle formed by the squatting councillors, and as one man they leaped to their feet in consternation. Expressions of surprise, awe, or terror were registered upon every countenance. They turned affrighted glances upward into the tree, but nothing was visible there among the dark shadows; then they looked down at the thing lying at their feet. It was the corpse of a man, its wrists and ankles bound, its throat cut from ear to ear.

'It is Lupingu, the Utenga,' whispered Gato Mgungu. 'He brought me word of the coming of the son of Lobongo and his warriors.'

'It is an ill omen,' whispered one.

'They have punished the traitor,' said another.

'But who could have carried him into the tree and thrown him down upon us?' demanded Bobolo.

'He spoke today of one who claimed to be the "muzimo" of Orando,' explained Gato Mgungu, 'a huge white man whose powers were greater than the powers of Sobito, the witch-doctor of Tumbai.'

'We have heard of him from another,' interjected a chief.

'And he spoke of another,' continued Gato Mgungu, 'that is the spirit of Nyamwegi of Kibbu, who was killed by children of the Leopard God. This one has taken the form of a little monkey.'

'Perhaps it was the "muzimo" that brought Lupingu here,' suggested Bobolo. 'It is a warning. Let us take the white man to the high priest to do with as he sees fit. If he kills him the fault will not be ours.'

'Those are the words of a wise man.' The speaker was one who owed a debt to Bobolo.

'It is dark,' another reminded them; 'perhaps we had better wait until morning.'

'Now is the time,' said Gato Mgungu. 'If the "muzimo" is white and is angry because we have made this white man prisoner, he will hang around the village as long as we keep the other here. We will take him to the temple. The high priest and the Leopard God are stronger than any "muzimo."'

Hidden amidst the foliage of a tree Muzimo watched the blacks in the palisaded village below. The Spirit of Nyamwegi, bored by the sight of black men, disgusted with all this wandering about by night, had fallen asleep in his arms. Muzimo saw the blacks arming and forming under the commands of their chiefs. The white prisoner was dragged from the hut in which he had been imprisoned, the bonds were removed from his ankles, and he was hustled under guard toward the gateway through which the warriors were now debouching upon the river front. Here they launched a flotilla of small canoes (some thirty of them), each with a capacity of about ten men, for there were almost three hundred warriors of the Leopard God in the party, only a few having been left in the village to act as a guard. The large war canoes, seating fifty men, were left behind, bottom up, upon the shore.

As the last canoe with its load of painted savages drifted down the dark current, Muzimo and The Spirit of Nyamwegi dropped from the tree that had concealed them and followed along the shore. An excellent trail paralleled the river; and along this Muzimo trotted, keeping the canoes always within hearing.

The Spirit of Nyamwegi, aroused from sound sleep to follow many more of the hated Gomangani than he could count, was frightened and excited, 'Let us turn back,' he begged. 'Why must we follow all these Gomangani who will kill us if they catch us, when we might be sleeping safely far away in a nice large tree?'

'They are the enemies of Orando,' explained Muzimo. 'We follow to see where they are going and what they are going to do.'

'I do not care where they are going or what they are going to do,' whimpered The Spirit of Nyamwegi; 'I am sleepy. If we go on, Sheeta will get us or Sabor or Numa; if not they, then the Gomangani. Let us go back.'

'No,' replied the white giant. 'I am a "muzimo." "Muzimos" must know everything. Therefore I must go about by night as well as by day watching the enemies of Orando. If you do not wish to come with me climb a tree and sleep.'

The Spirit of Nyamwegi was afraid to go on with Muzimo, but he was more afraid to remain alone in this strange forest; so he said no more about the matter as Muzimo trotted along the dark trail beside the dark, mysterious river.

They had covered about two miles when Muzimo became aware that the canoes had stopped, and a moment later he came to the bank of a small affluent of the larger stream. Into this the canoes were moving slowly in single file. He watched them, counting, until the last had entered the sluggish stream and disappeared in the darkness of the overhanging verdure; then, finding no trail, he took to the trees, following the canoes by the sound of the dipping paddles beneath him.

It chanced that Old Timer was in the canoe commanded by Bobolo, and he took advantage of the opportunity to ask the chief whither they were taking him and why; but Bobolo cautioned him to silence, whispering that at present no one must know of his friendship for the prisoner. 'Where you are going you will be safer; your enemies will not be able to find you,' was the most that he would say.

'Nor my friends either,' suggested Old Timer; but to that Bobolo made no answer.

The surface of the stream beneath the trees, which prevented even the faint light of a moonless sky from reaching it, was shrouded in utter darkness. Old Timer could not see the man next to him, nor his hand before his face. How the paddlers guided their craft along this narrow, tortuous river appeared little less than a miracle to him, yet they moved steadily and surely toward their destination. He wondered what that destination might be. There seemed something mysterious and uncanny in the whole affair. The river itself was mysterious. The unwonted silence of the warriors accentuated the uncanniness of the situation. Everything combined to suggest to his imagination a company of dead men paddling up a river of death, three hundred ebon Charons escorting his dead soul to Hell. It was not a pleasant thought; he sought to thrust it from his mind, but there was none more pleasant to replace it. It seemed to Old Timer that his fortunes never before had been at such low ebb.

'At least,' he soliloquized, 'I have the satisfaction of knowing that things can get no worse.'

One thought which recurred persistently caused him the most concern. It was of the girl and her fate. While he was not convinced that she had not been in the village while he was captive there, he felt that such had not been the case. He realised that his judgment was based more upon intuition than reason, but the presentiment was so strong that it verged upon conviction. Being positive that she had been brought to the village only a short time before his arrival, he sought to formulate some reasonable conjecture as to the disposition the savages had made of her. He doubted that they had killed her as yet. Knowing, as he did, that they were cannibals, he was positive that the killing of the girl, if they intended to kill her, would be reserved for a spectacular ceremony and followed by a dance and an orgy. There had not been time for such a celebration since she had been brought to the village; therefore it seemed probable that she had preceded him up this mysterious river of darkness.

He hoped that this last conjecture might prove correct, not only because of the opportunity it would afford to rescue her from her predicament (provided that lay within his power) but because it would bring him near her once more where, perchance, he might see or even touch her. Absence had but resulted in stimulating his mad infatuation for her. Mere contemplation of her charms aroused to fever heat his longing for her, redoubled his anger against the savages who had abducted her.

His mind was thus occupied by these complex emotions when his attention was attracted by a light just ahead upon the right bank of the stream. At first he saw only the light, but presently he perceived human figures dimly illuminated by its rays and behind it the outlines of a large structure. The number of the figures increased rapidly and more lights appeared. He saw that the former were the crews of the canoes which had preceded his and the latter torches borne by people coming from the structure, which he now saw was a large building.

Presently his own canoe pulled in to the bank, and he was hustled ashore. Here, among the warriors who had come from the village, were savages clothed in the distinctive apparel of the Leopard Men. It was these who had emerged from the building, carrying torches. A few of them wore hideous masks. They were the priests of the Leopard God.

Slowly there was dawning upon the consciousness of the white man the realisation that he had been brought to that mysterious temple of the Leopard Men of which he had heard frightened, whispered stories from the lips of terrified blacks upon more than a single occasion, and which he had come to consider more fabulous than real. The reality of it, however, was impressed upon him with overpowering certainty when he was dragged through the portals of the building into its barbaric interior.

Lighted by many torches, the scene was one to be indelibly impressed upon the memory of a beholder. Already the great chamber was nearly filled with the black warriors from the village of Gato Mgungo. They were milling about several large piles of leopard skins presided over by masked priests who were issuing these ceremonial costumes to them. Gradually the picture changed as the warriors donned the garb of their savage order, until the white man saw about him only the black and yellow hides of the carnivores; the curved, cruel, steel talons; and the black faces, hideously painted, partially hidden by the leopard head helmets.

The wavering torchlight played upon carved and painted idols; it glanced from naked human skulls, from gaudy shields and grotesque masks hung upon the huge pillars that supported the roof of the building. It lighted, more brilliantly than elsewhere, a raised dais at the far end of the chamber, where stood the high priest upon a smaller platform at the back of the dais. Below and around him were grouped a number of lesser priests; while chained to a heavy post near him was a large leopard, bristling and growling at the massed humanity beneath him, a devil-faced leopard that seemed to the imagination of the white man to personify the savage bestiality of the cult it symbolised.

The man's eyes ranged the room in search of the girl, but she was nowhere to be seen. He shuddered at the thought that she might be hidden somewhere in this frightful place, and would have risked everything to learn, had his guards given him the slightest opportunity. If she were here her case was hopeless, as hopeless as he now realised his own to be; for since he had become convinced that he had been brought to the temple of the Leopard Men, allowed to look upon their holy of holies, to view their most secret rites, he had known that no power on earth could save him; and that the protestations and promises of Bobolo had been false, for no one other than a Leopard Man could look upon these things and live.

Gato Mgungo, Bobolo, and the other chiefs had taken their places in front of the common warriors at the foot of the dais. Gato Mgungu had spoken to the high priest, and now at a word from the latter his guards dragged Old

Timer forward and stood with him at the right of the dais. Three hundred pairs of evil eyes, filled with hatred, glared at him – savage eyes, hungry eyes.

The high priest turned toward the snarling, mouthing leopard. 'Leopard God,' he cried in a high, shrill voice, 'the children of the Leopard God have captured an enemy of his people. They have brought him here to the great temple. What is the will of the Leopard God?'

There was a moment's silence during which all eyes were fixed upon the high priest and the leopard. Then a weird thing happened, a thing that turned the skin of the white man cold and stiffened the hairs upon his scalp. From the snarling mouth of the leopard came human speech. It was incredible, yet with his own ears he heard it.

'Let him die that the children of the Leopard God may be fed!' The voice was low and husky and merged with bestial growls. 'But first bring forth the new high priestess of the temple that my children may look upon her whom my brother commanded Lulimi to bring from a far country.'

Lulimi, who by virtue of his high priestly rank stood nearest to the throne of the high priest, swelled visibly with pride. This was the big moment for which he had waited. All eyes were upon him. He trod a few steps of a savage dance, leaped high into the air, and voiced a hideous cry that echoed through the lofty rafters far above. The lay brothers were impressed; they would not soon forget Lulimi. But instantly their attention was distracted from Lulimi to the doorway at the rear of the dais. In it stood a girl, naked but for a few ornaments. She stepped out upon the dais, to be followed immediately by eleven similarly garbed priestesses. Then there was a pause.

Old Timer wondered which of these was the new high priestess. There was little difference between them other than varying degrees of age and ugliness. Their yellow teeth were filed to sharp points; the septa of their noses were pierced, and through these holes were inserted ivory skewers; the lobes of their ears were stretched to their shoulders by heavy ornaments of copper, iron, brass, and ivory; their faces were painted a ghoulish blue and white.

Now the Leopard God spoke again. 'Fetch the high priestess!' he commanded, and with three hundred others Old Timer centred his gaze again upon the aperture at the back of the dais. A figure, dimly seen, approached out of the darkness of the chamber beyond until it stood in the doorway, the flare of the torches playing upon it.

The white man stifled a cry of astonishment and horror. The figure was that of the girl whom he sought.

CHAPTER TEN
While the Priests Slept

As Kali Bwana was pushed into the doorway at the rear of the dais by the old hag who was her chief guardian, she paused in consternation and horror at the sight which met her eyes. Directly before her stood the high priest, terrifying in his weird costume and horrid mask, and near him a great leopard, nervous and restless on its chain. Beyond these was a sea of savage, painted faces and grotesque masks, discernible vaguely in the light of torches against a background of leopard skins.

The atmosphere of the room was heavy with the acrid stench of black bodies. A wave of nausea surged over the girl; she reeled slightly and placed the back of one hand across her eyes to shut out the terrifying sight.

The old woman behind her whispered angrily and shoved her forward. A moment later Imigeg, the high priest, seized her hand and drew her to the centre of the smaller, higher dais beside the growling leopard. The beast snarled and sprang at her; but Imigeg had anticipated such an emergency, and the leopard was brought to a sudden stop by its chain before its raking talons touched the soft flesh of the shrinking girl.

Old Timer shuddered as the horror of her position impressed itself more deeply upon his consciousness. His rage against the blacks and his own futility left him weak and trembling. His utter helplessness to aid her was maddening, as the sight of her redoubled the strength of his infatuation. He recalled the harsh and bitter things he had said to her, and he flushed with shame at the recollection. Then the eyes of the girl, now taking in the details of the scene before her, met his. For a moment she regarded him blankly; then she recognised him. Surprise and incredulity were written upon her countenance. At first she did not realise that he, too, was a prisoner. His presence recalled his boorish and ungallant attitude toward her at their first meeting. She saw in him only another enemy; yet the fact that he was a white man imparted a new confidence. It did not seem possible that even he would stand idly by and permit a white woman to be imprisoned and maltreated by negroes. Slowly, then, it dawned upon her that he was a prisoner as well as she; and though the new hope waned, there still remained a greater degree of confidence than she had felt before.

She wondered what queer trick of fate had brought them together again thus. She could not know, nor even dream, that he had been captured in an effort to succour her. Perhaps had she known and known, too, the impulse that had actuated him, even the slight confidence that his presence imparted to her would have been dissipated; but she did not know. She only realised that he was a man of her own race, and that because he was there she felt a little braver.

As Old Timer watched the slender, graceful figure and beautiful face of the new high priestess of the Leopard God, other eyes surveyed and appraised her. Among these were the eyes of Bobolo – savage, bloodshot eyes; greedy, lustful eyes. Bobolo licked his thick lips hungrily. The savage chief was hungry, but not for food.

The rites of installation were proceeding. Imigeg held the centre of the stage. He jabbered incessantly. Sometimes he addressed an underpriest or a priestess, again the Leopard God; and when the beast answered, it never failed to elicit a subdued gasp of awe from the assembled warriors, though the white girl and Old Timer were less mystified or impressed after their first brief surprise.

There was another listener who also was mystified by the talking leopard, but who, though he had never heard of a ventriloquist, pierced the deception with his uncanny perceptive faculties as, perched upon a tiebeam of the roof that projected beyond the front wall of the building, he looked through an opening below the ridgepole at the barbaric scene being enacted beneath him.

It was Muzimo; and beside him, trembling at the sight of so many leopards, perched The Spirit of Nyamwegi. 'I am afraid,' he said; 'Nkima is afraid. Let us go back to the land that is Tarzan's. Tarzan is king there; here no one knows him, and he is no better than a Gomangani.'

'Always you speak of Nkima and Tarzan,' complained Muzimo. 'I have never heard of them. You are The Spirit of Nyamwegi and I am Muzimo. How many times must I tell you these things?'

'You are Tarzan, and I am Nkima,' insisted the little monkey. 'You are a Tarmangani.'

'I am the spirit of Orando's ancestor,' insisted the other. 'Did not Orando say so?'

'I do not know,' sighed The Spirit of Nyamwegi wearily; 'I do not understand the language of the Gomangani. All I know is that I am Nkima, and that Tarzan has changed. He is not the same since the tree fell upon him. I also know that I am afraid. I want to go away from here.'

'Presently,' promised Muzimo. He was watching the scene below him intently. He saw the white man and the white girl, and he guessed the fate that awaited them, but it did not move him to compassion, nor arouse within him any sense of blood-responsibility. He was the ancestral spirit of Orando, the black son of a black chief; the fate of a couple of strange Tarmangani meant nothing to him. Presently, however, his observing eyes discovered something which did arouse his keen interest. Beneath one of the hideous priest-masks he caught a glimpse of familiar features. He was not surprised, for he had been watching this particular priest intently for some time, his attention having been attracted to him by something familiar in his carriage and conformation. The shadow of a smile touched the lips of Muzimo. 'Come!' he whispered to The Spirit of Nyamwegi, as he clambered to the roof of the temple.

Sure-footed as a cat he ran along the ridgepole, the little monkey at his heels. Midway of the building he sprang lightly down the sloping roof and launched himself into the foliage of a nearby tree, and as The Spirit of Nyamwegi followed him the two were engulfed in the Erebusan darkness of the forest.

Inside the temple the priestesses had lighted many fires upon the large clay dais and swung cooking pots above them on crude tripods, while from a rear room of the temple the lesser priests had brought many cuts of meat, wrapped in plantain leaves. These the priestesses placed in the cooking pots, while the priests returned for gourds and jugs of native beer, which were passed among the warriors.

As the men drank they commenced to dance. Slowly at first, their bodies bent forward from the hips, their elbows raised, they stepped gingerly, lifting their feet high. In their hands they grasped their spears and shields, holding them awkwardly because of the great, curved steel talons affixed to their fingers. Restricted by lack of space upon the crowded floor, each warrior pivoted upon the same spot, pausing only to take long drinks from the beer jugs as they were passed to him. A low, rhythmic chant accompanied the dance, rising in volume and increasing in tempo as the tempo of the dance steps increased, until the temple floor was a mass of howling, leaping savages.

Upon the upper dais the Leopard God, aroused to fury by the din and movement about him and the scent of the flesh that was cooking in the pots, strained at his chain, snarling and growling in rage. The high priest, stimulated by the contents of a beer pot, danced madly before the frenzied carnivore, leaping almost within reach of its raking talons, then springing away again as the infuriated beast struck at him. The white girl shrank to the far side of the dais, her brain reeling to the hideous pandemonium surrounding her, half numb from fear and apprehension. She had seen the meat brought to the cooking pots but had only vaguely guessed the nature of it until a human hand had fallen from its wrappings of plantain leaves. The significance of the grisly object terrified and sickened her.

The white man watching the scene about him looked most often in her direction. Once he had tried to speak to her; but one of his guards had struck him heavily across the mouth, silencing him. As the drinking and the dancing worked the savages into augmented fury, his concern for the safety of the girl increased. He saw that religious and alcoholic drunkenness were rapidly robbing them of what few brains and little self-control Nature had vouchsafed them, and he trembled to think of what excesses they might commit when they had passed beyond even the restraint of their leaders; nor did the fact that the chiefs, the priests, and the priestesses were becoming as drunk as their followers tend but to aggravate his fears.

Bobolo, too, was watching the white girl. In his drunken brain wild schemes were forming. He saw her danger, and he wished to save her for himself. Just how he was going to possess her was not entirely clear to his muddled mind, yet it clung stubbornly to the idea. Then his eyes chanced to alight on Old Timer, and a scheme evolved hazily through the beer fumes.

The white man wished to save the white woman. This fact Bobolo knew and recalled. If he wished to save her he would protect her. The white man also wished to escape. He thought Bobolo was his friend. Thus the premises formed slowly in his addled brain. So far, so good! The white man would help him abduct the high priestess, but that could not be effected until practically everyone was too drunk to prevent the accomplishment of his plan or remember it afterward. He would have to wait for the proper moment to arrive, but in the meantime he must get the girl out of this chamber and hide her in one of the other rooms of the temple. Already the black priestesses were mingling freely with the excited, drunken warriors; presently the orgy would be in full swing. After that it was possible that no one might save her; not even the high priest, who was now quite as drunk as any of them.

Bobolo approached Old Timer and spoke to his guards. 'Go and join the others,' he told them. 'I will watch the prisoner.'

The men, already half drunk, needed no second invitation. The word of a chief was enough; it released them from all responsibility. In a moment they were gone. 'Quick!' urged Bobolo, grasping Old Timer by the arm. 'Come with me.'

The white man drew back. 'Where?' he demanded.

'I am going to help you to escape,' whispered Bobolo.

'Not without the white woman,' insisted the other.

This reply fitted so perfectly with Bobolo's plans that he was delighted. 'I will arrange that, too; but I must get you out of here into one of the back rooms of the temple. Then I shall come back for her. I could not take you both at the same time. It is very dangerous. Imigeg would have me killed if he discovered it. You must do just as I say.'

'Why do you take this sudden interest in our welfare?' demanded the white, suspiciously.

'Because you are both in danger here,' replied Bobolo. 'Everyone is very drunk, even the high priest. Soon there would be no one to protect either of you, and you would be lost. I am your friend. It is well for you that Bobolo is your friend and that he is not drunk.'

'Not very!' thought Old Timer as the black staggered at his side toward a doorway in the rear partition of the chamber.

Bobolo conducted him to a room at the far end of the temple. 'Wait here,' he said. 'I shall go back and fetch the girl.'

'Cut these cords at my wrists,' demanded the white. 'They hurt.'

Bobolo hesitated, but only for a moment. 'Why not?' he asked. 'You do not have to try to escape, because I am going to take you away myself; furthermore you could not escape alone. The temple stands upon an island surrounded by the river and swamp land alive with crocodiles. No trails lead from it other than the river. Ordinarily there are no canoes here, lest some of the priests or priestesses might escape. They, too, are prisoners. You will wait until I am ready to take you away from here.'

'Of course I shall. Hurry now, and bring the white woman.'

Bobolo returned to the main chamber of the temple, but this time he approached it by way of the door that let upon the upper dais at its rear. Here he paused to reconnoitre. The meat from the cooking pots was being passed among the warriors, but the beer jugs were still circulating freely. The high priest lay in a stupor at the far side of the upper dais. The Leopard God crouched, growling, over the thigh bone of a man. The high priestess leaned against the partition close to the doorway where Bobolo stood. The black chief touched her upon the arm. With startled eyes she turned toward him.

'Come!' he whispered, and beckoned her to follow.

The girl understood only the gesture, but she had seen this same man lead her fellow prisoner away from the foot of the dais but a moment before; and instantly she concluded that by some queer freak of fate this black man might be friendly. Certainly there had been nothing threatening or unfriendly in his facial expressions as he had talked to the white man. Reasoning thus, she followed Bobolo into the gloomy chambers in the rear of the temple. She was afraid, and how close to harm she was only Bobolo knew. Excited to desire by propinquity and impelled to rashness by drink, he suddenly thought to drag her into one of the dark chambers that lined the corridor along which he was conducting her; but as he turned to seize her a voice spoke at his elbow. 'You got her more easily than I thought possible.' Bobolo wheeled. 'I followed you,' continued Old Timer, 'thinking you might need help.'

The black chief grunted angrily, but the surprise had brought him to his senses. A scream or the noise of a scuffle might have brought a guardian of the temple to investigate, which would have meant death for Bobolo. He made no reply, but led them back to the room in which he had left Old Timer.

'Wait here for me,' he cautioned them. 'If you are discovered do not say that I brought you here. If you do I shall not be able to save you. Say that you were afraid and came here to hide.' He turned to go.

'Wait,' said Old Timer. 'Suppose we are unable to get this girl away from here; what will become of her?'

Bobolo shrugged. 'We have never before had a white priestess. Perhaps she is for the Leopard God, perhaps for the high priest. Who knows?' Then he left them.

' "Perhaps for the Leopard God, perhaps for the high priest," ' repeated Kali Bwana when the man had translated the words. 'Oh, how horrible!'

The girl was standing very close to the white man. He could feel the warmth of her almost naked body. He trembled, and when he tried to speak his voice was husky with emotion. He wanted to seize her and crush her to him. He wanted to cover her soft, warm lips with kisses. What stayed him he did not know. They were alone at the far extremity of the temple, the noises of the savage orgy in the main chamber of the building would have drowned any outcry that she might make; she was absolutely at his mercy, yet he did not touch her.

'Perhaps we shall escape soon,' he said. 'Bobolo has promised to take us away.'

'You know him and can trust him?' she asked.

'I have known him for a couple of years,' he replied, 'but I do not trust him. I do not trust any of them. Bobolo is doing this for a price. He is an avaricious old scoundrel.'

'What is the price?'

'Ivory.'

'But I have none.'

'Neither have I,' he admitted, 'but I'll get it.'

'I will pay you for my share,' she offered. 'I have money with an agent at rail-head.'

He laughed. 'Let's cross that bridge when we get to it, if we ever do.'

'That doesn't sound very reassuring.'

'We are in a bad hole,' he explained. 'We mustn't raise our hopes too high. Right now our only hope seems to lie in Bobolo. He is a Leopard Man and a scoundrel, in addition to which he is drunk – a slender hope at best.'

Bobolo, returning slightly sobered to the orgy, found himself suddenly frightened by what he had done. To bolster his waning courage he seized upon a large jug of beer and drained it. The contents exercised a magical effect upon Bobolo, for when presently his eyes fell upon a drunken priestess reeling in a corner she was transformed into a much-to-be-desired houri. An hour later Bobolo was fast asleep in the middle of the floor.

The effects of the native beer wore off almost as rapidly as they manifested themselves in its devotees, with the result that in a few hours the warriors commenced to bestir themselves. They were sick and their heads ached. They wished more beer; but when they demanded it they learned that there was no more, nor was there any food. They had consumed all the refreshments, liquid and solid.

Gato Mgungu had never had any of the advantages of civilisation (he had never been to Hollywood); but he knew what to do under the circumstances, for the psychology of celebrators is doubtless the same in Africa as elsewhere. When there is nothing more to eat or drink, it must be time to go home. Gato Mgungu gathered the other chiefs and transmitted this philosophical reflection to them. They agreed, Bobolo included. His brain was slightly befogged. He had already forgotten several events of the past evening, including the houri-like priestess. He knew that there was something important on his mind, but he could not recall just what it was; therefore he herded his men to their canoes just as the other chiefs and headmen were doing.

Presently he was headed down river, part of a long procession of war canoes filled with headaches. Back in the temple lay a few warriors who had still been too drunk to stand. For these they had left a single canoe. These men were strewn about the floor of the temple, asleep. Among them were all of the lesser priests and the priestesses. Imigeg was curled up on one corner of the dais fast asleep. The Leopard God, his belly filled, slept also.

Kali Bwana and Old Timer, waiting impatiently in the dark room at the rear of the temple for the return of Bobolo, had noted the increasing quiet in the front chamber of the building; then they had heard the preparations for departure as all but a few made ready to leave. They heard the shuffling of feet as the warriors passed out of the building; they heard the shouts and commands at the river bank that told the white man that the natives were launching their canoes. After that there had been silence.

'Bobolo ought to be coming along,' remarked the man.

'Perhaps he has gone away and left us,' suggested Kali Bwana.

They waited a little longer. Not a sound came from any part of the temple nor from the grounds outside. The silence of death reigned over the holy of holies of the Leopard God. Old Timer stirred uneasily. 'I am going to have a look out there,' he said. 'Perhaps Bobolo has gone, and if he has we want to know it.' He moved toward the doorway. 'I shall not be gone long,' he whispered. 'Do not be afraid.'

As the girl waited in the darkness her mind dwelt upon the man who had just left her. He seemed changed since the time of their first meeting. He appeared more solicitous as to her welfare and much less brusque and churlish. Yet she could not forget the harsh things he had said to her upon that other occasion. She could never forgive him, and in her heart she still half feared and mistrusted him. It galled her to reflect that in the event of their escape she would be under obligations to him, and as these thoughts occupied her mind Old Timer crept stealthily along the dark corridor toward the small doorway that opened upon the upper dais.

Only a suggestion of light came through it now to guide his footsteps, and when he reached it he looked out into an almost deserted room. The embers of the cooking fires were hidden by white ashes; only a single torch remained that had not burned out. Its smoky flame burned steadily in the quiet air, and in its feeble light he saw the sleepers sprawled upon the floor. In the dim light he could not distinguish the features of any; so he could not know if Bobolo were among them. One long searching look he gave that took in the whole interior of the chamber, a look that assured him that no single conscious person remained in the temple; then he turned and hastened back to the girl.

'Did you find him?' she asked.

'No. I doubt that he is here. Nearly all of them have left, except just a few who were too drunk to leave. I think it is our chance.'

'What do you mean?'

'There is no one to prevent our escaping. There may be no canoe. Bobolo told me that no canoe was ever left here, for fear that the priests or priestesses might escape. He may have been lying, but whether he was or not we may as well take the chance. There is no hope for either of us if we remain here. Even the crocodiles would be kinder to you than these fiends.'

'I will do whatever you say,' she replied, 'but if at any time I am a burden, if my presence might hinder your escape, do not consider me. Go on without me. Remember that you are under no obligations to me, nor—' She hesitated and stopped.

'Nor do I wish to be under obligations to you. I have not forgotten the things that you said to me when you came to my camp.'

He hesitated a moment before replying; then he ignored what she had said. 'Come!' he commanded brusquely. 'We have no time to waste.'

He walked to a window in the rear wall of the room and looked out. It was very dark. He could see nothing. He knew that the building was raised on piles and that the drop to the ground might prove dangerous; but he also knew that a verandah stretched along one side of the structure. Whether it continued around to the rear of the building where this room was located he could not know. To go out through the main room among all those savages was too fraught with risk. An alternative was to find their way to one of the rooms overlooking the verandah that he knew was there on the river side of the building.

'I think we'll try another room,' he whispered. 'Give me your hand, so that we shall not become separated.'

She slipped her hand into his. It was tender and warm. Once again the mad urge of his infatuation rose like a great tide within him, so that it was with difficulty that he controlled himself, yet by no sign did he betray his passion to the girl. Quietly they tiptoed into the dark corridor, the man groping with his free hand until he found a doorway. Gingerly they crossed the room beyond in search of a window.

What if this were the apartment of some temple inmate who had left the orgy to come here and sleep! The thought brought cold sweat to the man's brow, and he swore in his heart that he would slay any creature that put itself in the way of the rescue of the girl; but fortunately the apartment was uninhabited, and the two came to the window unchallenged. The man threw a leg over the sill, and a moment later stood upon the verandah beyond; then he reached in and assisted the girl to his side.

They were near the rear of the building. He dared not chance detection by going to the stairway that led to the ground from the front entrance to the temple. 'We shall have to climb down one of the piles that support the building,' he explained. 'It is possible that there may be a guard at the front entrance. Do you think that you can do it?'

'Certainly,' she replied.

'I'll go first,' he said. 'If you slip I'll try to hold you.'

'I shall not slip; go ahead.'

The verandah had no railing. He lay down and felt beneath its edge until he found the top of a pile. 'Here,' he whispered, and lowered himself over the edge.

The girl followed. He dropped a little lower and guided her legs until they had found a hold upon the pile, which was the bole of a young tree about eight inches in diameter. Without difficulty they reached the ground, and again he took her hand and led her to the bank of the river. As they moved downstream parallel with the temple he sought for a canoe, and when they had come opposite the front of the building he could scarce restrain an exclamation of relief and delight when they came suddenly upon one drawn up on the shore, partially out of the water.

Silently they strained to push the heavy craft into the river. At first it seemed that their efforts would prove of no avail; but at last it started to slip gently downward, and once it was loosened from the sticky mud of the bank that same medium became a slippery slide down which it coasted easily.

He helped her in, shoved the canoe out into the sluggish stream, and jumped in after her; then with a silent prayer of thanksgiving they drifted silently down toward the great river.

CHAPTER ELEVEN
Battle

Into the camp of the sleeping Utengas dropped Muzimo and The Spirit of Nyamwegi an hour after midnight. No sentry had seen them pass, a fact which did not at all surprise the sentries, who knew that spirits pass through the forest unseen at all times if they choose to do so.

Orando, being a good soldier, had just made the rounds of his sentry posts and was still awake when Muzimo located him. 'What news have you brought me, O Muzimo?' demanded the son of Lobongo. 'What word of the enemy?'

'We have been to his village,' replied Muzimo, 'The Spirit of Nyamwegi, Lupingu, and I.'

'And where is Lupingu?'

'He remained there after carrying a message to Gato Mgungu.'

'You gave the traitor his liberty!' exclaimed Orando.

'It will do him little good. He was dead when he entered the village of Gato Mgungu.'

'How then could he carry a message to the chief?'

'He carried a message of terror that the Leopard Men understood. He told them that traitors do not go unpunished. He told them that the power of Orando is great.'

'And what did the Leopard Men do?'

'They fled to their temple to consult the high priest and the Leopard God. We followed them there; but they did not learn much from the high priest or the Leopard God, for they all got very drunk upon beer – all except the Leopard, and he cannot talk when the high priest cannot talk. I came to tell you that their village is now almost deserted except for the women, the children, and a few warriors. This would be a good time to attack it, or to lie in ambush near it awaiting the return of the warriors from the temple. They will be sick, and men do not fight so well when they are sick.'

'Now is a good time,' agreed Orando, clapping his palms together to awaken the sleepers near him.

'In the temple of the Leopard God I saw one whom you know well,' remarked Muzimo as the sleepy headmen aroused their warriors. 'He is a priest of the Leopard God.'

'I know no Leopard Men,' replied Orando.

'You knew Lupingu, although you did not know that he was a Leopard Man,' Muzimo reminded him; 'and you know Sobito. It was he whom I saw behind the mask of a priest. He is a Leopard Man.'

Orando was silent for a moment. 'You are sure?' he asked.

'Yes.'

'When he went to consult the spirits and the demons, and was gone from the village of Tumbai for many days, he was with the Leopard Men instead,' said Orando. 'Sobito is a traitor. He shall die.'

'Yes,' agreed Muzimo, 'Sobito shall die. He should have been killed long ago.'

Along the winding forest trail Muzimo guided the warriors of Orando toward the village of Gato Mgungu. They moved as rapidly as the darkness and the narrow trail would permit, and at length he halted them at the edge of the field of manioc that lies between the forest and the village. After that they crept silently down toward the river when Muzimo had ascertained that the Leopard Men had not returned from the temple. There they waited, hiding among the bushes that grew on either side of the landing place, while Muzimo departed to scout down the river.

He was gone but a short time when he returned with word that he had counted twenty-nine canoes paddling upstream toward the village. 'Though thirty canoes went down river to the temple,' he explained to Orando, 'these must be the Leopard Men returning.'

Orando crept silently among his warriors, issuing instructions, exhorting them to bravery. The canoes were approaching. They could hear the paddles now, dipping, dipping, dipping. The Utengas waited – tense, eager. The first canoe touched the bank and its warriors leaped out. Before they had drawn their heavy craft out on the shore the second canoe shot in. Still the Utengas awaited the signal of their leader. Now the canoes were grounding in rapid succession. A line of warriors was stringing out toward the village gate. Twenty canoes had been drawn up on the shore when Orando gave the signal, a savage battle cry that was taken up by ninety howling warriors as spears and arrows showered into the ranks of the Leopard Men.

The charging Utengas broke through the straggling line of the enemy. The Leopard Men, taken wholly by surprise, thought only of flight. Those who had been cut off at the river sought to launch their canoes and escape; those who had not yet landed turned their craft downstream. The remainder fled toward the village, closely pursued by the Utengas. At the closed gates, which the defenders feared to open, the fighting was fierce; at the river it was little better than a slaughter as the warriors of Orando cut down the terrified Leopard Men struggling to launch their canoes.

When it was too late the warriors left to guard the village opened the gates with the intention of making a sortie against the Utengas. Already the last of their companions had been killed or had fled, and when the gates swung open a howling band of Utengas swarmed through.

The victory was complete. No living soul was left within the palisaded village of Gato Mgungu when the blood-spattered warriors of Orando put the torch to its thatched huts.

From down the river the escaping Leopard Men saw the light of the flames billowing upward above the trees that lined the bank, saw their reflection on the surface of the broad river behind them, and knew the proportions of the defeat that had overwhelmed them. Gato Mgungu, squatting in the bottom of his canoe, saw the flames from his burning village, saw in them, perhaps, the waning of his savage, ruthless power. Bobolo saw them and, reading the same story, knew that Gato Mgungu need no longer be feared. Of all that band of fleeing warriors Bobolo was the least depressed.

By the light of the burning village Orando took stock of his losses, mustering his men and searching out the dead and wounded. From a tree beyond the manioc field a little monkey screamed and chattered. It was The Spirit of Nyamwegi calling to Muzimo, but Muzimo did not answer. Among the dead and wounded Orando found him like mortal clay stretched out upon his back from a blow upon the head.

The son of the chief was surprised and grieved; his followers were shocked. They had been certain that Muzimo was of the spirit world and therefore immune from death. Suddenly they realised that they had won the battle without his aid. He was a fraud. Filled with blood lust, they would have vented their chagrin through spear thrusts into his lifeless body; but Orando stopped them.

'Spirits do not always remain in the same form,' he reminded them. 'Perhaps he has entered another body or, unseen, is watching us from above. If that is so he will avenge any harm that you do this body he has quitted.' In the light of their knowledge this seemed quite possible to the Utengas; so they desisted from their purposed mutilation and viewed the body with renewed awe. 'Furthermore,' continued Orando, 'man on ghost, he was loyal to me; and those of you who saw him fight know that he fought bravely and well.'

'That is so,' agreed a warrior.

'Tarzan! Tarzan!' shrieked The Spirit of Nyamwegi from the tree at the edge of the manioc field. 'Tarzan of the Apes, Nkima is afraid!'

The white man paddled the stolen canoe down the sluggish stream toward the great river, depending upon the strong current for aid to carry him and the girl to safety. Kali Bwana sat silent in the bottom of the craft. She had torn the barbaric head-dress from her brow and the horrid necklace of human teeth from her throat, but she retained the bracelets and anklets, although why it might have been difficult for her to explain. Perhaps it was because, regardless of her plight and all that she had passed through, she was still a woman – a beautiful woman. That is something which one does not easily forget.

Old Timer felt almost certain of success. The Leopard Men who had preceded him down the stream must have been returning to their village; there was no reason to expect that they would return immediately. There was no canoe at the temple; therefore there could be no pursuit, for Bobolo had assured him that there were no trails through the forest leading to the temple of the Leopard Men. He was almost jubilant as the canoe moved slowly into the mouth of the stream and he saw the dark current of the river stretching before him.

Then he heard the splash of paddles, and his heart seemed to leap into his throat. Throwing every ounce of his muscle and weight into the effort, he turned the prow of the canoe toward the right bank, hoping to hide in the dense shadows, undiscovered, until the other craft had passed. It was very dark, so dark that he had reason to believe that his plan would succeed.

Suddenly the oncoming canoe loomed out of the darkness. It was only a darker blur against the darkness of the night. Old Timer held his breath. The girl crouched low behind a gunwale lest her blonde hair and white skin might be visible to the occupants of the other boat even in the darkness that engulfed all other objects. The canoe passed on up the stream.

The broad river lay just ahead now; there, there would be less danger of detection. Old Timer dipped his paddle and started the canoe again upon its interrupted voyage. As the current caught it, it moved more rapidly. They were out upon the river! A dark object loomed ahead of them. It seemed to rise up out of the water directly in front of their craft. Old Timer plied his paddle in an effort to alter the course of the canoe, but too late. There was a jarring thud as it struck the object in its path, which the man had already recognised as a canoe filled with warriors.

Almost simultaneously another canoe pulled up beside him. There was a babel of angry questions and commands. Old Timer recognised the voice of Bobolo. Warriors leaped into the canoe and seized him, fists struck him, powerful fingers dragged him down. He was overpowered and bound.

Again he heard the voice of Bobolo. 'Hurry! We are being pursued. The Utengas are coming!'

Brawny hands grasped the paddles. Old Timer felt the canoe shoot forward, and a moment later it was being driven frantically up the smaller river toward the temple. The heart of the white man went cold with dread. He had had the girl upon the threshold of escape. Such an opportunity would never come again. Now she was doomed. He did not think of his own fate. He thought only of the girl. He searched through the darkness with his eyes, but he could not find her; then he spoke to her. He wanted to comfort her. A new emotion had suddenly taken possession of him. He thought only of her safety and comfort. He did not think of himself at all.

He called again, but she did not answer. 'Be quiet!' growled a warrior near him.

'Where is the girl?' demanded the white man.

'Be quiet,' insisted the warrior. 'There is no white girl here.'

As the canoe in which Bobolo rode swung alongside that in which the girl and the white man were attempting to escape, it had brought the chief close to the former, so close that even in the darkness of the night he had seen her white skin and her blonde hair. Instantly he had recognised his opportunity and seized it. Reaching over the gunwales of the two canoes he had dragged her into his own; then he had voiced the false alarm that he knew would send the other canoes off in a panic.

The warriors with him were all his own men. His village lay on the left bank of the river farther down. A low-voiced command sent the canoe out into the main current of the river, and willing hands sped it upon its course.

The girl, who had passed through so much, who had seen escape almost assured, was stunned by the sudden turn of events that had robbed her of the only creature to whom she might look for aid and crushed hope from her breast.

To Old Timer, bound and helpless, the return journey to the temple was only a dull agony of vain regrets. It made little difference to him now what they did to him. He knew that they would kill him. He hoped that the end would come speedily, but he knew enough about the methods of cannibals to be almost certain that death would be slow and horrible.

As they dragged him into the temple he saw the floor strewn with the bodies of the drunken priests and priestesses. The noise of their entrance aroused Imigeg, the high priest. He rubbed his eyes sleepily and then rose unsteadily to his feet.

'What has happened?' he demanded.

Gato Mgungu strode into the room at the moment, his canoe having followed closely upon that in which Old Timer had been brought back. 'Enough has happened,' he snapped. 'While you were all drunk this white man escaped. The Utengas have killed my warriors and burned my village. What is the matter with your medicine, Imigeg? It is no good.'

The high priest looked about him, a dazed expression in his watery eyes. 'Where is the white priestess?' he cried. 'Did she escape?'

'I saw only the white man,' replied Gato Mgungu.

'The white priestess was there, too,' volunteered a warrior. 'Bobolo took her into his canoe.'

'Then she should be along soon,' offered Gato Mgungu. 'Bobolo's canoe cannot have been far behind mine.'

'She shall not escape again,' said Imigeg, 'nor shall the man. Bind him well, and put him in the small room at the rear of the temple.'

'Kill him!' cried Gato Mgungu. 'Then he cannot run away again.'

'We shall kill him later,' replied Imigeg, who had not relished Gato

860

Mgungu's irreverent tone or his carping criticism and desired to reassert his authority.

'Kill him now,' insisted the chief, 'or he will get away from you again; and if he does, the white men will come with their soldiers and kill you and burn the temple.'

'I am high priest,' replied Imigeg haughtily. 'I take orders from no one but the Leopard God. I shall question him. What he says I shall do.' He turned toward the sleeping leopard and prodded it with a sharp-pointed pole. The great cat leaped to its feet, its face convulsed by a horrid snarl. 'The white man escaped,' explained Imigeg to the leopard. 'He has been captured again. Shall he die tonight?'

'No,' replied the leopard. 'Tie him securely and place him in the small room at the rear of the temple; I am not hungry.'

'Gato Mgungu says to kill him now,' continued Imigeg.

'Tell Gato Mgungu that I speak only through Imigeg, the high priest. I do not speak through Gato Mgungu. Because Gato Mgungu had evil in his mind I have caused his warriors to be slain and his village to be destroyed. If he thinks evil again he shall be destroyed that the children of the Leopard God may eat. I have spoken.'

'The Leopard God has spoken,' said Imigeg.

Gato Mgungu was deeply impressed and thoroughly frightened. 'Shall I take the prisoner to the back of the temple and see that he is safely bound?' he asked.

'Yes,' replied Imigeg, 'take him, and see to it that you bind him so that he cannot escape.'

CHAPTER TWELVE
The Sacrifice

'Tarzan! Tarzan!' shrieked The Spirit of Nyamwegi from the tree at the edge of the manioc field. 'Tarzan of the Apes, Nkima is afraid!'

The white giant lying upon the ground opened his eyes and looked about him. He saw Orando and many warriors gathered about. A puzzled expression overspread his countenance. Suddenly he leaped to his feet.

'Nkima! Nkima!' he called in the language of the great apes. 'Where are you, Nkima? Tarzan is here!'

The little monkey leaped from the tree and came bounding across the field of manioc. With a glad cry he leaped to the shoulder of the white man and throwing his arms about the bronzed neck pressed his cheek close to that of his master; and there he clung, whimpering with joy.

'You see,' announced Orando to his fellows, 'Muzimo is not dead.'

The white man turned to Orando. 'I am not Muzimo,' he said; 'I am Tarzan of the Apes.' He touched the monkey. 'This is not The Spirit of Nyamwegi; it is Nkima. Now I remember everything. For a long time I have been trying to remember but until now I could not – not since the tree fell upon me.'

There was none among them who had not heard of Tarzan of the Apes. He was a legend of the forest and the jungle that had reached to their far country. Like the spirits and the demons which they never saw, they had never expected to see him. Perhaps Orando was a little disappointed, yet, on the whole, it was a relief to all of them to discover that this was a man of flesh and blood, motivated by the same forces that actuated them, subject to the same laws of Nature that controlled them. It had always been a bit disconcerting never to be sure in what strange form the ancestral spirit of Orando might choose to appear, nor to know of a certainty that he would not turn suddenly from a benign to a malign force; and so they accepted him in his new role, but with this difference: where formerly he had seemed the creature of Orando, doing his bidding as a servant does the bidding of his master, now he seemed suddenly clothed in the dignity of power and authority. The change was so subtly wrought that it was scarcely apparent and was due, doubtless, to the psychological effect of the reawakened mentality of the white man over that of his black companions.

They made camp beside the river near the ruins of Gato Mgungu's village, for there were fields of manioc and plantain that, with the captured goats and chickens of the Leopard Men, ensured full bellies after the lean fare of the days of marching and fighting.

During the long day Tarzan's mind was occupied with many thoughts. He had recalled now why he had come into this country, and he marvelled at the coincidence of later events that had guided his footsteps along the very paths that he had intended treading before accident had robbed him of the memory of his purpose. He knew now that depredations by Leopard Men from a far country had caused him to set forth upon a lonely reconnaissance with only the thought of locating their more or less fabled stronghold and temple. That he should be successful in both finding these and reducing one of them was gratifying in the extreme, and he felt thankful now for the accident that had been responsible for the results.

His mind was still not entirely clear on certain details; but these were returning gradually, and as evening fell and the evening meal was underway he suddenly recalled the white man and the white girl whom he had seen in the temple of the Leopard God. He spoke to Orando about them, but the black knew nothing of them.

'If they were in the temple they probably have been killed by now,' he volunteered.

Tarzan sat immersed in thought for a long time. He did not know these people, yet he felt a certain obligation to them because they were of his race. Finally he arose and called Nkima, who was munching on a plantain that a warrior was sharing with him.

'Where are you going?' asked Orando.

'To the temple of the Leopard God,' replied Tarzan.

Old Timer had lain all day securely bound and without food or water. Occasionally a priest or a priestess had looked in to see that he had not escaped or loosened his bonds, but otherwise he had been left alone. The inmates of the temple had stirred but little during the day, most of them being engaged in sleeping off the effects of the previous night's debauch; but with the coming of night the prisoner heard increased evidence of activity. There were sounds of chanting from the temple chamber, and above the other noises the shrill voice of the high priest and the growls of the leopard. His thoughts during those long hours were often of the girl. He had heard the warrior tell Imigeg that Bobolo had captured her, and supposed that she was again being forced to play her part on the dais with the Leopard God. At least he might see her again (that would be something), but hope that he might rescue her had ebbed so low that it might no longer be called hope.

He was trying to reason against his better judgment that having once escaped from the temple they could do so again, when a priest entered the room, bearing a torch. He was an evil-appearing old fellow, whose painted face accentuated the savagery of the visage. He was Sobito, the witch-doctor of Tumbai. Stooping, he commenced to untie the cords that secured the white man's ankles.

'What are they going to do with me?' demanded Old Timer.

A malevolent grin bared Sobito's yellow fangs. 'What do you suppose, white man?'

Old Timer shrugged. 'Kill me, I suppose.'

'Not too quickly,' explained Sobito. 'The flesh of those who die slowly and in pain is tender.'

'You old devil,' exclaimed the prisoner.

Sobito licked his lips. He delighted in inflicting torture either physical or mental. Here was an opportunity he could not forego. 'First your arms and legs will be broken,' he explained; 'then you will be placed upright in a hole in the swamp and fastened so that you cannot get your mouth or nose beneath the surface and drown yourself. You will be left there three days, by which time your flesh will be tender.' He paused.

'And then?' asked the white. His voice was steady. He had determined that he would not give them the added satisfaction of witnessing his mental anguish, and when the time came that he must suffer physically he prayed that he might have the strength to endure the ordeal in a manner that would reflect credit upon his race. Three days! God, what a fate to anticipate!

'And then?' repeated Sobito. 'Then you will be carried into the temple, and the children of the Leopard God will tear you to pieces with their steel claws. Look!' He exhibited the long, curved weapons which dangled from the ends of the loose leopard skin sleeves of his garment.

'After which you will eat me, eh?'

'Yes.'

'I hope you choke.'

Sobito had at last untied the knots that had secured the bonds about the white man's ankles. He gave him a kick and told him to rise.

'Are you going to kill and eat the white girl, too?' demanded Old Timer.

'She is not here. Bobolo has stolen her. Because you helped her to escape, your suffering shall be greater. I have already suggested to Imigeg that he remove your eyeballs after your arms and legs are broken. I forgot to tell you that we shall break each of them in three or four places.'

'Your memory is failing,' commented Old Timer, 'but I hope that you have not forgotten anything else.'

Sobito grunted. 'Come with me,' he commanded, and led the white man through the dark corridor to the great chamber where the Leopard Men were gathered.

At sight of the prisoner a savage cry broke from a hundred and fifty throats, the leopard growled, the high priest danced upon the upper dais, the hideous priestesses screamed and leaped forward as though bent upon tearing the white man to pieces. Sobito pushed the prisoner to the summit of the lower dais and dragged him before the high priest. 'Here is the sacrifice!' he screamed.

'Here is the sacrifice!' cried Imigeg, addressing the Leopard God. 'What are your commands, O father of the leopard children?'

The bristling muzzle of the great beast wrinkled into a snarl as Imigeg prodded him with his sharp pole, and from the growling throat the answer seemed to come. 'Let him be broken, and on the third night let there be a feast!'

'And what of Bobolo and the white priestess?' demanded Imigeg.

'Send warriors to fetch them to the temple that Bobolo may be broken for another feast. The white girl I give to Imigeg, the high priest. When he tires of her we shall feast again.'

'It is the word of the Leopard God,' cried Imigeg. 'As he commands, it shall be done.'

'Let the white man be broken,' growled the leopard, 'and on the third night let my children return that each may be made wise by eating the flesh of a white man. When you have eaten of it the white man's weapons can no longer harm you. Let the white man be broken!'

'Let the white man be broken!' shrieked Imigeg.

Instantly a half dozen priests leaped forward and seized the prisoner, throwing him heavily to the clay floor of the dais, and here they pinioned him, stretching his arms and legs far apart, while four priestesses armed with heavy clubs rushed forward. A drum commenced to boom somewhere in the temple, weirdly, beating a cadence to which the priestesses danced about the prostrate form of their victim.

Now one rushed in and flourished her club above the prisoner; but a priest pretended to protect him, and the woman danced out again to join her companions in the mad whirl of the dance. Again and again was this repeated, but each succeeding time the priests seemed to have greater difficulty in repulsing the maddened women.

That it was all acting (part of a savage ceremony) the white man realised almost from the first, but what it was supposed to portray he could not imagine. If they had hoped to wring some evidence of fear from him, they failed. Lying upon his back, he watched them with no more apparent concern than an ordinary dance might have elicited.

Perhaps it was because of his seeming indifference that they dragged the dance out to great lengths, that they howled the louder, and that the savagery of their gestures and their screams beggared description; but the end, he knew, was evitable. The fate that Sobito had pictured had been no mere idle threat. Old Timer had long since heard that among some cannibal tribes this method of preparing human flesh was the rule rather than the exception. The horror of it, like a loathsome rat, gnawed at the foundations of the citadel of his reason. He sought to keep his mind from contemplation of it, lest he go mad.

The warriors, aroused to frenzy by the dancing and the drum, urged the priestesses on. They were impatient for the climax of the cruel spectacle. The high priest, master showman, sensed the temper of his audience. He made a signal, and the drumming ceased. The dancing stopped. The audience went suddenly quiet. Silence even more terrifying than the din which had preceded it enveloped the chamber. It was then that the priestesses, with raised clubs, crept stealthily toward their helpless victim.

CHAPTER THIRTEEN

Down River

Kali Bwana crouched in the bottom of the canoe; she heard the rhythmic dip of the paddles as powerful arms sent the craft swiftly downstream with the current. She knew that they were out on the bosom of the large river, that they were not returning to the temple nor upstream to the village of Gato Mgungu. Where, then, to what new trials was fate consigning her?

Bobolo leaned toward her and whispered, 'Do not be afraid. I am taking you away from the Leopard Men.'

She understood just enough of the tribal dialect that he employed to catch the sense of what he had said. 'Who are you?' she asked.

'I am Bobolo, the chief,' he replied.

Instantly she recalled that the white man had hoped for aid from this black, for which he was to pay him in ivory. Her hopes rose. Now she could purchase safety for both of them. 'Is the white man in the canoe?' she asked.

'No,' replied Bobolo.

'You promised to save him,' she reminded him.

'I could save but one,' replied Bobolo.

'Where are you taking me?'

'To my village. There you will be safe. Nothing can harm you.'

'Then you will take me on down river to my own people?' she asked.

'Maybe so after a while,' he answered. 'There is no hurry. You stay with Bobolo. He will be good to you, for Bobolo is a very big chief with many huts and many warriors. You shall have lots of food; lots of slaves; no work.'

The girl shuddered, for she knew the import of his words. 'No!' she cried. 'Oh, please let me go. The white man said that you were his friend. He will pay you; I will pay you.'

'He will never pay,' replied Bobolo. 'If he is not already dead, he will be in a few days.'

'But I can pay,' she pleaded. 'Whatever you ask I will pay you if you will deliver me safely to my own people.'

'I do not want pay,' growled Bobolo; 'I want you.'

She saw that her situation was without hope. In all this hideous land the only person who knew of her danger and might have helped her was either dead or about to die, and she could not help herself. But there was a way out! The idea flashed suddenly to her mind. The river!

She must not permit herself to dwell too long upon the idea – upon the cold, dark waters, upon the crocodiles – lest her strength fail her. She must act instantly, without thought. She leaped to her feet, but Bobolo was too close. Upon the instant he guessed her intention and seized her, throwing her roughly to the bottom of the canoe. He was very angry and struck her heavily across the face; then he bound her, securing her wrists and her ankles.

'You will not try that again,' he growled at her.

'I shall find some other way then,' she replied defiantly. 'You shall not have me. It will be better for you to accept my offer, as otherwise you shall have neither me nor the pay.'

'Be quiet, woman,' commanded the black; 'I have heard enough,' and he struck her again.

For four hours the canoe sped swiftly onward; the ebon paddlers, moving in perfect rhythm, seemed tireless. The sun had risen, but from her prone position in the bottom of the craft the girl saw nothing but the black, sawing bodies of the paddlers nearest her, the degraded face of Bobolo, and the brazen sky above.

At last she heard the sound of voices shouting from the shore. There were answering shouts from the crew of the canoe, and a moment later she felt its prow touch the bank. Then Bobolo removed the bonds from her wrists and ankles and helped her to her feet. Before her, on the river bank, were hundreds of savages: men, women, and children. Beyond them was a village of grass-thatched, beehive huts, surrounded by a palisade of poles bound together with lianas.

When the eyes of the villagers alighted upon the white prisoner there was a volley of shouts and questions; and as she stepped ashore she was surrounded by a score of curious savages, among whom the women were the most unfriendly. She was struck and spat upon by them; and more serious harm would have been done her had not Bobolo stalked among them, striking right and left with the haft of his spear.

Trailed by half the village, she was led into the compound to the hut of the chief, a much larger structure than any of the others, flanked by several two-room huts, all of which were enclosed by a low palisade. Here dwelt the chief and his harem with their slaves. At the entrance to the chief's compound the rabble halted, and Kali Bwana and Bobolo entered alone. Instantly the girl was surrounded again by angry women, the wives of Bobolo. There were fully a dozen of them; and they ranged in age from a child of fourteen to an ancient, toothless hag, who, despite the infirmities of age, appeared to dominate the others.

Again Bobolo had recourse to his spear to save his captive from serious harm. He belaboured the most persistent of them unmercifully until they fell back out of reach of his weapon, and then he turned to the old woman.

'Ubooga,' he said, addressing her, 'this is my new wife. I place her in your care. See that no harm comes to her. Give her two women-slaves. I shall send men-slaves to build a hut for her close to mine.'

'You are a fool,' cried Ubooga. 'She is white. The women will not let her live in peace, if they let her live at all, nor will they let you live in peace until she is dead or you get rid of her. You were a fool to bring her, but then you were always a fool.'

'Hold your tongue, old woman!' cried Bobolo. 'I am chief. If the women molest her I will kill them – and you, too,' he added.

'Perhaps you will kill the others,' screamed the old hag, 'but you will not kill me. I will scratch out your eyes and eat your heart. You are the son of a pig. Your mother was a jackal. You, a chief! You would have been the slave of a slave had it not been for me. Who are you! Your own mother did not know who your father was. You—' But Bobolo had fled.

With her hands on her hips the old termagant turned toward Kali Bwana and surveyed her, appraising her from head to feet. She noted the fine leopard skin garment and the wealth of bracelets and anklets. 'Come, you!' she screamed and seized the girl by the hair.

It was the last straw. Far better to die now than to prolong the agony through brutal abuse and bitter insult. Kali Bwana swung a blow to the side of Ubooga's head that sent her reeling. The other women broke into loud laughter. The girl expected that the old woman would fall upon her and kill her, but she did nothing of the kind. Instead, she stood looking at her; her lower jaw dropped, her eyes wide in astonishment. For a moment she stood thus, and then she appeared to notice the laughter and taunts of the other women for the first time. With a maniacal scream she seized a stick and charged them. They scattered like frightened rabbits seeking their burrows, but not before the stick had fallen heavily upon a couple of them as Ubooga, screaming curses, threatened them with the anger of Bobolo.

When she returned to the white girl she merely nodded her head in the direction of one of the huts and said 'Come' again, but this time in a less peremptory tone; in other ways, too, her attitude seemed changed and far less unfriendly, or perhaps it would be better to say less threatening. That the terrible old woman could be friendly to anyone seemed wholly beyond the range of possibility.

Having installed the girl in her own hut, under the protection of two women slaves, Ubooga hobbled to the main entrance of the chief's compound, possibly in the hope of catching a glimpse of Bobolo, concerning whom she had left a number of things unsaid; but Bobolo was nowhere to be seen. There was, however, a warrior who had returned with the chief from up river squatting before a nearby hut while his wife prepared food for him.

Ubooga, being a privileged character and thus permitted to leave the sacred precincts of the harem, crossed over and squatted down near the warrior.

'Who is the white girl?' demanded the old woman.

The warrior was a stupid fellow, and the fact that he had recently been very drunk and had had no sleep for two nights lent him no greater acumen. Furthermore, he was terribly afraid of Ubooga, as who was not? He looked up dully out of red-rimmed, bloodshot eyes.

'She is the new white priestess of the Leopard God,' he said.

'Where did Bobolo get her?' persisted Ubooga.

'We had come from the battle at Gato Mgungu's village, where we were defeated, and were on our way with Gato Mgungu back to the temp—' He stopped suddenly. 'I don't know where Bobolo got her,' he ended sullenly.

A wicked, toothless grin wrinkled Ubooga's unlovely features. 'I thought so,' she cackled enigmatically and, rising, hobbled back to the chief's compound.

The wife of the warrior looked at him with disgust. 'So you are a Leopard Man!' she whispered accusingly.

'It is a lie,' he cried; 'I said nothing of the sort.'

'You did,' contradicted his wife, 'and you told Ubooga that Bobolo is a Leopard Man. This will not be well for Bobolo or for you.'

'Women who talk too much sometimes have their tongues cut out,' he reminded her.

'It is you who have talked too much,' she retorted. 'I have said nothing. I shall say nothing. Do you think that I want the village to know that my man is a Leopard Man?' There was deep disgust in her tone.

The order of Leopard Men is a secret order. There are few villages and no entire tribes composed wholly of Leopard Men, who are looked upon with disgust and horror by all who are not members of the feared order. Their rites and practices are viewed with contempt by even the most degraded of tribes, and to be proved a Leopard Man is equivalent to the passing of a sentence of exile or death in practically any community.

Ubooga nursed the knowledge she had gained, metaphorically cuddling it to her breast. Squatting down before her hut, she mumbled to herself; and the other women of the harem who saw her were frightened, for they saw that Ubooga smiled, and when Ubooga smiled they knew that something unpleasant was going to happen to someone. They could only hope that it was not to them. When Bobolo entered the compound they saw that she smiled more broadly, and they were relieved, knowing that it was Bobolo and not they who was to be the victim.

'Where is the white girl?' demanded Bobolo as he halted before Ubooga. 'Has any harm befallen her?'

'Your priestess is quite safe, Leopard Man,' hissed Ubooga, but in a voice so low that only Bobolo might hear.

'What do you mean, you old she-devil?' Bobolo's face turned a livid blue from rage.

'For a long time I have suspected it,' cackled Ubooga. 'Now I know it.'

Bobolo seized his knife and grasped the woman by the hair, dragging her across one knee. 'You said I did not dare kill you,' he growled.

'Nor do you. Listen. I have told another, who will say nothing unless I command it, or unless I die. If I die the whole village will know it and you will be torn to pieces. Now kill me, if you dare!'

Bobolo let her fall to the ground. We did not know that Ubooga had lied to him, that she had told no one. He may have surmised as much; but he dared not take the chance, for he knew that Ubooga was right. His people would tear him to pieces should they discover he was a Leopard Man, nor would the other culprits in the tribe dare come to his defence. To divert suspicion from themselves they would join his executioners. Bobolo was very much worried.

'Who told you?' he demanded. 'It is a lie, whoever told you.'

'The girl is high priestess of the Leopard God,' taunted Ubooga. 'After you left the village of Gato Mgungu, following the fight in which you were defeated, you returned to the temple with Gato Mgungu, who all men know is chief of the Leopard Men. There you got the girl.'

'It is a lie. I stole her from the Leopard Men. I am no Leopard Man.'

'Then return her to the Leopard Men, and I will say nothing about the matter. I will tell no one that you are such a good friend of Gato Mgungu that you fight with him against his enemies, for then everyone will know that you must be a Leopard Man.'

'It is a lie,' repeated Bobolo, who could think of nothing else to say.

'Lie or no lie, will you get rid of her?'

'Very well,' said Bobolo; 'in a few days.'

'Today,' demanded Ubooga. 'Today, or I will kill her tonight.'

'Today,' assented Bobolo. He turned away.

'Where are you going?'

'To get someone to take her back where the Leopard Men can find her.'

'Why don't you kill her?'

'The Leopard Men would kill me if I did. They would kill many of my people. First of all they would kill my women if I killed theirs.'

'Go and get someone to take her away,' said Ubooga, 'but see that there is no trickery, you son of a wart hog, you pig, you—'

Bobolo heard no more. He had fled into the village. He was very angry, but he was more afraid. He knew that what Ubooga had said was true; but, on the other hand, his passion still ran high for the white girl. He must try to find some means to preserve her for himself; in case he failed, however, there were other uses to which she could be put. Such were the thoughts which occupied his mind as he walked the length of the village street toward the hut of his old crony Kapopa, the witch-doctor, upon more than one occasion a valuable ally.

He found the old man engaged with a customer who desired a charm that would kill the mother of one of his wives, for which Kapopa had demanded three goats – in advance. There was considerable haggling, the customer insisting that his mother-in-law was not worth one goat, alive, which, he argued, would reduce her value when dead to not more than a single chicken; but Kapopa was obdurate, and finally the man departed to give the matter further thought.

Bobolo plunged immediately into the matter that had brought him to the witch-doctor. 'Kapopa knows,' he commenced, 'that when I returned from up the river I brought a white wife with me.'

Kapopa nodded, 'Who in the village does not?'

'Already she has brought me much trouble,' continued Bobolo.

'And you wish to be rid of her.'

'I do not. It is Ubooga who wishes to rid me of her.'

'You wish a charm to kill Ubooga?'

'I have already paid you for three such charms,' Bobolo reminded him, 'and Ubooga still lives. I do not wish another. Your medicine is not so strong as Ubooga.'

'What do you wish?'

'I will tell you. Because the white girl is a priestess of the Leopard God, Ubooga says that I must be a Leopard Man, but that is a lie. I stole her from the Leopard Men. Everyone knows that I am not a Leopard Man.'

'Of course,' assented Kapopa.

'But Ubooga says that she will tell everyone that I am a Leopard Man if I do not kill the girl or send her away. What can I do?'

Kapopa sat in silence for a moment; then he rummaged in a bag that lay beside him. Bobolo fidgeted. He knew that when Kapopa rummaged in that bag it was always expensive. Finally the witch-doctor drew forth a little bundle wrapped in dirty cloth. Very carefully he untied the strings and spread the cloth upon the ground, revealing its contents, a few short twigs and a figurine carved from bone. Kapopa set the figurine in an upright position facing him, shook the twigs between his two palms, and cast them before the idol. He examined the position of the twigs carefully, scratched his head for a moment, then gathered them up, and cast them again. Once more he studied the situation in silence. Presently he looked up.

'I now have a plan,' he announced.

'How much will it cost?' demanded Bobolo. 'Tell me that first.'

'You have a daughter,' said Kapopa.

'I have many of them,' rejoined Bobolo.

'I do not want them all.'

'You may have your choice if you will tell me how I may keep the white girl without Ubooga knowing it.'

'It can be done,' announced Kapopa. 'In the village of the little men there is no witch-doctor. For a long time they have been coming to Kapopa for their medicine. They will do whatever Kapopa asks.'

'I do not understand,' said Bobolo.

'The village of the little men is not far from the village of Bobolo. We shall take the white girl there. For a small payment of meal and a few fish at times they will keep her there for Bobolo until Ubooga dies. Some day she must die. Already she has lived far too long. In the meantime Bobolo can visit his wife in the village of the little men.'

'You can arrange this with the little men?'

'Yes. I shall go with you and the white girl, and I will arrange everything.'

'Good,' exclaimed Bobolo. 'We will start now; when we return you may go to the harem of Bobolo and select any of his daughters that you choose.'

Kapopa wrapped up the twigs and the idol and replaced them in his pouch; then he got his spear and shield. 'Fetch the white girl,' he said.

CHAPTER FOURTEEN
The Return of Sobito

The wavering light of the smoky torches illuminated the interior of the temple of the Leopard God, revealing the barbaric, savage drama being enacted there; but outside it was very dark, so dark that the figure of a man moving swiftly along the river bank might scarcely have been seen at a distance of fifty feet. He stepped quickly and silently among the canoes of the Leopard Men, pushing them out into the current of the stream. When all had been turned adrift save one, he dragged that up the river and partially beached it opposite the rear of the temple; then he ran toward the building, scaled one of the piles to the verandah, and a moment later paused upon the tiebeam just beneath the overhanging roof at the front of the building, where, through an opening, he could look down upon the tragic scene within.

He had been there a few moments before, just long enough to see and realise the precarious position of the white prisoner. Instantly his plan had been formed, and he had dropped swiftly to the river bank to put a part of it into immediate execution. Now that he was back he realised that a few seconds later he would have been too late. A sudden silence had fallen upon the chamber below. The black priestesses of the Leopard God were sneaking stealthily toward their prostrate victim. No longer did the lesser priests make the purely histrionic pretence of protection. The end had come.

Through the aperture and into the interior of the temple swung Tarzan of the Apes. From tiebeam to tiebeam he leaped, silent as the smoke rising from the torches below. He saw that the priestesses were almost upon the white prisoner, that, swift as he was, he might not be able to reach the man's side in time. It was a bold, mad scheme that had formed in the active brain of the ape-man, and one that depended for success largely upon its boldness. Now it seemed that it was foredoomed to failure even before it could be put into execution.

The sudden silence, following the din of drums and yells and dancing feet, startled the tense nerves of the pinioned prisoner. He turned his eyes from side to side and saw the priestesses creeping toward him. Something told him that the final, hideous horror was upon him now. He steeled himself to meet the agony of it, lest his tormentors should have the added gratification of witnessing the visible effects of his suffering. Something inherent, something racial rebelled at the thought of showing fear or agony before these creatures of an inferior race.

The priestesses were almost upon him when a voice high above them broke the deathly silence. 'Sobito! Sobito! Sobito!' it boomed in hollow accents from the rafters of the temple. 'I am the "muzimo" of Orando, the friend of Nyamwegi. I have come for you. With The Spirit of Nyamwegi, I have come for you!'

Simultaneously a giant white man, naked but for a loin cloth, ran down one of the temple pillars like an agile monkey and leaped to the lower dais. The startling interruption momentarily paralysed the blacks, partially from astonishment and partially from fear. Sobito was speechless. His knees trembled beneath him; then, recovering himself, he fled screaming from the dais to the protection of the concourse of warriors on the temple floor.

Old Timer, no less astonished than the blacks, looked with amazement upon the scene. He expected to see the strange white man pursue Sobito, but he did nothing of the sort. Instead, he turned directly toward the prisoner.

'Be ready to follow me,' commanded the stranger. 'I shall go out through the rear of the temple.' He spoke in low tones and in English; then, as swiftly, he changed to the dialect of the district. 'Capture Sobito and bring him to me,' he shouted to the warriors below the dais. 'Until you fetch him I shall hold this white man as hostage.'

Before there could be either reply or opposition, he leaped to the side of Old Timer, hurled the terrified priests from him, and seizing him by the hand jerked him to his feet. He spoke no further word but turned and ran swiftly across the lower dais, leaped to the higher one where Imigeg shrank aside as they passed, and disappeared from the sight of the Leopard Men through the doorway at its rear. There he paused for a moment and stopped Old Timer.

'Where is the white girl?' he demanded. 'We must take her with us.'

'She is not here,' replied Old Timer; 'a chief stole her and, I imagine, took her down river to his village.'

'This way, then,' directed Tarzan, darting into a doorway on their left.

A moment later they were on the verandah, from which they gained the ground by way of one of the piles that supported the building; then the ape-man ran quickly toward the river, followed closely by Old Timer. At the edge of the river Tarzan stopped beside a canoe.

'Get into this,' he directed; 'it is the only one left here. They cannot follow you. When you reach the main river you will have such a start that they cannot overtake you.'

'Aren't you coming with me?'

'No,' he replied and started to shove the craft out into the stream. 'Do you know the name of the chief who stole the girl?' he asked.

'It was Bobolo.'

Tarzan pushed the canoe away from the bank.

'I can't thank you, old man,' said Old Timer; 'there just aren't the right words in the English language.'

The silent figure on the river bank made no reply, and a moment later, as the current caught the canoe, it was swallowed up in the darkness. Then Old Timer seized the paddle and sought to accelerate the speed of the craft, that he might escape as quickly as possible from this silent river of mystery and death.

The canoe had hardly disappeared in the darkness when Tarzan of the Apes turned back toward the temple. Once again he scaled a pile to the verandah and re-entered the rear of the building. He heard screaming and scuffling in the fore part of the temple, and a grim smile touched his lips as he recognised the origin of the sounds. Advancing quickly to the doorway that opened upon the upper dais he saw several warriors dragging the kicking, screaming Sobito toward him; then he stepped out upon the dais beside the Leopard God. Instantly all eyes were upon him, and fear was in every eye. The boldness of his entrance into their holy of holies, his effrontery, the ease with which he had taken their prisoner from them had impressed them, while the fact that Sobito, a witch-doctor, had fled from him in terror had assured them of his supernatural origin.

'Bind his hands and feet,' commanded Tarzan, 'and deliver him to me. The Spirit of Nyamwegi watches, waiting whom he shall kill; so delay not.'

Hastily the warriors dragging Sobito secured his wrists and ankles; then they lifted him to their shoulders and carried him through the doorway at the side of the dais to the rear chambers of the temple. Here Tarzan met them.

'Leave Sobito with me,' he directed.

'Where is the white prisoner you seized as hostage?' demanded one more courageous than his fellows.

'Search for him in the last room at the far end of the temple,' said the ape-man; but he did not say that they would find him there. Then he lifted Sobito to his shoulder and stepped into the room through which he had led Old Timer to freedom, and as the warriors groped through the darkness in search of their victim the ape-man carried Sobito, screaming from fright, out into the forest.

For a long time the silent, terrified listeners in the temple of the Leopard God heard the eerie wails of the witch-doctor of Tumbai growing fainter in the distance; then the warriors returned from their search of the temple to report that the prisoner was not there.

'We have been tricked!' cried Imigeg. 'The "muzimo" of Orando, the Utenga, has stolen our prisoner.'

'Perhaps he escaped while the "muzimo" was taking Sobito,' suggested Gato Mgungu.

'Search the island,' cried another chief.

'The canoes!' exclaimed a third.

Instantly there was a rush for the river, and then the Leopard Men realised the enormity of the disaster that had befallen them, for not a canoe was left of all those that had brought them to the temple. Their situation was worse than it might appear at first glance. Their village had been burned and those of their fellows who had not accompanied them to the temple were either dead or scattered; there was no path through the tangled mazes of the jungle; but worse still was the fact that religious superstition forbade them from entering the dismal stretch of forest that extended from the island to the nearest trail that they might utilise. The swamps about them and the river below them were infested with crocodiles. The supply of food at the temple was not sufficient to support them for more than a few days. They were cannibals, and the weaker among them were the first to appreciate the significance of that fact.

The warriors of Orando squatted about their fires in their camp beside the manioc field of Gato Mgungu. Their bellies were full, and they were happy. Tomorrow they would start upon the return march to their own country. Already they were anticipating the reception that awaited victorious warriors. Again and again each, when he could make himself heard, recounted his own heroic exploits, none of which lost dramatic value in the retelling. A statistician overhearing them might have computed the enemy dead at fully two thousand.

Their reminiscences were interrupted by the appearance of a giant figure among them. It appeared to have materialised from thin air. It had not been there one moment; the next it had. It was he whom they had known as Muzimo; it was Tarzan of the Apes. Upon his shoulder he bore the bound figure of a man.

'Tarzan of the Apes!' cried some.

'Muzimo!' cried others.

'What have you brought us?' demanded Orando.

Tarzan threw the bound figure to the ground. 'I have brought back your witch-doctor,' he replied. 'I have brought back Sobito, who is also a priest of the Leopard God.'

'It is a lie!' screamed Sobito.

'See the leopard skin upon him,' exclaimed a warrior.

'And the curved claws of the Leopard Men!' cried another.

'No, Sobito is not a Leopard Man!' jeered a third.

'I found him in the temple of the Leopard Men,' explained Tarzan. 'I thought you would like to have your witch-doctor back to make strong medicine for you that would preserve you from the Leopard Men.'

'Kill him!' screamed a warrior.

'Kill Sobito! Kill Sobito!' was taken up by four score throats.

Angry men advanced upon the witch-doctor.

'Wait!' commanded Orando. 'It will be better to take Sobito back to Tumbai, for there are many there who would like to see him die. It will give him time to think about the bad things he has done; it will make him suffer longer, as he has made others suffer; and I am sure that the parents of Nyamwegi would like to see Sobito die.'

'Kill me now,' begged Sobito. 'I do not wish to go back to Tumbai.'

'Tarzan of the Apes captured him,' suggested a warrior. 'Let him tell us what to do with Sobito.'

'Do as you please with him,' replied the ape-man; 'he is not my witch-doctor. I have other business to attend to. I go now. Remember Tarzan of the Apes, if you do not see him again, and because of him treat white men kindly, for Tarzan is your friend and you are his.'

As silently as he had come, he disappeared; and with him went little Nkima, whom the warriors of the Watenga country knew as The Spirit of Nyamwegi.

CHAPTER FIFTEEN
The Little Men

Bobolo and Kapopa dragged Kali Bwana along narrow forest trails away from the great river that was the life artery of the district, back into the dense, dismal depths of the jungle, where great beasts prowled and the little men lived. Here there were no clearings nor open fields; they passed no villages.

The trails were narrow and little used and in places very low, for the little men do not have to clear their trails to the same height that others must.

Kapopa went ahead, for he knew the little men better than Bobolo knew them; though both knew their methods, knew how they hid in the under-brush and speared unwary passers-by or sped poisoned arrows from the trees above. They would recognise Kapopa and not molest them. Behind Kapopa came Kali Bwana. There was a fibre rope around her fair neck. Behind her was Bobolo, holding the rope's end.

The girl was in total ignorance of their destination or of what fate awaited her there. She moved in a dumb lethargy of despair. She was without hope, and her only regret was that she was also without the means of ending her tragic sufferings. She saw the knife at the hip of Kapopa as he walked ahead of her and coveted it. She thought of the dark river and the crocodiles and regretted them. In all respects her situation appeared to her worse than it had ever been before. Perhaps it was the depressing influence of the sombre forest or the mystery of the unknown into which she was being led like some dumb beast to the slaughter. Slaughter! The word fascinated her. She knew that Bobolo was a cannibal. Perhaps they were taking her somewhere into the depths of the grim wood to slaughter and devour her. She wondered why the idea no longer revolted her, and then she guessed the truth – it postulated death. Death! Above all things now she craved death.

How long they plodded that seemingly endless trail she did not know, but after an eternity of dull misery a voice hailed them. Kapopa halted.

'What do you want in the country of Rebega?' demanded the voice.

'I am Kapopa, the witch-doctor,' replied Kapopa. 'With me are Bobolo, the chief, and his wife. We come to visit Rebega.'

'I know you, Kapopa,' replied the voice, and a second later a diminutive warrior stepped into the trail ahead of them from the underbrush at its side. He was about four feet tall and stark naked except for a necklace and some anklets and armbands of copper and iron.

His eyes were small and close set, giving his unpleasant countenance a crafty appearance. His expression denoted surprise and curiosity as he regarded the white girl, but he asked no questions. Motioning them to follow him, he continued along the crooked trail. Almost immediately two other warriors, apparently materialising from thin air, fell in behind them; and thus they were escorted to the village of Rebega, the chief.

It was a squalid village of low huts, bisected ovals with a door two or three feet in height at each end. The huts were arranged about the periphery of an ellipse, in the centre of which was the chief's hut. Surrounding the village was a crude boma of pointed sticks and felled timber with an opening at either end to give ingress and egress.

Rebega was an old, wrinkled man. He squatted on his haunches just outside one of the entrances to his hut, surrounded by his women and children. As the visitors approached him he gave no sign of recognition, his small, beady eyes regarding them with apparent suspicion and malice. His was indeed a most repellent visage.

Kapopa and Bobolo greeted him, but he only nodded once and grunted. To the girl his whole attitude appeared antagonistic, and when she saw the little warriors closing in about them from every hut she believed that Kapopa and Bobolo had placed themselves in a trap from which they might have difficulty in escaping. The thought rather pleased her. What the result would be for her was immaterial; nothing could be worse than the fate that Bobolo had intended for her. She had never seen pygmies before; and, notwithstanding her mental perturbation, her normally active mind found interest in observing them. The women were smaller than the men, few of them being over three feet in height; while the children seemed incredibly tiny. Among them all, however, there was not a prepossessing countenance nor a stitch of clothing, and they were obviously filthy and degraded.

There was a moment's silence as they halted before Rebega, and then Kapopa addressed him. 'You know us, Rebega – Kapopa, the witch-doctor, and Bobolo, the chief!'

Rebega nodded. 'What do you want here?' he demanded.

'We are friends of Rebega,' continued Kapopa, ingratiatingly.

'Your hands are empty,' observed the pygmy; 'I see no presents for Rebega.'

'You shall have presents if you will do what we ask,' promised Bobolo.

'What do you want Rebega to do?'

'Bobolo has brought his white wife to you,' explained Kapopa. 'Keep her here in your village for him in safety; let no one see her; let no one know that she is here.'

'What are the presents?'

'Meal, plantain, fish; every moon enough for a feast for all in your village,' replied Bobolo.

'It is not enough,' grunted Rebega. 'We do not want a white woman in our village. Our own women make us enough trouble.'

Kapopa stepped close to the chief and whispered rapidly into his ear. The sullen expression on Rebega's countenance deepened, but he appeared suddenly nervous and fearful. Perhaps Kapopa, the witch-doctor, had threatened him with the malign attentions of ghosts and demons if he did not accede to their request. At last he capitulated.

'Send the food at once,' he said. 'Even now we have not enough for ourselves, and this woman will need as much food as two of us.'

'It shall be sent tomorrow,' promised Bobolo. 'I shall come with it myself and remain overnight. Now I must return to my village. It is getting late, and it is not well to be out after night has fallen. The Leopard Men are everywhere.'

'Yes,' agreed Rebega, 'the Leopard Men are everywhere. I shall keep your white woman for you if you bring food. If you do not I shall send her back to your village.'

'Do not do that!' exclaimed Bobolo. 'The food shall be sent you.'

It was with a feeling of relief that Kali Bwana saw Bobolo and Kapopa depart. During the interview with Rebega no one had once addressed her, just as no one would have addressed a cow he was arranging to stable. She recalled the plaints of American negroes that they were not treated with equality by the whites. Now that conditions were reversed, she could not see that the blacks were more magnanimous than the whites. Evidently it all depended upon which was the more powerful and had nothing whatsoever to do with innate gentleness of spirit or charity.

When Bobolo and Kapopa had disappeared in the forest, Rebega called to a woman who had been among the interested spectators during the brief interview between him and his visitors. 'Take the white woman to your hut,' he commanded. 'See that no harm befalls her. Let no stranger see her. I have spoken.'

'What shall I feed her?' demanded the woman. 'My man was killed by a buffalo while hunting, and I have not enough food for myself.'

'Let her go hungry, then, until Bobolo brings the food he has promised. Take her away.'

The woman seized Kali Bwana by the wrist and led her toward a miserable hut at the far end of the village. It seemed to the girl to be the meanest hut of all the squalid village. Filth and refuse were piled and strewn about the doorway through which she was conducted into its gloomy, windowless interior.

A number of other women had followed her guardian, and now all these crowded into the hut after them. They jabbered excitedly and pawed her roughly in their efforts to examine and finger her garments and her ornaments. She could understand a little of their language, for she had been long enough now with the natives to have picked up many words, and the pygmies of this district used a dialect similar to that spoken in the villages of

Gato Mgungu and Bobolo. One of them, feeling of her body, remarked that she was tender and that her flesh should be good to eat, at which they all laughed, exposing their sharp-filed, yellow teeth.

'If Bobolo does not bring food for her, she will be too thin,' observed Wlala, the woman who was her guardian.

'If he does not bring food, we should eat her before she becomes too thin,' advised another. 'Our men hunt, but they bring little meat. They say the game has gone away. We must have meat.'

They remained in the small, ill-smelling hut until it was time to go and prepare the evening meal for their men. The girl, exhausted by physical exertion and nervous strain, sickened by the close air and the stench of the hut's interior, had lain down in an effort to secure the peace of oblivion in sleep; but they had prodded her with sticks, and some of them had struck her in mere wanton cruelty. When they had gone she lay down again, but immediately Wlala struck her a sharp blow.

'You cannot sleep while I work, white woman,' she cried. 'Get to work!' She pressed a stone pestle into the girl's hand and indicated a large stone at one side of the hut. In a hollow worn in the stone was some corn. Kali Bwana could not understand all that the woman said, but enough to know that she was to grind the corn. Wearily she commenced the work, while Wlala, just outside the hut, built her cooking fire and prepared her supper. When it was ready the woman gobbled it hungrily, offering none to the girl. Then she came back into the hut.

'I am hungry,' said Kali Bwana. 'Will you not give me food?'

Wlala flew into a frenzy of rage. 'Give you food!' she screamed. 'I have not enough food for myself. You are the wife of Bobolo; let him bring you food.'

'I am not his wife,' replied the girl. 'I am his prisoner. When my friends discover how you have treated me, you will all be punished.'

Wlala laughed. 'Your friends will never know,' she taunted. 'No one comes to the country of the Betetes. In my life I have seen only two other white-skinned people; those two we ate. No one came and punished us. No one will punish us after we have eaten you. Why did Bobolo not keep you in his own village? Were his women angry? Did they drive you out?'

'I guess so,' replied the girl.

'Then he will never take you back. It is a long way from the village of Bobolo to the village of Rebega. Bobolo will soon tire of coming so far to see you while he has plenty of wives in his own village; then he will give you to us.' Wlala licked her thick lips.

The girl sat dejectedly before the stone mortar. She was very tired. Her hands had dropped to her sides. 'Get to work, you lazy sow!' cried Wlala and struck her across the head with the stick she kept ever ready at hand. Wearily, Kali Bwana resumed her monotonous chore. 'And see that you grind it fine,' added Wlala; then she went out to gossip with the other women of the village.

As soon as she was gone the girl stopped working. She was so tired that she could scarcely raise the stone pestle, and she was very hungry. Glancing fearfully through the doorway of the hut, she saw that no one was near enough to see her, and then, quickly, she gathered a handful of the raw meal and ate it. She dared not eat too much, lest Wlala discover the theft; but even that little was better than nothing. Then she added some fresh corn to the meal in the mortar and ground that to the same consistency as the other.

When Wlala returned to the hut, the girl was fast asleep beside the mortar. The woman kicked her into wakefulness; but as by now it was too dark to work and the woman herself lay down to sleep, Kali Bwana was at last permitted undisturbed slumber.

Bobolo did not return the following day, nor the second day, nor the third; neither did he send food. The pygmies were very angry. They had been anticipating a feast. Perhaps Wlala was the angriest, for she was the hungriest; also, she had commenced to suspect the theft of her meal. Not being positive, but to be on the safe side, she had beaten Kali Bwana unmercifully while she accused her of it. At least she started to beat her; then suddenly something quite unexpected had happened. The white girl, leaping to her feet, had seized the pygmy, torn the stick from her hand, and struck her repeatedly with it before Wlala could run from the hut. After that Wlala did not again strike Kali Bwana. In fact, she treated her with something approximating respect, but her voice was raised loudly in the village against the hated alien and against Bobolo.

In front of Rebega's hut was a concourse of women and warriors. They were all angry and hungry. 'Bobolo has not brought the food,' cried one, repeating for the hundredth time what had been said by each.

'What do we want of meal, or plantain, or fish when we have flesh here for all?' The speaker jerked a thumb meaningly in the direction of Wlala's hut.

'Bobolo would bring warriors and kill us if we harmed his white wife,' cautioned another.

'Kapopa would cast a spell upon us, and many of us would die.'

'He said he would come back with food the next day.'

'Now it has been three days, and he has not returned.'

'The flesh of the white girl is good now,' argued Wlala. 'She has been eating my meal, but I have stopped that. I have taken the meal from the hut and hidden it. If she does not have food soon, her flesh will not be so good as now. Let us eat her.'

'I am afraid of Kapopa and Bobolo,' admitted Rebega.

'We do not have to tell them that we ate her,' urged Wlala.

'They will guess it,' insisted Rebega.

'We can tell them that the Leopard Men came and took her away,' suggested a rat-faced little fighting man; 'and if they do not believe us we can go away. The hunting is not good here, anyway. We should go elsewhere and hunt.'

For a long time Rebega's fears outweighed his natural inclination for human flesh, but at last he told them that if the food Bobolo had promised did not arrive before dark they would have a dance and a feast that night.

In the hut of Wlala. Kali Bwana heard the loud shouts of approval that greeted Rebega's announcement and thought that the food Bobolo had promised had arrived. She hoped that they would give her some of it, for she was weak from hunger. When Wlala came she asked her if the food had arrived.

'Bobolo has sent no food, but we shall eat tonight,' replied the woman, grinning. 'We shall eat all that we wish; but it will not be meal, nor plantain, nor fish.' She came over to the girl then and felt of her body, pinching the flesh slightly between her fingers. 'Yes, we shall eat,' she concluded.

To Kali Bwana the inference was obvious, but the strange chemistry of emotion had fortunately robbed her of the power to feel repugnance for the idea that would have so horribly revolted her a few short weeks ago. She did not think of the grisly aftermath; she thought only of death, and welcomed it.

The food from Bobolo did not come, and that night the Betetes gathered in the compound before Rebega's hut. The woman dragged cooking pots to the scene and built many fires. The men danced a little; but only for a short time, for they had been too long on short rations. Their energy was at low ebb.

At last a few of them went to the hut of Wlala and dragged Kali Bwana to the scene of the festivities. There was some dispute as to who was to kill her. Rebega was frankly afraid of the wrath of Kapopa, though he was not so much concerned about Bobolo. Bobolo could only follow them with warriors whom they could see and kill; but Kapopa could remain in his village and send demons and ghosts after them. At last it was decided that the woman should kill her; and Wlala, remembering the blows that the white girl had struck her, volunteered to do the work herself.

'Tie her hands and feet,' she said, 'and I will kill her.' She did not care to risk a repetition of the scene in her hut at the time she had attempted to beat the girl.

Kali Bwana understood, and as the warriors prepared to bind her she crossed her hands to facilitate their work. They threw her to the ground and secured her feet; then she closed her eyes and breathed a prayer. It was for those she had left behind in that far away country and for 'Jerry.'

CHAPTER SIXTEEN

A Clue

The night that Tarzan had brought Sobito to their camp the Utengas had celebrated the event in beer salvaged from the loot of Gato Mgungu's village before they had burned it. They had celebrated late into the night, stopping only when the last of the beer had been consumed; then they had slept heavily and well. Even the sentries had dozed at their posts, for much beer poured into stomachs already filled with food induces a lethargy difficult to combat.

And while the Utenga warriors slept, Sobito was not idle. He pulled and tugged at the bonds that held his wrists, with little fear that his rather violent efforts would attract attention. At last he felt them gradually stretching. Sweat poured from his tough old hide; beads of it stood out upon his wrinkled forehead. He was panting from the violence of his exertions. Slowly he dragged one hand farther and farther through the loop; just a hair's breadth at a time it moved, but eventually it slipped out – free!

For a moment the old witch-doctor lay still, recouping the energy that he had expended in his efforts to escape his bonds. Slowly his eyes ranged the camp. No one stirred. Only the heavy, stertorous breathing of the halfdrunk warriors disturbed the silence of the night. Sobito drew his feet up within reach of his hands and untied the knots of the cords that confined them; then very quietly and slowly he arose and slipped, bent half-doubled, down toward the river. In a moment the darkness had swallowed him, and the sleeping camp slept on.

On the shore he found the canoes that the Utengas had captured from the forces of Gato Mgungu; with considerable difficulty he pushed one of the smaller of them into the river, after satisfying himself that there was at least one paddle in it. As he leaped into it and felt it glide out into the current, he felt like one snatched from the jaws of death by some unexpected miracle.

His plans were already made. He had had plenty of time while he was lying working with his bonds to formulate them. He might not with safety return to the temple of the Leopard God, that he knew full well; but down the river lay the village of his old friend Bobolo, who by the theft of the white priestess was doubtless as much anathema in the eyes of the Leopard Men as he. To Bobolo's village, therefore, he would go. What he would do afterward was in the laps of the gods.

*

Another lone boatman drifted down the broad river toward the village of Bobolo. It was Old Timer. He, too, had determined to pay a visit to the citadel of his old friend; but it would be no friendly visit. In fact, if Old Timer's plans were successful, Bobolo would not be aware that a visit was being paid him, lest his hospitality wax so mightily that the guest might never be permitted to depart. It was the white girl, not Bobolo, who lured Old Timer to this rash venture. Something within him more powerful than reason told him that he must save her, and he knew that if any succour was to avail it must come to her at once. As to how he was to accomplish it he had not the most remote conception; all that must depend upon his reconnaissance and his resourcefulness.

As he drifted downward, paddling gently, his mind was filled with visions of the girl. He saw her as he had first seen her in her camp: her blood-smeared clothing, the dirt and perspiration, but, over all, the radiance of her fair face, the haunting allure of her blonde hair, dishevelled and falling in wavy ringlets across her forehead and about her ears. He saw her as he had seen her in the temple of the Leopard God, garbed in savage, barbaric splendour, more beautiful than ever. It thrilled him to live again the moments during which he had talked to her, touched her.

Forgotten was the girl whose callous selfishness had made him a wanderer and an outcast. The picture of her that he had carried constantly upon the screen of memory for two long years had faded. When he thought of her now he laughed; and instead of cursing her, as he had so often done before, he blessed her for having sent him here to meet and know this glorious creature who now filled his dreams.

Old Timer was familiar with this stretch of the river. He knew the exact location of Bobolo's village, and he knew that day would break before he came within sight of it. To come boldly to it would be suicidal; now that Bobolo was aware that the white man knew of his connection with the Leopard Men, his life would not be safe if he fell into the hands of the crafty old chief.

For a short time after the sun rose he drifted on downstream, keeping close to the left bank; and shortly before he reached the village he turned the prow of his craft in to shore. He did not know that he would ever need the canoe again; but on the chance that he might he secured it to the branch of a tree, and then clambered up into the leafy shelter of the forest giant.

He planned to make his way through the forest toward the village in the hope of finding some vantage point from which he might spy upon it; but he was confident that he would have to wait until after darkness had fallen before he could venture close, when it was in his plan to scale the palisade and search the village for the girl while the natives slept. A mad scheme – but men have essayed even madder when spurred on by infatuation for a woman.

As Old Timer was about to leave the tree and start toward the village of Bobolo, his attention was attracted toward the river by a canoe which had just come within sight around a bend a short distance upstream. In it was a single native. Apprehending that any movement on his part might attract the attention of the lone paddler and wishing above all things to make his way to the village unseen, he remained motionless. Closer and closer came the canoe, but it was not until it was directly opposite him that the white man recognised its occupant as that priest of the Leopard God whom his rescuer had demanded should be delivered into his hands.

Yes, it was Sobito; but how had Sobito come here? What was the meaning of it? Old Timer was confident that the strange white giant who had rescued him had not demanded Sobito for the purpose of setting him free. Here was a mystery. Its solution was beyond him, but he could not see that it materially concerned him in any way; so he gave it no further thought after Sobito had drifted out of sight beyond the next turning of the river below.

Moving cautiously through the jungle the white man came at last within sight of the village of Bobolo. Here he climbed a tree well off the trail where he could overlook the village without being observed. He was not surprised that he did not see the girl who he was confident was there, knowing that she was doubtless a prisoner in one of the huts of the chief's compound. All that he could do was wait until darkness had fallen – wait and hope.

Two days' march on the opposite side of the river lay his own camp. He had thought of going there first and enlisting the aid of his partner, but he dared not risk the four days' delay. He wondered what The Kid was doing; he had not had much time to think about him of late, but he hoped he had been more successful in his search for ivory than he had.

The tree in which Old Timer had stationed himself was at the edge of a clearing. Below him and at a little distance women were working, hoeing with sharpened sticks. They were chattering like a band of monkeys. He saw a few warriors set out to inspect their traps and snares. The scene was peacefully pastoral. He had recognised most of the warriors and some of the women, for Old Timer was well acquainted in the village of Bobolo. The villagers had been friendly, but he knew that he dared no longer approach the village openly because of his knowledge of Bobolo's connection with the Leopard Men. Because of that fact and his theft of the white girl the chief could not afford to let him live; he knew too much.

He had seen the village many times before, but now it had taken on a new aspect. Before, it had been only another native village inhabited by savage blacks; today it was glorified in his eyes by the presence of a girl. Thus does imagination colour our perceptions. How different would the village of Bobolo have appeared in the eyes of the watcher had he known the truth, had he known that the girl he thought so near him was far away in the hut of Wlala, the Betete pygmy, grinding corn beneath the hatefilled eyes of a cruel task-master, suffering from hunger!

In the village Bobolo was having troubles of his own. Sobito had come! The chief knew nothing of what had befallen the priest of the Leopard God. He did not know that he had been discredited in the eyes of the order; nor did Sobito plan to enlighten him. The wily old witch-doctor was not sure that he had any plans at all. He could not return to Tumbai, but he had to live somewhere. At least he thought so; and he needed, if not friends, allies. He saw in Bobolo a possible ally. He knew that the chief had stolen the white priestess, and he hoped that this knowledge might prove of advantage to him; but he said nothing about the white girl. He believed that she was in the village and that sooner or later he would see her. They had talked of many things since his arrival, but they had not spoken of the Leopard Men nor of the white girl. Sobito was waiting for any turn of events that would give him a cue to his advantage.

Bobolo was nervous. He had been planning to take food to Rebega this day and visit his white wife. Sobito had upset his plans. He tried to think of some way by which he could rid himself of his unwelcome guest. Poison occurred to him; but he had already gone too far in arousing the antagonism of the Leopard Men, and knowing that there were loyal members of the clan in his village, he feared to add the poisoning of a priest to his other crime against the Leopard God.

The day dragged on. Bobolo had not yet discovered why Sobito had come to his village; Sobito had not yet seen the white girl. Old Timer was still perched in the tree overlooking the village. He was hungry and thirsty, but he did not dare desert his post lest something might occur in the village that it would be to his advantage to see. Off and on all day he had seen Bobolo and Sobito. They were always talking. He wondered if they were discussing the fate of the girl. He wished that night would come. He would like to get down and stretch his legs and get a drink. His thirst annoyed him more than his hunger; but even if he had contemplated deserting his post to obtain water, it could not be done now. The women in the field had worked closer to his tree. Two of them were just beneath its overhanging branches. They paused in the shade to rest, their tongues rattling ceaselessly.

Old Timer had overheard a number of extremely intimate anecdotes relating to members of the tribe. He learned that if a certain lady were not careful her husband was going to catch her in an embarrassing situation, that certain charms are more efficacious when mixed with nail parings, that the young son of another lady had a demon in his belly that caused him intense suffering when he over-ate. These things did not interest Old Timer greatly, but presently one of the women asked a question that brought him to alert attention.

'What do you think Bobolo did with his white wife?'

'He told Ubooga that he had sent her back to the Leopard Men from whom he says that he stole her,' replied the other.

'Bobolo has a lying tongue in his head,' rejoined the first woman; 'it does net know the truth.'

'I know what he did with her,' volunteered the other. 'I overheard Kapopa telling his wife.'

'What did he say?'

'He said that they took her to the village of the little men.'

'They will eat her.'

'No, Bobolo has promised to give them food every moon if they keep her for him.'

'I would not like to be in the village of the little men no matter what they promised. They are eaters of men, they are always hungry, and they are great liars.' Then the women's work carried them away from the tree, and Old Timer heard no more; but that which he had heard had changed all his plans.

No longer was he interested in the village of Bobolo; once again it was only another native village.

CHAPTER SEVENTEEN

Charging Lions

When Tarzan of the Apes left the camp of the Utengas, he appropriated one of the canoes of the defeated Leopard Men, as Sobito was to do several hours later, and paddled across the broad river to its opposite shore. His destination was the village of Bobolo; his mission, to question the chief relative to the white girl. He felt no keen personal interest in her and was concerned only because of racial ties, which, after all, are not very binding. She was a white woman and he was a white man, a fact that he sometimes forgot, since, after all, he was a wild beast before everything else.

He had been very active for several days and nights, and he was tired. Little Nkima also was tired, nor did he let Tarzan forget it for long; so when the ape-man leaped ashore from the canoe he sought a comfortable place among the branches of a tree where they might lie up for a few hours.

The sun was high in the heavens when Tarzan awoke. Little Nkima, snuggling close to him, would have slept longer; but the ape-man caught him by the scruff of the neck and shook him into wakefulness. 'I am hungry,' said Tarzan; 'let us find food and eat.'

'There is plenty to eat in the forest,' replied Nkima; 'let us sleep a little longer.'

'I do not want fruit or nuts,' said the ape-man. 'I want meat. Nkima may remain here and sleep, but Tarzan goes to kill.'

'I shall go with you,' announced Nkima. 'Strong in this forest is the scent of Sheeta, the leopard. I am afraid to remain alone. Sheeta is hunting, too; he is hunting for little Nkima.'

The shadow of a smile touched the lips of the ape-man, one of those rare smiles that it was vouchsafed but few to see. 'Come,' he said, 'and while Tarzan hunts for meat Nkima can rob birds' nests.'

The hunting was not good, for though the ape-man ranged far through the forest his searching nostrils were not rewarded with the scent of flesh that he liked. Always strong was the scent of Sheeta, but Tarzan liked not the flesh of the carnivores. Driven to it by the extremity of hunger, he had eaten more than once of Sheeta and Numa and Sabor; but it was the flesh of the herbivores that he preferred.

Knowing that the hunting was better farther from the river, where there were fewer men, he swung deeper and deeper into the primeval forest until he was many miles from the river. This country was new to Tarzan, and he did not like it; there was too little game. This thought was in his mind when there came to his nostrils the scent of Wappi, the antelope. It was very faint, but it was enough. Straight into the wind swung Tarzan of the Apes, and steadily the scent of Wappi grew stronger in his nostrils. Mingling with it were other scents: the scent of Pacco, the zebra, and of Numa, the lion; the fresh scent of open grassland.

On swung Tarzan of the Apes and little Nkima. Stronger grew the scent spoor of the quarry in the nostrils of the hunter, stronger the hunger-craving gnawing in his belly. His keen nostrils told him that there was not one antelope ahead but many. This must be a good hunting ground that he was approaching! Then the forest ended; and a rolling, grassy plain, tree dotted, stretched before him to blue mountains in the distance.

Before him, as he halted at the forest's edge, the plain was rich with lush grasses; a mile away a herd of antelope grazed, and beyond them the plain was dotted with zebra. An almost inaudible growl rumbled from his deep chest; it was the anticipatory growl of the hunting beast that is about to feed.

Strong in his nostrils was the scent of Numa, the lion. In those deep grasses were lions; but in such rich hunting ground, they must be well fed, he knew, and so he could ignore them. They would not bother him, if he did not bother them, which he had no intention of doing.

To stalk the antelope amid the concealment of this tall grass was no difficult matter for the ape-man. He did not have to see them; his nose would guide him to them. First he noted carefully the terrain, the location of each tree, an outcropping of rock that rose above the grasses. It was likely that the lions would be lying up there in the shadow of the rocks.

He beckoned to Nkima, but Nkima held back. 'Numa is there,' complained the monkey, 'with all his brothers and sisters. They are waiting there to eat little Nkima. Nkima is afraid.'

'Stay where you are, then; and when I have made my kill I will return.'

'Nkima is afraid to remain.'

Tarzan shook his head. 'Nkima is a great coward,' he said. 'He may do what he pleases. Tarzan goes to make his kill.'

Silently he slid into the tall grasses, while Nkima crouched high in a great tree, choosing the lesser of two evils. The little monkey watched him go out into the great plain where the lions were; and he shivered, though it was very warm.

Tarzan made a detour to avoid the rocks; but even where he was, the lion scent was so strong that he almost lost the scent of Wappi. Yet he felt no apprehension. Fear he did not know. By now he had covered half the distance to the quarry, which was still feeding quietly, unmindful of danger.

Suddenly to his left he heard the angry coughing growl of a lion. It was a warning growl that the ape-man knew might presage a charge. Tarzan sought no encounter with Numa. All that he wished was to make his kill and depart. He moved away to the right. Fifty feet ahead of him was a tree. If the lion charged, it might be necessary to seek sanctuary there, but he did not believe that Numa would charge. He had given him no reason to do so; then a cross current of wind brought to his nostrils a scent that warned him of his peril. It was the scent of Sabor, the lioness. Now Tarzan understood; he had nearly stumbled upon a mating lion, which meant that a charge was almost inevitable, for a mating lion will charge anything without provocation.

Now the tree was but twenty-five feet away. A roar thundered from the grasses behind him. A quick backward glance, showing the grass tops waving tumultuously, revealed the imminence of his danger; Numa was charging!

Up to that time he had seen no lion, but now a massive head framed by a dark brown mane burst into view. Tarzan of the Apes was angry. It galled him to flee. A dignified retreat prompted by caution was one thing; abject flight, another. Few creatures can move with the swiftness of Tarzan, and he had a start of twenty-five feet. He could have reached the tree ahead of the lion, but he did not attempt to do so – not at once. Instead he wheeled and faced the roaring, green-eyed monster. Back went his spear arm, his muscles rolling like molten steel beneath his bronzed skin; then forward with all the weight of his powerful frame backed by those mighty thews. The heavy Utenga war spear shot from his hand. Not until then did Tarzan of the Apes turn and fly; but he did not run from the lion that was pursuing him. Behind Numa he had seen Sabor coming, and behind her the grasses waved in many places above the rushing bodies of charging lions. Tarzan of the Apes fled from certain and sudden death.

The spear momentarily checked the charge of the nearest lion, and in that fraction of a split second that spelled the difference between life and death the ape-man swarmed up the tree that had been his goal, while the raking talons of Numa all but grazed his heel.

Safe out of reach Tarzan turned and looked down. Below him a great lion in his death throes was clawing at the haft of the spear that was buried in his heart. Behind the first lion a lioness and six more males had burst into view. Far out across the plain the antelopes and the zebras were disappearing in the distance, startled into flight by the roars of the charging lion.

The lioness, never pausing in her charge, ran far up the bole of the tree in her effort to drag down the man-thing. She had succeeded in getting one forearm across a lower branch, and she hung there a moment in an effort to scramble farther upward; but she could not get sufficient footing for her hind feet to force her heavy weight higher, and presently she slipped back to the ground. She sniffed at her dead mate and then circled the tree, growling. The six males paced to and fro, adding their angry roars to the protest of Sabor, while from above them the ape-man looked down and through snarling lips growled out his own disappointment and displeasure. In a tree top half a mile away a little monkey screamed and scolded.

For half an hour the lioness circled the tree, looking up at Tarzan, her yellow-green eyes blazing with rage and hatred; then she lay down beside the body of her fallen mate, while the six males squatted upon their haunches and watched now Sabor, now Tarzan, and now one another.

Tarzan of the Apes gazed ruefully after his departed quarry and back toward the forest. He was hungrier now than ever. Even if the lions went away and permitted him to descend, he was still as far from a meal as he had been when he awoke in the morning. He broke twigs and branches from the tree and hurled them at Sabor in an attempt to drive her away, knowing that wherever she went the males would follow; but she only growled the more ferociously and remained in her place beside the dead lion.

Thus passed the remainder of the day. Night came, and still the lioness remained beside her dead mate. Tarzan upbraided himself for leaving his bow and arrows behind in the forest. With them he could have killed the lioness and the lions and escaped. Without them he could do nothing but throw futile twigs at them and wait. He wondered how long he would have to wait. When the lioness waxed hungry enough she would go away; but when would that be? From the size of her belly and the smell of her breath the man-beast squatting above her knew that she had eaten recently and well.

Tarzan had long since resigned himself to his fate. When he had found that hurling things at Sabor would not drive her away, he had desisted. Unlike man he did not continue to annoy her merely for the purpose of venting his displeasure. Instead, he curled himself in a crotch of the tree and slept.

In the forest, at the edge of the plain, a terrified little monkey rolled himself into the tiniest ball that he could achieve and suffered in silence. If he were too large or too noisy, he feared that he might sooner attract the attention of Sheeta, the leopard. That Sheeta would come eventually and eat him he was certain. But why hasten the evil moment?

When the sun rose and he was still alive, Nkima was surprised but not wholly convinced. Sheeta might have overlooked him in the dark, but in the daylight he would be sure to see him; however, there was some consolation in knowing that he could see Sheeta sooner and doubtless escape him. With the rising sun his spirits rose, but he was still unhappy because Tarzan had not returned. Out on the plain he could see him in the tree, and he wondered why he did not come down and return to little Nkima. He saw the lions, too; but it did not occur to him that it was they who prevented Tarzan returning. He could not conceive that there might be any creature or any number of creatures which his mighty master could not overcome.

Tarzan was irked. The lioness gave no sign that she was ever going away. Several of the males had departed to hunt during the night, and one that had made a kill nearby lay on it not far from the tree. Tarzan hoped that Sabor would be attracted by it; but though the odour of the kill was strong in the ape-man's nostrils, the lioness was not tempted away by it.

Noon came. Tarzan was famished and his throat was dry. He was tempted to cut a club from a tree branch and attempt to battle his way to liberty; but he knew only too well what the outcome would be. Not even he, Tarzan of the Apes, could hope to survive the onslaught of all those lions, which was certain to follow immediately he descended from the tree if the lioness attacked him. That she would attack him if he approached that close to her dead mate was a foregone conclusion. There was nothing to do but wait. Eventually she would go away; she could not remain there forever.

Nor did she. Shortly after noon she arose and slunk toward the kill that one of the males had made. As she disappeared in the tall grass, the other males followed her. It was fortunate for the ape-man that the kill lay beyond the tree in which he had taken refuge, away from the forest. He did not wait after the last male disappeared among the waving grasses, but dropped from the tree, recovered his spear from the carcass of Numa, and started at a brisk walk toward the forest. His keen ears took note of every sound. Not even soft-padded Numa could have stalked him without his being aware of it, but no lion followed him.

Nkima was frantic with joy. Tarzan was only hungry and thirsty. He was not long in finding the means for quenching his thirst, but it was late before he made a kill and satisfied his hunger; then his thoughts returned to the object of his excursion. He would go to the village of Bobolo and reconnoitre.

He had gone far inland from the river, and his hunting had taken him down the valley to a point which he guessed was about opposite the village where he hoped to find the girl. He had passed a band of great apes led by Zu-tho, whom he had thought far away in his own country; and he had stopped to talk with them for a moment; but neither the great apes nor Tarzan, who was reared among them, are loquacious, so that he soon left them to pursue the purpose he had undertaken. Now he swung through the trees directly toward the river, where he knew that he could find landmarks to assure him of his position.

It was already dark; so Nkima clung to the back of his master, his little arms about the bronzed neck. By day he swung through the trees with Tarzan; but at night he clung tightly to him, for by night there are terrible creatures abroad in the jungle; and they are all hunting for little Nkima.

The scent spoor of man was growing stronger in the nostrils of Tarzan, so that he knew that he was approaching a village of the Gomangani. He was certain that it could not be the village of Bobolo; it was too far from the river. Furthermore, there was an indication in the odours wafted to his nostrils that the people who inhabited it were not of the same tribe as Bobolo. The mere presence of Gomangani would have been sufficient to have caused Tarzan to investigate, for it was the business of the Lord of the Jungle to have knowledge of all things in his vast domain; but there was another scent spoor faintly appreciable among the varied stenches emanating from the village that in itself would have been sufficient to turn him from his direct path to the river. It was but the faintest suggestion of a scent, yet the ape-man recognised it for what it was; and it told him that the girl he sought was close at hand.

Silently he approached the village, until from the outspreading branches of a great tree he looked down upon the compound before the hut of Rebega, the chief.

CHAPTER EIGHTEEN

Arrows out of the Night

The Kid had returned to his camp after a fruitless search for elephants. He hoped that Old Timer had been more successful. At first he thought that the other's protracted absence indicated this, but as the days passed and his friend did not return he became anxious. His position was not an enviable one. The faith and loyalty of his three black retainers had been sorely shaken. Only a genuine attachment for the two white men had kept them with them during the recent months of disappointment and ill fortune. How much longer he could expect to hold them he did not know. He was equally at a loss to imagine what he would do if they deserted him, yet his chief concern was not for himself but for his friend.

Fortunately he had been able to keep the camp well supplied with fresh meat, and the natives, therefore, reasonably contented; but he knew that they longed to return to their own village now that they could not see any likelihood of profiting by their connection with these two poverty-stricken white men.

Such thoughts were occupying his mind late one afternoon upon his return from a successful hunt for meat when his reveries were interrupted by the shouts of his 'boys.' Glancing up, he saw two of the men who had accompanied Old Timer entering the camp. Leaping to his feet, he went forward to meet them, expecting to see his friend and the third black following closely behind him; but when he was close enough to see the expressions upon their faces he realised that something was amiss.

'Where are your bwana and Andereya?' he demanded.

'They are both dead,' replied one of the returning blacks.

'Dead!' ejaculated The Kid. It seemed to him that the bottom had suddenly dropped from his world. Old Timer dead! It was unthinkable. Until now he had scarcely realised how much he had depended upon the older man for guidance and support, nor to what extent this friendship had become a part of him. 'How did it happen?' he inquired dully. 'Was it an elephant?'

'The Leopard Men, Bwana,' explained the black who had made the announcement.

'The Leopard Men! Tell me how it happened.'

With attention to minute details and with much circumlocution the two boys told all that they knew; and when at last they had finished, The Kid saw a suggestion of a ray of hope. They had not actually seen Old Timer killed. He might still be a prisoner in the village of Gato Mgungu.

'He said that if he had not returned to us by the time the shadow of the forest had left the palisade in the morning we should know that he was dead,' insisted a black.

The youth mentally surveyed his resources: five discontented blacks and himself – six men to march upon the stronghold of the Leopard Men and demand an accounting of them. And five of these men held the Leopard Men in such awe that he knew that they would not accompany him. He raised his eyes suddenly to the waiting blacks. 'Be ready to march when the sun rises tomorrow,' he snapped.

There was a moment's hesitation. 'Where do we march?' demanded one, suspiciously.

'Where I lead you,' he replied, shortly; then he returned to his tent, his mind occupied with plans for the future and with the tragic story that the two 'boys' had narrated.

He wondered who the girl might be. What was Old Timer doing pursuing a white woman? Had he gone crazy, or had he forgotten that he hated all white women? Of course, he reflected, there was nothing else that his friend might have done. The girl had been in danger, and that of course would have been enough to have sent Old Timer on the trail of her abductors; but how had he become involved with her in the first place? The 'boys' had not been explicit upon this point. He saw them now, talking with their fellows. All of them appeared excited. Presently they started across the camp toward his tent.

'Well, what is it now?' he asked as they stopped before him.

'If you are going to the village of the Leopard Men, Bwana,' announced the spokesman, 'we will not follow you. We are few, and they would kill us all and eat us.'

'Nonsense!' exclaimed The Kid. 'They will do nothing of the sort. They would not dare.'

'That is what the old bwana said,' replied the spokesman, 'but he did not return to us. He is dead.'

'I do not believe that he is dead,' retorted The Kid. 'We are going to find out.'

'You, perhaps, but not we,' rejoined the black.

The Kid saw that he could not shake them in their decision. The outlook appeared gloomy, but he was determined to go if he had to go alone. Yet what could he accomplish without them? A plan occurred to him.

'Will you go part way with me?' he asked.

'How far?'

'To the village of Bobolo. I may be able to get help from him.'

For a moment the blacks argued among themselves in low voices; then their spokesman turned again to the white man. 'We will go as far as the village of Bobolo,' he said.

'But no farther,' added another.

Old Timer waited until the women hoeing in the field had departed a little distance from the tree in which he was hiding; then he slipped cautiously to the ground on the side opposite them. He had never been to the village of the little men. He had often heard the natives of Bobolo's village speak of them and knew in a general way the direction in which the pygmy village lay, but there were many trails in this part of the forest. It would be easy to take the wrong one.

He knew enough of the Betetes to know that he might have difficulty in entering their village. They were a savage, war-like race of pygmies and even reputed to be cannibals. The trails to their village were well guarded, and the first challenge might be a poisoned spear. Yet, though he knew these things to be true, the idea of abandoning his search for the girl because of them did not occur to him. He did not hesitate in reaching a decision, but the very fact that she was there hastened it instead.

Dark soon overtook him, but he stopped only because he could not see to go on. At the first break of dawn he was away again. The forest was dense and gloomy. He could not see the sun, and he was haunted by the conviction that he was on the wrong trail. It must have been about midafternoon when he came to a sudden halt, baffled. He had recognised his own footprints in the trail ahead of him; he had walked in a great circle.

Absolutely at a loss as to which direction to take, he struck out blindly along a narrow, winding trail that intercepted the one he had been traversing at the point at which he had made his harrowing discovery. Where the trail led or in what direction he could not know, nor even whether it led back toward the river or farther inland: but he must be moving, he must go on.

Now he examined carefully every trail that crossed or branched from the one he was following. The trails, some of them at least, were well worn; the ground was damp; the spoor of animals was often plain before his eyes. But he saw nothing that might afford him a clue until shortly before dark; then careful scrutiny of an intersecting trail revealed the tiny footprint of a pygmy. Old Timer was elated. It was the first sense of elation that he had experienced during all that long, dreary day. He had come to hate the forest. Its sunless gloom oppressed him. It had assumed for him the menacing personality of a powerful, remorseless enemy that sought not only to thwart his plans but to lure him to his death. He longed to defeat it – to show it that he was more cunning, if less powerful than it.

He hastened along the new trail, but darkness overtook him before he learned whether or not it led to his goal. Yet now he did not stop as he had the previous night. So long had the forest defeated and mocked him that perhaps he was a little mad. Something seemed to be calling to him out of the blackness ahead. Was it a woman's voice? He knew better, yet he listened intently as he groped his way through the darkness.

Presently his tensely listening ears were rewarded by a sound. It was not the voice of a woman calling to him, but it was still the sound of human voices. Muffled and indistinct, it came to him out of that black void ahead. His heart beat a little faster; he moved more cautiously.

When he came at last within sight of a village he could see nothing beyond the palisade other than the firelight playing upon the foliage of overspreading trees and upon the thatched roofs of huts, but he knew that it was the village of the little men. There, behind that palisade, was the girl he sought. He wanted to cry aloud, shouting words of encouragement to her. He wanted her to know that he was near her, that he had come to have her; but he made no sound.

Cautiously he crept nearer. There was no sign of sentry. The little men do not need sentries in the dark forest at night, for few are the human enemies that dare invite the dangers of the nocturnal jungle. The forest was their protection by night.

The poles that had been stuck in the ground to form the palisade were loosely bound together by lianas; there were spaces between them through which he glimpsed the firelight. Old Timer moved cautiously forward until he stood close against the palisade beside a gate and, placing an eye to one of the apertures, looked into the village of Rebega. What he saw was not particularly interesting: a group of natives gathered before a central hut which he assumed to be the hut of the chief. They appeared to be arguing about something, and some of the men were dancing. He could see their heads bobbing above those of the natives who shut off his view.

Old Timer was not interested in what the little men were doing. At least he thought he was not. He was interested only in the girl, and he searched the village for some evidence of her presence there, though he was not surprised that he did not see her. Undoubtedly she was a prisoner in one of the huts. Had he known the truth he would have been far more interested in the activities of that little group of pygmies, the bodies of some of which hid from his sight the bound girl at its centre.

Old Timer examined the gate and discovered that it was crudely secured with a fibre rope. From his breeches' pocket he took the pocket knife that the Leopard Men had overlooked and began cutting the fastening, congratulating himself upon the fact that the villagers were occupied to such an extent with something over by the chief's hut that he could complete his work without fear of detection.

He planned only to prepare a way into the village, when he undertook his search for the girl after the natives had retired to their huts for the night, and a way out when he had found her. For some unaccountable reason his spirits were high; success seemed assured. Already he was anticipating his reunion with the girl; then there was a little break in the circle of natives standing between him and the centre of the group, and through that break he saw a sight that turned him suddenly cold with dread.

It was the girl, bound hand and foot, and a savage-faced devil-woman wielding a large knife. As Old Timer saw the hideous tableau revealed for a moment to his horrified gaze, the woman seized the girl by the hair and forced her head back, the knife flashed in the light of the cooking fires that had been prepared against the coming feast, and Old Timer, unarmed save for a small knife, burst through the gates and ran toward the scene of impending murder.

A cry of remonstrance burst from his lips that sounded in the ears of the astonished pygmies like the war cry of attacking natives, and at the same instant an arrow passed through the body of Wlala from behind, transfixing her heart. Old Timer's eyes were on the executioner at the moment, and he saw the arrow, as did many of the pygmies; but like them he had no idea from whence it had come – whether from friend or foe.

For a moment the little men stood in stupid astonishment, but the white man realised that their inactivity would be brief when they discovered that they had only a lone and unarmed man to deal with; it was then that there flashed to his fertile brain a forlorn hope.

Half turning, he shouted back toward the open gate, 'Surround the village! Let no one escape, but do not kill unless they kill me.' He spoke in a dialect that he knew they would understand, the language of the people of Bobolo's tribe; and then to the villagers, 'Stand aside! Let me take the white woman, and you will not be harmed.' But he did not wait for permission.

Leaping to the girl's side, he raised her in his arms; and then it was that Rebega seemed to awaken from his stupor. He saw only one man. Perhaps there were others outside his village, but did he not have warriors who could fight? 'Kill the white man!' he shouted, leaping forward.

A second arrow passed through the body of Rebega; and as he sank to the ground, three more, shot in rapid succession, brought down three warriors who had sprung forward to do his bidding. Instantly terror filled the breasts of the remaining pygmies, sending them scurrying to the greater security of their huts.

Throwing the girl across his shoulder, Old Timer bolted for the open gate and disappeared in the forest. He heard a rending and a crash behind him, but he did not know what had happened, nor did he seek to ascertain.

CHAPTER NINETEEN

'The Demons are Coming!'

The sight that met the eyes of Tarzan of the Apes as he looked down into the compound of the village of Rebega, the Betete chief, gave him cause for astonishment. He saw a white girl being bound. He saw the cooking pots and the fires, and he guessed what was about to transpire. He was on his way to the village of Bobolo in search of a white girl imprisoned there. Could there be two white girls captives of natives in this same district? It scarcely seemed probable. This, therefore, must be the white girl whom he had supposed in the village of Bobolo; but how had she come here?

The question was of less importance than the fact that she was here or the other still more important fact that he must save her. Dropping to the ground, he scaled the palisade and crept through the village from the rear, keeping well in the shadow of the huts; while little Nkima remained behind in the tree that the ape-man had quitted, his courage having carried him as far as it could.

When the pygmies had cleared a space for their village they had left a few trees within the enclosure to afford them shade, and one of these grew in front of the hut of Rebega. To this tree Tarzan made his way, keeping the bole of it between him and the natives assembled about the fires; and into its branches he swung just in time to see Wlala seize the girl by the hair and lift her blade to slash the fair throat.

There was no time for thought, barely time for action. The muscles of the ape-man responded almost automatically to the stimulus of necessity. To fit an arrow to his bow and to loose the shaft required but the fraction of a split second. Simultaneously he heard the noise at the gate, saw the white man running forward, heard him yell. Even had he not recognised him, he would have known instinctively that he was here for but one purpose – the rescue of the girl. And when he heard Rebega's command, knowing the danger that the white man faced, he shot the additional arrows that brought down those most closely menacing him and frightened the rest of the pygmies away for the short time that was necessary to permit the removal of the captive from the village.

Tarzan of the Apes had no quarrel with the little men. He had accomplished that for which he had come and was ready to depart, but as he turned to descend from the tree there was a rending of wood, and the limb upon which he was standing broke suddenly from the stem of the tree and crashed to the ground beneath, carrying the ape-man with it.

The fall stunned him momentarily, and when he regained consciousness he found his body overrun by pygmy warriors who were just completing the act of trussing his arms and legs securely. Not knowing that they had completed their job, nor how well they had done it, the ape-man surged heavily upon his bonds, the effort sending the pygmies in all directions; but the cords held and the Lord of the Jungle knew that he was the captive of as cruel and merciless a people as the forests of the great river basin concealed.

The Betetes were still nervous and fearful. They had refastened the gates that Old Timer had opened, and a force of warriors was guarding this entrance as well as the one at the opposite end of the village. Poison-tipped spears and arrows were in readiness for any enemy who might approach, but the whole village was in a state of nervous terror bordering upon panic. Their chief was dead; the white girl whom they had been about to devour was gone; a gigantic white man had dropped from the heavens into their village and was now their prisoner. All these things had happened within a few seconds; it was little wonder that they were nervous.

As to their new captive there was a difference of opinion. Some thought that he should be slain at once, lest he escape. Others, impressed by the mysterious manner of his entrance into the village, were inclined to wait, being fearful because of their ignorance of his origin, which might easily be supernatural.

The possible danger of an attack by an enemy beyond their gates finally was a reprieve for the ape-man, for the simple reason that they dared not distract their attention from the defence of the village to indulge in an orgy of eating. Tomorrow night would answer even better, their leaders argued; and so a score of them half carried, half dragged the great body of their prisoner into an unoccupied hut, two of their number remaining outside the entrance on guard.

Swaying upon the topmost branch of a tree, Nkima hugged himself in grief and terror, but principally terror; for in many respects he was not greatly unlike the rest of us who, with Nkima, have descended from a common ancestor. His own troubles affected him more than the troubles of another, even though that other was a loved one.

This seemed a cruel world indeed to little Nkima. He was never long out of one trouble before another had him in its grip, though more often than not the troubles were of his own making. This time, however, he had been behaving perfectly (largely through the fact that he was terror-stricken in this strange forest); he had not insulted a single creature all day nor thrown missiles at one; yet here he was alone in the dark, the scent of Sheeta strong in his nostrils, and Tarzan a prisoner in the hands of the little Gomangani.

He wished that Muviro and the other Waziri were here, or Jad-bal-ja, the Golden Lion. Either of these would come to the rescue of Tarzan and save him, too; but they were far away. So far away were they that Nkima had long since given up hope of seeing any of them again. He wanted to go into the village of the little Gomangani that he might be near his master, but he dared not. He could only crouch in the tree and wait for Sheeta or Kudu. If Sheeta came first, as he fully expected him to do, that would be the last of little Nkima. But perhaps Kudu, the sun, would come first, in which event there would be another day of comparative safety before hideous night settled down again upon an unhappy world.

As his thoughts dwelt upon such lugubrious prophecies, there rose from the village below him the uncanny notes of a weird cry. The natives in the village were startled and terrified, because they only half guessed what it was.

They had heard it before occasionally all during their lives, sounding mysterious and awe-inspiring from the dark distances of the jungle; but they had never heard it so close to them before. It sounded almost in the village. They had scarcely had time to think these thoughts when they learned that the terrible cry had been voiced from one of their own huts.

Two terrified warriors apprised them of this, the two warriors who had been placed on guard over their giant captive. Wide-eyed and breathless, they fled from their post of duty. 'It is no man that we have captured,' cried one of them, 'but a demon. He has changed himself into a great ape. Did you not hear him?'

The other natives were equally frightened. They had no chief, no one to give orders, no one to whom they might look for advice and protection in an emergency of this nature. 'Did you see him?' inquired one of the sentries. 'What does he look like?'

'We did not see him, but we heard him.'

'If you did not see him, how do you know that he has changed himself into a great ape?'

'Did I not say that I heard him?' demanded a sentry. 'When the lion roars, do you have to go out into the forest to look at him to know that he is a lion?'

The sceptic scratched his head. Here was logic irrefutable. However, he felt that he must have the last word. 'If you had looked, you would have known for sure,' he said. 'Had I been on guard I should have looked in the hut. I should not have run away like an old woman.'

'Go and look, then,' cried one of the sentries. The sceptic was silenced.

Nkima heard the weird cry from the village of the little men. It thrilled him, too, but it did not frighten him. He listened intently, but no sound broke the silence of the great forest. He became uneasy. He wished to raise his voice, too, but he dared not, knowing that Sheeta would hear. He wished to go to the side of his master, but fear was stronger than love. All he could do was wait and shiver; he did not dare whimper for fear of Sheeta.

Five minutes passed – five minutes during which the Betetes did a maximum of talking and a minimum of thinking. However, a few of them had almost succeeded in screwing up their courage to a point that would permit them to investigate the hut in which the captive was immured, when again the weird cry shattered the silence of the night; whereupon the investigation was delayed by common consent.

Now, faintly from afar sounded the roar of a lion; and a moment later out of the dim distance came an eerie cry that seemed a counterpart of that which had issued from the hut. After that, silence fell again upon the forest, but only for a short time. Now the wives of Rebega and the wives of the warriors who had been killed commenced their lamentations. They moaned and howled and smeared themselves with ashes.

An hour passed, during which the warriors held a council and chose a temporary chief. It was Nyalwa, who was known as a brave warrior. The little men felt better now; there was a recrudescence of courage. Nyalwa perceived this and realised that he should take advantage of it while it was hot. He also felt that, being chief, he should do something important.

'Let us go and kill the white man,' he said. 'We shall be safer when he is dead.'

'And our bellies will be fuller,' remarked a warrior. 'Mine is very empty now.'

'But what if he is not a man but a demon?' demanded another.

This started a controversy that lasted another hour, but at last it was decided that several of them should go to the hut and kill the prisoner; then more time was consumed deciding who should go. And during this time little Nkima had experienced an accession of courage. He had been watching the village all the time; and he had seen that no one approached the hut in which Tarzan was confined and that none of the natives were in that part of the village, all of them being congregated in the open space before the hut of the dead Rebega.

Fearfully Nkima descended from the tree and scampered to the palisade, which he scaled at the far end of the village where there were no little men, even those who had been guarding the rear gate having deserted it at the first cry of the prisoner. It took him but a moment to reach the hut in which Tarzan lay. At the entrance he stopped and peered into the dark interior, but he could see nothing. Again he grew very much afraid.

'It is little Nkima,' he said. 'Sheeta was there in the forest waiting for me. He tried to stop me, but I was not afraid. I have come to help Tarzan.'

The darkness hid the smile that curved the lips of the ape-man. He knew his Nkima – knew that if Sheeta had been within a mile of him he would not have moved from the safety of the slenderest high-flung branch to which no Sheeta could pursue him. But he merely said, 'Nkima is very brave.'

The little monkey entered the hut and leaped to the broad chest of the ape-man. 'I have come to gnaw the cords that hold you,' he announced.

'That you cannot do,' replied Tarzan; 'otherwise I should have called you long ago.'

'Why can I not?' demanded Nkima. 'My teeth are very sharp.'

'After the little men bound me with rope,' explained Tarzan, 'they twisted copper wire about my wrists and ankles. Nkima cannot gnaw through copper wire.'

'I can gnaw through the cords,' insisted Nkima, 'and then I can take the wire off with my fingers.'

'You can try,' replied Tarzan, 'but I think that you cannot do it.'

Nyalwa had at last succeeded in finding five warriors who would accompany him to the hut and kill the prisoner. He regretted that he had suggested the plan, for he had found it necessary, as candidate for permanent chieftainship, to volunteer to head the party.

As they crept slowly toward the hut, Tarzan raised his head. 'They come!' he whispered to Nkima. 'Go out and meet them. Hurry!'

Nkima crept cautiously through the doorway. The sight that first met his eyes was of six warriors creeping stealthily toward him. 'They come!' he screamed to Tarzan. 'The little Gomangani come!' And then he fled precipitately.

The Betetes saw him and were astonished. They were also not a little fearful. 'The demon has changed himself into a little monkey and escaped,' cried a warrior.

Nyalwa hoped so, but it seemed almost too good to be true; however, he grasped at the suggestion. 'Then we may go back,' he said. 'If he has gone we cannot kill him.'

'We should look into the hut,' urged a warrior who had hoped to be chief and who would have been glad to demonstrate that he was braver than Nyalwa.

'We can look into it in the morning when it is light,' argued Nyalwa; 'it is very dark now. We could see nothing.'

'I will go and get a brand from the fire,' said the warrior, 'and then if Nyalwa is afraid I will go into the hut. I am not afraid.'

'I am not afraid,' cried Nyalwa. 'I will go in without any light.' But he had no more than said it than he regretted it. Why was he always saying things first and thinking afterward!

'Then why do you stand still?' demanded the warrior. 'You cannot get into the hut by standing still.'

'I am not standing still,' remonstrated Nyalwa, creeping forward very slowly.

While they argued, Nkima scaled the palisade and fled into the dark forest. He was very much afraid, but he felt better when he had reached the smaller branches of the trees, far above the ground. He did not pause here, however, but swung on through the darkness, for there was a fixed purpose in the mind of little Nkima. Even his fear of Sheeta was submerged in the excitement of his mission.

Nyalwa crept to the doorway of the hut and peered in. He could see nothing. Prodding ahead of him with his spear he stepped inside. The five warriors crowded to the entrance behind him. Suddenly there burst upon Nyalwa's startled ears the same weird cry that had so terrified them all before. Nyalwa wheeled and bolted for the open air, but the five barred his exit. He collided with them and tried to claw his way over or through them. He was terrified, but it was a question as to whether he was any more terrified than the five.

They had not barred his way intentionally, but only because they had not moved as quickly as he. Now they rolled out upon the ground and, scrambling to their feet, bolted for the opposite end of the village.

'He is still there,' announced Nyalwa after he had regained his breath. 'That was what I went into the hut to learn. I have done what I said I would.'

'We were going to kill him,' said the warrior who would be chief. 'Why did you not kill him? You were in there with him and you had your spear. He was bound and helpless. If you had let me go in, I would have killed him.'

'Go in and kill him then,' growled Nyalwa, disgusted.

'I have a better way,' announced another warrior.

'What is it?' demanded Nyalwa, ready to jump at any suggestion.

'Let us all go and surround the hut; then when you give the word we will hurl our spears through the walls. In this way we shall be sure to kill the white man.'

'That is just what I was going to suggest,' stated Nyalwa. 'We will all go; follow me!'

The little men crept again stealthily toward the hut. Their numbers gave them courage. At last they had surrounded it and were waiting the signal from Nyalwa. The spears with their poisoned tips were poised. The life of the ape-man hung in the balance, when a chorus of angry growls just beyond the palisade stilled the word of command on the lips of Nyalwa.

'What is that?' he cried.

The little men glanced toward the palisade and saw dark forms surmounting it. 'The demons are coming!' shrieked one.

'It is the hairy men of the forest,' cried another.

Huge, dark forms scaled the palisade and dropped into the village. The Betetes dropped back, hurling their spears. A little monkey perched upon the roof of a hut screamed and chattered. 'This way!' he cried. 'This way, Zu-tho! Here is Tarzan of the Apes in this nest of the Gomangani.'

A huge, hulking form with great shoulders and long arms rolled toward the hut. Behind him were half a dozen enormous bulls. The Betetes had fallen back to the front of Rebega's hut.

'Here!' called Tarzan. 'Tarzan is here, Zu-tho!'

The great ape stooped and peered into the dark interior of the hut. His enormous frame was too large for the small doorway. With his great hands he seized the hut by its doorposts and tore it from the ground, tipping it over upon its back, as little Nkima leaped, screaming, to the roof of an adjacent hut.

'Carry me out into the forest,' directed the ape-man.

Zu-tho lifted the white man in his arms and carried him to the palisade, while the pygmies huddled behind the hut of Rebega, not knowing what was transpiring in that other part of their village. The other bulls followed, growling angrily. They did not like the scent of the man-things. They wished to get away. As they had come, they departed; and a moment later the dark shadows of the jungle engulfed them.

CHAPTER TWENTY
'I Hate You!'

As Old Timer carried the girl out of the village of the Betetes into the forest, every fibre of his being thrilled to the contact of her soft, warm body. At last he held her in his arms. Even the danger of their situation was forgotten for the moment in the ecstasy of his gladness. He had found her! He had saved her! Even in the excitement of the moment he realised that no other woman had ever aroused within him such an overpowering tide of emotion.

She had not spoken; she had not cried out. As a matter of fact she did not know into whose hands she had now fallen. Her reaction to her rescue had been anything but a happy one, for she felt that she had been snatched from merciful death to face some new horror of life. The most reasonable explanation was that Bobolo had arrived in time to snatch her from the hands of the pygmies, and she preferred death to Bobolo.

A short distance from the village Old Timer lowered her to the ground and commenced to cut away her bonds. He had not spoken either. He had not dared trust his voice to speak, so loudly was his heart pounding in his throat. When the last bond was cut he helped her to her feet. He wanted to take her in his arms and crush her to him, but something stayed him. Suddenly he felt almost afraid of her. Then he found his voice.

'Thank God that I came in time,' he said.

The girl voiced a startled exclamation of surprise. 'You are a white man!' she cried. 'Who are you?'

'Who did you think I was?'

'Bobolo.'

He laughed. 'I am the man you don't like,' he explained.

'Oh! And you risked your life to save me. Why did you do it? It was obvious that you did not like me; perhaps that was the reason I did not like you.'

'Let's forget all that and start over.'

'Yes, of course,' she agreed; 'but you must have come a long way and faced many dangers to save me. Why did you do it?'

'Because I—' He hesitated. 'Because I couldn't see a white woman fall into the hands of these devils.'

'What are we going to do now? Where can we go?'

'We can't do much of anything before morning,' he replied. 'I'd like to get a little farther away from that village; then we must rest until morning. After that we'll try to reach my camp. It's two days' march on the opposite side of the river – if I can find the river. I got lost today trying to locate Rebega's village.'

They moved on slowly through the darkness. He knew that they were starting in the right direction, for when he had come to the clearing where the village stood he had noted the constellations in the sky; but how long they could continue to hold their course in the blackness of the forest night where the stars were hidden from their view, he did not know.

'What happened to you after Bobolo dragged me from the canoe at the mouth of that frightful river?' she asked.

'They took me back to the temple.'

The girl shuddered. 'That terrible place!'

'They were going to – to prepare me for one of their feasts,' he continued. 'I imagine I'll never be so close to death as that again without dying. The priestesses were just about to mess me up with their clubs.'

'How did you escape?'

'It was nothing short of a miracle,' he replied. 'Even now I cannot explain it. A voiced called down from the rafters of the temple, claiming to be the "muzimo" of some native. A "muzimo," you know, is some kind of ghost; I think each one of them is supposed to have a "muzimo" that looks after him. Then the finest looking white man I ever saw shinned down one of the pillars, grabbed me right out from under the noses of the priests and priestesses, and escorted me to the river where he had a canoe waiting for me.'

'Hadn't you ever seen him before?'

'No. I tell you it was a modern miracle, not unlike one that happened in the pygmy village just as I busted in to head off that bloodthirsty, old she-devil who was going to knife you.'

'The only miracle that I am aware of was your coming just when you did; if there was another I didn't witness it. You see I had my eyes closed, waiting for Wlala to use her knife, when you stopped her.'

'I didn't stop her.'

'What?'

'That was the miracle'

'I do not understand.'

'Just as the woman grabbed you by the hair and raised her knife to kill you, an arrow passed completely through her body, and she fell dead. Then as I rushed in and the warriors started to interfere with me, three or four of them fell with arrows through them, but where the arrows came from I haven't the slightest idea. I didn't see anyone who might have shot them. I don't know whether it was someone trying to aid us, or some natives attacking the Betete village.'

'Or someone else trying to steal me,' suggested the girl. 'I have been stolen so many times recently that I have come to expect it; but I hope it wasn't that, for they might be following us.'

'Happy thought,' commented Old Timer; 'but I hope you're wrong. I think you are, too, for if they had been following us to get you, they would have been on us before. There is no reason why they should have waited.'

They moved on slowly through the darkness for about half an hour longer; then the man stopped. 'I think we had better rest until morning,' he said, 'though I don't know just how we are going to accomplish it. There is no place to lie down but the trail, and as that is used by the leopards at night it isn't exactly a safe couch.'

'We might try the trees,' she suggested.

'It is the only alternative. The underbrush is too thick here – we couldn't find a place large enough to lie down. Can you climb?'

'I may need a little help.'

'I'll go up first and reach down and help you up,' he suggested.

A moment later he had found a low branch and clambered on to it. 'Here,' he said, reaching down, 'give me your hand.' Without difficulty he swung her to his side. 'Stay here until I find a more comfortable place.'

She heard him climbing about in the tree for a few minutes, and then he returned to her. 'I found just the place,' he announced. 'It couldn't have been better if it had been made to order.' He helped her to her feet, and then he put an arm about her and assisted her from branch to branch as they climbed upward toward the retreat he had located.

It was a great crotch where three branches forked, two of them laterally and almost parallel. 'I can fix this up like a Pullman,' he observed. 'Just wait a minute until I cut some small branches. How I ever stumbled on it in the dark gets me.'

'Another miracle, perhaps,' she suggested.

Growing all about them were small branches, and it did not take Old Timer long to cut as many as he needed. These he laid close together across the two parallel branches. Over them he placed a covering of leaves.

'Try that,' he directed. 'It may not be a feather bed, but it's better than none.'

'It's wonderful.' She had stretched out on it in the first utter relaxation she had experienced for days – relaxation of the mind and nerves even more than of the body. For the first time in days she did not lie with terror at her side.

He could see her only dimly in the darkness; but in his mind's eye he visualised the contours of that perfect form, the firm bosom, the slender waist, the rounded thigh; and again passion swept through him like a racing torrent of molten gold.

'Where are you going to sleep?' she asked.

'I'll find a place,' he replied huskily. He was edging closer to her. His desire to take her in his arms was almost maniacal.

'I am so happy,' she whispered sleepily. 'I didn't expect ever to be happy again. It must be because I feel so safe with you.'

The man made no reply. Suddenly he felt very cold, as though his blood had turned to water; then a hot flush suffused him. 'What the devil did she say that for?' he soliloquized. It angered him. He felt that it was not fair. What right had she to say it? She was not safe with him. It only made the thing that he contemplated that much harder to do – took some of the pleasure from it. Had he not saved her life at the risk of his own? Did she not owe him something? Did not all women owe him a debt for what one woman had done to him?

'It seems so strange,' she said drowsily.

'What?' he asked.

'I was so afraid of you after you came to my camp, and now I should be afraid if you were not here. It just goes to show that I am not a very good judge of character, but really you were not very nice then. You seem to have changed.'

He made no comment, but he groped about in the darkness until he had found a place where he could settle himself, not comfortably, but with a minimum of discomfort. He felt that he was weak from hunger and exhaustion. He would wait until tomorrow. He thought that it might be easier then when her confidence in him was not so fresh in his mind, but he did not give up his intention.

He wedged himself into a crotch where a great limb branched from the main bole of the tree. He was very uncomfortable there, but at least there was less danger that he might fall should he doze. The girl was a short distance above him. She seemed to radiate an influence that enveloped him in an aura at once delicious and painful. He was too far from her to touch her, yet always he felt her. Presently he heard the regular breathing that denoted that she slept. Somehow it reminded him of a baby – innocent, trusting, confident. He wished that it did not. Why was she so lovely? Why did she have hair like that? Why had God given her such eyes and lips? Why? Tired Nature would be denied no longer. He slept.

Old Timer was very stiff and sore when he awoke. It was daylight. He glanced up toward the girl. She was sitting up looking at him. When their eyes met she smiled. Little things, trivial things often have a tremendous effect upon our lives. Had Kali Bwana not smiled then in just the way that she did, the lives of two people might have been very different.

'Good morning,' she called, as Old Timer smiled back at her. 'Did you sleep in that awful position all night?'

'It wasn't so bad,' he assured her; 'at least I slept.'

'You fixed such a nice place for me; why didn't you do the same for yourself?'

'You slept well?' he asked.

'All night. I must have been dead tired; but perhaps what counted most was the relief from apprehension. It is the first night since before my men deserted me that I have felt free to sleep.'

'I am glad,' he said; 'and now we must be on the move; we must get out of this district.'

'Where can we go?'

'I want to go west first until we are below Bobolo's stamping grounds and then cut across in a northerly direction toward the river. We may have a little difficulty crossing it, but we shall find a way, At present I am more concerned about the Betetes than about Bobolo. His is a river tribe. They hunt and trap only a short distance in from the river, but the Betetes range pretty well through the forest. Fortunately for us they do not go very far toward the west.'

He helped her to the ground, and presently they found a trail that seemed to run in a westerly direction. Occasionally he saw fruits that he knew to be edible and gathered them; thus they ate as they moved slowly through the forest. They could not make rapid progress because both were physically weak from long abstinence from sufficient food; but necessity drove them, and though they were forced to frequent rests they kept going.

Thirst had been troubling them to a considerable extent when they came upon a small stream, and here they drank and rested. Old Timer had been carefully scrutinising the trail that they had been following for signs of the pygmies; but he had discovered no spoor of human foot and was convinced that this trail was seldom used by the Betetes.

The girl sat with her back against the stem of a small tree, while Old Timer lay where he could gaze at her profile surreptitiously. Since that morning smile he looked upon her out of new eyes from which the scales of selfishness and lust had fallen. He saw now beyond the glittering barrier of her physical charms a beauty of character that far transcended the former. Now he could appreciate the loyalty and the courage that had given her the strength to face the dangers of this savage world for – what?

The question brought his pleasant reveries to an abrupt conclusion with a shock. For what? Why, for Jerry Jerome, of course. Old Timer had never seen Jerry Jerome. All that he knew about him was his name, yet he disliked the man with all the fervour of blind jealousy. Suddenly he sat up.

'Are you married?' He shot the words as though from a pistol.

The girl looked at him in surprise. 'Why, no,' she replied.

'Are you engaged?'

'Aren't your questions a little personal!' There was just a suggestion of the tonal frigidity that had marked her intercourse with him that day that he had come upon her in her camp.

Why shouldn't he be personal, he thought. Had he not saved her life; did she not owe him everything? Then came a realisation of the caddish-ness of his attitude. 'I am sorry,' he said.

For a long time he sat gazing at the ground, his arms folded across his knees, his chin resting on them. The girl watched him intently; those level, grey eyes seemed to be evaluating him. For the first time since she had met him she was examining his face carefully. Through the unkempt beard she saw strong, regular features, saw that the man was handsome in spite of the dirt and the haggard look caused by deprivation and anxiety. Neither was he as old as she had thought him. She judged that he must still be in his twenties.

'Do you know,' she remarked presently, 'that I do not even know your name?'

He hesitated a moment before replying and then said, 'The Kid calls me Old Timer.'

'That is not a name,' she remonstrated, 'and you are not old.'

'Thank you,' he acknowledged, 'but if a man is as old as he feels I am the oldest living man.'

'You are tired,' she said soothingly, her voice like the caress of a mother's hand; 'you have been through so much, and all for me.' Perhaps she recalled the manner in which she had replied to his recent question, and regretted it. 'I think you should rest here as long as you can.'

'I am all right,' he told her; 'it is you who should rest, but it is not safe here. We must go on, no matter how tired we are, until we are farther away from the Betete country.' He rose slowly to his feet and offered her his hand.

Across the stream, through which he carried her despite her objections that he must not overtax his strength, they came upon a wider trail along which they could walk abreast. Here he stopped again to cut two staffs. 'They will help us limp along,' he remarked with a smile; 'we are getting rather old, you know.' But the one that he cut for himself was heavy and knotted at one end. It had more the appearance of a weapon than a walking stick.

Again they took up their weary flight, elbow to elbow. The feel of her arm touching his occasionally sent thrills through every fibre of his body; but recollection of Jerry Jerome dampened them. For some time they did not speak, each occupied with his own thoughts. It was the girl who broke the silence.

'Old Timer is not a name,' she said; 'I cannot call you that – it's silly.'

'It is not much worse than my real name,' he assured her. 'I was named for my grandfather, and grandfathers so often have peculiar names.'

'I know it,' she agreed, 'but yet they were good old substantial names. Mine was Abner.'

'Did you have only one?' he bantered.

'Only one named Abner. What was yours, the one you were named for?'

'Hiram; but my friends call me Hi,' he added hastily.

'But your last name? I can't call you Hi.'

'Why not? We are friends, I hope.'

'All right,' she agreed; 'but you haven't told me your last name.'

'Just call me Hi,' he said a little shortly.

'But suppose I have to introduce you to someone?'

'To whom, for instance?'

'Oh, Bobolo,' she suggested, laughingly.

'I have already met the gentleman; but speaking about names,' he added, 'I don't know yours.'

'The natives called me Kali Bwana.'

'But I am not a native,' he reminded her.

'I like Kali,' she said; 'call me Kali.'

'It means woman. All right, Woman.'

'If you call me that, I shan't answer you.'

'Just as you say, Kali.' Then after a moment, 'I rather like it myself; it makes a cute name for a girl.'

As they trudged wearily along, the forest became more open, the underbrush was not so dense, and the trees were farther apart. In an open space Old Timer halted and looked up at the sun; then he shook his head.

'We've been going east instead of south,' he announced.

'How hopeless!'

'I'm sorry; it was stupid of me, but I couldn't see the sun because of the damned trees. Oftentimes inanimate objects seem to assume malign personalities that try to thwart one at every turn and then gloat over his misfortunes.'

'Oh, it wasn't your fault,' she cried quickly. 'I didn't intend to imply that. You've done all that anyone could have.'

'I'll tell you what we can do,' he announced.

'Yes, what?'

'We can go on to the next stream and follow that to the river; it's bound to run into the river somewhere. It's too dangerous to go back to the one we crossed back there. In the meantime we might as well make up our minds that we're in for a long, hard trek and prepare for it.'

'How? What do you mean?'

'We must eat; and we have no means of obtaining food other than the occasional fruits and tubers that we may find, which are not very strengthening food to trek on. We must have meat, but we have no means for obtaining it. We need weapons.'

'And there is no sporting goods house near, not even a hardware store.' Her occasional, unexpected gaieties heartened him. She never sighed or complained. She was often serious, as became their situation; but even disaster, added to all the trials she had endured for weeks, could not dampen her spirits entirely nor destroy her sense of humour.

'We shall have to be our own armourers,' he explained. 'We shall have to make our own weapons.'

'Let's start on a couple of Thompson machine guns,' she suggested. 'I should feel much safer if we had them.'

'Bows and arrows and a couple of spears are about all we rate,' he assured her.

'I imagine I could make a machine gun as readily,' she admitted. 'What useless things modern women are!'

'I should scarcely say that. I don't know what I should do without you.' The involuntary admission slipped out so suddenly that he scarcely realised what he had said – he, the woman-hater. But the girl did, and she smiled.

'I thought you didn't like women,' she remarked, quite seriously. 'It seems to me that I recall quite distinctly that you gave me that impression the afternoon that you came to my camp.'

'Please don't,' he begged. 'I did not know you then.'

'What a pretty speech! It doesn't sound at all like the old bear I first met.'

'I am not the same man, Kali.' He spoke the words in a low voice seriously.

To the girl it sounded like a confession and a plea for forgiveness. Impulsively she placed a hand on his arm. The soft, warm touch was like a spark to powder. He wheeled and seized her, pressing her close to him, crushing her body to his as though he would make them one; and in the same instant, before she could prevent it, his lips covered hers in a brief, hot kiss of passion.

She struck at him and tried to push him away. 'How – how dared you!' she cried. 'I hate you!'

He let her go and they stood looking at one another, panting a little from exertion and excitement.

'I hate you!' she repeated.

He looked into her blazing eyes steadily for a long moment. 'I love you, Kali,' he said, 'my Kali!'

CHAPTER TWENTY-ONE
Because Nsenene Loved

Zu-tho, the great ape, had quarrelled with To-yat, the king. Each had coveted a young she just come into maturity. To-yat was a mighty bull, the mightiest of the tribe, for which excellent reason he was king; therefore Zu-tho hesitated to engage him in mortal combat. However, that did not lessen his desire for the fair one; so he ran away with her, coaxing some of the younger bulls who were dissatisfied with the rule of To-yat to accompany them. They came and brought their mates. Thus are new tribes formed. There is always a woman at the bottom of it.

Desiring peace, Zu-tho had moved to new hunting grounds far removed from danger of a chance meeting with To-yat. Ga-yat, his life-long friend, was among those who had accompanied him. Ga-yat was a mighty bull, perhaps mightier than To-yat himself; but Ga-yat was of an easygoing disposition. He did not care who was king as long as he had plenty to eat and was not disturbed in the possession of his mates, a contingency that his enormous size and his great strength rendered remote.

Ga-yat and Zu-tho were good friends of Tarzan, perhaps Ga-yat even more than the latter, for Ga-yat was more inclined to be friendly; so when they saw Tarzan in the new jungle they had chosen for their home they were glad, and when they heard his cry for help they hastened to him, taking all but the two that Zu-tho left to guard the shes and the balus.

They had carried Tarzan far away from the village of the Gomangani to a little open glade beside a stream. Here they laid him on soft grasses beneath the shade of a tree, but they could not remove the wires that held his wrists and ankles. They tried and Nkima tried; but all to no avail, though the little monkey finally succeeded in gnawing the ropes which had also been placed around both his wrists and his ankles.

Nkima and Ga-yat brought food and water to Tarzan, and the great apes were a protection to him against the prowling carnivores; but the ape-man knew that this could not last for long. Soon they would move on to some other part of the forest, as was their way, nor would any considerations of sympathy or friendship hold them. Of the former they knew little or nothing, and of the latter not sufficient to make them self-sacrificing.

Nkima would remain with him; he would bring him food and water, but he would be no protection. At the first glimpse of Dango, the hyena, or Sheeta, the leopard, little Nkima would flee, screaming, to the trees. Tarzan racked his fertile brain for a solution of his problem. He thought of his great and good friend, Tantor, the elephant, but was forced to discard him as a possibility for escape as Tantor could no more remove his bonds than the apes. He could carry him, but where? There was no friend within reach to untwist the confining wires. Tantor would protect him, but of what use would protection be if he must lie here bound and helpless. Better death than that.

Presently, however, a solution suggested itself; and he called Ga-yat to him. The great bull came lumbering to his side. 'I am Ga-yat,' he announced, after the manner of the great apes. It was a much shorter way of saying, 'You called me, and I am here. What do you want?'

'Ga-yat is not afraid of anything,' was Tarzan's manner of approaching the subject he had in mind.

'Ga-yat is not afraid,' growled the bull. 'Ga-yat kills.'

'Ga-yat is not afraid of the Gomangani,' continued the ape-man.

'Ga-yat is not afraid,' which was a much longer way of saying no.

'Only the Tarmangani or the Gomangani can remove the bonds that keep Tarzan a prisoner.'

'Ga-yat kills the Tarmangani and the Gomangani.'

'No,' objected Tarzan. 'Ga-yat will go and fetch one to take the wires from Tarzan. Do not kill. Bring him here.'

'Ga-yat understands,' said the bull after a moment's thought.

'Go now,' directed the ape-man, and with no further words Ga-yat lumbered away and a moment later had disappeared into the forest.

The Kid and his five followers arrived at the north bank of the river opposite the village of Bobolo, where they had no difficulty in attracting the attention of the natives upon the opposite side and by means of signs apprising them that they wished to cross.

Presently several canoes put out from the village and paddled upstream to make the crossing. They were filled with warriors, for as yet Bobolo did not know either the identity or numbers of his visitors and was taking no chances. Sobito was still with him and had given no intimation that the Leopard Men suspected that he had stolen the white priestess, yet there was always danger that Gato Mgungu might lead an expedition against him.

When the leading canoe came close to where The Kid stood, several of the warriors in it recognised him, for he had been often at the village of Bobolo; and soon he and his men were taken aboard and paddled across to the opposite bank.

There was little ceremony shown him, for he was only a poor elephant poacher with a miserable following of five blacks; but eventually Bobolo condescended to receive him; and he was led to the chief's hut, where Bobolo and Sobito, with several of the village elders, were seated in the shade.

The Kid's friendly greeting was answered with a surly nod. 'What does the white man want?' demanded Bobolo.

The youth was quick to discern the altered attitude of the chief; before, he had always been friendly. He did not relish the implied discourtesy of the black's salutation, the omission of the deferential 'bwana'; but what was he to do? He fully realised his own impotency, and though it galled him to do so he was forced to overlook the insulting inflection that Bobolo had given the words 'white man.'

'I have come to get you to help me find my friend, the old bwana,' he said. 'My "boys" say that he went into the village of Gato Mgungu, but that he never came out.'

'Why do you come to me, then,' demanded Bobolo; 'why do you not go to Gato Mgungu?'

'Because you are our friend,' replied The Kid; 'I believed that you would help me.'

'How can I help you? I know nothing about your friend.'

'You can send men with me to the village of Gato Mgungu,' replied The Kid, 'while I demand the release of the old bwana.'

'What will you pay me?' asked Bobolo.

'I can pay you nothing now. When we get ivory I will pay.'

Bobolo sneered. 'I have no men to send with you,' he said. 'You come to a great chief and bring no presents; you ask him to give you warriors and you have nothing to pay for them.'

The Kid lost his temper. 'You lousy old scoundrel!' he exclaimed. 'You can't talk that way to me and get away with it I'll give you until tomorrow morning to come to your senses.' He turned on his heel and walked down the village street, followed by his five retainers; then he heard Bobolo yelling excitedly to his men to seize him. Instantly the youth realised the predicament in which his hot temper had placed him. He thought quickly, and before the warriors had an opportunity to arrest him he turned back toward Bobolo's hut.

'And another thing,' he said as he stood again before the chief; 'I have already dispatched a messenger down river to the station telling them about this affair and my suspicions. I told them that I would be here waiting for them when they came with soldiers. If you are thinking of harming me, Bobolo, be sure that you have a good story ready, for I told them that I was particularly suspicious of you.'

He waited for no reply, but turned again and walked toward the village gate, nor was any hand raised to stay him. He grinned to himself as he passed out of the village, for he had sent no messenger, and no soldiers were coming.

As a gesture of contempt for the threats of Bobolo, The Kid made camp close to the village; but his men were not a little perturbed. Some of the villagers came out with food, and from his almost exhausted stores the white extracted enough cloth to purchase a day's rations for himself and his men. Among his callers was a girl whom he had known for some time. She was a happy, good-natured creature; and The Kid had found amusement in talking to her. In the past he had given her little presents, which pleased her simple heart, as did the extravagant compliments that The Kid amused himself by paying her.

Bring a girl presents often and tell her that she is the most beautiful girl in the village, and you may be laying the foundation for something unpleasant in the future. You may be joking, but the girl may be in earnest. This one was. That she had fallen in love with The Kid should have worked to his detriment as a punishment for his thoughtlessness, but it did not.

At dusk the girl returned, sneaking stealthily through the shadows. The Kid was startled by her abrupt appearance before his tent, where he sat smoking.

'Hello there, Nsenene!' he exclaimed. 'What brings you here?' He was suddenly impressed by the unusually grave demeanour of the girl and her evident excitement.

'Hush!' cautioned the girl. 'Do not speak my name. They would kill me if they knew I had come here.'

'What's wrong?'

'Much is wrong. Bobolo is going to send men with you tomorrow. He will tell you that they are going to the village of Gato Mgungu with you, but they will not. When they get you out in the river, out of sight of the village they will kill you and all your men and throw you to the crocodiles. Then when the white men come, they will tell them that they left you at the village of Gato Mgungu; and the white men will go and they will find no village, because it has been burned by the Utengas. There will be no one there to tell them that Bobolo lied.'

'Gato Mgungu's village burned! What became of the old bwana?'

'I know nothing about him, but he is not at the village of Gato Mgungu, because there is no village there. I think he is dead. I heard it said that the Leopard Men killed him. Bobolo is afraid of the Leopard Men because he stole their white priestess from them.'

'White priestess! What do you mean?' demanded The Kid.

'They had a white priestess. I saw her here when Bobolo brought her to be his wife, but Ubooga would not have her around and made Bobolo send her away. She was a white woman, very white, with hair the colour of the moon.'

'When was this?' demanded the astonished youth.

'Three days ago, maybe four days. I do not remember.'

'Where is she now? I should like to see her.'

'You will never see her,' replied Nsenene; 'no one will ever see her.'

'Why not?'

'Because they sent her to the village of the little men.'

'You mean the Betetes?'

'Yes, the Betetes. They are eaters of men.'

'Where is their village?' asked The Kid.

'You want to go there and get the white woman?' demanded Nsenene suspiciously.

There was something in the way the girl asked the question that gave The Kid his first intimation that her interest was prompted by more than friendship for him, for there was an unquestionable tinge of jealous suspicion in her tone. He leaned forward with a finger on his lips. 'Don't tell anybody, Nsenene,' he cautioned in a whisper; 'but the white woman is my sister. I must go to her rescue. Now tell me where the village is, and next time I come I'll bring you a fine present.' If he had felt any compunction about lying to the girl, which he did not, he could easily have salved his conscience with the knowledge that he had done it in a good cause; for if there was any truth in the story of the white priestess, captive of the Betetes, then there was but one course of procedure possible for him, the only white man in the district who had knowledge of her predicament. He had thought of saying that the woman was his mother or daughter, but had compromised on sister as appearing more reasonable.

'Your sister!' exclaimed Nsenene. 'Yes, now that I remember, she looked like you. Her eyes and her nose were like yours.'

The Kid suppressed a smile. Suggestion and imagination were potent powers. 'We do look alike,' he admitted; 'but tell me, where is the village?'

As well as she could Nsenene described the location of the village of Rebega. 'I will go with you, if you will take me,' she suggested. 'I do not wish to stay here any longer. My father is going to sell me to an old man whom I do not like. I will go with you and cook for you. I will cook for you until I die.'

'I cannot take you now,' replied The Kid. 'Maybe some other time, but this time there may be fighting.'

'Some other time then,' said the girl. 'Now I must go back to the village before they close the gates.'

At the first break of dawn The Kid set out in search of the village of Rebega. He told his men that he had given up the idea of going to the village of Gato Mgungu, but that while they were here he was going to look for ivory on this side of the river. If he had told them the truth, they would not have accompanied him.

CHAPTER TWENTY-TWO
In the Crucible of Danger

For a long time Old Timer and the girl walked on in silence. There were no more interchanges of friendly conversation. The atmosphere was frigid. Kali Bwana walked a little behind the man. Often her eyes were upon him. She was thinking seriously, but what her thoughts were she did not reveal.

When they came to a pleasant open stretch through which a small stream wound, Old Timer stopped beneath a great tree that grew upon the bank of the stream. 'We shall remain here for a while,' he said.

The girl made no comment, and he did not look at her but started at once to make camp. First he gathered dead branches of suitable size, for a shelter, cutting a few green ones to give it greater strength. These he formed into a framework resembling that of an Indian wickiup, covering the whole with leafy branches and grasses.

While he worked, the girl assisted him, following his example without asking for directions. Thus they worked in silence. When the shelter was finished he gathered wood for a fire. In this work she helped him, too.

'We shall be on short rations,' he said, 'until I can make a bow and some arrows.'

This elicited no response from the girl; and he went his way, searching for suitable material for his weapon. He never went far, never out of sight of the camp; and presently he was back again with the best that he could find. With his knife he shaped a bow, rough but practical; and then he strung it with the pliable stem of a slender creeper that he had seen natives use for the same purpose in an emergency. This done, he commenced to make arrows. He worked rapidly, and the girl noticed the deftness of his strong fingers. Sometimes she watched his face, but on the few occasions that he chanced to look up she had quickly turned her eyes away before he could catch them upon him.

There were other eyes watching them from the edge of a bit of jungle farther up the stream, close-set, red-rimmed, savage eyes beneath beetling brows; but neither of them was aware of this; and the man continued his work, and the girl continued to study his face contemplatively. She still felt his arms about her; his lips were still hot upon hers. How strong he was! She had felt in that brief moment that he could have crushed her like an egg shell, and yet in spite of his savage impulsiveness he had been tender and gentle.

But these thoughts she tried to put from her and remember only that he was a boor and a cad. She scanned his clothing that now no longer bore even a resemblance to clothing, being nothing but a series of rags held together by a few shreds and the hand of Providence. What a creature to dare take her in his arms! What a thing to dare kiss her! She flushed anew at the recollection. Then she let her eyes wander again to his face. She tried to see only the unkempt beard, but through it her eyes persisted in seeing the contours of his fine features. She became almost angry with herself and turned her eyes away that she might not longer entertain this line of thought; and as she did so she stifled a scream and leaped to her feet.

'God!' she cried; 'Look!'

At her first cry the man raised his eyes. Then he, too, leaped to his feet. 'Run!' he cried to the girl. 'For God's sake, Kali, run!'

But she did not run. She stood there waiting, in her hand the futile staff he had cut for her that she had seized as she leaped to her feet; and the man waited, his heavier cudgel ready in his hand.

Almost upon them, rolling toward them in his awkward gait, was an enormous bull ape, the largest that Old Timer had ever seen. The man glanced quickly sideways and was horrified to see the girl still standing there near him.

'Please run away, Kali,' he implored. 'I cannot stop him; but I can delay him, and you must get away before he can get you. Don't you understand, Kali? It is you he wants.' But the girl did not move, and the great beast was advancing steadily. 'Please!' begged the man.

'You did not run away when I was in danger,' she reminded him.

He started to reply; but the words were never spoken, for it was then that the ape charged. Old Timer struck with his club, and the girl rushed in and struck with hers. Utter futility! The beast grasped the man's weapon, tore it from his hand, and flung it aside. With his other hand he sent Kali Bwana spinning with a blow that might have felled an ox had not the man broken its force by seizing the shaggy arm; then he picked Old Timer up as one might a rag doll and rolled off toward the jungle.

When the girl, still half dazed from the effect of the blow, staggered to her feet she was alone; the man and the beast had disappeared. She called aloud, but there was no reply. She thought that she had been unconscious, but she did not know; so she could not know how long it had been since the beast had carried the man away. She tried to follow, but she did not know in which direction they had gone; she would have followed and fought for the man – her man. The words formed in her mind and brought no revulsion of feeling. Had he not called her 'my Kali' – my woman?

What a change this brief episode had wrought in her! A moment before, she had been trying to hate him, trying to seek out everything disgusting about him – his rags, his beard, the dirt upon him. Now she would have given a world to have him back, nor was it alone because she craved protection. This she realised. Perhaps she realised the truth, too; but if she did she was not ashamed. She loved him, loved this nameless man of rags and tatters.

Tarzan of the Apes stoically awaited his fate, whatever it might be. He neither wasted his strength in useless efforts to break bonds that he had found unbreakable, nor dissipated his nervous energy in futile repining. He merely lay still. Nkima squatted dejectedly beside him. There was always something wrong with the world; so Nkima should have been accustomed to that, but he liked to feel sorry for himself. Today he was in his prime; he could scarcely have been more miserable if Sheeta had been pursuing him.

The afternoon was waning as Tarzan's keen ears caught the sound of approaching footsteps. He heard them before either Nkima or the great apes heard them, and he voiced a low growl that apprised the others. Instantly the great, shaggy beasts were alert. The shes and the balus gathered nearer the bulls; all listened in absolute silence. They sniffed the air; but the wind blew from them toward whatever was approaching, so that they could detect no revealing spoor. The bulls were nervous; they were prepared either for instant battle or for flight.

Silently, notwithstanding its great weight, a mighty figure emerged from the forest. It was Ga-yat. Under one arm he carried a man-thing. Zu-tho growled. He could see Ga-yat; but he could not smell him, and one knows that one's eyes and ears may deceive one, but never one's nose. 'I am Zu-tho,' he growled, baring his great fighting fangs. 'I kill!'

'I am Ga-yat,' answered the other, as he lumbered toward Tarzan.

Presently the others caught his scent spoor and were satisfied, but the scent of the man-thing annoyed and angered them. They came forward, growling. 'Kill the Tarmangani!' was on the lips of many.

Ga-yat carried Old Timer to where Tarzan lay and threw his unceremoniously to the ground. 'I am Ga-yat,' he said; 'here is a Tarmangani. Ga-yat saw no Gomangani.'

The other bulls were crowding close, anxious to fall upon the man-thing. Old Timer had never seen such a concourse of great apes, had never known that they grew so large. It was evident that they were not gorillas, and they were more manlike than any apes he had seen. He recalled the stories that natives had told of these hairy men of the forest, stories that he had not believed. He saw the white man lying bound and helpless among them, but at first he did not recognise him. He thought that he, too, was a prisoner of these man-like brutes. What terrible creatures they were! He was thankful that his captor had taken him rather than Kali. Poor Kali! What would become of her now?

The bulls were pressing closer. Their intentions were evident even to the man. He thought the end was near. Then, to his astonishment, he heard savage growls burst from the lips of the man near him, saw his lip curl upward, revealing strong, white teeth.

'The Tarmangani belongs to Tarzan,' growled the ape-man. 'Do not harm that which is Tarzan's.'

Ga-yat and Zu-tho turned upon the other bulls and drove them back, while Old Timer looked on in wide-eyed astonishment. He had not understood what Tarzan said; he could scarcely believe that he had communicated with the apes, yet the evidence was such that he was convinced of it against his better judgment. He lay staring at the huge, hairy creatures moving slowly away from him; even they seemed unreal.

'You are no sooner out of one difficulty than you find yourself in another,' said a deep, low voice in English.

Old Timer turned his eyes toward the speaker. The voice was familiar. Now he recognised him. 'You are the man who got me out of that mess in the temple!' he exclaimed.

'And now I am in a "mess,"' said the other.

'Both of us,' added Old Timer. 'What do you suppose they will do with us?'

'Nothing,' replied the ape-man.

'Then why did they bring me here?'

'I told one of them to go and get me a man,' replied Tarzan. 'Evidently you chanced to be the first man he came upon. I did not expect a white man.'

'You sent that big brute that got me? They do what you ask? Who are you, and why did you send for a man?'

'I am Tarzan of the Apes, and I wanted someone who could untwist these wires that are around my wrists; neither the apes nor Nkima could do it.'

'Tarzan of the Apes!' exclaimed Old Timer. 'I thought you were only a part of the folklore of the natives.' As he spoke he started to work on the wires that confined the ape-man's wrists – copper wires that untwisted easily.

'What became of the white girl?' asked the latter. 'You got her out of the Betete village, but I couldn't follow you because the little devils got me.'

'You were there! Ah, now I see; it was you who shot the arrows.'

'Yes.'

'How did they get you, and how did you get away from them?'

'I was in a tree above them. The branch broke. I was stunned for a moment. Then they bound me.'

'That was the crash I heard as I was leaving the village.'

'Doubtless,' agreed the ape-man. 'I called the great apes,' he continued, 'and they came and carried me here. Where is the white girl?'

'She and I were on our way toward my camp when the ape got me,' explained Old Timer. 'She is alone back there now. When I get these wires off, may I go back to her?'

'I shall go with you. Where was the place? Do you think you can find it?'

'It cannot be far, not more than a few miles, yet I may not be able to find it.'

'I can,' said Tarzan.

'How?' inquired Old Timer.

'By Ga-yat's spoor. It is still fresh.'

The white man nodded, but he was not convinced. He thought it would be a slow procedure picking out the footprints of the beast all the way back to the spot at which he had been seized. He had removed the wires from Tarzan's wrists and was working upon those on his ankles; a moment later the ape-man was free. He leaped to his feet.

'Come!' he directed and started at a trot toward the spot at which Ga-yat had emerged from the jungle.

Old Timer tried to keep up with him, but discovered that he was weak from hunger and exhaustion. 'You go ahead,' he called to the ape-man. 'I cannot keep up with you, and we can't waste any time. She is there alone.'

'If I leave you, you will get lost,' objected Tarzan. 'Wait, I have it.' He called to Nkima, who was swinging through the trees above them, and the monkey dropped to his shoulder. 'Stay near the Tarmangani,' he directed, 'and show him the trail that Tarzan follows.'

Nkima objected; he was not interested in the Tarmangani, but at last he understood that he must do as Tarzan wished. Old Timer watched them chattering to one another. It seemed incredible that they were conversing, yet the illusion was perfect.

'Follow Nkima,' said Tarzan; 'he will guide you in the right direction.' Then he was off at a swinging trot along a track that Old Timer could not see.

Kali Bwana was stunned by the hopelessness of her position. After the brief sense of security she had enjoyed since the man had taken her from the village of the pygmies her present situation seemed unbearable by contrast, and in addition she had suffered a personal loss. To the burden of her danger was added grief.

She gazed at the crude shelter he had built for her, and two tears rolled down her cheeks. She picked up the bow he had made and pressed her lips against the insensate wood. She knew that she would never see him again, and the thought brought a choking sob to her throat. It had been long since Kali Bwana had wept. In the face of privation, adversity, and danger she had been brave; but now she crept into the shelter and gave herself over to uncontrolled grief.

What a mess she had made of everything! Thus ran her thoughts. Her ill-conceived search for Jerry had ended in failure; but worse, it had embroiled a total stranger and led him to his death, nor was he the first to die because of her. There had been the faithful Andereya, whom the Leopard Men had killed when they captured her; and there had been Wlala, and Rebega, and his three warriors – all these lives snuffed out because of her stubborn refusal to understand her own limitations. The white officers and civilians along the lower stretch of the river had tried to convince her, but she had refused to listen. She had had her own way, but at what a price! She was paying now in misery and remorse.

For some time she lay there, a victim of vain regrets; and then she realised the futility of repining, and by an effort of the will seized control of her shaken nerves. She told herself that she must not give up, that even this last, terrible blow must not stop her. She still lived, and she had not found Jerry. She would go on. She would try to reach the river; she would try in some way to cross it, and she would find Old Timer's camp and enlist the aid of his partner. But she must have food, strength-giving flesh. She could not carry on in her weakened condition. The bow that he had made, and that she had hugged to her breast as she lay in the shelter, would furnish her the means to secure meat; and with this thought in mind she arose and went out to gather up the arrows. It was still not too late to hunt.

As she emerged from the frail hut she saw one of the creatures that she had long feared inwardly, knowing that this forest abounded in them – a leopard. The beast was standing at the edge of the jungle looking toward her. As its yellow eyes discovered her, it dropped to its belly, its face grimacing in a horrid snarl. Then it started to creep cautiously toward her, its tail weaving sinuously. It could have charged and destroyed her without these preliminaries; but it seemed to be playing with her, as a cat plays with a mouse.

Nearer and nearer it came. The girl fitted an arrow to the bow. She knew how futile a gesture it would be to launch that tiny missile at this great engine of destruction; but she was courageous, and she would not give up her life without defending it to the last.

The beast was coming closer. She wondered when it would charge. Many things passed through her mind, but clear and outstanding above all the rest was the image of a man in rags and tatters. Then, beyond the leopard, she saw a figure emerge from the jungle – a giant white man, naked but for a loin cloth.

He did not hesitate. She saw him running quickly forward toward the leopard; and she saw that the beast did not see him, for its eyes were upon her. The man made no sound as he sprang lightly across the soft turf. Suddenly, to her horror, she saw that he was unarmed.

The leopard raised its body a little from the ground. It gathered its hind feet beneath it. It was about to start the swift rush that would end in death for her. Then she saw the running man launch himself through the air straight for the back of the grim beast. She wanted to close her eyes to shut out the horrid scene that she knew must ensue as the leopard turned and tore his rash antagonist to ribbons.

What followed after the bronzed body of the white man closed with that of the great cat defied her astonished eyes to follow. There was a swift intermingling of spotted hide and bronzed skin, of arms and legs, of talons and teeth; and above all rose the hideous growls of two blood-mad beasts. To her horror she realised that not the cat alone was the author of them; the growls of the man were as savage as those of the beast.

From the midst of the whirling mass she saw the man suddenly rise to his feet, dragging the leopard with him. His powerful fingers encircled the throat of the carnivore from behind. The beast struck and struggled to free itself from that grip of death, but no longer did it growl. Slowly its struggles lessened in violence, and at last it went limp; then the man released one hand and twisted its neck until the vertibrae snapped, after which he cast the carcass to the ground. For a moment he stood over it. He seemed to have forgotten the girl; then he placed a foot upon it, and the forest re-echoed to the victory cry of the bull ape.

Kali Bwana shuddered. She felt her flesh turn cold. She thought to flee from this terrible wild man of the forest; then he turned toward her, and she knew that it was too late. She still held the bow and arrow ready in her hands. She wondered if she could hold him off with these. He did not appear an easy man to frighten.

Then he spoke to her. 'I seem to have arrived just in time,' he said quietly. 'Your friend will be here presently,' he added, for he saw that she was afraid of him. That one should fear him was no new thing to Tarzan of the Apes. There were many who had feared him, and perhaps for this reason he had come to expect it from every stranger. 'You may put down your bow. I shall not harm you.'

She lowered the weapon to her side. 'My friend!' she repeated. 'Who? Whom do you mean?'

'I do not know his name. Have you many friends here?'

'Only one, but I thought him dead. A huge ape carried him away.'

'He is safe,' the ape-man assured her. 'He is following behind me.' Kali Bwana sank limply to the ground. 'Thank God!' she murmured.

Tarzan stood with folded arms watching her. How small and delicate she looked! He wondered that she had been able to survive all that she had passed through. The Lord of the Jungle admired courage, and he knew what courage this slender girl must possess to have undergone what she had undergone and still be able to face a charging leopard with that puny weapon lying on the grass beside her.

Presently he heard someone approaching and knew it was the man. When he appeared he was breathing hard from his exertion, but at the sight of the girl he ran forward. 'You are all right?' he cried. He had seen the dead leopard lying near her.

'Yes,' she replied.

To Tarzan, her manner seemed constrained, and so did that of the man. He did not know what had passed between them just before they had been separated. He could not guess what was in the heart of each, nor could Old Timer guess what was in the heart of the girl. Being a girl, now that the man was safe, she sought to hide her true emotions from him. And Old Timer was ill at ease. Fresh in his mind were the events of the afternoon; ringing in his ears her bitter cry, 'I hate you!'

Briefly he told her all that had occurred since the ape had carried him away, and then they planned with Tarzan for the future. He told them that he would remain with them until they had reached the man's camp, or that he would accompany them down river to the first station; but to Old Timer's surprise the girl said that she would go to his camp and there attempt to organise a new safari, either to accompany her down river or in the further prosecution of her search for Jerry Jerome.

Before night fell Tarzan had brought meat to the camp, using the bow and arrows that Old Timer had made, and the man and the girl cooked theirs over a fire while the ape-man sat apart tearing at the raw flesh with his strong, white teeth. Little Nkima, perched upon his shoulder, nodded sleepily.

CHAPTER TWENTY-THREE
Converging Trails

Early the next morning they started for the river, but they had not gone far when the wind veered into the north, and Tarzan halted. His delicate nostrils questioned the tell-tale breeze.

'There is a camp just ahead of us,' he announced. 'There are white men in it.'

Old Timer strained his eyes into the forest. 'I can see nothing,' he said.

'Neither can I,' admitted Tarzan; 'but I have a nose.'

'You can smell them?' asked Kali.

'Certainly, and because my nose tells me that there are white men there I assume that it is a friendly camp; but we will have a look at it before we go too close. Wait here.'

He swung into the trees and was gone, leaving the man and the girl alone together; yet neither spoke what was in his heart. The constraint of yesterday still lay heavily upon them. He wanted to ask for her forgiveness for having taken her into his arms, for having dared to kiss her. She wanted him to take her into his arms again and kiss her. But they stood there in silence like two strangers until Tarzan returned.

'They are all right,' announced the ape-man. 'It is a company of soldiers with their white officers and one civilian. Come! They may prove the solution of all your difficulties.'

The soldiers were breaking camp as Tarzan and his companions arrived. The surprised shouts of the black soldiers attracted the attention of the white men – two officers and a civilian – who came forward to meet them. As his eyes fell upon the civilian, Old Timer voiced an exclamation of surprise.

'The Kid!' he exclaimed, and the girl brushed past him and ran forward, a glad cry upon her lips.

'Jerry! Jerry!' she cried as she threw herself into The Kid's arms.

Old Timer's heart sank. Jerry! Jerry Jerome, his best friend! What cruel tricks fate can play.

When the greetings and the introductions were over, the strange combination of circumstances that had brought them together thus unexpectedly were explained as the story of each was unfolded.

'Not long ago,' the lieutenant in command of the expedition explained to Kali, 'we heard rumours of the desertion of your men. We arrested some of them in their villages and got the whole story. Then I was ordered out to search for you. We had come as far as Bobolo's yesterday when we got an inkling of your whereabouts from a girl named Nsenene. We started for the Betete village at once and met this young man wandering about, lost, just as we were going into camp here. Now you have assured the success of my mission by walking in on me this morning. There remains nothing now but to take you back to civilisation.'

'There is one other thing that you can do while you are here,' said Old Timer.

'And that?' inquired the lieutenant.

'There are two known Leopard Men in the village of Bobolo. Three of us have seen them in the temple of the Leopard God taking active parts in the rites. If you wish to arrest them it will be easy.'

'I certainly do,' replied the officer. 'Do you know them by sight?'

'Absolutely,' stated Old Timer. 'One of them is an old witch-doctor named Sobito, and the other is Bobolo himself.'

'Sobito!' exclaimed Tarzan. 'Are you sure?'

'He is the same man you carried away from the temple, the man you called Sobito. I saw him drifting down the river in a canoe the morning after I escaped.'

'We shall arrest them both,' said the officer; 'and now as the men are ready to march, we will be off.'

'I shall leave you here,' said the ape-man. 'You are safe now,' he added, turning to the girl. 'Go out of the jungle with these men and do not come back; it is no place for a white girl alone.'

'Do not go yet,' exclaimed the officer. 'I shall need you to identify Sobito.'

'You will need no one to identify Sobito,' replied the ape-man, and swinging into a tree, he vanished from their sight.

'And that is that,' commented The Kid.

On the march toward Bobolo's village the girl and The Kid walked close together, while Old Timer followed dejectedly behind. Finally the Kid turned and addressed him. 'Come on up here, old man, and join us: I was just telling Jessie about a strange coincidence in something I said in Bobolo's village last night. There is a girl there named Nsenene. You probably remember her, Old Timer. Well, she told me about this white girl who was a captive in the pygmy village; and when I showed interest in her and wanted to know where the village was so that I could try to get the girl away from them, the little rascal got jealous. I discovered that she had a crush on me; so I had to think quickly to explain my interest in the white girl, and the first thing that entered my head was to tell her that the girl was my sister. Wasn't that a mighty strange coincidence?'

'Where's the coincidence?' demanded Old Timer.

The Kid looked at him blankly. 'Why, didn't you know?' he exclaimed. 'Jessie is my sister.'

Old Timer's jaw dropped. 'Your sister!' Once again the sun shone and the birds sang. 'Why didn't you tell me you were looking for your brother?' he demanded of Kali.

'Why didn't you tell me that you knew Jerry Jerome?' she countered.

'I didn't know that I knew him,' he explained. 'I never knew The Kid's name. He didn't tell me and I never asked.'

'There was a reason why I couldn't tell you,' said The Kid; 'but it's all right now. Jessie just told me.'

'You see—' she hesitated.

'Hi,' prompted Old Timer.

The girl smiled and flushed slightly. 'You see, Hi,' she commenced again, 'Jerry thought that he had killed a man. I am going to tell you the whole story because you and he have been such close friends.

'Jerry was in love with a girl in our town. He learned one night that an older man, a man with a vile reputation, had enticed her to his apartment. Jerry went there and broke in. The man was furious, and in the fight that followed Jerry shot him. Then he took the girl home, swearing her to secrecy about her part in the affair. That same night he ran away, leaving a note saying that he had shot Sam Berger, but giving no reason.

'Berger did not die and refused to prosecute; so the case was dropped. We knew that Jerry had run away to save the girl from notoriety, more than from fear of punishment; but we did not know where he had gone. I didn't know where to look for him for a long time.

'Then Berger was shot and killed by another girl, and in the meantime I got a clue from an old school friend of Jerry's and knew that he had come to Africa. Now there was absolutely no reason why he should not return home; and I started out to look for him.'

'And you found him,' said Old Timer.

'I found something else,' said the girl, but he did not catch her meaning.

It was late when they arrived at the village of Bobolo, which they found in a state of excitement. The officer marched his men directly into the village and formed them so that they could command any situation that might arise.

At sight of The Kid and Old Timer and the girl Bobolo appeared frightened. He sought to escape from the village, but the soldiers stopped him, and then the officer informed him that he was under arrest. Bobolo did not ask why. He knew.

'Where is the witch-doctor called Sobito?' demanded the officer.

Bobolo trembled. 'He is gone,' he said.

'Where?' demanded the officer.

'To Tumbai,' replied Bobolo. 'A little while ago a demon came and carried him away. He dropped into the village from the sky and took Sobito up in his arms as though he had no weight at all. Then he cried, "Sobito is going back to the village of Tumbai!" and he ran through the gateway and was gone into the forest before anyone could stop him.'

'Did anyone try?' inquired Old Timer with a grin.

'No,' admitted Bobolo. 'Who could stop a spirit?'

The sun was sinking behind the western forest, its light playing upon the surging current of the great river that rolled past the village of Bobolo. A man and a woman stood looking out across the water that was plunging westward in its long journey to the sea down to the trading posts and the towns and the ships, which are the frail links that connect the dark forest with civilisation.

'Tomorrow you will start,' said the man. 'In six or eight weeks you will be home. Home!' There was a world of wistfulness in the simple, homely word. He sighed. 'I am so glad for both of you.'

She came closer to him and stood directly in front of him, looking straight into his eyes. 'You are coming with us,' she said.

'What makes you think so?' he asked.

'Because I love you, you will come.'

Edgar Rice Burroughs (1875–1950)

Edgar Rice Burroughs was a prolific American author of the 'pulp' era. The son of a Civil War veteran, he saw brief military service with the 7th U.S. Cavalry before he was diagnosed with a heart problem and discharged. After working for five years in his father's business, Burroughs left for a string of disparate and short-lived jobs, and was working as a pencil sharpener wholesaler when he decided to try his hand at writing. He found almost instant success when his story 'Under the Moons of Mars' was serialised in *All-Story Magazine* in 1912, earning him the then-princely sum of $400.

Burroughs went on to have tremendous success as a writer, his wide-ranging imagination taking in other planets (John Carter of Mars and Carson of Venus), a hollow earth (Pellucidar), a lost world, westerns, historicals and adventure stories. Although he wrote in many genres, Burroughs is best known for his creation of the archetypal jungle hero, Tarzan. Edgar Rice Burroughs died in 1950.